WITHDRAWN
L R COLLEGE LIBRARY

SOME CAME RUNNING

FROM HERE TO ETERNITY

BY THE SAME AUTHOR

FROM HERE TO ETERNITY

SOME

CAME

RUNNING

BY *James Jones*

"One Book among the rest is dear to me;
As when a man, having tired himself in deed
Against the world, and falling back to write,
Sated with love, or crazed by vanity,
Or drunk with joy, or maimed by Fortune's spite,
Sets down his Paternoster and his creed."

—SIR WALTER RALEIGH

CHARLES SCRIBNER'S SONS · New York

Carl A. Rudisill Library
LENOIR RHYNE COLLEGE

© Copyright 1957 by James Jones

A·10-57 [H]

All rights reserved. No part of this book
may be reproduced in any form without
the permission of Charles Scribner's Sons.

Printed in the United States of America

Library of Congress Catalog Card Number 57-8932

The quotations appearing on the dedication page
are from COLLECTED POEMS, Harper & Brothers
Copyright © 1928 by Edna St. Vincent Millay
Copyright renewed 1956 by Norma Millay Ellis

> "At last he was free
> of the damnable books of Romance."
>
> DON QUIXOTE

"17 And when he was gone forth into the way, there came one running, and kneeled to him, and asked him, Good Master, what shall I do that I may inherit eternal life?

18 And Jesus said unto him, Why callest thou me good? *there is* none good but one, *that is,* God.

19 Thou knowest the commandments, Do not commit adultery, Do not kill, Do not steal, Do not bear false witness, Defraud not, Honour thy father and mother.

20 And he answered and said unto him, Master, all these have I observed from my youth.

21 Then Jesus beholding him loved him, and said unto him, One thing thou lackest: go thy way, sell whatsoever thou hast, and give to the poor, and thou shalt have treasure in heaven: and come, take up the cross, and follow me.

22 And he was sad at that saying, and went away grieved: for he had great possessions."

—MARK, 10

Down, down, down into the darkness of the grave
Gently they go, the beautiful, the tender, the kind;
Quietly they go, the intelligent, the witty, the brave.
I know. But I do not approve. And I am not resigned.
                                        —EDNA ST. VINCENT MILLAY,
                                        IN *Dirge Without Music*

THIS NOVEL IS DEDICATED TO

THE MEMORY OF MY SISTER

MARY ANN JONES

WHO DID NOT LIVE TO FINISH HER OWN

IN THE HOPE THAT TIME

WILL NOT OBLITERATE FROM HUMAN THOUGHT

THE NAME USED TO DESIGNATE

THIS PARTICULAR HUMAN PERSONALITY WHICH,

HAD IT LIVED, WOULD SURELY HAVE MADE

ITSELF REMEMBERED

Lovers and thinkers, into the earth with you.
Be one with the dull, the indiscriminate dust.
A fragment of what you felt, of what you knew,
A formula, a phrase remains,—but the best is lost.
                                        2ND STANZA, *Dirge Without Music*

SPECIAL NOTE

In this book, which is entirely fiction, the macabre imaginings of a novelist's mind, whose characters and situations are completely imaginary, and any resemblance to actual persons is accidental, as everyone can see, nobody like that ever lived, the fanciful workings of a perfervid brain,—in this book then, the author has taken certain deliberate liberties with time and space and geography, and with certain factual if minor events which did not always occur in the years stated, but were called so in order to gain proper effect. These were done with the author's full awareness and are not mistakes. So no one need write the author to point them out.

Anyone driving along Route 40 will find there is no town of Parkman on it in Illinois. Nor is there any town of Israel. The River is not the State boundary on Route 40. There is no interstate bridge to Indiana upon Route 40. The interstate bridge, enhanced and modified, might be seen at Hutsonville; but Hutsonville is not Israel. Israel does not exist. Neither does Parkman. Both are composite results, results of the author's observation of the Illinois landscape and personality, an observation which has lasted some thirty odd years, with five years off for good behavior, in the Army.

One more thing. There is a character in this novel which may cause surprise, or consternation, or even disbelief, among certain types of readers: that of the lady school teacher. In this connection, the author would like to point out that this character is—though changed and modified and personalized to suit the author's need, of course—the result of the author's fascination with, and great admiration for, Miss Emily Dickinson. The author would like to, and chooses to, believe that such ladies could exist in 1950 as well as 1850.

And now in fine, the author also wishes to take this opportunity to thank all those kind people who wrote him letters telling him everything that was wrong with his last book. Also to thank those others, who wrote him letters telling him what was good about it. And he sincerely hopes that this book now will wholly and completely please and satisfy everyone in the whole world.

Readers should also remember that the opinions expressed by the characters are not necessarily those of the author.

PROLOGUE

They came running through the fog across the snow, lumbering, the long rifles held up awkwardly high, the pot helmets they were all so proud of and never seemed to camouflage gleaming dully, running fast, but appearing to come slowly, lifting their feet high in the big thick boots, foreign, alien, brain-chilling. They came that way again and again, and then again, and when you thought there could not be any more of them left on earth to come, they came still again, and still again. Dave knelt behind the wall at the end of the field, his knees soggy wet and numb cold in the snow, and fired carefully and mechanically at them with the carbine he had taken (like the Torch! ha ha) from the dead man whose face he would always see but never be able to recognize as human because the open mouth and the nostrils and eye sockets and ears were all filled with snow. Sometimes when he fired one of them would fall but there was no way of knowing whether it was himself who hit him or one of the other men behind the wall kneeling in the snow that the sun had not melted and firing too. The other men of the 3615th QM Gas Supply Company. At least, he was quite sure, some of them must be.

At other times they came with the tanks, riding, or running along behind them, and it was no longer the wall but a road ditch where there was no snow, and where the land sloped down and away from him, that he fired from behind, and then behind him he could hear the armor and the TDs firing too. Most of the tanks would stop and disgorge their unhuman contents smoking and running, and finally the others would turn back. Even so, sometimes the running figures would still come on, lumbering through the fog across the snow, the long rifles held up awkwardly high, the pot helmets they were all so proud of and never seemed to camouflage gleaming menacingly, dangerously, and lifting their feet high in the big thick boots. Sometimes it was snow they came across, and sometimes it was only mud, and at other places it was through the woods, and at one place it was broken buildings that he stood behind and fired at them from, the white Red Cross brassard (because he was the medic of the 3615th QM Gas Supply Company) still on his arm forgotten, though he had meant to take it off. Dave was never just quite sure how he got from one of these places to another. Four days, eight days, ten days, twelve days. And *in all this time they never stopped coming. They might have been mechanical, electric robots; or they might have been little bandy-legged Japanese men; or they might have been strange, alien man-creatures disgorged and dropped by the thousands and the millions with all their ammunition and vehicles and equipment from giant cigar-shaped space ships hovering in the stratosphere to conquer this foreign planet for their race, their civilization and their leaders. The broken rubble of buildings he stood behind as he fired at them was, somebody said, called Malmédy; or was it Stavelot? He was at both, at different times. Most of the time he did not know the faces of any of the men he was with. But sometimes, at other times, usually when he least expected it, he would see the face of a man he recognized from the 3615th QM Gas Supply Company. . . .*

. . . The lonely, solitary, unexpected MP carrying a slung rifle had stopped the convoy at the crossroads, standing in the road his gloved hand held up high, and directed them to turn back north away from St Vith toward Spa. Dave was riding in the cab of the second truck, behind Lt Perry.

"Theyre comin in all through around here," the MP yelled over the motors. "Nobody knows all just where. Everythings to circle back north. If you get to Spa youll probably be all right. I dont know if you can make it."

It was the first that any of them had ever heard about the Battle of the Bulge. Which, in fact, was not even called that yet, then.

"But we're supposed to deliver this gas in St Vith," Lt Perry yelled back. "We've got twelve bays of cans here. They may need it in St Vith."

"Then you better burn it. There probably wont be anybody in St Vith when you get there except Jerry. My orders are to send everything back north to report to V Corps."

"Well, maybe we can get it through to the dump at Spa," Lt Perry yelled.

"You better burn it. Youre more liable to get cut off from Spa than not before you get there. And for that matter there may not be no dumps left in Spa by the time you get there. Just try and get it off the road to burn it, thats all I ask."

So they had left him there, solitary, alone, and—to Dave's eyes at least—incredibly valiant, a lone MP set down from some passing truck to direct traffic at a nameless crossroads during the end of the world, and a mile further on they pulled the carrier trucks off into a patch of field and pulled the distributor caps and sloshed the gasoline around and set fire to it, and then went on in the two personnel trucks. They never did get to Spa. At Stavelot they were shuttled along into the line by a frantic irate Major.

"What outfit?" he yelled.

"3615th QM Gas Supply Company," Lt Perry answered.

"What?!" the Major yelled incredulously. "The 3615th QM Ga—Well, go along north and east and report to the first line colonel you see."

"We havent got any rifles, except two or three."

"Pick some up off the dead casualties," the Major had yelled disgustedly. "Theres plenty around. Dont stand on ceremonies. And dont forget to get the bandoliers!" he had bellowed after them as they had moved away. . . .

. . . It was that same afternoon, they learned later, that Battery B of the 283rd Field Artillery Observation Battalion, together with the MP who was directing traffic at the crossroads where they stopped, were ambushed and most of them massacred, three miles south of Malmédy. . . .

. . . The strange thing was that you did not really feel anything much at all, after the first two hours. The first two hours of being scared. When the bullet that clipped the big arm muscle below his left shoulder knocked him down and he got back up and found he could still move the arm, he went right on firing the dead man's carbine without thinking much about it one way or the other and before very long forgot all about it. At least it took care of that Red Cross brassard. It wasnt that he was brave, it was just that there wasnt anywhere really to go it seemed, or anyone to go to. No place in the world was there anyplace, or anyone, to go to. No one to appeal to. No Supreme Court anymore. No President, no Congress, no FBI, no police who had used to pick him up for vagrancy to protect the citizenry. No nothing. And it was important to keep firing at them as they came, and kept on coming, and did not stop coming, running big-footed in the big thick boots, the pot helmets gleaming cruelly and inhumanly through the fog. They hadnt wanted him for an Infantryman when they drafted him because he was fat and over thirty. But now he was an Infantryman anyway in spite of them. Once he saw Lt Perry, somewhere, with blood running all down one side of his head, his big thick glasses lost and broken somewhere evidently, and looking very disbelieving at finding himself a Lieutenant of Infantry at last finally, as someone led him away.

It was a strange way to live—without lawyers, and without judges, and without Courts of Appeal any more. Without mealtimes, and without bedtimes, without a morning crap somewhere, without running water. Strange, very strange. And still they seemed to keep on coming. Where did they all come from? They had told you that there werent even that many of them left everywhere, any more. That they were all *on the run, back to Berlin. That everything was practically over, the war was practically over.*

Sometimes when they came they got real close. Close enough you could see that they were men after all, with the same strained numb disbelieving hopefully-cruel faces as the faces all around you up and down the ditch, and then it was great fun and a real satisfaction to shoot them and see their faces as they fell twist with pain you were glad they felt, and know that it was you who definitely hit them.

Four days, eight days, ten days, twelve days. And he had eleven definites and two or three very probables, of which he kept careful track. One time, coming with and behind a tank that was not stopped, they got so close that with the tank some of them overran the wall and then someone finally got the tank stopped and a man near him tripped up one of them and Dave jumped and smashed his face in with the butt of the dead man's carbine which had no bayonet, but that was the only time he ever really touched one of them. All the other definites were carbine shots—at twenty feet, at ten yards, at twenty yards. And still they seemed to keep on coming. Like ants or spiders. That when you tramped a mess of them, the others only ran on up over your shoe top and up inside your pants leg on your leg itself.

Four days, eight days, ten days, twelve days. And it appeared as though it was never going to stop. Then, finally, he knew definitely it was never going to stop.

It was the new way of life—without lawyers, without judges, without Courts of Appeal. No Supreme Court, no President, no Congress, no FBI. It was the new way of life, and he knew, definitely, at last, that it would never stop.

BOOK ONE

THE INVESTMENT

with, he would never have come back here. They had put him on the bus at six AM, after he had suddenly made up his mind. Sober now, he knew it was a damn fool thing to do. He wanted to go back, not after the way hed left, he felt bad, a deep depression. When the bus stopped, he got his issue overcoat and canvas ful[bag]

CHAPTER 1

Of course, he knew the town when the bus slowed coming into it. He had known it nineteen years ago when he left it, and he would know it again nineteen years from now, if he should ever happen to come back a second time. A man's home town, the one where he was born and raised, was always special. It was as if secretly all those years your senses themselves had banded together on their own and memorized everything about it so thoroughly that they remembered them even when you didnt. Even with the things you did remember, your senses kept remembering them first a split second sooner without permission and startling you. And it didnt matter whether you loved the thing or hated it. He shifted a little in his seat, suddenly selfconscious of the person, a man, beside him. Your senses didnt feel. They just remembered. He looked out again.

The long S curve wound across a little rise and then dropped to the little wooded creek and crossed a bridge, before it became a brick street and began to climb the long hill between the houses. He looked out upon the estate of the town's richest doctor, nestled in the arm of the first curve. Further west behind it were the well-treed grounds of the little denominational college. A mile off east were the thin stacks and complicated towers of the Sternutol Chemical. Then the bus went on around the second curve through the woods and crossed the bridge, still slowing.

"Parkman!" the driver called, working his brake.

It had been visible off across the flat sand prairies of the Southern Illinois landscape long before they ever got there. He had even known beforehand the exact spot where it would become visible. The last rise which when you topped it out onto the flat, suddenly there it was, miles away yet, its trees that hid the houses rising slowly up the sides of the hill that was crowned with the county courthouse, the whole an island in the middle of its gray sea of winter farmland, and on the left five miles away the thick woods of the Wabash River bottoms. Under the November sky, it had made him think of El Greco's View of Toledo, and he had had that same devilish weird unearthly feeling of foreboding. Suddenly he had thought that The Greek must have really hated that town. Or else feared it.

The driver stopped using his brake and ground the bus on up the mile long hill toward town, Dave watching the houses along North Main Street and remembering most of them. If he hadnt got drunk yesterday in Chicago with that bunch of guys hed been discharged

3

with, he would never have come back here. They had put him on the bus at six AM, after he had suddenly made up his mind. Sober now, he knew it was a damn fool thing to do. He never should have come back, not after the way hed left, he felt bad, a deep depression.

When the bus stopped, he got his issue overcoat and canvas furlough satchel off the rack and followed the driver down out of the whistling fan heat into the cold air outside and set the furlough satchel firmly on the wet bricks of his destination.

He was here, and he was staying. Youre a creature of as many moods as you have dollars. No wonder you can never make up your mind.

Across the square of the town with the courthouse of the county seat in its center a light November snow, granular and dispersed, was falling and melting. It had wet everything just as confidently as if it had been rain, streets sidewalks lampposts, the solid blocks of storefronts, and the echelon of parked cars with Illinois plates alongside of which the bus had pulled up in the street. At a distance under the low gray of the early afternoon sky the wind blew the invisible snow in invisible patterns against the lighted windows of the courthouse offices.

Dave's heart knocked suddenly against the backs of his eyes and he wanted to laugh. No man his age had a right to be this much excited over anything except a woman.

The immaculate bus driver had put on black gloves and was squatting carefully and immaculately on the wet bricks in front of the baggage compartment in the side. Across the square two cars started up, exhaling their white winter exhausts, and backed out and pulled away out of sight behind the treeless courthouse.

Watching them, the whole feel of winter Illinois in a small town flooded back over Dave and he grinned slightly with the sense of humor of a man about to explode a stink bomb in a crowded hall of enemies. When he had left Parkman Illinois nineteen years ago, it had been under very unsavory circumstances: As a senior in high school he got a girl from down in the country pregnant and ran off with a carnival upon the advice of his family. That had been in 1928, and he was 17. Now he was 36, and it was 1947. A long loop of years . . . a long loop of living . . . lay scattered in between. None of his relatives, not even his immediate family, knew he was coming. It wasnt hard to imagine the furor it was going to create.

"Hirsh, David L.," the driver said, reading the stencil on the bulging B-4 bag he had dragged out to the edge of the baggage hole.

"Thats me," Dave said. He turned back from the townscape, still savoring the malices he would activate, and hung the overcoat over his left arm carefully so the bottle in the pocket would not fall out.

The driver swung the big bag to the pavement. "Ive only got four of these things this trip," he said with wry complaint.

"Lots of guys coming home," Dave grinned. He took the bag and set it with the furlough satchel. The driver, watching him, began to laugh silently.

"That was sure some little farewell speech you made those other soljerboys just before we left Chicago."

"Well, they came to see me off. I had to tell them something."

"You told them. I just wish my wife could of heard that little bit about kickin the 4Fs out of their beds. That war was hard on us bus drivers, too."

"I bet it was also hard on bus drivers' wives," Dave said, looking at the immaculateness.

The driver laughed, flashingly and arrogantly, and pushed back his cap with a thumb in the spitting snow and put the backs of his palm soiled gloves carefully, immaculately on his hips. "You know, I was born and raised about fifteen miles from here myself," he said disparagingly.

"Where?"

"West Lancaster." It was a muddy little community, weathering away on the river bank beside a discontinued ferry that constituted one end of the single street.

"Sure. I know West Lancaster." Dave hadnt heard the words in years.

"You dont see me going back," the driver offered. He looked around him at the square of business houses and grinned contemptuously. "I know these towns. No bars. No shows. No burlyque. No nightclubs. No racetracks." He bent down again at the luggage compartment in the side. "You cant even buy whiskey, except in a package. Gimme Chicago."

"They still sell beer," Dave said, looking at the sign over a tavern. He kept his face deadpan: "And theres always the church socials."

The driver looked up, his face pained. "Jesus God! You mean they still have those?"

Dave laughed, looking again around the square with its business houses.

"Well, you can always learn to play golf," the driver said sympathetically, bending his head again to the compartment. "Parkman's got a snazzy Country Club."

"My brother's a wheel in the Country Club," Dave said.

The driver didnt hear it. But then, Dave didnt really care. The driver had been joking. Perhaps he hadnt even said it to the driver, perhaps hed said it to himself. Or to the town.

The driver had his head in the baggage compartment. Dave was still looking off across the town. It was curious, that association of golf and his brother Frank and how they always went together in his mind. Out on the West Coast where he had been living when he was drafted, there were almost as many golf courses as golfers; and he never passed one that it wasnt immediately, and at once, Frank he thought of first. Dear Frank, Dear Brother Frank, Brother Frank the little breadwinner, Brother Frank the family father. Brother Frank the jeweler. Across the square on the east side he could see the building. He couldnt read the words painted on the two plateglass windows, but he knew by heart what they said, in their gold-and-black jeweler's script which he also knew: FRANK HIRSH, JEWELER and FRANK HIRSH'S JEWELRY STORE. The building had not changed any in nineteen years, and neither had the business block it was a part of, and they would not be changed either, the words, and the window displays would still be arranged carefully and tastelessly with that racial trait of Germanic thoroughness that was as natural to the Hirshes as their ball-like heads and blocky bodies. Only now there would be clerks, instead of just Frank and his wife Agnes. Agnes was probably still meaning to re-decorate the interior and still hadnt got to it. Brother Frank would probably be back in the back in the office, right now smooching around with his office girl. As he watched from across the square, a woman in a coat with a fur collar went inside between the display windows. Dave had worked there all through high school. It was hard to believe. And yet you were never really free of a thing like that either.

The bus driver had pulled two big bundles of magazines to the lip of the opening. "Well, I had best get on with my chores," he said. "Ive already got your checks. Youre loose."

"Its too bad you dont get off duty here," Dave said suddenly. "You and me would throw a party. Ive got the money. Ive got plenty of money."

If his voice was harsh (was it?) the driver didnt notice. "Well I aint," he said ruefully. "And these people want to get on down the road." He pulled off his black gloves and touched up his tie meticulously with his fingers. Then he put the gloves back on with satisfaction and picked up the bundles. "But you ever get back up to Chi look me up the Randolph Street Station. Name's O'Donnell." He carried the bundles through the parked cars and across the sidewalk and inside where probably a woman worked, holding them carefully away from his slick lady-slaughterer's uniform.

Dave watched him go in under the sign over the store front that read PARKMAN NEWS AGENCY; on the window was painted another sign BUS STATION PARKMAN ILLINOIS. The place was both. It had been both nineteen years ago, too.

He turned back to his bags, wishing momentarily that they could have gone on talking. But when he asked himself why or what about, there wasnt any answer. Two strange men who didnt give a damn about each other standing and trading quips that tried to top each other, each trying to use the other as a mirror for his own ego. He was horrified when he thought that driver might actually have been getting off duty here. Then he would have had him on his hands for a two- or three-day drunk, boring hell out of him. And for what? He looked down the street again at "the store", Frank's store. Why did he do it? things like that offer to the driver. He didnt know. But he always did. Half angry, he picked up his bags and crossed to the sidewalk and started down the street to the hotel.

It would have ruined all his plans for a triumph that he had worked out so carefully on the way down on the bus and he would have gone right ahead and done it anyway just like that. All around him as he walked the town lay spread out seemingly quiet and peaceful under the winter sky. He grinned. He was not fooled. Behind this misleading facade telephones still lurked, bells poised and waiting. Unless the lines suddenly went out in an unanticipated storm, the whole town would know he was here before suppertime.

The Hotel Francis Parkman was Parkman's finest. There were two others. But The Parkman—named after the same historian and Indian student and author of *The Oregon Trail* whom the founding fathers had chosen to name their town for in 1850—was the only one that had a kitchen and dining room. It was where all the corporation executives, factory officials and other visiting dignitaries stayed when they came to town and Dave Hirsh was not going to stay anywhere else either. The cold wind touched its tongue of melting snow grains to the store fronts as he passed.

In the lobby it was warm and easeful, after outside. An unneeded, luxurious wood fire was burning brightly in the old style marble fireplace and three men in suits and ties and one carefully dressed woman sat in deep chairs near it, in that part of the long bare lobby which the arrangement of the furniture on rugs had constricted into a sort of separate lounging room. When the people talked they didnt look at each other but stared out the big window at the weather as if fascinated by it.

Dave felt his chest swelling deeply with excitement as he set his bags down. It was the first time in some months that he had been vain about his uniform. A uniform was like anything else, when you were around where everyone else had the same thing it didnt mean nearly as much to you.

The clerk left his work and came to the register. He was a chubby blond young man in a suit that looked too big for him. There was a Purple Heart button in his lapel and a glass eye in his face.

"Yes, sir?" With his good eye he scanned Dave's ribbons expertly.

"I want the best room in the house," Dave said. He had been aware of the four loungers eyeing him. Now he could feel their gazes converge upon him like four columns of infantry.

"Yes, sir," the clerk said. "We have a corner suite of two rooms, over the foyer. Thats our best."

"Ill take it," Dave said. "If its empty."

"Yes, sir, its empty. If you will just register, please." He turned the card holder and pushed it forward, while the glass eye continued to stare out of his chubby face like a bright blue marble pressed into a piepan of dough. "Price is ten dollars."

Dave printed his name carefully. He wanted to be sure everyone could read it. Under it he put his old California address in North Hollywood.

Then he stuck the pen back, looked up, and found himself staring deep into the cold reserve of the clerk's glass eye. Time seemed to hang. Then the clerk blinked. This seemingly unnatural act, a direct violation of the laws of motion of inanimate bodies, while freeing him, shocked him like a blow from a fist, he felt the eyelid should have clicked. Or at least made a grating noise. Momentarily, the soldier in him re-asserted itself. Christ what a way to get it. In the eyes. And what a job.

"Have the boy bring my bags up, will you?" he said, trying desperately to look in the real eye.

"Ill bring them, sir," the clerk said. "Our bellboy isnt home from school yet." He turned the register and read the card. "Hirsh?" he said politely. "We have a Mr Frank Hirsh in our town. Who owns the jewelry store."

"Yes, I know," Dave said, again aware of the loungers now. "Im his brother."

It meant nothing to the clerk. He was too young anyway. But Dave was sure it meant something to the four loungers. You could almost feel it, in the air. He started for the back of the lobby, where the stairs were.

"Just a minute, Mr Hirsh, and Ill show you the way," the clerk said.

"I know the way," Dave said, not stopping, "I was born and raised here," as he rounded the corner of the little private dining room where the Rotary Club held its meetings every Thursday. At least that *was* where, nineteen years ago.

It was all just exactly like he had invented it so many times, and played it out in his mind. Except for that damned glass eye. It was almost occult, how like it was. Sometimes there had been just two loungers, sometimes six or seven. But there were always loungers. He just knew it. He had thought about it a lot, this homecoming, in a lot of different places—with the carnival and the circuses he worked for after, later on on the bum, still later when he lived with his sister Francine, who was Frank's twin, in North Hollywood.

At the top of the stairs he looked back and saw the clerk struggling up with the heavy B-4 bag and the satchel. He had completely forgotten all about him. He ran back down the stairs and held out his hand for the small bag.

"Here, give me that."

"I can manage it," the clerk said coldly.

Dave took it anyway.

The clerk shrugged elaborately.

Again, Dave felt that psychic trauma of reasonless fear for his own eyes. "I dont want you to strain yourself on that thing," he joked, striving to make conversation.

"A man can stuff everythin but a ten room house in one of these things," the clerk countered indifferently.

"This war has ruptured a lot of redcaps," Dave said. "What if the VA had to pay them compensation?"

"Do you want the country to go broke," the clerk countered, but he did not laugh. He was apparently used to this trick of people having to make conversation with him. He led the way on down the hall. "Here we go, Mr Hirsh," he said, opening the door. "The bedroom is on in here." He carted the big B-4 bag into it. Dave could hear him opening the zippers and hanging it up on the closet door.

He disposed of his overcoat and got the bottle out of it. He had it open in his hand, almost desperately, when the boy came back in, smiling with half of his face and staring unconcernedly with the other where the bright blue eye reposed in solitary splendor like a turquoise set into the center of a big white silver plate. It was the first really good look, undistracted look, Dave had got at it and it made him want to wince. It was a botched up job, even for the Army.

"How about a drink after all that exertion?" he said, holding it out. He tossed a half dollar on the daybed, deliberately dispassionate.

The clerk pocketed it. "I didnt hear you. Sure. I can awys use a drink."

When he spoke this time Dave detected the accent he had been trying to put his finger on. He handed him the open bottle. "Youre not from around here, are you? Where you from, Jersey?"

"Yeah, Jersey City." He did not quite say Joisey.

"We had a bunch of Jersey boys in my outfit," Dave said. "Whats your name?"

"Barker. Freddy Barker. I was station down at George Field near Vincennes and married a girl from here. Came back out here after I got discharge."

He took a sparing drink from the bottle and made as if to hand it back, but Dave made a gesture, a too big gesture, for him to have another. Instead, the clerk set it gently on the end table.

"Thanks for the drink," he said distantly. "Is there anything else I can get you right now, Mr Hirsh?"

"Yes, there is. As a matter of fact," Dave said. He opened his left blouse pocket. "Id like to have some ice. And Ive got a bank draft here for fifty-five hundred dollars that Id like for you to take over to the Second National Bank and deposit for me."

There was just a second's pause. "Why you want me to deposit it for you?"

"Because I dont want to go over there myself," Dave said. "Its simple. And while youre gone, pick me up a couple bottles of whiskey."

"Okay." The clerk was looking at him curiously with his good eye. The other, as always, was aloof and cold. "Its got to be signed, doesnt it?"

Dave nodded and got out his pen. "Ill sign it right now. Itll be worth a couple of bucks to you to get it in before the bank closes."

"The banks dont close till three. Theres plenty time."

"Its important to me to get it in today," Dave said.

"All right, Ill do it right away. Okay?"

Dave handed him the check and a $20 bill. "Instead of whiskey, why dont you get me a fifth of Gordon's gin and a bottle of Noilly Prat vermouth."

"I doubt if anybodyll have that kind, in this town."

"Okay, then just get the whiskey. Any good blend."

The clerk nodded. "Thats a lot of money to trust a stranger with," he said casually.

"I know, cant you see how worried I look?"

The clerk grinned, a little. It wasnt much of a grin. And anyway, it was a lop sided weird grin because his left eye did not join in and grin with the rest of him.

"You said the Second National, didnt you?" he asked. "A checking account?"

"Thats right. Dont you want another drink?"

"Yes. Ill take one." He picked the bottle up off the table where he had set it. He used the word take as if it meant accept. "Your brother Frank is a member of the Board at the other bank, isnt he?" he said. "At the Cray County Bank?"

"I believe he is," Dave said. "I believe thats right."

The young clerk drank the raw whiskey easily. Then he folded the check and bill and put them in his jacket pocket. If he thought there was anything unusual about it, he didnt show it. When he got up the expression of his good eye was as veiled as that of the glass one. "Ill get this done for you right away, Mr Hirsh."

"Have another drink before you go if you want," Dave said.

"If I have another drink, Ill wind up spendin the afternoon here," the clerk said. There was no humor in his face. He went to the door.

"Ill bring you back a deposit slip," he said.

Dave sat still a moment or two, thinking about the clerk. He liked him. But then he liked most everybody. But he hadnt handled him right. He got up and walked over to the window, taking the bottle with him. But he did not drink, and by the time he reached the corner windows a big arrogant grin had spread over his face. He was thinking about the faces of the people in the bank, when they saw his name on that check. And he was thinking about his brother Frank's face, when he heard about it, which he would soon enough.

Down below him Freddy came out from under the hotel marquee in a topcoat now but still blond bareheaded in the spitting snow whose wetness threw up highlight glints from the brick paved street. Dave watched him cross the street diagonally and go up the other side to the square.

Standing at the window, for a moment he forgot the town. He seemed to go back into the Army. You didnt get over it all at once. And the one eyed clerk had brought out a singularly strong emotion in him. He had just finished spending four years of his life, years he couldnt spare, with boys like that. They called him Pop. And they brought their troubles to him. They believed that, being nearly thirty-five, he by rights ought to know more about life than they did. He had wound up as a sort of elected father of the outfit, and now he missed that. Wherever they were. Wherever they were now. All scattered out. A lot of them dead. And a lot of them crippled too, like Freddy.

It seemed that in the last few years the cripples had become a normal part of everyday life, a steady stream of them, rolling back from over both seas, hardly anyone even noticed them any more. He was suddenly reminded of Falstaff's speech about the maimed and crippled rabble, that had come home with him, from the Continental Wars.

It must have been a lot like this in Rome, too, during *her* great days of world leadership. Except now the government bought them cars which the tax payers paid for. Well, as everyone knew, civilization had advanced a lot. The only thing was he, Dave, had about got to the place where he didnt much give a damn about civilization any more. Except of course for the comforts. You mustnt forget the comforts. Thats what kept us all going wasnt it: the comforts.

Sometimes, and increasingly the past year and a half that hed served with the Occupation Army in Germany, Dave got the feeling he was living in a dying age. It was the same feeling he got when he listened to Stravinsky's The Rite of Spring, a picture not of the birth of the world but the death, and the now primitive tribes that sang hauntingly of the former greatness of their people and put the rusted gun and the wrecked auto upon their stone altars and worshipped them as gods because they no longer knew how to operate them, while they sang to them their haunting songs of a dying race.

Along roads and streets no longer plainly marked, amongst courthouses and buildings turned into grass grown piles of masonry, filled with the rotting papers and unreadable records of an entire civilization, gone.

And in Germany it was not hard to believe it completely. Here it was a little harder.

At such times, it was not too difficult to believe that a man of his own years if he learned to throw a knife and fight with it and taught himself the intricacies of archery he could plan ahead upon someday making himself Chief of the Wabash Valley, or even Chief of All Illinois.

Except the man was always too lazy. And he wasnt getting any younger either. He was getting noticeably older, in fact, the man. Getting bald and until the Army took him and worked it off him had been getting rounder and more waistless with the unhealthy fat of eating too much and drinking too much. The comforts. It appeared to be a toss up, which would outlast the other, he thought, the world or the man.

But either way the man would lose. Lose the bodies of women, lose the physical health, lose the witty intelligence, lose all the great loves the man might have had.

That seemed to be what the emotional progression always ended up at. All his life, he thought, he had been afraid of getting syphilis. Well, it was a wild, weird, melancholy thing, when it took him, and the only thing to do was wear it out. Probably thinking about all the cripples was what had brought it on.

Still holding the bottle, he left the window and went into the bedroom to the closet and from one of the sidepockets of the B-4 bag hanging on the door fished out his books. There were five, all Viking Portables. FITZGERALD, HEMINGWAY, FAULKNER, STEINBECK, WOLFE—the five major influences his sister Francine had called them. She had sent them to him in Europe from Hollywood one by one as they came out.

Dave grinned. Sister Francine. It was her address he had put on the hotel register. It was she he had been living with—and, he was forced to admit, largely off of—in Hollywood when he got drafted. She was a good old gal but she just couldnt get over being an English teacher it had given her an abnormal love for literature she had to feel that what she did was important.

Well, a lot of people labored under that self delusion. He grinned derisively at the five major influences, the biggest mark of his time spent with her—what was it? eleven, almost twelve years. Off and on.

Nevertheless, the sight of the five books there on the dresser, their pages swelled with too much reading, their covers dog eared and warped from too many barracks bags and afflicted with a rash of water and mold spots, really touched him deeply. He had dragged them half way across Europe, they had seen a lot of country with him.

Affectionately, he arranged them between hotel water glasses for bookends and then, still holding the bottle from which he had not drunk yet, went back into the other room to the windows. Freddy was just coming back around the corner carrying a paper sack. Dave watched him come back down the block and go in under the marquee, feeling a strange sense of loss for that imposed fatherhood he had suffered in the 3615th QM Gasoline Supply Company. He had never quite realized he would miss it so much. When the knock came on the door he went over and opened it.

The clerk set the ice bowl down on the table and immediately reached for his pocket.

"They didnt give me a deposit slip. They wrote it down in a bank book. Its in the slot."

He looked at Dave questioningly.

Dave nodded and went through the motions of opening the checkbook and checking the amount because he knew that was what the other wanted. Freddy appeared satisfied and handed him his change.

"I had to get the whiskey," he said.

"Thats okay. Thats fine," Dave said, and handed him back a five dollar bill.

"Thanks," the clerk said without warmth. He looked at it and stuck it in his pocket.

"Do you want another drink?" Dave said.

"Well, I might have just one." His face was already liquor-flushed, and he did not look like a tough ex vet any more. Nowhere, that is, except for that one icily dispassionate, flintily unrelenting, bright blue old soldier's eye that some Army doctor had stuck in his face by way of replacement, either through some horrible mistake of character judgment or else as a macabre joke.

Hes just a kid, Dave thought with surprise. Hes no more of a tough ex vet than I am.

"That air kind of hit me outside," Freddy said, picking up the bottle and studying it pleasurably. "Say, do you know Ned Roberts, the Second National cashier?"

"Ned Roberts?" Dave said. "Ned Roberts. Yeah. Sure. He was two years ahead of me in school. Is he their cashier?"

Freddy nodded, and again that look of unadmitted curiosity came over his face. "He remembered you."

"He did, hunh?"

"He looked funny," Freddy said. It was clear he knew there was something a little out of the ordinary that he was not in on and was not getting. "I couldnt tell if he was surprised because it was you, or if he was surprised because it was that much money."

Dave grinned. "Probably both. Maybe he was thinking about my brother on the board of the other bank."

The clerk nodded, elaborately indifferent. But he was still looking at Dave curiously. "You know, Ive lived in this town almost four years, and I still dont know anything about it," he said. It sounded like a non sequitur. "Its a funny kind of town."

"Not so funny," Dave said. "Probably not much like Jersey City though."

"No. Not much. Well, Ill see you later," Freddy said. He went to the door, where he hesitated, and then turned back, his face closed up tight like a poker player making a big raise. "Mind if I ask you something?"

"No. Shoot."

"You was in the QM." He nodded at Dave's shoulderpatch.

Dave nodded. "3615th QM Gas Supply Company. I was Company Medic."

"If you was in the QM, howd you get that Combat Infantryman's Badge?" He nodded again, at the nationally familiar emblem of the Kentucky rifle on its blue field with the silver wreath around it.

"My outfit fought as Infantry during the Bulge," Dave said. "They gave it to us by Division Special Order. We were up there gasing tanks, when the breakthrough came."

"That was a rough go," Freddy said non-committally.

"I didnt get it in any Army store," Dave smiled, "if thats what youre thinking. Nor any of the rest of these."

"Well," the clerk said, "thanks for them drinks." It sounded awkward, as if he felt he had gotten out of line.

"What were you in?" Dave said. "Infantry?"

"No. Air Corps," Freddy said awkwardly. "But my brother was. He got his in the Huertgen Forest." He went out before Dave could answer, his last sentence hanging in the air, an awkward attempt at explanation, embarrassed.

Dave mixed himself a whiskey and water and sat down in the chair of the desk which had been placed in the corner between the windows. Tilting it back on two legs he looked out the side window up the street to the square.

It was such a funny thing, about soldiers. Funny, in a way that made you want to cry. Everybody always assumed the other guy had had it tougher than he did. The men in Europe thought the men in the Pacific had it tougher because of the jungle. The men in the Pacific thought the men in Europe had it tougher because of the firepower. And it carried right on down, all along the line.

Its like some kind of a mass male guilt psychosis, he thought. Nobody thinks he has as much guts as he should, and the man who only lost one hand drops his eyes before the man who lost them both.

He and Freddy had just made the same mistake, about each other. Now Freddy thought he had it tough. Well, ordinarily—except that he had been coming home to Parkman—he didnt wear them, any of them. (his Purple Heart was purely a technicality) But that could become a pose, too. Everything could become a pose. And usually did.

Except for the Combat Infantry Badge. That he was really and truly proud of. But why? Because he had never been Infantry, of course.

Will we ever get free of it all? Will we ever live it down? and get far enough away from it so we will be able to digest it? look back at it with tolerant amusement and condescension? He doubted it. And then the next war would come along, with its crop of cripples, and oust us from our place we are reluctant to give up.

From the window he could see, up the street in the corner of the courthouse yard a block away, the Cray County Honor Roll. With the war over almost two years, it was beginning to smudge and flake its paint just like all the rest. The Scoreboard, he thought, jocosely. In another year theyd take it down. Moved by a sudden impulse, he wanted very badly suddenly to walk back up town and see if his name was on it, although he already knew it wasnt. He had been drafted from Hollywood.

Curious, wasnt it? that though youd lived in Hollywood eleven years you would still give your home address as Parkman Illinois? That was the reason he had been discharged in Chicago.

And so now he was here, who had never had any real intention of ever coming back here. By a series of snap decisions made hastily and without thought on the spur of the moment. And yet all leading in the same direction. Well, he would give it a week, and one only. It wasnt worth any more than that.

Suddenly he grinned with a sly heavy levity not unlike the looks on the faces in a poolroom when a pretty woman passes. So old Ned Roberts was Cashier of the Second National Bank. Who would ever have thought little old Ned Roberts would have wound up as Cashier of the Second National Bank? Prissy little old Ned.

At the same time he was wondering why he had ever convinced

himself into coming back here. It would only make for unpleasantness, and basically he was not a man who liked unpleasantness.

Well, a week was all he was going to give it.

CHAPTER 2

HE sat there for perhaps twenty minutes. Once he got up to go and mix himself another drink. Then he came back and watched the wet scene of the town from the window, teetering a little on the chair legs now and then to keep his balance. What he planned to do was wait until he was sure Brother Frank had had plenty of time to find out the news. Then he was going to call him at the store. Right now the phones were probably ringing all over the town he was watching, or would be before long. He wanted to give Frank plenty of time to stew and worry over his reputation, the son of a bitch, it might be better to call him just before closing time.

That was what he planned. But when he finally got up again, just as he went across the room to mix himself a third drink, his own phone rang shrilly.

It was so unexpected it startled him and he jumped. Who in hell in Parkman Illinois would be calling him? He couldnt think of a soul. Maybe it was the police. Now what the hell made you think that? he thought angrily; youve broken no law. He was so surprised as the phone continued ringing that he almost didnt answer it.

"Hello, Dave," the voice said.

"Who is this?"

The phone laughed heartily in his hand. "Hes been away so long he dont even recognize his own brother."

"Who. Frank?" There were, as a matter of fact, three other brothers, one in Milwaukee, one in New York, one in St. Louis. The one in New York he had not even bothered to call when he was there.

"You got any other brothers in Parkman?" the voice said.

"No," Dave said, "Well, what do you want?"

"Why I wanted to find out why you hadnt called me. I just this minute found out you were in town."

"You did, hunh?"

"Ned Roberts at the Second National called me."

"I just got in this afternoon," Dave said.

"But why didnt you let us know ahead of time you were comin'?"

"I just decided to come on the spur of the moment."

"You could have called long distance or wired," the voice said.

"I never thought about it."

"Yes, and thats a fine way to act, after three years in Europe."

Dave could feel himself grinning a little, slyly, stiffly. "Well, I wasnt sure youd want to see me, Frank."

"Not want to see you!" the phone said. "Listen, what are you doin' tonight? Nothin'? Good. Why dont you come out to the house for dinner?"

"Well," Dave said. "What for?"

The invitation astounded him speechlessly.

"We wont have nothin' special, because Agnes didnt know you were comin' " the phone said. "But you can take potluck with us and have a deep freeze steak. I know Agnes and little Dawn will be excited to see you." There was a pause, "How about it. Youll come?" the phone said almost sharply.

"Well, Frank, I—"

"Good," the phone said. "Ill pick you up."

"God damn it I cant!" Dave burst out.

"Nonsense! You cant? Why cant you? Of course you can. I tell you what. Its only three now. I cant possibly get away from the store but we close at five thirty in winter. Ill be over for you soon as we close."

Dave grinned slyly. "I could just as easy come down past the store."

"No, no, Ill pick you up. Dont want you havin' to walk in this weather."

"Oh, I dont mind coming by the store at all, Frank."

"Wont hear of it. Pick you up right the hotel. Besides, I might not be here," this time there was no pause, "better yet, why dont you just pack your stuff and move on out here with us? We got plenty room."

"What!"

"I said, move in with us."

"No," Dave said sharply. "I mean thanks, Frank, but Im all settled in here now. Got me a nice little suite of rooms. Anyway, Im only in town for a week."

"Is that all?" the voice said. "Youll wanta stay longer'n that. Anyway you could spend the week with us."

"No!" Dave said desperately.

"Well, all right," the phone said. "But youre sure welcome, Dave, you know that."

"Sure," he said, "sure."

"Ill pick you up at five thirty."

"All right," he said, vaguely feeling he had won a point.

As soon as he had hung up, he began to think of all the things he could have said. He could have said coolly sorry Frank Ive got another dinner date tonight. Or he could have said not from the way you wrote to Francie you didnt want to see me Frank. Or if you want me to come Ill come by the store, in fact Ill drop right over now. He hadnt really

won a point at all, about moving in, Frank had just donated him that
to insure the other.

What he ought to do was just not be here when he came. But you
couldnt do that. What he *should* have done was not accepted.

Dave lit a cigarette. His hands were trembling perceptibly, he
noticed objectively. You wouldnt think it would have bothered him that
much. He smoked deeply. Hungrily. Gradually it sorted itself all out.

In the first exchange he had come off a good bit less than second
best. He hadnt even finished. Even in his fondest hopes of success
he had not anticipated so much success that it would make Frank
call him first. That was the first mistake. And was why Frank had
called of course, instead of waiting to be called. And then when he
had him off balance, he hit him with this unexpected invitation to
dinner. It stole the offensive right out from under him. And Dave
had not only been outsmarted, but completely out-generaled too.

Suddenly Dave laughed out loud happily. It was a deep throaty
chuckling laugh of sheer pleasure. By God, you had to hand it to the
little son of a bitch. It was no fluke that he had run all the other
jewelry stores in town out of business except two, and relegated these
to the position of tolerated competitors. It had been so long, so very
long, since Dave had listened to that flat voice with its twanging nasal
Midwest drawl with all the Gs so conspicuously missing. He had
almost forgotten what it was like. The little lying cheating mean no-
good bastard he thought happily and with a kind of tumultuous
tight-lipped rancor. Maybe it was because Frank had always been the
father in the family, from the time the old man had run off when Dave
was a small boy in grade school. The authority. Maybe it was because
it was Frank who had suggested—suggested? ordered!—him to run off
with that carnival when he got that girl pregnant. He had given him
five dollars. Five lousy dollars. Anyway the others never seemed to
mean anything. And that included Francine; though he oughtnt to
say that, and felt guilty because he did. After all shed done for him.
But they none of them meant anything. One way or the other. Except
Frank, he thought malevolently, the son of a bitch, his eyes narrowing
maliciously.

Dave looked at his watch. It was silly for his hands to be trembling.
He was glad he had saved back a clean, pressed pair of o.d.'s and
some clean shirts. He poured himself a quick drink and went to lay
them out. At least he had gotten out of moving in with them in their
house. He had done that.

Who you kidding? he asked himself. He never had any intention of
you moving in with them. What you should have said was sure Ill
pack and be right out. That would have scared the living daylights
out of him. Agnes would flay him alive.

When he had laid out the clothes, he walked back into the living room. But suddenly he could no longer stand the thought of spending two and a half hours in this hotel room.

Anyway, he was hungry. He hadnt realized it. A guy should eat, shouldnt he?

He looked at the overcoat and decided not to take it. What he wanted was some cold air on him. It was far too hot in here anyway, all of a sudden, and his face felt flushed. There was a beertavern-restaurant half a block up the street toward the square, he remembered. He looked in the mirror to see if his ribbons were on straight.

—and suddenly for no reason he was thinking of Harriet Bowman. Miss Harriet Bowman of Greater Los Angeles. Did live in Santa Monica. Only now she was married. Got married before he even left there. Didnt know where she lived now. But Francie had written him that she had had a baby. Then she had written that she had had another baby. Four years was a long time. Maybe by now she had had still another baby. To a lawyer. To of all things a goddam lawyer. Promising young attorney. And to not ever have laid her even! He looked in the mirror. Oh Harriet Bowman if only you knew now what you missed, if only you knew now what you threw away. I wouldnt care so much. It would make me feel much better. If I knew you knew. Who the hell gives a damn about marriage? Anger helped combat the sickness in his belly. What the hell had started him thinking about *her*? Maybe it was looking at himself in the mirror. He didnt much like what he saw. But it looked a lot better than it did four years ago, when the Army took him.

Buttoning up his collar and tightening his tie, without bothering to check these in the mirror, he went out and locked the door behind him.

Outside the hotel it was still raining its drizzle of snow, but it was beginning to slack off a little. He stood under the marquee a few moments, breathing the cold wet air. It felt good on the flushedness of his face. Up the street in the same block as the bus station was the beer tavern. It was named Ciro's. He remembered it from his youth, but the name had been different then, of course. The neon of its sign shone bright red and green merrily, invitingly in the gray afternoon, but now that he was outside he didnt feel much like going there. After a moment of indecisiveness, he walked up to it slowly through the tiny granules of dropping snow.

A tall gray headed long nosed man was behind the marble top bar cleaning the sinks in an odor of ammonia, as he went up to it. Back in one corner was a griddle and a glass topped contraption for cooking hot dogs. On one wall hung the Anhauser-Busch reproduction of Custer's last stand. A home made crayon picture of one of those big old fashioned beer goblets was scotch taped to the backbar with the words HAVE A SCHOONER! under it. The gray headed man listened dourly to his order for two hot dogs and a schooner and went back without enthusiasm to fix it.

The place had been re-furnitured since hed seen it last, but that hadnt changed it any. Feeling suddenly excited, Dave upended the heavy schooner the man brought him and drained half of it. Then he took a big bite of one of the hot dogs. His mouth watered copiously. He was suddenly enthusiastic, and genuinely hungry—tremendously so. Back at the hotel he hadnt been.

Except for three young men in one of the booths drinking beer there was nobody in the place at this hour of the day. Dave caught them looking at him. One wore a natty light gray suit and pearl semi-Western-style hat. The other two wore their old Army clothes. Quiet seemed to ooze into the place from the walls, with nobody there. It was like stepping clear back into 1910. You felt there should be sawdust on the floor. The three young men looked as if they might have been out all night and just gotten in and were now tranquilizing themselves over a beer in that lazy middle of the afternoon when everyone else was working, before starting out again tonight.

Dave caught them looking at him again, and when he ordered his second schooner the one in the suit and hat said something to the others and got up and came walking lazily over to him at the bar, a cigarette dangling from his mouth. Tall, thin, sway-backed, with a hanging belly due more to the abnormal curve of his spine than to paunch, setting his feet down with that same slow jerky lift and drop a horse has in its hind legs, letting all the weight strike straight up to the buttocks. He stopped in front of him, languid, arrogant, insulting, and apparently congenitally disrespectful and Dave tensed himself. Then carefully with the ball of his thumb the man pushed his hat back just exactly to his hairline exposing a widow's peak. Only then did Dave realize that the man was ill at ease.

"Hello, Miste' Hirsh," he sneered lazily. "Welcome home." Behind the biting Hoosier nasality was a trace of Southern accent. "Im 'Bama Dillert." He did not offer to shake hands.

"Hi," Dave said non-committally, looking him over. He was well over six feet, with dark circled eyes in a pallid face. Maybe thirty-three. The suit, in spite of looking expensive, nevertheless managed because of its narrow cut to look smalltownish and countrified. It was badly wrinkled. Also he hadnt shaved today and his cuffs and collar were grubby. It looked like a real bender. But over and above all of this, seeming to disdain all of it, the pearl hat stood out like a living jewel. There was not a smudge on it, or on its sharply snapped brim, and above the narrow Western-style band its creases were as sharp and distinct as if theyd been steamed into it when it was bought and never touched again. It was obviously a Stetson.

"How you like bein back in Parkman Illinoiz by now?" he asked sardonically.

"How did you know who I was?" Dave said.

"Hell, anybody could look at you and tell yore a Hirsh," the other grinned. "Besides, I already heard you were in town."

"Already?"

"News travels fast in this burg," the tall man sneered cheerfully as if he didnt seem to mind.

"I know. But I didnt think it was that fast."

"I happen to go by the bank. Why dont you come on over and sit with us?" the tall man sneered. Apparently the sneer was ingrained. "Seeing as how you dont know anybody. If you want to, that is."

"Sure," Dave said. "Why not?"—"Bring me two more hot dogs," he called to the gray headed man. He got his beer and followed the tall horse walking Southerner over to the booth. He was really quite tall.

"Dave Hirsh meet Dewey Cole and Hubie Murson. You dont mind if I call you Dave?" 'Bama Dillert said as they sat down.

"No," Dave said. "Hi."

"Hi," the other two said in unison. They were younger. They were all three drinking Griesedieck out of the bottle.

'Bama had leaned himself back into the corner easily, so he could face Dave beside him as well as the other two across. "You seen Frank yet?" he sneered in a friendly way.

"Not yet," Dave said. "I talked to him on the phone."

"He ought to be right glad to see you," 'Bama grinned knowingly. "Dont he look like Frank?" he said, "he looks just exactly like him."

"Yeah," Dewey Cole said sourly, "but thats no compliment in my book."

"Dewey here use to caddy for Frank out the Country Club," 'Bama grinned.

"He never did learn to play golf," Dewey said sourly. "He beat himself to death every day and he never did learn."

"Frank aint learned nothin' about it yet. Frank still flubs his way around ever' day," Hubie Murson said as if he were an echo; he spoke in a naturally high complaining nasal from which the Gs were noticeably absent. Dewey gave him a disgusted look.

"He always won his bets though," Dewey said. "He made them give him enough strokes so he could win. Or he wouldnt bet."

'Bama laughed softly. "Plays poker the same way. Only hes a good poker player."

Dewey apparently did not even hear him. He was looking hard at

Dave. "I used to beat Frank's scores all the time when I was caddyin out there," he said as if 'Bama had not spoken. "I could do it again too in a week. But of course Im not a member of the Country Club. And Im grown up now. I dont caddy any more."

"No, now hes a plasterer," 'Bama said. "Among other things. You know your old girl friend still lives down at New Lebanon," he grinned at Dave. New Lebanon. It was a country community, ten miles south of Parkman by a gravel road. Back here in Illinois they pronounced it Lebanon, New Lebanon.

"Not my girl friend," Dave said. "She never was."

"If you seen her, buddy, youd double that," Dewey said. "In spades."

"Yeah, matter fact, shes got *seven* kids now," Hubie Murson drawled.

'Bama laughed delightedly. "Yeah. A very respectable lady now. If a little dowdy. But very respectable. She married one of them other two guys who were sleeping with her the same time you were. Did you know?"

"Yeah, I know," Dave said. "Frank wrote my sister. I know all about it." So did they apparently. The pregnant girl, the departure, probably the carnival too. I wonder if they know about the goddamned five dollars too, he thought.

"I spent four months with a carnival myself once," 'Bama grinned. "For a different reason. I didnt much like it."

"Neither did I," Dave said, wishing now he hadnt come over. The sense of anticipation ran down out of him as suddenly and as reasonlessly as it had come. Women. He was thinking about a woman all right, but not the one they thought. They had never heard of Harriet Bowman. To a lawyer! To a goddam stinking lawyer! Hell, think about that German woman. Or that girl in—Well, you figured the whole town knew about it, didnt you?

"What the helld you ever want to come back to this dump for?" Dewey Cole said contemptuously.

"Oh—I got drunk up in Chicago," he said.

"Well it was sure a loaded man's idea all right, Ill say that," Dewey said contemptuously. "Dont you think?"

"What do you stay here for?" Dave said.

"Hell, I live here," Dewey said. He shrugged. "Me and your brother Frank, we live here."

"Well, I used to," Dave said.

"Yeah," Dewey snorted.

Dave looked at him, thinking about all three of them, thinking hed probably guessed right when he guessed theyd been out all night and were loafing getting ready for another.

What he saw was an incredibly handsome young man of twenty-four or -five, with curly black hair and beautiful long lashes over astonishingly innocent blue eyes, especially when you heard him talk. It was a Midwest type that Dave remembered, slim and light, with that long narrow fine-boned skull that had come from England to Virginia to Kentucky to Illinois finally, and had taken many generations to develop. Dewey carried it proudly, in the same way the Scottish Stuarts must have carried it proudly, Dave thought, before they lost it. He was wearing an open GI shirt and an old field jacket with the collar up and which had had staff sergeant's stripes daubed in black paint on the sleeves; and he was aware of Dave's scrutiny and was staring back.

Hubie Murson was a chunky blond youth with a big blade-like nose, about that same age. He wore an Eisenhower jacket and khaki pants and combat boots.

There was that same quality about all of them, something not exactly dangerous exactly, something not menacing, something that just gave the impression of dangerousness, the dangerousness in just living, which most of us managed to forget, some intangible proof of hard living and wild midnight revels and a complete lack of social consciousness, responsibility, God damn the hindermost. That something, that kind of a something, quality, always attracted him.

The only way you could say it, he thought, was that the life they lived still had fist fights in it. Most men never fought in fist fights after they were twenty five, not civilians. Every town had a group like that, living on the fringes, always within the law, always strictly within the law, not criminal, but at the same time not respectable. A little wild. It always did attract him. Probably mainly because the respectables always bored the hell out of you, with their lies about themselves theyd convinced themselves of finally. Why shouldnt it attract you he thought miserably, youre one. She always said you were one, didnt she? He still wished he hadnt come over.

"I take it apparently you guys dont think so much of Brother Frank," he said wryly.

For a moment Dewey Cole's face looked almost startled. Then he said, "I guess I been running on too much."

"No more'n usual," Hubie Murson drawled.

Dewey gave him a dirty look. "Frank's all right," he said charitably. "Hes a good boy. Its just that he wants to be a goddam institution." He took a drink of his beer and set it down, and then he grimaced. "Yeah. An operator. Like old Wernz." He moved his head vaguely behind him, and Dave knew what he meant and looked out through the plateglass window at the Second National Bank building across the street, which Anton Wernz III, still living, had built back in 1924. There were two other store fronts with it, and the whole was labeled WERNZ BLOCK—1925 in concrete. It was Anton III's only stab at competing with his father, Dave thought, with Old Anton II, now dead. Anton III just didnt have it. Probably because Anton II who made the money had managed to beat it out of him, before he died.

"I guess everybody that aint," Dave said jocosely, "wants to be an institution."

"Not me," Dewey said contemptuously.

"Yore one already," Hubie grinned, "in a kind of a way."

This pleased Dewey and he grinned suddenly, his light blue eyes flashing with a shy charm. It was impossible not to like him simply because he was so handsome. "Look," he said to Dave. "I apologize to you. I didnt mean to get onto your brother like that with you."

"Thats all right," Dave said, "as a matter of fact I guess Im inclined to agree with you; somewhat."

"Well, what I said about Frank, that dont mean I got anything against you or your family, you know?"

"I didnt figure you did."

"Well I dont," Dewey said, suddenly explosive, his eyes taking on a pugnacious glitter. Pride. "And if I ever do, youll know it. Because Ill tell you. Myself."

"Fair enough," Dave said, and looked up to see the gray headed bartender approaching. A sort of pause developed. Everybody looked down at the table. The gray head carried hot dogs and another round of beers; but it was not just the two hot dogs Dave had ordered, it was a full platter of a dozen. As far as Dave knew, nobody had solicited it. But the man set them down and started serving the beers and picking up the empties. Nobody said a single word until he had gone away. He didnt say a word either. Nobody paid him.

In the silence Dave became aware of the personality of the wet, cold, dull afternoon making itself felt again, flowing in from outside and loafing audibly along around them. Like him, the others all seemed to be savoring it momentarily, but he suddenly felt more lonely and more miserable anyway.

Dewey reached for a hot dog. So did the others. "You know I can remember when you left town," Dewey said. He shifted a little in his seat, the blue eyes getting shy. "You dont know me, but I remember you. I was just a little kid at the time. But I can remember you from the high school football team."

"Yeah," Dave said, "we had the distinction of being the poorest team in Parkman's history. I got kicked off my junior year."

"Yes, I remember that," Dewey said, his eyes taking on a curiously hateful glint of pleasure. "You and a bunch of other guys, for drinking."

"It like to broke Frank's heart I guess."

"I bet it did. I just bet it did. Frank the star punter," Dewey grinned again, his eyes glinting again, in that same way. "I remember all about how you left town too. Or if I dont, Ive heard about it so many times I think I do."

"Well I dont remember it," 'Bama grinned. "Because I wasnt here then. But Ive been told about it enough goddam times, one place or another."

"Well, you havent been told about it as many times as I have," Dave said dryly.

It got a laugh from all of them, especially Dewey, and Dave supposed he ought to be enjoying it and taking some pride in his fame, basking a little in the glory they were deflecting him, but the only thing he could think of, had been thinking of progressively, was to get away without hurting their feelings, away from them away from everybody, off to himself and sit, just sit completely alone and be miserable. All he wanted to do now was get away and inside his clothes his muscles were almost twitching with it, to get away. This, though he knew beforehand the moment he got away he would be aching to be where there were people.

It was strange, strange and almost horrifying, coming back here this way, and getting involved with all these personalities and immersed in all these subtle undercurrents that he was not wise to. If he had gotten on the Super Chief for LA like he originally planned, he wouldnt have known any of them, wouldnt have even known they existed.

"Have you seen your mother yet?" Dewey asked.

"No," he said, "not yet."

"Your old man's still around town, too," Dewey said, as if this were a sudden afterthought. He was grinning in that peculiar way people always grinned whenever they mentioned Dave's father, who had run off and then come back. Dave had forgotten it completely, that way of grinning, living out on the West Coast, but now he remembered it again from his high school days except that now it no longer embarrassed him.

"The old son of a bitch," he said with a grin. "I havent seen him yet either."

"Him and your mother still aint speakin," Dewey grinned.

Dave suddenly felt like laughing, but then thought better of it. Anyway, at that moment the outside door slammed open disrupting the conversation, and a stolid faced young man in civilian clothes and an Army Air Force fleece lined jacket burst into the place at a fast running walk. He headed straight for the booth, apparently in a great state of excitement, which didnt show at all on his broad flat face, only in his movements.

Dave noted 'Bama and the others were grinning at him friendlily.

Here comes another one, he thought, a little sickly. I wonder how many other personalities Im going to get involved with before I get away from this town.

CHAPTER 3

"Howdy, men, howdy," the newcomer said stolidly, stopping his running walk just at the edge of the booth. He seemed to deliberately not look at Dave. Below the Air Force jacket, which he wore proudly although he obviously was not old enough to have been in the war, he had on a loose cut expensive pair of gray covert trousers which were mud splashed and rolled up two turns to expose high heeled Western cowboy boots.

"Hope you men havent drunk up all the brew today. Im sure ready for my brews today," he said lugubriously, and swept the heavy jacket off his back, hung it on the post, and slid into the already crowded booth beside Dewey Cole. Under the jacket he was wearing a fine wool Pendleton shirt.

"Did real great today, man," he announced stolidly. "Real great. Practically finished a chapter." He still studiedly did not look at Dave.

"Hi, Wally," Dewey said indulgently. He elbowed Hubie. "Move over."

"Where?" Hubie said.

"Hello, Wally," 'Bama sneered in the same indulgent tone. "Dave Hirsh meet Wally Dennis." He sounded as if he were trying hard to make it sound like he was used to introducing people formally. "Wally's writing a novel," he said. "Hes a writer."

"Is that right?" Dave said politely.

Wally, for answer, looked up at him suddenly and stuck out his hand. It was as if he had just noticed Dave sitting there. He had a huge knot on his short nose, around which he seemed to be peering.

"Wallace Dennis. Wallace *French* Dennis," he said. "For my mother."

He quite obviously was not old enough to be of beer-drinking age (21 in Illinois), but he couldnt very well have fudged in Parkman where the bartenders knew everybody. He must have worked some angle. His hair was cut very long, cat-musician style.

"Hello, Wally," Dave grinned, taking the hand.

Wally pumped his hand solemnly, eyeing him. "Know you, man, know you," he said agitatedly in his flat voice out of his stolid face, "knew you all along. *D. Hirsh*. Ive read your stuff. Some of its real cool. But it smacks a little too much of Saroyan."

Dave's grin faded. He could feel consternation spreading all over him, making his nerves jangle dangerously, and his stomach quiver. Panicky indignation followed upon its heels, making his whole head feel red.

Dewey had snapped his fingers. "By god, now I know what it was. I knew there was something else about you I couldnt remember. Youre a writer!"

"No Im not!" Dave said stiffly. He could gladly have kicked the innocent Wally right square in the tail. "Did you read the later stories and the novel?" he asked him instead.

Wally nodded in his stolid way. "Read it all, man. All the stories. Both novels. Later stuff's better. —Hey, Jake!" he called, "bring me two brews one right after the other so they wont get warm!—Still too much Saroyan," he said. "But better."

"Im not a writer," Dave said emphatically to Dewey. "I dont know what you heard. But Im not a writer. I just did some writing once.

"Theres only one novel," he said to Wally. "The first one dont count. Youre probably right. In the 'Thirties we all copied Saroyan, out on the West Coast. He was the only one who was selling."

He was still wanting to holler No! No! and keep on hollering No! like a man confronted by his wife with his own damning nude photograph I didnt! Im not! Dont talk about it!

"I was beginning to outgrow all that," he said.

"Good, man, good," Wally said solemnly. "Glad to hear it."

It was a chaotic reaction a completely chaotic reaction he knew it he still couldnt help it. Simmer down. Lets get out of this.

"With us, it was Saroyan," he said angrily. "In the East it was Thomas Wolfe."

"Now theres a real great writer, man," Wally said excitedly.

—yes and now we have to go through all that Dave thought the young always think that—

"Real cool," Wally said excitedly. "That man's way out. Hes the only American writer whos ever written a really accurate picture of what its like to be a young man, what a hell a young man's life is really like. —Only trouble is," he said, "he never got any older."

Dave was brought up short, startled by the perception. Interest gnawed at him. "Is that your own idea? About Wolfe?"

Wally shook his head. "It aint original. My teacher said it. —The point is," he explained stolidly, "even if he didnt do no better, you still cant take away from him what he did do, which nobody else's ever done."

"Yeah," Dave said. "Whos your teacher?"

"Guinevere French," Wally said. "Miss Guinevere French. She teaches English out the College."

"You mean Parkman College?"

"Yes, man. Where else. But I aint no Parkman College student," he added quickly. "Im unclassified. Just takin a few courses of my own choosing, mostly English."

"Guinevere French. Is that any relation to Old Man French the English teacher?"

"Sure, man, the poet. Robert Ball French. Shes his daughter. Theyre relations of mine."

"He taught me English in high school," Dave said. "He used to act out both sides of the duel scene in Hamlet with a yardstick."

"Thats him. He moved up to the College, after you left. But hes retired now." Wally took a drink of the first of his two beers which Jake had brought him. "You ought to meet them. Hell, man! That's where I got hold of all that stuff of yours. You know Ive read everything you ever wrote, man, you know that? Even them two little articles in that little magazine. What was its name?"

Again Dave felt that flickering wave of dismay, that wanting to push it away with both hands, to not think about it, any of it. If theyd just shut up about it. If they were just goddam sensitive enough to realize he didnt want to talk about that. 'Bama and the others were listening with silent interest.

"nous neurotiques," he said, looking down at his glass.

"Thats the one. Without the caps. It folded later. I even read them," Wally said. "They wasnt very good." He kept on looking at Dave, sort of hungrily, as if he expected him to do something miraculous.

Dave didnt look up from his glass. "Whered you ever get hold of all that old stuff?"

"From Gwen French," Wally said indifferently. "Shes collected all your stuff. Partly because you was from here, I guess. But she collects lots of little known writers like you. Uses them in her classes. Says you can learn more off them than the big ones. You know George Blanca?"

"Sure, he used to be my best buddy out on the Coast, years ago," Dave said faintly.

Wally nodded stolidly. "I know. Shes got all his stuff too. Even his screenplays. Also that other guy you knew, the one who committed suicide."

"Kenny McKeean," Dave said. The consternation and dismay flooded back over him full force, stronger than before, rendering him totally inadequate, wanting to talk about it and not wanting to talk about it, and making the insides of his elbows and fingers twiddle alarmingly inside the skin. In Parkman Illinois, of all goddam places! He had not thought about any of them for a long time now, especially Kenny. He and George were the ones who found him. They had gone up drunk to get him to go on a party. It was such an easy thing to forget things, if you wanted to, that had happened a long time ago. Particularly if they belonged in a period of your life you yourself were no longer in.

But then something happened to make them come back full force, fuller than full force, more real and more tangible, fists in the face.

"Thats the guy," Wally Dennis said from a long way off. "Wrote two novels that didnt sell and blew his brains out."

"He hung himself," Dave corrected. "And there was more to it than that. There was a dame involved in it."

The others sat listening silently, as if they seemed to sense he had gone back into a past, recreating it here.

"You mean he killed himself for love?" Wally asked disbelievingly.

"Yeah," David said, "sort of. Love, or the lack of it."

"I didnt know people did that any more," Wally said incredulously. "Especially writers. Well, anyway, shes got all his stuff too. I think what started her out was you, your bein from here and all. And then she moved on to them two, because they was sidekicks of yours. And another guy: I dont remember. Shes got lots more of them now."

"Say!" 'Bama said in his sneering way. "You ought to look into this, Dave. This broad seems to think a lot of you. Might be something in it for you wholesale."

"Naw, man," Wally said. "Its all strickly professional. You got it all wrong. This aint hero worship. Strickly aboveboard. This gal aint got no sex."

"You think so?" 'Bama said confidently. The spell of the past that had come into the room had been broken now, for everyone except Dave at least. The others began to talk.

"I got news for you, son," Dewey said, grinning. "Women do like sex. I know. I use to think like you do, when I was your age and wasnt gettin any."

"Not very many of them dont," Wally said, undisconcerted. "Shes doin all this here for a book shes doin, man. Book on writers and writing. She wrote her doctorate paper on it three years ago."

"What the hells a doctorate paper?" Hubie drawled in his Midwest twang. "Im igerant. You mean shes learnin' to be a doctor too?'"

Dave got up out of the booth. Wally was grinning sheepishly at Hubie; he knew when he was being ridiculed. Dave reached back down and finished off the rest of his schooner. It was about half full. "Excuse me," he said. "Got to go to the head."

"Its right straight back there, Dave," 'Bama said helpfully.

He went back past the empty booths to the door. Beyond the door was a narrow corridor with the two doors on the left side, the first marked SHES' and the second HES' and whoever had painted the signs had put the apostrophes after the S. He entered the HES' and lit a cigarette but it was unpleasant in there with the smell of the disinfectant blocks in the urinal in the small room and he went on down the narrow corridor to the back door and opened it and stood in it remembering to smoke. He didnt do anything. He didnt even think anything really. He just stood there while it welled up in him and looked out at the wet. It was very grimy out in back and the bricks were black with soot on the two buildings on each side. Whatever natural dirt had been in the ground had long since been mingled with or completely covered by ashes, and the little brick building out behind looked fusty with old slop water. After a minute he turned around and started back up the narrow corridor.

Now it will be coming he thought desperately all that old literary crap and hed quit that he was through with all that thanks to you Harriet Bowman but no. That wasnt strictly true. Not the whole truth anyway. That was only part of the whole truth, which covered everything every experience every association and it was all foredoomed to what it became. —But to a goddamned lawyer! Protest filled him.

We were all in love out there, he thought. Every one of us. Each and every one of us. In love. Did anybody understand that really? and why? God bless us every one cried Tiny Tim. Every Godblessed one of us was in love. And everyone of us, in a different way, got

maybe Kenny McKeean got off lightest of us all, afterall, the simple bastard.

They were still talking at the booth, and Wally was on his second beer.

"Was that who told you I wrote too much like Saroyan?" he said as he sat down.

"Gwen? Yes, man. But I thought of it myself first. I just didnt say it." He took a drink of his beer. "You ought to meet them, man. Gwen and Old Bob."

"No thanks," David said. "Im not volunteering as anybody's literary guinea pig."

"Oh, no, man!" Wally protested. "Nothin like that! Theyd just like to meet you is all. We dont get to talk to many writers around here."

"How do you know theyd like to?" Dave said.

"Well, I just know. You see, my mom was a French. Her and Old Bob are cousins. Old Bob's a great guy. Pretty good poet too. Little old fashioned."

"Ive never read him," Dave lied.

"What! Youve never read Old Bob? From your own home town? Hell, man! Hes one of our nation's major minor poets. You really ought to meet them; you ought to meet her, anyway, while youre here." He took another drink of his second beer. "How long you going to be in town? Maybe I could arrange it."

"Not long. Only a week," Dave said. "And I dont want to meet anybody." But then he could not help adding, "I think I went to school with Gwen French."

"Same one," Wally said. "Shes pretty old. Thirty-five or -six. About your age."

"Shes a good looking broad," 'Bama said suddenly from his corner. "In a funny, frightened kind of a way. Its attractive," he said in the voice of a connoisseur.

"She aint interested in sex," Wally said. "Her fiance was killed at the start of the war. All shes interested in is literature, man. Not men."

"Im not interested in men, either," Dewey said.

"Well I am!" Hubie Murson drawled in a high nasal falsetto, from where he sat squeezed back into the corner of the booth. He put his hand up delicately to the back of his blond head.

Grinning, Dewey elbowed him in the ribs. "All right, shut up and sit still. Ill see if I can find you one someplace."

"I aint got any choice but to sit still," Hubie said, in his Midwest twang. "You *prom*ise?" he said in falsetto.

Wally looked at them briefly and emitted an appreciative snort as he turned back to Dave.

Dave looked from one to the other. "You mean shes a lesbo?"

"A what?" Wally said.

"A lesbian."

"Oh," Wally said. "Oh, no. I don't think so. A dyke, you mean. Ive heard it said, but I dont believe it myself. We got some out there that are though," he grinned.

"That gal's no lesbo," 'Bama sneered from his corner. "I seen her too many times. I know a dyke when I see one. That gal's a gal that needs a man about as bad as I need a woman. Her and me ought to get together." He sounded almost hungry, in spite of the joking manner, and Dave turned to look at him.

"Shes nice," 'Bama said to him, as if they two understood each other.

"You wouldnt stand a chance," Wally said disdainfully. "She says shes had all the sex in her life shell ever be interested in."

"She said that?" Dave said quickly. He could feel the old pin, pricking him again. The old hat pin. Sit up and take notice. Wake up, young man. Get up and give the lady a seat, young man. God damn it why cant you let it alone. The only thing that kept him there was the talk about the woman.

"Well I dont reckon itll kill me," 'Bama said. "One more or less. But that gal's no dyke, boys. Thats a gal thats hungry. Only she dont know it."

"No, man," Wally said earnestly. "Man, you got it all wrong. She knows it. Shes had it. Practically the same as told me so, in so many words practically. It bores her. All shes interested in is literature, man."

"Okay," 'Bama said boredly. "This bores me. Im wrong." He sat up straight suddenly.

"You say her fiance got killed?" Dave said.

"Yeah," Wally said, "but he wasnt much of a fiance. Theyd been engaged to each other for five years."

"Lemme out of here," 'Bama said, standing up. "I got to go piss," he sneered. Dave had to move quickly to get out of his way as he slid out. Standing by the booth the tall man looked down at them. "But I aint wrong," he said. He started for the back in that hanging bellied long legged horse walking gait of his, taking his time, languid, arrogant, insultingly confident. His sudden eruption out of the booth, and then his comment, had startled the whole conversation out of them and changed the tone and made it all look ridiculous.

"You say he wasnt much of a fiance?" Dave said anyway, cursing himself, still standing.

"No, man," Wally said. "He was a real sister. What she got she must of got someplace else. Out of town. College, maybe. She took her doctorate at Columbia in New York." Both he and Dewey were smiling fondly after 'Bama.

Dave sat back down. "If shes so goddamned good, whats she doing here?"

Wally cocked his outside leg up over the other knee and smilingly ran his finger over the heavily ornate stitching on the cowboy boot, caressingly and thoughtfully.

"She likes it," he said. "I guess. Her and Old Bob's always lived here. Old Bob's no crud, you know. Hes no Allen Tate. But hes well known. Even the Kenyon Critics wrote about him. They panned him, but they wrote about him." He finished off the rest of his beer. "Well, I got to go, men. Got a class in forty minutes. Listen, man," he said to Dave earnestly. "Why dont you let me fix it for you to meet them?" He stood up and got the heavy fleece-lined jacket off the post. "We could make it a party. A regular party, see? And Ill bring your niece along, and therell just be us five. We can hoist a few brews and just talk."

Dave listened, astounded. "Who do you mean?" he said. "You dont mean Dawn?"

Wally nodded, shouldering into the jacket. "Sure. Your brother Frank's girl. Shes a senior in high school this year and I been running around with her some. Shes a pretty artistic kid. Shed fit in."

"What kind of art?" Dave said disbelievingly.

"Oh, she acts. Paints a little, too. On the side. You be surprised. Look," he said, "what do you say? We could have a real flipped time, man."

"No thanks," Dave grinned. "Ive quit writing. And Ive quit meeting literary people. I dont even talk that language any more. So theres no point in it."

"You what?" Wally said. He was entirely in the jacket now. "Youve quit writing!" He looked utterly and completely shocked. If he had heard the former allusion made to Dewey, he had been too obsessed with something else for it to penetrate, because he looked as if the thought had never entered his head.

"Thats right," Dave said. "The whole shebang." Wally was still looking at him, an odd look beginning to come over his face. Dave winked at him merrily. "Gave it all up," he grinned.

"I thought it was a long time since youd published anything," Wally said in a funny odd voice.

"I havent published anything for ten years," Dave said, explicitly. "I havent written anything for six years, almost seven."

"But of course youve been in the Army," Wally said coldly.

"Ive only been in the Army four years," Dave said, covering all the loopholes, gladly, and with a kind of lefthand enjoyment.

"And youve really quit?" Wally said slowly.

"Thats right," Dave said blithely. "Really have."

"Well, its your business," Wally said, just as blithely.

"Thats the only one whose business it is."

"You mind if I ask you one question? Was there a woman involved in that, too?" Wally said.

Once more, Dave was surprised at the depth of perception that could flash out of him occasionally.

"No," he grinned. "No woman." Just a pig, he added to himself, a fat acorn chewing pig. Who turned into a cow. Now thered be a hell of a good story title. The Pig Who Turned Into A Cow. He was aware he was being bitter, but he enjoyed it. Hed had a rough afternoon. You could sub title it, too. The Pig Who Turned Into A Cow; or The Short, Happy Life Of Harriet Bowman. Apologies, Ernest old boy, he thought. "Now what do you say we drop it and have another beer?"

"Oh, I cant," Wally said. "I always limit myself to two." Then he turned to the others, Dewey and Hubie, like a man whos just remembered his manners. "Well, men, I will see you," he said in that same lugubrious voice hed used when he came in, and the agitated excitement seemed suddenly to pop out through his pores, as if he were pushing himself up to it. "This here beer and talk really bugs me, but you know how it is. Got to go, men. Got to go. See you. See you."

"Give my love to all the college professors," Hubie drawled, "and professorettes."

"Dont take any wooden typewriters," Dewey grinned.

"Great," Wally said solemnly. "Great, men. Youre very witty today. He zipped up the jacket. "Listen," he said to Dave, in that same agitated, stolid lugubriousness, as if he couldnt stop it once hed turned it on. "Listen, the party's out. But Id like to call you up while youre in town?"

"Sure," Dave said. "I'm staying at The Parkman."

"Great," Wally said, his face still stolid, his voice still flat. "Great, man. Ill call you. I really did great today. Really great, man. Im high as a kite. Every now and then I get so I think Im not a writer, you know?" He turned away. "See you. See you, all." He took off for the door in the same fast running walk with which hed entered, the high heeled cowboy boots thudding on the floor.

He seemed to leave in a flurry of whirling air, and Dave thought how many times in his life he had done that same thing. It was all right to be a writer. But you cant act like a writer. You must act like a regular guy. He thought that Wally must be terribly tired and exhausted every time he got home, after he had been out where there were people.

"Hes some boy," he said.

"Hes always like that," Hubie said.

"No hes not either," Dewey contradicted. "All depends on the mood hes in. Sometimes hell sit for hours and not say nothin but screw you, man. Hes real high today."

"He sounds like a writer," Dave said. "He has all the symptoms."

"Him?" Dewey said. "Hes not a writer. Ive known him all my life."

"You mean he couldnt be a writer because you knew him all his life?" Dave asked.

Dewey grinned sheepishly, and ducked his head. "I guess that did sound—insular." It was an unexpected, strange word for him to use. "No, I meant he just didnt seem like a writer."

"How should a writer seem?" Dave said.

"Oh, you know. Different."

"Strange?" Dave said.

"Yeah. Strange. Sort of," Dewey grinned, and then picked up his beer bottle and drank, and Dave realized suddenly that he was not going to say any more; and he knew simultaneously that 'Bama would not say anything more either, about him or his writing. Because men who lived their kind of lives learned early that incuriosity is, at certain times, just as important or moreso than curiosity is at others.

"How come theyll sell him beer?" Dave said, nodding at the door, and Dewey grinned with that look of malicious relish that he was beginning at last to recognize. It came whenever anything was said or done against the social order, or the current moral code.

"Because officially hes twenty-two," Dewey grinned. "He fixed his driver's license up himself last year when he was nineteen. Changed it to twenty-one. He says now he'll be two years older than himself the rest of his whole life."

Dave laughed. He could hear 'Bama horse walking lazily up behind him toward them, down the long room. "They really know how old he is, dont they?"

"Sure but hell, they dont care. You know that. Long as the law cant get them. See, he plays a trombone in a dance band around here, thats how he gets spending money. Them kids get around. His old lady's got a fair chunk of dough, I guess. But I guess she holds on to it. Her husband's dead. He was an oil man. Owned his own company during the oil boom."

"The trombone accounts for the long hair," Dave said, getting up to let the tall man in. Dewey nodded.

'Bama did not sit down. Instead he leaned on his hands on the edge of the table, one leg stiff throwing the buttocks out so far at the tail of the deep curved spine that they seemed disjointed, and looked down into the booth sardonically. "Well, are you guys all through di-secting love and women?" he sneered.

"All through," Dewey said. "Sit down."

'Bama shook his head. "Wheres the kid? He didnt get mad did he?" There was almost a tone of anxiety in his voice.

"Naw, he just left."

"Without payin' for them beers, incidentally," Hubie said dryly.

"He never does," 'Bama said. "I didnt aim for him to."

"Come on, sit down," Dewey said.

'Bama shook his head, grinning. "I got to make my rounds." Then he seemed to think better of it and slid into the booth temporarily. "Wait just a minute," he said to Dave. "Whats on the agenda for tonight?" he asked the others. "Theres a good hockey game on over at Indianapolis."

"Yeah and I wanted to see that game," Dewey said.

Hubie poked him in the arm. "Weve got that paperin' job weve got to get at for those people, Dewey," he cautioned. "That job's past over-due now."

Dewey looked at him disgustedly.

"Well, you told me to remind you."

"Hes right," Dewey said reluctantly. "We got this papering job we ought to get on tomorrow. Ive been putting it off for a month. The people are beginning to get on me."

"Then I guess you stay home," 'Bama said. "Anyway, we dont have to decide it now. Youll be down at Smitty's later, wont you? I thought we might go over there to the game and take Dave here with us."

Once again, as he had before, Dave had that curious feeling of something conspicuous that he couldnt put his finger on, in the way 'Bama used his first name so familiarly.

"Can you get me a woman too?" he asked suddenly, leaning on the booth back.

"Hell yes, two if you want em," 'Bama sneered. "What flavor do you prefer?"

"Ones plenty," Dave grinned. "But I really cant go. Im supposed to go out to Frank's for dinner, and I wont get away from there in time to make the game."

'Bama shrugged. "It dont matter if we go to the game or not. The thing is to go. They got some nice after hours places over there."

"Ill try to get away by ten," Dave said. His palms felt sweaty suddenly at the thought of a woman. Any woman. He hadnt thought to stock up a little, back in Chicago before coming down here. And he had had a bad afternoon. A woman helped. For a while, at least.

"All right, lets figure Ill meet you at the Athletic Club," 'Bama said. "Thats a poolroom up the street."

"Okay," Dave said, but suddenly depressed at the prospect now, "and if Im not there you go ahead."

"Right," 'Bama said, and made as if to get out of the booth. He seemed suddenly jitterish to get going, moving, some other place. "And well go from there to Smitty's." He got up and out so Dave could sit back down. He did not have a topcoat.

"Wheres Smitty's?" Dave said.

"Another bar. Out north." 'Bama had abruptly stopped and was now standing motionless, his hands jammed under his coat skirts in his pants pockets, looking out through the window up front at the wet streets and damp cars, the shining Stetson still just exactly where it had been ever since hed pushed it back with his thumb when Dave first met him and exposed the widow's peak.

Dave had again that strange feeling of having been dumped unceremoniously into the middle of this town, right square into the middle of its personalities and conflicts and allegiances and cherished stimulations. Dumped like a chunk of beef, down into a yowling pack of cats. He sat down.

"Its funny," he said aloud, "me showing up back here, and meeting people, and finding out so much about so many others. I never had any idea there was as much going on in this town as there seems to be, I guess."

"Oh this is quite a town," Dewey said almost protectively. It was not sardonic. "Theres a lot more goes on in this town than an out of stater drivin through might think. And sooner or later, this place right here is where it all winds up and where the business all gets done.

"Unless of course you belong to the Elks or Country Club," he said contemptuously.

"Here or Smitty's," the standing 'Bama said indifferently without moving.

"There dont seem to be much winding up here right now," Dave said.

"This is working hours now. Waitll this afternoon. And after supper," Dewey said. "—This is where your old man hangs out most the time," he added.

Dave grinned. "Pop?" Again he felt that pointless desire to laugh. "Has he ever changed his name yet?" he asked.

"Nope, not yet," Dewey said. "Its still Herschmidt. Old Man Herschmidt, thats what everybody calls him."

"I figured he hadnt," Dave said. "The last time I heard, he hadnt. —I bet that makes Frank happy," he said.

"I bet it does," Dewey said maliciously. "After he went to all that trouble to get it changed. Why the hell would anybody want to get his name changed? like that. I might could see changing it to something different maybe. But to change it from Herschmidt to Hirsh!"

"He did that when pop ran off," Dave said. He grinned. "And I guess he thought it sounded higher class, too. —And you say this is where the old man hangs out, hunh?"

"Yeah. Whenever he can scrounge up the price of a beer," Dewey said. "Hes on the old age pension now."

What a family Dave thought helplessly, and me Im part of it.

"As a matter of fact," 'Bama said carelessly from where he still stood, still motionless, in the same position, "I think thats him coming in the door right now." He took his hands out of his pockets and turned on the balls of his feet and leaned on his arm over the booth back facing the room, impassive, languidly at ease, and all ready to watch.

Oh no, Dave thought, Oh no. Not now. Not right on top of all that other. All the old hate, and the child's hurt inability to understand, that was all gone. But what a fitting climax to a lovely afternoon and he even had an audience.

He had not been watching, and his first inclination was to jerk his head around to look. But something in 'Bama's voice stopped him, some deliberate understatement, like a poker player making a larger bet. Casually, after a moment, he turned his head slowly toward the door, where the stooped stringy looking figure dressed in overalls, work shoes, high railroader's cap and a redblanket mackinaw was coming in out of the light. The others were looking too.

"I dont think Ive ever heard his first name," Dewey said. "What is it?"

"Victor," Dave said, watching his father. "But I dont think I ever heard him called that," he said. "Except maybe by the old lady when I was a kid."

"Id never heard it," Dewey said. "I guess I told you they still werent speaking, didnt I?"

"Yeah," Dave said, "I think you did, but then thats been goin on for twenty years or more. They werent speaking when I left here."

His father stumped straight to the bar without looking around, took off the blanket mackinaw and put it on a stool and sat down beside it. He ordered a beer. Under the overall straps he wore a light blue workman's shirt, much washed and scrupulously clean. In fact all his clothes were clean Dave noted with surprise, all except the weathered red mackinaw. They didnt look like the clothes of a workingman. But then why should they? he thought, hes been living on the old age pension almost ten years.

It was hard to believe, sitting here and looking at him (and aware of the others watching me) that this old man sitting there was his father, his flesh and blood parent. He had to *work* at believing it. They really had had so very little to do with each other, and Dave didnt really feel anything about him one way or the other, nothing at all. Nothing except that the thought of the word FATHER, the abstraction, sent the blood of excitation pounding up into his throat and temples to pump against the backs of his eyeballs. Thinking about the old man coldly was one thing, but seeing him in front of you was another, not so objective.

Of course part of the emotion was due to knowing these three men were sitting here watching him intently.

Actually, to all intents and purposes, he had never really had a father. From the time he was in the fifth grade, Brother Frank the eldest, Brother Frank the breadwinner, had been the only father he had had. But even before that he had known he hadnt had one. A lot of times he had surprised upon the face of the old man that look that he the child couldnt make out but intuitively understood. Later on he the adult had seen the same look on the faces of other men *many others, a great many more than our civic leaders are willing to admit, he thought* and remembering had been able to understand it intellectually. They *these other men, these many others* would sit and tell him all about their wonderful sons and daughters and display their photographs, and upon their faces would be the same look that once had been on the old man's face, when he would sit around the house in the flimsy (but comfortable) workingman's house in the evening after work and stare disbelievingly at his yowling progeny his six offspring with a look of bewildered ire as if wondering irascibly where they had come from, and how in hell he had ever come by them, and what connection could they possibly have with such a simple thing as a Saturday night lay.

But at least, Dave thought, he didnt pretend to love us with that mealy mouthed virtue, or put on pompous airs about his family responsibility, or expect us to love him—all of which Brother Frank had immediately done when, hating them all for cramping him, he had been forced by their existence and by the circumstances of social approval to become the family's sole support and caretaker.

From the corner of his eye he suddenly became aware of Dewey Cole opening his mouth to say something further and he turned back to him.

"What I dont see is why they never got a divorce," Dewey said.

For a moment Dave couldnt figure out what he was talking about.

He had to think back, way back, to what he himself had last said, before he realized that Dewey was only carrying on the conversation.

"Why?" he said. "They both seem to be satisfied as they are. Besides, the old lady dont believe in it."

"Hell, I thought that was only Catholics," Dewey grinned. "Thats no kind of woman to be married to."

"There used to be a lot more of them," Dave said. "They were just products of their time. —I think Ill go over and say hello to the old son of a bitch," he said with a grin, and got up, and walked over to the bar. He said the first thing that came into his head. "Hello. Hows the welding business?"

The old man at the bar, who resembled a cartoonist's caricature of his father, looked up at him piercingly. He is over seventy, Dave thought. He had been stocky once, like the rest of them, but age had wizened him and made him look birdlike. The long scrawny neck and beak of a German nose and the unwinking piercing eyes under the domed railroader's cap all made him look like a topknotted kingfisher.

"I aint in it no more," he said balefully. "Im retard." If he recognized his youngest son he hid it well. Even his bushy eyebrows looked feathery.

"Do you remember me?" Dave asked grinning, as if talking to a child. "You know who I am?"

"I remember ye," his father said. "Well, whatta you want?"

"I just got in town. Thought Id say hello."

"All right, hello. If its money ye want, I aint got any. If youre wantin' me to change my name, I wont do it. Now, what else do you want?"

"Nothing," Dave said. "Not a thing. I dont want anything, I just thought Id buy you a beer."

The old man jerked his head at the gray headed bartender. "Tell him. Hes the one youll have to pay for it."

"Bring Mr Herschmidt here another beer," Dave said, "and put it on my check."

"And ye can tell Frank Im never goin' to change it. Itd give the son of a bitch too much pleasure. He he." Greedily he pulled at the beer he obviously had been nursing.

"All right, Ill tell him," Dave said. "Im goin out to his house tonight."

"You are, hunh? Then tell him for me that the next time he sends somebody around they should buy me a pint of whiskey instead of a beer and not make it so obvious."

"Okay," Dave said, "Ill tell him."

"Dont baby me, you son of a bitch," his father said balefully. He was watching Dave in the mirror, grinning malevolently, like a predatory bird. "It wont do you any damn good. Agnes already tried it."

"Okay, pop," Dave said lightly. "Get him another beer when he wants it," he said to the gray head, who was standing down the bar listening without interest. "And give him a fifth of whiskey."

"Go to hell," his father said balefully. "You just tell Frankie what I said. He he." Frankie was a nickname Frank hated.

"Ill tell him," Dave grinned. His face was flushed. He turned away from the bar. "See you later."

The old man took another long greedy drink of his beer without looking around.

Dave sat down in the booth and grinning looked at the three men and shook his head ruefully. "Whatre you gonna do?"

It was a reasonably good act. They all grinned back. There wasnt really any malice in them. They had just wanted to watch.

"Hes a mean old bastard," 'Bama said admiringly from where he leaned against the booth, as if voicing Dave's thought for him. "Well, I got to go and make my rounds." He straightened up and turned, and then stopped and put his hands in his pants pockets under his coat skirts and stood motionless facing the window, like he had done before.

Up at the bar Dave's father was having the barman put six bottles of beer, instead of one, in the sack with his fifth of whiskey. Without paying he clutched the sack and stumped stringily to the door, looking neither right nor left.

'Bama pulled his hands out of his pockets and lit a cigarette, tilting his head on one side to the match, and then stepped over and held the door open for the old man with his sack. Old Man Herschmidt stumped on through, holding his sack, and 'Bama holding the door with one swayedback buttock as if it were a usable appendage jerked his head at the bartender and made a motion as if writing on his cuff with a pencil, then pointed his finger at himself. Then he turned out and was gone, up the street.

"Hes not paying for all that!" Dave protested.

"Hes done done it," Hubie drawled wryly.

"Whats he do for a living?" Dave asked, looking after him.

"He gambles," Dewey grinned.

"Is that all?"

"Thats enough. If you gamble like he gambles," Hubie said.

"Hes pretty good," Dave said.

"Good enough to make a lot of money around here. When he works," Dewey said. "But half of what he wins he donates to the bookies in Terre Haute or Evansville or Indianapolis."

"The rest he spends," Hubie drawled.

"Hes a hell of a pool player," Dewey said. "Makes a lot, that way. Ats where hes goin now."

"Has he got a name? Ive never heard anybody call him anything but 'Bama," Dave said.

Dewey grinned boyishly and his incredibly handsome blue eyes shaded by the long silky lashes lit up with relish. "His name is William Howard Taft Dillert. He was born in 1912."

"But you dont never want to call him that," Hubie grinned. "Specially Howard. Thats what his mother calls him."

"See, theyre from down around Florence Alabama," Dewey grinned. "Thats why the nickname. His sister use to work in a plant in Birmingham as a lab technician and took the family there. Then she moved up here to Parkman to work for Sternutol Chemical and brought them here. Now the other brother works for Sternutol, too. 'Bama came along with him for a visit and just stayed."

"They dont much like it either," Hubie said. "That was ten years ago. I dont bet theres fifteen people in town knows what his real name is. Countin' his family. Dewey just happen to go up the same day he did to register for the draft, is how he found out."

"He hates that name like poison," Dewey grinned.

"Dillert's a good old Southern name," Dave said.

"Yeah, but William Howard Taft isnt," Dewey said. "'Bama says his old lady sure wouldve done him a big favor if shed only waited six months to have him."

"Yeah, at least Woodrow Wilson was a good Democrat," Hubie said.

Dave laughed. It was the first good laugh real laugh hed had all day since he came back to this place, and it was a short one. And immediately it had stopped he abruptly felt exhausted, depleted, completely empty. He felt as though if it hadnt stopped he might go on laughing and laughing until it turned into crying hysterics. The kind where you lie on the floor weeping and listening to yourself and wondering why. Thinking about it now, he felt it bubbling up in him, like that, and he choked it off.

"Well, Ive got to go," he said. "Got to get back to the hotel and get cleaned up to go out to Frank's tonight. You tell 'Bama thanks for all that beer and stuff."

"We see you down at Smitty's later," Dewey said. He looked at his watch. "My girl'll be gettin off at the brassiere factory before long. Were gonna meet her here." He grinned with the long lashes and boyish eyes. "She gets two weeks pay today."

"Yes," Dave said vaguely, "sure." He nodded and got up and went toward the door. He felt too full of beer, and he was hungry for food again already. But he couldnt stay here and eat it. He had to get out.

He went out and turned the other way from 'Bama, down the hill away from the square toward the hotel. He had to get cleaned up to go to Frank's. It was still dribbling its spit of snow, and this surprised him.

He thought that had been a long time ago. Before all this life had started coming rushing back at him, from all sides, zeroing on him, like a man standing in the middle of a maze of railroad junctions, trains shooting at him from first this side and then that side, whistling past, and the blinding lights, and the smell of coal smoke and vitality.

CHAPTER 4

THE *streets were almost deserted. Not busy at all.*

It was strange he didnt remember the day the old man left or the day he returned but it didnt work like that. It worked like this: one day they discovered he was missing but they didnt know how long he had been missing it might have been four days or one because sometimes when he got drunk enough he didnt come home and just slept at the shop the welding shop which was really a converted shack of a garage and when he did they never bothered him there and left him alone though sometimes the fire went out on him and he would almost freeze but this was rare because it was rare for him to get drunk like that only once or twice a year maybe but still it was enough for them not to realize he was missing no letter no farewell note no good byes just suddenly began to realize he was missing; then they started living their lives without him being there; a long time later when they had about got used to it he suddenly reappeared in town they began to see him somewhere on a street or in a store silent irascible and morose finally they realized he was back to stay they never spoke to him and he never spoke to them.

Not for a long time anyway.

Of course by then they all knew the story. Their father had run off from Parkman with the wife of the family doctor and a large part of the doctor's savings. Five years later, Old Man Herschmidt came back. Minus the doctor's wife, minus the doctor's savings. He proceeded to settle down in Parkman again. He moved in on the other side of town and morosely went back to his welding, and he and his lawful wife never spoke to each other again. It was rumored in Parkman that the doctor's wife had forsaken him and expended the remainder of the doctor's savings upon becoming the mistress of Samuel Insul. No one ever knew though because Old Man Herschmidt he was already Old Man Herschmidt never said anything spoke one word about it; or her; or the doctor's savings.

Up to then they had been an ordinary family of an ordinary welder who did not get drunk over ordinarily much.

He remembered the night they finally realized he was missing. Frank called them all of them Francine the other three brothers Dave and himself all in while their mother remained alone in her bedroom they sat down around the kitchen table and Frank said we must never ever mention this to mother again we must never mention that name his name again even to ourselves he is dead he no longer exists we bury him by the Grace of God and our own ingenuity we will make out we will get along it will probably kill her and that was when Francine who was already an intellectual even then in high school said scornfully nuts! to both counts and Frank said all right its going to be embarrassing and whos going to be making the money? it looks like I am and you take it or leave it. Frank was then a senior in high school. So was Francine, since they were twins.

So they never mentioned it, or him, again even when he came back to town. Especially their mother never mentioned either and it was as if he really was dead, as if he really did no longer exist even when he did exist and they saw him on the street. It never seemed to bother him. Nothing did. He was already Old Man Herschmidt. The only time he was ever mentioned, or even referred to, that he could remember was when he himself was packing up and preparing to leave and Frank said less didactically and more ruefully than he would have five years ago Like father like son! Frank was then already married and his wife pregnant to the daughter of the man who owned the cheap notion-semi-jewelry store he worked for which he later developed with his own blood into exclusiveness and was already having his own girl friends on the side one of them the store's bookkeeper whom his wife's father now dead had slept with for years. Like father like son! he told him with some little ruefulness and gave him the five dollars.

The girl herself was a nice enough girl. A country girl. Who had filled out at thirteen and been bewildered by it since she discovered (probably by accident) that she liked sex when she hadnt ought to. The three of them, all seniors and all good buddies in each other's confidence, had been serving her night after night each with a good bit of friendliness among the four but her father with a farmer's necessary business acumen decided on him because Frank was a townman and owned a prosperous business, prosperous at least by the standards of New Lebanon, Dark Bend River farmers from down the bottom of the county which the other two seniors also were.

He himself had lost his own virginity in the eighth grade. And wasnt that about the time Frank had changed the family name? how did they know the old man would come back?

the eighth grade was also the year that Francine her sensitive nature no longer able to suffer the continuing embarrassment which Frank had warned of flounced out in a fury and left town on her own and began putting herself through teacher's college wasnt it?

God how it jumbled and tumbled out no continuity almost no con-
nection even How long had it been since hed thought about it? and
only those three main threads to give it any semblance of reason at all!

The old man was back of course by that time the time he left and he
had gone up by to see him on his way out of town but then he hadnt
had nerve enough to go in. So he stood outside and looked in through
the grimy window at the alien world figure in the dark glassed mask
holding the torch to the red welt of a weld on a model T chassis and
went away without either speaking or the couple of bucks he might have
been able to milk him for, not because he was afraid or hated to speak
to him he had spoken to him many times since he got back talked to him
even, but because he was embarrassed to be leaving town in disgrace.

His mother had said with her laboriously acquired religious sorrow,
only: you have sinned, son, sinned very bad, but God will forgive you
if you ask him to ask him ask God write me often youre my son. Funer-
ally.

Christ the things you think of Remember.

A year of acute physical discomfort with that carnival.

Another with circuses.

and no meaning no meaning anywhere

Except to work up from hammerhead to peewee gandy dancer. That
means assistant to a seller of cheap novelties, that does. Definition Amer
slang Thesaur section Carnival. More money for more broads. He
learned to short change fairly well. And of course he drew upon that
material later for those short stories.

the meaning of meaning

After that he traveled the South with a magazine subscription gang,
where his short changing ability immediately endeared him to the
heart of his boss, a lean hard hunch-shouldered little man from Ohio
who could not read but who had learned to tell apart the names of the
magazines, and who had an uncanny ability to pose as an awkward
embarrassed Bible student working his way through the nearest seminary
whatever name which was almost universally infallible with farm wives.
He quit after three weeks because he was no good, he made no money,
he did not eat, he could not convince himself that they ought to buy
magazines and hence could not possibly convince them, but he would
not confess this because he hated to admit to anyone, especially the
boss, that he was an abysmal failure at so simple a thing in which the
boss, an ignorant man who could not even read, succeeded so brilliantly.

Ha wonder what ever happened to Leach? George Leach?

Once, for a short period of comparative prosperity, he had dealt blackjack in a Kansas City game while he and a buddy worked a short con
game, usually the gold brick or a variation, for a few damn few bucks
on the side. But this did not last. He, who still had his morbid dislike

of being disliked, did not have the makings of a successful con man. He came out of it with a hundred bucks cash clear, this ambition to be a big gambler as distinguished from con man, and his ex buddy's undying disdain.

With this hundred, and two suitcases full of the meaning of meaningless or should I say the meaninglessness of meaninglessness? all right two suitcases full of clothes, he moved in on Sister Francine teaching high school English in Greater Los Angeles.

Ha wonder what ever happened to George Leach a talented man?

Ha wonder what ever happened to Sister Francine?

He had been there before. But this time, when he fell in love with an educated girl named Harriet Bowman who would not sleep with him, he moved there permanently.

All his life he had probably been horrified at the indifference the rest of the human race showed him. Even as a small boy, he was probably constantly being shocked at the way people went about their lives as if his existence meant nothing at all to them. Long before he ever fell in love, he would probably nevertheless still wake in terror in the middle of the night from the awareness that *no*body loved him enough to sacrifice everything for him, an experience probably usually reserved for lovers.

So when love came, man it was *really* something!

He did not know if he loved her because she was educated, or because she would not sleep with him; but he decided it was because she basically was such a wise, good, sweet, kind person; she could not even kill a moth but would catch it and carry it outside and let it loose. If he killed it, she would cry. It was his first great love He was deeply thrilled by the violence of his own emotions He had not believed himself capable of such violence of emotion He was glad to find out. He was also often discomfited. But he even enjoyed this too. When he was drafted in 1943, nine years later, she still would not sleep with him. Married.

She was, in fact, married, was she not? To a lawyer. A lawyer who did not belong to, and had not ever even been introduced to, Francine's circle.

because in order to be near her he himself had had to associate with Francine's circle of artist and intellectual friends, of which the educated girl Harriet Bowman was what you might say an inactive member. She was of the type who did not have to read, talk, or think, she just sat on her magnet and let it attract. She was graduating from UCLA in the spring, a psychology major. She sat in the middle of every gathering, contributing nothing, and knowing with a sure generationsold instinct that she did not have to, that the world was full of iron filings, and that everyone admired her for her brains. This was what he fell in love with. He was an iron filing. Ergo.

So, he associated. That was how he met George Blanca. How he met Kenny McKeean. How he started writing. And how he met that another guy: I dont remember Wally French Dennis said, who was now dead in the war.

Why remember? Trees to you, Joyce Kilmer, trees! Alan Seeger dead behind some disputed barricade. Do you know what my dog's favorite song is? He was getting bitter, really bitter. That was bad. Be glibly bitter, literarily bitter, bonmotly bitter. Okay. But dont be really bitter, dont do your thinking remembering really bitter. Thats no good. My, but the streets were deserted, werent they?

He remembered him as he was then. He believed her a virgin. And nothing would convince him otherwise, the then he insisted to the then himself stoutly; though no one had ever suggested she was not. But his ego just couldnt stand the thought that she had been slept with before and could still resist him so absolutely stoutly. It really became a sort of polemic argument with the then him, he remembered. And as far as she was concerned, he never resolved it.

Francine, who had given up prose for poetry, helped him write several poems to her (one of which he even liked well enough to keep) (still had it) which he read her. God, no one would ever know how he worked at that! When he discovered *Martin Eden* he read the entire book to her. He even descended to the level of explaining to her what she was missing out of life. It availed him nothing. She was as immovable as a rock. He suffered a profound amazement that anyone as wise, good, kind, and sweet as she, who could not kill a moth, could be so unwaveringly unkind, unfeeling, and rock hard about him and his agony. It was not as if she were uneducated. He just could not believe it. UCLA? He began to lose his faith in education. Once, he so lost control of himself that he abruptly asked her to marry him. He returned the next day intensely relieved that she only had smiled sweetly and sadly, and shaken her head without speaking.

The more she refused it him, the more he respected her integrity which, though he knew of course it was completely misled and in error, he held in great reverence and loved her the more for, while his nervous system screamed with a perpetual rage at her supreme self confidence that knew he would keep coming back.

Back up the street a car honked. A young girl squealed. And another young girl squealed back. High school must be out already.

He remembered it finally got to be a vague disquieting impression he carried with him all the time that nothing none of the actions none of the people was what you could actually call real neither Francine George Kenny and his death that another one none except himself and the educated girl Harriet Bowman who would not sleep with him and sometimes even she was not real and only his love for her was real.

Everything else, including the buildings and sidewalks, was tenuous and unreal. It was as if he talked to people and people talked to him he could see their mouths move but the words had no meaning no meaning of meaning when he reached out to touch them the people his hand seemed to go through them like fog but when he pulled it back it was not bloody he could not wake up he tried and tried sleep would not go away. He got really frightened. Then she got married and he did not see her any more, except once downtown in LA with a tall dark man he assumed to be her husband the promising young attorney. It was only a few years after that he was drafted.

It was the love of a life time, it. O A O

And of course all that time he was writing wasnt he? George Blanca helped him most, together with Francine, who was supporting all three of them but only sleeping with George. George also suffered from the fact that his existence meant nothing to people, and he had determined to avenge himself upon them by becoming a great writer. He had already published one novel which received good reviews but did not sell enough to support him and was working hard on another between attempts to get into the movie studios as a script writer in order to be financially free to write seriously. George came from El Paso, and claimed to be Creole French and Spanish of a family that had moved west from New Orleans. It was recorded so on his book jacket. In reality, he was a handsome composite of Italian and Mexican and came straight from the Paso yards. Like the rest of the circle he himself knew this about George but would nod seriously and sedately while George stared at him from his handsome face with torment haunted eyes and explained carefully to him his extraction another time. They got to be best buddies, probably because George also had an unrequited love (in addition to Francine) a Japanese waitress in a cheap beer lunch joint downtown in the skid row section. Apparently she would sleep with everybody but George, and he tried to explain to George that it was simply and solely because George so obviously wanted her so badly, and all George had to do was act like he did not care. But George could not do this. In fact he was no better at it than he himself was with the educated girl Harriet Bowman whom he unrequitedly loved, so he and George would go together to the proper places George knew and speak to the proper people, in order to get their discomfitures taken care of with Francine's money, and afterwards they would go to a joint and drink beer with the remainder of Francine's money while they consoled each other on their unrequitals in love, George's was the subject of his new novel the second one a Japanese girl, he read parts of it to Dave, Dave thought it was good, Francine thought it was good too.

And all the time he was writing writing writing writing for dear life he wrote a number of short stories and part of a novel he could not find the end for and sold several of the stories usually for around ten dollars to small West Coast reviews. One of them was about a man in a circus in love with an elephant but they would not let him marry her. It received such favorable comment around it gave him new determination. William Saroyan was reputed to have said he thought it remarkable and showed great promise. George and Francine were both proud of him. So was the educated girl Harriet Bowman, very proud but it did not change her indehiscence. Nevertheless he found the end and finished the first novel which was published and died and wrote more stories with a sense that they were changing somehow, a little, and started the second novel. This was about the time that George, his second novel about a Japanese girl in a cheap beer lunch joint out and not selling, got his first job with a major studio.

A strange man passed him on the wet street and said hello Dave. Hello he said. Somebodys tires swished on the wet brick rounding the corner.

That was really when it all started to go to hell, really. Kenny was dead of course. The another one: I dont remember, he had gone. Somewhere. Francine heard from him. Francine was a great letter writer. And then the educated girl Harriet Bowman got married. And after a while George had enough pull to get him a few jobs on Westerns he had some dollars now he even helped Francine out with the bills some. He finished the second novel just sort of on impetus. There was no elephants in it. It was about a West Coast ball player who could field but would never hit good enough to make the big leagues and his girl who was a successful starlet in a studded sky wanted to go back to New York and try and make a real break there and she left him. It was published. When the Army took him he was almost grateful.

and there it was

full circle

the meaning of the meaning

He went up to the Writers' Building to say goodbye to George. George looked very well since he had married his very beautiful, and very blonde, wife whose father owned about fifteen per cent of the smog down in Southgate. Just recently he had been working for De Mille since Young Jesse Lasky left him, on some of them Technicolor epics. Gee kid Im sorry George said things are going all right with me though but gee baby thats tough wish you had time to come out the house baby see the wife and kid most beauti-kid in the world Davebaby the little blond bastard and that pools only thing that keeps me lean but gee kid Im sorry to hear it youll look me up when you get back?

A cigar butt lay on the sidewalk in the wet just ahead of his moving feet. He kicked it off into the gutter. It looked unpleasant laying there wet.

Cigar George said take another hell take some more take a flock with you them aluminum containers keeps them fresh

even if they are too damn big

and Dave Hirsh, thats me, was grateful the Army took him. Why? He was even grateful for getting to be in the Battle of the Bulge as Infantry, Dave Hirsh was—after it was over. And getting the Combat Infantryman's Badge. But most of all he was grateful for getting to be the adopted father of the 3615th QM Gas Supply Company. Pop Hirsh. And maybe that was why Dave Hirsh, cynical combat veteran being discharged in Chicago, after a no longer counted number of drinks, began to imagine he believed these young tough smooth faced boys drinking with him who also called him Pop were them, those others, so that at 6 AM in the morning, carried on the shoulders of two of his stranger-friends and cheered on by the others, Dave Hirsh entered the Randolph Street Depot across from Marshall Field's and mounted his bus, slung his canvas furlough satchel up on the rack, and stepped to the open window to deliver them his farewell oration.

"Friends," he yelled at them, some tears of genuine love carefully hidden behind the sly levity of his eyes, "brothers in arms, compatriots! We have just finished winning for our people the greatest war of world history, and now we are preparing to pay for it. Men do not win wars without having to pay for it. Dont believe it! Thats propaganda! Thats indoctrination! . . . All I got to say to you, brothers, in this hour of great travail is—let us all go with God, to the arms of our loved ones and the beds of our sweethearts. And if they any 4Fs in those beds, kick them the hell *out!*"

He sat down, complacently bouncing a little, amid a volley of cheers from the small mob of uniforms on the pavement, while the laughing driver started the motor, and looking back down at them in the dimness of the station as the bus pulled out his throat choked on him, and he was doubly glad he had had the foresight to put his money into a bank draft, otherwise he would probly of made a full week of it and spent it all on them. God knew, they deserved it.

Was he back at the hotel already?

CHAPTER 5

FRANK HIRSH had had lunch with George Walters that day. George owned the men's apparel next door to the jewelry store. Usually they walked back from lunch together but today George had an appointment and so he walked back by himself, feeling good, perhaps even a little complacent. Certainly social embarrassment and his kid brother Dave were the two furthest thoughts from his mind.

What he was thinking was that they had had with Doc Cost a late good lunch, enjoyable, and that he had won the game of 14 ball theyd played to see whod pay, and that he did not have to be anywhere at any given time and did not even have to go back to the store at all if he didnt want because it was his store and he was the boss.

Winning the pool game was a silly thing to be proud of. As a matter of fact, he usually won it. He was a good pool player, a damned good one, and with his training in pool as a kid he ought to win it more often than the other guys although George was pretty good and getting better. But it always made him feel good when he won it.

Of course, it worked both ways. When he lost it depressed him. Day before yesterday, one of the few days he lost, he had existed in a foul depression all afternoon which he found himself trying to blame on the weather.

Frank knew what it was, of course. It wasnt just pool. He just happened to have a stronger competitive instinct than the average man. He had a fetish about winning because he had been competing for things with people all his life. He had had to have it it was the only way he had of getting what he got. He didnt have any rich relatives to leave it to him, like certain people he knew. He was aware that certain people looked down their nose at Frank Hirsh's strong sense of competition, but he noticed they were always successful people who had already got their heads in the trough. The others didnt.

As he walked along, luxuriously aware of the raglan shouldered camel's hair top coat and dark Dobbs winter hat he was wearing, several people spoke to him on the street and in his complacent mood he took their perfunctory greetings as recognition of the universal respect he Frank Hirsh enjoyed in Parkman.

And when he did that a sudden strong emotional apprehension of the town hit him hard in the stomach with the things he saw. The familiarity of the old brick courthouse in the treeless square, the look of the wet dirty old hand laid brick streets badly in need of repairs since before the war, the for him peculiarly unique street lamps like no others in the world. He looked at the blocks of store fronts each with its date of erection and the erector's name. PARKER BLOCK—1907 and McGEE BLOCK—1904 and WAYNE BLOCK—1899 and WERNZ BLOCK—1900 and on and on not forgetting Anton III's WERNZ BLOCK—1925, he thought with a smug grin. The Second National Bank.

It was his town, and he loved it. He knew every street of it. And every house on those streets and usually the antecedents of most of the occupants. He had lived in it all his life, and he wouldnt live anywhere else. He didnt even enjoy a vacation particularly, except to come back.

And he still had to have it, he thought suddenly, the competitive sense. Unless he meant to stop his life with one jewelry store, and then just sit there in it till he died. Someday well, there was no HIRSH BLOCK, was there? If he had the money he would like to buy one of these already too old business blocks and tear it down and build a new modernistic one and so inscribe it. It was one of Frank's dreams. The HIRSH BLOCK—1949 or 1950 named for the boy who had worked nights in a poolroom all four years of high school, and paid for his single year of college by playing pea pool.

He didnt have that kind of money, yet. The war had been good to him, as it had to most businessmen, and it had raised him from a simple owner of a jewelry store to where he owned investments in more than one money making local thing, but it still hadnt given him that kind of money. It had given him the means to get it, though.

—Short, blocky, neckless, and ball headed like his brothers, all of them plainly German Dutchmen, and all built as exactly alike as peas in pods, so that anyone in Parkman could tell him, from as far as they could see him, as one of the five Hirsh boys, he strolled along back to his store, thinking of his dream.

There were several customers in the store, most of them country people, and Frank nodded to them benignly, feeling a sort of paternal warmth for them shopping in his store. Al Lowe was already back from lunch and helping the new girlclerk wait on them.

Since hiring Al six months ago and breaking him in to sell Frank himself had almost ceased waiting on customers except on rare occasions when he just felt like it. It gave him a good feeling not to. Al was going to make him a good manager for this store someday, when he started branching out; young, personable, willing, still inexperienced but learning fast, almost too eager, but time would fix that.

The girl of course was green, thick waisted and unable to talk like all girls from the country who come into town always are, she would never be any more than just a clerk, but she would make him a good one of those in time.—unless her boy friend came home from Japan and married her out from under him.

He had a good crew, all three of them, Frank thought complacently as he went on through the showroom and started across the long store-room behind it to the little half glassed half paneled office at the very back where his office girl sat working at her desk.

Al Lowe, coming quickly from up front behind him, caught him half way across the storeroom.

"Frank, Tom Alexander's wife is here for that new watch we ordered for her."

"Whats the matter, aint it come in yet?" He walked on back toward the office, Al following, shame faced.

"Well, thats it. Theres been a mixup on that, Frank. I knew it ought to be in by now, so I checked on it thinking somebody might of put it away. Theres no record on it being ordered, Frank."

"Oh-oh. Thats bad."

"I know it," Al said dismally. He was very upset. He said, "I made the sale myself. I know I made out an order slip on it." He went on talking as they reached the office door.

The girl looked up from her desk smiling, then saw Frank was busy and went back to work without speaking. Usually, she would say something friendly when he came from lunch, like Hello, Mr Hirsh; and then ask him how the pool game had gone, and if hed won congratulate him and if hed lost commiserate, all sort of half bantering and friendly. But respectful. And Frank found he sort of looked forward to the exchange.

He listened to Al politely as he hung up the camel's hair coat and Dobbs hat carefully. It was not a very major crisis. On the other hand it wasnt good policy to go around losing orders either. Made the store look bad. But it irritated him that Al hadnt gone ahead and handled it by himself, without mentioning it to his boss. That was what a smart man would have done. That was what he Frank would have done. What the boss didnt know never hurt him. But Al had brought it to him wanting to be told something, to be reassured probably, or else wanting to be chastened. Over his rising irritation, Frank kept his voice patient.

"Al, you know a business cant be run sloppy that way, not and have customers. Thats one of the main things Ive tried to—" he hunted for the right word.

"Instill?" Al suggested.

Frank nodded. "—instill in everybody in this store. Efficiency," he said. "Service."

Al nodded wretchedly.

"Well, make out another order slip in duplicate and date it back and show her the carbon of it. Thatll prove youre not lyin' when you tell her you dont know whats holdin' it up but that we'll put a letter on it today. That ought to fix it."

Al looked at him admiringly. "I thought of that," he said; "but I wasnt sure I ought to do that."

"What else could you do?" Frank said patiently. "Tell her the truth? that we lost it? You want people to think we run our store sloppy that way?" Sometimes he despaired of Al ever learning anything about business. "Now you go get that duplicate fixed up. And remember that, if the same thing ever comes up again."

After he had gone nodding happily, Frank got a pack of Luckies out of the catch all drawer of his desk and lit one and leaned back in the Mission oak swivel chair. Well, that little crisis was taken care of. He did not doubt that Tom Alexander's wife would disbelieve every word Al told her and go away and talk about the store, but he didnt care. If

he had wanted Tom Alexander's wife to believe it, he would have talked
to Tom Alexander's wife himself (she would probably have gone away
and talked about the store anyway) it was good training for Al that was
what was important. Frank suddenly felt a great fatherliness for Al
whom he had taken out of the local Sternutol Chemical plant as a
laborer. It was hard to believe sometimes the kid was thirty-two years
old; or that he had just spent four years as a Combat Infantryman.

Well, he owed it to Al Lowe to train him. Simply because of Al's
wife, if for no other reason. He remembered suddenly that Geneve
had not called him for quite a while now, then shrugged it off and forgot
it. But—curiously—he was getting to think a lot of Al himself. He was
a good boy. His main trouble was he was too goddamned open hearted—
and open faced. Of course, this whole thing might not have been Al's fault.

"You know anything about that misplaced order, Edith?" he asked
the girl leisurely, still studying the ceiling.

"No sir, Mr Hirsh," the girl said crisply.

She was a young local girl of twenty-three or -four, just out of the
business college at Terre Haute, with bright lipstick and fingernails
and competent eyes in an attractively uneven face, laconic, trenchant,
and efficient, and with a lithe independent swing to her shoulders when
she walked that she must have practiced a long time, Frank thought,
before it became so natural and attractive.

"Well, maybe we can get on with those letters then," Frank said
indulgently, swinging back up level, "if theres no more other little things
around here for me to take care of."

"Yes, sir," Edith said, and left the adding machine to get her notebook.
Frank did not doubt she had told him the truth, as he started to dictate.
He was her first boss, and she had been with him almost a year, and her
professional loyalty was fiercely and unquestionably his. That was what
came of taking your help from the bottom, from the laboring class, and
raising them a step into the white collar. You got their undying devotion. Edith's father John Barclay worked for the Sternutol too like Al had.

—Feeling a little smug over this evidence of his cleverness, and looking forward to the pleasant animal security of a winter's afternoon of
easy work with the lights and heat turned on against the dimness and
the chill outside, Frank settled down into dictating the letters which
didnt actually need to be dictated because Edith knew the form as well
as he did, but which he nevertheless always liked to do himself one by
one because it made him feel educated.

That was when the first phone call came. With the news of Dave's
arrival.

"Just a minute, theres the phone," Edith Barclay had said and swung
around in her chair to answer it. "For you, Mr Hirsh."

Frank had taken it nodding, being careful not to let his hand touch hers as he took the phone from the slender manicured fingers. He always did that with his female help. He took no chances, he was too big a man any more to either have to or to allow himself to fool with the help, like it had used to be.

And she was a good looking girl. "Hello?" he said and immediately the afternoon changed. From a low geared slow rolling rhythm like a truck on a long grade it leaped without warning into the hectic churn and jugglery of a motorcycle hill climb. And it stayed that way.

This was the first of the friendly calls he would be getting the rest of the afternoon. The caller did not try to conceal his malice. At first Frank could not think who it was about. He had not thought about Dave, except vaguely, since Francine had written him Dave was being shipped overseas. Dave who. Your brother Dave. Oh Dave. He selected quickly the least embarrassing and at the same time least disprovable lie he could tell and stick by. He let on he knew all about it and had invited Dave himself. Everyone in Parkman would know this was not true, but the only way they could prove it would be ask Dave pointblank and none of them would venture that.

With the small remaining part of his mind not shocked to a standstill, he noted that he must have carried it off, at least partially, because the caller sounded a little piqued when he hung up.

Nevertheless, it did not put him at ease, or relieve him, or free him from a sudden vague feeling of fear and embarrassment. It was as if he were suddenly all at once endangered with the public exposure of secret shameful acts of his which, if asked, he could not have named. The effect upon Frank, as he put the phone back on its cradle and leaned back to consider, was the same as if a band of vigilantes or Kluxers had seized him and stripped him naked and tied him to a lamp post in the square for all to come and look at titteringly.

Edith, who evidently hadnt even been listening, was waiting with her head down and pencil poised for him to go on. She had a very pretty neck, he thought, bent as it was under the soft dark hair. When he didnt go on dictating, she looked up.

"You can handle the rest of those yourself, cant you, Edith?" he said heavily.

"Sure; of course," she said. "Is something wrong, Mr Hirsh?"

"No," Frank said.

"You arent sick, are you?"

"Its my liver," Frank said absently.

"Do you want me to call Doc Cost?"

Frank smothered an intense desire to swing on her angry eyed and cuss the hell out of her. He said instead:

"No. Edith, you go ahead with the letters. I got some other things to do." and got up and went out into the storeroom to get away from her solicitude. He had to think. The first thing was to figure out why Dave hadnt called him. He evidently must have something up his sleeve.

As if in answer, the phone in the office rang again.

"Mr Hirsh? Its for you?" Edith sounded faintly disapproving, as if she thought in his condition he ought not to answer.

Frank went back into the office. His mind was going so hard he hadnt even had time to think of getting mad.

"Its the judge, Mr Hirsh," Edith whispered, her hand over the mouthpiece. Frank felt another surge of anger, which he also smothered, that she should have tried to imply by her tone of voice that he ought not to answer. The judge was Steve Deacon. But in Parkman no one called him that, it was always the judge. He had served a term on the county bench in his youth. The judge was Chairman of the Board of the Cray County Bank, of which Frank was a member, the most recent member. The judge was also principal stockholder in the Parkman Building & Loan, into which Frank had at his suggestion recently bought himself with a substantial number of voting shares. Did she think he should refuse to answer a call from the judge? he thought angrily, wondering what the judge wanted.

Sitting up in the dim dirty Deacon & Deacon Law offices across the square over the Kroger store, breathing hard through his deep unhealthy fat and wheezing phlegmily and scornfully into the phone, Judge Deacon did not let him wonder long.

"You know your worthless brother's back in town?"

"So I just been told," Frank said wryly. "Twice."

The judge did not laugh. He had a one track mind and humor rarely affected him unless it was dirty. "You know he just deposited $5500 in the Second National Bank?"

"No," Frank said in a small voice. "I sure didnt know that."

"Well you know it now," the judge said witheringly.

Frank felt the dart prick open a small wound of vanity, in spite of his upset. He tried to ignore it. He was getting valuable information. The judge had never been one, even before he retired from practice to take over the Cray County Bank, and other interests, to be especially careful of others' feelings. He always said he didnt have to if he had the money. But he neednt get snotty with me, he thought angrily.

"I guess that makes us look kind of foolish," he said.

"It wont kill us," the judge wheezed, "I dont reckon. It dont make us look good. You never seen any my relatives doin' something like that." This was, Frank reflected, quite true; the judge, as the eldest and only brother of eight sisters and numerous cousins throughout the county, directed all of their estates. That was part, a substantial part, of his other interests.

"Your relatives live here," Frank said. "Where you can keep a tab on them. Also, they are more or less sane."

"Not so sane," the judge snorted. "Like to see you try to handle them."

"Well, I appreciate you callin' and tellin' me, anyway. I didnt even know he was here till just now. He hasnt called me."

"I didnt call you for you to appreciate it," the judge said scathingly. "I called you to put you wise. Somebody better get ahold of that boy and teach him some common sense."

"You got any suggestions who?" Frank said.

"Well, youre his brother. And head of the fam'ly."

"I been tryin' to teach him common sense for thirty-five years," Frank said.

"Try, hell," the judge said; "well, try harder. And also, Ned Robertsll probly be callin' you up before long, I would reckon. So be prepared. Its a good thing for us I got to you first, aint it?" he wound up with grinding scorn, and hung up before Frank could answer. The judge was never much of a one for amenities, either.

Frank replaced his own phone, feeling more angry at the judge's blunt incivility than grateful for the information hed given him. It was all right to be individual, but he didnt have to run it into the ground. Irately, he wondered where in hell Dave had ever managed to get $5500 together at one time. That was not the Dave he remembered.

The judge was a mighty good man to have on your side in a business deal, but you sure couldnt say it was exactly pleasant to work with him.

Edith Barclay had her head down working at her desk. But it was plain from the very set of her head that shed been listening hard.

"Well," he said irritably, "did you learn all about it?"

"No, sir," Edith said calmly, and went on working. "I hope it isnt any bad trouble."

Frank stared at her, angrily wanting to say something cutting, but she was just too good a help to get her mad at you. "If any more calls come in for me," he said stolidly, "I want to talk to all of them. No matter how many, or who it is."

Well, he knew now what it was Dave had had up his sleeve.

"Im going up front," he lied. He wasnt going up front, he was going back out into the storeroom. He wanted to think this thing out, and the dimness and quiet there ought to be reassuring.

"Yes, sir," Edith said quietly.

But the storeroom wasnt helpful. The crusty old watch repairman in his cubicle workshop did not look up; and his nose, which he never raised for anything unless a woman went by, was stuck down in a watch as if he were trying to smell its trouble; and yet he managed somehow to make himself strongly felt as a presence. He always did that. Frank went back into the office.

Edith, with the sure sensitivity to her boss of a private secretary, did not even look up from her work, and he sat down at his desk to think it out. If he had been at home, or by himself in the office with the girl gone, he would have turned on the radio. He would not have listened to it, but the presence of the sounds of talking voices would have helped him think.

Frank's attitude toward the youngest of his brothers had always been one of indignant disbelief. You could not run over customs and usages the way that boy thought he could. Not if you wanted to live with people. The indignation was coupled with a contempt for the boy's complete inability to do anything and a kind of awed pride because Dave had turned out to be an artist, a writer. Frank did not read a book a year and said it was because he was too busy making a living, but the truth was books frightened him. He would never learn to read them easily. It did not help any that his wife Agnes, who was literary minded, was able to read into books a spiritual, religious and intellectual significance that he himself could never find there, and felt ignorant because of. So secretly he was proud to have an artist, a writer, in the family because he did not count Francine. But he also felt Dave ought to make a little money at it. Otherwise what was the point? Besides, that would at least prove it to Agnes, who had absolutely no use for Dave. This dabbling in the arts stuff was all right for women who had husbands to support them and nothing better to do with their time, he didnt begrudge Agnes her art. But a grown man had to support himself. Or else suffer the ridicule of his associates. He had written as much to Sister Francine, who all during Dave's years in Hollywood had kept him posted on Dave's development; Francine had immediately written back defending Dave with fire, and the statement that there was no place for the creative artist in America. Frank was willing to concede that this might be true, though he did not see why it should be true in America and not in other places. He had followed Dave's career closely, a lot more closely than anyone knew, except possibly Francine, and he had carefully read all the stories and both books when she sent them, and he couldnt see where there was much sense in any of them, no wonder people didnt buy them. For instance, who the hell ever heard of a man falling in love with an elephant? And yet the publishers in New York took them. The only thing of it all that touched him any, was that second book about the ball player and its main effect was surprise that Dave knew that much about baseball. Frank would never have suspected it. But then, back not long before the war, Francine had written with malicious triumph to say that Dave was working on some movie scripts and as proof listed the titles. Frank, who was no movie-goer and had only the vaguest ideas of Hollywood, went to see every one of them religiously. He had never given up hope of bayoneting the inflated bladder of Dave's scandal, for his own sake if Dave didnt care or give a damn. Once more, he was disappointed. All of them were Westerns but two, those two were light comedies, all of them were bad movies, horribly bad, atrocious, even he could tell that, and in addition he did not find Dave's name mentioned anywhere in any of them. Luckily, just luckily, he had not told anybody else about the list, not even Agnes. He had no choice but to conclude Francine had been lying, and he wrote her so. He got no answer at all. Nevertheless later on he had been glad when Francine, after her long and injured silence, had written worriedly to tell him Dave was being inducted and asked if he couldnt do something about it. He was glad to hear about Dave, and he was glad about the Army. He felt the Army might be damned good for Dave. He sincerely doubted if it would and yet he still could not give up hope that something good might come of it.

Well, evidently it hadnt.

Now obviously, Dave's reason for not calling him was because Dave knew the news of the deposit would reach him. One way or another. Almost as soon as it was made. That could only mean he was out to make trouble.

It left two alternatives: either Dave would call him later, or he wouldnt call at all. With a sure swift instinct that amounted almost to instantaneous intuition, sitting at his desk in his office, he felt out and reconstructed Dave's plan. Dave intended to call him later. He knew it. Probably the idea was to let him sweat a while over the deposit. And if this was true, and Frank knew it was true, by some sure subconscious method (its what you wouldve done, aint it?) then his countermove was to call Dave first. Catch him off his guard. Dave would expect him to be angry. So he would not be angry. He would invite Dave out to the house for dinner.

Then we'll see what happens.

Finding his eyes staring at the back of Edith Barclay's prettily bent neck and feeling not much better over what hed just worked out he sat back up and reached his hand out for the phone when suddenly another aspect hit him which he had not thought about Oh Jesus Christ the Old Man son of a bitch.

It was a very lovely neck, half of his mind was thinking, especially bent over low like that. The two cords or tendons or whatever they were that ran up to the base of the skull stood out in high relief, yet mellowly, making very feminine very fragile very kissable hollows. For some young guy to enjoy, the half of his mind added quickly.

Yes the Old Man. It was a subject he very rarely allowed there. Even when they met on the street or in the poolroom, and spoke he coldly the old man irascibly, as often happened. He had trained his mind to ignore it all completely all of it the handicap to his reputation the perpetual drawback to surmount in the town the constant affront to himself. This old bastard who was too old to weld any more, so now he lived on the old age pension, in a room in one of those homes for pensioners that middle aged widows without incomes were starting all over, $30.00 a month! that got him his room and board in the home, and his liquor he had to scrounge for. But he seemed to do pretty god-damned well, because he never seemed to be sober. What was this going to do to that situation?

Dave's coming home would re-awaken all that old stuff about him and Doc Cost's first wife and the money and Samuel Insul, as well as Dave's own scandal. And himself had become one of Doc Cost's best friends! All that old mud and dirt stirred up from the bottom of the pool, and himself expecting to be elected Secretary of the Country Club at the annual meeting next spring.

Frank had offered him four times as much as his pension, if he would move clear out of the county. Up to Danville. Or over to Terre Haute. But the old son of a bitch refused to leave Parkman, just out of sheer cussedness, just as hed refused to drop the c and midt off his name and change e to i all these years, just so he could continue to wander up and down town and display himself unshaven unwashed and unsober a worthless poolroom drunken bum and listen to people say There goes Old Man Herschmidt Frank Hirsh's father and then cackle over it, the no good bastard.

No wonder Mother's life had been ruined and she had nothing but sadness and had become practically a recluse except for her Holiness Church friends.

He sat at his desk and thought about it, and burned. Burned help-lessly. With a furious eyed frustration of useless hatred that threatened to explode his whole head like a bomb.

What he should have done, obviously, was offered him the $120.00 a month if hed promise *not* to leave Parkman, then the old reprobate would have insisted on moving to Terre Haute.

Through the half glassed wall of the office cubicle beside his desk he saw Al Lowe bearing down on him excitedly across the storeroom. What now? he wondered with a muffled sigh, and ran his hand over his face in an effort to clear some of the congestion off it.

Al was bright eyed in the doorway. "Frank, Mrs Stevens and her daughter Virginia just came in. You know, the Stevens-Bookwright marriage."

Frank spoke with slow stolid patience:

"And why should I care if Mrs Stevens and her daughter Virginia come in any more than other people?"

"Well, the marriage," Al said. "Theyre looking at silver. Big wedding. You know the story. I thought youd want to know they came in?"

Frank did indeed know the story. More of it than Al knew. He was a friend of Arthur Bookwright's father who was Harold Bookwright the Sales Manager for The Sternutol Chemical Company's local marketing division. It was one of the biggest weddings Parkman would see in some years, and a triumphant tribute to the tenacity and ingenuity of Mrs T L Stevens.

During the war Virginia Stevens had been in love with a nameless Air Force Private from Arkansas whom she had met at Bloomington where she was finishing Indiana University. When she came home with her diploma and plans to marry him, Mrs Stevens who had not thought it was that serious leaped into the arena armed with the weapon that Virginia was too young to marry. She had checked the Arkansas Private's background and found there was none unless you wanted to call ten or twelve generations of sharecropping a background. She got Virginia to promise she would wait a year and date some other boys, and as a starter she had suggested Arthur Bookwright who lived a few doors down the street, since he was an old friend. Arthur was then attending West Point, where his father had got him appointed to keep him honorably out of the war, as Frank knew because Frank had helped Harold Bookwright plan it one night over the Country Club bar shortly after Pearl Harbor. Virginia and Arthur had played together since childhood but this was before Harold Bookwright got to be Sales Manager and was still working in Accounting; T L Stevens only ran the local Western Auto Store. So, to please and convince her mother of her maturity, Virginia dated Cadet Bookwright when he was home on leaves, and after the war Virginia went on dating Arthur, now a graduated 2nd/Lt attending an Army flying school somewhere in Texas. That removed one obstacle. The other obstacle was Mrs Bookwright. Mrs Bookwright was a married lady, too, and she possessed the same intensely realistic attitude and instincts Mrs Stevens had, that feminine intuition over which Frank and Harold Bookwright often had shaken their heads in awe and fear at the Country Club bar after seeing it in operation among the ladies. Both ladies seemed to know without ever having studied psychology that love per se was a definitive stage of biological development in the individual and as such, as easily forecastable to appear at a certain period as was pubic hair. While he was at West Point, Mrs Bookwright urged Arthur to associate with Generals' daughters, and when he was home on leave she tried always to have him in the presence of at least one daughter of a Sternutol Chemical executive. Arthur's time however came in Texas where he fell in love with a waitress in the PX. When this news reached Parkman, Mrs Stevens hastened across the street to commiserate with her dear friend Mrs Bookwright. Mrs Bookwright was no fool either. Between them the ladies cooked up a deal, the details of which were still as unknown in Parkman as was the method they had used to handle Arthur. But

Harold Bookwright while in his cups at the Country Club bar one night had told Frank confidentially that they were all more-or-less-sort-of-aware that Arthur had been sleeping with Virginia when he was home, ever since the latter West Point days and Mrs Stevens, Harold said, had them by the short hair because anything was better than a Texas PX waitress. Arthur had been led, or rather misled, to believe (without Virginia's knowledge of course) that he had gotten Virginia pregnant. This was the two ladies' deal.

Naturally Arthur had to do the honorable thing and would marry her. Harold was going to support them both while Arthur studied aeronautical engineering on the GI Bill after he graduated from flying school and resigned his commission.

Frank, who sympathized with Harold, and also valued Harold's friendship because of a couple business deals, had divulged none of this. Frank was a secret partner in the Parkman Dodge Agency, which thanks to Harold anyway partially thanks to Harold had sold Sternutol Chemical some replacement pickups for their old ones. Frank did not even tell his wife, although Agnes tried hard enough to pump him. Now he said to Al with the same slow patience:

"Al, T L Stevens runs the Western Auto Store. His daughter is marryin' up into the executive bracket of Sternutol Chemical. His wife aint goin' to pick her daughter's silver pattern, or her china pattern, here in Parkman. For the same reasons shes goin' to have a big wedding —if it takes T L two years to pay for it.

"And if they did pick a pattern in my store, or even one someplace else, that I carried, there wouldnt be enough money in it for us to even get excited because at least fifty per cent of the guests will be Sternutol people and such, from out of town, and will buy their presents someplace else."

"Well, it would be a big piece of prestige, not to mention advertising, if they did pick her patterns in our store, not to mention the extra money."

With his infuriatingly slow German patience Frank said:

"Sure it would. But they just wont, Al. Theyre just shoppin'. Hell, theyll go to Terre Haute, and Danville, maybe even to St Louis and Indianapolis, and probly wind up in Chicago at Marshall Field's; before theyre done." He got up from the desk and steered Al out into the storeroom.

"But Virginia just might happen to see one of our patterns she liked?" Al said.

"Virginia wont have a damn thing to say about it, Al."

Al nodded gravely. "You mean her motherll do all the picking. I guess thats right." His voice was quite calm now. Somehow, while theyd talked, Frank's stolid unwavering patience had gradually penetrated his excitement, bringing it down and down a bit at a time until now they were both talking in identical tones of indifference, Frank reaching up his hand on the tall Al's shoulder, rather like a small coach exhorting a large substitute he is about to send in. In fact it rather made Frank think of that, he felt very paternal.

In the office the phone rang.

"Mr Hirsh!" Edith Barclay called from the office door. "Telephone!"

The watch repairman, for the first time since noon, looked up from his bench. He looked at Edith standing in the door, and continued to look at her.

"Yes?" Frank said. "Who is it."

"Mr Roberts of the Second National," Edith said.

"Ill be right there," Frank said.

She went back in.

The watch repairman looked back down.

"Now you go on back up there," Frank said with his hand on Al's shoulder. "And be nice and polite, and show them everything they want to see. Just like you really thought they might take somethin'. We might sell them a good watch for T L for Christmas, later on."

Al nodded with a solemn patience and responsibility that mirrored Frank's voice. Frank stood a moment watching him go. Sometimes Frank wondered how Al had ever managed to survive four years of war as a Combat Infantryman. It seemed impossible. Yet he had. And had the ribbons and medals to prove it. Had even made Corporal. And yet he didnt show any more effects of it than if he had been away four years at the University of Illinois up in Champaign. Four years away from his wife had rolled off him like water off a duck's back. Frank did not think he himself could have stood that. If all veterans were as well adjusted as Al Lowe, there wouldnt be any veterans' problem. Al was thirty-two, Frank calculated, that was just about four years younger than Dave, wasnt it? He went on back to get the phone.

The watch repairman did not look up as he passed.

CHAPTER 6

FRANK, however, was not aware of the repairman this time because he was thinking about Al Lowe's wife. He did not allow himself to think about Geneve usually. But he was beginning to wonder why she hadnt called him. It was because of Geneve that he had hired Al for the store when Al who had had two years at Illinois was working as a laborer for the Sternutol after he got back from the Army. She had suggested him. It was one time when he was explaining to her some of his plans for expansion. And had sold him on it. He would never have thought of it. Geneve was twenty-nine, three years younger than Al, and looked a lot like a Vogue Magazine model, and smart. Those four years in the Army had rolled off her back too, Frank thought, feeling a little sly. She had worked at the Mode Shop across the square all during the war as a sort of head salesgirl and assistant buyer for Dotty Callter, and then had just kept on working there, she was a good girl, she and Al were pooling their incomes to save. She was a smart girl, too. He would never have thought of Al himself. She ought to be calling him again now in a few days, Frank calculated, it had been over a month since her last buying trip to Chicago for Dotty.

He stopped in the door of the office and looked at his watch, thinking he ought to call Dave right away, before the opportunity slipped. He would call him as soon as he got through with Ned Roberts, he thought, and became aware of the watch repairman and looked over at him. It might be a good idea to have a small radio put in the watch repairman's cubicle. Working by himself alone all day as he did. Be good for his morale. He could buy it and put it in some evening after closing so it would be there unobtrusively the next morning and show he was a good thoughtful employer. For that matter it wouldnt be a bad idea to have one up front for the clerks. Then the thought came into his mind suddenly from nowhere that he ought to go to church with Agnes when she went next Sunday. He hadnt been for a long time now. And it would please her. And it couldnt hurt anything. But then the very idea of having to sit for two hours in the midst of so many people who knew Dave was back and had deposited money in the Second National made him cringe inside.

He took the phone stolidly, and carefully, from Edith's hand. "Hello?"

"Hi, Frank," Ned Roberts' tenor voice said in his ear. "I just wanted to call and congratulate you on Dave's safe return from the wars, Frank."

"Well thanks Ned," he said. "Were real glad to have him back."

"I didnt even know he was in town until a half hour ago, Frank."

"Yes it was sort of sudden," he said. "We werent even sure he was goin' to be able to make it down here at all."

"He sent the clerk over from The Parkman to make a rather substantial deposit. That was how I found out he was here."

"You mean that fifty-five hundred," he said stolidly. "Yes, he asked me about that."

There was just a tiny, almost imperceptible, pause at the other end. But Frank did not go on. Let him hold the ball. The voice said, "I dont suppose he'll be staying long?"

"Well Ned we dont know. We're hopin' he'll decide to stay quite a while. After all, we havent seen him for a long time. But you know how Dave is."

"Ha ha ha yes quite a fellow but I understood the clerk to say he was staying at The Parkman?"

"Yes," he said. "I did that. You know how Agnes has been feelin' so damned poor lately. I just didnt feel like I ought to have him stay at the house. He understood that." It was an unturnable flank. Agnes had been feeling bad. She always was.

"Yes, thats right," the voice said. "Of course its better."

"Besides, shes been redecoratin' lately, you know," Frank said stolidly. "You know how women are with decoratin'. House always in an uproar. Everything messed up, and them ready to cry. Dave's comin' out the house for dinner tonight though, of course."

"Yeah, this decorating's rough," Ned Roberts' voice said sympathetically. His wife had just finished their living room. "Well, dont let her overwork herself doing it. We dont want her getting down bad-sick again."

"Im holding her down some," he said stolidly. "Much as I can. But you know how Agnes is."

"Yes, thats right. Always driving herself."

"Well, I got to get back, Ned. Some people out front."

"Yes," the voice said smugly, "Mrs Stevens was in a short while ago and said she and Virginia were going to stop by your place to look at silver. She said they were going over to Indianapolis to look tomorrow."

"Yes, so I understand," Frank said stolidly. "We never expected them to pick a silver pattern for a marriage like that in Parkman. Well thanks for callin', Ned."

"Forget it, Frank. Just wanted you to know how happy I was over Dave getting back safely."

"Yes. And thanks." He hung up and stood looking down at the phone too outraged too infuriated, to think rationally. Did he actually expect he was going to get me to admit anything? Get back safely! The war's been over almost two years. A hot flame of pure rage soared up through him, consuming Ned Roberts and his goddamned Second National, charring beyond all recognition the Stevens women with their monstrous gall to come in his store with no intention of buying, and continued on burning Parkman Illinois to the ground entire with all its environs like a conflagration, while he stood slack faced and thought-less, staring loosely.

Gradually he became aware of the girl who was not looking at him curiously from her desk but who might as well have been. Resisting an impulse to turn on his heel and go out in the storeroom, he sat down at his own desk and put an expression on his face. He had no mirror but it felt like it must look ghastly. He took it off and put on another which was no better. He was glad Edith still had not looked up. She was a good girl. *He* was the laughingstock of Parkman Illinois. He was also the brother of Dave Hirsh, Army veteran.

and, he decided, he was very likely to remain very publicly both until such time as something both public and embarrassing happened to somebody else and changed the focus of public attention.

and there was nothing he could do, now, about it. It was done. If Dave didnt even stay in town overnight, it would still serve to stir up all the old mud and dirt, and recall to everyone's mind that Frank Hirsh was the son of Old Man Herschmidt of Mrs Rugel's pensioners' home. He wondered how the judge had found out about the deposit, that had sure been a godsend. But he knew hed never find out, not from the judge anyway.

It was so bad, really, that he could almost afford to feel hopeful because it could not possibly get any worse. Who knew? $5500 was a lot of money for a discharged soldier to be throwing around recklessly. He might be able to talk him into investing it, before he threw it away. If he Frank had had that much unattached capital to invest when he started out God only knew what hed be worth today. Of course money was worth a lot more then. But the inflation was going to get worse. And $5500 invested now in 1947 would count for as much as $10,000 by 1950. If he turned Dave's money over once for him and then matched it with an equal amount of his own theyd have enough to incorporate as an investment firm. Hirsh & Hirsh, Inc. Wouldnt that make the judge's neck rigid! If this new factory came in, and a man could find out just where the new highway bypass was going to be laid, Christ thered be plenty of opportunities for good investment in this town, you couldnt have enough capital. Maybe Hirsh Bros, Inc would be better. Why there was no limit to what they might do. It would sure break it off in the judge. —Frank's mind went on by itself, without Frank this time, building empires of wealth and honor and fame that did not include the judge, creating between brothers and partners a great love and friendship and loyalty where there was none, and amassing respect until it weighed more than a mountain and displaced as much space, all out of Dave's measly $5500.

Then the balloon burst, overinflated by his own treacherous breath, leaving him with his mouth dangling the shreds of rubber that had exploded in his face and staring off at the wall across the space that a moment before had been a solid opaque bubble.

His own violated sense of reality told him it was an impossibility. Not because he couldnt have done that for Dave he could have but because Dave wouldnt let him do that. What dumbfounded Frank was that he should even have tried to imagine it.

Al Lowe was standing agitatedly in the office doorway.

"Yes, Al," he said patiently. "What is it." Still, it was nevertheless an idea to consider.

"Mrs Stevens wants to see you," Al said, emphasizing the last word.

"Ive shown her every piece of silver weve got in the store. Now she wants to see you."

Frank sighed. Must have been sitting here quite a while. "Okay," he said stolidly. "Ill be right there." He got up and followed Al out into the storeroom.

Al turned around. "I tried everything I could, Frank," he said, his voice agitated. "I ran up and down and showed her everything she asked for and a lot that she didnt and I was as nice and polite and she just stood there. Kept looking and looking and staying and staying. Then she asked to see you."

"Thats all right," Frank said. "She didnt ask for me because shes dissatisfied with your service." He put his hand gently on Al's back and started him toward the front. "This is her big day, and she wants to take advantage of it."

Al went a few steps, and then stopped and turned again. This time his eyes were big with sympathy, and his voice had that lugubrious quality of a man trying to console a friend on the death of a dear one:

"I just heard, Frank. Mrs Stevens told me."

"Mrs Stevens?"

"Yes. She must have picked it up at the bank."

"Picked up what."

"About Dave," Al said. He looked as if he would have liked to say he was sorry, but could not be sure this was proper. Unlike Edith Barclay, Al Lowe was not too young to remember Dave Hirsh.

"Oh." Frank rubbed his hand over his face thoughtfully. Then he said:

"You were in high school with him, werent you?"

"No. He graduated—" Al said. "He left—" He tried once more, with an indirection. "I was in the eighth grade when he was a senior."

"Thats right," Frank said, "you were younger." He thought some, and then said: "I havent seen Dave for nineteen years. Hes probably changed some." He put his hand on Al's back again. "Lets get on up there."

"Okay," Al said. "I wonder why he put his money in the Second National?"

Frank stopped and looked at him. "She tell you that too?"

Al nodded.

"Because he wanted to save it, I reckon," Frank said, and put his hand back on Al's back. "Better get on up there."

"I can tell her youre busy if you want?" Al offered.

"No. The customer is always right. And anyway shed know better. You go ahead of me though, and Ill wait a minute. Dont want to look—" he hunted for the correct word.

"Solicitous?" Al suggested.

"Thats it," Frank said. "You go ahead. I got to make a phone call anyway," he said, and went back into the office and picked up the phone and called the hotel for Dave. Two things: dont get mad, and invite him to dinner.

Edith listened to this conversation too, her head tilted stiffly, but working away and not looking up. After he hung up, feeling a little better, it was the best he could do under the circumstances anyway, Frank looked at her thoughtfully for a moment and turned on his heel to go up front.

When you came up from the office, the front, the display room was separated from the storeroom by an ancient near-to-ceiling-high cupboard with glass doors above and a shallow counter top. Similar cupboards lined the two side walls and glass cases were fixed to the floor around the three sides with a walkway behind them, encroaching upon the floor space still further. The fourth side of course was the two big display windows with the door between them, and a widening entryway that ran out to the sidewalk. The huge wall safe. Two filing cabinets. The even more ancient roll top desk fixed up as a work bench where Frank had once used to do minor repairs and adjustments on watches and which Al Lowe now used. The stock of silverware, flatware and hollow, the china, figurines, timepieces, jewels; fountain pens, lighters, cuff links, toilet articles; some of it expensive and some of it cheap; was distributed around in the glass cases and the glassed in shelves of the cupboards. A simple square cornered U of enticement facing the door. That was all.

This was Frank's jewelry store the heart of it familiar to him as the operating room to the surgeon and, he often thought, he was just as sentimental about it and its social service and as cold blooded about the money it made.

Anyway he never failed to get a small prickle of pride when he walked into it as well as a slight sense of astonishment that he should be in the jewelry business, instead of some other.

It wasnt much. Except for its stock, there was almost nothing to distinguish the place itself from almost any other store on the square. He had inherited both the furnishings and their arrangement from the tenant before him, who had been a druggist but who might as well have been a haberdasher or grocer, who had likewise inherited it, but Frank had had it so long now that it would have been a constant source of annoyance to everyone in Parkman if it had been changed to anything but a jewelry store. Ever since getting it he had intended to do it all over (with Agnes' redecorating help) in modernistic style, but had never felt quite flush enough to lay out the dough, even as the druggist before him, although he always had dough for some other project, so the store remained, comfortably dingy and undistinguished, like an abused old friend who can always be abused because he is an old friend, but a stranger in town would have been hard put to find anything at all individual about it.

In this familiarity, then, stood Mrs Stevens and her about-to-be-married daughter Virginia, surrounded by silverware place settings strewn up and down the glass cases, their coats lying on the counter, and only one of them talking to Al, as Frank came up.

"Hello, Mrs Stevens?" he smiled. "And Virginia. How are you."

Al moved back out of the way.

"We werent really meaning to select anything definite today, Frank," Mrs Stevens, who plainly had no intention of giving up all this pleasure in one afternoon, told him coquettishly and immediately. "We were just looking, weren't we, Virginia."

"Yes," Virginia said levelly.

"Thats quite all right," Frank said. "Look all you want. Make yourselves right at home."

"We did want to see what you had," Mrs Stevens said. "As I told Virginia, if its available in Parkman, Frank Hirsh will have it. But we didnt want to bother you. Did we, Virginia."

"No," Virginia said quietly.

"You didnt bother me," Frank protested. "Thats what Im here for. I was sittin' back in the office bored to death." He turned to the girl. "I havent had a chance to offer my best wishes yet, Virginia."

"Thank you, Mr Hirsh," she said in that same level, quiet and peculiar tone—as if she were concentrating hard on producing every word and gesture required of her, and jealously intent upon not showing one thing more.

"You dont carry the Towle line, do you, Frank?" Mrs Stevens asked.

"No, I sure dont, Mrs Stevens."

Al had waited a minute, like Frank had taught him, and then moved off to wait on some of the other customers.

"We were interested in seeing some Towle," Mrs Stevens said.

"Well now if its Towle youre interested in," Frank said, "old Simon Clatfelter across the square carries Towle, Mrs Stevens. I be glad to call him up for you?"

"Simon Clatfelter?" Mrs Stevens murmured. "He carries Towle?"

"Yes; fact is, thats one of the reasons I havent been able to stock it. Towle feels the town's too small for two dealers."

"I had supposed only the really big stores in the cities carried Towle," Mrs Stevens said.

"No, as a matter of fact, Mrs Stevens," Frank said pleasantly, "they carry quite a few dealers in small towns. Towle's a very particular, very fussy old fashioned outfit though, you know. And I think old Simon's grandfather started theirs; years ago; when he first started the store. It was the best store in Parkman then, you know. Id be glad to call Simon for you, if youd like to see what he has in it?" he offered.

"Oh no," Mrs Stevens said. "Not today. Im afraid its too late today."

"Well Ive got a leaflet of Towle patterns around here someplace, if youd like to look at it."

"Oh no," Mrs Stevens said and looked at her watch. "Well yes. Perhaps for just a minute. If it wouldnt be too much trouble?" she said sweetly.

"Why no trouble at all," Frank said. "I picked it up at the Chicago Gift show last fall, when I was hopin' to get Towle in. Ill get it for you." He turned around to a drawer.

"Well. All right. Yes, that would be nice," she said. "Well just glance at it. Dont you think that would be nice, Virginia."

Virginia appeared to be lost in some bitter (or sweet, Frank suddenly thought) reminiscence or dream of her own. "Yes, that would be nice," she said levelly.

"Here we are," Frank said, and spread it out on the counter. Covertly, he looked Virginia over. She was a rather attractive, wide hipped girl. Slender but widely hipped. He did not remember having seen her since she started at Indiana. It was funny how little girls you had known all their lives and paid no attention to suddenly became big girls with wide hips and you noticed them. Virginia didnt look too awfully hepped up about her forthcoming marriage he thought.

"Oh, they have some lovely Traditional patterns," Mrs Stevens said without looking up. "Why— Heres Old Colonial. Why I had an aunt who had that," she said looking up with some surprise, as if she hadnt realized it was important at the time.

"You like the Traditional?" Frank asked her, but looking at Virginia's black hair parted in the middle which fell loosely from both sides of her bent face as she looked, and thinking about young Arthur Bookwright and the Arkansas private. He was suddenly aware of the rhythmic moisture-warmth of her breathing as she studied the pamphlet. Harold Bookwright had (privately, of course) said that she looked like an awfully good piece. And he had not believed it.

Out in the office, the phone rang again. And he remembered Dave.

When it rang, everyone in the store instinctively stopped moving and stopped talking, with that intent self absorption Americans always get when a phone rings and they hope or dread it is for them. Al Lowe went back to ask the girl who it was for.

"For you, Frank!"

"Be right there!"

The people in the store started living again.

"Modern is so plain," Mrs Stevens answered him. "Silver should call up lovely visions, of court banquets, and powdered hair, and silver knee buckles, and lighted candles and romance."

"I," Virginia said suddenly, in a low but quite clear and penetrating voice, "think I am more attracted to the plainness of the Modern."

The sudden murderousness of it with its deliberate implications startled all of them, even Virginia. Then the start faded off her face and was replaced by a bold look of audacity, with which she stared at her mother in the silence.

"Well, a lot of discriminating young people are buyin' Modern nowadays," Frank said.

"Yes, thats true," Mrs Stevens said quickly, and smiled. "I guess its just we old dogs who cant change our spots," she laughed nervously.

"For one thing, the Modern's very easy to keep clean," Frank said. "Will you excuse me a minute, Mrs Stevens? Virginia? I have to get that phone."

Mrs Stevens smiled graciously. "Why, of course, Frank. You go right ahead."

He half bowed to them, cavalierly, and went out back, hoping the call wasnt about Dave, but thinking more about Virginia Stevens and her Arkansas private. That Arkansas boy must have had an extra special something he thought. The way Virginia still seemed to miss him after two years.

Whatever he had, it was evidently what Virginia liked and appreciated. He must have really satisfied her. She had sure peeled the old lady.

Frank suddenly felt king-like; and there was a diffusion of excitement all through his stomach as he answered the phone.

The call was another friendly call congratulating him on Dave's safe return. This caller did not conceal his malice either. But Frank hardly noticed this time because he was preoccupied with a bewitching picture of Virginia Stevens being satisfied.

He was careful not to look at Edith Barclay when he hung up. He sometimes had the feeling she could read his mind. He went back out front. He could hardly wait to get back up front and start looking at Virginia again.

The two women, mother and daughter, —their faces cut from the same long boned sharp jawed pattern, so that at this distance they suddenly and surprisingly looked almost identical except for twenty-five years and some 28,000 meals— were still at the counter where their coats lay, and talking to each other animatedly. As he approached down the counter, he overheard Virginia:

"and you heard him say its easier to clean."

and then Mrs Stevens, dryly: "Thats an important consideration for a bride."

and Virginia, flashing back: "For this bride it is."

and Mrs Stevens, sharply: "Lets have no more of that."

then they shut up, as he came closer. Mrs Stevens turned to him charmingly.

"We really must run along," she smiled graciously. "Thanks so much, Frank. Youve been very helpful and I know weve taken up your time."

"Not at all," Frank said, carefully restraining himself from looking at Virginia more than casually. "Glad to be of service."

"Thank you, Mr Hirsh," Virginia said in that same defiant eyed peculiar voice, which seemed to say she was aware he (and the rest of Parkman) knew all about her and her marriage but they didnt care to say it to her face; and which at the same time, sounded like a small child whos been pinched to remind it of its manners.

"Youre quite welcome, Virginia," he said gravely. "And I want to wish you the greatest happiness."

He stood at the counter as they went to the door, smiling after them in case they should look back, and beginning to feel exultant, not only because of having handled them so well, but also because he was now free to look his fill at and to study the Arkansas private's conquest, —at least until they had got into their coats and opened the door and gone.

What interested Frank was not so much that she was an attractive girl, he looked at every woman. It was that she was not virgin. He was not intrigued because she was disreputable, but because he knew she was just the opposite. She was a respectable young woman, very respectable, who had succumbed to conquest twice and was known to have been unvirtuous. He was fascinated by her.

At the door, struggling agitatedly into her coat with a perfectly serene calm face, Virginia said in a low voice:

"I dont care *what* you *say*, mother. Ive *made* up my *mind*."

To which Mrs Stevens answered firmly: "Well discuss it later. At home."

"It wont do any *good*. Its *my* wedding."

"I said wed discuss it later."

There was no one near them, and Virginia had spoken in a low voice, which Frank managed nevertheless to overhear, and now with the exchange over, tears of frustration welled indignantly and incongruously in her eyes in the carefully serene calm face.

Frank watched her struggling into the coat, the long legs throwing first one wide hip out into relief then the other as she worked her arms into the sleeves. He was filled with an almost uncontainable exuberance. She was living proof of a theory dear to his heart, and which he had been trying to convince himself of for years. Exultantly letting his eyes run themselves up and down the young woman lines of her, long

thighs and the small breasts in the sweater as she turned sideways getting into the coat, he dwelt with savor upon some of those
old gems of poolroom folklore which also proved his theory, but which
he could almost never believe.

Women, the poolroom sages maintained and Frank now believed,
loved only one thing more than bed, and that was the fiction that they
did not love it at all.

In a lot of ways she made him think of Al Lowe's wife. But then he
knew what Geneve was like. And besides, Geneve did it for what she
could get out of it. Maybe she liked it, but basically she did it for
what she could get out of it, and that disqualified her. And anyway
he did not consider Geneve respectable. Virginia Stevens, he did. Frank
suddenly wanted badly to go to bed with his wife.

Virginia was still crying bitterly (if such controlled precipitation
could be called crying) out of the defiant eyes in the serenely calm
face. It was plain even to her that she was not going to get the Modern
pattern, and would have to think up a new way to frustrate her
mother.

When they had left, he went out in the back elatedly, to call the
judge the information about his invitation to Dave. He felt so king-
like, he even believed he could handle that problem without too much
undue publicity. He wished Virginia would rebel and refuse to marry
Arthur Bookwright; that would sure take the attention off Dave. But
of course she wouldnt.

After the call, he hurried into his topcoat, and winked at Edith
Barclay who was still at her desk working, and told her to take the rest
of the afternoon off. Short, stocky, neckless and ball headed like his
brothers, he left the store to go home and brief his wife about tonight's
dinner for Dave. By the time he got there, and pulled the car into the
drive, the passionate desire for her was no longer with him.

CHAPTER 7

EDITH BARCLAY, after her boss left, did not take the rest of the afternoon off. Instead she stayed on in the office, clean slim capable and
immaculate, and worked on up to closing time.

There wasnt really much work to do. No real reason to stay. But
had she taken the afternoon shed only have spent it loafing in McGee's
Pharmacy drinking cokes or coffee by herself with no one to talk to
till the girls in the courthouse got off; or else in a shopping expedition
she didnt need and could ill afford; or in going home. It was too late for
the matinee, and anyway she had a date for that tonight and had
planned to stay after work and re-do her nails.

Besides, she was upset about the boss. She knew a lot more about her boss than he gave her credit for knowing. More than once during the past year without the boss ever knowing it, she had discreetly saved his goose with his wife when that lady called the store for him and he was gone. Maybe she was only twenty-four, but women grow up quicker than men, and besides for three years after she got out of high school she had worked at the telephone company as an operator to save the money to go to Terre Haute to Business College. It hadnt taken much accidental listening to the boss's phone conversations today for her to know what had happened.

Edith knew all about Brother Dave's scandal. Edith's grandmother had been the Hirshs' cleaning woman for years and hated Frank Hirsh (and his success) unconditionally and passionately, as only an unsuccessful old woman could; it was her favorite topic, and one of her two favorite stories (the other was how Frank married Agnes for her father's variety store) was the story of Brother Dave's youthful scandal, appropriately colored up to fit her thesis, which in her own words was that all the Herschmidts—she always used the earlier spelling—were bums. Edith herself refused to have any truck with such insane jealousy. But she couldnt very well without leaving home avoid hearing the stories. Or knowing all about Brother Dave.

It was a silly scandal, Edith thought, one that could have happened to any two high school kids who didnt know how to take care of themselves, but it could cause the boss a lot of embarrassment, especially if you took things like that hard, the way the boss did.

At five-thirty Al Lowe came back to the office with the cash to lock up in the big square floor safe they both had access to. Edith heard him coming. She started filing some colored ad circulars.

"You staying late again?" Al said as he closed the safe and twirled the knob.

"I have a few little things I want to get finished up before I leave," she said without looking up.

"Well," Al said, rising and leaning on the safe. "See you then, Edith."

"See you tomorrow," Edith said indifferently and continued filing.

Standing there looking at her the second or two he did, just long enough actually to make the last remark, the same remark he always made when she stayed late, she could sense hidden in his voice the same hurt bafflement, bafflement at anyone who would want to stay after hours when they didnt have to, the hurt directed at her because she would never offer to explain why, just as at the rare times she looked at him (in order not to appear to be avoiding looking at him) she could sense the same thing hidden in the arrangement of his features but he never said anything, and by the time the sensing reached her ears (or eyes) and traveled its message of hurt and bafflement to her brain, he was always already gone, back up front to finish closing and lock up. He never asked her to tell him why she stayed. And even if he did shed be damned if shed tell him, she thought angrily, because it was none of his damned business why.

Another of the things she knew about her boss that he did not guess she knew was that in her year there the boss had been carrying on a sporadic affair with Al Lowe's wife. This had the effect of always making her dislike Al and feel irritated with him. She also knew (this from her grandmother, whose purpose in life was the acquisition of such things, whether on Frank Herschmidt or on anybody) that the affair had been going on sporadically since 1942, Al's first year in the Army, and was the reason (her grandmother said) for Al's job with Frank Herschmidt—a kind of sop, her grandmother said, a herring, a marinated herring (her grandmother always insisted vehemently that Frank Herschmidt was Jewish, although the whole town knew for a fact the family was German) to draw Al's big fat nose off the trail. Al's nose was neither big nor fat. The adjectives were purely rhetorical. But Edith had to admit (to herself; she admitted it to no one else) that as to facts this time, wherever it was Jane her grandmother got her information, for once the old bag was right. They were having an affair, all right. Just where Al figured in it Edith wasnt sure. If he didnt know about it, he was just plain dumb. If he did know, he was pretty smart and quite an opportunist. It was always possible he knew and just didnt care; however, Edith was inclined to think he didnt know and was dumb. He just looked dumb. Whichever the case, she certainly had no intention of ever giving Al Lowe any opportunities for considering her as a possible consolation prize.

Self conscious and angry, she went on with her filing (Al was already gone, aware of her own stiffened spine and taut neck) deeply offended by his mere presence in some strange way as if it personally jeopardized her whole future existence, and filled with a disgust for him which wasnt really disgust but her own fear that she might someday marry a man who would love and appreciate her so little he would allow her to step out on him if she wanted to or worse yet, would not even know about it.

Up front the oblivious Al finished locking up. There was the mild confusion as he and the repairman and the countrygirl (Edith, too, always thought of her as the countrygirl; everyone did, she guessed; they couldnt help it) got into their winter coats and rubbers and left to go home, all of it suddenly shut off by the last click of the door and then she was alone, by herself in the lighted office in the darkened store lit only by the florescent night light up front and the two display windows that the night cop would switch off from outside at ten oclock all around the square.

In the silence which assailed her eardrums, Edith finished filing the circulars without haste. She did one last letter on her desk, sealed and stamped it and put it with the others, and then leaned back and lit a cigarette, sprawling mannishly in the spring backed chair in a very female way that would have been very attractive to a man, had one been there to see it.

That damned Al. Edith knew a lot of other things about her boss, too. She knew all about Old Man Herschmidt, his departure, his return, and subsequent refusal to change his name. She knew about Frank's numerous affairs through the years since he married Agnes, and she knew all about Agnes herself. She couldnt very well help knowing, living day in day out in the same house with Jane her grandmother. There wasnt much she could do to help about Brother Dave, anyway hed be leaving in a week or so, but she did wish she could get the boss out of the clutches of that female golddigger Geneve Lowe. He was such an easy mark, even if he did think he knew it all. Edith was new to the chronic disease of boss-fever, the occupational hazard of unmarried office girls, and sometimes the loyalties that possessed her concerning the boss got so violent they surprised her.

It wasnt only that he had hired her to replace the girl who married, advanced her money, helped her with the work at first, all this at a time when she thought shed have to go back to her old job at the telephone company, School diploma or no School diploma. That was only part of it, and largely because he had this positive phobia about being disliked. He had a driving need to feel he was a benevolent employer. That was why that lecherous old bastard of a watch repairman could get his goat so easily. Edith understood all that. But, it was a lot more than that. She felt protective. He was so incredibly, unbelievably innocent. Anybody could hurt him. Even though he thought he could hide it. And even though he thought he was cynically impervious to hurt.

Actually of course all the boss's trouble lay at home, and that wasnt her department. But a smart businessman like the boss should know better than to fool around with a she tiger like Geneve Lowe. Edith had seen her often enough in the store, and taken enough sweet voiced arrogant phone calls, to get her number. A thin exquisite-featured girl with that thin, exquisitely turned out look of a *Vogue* model, always looking as if she never wore her clothes but had just put them on long enough to be photographed. Edith followed the styles pretty closely herself. Enough to recognize the Chicago- and New York-bought clothes Geneve got through Dotty Callter (always at wholesale) when she saw them. And always that exquisite, greedy-bright, acquisitive look in the dark eyes in the thin face. Edith's sympathy was all with the boss instead of Al. Al was lucky. Lucky somebody, anybody, had taken her off his hands for a while.

Sitting sprawled in the tailored suit, one arm over the chair back, her legs straight out in front of her like a boy, feet flat on the floor, skirt hiked up to her knees by the movement of the sprawling, Edith smoked and let the feel of the silent store seep over her, soothe her. This was the time of the day she liked best. She stayed after work a couple of evenings every week, doing a lot of her real work her book work then, alone in the empty store. It was her store, then. It belonged to her. She was its nervous system, circulatory system, and digestive tract all rolled into one; without her the organism would cease to exist and that was good to know. But the real treasure of it was in the being alone, completely alone for an hour, a thing which because of her grandmother who kept house for her father she could never accomplish at home. She would have stayed a lot oftener, if she hadnt felt it would be conspicuous to the others. She didnt want to give the impression she had to stay to keep her work up.

Anyway, as she often told herself, if she stayed late every night the treasure of it would soon pall probably. That was the way things always did with her, she thought ruefully.

she was one of those who always had to ration life to herself.

She snuffed out the cigarette end and got out her leather bound manicure set.

While the last coat dried she smoked another cigarette, holding it carefully, then put the set back in the desk and got out her draw-string top sewing bag and worked on a blouse she had bought on sale her last trip to Terre Haute and was altering. By staying late, she had missed her regular ride home and would have to walk it. She didnt mind.

Edith's home was in the east end of town near the Sternutol plant where her father worked, in a section that had been just outside the city limits up to 1943 when Parkman had extended its boundaries to accommodate the war boom. Two short streets of identical bungalows at right angles to the highway-mainstreet, a former adventure in real estate development by Mr Anton Wernz III who owned the land and built the rest to sell in '30, formerly called The Wernz Addition, and re-named by the city in 1943 to Roosevelt and Hull Drives, respectively. Edith, whose father had bought one on time and was still paying for it out of his salary, had lived there since she was six and could never get used to not seeing the white city limits sign as she crossed on the sidewalk the line where the mainstreet brick pavement ended and the highway slab began. The mayor and city council might move the city limits from the end of the brick the whole five miles to the

Wabash River; the end of the brick would still be the city limits to Edith. There were no railroads in the east end of town so there couldnt very well be a wrong side of the tracks, but the old city limits line served the same purpose in the east end of Parkman and all her life Edith had lived about twenty-five yards on the wrong side of it. In fact, the Barclay backyard ended right at the line, so that a small girl could stand at the fence and look across to untainted ground just a few feet away. You do not give up a demarcation like that easily, and the fact that she lived so close to it may have had a great influence on her subsequent life. She sometimes thought that if she had lived out on the far side of Hull Drive, instead of on the near side of Roosevelt, she probably would have remained a telephone operator and never gone to Business College in Terre Haute and become Frank Hirsh's office girl.

Outside, it had turned colder. The drizzle of snow had stopped. The sidewalks gleamed wet under the light of the streetlamps. There were no stars. Winter was moving in.

Edith checked the locked door after her carefully, and then stopped on the sidewalk and looked back at the store. She stood maybe thirty seconds, looking it right square in its display windows.

It represented a triumph, and her trick of staying late was partly a habit left over from her first months there, months of unsureness and doubtful worry working always with the uncertainty hanging over her whether she would make the grade or be let go tomorrow and she had had to unlearn every thing they had taught her at the School and create for herself out of whole cloth a practical system, one that would work, to replace the theoretically perfect (but completely unpracticable) system the School had drilled into its pupils well enough but which would not work because its precision left no room for the mistakes of bosses or salesclerks, or of office girls, and in addition at the same time she had had to straighten out the mess left by the girl who had quit to get married she had done it in those evenings, staying late night after night, working alone in that office, quietly and without telling anyone, because she was afraid if she did theyd find out how little she knew and can her

and as the months of uncertainty gave way slowly to the months of competence and success when she knew shed made the grade and wouldnt be let go she began to look back on those evenings of struggle and worry as the happiest time of her life though she knew they werent were probably the worst but the feeling persisted and so did the staying late habit a battle fought and won against not only order and system but against herself and her own misgivings, and of which, she thought, she was just as proud as if it were something important.

The face of the store always said all this to her every time she looked it in its display windows. And having looked at it, she turned and started home with a glance up at the lighted courthouse clock, which was never right, to get some vague approximate idea of the time, and feeling one word in her mind. History.

The courthouse of Parkman had been built upon this small eminence which rose up out of the flat river prairie, so that the town flowed back down to the prairie away from it in all directions as if reluctant to leave it there, the town which had been laid out by some unsung Greek scholar come overland with his lexicon and Homer in his pack they did that then I cant read Latin Caesar French who probably would have preferred a real hill but did the best he could with what he had as the porticoes around the four sides of the belfried-Parthenon of the courthouse showed though the effect would have been a little better if they had used marble, or even granite, instead of brick or at least made the columns brick like the walls instead of covering them with cement fluted eliptically to resemble Doric columns but granite was too far off to haul then and nobody would pay for marble and anyway the old men with the weathered hats who sat around under the architrave on the good days were not philosophers. At least, not professionally. And anyway old brick aged beautifully.

Edith walked on along down the gentle slope to the prairie on East Wernz Avenue, the mainstreet which became the highway at the end of the brick, and had all the best homes on it. Parkman was a moneyed town. Oil as well as farming. And East Wernz Avenue proved it. She passed them all, the big old homes of two and three generations ago interspersed with newer ones, all with their deep wide lawns and old trees, getting noticeably a little less big as you worked out toward the edge of town, until right at the end of the brick were the two or three biggest of all but built only half a generation ago, walking confidently in her heavy coat and calf length cowboy style white rubbers, moving among them with complete safety, self reliant and positive, not feeling put upon either by the houses or the necessity of walking because now all that was carefully buried in the years of her young childhood in The Wernz Addition. And because she was Edith Barclay of Parkman Illinois whose permission they must have to be there.

At the corner where she turned on Roosevelt she could see down the line to the house and the lights were on in it, and when she came in the door it was the same as if a day had not passed and her father was sitting with his shoes off, still in his work clothes, reading the Parkman evening paper through the horn rimmed glasses he had selected for himself out of a bin at Woolworth's when his eyes started getting weaker.

John Barclay did not look up. The hard, brassy smell of chemicals— which was the trademark of the Sternutol plant throughout town when the wind was right—hung faintly in the room.

"Daddy, go take your bath," Edith said as she took her coat off.

"Aw now Edith honey," John Barclay said. "I just wanted to read the paper."

"You can read the paper after your bath," Edith said, sitting down to take off the white rubbers.

John Barclay folded the paper and put it on the footstool where his feet had been, and folded his Woolworth glasses and put them carefully on the end table.

"All right Edith honey."

He stood up, and the nose-numbing, penny-in-the-mouth taste of chemicals eddied about the room like a visible blood-colored wind. A big balding meaty man, his chest still well-muscled beneath the under-shirt that hung on him loosely, he picked up his denim shirt off the floor and went off with it walking stiff-jointedly to the bathroom in his stocking feet.

Edith went around the room after him, straightening it up. She put his glasses in their imitation-leather envelope and put them on top the imitation-walnut bookcase where they belonged. She took the paper off the footstool and placed it on the imitation-mahogany wall table where it should be. She emptied the home-turned ashtray stand John had made for himself in the shop at the plant and wiped up the cigar ashes he had spilled on the rug. She took the heavy work shoes and put them inside the door to his room. From the kitchen came the smell of liver and onions frying.

"Edith? Is that you, Edith?" her grandmother called apprehensively, pretending she did not know who it was.

The voice, deep-throated and gravelly, charged with immense vitality, was a very paean of querulosity, floating mournfully out of the kitchen on the hot cooking smell.

"Yes, Jane." She collected her own things, the coat and the rubbers, to take to her room. "Whats for supper?"

"I tried to git him to take his bath," her grandmother hollered, "but he wont pay any attention to whatever I tell him."

It was a shameless lie. The huge figure—whom no one on earth ever would dare not pay attention to, if she demanded it—came slowly into eye range through the kitchen door, clad in the habitual faded-but-flowered wrapper which covered but could not contain her bulk. She was holding a cooking fork.

"You ought to dust in here," Edith said.

"I been meanin' to," Jane said, "but I been too tired. I didnt know if you was comin' home for supper or not," she said. "Youre so late gettin' home."

Edith, who never failed to call home when she stayed downtown for supper, refused to be taken in. She said only: "I stayed after work to fix my nails."

"Well, I didnt know whether to fix you any food or not," Jane said.

"Im not very hungry. Ill fix myself something."

"Well, maybe therell be enough," Jane said charitably. "You say you got a date tonight?"

"Yes."

"So have I," Jane said brightly.

Edith wanted to swear. She was always a little disconcerted by her sixty-two-year-old grandmother's dates, though she tried hard to hide it and be broadminded. It was dismaying to go into a local pub with a date and find Jane installed in a corner booth with a couple of old lechers, coyly egging them on in a loud contest for her affections. "Who with this time?" she said.

"Ohhh—a feller," Jane said archly. She grinned obscenely and put her gnarled hand on her great hip. "Maybe two fellers."

"Well, have a good time." It wouldnt be so bad if she werent so big and fat, with those huge breasts and buttocks. A brassiere, Edith felt, did Jane more harm than good. She would be better off to let them just hang. Either they didnt make brassieres that big, or else Jane bought hers too small—Edith never felt up to discussing it with her—but the result was always that a great deal of Jane's breasts was pushed clear up under her chin, where they bulged forth from the neck of her dress like some sort of fleshly muffler on an old woman with a bad cold. The sight always embarrassed Edith.

"I aim to," Jane said, and the obscene grin slowly faded away into a look of worn pain. "You want to finish gettin' supper for me? My feetre killin' me."

"I would but I havent washed yet," Edith said.

"My kidneys are goin' bad on me too again I think," Jane said painfully. "I believe Im gettin' the gravels again."

"Have you been taking your medicine?"

Jane snarled, suddenly, like a voracious wolf. "Ahh, that crap! That bastard is only bleedin' me for my money I have to work so goddam hard to earn."

Edith remained unworried. "Then you ought to go to somebody else."

"Theyre all alike," Jane snarled. Her voice got muted. "Theys nothin' wrong with me a little rest wouldnt cure."

"And rest is what you never get."

"Thats right," Jane said. "And you know its the truth, too." She went back into the kitchen to stir the mess of calf's liver and browning onions pugnaciously with her weaponlike fork. Perpetually wan-faced, always sick, forever in pain, at sixty-two she had more energy than ten men, could do almost as much work, and spent all her cleaning money that she didnt spend on beer, on doctoring, in much the same way that some ladies have their breasts or organs removed in order to become invalids and get a little attention. Edith understood all that; the only times she was ever *really* ashamed of her was when she came in the store, to buy some worthless trinket for a birthday present to give some equally worthless birthday-having crony, and haggle over the price. Jane came back to the door of the kitchen, still holding the fork, as Edith was about to go into her room. Her face had lighted up with happy malice, the intensity of her pain since it was obviously doing her no material good, forgotten. Whatever else she might be, Jane was a realist.

"Have you heard the latest big news? Today was my day at Miz Smith's, and I got it first hand. Miz Harry Appel called her up to tell her."

Edith stopped in the doorway. "You mean about Frank Hirsh's brother coming home?"

"Haw!" Jane cried exuberantly. "That son of a bitch! I bet hes sweatin' blood right now!"

"If he is, I certainly didnt notice it at the store this afternoon."

"You!" Jane hooted. "You aint dry behind the ears yet. You wouldnt recognize it if he was. And if you did, you wouldnt admit it."

"Thats right. I sure wouldnt. But it just so happens there wasnt anything to admit."

"Then he dont know about it yet, thats all."

"How did you think I found out about it?"

"You could of found out lots of places. The whole damn town's buzzin' with it. Its bettern Virginia Stevens's marriage. Brother Dave's moved into the corner suite at The Parkman, and deposited $5500 in the Second National Bank. Not the Cray County Bank, mind you. The Second National. And you stand there and try to tell me that damned Frank Herschmidt dont even care."

"All I said was, if he was upset he didnt show it at the store."

"Course he wouldnt show it at the store, you ninny."

Edith wanted to laugh, remembering just how unsuccessful the boss had been at hiding it.

"Oh, hes a sly fox, all right," Jane said. "You neednt grin. How else you think he got that store? and all that money? Waitll youve worked for him as long as I have."

"Youd better watch the liver," Edith said. "Youll burn it. And I have to wash." She went on in her room, still carrying the coat and rubbers.

"Waitll next Friday," Jane called after her. Friday was her day at the Hirshs'. "Ill be able to give you the straight dope then. Agnes never can hide her upset."

She turned back into the kitchen, still holding the fork, the pleased malice on her face replaced by disappointment. She had thought surely this time she could get her goat. Many more times than not a great many more Jane was convinced her granddaughter had no more emotions or sensibilities in her than her damned stupid father. It seemed the only person around this house who had the ability to feel anything anything at all was herself. Forgetting momentarily that she herself had also married for security as well as love (and with much less luck), Jane wondered again with renewed amazement what in the name of God had ever possessed her daughter Frances to marry a clod like John Barclay. Life ought to be exciting. People liked to turn up their nose at older women because they gossiped, but if older women could ever have some excitement in their own life, instead of spending it cleaning up some damned grandson's house, they wouldnt have to get it secondhand by talking about other people's. And Edith. Jane was becoming increasingly convinced that Edith was going to turn out to be a cold-blooded old maid of a virgin. Disdainfully, she thrust the fork down in the skillet. She had a heavy date tonight, herself. Someday shed get married again and let them see how good they got along without her around here.

In her room Edith hung up her coat pleased she hadnt gotten angry. Wait till shed worked for him as long as Jane had! She already knew him better, in less than one year, than Jane did in over twenty. But then it was Agnes Jane really worked for, wasnt it? Edith stopped her mind. That wasnt her department. She put the rubbers away and got out of her office clothes. She inspected the armpits of the suit blouse minutely before she hung it away. She had had to change her deodorant lately because the old one was beginning to fade the armpits of her clothes, and she had an abhorrence of it happening again and perhaps embarrassing her publicly. Besides she couldnt afford it, in clothes. Wishing she didnt sweat so much, she got out of the bra and panty girdle which had ridged her flesh, and massaged the welts with her palms. She didnt look at her nude self in the lyre shaped dresser mirror, not so much because of modesty as because she wasnt interested. It didnt occur to her to look. Having eased the itch of her armor, she put on a housecoat to wait for her father to be through in the bathroom.

Edith, contrary to her grandmother's wishful thinking, was not only not a virgin, she was twice-removed. Her first affair, but you could hardly call it an affair, she thought, was with a boy in high school. Rather like the scandal of Dave Hirsh, except that she and her high school boy did not get caught. She supposed it happened to practically every one. This one was the result of two things—one, a deliberate rebellion against the persistent advice and furrow headed worry of her widowed father, who kept warning her to beware of boys; and two, a strong curiosity aroused by all sorts of half-allusions from all sorts of sources (movies, perfume ads, overheard conversations, conversations participated in) as if sex were one of those faint stars seen indistinctly from the corner of the eye but which when looked at straight, disappears.

The concrete fact itself came as something of a surprise, she guessed, at once an inelegant and too personal exposure (like the discolored armpits) and an overrated activity disappointingly devoid of interest. At first she thought there must be something not like other people about her, but after three identical experiences with him over a period of weeks she trusted her judgment and thereafter refused the puzzled boy who mistakenly believed that once you got in you were in to stay, though she was willing to go on dating him. Her second—this *was* an affair, and lasted several months—was with a wounded veteran returned from the European Theater, during the time she was working at the telephone company. The main reason for this one was that she was beginning to feel that reasonless loneliness which comes with adulthood, and also because she felt sorry for him, not because he was wounded though he tried to use that, but because he was so anxious and so desirous of that in her which seemed so vastly overrated to herself. Magnanimous was perhaps a better word than sorry, for the way she felt. It was like giving old clothes to the Salvation Army; you lose nothing, and yet get to feel generous. She supposed she did like it, in a way, but it was mainly because she felt she was giving him pleasure. Feeling that way, she supposed, it might well have blossomed into something finer. But when the veteran tried to teach her some of the more unusual ways of making love (she figured it out later that he must have learned them while in Paris) she realized all her sympathy had been misplaced. And that was when the affair began to teach her something, something curious. A woman should be careful who she has an affair with, because once she enters it something strange happens to her and she will cling to it through hell and high water for some reason and put up with almost anything before she can bring herself to break it off. With her veteran, in spite of his Paris-wrought degeneracy, she found herself hanging on and on to an unhappy association, hoping and rationalizing for some months before she got up courage enough to finish it, when he would not change. Since then she had not had a lover, and did not feel the lack, except that sometimes that peculiar pointless loneliness overwhelmed her. But dates helped take care of that.

She didnt know why she was thinking about all this junk tonight. Probably the only reason it came into her mind this evening was because she had a date tonight. That, and because Dave Hirsh's return had recalled all that silly high school scandal stuff.

Sitting on the bed in her housecoat waiting for her father to finish his bath, she took up her earrings from the coverlet where shed tossed them and carried them over to her jewel box on the dresser.

The moment she opened the lid, Edith saw Jane had been into her jewelry again. The earrings, which she kept separated in their pairs on the felt of the tray, had been taken out and cunningly replaced, but not quite perfectly enough. The same was true, when she snatched up the tray and looked, of the other things in the bottom. What had happened was Jane had had it all out trying it on in front of the mirror again. Stung to tearful indignation, she seized the box and charged down on the kitchen.

She didnt have much jewelry. She couldnt afford much, on her pay. But what she had was hers. She had paid for it. Most of it was only costume jewelry, but she had selected it painstakingly. And she had two prize possessions, both bought at the store since she went to work there: one a matched set of Mexican amethyst set in roped silver— bracelet, ring, earrings, and the pin made in the shape of an owl with big amethyst eyes; and the other a pair of apple green jade earrings for which she had paid thirty dollars. But more than that, it was the invasion of her privacy. She had no place in this house, no drawer, no cupboard, no closet, no room, which was hers and no one else's. Not even her own jewelry box.

Jane looked up startled from the stove, but she recovered quickly when she saw the box, and her face set in iron defense.

"Youve been in my room again!"

"I have not."

"You have too!"

"I have not!"

"You have so, you have. Youve been in my jewelry again."

"No I aint," Jane said stoutly. Her guilt was spread all over her face. "I aint any such a thing."

Edith was beginning to cry, from pure anger. "God damn you," she said. "God *damn* you. Why dont you admit it? You ruin everything I ever get. It isnt yours. Its mine. You have no right to go in my room. I dont go in yours. I have no privacy at all!"

"Edith, I aint," Jane said guiltily. "Honest to God I aint."

"You have! Youve been in my room trying on my jewelry again. Damn you to hell," she said. It was useless. She knew Jane would never admit it. You could put her on a torture rack, and she would lie there, screaming when it hurt, guilty faced when it didnt, and continue to swear she had not.

Crying hard with frustration and outrage because she could not at least make her admit it, Edith shook the box at her inarticulately, unable to think of anything strong enough, hurtful enough, to say to her. "You old whore, you," she said, and stormed back to her room, still clutching the precious box, and slammed the door as hard as she could fling it. It rattled in its frame, drowning Jane's answer: "Honestly, Edith. You must of moved them yourself, and then forgot about it."

John Barclay chose this moment—with the slammed door rattling the whole house, and Jane calling apologetically—to emerge from the bathroom, his face shining and the smell of chemicals gone, though he could not erase the callus and stain of them off his hands. He had expected to be complimented.

"Whats the matter with her?" he said.

Jane shrugged. "Oh, she thinks I been in her jewelry tryin' it on."

She wasnt hurt—or even angry, really—at being called an old whore. Just melancholy. Gradually, during the past eight or ten years, she had, with great guilt and unhappiness, been forced to come to about that same conclusion herself. Her husband, an oil driller, had run off and left her years before Edith's mother had married, and she hadnt needed—or wanted—men then. But in the past ten years or so something had changed somewhere. That was what she was, all right. But if that was what she was, that was what she was and she might as well enjoy it where she could, by God. Besides, Edith was upset.

"Well, did you?" John said, after he had digested what she said.

"Course I didnt," Jane said. "Why would I want to try on her damned old jewelry?" But shed be damned if shed admit it to any-body else. Trying on her damned old jewelry, just to see for a minute how it looked on you in the mirror, didnt hurt it any. Calling her own grandmother an old whore!

"Well, even so, you ought to be more careful how you handle the girl," John Barclay said, after considerable deep thought. "I know she gets on your nerves. But shes a bright girl. And bright people like that are extra sensitive. She aint rough like you and me, and you cant treat her like she was."

What a hell of a smart man to have for a son-in-law, Jane thought disgustedly. You could tell him jam was polish, and hed rub it on his shoes. She said shortly: "What she needs is to get married." Then some malicious devil in her made her add: "Or at least, a man."

John looked deeply shocked. "When she needs a man, shell find one for herself. And shell marry him, I warrant."

Jane snorted. "Supper's about ready," she said.

"The girl aint had her bath yet," John Barclay said. "Youll have to put it back a while." He trod across the room slowly in his sock feet and sat down at the kitchen table to wait for supper.

In her room, the object of this discussion had put the box back on the dresser and flung herself facedown on the bed. Gradually, in direct ratio to the cessation of her angry crying—which was swift now she was alone—the old hopelessness settled over her like a falling tent. The slamming of the door had helped a little. But not much. Whoever said a man's home was his castle must surely have lived without his rela-tives. Otherwise, he would have said instead that a man's home was his fishbowl. Or his prison. The only times Edith had ever actually seriously considered marrying the degenerate veteran had been to deliberately get out of this house, after a fight with Jane, and that was a horrible thing to have to admit.

She wished she hadnt called Jane an old whore, even if it was true. Besides Jane wasnt *act*ually a whore. She didnt take money.

She knew she would have to get up in a minute and go take her bath. They would be waiting supper on her. John would see to that. He was a sweet thing—if only he wasnt so damned *dumb*.

Using considerable more energy than she believed she possessed, she made herself get up off the bed, and went to the dresser to examine her jewelry to see if any of it was scratched by the violent shaking. Quietly as possible, she went out through her door and down the tiny hall to the bathroom.

That was the trouble. If she just didnt like them, if she only just hated them, it wouldnt be such a terrible, painful thing. But damned family loyalty had to come into it.

The bathroom was at the very back of the house. After she shut the door, Edith went to the window and looked out across the back yard and the fence across the deep side lawn of the Frederic place. The big old ugly three storey house was ablaze with light, and the lights were on in Doris's room. For a moment she debated calling her. She badly needed somebody to talk to for a while. But she had this damned date tonight.

The window was high, and up behind the lavatory, and she had to lean on the bowl and stand almost on tiptoes to see out. The house was really lighted up. But then they always did that. Paul Frederic had married Anton Wernz the 3rd's only female offspring Antonia late in life and gone into the Wernz's real estate business and entered the Wernz-owned Second National Bank. They could afford the lights, and Doris was their only child. She was two years older than Edith, twenty-six.

Edith grinned ruefully and relaxed her toes and came down from the window. She and Doris had been chums sort of all through school, used to bring each other all their more emotional problems, Doris in a sort of magnanimous older person's way after all she was two years older, Edith more as a satellite seeking advice she also used to get all the clothes Doris had outgrown. Even after Doris had gone away to college. During her college summers home Doris would come over and read her the letters and tell her the troubles of her various heavy love affairs. She still did. They hadnt grown apart, they still called each other, though perhaps not as often now because their lives had taken different paths was all. Doris had come home to teach ninth and tenth grade math in the high school, this in spite of the fact that her father was still president of the largely-Wernz-owned Second National Bank and still lived in one of the Wernz-built family mansions. A strange girl. Edith suddenly felt warm toward her. If she didnt have this date tonight, she would still call her. But then, she thought, what in hell was there to tell her, really?

She turned away from the window and looked at herself critically in the medicine chest mirror. Her face was a sight. And her with a date tonight. She wet a cloth with cold water and bathed her eyes. Harold would want to stop for a beer after the show, and that would mean they might run into Jane with one—or several—of her boyfriends. The other alternative was to drive over to Terre Haute for a drink, and that meant she would have to fight Harold off all the way there and back. She had put off going there for dinner and a better show for just that very reason.

It was embarrassing not to be able to go into one of Parkman's three bars for a beer without running into your own grandmother with some of her decrepit lovers. Edith giggled. They didnt any of them look like they could do any good.

She put the cloth away and commenced to wash out the tub which, as usual, John had forgotten to clean. Harold, the poor dope, thought he was in love with her and wanted to marry her because she wouldnt sleep with him. Why did it always have to be the dopes, who fell in love with her?

She drew the water, wishing there was some way to get out of eating supper without hurting them. Supper would be strained and unpleasant, with everybody trying to pretend nothing had happened, Jane forcing food on her in a pathetic effort to be friendly, and herself unable to digest it from trying so hard to show them she was no longer angry, which she had every right to be, and for that matter still was, but would rather die than have them suspect it meant that much to her.

She tested the water with one foot, wishing now shed never brought it out in the open. She wished a lot of things

she didnt like these wishing moods that came over her from time to time, they only made for dissatisfaction, nevertheless she went ahead and wished laughing to herself ruefully for doing it that some big handsome man (handsome in an ugly, masculine way) who was forceful (but only tenderly so) and rich and sophisticated (without being snobbish) would come along and seize her and carry her off (against her will or no) from this Cinderella's hovel of a place she herself did not want to assume the responsibility of leaving.

Such a wish was maybe excusable in a high school sophomore. Not in Edith Barclay of Parkman Illinois, who earned her own way, living, paid her own way, and knew at least somewhat about men.

Anyway, that wasnt what she wanted.

All she wanted was a normal home and family, and a husband who would love her forsaking all others as much as she felt she ought to be loved.

Gingerly, she shed the housecoat and stepped into the scalding hot water and let herself down into it gracefully, a very nubile female who would make some man a fine wife someday, provided she could only find the kind of man she was looking for, which was one who would dominate her; and whom, if she ever did find him, she would immediately begin to fight to the last breath, to keep him from doing it.

Absorbing and enjoying the nourishment of the hot bath, she wondered how the boss was making out with his dinner for Brother Dave.

CHAPTER 8

As he sat in his car in the driveway, after the trip home from the store, Frank turned off the ignition and sat watching the fading afternoon light. He had no desire, absolutely none, to go into the house.

The human mind was a funny thing, he thought. He was no longer the crisp decisive businessman who had left the store, and he knew it. His mind seemed to freeze up stiff into a complete blank of nervous anxiety before the prospect of getting Agnes to cook a steak dinner for Brother Dave.

At the store, he had seen fit to ignore the problem of Agnes and had pretended she would do whatever he told her to. Now, he could not. Agnes was known on several occasions to have made the remark publicly that she would not even allow Dave Hirsh in her house. Obviously, if he could not get Dave into the house he could not very well feed him a steak dinner to show the town how happy they were to see him. But he had not thought about this then, and now it was too late, he had to ask her, and his mind was completely bereft of inspiration, not an idea in his head, no emotion in his belly except emptiness, he wished some brilliant lie would come to him.

It wouldnt be so bad if she were just logical. And she was going to be doubly angry when she found out he had invited him without consulting her first. If there was anything Agnes didnt take to, it was not being consulted. The more he thought about it, the more he felt sure he should have asked her first, the more he was convinced that if he had just asked her first she would have cheerfully agreed to having Dave instead of flatly refusing. It was all his fault for not giving her credit for any understanding. He felt an obscure but nonetheless strong sense of guilt for having failed his wife, for having let her down, by inviting Dave to dinner without asking her.

Reluctantly, he pulled the key and put it in his pocket and got out and walked toward the porch. He had to go into the house sometime. What he expected, what he feared, was that shortly he would find himself on the phone calling Dave to tell him the dinner was off because Agnes unbeknownst to him made another date for them tonight. And then the fat would be in the fire and the town could all look wise and snicker.

It didnt turn out that way, though. The way it turned out was that at five-thirty Frank, in a state of near nervous collapse and feeling beaten about the head and ears but full of gratitude for his wife's immense understanding, drove down to the hotel to pick Dave up. And Agnes, equally nervously exhausted and quite sure she would never be able to get up off her bed again, went into their room and lay down on it for about one minute wondering irately why he wanted to make her say such terrible things, before she got up to lay the steaks out to thaw and hurried to bathe and dress in order to look fresh and bright and happy when Dave arrived.

She thought she never in her life had seen such a selfish, inconsiderate person as Frank Hirsh. Frank on his way downtown was thinking the same thing about Frank, in a more affectionate way.

She had been in the utility room off the kitchen (re-converted for her from a former extra guest room when they remodeled) ironing sheets on the beautiful big mangle he had bought her, when he came in the front door treading nervously like a man in a carnivorous jungle across the highly polished floor of the living room past the concert grand he had bought for little Dawn's piano lessons, him glad when he saw it that little Dawn was at the high school practicing for a Senior Class Glee Club Festival and wasnt home to witness this because it was bad for kids to see their parents not being happy, and had passed through the dining room where he saw on the buffet a new novel propped open on Agnes's lovely hand carved curly maple bookholder he had had made up special for her their last anniversary.

"Frank?" the voice said. It had the shrill but plaintive note of a bent saw struck with a hammer.

"Yes," he said. "Yes, Agnes."

"Ive just had four phone calls," she said from the utility room penetratingly. "All from friends of mine," she said, twisting the word bitterly.

"Ive had a few myself," he said heavily.

"Then you know about it!"

"Yes."

"Well, what are you going to do about it?"

He went on into the kitchen he had bought for her when they remodeled, the best in Parkman with its combination disposall-sink-and-automatic-dishwasher, its six-burnered double-ovened glass-doored stove with airplane switchboard panel and built-in blower, its six-foot compartment-doored refrigerator with separate butter temperature, its big bin-type deep-freeze, its airy breakfast nook, its tiled serving peninsula built out into the room, and the complete list of Sunbeam Electric accessories no wife should be without, but which most are.

"Well, I dont know exactly, yet," he said. "Im workin' on it. I—"

"Well you had better do something and do it damned quick!"

"I—"

"It may not have occurred to you," the voice cut at him, "that I have to live in this town."

"So do I," he said patiently, "so do I. I said Im workin' on it. I—"

"Youd better get him out of this town and get him out QUICK. Thats all Ive got to say."

He did not go on into the utility room where in addition to the mangle reposed the Bendix automatic washingmachine, the spindry dryer, and the special low ironing board with built-in seat, and the de luxe steam hand iron which he had bought for her too, but instead stopped at the icebox and pretended he wanted a coke and got one out and opened it.

"I cant do that. I have to handle it my own way," he said, then he took a deep breath. "Ive invited him out the house for dinner tonight."

"Youve what!" the voice cracked.

"Ive invited him to dinner," he repeated. "I—"

"In my house? You certainly will not!"

"Now just wait a minute."

"Ill not have that Hollywood degenerate coming into my house! I wont have it!"

"Now you just shut up a minute!" Frank half yelled, "—and let me talk a minute?"

A stony silence met his ear.

"You hear me?"

Again, silence.

"Im workin' on it," he said. "And Ive got to handle it so that it looks right. Do you trust my judgment or not? Ive got to make it look friendly. Thats the only way."

"Its your brother," the voice said like a knife blade, a frozen knife blade. "Just dont expect me to be here when you bring him."

Feeling panic although his mind was positively sure she didnt mean it, Frank set the untouched coke on the counter and charged the utility room door. "Now look!" he protested. "Be reasonable!"

She was sitting there before the mangle, an attractive woman still although thickening considerably, angry faced, with that intangible heavy-armored safeguardian look of a wife and matron on her face, where once there had been the eager look of a young girl.

"Reasonable!" she said.

"Yes, reasonable!" Frank said desperately. "You know we cant keep him from comin' into town if he wants to. And you know we cant make him leave if he dont."

"Did I say we could? You think Im dumb?"

"No. But you—"

"You ask me to be reasonable!" Agnes said. "Why didnt you call me from the store?"

Frank wanted to say Because I didnt want a scene over the phone, but he had enough control left to know better than to say that. "Why didnt you call me?" he countered.

"Because Ive been let know often enough, in enough subtle ways, that Im not welcome to call the store in business hours," Agnes said. It was a double entendre, an allusive remark, and there was that half-haunted look in her eyes behind the matronness, a slapped-face look.

"Oh now, Agnes, thats not true," Frank started. "And you—"

"What did Al Lowe think about it?" she interrupted.

"Al? Nothing. He was sorry, I guess."

"Did you call his wife? Geneve's a smart girl. Maybe she could help you?"

"Of course not," Frank said. "Why should I call her?"

"Hasnt she been in the store lately?" Agnes said.

"Who. Geneve Lowe?" Frank said. "I dont think so. I havent paid any attention. Why should I pay any attention to whether—"

"Well, Im not going to have that madman brother of yours in my house, and thats final!" Agnes said. She bent back down to her mangle.

It was cruel, and she knew it, but she didnt care. He had it coming. He shouldnt act so much like a sheep-killing dog. She wasnt that terrifying. The truth was, she didnt care a fig about Dave one way or the other. When she heard on the phone of Dave's arrival, she had immediately penetrated by inference to the dinner invitation too, because that was what she would have done, it was the only thing to do. But she was not going to let him know it.

It was true she had stated publicly (it was at the Elks Grille, and shed had several) that she would not allow Dave in her house, and had meant it. Drinks or not. She did not like him, she thought him lazy and no-good, and felt he had proved conclusively by running off from the girl he had got pregnant that he was entirely lacking in moral fibre and responsibility; and after his living in Hollywood for years, she was quite sure he was some kind of a degenerate and would not have been surprised if he were arrested for molesting little girls his first night in town. But all of this was *per*sonal feeling, and had nothing to do with the situation he had created for them in the town, and she was as well aware as Frank what they had to do to rectify it. She was quite willing to have him for dinner. Or even as a house guest the rest of his stay, if she had to.

"Take him over to Al and Geneve's for dinner," she said, looking up for a moment. "Hed have a good time there." If he acted like a frightened moron, he could expect to be treated like one.

"Oh now look," Frank said. "Dont talk silly. This is an important decision."

"You think Im being silly?" she flared. "I meant just *exactly* what I said! And still mean it! Take him to Al and Geneve's for his damned dinner."

He apparently thought she was the world's worst kind of a fool, and that was what she resented more than anything else. Did he think she didnt know? A wife always knows. But if he thought he was going to make her give him the satisfaction of talking about it he was the fool, and had another think coming.

"What kind of a fool do you think I am!" she said shrilly, feeling it begin to take hold of her. "I know you didnt think I was beautiful when you married me. But the store you got more than offset that. I knew that, but I never thought youd think I was a *fool!*"

"Dont *say* things like that, Agnes," Frank said. "On the contrary, I dont think youre a fool. I know what all youve done for me and how much help youve been to me. I would never have been a success at all if it hadnt been for you!"

He knew, too, what was coming. And as far as he had ever found, there was no way of avoiding it. She wasnt going to block him about having Dave, she was as smart about that as he was, but she would go on pretending that she would, and it would unnerve and upset and mangle him mentally just as much as if he believed it, even when he knew all the time that he didnt.

So for the next hour, until he went to get Dave, with that singular and ferocious talent she alone had for separating him cell from cell and nerve from nerve, in a quiet but deadly scene that was not confined to the utility room but ranged over the whole downstairs of the house and wound up in the kitchen which was the envy of nearly every housewife in Parkman, she assured Frank she would not allow Brother Dave on the premises for any reason invitation or no invitation, just on moral grounds alone, while at the same time she upbraided him sorely for not calling her first and at least giving her credit for sufficient intelligence to understand the situation and agree to the invitation, and then went on to bring up also every single thing that he had ever done to her in their married life, over the whole twenty some odd years, she had a memory like an elephant; and the real reason behind it all and all the previous reasons were not even mentioned at all, by either of them.

Frank, who had anticipated exactly what she would say and had not missed the contradiction in it, but who in spite of this could not prevent himself from believing she meant every word she said, was scattered all over the floor in small fragments and nearly in tears of apprehension and anxiety by the time she suddenly changed her mind, which was just a few minutes before five-thirty.

"and if you ever so much as let him set his foot on the driveway," she wound up, "let alone walk into the yard, Ill leave this place so quick itll make your head swim and Ill never come back and youll never find me!"

Frank did not say anything. He was afraid she really might go. She had a sister out in Kansas City and she had gone before.

"Well?" she said matter of factly, "arent you going to go down and get him? Its five-thirty now. Youre going to be late as it is. And he may not wait on you."

"Yes," he mumbled, "Ill go get him."

"Well?" she said. "Then move."

He got up.

"By the way," Agnes said crisply, "Ive invited Old Bob French and Gwen to come for dinner too. Theyre to come at seven-thirty."

"But dont you think thats sort of—inadvisable?" Frank said weakly.

"Well, theyre writers, arent they?" Agnes said. "At least theyll be able to talk to him. Maybe they even admire him, at least they wont already have their minds made up against him like a normal person would."

"All right," Frank said weakly.

"Youd better go," she said crisply.

He left visibly shaken, in abject gratitude, —his guilt was as real to him as it seemed feigned to her— and Agnes, unsatisfied, suddenly ashamed, but having acted the part so well she now believed it herself, crept to her bed exhausted, convinced that Frank had deliberately driven her into making a scene and hating him for it, until she suddenly remembered the steaks had not been taken out of the freezer yet and jumped up to go get them out to start thawing before she started to dress while wondering what in the Name of God she had been talking about all afternoon.

Frank, driving downtown cautiously on the icing streets with both front windows rolled down wide open in the cold air, breathed great lung-freezing draughts of it and stared straight ahead vacantly, momentarily content with pure physical freedom.

He let his mind think about Geneve Lowe. It soothed him. He wondered when the hell she was going to call him about her next buying trip to Chicago, so he could arrange a business trip himself and meet her. He was getting damned impatient, suddenly.

Geneve was a good girl, in a lot of ways. She liked (or pretended to like, he amended cautiously) the same things he liked, that men liked. Drinking parties at the hotel, to nightclub at the Chez Paree, to eat in the big restaurants, to buy things, to spend money, to go to ball games, and she was always meticulously careful never to let herself or him either step over the fun line into anything like seriousness. Frank could hardly conceive of two women, members of the same sex, being so completely unlike.

As a matter of fact, he thought, he had lived with Agnes so long he found it almost impossible to believe there were women like that like Geneve even when he knew it.

As he pulled up the hill onto the courthouse square, hoping Agnes would not go lie down on her bed and forget to take the steaks out of the freezer, he let his mind run over the last Chicago trip as a sort of palliative for his ego which had gone into deep shock from its terrible injury. If he paid for all this Chicago fun, Geneve was smart enough never to ask for more than she could equitably get. And she was sexy, or else (he amended cautiously) made a damned good show at acting like she was. And it was reasonable to assume she was, he thought. Her father, Old Doc Callaghan, had achieved local renown as being the horniest man ever to live in Cray County. That was what lost him his practice, the husbands got so they wouldnt send their wives to Doc and Doc died a drunk. Life was funny. Strange. Who would have thought when as a grown young man of seventeen he used to be sent to Doc Callaghan for his gut aches and sundry ills that he would someday be laying Doc's daughter, then a tiny baby. He knew she was an avaricious little flip, and that she led Al by the nose and dominated him completely, and that she was as cold blooded a little tiger as existed anywhere. He knew all that as well as anyone in Parkman knew it. And everyone in Parkman knew it. But if Al Lowe couldnt control his own wife enough to keep her from dominating him, that was his lookout the damned jerk. And if Geneve was ambitious, it was the long range ambition that would someday make her the respected owner of Dotty Callter's Mode Shop and her husband the respected manager of Hirsh's Jewelry Store. It was not the short range ambition of the gold digger or the blackmailer. Her cold bloodedness was the absolute hundred per cent variety that would never make an enemy of someone who could help her. Like Frank Hirsh. That kind of cold bloodedness you could trust. And he never had to worry about her being careful. She was always careful. Sometimes he thought she was almost too careful.

The infuriating thing about Agnes, he thought, the almost apoplectic thing, was that she never let logic or facts bother her a bit.

It made him feel some better thinking about Geneve but when he pulled up at the hotel and went inside he was still flat eyed and dead faced, his neck pulled in, from the hiding he had taken. Staring straight ahead of him as he got out of the car, he did not see his brother jump back savagely from the lighted corner window.

Upstairs, in his two room corner suite, Dave Hirsh had shaved, and showered, anointed himself with lotion, and donned the clean pressed o.d. pants and khaki shirt. He dressed carefully and fully. He even removed the set of everyday ribbons that were smudged and dingy and replaced them with the new set that he kept back for state occasions, pinning them carefully onto his blouse laid out on the bed so they would be perfectly straight and centered properly. Then, smelling good, clean and shining, he went out into the sitting room and sat down with the nail file from his kit. As usual, he had hurried so as not to be late and had gotten done far too soon so that there was nothing left to do but wait.

It was typical, he thought, depression overwhelming him. He put the nail file away and mixed himself one more drink and sat down to wait.

It was already dark outside. If there was anything he hated to do it was to wait. Waiting was always bad, especially waiting dressed and alone for it to be time to go to a party. Dusk was the worst time of day for it too and that was always when you did it. He wondered how many times in his life he had sat in rented furnished rooms at dusk, waiting alone for a party to start somewhere. He hoped suddenly that 'Bama had not been kidding him about that woman.

Feeling miserable and fearing for the crease in his pants in the warm room, he got up and took his drink with him to the window. The street lamps and the colored signs were on now all around the square, and he stood looking at them with that same melancholy feeling of the outsider who has tried to return to something he left too long ago. It was a silly damn thing to have done, he thought sadly.

Below him a Buick sedan drove in diagonally to the curb and turned off its lights. Dave stepped back from the window quickly, cursing furiously.

When the phone rang on its little table, he was waiting for it. "Frank? Okay!" he said jubilantly. "Be right down, boy!" He hung up and got his issue overcoat and turned off the lights, hoping his voice sounded carefree enough.

Frank was waiting at the desk. It had been nineteen years since they had seen each other, since they had spoken, since they had shaken hands. It had been a nineteen years of implacable and unrelenting warfare, a nineteen years of each trying to make the other admit he was the one who was and had been wrong, and of each nursing secretly the resentment that the other could treat him such a way. For nineteen years there had been only the occasional word heard and then long periods of silence. And all that time each had displayed publicly his violent and acid contempt for the other's personality and way of life. A stranger from an alien planet who did not know much about the human race might reasonably have expected them to fall upon each other with knives or clubs, right there in the lobby. Instead, both had trouble keeping the tears of affection out of their eyes.

They shook hands awkwardly, and looked each other over eagerly for the changes nineteen years had effected, saying the usual awkward words of greeting to cover the inspection. Then they went out the door talking friendlily and grinning, each carefully on his guard now that the moment of emotion had been successfully weathered.

If any of the people sitting in the lobby had hoped to see a scene when they saw Frank Hirsh enter, they were badly disappointed.

As they walked to the door Dave's ego bloomed. He had come off best by far in the mutual inspection, and both knew it. Frank, who had still been young enough to look like an ex-athlete when Dave left, and whom Dave had seen no pictures of since then, had at forty-five thickened considerably in facial features and in belly, and simultaneously seemed to have grown smaller in shoulders and legs. He had also acquired that sanguine complexion and slightly self satisfied air of a successful businessman, and in the acquiring of it had lost a good bit of hair off his head. On the other hand, the Army had toughened Dave considerably and Frank, who had seen pictures of him in Hollywood, was unprepared for it. The result was that Dave felt elatedly magnanimous.

Outside they stopped on the steps under the marquee in the cold air and lit cigarettes, cupped palms holding the matches against their faces in the dark.

"Its a shame you had to come down and pick me up like this," Dave said.

"Hell, its a privilege," Frank said. "Dont think about it. Dont even mention it. The Army's been good for you."

"Yeh. Youd think this townd be big enough to support a taxi service, wouldnt you?" Dave said, looking all around disdainfully. "Then you wouldntve had to come get me."

Frank felt suddenly as if somebody had exploded a bomb inside of him. He didnt answer immediately. Why the hell hadnt he ever thought about a taxi service in this town? Why hell that might be the very investment hed been looking for to get Dave into. It would be one hell of a fine investment in this town, growing like it was.

"Yes, youd think itd be big enough," he said cautiously. "And we need one too. Come on, lets go," he said and started down the steps.

They climbed into the dimly lit front seat of last year's Buick and Frank drove along slowly west away from the hotel and from town although he had meant to turn back east toward home at the next corner, running down the slope of the wet brick street between the rows of spaced and lighted streetlamp globes for several blocks before he spoke. He was still thinking about that taxi service. An idea like that ought to be taken advantage of right away, before somebody else thought of it and beat you to it.

Dave didnt speak either. Aware that he had come off best in the inspection and ready to utilize his advantage as soon as he got the chance, he had slid into the front seat of the car to find his nose suddenly assailed by an olfactory memory so strong it threatened to completely suspend his time-sense and make non-existent the war and Hollywood and everything else that had happened to him since he was seventeen. Sniffing the odor of the car—composed of equal parts dusty upholstery, stale cigar smoke, barber's witch hazel, old raincoats, and spilled powder from Agnes's compact, the same smell in this '46 Buick as in Frank's old '26 Studebaker sedan that he remembered—he felt again the luxurious sense of security he had always felt with his older brother, and had not felt anywhere else in the world since. He was suddenly hit with a jaw tightening, almost eye moistening emotion. Even at twenty-six Frank had smoked those cigars. Wanting to laugh, wanting to cry, feeling luxuriously safer than he had felt in years, he sat back grimly and said nothing and looked out at the town which had changed so incredibly little, still determined to use his advantage as soon as he got the chance. You cant let your damned emotions run away with you, by God. Quite suddenly he hated Frank.

"I didn't know you lived out in this end of town now?" he said finally.

"No. No," Frank said, putting the taxi service out of his mind, "as a matter of fact, we live back east. I just thought Id drive around a little bit so wed sort of get used to each other a little before we went back to the house. You havent seen our new house, have you?"

"No," Dave said. "Nor the last two before that. Whats to get used to?"

"Oh," Frank grinned, "I guess weve both changed a little, since we saw each other. A little older. A little smarter."

Dave laughed out loud. "Were both older all right. Especially you. And you may be smarter. I dont guess I am. In fact I know Im not."

"Maybe you dont want to be," Frank said. "Anyway, youre lookin' awful good." This was certainly not the time to talk to him about that taxi service.

"Yeah, thats the Army," Dave grinned cockily. "I feel in better shape than Ive felt in years."

Frank cleared his throat. "I didnt know you were in the Infantry?" he said, nodding at the Combat Badge.

"I wasnt. I was in the QM. My outfit was awarded the Badge for voluntarily fighting as Infantry during the Bulge."

"I didnt know you were in the Battle of the Bulge."

"Yeah," Dave said. "I was there."

Frank drove on another block.

"I see youve got the Presidential Citation ribbon, too."

"Yeah. Got that for the same deal."

Frank nodded. "Did you know that I bought more war bonds than any other man in Cray County durin' the war?"

"No!" Dave said. "Is that right?"

Frank gave him a sidelong glance. He drove on another block or so. "Werent you scared of gettin' killed all the time?" he asked.

"Sure but once you get used to it, thats not so bad," Dave said. "Its kind of fun. After you get used to the idea of people dying, of you dying, and realize its nothing abnormal or supernatural under the circumstances," he explained knowledgeably. "The only hard thing," he explained, "is right at first while youre getting accustomed to this idea that a person dying is normal and common everyday, and not something weird and unusual." He grinned at Frank. He had once thought about writing a novel on this theme, in France.

Frank didnt say anything but his acute distaste showed on his face.

"Its just a simple problem in adjustment," Dave said nonchalantly. "If youre an integrated personality, you adjust."

Frank nodded. He had driven to within a block of the railroad and the end of the brick without knowing it. He turned right, to the north, and went on around the block back east toward town. "We better get on home," he said. "I guess youd rather not talk about it anyway."

Over here off the mainstreet Wernz Avenue the houses were smaller and there were no rows of streetlamps, only the street lights—bare bulbs in reflectors hung over the center of the street at corners—and the light would come and then be gone, come and then be gone, on their faces through the windshield.

"No," Dave said somberly, "as a matter of fact I wouldnt. I want to forget all that."

Frank nodded solemnly and drove on a piece. "I guess you think I did wrong," he said suddenly, "makin' you leave town that time?"

"Why no," Dave said. "As matter of fact, Ive always felt you did me a favor. Otherwise Id probly still be here, married to that little gal, or some other little gal, workin in some office, goin home to the same house every night of the world, payin the electric bill every month."

"There are a lot of worse ways of spendin' your life than that," Frank said.

"Not for me there aint."

"I guess you were right a while ago," Frank said. "I guess you havent got any smarter."

"I guess not," Dave said. Then suddenly he couldnt go on with it any more. Maybe it was too easy. "I didnt mean to go casting aspersions on your way of life," he said.

Youre a chameleon, he told himself, feeling in him the liquor he had drunk back at the hotel to ward off his loneliness. Back there he could hardly stand it. An emotional chameleon, thats what you are. You can be anybody. You become somebody else with everyone youre with. That may be a good thing in a writer, but its a damn poor trait in a human being.

"Oh, sure," Frank said. "I know that."

"What we need is a drink," Dave suggested gently.

"Thats a damn good suggestion," Frank said, and suddenly remembered Agnes was waiting for them at home. His nervous anxiety was at once restored to him full blown. He even forgot his plans for the taxi service with Dave. He had forgotten all about Agnes in his guilty talk of war. It was like sex. It seemed to him suddenly that he never felt anything but either anxiety or guilt or fear anymore. Even when he was with Geneve in Chicago, fear of meeting someone who knew them was what dictated most of his movements.

But of course that wasnt true either. He felt all kinds of happy things. All the time. Didnt he.

"This is our street," he said cheerfully, and swung the wheel with his shoulders turning the corner. "Its only a few blocks from here. Then well get that drink."

"Great," Dave said gently, but already beginning to be mad at himself for chickening out.

They drove the rest of the way in silence, Frank worrying about the reception Agnes would give Dave and trying to decide whether to have him go up to the door alone or not, Dave worrying because he had chickened out on his advantage over Frank and thinking there sure must be something wrong with him somewhere. Neither of them, at this long postponed moment of meeting, was even considering how strange it was that of all the men alive in the world to choose from, they two should be brothers; or gave the slightest thought to the two persons responsible for this, namely their parents, who—with monumental sang-froid, with complete lack of forethought, perhaps even with indifference, certainly unwittingly and uncarefully, with absolutely no scientific objectivity, driven and harried by that biological loneliness characteristic of the Mammalia as a man is driven and harried into shelter by the weather since he cannot control it either—had, with the sanction of religion and politics and in the name of human good, engaged in an attempt (largely unsuccessful) to relieve themselves of loneliness and labeled it virtue after the fashion of their species, but which actually resulted mainly only in the making of their offspring relatives; and who, of all the people in the world were the most nearly responsible for having made them the singular, and largely unhappy individuals, that they were. Neither of them thought of this. But when the car pulled in the driveway and stopped, they both thought sentimentally that it had been a nice ride together, a fine way to meet after nineteen years.

CHAPTER 9

FRANK neednt have worried about Agnes at all. Agnes was positively radiant. She had bathed, fixed her hair, and dressed, and she looked fresh and happy and expensive and at least ten years younger. There were no signs whatever that less than an hour before she had been either exhausted or tearful, or furious. She led Dave inside with such honest welcome and charming grace that it appeared she had been waiting this whole nineteen years, just for him to return to Parkman.

Not only that, little Dawn who had got home from the Glee Club rehearsal was right there with her, equally dressed up and part of the welcoming committee. Dawn was at that age where she felt it unworthy of her new-found intelligence to have anything to do with her parents except at mealtimes. So this could only, Frank knew, have been Agnes's doing.

The house was shiningly immaculate and looked lovely in the light of the lamps and the subdued indirect lighting he had had put in. The big table in the small dining room had been laid with full service for six, dazzling white and bright silver. The cocktail things were laid out invitingly on the buffet.

It was a fine home Frank thought and went straight to the buffet and nervously poured himself a stiff shot of the rye for the Manhattans. Then and only then, he followed them on out to the kitchen.

Agnes was proudly showing Dave how the automatic dishwasher worked. Dawn had already gone back into the living room and gotten herself a book.

"Thats all there is to it!" Agnes said. "When you take them out, theyre done. Washed, rinsed, and dried. Its one of the first ones in town. The only thing you have to be careful of is to rinse all the food off under the faucet before you put them in."

"Its amazing," Dave said.

From the way she bragged it up in company, Frank thought wistfully, you could almost believe it actually meant something to her. In spite of his anger, which still hurt his ears and which the liquor had not helped yet, he decided proudly that for a woman of her age his wife was a remarkably beautiful woman when she wanted, in spite of the thickening around her middle. He walked over to her from the door and draped his arm around her waist.

"Maybe Dave's not interested in our domesticity, mama."

"Oh, no!" Dave said. "Im interested." He was beginning to recover a little from his embarrassment at the effusive welcome he had not expected.

"Of course it probably doesnt mean much to you men," Agnes smiled lovingly, taking Frank's hand that was on her flank into her own. "But it means an awful lot to a housewife."

"Ill bet it does," Dave nodded eagerly. He was determined to be a superlative guest and get along with all of them, especially Agnes, so that nobody especially Agnes could run him down afterwards.

"You men would probably rather talk about some old car or a business deal," Agnes said girlishly. "But I did want to show off my pretty house." She gave Frank an open sidelong smile, her eyes alight with a great deal of love that had not been there earlier today before Dave came on the scene. And which, Frank thought matter of factly, would not be there again later after Dave left.

"Well, we will certainly show it to him, mama," he said heartily. "All of it."

"I want to see it," Dave said.

"First wed better get him a drink," Agnes said turning her warm smile on Dave. "I ought to be ashamed, running him all over the house before he even gets a drink."

"A capital idea," Frank said.

"You didnt run me all over the house," Dave said.

"Now you just be still, Dave," she smiled. "I dont want any back talk from you."

"—and thats orders from headquarters!" Frank winked.

"Will you mix them, poppy?" Agnes said.

"I sure will. Gladly," Frank grinned, rubbing his hands together. "Are you goin' to have one, mama?"

"Well, maybe just one," Agnes said. "Since this is a special occasion." She smiled at Dave modestly, with girlish excitement. "I hope you like Manhattans, Dave?"

"Love Manhattans," Dave said.

"We're Manhattan drinkers," she said. "Poppy's famous for his Manhattans. Besides we're too old to be changing back and forth from gin to whiskey, we're exclusively whiskey."

"Im an old whiskey drinker myself," Dave said. He wondered how long it was going to go on? Would it be like this all evening?

"Lets go on in and watch him make them," Agnes suggested. "Its really a treat to see."

"Swell!" Frank said, leading the way and winking at Dave. "Mama knows I always do better when Ive got an audience."

"Now, poppy," Agnes chided. "He really makes the best Manhattans you ever tasted," she said to Dave.

Carl A. Rudisill Library
LENOIR RHYNE COLLEGE

Together, after Frank had mixed the drinks and handed them round, they showed Dave over the rest of the house, explaining how they had redesigned the closets for more space, showing how they had added the bathroom to the two half-storey upstairs rooms which were Dawn's by placing it directly over their own, all of them carrying their drinks as they went. They pointed out how they had torn out the wall between the living room and the dining room, so that there was now a wide arch there instead of a single door, and they showed him how they had added onto the small furnace-basement for a small rumpus room by digging out under a portion of the house that wasnt basemented, and as a sort of pièce de résistance they took him last to the Parkman-envied utility room. Then they came back to the dining room for another drink.

Frank needed one badly. As he had moved around the house conducting the tour he gradually descended from the ear-hurting anger of earlier down into an acute depression. It was a good act they put on for guests, he and Agnes, and he was proud of it. He considered it much better than the acts of their friends. But he wished that sometime they could just continue to play the act for a little while when they were alone by themselves.

What depressed him was not so much that they were dishonest, he did not mind lying to Dave, he had no moral qualms about lying to anybody when it was necessary, neither did Agnes, though she professed to, and rightly. What depressed him was that the act would not continue to go on between them after the guests were gone.

"Are you goin' to have another one with us, mama?" he asked.

Agnes was, under Dave's gaze, delicately inspecting the layout of the dinner table. She straightened a salad fork a sixteenth of an inch and turned back and smiled at Dave sweetly before she answered.

"Well, do you really think it would be all right?" she said coquettishly. "I might get giggly."

"Go right ahead!" Frank boomed, and winked at Dave. "Go right ahead! Youre among friends."

"Well all right," Agnes laughed blushing girlishly. "Just one more then. I dont ordinarily, but I will this once."

She turned back to the table. "Were having a couple of other people in to dinner to meet you," she said to Dave. "Thats why the six places."

"Yes," Frank said. "Theyre Robert Ball French and his daughter Gwen. You remember them, Dave?"

Oh no, Dave thought dismally, oh no. "Just barely," he said. "I went to school to Bob French."

"Theyre both writers," Agnes said. "Thats why I asked them. I thought youd have something in common to talk about that way. Bob French is really quite well known nationally as a poet."

"Yes," he said. "Ive heard of him." Oh no, he thought again, oh no.

Carl A. Rudisill Library
LENOIR RHYNE COLLEGE

"Well. Now you boys just go on in the other room and sit down and have your drinks," Agnes said. "Im going out in the kitchen and get things started. You bring my drink out there for me, poppy."

"Sure thing," Frank said. "I sure will." He had just sneaked another shot of the straight rye.

"Thats sure a beautiful table youve got laid there," Dave said. He was in it now, all the way, might as well play it out to the bitter end. Even with the literary Frenches dragged into it, he was still determined to be a superlative guest.

Agnes stopped in the kitchen doorway indifferently. "Oh, Dawn and I didnt have much time. We would have fixed a real dinner if wed known you were coming."

"I tried to call her all afternoon, Dave," Frank said, "after I talked to you. But she was out gallivantin' someplace."

"So youll just have to take pot luck with us," Agnes said demurely. She went on into the kitchen. Her dark eyes were bright with party-excitement and pleasure. Nobody knew the initial energy that had been required of her to lift herself into this state of party-excitement. It had been tremendous, almost heart-bursting, and its expenditure and loss would almost certainly show itself later. But right now, like a space ship that had almost exploded itself to reach escape velocity, she could shut off and just coast the rest of the way on her own previously expended fuel.

"Here, Dave," Frank said, "you take this on in the other room and talk to little Dawn. Ill join you in a minute, soon's I fix mama's."

Dutifully, Dave wandered into the front room through the archway which once had been a single door, holding his glass carefully. He was tiring fast from being a superlative guest. Everything had moved so fast and frenetically. And now the damned Frenches, who wanted to do a book on lesser writers, such as D. HIRSH, were being hauled into it. He might just as well have gone ahead and gone out with Wally Dennis. Dawn was curled up with her book in the big, leather easy chair. He sat down in the lesser, upholstered one.

Dawn looked up briefly with wide eyes that stared straight into the center of his forehead, smiled at it distantly, and then looked back down her young hair falling about her young face and hiding its sternly adult expression.

Dave cleared his throat and took a swallow of his drink. She had been his niece for over seventeen years, he calculated, although he did not feel like an uncle. She was born two years after he left and he had never seen her in the flesh. He had seen pictures of her—as a fat baby, as a less fat little girl, as an extremely unfat big girl (as if the fat had all receded inward, gathering its forces for the onslaught of womanhood when it would suddenly swell out again at the particular right places over-night)—but since going overseas he hadnt even seen pictures of her.

In those two years the transformation had taken place. Curled with supple joints in the chair with her high school girl's haircut and the tightish cashmere sweater, pleated thick wool skirt, bobbysox and red moccasin-toed loafers—The Uniform, as it were—her breasts were not budding, but had budded; and her thighs were not swelling, but had swelled. And by some curious mechanism in him which cropped up at times and carried him forcibly into the mind of the person he was facing, he knew that at this moment she was intensely aware of it and expected him to be aware of it too. Dave shifted uneasily in his chair. He was aware of it all right. She had the same short stocky body all the Hirshes had only on her it looked good he thought, and everything about her shouted eloquently that she was just waiting, putting in time, confidently and with supreme assurance, until somebody or other came along and adored her, as she knew it was her inalienable right to be adored.

He cleared his throat again.

"I met a friend of yours uptown today," he said tentatively.

"Oh?" Dawn said, raising her head on her pretty neck slowly. "Who was that?"

"Boy named Wally Dennis," Dave said.

"Oh, Wally," Dawn smiled patronizingly. "Yes. Ive had a few dates with him. He thinks he wants to become a writer, someday maybe. Hes a nice enough fellow." She looked back down at her book.

That seemed to have closed that subject. Dave cleared his throat again.

"Whatre you reading?" he asked conversationally.

Dawn looked up—at his forehead, with widened eyes—without closing the book. "The Remembrance of Things Past," she said, and looked back down primly.

"Proust?" Dave said. "Have they got a course in him in high school now?"

"Oh no," she said, looking up at his forehead again and still not closing the book. "My dramatics teacher recommended it to me."

"Thats kind of heavy reading for a high school girl."

Dawn smiled. "Oh, do you think so? I didnt think so, I like him very much."

"I never could get much out of him, myself," Dave said. "He always seemed a little bit too sensitive for me."

Dawn's face took on a look of genuine horror. "Oh, no! Thats the very thing thats so wonderful about him! You dont really think that, do you!"

"About Proust?" Dave said hastily, "well, maybe I put it a bit too strongly."

"He has one of the most exquisite sensibilities of any man Ive ever read," Dawn said.

"Yes, he certainly has a great sensibility," Dave agreed. "Well. See, I knew so many third rate intellectuals out in Hollywood, you see. Who made such a fetish of Proust. I guess it turned me against him."

"But do you think thats fair? Its hardly fair to blame Proust for that, is it?"

"No. Of course it isnt. That was just what I was going to say." Dave took another tentative swallow of his drink, wondering what the hell was keeping Frank. From where he sat he could see the kitchen door where Frank had gone.

As if mollified by his last remark, Dawn closed her book with finality, and with all the seductiveness of a thirty-year-old siren turned upon Dave a brilliant lovely smile, her eyes kindling and changing inwardly with a half-bold, half-shy knowledge of her own attractiveness. It was at once an innocently girlish, and an artfully womanish, gesture and it made him mad.

He was already half mad. What with the painful discussion of Proust, and the abortively affectionate turn the whole evening had taken. He tossed off the rest of his drink savagely, and was not relieved.

Smiling lovingly, although more at herself than at him, Dawn laced her fingers on the chair arm and squirmed around in the chair facing him and settled herself to talk unaware she was exposing as she did so a portion of young thigh still faintly colored by summer tan.

"You were a protégé of Saroyan, werent you?" she said, "out *there*."

Dave could not keep his eyes from looking covertly at the line of his niece's skirt hiding the rest of her bare athletic thigh. Outwardly embarrassed, inwardly raging, he toyed with his empty glass and tried to stare fixedly at the cherry in it.

"Lord no, I never met the man."

"I read your stories and the books. You know, the ones Aunt Francine sent us. They sounded a lot like Saroyan."

"Oh, we all copied him," Dave said abortively, "during the 'Thirties. Him or Steinbeck, if you lived in California. In the East it was Thomas Wolfe. They were the only ones that sold." Ought to make a recording.

He had not had a woman since a week before he was discharged. He wished now he had thought of that last night in Chicago when he had the chance, before coming down here where there werent any whorehouses. There used to be some down in Terre Haute when he was a kid, he remembered. But doubtless the war had closed all those.

He sure hoped 'Bama wasnt kidding about that woman.

"Whats it really like," Dawn asked eagerly, "out *there*? Is it really as fabulous as they say it is?"

Her face eager, Dawn shifted her bottom in the chair and pulled her skirt down, unthinkingly and instinctively, without even looking down or realizing it had been up. In spite of the relief he felt Dave suffered a tender regret, it was like watching the curtain come down on a play you had enjoyed.

"I dont know what its like if youve got money. Without money, its just like everyplace else."

"But youre going back out there, though. Arent you?" Dawn said, smiling that brilliant seductive smile. All her former distance and reserve seemed suddenly to have evaporated, as if shed forgotten.

"Only because Ive got a job waitin for me," Dave lied, rolling the cherry around in the glass.

"At the studios?"

Dave nodded. If he had of had one, hed be damned if hed take it.

"Which studio did you work for?"

"Universal, mostly. RKO a little while." It sounded almost good, when you said it that way. Seven class Z westerns was what it really was, as a junior writer, and then they had never used a single line he had written.

"Oh, sometimes I wish I were a man!" Dawn said. "Men get to do so many more things than women do. I dont think its fair."

"Well, women can do lots of things men cant, too," Dave said wistfully. "Ive often wished I was a woman."

"What," Dawn demanded. "Name one."

He at once realized hed dug himself into a hole. "Oh, lots of things," he said vaguely. Awkwardly.

"If youre referring to sex," his seventeen-year-old niece said incisively and without embarrassment, "even that isnt true. Thats a myth. Men get to go out and sleep with all kinds of women whenever they want, and nobody but their wives thinks a thing about it. But women arent made like that. They cant do that."

"I guess thats right," Dave said difficultly, "except that some of them do." He wished to hell Frank would come back.

"Oh, well! That kind," Dawn said contemptuously, and shifted her woman's bottom girlishly in the chair again with disdain, and went back to her point.

"Men get to do all kinds of things women dont. You left home and went on your own when you were my age. You bummed around the country and worked at lots of different jobs and lived your own life and had experiences. Thats what made you an artist. But what about me? What if I wanted to write? You think Id ever get a chance to do that? Even if Frank and Agnes would let me, which they wouldnt, I still couldnt do it because Im a female."

"Are you writing?" Dave said, with relief.

"Oh, no. I dont write. Except for a few little things. I thought you knew. Acting is my field. Didnt Wally tell you?"

"Yes," Dave said. "Yes as a matter of fact he did. What I meant was did you write, *too*?"

"No. Only a few little things. Acting is my love."

"Movies?" Dave said.

"Heavens, no! I dont want to go to Hollywood," Dawn said. "I want to really act."

Dave nodded. "New York, then."

"From what I understand," Dawn said seriously, "the only way to go to Hollywood is to go there direct from New York, anyway. With a name."

"I guess it helps," Dave said. He was suddenly aware that he was being complimented—complimented?—with the bestowal of confidences the rest of the family probably never had heard.

"Ive made plans," Dawn said secretively. "I may not even go to college."

"College never helped any kind of an artist," Dave said didactically, and instantly.

"There, you see? I know. You just proved my point. Thats why I mean to go to New York on my own, and make my own break. But dont tell the folks."

"Well now wait a minute," Dave hedged. "Thats a pretty tough row to hoe in New York. Theres lots of competition."

"Not if youve got what it takes," Dawn said.

"Well, a little college training wouldnt hurt you there," he hedged. He suddenly felt very inadequate to advise anybody, especially a seventeen-year-old niece with such a passion for acting it would allow her to tear up roots like a man furiously clearing and burning a pasture. To talk about the theories he had evolved about art and artists was one thing. But it was something else again to advise a girl to go out among all the producers, stage managers, actors, and messenger boys (not to mention female actors) whom she would probably have to test her determination to become a star by sleeping with, in order to get on a stage at all. Some girls it didnt bother. Whenll you learn to keep your big fat mouth shut?

"Well, if a person wants to do a thing," Dawn said, looking pleased that she had frightened him, "he or she ought to do it, without trying to hedge or be safe."

Out of the corner of the eye he had kept peeled at the kitchen door, Dave saw Frank come through it into the dining room still holding his drink. Dawn heard him, and rearranged her face. Frank's face looked congested Dave noticed, as if there must have been quite a scene in the kitchen. Probably over himself. Frank gulped off part of his drink greedily and came into the living room smiling heartily.

The scene in the kitchen had not been over Dave. It had been over the fact that Agnes had caught him sneaking drinks of the straight rye and had taken him to task for it with a whip-tongued vengeance all out of proportion to the way she looked and had been acting. The result of course was, he wanted to drink more.

"Whatre you two gabbin' about?" he said cheerfully, taking Dave's glass.

"Weve been discussing Marcel Proust," Dawn said.

"Whos he?" Frank said cheerfully.

"Oh, Daddy!" Dawn said, flushing.

"Whats the matter? Did I say the wrong thing?"

"You do know who Proust is," Dawn said exasperatedly. "The writer. I was just talking to you about him the other night." She hadnt been. She had never read him.

"I dont remember it." Frank's hearty laugh was a little too hearty, especially for a man with his embarrassed face. "My God, child. I cant remember all the writers you talk to me about. I got to make a livin for this family." He laughed again, with Rotarian heartiness.

"He always acts like that," Dawn said, smiling at Dave with desperate levity. "Youd think he never read a book in his life."

"Well, I havent, except for one or two," Frank grinned.

"Oh, Daddy! Please stop acting like a country farmer! It doesnt become you!" Under the light smile on her face there was an edge in her voice. She got up suddenly from the chair, smiling that desperate light smile, collected her book and walked with her woman's body above which floated the desperate child's face across the room to the door into the hall where the stairway was.

"Wait a minute. Where you think youre going?" Frank said.

"Why, upstairs. To read," Dawn said lightly. "I cant concentrate here with you men talking."

"But supperll be ready in a little bit," Frank said. "I mean dinner."

"Well? Cant you call me, silly?" Dawn said lightly. "Youll want your big chair. And I cant read on the davenport." She turned her desperate, bright, shamed smile upon Dave, whereupon it became again that brilliant, lovely and incredibly sexy smile of before which kindled her eyes, then changed back just as suddenly to the other one as she turned away and was gone before Frank had a chance to answer.

Frank looked for a moment as if he wasnt sure whether he should order her back and reprimand her but if so what for and also that if he did there was sure to be a row. Then he sank into the big leather armchair with an affected "Ahhh!" of satisfaction.

"Shes an awful tempermental kid," he said proudly, and then realized he still had Dave's glass in his hand. "Wait, Ill get you another drink."

"Thanks," Dave said. He was debating whether he should ask Frank about the possibility of getting a woman in Parkman, and wondering if he did whether Frank would guess it was his daughter's figure which had brought it on. He decided against. Frank would probably let on he didnt know anyway.

On his way to the buffet Frank furtively drank off the rest of his own drink. As he mixed them both new ones he kept on talking about Dawn back over his shoulder to Dave in the living room.

"Shes really a very talented girl. I dont say that just because shes my kid. Her teachers all say it. But shes awful headstrong. And now shes got this idea about bein' an actress. I dont mind her bein' an actress. Shes always more or less wanted to be an actress. Myself, I think she ought to do somethin' in the artistic line like that. Shes too smart and too egotistical to ever be happy as just a housewife. But now I think shes got the idea that four years at college would just be wastin' her time. Every time we try to talk to her about college she just clams up and gets vague on us. And shell graduate next June. Its time she ought to be thinkin' about her college."

Frank left off working on the drinks to peek at the kitchen door, and then took a stiff shot of the straight rye. Then he went on talking about the colleges. He had looked into it, and he had done a thorough job of it. He knew his ground as he talked. There were all kinds of good schools for dramatic training. Western Reserve in Cleveland, Arthur Jordan in Indianapolis, Northwestern University. She could go to any of them she wanted. If that was what his daughter wanted, by God that was what she was going to have. But she was going to have to go to school, and that was all there was to it, and he was afraid he was going to have to set his foot down.

From the kitchen came the steel and pottery and mechanical sounds of someone preparing to cook with a multitude of intricate equipment, and the faint sounds of the foodstuff itself—the wet crisp whisper of the salad lettuce, the rich clinging slap of the uncooked meat as it was moved on the counter, the murmur of the grease boiling in the french-frier.

—and upstairs in the two little sloping-roofed rooms and bath which she had decorated herself and liked to call her apartment Dawn, who had always hated her name even though she knew the history of it which was as her mother who had picked it always said that she was born just at daybreak, Dawn lay face down on her bed in a misery so overwhelming it made suicide seem enjoyable. She should never have let out her secret to Dave, he would almost certainly tell Frank. And she should *never* have taken The Remembrance of Things Past down there in order for Dave to see her reading it when he came. She should have *known* better. But how was she to know the only artist in the family would think Proust was passé. Oh what a fool. Almost any other book would have been better. And Frank. Frank had made it ten times worse. And Agnes acting like a giggly school girl. The book lay on the floor where she had dropped it and she had no inclination to pick it up, now or ever again, who the hell wanted to read Proust, and she looked around her place which she had done herself, at the larger bedroom done very femininely in fuchsia with its head- and foot-less Hollywood bed and the overstuffed chaise longue, at the smaller study done very masculine and businesslike in white with its panel desk and typewriter and the tacked up book jackets and dance programs and painting reproductions covering the walls and ceiling, and it all seemed horrible, horrible and crappy and middle class. Just like she herself, who had made it. Just like the crappy high school dramatics training, and all the crappy middle class middlewestern colleges where the myriads of horrible and crappy and middle class girls congregated reverently with their horrible crappy middle class dramatics ambitions, horrible and crappy and middle class, well she was not going to any crappy middlewest college and study horrible dramatics, they could say what they wanted, and they could just wait, by God son of a bitch, and see. Swearing didnt help. She wanted to die.—

Downstairs, Frank brought the fresh drinks back into the living room. "As a matter of fact, Im just as glad the girl did go upstairs," he said, "because Ive got somethin' I want to talk to you about. Before the Frenches get here."

"Yes? Whats that?" Dave said. He already knew though.

"Well," Frank said, sitting down again in the big leather chair with that same affected "Ahhh!" of satisfaction, "its about your plans. For the future."

"Thats simple," Dave said. "I havent got any."

It had suddenly gotten like a poker game between them, in the room, and that stark hushed alertness, of a poker game, had manifested itself all over the room as if it were the back room at the Elks or the American Legion. There should have been a few steel gray cones of tobacco smoked light coming down from the ceiling, Dave thought, remembering what a good poker player Frank always had been.

"Its also about this money of yours youve got deposited in the Second National Bank," Frank said, sipping his drink.

"What about it?" Dave said casually.

"Theres no sense in us beatin' around the bush with each other," Frank said. "I happen to know how much youve got. A good friend of mine called me up and told me you deposited $5500 in the Second National not ten minutes after you did it. And if you didnt know that was what would happen, youre a lot dumber than I think you are." He grinned at Dave without rancor.

"I didnt think anything about it one way or the other," Dave said. "It just happened to be the bank nearest the hotel."

"Well, its none of my business where you put your money. Its not goin' to break me, or seriously injure the bank Im with, if you put it in the Second National. But I think you ought to plan to do somethin' with that money."

"Im planning to live on it," Dave said.

"Id hate to see you just throw it away."

"Im not figuring on throwin it away, just live on it."

"Theres an old saying that it takes money to make money. You cant live on it forever," Frank said. "You mind if I ask how you got it?"

"I won it. On the boat comin home from Europe," Dave said.

"Thats a lot of money to win at poker."

"They have some pretty big games, on those boats. Thats all there is to do."

Frank sipped his drink easily. "Well, Ive given that money of yours a considerable lot of thought in the last six hours," he said. "And Ive got an idea. As a matter of fact, you gave me the idea."

"I did?" The poker tension was getting deeper. As Frank had intended it should, Dave thought. Youve got to watch him, hes got something up his sleeve, and hes going to use it on you, just to get that money out of that bank. If for nothing else.

"And thats one reason I figured Id give you a chance to get in on it first."

"Well," Dave said, "I dont—"

"Its one of the best deals for a good investment Ive seen in some time," Frank interrupted. It reminded Dave of a heavy-tank he had seen in France once, outside St Lô, rolling steadily and peacefully over a forest of young saplings. "You said something in the car tonight, Dave, that struck home to me," he said. "About how this town was big enough any more it ought to be able to support a taxi service. I never thought of it before, and neither has anybody else I know of, but its true."

"Well the only reason I said that—" Dave said.

Frank waved his hand. "Its not important why you said it. I know why you said it. You were showin' off. The point is its a helluva good idea. I dont know why I never thought of it myself. So why cant the two of us go into it? Ive got a little loose money to invest and if you want to put your $5500 in, Ill put up $7000 to go with it and make you a junior partner. Im makin' you an offer. I think thats a fair deal."

"I think its a lot more than fair," Dave said. He meant it. Once more, he had been caught completely off balance by that wide-ranging, quick-shifting mind, strangely unvindictive in anything that had to do with money. "But Im just not interested in anything like that. A business."

"And why not? We buy three or four good used cars," Frank said complacently, "(I think I know where I can get us a deal on those. Im a silent partner in the Dodge-Plymouth agency.) and hire some drivers cheap and rent one of those little buildings just off the square for a taxi stand, put in a phone, and we're in business. Not too much capital outlay. And itd be a good little money maker from now on."

"Im sure it would be," Dave said, he was having difficulty remembering that Frank was trying to trick him with some kind of deal, "but I dont know anything about business, Frank. Why dont you put up the same as me and make me a full partner?"

"I dont think $11,000 will be enough to swing it," Frank said easily, sipping his drink. "Cars are awful high right now. Probably need runnin' capital for the first two three months, too."

"So for $1500 extra you get control of the business," Dave said.

"Well, you said yourself you dont know anything about business," Frank said. "I do."

"Thats true," Dave said thoughtfully. "Youre right there. I guess."

"On the other hand, youd be gettin' a little over two-fifths of the profits," Frank said. He paused a second, "Eleven-twentyfifths, to be exact. Thats more than a third. And you get none of the headaches."

Dave nodded. "You mean youd actually do all that for me? Just because Im your brother? and I gave you the idea?"

"Well, no," Frank said. "But I do need a partner. And I dont want to sink that much money in it by myself. And it was your idea. I dont see why you shouldnt profit by it." Frank was beginning to feel high. And it wasnt due to the liquor either. Even if he was beginning to feel it a little.

"I dont know," Dave said. He shook his head, thoughtfully. "Im no businessman and I know it." He looked up at his brother who was sipping at his drink, and watching him over the rim of the glass. "Youre not just doin all that to get my money out of that bank?"

"Jesus Christ," Frank said. "You think Id throw away $7000 just to get your money out of the Second National Bank?"

"Well no, but I could see where you might invest into a profitable thing like that, in order to do it. Itd get you back whatever prestige you lost, and still make you a profit too. Especially if people knew Id invested it with you?"

"I aint lost any prestige," Frank said. "Is that why you did it?"

"No," Dave said. "I told you. It just happened to be the closest bank to the hotel. I sent the bellboy over with it."

"Well," Frank said, sipping his drink, "youll never find a better deal to invest that money in."

"Well. I dont know," Dave said doubtfully.— "I dont see how I can do it," he said finally. "Ill need that money to get me back out to the Coast and to live on."

"Then dont go," Frank said, crossing his legs. "Stay here."

"Stay here! In this goddam town?"

"Well, sure," Frank said. "Why not? Now just wait a minute, just hold your horses till I tell you what I been thinkin' about."

—it was at moments such as these that he felt most alive he thought because he was seeing in his mind a deal like this and elaborating it and it was these moments that he lived for, but not because during them and out of them he had developed his best money-making schemes that were now paying him dependable profits and someday the profits would be bigger a lot bigger, no. The thing itself was the thrill—

—and if at other times like the unnerving scenes with Agnes and battles with Dawn and the times he thought Agnes had found out about Geneve Lowe or some other woman if then depression gripped him and fear ate at him these times like now made up for it and restored him and filled him back up again with the vitality and the enthusiasm—

Frank could see his life laid out straight ahead of him, happily married, a fine home and family, a prospering business, and unlimited prospects of success. Of ownership. Someday hed own the whole damned town.

"Look here," he said. "You need your money to get out to the West Coast, right? So if you go you cant put it in the taxi service, right? And if you do put it in, youll have to have something to live on, wont you? All right, weve got to have somebody to run the taxi service. I cant do it. Why pay a stranger? You stay here and run it. We pay you a livin' wage out of the profits. You run the taxi stand and check the drivers in and out and handle the money. You live off your salary, and save all of your share of the profits.

"Hell, no young man startin' out in business could ask for a better deal than that!" he said.

"What the hell," Dave said savagely. "I aint about to be startin out in business. And I aint about to be stayin in this damned hick town either. Is that what you been workin it toward?"

"But why not?" Frank said easily.

"Because I never had to yet and I dont want to now and I aint about to start. Thats why. Im here for a week and then Im takin my money out of that bank and Im off for California. And you can get your lost prestige back some other way."

"You think if I felt youd lost me any prestige, Id be tryin to make money for you?" Frank said.

"I dont know," Dave said. "You might. I never know what the hell you might do. What it amounts to is that Id be your employee, isnt it? Thatd look good in the town. No thank you."

"Not mine," Frank said. "The firm's. Of which youll be over two-fifths owner. And as such draw down over two-fifths of the firm's profits. In addition to your salary. Eventually, in time, you could quit the job part altogether someday."

"In how many years?" Dave said with a grin that was almost a snarl. "Fifty? And in addition youd have me right here where you could keep me under your thumb, workin for you, and let everybody see how you handled Brother Dave. Huh!"

"Well, it would take you a while," Frank said. "Naturally. You couldnt do it in a year. Ive been at it over twenty years myself and Im not quite ready myself. But with you, Id say in about five years youd have enough to quit the workin' and concentrate on the money-makin', if you really worked at it and put everything back into it. This town's boomin', boy, and anybody who gets in on the ground floor of it now— Theres no limit to what the two of us together could do."

"Yeah, with you as the boss, and me as the yesman."

"No, as partners," Frank said.

"And so what would I have then?" Dave said, grinning. "No thank you. I have no desire to be a bourgeois middlewestern businessman. And if I did, Im sure not goin to run any monotonous crappy little taxi stand for five years to do it. Sittin on your dead ass in some dinky little shack at some homemade desk of a table day in day out, hugging an Army-surplus space heater in the winter and a rotating electric fan in the summer, writin out trip tickets for drivers and takin phone calls. No sir. Not me. No thank you. I never lived like that yet, and I dont intend to start now."

"You dont expect to get anywhere in the world with that kind of an attitude, do you?" Frank said easily, sipping his drink. "You dont expect to make a fortune without workin' at least a little bit for it, do you?"

"I dont know," Dave said. "I dont care. Maybe not. The point is, I just misunderstood you. Hell, I could have done all that years ago if Id wanted to do that." Suddenly, just thinking about it, about being caught like that, he wanted to get up and run out somewhere, anywhere. Only there wasnt any place to run to. Or any one.

"Whatll you do when you get back to Hollywood?" Frank said. "You havent written anything at all for six years, have you?"

"I dont know!" Dave half yelled frenetically. "That doesnt matter! Thats not what we're talkin about!"

Behind them, in the hall, the four-chimed doorbell rang, seeming to take an eternity to get through its rigmarole of notes.

"Thats the Frenches," Frank said. "You think it over."

"I dont have to think it over," Dave said. "I know my answer right now."

Agnes came through from the kitchen, going to answer the door. Apparently very carefully, she did not look at either of them, as if she sensed her discretion was important right now.

"Listen to me," Frank said sincerely, and his voice was clear and stable but when he stood up he swayed a little. "Im not bullin' you.

Theres goin' to be a lot of big things come up in this town in the next few years. If I had time I could tell you about some of them I know about. Its goin' to boom. You and me could get in on it, and with some hard work and careful savin' and investin' we could the two of us take this town away from some of those snotty bastards like the Wernzes. And relieve them of a large part of their capital in the bargain. And I for one aim to do it. And if youre smart you will too."

"And whatll you have?" Dave said, "when you do it?"

"Ill have respect, and friendship, and the love," Frank said distinctly. "All the respect and friendship and the worship they always give the big boy, and that you and me never got in our whole lives because our old man ran off with the doctor's wife. Thats what."

"No you wont," Dave said. "Theyll just hate you more and laugh at you more." He got up, too.

"Oh yes I will," Frank said. "Oh yes I will. Because when youre the man with the money and the success everybody bows down to you, see? Now Ill go mix us all a little drink."

"Just dont count on me," Dave said. "I dont like this kind of life, and I never did, and Im not going to try to start now," he said after Frank as Frank swayed off toward the buffet to mix the drinks. Behind him he could hear the voices of them as they came toward the living room door and in through it, and he turned around to look at them and look them over feeling bull-ish and glowering and half-drunk and unhappy. How were you supposed to feel when you met somebody who wanted to dissect your private life for a book to explain why writers are writers?

He was sure Frank had been trying to put it over on him, he reflected, pull something. He was sure because Frank hadnt gotten mad or angry at a single thing he said.

They came through the door toward him, the three of them, Agnes leading and talking back over her shoulder in that party voice, then the woman smiling, and finally the man, and it was the man who caught and held his eyes and all of his attention.

He was a tall man, spare and very straight and he had close cropped snow white hair, very snug to the small beautifully rounded head, and with it an unusually full, heavy irongray mustache that was incongruous and out of place with such a short haircut and yet on this man belonged there, was the only way you could conceive him wearing it. He was probably sixty-eight. But most of all it was the eager mobility of the features, the almost childishly bright expectancy of the eyes, that demanded and captured, caught and held you, as if in a crowded room you suddenly saw him and for no reason with an unaccustomed warmth were just glad that he existed. Dave remembered him from high school with a different picture, doing both sides of the Hamlet duel scene with the yardstick, and wondered suddenly at the self-centered ignorance of youth that does not see.

But then thats probably all that keeps the young alive.

The woman, when he finally thought of her and looked, was different and yet the same. Sort of as if she had been consciously compounded, balanced mathematically of a given number of salient ingredients both of him and of her mother, whom Dave remembered as a large raw-boned woman. She was tall too, but there was more weight of bone in her, less fragility, yet a long-thighed delicacy of muscle too that the heaviness of the mother had not had, high wide square shoulders solidly under the slender neck, rawboned, with long hair—so long as to be unstylish—to the shoulders, but looking good in it, and Dave saw the thing in her that the gambler 'Bama Dillert had commented so positively upon that had impressed him too, a tension, a quietly held in restraint that did not let the inner eagerness out like her father, and in the very deepest bottom of the eyes where she no doubt thought that it was hidden this look of sexual (or would you say spiritual) expectancy, as if she unconsciously viewed every man she met in the world, not so much thinking as feeling, Perhaps this is him? Perhaps this is the one? and if she was smiling at Agnes at all, which you were positive she was, it was hard to be sure because it was such a small smile. Not beautiful. Not beautiful at all. Very uneven, irregular features, a completely unmatched face under masculine eyebrows that were unplucked. Two halves of two different faces, almost. Yet giving a strangely unlogical illusion of beauty in a boyishly female way that you knew was an illusion but couldnt help feeling anyway.

Dave was instantly and immediately positive he was going to like both of them, and felt even more bull-ish and glowering because he hadnt wanted to.

Agnes introduced them all to each other.

"Of course, of course," Bob French said delightedly, clasping his hand strongly, running those eyes openly and eagerly back and forth over his face, a blotter, an emotional blotter, getting impressions. Impressions that would be accurate, Dave thought. "I taught you your Shakespeare in high school. Not a very successful job of it though, Im afraid."

"You cant get blood out of turnips," Dave said. "Or pump it into them either."

"Its sad," Bob French said, "but its true. I might also say Ive read all of your work but I wont. Although I have."

Dave said nothing.

"How do you do?" Gwen French said. Her father had not bothered to wait for her to speak first. Her voice was low and very quiet, with a kind of quivering quality like a softly tapped drumhead stretched to the splitting point. She had much assurance. Selfcontained. She hardly seemed to be looking at him at all, not out of shyness, out of assurance, but he knew she was carefully studying him.

For the book no doubt, Dave thought bull-ishly, the goldfish. Hirsh the goldfish.

"I understand you teach creative writing," he said to her.

She smiled, the slight, slightly belligerent dig not lost on her, and did not answer. There was no need to. Her father laughed delightedly.

"Maybe you would teach me," Dave persisted. He knew it was bullish, but her father laughed delightedly again.

"She needs that," he said. "Give her more."

"Im afraid my courses are all filled for the rest of the semester," Gwen French said amiably. "Maybe next year?"

"Manhattans?" Frank called in a clear voice from the buffet where he stood swaying slightly, very slightly, every now and then.

The tableau broke up then and they all moved out into the dining room, Dave following the wide but boyish hips and long-boned thighs of Gwen French in the tailored suit.

"A Manhattan will be fine, Frank," she said in that voice. Self contained. Assurance.

"Well I want a Martini," Bob French said delightedly, as if anticipating one for the very first time. "And dont tell me you havent got the stuff."

"You!" Frank said, grinning. "You would," and bent down to the buffet door. "Youre too old to drink Martinis, Bob, you know that."

"Of course!" Bob French said, in that delighted, selfoblivious voice which was apparently always as eager as his face. "Thats why I drink them! They give me a distinct illusion of youth. Erroneous, perhaps," he grinned boyishly under the heavy mustache, "but nonetheless, distinct."

His daughter smiled at him tolerantly.

"Its quite true, Guinevere," he said. "Dont grin."

He was, Dave thought, the youngest one in the room.

He hoped dinner would sober him up a little.

CHAPTER 10

THE Frenches did not actually live in Parkman at all, it turned out at dinner. They lived in the little town of Israel five miles east on the banks of the river. When Robert Ball French retired from teaching two years before, he had astounded everyone by selling his home out by the College and buying in Israel this big old square three storey mansion built during the last days of the river trade, getting it for a little of nothing, and had proceeded to move himself and his daughter into it lock stock and barrel and live there. The house itself, as he described it for Dave at dinner, was down on the mainstreet of the town the business street with its back to the river, set off from the two small blocks of businesses by a yard full of huge black oaks and sycamores. The last retreat Bob French had called it jokingly, and having called it that to everyone for so long, finally named it that officially: *Last Retreat,* and had a sign with that name made of wrought iron and mounted it over the gate.

"Guinevere didnt much like the idea at first," he smiled gently under the heavy mustache. "Especially the name, she didnt like the name."

"I still dont," Gwen French said tolerantly. "I think its mawkish sentimentality."

"Well, you must allow an old man his little foibles, my dear," Bob French said. "I think the name is very apropos, both for Israel and myself."

Israel was one of the oldest towns in either State and had once been an important call in the heyday of the riverboats, a place where Abe Lincoln had stopped in on his way north; but now it weathered away on its riverbank, nestling under the new bridge and its approach where the highway (which ran straight through Parkman like a knife bisecting a cake) left the State in a soaring leap across the new bridge as if glad to get into Indiana. The bridge changed everything for Israel, what little there was to change, and the roaring truck and tourist traffic along the National Pike bypassed it completely in spite of the sign telling its history which the Parkman DARs had caused to be erected up on the right of way.

"Thats why I moved there when I retired," Bob French said. "I rather felt the two of us sort of belonged together, Israel and I."

"Its nothing of the sort," his daughter contradicted emphatically. "He moved there because he liked the river, and to get away from people and concentrate on his work."

Bob French smiled at her gently. "What work? You mean my work for the *Partisan Review?* And incidentally, the name Israel is an old one, a Biblical name, and was not named in honor of the Haganah and the Irgun."

Dave, whom the shrimp cocktail and chopped salad and now the deliciously rare steak he was still working on had sobered up considerably, watched them both affectionately amused, thinking melancholily that always everybody who lived their lives in on the prairies always loved the river. Even back in the 'Twenties, when he was in high school, they had used to drive over to Israel and park along the bank and get drunk and throw the empty home brew bottles (which they should have saved) in the river and watch with satisfaction as they would float away. Why it satisfied them so he didnt know. But it was always better than breaking them, or throwing them out the windows at the moving signs and phone poles.

He remembered the town. The new bridge hadnt been there then, of course. The old bridge was there. And to cross you had to drive through town. Big old trees, a single dusty weathering business street of one storey buildings which looked like they still should have hitching racks out in front and sometimes did, a number of big old Southern Colonial houses left over from the riverboat days scattered around town, dry rotting away, and from the high bank back of the business street the river, the Wabash, curving away into the east and mist. Bob French's house would have that same view, situated as it was.

—You always got that feeling that you were looking at history, when you watched the river. And you wondered if maybe it had looked the same to them then as it did to you now, those first ones, when they first came up it. Well, it ought to be a good place for a poet to live, he thought bitterly.

Even before Dave's time the Parkman DARs had bought up the ancient courthouse left over from the old days when Israel was the county seat before it was moved to Parkman, and had converted it into a museum which almost no one ever bothered to visit. The Parkman DARs sort of claimed squatters' rights on Israel. As the third or fourth oldest town in the State.

Apparently, now, it had become little more than a suburb of Parkman. Over half its people now drove the five miles into Parkman to work at Sternutol Chemical or the brassiere factory, shuttling their way in and out among the heavy diesels that never ceased spluttering through along Route 40 day and night around the clock. And even the rest of them who didnt work there did most of their shopping there, even the farmers.

"Doesnt the DAR ever bother you?" he said.

Bob French's eyes glinted gently with amusement. "No. I bought a shotgun. I am not quite that old yet.

"—Guinevere really wanted to live here in town," he went on. "But she also wanted to keep a weather eye on me, so I was able to out bluff her. Quite honestly, I think it was mainly because she was afraid I might walk off the bank in a brown study and fall in the river, if she wasnt there."

"I never know what youre liable to do," his daughter said tolerantly.

"I still think youre both crazy," Frank said decisively. He was sobered some, too. "You have to drive over here every day to get somethin' you want. Its impractical. But then youre a poet."

"Quite true," Bob French said under his heavy mustache. "I am allowed to do things sane citizens cannot." Then he grinned. It would have been bitter if he had not grinned, Dave thought.

"Oh, daddy!" Dawn said exasperatedly from her end of the table. "Havent you got any feeling for beauty at all? If Professor French wants to live by the river, he has a perfect right to."

"Thank you, my dear," Bob French said to her gravely. "Im glad to see I have some support here. If you ever want to come live with me when you get out of school, youll be most welcome. You have a standing invitation. Beauty should only be for those who appreciate it."

"Thank you, Professor French," Dawn said with great dignity. "I may avail myself of your kindness someday," she said with a look at her father.

"You could live a lot worse places," Frank said.

"Im sure you would be a most gratifying guest to have," Bob French said to her gravely. "—Anyway, I think Guinevere is pretty much inured to it now," he continued to Dave. He grinned impishly at his daughter. "In fact, I think she has become so inured that Im really afraid shes going to try and move me out and take over herself. Any time."

"Its really a lovely place to live," Gwen French said to Dave, ignoring her father. "Peaceful and quiet. Im really glad we moved there, now. Though my vanity hates to admit he was right. Its just far enough back from the street that people going by on the sidewalk dont bother you unless you want them to. And theres always the river. Its very good for his work. Thats whats important. Even if there are cracks in all the walls and the wind does blow through," she said with that small smile. Selfassured. You couldnt say it was smug, actually.

"Nonsense!" Bob French exclaimed. "Fresh air! We none of us get enough fresh air! I dont mind living in a dressing robe and wool scarf. Why should you?"

It was comical, not only the picture he evoked of them hunching around a windswept house blowing on their hands in heavy robes and wool scarves, but also especially the explosive way he said it, and Dave laughed. They had all sat around in the living room having drinks and talking as was customary and proper and that was why they did it, apparently, and then Frank had called Dawn down and she had come glumly and miserably and they had all gone in to the dining room to eat and all that time the woman, this Gwen French, had rankled him with her selfassured almost but not quite smugness and the small smile. Now he turned to her. She still rankled him, and made him irritable, with that apparently unpuncturable armor of serenity and selfcontained assurance.

"What about your work?" he asked her. "Isnt it good for your work, too?"

"Oh, I can do my kind of writing anywhere," Gwen French said.

"She does all her writing when shes in charge of Study Hall at the College in the afternoon," Bob French smiled—an obviously outlandish lie.

"I suppose you can do that," Dave grinned at Gwen. "Since youre a critic."

"It keeps me from being bored," Gwen countered, smiling that small tolerant smile. "Who told you I was a critic?"

"You mean your writing keeps you from being bored by the students?" Dave grinned at her. "Or is it the students keep you from being bored by your writing? —Oh, I just heard that you were," he said.

He was hoping she would ask again so he could keep on evading, and string her along. Just enough to see if he couldnt make her mad, enough at least to see if there wasnt somewhere some real blood of feeling in this smug selfconfidence. But she didnt ask. She looked at him levelly and then smiled again, as if she already understood what he was doing, and saw through him as clear as glass and, worse yet, did not hold it against him.

"Students never bore me," she said amiably. "Especially those ones of them who really want to learn. Thats my job, you know. To teach them."

"I suppose somebody has to teach them," Dave said.

"Yes. If I had your talent, I wouldnt have to be a teacher," Gwen French said gently, gazing at him levelly.

"My talent!" Dave exploded, and then laughed out loud pointedly. —here we go with that crap again that let me help you to help yourself woman crap again they always do it dont they— She wasnt going to get at him that way. "You mean its really the writing that bores you then?" he grinned. "If its not the students?"

Gwen French looked down at the table, seriously and thoughtfully, and traced her finger on the cloth. "No-o. The writing doesnt bore me either." She looked up at him quite honestly. "But I sometimes think one of my troubles is that it isnt painful enough for me, doesnt really cause me enough real agony."

Irritation surged up in Dave. It was an unusually perceptive statement for her to make, one that showed a pretty thorough knowledge of the workings of the creative mind—at least as he had come to understand it. He hated to think she knew that much, was that smart.

"It would, if you were writing a novel," he said shortly.

"I expect," she smiled amiably. "Anyway, I think that thats an important factor to all good writing."

"Maybe you dont want to feel agony?"

"Probably I dont," she said honestly. "But I think that the agony that goes before, in living, is what is later transmuted—transmuted in the same sense the old alchemists used it—into the agony of trying to express, get it down on paper. Nothing else could make a person attempt it. Human beings were not originally constructed to think. I think if you dont have the first agony, you wont have the second. Thats why I said I lacked your talent. I dont have the first. I lack your talent for misery."

"You ought to try falling in love some time," Dave said sourly.

Instead of being irked or embarrassed as he had expected—expected?

hoped—Gwen French's eyes lit up eagerly and she leaned forward in her chair (twisting her bottom in the chair, he noticed, a little eager squirming motion) and put her elbows on the table and folded her hands against her cheek.

"Thats exactly the same theory Ive been working along," she said eagerly. "I just completed a paper on it not too long ago. Im glad to hear you say that. My thesis was that its this unique and abnormally high potential for the falling in love process, the really abnormal need for it and the inability to escape it, that largely both makes and destroys the creative personality in any given individual."

"Thats a large mouthful," Dave said sardonically.

"—Dowson, with his Cynara, is the classic example," she went right on unmindfully. "Why did he pick a middleclass barkeep's daughter to fall in love with?"

"Probly because he couldnt get ahold of anything else at the time," Dave said sourly. Shades of Harriet Bowman!

"I dont think so. I thought of that," Gwen French said. "He could have had a lot of loves, then or later. I think he picked her because this was the surest bet he had of causing himself agony enough to have an excuse to destroy himself. Stendhal is another classic example of it."

"Stendhal wasnt destroyed by it," Dave said quickly. Here she was on familiar ground. Stendhal was his favorite.

"No!" Gwen French said, "but why? Only because he was a little less of a romantic masochist. He destroyed himself every time he loved, though. And ultimately, in the last analysis, that was where all his material he later wrote about came from."

Dave watched her, listening but hardly taking in what she was saying from preferring to watch. Here was all that old literary crap again, he thought, that hed promised himself to avoid, and yet he couldnt even feel disgusted. It was impossible, when she looked like this, her face alive and vibrant. It was impossible not to like her, impossible not to be attracted to her, —impossible not to be in love with her, really. Oh, hell, he thought, here we go. But he still had a sudden vision of them lying together in a bed, in half light, and her telling all this there, lying on her side her head propped on her elbow talking excitedly, —instead of here across a dinner table of strangers, because all of them did seem like strangers suddenly, people he did not know. The thought he had been trying to put down all afternoon rose up irresistibly now: that this woman could understand him, could love him, could really understand him. He wanted to clutch at her. And yet how? *But* how? Tell her that.

For some reason this rankled him still more, that he should feel all this, that he should not feel rankled. He had known all along what would happen when he met her, he told himself, he could smell it, from the moment Wally Dennis and 'Bama started talking about her, that was why hed refused to meet her with Wally, he had known he would want to make her—make her? no, more than that. Have a love affair with her. A long, rich, exchangeful, reaching out, and perhaps even sometimes touching, making contact, love affair. But why? Irritation washed up in him even higher. Who the hell was she, anyway? Who is Sylvia? What is she-ee?

All right, hed settle for one good romp with her, he told himself, before he went back to California. If he could make it. In a week. And if he couldnt the hell with it.

"You remember the Contessa-or-whatever-she-was, in Italy?" Gwen French said. "It was in Milan, and Stendhal lived there with her for two years. She wouldnt have an affair with him and she wouldnt marry him. She even thought him something of a buffoon. He kept himself celibate for her for two years, until he left."

"Then she was right," Dave said sourly. "He was a buffoon."

"Oh I dont know. Not any more than all writers are buffoons," Gwen French smiled.

"Hear, hear!" her father said. "Poets are writers!"

"The statement still stands," Gwen French grinned at him.

Someone set Dave's dessert in front of him. It was Agnes. He looked up at her for a moment, almost not recognizing who she was from the force of his absorption with the other woman, with Gwen French. It was all only light dinner conversation really, meaningless, deliberately and calculatedly meaningless, he told himself, to go with the meal. But all the unspoken undercurrents were there, too, just the same. Irritation surged up in him again. He went back to his dessert.

It wasnt what she said so much as the way she said it that made him mad. That infuriating quality of complete selfcontainment, that would not allow you to get inside. It was as if she were hugging herself to herself with her both arms. It was like she was some kind of hermetically sealed capsule full of powerful vitamins that she was aware of but would not allow anybody to digest. Because she didnt need to. Because she didnt need someone. Anyone. That was Gwen French, the woman: She didnt need proof.

—and he was Dave Hirsh, the man, who all his life had always needed more someones than he happened to have however many that might be at the time.

—and all the time in her this other thing, that half frightened half eager lover hungry look, which 'Bama had been irked by too and had commented on, peeping out at you out of the very bottom depths of the eyes, giving the lie to everything else. But how to reach it? You might almost think she was a damned virgin if you didnt already know better.

A great situation.

He always picked them.

He swallowed the icecream chokingly, his jaws taut and the palms of his hands dampening. Something in her that reached him—if not actually reached out to him, because you certainly couldnt say that—made him want to take hold of her and lay her back across a bed, or a couch, or a chair arm, or the backseat of a car. That was what she wanted, and what she most certainly would fight.

—but that would take a lot of arrogance to do. Because maybe it was all his own imagination. Wishful thinking? It would take a lot more arrogance than he had—except in certain moods, like now. The trouble with him was his vanity made him afraid of being rebuffed. And he could hear her laughing answer as clearly as if she were speaking it right now:

Yes, you men. Whenever you cant dominate a woman any other way, you want to throw them back on a bed and pretend to dominate them that way, by pretending youre a great big male and that they the poor little women need what youve got and have to have it, and then you can swell your chest and drum the gorilla call the Tarzan call on it, sweet music to no one's ears except your own.

—he could hear her—

—and maybe she was right? Agnes was getting the coffee. He had not said a word for some minutes, bullishly. The conversation had gone on without him well enough, he noticed. Without turning his head, his eyes slitted and his face set, masked, he turned his gaze back slowly and covertly to her, to the woman. Gwen French. With surprise, he found she was looking at him with concern. His heart leaped. Hopefully. For a moment their eyes met and locked, his slitted and angry, hers widened with concern, and held. Then her father said something to her. She turned carefully to smile at him tolerantly and laughed at his joke.

In spite of his anger, the very real and very deep affection between father and daughter came through to Dave strongly. And because of that—if not quite only for that, eh?—he couldnt help liking both of them. He was quite sure that Bob French had dug everything that had passed, had dug the whole situation. Christ, he thought, youre getting to sound like Wally Dennis. He looked up angrily as Agnes set his coffee in front of him.

—and yet Bob French had said or done nothing, given no sign, had passed no judgment, no apparent judgment; even if it was his own daughter.

During dinner Dave had gotten another, and entirely different picture of Robert French.

The older man had gotten his Martini when they first entered, in spite of Frank's demurrings, and drunk it sitting in the living room during that awkward period of first meeting. Then he had had two more, which

Frank obligingly mixed for him, with the shrimp cocktail and Agnes's chef's salad. The effect of three Martinis, instead of exhilarating him, was to slow him down visibly. The youthful excitement and exuberance with which hed entered were gradually replaced by a deep and abiding gentleness and calm which exuded from him quietly in an aura so unobtrusive as to make you suddenly aware that you had been for some time without knowing it in the presence of a true gentlemanliness such as was rarely found anywhere any more. Not in our generation, Dave thought. He realized now that this was probably Bob's more nearly natural state, and the childish exuberance—which was vital and not feigned, though—only a protective party attitude. And it was a gentlemanliness so deep and so ingrained that it had absolutely nothing to do with good manners at all, and made its possessor's first and foremost concern—most natural and only concern you almost might say—the feelings of whatever person he was addressing; good manners a la Emily Post were a superfluity in such a man. His wit and humor were unchanged, but there was a gentleness there that left no sting in them, they did not hurt. Dave remembered enough about him from childhood to recall that after attending Harvard he had lived in Europe, studied at Heidelberg and Cambridge, and had once met Swinburne on the street in London. It was a background that just didnt exist any more. They just didnt make gentlemen like that any more. Of the old school, truly. Not in our time, not in our generation, Dave thought, envying him. It was a byproduct of a world that had died just a little bit too long ago, and only a few of them were left now and getting fewer, probably feeling unused and out of place, but serving to remind today of some of yesterday's important luxuries which today's forces, too powerful to be controlled, had caused to be destroyed, junked. And who will remind us of gentlemanliness when these are gone? In spite of the excitement and the three Martinis, Dave noticed, he ate sparingly and very slow.

There was some quality about him that made you know he was an entity, a unit, complete in himself—or as near to that as any human ever gets—in a way perhaps that his daughter wanted to be but probably never would be. And perhaps that was why, or partly why—that inner knowledge that she wouldnt be and wasnt—that Dave was drawn more and more to her, to Gwen, as they finished up and left the table and all moved with that carefully prescribed precision of Middlewest propriety into the living room where they would not have to look at the congealing dirty plates of their own surfeited appetites. So that in the end he and she, Gwen, wound up sitting by themselves off in the corner on Agnes' antique loveseat—symbolic piece, eh? he thought bitterly—while the others talked amongst themselves across the room. But of course Dave Hirsh, he told himself, that was only partly why, ey? Women women women. God damn women.

All of them did this, that is, with the exception of little Dawn, he amended, who betook herself quietly off upstairs in a moody misery-laden silence. One of the things Dave had loved most about Bob French was the gravely serious way hed handled the girl at dinner, as if she were as adult as anybody there.

Which she probably was, he added.

The dinner had been heavy, the typical Midwestern party meal, canned shrimp in a cocktail of bitey sauce, the chopped fresh vegetable salad with a French type roquefort dressing, the thick frozen steaks and the frenchfries and stringbeans, icecream for dessert and coffee, and brandy if you wanted it, the whole a fare so typical they could have eaten the exact same meal that same evening at the Country Club or the Elks except that this perhaps tasted a little better, or practically any other place road house or dinner joint where they might have gone, a ritual almost, a Middlewest ritual of affluence, and everyone with the exception of Bob French, and perhaps his daughter who nevertheless seemed to put away an awful lot, had eaten far too much, and Dave felt uncomfortable. He had to sit up straight to breathe easily, and the tight uniform bound him. He was damp from sweating in the heavy blouse in the warm room and the heat of the food inside him, and from time to time he wiped his palm across his forehead. And beside him, sweatless, sat the woman, Gwen, looking cool and comfortable and as unladen in the belly as if she hadnt eaten anything, a cool slim appari-tion on a loveseat, an an*tique* loveseat.

Finally he got around to asking. He had hoped she would volunteer it. She hadnt.

"I understand youre doing a book on writers now?" he said.

"Well," Gwen said, "yes, I am. Its really only an extension and de-velopment of that paper I told you about earlier."

"I understand Im in it," Dave said, "more or less."

"Thats true, you are. Who told you?"

"Also a lot of my old buddies," he said. "George Blanca, Kenny Mc-Keean who committed suicide, and another guy."

"Herman Daniel," Gwen said.

"Yes, thats right. I couldnt remember his name. He was killed in the war, you know."

"I know," Gwen said softly.

"He left early, several years before it all broke up."

"I know."

"You just about know it all, dont you? Well, look. Can I ask you a favor please?"

"Yes?"

"Will you please leave me the hell out of it please?" he said gently.

"Well I hardly think thats a fair favor to ask," she said. "After all, its

public information. Im not exposing anything private. Im only doing
an analysis of the published work all of you did, coupled with whatever
biographical material Ive been able to read and pick up, and through
that hoping to arrive at a real understanding of your personalities, and
the group personality, and what made you tick."

"Fine. Great," Dave said, "an admirable project. Only, I wish youd
please keep me out of it, hunh?"

"Why," she said.

"Because it happened a long time ago, and its a period of my life thats
past, and Im done with it," Dave said irritably. "Done with writing. So
I figure the less said about it the better. Maybe I dont want my personality understood."

"Well, I think you must be more or less prepared to accept that sort
of critical publicity when you publish," Gwen smiled at him. That
small smile. "Otherwise you shouldnt publish. You become public
property then. I couldnt very well do a critique of a group and then
leave one of its main members completely out. Now could I?"

"Did you know that George Blanca had an affair with my sister
Francine?" Dave sad bluntly.

"No, I didnt," Gwen said. "I didnt know. I suspected it."

"Theyre both married now. It would only cause them both embarrassment to bring something like that back up publicly."

"Are you worrying about them? or about yourself?" Gwen smiled.

Across the room they were talking about something about the
Kenyon Review and a book review Agnes was doing for the Tuesday
Literary Club. Agnes was doing most of the talking, to Bob French, and
Frank who had mixed them all scotch drinks was just sitting drinking,
while pretending to listen. Bob French had gathered himself as if
preparatory to getting up from the divan.

"Why do you want to do it?" Dave said. "And what made you pick on
this group, our group, anyway? for your criticizing? We werent even
important."

Gwen French—he still always thought of her like that, both names,
he couldnt help it—Gwen French paused to light another cigarette and
then settled back, placing the elbow of the arm which held it in her
other palm reflectively. It gave her an at ease, sophisticated look in addition to the sweatless, unladen belly look, and made Dave feel even
more loutish and uncomfortable.

"I suppose it came from knowing you, actually—at first anyway,"
she said. "You may not remember, but I was in high school with you.
Two years behind you."

"Vaguely," Dave said; "you wrote an awful lot of poetry."

"Very bad poetry," Gwen said shortly, and she did not smile proudly.
"I knew all about you and all about your leaving town when you did.

Why you did. Before you graduated. Then about the time I first began to get really interested in literature your first stories began to come out. I was surprised; I would never have thought of you being a type that would make a writer. And I was interested. So I started following you. Through you I got acquainted with the rest of that group. The ones who were writing. I started collecting everything any of you wrote."

She took a drag from her cigarette held in the hand of the arm whose elbow still rested in her other palm, then flipped her hand to clear the smoke and it looked like a gesture of dismissal.

"That was all it was. Just a sort of interest. And I kept it up. But then after a long time of watching what happened I thought I began to see—I thought I could see—a sort of definitive relationship, a logical pattern, emerging from what happened to all of you. I think what intrigued me most was the failure. All of you failed. And all about the same time. All of you had high resolves and all of you failed. First Herman Daniel left, and went home, and finally married his schoolgirl sweetheart, and settled down. Did you know that?"

"No," Dave said. "I didnt. But I didnt fail. Lets just say I grew up. Outgrew it."

She smiled. "Then Kenneth McKean committed suicide over a girl. George Blanca started writing fairly good movie scripts which got better and better and married a rich girl. And then you stopped writing altogether," she said. "You havent written anything since that second novel, have you." It was not a question.

"No," Dave said stiffly. "Nothing."

"I had high hopes of you," Gwen French said reminiscently. "Especially after I watched what happened to the others and it didnt happen to you. But you didnt write any more."

If she was hurting him, disturbing him, and she was, she certainly wasnt doing it on purpose he thought objectively and didnt have any idea that she was doing it. He realized that, watching her.

"Finally," she said, "later, I decided that you must have had some kind of a very deep or very unhappy love affair, which obviously must not have come off since you didnt marry, but somehow or other affected you badly enough to make you quit writing." She looked at him questioningly.

"I guess Im not over it yet," Dave said abortively.

She nodded. "No, and you probably never will be." She took another drag of her cigarette and flipped her hand again. It was as if she were dismissing the whole episode. "Well, you can see why I was intrigued. In every case a girl—sex—was involved in the failure."

"How did you figure that out about me, though?" Dave asked stonily.

"It was the only possibility that fitted in with my theory," Gwen

French said ingenuously. "But I didnt know. I wasnt sure. —Until just now.— But I knew it had to be that. You see, in each case each of you arrived at a crisis with a woman in which you either got what you wanted—not only from her, but from life—or else didnt get it. But either way, it destroyed you as writers. By destroying in you the hunger *to* write."

"Maybe we just didnt any of us have the talent," Dave said. "Or is that too easy an out for you?"

"No, all of you had talent—in varying degrees."

"The degree," Dave said. "Thats the rub."

Gwen shook her head positively, stubbornly. It was a very female gesture. She had them every now and then, he thought, in spite of her irregular mannish face and figure. Perhaps that was the thing, the contrast, that made them seem more lovable. Oh she was a woman all right, he thought, in spite of that act she put on. It was strange. All those years out there, with all those people, who hardly seemed real any more, and Harriet Bowman, and living only day to day really. And all that time what was it? ten? twelve? thirteen years? this woman back here watching, studying, following it all. All her young years really and he hadnt known. Very strange.

"I dont believe talent is born in people," Gwen said, still shaking her head stubbornly. "Or rather, lets say I believe talent is born in everyone. Only its usually unrealized. We're all animals, you know. Lazy. We'd rather sleep. Only when it is more painful not to, are we willing to suffer enough to develop the talent. But in your cases, this hunger to be loved—which all of you had because of some thing in your environment—caused enough drive in all of you to push you out of the usual and sent you to Los Angeles on some pretext or other, and then made you work hard enough and painfully enough to develop the talent that was already in you. In fact," she said scientifically, like a researcher dissecting a dog in a lab, "I should say you all had talent. In varying degrees and in this order: Kenneth McKeean first, you second, Blanca third, Herman Daniel last.—"

She stopped a moment, thoughtfully, and then looked back up at him with a look of mild astonishment on her face. "—You know, there might be another general principle for me there to cabbage onto," she said in a surprised voice. "McKeean with the greatest—and the most developed— talent couldnt stand losing his love and killed himself. You with the next highest stopped writing, but didnt kill yourself.—"

"I thought about it a lot of times," Dave interposed.

"But you didnt," she said; "—and George Blanca, the third highest, married what he wanted: money.—"

"And a blonde," Dave interjected.

Gwen looked at him questioningly.

"He was part Mexican," Dave said.

"I never thought of that," she nodded. "Of course. —And then stayed there," she went on, "writing things he would never have written before, and believing them. Things McKeean and you," she said analytically, "could never have written, were incapable of writing, because you could never have believed them. Because you were both too neurotic to believe them; the greatest test of normalcy, you know, is how much you can lie to yourself and believe. And Herman Daniel, with the least talent and therefore the most normal, gave it up completely and went into business back home."

"You havent got a critical piece there," Dave said. "Youve got a novel."

"Oh, no," she said seriously. "Im no creative writer. I learned that a long time ago, the hard way. I dont have that drive, that abnormal hunger to be loved so badly. I guess my childhood was too normal, too happy."

"Maybe you have it and dont admit it," Dave said sharply.

Gwen nodded thoughtfully. "Thats very possible. But if I do, it does me no good. Then Im lying, too. That makes me even less creative than if I really didnt have it at all. —Anyway," she said happily, "I really think Ive stumbled onto a valid principle to use, there. I can already see how I can work it in."

"How did you find out so much about Herman?" Dave said.

"Oh, I checked into it," she said abstractedly.

"Youve got a mathematical mind. Youre too goddamned clinical about it for me," Dave said irritably. "I have to look at it in a personal, emotional way myself. Im sorry." He was trying to be sarcastic. It was wasted.

"Of course you do," she said abstractedly, then brought herself back: "you were part of it. My theory is that this thing that drove you all out there and into the field of creative endeavor in the first place, this hunger, otherwise youd never have wound up there, all of you, was the same hunger that when pushed to a climax—as, it must always be in life finally: when you finally have a chance at getting the thing you want— took away from all of you the thing, the drive, it had given you in the first place. The thing, the drive, I never had."

"Maybe youre just unwilling to expose yourself," Dave said angrily. "Writing is a lot like sex exhibitionism. Like the man on the street who is under a compulsion to take his genitals out and show them to people. Especially to women," he said angrily.

"Youre right," Gwen French nodded, "and what you say is very possibly true of me, too. That unwillingness to expose is one of the biggest trouble women writers always have. Oh, we could go on talking about it for hours. The thing with me is I just have no desire to be a creative writer. Whatever the reason."

"No," Dave said. "And neither do I."

Across the room Bob French had relaxed and re-gathered himself several times. Now he re-gathered himself again, and this time he actually got up. Agnes was still talking.

"Oh, you have it all right," Gwen smiled tolerantly. She seemed to come back into herself from a long way off, thinking, and looked at him. "The only thing I worry about is that in not writing for so long a time you may seriously retard your later development so that you never become as good as you might have done."

"Oh balls!" Dave said angrily, wanting to shock her, and feeling frustrated and mean. How the hell were you going to argue with someone, with a woman, who wouldnt even admit that what you said was what you meant?

But he might have known. She wasnt shocked. She just smiled tolerantly—that small smile—as if she understood him completely, and then crushed out her cigarette in the coffee table ashtray and picked up her nearly untouched scotch drink, and looked up expectantly at her father who having listened politely while standing until Agnes stopped talking was now coming over toward them. "Dont get up," Bob French smiled, as if anticipating his daughter's intention. "Ive got to run along. You go ahead and talk. —A couple of old cronies and I are going over to Terre Haute to see the late movie," he explained to Dave, "thats why Gwen and I both brought our own cars.— You stay as long as you want," he said to her. "You two seem to be having a considerable conversation."

"I have to be going too," Gwen said quickly. "Ive got some papers to grade yet tonight."

—It was almost as if she had suddenly become frightened. As if she could not stand the thought of being left here. If he were gone. Without him. Or else as if she didnt like the idea of him going out so late and was already beginning to worry. —Because certainly it could not be me she was afraid of, Dave thought bitterly.

"You dont have anything to do that wont keep a while, if you want to stay," Bob French said gently.

"It just means Ill have to stay up that much later, is all," Gwen said. "You know you oughtnt to be going anyplace so late," she said, her voice changing, harshening. She had moved on the loveseat, gathering her weight together over her feet as if to get up. Frank and Agnes had gotten up also, Frank holding onto his glass which he had refilled several times already.

"Dont start mothering me, Gwen," her father smiled gently. "Eventually, when Im dead, youre going to have to find some other object for your frustrated mother instincts."

"Of course," she said; "youre quite right," and relaxed back into the loveseat.

Still smiling gently Bob French turned away, Frank and Agnes following him to the hall to see him out, to get him into his coat. Their voices, saying all the usual customary things, you could tell by their very inflections, drifted back through the doorway behind them as they went.

"Sometimes," Gwen said to Dave, "sometimes I almost think he throws me at the head of every man we meet. Almost as if he wanted to get rid of me. But he couldnt get along without me. What would he do without me to take care of him?"

"Probably find himself an elderly housekeeper and get along quite well," Dave said.

"She might not enjoy looking to see if he had his head on every time he leaves the house. Hes the most forgetful man who ever lived."

"I didnt mean to insult you," said Dave, who had been trying to do just that all evening. Then he had to laugh: the picture of old Bob French going off without his head and his daughter running down the walk after him with it, or else looking around all over for it until his daughter reminded him that it was on his shoulders, was too much. The spasm of laughter tickled up through his chest into his throat and burst out in a series of guffaws.

Gwen French continued to stare at him soberly, as if she hadnt the least idea what on earth he was laughing at, and expected a proper explanation.

"Im sorry," he said, when the spasm ceased. "It was just that it was the way you described it. —Look," he said, "theres just one thing I want to tell you about us. About that group of ours, when we were out in California.

"We didnt any of us have any idea that it was going to turn out to be history," he said. "Literary history. You know? Or that anybody was going to be interested. We were just living. Or trying to. All of us had romantic pictures about writing, and writers. —Which we subsequently had beaten out of us," he added.

Gwen nodded, as if wondering why such an obvious and pointless statement.

"In all fairness, you ought to take that into account," he said.

"But that was one of the most important things to me," she said with surprise that he apparently didnt know this. "That was one of the main reasons I wanted to do it." She seemed to have completely forgotten her coldness of a moment before. "That, and the fact that you were all small writers, lesser writers. Those were my main points of force: You werent trying to hide anything. Big writers always start covering up their tracks, or else someone does it for them, the moment they start to get big. That, together with all the myths about them, makes it doubly hard. You dont know whats true and what isnt and besides, its harder to isolate what makes the big writers fail. They all succumb to their own particular romanticisms, especially when they get older, but its much harder to pick out and show."

"The realists, too?" Dave grinned.

"Especially the realists," Gwen smiled. They looked at each other for a moment and it suddenly became a long moment, one of agreement, of understanding, one of those rare ones which need no words, perhaps the first real such moment they had had. Then Frank and Agnes came back into the room and Gwen got up off the loveseat.

Dave did not get up, and picked up his scotch drink which Frank, as if to assuage a guilt, had kept refilling whenever he refilled his own. He was getting a little drunk again. Gwen French wasnt, though. She had had only one Manhattan before dinner, and her glass which remained sitting on the coffee table was her first drink after, and over two thirds of it remained untouched. It took her several minutes to get said all the necessary talking to Frank and Agnes preparatory to leaving. Dave remained seated, out of it, finishing off his drink. Then he finished off her glass too. Hell with it. When they were about done talking, he got up too.

"Ive got to go too, Frank," he said. "Meetin some guys downtown."

"Who?" Frank said immediately. He was pretty tight too, but his eyes were sharp.

"Fellow named 'Bama Dillert. Maybe you know him? And a couple guys named Dewey Cole and Hubie Murson."

"'Bama?" Frank said. "The gambler and pool player?"

"Oh, not Dewey Cole," Agnes said. "Not those two."

"Why not?" Dave said quickly. "Whats wrong with them? I met them all today and we going to have a couple drinks together." He could hear his voice dropping back into Army contractionism, now he was tight, and he was aware also of Gwen French watching him.

Frank did not say anything, did not commit himself. He had been in a lot of poker games with 'Bama Dillert.

"Because theyre no good," Agnes said. "Why dont you meet some decent people? instead of running around with bums."

"Because decent people bore me, Agnes," Dave said. "Usually." He couldnt resist it. Her tone made him mad.

—But you could have quoted beforehand what shed answer, couldnt you? he told himself, quoted it verbatim. You knew ahead of time just exactly what shed say. Was that fair? He didnt care. She didnt like him anyway. He felt suddenly quite dangerous.

"Ill get the car out," Frank said, "and run you down."

"Oh, theres no need to do that," Gwen French said. "He can ride down with me."

Dave allowed himself to look at her, but indifferently. This was what he had been angling for all along. "Oh, I dont want to put you out," he said. "Youve got things to do yourself, Im sure."

"Its no trouble at all," she said.

"All right," he said, "then Ill ride with you. If youre sure you were going through town anyway."

"Im sure," Gwen smiled.

As if that settled it, they all moved and started toward the hall doorway. As the women went ahead Frank took hold of Dave's arm and held him back. Dave turned around.

"Look, I dont want you to forget that deal we were talkin' about," Frank said conspiratorially. "You made all that money. Now I dont want to see you squander it and throw it away. I know what I want you to do with it. You think it over and let me know."

"No deal," Dave said contemptuously, disdaining to lower his voice. "I don't have to think it over. I already have. Theres nothing to let you know. I am not a businessman and anyway I am leavin for California Thursday."

"All right, I wont argue with you," Frank said in a low voice. "Only dont talk so loud. This is q t. But Ill tell you one thing." He put his arm around his brother. "At your age and with no more than that much capital, youll never get a chance at a better proposition."

"I dont aim to," Dave said, refusing to lower his voice.

"Dont make up your mind yet," Frank said. "Ive got some other little things in mind too that I didnt tell you about tonight. Theres several pretty big things goin' to be happenin' in this town in the next couple years." With his arm still around Dave, he moved him on along into the hallway where the two women were waiting. "Ill tell you about that later."

"Its no use. I dont care. I wont do it," Dave said loudly. "And Im leavin in a week."

"Well, you think it over anyway," Frank said unctuously. He helped him into his greatcoat. Then he laid both hands on his shoulders. "And come see me." He smiled at Dave slyly.

"Im sorry. Its already decided," Dave said loudly. Then he followed the woman in her beautifully soft deadyellow tweed sportcoat out and across the porch without saying goodby to Agnes and down the steps and out across the yard toward her car on the driveway. Outside, it had begun to snow heavily. Damn woman. Damn all women, anyway. Why didnt they ever want to sleep with you.

Behind them the wide open door closed, shutting off the big rectangular beam of yellow light that had slanted across the yard exposing the big wet thickly falling flakes, turning them yellow. They were already beginning to pile up thickly on the grass under the trees.

When they got in the car by God he would ask her. Just come right out and ask her. That was all. Who could tell. Maybe she might even say yes, might do it.

Poor old Frank, he thought.

Inside the house Frank turned away from closing the door and went back into the living room where Agnes was sitting exhaustedly and straight on through to the buffet in the dining room where the bottles were.

"Im gettin' myself a big stiff shot," he announced belligerently before Agnes could say anything. "Then Im goin' to have a big stiff scotch and soda to chase it with."

"Youd better go to bed," Agnes said wearily, her party excitement suddenly all gone now. She had talked too much, far far too much. Like an ass. "Youve had enough to drink."

"And youd better have a drink, with me," he said.

"Ive had too much already," Agnes said sharply. "And so have you. Im going to bed." But she did not get up.

"Well, you can do whatever you want," Frank said. "Im goin' to sit here and have a couple of drinks to quiet my nerves."

He came back into the living room carrying the glass and sank down in the big leather easy chair so badly let down, and beat, he did not even bother to emit his customary "Ahhh" of satisfaction.

"God damn it!" he said.

Agnes was looking at him from the divan. "Hes not going to take your offer, is he?"

"If you hadnt invited Bob French and his daughter, I might have had some chance to at least talk to him!" Frank said. "As it was, he and Gwen were holed up on the loveseat all damned evening!"

"Yes, and I wonder what kind of a pleasant evening it would have been if I hadnt invited them!" Agnes said sharply. "—He and Gwen certainly did seem to take to each other, didnt they?" she said speculatively. "You suppose shes really attracted to him?"

"I couldnt care less," Frank said.

"You dont think he'll take your offer?" Agnes said.

"Id rather not talk about it," Frank said. "Im too tired."

"But you *dont* think he'll take it. Do you," she persisted.

"How do I know! He might. You never can tell. I wouldnt be at all surprised, if he took it."

"I dont see why you ever offered it to him in the first place."

"To get his money out of the Second National and in with us! And get you and me out of this embarrassment! like you wanted! What else would I ever offer it to him for."

"I dont know," Agnes said, intuitively. "I just felt you might have had some other reason."

"Sure, I did it because I love him."

"Well, it isnt really important. It seemed to me an awfully great length to go, just to get his money out of the Second National Bank," Agnes said sharply. "He might be a lot more trouble and embarrassment as your partner. You heard what he said. Hes going out and get drunk with those drunken loafers and gamblers. God only knows what theyre liable to do. He didnt even say goodby to me. —I couldnt for the life of me see what she *could* be attracted to him for," she added.

"Please," Frank said. "I really dont want to talk any more about it, dear. Im tired. I want to relax."

"I only wanted to try and show you you shouldnt worry," Agnes said gently. "This way, he'll be gone in a week and itll all blow over after a while. If he had taken your offer, he might have been no end of trouble. Dont worry about it. You did all you could."

Agnes got up from the divan. "Well, Im going to bed. Are you coming? Or not."

"No."

She stopped in the hall doorway a moment and looked back. For a long moment she did not speak. "Good night then."

"Good night," Frank said.

But she didn't go. And they stayed that way almost a full minute, looking frankly into each other's faces, he from the chair across the glass in his hand, she in the doorway, somehow caught, and held. And for that near minute both their faces were wide open and without disguise. It was a rare thing with them any more. It was almost as if each was waiting for something to happen but nothing happened. As if each was waiting for the other to say something, or else each himself wanted to say something but either had forgotten what it was or else how to say it. Forgotten it all. It was a look of rare understanding. Full understanding.

"Please dont drink any more, Frank!" she said irritably.

Then she went on across the hall into the master bedroom with its oversize twin beds, separated by a big bed table, which they had had put in in place of the double bed years ago.

Frank waited till she was gone, then turned off all the lights except the floorlamp beside the buffet where he mixed himself still another stiff drink. He was getting pretty tight. But to hell with it. He took the new drink back to the living room and sat down in the dark.

His wife. His wife Agnes. Goddam her, she had divined like she usually did that there was something more he hadnt told her. But he couldnt tell her the dreams hed had for using Dave and the taxi service to build a Hirsh dynasty in Parkman. Especially now. They even seemed silly to *him* now. She would have been angry and sarcastic. Or else would have hooted laughter at him, which would have been even worse. He couldnt tell her the dreams any more than he could ask her to go to bed with him when she stood waiting in the doorway. He wished he had a son.

Well, he had flopped. Failed miserably. And he might as well admit her, he thought. Whatever else he pretended to Agnes—or anybody else, now or in future—he wasnt going to kid himself. He knew damn well there wasnt a snowball's chance in hell of Dave accepting the taxi offer now. There was nothing working on him now. If he was going to, he would have.

He could not figure where it had gone wrong, what it was he had not done right. He had not thought anyone alive would be fool enough to turn down a deal as nice as that. Especially a man like Dave with no investments or prestige or connections and damn small chance of getting any. It was the best possible deal he could have offered him. Dave could spend the rest of his life looking for a deal as attractive as that and never get a smell of one, he told himself. Maybe he should have offered him a full partnership, after all? —well, if he came back around he would, by God.

But that wouldnt have made any difference, he told himself. Dave wouldnt have accepted anyway. And somehow he knew it. He couldnt understand it. And at the moment his mind was too numbed by liquor, fatigue and failure to even try. There just wasnt any answer, and a kind of deep fright at the inconsistencies of things, at the complete unreliability of human beings and their reactions, at his own inadequacies, came over him with a feeling of frightening bottomlessness. He wished theyd had a son.

—The judge was sure going to be unhappy. The judge was going to be unhappy as hell. Well, the hell with the judge. He knew a lot of people in Parkman whod be happier than hell.

He got up to mix himself another drink. It had been some day, really some day, and he found with a feeling of strangeness that he could hardly remember what yesterday had been like, as if it were another world or life.

He had already drunk a lot, and now he drank fast, thirstily, getting up to go back and forth to the buffet. Consequently, he was still sitting there some little time later, defeated and waveringly drunk and aware that shortly he would be sick, when the phone rang and he got up to go waveringly and answer it and discovered that it was Dave calling him from downtown to say that he was going to take him up on his offer and go into the taxi service.

CHAPTER 11

WHEN Dave left Frank's house to ride downtown with Gwen French, he had felt sad momentarily. Especially when the door closed as they were going across the yard. It seemed to him to have a finality. It seemed to him to be a symbol of all finality, actually. One moment it was open its yellow rectangular beam bearing on them, the next it was closed the beam cut off suddenly and the latch clicked in the stillness: locked out. He wished he had not started this whole thing about the banks. He did not expect to see Frank again before he left, and for a moment he half drunkenly felt like weeping. Inside, Frank had put both hands on his shoulders in the hall. And he had felt that sudden rush of warmth he always felt when he had that sort of physical contact with people that he liked. Or wanted to like him. —And at the same time, at that same exact moment, he had been making his loud arrogant pitch about refusing the deal. Deliberately to break it off in Frank. He did not understand it and walking across the yard in the thickening snow he wished it had not been that way, that he had done something else, and felt sad, while at the same time an egotistical triumph flamed in him at having out maneuvered Frank and kept his money in the Second National Bank.

But these feelings, the sadness and the triumph only lasted until he slid into the seat of the Chevrolet coupe beside the woman, beside Gwen French. Then he promptly forgot them.

He sat watching her as she turned on the dash light and put in the key, trying to figure out the best way to approach her. It seemed to him now too sudden, to just come out and ask her to sleep with him without at least preparing her a little first and giving her some warning of what was coming.

It was cold in the car as she turned on the motor, leaning forward a little to reach the key, and the snow had already begun to feather the windshield. She turned on the wipers. He sat watching her until she swung her head around toward him to see to back out the drive.

"Thats a very beautiful coat," he said, in his best seducer's voice.

"Yes, it is, isn't it?" Gwen French said, looking sort of surprised. She took hold of the wide collar with her hand and gave it a little tug. "Ive had it an awful long time though." His seduction tone was apparently completely lost on her.

She backed them out into the street. She started off in low gear.

"I like the way you do your hair," Dave said, making the seducing tone heavier.

"It isnt very stylish," she said. She shifted into second. "I bet that street's slipperier than the devil," she said, peering out.

138

"It doesnt matter whether its stylish," Dave said, striving his best to sound Continental. "As long as its becoming."

"I dont think Id better shift into high," she said; it was easy to see she was a very cautious driver. "Hair's a lot of trouble. So I usually dont do anything with it. Just let it hang. It doesnt matter at school. If it wasnt for making concessions to the damned school board, Id have it all cut off.

Ahead of them under the first street light the snow was white on the pavement. Only a few car tracks showed on it. Dave tried to think of something else to say. Under the cone of light the thickly falling snow made a live, undulating curtain. "Isnt it lovely!" she said. "Yes," he said. They were big thick wet flakes, and whole clusters of flakes, not like the hard granular melting snow of this afternoon.

"You have beautiful eyes, too," Dave said.

This time she caught it. She turned to look at him "Theyre green," she said. "But not very green. A washed out green. And my nose is crooked. And my face irregular. And my shoulders are too high and too rawboned. And my legs too long for their size. Usually when men compliment me, they only compliment me on my brain. If on that."

"Maybe you dont give them a chance," Dave said.

"Not in this town I dont."

"What if theyre in this town, but not from this town?"

She looked at him again. "Theyre still in the town."

Dave suddenly felt relieved. "Well, your coat *is* beautiful, anyway," he laughed. As long as there was a chance, a doubt, he had been on edge and nervous. Now that he knew there wasnt he felt better. Relaxed. But the hunger still gnawed at him down deep in his crotch and belly. He left it gnaw. Sometimes a man almost wished he could get free of it completely, just have no sex. It would certainly save a lot of time and energy spent in chasing. And a lot of misery. Ahead of them now he could see the streetlamps lining the street up the hill on the square through the snow. It had warmed up some in the car.

Gwen French had turned to look at him again, and smiled. "School teachers have to be very careful in their hometown," she said, and it was plain that she really liked him, probably because he had laughed, he thought, but there was also he noted a strange indefinable ring of what for lack of a better word he could only call falseness, a subtle falseness, in what she said.

"Of course when Im away in the city, like in New York, its quite different," she said. "Then Im my own boss."

"You took your PhD at Columbia, didnt you?" Dave said.

"Yes, two years ago. How did you know that? And another thing I asked you before. How did you know about me doing this book on your group?"

"I learned them both from the same source. A student of yours," Dave grinned. "A young man named Wally Dennis."

"Oh, Wally. Yes," she smiled. "Isnt he a strange boy? But hes a very talented boy I think. Hes doing some really excellent writing in a couple of courses of mine. He absolutely refuses to attend college as a regular student. He says its a violation of his ethical principles."

"He also told me you said you werent interested in sex. That youd had all the sex in your life youd ever be interested in," Dave said.

"That quite true. I did tell him that," Gwen smiled. "I was afraid he was getting interested in me. —But its the truth, all the same. I didnt lie to him," she added quickly. "After all, sex is only one way of trying to escape from loneliness. After youve had it you wonder why you worried about it so, and why you ever thought it would help you. It doesnt."

"You seem to know all about it," Dave said.

"Oh, Ive had my little troubles. If you let your loneliness control you that way, or any other way, youd never get anything important done."

"Important like what?"

"It just drives you on and on," she said, not answering him.

"Yes. Its driven me most of my life," Dave said sourly.

They passed another streetlight cone of snow, the third.

"You just have to learn to stay outside of it and control *it*," Gwen smiled.

"Thats great advice. But maybe its a lot easier to do when you have a home and a father to take care of," Dave said stonily. "And, if youre a woman."

"I wont always have them," Gwen said amiably. "But its you we're talking about, not me. You are the one with the gnawing loneliness."

Dave grimaced. "You know so much about love. Its a shame youve never experienced it."

"Oh, Ive experienced it enough times to know Ive learned all Ill ever need to know about it," Gwen said airily. "When I said sex before, I was meaning love."

"You have the advantage over me," Dave said sourly. Then he said, "What about this Casper Milquetoast guy you were engaged to? Were you in love with him?"

"I dont think thats any of your business," Gwen said, her eyes flashing. She turned to stare at him indignantly.

"I guess youre right," Dave said meekly, startled. "I guess its not." Killed in the war. In love with a dead war hero, he thought bitterly. He would like to have said it.

"You seemed to have learned quite a bit about me," Gwen said.

"We talked about you," he said. "That was all. There was nothing compromising or disrespectful. Wally thinks the sun rises and sets on you."

"Hes a dear boy," Gwen said warmly. "I think a lot of him. Hes liable to turn into a very fine writer some day." It was as if this was the highest compliment she could pay.

They were pulling up the hill through the snow, much trackier with cars now, to the square. There was a very real warmth and generosity in her, as she spoke about Wally Dennis, and Dave could not help feeling a pang of childish jealousy.

"You know," she went on, "Ive really enjoyed talking to you tonight. There arent very many adult people around here whom one can talk writing with. Mostly, theyre all youngsters like Wally. If you ever feel like coming over to see us in Israel while youre here, I hope you will. If youd like to come for a visit and spend a few days before you leave, you have a carte blanche invitation."

Dave's heart bounced once. Here was the opportunity. "If I do, will you sleep with me?" he said casually.

"Certainly not," Gwen French said. "Of course not."

"Why not?"

"Why, I hardly know you."

"Then theres not much point in my coming, is there?"

"No. Not if thats what youre coming for."

"Whats wrong with me?"

"Whats wrong with you! Why, nothing." Then she laughed, the first time he had ever actually heard her laugh, a sudden short trilling little nervous laugh, quite suddenly come and quite suddenly gone, then a silence. "It would take me a lot more time than I have to spare right now to tell you."

"I mean, as far as sleeping with me. That makes me unattractive."

"Nothing."

"I mean, youd sleep with Casper Milquetoast, and all these guys in New York youre telling me about, whats wrong with me?"

Gwen turned the corner off of North Main Street onto the one way square in front of the corner drugstore and a line of business houses. "By the way, where do you want me to let you off?"

"Right here is good enough," Dave said depressedly. He should never have asked her. He felt like a fool. She slanted the coupe into one of the diagonal parking spaces in the thickening snow and stopped it, and he stared out at the drugstore's lighted display window of patented remedies and its cardboard figure of a rather unappetizing dumpy young woman with a rather uninspired hairdo wearing a double truss belt. Beside her was her mate, an equally unappetizing not very athletic looking dumpy young man with no hairdo at all just slicked back wearing a single truss belt. Neither of them appeared to have genitals. Or muscles. Or brains. A eulogy to Modern Man. Stop hernia!

Gwen French leaned forward and switched off the lights and the motor, then leaned back and turned to face him resting her elbow on the back of the seat.

"I realize it may sound strange to you, and I have no idea what kind of women youve been used to," she said succinctly, but amiably, "but I cant sleep with a man without getting personally involved with him. Im just made that way. And right now I dont want to get personally involved with a man."

"Youre still in love with the dead war hero?" Dave said, still looking out.

"No. Not at all. For your information, I was never in love with him. He was just convenient. And also, I never slept with him."

"You expect me to believe that?"

"I dont care whether you believe it or not," she said amiably. "And as for you. If I were going to sleep with a man right now, and get involved with one, I certainly wouldnt pick you. In the first place, youre not in love with me; youre still in love with that girl in California. And probably always will be. Youre a cripple. And in the second place, youre only going to be here for a week; I heard you tell Frank. I should sleep with you, and get involved with you, and start a love affair, and then have you leave in a week and probably never set eyes on you again. If I wanted a love affair now, which I dont, youre just about the worst bet I could pick." She smiled at him.

"What if I should stay around longer?" Dave said still looking out. Why should it have become so important to him? Hell, he hardly knew her. And she was obviously a jerk anyway. And now he was beginning to plead with her! That was the one thing he would *not* let himself do. But why should it be so important suddenly? Ego? Vanity?

"No." She shook her head. "It wouldnt make any difference. Anyway, in the end it would be the same: you would leave. Why, youve only known me a matter of three or four hours!"

"You may have missed something very valuable," he said arrogantly. "Even if it only did last a while."

"I doubt it. I doubt if theres anything you could teach me I dont already know and havent already experienced. After all, there are only so many ways to have sex and so many feelings you can have about it," she said scientifically. "And once youve had them all, youve had them, and anything else is repetitious"

"Maybe you should be teaching me," Dave said sourly.

"Excuse me," she said; "youre wrong. Any teaching I do I get paid for by the College, and at the present time they do not have any courses in sex. Someday they may have."

"Youre a very unusual woman, you know it?" Dave said lowly, and regretfully.

"Not so unusual as you might think," Gwen French said, darkly.

"Not nearly so. —Oh, Dave!" she cried. —he enjoyed hearing her use his name like that, valued it immensely. what difference did it make? why the hell should it be so important— "Oh, Dave! Youre in love with love. I understand you so well. Im the last one you should pick. My whole life has been spent studying the lives of people just like you. —Besides, I have my own problems," she said darkly.

"Look," she said, more calmly. "In the first place, I couldnt trust you; youre an artist, a writer; whether you believe it or not, you are; and always will be; you might have the best intentions and meaning in the world, but the moment some little thing upset you youd up and take off for God knows where; running. And in the second place, you dont want to love; you want to be loved; you go around making all these women fall in love with you; you suffer if they dont; and the moment they do fall in love with you, and begin to clutch at you, you get frantic and leave them, and what? immediately begin looking for another right away."

"That might not be such a bad life," Dave said sourly, "if it were only true."

"If it isnt, its only because up to now all the women youve met have been smarter than you are."

Dave opened the door of the coupe. "Well anyway, it would make me a great epitaph," he said. "True or not." He got out. "Like Stendhal's."

Gwen leaned over in the seat so she could see him outside.

"Youre not angry, are you?" she said anxiously. "Dont be angry at me?"

"No. Im not angry."

"The invitation still holds?" she said, still leaning over to look up at him, "if you want to take it?"

"Maybe I will," Dave said sardonically. "I wanted a chance to get to talk to your father, anyway."

She straightened up. "Come any time," she said. "Call first." She started the motor. Dave stepped back up on the sidewalk, and stood in the shoedeep snow, and watched her drive off cautiously, carefully.

He moved back and stood in the shoedeep snow back against the building, back against the drugstore's lighted hernia display and watched her car until the tail lights disappeared. It was ten o'clock by the old courthouse clock with its Roman numerals. The drugstore was already closed. Almost everything was closed. Everything except the three bars and the two poolrooms. There was only one other set of tracks in the shoedeep snow, he noticed. Then the anger began to hit him.

Standing there, he considered coldly, and furiously. He was satisfied that she could be had. She could be made all right. He was sure of that. It was, therefore, just a question of the time it would take. He calculated. It might take six months, it might take a year. With her.

You would have to stay around long enough to convince her that you loved her exclusively. But it could be done.

That was the trouble with a guy, living like he did, moving all the time. You were never around long enough to make the really hard ones, the challenges, the ones you could be proud of.

That lover hunger that was in her eyes—hidden, she thought?—had showed up again in that last remark she made, anxiously, was he angry? Why the hell should she care if he was angry? That in itself proved she was insecure, he thought coldly. Insecure meant ripe.

All right well okay so what if it took him six months. What if it took him a whole year. A kind of wild, crazily indignant enthusiasm swept up through him. He could go into that taxi business with Frank and work for him in the taxi stand. That would pay expenses. It would cost him the $5500, but who cared? A man ought to be willing to pay that much, $5500, to make a woman he really wanted to make, he thought with a powerful kind of elation. The hell with the money. Come easy go easy. It would be worth it. It would be more than worth it, it would be something to be proud of. How many people in the world would throw away $5500, all they had, just to make one woman? he asked himself with a powerful kind of selfdestructive exultation.

The melting drizzle that had slacked off earlier in the day had fled on to the eastward, and it had begun to really snow, just about the time they sat down to dinner. Moving in from the northwest across the town, it came down in big fat clusters of flakes with the points of crystals sticking out all over them like quills, falling fast, and enveloping the world in the insulated stillness of white rock wool. Already the ground was covered white shoe deep, and the bushes and limbs of trees beginning to collect the blanket that when you looked at them would almost convince you you were seeing double, and far off the sounds of cars and voices seemed in another world. He could not hear his own footfalls. It was a real snow, the first one of the winter.

Walking along in it, he put out feelers of sensation to taste the excitement of it. Large clusters of flakes caught in his lashes and licked wetly at his unprotected face under the overseas cap. He was reminded of Europe, how it had snowed like this in Belgium during the Bulge, how it had snowed this way all on through the forests. And the dead bodies lying half covered in it. Fresh blood was electrifying when spattered in snow, but afterwards it turned brown. Oh, it was a shame, a shame.

Did you know it was a shame, Gwen French? Or would you, Gwen French, be scientific about it? Gwen French. Gwen French Gwen French Gwen French! You and your writers.

He had had an idea for a combat novel once himself, he remembered all at once. In France. He had not thought about it for a long time. His combat novel was to be a comic novel. A comedy. The writers after the last war had all written and written and written about the horrible horrible horrors of war until it had become a literary tradition. But nobody had ever thought of writing a comic combat novel. And really, if you could divorce yourself from imagining it was you, there was nothing funnier in the world than the way a man whos been shot tumbles loosely and falls down. Unless its watching someone slip on a banana peel and fall and break their arm. Besides, he knew why the old ones had written like they did. They pretended that horror stuff. It was not because they especially hated war or felt sorry for the men and animals who got killed. And it was not particularly because of fear, either, everybody was afraid when he was being shot at. The comical thing was how unafraid it made you to do the shooting. No, they had written like they did because their egos could not support this hated indignity of personal death, any kind of death, which they feared they might have to suffer and were so vain they could not stand the thought of. That, and also because they were hungry starved for sympathy. He knew, because he had felt that way himself. But your typical Infantryman's vanity took quite another form. He had got a glimpse of that, too, when he killed his first three Germans and felt so pleased and powerful and Godlike. Once youd killed a couple war wasnt nearly so horrible. He wanted to write a pleased delighted comical novel about killing and combat and bust up their old monopoly why should they have a monopoly on war? and at the same time force the human race for once to take an unvarnished unsugarcoated look at itself for a change. That was to be the theme of his combat novel, and its purpose, and the reason he wanted to do it was because he was as vain as they were, and because maliciously he would love it if he could just once make the human race for once look at itself. He would enjoy that more than anything else in the world. They would recoil in such shock and horror at themselves that foreverafter never again would the name of D. HIRSH be mentioned in polite society.

Except that he wasnt going to write it.

Why should he write it?

He walked along looking in the store windows, the big snow playing upon him as if it were a musician, drawing from him not one or two successive emotions, but whole chords of them, like a pianist playing many notes simultaneously.

Wally, if you and I love the world too much, remember, its not the world's fault; its our own. Why the hell should he write it? He was going to make this woman, if it took him every last dime he had, and then he was going out to the West Coast and live it up a little. The world didnt ask us to love it that way, Wally, did it?

He passed one of the old oldfashioned cast iron water fountains, its basin filled with snow, that did not appear to have changed a bit since he used to play in them, and he loved it. The windshields of the late parked, swiftly whitening cars were plastered with it too, and he loved them too, and he loved the people who owned them. The sidewalk was still uneven in the same spots, from where they had set the fountain in.

He was not tight any more, and the skin of his face felt drawn around the eyes from the liquor. Like your fingers when theyve been left too long in water.

The courthouse and its square of yard were completely dark save for the four faces of the clock with their Roman numerals in the tower and the public toilet night lights at the basement entrance under the stairs, and across the square he could make out the dark figure of the night cop making his rounds and switching off the lights in the display windows.

Gwen French Gwen French Gwen French. We will see, Gwen French, we'll see.

He passed Dorothy Callter's Mode Shop where there was a lingerie display on mannequins and stopped to look at it. It made him think of his niece "little" Dawn, with that body of hers and a picture of her walked across the projector screen of his mind. Desire and guilt tormented him simultaneously. Mentally—that is, in words rather than in pictures—he undressed her. He speculated. Well, he would never know. Dressed again, this time in pictures, he gently removed her head and replaced it with the face of his ideal woman who would love him more than herself, or life. Where was she? Ah yes, where? As the picture was no longer his niece "little" Dawn now, although it still had her body, he could legitimately imagine himself going to bed with it. He did so. He would worship her in a way it was given to few women to be worshipped.

The knowledge and awareness of his own ugliness, his physical unattractiveness, which he never thought about unless he had been drinking, flooded over him like the curling waters of an upriver cloudburst creeping over a delta swamp. He did not itemize them.

It was really all only sex. All. Everything. The game and the profession of the universe. Money was made, and music written, books were written, statues, poems, governments fell. All. All for sex. Love me, love my horse. Here, Trigger.

He stopped before the Athletic Club poolroom and looked inside. It was a huge place with big plate glass windows clear across the front that he remembered had once been a bank, the Prairie Farmers & Growers Bank & Trust Company, but had gone under in the Depression. The light from the windows cast yellowish pools on the white mat at his feet where only two other sets of footprints showed in front of him. Inside, a bunch of men holding cues stood around one of the tables near the back, first one then another of them bending over to shoot. He could recognize the tall 'Bama in his hat. One of them said something, and they all laughed heartily. They had evidently been there a long time, playing. Since before the snow, by the footprints. He went inside. It had been a long walk.

CHAPTER 12

IN the poolroom two old men with tobacco stained whiskers sat on the mahoganystained benches against the wall, reading the papers. The owner—or manager, whichever he was—stood behind the glass cigar counter turning the pages of a Motor Sports Magazine. All three looked up guardedly when Dave came in. Dave took off his great-coat, suddenly selfconscious under the stares about his ribbons which hed worn to impress Frank and Agnes, and hung it on one of the mahoganystained coat racks on the wall and went directly to the telephone on the corner of the counter to do it now. He might forget it later. Besides now that he had made up his mind he wanted to be committed. He dialed Frank's number and cupped his hand around the mouthpiece so the man behind the counter could not hear him. It was several long moments before there was an answer.

"Frank?"

"'Lo?" His brother's voice sounded thick, mumbly.

"This Dave."

"Dave?" Frank murmured.

"Yeah. Im downtown. Listen, Ive been thinking about that deal, you know? And Ive changed my mind. Ive decided to take you up on it."

"Tha' good," Frank mumbled vaguely. "Tha' fine, Dave. But I knew all 'long youd take it. A' you needed was a chance to think it over 'n see wha' a good deal i' was. Knew it all 'long."

"Fifty five hundred, that right? That was what we said."

"Tha' right," Frank mumbled.

"And course I suppose the job has to go with it," Dave said, slyly. "Okay. Ill stop by the store and see you tomorrow about the details."

"Tha' right," Frank mumbled. "Job go wi' i'."

"Say, whats the matter with you?" Dave said. "Are you drunk?"

"No," Frank mumbled. "Lor', no. A' this time o' night? You jus' woke me up, thas all. I was in bed 'sleep."

"Okay," Dave said. "Ill see you tomorrow then."

He hung up and turned around toward the single pool game at the back, feeling satisfied like a man who has accomplished a job of work. "Thanks," he said to the man behind the counter.

"Okay," the man said indifferently, turning the pages of his motor magazine without looking up.

Dave walked on back to the table, threading his way amongst the empty darkened ones. He did not know any of them except 'Bama. And while he used to be a good pool shooter in his youth, he knew he was not in their class. He suddenly felt embarrassed and ill at ease, and felt his face set itself in that stiff retracted look of elaborate expressionlessness.

There were seven players in the game. They were playing pea pool like he had figured when he saw so many. A dollar a game. Four of them were dressed in overalls or work clothes and a couple of these wore those pleated "railroader" workcaps. Two others wore the nondescript uniforms of store clerks from around the square: nondescript slacks, nondescript white shirts and nondescript ties, all looking as though they had been chosen and bought hastily with an eye to utility once during a rushed lunch hour, and all slightly soiled from the day's trade. They were all six of them young—that is, below middle age—and they all appeared to be thoroughly enjoying a slightly expensive night off from the wife and kiddies.

By contrast, 'Bama Dillert stood out like a thief in church. He did not have that married look of the others, and he had changed his clothes to a sharply pressed suit of a slightly different shade, the coat of which he did not take off to play, and which had the exact same narrow smalltownish cut as the other while still managing to look expensive. He also wore, pushed carefully back just to his widow's peak, another semi Western thin banded hat of a very light tan, this one, with the same deeply snapped brim and creases as sharp and meticulous as the press in the suit. He had shaved, and bathed, and evidently even cleaned his fingernails, and had on a dazzling clean white shirt and a tie that was a futuristic print maker's dream, all dots and radial stripes and triangles, but which nevertheless blended well with the suit. He obviously felt it to be a sophisticated outfit.

As Dave came up and leaned against the next table, 'Bama chalked his cue, studied the table, wrapped long fingers lovingly around the stick in a small tight bridge, bent to shoot exposing cuffs unsoiled by what was apparently hours of playing, made a crisp hard but accurate kiss shot across the end of the table, and stood up throwing out across the felt the small ivory pea whose number corresponded to the one on the ball he had just pocketed—all of this in what seemed to be one short swift concerted, and inexorable, movement.

"Read it and weep," he sneered in his high contemptuous nasal.

"You son of a bitch," one of the men in overalls said good naturedly.

"I said weep," 'Bama said in the same contemptuous nasal. "Go ahead and cry, you sad bastard. Get it off yore chest."

As he spoke, he went around the table and collected the six dollar bills the others had laid out on the edge; tall, thin, sway backed, with that hanging belly appended to the abnormally curving spine, setting his feet down in that same slow jerky horsewalk, languid, arrogant, hateful of even the money. He shoved the bills contemptuously in a wad in his front pants pocket. "Rack em up!" he bawled, and banged with the butt of his cue on the floor several times, and walked over to stand by Dave. "Hows it goin, Dave?" he smiled sneeringly.

The houseman, the same one who had been reading Motor Sports, was already there with the rack before he even yelled, appearing suddenly the instant the game was over as if he had divined the end ahead of time by telepathy and then moved himself there from the pages of his magazine by teleportation rather than walking. But the cry and the banging of the cue butt, as well as the putting of the money in the pocket, seemed to serve as a sort of official end to the game and a kind of silent collective sigh went up from around the table, as if they were all playing with money they could not really afford, and then they relaxed and began to get ready for the next game. 'Bama paid for the game, as winner.

"You ought to know you cant leave that 'Bama have a set up shot," one of the men in overalls said amicably to one of the clerks.

"You got to leave him safe," another said sociably.

"You want to shoot in front of him?" the clerk said coldly.

"Id rather shoot in front of him than behind," one of the men in railroader caps said.

"If I played that bastard safe," the clerk said coldly, "Id never get to shoot for my ball all night but that wouldnt keep you from winnin."

" 'Bama, are you payin him to shoot that way in front of you?" the second clerk said.

"Course Im payin him," 'Bama said shortly, pocketing his change from the houseman. He said it so quickly and matter of factly, and with such offhand surety, that even though you knew it wasnt true you had a momentary impulse to believe him. As if he knew this, for the first time facing them something other than the sneer showed a little on his face. A hint of a selfsatisfied sly grin crept over the sneer, then crept off.

"Ive been a-anticipatin' all along that was what you was doin'," another of the overalls said.

"Id be glad to accept some of my pay now," the first clerk said coldly.

'Bama ignored both of them. He leaned back against the table beside Dave with his hands propped on the rail and the fingers of one of them holding his cue, waiting for the houseman to collect all the peas and pass out new ones, and turned his narrow hazel eyes on Dave.

"Howd the dinner turn out?" he asked privately. Once again, there was that strange incongruous intimacy of friendliness that was too great for the time theyd known each other, and was out of place in 'Bama's character, in his voice. Dave wondered again why it was. Could Frank be that important in this town?

"All right," he said.

"You get enough to eat?" 'Bama grinned.

"Too much," Dave said. He was watching the other men moving around the table waiting to get their peas from the houseman. "I met our girl," he said.

"Who?"

"Gwen French. She was there for dinner."

"Ohhhh! Yeah?" 'Bama said quietly. "You make her?"

"I didnt try," Dave said. "I think Wally's right. I dont think it would be worth it."

"Look, dont tell me," 'Bama grinned quietly. "Ive looked at them eyes. It might be hard work. I grant you that. But itd be worth it plenty."

"I dont think so," Dave said stiffly. He discovered that he did not like 'Bama talking about Gwen like that. Even privately.

"Okay," 'Bama grinned understandingly. "You shoe yore own horse. Aint you gettin in on this one?" he nodded at the table.

Dave's embarrassment came back, "Im just watchin," he said. "But I might play one. Later on."

"Youd better get in now if you aim to. Because theyll be closing up before long. They close at eleven so they quit at ten thirty."

"Why, perhaps I will play a game then," Dave said profoundly. "If theres room."

"Plenty of room, Mr Hirsh," one of the clerks said politely.

"Why, thank you," Dave said. He went to the nearest wall rack for a cue, cursing himself savagely for sounding so pompous and wondering why he did when he didnt mean to, and feeling a fool. He relieved himself by hunting with great diligence for a cue that felt good. He was committed to it now.

When he came back to the table 'Bama came over and stood beside him. "You follow me," he said protectively, some kind of an eagerness in his voice. "I was the last man to get in, so youll follow me. And since I won the last game that means I break, so you shoot second." He actually sounded gentle and solicitous. Dave wondered if the jerk thought he didnt know anything about pool at all. But it wasnt that; 'Bama sounded more like a pleased host who was proudly and somewhat pathetically showing one of his rare visitors around his unfrequented estate.

The houseman, having racked the balls and collected all the peas, began to rattle the black leather bottle. He held it in his right hand stopping the neck and shaking it, while he turned it around and around in a great and evidently prescribed style with his left. Occasionally he banged the bottom of it down flat on the table rail. Finally, he began to let the peas out the neck of the bottle into his hand one at a time and shot them across the green expanse of felt to the players, who caught them, peered at them secretively and expressionlessly, and then hid them. When they all had their peas, he put the bottle up and abruptly disappeared again, as suddenly and silently as he had appeared, without having said a word the whole time.

'Bama broke the rack, standing bent over down at the other end of the table, his weight all on his right hip and left hand, his left elbow crooked high in the air over the tight little bridge of his big left hand through which the cue slid so smoothly, his right buttock jutting out behind him so far in the air that it appeared to be completely dislocated from his pelvis. It was unbelievable that he had not even gotten his white cuffs dirty all evening. His break was a snapping hard very clean shot like a striking snake that sent colored balls squirting out from the triangle in all directions and sank two of them into pockets. One of these belonged to the first clerk, who cursed coldly, and 'Bama grinned at him. He went on shooting and sank three other balls before he missed.

Dave, whose turn it was to shoot next, did not sink three balls during the entire game. Nor did he sink a total of three balls in any one of the other four games they played before quitting time. These games didnt last long, not the way these people played, and nervousness plus extreme selfconsciousness plus a great embarrassment at his poor playing plus a tense wild hunger to win every game all combined to make him play even worse than the poor game he should have played with no more practice than hed had. His muscles refused to coordinate and the balls would not go where he aimed them. He played increasingly in a grim, black, deadfaced silence intended to conceal the way he felt but which instead only served to expose and call attention to it.

Nobody offered him any encouragement. To have done so, the way he was playing, would have been fatuous. Or else deliberate misrepresentation. Sucker fleecing. Neither did anyone offer him any sympathy. Cold, hard, perennial dollar a game players, they did not have any sympathy for anyone. They probably did not like to be made to look like sucker fleecers, and the difference between their games and his perhaps embarrassed them, but they were not going to refuse to take the extra dollar either. 'Bama was the only one who spoke to him at all, and he only between games. The rest did not look at him and maintained a neutral, blank faced silence, leaning on their cues. He was twice as lonely as he had been outside walking around the square.

'Bama won three of the five games, collecting as insolently for them as he had for the other one, before the houseman finally came back and closed them down. One of the clerks won one, and one of the country men won the other. Dave played along in all of them, actively hating every moment of it, wishing he could make himself quit but unable to because his pride wouldnt let him, and getting more and more inflamed every minute. When they stopped, all he felt was relief. By the time it took him to walk up front his anger broke and was replaced by an unutterable, almost unendurable melancholy. In this state, he thought about Gwen French.

The whole project did not seem near so appetizing nor near so much of a lark as it had when he first thought about it and he wished to God he had not called Frank and committed himself now. She really wasnt a very appetizing woman at all, when you thought about it objectively. And $5500!

'Bama had gone back to the men's room, and he sat down on one of the mahoganystained benches to wait and lit a cigarette. The two whiskered old men had left, shuffling off to whatever miserable homes. He would have to look the Old Man up, he thought. He sat watching the falling snow through the big plate glass windows. Beyond the windows it filled the air between him and the courthouse, making it tangible. His own footprints outside were no longer sharp and clear cut, were already dusted over.

Behind him, the others still were talking as the houseman continued turning the lights off. Then the four men in work clothes came past him and went out together, a unit, going up to the restaurant for coffee. "Christ," one of them said, "it sure is snowin."

A moment later the two clerks followed, but not as a unit, as two separate unconnected entities, not talking, each going his own way toward his own car which would take him to his own separate home. —and presumably, to his own separate wife, Dave thought wryly— They looked as if they were two utter strangers who had never met. Then they were gone too, adding more footprints to the growing web.

'Bama came up behind him.

"Ready to go?" he said. He was folding a big sheaf of bills in half. He rolled it into a roll and snapped a rubber band around it. "All ones," he laughed, and put it in his pocket.

"How much did you win?" Dave said.

'Bama studied him narrowly a moment, as if debating whether to tell him the truth. "Bout thirty bucks."

"Thats not a bad night's work."

'Bama studied him again. He had his topcoat on, a conventional ordinary light gray gabardine that you saw millions of, and his hat was pulled forward now. He wore it about three quarters of the way down his forehead, a lot like a soldier wears a campaign hat, except for the long Western crease and sharp snapped brim. "It aint bad," he admitted; "for pool. But if I had to live on that Id starve to death damn quick."

"You look like you do all right."

'Bama grinned. "Well, it aint because Im holding down no high payin job at the damned Sternutol Chemical."

"I thought it was," Dave said.

'Bama grinned again. The word gambler had not been mentioned, but he was still obviously flattered. He put his foot languidly up on the next bench and leaned on it, lit a cigarette from a pack in his topcoat pocket. "I had a heavy date over at the Eagles Lodge tonight with a poker game until I met up with you," he grinned. "I figure I just about made my ante money."

"It must be a good game."

"We have some good ones around here. Now and then." He grinned in that style he evidently thought was wicked. Then he moved his head. "Well, you ready to go?"

"Sure. Any time. Ive just been sitting here watching it snow."

Without moving his feet 'Bama swung his torso around to look. "Yeah, it is pretty, aint it?" he said, trying to sound interested, dutifully. He took his foot down and crushed the half smoked cigarette under a sharp pointed toe jitterishly. Then he walked over to the windows and stood looking out. "Use to snow some down in Alabama where I come from, but never nothin like it does up here sometimes." He stood there with his hands in his topcoat pockets, tall, sallow, sway backed, narrow rather than thin. He had big feet. "I figured youd never get up here tonight," he said to the windows. "I figured youd still be down to yore brother's, to Frank's, having that big shindig welcoming home party."

"Well, Im not," Dave said.

"Yeah," 'Bama grinned, swinging around. "I can see that yore not."

"I came straight here from there," Dave amended.

"Whats the matter?" 'Bama said, coming back grinning to the bench. "You have an argument?"

"No. Me and Frank never argue. We understand each other."

"If you do, yore the first two brothers ever did," 'Bama said. "Me and my brother been fightin about the goddamned Sternutol Chemical for ten years ever since I come here."

Dave looked at him questioningly and he moved his head toward the east.

"He works out there."

"Oh."

"And he thinks I oughta work there," 'Bama grinned. "But I aint about to."

"You dont look like you need to."

"Damn right I dont."

"Then whyre you worrying?" He could hear the houseman behind them in the back.

"Awww," 'Bama said. "Hes a poker player himself. Used to live off of it till he got married. Now he plays over at the Moose Lodge all the time. I play there. But he thinks I ought to have a steady job. Its his wife. He thinks it aint respectable, now, unless you work." He stopped, inconclusively.

The lights were all off now except the one above them, had been off for some time, and the houseman pottering around back in the dark interior behind them, probably putting the rubberized covers on the tables. Now he came up over on the other side by the cigar counter carrying a case of cokes from the back room and began replenishing the soft drinks chest.

"I guess wed better get out of here," Dave said. He looked up at the near wall where there was a big blackboard with the collegiate basketball scores and the high school scores for the Wabash Valley and Eastern Illinois Leagues. Indiana had won. Bradley had won. So had Parkman won, but so had its two arch rivals, Paris further north and Robinson further south. The benches which lined the one wall and were also placed back to back across the center of the floor, were all strewn with all kinds of daily papers but the sports sections looked the most read. "Before we get thrown out," he said.

"Sit still," 'Bama sneered contentedly, "yore all right." He opened his topcoat exposing a pint bottle in the side pocket. "I just bought him a drink. I got to stay on the good side a my business acquaintances. He wont throw us out."

"But does that include me too?" Dave grinned.

"It does as long as yore with me. We kin sit here till two," 'Bama boasted. "If we want to. Although I dont know why the hell wed want to."

"I dont either," Dave said. "To keep from going home, I guess. Lets get on down to Smitty's."

'Bama snorted. "Its always the same old answer, aint it? Evi-dently, what you need is a woman. Well, thats where we'll find them."

"Only about like I need to breathe, is all," Dave said.

"Hell, what you need is a wife. Why dont you get married?"

"Why dont you?"

"I am," 'Bama said.

When Dave didnt answer, couldnt think of an answer, because he had been so sure all along that 'Bama was single, the tall Southerner said:

"I been married since I was nineteen down in Alabama. I got two kids."

Dave still couldnt think of anything to say. "I always just figured you were single," he said finally.

"Why? Because I run around?" The tall man snorted; then went on with cheerful cynicism, philosophizing from the particular to the general. "Way I see it, a guy almost has to be married. The trouble with women is the nice women wont put out and the others dont do you any good when they do. They put out to everybody. And if the nice ones do put out to you, something happens to them and they seem to stop being nice ones after a while. I didnt make the rules."

"Maybe its that something happens to you?" Dave said.

"Naw. Not me. 'Bama stays the same. What is it makes men chase after women. An instinct of nature, I guess. Well, nature's all fouled up then. Why didnt it give women an instinct to chase after men."

"It did," Dave said. "They do. Only as soon as the men start chasing back, they quit."

'Bama laughed. "Yeah but they always call it by another name. Men like sex but women dont. They can take it or leave it alone. Mostly they leave it alone. For them its only what you call—a means to an end. And if the men dont mostly leave it alone too they think all you want from them's to lay them which is mostly true but if the men do leave it alone too, then they think you dont love them. For women, it seems to me sex is only just the one available means of getting children that they know of. And society says they got to have children."

But it wasnt true, it wasnt all sex like he said, Dave thought desperately, was thinking desperately, all the time 'Bama was talking. If it only were that! It was this wanting to be loved, Gwen French was right. Loved more than anything else in the world. Loved more than self. Loved more than life. He wanted to be loved by every woman he encountered. Every woman he passed on the street, every woman he saw in a bus. All of them. The more the merrier. He didnt want them to fight and dispute over him. He wanted them to share him lovingly. It was the lack of all that love that had made him write what little he had written. She was right there, too. So that he would be loved. Loved by many women in general, and by one woman in particular— Harriet Bowman in Los Angeles. Used to be when he was thinking about his writing, figuring on it, he was thinking about them too; and about her. When he was finishing up that second novel after she had married, he thought about her a lot—About how she would pick it up someday in a bookstore, read it, see his name on it, regret, be sorry for what she had missed. By *God*, he would make her regret marrying that lawyer!

Sitting there, dazed into near deafness by the violence of his own emotion, he laid at her doorstep the heavy load of blame. If she had given him the love he needed, the kind of love of which he knew she was capable, and which only he could have returned, he would not be here now, going through this idiocy of this damned $5500 and the taxi service.

Once again, as it had earlier, the knowledge of his own personal ugliness, his purely physical unattractiveness, swept over him like a high sea over a freighter carrying away everything that was not lashed down.

"You know," he said, "Ive got a theory. I think its all due to popular music. You know how you can sit around and listen to some love ballad on a jukebox or a radio and it twists you all up inside and makes you dream unreasonable dreams?"

"Never bothers me," 'Bama said.

"It dont. Well it bothers me. And I think its these damned songs that make us romanticize sex and love and women so much. Whether we want to or not. They dont do it in Europe. Not like we do here."

"Listen," 'Bama said. "I didnt mean to give you the i-dea I was talkin about *my* wife a minute ago. I didnt, did I?"

"What?" For a moment he couldnt grasp it, what he meant. "Oh," he said. "Why no," he lied. "I assumed you were just talkin in general."

'Bama looked relieved. "Well, thats good. Because I dont talk about *my* wife. At all. To nobody. I dont have to. *My* wife stays at home where she belongs like a wife's supposed to. I wear the pants in my family. She does what I tell her, when I tell her. If she didnt she wouldnt be there long."

Dave felt like laughing. "Well, thats the way it ought to be, isnt it?"

"You damned right," 'Bama sneered. "And thats the way its gonna stay. —Come on, lets blow this joint and go on out to Smitty's. Thats where all the stuff is."

"Right," Dave said. "Why not?" He went to get his greatcoat.

'Bama was waiting for him, holding the door open. "See you later, Curly!" he called to the near bald houseman. He led the way to the axblade nose and sharp sided hood of a 1937 Packard sedan sitting a few doors down near the restaurant. Dave looked it over, the snow soft and mattressey under foot, mildly surprised. He had figured him for a Chevie or a Plymouth. This car was all black and nicely chromed and had the big radiator ornament of the woman in flowing drapes holding aloft a silvered wheel. It was still expensive looking in spite of being an old model. It looked nicely kept. 'Bama went up to it and began shoveling snow off the windshield with his bare hands.

"Let me do that," Dave said. "Ive got gloves on."

'Bama shook his head. "Snow ruins leather. I got gloves." He went on pulling the snow off with his bare hands, first the windshield, then the hood, then the back window, keeping up a running fire of conversation as he worked.

"Sonabichll be coldern hell. Probly hard to start. I got cold plugs and the mixture set down lean for high speed drivin. Got this bastard off a used car dealer in Indianapolis that didnt know it had a good motor in it. Rather have it than one of them crappy new postwar ones theyre puttin out. Guy charged for all his cars as if they had good motors in them. Hed a known this one really had one hed a charged a lot more. All it needed was a little work on the carburetor."

There was a great affection in his hands as he worked on it, an affection that seemed out of character and incongruous to the cynical gambler he professed to be. It was almost domestic. He did not have any trouble starting it.

"Let her warm up a little," he sneered lovingly after they were inside and it was started. "Youre not drivin, are you? You dont have a car?"

"No."

"Good. Then we wont have to worry about pickin your car up if we line something up and decide to go someplace else. Dewey and Hubie will be out there and we'll see what they got planned."

"Where is this Smitty's?" Dave said.

"Out north by the railroad, in that block of buildings. Its the first one by the tracks."

"Oh, I remember that place. There used to be a confectionery there."

"I dont know," 'Bama said. "Its been a bar ever since I come here. If you can call them bars in this county when they dont serve hard liquor." He put the car in gear and peered at the temperature gauge. "Almost normal. You know, you ought to get rid of that uniform. As soon as you can. The chicks around dont dig uniforms much anymore since the war's over."

"Yeah, I mean to," Dave said, "I just havent had a chance to get any civilian clothes yet."

"Thats quite a parade of ribbons you got there," 'Bama sneered friendlily as he backed the Packard out in the street. "Thats a lot of fruit salad for a QM, when you top it off with a Combat Infantryman's, too. I noticed it earlier. You must of been in a good outfit."

Dave named his division. "They drafted our company as Infantry during the Bulge, or we wouldnt of had anything but the Good Conduct."

"I was in the First Army," 'Bama said indifferently. "Ninth Armored. Im an old tank jockey. I was on your left flank then."

"Then you were at Aachen."

"Yeah, Aachen. Remagen, Seigen, all them places," 'Bama said indifferently, peering behind him.

"So was I. They shifted us around all over," Dave said, "you know: A QM Gas Supply Company."

"Yeah," 'Bama said, turning around and shifting into low. "Maybe you gassed our tank sometime." He looked at his temperature gauge again.

Watching him, Dave was surprised again. Somehow he had not envisioned 'Bama ever being in the Army. Dewey had said he registered for the draft with him. But he had assumed that 'Bama had got out of it some way or other. He seemed more like a perpetual civilian, one of those cynics who spent the whole war scoffing and with reason from the sidelines. Not an exGI. There was certainly nothing of the professional veteran about him. He waited for 'Bama to go ahead, to tell him something else.

Instead, 'Bama began to tell him about the bar they were going to. Rather than being proud of being in the Army, he gave the impression he was embarrassed by it and had a slight sense of shame, as if in catching him the Army had pulled a fast one, out smarted him and out foxed him all the way around, and that such a fiasco was better left in the closet with the other skeletons.

"Smitty's Bar they call it because a guy named B H Smith runs it. The real name is Drop Inn Dram Shop. Smitty named it that. Its the only decent bar in town and thats where all the loose stuff in town hangs out. They most all work at the brassiere factory. Maybe we can find us a couple there tonight. Theres sure to be some around."

As he talked, he swung the Packard on around the one way square, deftly following the few cut tread marks in the fresh snow that was still falling and not packed yet, skinned it around the corner heading north, and ran on out, down the long hill, accelerating fast on the slick street, but completely in control with just the foot accelerator and the rear wheel traction. Dave realized belatedly that he was in the hands of the best driver he had ever ridden with.

Across the railroad they pulled into the tracked snow of the cinder parking lot beside the bar, and the lights and music coming from inside promised excitement. Something doing. Laughter, love, and entertainment.

"Come on, lets go on in," 'Bama said, lighting a cigarette from the pack in his topcoat pocket.

CHAPTER 13

SMITTY'S Bar was located in the south corner of a four place business block which was known as the Madin Block chiefly because that title had been worked in concrete letters two feet high on its brick front by a man named Madin who had built it.

The Illinois Northern Railroad which was almost universally referred to as the I.N. passed through Parkman about half a mile north of the courthouse, which put it just about half way out to the edge of town. Out there, where it crossed North Main Street—the street which with Wernz Avenue the real mainstreet form a cross of thoroughfares in to the square—a little business district had grown up around its depot. A grocery, a barbershop, a restaurant, two filling stations and a bar (Smitty's), with a couple of lumber yards across the tracks, it clustered around the depot and tracks as though for nourishment in much the same way that the much larger West End business district huddled around the junction of Wernz Avenue and the Big 4 Railroad out at the western edge of town.

Although never much as a railroad, at one time the I.N. had been a powerful social force in Parkman. Running east and west clear across town the I.N. tracks had formed a convenient separation line, even as had the Big 4 in the west end. But the I.N., being nearly half way to town instead of out at the edge, gave a much greater opportunity for superiority since so many more people could live on the wrong side of it. In the 1900s it was only about a third of the way to town instead of half, and the Biblically learned civic leaders of Parkman, who wanted so badly to be aristocrats, referred contemptuously to everything north of the I.N. tracks as *Pisgah*. But as Bible reading gradually passed out of general fashion and a new generation of civic leaders who badly wanted to be aristocrats grew up to replace the old, the nickname gradually fell into disuse until it came to mean only the little business district at the tracks, and no longer carried an especially bad connotation since almost no one in the present generation knew what *Pisgah* meant. Few even knew how it originated. Also, building space was getting harder to find and more and more people who could afford it were building nice homes on the north side of the I.N. tracks, a thing which no selfrespecting citizen who could afford it would have thought of doing forty years ago.

But just the same certain echoes of this former derogation, probably aided by coal dust and smoke cinders, still clung to the tracks themselves and to locations near them. B H Smith, Smitty, had overcome this liability with his own peculiar brand of fake heartiness, the judicious use of what he called "atmosphere", and by buying an expensive home in a respectable section of town out of his profits. So that now Smitty's was considered the bar to go to in Parkman and was even occasionally visited by some of the people who belonged to the Country Club, which Smitty had lately joined. He had also joined the Trap & Skeet Club.

The Madin Block itself was a great aid in Smitty's policy of atmosphere. Soot grimed and tear stained by the rain after years of sitting almost astride the railroad, it had hung on to existence grimly until it finally achieved the sort of humorous veneration accorded a bearded tobaccojuicestained octogenarian.

Smitty himself, whom Dave had never met, was a big bluff excessively hearty man who laughed a lot, loudly and often, as if he thought he might in this way secretly hold off at arm's length all the slavering problems of his life which were threatening to devour him. He had shrewdly decorated the bar to look like a pre-Prohibition tavern, but he still could not, Dave learned from 'Bama as they left the Packard and went inside, make enough off of it to afford the Country Club and the Skeet Club and the Elks and the cabin which he like the rest of the well off people had built out at South Lake, mainly because his wife had always felt degraded and looked down upon because of the business he was in. He had two boys in service too and the Russians were giving us trouble. He also had once run for mayor, 'Bama said, on a reform ticket to try and get hard liquor and mixed drinks sold over the bar but his landlady Mrs Madin the secret drinker had been instrumental in defeating him in the name of the Temperance League and even his own wife had felt morally bound to work against him in the election.

'Bama, Dave found out immediately they were inside, also was counted as part of the atmosphere of the place, apparently. He also saw that 'Bama seemed well aware of this and relished it. Smitty, who was standing just inside the door talking on the phone behind the bar, treated him with the complaisance of a privileged character that he wanted to keep hanging around so as to amuse the more respectable customers, who evidently came partly for that reason. It wasnt exactly snobbery, which the prideful 'Bama obviously would never have tolerated. It was more like a sort of tacit business agreement between them.

The same tolerance apparently held true for a group of five tittering young women sitting by themselves in a booth across from the bar drinking beer; and for Dewey and Hubie and two other men whom Dave saw sitting sprawled at a table in the back near the jukebox.

The front of the place, narrowed by the bar and a string of booths along the wall, was fairly well crowded. 'Bama moved into all of this with Dave in tow and the air of a man who has been in a place often enough to feel safe and familiar there. He nodded to several people who spoke to him, and gave the booth of young women a searching look.

"Whats the matter, Dewey," he called from the front, and headed straight back for the table past the girls. "You and the brassiere factory on the outs again?"

There was a small titter of laughter from the booth of girls, which 'Bama ignored.

"Ah, that Lois," Dewey's voice carried up from the table. In the dimness Dave could hardly see what he looked like from this far away. "Shes teed off and up on her high horse again. All over some little old thing or other. Shes gettin tempermental as some prima donna. Youd think she was a movie star or somethin."

There were several laughs from the men at the bar. While he was speaking they continued moving to the back and the table. There were five small tables out in the wider floor space of the back, which could have been a dance floor but never had been (there was a city ordinance against this: drinking and dancing together in the same place) but all of them were empty except the one the four men sat at. The back of the place was fairly well crowded too, though. A number of couples and two parties of four, the men all wearing suits and ties for these dates, sat in the booths around the edge. Dewey and Hubie still had on the same old Army clothes they had worn this afternoon. The two men with them were equally sloppily dressed. One of them, a pus-y but well muscled tough looking man with a beat up face, very much so. Smitty was still talking on the phone up front and his bluff booming laugh, which must have been very hard on the ear at the other end, periodically penetrated the jukebox music.

"Thats not his wife," 'Bama said, listening. "He always talks very soft when its his wife."

He introduced Dave to the two new men, pointing to the men as he named them. They were Gus Nernst, and Raymond Cole Dewey's brother. He was the tough looking one. Somebody reached out and pulled up two more of the oldfashioned wire drugstore chairs from another table.

"Whats she mad at you about now, Dewey?" 'Bama grinned, sitting down.

Dewey grunted. "Shell get over it."

"Thats his girl Lois," 'Bama said to Dave, indicating one of the girls in the booth, the one on the end facing them. "Lois Wallup. The one with the body. Aint she got a body?" He grinned. "She wants to get married to Dewey and she gets mad at him all the time because he wont."

Dave turned around to look and another titter of laughter rose from the booth of girls.

"Why should I marry her to get somethin Im already gettin," Dewey said.

She did indeed have a body. Big boned and meaty, beautiful legs, voluptuous breasts and hips separated by a small waist, above which was a very small rather unsightly pugdog face framed in long black hair. With this face she scowled furiously back toward the table, although she had just joined in the titter of laughter.

"Whatd you do this time?" 'Bama said.

Dewey merely grunted.

"First, he tried to cop a feel off her while we were all sittin' there in the booth," Hubie said in his high complaining nasal. "And she wouldnt let him and got mad."

Dewey grinned a little.

"Then when Raymond and Gus come in, he told her he wanted her to give Raymond a piece," Hubie said thinly. "Because Raymond was his brother and he looked hard up."

Dewey grinned boyishly with his handsome blue eyed face. "I dont see why that should make her so mad."

"You mean that made her mad?" 'Bama said with mock surprise.

Dewey grinned sheepishly. "Yeah."

"I dont need anybody to get none for me," Raymond Cole said with a black scowl. "I can get all I need for myself. And if I cant Ill go home and use my wife." He did not lower his voice, either. Dave looked at him, vaguely remembering him from a tough kid. He was six or eight years older than Dewey, a man of middle height but very big, with arms that bulged out the sleeves of his badly worn blue work shirt, but beginning to go badly to fat, with that face, round and fat and ugly, that had been hit very hard many times. He had none of the innocent open boyishness of Dewey.

"All the outside stuff youve had in the past six months, Raymond," Dewey said contemptuously and explicitly, "you could count up on the fingers of an armless man."

Raymond's often beaten face congested and his eyes went suddenly wild and crazy. "Lissen, you punk!" he said loudly, shoving back in his chair and starting to get up.

As one man, 'Bama on one side and Gus Nernst a tall lean horse-faced man the age of Dewey on the other each grabbed an arm of Raymond by the wrist with practiced efficiency and with their other hands pressing down on his shoulders held him down in his seat between theirs. His arms at his sides, he was off balance and could not get up. They bobbed up and down and back and forth with the silently struggling Raymond who breathed in whistles.

"So what else?" 'Bama asked Hubie a little breathlessly, as he bobbed up and down with Raymond. "Is Martha mad at you too?"

"Nah," Hubie said. "But I come back to sit with Dewey. So now we been sittin' here three quarters of an hour."

"To hell with her," Dewey said without resentment. "Let her make up. She started it. Wait a while and shell make up."

All during the episode with Raymond he had regarded his brother coolly and with a kind of innocent indifference, and he continued to look at him the same way now while Raymond struggled silently against the two men holding him. Each had planted a foot behind one of Raymond's ankles to keep him from getting any leverage with his legs.

"Martha Garvey is Hubie's girl," 'Bama, bobbing with Raymond, explained to Dave. "Shes the one next to Lois."

Dave took his eyes off Raymond long enough to see a small petite ravenblack haired girl with very big eyes and a great deal of selfpossession. He couldnt see her legs as they were inside the booth. Again, the booth of girls tittered.

"Come on, Raymond," Gus Nernst complained breathlessly. "Quit it, now."

Raymond, whistling air, made one more titanic struggle to get up. Then he relaxed so suddenly that both men lurched toward the table and almost fell on it. "Leave go of me," he said in a choked voice. "Im all right. I aint mad no more."

They relaxed their grips and turned back to the table without so much as a word or look, apparently seeming to have completely forgotten him.

"Lets have another round," 'Bama said.

"Thats a good idea," Gus said. "But we're about broke."

"Im buyin'," 'Bama said. "Raymond? Want one?"

For answer Raymond launched a tremendous powerhouse punch with his right arm. It swept along the edge of the table at 'Bama on his left with the force of a hurricane, the big fist traveling with all the power of the big arm behind it. 'Bama, who evidently knew him well and hadnt forgotten him at all, as neither had Gus, moved with the speed of greased light, putting his left hand on the table for balance and leaning away to his left. Consequently, Raymond's fist exploded into the springwire back of the chair, tearing skin and fingers and knuckles in a wild flurry of flesh, while Raymond grunted in surprised and unexpected pain and then retrieved his damaged hand to inspect it in the dim light and nurse it with his other one.

"God damn it," he said. "Now Ive hurt my hand."

"Serves you right, Raymond," 'Bama said. "Bring us another round!" he called to the bar.

Up at the bar Smitty's helper and extra bartender, a one armed youth of twenty-one or -two wearing one of those double claw hooks the Army gives you on his right arm and a faded GI suntan shirt, nodded at 'Bama and began opening beers, six of them, which he put on a round tray and carried over to them in his powerful left hand, disdaining the dangling hook.

"Helpyerselves, gents," he said, hanging the hook in his apron string. "How you, 'Bama?"

"Okay, Eddie," 'Bama said mildly, "Well enough to pay." He gave him the money.

The young bartender took it and grinned and went away, clicking his hooks absentmindedly, the way a man snaps his fingers.

"You oughtnt to treat Raymond like that, Dewey," Hubie said mildly.

"Treat him how?" Dewey said. "Why not?"

"Well, he is your brother," Hubie said.

"How long since you been home, Raymond?" 'Bama said.

"A week," Raymond said absently, nursing his hand.

"Yore wifell be gettin hungry pretty soon, wont she?" 'Bama said.

"Let her work," Raymond said. "I work when I get hungry."

"Youd think he was a punchdrunk fighter," Dewey said. "The way he acts." They were all talking in normally loud voices, and had been all this time, all during the discussion of Lois's figure and Raymond's lack of females. The people in the booths around the wall were watching them, rather excitedly and hopefully, almost as if they were a floor show or a movie. Dave realized suddenly why there was nobody sitting at the tables near them. It was undoubtedly because they did not want to get hit with a flying chair.

"Well, hes had a lot of fights," Hubie said to Dewey cautiously.

"Not with me," Dewey said.

"More with you than anybody else," Gus Nernst said. "Drink your beer, Dewey. Leave him alone."

"Hes had fights. Look at his face," Dewey said, still looking at Raymond coolly with his innocent eyed handsome face. "So many theyve scrambled his brains."

"God damn you, Dewey, leave my face out of this," Raymond said. "Come on outside and Ill beat your goddamned head in."

"Come on," Dewey said without moving, "lets go. Ill put a couple more scars on that head of yours for you."

"Hand or no hand!" Raymond bellowed. This time he jumped up so quickly they couldnt grab him. Dewey, who had been sitting scrounged down on his tailbone, straightened up lazily in his chair a little and watched his brother coolly, alertly.

"Do you think Dewey could really take him?" Dave asked 'Bama quietly.

"I dont know," 'Bama said. "It usually winds up as a kind of a draw."

"Sit down, sit down," Gus Nernst said, rising between them and holding up his bottle of beer for Raymond to look at. "Sit down and drink. I want to propose a toast first."

It looked like a foolhardy thing to have done, but he evidently knew how to handle Raymond.

"A toast?" Raymond said, looking at the bottle. "A toast to what?"

"To what? To the next war. Sit down."

"To hell with that," Raymond said.

"Sit down," Gus said.

Raymond stood, looking around indecisively.

"Come on, Raymond," Gus said. "Lets you and me blow this place. Lets go someplace else."

"Thats a good idea," Raymond said happily, sitting down and reaching for his beer. "By God it is. Lets go over to Terre Haute in my car or someplace." He wiped his mouth with his hand and got up, this time putting on his leather coatjacket his eyes glittering with some hidden fever in his fat round ugly face.

He started off, then came back and drained off the rest of the beer 'Bama had bought him. "Ill see *you* later, punk," he sneered at Dewey, and went off again, down past the near end of the bar where Smitty was standing alertly, ready to stop any trouble that happened inside. "See you later, Smitty," he said benignly.

"Good night, Raymond," Smitty said; and Raymond waved and went on, jauntily, a haunting figure.

Dave watched him go, feeling as if a huge black hand had reached inside of him and squeezed his heart. The hand of God. The black hand of God. Warning him. There goes all of us, he thought, watching him. In Raymond Cole, imbued with an almost classical Greek inevitability of selfdestruction and carrying that same sense of tragic fitness. Which everyone could enjoy the poignancy of, instead of fear, because in this case like in a novel they were not intimately involved and did not stand to suffer. Ah, yes, but what about those cases where you are intimately involved, eh? It was all so mathematical. That was what was so frightening. Given a man who persistently drinks too much and you come up with permanent liver damage. Given a man who fist fights all the time and you arrive at scar tissue and permanent punchdrunkards. Raymond could blame no one but himself and neither can we. He fought and drank his way through his life looking for something. Hoping to have something. Love. Admiration? Respect. And he got scars and liquor fat. And an addled head. And those people over there in those booths watching so avidly, they hedged and qualified their lives and then came here to watch, and got nothing. Dave reached for his bottle of beer frantically. Raymond had stopped by the door and was looking round anxiously for Gus.

"Ill take him off someplace and get rid of him," Gus Nernst said to the rest of them, "and then come on back."

"Why dont you take him home?" 'Bama said.

"Him? Hes been sleepin in the back seat of his car for the past week."

"Its a wonder he dont freeze to death," Hubie said.

"Him?" Gus said. "Ill be back in a little while."

"Him and that old beatup '34 Dodge of his," Dewey said contemptuously as they left. "It looks as bad as his face. But he thinks hes really got somethin because hes got a car."

"Slip me a drink from that bottle," Dave said to 'Bama.

"You oughtnt to deliberately go makin' him mad like that," Hubie said.

"Why not?" Dewey said. "He makes me mad."

"Yeah, but he dont do it on purpose."

"I get sick of seein him hangin around."

"He used to be a damned good man," Hubie said.

"He still is," Dewey said quickly. "And dont you forget it. But I can take him. And he knows it."

"Was he in the Army?" Dave said, still holding onto 'Bama's whiskey tightly, as if that would help him. "Was that it?"

"Yeah, he got shot up two or three times. You ought to see his legs," Dewey said. "He was in the 132nd Infantry. Illinois National Guard. Americal Division. Guadalcanal and points west."

"But he was like that before he ever got in the Army," Hubie said. "Too many drunk fights. Too many times of havin' his head bounced on the sidewalk."

Dewey nodded. "Yeh."

"You ought to seen the fights those two had as kids," Hubie said, indicating Dewey with his head. "But then they was just kid fights."

"But I bet he was a good combat soldier wasnt he?" Dave said hopefully, and then took another long drink of whiskey straight out of the bottle. Go away go away.

"As a matter of fact, he was," Dewey said. "Damned good. You wouldnt believe it now, but he really used to be a damned good looking guy. All the women in this town used to be nuts about him. As a matter of fact, one of the Scott girls was crazy about him in high school. She probably would of married him before they graduated," Dewey said. "If he hadnt quit school his sophomore year and gone to work in a garage."

"So instead she married Van Crowder," 'Bama sneered with amusement, "after they both got out of college." He stared at Dewey disgustedly.

But Dewey only nodded, quite innocently. "Thats right. Shes missis richbitch in town now."

Dave laughed wildly. "Cherchez la snatch," he said. He took another big drink. "Oh, no," he said. "Oh, no.—Wouldnt you know it."

"Naw, nothin like that," Dewey said. "He never cared. She was more in love with Raymond than he was in love with her. He never give a damn.—"

—"Thats something, anyway."—

Dewey looked at Dave earnestly. "You know when Raymond was with the 'Merical on Guadalcanal, he was—"

"Look! I don't feel like refightin no war," 'Bama sneered, "tonight. What about these women up there? Are you goin back up or not?"

"Hell with them," Dewey said. "Let them come back here."

"Yeah. Hell with them," Hubie said loyally.

And with that Raymond Cole was dropped completely out of the conversation and forgotten. By everyone except Dave.

"Here, give me a drink of that," 'Bama said to him. "Before you drink it all up."

"We can get more. Plenty more," Dave said, handing it back.

"Sure," 'Bama said, taking it anyway. He poured some in an empty glass and handed the bottle back to Dave. "Now wait a minute," he said to Dewey. "I promised Dave here I'd get him fixed up tonight. We cant get him fixed up with any of those women if theyre on the outs with you guys."

"You dont need us to get him fixed up," Dewey said.

Hubie was looking wistfully up at the booth of girls. "Naw, you dont need us."

"Damn it, you know how these women stick together," 'Bama said.

"We cant go out anyway," Hubie said. "We got to work tomorrow."

"Yeah," Dewey said irritably. "I wish youd quit remindin me of it."

"It doesnt matter whether I get laid," Dave said to all of them. "Ive changed my mind. I dont even feel like getting fixed up. I dont care. Why dont you just drop the whole thing?"

"Now you just let me handle this," 'Bama said to him.

"We'll get you fixed up," Dewey said.

"Im going up and get us another bottle," Dave said suddenly, handing the almost empty one back to 'Bama. "Or two."

He got up from the table and went up to the near end of the bar where the one armed youth Eddie was pulling the caps of beer bottles with his double hook. Right along here Raymond Cole had walked so jauntily.

"This damned thing makes the best damn bottle opener," the boy grinned. He was half tight. "Whatll you have?" he said, "Pabst Blue Ribbon?"

"No," Dave said. "Two pints of Seven Crown."

"Sure thing," the boy grinned. "But you cant drink em in here." He winked.

"Course not."

The boy chuckled and went away up the bar. Dave watched him go, absently clicking his hooks. Everywhere you saw them. Fingers. Hands. Arms. Legs. Feet. Eyes. What a nation we were turning into. It was like living in the last wild days of the Roman Empire. Everybody drinking and discussing and destruction sweeping down in hordes from the north. We will maintain our policy of Business As Usual.

He turned around and looked back into the dimness at the table. They were arguing.

CHAPTER 14

FOR him the wildly grotesque episode of Raymond Cole seemed to have changed the complexion of the entire evening. He noticed it did not seem to have bothered any of the others. But he could not get free of it. Coupled with everything else that had happened to him today, it was too much. Raymond—without knowing it—seemed to him to have left himself behind him, and to have set the tone for everything that followed. What had started out as an ordinary evening in search of entertainment and of getting fixed up, seemed suddenly to have become one of those Walpurgis Nights that he had had before when nothing at all seemed real, a Witches' Sabbath of an evening, wild and frightening and insane, in which liquor and fatigue combined with a vague but piercing hunger and overwrought emotions drove both the mind and the personality into turning faster and faster and faster, until they seemed unable to partake of anything happening around them, seemed only to register half of what they saw, and just sat there arm in arm like the two joined halves of a gyroscope wheel whirling themselves into invisibility, suspended between the twin axles of fear and vanity, out at the very outer rim of existence. And he himself was trapped, trapped behind his own barrier of centrifugal force which threatened to whirl him off into space piecemeal an arm or leg at a time, but from which he could not break forth and take part. And everybody in the world was a stranger.

The four of them sat on at the little table drinking beers which now and then they laced liberally with Dave's new whiskey and discussing the intimate private lives of various persons whom Dave did not know but who were all evidently members of their coterie their gang their group, both boys and girls. They discussed both. All of them seemed to have problems, largely sexual. Dewey was apparently the unofficial (and unacknowledged) leader of the group. 'Bama enjoyed a unique position of being sort of senior advisor to them while not actually one of them. Every now and then they arrived back at the current problem of the girls up front in the booth. Dave noticed the people around the walls in the booths were still watching them hopefully, and trying to listen.

"What the hell do you think theyre sittin there for?" 'Bama sneered disgustedly. "Theyre just sittin up there waitin for you to come back."

"Let em sit," Dewey said serenely. "Im happy."

"Didnt Lois get paid, out at the brassiere factory today?" 'Bama asked slyly.

"Yeah, she got paid," Dewey said. "Hell with her. I dont need her money. At least not tonight."

"Well, you need somebody's," 'Bama said. "And Id a lot rather you had hers, than mine."

"I can go up and get some off of Martha," Hubie offered. "If youre runnin' short."

'Bama transfixed him with a withering look and Hubie looked away. "Well I could get some off of her," he said defensively. "I wasnt bein' snotty."

'Bama ignored him. "Look, Dewey," he said slowly and carefully, as if explaining something incomprehensible to a child, "heres the thing. I promised Dave here Id get him fixed up tonight. Hes hard up and dont know anybody around here. So I told him Id help him out. But we cant go up there by ourselves while you guys are sittin back here."

"I dont care if you go up there," Dewey protested. "Go ahead. Hell, I wont be mad. What kind of a guy do you think I am?"

"That aint the point," 'Bama said patiently.

"Hell, take Lois and Martha out if you want to," Dewey said. "Theyre the best romps in the bunch."

Hubie looked a little uncomfortable at this suggestion, and it was plain he wasnt very happy at the idea, but he loyally didnt say anything. Dave listened to them indifferently. He no longer cared at all whether he got fixed up or not, the mood he was in. He sat quietly, but surcharged with an energy of misery, of soul hunger, that he knew might burst out of him at any moment like a sky rocket into something ridiculous, looking at a young unpretty but very nubile and because of it very lovely young woman who was sitting in a booth almost directly across from him and had been watching him—or at least, their table— to the point of practically ignoring her boy friend.

"You know, I suppose," 'Bama said. "Because youve laid them all."

Dewey grinned sheepishly with his handsome boy's face. "Well, Ive been out with Ginnie."

"Everybody's been out with Ginnie," 'Bama said, unimpressed.

Dave continued to look quietly at the unpretty but very lovely young woman who had turned back after he caught her looking at him, and was now talking animatedly to her boy friend. The more he looked at her the more lovely she seemed. In spite of the fact that she wasnt pretty at all. Her nose was too big and too sharp, her face was too thin, her neck was too thin too, and too long. And yet something behind her face and in her eyes, some warmth of love to give, some look of love there to be given, and obviously it was not for her boy friend who apparently could not incite it, made her not only lovely, but almost beautiful. By God, she was beautiful. So many, he thought, so many. There were so many women in the world like that, who had so much unincited love to give, and were aching to give it. Why couldnt any of them stumble on him? He could love that girl over there.

"I *could* put it on the basis of personal friendship," 'Bama said, "and *ask* you to go back up there. As a favor to me."

"Well, if you did that," Dewey said reluctantly, "Id have to go. But Id sure hate to."

"Well, I wont do that," 'Bama said. "I wouldnt do that. But how about this? How about if I go up to the booth and talk to the girls a while and tell them youll come back, if Lois and Martha will move over into the next booth?

"If I can get them to move over into the empty booth first, will you and Hubie walk up there and sit down with them in the empty booth?"

Dewey shrugged sheepishly and grinned a little. "Sure. I guess. We'll do it for you. But, quite frankly, Id just as soon sit right here. Im having a good time," he said. And he was. "I can have a good time anywhere."

"But youll do it?" 'Bama said.

"—if youll get them to move first," Hubie amended.

"We'll do it," Dewey grinned.

"Okay," 'Bama said. "Im off."

They all of them including Dave watched the tall gambler push back his chair and rise and go languidly up front to the booth of girls, his hat pushed back just to his widow's peak, moving in that lazy horse like walk of his. He slid into the empty space next the two girls on this side, his back to their own table and facing Lois and the other two, and began to talk. They could no longer look at Lois's legs because he had blocked the view, and Dave turned back to look across at his unpretty but very nubile young woman, who had looked up to watch the outcome of this new movement at the table. She looked away quickly. He would have sworn she was watching mostly him.

"I didnt know he was married," he said, turning his head back to the table, "until he told me just a while ago."

"He doesnt *look* married," Hubie agreed.

"Yeah, hes married," Dewey grinned, watching 'Bama affectionately. "He bought himself a farm down in the south end of the county out of his first big killing after he came here—down in the Dark Bend River region—and installed his wife and two kids there and left them. He goes back down there once every couple of weeks or so. Most of the time he stays in town here. Rents a room."

"—but hes seldom there," Hubie said. "I heard shes pregnant again," he said to Dewey.

"Who told you?"

"Martha. She heard it."

Dewey laughed. "She probly is."

"You mean she stays there and farms the place all by herself?" Dave asked, looking again at his nubile young woman.

"Naw," Dewey said. "Hes got a man and his wife living there too, in another house. They farm it on shares. She just stays down there, and keeps an eye on them. Manages it, sort of. His old mother lives down there too part of the time, I guess; when shes not at his brother's."

"Have you ever been down there?" Dave asked. He took another drink, quietly, almost placidly, in spite of the churning energy of misery and frustration and malice—of fright, abstract and objectless—boiling inside of him, and turned to look at the young woman again. She had just crossed her legs. They were too thin too. It didnt matter.

"Yeah we been down there a couple of times," Dewey said. " 'Bama wanted me and Hubie to paint it for him once but weve never got around to it."

"What kind of place is it?" Dave said listlessly. "Nice place?"

"Naw, just one of them old oldtime houses. The land's good. He knows farmin, 'Bama."

"Must be a fine life for her," Dave said.

"She doesnt seem to mind it. Just lives there. Kids go to a country school. Shes not a bad lookin woman. If shed just fix herself up a little. Take care of herself."

"She probly doesnt have much reason to," Dave said.

"I guess not," Dewey said. "Say, you knew my brother Raymond in high school, didnt you." It was not so much a question as an assumption.

"Yeah. That is, I knew of him. He was three years behind me. I remember him as a tough kid who was always getting into fights, even then," he said, looking across at his girl again. His eyes themselves just wouldnt stay away.

"Did you know that Scott girl who was in love with him?"

"No. Just by sight is all."

"She was really hung on him," Dewey said.

"I never knew any of those rich kids," Dave said.

Dewey's assumption had touched something deep inside of him, somehow or other. It made him aware that, historically at least, he was as much a part of Parkman as were Dewey and Hubie, or 'Bama, or Brother Frank. Or as that girl over there. Momentarily this gave him an unexpectedly powerful emotion, before he quickly rationalized it. It meant he existed here—if only as a birth certificate in the County Clerk's office, and a record of grades (usually poor) at the high school, and a rarely remembered bit of scandal—in a way he could never exist in Greater Los Angeles. And he needed that. But such existence was hardly compensation for a man who had an almost physical need to be loved by the whole world, either.

"As a matter of fact, I was always a sort of a black sheep," he said slowly. "Like you. A neerdowell. The guys I ran around with were mostly all wild boys from down in the country who stole their old man's homemade whiskey, or else stole his corn to make it themselves." Prohibition, he thought, what a strange thing it had been for them.

With everything colored by his emotion, he thought he could sense that same sense of existence-in-Parkman in everyone else as he looked at them around the wall booths. They all knew they existed here, but were unsure they would exist elsewhere. That was why they stayed. That was why they enjoyed Dewey's gang's escapades like they did, with a sense of partisanship. It was a part of the town. And besides Dewey had the same thing in him. That was why he stayed. They were all obviously disappointed by Raymond's exit, he thought, and were still hoping for some event or other to happen that they could carry home with them to talk about, but there was an affection in their scrutiny, too. Of a sort. Dewey sort of belonged to them along with other civic property and they felt a sort of sense of civic possession for Dewey. They had known him all their lives. His father had been one of the town bums when they were kids. When Dave's sweeping eyes came to the nubile girl across from him, she dropped hers, sliding them away again as if she were looking at something else just past him, and then began talking animatedly to her ignored boy friend.

"Yeah, I remember," Dewey answered him, his eyes glinting curiously with a private malicious pleasure. "That was the same bunch that you got kicked off the football team with."

Dave nodded, feeling both choked up and a wild driving energy to kick over tables, to smash. If Raymond were still here, right now, hed be pleased and happy to fight him himself, love it. And for no reason. No reason at all. Just because he was miserable. Miserable with a self biting, self lashing, hacklebackrising tooth gnashing misery that would have made being beaten up actually enjoyable.

"What I still dont see," Hubie said disgustedly, "is why the hell you ever come back here."

"For the same reason that you did, probly," Dave said, looking at him belligerently; then he looked away, "Im only here for a week," he said. "Say, who is that girl over there against the wall across from us?"

Dewey swung around in his chair to look. The girl seemed to flush in the dim light but she did not look at them or stop talking. "Thats your brother Frank's office girl," Dewey said. "Name's Edith Barclay. Use to be a phone operator."

"No kidding," Dave said ominously, he looked at her again, "Is that right."

"Yeah; I thought you already knew her," Dewey said. "You been lookin at her like you did."

"Nah," Dave said forebodingly. "I dont know her. Brother Frank's office girl, hunh?" That was why shed been watching him.

"Nice lookin girl, isnt she?" Dewey said decently—that is, not suggestively. "Guy shes with is Harold Alberson. Works for Sternutol in the Sales Department. White collar kid."

"They engaged?" Dave said.

"Naw," Dewey drawled. "Edith goes out with—dates, that is—a lot of different guys. The way we hear it is Harold is nuts about her and wants to marry her but she wont give him a tumble. Or anybody else, we hear. But of course we dont run in their circle."

"What circle?" Hubie demanded. "Her old man works for the Sternutol just like mine."

"I wonder if Brother Frank could be getting a little of it?" Dave said. His pulse was beginning to move from his chest up into his ears, wildly. He was contemplating doing something extravagant.

"I dont know," Dewey said, scrupulously honest. "I kind of doubt it. I never heard that. And I probly would have. —But then again," he said, letting his more natural inclination loose, "I wouldnt be surprised. Would you? Because shes really a looker. Aint she? Beautiful really."

Dave studied her again, male ego rising and engulfing him in wild vanity without any legitimate reason. Except that he wanted to do something, something wild. She was still talking selfconsciously to Harold. Dewey thought she was beautiful, too. It wasnt just him. She had almost no breasts at all and what were obviously overwide hips, even sitting down. But that glow of nubility from her changed them all into beauty.

"I think Ill just step over and say hello to her," he leered at Dewey. "After all, shes practically one of the family."

"Go ahead," Dewey grinned, and his eyes lit up again with that curious pleased glint of malice they got, every time something was said or done that might conceivably flaunt the proprieties of Parkman.

Dave took a lastminute gulp of beer and got up and sauntered across the room toward her booth, the old sourmash liquordriven arrogance rising higher and consuming his timidity completely. It was one of the few confident emotions he ever got the pleasure of feeling in his life. Besides, he was committed now.

She saw him coming and her eyes widened, slightly, and she turned and quickly began talking to Harold. That pleased him. He felt very powerful. She must have been twenty-four or -five but looked at least twenty-seven. Harold was twenty-three or -four and looked it. Dave leaned one arm across the back of their booth behind Edith and grinned down at them arrogantly.

"Hello," he said insultingly. "Youre Edith Barclay, arent you? That works for my brother Frank."

"Why, yes," she said, "I am. Hello, Mr Hirsh, how are you?" and introduced him to Harold Alberson. Her voice was naturally low, sexily nubile just like hed guessed, and now it was troubled and her face uncomfortable.

Dave felt even better. "Hi, bud," he said magnanimously to Harold, still grinning insultingly. "I thought it was you," he said to Edith, ignoring Harold's hand. "Sooo, I just thought Id come over and say hello."

Behind him over the noise of conversation, music and drinking he could feel just about every eye in the other booths upon his back, watching speculatively and intently. They knew who he was all right.

"How did you know who I was?" she said in the same low voice. Apparently she was well aware of the watchers, too.

Dave grinned disparagingly, and said the first thing that came into his head. "I was in the store a few minutes this afternoon."

"Oh, I didnt know that!" she said. Then she said, more thoughtfully, "But I work back in the office . . ."

Dave slowly closed and opened his eyes arrogantly. "I know that. You happened to come out front a minute with some papers and I saw you. You didnt notice me."

Her eyes, watching him with the hollow fortitude of the deeply embarrassed, flinched a little and betrayed she knew he was lying.

"Its still the same old store, aint it?" he said insolently.

She nodded. "I didnt know youd ever seen it."

"I never had. Till today. But then Frank's sent us pictures of it," Dave grinned. "Whens he going to redecorate it?"

This was evidently an unintended lucky shot, because her eyes showed surprise. She evidently wasnt sure just how much of Frank's confidence he had.

Edith smiled at him tentatively, evidently hoping she had at last found some common ground. "Well, hes been talking about it for a long time. He wants Agnes to do it for him. Agnes is awfully good with colors. Someday theyll get around to it."

Dave raised one eyebrow and grinned insultingly. "I doubt it. I seriously doubt it, Edith. I doubt if theyll ever get around to it. Theyll just go on talking about it the rest of their lives. But then it wont make much difference, will it, Edith?"

She did not say anything to that, one way or the other, and merely sat looking at him with those troubled, marriageable eyes. (He swore he could smell her, the marriageableness of her, a delicious ruttish female smell compounded of damp female flesh and hair seasoned liberally with cologne or perfume. Oh, Christ, Hirsh. Cut it out. Get away from here.)

"Well, Ive got to be getting back to my friends," he grinned at them arrogantly. "You know my friends, dont you? But Im glad I came over.

Ill see you tomorrow. Im coming up to the store again tomorrow. See Frank. I was out to the house tonight, for dinner."

"Its nice to have met you," Edith said in that low voice, her eyes not only embarrassed now but somehow vaguely guilty too, as if all this were somehow her fault. She did not mention she already knew he was going to be at the house tonight.

"Pleasure's all mine," Dave grinned, "I assure you. The pleasure's all mine. I thought I ought to come over when I saw you watching me."

"I wasnt watching you!"

It was an instinctive exclamation, and a guilty one, torn out of her without thought as if she had been jabbed with a pin and said Ow!

"You werent?" Dave grinned. "Well, I wouldnt contradict a lady. But when you sit and stare at someone, you shouldnt try and act surprised when they come over and speak to you. Bye, Harold."

He made a little bow with his head and turned on his heel and walked off, but not before he had seen the outraged start on her face and the look of mingled puzzlement, anger and hurt at why he should want to come over here and deliberately embarrass her when she had not offended him or done anything to deserve it.

The truth was, he didnt really know why himself. Except that she was so damned nubile, so marriageable, and because he was so filled up with such a goddamned churning driving energy of misery and lack of love that it had to come out someplace and anyway he resented her.

He took his time going back to the table, although he didnt want to, very much aware of all the eyes in the booths upon him, but in every booth he looked at and he tried to look at them all the eyes all dropped away leaving him staring at nothing.

the eyes have it

"Whatd she have to say?" Dewey grinned as he sat down. He had thoughtfully ordered another beer for Dave.

"Said she was glad to meet me," Dave said shortly, and proceeded to drink off most of his fresh beer. He was breathing a little fast and the interiors of his wrists where the blood vessels ran were trembling, but the feeling of hilarious superiority had not left him. Neither had the vague but piercing hunger and the misery. These were stronger. Than ever. It was a relief to get back to the table with Dewey and Hubie who he knew would not censure him, even if he didnt like them very well because he felt they were wastrels.

Hubie snorted. "Yeah, she looked like she was glad to meet you. She looked like she could of killed you."

Dave grinned, the acidulous tightfitting puckery mouthed—too much drinking too much drinking—arrogance washing about him—too much *living!*—in heady waves. He knew he had made a colossal ass of himself, a real violent fool, but he didnt feel badly about having done it.

Rather he felt glad, very glad. He liked doing it. It was his business if he liked making a fool of himself wasnt it?

"She sure smelled good," he said, grinning grimly.

"—and thats all the good itll do you," Hubie snorted. Hubie was getting more argumentative as he drank more.

"Dont you worry, Dave," Dewey grinned understandingly. "She aint so lily white all over. See that old dame up front in the corner booth smoochin with the old guy? Well, thats Edith's grandmother. Jane. Jane Staley. Jane's a good old gal; shes one of the best friends I got in town; shes always good for a buck loan for a beer. But nobody knows what the old guys in this town would do for lovin if it wasnt for Jane. So dont let Edith crap you shes no saint descended from no Virgin Mary."

"They dont even speak to each other hardly in here or up town," Hubie said indifferently.

Dave looked up at the front booth, although he didnt want to, didnt care, where an old gal of sixty-some was somewhat prevented from cuddling any closer to her stringy aged companion by the unbelievable enormity of her breasts. Then he remembered her, startled. It was the same old Janie who used to take care of him as a kid. But shed put on an awful lot of weight. He wanted suddenly to laugh out loud wildly. They didnt any of them, anywhere, noplace, understand a bit of it, even a littlest bit. What a way to introduce yourself to a woman you wanted to fall in love with! To make fall in love with you! He had sure picked himself a couple of great ones today hadnt he! And played them well! Played them so well! He felt, suddenly, exuberantly destructive. He just barely restrained himself from throwing back his head and roaring with laughter.

"Old Jane works for Frank, too," Dewey said, looking at him curiously. "Or for Agnes rather. Does their housework."

"I know. Maybe I ought to go over and say hello to her, too." He laughed out loud. While he was still looking at the ancients, 'Bama got up from the booth of girls and walked languidly back toward them, cool, selfpossessed, a cigarette hanging out of the corner of his pulled down mouth, his hat still riding just at his hairline exposing the widow's peak. Dave's sudden and overwhelming exuberance included him too. What a book these characters would make someday! —For some writer. Somebody. Somebody, like Wally Dennis, ought to do it.

"Hi, 'Bama!" he cried exuberantly.

From the booth Edith, too, watched the tall 'Bama come back down the room to the little table. He had evidently succeeded in patching up the squabble between Dewey Cole and his girl friend Lois Wallup. Now they would all get back together. Until some other argument started.

It had been an interesting diversion to watch, an amusing development, and she had more or less enjoyed it. Rather like going to a movie you dont especially like or dislike there were so many of them like that but you stayed to the end anyway just to see what would happen in the end. But she was still embarrassed about Dave, and therefore angry, and now it seemed to her suddenly a disgustingly fruitless and unedifying way of spending an evening: To go to Smitty's after the show and drink beer and watch an argument between Dewey Cole and his girl friend.

And with Harold Alberson!

She looked over at Harold for a moment, and because he was watching her with his large eyes, smiled, then looked back down at her beer, from which she drank unconcernedly, and then looked back over at the table, putting a conscious look of interest on her face.

Poor Harold. They had only spoken once since Dave Hirsh had come over to the booth, which was when Harold asked her if she would like another beer, and she had said no.

She had been terribly embarrassed, and she had been hurt. Mostly of course it was just the being made conspicuous. It really had nothing to do with her at all and he was pretty drunk and she understood that. But it was all so sanguinary and uncalled for. Why on earth would he want to *do* something like that to her. She had never even met the man.

She had wanted to run away, leave, blindly and without forethought, and even now her body was still sending her frantic signals to move, but she was confident none of it showed on the outside of her.

She watched the gambler 'Bama slide into his chair. She had never heard his last name, just 'Bama. And she listened coldly and analytically to Dave's euphoric yelp of greeting. It was amazing how much he really did look like the boss. Like Frank. It was unbelievable two people could look so much alike and be so completely and utterly different.

"What is 'Bama's last name?" she asked Harold pleasantly.

"Dillert, I think it is," Harold said hollowly. He cleared his throat.

"Dillert," she said, saying it aloud to herself.

"Yes," Harold said hollowly. "He came up here from Alabama." He cleared his throat again. "Thats why the nickname."

"Yes, I had heard that," Edith smiled. He was supposed to be a very successful seducer of women. She could see where there might be—for certain types—a certain quality about him of iciness that might seem dangerous and attractive. —if not very sensible. But he was so unattractive physically with that hanging belly and that strange way of walking, and that sneering cockiness as if he expected every woman to lie down for him, that she would have thought any woman would refuse to go to bed with him if only to show him all women werent easy. Who wanted to be just another jewel in some man's crown?

Besides, he looked sallow and not very healthy, as if he perpetually never got enough rest, and only ate whenever he happened to think about it, and drank far too much, and as if his bowels had not moved regularly for years. That belly. You just couldnt have good elimination without regular meals.

In front of her Harold cleared his throat again. "I think I better go over there and say something to him," he said hollowly. "Dont you think I should?"

"Say something to who?" Edith said.

"To Dave Hirsh. I think Id better go over and speak to him," Harold said hollowly. "Ask him to go outside with me or something. Dont you think I ought to?"

"Youll do no such a silly idiotic damned thing!" Edith said curtly. "Youll sit still and drink your damned beer!"

"Well, I didnt like him coming over and talking to you like that," Harold said hollowly. "And I think I ought to do something about it. Even if he is your boss's brother."

"I think youre talking like an idiotic damned fool," Edith said. "Do you want to make us even more conspicuous?" Jesus! Jesus Christ! she said to herself, feeling ashamed for saying it about Harold. And he wants to marry me! None of those men over at that table would have asked your permission. Certainly not your advice. They would have jumped up, perhaps too eagerly, and hit somebody if they were going to do anything at all. Poor Harold. Jesus!

"After all, he cant be that tough," Harold said hopefully. "I think I should ask him to apologize or go outside with me," he said hollowly. He looked at her beseechingly. "Maybe you would like me better if I did."

"Id like you a lot less," Edith said irritably. "And youll do no such a thing. The thing I like about you the best is that youre a gentleman."

"I think I ought to do something," Harold said.

"Harold, you wouldnt stand a chance with any of those men in a fight," Edith said crisply. "Quit being a romantic damned fool."

"Oh, I dont know," Harold said. "I used to box a little."

"Those men are not boxers. Theyre knock down drag outers. And theyre crazy. They dont care if they get hurt. Now stop it and shut up," she said. "I can defend my own virtue. When it needs it. It doesnt need it now."

Harold looked away, perhaps mildly relieved, but mostly wretchedly miserable. Edith felt sorry for him. Maybe she ought to let him go over there. And get his block knocked off. But it was stupid. Stupid and foolish, and she could not endure the thought of being the cause of a fight. She had seen too many fights between men and almost always they were started by some woman. Some woman who then screamed and looked frightened, and *then* sat back and swelled up like a poisoned

pup with pleased vanity, while the poor idiot men beat each other sense-
less. Women! She was having increasingly less use for women.

She turned back to watch the table, where 'Bama was talking volubly,
and the others listening. —Except for Dave, who was staring off into
some space and apparently not listening to anything. It was amazing
how much he looked like the boss, with a little less hair and the littlest
bit more paunch it could *be* him. She supposed she should be flattered.
But she wasnt.

It wouldnt be so bad, watching them, if the whole wild bunch of them
werent all so obviously aware they were being watched, so obviously
playing to their audience like a bunch of ham actors. They loved it.
—And yet, to be honest, she had to admit there was something menacing
that made it exciting to come here and watch their antics—those evenings they were here, showed up. Not a month ago, with another date,
she had watched Dewey Cole and Hubie Murson throw back their
chairs and fall to the floor and begin punching each other in the face
and body in a frightening dead silence of concentration until Smitty
and Eddie collared them and got them outside. Half an hour later
they were back, their clothes torn, laughing and drinking together, as
great buddies as ever. When they werent here, the place was dead as
hell, that was the truth. No wonder Smitty catered to them. Edith felt
sorry for them. It was almost like going back to the Middle Ages, or to
the days of Queen Elizabeth in England. It was as if they didnt care at
all about their bodies, or about their reputations —And why should
they? she thought, never having had any? She knew about that herself.—
or else were haunted beyond endurance, beyond caring, by something.

In front of her, Harold cleared his throat again. "Sometimes I think
you would like me a very lot better if I were more like guys like that,"
he said hollowly.

"Harold, you can without doubt make some of the stupidest remarks
I have ever heard from a human being!" Edith said irately. "I like you
better than *all* of them."

She snapped her head away, and looked back at the table. God! And
Dave Hirsh could go and nut himself—as Jane would undoubtedly
have said; Jane had probably seen the whole thing and was sitting up
there chortling to herself. She had heard bad stories about Dave Hirsh
all her life from Jane, all told with too much relish, and plenty of
veiled allusions from both Frank and Agnes. Certainly, whether they
were true or not, she had never seen a man who could make himself so
thoroughly and completely unattractive and disliked in so short a time.
In spite of that he certainly did look an awful lot like the boss, she
thought, and in a different way he had that same childish bumbling way
about him that made you want to mother him. Poor Harold was worth
five of him.

"Order us another beer!" she commanded curtly.

Oh, hell! she thought. Oh, damn damn hell!

CHAPTER 15

'BAMA had slid lithely into his seat at the table grinning triumphantly, when he came back from the girls' booth.

"Well, its all fixed up. Theyre goin to move over into the empty booth. But they want to wait ten minutes so it wont look like me talkin to them had anything to do with it. Lets have another beer.

"God," he said leaning back in his chair, "the things I have to go through to get my friends fixed up—Eddie!" he called.

The one armed young bartender—one handed actually, since he had retained most of his right arm almost down to the wrist—looked up and grinned and held up four of his five fingers.

'Bama nodded at him. "Now, look," he said to Dewey, leaning forward again. "All I want is for you to give us fifteen minutes to get us established with the other three. Then you can do anything you want: get up and leave, kick them in the jaw, pour beer on them. But give us that fifteen minutes so our three wont feel honor bound to side in with them like theyre doing now. In fifteen minutes they can legitimately feel like a separate party. So please sit and talk to them that long." He paused. "Okay?"

"Sure," Dewey said, unperturbed. "I said we would. But if youd of just waited theyd of come back here finally."

"Yes," 'Bama said, "but by that time it would of been five minutes of closing and we wouldnt of had any time left to make our pitch."

Dewey shrugged. "We're goin to do it for you."

"Okay," 'Bama said. "Now as for you," he said, turning to Dave.

Dave, who would at this moment have felt highly flattered if he could have heard Harold Alberson's opinion of his fighting prowess, nodded. But he could not make himself really listen. All he could think of was what an operation it had turned out to be, what a tremendous amount of thought and energy was being expended, wasted—all because he had inadvertently said something earlier about wanting to get fixed up. It had set all kinds of unanticipated conflicts and emotions and problems to be solved into furious motion. And now he didnt care. But he couldnt say anything, not now after 'Bama had gone to all this trouble. He felt trapped. He tried to make himself listen.

"First I made sure they understood you werent a soldier, you were a civilian guy who just got his discharge," 'Bama said. "Then I told them some stuff all about you: how you live in Hollywood, are a writer for the movies, and are just visiting your brother here a week or so. And you dont know anybody and want to meet someone."

"Oh, Christ," Dave said. "You didnt tell them I was a writer."

'Bama paused to look at him. "Sure. Why the hell not?"

"But Im not one any more."

"So what? What difference does that make? As long as you can make it work for you," 'Bama said, looking at him. "I told them you were a movie writer, and then later on I let it drop that you werent workin on nothin now, but that when you got back out there and got to workin on some new ones, if you saw some part that might fit one of them, should any of them happened to of caught your fancy, you might very easily get her out there and get her started in a couple jobs.

"I figured we might as well use everything."

"Oh, Christ," Dave said.

"What the hell, why not use it on them. Theyll never know the difference anyway. Whats wrong with that?" 'Bama demanded.

Eddie brought their beers. 'Bama paid him. "Now look," he said. "Theres three of them. You can have yore choice. Ive had them all one time or another I guess, so it dont make me no difference."

"Why dont we take all three," Dave said. He laughed uproariously.

'Bama looked at him curiously. "Thatd be all right with me," he said, "but I dont think these gals would play along. You got to remember these gals are country gals. We'll have to go to the city for that. Chicago or someplace."

"Then I guess we better not," Dave said, grinning sillily.

"I dont think we better chance it," 'Bama said. "Now look. Ill brief you on them. Two of them work out at the br—" He paused. "Wait a minute. Howd you make out over there?" he asked, nodding his head toward Edith Barclay.

Dave grinned. "No good."

"Because I can always break this off quick, if you find somethin better."

"No," Dave said. How to explain it? "I didnt—"

"He wasnt tryin'," Hubie volunteered helpfully.

"Well, I didnt figure youd make out anyway," 'Bama said. "With her. Especially when shes got a date. —Now look: Two of these work out at the brassiere factory with Lois. Thats Ginnie and Mildred. The other one—"

"Look, theyre movin'," Hubie said suddenly. "Theyre gettin' up. Theyre goin' over to the other booth. Come on, Dewey," he said eagerly, "lets go."

"Let them sit a spell," Dewey said sourly. "Whats your hurry? We dont want to go runnin up there like a couple of dogs."

"—the third one, is Rosalie Sansome. Shes the big, well built one.

Shes the niece of the woman who runs one of the bars up at West Lancaster. You know about West Lancaster?"

Dave nodded, absently.

"West Lancaster's the only place in the county can sell hard liquor over the bar," 'Bama said anyway. "The county's dry so they got themselves incorporated so they could pass a city ordinance permitting liquor by the drink because thats where they get all their income. Theyve got five buildings there, on the river bank, and one of them's a grocery; the other four are bars. Her aunt's a tough old gal, used to run a whorehouse in Terre Haute, and Rosalie's pretty rugged herself. She can get pretty huffy—because her aunt's made all that money, see; Rosalie works for her in the bar sometimes—but she can be made, on the first time out, if you handle her right and baby her along. For instance, you dont want to ever call her Rosie, she hates it. But shes the best lookin one by far of the bunch."

"Except for Lois," Dewey said.

"Except for Lois and Martha," Hubie said.

"Naturally," 'Bama said tiredly. "You dint think I was counting them."

"Which one do you think I ought to take?" Dave said, trying to sound interested. The Walpurgis Night feeling was on him again, with its agonizing sense of complete separation, of being unable to partake, of being painfully aware of being so different all the time. Arrogance boiled up in him again: Why the hell should he have to cater to some goddamned woman, just to make her.

'Bama scratched his head alongside his hat and back over his ear without touching the immaculate brim. "Well, I dont know. It all depends on what youre lookin for most. Ginnie is the easiest made; and she really likes her sex; but shes hard to get along with sometimes; and she looks horrible, looks like a regular pig.—"

"Looks like just what she is," Dave said with drunken profoundness.

"Yeah, and Mildred's the easiest to get along with; and shes not bad lookin; and she can be a lot of fun, good sense of humor; but when you get her in bed shes no good at all, gets all tightened up, doesnt really like it.—

"And Rosalie," he wound up. "Shes the best looking; and shes pretty damn good in the hay; but shes awful damned hard to get along with. But shes really almost beautiful," 'Bama added, "if youre a breast man. —But Id say shes the hardest one of the bunch to make.

"So there you are."

"Ill take Rosie," Dave said after a pause, in the voice of a man accepting a challenge.

'Bama shook his head. "Dont never call her Rosie. I mean it. Really. She hates it like poison. And she aint got that red hair for nothin.

—And dont call her Red either," he said. "Look, why dont you wait," he said cautiously. "Until you get up there and look them over and talk to them a little bit."

Dave was about to say No by God! Im not scared of any two-bit madam's niece! but he decided not to. Something about 'Bama's face. The earnestness. It was 'Bama's show wasnt it?

"All right Ill wait," he said.

"Come on, Hubie," Dewey said sourly. "We might as well get on up there." He got up disgustedly.

"Stay with them," 'Bama said like a man cheering on the home team, and looking up. "Do you all want to figure on goin long with us later?"

"Nah," Dewey said.

"We got to work tomorrow," said Hubie, who had gotten up also.

"God damn it!" Dewey said irately, glaring at him. "Where you goin to take them?" he asked 'Bama defiantly, and looked at Hubie as if daring him to say anything.

"Indianapolis."

"In this snow?"

"Hell yes," 'Bama said. "Snow doesnt bother me. We could go up to West Lancaster, only we wouldnt have any place to bed down unless the ferry was runnin to take us across the river where them fishin resorts are."

"I doubt if it will be," Dewey said, looking up at the front window.

They walked away, up toward the now no longer empty booth that had been under discussion, and that now had the two girls in it. Everyone in all the booths watched them to see what they would do. When they merely sat down with the girls, and ordered beer, there was a sort of unheard sigh of disappointment went around the room.

"We give them a couple minutes," 'Bama said, apparently completely unaware of the audience. "To get settled in." He looked at his watch suddenly, and nervously, as if he were expecting to time them for two minutes to the second.

Dave thought he looked worn and tired out, with those perpetual purple circles under his eyes, outlining their present haggardness, and the drawn look around the corners of his no longer youthful jaw. And yet there was an old time kind of life-eagerness in him, on his face, a sort of ardent interest in everything he looked at, that should have been incompatible with that perpetual sneer of his but evidently wasnt. Looking at Dave, he suddenly grinned that twisted sarcastic grin, and there flooded up from behind it such a shy look of liquid warmth so filled with pure animal magnetism and unselfconscious charm that it seemed to drive his personality into the other man like a stake. It was almost as if he had deliberately turned on a switch, or opened a floodgate.

He must really be a woman breaker Dave thought, when he wants to.

"Why are you doing all this for me?" he asked him.

"Why! You wanted to get fixed up, didnt you?"

"Yeah but, you dont go all out like this for every stranger you meet who wants to get fixed up, do you? Is it," Dave said, thinking of how the other had used his first name Dave so strangely, "is it,"—he fumbled, unable to express the subtlety he felt into the simple gross crudities of Words: c-a-t cat, d-o-g dog, human beings he thought millions and millions and millions of them, m-a-n man, intelligent human beings, they went to school, most of them even graduated from high school, s-c-h-double-o-l school. Now, children, say after me: Cats do not have schools. Dogs do not have schools. Only m-a-n has schools. Arent you proud that only m-a-n has schools!

s-m-u-g smug

We cant even talk. We think we can think though. Oh nuts.

'Bama was still watching him expectantly. "Is it what?" he said. "Is what what?"

"Well, is it because Frank Hirsh is a big shot in this town? Does that impress you?"

'Bama seemed to draw back haughtily. "Impress me? Why the hell should *that* impress *me*?"

"I mean, because it was Frank Hirsh. Frank Hirsh's brother?"

'Bama stared at him coldly, with a greater contempt in his eyes than there had ever been in his sneer. "Hell, buddy, Frank Hirsh dont impress me. Why the hell should *he* impress *me*? I knew him when he didnt have but one pot to pee in—back before the war."

Dave moved his shoulders awkwardly, wishing he hadnt spoken. He hadnt meant to offend him, only understand, curiosity. "Well, you seemed awful nice to me, that was all. It surprised me, I guess."

'Bama drew up his lip in a contemptuous sneer of real magnitude this time, his eyes showing both disbelief and outrage. "I guess you dont know me very well. Nothin in this town impresses *me*. I wasnt nice to you. I just thought you wanted to get laid and didnt know nobody. It dont make one good goddam to me if yore Frank Hirsh's brother or not," he said coldly. "Or anybody else's brother. As far as that goes—"

Dave held up his hand palm out in a sign to slow down. "It dont make one to me either," he grinned soothingly.

'Bama stared at him narrowly. Then he laughed suddenly. "I guess you dont know me very well yet." The semi Western hat, evidently worn Dave thought suddenly to show he was not a native of this country but had come here from Alabama, looked both virile and energetic on him, but somehow ludicrous, but also dangerous, as he leaned on his elbow on the table. "I was about to ask you if you wanted to go on up there now. But I dont want you to think Im suckin Frank Hirsh's nose."

He leaned back in his chair and looked around the booths sneeringly and said nothing further.

"Well, are you askin me or not?" Dave said.

'Bama sneered scornfully. There was a hurt sullenness in his voice as he ignored the question. "This is the goddamnest town," he said, looking around the booths. "Theres never nothin to do in this damned town. And nobody to do it with. I dont know why the hell I ever moved back here in the first place, after I got out of service."

"If youre askin me, lets go," Dave said. "If youre not, lets just sit here." It was the exactly right thing to have said, probably the only right thing.

"Well, come on," the tall man said contemptuously, "what the hellre you waitin on? —We might as well, I guess. Theres nothin else to do around here."

To Dave hearing the words, it was as if a great knell of relief had tolled somewhere, informing him that he had been saved by the bell from a great catastrophe. He felt correspondingly gay.

"Okay, lets go," he said. When are you going to ever learn that you cant talk the truth with people about themselves? About other people, yes. Yes, and of course. Yes, gladly. But not themselves. Its not that theyre lying. Its that they dont know. They make damn sure they dont know. Did you ever see a whore who believed she was a whore? did you ever see a Scrooge who thought he was one? did you ever see a mother who didnt believe she was Mary?

"Wait a minute," 'Bama said, in an entirely different, amiable, almost eager, tone. "Theres Wally."

Wally Dennis was just coming in the front door, complete with cowboy boots, rolled up pants, Air Force fleecelined jacket and glints of snow glistening on his bare head. Smitty's seemed suddenly warm and cozy, as he shut the door on the blast of cold air. Wally spoke happily to Dewey and Hubie sitting in the low backed booth with Lois and Martha, but he did not even slow his stride. He came on back, smiling happily, to 'Bama and Dave at the table, and it was as if 'Bama had known he would.

"Howdy, men, howdy," he said, nodding and nodding. "Whats the matter? you and the men got a mad on?"

"Yore out late," 'Bama said, grinning. "Are you ridin that damned motorcycle in this weather?"

"God, no," Wally said. "Im not that good! Id have her down every fifteen feet, in snow like this. Shes locked up in the garage. I walked. Mr Hirsh," he said.

"Wallace Dennis," Dave said maliciously. "Wallace *French* Dennis."

"Thats right," Wally said. "You got it *right,* man. And Ive got a bone to pick with *you.*"

"Yes? Whats that?"

"Aw, nothin. Just kiddin," Wally said. He swept off the jacket, hung it on the chair back, and sat down holding up one finger to the grinning Eddie. "Everybody grins at me. That is because they know I am a writer. In this town everybody grins at writers. Not only do they expect them to be eccentric, but they do not think I can be one. I resent it. —No," he said to Dave, "all I meant was I had a date with that chick niece of yours tonight and she stood me up. What did you do to her? She wouldnt even come downstairs but sent her mother to tell me to go to hell. Or words to that effect."

"She had an argument with her daddy," Dave said.

"Thats what I figured. About going to school. You know how I figured? Because every time that happens she wont come downstairs and stands me up. See, Frank wants her to go to school but she wants to go to New York and—"

"I know all about it," Dave said. "But this argument was about literature."

Wally nodded. "Well, she asked me and I advised her to go to New York, if she felt like that and wants to be an artist. And not go to school. Run off if she had to."

"I didnt advise her anything," Dave said profoundly. "Its a pretty tough proposition, to break into the stage in New York."

"True," Wally said. "True, true. On the other hand, lots of other girls have done it though, Mr Hirsh."

"Yes," Dave said. "By sleeping with all the stage managers, and assistant stage managers, and producers, and male leads and female leads and coaches, that they have to sleep with first."

"You forgot the agents," Wally said.

"And agents," Dave nodded. "And producers' brother in laws, too, for that matter."

"I really dont see what difference all that makes, though," Wally said. "If a girl really wants to act. If she has that drive to greatness. Girls all get had sooner or later. It seems to me youre getting old, and conservative. Mr Hirsh."

"Perhaps youre right," Dave said.

"Well, if *we* intend to get laid——sooner *or* later——" 'Bama said, "we better get to movin on it."

"You getting Dave here all fixed up with something?" Wally grinned at him. "Hey Hey."

"Well, Im tryin" 'Bama said. "Its them three up in that booth alone. We cant decide which two. Whynt you come on and go along with us and take one?"

"Noo, I guess not," Wally said, a little wistfully. "Not tonight. I got to work tomorrow. I know your parties. Anyway, I know that Ginnie.

She was in the same grade with me in school. She was sleeping with everybody in our class in the sixth grade and even grown men, before I ever knew what it was all about."

"I admit they aint a whole hell of a lot," 'Bama said. "But its the best I could do under the circumstances, on such short notice."

" 'Tisnt much, but I give it to you in the name of the Lord'," Wally said, "as my grandmother used to say when she handed her leftovers out the back door to the bums. You know, there dont seem to be near as many bums looking for meals as there used to be thirty forty years ago when my grandmother used to feed them," he said with the surprised air of a discovery. "I wonder why?"

Dave sat silent, listening to the two of them talk, 'Bama with that strange pleased happiness that seemed to come over him whenever Wally was around, Wally with that same strained almost painful effort to be amenable to be *regular* that he had noticed before, earlier in the day. —My God, had that been today? It didnt seem possible!— Perhaps Wally was right: Maybe he *was* getting old, and conservative. Mr Hirsh. It made him mad. Not mad at Wally. But mad at the idea that anybody could think that about him. He looked at him; Wally was still talking frenetically to 'Bama, who was grinning.

"You know, Wally, if you and I love the world too much," he said suddenly, "thats not the world's fault, its our own." Pompous, he thought, pompous.

Wally stopped talking and looked at him thoughtfully. "Thats true," he said simply.

"The world didnt ask us to," Dave said.

Wally nodded. "Thats right, it didnt," he said. "And its unnatural of us. Its neurotic. Isnt it? And anybody who has this need to love—"

"—and be loved by—" Dave said.

"—the world, I mean really love," Wally defined, "not just pretend and give it lip service, like by going to church Sundays say, a real need," he said, thinking it out as he went along, "I dont know how to say it, love to the point of selfdestruction I guess, is really, when the world hasnt asked us for it, and doesnt want or need it, has no place for it really, is really a real neurotic. Neurotic in the sense of being contrary to nature. An unnatural organism. How far would an amoeba or a lion get on love?"

"Not far," Dave said.

"I dont understand all this hifalutin crap," 'Bama said, "but if we want to make them women, wed better get our tails up there. You want to come on up and just sit with us, Wally?"

"No. I dont think so. Thanks. I think Ill just sit here and drink my beer. Ive got some things I want to think about," he said. He turned to look at Dave, who was getting to his feet laboriously. "I take back everything I said this afternoon, Mr Hirsh," Wally said. "Even though I meant it. Its your affair. You have to work your own way out of the hole. Everybody does."

"Sure," Dave said, vaguely. "From the frying hole into the pan. See you later, Wallace Dennis," he said, "Wallace French Dennis."

Wally grinned ruefully. "Guess Ill have to change my pen name."

"Come on," 'Bama said. "Dave. If were goin."

He had used the name again, in that same way. Dave followed him, disconnectedly, moving in that frightful boiling energy of arrogant frustration that made everything seem perspectiveless, without continuity and therefore unconnected, but having drunk enough now to have dulled the painful down into the only dully malicious, followed him up along the bar to the booth, where the three young women sat of whom he was to choose just one.

It did not take him long. With the same sense of belligerent challenge he had felt before at the table he chose, and chose the same one he had picked before sight unseen as we used to say with marbles he thought uproariously: Rosalie. And immediately he had picked her, began to ignore her and to antagonize her in just about every way available. He happened to be sitting beside her, just happenstance, with 'Bama sitting across from him with the other two. It suddenly seemed to him too much effort to keep swinging his head around to include her, it made his neck stiff, and it was either that or swing clear around and put his knee up in the booth. Why should he make himself uncomfortable? He directed all his conversation across the table.

'Bama, who was no inexperienced slouch at this game, had understood immediately which one hed picked, and at once had started subtly directing everything toward that end, committing them as soon as possible to the two, to Rosalie and Mildred, and letting Ginnie know she was out.

—Its never a good idea he said before they left the table to try and play two of them along while yore seein which one you want; pick one attach yourself to her then stay with her, the one you pick likes that.—

'Bama kept signalling him with his forehead and eyes and eyebrows to let up a little, take it easy. Dave ignored it. He might as well, he couldnt help it.

He had got off to a very slow start, anyway. When 'Bama had introduced them, and named Mildred's last name as Pierce, he had grinned with heavy levity:

"Sure, I know you. Theres a novel about you by James M Cain."

Mildred had laughed rather weakly; she was evidently used to this. "I saw the movie," she said. "I didnt know there was a book."

"Sure. Jim Cain's a good friend of mine out on the coast. Do you know Jim?" he said with heavy humor.

"Not really," Mildred smiled, though with a good deal less interest. "You see, that movie's not really about me."

"Ill have to tell old Jim I saw you," he said with the same heavy levity, ladling it on.

Mildred laughed, a little coldly. "Please do. Im sure he'll be glad to know."

"Ill make a note of it," he grinned, and sat down heavily.

—Beside Rosalie.—

Rosalie had already been introduced to him, before the tremendously humorous exchange on James M Cain. She had, leaning back in her booth corner easily, met him with the thin smile and raised brows of a very superior person and said Hello as if she were dropping a pearl of rarest price. After that, sitting by her, tonguetied and irritable, he made three abrupt short remarks to her, which she answered in a similar vein and even more shortly and then sat back and waited, looking at him expectantly as if he had been hired to entertain her. When he stopped talking to her, she lapsed into silence and, leaning back in her corner, hurt and still superior, drank her beer and smiled thinly and listened with raised eyebrows. She was a husky girl with beautiful breasts and brusque in character. It was an old pattern. He had known all along what would happen. She was really a very good looking girl. Except for her face which was not good looking. But not ugly. Just plain. If her height sitting in the booth was any indication of her height standing, she was probably three or four inches taller than him.

With 'Bama still signalling at him with his forehead and eyes and eyebrows, he began to talk with the other one. Ginnie. Ginnie Moorehead, she had been introduced as. Both of the other two, Ginnie and Mildred, were apparently trying to be nice to him. Especially Ginnie.

She was a horror, all right. But not quite the horror 'Bama had described. Or maybe Im drunk he thought. She wasnt really fat, just dumpy, round and dumpy. Her breasts were of that type which before very long would appear to be one solid roll of flesh across her chest from armpit to armpit, rather than two separate entities. They were almost there now. She had a moon face with almost no nose, which was considerably enhanced by a double chin which ran from jaw hinge to jaw hinge. Her shoulders were round, and to all intents and purposes she was waistless. She hunched. But all of that was not so especially bad, if it had not been for her eyes. They were as blue as Dewey's, but washed out and vague instead of icy, and they had an intensely intent look in them of inarticulate, frightened dullness.

"So you live in California? In Hollywood?" Ginnie said, evidently trying to play along with 'Bama's suggestion that they not let on they knew about Dave. She had apparently accepted the fact that she wasnt going.

"Yes," Dave said, "that is I used to before I got drafted."

"Im a singer myself," Ginnie said.

"Oh, is that right? Where?"

"Well, not now, so much. Just a little, locally. But before— Oh, Terre Haute, Vincennes, Danville. Durin the war I lived in Ind'ana-polis, you know where Camp Atterbury is, I knew a lot of boys from Camp Atterbury, and sang in two three clubs over there. I love to sing," she said anxiously.

"Well, it can be a great source of pleasure," Dave said.

"I dont suppose youre connected with the movies any way, or other," she said. "Out there."

"No," Dave grinned heavily. "As a matter of fact, a great many people live in Los Angeles who are not connected with the movies."

"I imagine thats true," Ginnie said blandly. "I figured you werent, anyway. —Ive always figured on movin out there myself someday," she said looking off at the bar, "and givin it a whirl. As a singer, you know."

Dave stifled himself from shouting with laughter. For a moment he did not trust himself to answer.

"Well, I reckon it would be an interesting experiment," he said. "But you know when you live out there you see so many movie stars you get to takin it all for granted." He drank from his beer.

"How you doing, Rosalie?" 'Bama asked. "Ready for another beer?"

"I dont know," Rosalie smiled thinly. "Its gettin pretty late."

"Thats right, it is," 'Bama said. He looked at his watch. "If we're goin to go anywhere, we better get movin. Dont you think, Dave?"

"Where you going?" Rosalie asked bluntly.

"Dont know," 'Bama said. "Indianapolis I guess."

"How long you going to be gone?"

"Dont know," 'Bama said. "All depends on how I feel. May come back tomorrow, may stay three four days."

"Okay," Rosalie said, smiling thinly. "Ill go."

'Bama nodded easily, indifferently; and Dave sat rooted, wondering how he did it. It was amazing. Absolutely and completely amazing. It was unbelievable.

"Well, Ginnie, I hate to break it up," 'Bama said easily, "but I guess if we're going to go wed better get started. If we want to get there before morning."

Again, Dave sat rooted, speechless.

"Yeah," Ginnie said, looking at the tall man with her washed out eyes, "Well, have a good time."

"I dont know if I ought to go or not," Mildred Pierce said doubtfully. "But Im going anyway and to hell with it," she added. "You tell the foreman I got some bad hamburger or somethin, Ginnie. We both work in C Cup," she explained to Dave.

"Tell him she came around," 'Bama said.

"Cant," Mildred said. "I used that last time, last week."

"Ill fix it some way," Ginnie said, somewhat wistfully.

They had all risen.

"You got another beer comin at the bar, Ginnie," 'Bama grinned.

Toward the front, in the next booth, Dewey and Hubie both had their arms around their girls, whispering, two closed couples rather than a foursome. They both looked up as 'Bama passed them.

"You sure you guys dont want to come and go along," 'Bama said. "We can find room. We have before."

Hubie made as if to speak, looking anxious, then thought better of it.

"Naw, I guess not," Dewey said. He had been waiting, glaring at the silent Hubie. "We got to do that job of work tomorrow."

Hubie looked greatly relieved. He did not say anything.

"Some other time, then," 'Bama grinned. He ushered the two girls out.

They went outside in single file, 'Bama first, then the two girls Rosalie and Mildred, and Dave bringing up the rear. Dave was aware that there were still other people, quite a few other people, still in the bar and yet at the same time it was as if he moved through a profound and frighteningly empty silence in a closed and empty bar where no one was, except the four of them. Dimly, he was aware of men sitting at the bar. Talking. Laughing. Drinking. Jukebox. He was aware, dimly. But it was as if his eyes and ears, all his senses, were locked up in the black box of his skull. Shut up in the dark closet of his head. Divorced. And not just from a wife. From everything. He followed them out and shut the door behind him.

Outside, the snow had slacked up some but it was still coming down, and still deepening on the street and sidewalk. 'Bama led the way to the Packard in the parking lot, the cinders beneath the snow crunching under their feet.

"You think we can *get* to Indi'napolis?" Rosalie asked him in her abrupt way. "In this snow?"

"Ive driven there worse nights than this," 'Bama grinned. "Besides, thisll all be worn off the highway already." He got in and started the heater confidently.

He was right, or at least partially so. When they got back downtown and on around the square to Wernz Avenue the mainstreet which was also the highway and headed on out east on 40, they found most of the snow was gone off the street just like he said, beaten off by the whirling tires and the through truck traffic, so that only a thin roll of slush remained between the tire tracks and on each side. Out of town on the pavement it was even better.

Nevertheless, for Dave, in his peculiarly locked up, sensitized state of mind, that wild, crazy, midnight ride to Indianapolis, dreamlike if not actually nightmarish with the snow falling in the light of the head-lights and the windshield wipers clicking and the tires whispering omi-nously in the slush and the heater roaring, remained forever afterwards the peak and the epitome of what a Walpurgis Night Witches' Sabbath could—could? should!— be. Never would there be such another. Not like that.

'Bama drove intently, peering forward over the wheel, hardly talking, pushing just as much as he could without taking chances —undue chances, Dave amended. Every time he pulled out to pass a spluttering diesel truck, the Packard slid dangerously for a split second as they crossed the slush roll from one set of tire tracks to the other. He drove expertly. Nobody passed him. And he passed just about every car on the road between there and the city.

In the back seat Dave tried to make some time with Rosalie. She allowed him to put his arm around her. He even was permitted to kiss her. It was awkward work in an Army greatcoat. He had never felt lonelier in his life. Finally he scared up enough nerve to put his hand in-side her coat; he was sitting behind 'Bama. She didnt do anything, didnt move. All she did was say in a loud voice:

"Please take your hand off my breast!"

He did. As quickly as if he had put it on a hot stove.

"Now damn it, Rosalie!" 'Bama said. "Cut out all this crap!"

"I just dont want anybody to think Im easy had," Rosalie said in her brusque way.

"Well, Im sure nobody does," 'Bama said. "So cut the crap."

"I dont like some joker happy-handing me in the back seat of a car just because I agreed to go on a party with him."

"Thank you," Dave murmured, not loud enough for anyone to hear. He had already withdrawn his arm from around her.

"Well," 'Bama sneered from the front seat, "thats fine, Rosalie. I respect your integrity. But you better cut the crap with my friend Dave because Id hate to have to stop at the first filling station and kick you out."

"Youd do it too, wouldnt you?" Rosalie said in a brassy voice.

"You know damn well Id do it."

Rosalie said nothing further. Dave had already withdrawn to his own corner behind 'Bama and lighted a cigarette and the hell with it. Rosalie looked at him once but he did not look back. Instead he watched the silhouette of 'Bama's hat, pulled forward now, against the light of the headlights. Outside the window the silent snow still fell. He felt a sudden warm uprush of such a powerful emotion for the sneering gam-bler it almost brought the tears to his eyes. He crushed out the cigarette and leaned forward and put his elbows on the back of the seat.

"How you doin, buddy?" 'Bama said, glancing back swiftly.

"Fine," Dave said. "Fine." He hesitated. "You know, Im going to stay on in Parkman," he said in a low voice.

"Is that right?"

"Frank and I got a business deal cooked up Im going to go into with him."

"How longll you stay?" 'Bama said. Ahead of them the tail lights of a car appeared.

"I dont know," Dave said. He looked around the car. Over on her side of the front seat Mildred Pierce was sound asleep. Rosalie was smoking a cigarette, staring out the window.

"We're going to start a taxi service in Parkman," he said softly and confidentially to 'Bama. He had no fear at all of telling him.

"Yeah? Well, if yore in with Frank youll do all right, believe me," 'Bama said. He began to slow a little as the brightening tail lights ahead slowly turned into the back end of a car. "Some poor bastard," 'Bama said as he swung out to pass and the Packard slid momentarily and sickeningly in the slush, "out on a night like this. What do you want to stay in Parkman for?"

"Oh. I dont know. No reason," Dave said. "Got nothin better to do right now." It seemed to him that 'Bama had taken the startling news awfully easily.

"That school teacher gal, hunh?" 'Bama said, swinging the Packard back in again and again it yawed.

"Christ, no!" Dave protested. "No, I just thought Id give the old home town a whirl for a while."

"Okay," 'Bama said.

"—Listen," Dave said quickly, "whatre we gonna do when we get to Indianapolis."

"Oh. Get some rooms at the Claypool," 'Bama said. "Or someplace. Throw a party," he said, raising his voice. "Dont mind that pig Rosalie back there. Shell come around. Remember I told you she was hard to get along with."

"Are you referrin to me?" Rosalie asked brusquely.

"Yas, Im referrin to you," 'Bama said sneeringly. "Who else is back there with you. Now shut up. You just earned yourself a pretty bad reputation, as far as Im concerned. —Dont mind them," he said to Dave. "We get over here and get to drinkin theyll be all right."

"I do not plan," Rosalie said brassily, "on doin any drinkin."

"Then Ill pour it over yore head," 'Bama sneered. "Or pour it down yore throat. Shut up.

"I figure we'll come on home tomorrow night," he said to Dave.

"Okay," Dave said. He took his elbows off the seat back and leaned back again, as 'Bama began to run up on another set of tail lights.

"Itll cost us a little money over here," 'Bama said after a moment, "with two girls. But I figure its a good investment."

"Yeah," Dave said. He lit another cigarette thinking this was certainly a propitious way of ending his first day back home in Parkman, an auspicious beginning. The Walpurgis Night feeling came over him again. God, had it only been one day? It seemed like years. Well, tomorrow—or next day rather, when they got back—hed go see Frank at the store . . . —and that Edith Barclay. Sign the papers and get that over with.

And then, once that was over with, hed go over to Israel to the Frenches', make his first sortie. He ought to have a car. Goddam her. And Goddam Harriet Bowman. Goddam them all, he thought looking at Rosalie, for making him stay here.

"Ive got plenty of money on me," he said out loud harshly. "Four hundred in cash."

"I didnt mean that," 'Bama said from up front. "This is my party. —Christ!" he said, "dont tell anybody. —That Rosalie back theres liable to knock you on the head and take it from you," he said laughingly.

"Damn you, 'Bama!" Rosalie said so furiously it almost sounded like she was crying, "you know Ive never rolled anybody in my life. You know it!"

Silence, a pause, the swishing of the wet tires.

"Hes a real son of a bitch, that guy," Rosalie said to him friendlily, "you know it?"

"Yeah," Dave said sympathetically, "he sure is."

Up front, 'Bama snorted with laughter approvingly, and swung out to pass the next car.

BOOK TWO

THE JOB

CHAPTER 16

DAVE and 'Bama did not get back from Indianapolis for five days in spite of the resolution 'Bama made in the car going over. When they did get back Dave found that Frank had been out of town the whole five days, gone to Chicago for a jewelry show Agnes said, and was expected back tomorrow, or before. Dave need not have worried about Frank and his promise to see him at all. But he had worried about it, for some strange reason, and felt guilty, all the time he was gone. Apparently Frank still had a stronger hold over him than he thought.

When they did come back to Parkman they were driving two cars. Because Dave had bought one. They had talked about it on the way over, the advisability of it, and 'Bama had promised to help him find one, a good buy. Bein without a car today 'Bama maintained was about like bein without feet a hundred years ago. But when they got over there and got settled in at the Claypool Hotel, the whole party turned into such a bout of drinking fornicating and nightclubbing that there never seemed to be enough time left over to do anything about the car. Twice 'Bama ran him out to used car places he knew for a few minutes, but they were both so liquored up if not actually drunk that the whole project seemed not only vague and unreal and a waste of valuable time but positively unnatural, a withdrawal from reality: it was unimportant, they were fooling themselves with trivia, what the hell did he need a car for, 'Bama had one didnt he? it was only conscience that had driven them out there anyway wasnt it? and to hell with conscience it was frightening. They wound up buying the car in Terre Haute on the way home.

Shortly after every noon—which was the time they all got out of bed and ordered breakfast sent up—'Bama would conscientiously ask Dave if he had to be back for anything special, and Dave would remember Frank and his promise to see him and as conscientiously say no, and they would stay another day. It went on like that for the whole five days. The two girls evidently knew beforehand what kind of a party to expect from 'Bama, which was why they had come. In the end it was 'Bama himself who as though he had finally fulfilled some particular need or necessity of his own and was finished, suddenly called the halt and sneeringly said it was time to get back to the unpleasant prospect of living.

And it was like that too, Dave thought. For five days nothing of the world they knew existed, neither national nor international, county State or Parkman, none of their responsibilities or embroilments or

197

entanglements, but especially: no close personal relations with people. They lived in a hotel; they spent money; they were waited on. It was all in the money. As long as you spent the money, people would do anything for you, wait on you, cater to you, carry you around on a chip, and not intrude on you. It was a vacation from life.

The tall countrified 'Bama with his country suits was apparently almost as well known in Indianapolis as he was in Parkman. His checks were cashed at the Claypool without credit cards or questions. All the desk clerks knew him. So did the bellboys and bartenders. And when they sat in the bar they actually seemed as much a part of it as did all the partying oil company executives and out of town businessmen who surrounded them. He had cards for all the private dinner and supper clubs and afterhour joints both in, and outside of, town and every night they went to a different one and after closing wound up at a different afterhours place where they sat and drank and were overcharged until six o'clock in the morning. Dave danced, with both girls. 'Bama did not dance. Some of the places had gambling and if they did 'Bama gambled. Otherwise he just sat. And drank. And paid, for everything. The girls had a wonderful time and even Rosalie, in her brusque brassy way, became almost pleasant.

And through all of this, through all of the five days, 'Bama remained as coarse and countrified and openly smalltownish as he had always been, as he was the first time Dave saw him in Ciro's in Parkman, as hickish as his country suits. These suits themselves he bought at L. Strauss where at his insistence they were specially tailored to his specifications, much to the distress of the salesperson, and paid a hundred dollars each for. And he ordered another new one while he was in town this time and took Dave there to shop for civilian clothes. He also took him to his bookmaker's.

Every afternoon (morning it was, to them) after they had eaten breakfast (washing it down with whiskey, the four of them)—the first of the large amount they would be consuming regularly the rest of the day—'Bama would give the girls some money (ten, fifteen, twenty) and send them out (to shop, he sneered, or go to a show) and then, fixing himself a fresh drink, he would prepare to begin his day.

He drank a lot, a tremendous amount. He never drank anything but bourbon and plain water. Except for some beer now and then. And he kept a bottle and a water carafe on the bed table beside him where he could reach it any time during the night. But yet he never seemed to get drunk.

Holding the fresh drink, he would first sit on the edge of the bed in his underwear with his hat on and call the valet to check on the progress of his suit which he always sent out to be sponged and pressed the first thing after he got up, even before ordering breakfast.

Then he would take the drink, which he may or may not have added whiskey to in the meantime, into the bathroom to shave and shower, bare footed and wearing nothing but his underwear and his hat. Coming out still holding the glass, usually empty, he would first replenish it and set it carefully on the table, then fresh socks and his shoes, fresh underwear for the undershirt of which, to get it on, he had to remove his hat momentarily, and finally a clean white shirt (he had immediately bought accessories and shirts the same day they arrived) and his tie, and like that he would remain, moving around leisurely with his drink, a man who lived in hotels so much he felt more at home there than he would in a house, until the valet's man arrived with his suit.

The girls of course would be gone by then. The first day Dave went with them. They went out and had drinks, then lunch, at the Canary Cottage on the Circle, then more drinks, then went across the street to a show, then more drinks. They talked a great deal, mostly about themselves. They got back just in time to go out for drinks and dinner. Dave could not have been more bored. The second day he elected to stay with 'Bama, and the girls went out alone, and 'Bama grinned at him sympathetically. They were nice girls, in their way, he said, but he just couldnt stand only so much of them in any one day. That was the day that 'Bama, muttering something about not wanting to ruin his civilian reputation by being seen out with no soldier, took him, still in uniform, to L. Strauss's for clothes and after ordering his own suit, left him there and went off alone.

So it was that that afternoon (morning) Dave was treated to the spectacle of watching, from the other bedroom of the two bedroom corner suite, 'Bama had taken, where he lay trying to keep from laughing out loud, 'Bama's morning (afternoon) ritual which never seemed to vary a penny'sworth and which he was to see so many times—especially after they leased the house—that it would remain deeply impressed on his brain as if stamped with metal foreverafter.

What the two girls did those afternoons (mornings), where they went, 'Bama neither knew nor asked. He apparently did not care. Whether they shopped, or went to shows, or picked up some other men, they were always back at the hotel in time to go out to some private club for dinner. 'Bama apparently did not even care whether they came back or not. And Dave found he did not care either. Rosalie had made herself more or less amenable in the bed with him, but while sufficiently active, it seemed to him to be pretty much of a mechanical variety, as if she were in this way deliberately and conscientiously paying her way on the party. He appreciated her honestness, but it did not help him any to know that she would also have come along on this party just the same, if 'Bama's stablemate had been Gargantua himself. He knew one thing for sure. If he ever went on any more brawls with 'Bama, Rosalie Sansome would not be his partner. If he was hungry for love, Rosalie was not for him. Rosalie admired nobody but herself.

It was on the third afternoon that, dressed now in a flamboyant and Hollywood cut gray-and-blue-tweed sport jacket and flannel slacks that he had had a very hard time locating amongst the dark conservative business suits at L. Strauss, 'Bama took him up to his bookmaker's. The unseasonable snow had melted off completely and it was a brisk sunshiny windy day, and wearing almost identical gabardine topcoats they walked from the Claypool over to the Circle and north on Meridian to one of the newer highpowered office buildings and took the elevator to the eighth floor. In a combination investment house and loan office which took up a full quarter of the eighth floor, 'Bama sneered hello to two girls working behind the counter and went on through a rugged looking door into the next room where one entire wall was covered with a lined blackboard and a number of people moved about, and as far as Dave could tell the door was not locked and there was no system of checking or identification.

Once inside, Dave was at first afraid they had made a mistake and blundered into some exclusive private men's club. He had patronized a few people who made book himself, out on the West Coast. Invariably, they either ran dingy little cigar stores or poolrooms, or else operated behind locked doors on the top floor of some foul tenement rooming house. Here, the carpeting was thick. Roomy comfortable chairs and ashtray stands and cocktail tables were scattered around facing the blackboard wall. Lithograph prints of famous horses decorated the other walls. Several expensively dressed (L. Strauss? he wondered) older men sat in chairs holding drinks which were served to them by a Negro man in a white coat. Three young men, excellently dressed in ultra conservative (L. Strauss, too?) business suits, walked up and down politely, holding sheaves of cards and pencils. Now and then one of the seated men would authoritatively but quietly tell them something and they would write it down obsequiously. Another conservatively dressed man stood by the blackboard holding an eraser and a piece of chalk. Occasionally he would erase something off the board and write something else in its place. Very little of the blackboard was in use. Dave knew enough to know this was because the main winter racing season in the South had not started yet. The feeling of the whole establishment was really that of a rich stock broker's office, rather than an illegal bookmaker's for gambling on the horses. Or at least like he imagined a rich stock broker's office to be. And behind the counter on their left where a few desks stood, still another conservatively dressed man sat beside a teletype ticker machine under a glass dome, completing the picture.

'Bama checked his topcoat with a girl behind the counter just inside the door, and Dave did likewise. She gave them checks and hung the coats on an open rack that ran back along the desks. 'Bama took a copy of the Racing Form and a red and a green sheet from stacks on the counter and, still wearing his hat, sat down with it. He ordered whiskey and plain water from the Negro man, pushed his hat back to his widow's peak, and began to study the form and the blackboard. Dave took copies too and sat down beside him, wondering idiotically if he was going to buy Tel & Tel today.

And yet, in spite of the conservative respectability and businesslike air of the place, there was also a hushed subdued note of secrecy and clandestineness that, for him, made it very exciting. Why was it always so much more fun to do something if it was against the law?

'Bama made some calculations on the margin of his form with a gold pencil, then studied the blackboard, then made some more calculations, then simply sat, studying them and looking back and forth to the blackboard. Dave just sat, holding his Racing Form laxly and awkwardly like a man holding a rifle who has never shot one before; he still could not get over this place, which 'Bama had not prepared him for. One of the young men came by, with his stack of cards and pencil, murmuring politely that it was almost post time, in a moment no more bets would be taken. Mr Dillert? 'Bama looked up at him a long moment as if expecting to find an answer there, during which the young man waited, and then gave him a bet. Then he laid down his form and picked up his drink. The man at the ticker tape left it and put a set of earphones on his head that made him look like an Air Force co-pilot, announced without feeling that they were off and began in absolute monotone to name the changing positions of the horses as they ran around the track, staring at the wall before him blankly. The men in the chairs sipped their drinks and listened silently. Dave listened too, feeling a tremendous excitement building up in him. When it was over, the young man with the cards came over and gave 'Bama a chit which the tall Southerner shoved in his pocket. Then he picked up his form again.

They stayed there the rest of the afternoon, listening to that bored, almost moronic, monotone, evaluating one race after another, and when they left, Dave left a confirmed horse player.

In addition, he had been treated to a display of 'Bama at work, and could feel nothing but unqualified admiration. Mostly, it was patience —a patience the like of which he had never seen before and would not have believed the jitterish 'Bama capable of, but which he was to see many times again whether it was with cards, dice or horses. 'Bama worked every race, studying his form and the blackboard, making some kind of private calculations, then revising them, then re-revising them, then re-re-revising them. He did all this with every race. But he placed only one other bet. It was on the next to last race. Again, the polite young man brought him a chit which he stuffed in his pocket. When they went to leave 'Bama presented the chits at the counter and from the man at the ticker tape received in exchange a stack of bills the size and denominations of which made it appear to Dave from what he could see of it that he had made enough money to more than pay for the whole trip. They got back to the hotel just in time to meet the girls, have drinks, and go out to dinner—and the usual evening.

The next day they were back. That was the fourth day of the trip. They went back the fifth day too, and it was late that night—or rather, early the next morning, because it was after five A.M.—that they started home. 'Bama had told them that morning (afternoon) that unpleasant as it might be to all concerned, it nevertheless looked like they were all going to have to start living again. Neither of the girls nor Dave felt like arguing with him, since he was paying the bills. So they had packed all the newly acquired purchases, including Dave's new clothes packed in his two new bags, loaded them in the Packard and checked out of the hotel, put the Packard in a parking lot, and then gone about the rest of the day just as usual—which was why they were leaving at five in the morning.

It was sad, in a way, Dave thought. Sitting beside 'Bama in the front seat—they had put the two girls in the back seat together; both were asleep already—he felt let down and worn out and half sick. And beside him 'Bama, driving, looked even more frail, thin skinned and sallow—with even bigger purple circles under those gambler's eyes—than he had looked at Smitty's before they started. Here they had been living for five days like a very great percentage of the American people dreamed of living, and went to a great many movies in order to live it vicariously when they themselves could not afford it, and look at them. The best dinner places, the best nightclubs, the best orchestras to dance to, the best gambling joints, afterhours places galore, the finest bookmaker's, shopping sprees, almost unlimited money to spend. And after only five days of it—five days, not five months—they all looked more dead than alive, and were about ready for collapse. The thought depressed him exceedingly, and his bowels had not moved for two days.

Driven by something. Driven by what. To the very *brink* of collapse. If 'Bama had achieved some obscure satisfaction, and he evidently had, he himself had not. He himself felt about the same as he had when he came, except tireder. It was worse than sad. It was frightening. A person could actually kill themselves that way. 'Bama looked even worse than he did. He offered to drive for him a while. 'Bama looked at him cheerily and declined No he was doing all right, he was fine.

'Bama had not done nearly so well the fourth and fifth days at the bookmaker's as he had on the third. He won some races, but he also lost on some. When he went to the ticker tape man at the counter to cash in his chits, instead of receiving bills in return, he wound up signing checks—though small ones, it is true—for his losses. He did not mind, though. Like he said, this was his hobby, not his profession. Before they left he introduced Dave to the ticker tape man who shook hands warmly and smiled while looking completely through him at the wall beyond blankly with his eyes and said Yes hed be glad to send him a card since Mr Dillert here recommended him Mr Dillert was one of our best members but we usually liked to keep the membership of the club pretty small and exclusive. Restricted.

Dave thanked him. He had already placed a few bets anyway. Three, to be exact. All of which he won. Unable to resist the second time he came, he had thought to follow 'Bama's lead with a five dollar bet just for fun. But then the smallness of the bet embarrassed him, he was not even sure one of the young men with the cards would accept such a small bet, and he had no idea of what the others including 'Bama were betting because they all whispered and he was embarrassed to ask, so he upped it to twenty. The young man accepted it; and he discovered suddenly he was involved. He could not afford to lose twenty dollars. Not with all the money hed spent on clothes. And luggage. But that was one of the times 'Bama's horse won. It paid three to two. Thirty bucks. He quit. But the next day, the last, he asked 'Bama again and bet the thirty on another horse that paid even money and won again and then he played a hunch. There was a horse in the last race named Haggard and the name caught his attention because he was feeling exactly that way and because 'Bama looked that way. He bet fifty dollars on it, and he leaned over and told 'Bama, who sneered at him disdainfully. However, Haggard won. He was a six to one shot. That was three hundred dollars. He noticed it was even more exciting to listen to that dead dull monotone unfolding the races, when you had some money bet on them. But it was also ticklish business, he knew, for him. Because he was dabbling in something he knew absolutely nothing about. What if he had made all the same three bets and had lost them all? It made him feel very ticklish, somehow, as if he were walking out on thin ice over a cold dark running river. Well, it had been the last race anyway, and now he was going home with almost as much money as the four hundred he had brought with him, in spite of having spent almost all of it on luggage and clothes.

Then suddenly he recognized what it was that felt so familiar. Since he had committed the $5500 to Frank he was back in the position of having to count pennies, with that feeling that if you didnt count right there was nobody to turn to. Anywhere. Nobody to make up the deficit.

In the car 'Bama looked over at him and grinned and started talking. Probably to keep himself awake. 'Bama had been to the bookie's every day they were there; that was where he had gone the second afternoon, when he left Dave to shop for clothes at Strauss's; "I should of stayed with you, I guess," he said, "from the look of those clothes." "Whats wrong with my clothes?" Dave demanded. "Nothin," he said looking at the Hollywood cut distastefully, "nothin at all, if I could just remember to wear my sunglasses when Im looking at you." But he had gone anyway. Making a total of five afternoons with the horses from which he had netted some four hundred dollars. He was counting the net, he told Dave, not the gross. The gross would have been something over twelve hundred dollars, but he only counted what he took home he said, not what he lost back. A wise policy, Dave told him grinning. 'Bama did not see the joke and went on talking. The point was: this was his hobby, not his profession. He expected to lose. He didnt expect to make money at it. His profession was gambling in Parkman. Cards and dice and the pool. That was where he made his money. He didnt count to make money on the horses, he just did that for fun, so anything he actually did make off of them was just extra gravy, see? He sounded almost defensive. They were riding out through Indianapolis west, on their way home, the streets virtually deserted now at five in the morning, almost no traffic present to heed the changing traffic lights which seemed much brighter in the city half dark now that almost all the neon was turned off. The girls were sound asleep in the back. 'Bama did not know exactly how he had gotten onto this particular bookmaker. He had been coming over here for some time and had heard a lot about it, before he ran into someone who could take him up there. Meanwhile he had patronized another place, a dinky little hole in the wall one man joint, but this place here was the best and the ritziest bookmaker in the city. The investment office and loan business was a good paying business in itself, and made a wonderful front for it. Actually, he was pretty sure, it was a syndicated place. *The* Syndicate? No, he didnt think so. He didnt mean that. Private owner. He grinned: actually, as a matter of fact, he didnt know a damn thing about The Syndicate. He had heard about it, sure, everybody had. But hed never met or seen it. And didnt especially want to. He didnt even know if there even was such a damned thing. He grinned again. Then shrugged.

Dave looked over at the cheerful 'Bama—as he had been doing ever since they had got in the car—and noticed for the first time something that once he had noticed it, seemed to be something he had been aware of for quite some time without knowing it, more like a memory than a discovery. 'Bama was wearing a gun. Had been wearing it since they got in town, Dave realized belatedly, but he had been so matter of fact and unobtrusive and casually careful about keeping it out of sight that Dave realized now hed been noticing it for several days without being aware of it. The Southerner's coat was unbuttoned and flapped open, and even in the dim light of the dash the black pistol butt was clearly discernible under his left arm.

'Bama noticed him looking and grinned at him cheerfully. It was just for protection. He wore it whenever he came to the city. A lot of times he carried so much cash money on him that he had gotten a sheriff's permit in Parkman to wear it. Here, if hed take the wheel a minute, hed get it off. Wouldnt need it now. And the damned thing was uncomfortable. While Dave held the wheel and watched him, he shrugged out of his coat sleeves and got his arms out of the double loop of leather that went across his back from shoulder to shoulder and handed it to him to put in the dash compartment and put his coat back on. Matter of fact, the sheriff's permit wasnt really valid any more. The previous sheriff—the one whod given it to him—had been a Democrat whom he played poker with. The new sheriff was a god-damned Republican, and anyway the new sheriff didnt like him. So hed not tried to get it renewed, but he still carried the old card.

Dave took it and held it. It was a little .32 six shot Smith & Wesson with a 3½ inch barrel, in a beautifully made little spring clip holster made with the front side open so the gun could be swept out instead of having to be drawn. The leather showed good care.

"Only cost me fifty bucks," 'Bama said cheerfully. "Had the holster made up special at S D Myers in El Paso."

Dave wrapped the straps around it carefully and put it in the dash and pushed the little spring latch door closed upon it.

"Now its legal," 'Bama said cheerfully. He wriggled his shoulders against the seat back as if glad to be free of the weight. "Whats the matter?" he said grinning. "Were you afraid youd fallen in with a member of The Syndicate?"

"No," Dave said.

It was funny. *Gun.* It was another word that had developed its own meaning apart from the object it was used to designate. In the Army you took a rifle or pistol for granted and cursed it because you had to clean it all the time and in combat you fired it when you got the chance and still worried about cleaning it because the Army used corrosive priming and the object beyond the sights you took for granted too. *Concealed weapon.* That was the phrase. *Carrying a concealed weapon.*

"Did you ever draw it on anybody?" he said.

"No," 'Bama said cheerfully, "never had to yet."

It was in Terre Haute that they bought the car. They arrived there just as the businesses were opening. They had talked about it again in the car, and 'Bama drove to a place he knew on Ohio Street. They had had no sleep at all and had been drinking all night long. 'Bama tramped around the frozen lot with the dealer looking at the cars that had just been rolled out, kicking tires, disappearing under hoods, even getting down to look underneath some of them. Finally he selected one a 1942 Plymouth of light green and said, "We'll drive it around the block." When they came back he said to Dave, "Take it. You got a good buy." The dealer wanted nine hundred and fifty. But by deriding the car itself, its maker, complaining about the tires, the motor, the interior, and even the windshield wipers which he insisted would have to be replaced, 'Bama jewed him down to eight hundred, then refused to take it and got another fifty knocked off. The dealer, complaining miserably, flatly refused to go any lower. With energetic disgust 'Bama told Dave he might as well take it, he had to have a car, and the guy had them by the throat. Dave paid him with two hundred fifty cash and a five hundred dollar check which, because the dealer did not know Dave, 'Bama had to countersign.

"You got a good buy," 'Bama grinned at him after they got the keys. "Its worth eight fifty easy. Youll probly need a valve job after six or eight thousand miles, but otherwise its in real good shape."

The two girls were still in the back of the Packard fast asleep. They decided to leave them there.

"Now dont go to sleep and smash it up," 'Bama admonished him. "If you get sleepy, take off your topcoat and open the window. You follow me in. If you have to stop for anything, flash your headlights at me."

Dave did not get sleepy. It was as a matter of fact the first time in his life he had ever owned his own car. The thoughtful 'Bama drove slow enough he did not have any trouble keeping up. He enjoyed the whole fifteen mile trip immensely.

He had been gone five days, and during it had spent something over a thousand dollars. Five hundred of it had come out of his $5500 capital. But Frank could either take or leave it. He had enough good clothes to last him a long time, some luggage, and a pretty good car. And he felt he had made perhaps the best friend he had ever made in his life, although he did not know what he especially had done to deserve it, or what 'Bama's motive had been.

Back in Parkman, whose winter business day was already well under way, 'Bama pulled up in the street in front of the hotel and waited for him. When Dave pulled up along side he rolled down his window and stuck his head out.

"Ill take these two on home," he called. "Dont worry about Mildred

Pierce losin her job." (It had become a private joke to them to always call her by her full name). "She wont. They need people too bad at the brassiere factory. She wouldnt of gone if she thought she would of. Ill call you in a couple days." He pulled his head in, the purple circled eyes looking like two blue covered wartime flashlights, then stuck it back out. "Or else you can look me up at the Ath Club poolroom."

The heavy Packard slid away smoothly and took the hotel corner expertly, still accelerating.

Dave parked his Plymouth in front of the hotel and made his way upstairs with his new luggage, his heart thumping heavily from lack of rest. But before he undressed he called the house and learned from Agnes that he neednt have worried about Frank at all while he was gone, Frank was Agnes said at a *very* important jewelers' show in Chicago, he would be back today or tomorrow at the latest. Dave hung up; why the hell did he feel so relieved?

That Rosalie. All the time hed spent with her, all the times hed had her, and not a bit of it had helped him a damned bit.

Loneliness like another living presence inside his skin, he got undressed and lay down to sleep.

CHAPTER 17

FRANK had already known Dave was out of town when Geneve Lowe called him at the store to tell him she was going to Chicago. So he did not have to worry about that conflicting.

But there were a couple of things he did have to worry about. One was about getting the contract drawn for the taxi service, which was going to be a considerable problem in itself on account of Judge Deacon; and it ought to be ready for Dave to sign when he got back. The other worry was the fact that Geneve hadnt given him any advance notice this time.

Geneve, as usual, was leaving just before lunch and Dotty Callter was driving her to Terre Haute to catch the train. They always had lunch at the Terre Haute House and talked, together with a few drinks to stiffen her for the train ride, and then Dotty would put her on the three o'clock train. Since it was in the neighborhood of two hundred miles to Chicago she didnt get in until around seven. Their usual procedure was for him to drive up some time during the day and meet her, either at the station or if he was later, in the bar of the hotel. He and Geneve always stayed at the same hotel on Michigan Boulevard because no one from Parkman ever seemed to go there, they always stayed at the Palmer House or the Drake. But usually she let him know a couple of days ahead of time.

"Thats pretty short notice," he said, peering around the phone at the office door. Edith Barclay had found something to do outside—she always did when a certain unnamed party called for him—he was sure she recognized the voice because Geneve called for Al too a lot of times. She was a good girl.

"I know, darling," the cool voice said sympathetically. "But I didnt find out about it till last night. —And I didnt want to call you at home," she said meaningfully. "Dotty sprang it on me yesterday evening after work."

"Well I dont know if Ill be able to make it today or not," Frank said, a little testily.

"Ahh, poor darling," the cool voice said cajolingly, "I know. But if you cant make it today, you can make it tomorrow, cant you?"

"Oh Ill make it today," he said, mollified. "Somehow. You go ahead and register. Because I may be late. But dont worry, Ill make it," he said, putting power into his voice.

"I knew you would," she said blithely. "See you tonight." She hung up.

Frank hung up too, grinning. She knew how to handle him. Sometimes he almost felt she did things like this on purpose, just to see how far she could push him and still make him comply. But he also liked having her make him comply like that. She couldnt do it on anything important, when he didnt want her to. It even made him hot for her, sometimes. To force him. Make him comply with her desires. Frank could feel his breath coming slow and deep and turgid into his chest; when he exhaled through his nose it burned his upper lip. Thin, yes; she was; but she had wide hips and plenty breasts—when you got those tight little brassieres off her that she wore to make them look tiny. Hed even tried to reason with her about it. And there were so many things they did together, too.

It was funny he thought suddenly, I was seventeen and a senior in high school when she was born. Think of it. Just really imagine that.

His lips felt heavy and full of blood, and aware of his lungs moving and the muscles of his body, Frank suddenly felt like getting up on top his desk and beating his swelling chest with his fist and shouting at the top of his lungs Im a *MAN!*

Half the fun was in the secretiveness, he thought, really. The slipping around and sneaking off to someplace like Chicago. The doing of something wrong—and putting it over. The thinking if they could only see this. —and yet at the same time it hurt his pride and selfrespect and made him angry that he had to do it that way. —He had had other women, plenty of them. Mostly waitresses, and office clerks, and factory workers, from Terre Haute and Indianapolis. He had even had a couple of short lived country club affairs; but these were always so difficult to find safe trysting places for that they didnt last long. But in Geneve he had found the kind of mistress that he really wanted. She was sophisticated, she was good looking, she was young— You could take her anywhere— And she wouldnt clutch at you. That was the kind of mistress he had wanted all along, when he had been fiddling around with those others. That was the kind of mistress a man in his position ought to have. That was the kind of mistress Wernz and Crowder and Paul Fredric, Wernz's son in law, and the rest had. Judge Deacon had been sleeping with that secretary of his for twenty years, and he had done a lot for her husband. Now that he had his, he could do the same. For Al. Someday hed have enough to be able to set some girl up in an apartment someplace, but until then he couldnt do better than with Geneve; hell, she was the best looking one of the bunch, everybody in town envied him, he thought grinning. He thought of her again, secretively, and perhaps even a little smugly he thought, seeing her in his mind's eye in that same mental picture he had of her, which was his private symbol for her and which he always saw in his mind whenever he thought of her: thin, little, narrowshouldered, with those tiny arms no bigger than his wrists, and that wide pelvis walking across a hotel room toward him. Everybody said she looked like a Vogue Magazine model. Well, he had better cut this and get moving, on those things he had to do, he thought energetically. If he got out of town by four o'clock he could be in Chicago before eight tonight.

He swung the swivel chair away from the telephone, and as he did Edith Barclay came back inside. He looked away from her so that she could not see the redness in his eyes which felt full of blood.

The first thing he wanted to do was to get that contract fixed up for Dave to sign, but he didnt know how to go about it yet. Edith had sat down and gone studiously back to work, blank faced. He looked at the back of her head. She was really quite some girl. If it wasnt for the absolutely ironbound rule he had made himself about female help, when he began to get into the upper brackets—it had been Edith who had told him this morning about Dave going to Indianapolis last night. Which, if he hadnt known, would have changed everything. When Geneve called. He wouldnt even have been able to go. . . .

She had been sitting at her desk working—she always got there first, of course—when he came in. He was still pretty shaky and badly hung over from all that drinking last night. God, why did a man do it. So he was a bit later than usual. And he felt lousy. He had stopped at the Rexall for a Bromo, but it hadnt had time to take effect yet, and his stomach was still fluttering in protest at all the alcohol that had been poured into it last night without its consent. Agnes had not known he got sick and was throwing up last night, and he did not dare eat any breakfast. After the hellos, and her customary sympathetic remark about him looking like he felt rotten that she made every time he came in hungover, Edith had gone quietly back to work for several minutes, and then had said suddenly in a half smothered subdued casual voice: "I met your brother last night."

"Who?" Frank said. "Dave? Where?"

"At Smitty's," she said, in that same strange voice. "He was there with that gambler 'Bama and Dewey Cole."

"He didnt get in any trouble?" Frank said.

"Oh, no, nothing like that."

"He didnt insult you or somethin'?"

"Oh, no. He just came over to the booth and introduced himself to me." She paused. "Talked a minute. I guess some of them had told him I worked for you."

"Then he was all right then?" Frank said, wanting to feel relieved. "I mean, he didnt do something?"

"Oh, hed been drinking a good bit," Edith said. "And you know that bunch he was with, always up to something or other. But he was perfectly all right. But he said hed been out to your house, and said something about seeing you tomorrow. But then when they left, he and that 'Bama left with two of that bunch of girls from the brassiere factory and were going to Indianapolis."

"In that snow!" Frank said.

"Oh, I didnt mean that!" Edith frowned. She shook her head. "I understand from Harold that 'Bama is a really excellent driver. The snow wasnt bad, out on the highway."

"Well what did you mean?" Frank asked. "What are you tryin' to tell me?"

"Well, they didnt look like theyd be back today," Edith said in that same half smothered, subdued, casual voice. "That was all. And I thought since hed said he expected to see you, if you were expecting to, youd better not look for him. That was all."

For the first time she turned around and looked him in the eyes, almost belligerently.

Frank merely sat and looked at her in puzzlement.

The truth was, she didnt know herself why she had told him, Edith thought. It had just popped out of her while she was working. And it wasnt important. It was not her custom to talk to the boss about unimportant things. She turned back to her desk to go on with her work, almost angrily, in what she recognized was more of a face saving gesture than anything else. Why *had* she told him? Had she wanted to *help* him? It was probably all due to the fact that she had recognized in Dave that peculiar something that was so much like Frank—that awkward little-boy-ness—though of course in the boss it was so entirely different. He looked terrible today, absolutely awful. He shouldnt try to drink with

Dave. And that wife of his, she thought angrily. Agnes was going to have to do something to help him out, aid him, some way. Instead of sitting around feeling sorry for herself all the time. Between the two of them—her and Geneve Lowe—they were ruining him. Destroying him. No wonder he drank so much. Couldnt they see how unhappy he was? She should never have mentioned Dave to him.

"Look!" Frank said intently, "Youre not gettin' interested in that bum, are you! Youre not fallin' in love with him?"

"With *that*?" Edith exclaimed. "Good God, no! Thats one thing youll never have to worry about!"

"Well youd better not," Frank said. "Youre just a bushleaguer, compared to that guy. Hes a pro."

"If hes a pro," Edith said, trying hard to keep at least some of the contempt out of her voice, after all it was the boss's brother, "he certainly doesnt handle women like hes one."

"What do you mean?" Frank said, looking at her angrily.

"Just that," Edith said crisply. "He doesnt know how to handle women."

"Did he try to proposition you?"

"No, no, no. Nothing like that."

"Well you just keep away from him," Frank said angrily.

"Dont worry about that, boss," Edith said. "But what ever gave you the idea Id even be interested in him?"

"I dont know," Frank said irritably, still looking angry. "I dont know what. You sounded awful funny. —You just stay away from him, thats all."

"Dont worry," Edith said again. Cheerfully. But for her part, she was a little indignant that Frank could even think that. She bent to her work.

"Im goin' back down to the Rexall for another Bromo," Frank said, still staring bleakly at the back of her head. "Ill be back in a minute."

It had upset him, upset him more than he liked to admit. He meant to speak to Dave about it. Christ, if he couldnt keep his own office girl safe from him. . . .

. . . But then after that, after he got back, Geneve had called and he had realized how important it was that shed given him the information.

"Im goin' to have to go out of town for a few days, Edith," he said from behind his desk, "it looks like. While you were out front, right after that other call, Jeff Miller of Miller's Jewelry in Terre Haute called me. Seems the Indiana Jewelers' is havin' some kind of a display-show shindig in Indianapolis, and he wants me to help represent the Wabash Valley at it."

"Yes, sir," Edith said, without raising her bent neck or looking up. She went on working. She was a good girl. That was a good enough story to tell Agnes, too, he thought with surprise. Sometimes his own versatility amazed him. Only hed better make it Chicago to Agnes instead of Indianapolis, in case she might try to get hold of him for something. But hed better make it Hammond, then, instead of Chicago, that was still in Indiana. He could say he was staying in Chicago, and driving over.

"Ill leave the store in yours and Al's care," he said happily, now that hed got his story for Agnes. He felt he could trust this girl with just about anything. He thought for a moment of making a humorous remark about finding himself a little girlfriend for while he was away. But then he thought better of it. She might take it the wrong way, and think it suggestive. "And if that no good half assed brother of mine comes around looking for me, you have Al tell him Ill be back in a few days. And *you* stay away from him."

"Okay, boss," Edith grinned. He was such a round, rollypolly little guy with that round head like a ball, and that pudgy face, and those eyes that were usually so mild but that became so flat whenever he was being a businessman. You wanted to laugh and cry over him at the same time—him with all his transparent little subterfuges and his deceptions he thought he was being smart and getting away with. He was comical yes, but he was also heartrendingly tragic. What he really needed was a wife who would really love him—and that was just exactly what he would probably never get.

"And dont laugh. I mean it," Frank said seriously; "if you want to keep on workin' for me. Somebodys got to look after you." Well, he had solved the problem of what to tell Agnes that would explain the short notice, but there was still the contract and as he sat at his desk thinking about it, he still didnt know what to do about it.

There was, actually, a choice of two or three things he *could* do. The whole thing centered around Judge Deacon. The minute the Judge heard about the taxi service he was going to want in on it. It wasnt much of a thing but that wouldnt stop the Judge. He would want to put in a piece of change and sit back and draw down part of the profits without doing any of the work, and he was going to feel he had a right to do it because of all the things hed put Frank onto in the last five years. On the other hand, if the Judge had got the idea first he would have gone right ahead and started it up himself, and not have let *any*body in on it.

Besides, Frank didnt want him in on it. He had been the Judge's satellite just about long enough. And anyway that would mean splitting ownership three ways, which meant that no one party would have control, and any two could gang up on the other one. And he didnt trust Dave that much. And yet he didnt want to antagonize the Judge. Not yet.

That was the crux of the thing. And the trouble was, the Judge was his lawyer. He had been doing all his legal documents and stuff like that for years.

The more he thought about it the best choice—best? the only—seemed to be to take it right to the Judge to draw, and then some way or other talk him out of wanting to invest in it. But how? He cast around. Why couldnt he say that Dave was timid about business and had absolutely refused to go into it if anybody else at all was allowed in? After all, he was only doing this to get Dave's money out of the Second National where it was embarrassing them, wasnt he? Heh heh.

Frank brought the chair back up level and got his cigarettes. The desk clock said eleven twenty which meant that he would have to wait till after lunch now. The Judge always left his office at eleven and went to Ciro's where he drank five or six bottles of beer before he ate his lunch—dinner was more the word—at Annie's Restaurant next door. Why in the name of God the Judge with his money wanted to hang out at crummy little dumps like Ciro's and Annie's Frank could never understand, but he knew it was because that bunch of girls from the brassiere factory hung out there. The Judge was sinking pretty low, he thought smugly. But then he had always been a sort of low type character. If it hadnt been for his wife's father in the State Senate—?

Well, he would have time to go down to the Elks and maybe get in a game of fourteen ball or two—the poker players wouldnt be there yet—have a drink or two for his aching head, eat lunch and catch him back at the office at one o'clock.

"I wont be back," he said to Edith in parting, as he got into the camelshair coat and Dobbs hat. "If anybody wants me for anything tell them Ive already left. Except my wife. Just tell her I plan to leave. But then Ill probably be home by then. —And *you* remember what I told you."

Outside, the snow was melting off fast under a bright winter sun, as he walked to the Elks. It gave him a deep satisfaction deep down in his belly, to know he walked this same path to the same place every day like this, and that he would continue to do so days without number. Uptown, he noticed, where there were only streets and buildings and no open earth—except for the treeless grassed courthouse yard—it seemed to melt much faster than it did in the residential sections where there were lawns. That was funny, wasnt it? A few patches which had once been drifts remained white on the wet brownness of the courthouse yard.

There was almost no trouble with the Judge. The old man—he *was* old Frank thought by God, looking at him in his office, hed never noticed it till now—sat behind his desk lumpishly in the long expanse of the room whose other end was legal library; looking with all his drooping edges of fat Frank suddenly thought rather like one of those less than half filled hydrogen balloons that they send up into the stratosphere. It was a tall high ceilinged room, with ornate moldings, and behind the desk the two very tall windows that looked out upon the courthouse and down upon the square, the windows framing the Judge who sat like an out of condition, badly winded and very possessive frog perched emphatically on a toadstool. The far end with its table and chairs in the center was literally lined, from floor to ceiling, with those bookcases with the push up glass doors, bookcase after bookcase of them, all filled with legal volumes which looked as though they had never been moved or opened or cleaned but just left to age, but which Frank was sure wasnt true, not with the legal stunts the Judge had pulled in the past thirty years, no sir! The whole of it looked like it had been dusted hastily and perfunctorily once a day for twenty years by the twenty-years-old secretary, using that feather duster which still hung from a nail on the wall, and that was all the cleaning it had had. The year by year increasingly stringy secretary had ushered him in from her cubicle outside and gone out and quietly closed the door.

The Judge (the old man) behind his desk did not have just a double chin, he had four of them, with the beginning of a fifth tacked on below the others, all of which ran in curved parallel lines around the outside of his head and faded off together somewhere in the vicinity of his ears as if they were beards. From behind the armor of this fat he peered forth out of his shrewd little eyes like a man looking out the porthole of a battleship. All his life he had doggedly and unrelentingly bucked the vested interests—the Wernzes, the Crowders, the Scotts, Frank Madin, with their Wernz-owned Second National Bank —all of whom had backed his wife's father as State Senator—because of which he hated them implacably—and he had never given up fighting them, and finally he had become Chairman of the Board of the competition opposition bank the Cray County, and made some few dents in them, and had become a vested interest in his own right— though never quite of the calibration they had. He belonged to the Country Club and the Elks Lodge they had built, and meticulously kept his dues paid, and never went inside of either. He steadfastly refused to move from his tacky office. He lived silently, and occasionally jovially, in his father in law's the Senator's—the *State* Senator's—big old three storey frame house, formerly a mansion, but the interior exterior and grounds of which he had meticulously and systematically allowed to run down into such nearly complete dilapidation that it looked like something out of the Deep South. Here he subsisted in ignored discomfort with his mad wife, some years older than himself, who still insisted that her friends (all dead now) were discriminating and conspiring against her for having married beneath her, and never set her foot out of the house—just as she had done a number of years ago when her assertion had been wholly, absolutely and unequivocally true. The Judge never talked about her; and kept on a housekeeper for her, until she attained the status almost of a family retainer, a slatternly former mistress of his. All this in a house which had once been one of the show places of Parkman—and still was, historically at least—one of the very oldest houses in town, whose solid curved stair rails had been made by the controlled warping of young walnut trees tied in shape until they grew to the desired dimension and curve. He dressed almost as sloppily as a bum—which was not difficult for him, with his figure—and spent his time and a small part of his money at Ciro's and Smitty's and the Eagles Lodge, jovially buying drinks for the brassiere factory girls whom he often took riding. As he said, it did not matter, as long as you had the money you did not have to worry about people's feelings, and he continued to direct the estates of his eight married and unmarried sisters, plus the estates of the widows of several of his friends, and two large estates left to minor children of divorces for whom he had contrived to get himself appointed guardian. As he said to Frank on numerous occasions, he handled them well enough to make all of us some money. In addition, he handled the bank and his own investments and enough shrewd legal work to make him a good bit right there.

Yes, and that was all the good it had done him, Frank thought smugly: four chins going on five, a hide that fit like a burlap suit, a mad wife, the right to ruin the Senator's property. He spent almost no money; not really. He enjoyed nothing. Not even the brassiere factory girls, Frank suspected, and his numerous relatives when he died childless would have no time to bury him for fighting over his financial bones. When he Frank finally broke him—broke his monopoly, rather, he amended, he didnt want to break *him*—he Frank was going to enjoy his money. He and Agnes. But then doubtless Judge had his compensations, he thought, thinking of that once beautiful old house. —And he knew how he was going to break it, too, already. —And it wouldnt be long.

Judge Deacon listened to him silently, looking at him shrewdly through the two portholes in his fat, as Frank explained what he wanted. He laid the whole thing out for him: how he had talked to Dave, how he had then cast around for an investment to use, and finally settled upon the taxi service, and how Dave had leaped at the idea. The story he told him was not the truth, but it served his purpose much better than the truth would have. Then, before the Judge could make any kind of an answer at all beyond a grunt, he quickly without seeming to be quick, pointedly without seeming to point, brought in his clincher: Dave refused to go into it if anybody else but the two was brought in; he distrusted businessmen.

The Judge nodded brusquely, asked no questions at all, and wheezed immediately in his scornful withering voice: "You may find, that youve got yerself in a lot more trouble, than just havin' that money in the Second Nash'nul would of made."

"Well, I didnt know what else to do," Frank said. "And I knew you wanted that money out of there?"

The Judge merely grunted at him.

"Now about the contract," Frank said. "I just want a regular partner-ship contract, sort of. You know. That calls him a junior partner. Just a regular contract form, except that theres one extra thing I want put in it. (Ive got to be out of town a few days," he said parenthetically, "and Id like to have it ready for me when I get back.")

"Itll be ready," the Judge grunted, without bothering to ask about the extra.

"Thanks. But about that extra thing: I want a regular 'Give or Take' partnership clause put in it. You know, the kind that says if for any reason either partner wishes to get out, his partner is then allowed to set the price and the partner who wishes to get out must then either buy his partner's share or sell his own at the price set by the other. You know what I mean. Give or Take. Youll know how to word it better than me."

"You dont need that clause in this contract," the Judge said scorn-fully, as if talking to an idiot. "That Give or Take thing is for full partnerships that are fifty-fifty. The partner who sets the price thus sets the price for both halves. Since that screwball brother of yours will own less than half, and youll have the controllin' interest, you dont need it."

"I know all that," Frank said politely, "but Id like to have it put in anyway, if its all right with you."

The Judge looked at him a long moment thoughtfully, peering out with those shrewd little eyes set very deep between the fat full cheeks and that broad forehead. He seemed to be making some mental note Frank thought.

"All right," the Judge grunted insultingly, "itll have to be worded so as to include two prices stead of one. Ill put it in. If it makes you feel better. If itll make you sleep better nights."

That seemed a strange thing for him to say Frank thought. He could not be sure what was going on in his mind. "The reason I did that," he explained carefully, "is that the business is liable to expand some. And it might be hard to appraise what a share of it is worth exactly. And besides we're relatives."

"I been writin' contracts for years," the Judge said witheringly.

Frank still did not know what he had in his mind. If anything. Maybe it was nothing.

"I got work to do," the Judge grunted abruptly, and swung his chair around to the little table full of papers beside him.

"Okay," Frank said. "Ill see you then. Youll have it ready for me when I get back?"

The Judge merely looked at him—with those shrewd little eyes—scornfully, witheringly, insultingly. He made no answer.

The obstinate, pigheaded, miserly, insulting old son of a bitch, Frank thought furiously as he went down the stairs from the office. Someday he would learn his goddamned lesson. If he ever lost his money and all those investments, there wouldnt be a single soul in town who would speak to him on the street, or give him a chunk of bread for a handout. —Still, in spite of his fury, he felt it had come off the way he wanted it. It was mid-afternoon outside. Almost all the snow was gone, even the drifts in the courthouse yard, and everything looked wet and dirty. Now all he had to do was go home and pack, which he dreaded.

Everything went all right at home, but then it always did. Agnes did not say anything, she never did. There wasnt any trouble, there never was. It was a dreadful experience just the same. Agnes had just got home from one of her club luncheons and was still all dressed up. She had her own car, a Ford. He packed the next to smallest of his three bags, a two suiter, in the bedroom, the bag lying spread open on his bed. She came and stood in the doorway. As he packed, he explained to her *why* he was going. He had already told her he *was* going, when he first came in the door. The call from Jeff Miller, the Indiana Jewelers' meeting in Hammond, his staying in Chicago because he liked that hotel——he went through them all. It was horrible. Agnes did not say anything. But he was positive she knew, and knew he knew she knew, he was sure from little things she had let drop at other times. She even knew who, he was quite sure. At that moment, as he finished packing the bag and closed it, he wondered—strangely, as if he were another man—why the hell he was doing it, and what the hell good there was in it, and if he had not already gone this far with it he would not even have gone. Chicago actually seemed nothing, nonexistent. And he was puzzled at himself wanting to go there.

But when he was free, and out in the Buick on the highway, he felt better. It was as if for an hour he had existed under some kind of a mental fog, a lapse, an amnesia. And that was strange, because that was exactly how he had felt about the other, about Geneve, when he had been home packing with Agnes there.

It was a good day to drive: sunny with the bright but weak sunshine of early winter, the highway already bone dry of the melted snow, the fields beautiful, beautifully damp, and here and there one with the thin green spikes of winter wheat showing. He settled down into the long haul to Chicago, enjoying the power of the car, and the being alone, and put his mind upon a rehearsal of his plans that were coming clearer every day now and would soon be at the time to put them into action.

The whole thing centered around the highway bypass. Since the war, they had already built the new bridge and the bypass around Israel. They were working on Route 40 all across the State, rebuilding it completely, widening and straightening it. All the new types of earthmoving equipment, like LeTourneau and Caterpillar, that had been developed during the war to build airstrips, were responsible for this. Nowadays they could make the earth conform to the road instead of fitting the road to the land, and the last time he had been in St Louis, not long ago, they were already preparing to build a long, angle shortening bypass that would cut off Vandalia. Come summer they would probably start it. And on all the other new sections of road they were doing the same thing: bypassing the towns. That meant that eventually, when they got around to it, they would build a bypass around Parkman. Right now the highway ran straight through the center of town, with stop signs, and stop lights, and one school zone, slowing the traffic, and the tourist trade in food and lodging on 40 in the summertime was an important item. The bypass would kill all that. The tourists would completely miss the business section.

If a man could find out exactly where that bypass was going to be built, and buy up some of the land it would cross before the price began to go up, not only would he own the land to which business must move when it moved out there, which he could then sell in small lots at a high price, but he could also build and invest in and own a couple businesses himself on his land which he had got cheap but which was now enhanced in value. Apparently no one in Parkman had thought of this as yet. That, with certain other basic additions, he thought fondly, was his plan.

He was pretty sure the bypass was going to go to the north of town. And if it did, he already owned a small farm there out in back of the College which he had bought up some time ago as a mortgage, and which the highway would if not actually cross almost certainly have to touch along somewhere. It all depended on just where the bypass went. That would put him in on the ground floor but he wanted more and if he started buying adjoining land it would look—at least for a while—like he was only adding to his farm. But first he had to know exactly where the bypass would go. Of course it was always possible it might go to the south, and if so he would lose that much headstart, but he didnt think so because out east of town, where they had also built new the five miles of highway from the bridge to the Parkman city limits, there was a long slow curve in to town which if it were only extended straight would throw the road naturally to the north side. And he figured that was what they would do. Ahhh, he had thought it all out very carefully. And so far he had not said a word to a soul, even his own wife.

The only man he knew who might get him the information was Clark Hibbard, who owned and edited the Parkman Oregonian & Evening News, a paper founded as a weekly by his grandfather who named it after the title of Francis Parkman's best seller "The Oregon Trail" and which Clark's father had changed into an evening daily. Clark, in his spare time, was also State Representative from this district. Frank was a staunch Republican and Clark was a Republican, and Frank had always supported Clark and worked hard for him in the last election, and also done a great deal of local politicking in order to get the ticket and a Cray County man elected. He had been one of the group who first got Clark to come out for office. Clark was still a young man, and had ambitions of someday going to Washington as Senator. He felt he could trust Clark. And Clark could get him the information. The new plans were probably right now being decided by the Highway Department in Springfield. It might even be remotely possible that Clark had enough influence to get that bypass laid just exactly whereever he wanted it. Heh heh.

Of course, that would mean tipping Clark off to the deal, but that couldnt be helped. Anyway, he wasnt greedy, he told himself proudly, he didnt want it all. And besides, he had another plan; a corollary.

This had to do with the new factory. An eastern glove concern had petitioned and been voted in and accepted by the City Council and Chamber of Commerce to build a new plant in Parkman. Naturally they would want to be near the railroad—one of them—and what would be a more ideal spot for them than out north of town, in the strip of land between the New York Central tracks where the freight depot was, a mile from the edge of town, and the new bypass highway! Then theyd have railway freighting and trucking both!

His vision began to mass up schemes and he could see clearly a whole new town tacked onto Parkman. There was a strip of land out there that would, depending on the position of the bypass, be anywhere from half to three quarters of a mile wide, and long enough to support five factories—all big ones. Part of that strip was already on his little farm— a small part—and he wanted the rest of it. In his mind's eye he could visualize them: five big, shining, modernistic factories—not just one— all in a row——and all built on land owned by Frank Hirsh. From there it was only a small jump to a subdivision clustering around them. What could be more natural than for people to want to live near where they work? And then the crowning glory: a huge, new, modernistic ten- or twelve-unit shopping center like they were beginning to build all over the country now: built Western style, in a long L, with a tremendous blacktop-marked-off-in-yellow-paint 150-car parking space in the angle, built right at the junction of northbound State Route 1 and the new bypass——and above it, in yellow brick set into red he could see it now the five foot high legend HIRSH BLOCK.

HIRSH BLOCK!

Why, not only his subdivision, but everybody in town would end up doing all their buying in a modern place like that.

In the car, driving almost seventy, his hands tightened nervously and exultantly on the wheel and swerved him clear over to the black line. He pulled it back. The shopping center would be a goldmine, just in itself! He had thought it all over carefully, very carefully, and the only thing he was not absolutely 100% sure of—outside of Clark Hibbard—was all the capital. A chance like this only came to a man once in a lifetime—if then. He had already begun converting his other holdings, and he had two or three rental houses scattered around town, he could float a loan on them. And he had $15,000 stashed away in war bonds. He could not borrow on his holdings at the bank and the Building & Loan on account of the Judge—at least, not until the news was out and the surprise over. Frank calculated—again—feeling like a parrot he had done it so many times: He was worth just a little bit over $75,000. And he could probably stretch it to $25,000 more. He probably had enough for the land—if they could get most of it before the price started rising. But projects like the shopping center were going to take more, a lot more, than he could put up alone. But once the thing was started and under way he was sure he could get all the capital he wanted, even if he had to go outside town, or even the State, to get it. —There was Fred Benson, in Indianapolis, always ready to invest in a good thing.—

He didnt care. One way or another it would come to him. He would get what he needed. This was the chance of a lifetime, and he was going to throw everything into it that he could scrape up. It was a gamble, sure. Okay, so it was a gamble. He loved to gamble.

He had put off approaching Clark about it up till now, until he had it worked out in his head, and on the theory that the less people there were who knew about a thing the more likely it was to be kept a secret. But now with Dave coming into the picture, and things beginning to develop—plus the strange way the Judge had acted—he was beginning to feel it was about time. He didnt want to put it off so long that somebody else got the idea too.

That Dave. He could do a lot for that boy if he would only play ball and work a little and do what was right. That boy would make him the best partner he could have. The very fact that the boy had changed his mind like he did about the taxi service was in itself a good sign. He was at last getting some gumption and some common sense.

But—the truth was—what Frank really wanted was a son. Taking Dave was only a substitute for a son, and a poor substitute at that because if he did build a dynasty there wouldnt be anyone to take over and handle it when he died—passed on.

It was not that he didnt love Dawn. Quite the contrary. Well, who knew, if the thing came off, maybe they might even adopt a son, who knew? It was not the first time he had thought of this, but he had never mentioned it to Agnes.

This bypass deal was his first real venture, big venture, away from the Judge, and he wanted it to come off. It had to come off. Because if it didnt the Judge would see to it that he never got an opportunity at another dollar outside his own store the rest of his life.

He thought about it all the way to Chicago, feeling high and excited and exultant. The more he thought about it the better he felt. About it, and about everything.

Only once, going through Monee, did he have a moment of panic, when he remembered hè had told Edith one thing and Agnes another —Edith that the meeting was in Indianapolis, Agnes that it was in Hammond—and wondered if Agnes mightnt call Edith and find out the discrepancy accidentally, and the wild feeling of helpless panic rose. But he put it down by telling himself that that Edith was a smart one, she never said anything, not one word, that she didnt absolutely have to. And anyway, Agnes knew he was *staying* in Chicago, and would probably think Edith had got her towns wrong—or else would think Edith didnt actually know the details, which was even better. So it was all right after all.

He did not go into it further than that (after all, he was in a hurry) and did not question himself as to why he should panic over Agnes finding this out when he already knew that she knew about Geneve anyway, and when he drove up in front of the hotel on Michigan after dark and turned the car over to the doorman to put away, after working over east at Chicago Heights and coming in up the Outer Drive, and the periodic streetlights, and the glow of lights and the lit windows in the tall buildings, and on the other side the complete and utter darkness of the Lake that was almost frightening, and then over on 26th Street and up Michigan, he was feeling in fine fettle and very high, and looking forward to a three or four day idyl with his mistress.

However, that was not what he found.

CHAPTER 18

SHE was waiting for him in her room—they always registered separately; took separate rooms—and as soon as he deposited his bag in his and got rid of the bellboy, he called her and went up there. It was on the next floor above, and she was waiting for him all dressed to go out except for her dress which was laid out carefully to keep it from wrinkling on one of the twin hotel doublebeds. The door was not quite latched and he went on in, and she was standing across near the corner by the desk-table waiting, just in her slip and stockings and shoes and under it you could see the raised ridges of the garter belt and her panty legs and that brassiere and the lumps of the garter heads attached to her stockings on her thighs. —Armor, he thought heavily, the armor of women, my clasp and my helm, in which they gird themselves to go forth and do battle with the males, and which becomes armorplate whenever they need it—He knew she had posed so for him to see her when he came in and admire her. So he stopped for a moment by the door and did so. Then he sat down in a chair by the door.

"Come here," he said, his hat still on his head forgotten, and his face and ears and other parts of him beginning to burn with excess blood. "Take off your clothes and walk across the room to me." It had become almost—if not actually quite one—a ritual with them.

This time she hesitated. For a moment there was a look of quite something else on her face, certainly not sex, but then she evidently thought better of it and put it down and began to comply, coolly smiling at him for admiration. Very slowly and gracefully she slid her slip up and off over her head, revealing that thin small almost child's body, smiling at him that smile which expected and required admiration; and which made him feel that if he didnt show enough of it to satisfy her she would suddenly go into reverse gear and begin putting everything back on in the exact same way, like a movie sequence stopped short and run backwards, and he himself would get back up helplessly and walk backwards out of the door.

Shes a real whore, he thought suddenly—

"Come here," he said thickly, "let me do somethin' to you," and then became aware of his hat still on his head and flung it off him to the floor. He was aware of the look on her face, a look that was always on her face in sex, which was a look not only of physical pleasure but also of something else, another pleasure, as if she closed her mind to everything except a slit eyed smug awareness of her power here, a passive domination, and he liked it, and he lifted her to him.

—Once again, and just as strangely as always, he thought again of the time his mother had almost caught him, and had tried to make him admit it, and he had wound up on the kitchen floor under the table, where she had jabbed and poked and tried to hit at him with the broom handle her face red and her eyes blooded, until he finally admitted it, and she had whipped him, and momentarily, but only for a moment, he had hated her, had hated his own mother.—

Finally, when all the thunders and lightnings and A-bombs were all over, they were lying side by side on the other bed where her dress wasnt, his clothes scattered as by a small whirlwind all over the floor, and after a minute he got up dazedly and began to pick them up and straighten them out, so that they wouldnt be more wrinkled than they already were if they were going to go out for dinner.

But they didnt go out to dinner. Geneve lay on the bed and leaned on her elbow and watched him pick up the clothes. She had bought him two fifths of whiskey, which he saw sitting on the dresser, and when he heard what she was saying as she began to talk he wanted a drink out of them so bad he did not even bother to pick up the rest of the clothes but went and got one and opened it without bothering to get a glass either and sat down with it, realizing now at last why it was she had hesitated so when he first came in.

"Ive got some pretty serious news for you," Geneve said by way of preamble. And she had. "Agnes has been talking about me."

The upshot of what she had to say, while he drank, and then drank again, and then continued drinking unintermittently, was that she had learned through several sources—one a young-married-couple friend of hers and Al's, another Dotty Callter her boss—that Agnes had been talking lately to more than one of her friends about her husband having an affair with Geneve Lowe and what should she do about it? When she had left this time to come to Chicago, at lunch in the Marine Room of the Terre Haute House, Dotty had laughingly asked her if there were any jewelry conventions on now in Chicago. Dotty was a good girl, and she could be trusted to keep her mouth shut, she got around plenty on her own since her divorce, but she always—or almost always—was careful to do it out of town and take care of her reputation. And just before they left Dotty had warned her, seriously this time, not laughingly, that she had better be careful, because several people —among them, Dotty had said, one who shall remain nameless except for the initial A.—had it in for her and were out to cause her trouble. It was all right with Dotty what she did on her own time, but the store could not stand that kind of publicity and, Dotty laughed, neither could Dotty. And if it ever broke out in the open, Dotty wanted her to know ahead of time she would have to let her go—even though she was her assistant manager, and she was coming to depend on her more and more, and they had become such close good friends.

Lying nude on the bed propped on her elbow and talking seriously, she looked very sweet. She was the most beautiful woman, Frank thought as he drank, that he had ever slept with, she really did look just like one of those models in Vogue Magazine—he didnt know just which one for sure because they all looked quite similar and he didnt read the magazine. And as a mistress she was just about as perfect, both in practicality and as a display piece, as a man could hope to run onto. And now Agnes and her goddamned gossiping friends were going to ruin it for him.

The other one, Geneve said, was the young married woman friend of hers, who merely told her she had heard it—about Agnes—and wasnt it ridiculous: she must really be deluding herself about her husband if she thought somebody as young and attractive as Geneve would go out with him. To which, of course, Geneve perforce agreed with her, and they laughed together over it, because Geneve didnt know whether she really meant it, or was just trying to find out what kind of a reaction she would get.

In spite of a slight pique to his vanity, Frank was forced to agree with her she had been smart and done right. She was going to be a pretty big and powerful element in Parkman, he thought, someday, if she kept on going as sharply as she was now.

But the point was, Geneve went on coolly, that it should not have ever even gotten around to this woman. She was not usually in the know. That in itself showed how dangerous it was and proved it was already getting around too much. What she would like to know was how Agnes had ever found out about it in the first place?

"It wouldnt be too hard. The whole town knows about it. Probably one of her *friends* told her," Frank said bitterly, and had another drink.

"Well, somethings got to be done about it," Geneve said coldly. "I cant take a chance on losing out with Dotty. Not after all these years Ive put in there."

"What the hell am *I* goin' to do about it?" Frank said angrily.

"Find some way to make her stop doing it," Geneve said. "Or else its going to keep on until it breaks us up. Neither one of us can stand a scandal like that, and you know it. —And I dont want us broken up," she added like an afterthought and smiled at him flatteringly.

"Well I dont know what *I* can do about it," Frank said.

"I dont either," Geneve said. "But you must think of something. If you want to keep on. —If she was any normal wife like she ought to be," she said coldly, "she wouldnt pull something like that. Shed keep her mouth shut in public and let her husband have his affairs and be satisfied she was his wife, and have an affair herself now and then if she felt like it."

Frank did not think so much of this idea. "Shes a good bit older than you," he said, and took another big drink of whiskey. It was beginning to hit him pretty hard. He discovered with surprise that he had drunk almost half of the bottle. "Her generation was brought up different than yours."

"Her generation, hell," Geneve said coldly. "I know lots of women her age whove lived like that for years. And they seem to make a pretty good life of it."

"I guess she just loves me," Frank said guiltily, and took another drink.

"Loves you, hell," Geneve said. "So do those other women love their husbands. I love my husband. That doesnt have a thing to do with it. Shes just not normal. —Going around weeping on all her friends' shoulders," she said contemptuously. "Youd think shed have some pride."

"Now, listen," Frank protested, and had himself another drink. "Shes a good wife. Shes been a damned good wife to me. As good as any man ever had. Dont talk about her." He looked at the bottle, wanting suddenly to throw his head back and drain it all. In the last minute and a half he had become drunk. Quite suddenly. It surprised him. And he could tell he was going to become drunker. A lot drunker. Whether he drank any more of the bottle or not. "Why cant you women ever get along?" he said thickly. He took another drink. "Im sleepy," he said.

He did not know or remember what happened to Geneve after that. He woke up the next morning suddenly at ten o'clock and found himself in the bed they had partied in, still feeling drunk, and with a splitting head, and feeling as if all the water in his system had evaporated. Geneve was not there, she had gone out on one of her buying expeditions for Dotty. He did not know whether she had gone out for dinner last night by herself or not. There were no dirty dishes in the room. He had vague mumbling memories of her going on talking about Agnes to him after she had helped him to bed. It was as if a curtain had come down in his mind in the middle of the second act. The other bed had been slept in, and the party dress, when he looked, was hanging meticulously in the closet. It did not look wrinkled. But then, Geneve never wrinkled. Like he did. The opened bottle sitting on the dresser with the full one was only a tiny fraction from being empty, and he wondered if he could have drunk all that? Christ, that was nearly a whole fifth, he thought, frightened. He went into her bathroom with its feminine things laid about and drank large quantities of water, which helped neither his stomach nor his head. Then he got dressed and went back down to his own room, feeling wrinkled and crummy, and had a shower which did not help him much either, and made himself open his bag and hang up his suits and dressed in a fresh one and sent the other one out, and then went downstairs to the cocktail lounge which had just opened for lunch to get a Martini. He had found by experience that a Martini was the best thing for you when you felt this bad. They eased you off gently, and stopped the headache, and also helped your digestion to where you could eat lunch. But he never drank them at home in Parkman—only Manhattans—as if in this in some way he could keep separated his two separate lives: at home, and away. It was as if the Martinis themselves were, in Parkman, both an unfair advantage and slap in the face to Agnes, and marks of guilty evidence which she might be able to read.

He had three of them, sitting at the modernistically shaped bar, although he had only meant to have one, and then got several good cigars—H Upmann Churchills—in aluminum containers at the drugstore across the foyer, and went for a walk up Michigan Avenue. It was a cold dry sunbright early-winter day, and he walked as far as the old waterworks which looked like a castle, and then turned around and walked all the way back, looking in the store windows as he walked, had another Martini and ate lunch, and went upstairs to take a nap and wait for Geneve, feeling much less guilty and frightened now that he had conscientiously exercised himself.

But he could not sleep, and while he thought of buying a magazine—an Argosy or a copy of Time—he did not feel like any heavy reading. So he wound up back down at the bar, there being nothing else to do, and when Geneve found him after having found the note hed left for her, he was already pretty well loaded, and well on his way. Well, what the hell? he thought wildly, this was a vacation wasnt it?

That night they did go out to dinner. Geneve had two cocktails in the lounge (she always drank Martinis) and he had two more Martinis with her, and then went upstairs with her while she dressed. He sat in the chair and watched her, and when she was naked, watching her, he suddenly and without pre-intention got up and began to take his own clothes off, and they went to bed again, but this time—although he was pretty excited, and pretty drunk too—he laid his clothes out neatly on the other bed beforehand, and there was that strange look of smug power on her face again that he liked, and then they showered and got dressed and went out, and he made a mental note that he would have to do something about Agnes, he would just have to, in order not to lose such a wonderful mistress. They went to the Pump Room at the Ambassador East, for dinner.

They went there because Geneve always liked to go there. She loved to go there. They had such wonderful service, she said. And those uniforms. And the little Negro boys with the turbans and long feathers. He also suspected she liked to go there because it was expensive. But that didnt matter. Because she belonged there, he thought, looking at her. In fact, when she made herself up, with the lipstick making another fuller mouth over her own, and the lines of eye pencil at the corners of her eyes that made them look much longer, and the darkened brows, and did her hair in that short tousled way, she looked exotic. Exotically beautiful; and enough like all these other women he saw in here to be one of them. In fact, he thought drunkenly and happily, looking around the room, it looked as though all the models of Vogue Magazine had all conspired to bring their escorts to the Pump Room together on this one particular night. That was one of the reasons he liked to go out with her. She was always in the height of fashion. She was a real display piece, and it made him proud, that she made them look like they belonged here. He wondered how many of them were wives and how many mistresses?

Geneve ordered for both of them, some French dish, (Men dont have to order for women anymore, she always said, Thats oldfashioned today, It dates them the minute they do it), and while they were having their drinks, looked over at a corner table where a rather heavy, large dark woman in a gold dress and big gold hat was seated with a number of men congregated around her and an unusual number of waiters hovering near. Geneve looked back at him, her eyes—dark in the thin face—bright.

"I think thats Dorothy Lamour over there," she said excitedly in a low voice. "The movie star. See the one with all the men and all the waiters?"

Frank puffed on his cigar and sipped his drink and looked, but he would not have recognized a movie star if it was one. "I really think it is," Geneve whispered excitedly. It tickled him complacently. It probably was this Dorothy Lamour. Geneve knew her movie stars. They planned to go on to the Chez Paree after dinner.

But it was during dinner that Geneve brought Agnes up again, and that he consequently got drunk again. He did not remember going to the Chez Paree, or what happened there, but Geneve told him later that they had gone.

Perhaps it was because she felt more secure there in the Pump Room, or perhaps it was because she had had several Martinis—two at the hotel lounge and three there at the Pump Room—but she had suddenly brought Agnes up again and insisted on talking about it, this time more forcefully and a great deal more outspokenly.

"I dont know what youre going to do about it," she said. "But youre going to have to do something. Youre going to have to stop her. If you want to keep on having a love affair with me." It was, openly and plainly, an ultimatum.

"Ill try," he said uneasily. "But I dont know what I can do. After all she is my wife you know, and that makes it a problem. I dont know."

"Well she certainly doesnt act like it," Geneve said spitefully. "She sounds more like she thought she was your mistress."

"Ill do what I can," Frank said, and signalled the waiter that he wanted another Martini, a double. He wanted to shake his ears, as if in some way or other that would stop the unceasing racket and noise that was going into them.

"I want to tell you something," Geneve said positively and force-fully. "Ive spent a long time on Dotty Callter. Shes made a lot of money on that shop, and shes getting ready to retire soon. Shes not getting any younger. She wants to retire and go to Florida and have some fun. And she wants me to manage the store for her. Not only that," Geneve said, "shes childless you know. If anything should ever happen to her, who do you think stands to inherit the store *and* the money?"

"You," Frank said. He finished his double Martini and ordered an-other.

"Thats right," Geneve said vigorously. "Do you think Im going to jeopardize that? For you or anybody? I wont jeopardize that. I *cant* jeopardize it."

"You better get her to put it in writin'."

"Do you think Im a fool?" Geneve said. "Its already in writing. She changed her will last year. Dottys a smart businessman. She knows what would happen; her relatives have hated her ever since she got her divorce. Its an ironbound will."

"Thats all right then," Frank said. "You got nothin' to worry about."

"Oh yes I have," Geneve disagreed. "Dotty and I see things a lot alike. Dotty's no prude. Ive been on more than one party with Dotty in New York, and Cincinnati, and Chicago.—"

"Were there any women in on any of those parties?" Frank asked suddenly.

Geneve looked at him a long moment. "Thats none of your busi-ness," she said, but her eyes lit up warmly at him. They were bright from drinking.

"I just wondered," he said, fingering his glass vaguely and wonder-ing why he had asked, had been interested. The thought excited him.

"Why do you want to know?" Geneve smiled smugly. "For your information, there were no women. The point Im making is, Dotty wouldnt hesitate a second to fire me, and to cut me off in her will, if there was any scandal. And I wouldnt blame her. She doesnt want a scandal. And neither do I. Scandals just arent good for business. Its sad, but its true."

"Dont I know," Frank said ruefully, thinking of the Old Man, and of Dave. He looked at his food and decided to order another double Martini instead. He could see the end. He would be meeting her some-day at the Country Club dances, perhaps he would even covertly watch her body dancing, and theyd meet and smile and be friends. Perhaps there would even be a certain pleasure in their secrecy as they looked at each other. Of course, he could always fire Al. But that would only make enemies of both of them. And to the town, which already knew it all anyway, it would only be an open gesture of malice. Besides, he had gotten to be very fond of Al. Of course, Al was no match for his wife,—but then, he thought bitterly, few men are. The last thing he remembered was paying the check and giving the waiter a very generous tip, which a part of his mind that was not drunk told him he would remember later and regret.

The next thing he knew he was lying on one of the beds in her room, his head hung down over the side, retching into a bath towel which Geneve in her dressing gown was anxiously holding for him.

He continued to retch, abstractedly, as if he were standing off somewhere watching himself, while his mind swam around sickeningly trying to find out where it was. He noted that there was next to nothing on the towel, only a few gobby gray strings of mucus. He also noted that it was morning, because it was daylight outside.

"Is it morning?" he mumbled through the thick desire to vomit in his throat, and fell to retching again, uncontrollably, into the towel she held for him although nothing came up but spittle. Over the loud and continued rasping of his own throat in his ears, he could hear her answer, her voice nervous and anxious:

"Morning! Its after noon. And youve been this way since five o'clock this morning."

The retching continued for what seemed an endless time, his stomach muscles convulsed and aching, then finally it ceased and he rolled over and lay back exhausted, his ears ringing and feeling stupefied. Under the stupefaction he felt scared.

"Whats the matter with me?"

"I dont know," Geneve said anxiously. "Youre sick. You keep trying to vomit, but nothing comes up now, for a long time, except this mucus." She laid the towel down on the floor beside the bed. "Your face is as red as fire."

Fright spread through him as full awareness gradually returned. "Ive heard of fellows havin' the dry heaves," he said. "But Ive never had them. I guess thats what Ive got."

"Ive never seen a man so drunk in his life and still stay on his feet," Geneve said. "Ive been trying to get you to talk for hours. But all youd do was lay there and throw up. Or try to. And just mumble. I was afraid you were going to die in my room," she said nervously.

Frank did not say anything and lay still, breathing deeply and heavily. His stomach muscles ached as if they had been beaten.

"Do you feel all right now?" she said anxiously.

"How the hell do I know?" he said heavily, anger rising over the stupefaction. "I dont know whats wrong with me. No, I dont feel all right. I feel sick." He could feel it coming on him again, and tried to hold it back down.

Geneve began suddenly to talk, nervously, almost babblingly. It had started at the Chez Paree. He was terribly drunk, and still drinking. At first she hadnt realized how drunk he really was. Then she had thought she had better get him out and get him home. But he refused to go. Finally, when they closed the joint, she had got him outside and into the cab. He had walked all right and had paid the check himself. Then in the cab he had started vomiting. He stuck his head out the window, and she held onto him, and he vomited almost all the way back to the hotel.

"I didnt know a stomach could hold so much," she laughed nervously and unfunnily.

The cab driver had been angry, and she had paid him and tipped him five dollars for what they had done to the side of his cab, and then had gotten him upstairs in the elevator and into her room.

"Why didnt you take me to my room?" Frank said thickly through the rising desire to retch.

"I was afraid youd die. And have a stroke. Every time youd try to bring up your face would get full of blood and red as fire. So I brought you here." And there, she said, they had remained—all night and until now, the next afternoon.

In the midst of her rush of talk he could no longer control his throat and he rolled over and began to retch again into the towel, which she grabbed and held for him, and heard no more.

"Do you want me to call the hotel doctor?" Geneve said anxiously, after he lay back exhausted.

"No," he said thickly, feeling panic rising in him. "No, no. Not while Im in your room. Ill be all right."

"I know you want to be secret," she said nervously, "but it may be something dangerous. You might die. The hotel people wont say anything. Thats their business. Besides, they wont know who we are."

"I said Ill be all right," Frank said dully. "Really. I know Ill be all right," he insisted, wondering how long it would last, and if he would die.

It lasted two more days. He did not die. Several times he almost wished he could, though. Geneve tried everything on him: orange juice, tomato juice, soup, water, Pepto-Bismal, soda. He could not keep anything down, even water. On the third day he was able to take a little soup and keep it down. The first day Geneve did not even leave the room. He felt a warm affection for her, when he was capable of feeling anything, even though he knew she was thinking more about herself and her own reputation than she was about his health. The next day she went out to do the rest of her buying for Dotty's stock.

"I dont know what to do," she said when she came back. "Ive already stayed longer than I was supposed to, or should have."

"Christ," he said, "I cant go home lookin' like this." He had lost around ten pounds. And he was very weak. His hands shook noticeably. Even his mouth trembled. His eyes were bloodshot badly from so much retching.

"You go on home by yourself," Frank said. "Ill stay on another day and eat and rest up, and then drive on home the next day."

"I hate to do that," Geneve said. "I dont like to go off and leave you here like this."

"Its okay," he said tiredly, wishing only that she would shut up, and leave him alone. "Im better, and Ill be able to get back to my own room, and youve got to get back home."

"Ill leave tomorrow then," she said, looking perhaps a little bit relieved.

That night she went out for dinner alone. It was very late when she got in, and she was three fourths tight, and her party dress was rumpled and her lipstick smeared. She giggled as she asked him softly how he was and slipped into the other bed. Frank lay awake and watched her after she had gone to sleep, feeling very melancholy and very sad. He could already see those Country Club dances clearly in his mind that someday he would meet her at. In the morning she left, and he moved back into his own room.

"When will I see you?" Geneve said.

"I dont know," he said. "Ill call you at the store in the next few days, after I get home."

"All right," she said although it was contrary to their policy, "you do that. And the first chance I get to go out of town, I'll let you know."

"Okay," he said.

The drive he made home was terrible. He was still weak and pretty shaky, and the nearer he got to Parkman the higher the level of panic in him rose, like water poured slowly into a beaker. Agnes would spout green applebutter, when she saw him. He made a mental note to ask Doc Cost what the hell it was had happened, and what was the cause of it. But after he got home he got so involved with Dave and getting the taxi service running that he did not get around to doing it, and besides he was ashamed. When he did get around to asking Doc it was a week later and he did it in a roundabout way, pretending that it was some third person he was asking about. Whats the matter Doc asked him, you been getting the dry heaves? Oh no he answered, not me, a guy I met at the meeting in Chicago, he asked me about it. Its acute gastritis Doc diagnosed, an acute inflammation of the stomach walls, usually from too much alcohol over a period of time, you better tell your friend if you ever meet him again to lay off the liquor—at least as much as he can, Doc who drank a lot himself amended ruefully, it could kill a man, though it doesnt very often.

But that was a week later.

When he got home that day, and pulled into the drive, and saw that Agnes's car was there, the panic beaker was finally full and even sloshing a little bit over the sides. He sat in the car a long minute and got hold of himself, and shakily opened the door and went inside.

Agnes was in the utility room.

"Great God!" she said, coming into the kitchen as soon as she saw him. "What on earth has happened to you?"

"Oh, nothing," Frank said easily, getting a drink of water from the kitchen tap. "A bunch of the boys got a little drunk last night after the last meeting, and Im a little hung over, thats all."

Agnes looked at him a long moment and then went back into the utility room. "You oughtnt to drink so much, Frank," she said angrily, and softly.

"I know it," he said. "Im seriously thinkin' of quittin' altogether."

He thought he had handled that pretty well.

CHAPTER 19

As a matter of fact, Frank had not handled anything. He had done no better and no worse than he usually did, which was to be reasonably adequate, under the circumstances.

The truth was, Agnes herself had let him off the hook. She had had him red handed, roped and tied and basted, and ready to put on the spit over a slow fire, and she had let him off the hook. She had felt sorry for him.

Agnes Marie Hirsh (Herschmidt), nee Towns, had been handling this kind of thing for some time. She had handled enough of it to have an instinct about it. She had only to look at her husband to know that she had won. She had enough proof on him to burn him down to the ground or send him up for life or hang him with his own rope, but she did not use it. There were times when you could push a man only so far and this was one of them. So instead, she filed it away with the rest for use at some future date when it would be more good to her than now. Now she did not need it. She did not want to confront him and leave him, she wanted only to keep him.

Looking at him standing there, she could tell he had been pretty sick. She could also tell by the smug look on his face just exactly what he was thinking: that he had handled it; and this made her angry. But when he turned to her from the sink, and repeated that he was pretty hung over, and then said he thought he would lay down for a while, she let him go. It was easy to see he had not had just an ordinary hangover, but she did not say anything. He obviously did not want her to know. And anyway it was good enough for him. She had been sick herself while he was gone.

She really did feel sorry for him, now that she was sure she had won. He was so transparent, when he thought he was being so smart. And he didnt know the first thing about women. He apparently had no idea that Geneve Lowe was merely using him for what she could get out of him for herself and her husband. He was probably quite convinced she was madly in love with him, the poor simp. Until today Agnes had never been sure that she would win; but after seeing how he looked, it was easy to see something had happened in Chicago. Agnes thought she knew what it was. —And it had nothing to do with her proof she had collected: that was another plan.

This proof that she had collected while he was gone, and was now filing away because she did not need, was her ace in the hole so to speak. Whether it would have stood up in a court of law, Agnes didnt know, but it didnt matter. It was evidence that would stand up with Frank Hirsh, and that was all she cared about. She knew him well enough—she ought to! after all these years of it—to know that once she proved to him with incontrovertible evidence, *material* evidence, that he was having a love affair, and backed him into a corner where he could not worm out but had to admit it to her, once she did that, then he would drop the love affair like he was holding a hot potato. And lick his burned fingers and look guilty. So she had done it, had fixed it all up, gotten it all arranged; and as soon as she had completed it she had gotten sick as she always did.

That was one of the reasons she always kept putting off doing it for so long. It always upset her and made her sick. And sometimes he got over them—the minor ones—by himself, without her having to step in. But this time, no.

The day after Frank left she had driven to Terre Haute on a shopping expedition, she had had some things shed been wanting to buy anyway for some time. While she was there she had suddenly decided to go into Miller's Jewelry to look at some imported glass she had been meaning to look at for some time anyway. Jeff Miller had waited on her himself. She was surprised and shocked. Obviously, Jeff could not be in Hammond to a meeting if he was in Terre Haute waiting on her. She had said nothing, and bought several pieces of the glass and paid cash, not a charge. When she got home she did not unwrap it but put it away in her closet. The dated carbon of the sales slip was inside. It gave her a strange sense of comfort to know it was all there on the shelf. It had all been the strangest coincidence; God must have been looking after her.

nee Towns—a long time ago that was, wasnt it? she thought—yes, it was. Agnes Marie. It had been a long time since anybody had called her that. Just Agnes. Agnes Hirsh.

Then, the next day, she had gone down to Dotty Callter's Mode Shop because there was a lingerie sale on. She had gone at a time when Geneve Lowe would be there because Geneve always waited on her, Frank being Al's boss. Geneve, however, was not there. Dotty herself waited on her. Dotty did not mention Geneve was on a buying trip to Chicago. Dotty did not mention Geneve at all. She had bought some sale lingerie, and two of their very best slips—why not?—and did not say anything, and had it charged. It would come in on the first of the month, to Frank, with the dated sales slip, when the account was rendered.

And when it did, she would have the glass. If she decided to wait that long. She did not expect to wait that long. She intended to break it open as soon as he got home. It was a shame it had to be like that. It was a shame she had to do it. But there you were. There it was.

—so she had gone ahead and done it, she thought, knowing she would get sick, and then had gone ahead and gotten sick, and called Doc Cost, because thusly she would have two strings to her bow, would have another plan, the infallible one, if the first plan should have failed—

But the moment she had seen him come into the kitchen, she had known the first plan, which was the gossip she had started among her friends, had not failed, had only been slow in starting.

She would not need the other plan—the infallible one—now, but she did not begrudge the energy spent on it. She anticipated ahead like any good field commander, that before it was all over, before the last shot was fired, the last capitulation given, she would probably need to bring in her reserves. So it was just as well that she mass them. This was the first time since it had started that she had known for sure she *had* won. The mopping up might take a while yet, but she *had* won. She had never been sure before. The other plan, the gossip amongst her friends, had taken so long to get started.

Contrary to what Geneve Lowe had said to Frank, Agnes was not without pride. She had thought a long time before deciding to embark upon a planned campaign of gossip among her friends. She did not relish at all the idea of weeping on her friends' shoulders and confiding to them that her husband was having an affair with Geneve Lowe and what had she ought to do? It gave her no pleasure; she was not that type, and had no use for women who were, and she did not like the idea of making her friends think she was that type. But she also knew—unpleasant or not—that it was the best way—if not the only way available!—to get at Geneve Lowe: In her still vulnerable position with

Dotty Callter she could simply not afford talk like that. It had hurt her pride terribly, to make those weeping visits—carefully spaced over a period of eight weeks: ten friends; eight weeks—and that was something else she was going to take up with Mr Frank Hirsh—at the proper time, which however was not now. Not only did it hurt her pride, it made her feel as though she had no integrity.

She did not know why it always made her sick. She supposed it must be because it was so embarrassing, that must be it, and because in a way it was like admitting that the only way she could keep her husband from sleeping with other women was by *force*. She didnt care if he never slept with her again, sex had always been a vastly overrated pastime, to her, she thought, her face burning with indignation, but she would be God damned to hell if he was going to go around sleeping with other women.

Men always made such a loud to do about sex. Well, apparently men were built that way. But more than half the time she was convinced it was all a put on. Like Pete Shaw at the Elks Grille or the Country Club every time he got tight, telling in a loud voice that he had to have his sex every night, every single night of the year, or he would get down sick, and his wife Mona sitting there smiling embarrassedly, what else could she do. Pete had been in the first war; Agnes was inclined to believe Mona Shaw did not have as much sex from her husband as most wives did, even. And she was pretty sure Mona felt about sex like she did, though theyd never talked about it. She did not think sex was evil. She did not think it was dirty. It was just that it was a transitory physical pleasure, soon gone, whose main purpose was still after all procreation, and she felt all the talk about it—except for other people's extramarital affairs; and possibly most of that—was largely wind.

Again, Agnes felt her face burning with indignation: She did not care if she got sick, and stayed sick—from now until Doomsday—as long as she was married to him Frank Hirsh was not going to step out on her with other women, not for very long anyway. After all as a wife she had some rights.

—she should have more rights than most. She wasnt so much a wife as a partner. When her father died suddenly and unexpectedly, leaving her as his only heir, she had signed the store over to Frank, lock stock and barrel. Had he left anything to Frank, who worked for him? He had Not! She had not asked for any recompense, had not expected any; and she had not gotten any. That entitled her to something. Of course, it had only been a cheap notion store then, in danger of being run out of business by Woolworth's, and everything that had been done with it and to it had been done by Frank. He had studied hard, and worked hard. She was willing to admit that. It had been his idea to convert to a jewelry store. Practically everything had been his idea. Nevertheless, he could not have done it without her and her store because he could have worked all his life and never made enough money to buy one. He owed her something. If not love, then at the very least, loyalty. And she intended to have it—whether collecting it made her sick or not.

Agnes got up from her seat at the mangle agitatedly—she did not feel like ironing any more damned sheets; she was going to start having old Jane Staley two days a week, instead of one, by God, from now on; if she could get the old harridan to come that often—and went into the dining room through the kitchen and sat down at the big table.

—she could have died! actually; actually gotten so sick shed have died; and hed not even have known it! and he had not even asked her whether she felt well.—

Agnes longed, with a deep and passionate longing, to go in the bed room and snatch him up off that bed and give it to him straight right now. But—she knew it wasnt wise, hed had enough to swallow for one dose, and she contained herself.

—but to not even notice that shed been sick!

When she had called Doc Cost, the big man had come right away. She had come home from Dotty Callter's shop, put the new lingerie and slips neatly away in her bureau, and then as regular as clockwork had gone in the bathroom and begun to vomit. When she was empty and had gotten over the dizziness and strain, she had gone to the phone and weakly called Doc Cost's new hospital. The girl on the switchboard informed her that Doctor Cost was not in now but young Doctor Hampton his son in law was, and would he do. Agnes, who had nothing against young Hampton but who had always doctored with Doc Cost, thought not, and wondered where she could reach him. Well, he would probably be at the Elks Club about now, the girl thought, since it was mid afternoon. So Agnes called for him there. He was in the bar. He came right out.

Agnes was in bed when he got there. In spite of being sick and dizzy, and this feeling of utter, complete flagging lassitude she always got, she had managed sketchily to get herself undressed, and into a nightgown, and in the bed, to which she went as though it were a redoubt into which she could safely retreat.

As if he expected that, Doc Cost only rapped lightly and perfunctorily once or twice and came on in, carrying his battered old black bag which, in spite of the new hospital and all the money he had made, he still carried. His various sons and daughters and their spouses, Agnes knew, had on numerous occasions such as Christmas or his birthday, tactfully presented him with new replacements for it, and he now owned a total collection of ten or twelve expensive modern

brand new doctor's bags; but he never used them because he still preferred his old one, not only for sentimental reasons it seemed, but also
because he apparently felt it was some kind of lucky talisman, a sort
of hostage to whatever rapacious gods of fate They were who ran this
Universe and he believed in, and that as though by continuing to use
it, and thus proving to Them he was not a snob in spite of his success
and all the money he had made, he hoped in future to escape Their
fiendish attentions. Agnes had never known another man who was so
ashamed of being a success. He was a big man, and he almost filled
the bedroom door as he came through it.

Dr Immanuel Calvin Cost was a Welshman—one who, however,
was not born there but here. An American Welshman, from Rhode
Island. He had been born in Newport, but without the money. As he
himself said, his parents had split the naming of him, his mother for
her religion, his father for his philosophy. It was one of his standard
jokes—delivered, like the others, with that same sort of sad, wistfully
wry smile—that his father had wanted to name him Kant, instead of
Immanuel, but since his mother insisted his middle name would be
Calvin, and that they address him as that, his father had decided it
would be a little too much of a pun, especially since they planned on
him being a doctor. In spite of this statement, he always seemed to
undercharge rather than overcharge. He was too big to look like a
doctor, with mild embarrassed eyes (which were nevertheless astute)
and which were always vaguely apologetic because he had made such
a lot of money in a profession which was—or was supposed, at least,
to be—a profession of service rather than of profit. He was—as he himself often said—on the wrong side of fifty five, though not yet nearing
sixty—and looked a great deal younger; and he drank a lot and showed
it. Right now he was something more than half drunk, and he sat
down on the in-side of the other bed and clasped his big hands awkwardly between his knees and wafted over Agnes a breath of partially
assimilated whiskey which for some years now had been one of the
most soothing, and comforting, and safest odors Agnes was aware of.

Doc Cost—almost no one called him anything but that—had been
the Hirshes' family physician since their marriage, and before. Ever
since, in fact, the time when Frank's father had run off with Doc's first
wife—the one reputed to have become the mistress of Samuel Insul—
and Doc's savings; which was when Frank had started to cultivate him
and had assiduously called him in on all the Hirsh family illnesses.
Doc had apparently understood this. He had been Frank's doctor ever
since. He had not apparently held it against Frank: what Frank's father
did; and they had become good friends.

Lately, he had built this new hospital on a small, heavily treed estate
on the outskirts of town, and for the past ten years—ever since a trip

to England—had been a sports car fan and owned two foreign cars which he tinkered with and an English MG which he drove around town. Through it all—sometimes, it almost seemed, in spite of himself—he had gone right on making the money that he hated; except for spending, and he really spent it.

She looked at him weakly from the bed.

"What is it this time, Agnes?" he said heavily, the breath of whiskey getting thicker and wafting pleasantly about her with a feeling of security. "Same old thing?"

Then, before she could answer, he suddenly for no reason got up and walked to the foot of her bed and stood, his arms folded and swaying ever so slightly, looking down at her. As if belatedly realizing he perhaps might be swaying a little, he took two or three steps backward and propped his back against the wall, and continued to look at her, arms folded. His eyes were wide open and slightly stary.

"Ive been vomiting," Agnes said weakly. "Dizziness and sick at my stomach. Nervous indigestion, I guess."

He nodded gravely and unfolded his arms.

"You havent been drinking too much?" he said gently.

"No more than usual," Agnes said, and shook her head weakly. It was strange that his having been drinking did not upset her any, but it had always been that way. The time or two he had operated on her a few years back, he had always been sober as a judge, and as calm and cool. You knew without thinking about it that whenever he needed to be sober, he would be—and would not be hungover, either. You also knew that even when he was a lot drunker than he was now, he would never fumble, never reach around in his bag and come out with the wrong pill. That was just Doc Cost. A big man and all meat except for his heavy stomach, with the sausage fingers of a big man that he always used very gently, as if he were always aware of them and afraid he might unwittingly squeeze too hard and break something, he inspired confidence in the same way that most other people inspire just the opposite. You knew he *knew*—whatever it was; and that he would never censure.

"Ill give you something to quiet you down and settle your stomach," Doc said, the mild, embarrassed, apologetic eyes looking at her gently and astutely. "I dont guess its anything to get worried about."

"Oh no; Im sure," Agnes said. "I thought I knew what it was. But I just thought I ought to call you anyway." She was sitting half up in the bed, with the covers tucked around her just under her breasts, and she was aware of him looking at them, and at her body under the covers, but she did not mind. The nightgown was not a very sheer one. She was not an unattractive woman, for her age, even if she was thickening a little; and if her breasts sagged a little, they were still ample and fairly shapely, she thought. And it was nice to know there were still *some* men who wanted to look at you. And besides, Doc would never do anything and you did not have to worry about him, he was always a perfect gentleman, she had known him for years. "I just wanted to be sure, you know," she said.

Again Doc nodded gravely, and gently. "Ill just take your temperature and your pulse," he said, coming around between the beds where his bag was. His hands were accurate and sure, reaching in it for the thermometer, and his big sausage fingers—so delicate and light of touch for their size—were gentle on her wrist as he felt the artery. "I suppose Frank must be out of town," he said casually, "or youd have called him."

"Oh, yes," Agnes said quickly. "Or I would have. But hes up in Chicago on a big Jewelers' Association convention."

Doc took the thermometer out of her mouth, read it, wiped it with an alcohol swab of cotton, and put it away. "Both normal. I dont think Ill need to check your heart. Our bellies are connected to our heads, Agnes," he said. "I guess nobody really knows just how much of our sickness is due to our mental attitude at the time. Maybe it all is. I dont know. Or why some people get tuberculosis when we all of us have the germs in our bodies all our lives. The AMA wouldnt much like me for saying that, I guess," he grinned. "Have you still got those sedatives I gave you?"

"Some," Agnes said. "I still use them to help me sleep, sometimes. —But Ive used them sparingly," she added quickly.

Doc nodded. "Guilts have a lot to do with our sicknesses, I think," he said, looking at her gently with the apologetic eyes. He poured a handful of sedatives out of a big mouthed bottle and slid them into an envelope. "But not like the head shrinkers think, I dont think." —He had disliked psychiatrists for years.— "Dont use any more than you have to," he said, handing it to her together with the medicine. "And never more than one at a time. Dont want to get to needing them."

"Thank you, Doctor," Agnes said.

"I guess the AMA wouldn't like that either," Doc grinned, closing the bag and getting up, "but then I dont do it with everyone." He smiled down at her, the wide open eyes seeming not even to be focused. Abruptly, he ran his hand back through his hair. Hes really a very big man, she thought, huge; and it always surprised you. "Guess I better get back to my poker game," he said, grinning again that strange grin which all seemed to take place on his mouth and face and the skin around his eyes, while leaving the eyes themselves still wide open and staring that way, semi focused. "Boys are takin me. Stay in bed a few days if you want to. It wont hurt you. That man who said A man's home is his castle was wrong. Theres always too many people around.

What he should have said was One's bed is one's fortress. If you feel like you want me again for anything, just call me."

"Thank you, Doctor," Agnes said.

"If I dont hear from you Ill figure youre all right," he said. "Goodby."

"Goodby, Doctor," Agnes said.

He was really very big. She listened to him go until she heard the door close, and then in a moment the sputtering of the little MG on the drive, backing out. He drove it winter and summer although he had a four car garage at home which in addition to the two foreign cars also contained a big Chrysler sedan. He was a strange man. She already felt much better. She had considered calling the new minister, too, earlier, but hadnt because he was a new man and she didnt know him very well. And anyway she didnt like his name. Fishhauser. Reverend Wilbur Fishhauser. But now she did not feel she needed to call him. Guilts, he had said: Doc. Thinking with comforting satisfaction of the packaged Swedish glass up on the shelf, and the lingerie and slips in the drawer, she turned over and went soothingly to sleep. The combed percale sheets were fresh and clean against her through the nightgown, and the weight of the cover safe and secure and sheltering like a heavy sweater on a chill day, though it was not cold in the house. The pillowslip smelled smooth and clean. She drifted.

She woke in the evening to the sound of a voice. It was Dawn on the telephone. She listened strengthlessly in the semi darkness of the bedroom.

"Where?" Dawn was saying. "No, Wally. Thanks, but I really cant tonight."

. . .

"Mother isnt feeling well. Yes. And I think I ought to stay around the house tonight. Anyway I have some work to do on my French."

. . .

"No. Nothing serious."

. . .

"No. She doesnt need me. When Mother's sick she likes to stay by herself and be let alone. But I want to stay around."

. . .

"No. Really, Wally. I dont *want* to go out tonight."

. . .

"Youll have more fun without me anyway."

. . .

"Well, there. You see?"

. . .

"Goodby."

The phone was hung up, softly, and then she came to the bedroom door, her shadow making a silhouette in the lighted door frame for a moment on the wall. Then she quietly went away. Happily, Agnes went back to sleep.

Sitting at the big dining room table, and looking toward the bedroom door where Frank had disappeared, Agnes loved her daughter. Loved her very deeply. So much so it almost made the tears come. Dawn understood her.

She had stayed in bed three days, getting up only to make herself some broth, or an egg and toast, a light meal, now and then. Dawn took care of herself, and cooked her own meals, and left her alone. She had been through these sessions before, Agnes thought; she understood. But the fourth day was the day Jane came to clean, and she did not want Jane to see her in bed, so she had gotten up, and getting up had stayed up.

Hadnt she.

Yes she had.

And she was reasonably proud of it.

That was the same day that Dave, with a strange urgent note in his voice, had called her about Frank. Evidently they were going to go ahead with it.

Again, she found herself looking toward the bedroom door where Frank had gone. After a moment, she got up from the table and went to get the new novel she was reading.

CHAPTER 20

It took several days to get the taxi service set up, almost another week to get it operating. There was the building and lot to rent. Then the cars to buy. Titles to be applied for, licenses to be applied for, corporate papers to be made out, the contracts to sign. It never failed to amaze Frank when he went into a new business deal, the voluminous amount of paper that had to be signed, re-signed, witnessed, notarized and recorded to keep honest people from cheating one another. He did almost all of the work himself. For a week they hardly saw him at the store and Edith and Al Lowe ran it. As he worked, he was already planning that if this worked out, if it paid for itself, paid at all well, he was going to get hold of a couple good secondhand buses in Indianapolis and start a city bus service in a year or two.

The building he finally rented was a block off the square on South Plum Street, one of a cluster of tacky little buildings right in there that had never been replaced by anything better. It had been a run down lunch counter, which had gone under a year ago, and had been in disuse since then and showed it. He did not care. He did not want a good building, he wanted a cheap one. He did not intend to put any work, or any money, on it. And this one was on an alley and had a back lot on the falling hillside which had been built up level with the cinders of several generations and would park several cars. He would rather have had a lot on Wernz Avenue the mainstreet but nothing was available there, and he would not have paid the price if any had been.

He enjoyed himself equally as much in getting the cars, but this was a different kind of enjoyment. He was, as he had told Dave, a silent partner in the Dodge-Plymouth Agency—not even Judge Deacon knew this; in fact no one did, except himself and Slim Carroll and Slim's attorney who drew the papers. Slim had needed money several times when Frank had happened to have it and he had advanced it against shares of the business. So he got good buys on cars he knew he could trust. The pleasure was in the getting of them cheap, and in the secrecy.

There was the matter of the drivers. When everything else was done, the leasing of the building, the buying of the cars, everything in short that required secrecy, he went out to hire them. It had somehow—by some occult osmosis, in spite of everything he could do—gotten around town that Frank Hirsh was starting a taxi stand, and several people had approached him for jobs. He turned them all down. He had given some little thought to this matter of drivers. He wanted to save money on the drivers. He had a choice of hiring reputable dependable men, in which case he would have to match the salaries paid by Sternutol or Kentucky Oil, or by the stores uptown. The stores didnt pay much, but it was more than he wanted to pay. Or he could hire kids just out of high school, who lived at home, had no families of their own to support, but were usually pretty wild drivers.

He did not want to—could not—pay the salaries required by the former; and he did not want to hire the latter because of their irresponsibleness. He thought briefly of hiring women drivers, but discarded this because of his feeling that women were too nervous to make good drivers; the kids would be better. —and also he had an intuitive feeling that women drivers would not sit too well in Parkman, somehow. In a city, maybe. But not here.

But there was still another element in the town he might draw from. These were the type of undependables and semi-disreputables to which Dewey Cole and Hubie Murson might be said to belong: younger fellows most of them, some of them married some unmarried, whose families had never amounted to much in town, but mainly men who were sort of misfits and would rather live and work cheap than to hold down steady respectable well paying jobs that they would have to go to every day.

Frank was aware of what he was getting into. Someone would always be quitting. Because his feelings had been hurt. A customer had insulted him. Or he wanted to go to St Petersburg and work on the docks for the winter. Or his kidneys were going bad on him from all this damned driving. Or he got drunk and forgot to come home from Terre Haute for a month. —or if he was more honest than most because he was just plain bored, disgusted because the novelty had worn off. Yeh, there would be a constant turnover of personnel. But there were several advantages on the other side. All of these young guys loved to drive cars; and rarely—if ever—did any of them ever get enough money to buy one. Also, there would always be quite a number of them hanging around town, no matter who happened to be gone, and replacements should be fairly easy to get—especially since the job was driving. Last, but most important, there was the money they could be hired for.

It was not at all the same as his store, where respectability of background was a necessary asset. Nobody cared who drove them down town in a taxi—as long as they didnt run into something.

Having made up his mind, Frank sallied forth to do his hiring. Shrewdly and wisely, he went to the Foyer. The Foyer was the other poolroom on the square. The chief difference between it and the Athletic Club was that the Foyer was the hangout of store owners and businessmen around the square and of the townsmen in general, while the Ath Club was more the hangout of the high school kids and the country men. Nobody knew why this was so. It had always just been that way.

Possibly, Frank thought as he ordered a beer, it was because the Foyer served beer and had a package liquor counter. That would account for the high school kids. But not the country men. They drank as much if not more than anybody. Matter of fact, the high school kids drank more than their fair share when they could get hold of it. It was just one of those things, he guessed. He drank two beers and played two games of pool. He went there at nine o'clock in the morning and before eleven he had all three of his drivers hired.

A good sample of one of them was Albin Shipe. Albie Shipe was 28 and had hung around Parkman all his life until he became a sort of fixture. His aged father had been Parkman's only garbage man from the time Frank could first remember up until five years before the war, when he died. Old Man Shipe had collected Parkman's garbage as a volunteer, rather than as a city employee. With an old wagon and an even older horse, he would make a part of his round every morning sitting under a filthy yellow umbrella that shaded the box, and the smell which had permeated the grease soaked boards of his wagon would hang in the air after him minutes after he had gone by. He collected only in the mornings, and spent the afternoons separating the edible garbage from the inedible. The edible he fed to a big gang of hogs he kept on his tiny place in the north end of town—(beyond the I.N. tracks; in Pisgah)—his sole source of income; the inedible he either threw in the steep ravine behind it (which was the reason he had been able to buy it cheap) or else used to build a new room on his shack for his numerous and constantly increasing progeny. Needless to say, as the town grew up around him, everybody tried to build as far away from Old Man Shipe's place as possible, but even that did not help when the wind was right. By the time he died he had filled in fifty yards of the ravine and owned a shack of fourteen rooms no longer filled with the grown up offspring. Judge Deacon, who held the mortgage Old Man Shipe had been paying interest on for some forty odd years, tore down the shack and bulldozed dirt over the whole stinking mess and built four modern houses upon it to rent.

He had had a plan, Frank sometimes liked to think, Old Man Shipe. Judge Deacon had told him about that part of it some time later. The Judge had seen it, and he said he had a plan; the only difference was, the Judge grinned, he was not as squeamish about fulfilling it as some people, Old Man Shipe. Old Shipe had had the place perhaps fifty years all told, the Judge said, from the time he married around twenty. And everything about it showed a plan. The fill in the ravine was well placed, and well packed; and the layout of the shack with all its added rooms was practical and efficient. It could have been a mansion except for the materials in it and the fact that they were not sturdy enough to support a second or third storey. And by the time the old man had filled up the little lot with added rooms, he was able to start building out over the fill which he had hand-shoveled a little dirt over. Almost certainly, the Judge grinned, the nearly uncountable offspring were part of the plan, too. With that many unhired hands they could almost certainly have added a second and third storey and eventually made a mansion of it, and Old Man Shipe used his wife and himself as unsparingly as he used his garbage. It apparently never occurred to him that they would not want to help. But as soon as they got big enough, one by one like logs rolling off the end of a battered platform, they all left him—and left town. The best laid plans of mice and men, the Judge quoted grinning, gang aft aglee.

All except Albie, Frank thought sipping at his second beer, after he had hired him; he was too young. Albie was the youngest and was born when the old man was 58. The mother died soon after Albie, so that no one was left except Albie and the old man, alone together in the shack of fourteen rooms, and the old man brought Albie up, and when he died—finally killed by the smell, people said—Albie took care of him for a week before he died and was the only one there for the funeral which Judge Deacon paid for, but a couple of the boys came back once, a year or so after, from Chicago where they lived, tall thin sharp faced young men, dressed in clean, nice, if cheap, suits, and with scrupulously clean fingernails, everyone noticed. They stayed three days and threw money around in the poolrooms, buying drinks and playing pea pool for a dollar a game, and then disappeared after giving Albie twenty dollars. None of the daughters ever came back at all.

But that was after the old man died. Frank remembered him well. He used to lean down off his wagon and give Frank and the other boys penny suckers which they never ate and always threw away as soon as he was gone because they were afraid they were dirty and would give them some disease. *Kids are comical little bastards, Frank thought grinning.* They had used to have a rhyme they taunted each other with: "Gripe, gripe, you little snipe! your only friend is Old Man Shipe!" But of course they never said it where the old man could hear them.

Albie himself had stayed on in Parkman. He had carried papers at the News Stand from the time he was ten anyway, and when the shack was bulldozed under, rented himself a cheap room in the house of a poor but honest woman who taught him to take a bath every other day. He continued to carry papers until he was twenty. In a family never conspicuous for brilliance in school, Albie was even below normal. Eventually reaching the sixth grade, he remained there—much in demand by the various sandlot football teams at recess—until being big for his age anyway he was able to whip not only all the eighth grade boys but also most of the teachers. He never whipped anyone, however, because he never fought, Frank thought. What a missed opportunity. At sixteen he left school and the sixth grade forever, and continued to carry papers until he got a job taking care of the court-house furnace for the janitor, and from there graduated to a series of similar jobs. Naturally, when the war came, he was naturally one of the first who could be spared. The draft board sent him to the Army, where he loaded, drove, and unloaded trucks for the duration, and was discharged with a total decoration list of one, the Good Conduct Medal, the ribbon of which he continued to wear, after he got home, in the lapel of his leather jacket. He was not a moron, or an idiot, or anything like that. He was just slow, and easily contented. He had always lived in the present moment and lacked the foresight to see where studying might have someday been important to him. He laughed a lot in a loud voice and never talked about his father and read a great many comic books. Frank felt very paternal when he hired him. Almost like what they called landed gentry in England. He had been meaning for a long time to get himself a small place where he could run some horses, when he got the money. Albie would make him a wonderful caretaker for it. Albie himself had been very pleased. It would be the first time he had driven a vehicle since the Army.

The other two men Frank hired were similar types. A lean little ferret faced youth named Fitzjarrald, whose family had come here from the East before 1860; and a tall blond boy named Lee, probably a distant poor relation of all the Virginia Lees, since his family had come to Parkman from the South, in 1870, after the Civil War.

He was really very pleased with his selection, and from there he went to see the owner of the filling station nearest to the cabstand— already he was beginning to think of it as that—where he arranged a deal to get gas and oil and service at a discount in return for doing all his business there.

. . . But of course, all of this—all the business manipulation—was done only after he had seen Dave and signed the contracts. He would never have gone ahead with doing it, if that had not been done first thing.

The day after getting home he had gone around to the Judge's office and picked up the contracts—while the Judge stared at him impassively as if reading the inside of his head, and made him mad again. They talked about a couple of other business deals briefly and passed the time of day just as if they were still friends. As soon as he got back to the store, he had called for Dave at the hotel.

His brother wasnt there, the clerk—Freddy Barker, that one eyed boy there—informed him. He had gone out early, and left word to tell anyone who called that he had gone for a ride down in the country and to take their names and he would call back later.

"Gone for a ride!" Frank said, instinctively thinking of the Judge, although he had just left him. "Gone for a ride with who?"

"By himself," Freddy said. "In his own car, Mr Hirsh."

Frank thanked him and hung up. In his own car! So now he had a car. Well, there was nothing to do but wait. Frank wished he had not stayed so long in Chicago. He wondered how much he paid for it? He wished he had not gone to Chicago at all. Shortly after noon, Dave called him back. He sounded a little more than half tight. Sitting at his desk and looking at the back of Edith Barclay's pretty head, Frank suddenly decided it might be better if he went over to the hotel. He had intended for Dave to come over here. Dave seemed perfectly amenable to the suggestion. He hung up and got the contracts out of his desk and put them in the pocket of his coat.

Dave ushered him into the suite wearing an expensive looking pair of flannel slacks and a garish Hollywood sport shirt. Frank found he was surprised, he had seen him only in his uniform and he had not thought about him ever changing it for civilian clothes. He decided he did not look so hard or tough, in civvies. Dave's face was red and his eyes a little wavery.

"Before we do anything else," Dave said belligerently, "I want to tell you something. I dont have fifty five hundred to put in any more. I only have five thousand. I bought a car."

"For five hundred dollars!"

"Well, no," Dave said, deliberately vaguely. "I had some other cash."

"Whatd you pay?" Frank felt a little relieved.

"Seven fifty."

"What was it?"

"A 1942 Plymouth," Dave said. "Good condition."

"Tires?"

"Good tires."

"I could of got it for you for six fifty," Frank said. "I told you I was a silent partner in the Dodge Agency. —Thats on the q t by the way."

"I didnt want to wait," Dave said belligerently. "I needed it then."

"Well, thats all right," Frank said, getting the contracts out of his pocket. "It just means youll have to take a little less percentage of the business."

"Thats all right with me," Dave said. "But I needed that car."

"Well, theres no need to get mad about it," Frank said. "Its your money. —I see you got some pretty nice clothes, too."

"I didnt have any. I told you. I had some other cash on me. And then I won a little on the horses."

"That 'Bama," Frank said. "Hes a very good pool player; and hes a crackerjack poker player. I dont know how he is with the horses." He looked up from the couch.

"Its his hobby," Dave said testily. "He makes his money on cards and pool. He just plays the horses for fun. He doesnt care whether he wins or not. Doesnt expect to."

"He sure drinks an awful lot," Frank said gently. "More thans good for him. —Well, heres the contracts," he said. He spread the several copies out on the coffee table.

"Dont those have to be changed now?" Dave said curiously.

"No. There arent any amounts mentioned," Frank said. "And I can have my office girl change the percentages later and we can both initial it."

"Dont they have to be notarized or something?" Dave said, in that same curious tone. From where he stood he was watching the papers gingerly with a kind of fascination, as if they were poisonous snakes, and trying to hide his curiosity. He looked ready to jump back if they moved.

"My office girl's a Notary," Frank said. "Shell do it for me later."

"Oh," Dave said. He nodded. "How come theres so many copies?"

"For filing," Frank said. "You get two, I get two, and one for the corporation files."

"Okay. Gimme a pen," Dave said. "Where do I sign?"

"Don't you want to read it first?"

"Hell, no. I wouldnt know what I was readin anyway."

"Well theres one thing I think I ought to read to you," Frank said, getting his pen out of his coat. He turned to the last page and read out loud the "Give or Take" clause he had had the Judge insert, and then explained it, looking up at his younger brother.

"Okay, okay," Dave said. "Gimme the pen. Now where do I sign?"

"This line," Frank said, "and then initial each page. Sign every copy the same way."

In silence, Dave got down on one knee by the coffee table and riffled through the various copies, signing and initialing.

"Sign my life away," he said with a malevolent grin.

He finished, capped the pen, and handed it back to Frank who signed them too.

"Well. Now that thats over with," he said, "what about a drink?"

"I might have *one*," Frank said. "To celebrate."

Dave nodded abruptly and went to the phone table where the liquor and ice were. "I took a trip down around New Lebanon this morning," he said. "Went down to the old farm."

"The Dark Bend River?" Frank said with surprise.

"Yeah." He came back with the glasses. "I almost wish granddad had never sold it."

"I havent been down there for years," Frank said.

Dave grinned malignantly. "I took a case of beer, and a couple sandwiches, and got in my car and went down to see the old family cemetery." He took a long drink from his glass. "But—the beer got warm; and the sandwiches got squashed; and the roads were muddy and I almost got stuck twice; and got all wet wading through the weeds; and then most all the tombstones were either all broken up or fallen over or gone and it was all grown up in bushes under the trees." He grinned again, that same wry, almost bitter, malevolent grin. "Always happens to me."

Frank studied his brother a moment. "Our family took up that land in 1887," he said sort of wonderingly. Then he said, "Grandad didnt sell it; he lost it. It wasnt good land."

"It still aint," Dave said.

Frank took a drink from his glass. "There was one thing I wanted to talk to you about, and that was the name of the cab company. I left it blank until we could talk about it. I think a good name would be Hirsh Brothers Taxi."

"Oh great Christ!" Dave said. "No."

"Well, why not?"

"Because," Dave said viciously.

"Well then, how about Hirsh and Hirsh Cab Company?"

"Look," Dave said. "Youre not startin a big city operation. You want everybody in town laughing at you?"

Frank looked angry. "All right, what would you call it?"

"Hell, I dont know. Red Checker Cab. Or Black and White Cab. Something like that. But dont give it a big pompous name so everybody will be laughin at you."

"I like that Red Checker Cab," Frank said. "We can have a red and black checkered band around the side like the black and white checkered ones in Chicago, you know?" He thought a moment. "Paint the cars yellow."

"Black," Dave said.

"But if we have red and black checkers—". Frank started, then thought again. "Okay. Black. We can run a little green stripe along the outside of the checkers."

"Keep it inconspicuous," Dave nodded, "now look. Now everythings settled, when do I start to work for you?"

"You wont be workin' for me," Frank protested immediately.

"All right then: us."

"Well, Ive got a lot of things to take care of. Rent a building. Get the cars. Hire some drivers. All the paper work. Itll take at least a week or ten days."

"That long?" Dave half-snarled. "Okay, look. Im going to move out of here and get a room in the other hotel. The Douglas. Start savin money, now Im poor again. So you can reach me there when youre ready for me."

"Okay. But theres a lot of these things you could help me with," Frank said.

"Okay. Anything you want me for, just call me at the Douglas," Dave said, as if anxious to have done. "Do you want me to write you a check for five thousand now? Ill have to close out my account. Five thousand's all I got in it."

"Why dont you get a bank draft instead?" Frank said. "Close out your account and have them give you a draft and then sign it over to me."

"Whats the difference?"

"Id just rather you do that," Frank said.

Dave grinned sourly. "So the draft will go through the Cray County Bank, hunh?"

"No," Frank said. "Not at all. Its just better business, thats all."

"All right," Dave said. "Ill send Freddy over to do it before the bank closes this afternoon."

Frank grinned. "Why? Dont you want to go over yourself?"

"No," Dave said. "Not at all. Its just better business, thats all." Again, he grinned that wry, malevolent, selfaccusative grin.

Frank looked at him a moment, and then ducked his head and chuckled. "Touché."

"Okay," Dave said briskly. "Is there anything else?"

"Yes," Frank said, looking up. Carefully he composed his face into an expression of sternness and displeasure. "Yes, there is. There is somethin' else. Just one more thing."

"Whats that?" Dave said, looking as though he wanted to sigh.

"Its about my office girl. Edith Barclay."

Dave turned to stare at him over his glass. "What about her?"

"I want you to stay away from her, thats what. And leave her alone," Frank said, his indignation almost getting away with him.

"Whats the matter?" Dave said, grinning evilly, "you rompin her yourself?"

"No," Frank said primly. "Of course not. Absolutely not. I make it a hard and fast rule never to get involved with any of my help."

"You do, hunh?" Dave said blackly. "Then its a rule you made since I left here."

"What Im tryin' to say is," Frank said, "is that Ive got a damned good office girl there. And I got no intention of losin' her because she gets in some kind of a mess with you."

"Okay," Dave said, still watching him. "But dont try to give me all this crap about you being such a damned plaster saint. Anyway, you flatter me unduly, I think."

"Its possible for some people to learn something from their previous mistakes," Frank said with stiffened dignity, "though you may not be used to people like that."

"Possible," Dave said. "But not probable. And not you. Or me. But you dont need to worry about me bein interested in your office girl. Im not. However, if I was nothin you could say would stop me from tryin. See?"

"I dont care about you," Frank said. "Or what you say. Or what you think. You just keep away from my office girl, you hear?" he said, staring at Dave.

"I hear you," Dave said. "And you heard me: If I want to, I will."

Frank turned and went to the door and then turned back. Dave was looking him coldly, and clearly, and malifically, in a way Frank had never in his life seen him look before. For a moment he was afraid he had gone too far, without somehow realizing it.

"Look," he said from the door. "I dont want us to get in an argument. Weve got a good deal here," he said shaking the contracts. "Im just askin' you to help me out with this girl, thats all," he said almost pleadingly.

"Then ask me," Dave said. "Dont try to tell me."

"I am askin' you."

"You dont need to worry," Dave said. "I got other fish to fry. I aint interested in your office girl."

"Okay, boy," Frank said and grinned and winked, opening the door. "Ill see you. Ill probably need you in the next day or two. Ill call you at the Douglas."

"Okay," Dave said sourly. "Just call me."

Frank nodded, and the last thing he saw as he closed the door was Dave—red faced and wavey eyed—heading for the table where the liquor was.

He walked back to the store. He did not know that after he left, his brother sat down staring blackly at the shuttered windows and let come into his mind what he had been feeling all morning and all afternoon during the interview: wondered, blackly, why in hell he had ever let his money, and himself, get tied up in this damned taxi service that tied him down to Parkman. Frank did know, however,—during the next week, when he was working himself frazzleassed—that his brother Dave was not being of much use to him. Whenever he tried to get in touch with Dave at the other hotel, the Douglas, where he had registered, Dave was not to be found. He was not there, was out somewhere, they didnt know where, could not be got hold of. He even called Dave one night at eleven thirty, and Dave still was not there. That was about the way Dave remembered all his promises, he reflected.

When he got back to the store, Edith was at her desk working. Without pausing to think about it—except to expect her to be deeply grateful to him for having done it—he told her about having talked to Dave. Instead of being grateful, she got madder than hell. Madder than he had ever seen her. And formal.

"If Id known you were going to do that, Mr Hirsh," she said crisply, "Id never have told you in the first place." Her eyes looked like a cloudy sky, threatening lightning flashes.

"I only did it to keep him from takin' advantage of the fact hes my brother and bothering you," Frank said.

"Nobody bothers me, Mr Hirsh," Edith said succinctly. "Ive been taking care of myself ever since my mother died, and that was when I was in high school. I dont need any help to do it, from you or anybody, sir."

"Well; Im sorry; then," Frank said, still taken aback. So she was interested in Dave after all, hunh?

"As long as my work at the store is satisfactory," Edith said, seeming to relent a little, "and I dont cause any talk that might be detrimental to you or the store, I think what I do outside of working hours is my own business. And doesnt need any assistance or looking after—or direction—from you, boss."

"Then you are interested in Dave, hunh?" Frank asked.

"No, sir, I am not," Edith said vehemently. "I told you that. I wouldnt lie to you about it." She softened, and smiled. "I just feel you havent any right to try and take my welfare in hand without consulting me first about it, and taking things which I told you in confidence and using them. After all, I only work at the store eight hours a day."

"I didnt know it was in confidence," Frank said.

"Well it was."

"Okay, Im sorry," Frank said. "Look, heres the contracts. Theres two or three small changes. And I want them notarized."

"Yes, sir," Edith said, taking them.

"Now about the changes," Frank said, thinking he had really put his foot into it that time, and wondering suddenly why the hell he had ever bothered his head about it in the first place?

Well, he would see what happened with Dave. What he was planning, what he hoped, was that once he got the building and lot rented—or leased—he would turn it over to Dave to get fixed up and cleaned up and get the phones in (Frank had decided he wanted two phones in it) and generally get it ready to start operating.

That was not the way it turned out, however, because when he finally got time to get around to calling Dave two or three days later he could not get him. He could not get him the second time he called, either. Nor the time after that. Nor the next time. Nor the next. Nor any other time he tried to reach him. So he finally wound up doing it all himself. As usual.

Dave, as a matter of fact, was having his own troubles. And he was spending a great deal of time at the Frenches' over in Israel trying to solve them. Trying to realize his investment. It was a real job.

CHAPTER 21

DAVE had sat for a long time by himself in the hotelroom, after Frank left with the contracts. As soon as Frank had closed the door he had got himself another drink and sat down in the chair with it. Then, not knowing what to do, he just sat, holding it, and because he happened to be facing that way, looking out the window. When he became aware of it, he got up and closed the venetian blind and sat back down.

It just didnt seem possible. He just couldnt believe he had really signed those contracts, those goddamned contracts. Everything in him had cried out to him not to sign them. Even when he knelt down on the floor by the coffee table with the pen already in his hand. But he had gone ahead and signed them just the same. Why? It was silly, but it was as if he felt he didnt have a right not to sign them after letting everything go this far, and letting Frank think he would sign them. Some obscure vague sense of—of justice, was the only word he could give it; of selfjudgment and selfpunishment. It had somehow forced him to sign them even when he hadnt wanted to. He hadnt wanted to sign them all along, from the very beginning, and yet every time he had found a loophole that might have saved him he had covered it up and plastered it over. It was as if he had made sure from the very beginning to get himself in this position, for the very reason that he hadnt wanted to, in order to punish himself for something. For living, maybe.

And now that he was in it he felt trapped like an animal. He was frightened. With no apparent reason, and without a specific object, he was afraid. Fright spread a network of small sensations over the outside of him, and panic was like another living presence inside his skin. It was himself he was afraid of. Any man who couldnt depend on himself more than that. A man who couldnt trust himself any further than that. A guy who deliberately did things to himself to hurt him in order to punish himself. Christ, he was liable to wind up like Van Gogh cutting off one of his ears or something. Fear made him want to jump up out of the chair and run.

Hell, a contract was like an oath! Once you took it you were bound by it. Even though you changed your mind two minutes later, you were still bound to it. And even if you didnt believe in that stuff yourself the law bound you to it anyway. And so Frank had outsmarted him. With the very thing he had come here not to do.

This was the first time in his life Dave had ever signed a real, bona fide contract, and he felt as if he had just lost another virginity. He had been losing one virginity after another all his life, it seemed, and now here was another one. How many more firsts were there going to be for him to lose? he wondered. Before he was allowed to quit.

There was a constant tendency in him, he found, a constant desire in his neck, to just keep continually shaking his head. To have turned over all his money that way, to have signed himself up to stay in Parkman like that—and for what, to work in a lousy three car taxistand—it was almost more than he could bear to think about. And all of it because he had convinced himself with some crazy logic momentarily that it was worth it—*would* be worth it—to seduce this one woman. Gwen French.

The horrible thing was he thought he had figured it all out logically. But if he had figured it all out coldly and logically beforehand, that night in the snow on the square, now he could prove just as coldly and logically that he had figured it out wrong and should not have done it. That was the horrible, the frightening thing. It didnt leave you *any*-where to stand. Logic. The ability to reason coldly. Heh heh. Yeh. It was a great trait in human beings.

Filled up with an unconsumed energy of disgust and misery and fright and selfaccusation that had suddenly boiled over into a scalding inability to sit still, Dave got up from the chair and began to march around the room, the untouched drink glass in his hand, forgotten.

Well, he had done it now; he was in it. He was hooked through the bag, the fishhook was in his scrotum. He might as well collect his prize. If you can, that is. There was a frenetic desire in him get on with it, get started, get the ball rolling. He was like a man who, having mistakenly agreed to get up on a stage before an audience and make a speech, now insists on going through with it down to the last bitter embarrassing dram of gall, even when everybody else—especially the audience—wishes that in God's name he would stop.

Prowling jitterishly about the room for all the world just like the caged animal he felt himself to be, he happened to look down at his hand and discover the drink glass in it. He stared at it a moment, as if wondering what it could be, and then set it down and went back and sat back down in the chair to think. Gwen French. It wasnt even sensible. But he had to seduce her now. He had to. If he didnt, he wouldnt have anything at all to show for his $5000. What up to now had been one big lark suddenly had become a matter of extreme desperation. Grimly, he set about preparing himself for the first onslaught of the citadel, Bob French's "Last Retreat" in Israel.

But then maybe—a thought which, strangely, had not occurred to him before; had not even been considered among the logic of the original decision—maybe a woman like that was, instead of being easier, actually the hardest type there was to make. She would know her way around, wouldnt she? She wouldnt lose her head, would she? She would be able to pick and choose, wouldnt she? And maybe after all she was really telling him the truth, when she said sex bored her and she wasnt interested in it any more.

Dave slumped down in the big chair, immersed in such a sense of defeat as he had not had in a long, long time. Oh, hell, what he ought to do was just give it all up as a bad job and take the hell off. Leave the money. Let Frank have it. He could always go back to Sister Francine's in North Hollywood—the oasis, he thought—and live off of her and her husband. It would be rough, leaving on the bum like that again, after all these years, with no money now, hitching out across country again, with no prospects. But he could do it. He had done it before. In fact, half of him—more than half—hungered desperately to do just that. Sneak away from this damned town in the black of night. And *never* come back.

There was a consolingly perverse satisfaction in the thought of embracing the defeat you loathed, hugging to you the failure you were ashamed of, and making both of them public by running off. A feeling that you were better off, because then nothing worse could happen to you.

Going back on the bum presented him with deceptively pleasing pictures: Cold nights in boxcars, newspapers wrapped around you under your clothes. Canned beans, which he loved. Wood fires in jungles on drizzling nights. Freedom. No responsibility. And the friendship of the outcast. It was the heritage of the Great Depression. There was a whole generation of men still floating around who had shared that experience.

No, sir! Not without a try, by God! he promised himself stoutly, getting up and striding back and forth across the room. A man had to be a man. A man had to have some spine. A man just couldnt just give up and quit. He wouldnt be a man. He would seduce Gwen French, or know the reason why.

It was over an hour since Frank had left, the signed contracts in his hand, and Dave was already exhausted. Anyway, it wasnt like that on the bum. It was dog eat dog and the devil take the hindmost. He would stay. Here-I-come-ready-or-not, like the kids hollered playing hide and seek. Olly-olly-ocks-in-free.

There were a number of things he had to do first, the packing, the checking out, the getting of the bank draft, mailing it to Frank, the checking in at the fleatrap called the Douglas, all the insufferable infuriating mosquitolike details of remaining alive, alive and solvent. He went about them grudgingly and grimly, with irritation, jealous of the time they took. And all the time his mind gnawed away at him like acid, or as if it were a hungry dog for whom he himself had become his own bone: Why did you do it? Why did you do it? The people whom he had to address he did not even see; and several persons who spoke to him on the street by name he was not even aware of.

Finally, ensconced in his grubby little room at the Douglas where he would live, all of it done, he sat down to call them in Israel. Only, there was no phone in this room. He had to go out in the dark grimy hall where beside a cobwebby unwashed-in-years window there was a box wall phone which you could hardly see to dial. It was a phone he was to become very familiar with in the next year, and he already had a premonition about that as he looked at it. His vision told him he would become as used to it as he would to the Douglas Hotel itself.

The Stephen A Douglas Hotel was a three storey frame structure with a brick front two blocks off the square on Apple Street. All the north-south sidestreets in Parkman were named for fruit trees, all the east-west ones for shade trees. —That is, he thought, the old ones were; but as the town had kept on growing they had run out of tree names and begun naming them for famous persons; so that it was as if there were a line, a demarcation anyone could point to, between the old town and the modern. Sandwiched in between two other business buildings, the Douglas possessed side yards which three men could walk abreast in, if they didnt mind the old tough but unproductive rosebushes, and out in front on the parking two big old laurel oaks whose roots were pushing up the sidewalk, and that had somehow escaped when the rest were cut down. It had once had big yards on both sides, one extending all the way to the corner, with lots of trees, but that was in its heydey. Built after the Civil War, it was the first real hotel in Parkman, and a wood and brick reminder to all that here in Cray County existed a loyal knot of diehard Douglas Democrats who, in spite of A Lincoln's martyrdom, still thought their man The Little Giant should have been elected. There it remained, a memorial to the bullheaded cussedness of a group of conservatives whose conservative descendants all turned into Republicans, for forty years the pride of Parkman, until after the turn of the century and the oil boom a new hotel was built to eclipse it on the site of what is now the Parkman and was called simply The Parkman Hotel until twenty years after that when it was remodeled and renamed the Hotel Francis Parkman and the Stephen A Douglas went still further into decline. Now it was the stopping place and hangout of tenth rate businessmen trying to sell the cheaper stores, down and out oil speculators and prospectors trying to recover the boom, a few people who did nothing, and Dave Hirsh, its big ground floor dining room—former scene of so much gaiety—long since converted into an insurance office. It had once had, also, the distinction of having been Parkman's one and only whorehouse for a while, back during the oil boom, and to the more respectable this aura had never left it. Most of it was still owned by Judge Steven A. Deacon, who had owned most of it then. There were only the two hotels in Parkman to choose from, and Dave could have gotten a much cheaper room at The Parkman but his pride would not let him. If he was going to have to move out of his two room suite, and use a hall phone, he might as well go to the Douglas and really save money.

It was Bob French whom he got on the phone in Israel, when he called. His first reaction was one of intense guilt, and an inability to decide what he should call him—Professor, or Mister, or just Bob. Of course Gwen wouldnt be there, she'd still be out at school. He hadnt thought of that.

"Is Gwen there, Mr French?" he asked respectfully. He didnt know whether to try and disguise his voice and lie about his name, or whether he should have just hung up, without speaking.

"No she isnt," Old Bob's cultured gentle voice came back. "Who is this speaking?"

"This is Dave Hirsh, Mr French," Dave said respectfully. Perhaps the respectfulness was enhanced a lot by his guilty feeling. Whatever it was, he felt very respectful. He hoped the guiltiness didnt sound in his voice.

"Oh, Dave!" Bob French said delightedly. "Weve been wondering what had happened to you. When are you coming over to Israel? —And whats all this Mister business?"

"Well, nothing, Bob," Dave said lamely, feeling even worse. "I just— Well, Gwen invited me over, you know. And I thought I might run over a while tonight," he said guiltily. "If thats all right of course." There was a strong tendency to say "sir."

"Of course its all right," Bob French said. "You must come for dinner. Ive been wanting to talk to you myself too anyway. Gwen isnt home from the school yet, so I dont know what we will be having, but whatever it is you can be sure it will be all right. Ill tell her you called and that youre coming."

"Well, if it will be all right, sir," Dave said lamely.

"But of course it will be all right!" Bob French said. "We usually eat at six thirty or seven. Thats a little early for sophisticated dining, I know," he apologized, "but—"

"*I* wouldnt know," Dave said.

Bob laughed delightedly. "Of course not. Or care. Come around six and we will have a drink or two before, eh?"

"Okay," Dave said, "if youre sure its all right."

"Of course, of course! See you then, then." He hung up.

Dave replaced the receiver of the wall phone in the Y of the hook, and went back into the dismal little room with its one oldfashioned window that looked as though it would always stick. He had turned on the light against the dim of the mid afternoon winter overcast, and a blunt wedge of bright yellow cut out sharply into the blackness of the hall floor at his feet.

He couldnt help wondering if Bob's signing off hadnt been a little abrupt, sort of a dismissal, and he chided himself for this feeling, but it didnt help him much. He felt like a perfect son of a bitch. There was always this feeling of guilt whenever you talked to the father of a girl you planned on making—or already were. It was always work to make yourself look them in the eyes, too. You didnt feel that way about the girl herself, and you didnt feel that way with her mother. But you always expected the father to be mad at you. It must be the old Southern Gentleman horsewhipping myth, he decided.

Feeling like a real son of a bitch, Dave pulled the single chair in the room, a cheap modern one with overstuffed back and seat and straight wood arms, to the window and put his feet up on the sill and sat looking out at the winter afternoon light that was imperceptibly but swiftly dwindling. He had to plan his campaign about Gwen. He was on the second floor—the third was almost never used now any more—and way back here at the back where you could look out behind the building alongside you could see trees. Minus their leaves, except for one or two oaks he could see, they spread their etched black filigree against the gray of the sky, moving with astonishing resilience in the wind that was rising.

If they would just understand that he had to do it, he burst out painfully in his mind. If they would just understand that. Why he had to do it. And what it meant. How important it was. His whole selfrespect and integrity was at stake. If they just knew that. But that wasnt it either. At all. He didnt want her to just give it to him. He didnt want her to just let him have it to save his integrity. That wouldnt save it. That would lose it.

There were two things he knew of that he could use on her with powerful effect, he felt. One of these was his writing. Not what he had written, but what he might write. She would give a good bit, he felt, to be able to feel it was she who had got him back to writing. And he still had this idea for this comic combat novel. Which he did not intend to write. But he could let her think he did. He was even willing to go clear to the point of actually doing some work on it—for a while—if it would help any. And not only that, it would give him an excuse to spend a lot more time with her. If she actually felt that she was responsible for him going back to work and writing a novel, it was going to have such a powerful effect on her affections for Dave Hirsh that even she the sexually blasé might have a hard time to keep from falling in love with him.

Because he was going to have to make her fall in love with him. He was convinced of that. Had been all along. Excitement welled up in him. It had been a long time since anybody was in love with him, desperately, dangerously in love with him. It was a wonderful feeling, to have someone in love with you like that. And she was capable of it, of that kind of love. And after all, it wasnt as if he were hurting her any.

The other thing was the poem. He had not thought about it in quite a while—not since France in fact, where he had been in the hospital a while after the Bulge and had used it on one of the Red Cross girls who was an intellectual. It was the best of all the poetry he had ever written and had been written in 1939 in Los Angeles. It was called Hunger and had been written to Harriet Bowman, during one of his last desperate efforts to seduce her at least once before she married her goddamned lawyer, and it hadnt worked. But it had worked a lot of times since then. He had never used it on another woman, outside of Harriet Bowman, that it hadnt worked with. It had never been published because only they two knew about it and he had wanted to keep it private, and then later, when he discovered how really valuable it was, he decided to keep it instead of publishing it someplace for five dollars and taking a chance that some woman he pretended to write it for later might already have seen it somewhere. Take Gwen French, for instance; if he had ever published it she would certainly have seen it.

It was funny, Dave thought, moving his feet on the windowsill and looking out at the trees, but it seemed that everything he had ever written in his life had been written to impress some damned woman or other.

It had always worked, and he had used it exactly seven times. Probably, he thought guessing, it was the sincerity in it. It had the sincerity. He didnt use it oftener because he didnt want to waste it, and he had a superstition that it was like a rifle with a clip in it and there were only just so many shots in the magazine.

He couldnt write a new poem like that about love now, he told himself somberly; and he really believed it. He couldnt do it because he didnt have the sincerity. You had to be young to have that sincerity about love, he told himself. Wally Dennis could write a poem like that.

Quite suddenly he was frightened again, a deep fright amounting almost to panic, at what he was doing. How here he was, in this town, this miserable dismal town, where he had never intended to be, in this crappy horrible little room in this ancient rundown hotel, with not enough money to last him a week, preparing himself carefully to attempt to seduce a woman whom he was not even interested in, who he was already more than half convinced was far too sophisticated for him to even have a chance with, who had slept around so much so long it would take a much smoother sharpy than himself to interest her. He hated cheap, crappy, horrible things and places, and he hated living cheap and crappy and horrible. It was a phobia left over from the years with carnivals and circuses. The whole thing was insane. He was insane. If Frank didnt come through with this taxi service thing now, he wouldnt even have a job.

He wasnt sure which way to go about using the poem on her. There were two, and he could not decide which. She was a pretty smart woman. The more powerful and dramatic method was to seem to write the poem right in front of them; get thoughtful, ask for paper and pencil, and— with proper hesitations every now and then for thinking—pretend to create the poem right there. But this called for a certain acting ability, and he was not sure he could bring that off in front of her; she might see through him. He had used this method four of the seven times, and it always created a very powerful and emotional effect; but Gwen French was smarter than most of the other intellectual women hed used it on. The other way was to—usually after some evening of particularly heavy lovemaking which ended in frustration—to show up with the poem next day and say hed written it that night when he got home, had sat up all night writing it; but she was so damned smart—and skeptical —she would probably immediately assume he had had it all along. He could not make up his mind which to do. He copied the poem over three times, and then said it over in his mind until he was sure he had even the punctuation, which was important, and the nearer it got to time for him to go the more nervous and upset he got. Outside, it had got completely dark by five o'clock, and he could not see the trees any more.

All he could see was the tailend of the next building, on his right, on whose second floor the lights were on. It was apparently an upstairs apartment. Further on toward the center of town he could see lights on second and third storeys of other buildings. He ought to unpack; he had unpacked nothing but the poem, not even his new bags. And he hadnt bathed today. But here the bath was up at the other end of the hall, so instead he turned off his own light and stood by the window, his heart giving a little jump when he thought he might perhaps see something sexual. What he saw instead was a woman with nice breasts and fairly nice figure but stringy hair cooking supper on an unclean stove in a stark unornamented room. She was frying potatoes and some meat unenthusiastically, and as he watched her husband came in and made a kissing motion at the side of her head dutifully and sat down at the table and looked at her expectantly. Dave could not help thinking of Thoreau's great line.

Most men lead lives of quiet desperation.

Yeh. Most men lead lives of desperate crappiness. He turned his light back on. He, like they, had a single bare bulb in the ceiling. Except for the little dime store bedtable lamp. He would have to get himself a reading lamp, if he stayed here very long.

It was five thirty and he decided he should call them at Israel again. He did not know why. Something just told him he should, and he went out in the hall. The moment the phone was answered at the other end he wondered why he had and wished he hadnt. It was Gwen who answered this time, and when she said hello with that quiet childlike eagerness that lay just under her voice, he suddenly remembered her. Remembered how she looked and the way her face moved and what she was like inside. It was as if he had forgotten her all this time.

"This is Dave," he said.

"Yes? What is it. Is something wrong?" Gwen said.

"Oh, no," Dave said lamely. "But I— Well, I— I just wanted to call and see if it was all right with you if I came over." It didnt sound reasonable, even to him.

"Why, of course its all right!" Gwen said in a surprised voice. "Didnt Dad tell you it was all right? We're both here."

"Yes. He told me. But I wanted to be sure it was all right with you."

"Of course its all right with me. I invited you to come over, didnt I?" She paused. "What are you doing?" she added alertly; "are you sitting over there stewing yourself into something? If you are, stop it right now."

"Oh, no," Dave said.

"You writers!"

"I just got through moving from the Parkman, you see," Dave said, "and I just wanted to call and see if it was still all right with you if I came."

"You moved from the Parkman? Where are you staying?"

"The Douglas."

"Oh, no! Not that place!"

"And whats wrong with the Douglas?" Dave demanded.

"Well, its shelter," Gwen French said. "But thats about all you can say for it."

"Do you like poetry?" Dave said suddenly.

There was a pause. "Of course. I love poetry." Another pause. "Though maybe not quite as much as I used to when I was younger. I never seem to have time to— Why?"

"I thought I might bring some of my poetry over with me to show you," Dave said abortively, some strange compulsion working in him to tempt fate; give fate a hostage; but the moment he said it he was sorry.

He was proud: If he could still work the poem on her after giving himself a handicap like this, he would know he was good. But he was also sorry: Because he might not be able to.

"I didnt know youd written very much poetry," Gwen said. "Ive scrounged up a few in old West Coast magazines but not many."

"I havent," Dave said, desperate now that he had been so foolish, and casting around for some way to save himself; maybe he could turn it to advantage? "And only a little bit of it was ever published. I just, you know. Every now and then when something hits me I just write it down —or used to—just so I can get rid of it," he said, and added, "Its not very good poetry."

"And you still say youre not a writer!"

"Im not."

"No. I can see clearly that youre not," Gwen said. "Well bring it along, by all means. Dad and I would both like to see it."

"Ill see how I feel when I come," Dave said. "Maybe Ill bring it and maybe I wont."

"I dont know whats eating on you," Gwen said. "But something is."

"I just remembered your dad was a poet," Dave said.

"Its more than that. Now dont you just sit over there and work yourself into some miserable stew. Its foolish. And it never does any good. How soon are you coming?"

"In just a little bit."

"All right," Gwen said. "Ill see you—in half an hour? Drive carefully."

"Do what?" Dave said dumbly. "Oh. Oh, I will."

He hung up slowly and went back in the room, where the wedge of yellow light still bit at him across the blackness of the hall, and took an old spiral Steno Notebook from one of the zippered pockets of the B-4 bag, and stood, riffling through it. It was pretty battered, and only a few pages short of being full. He did not know whether to take it now or not, now that he had mentioned it to her. Finally he decided, not to.

He put the notebook back in the pocket and carefully zipped it shut. Here was almost all the poetry he had written in his life, all of it written in the Army. All his other stuff, including copies of all his published work, he had left with Francine in Hollywood. Except the one poem, Hunger. He stood looking at the bulging zippered pocket for a moment, and then went and got the typed copy of the love poem off the rickety little table.

Standing in the center of the room, his eyes closed, he said it over to himself one last time and then checked it against the paper. It checked. He folded it back up carefully along the cracking folds and tucked it back in the Hemingway Portable between The Short, Happy Life of Francis Macomber and The Snows of Kilimanjaro. He put the book back with the others. Then he got his topcoat and turned off the light. Across the way, his friends were through with supper now because the dirty dishes sat on the table where they had left them.

He locked the door behind him and went down into the freshening wind to his car which he had had to park across the street this afternoon, facing back toward Wernz Avenue the mainstreet. Everything else had been full then.

CHAPTER 22

SLOWING gradually, he drove up the long high shallowrising earthen ramp that approached the new bridge. The towering, aluminum painted bridge members and supports caught the light from the little Plymouth's headlights, looming high on up above it into the dark. Down below him on the south side to his right he could see the miniature lighted windows of the houses in the town.

Behind him was the five miles to Israel from Parkman, which he would come to know so well, running out across the low sandy riverbottom plain flat as the palm of your hand from the hill where Parkman sat to the long-sweeping almost imperceptible rise where Israel perched on its bluff above the river. This inbetween had once been swampy bottomland, and even now in the latterdays of the levees the bigger floods would put it under a foot of water and get it wet. It was good farm land if it got enough rain. And if the river didnt get out of hand

and drown the corn. The Route 40 highway ran straight as a string across it, and the big diesels labored roaring over it, belching and gagging at the richness of their fuel, sighing disgustedly when they had to brake, a perpetual neverending shuttle of goods and merchandise. He passed three of them on his way over.

He had never seen the new bridge before, not to notice, anyway. Its construction had changed the whole face of the land. Nothing looked familiar any more. Not quite half way to the top of the approach, he turned off down the one lane Israel cutoff that ran down along its side, and it was suddenly like entering another world. As if you had driven your car through a time machine operated by the DAR that set you down in the exact same spot, only now it was a hundred and fifty years ago, when they hadnt had bridges like this, then. There were several discrepancies to the effect—a couple of grubby little filling stations trying to look modern, the DAR sign itself at the cutoff, the neon light of a little tavern advertising beer, the one lane mate to the cutoff that joined it at the bottom to form a Y and would take you back up to the world you knew when you were ready—but in spite of these he had an eerie feeling that this was the only automobile he would find down here and everybody else would be driving horses and every car he did see shocked him with surprise to see it. And the further in you went the stronger the feeling was.

Everything looked old. Old little houses, old big houses, a few of them Southern Colonials with porticoes, a number of the later 1880s ones gingerbreaded and with their own gingerbreaded livery barns with cupolas but converted to makeshift garages now. Old trees. Huge splayfingers elms, oaks four feet across, maples almost as big, dotting old lawns that sloped magnanimously down to the two lane street which had once been the highway. And always, over on the left, out at the north edge of town, towering over everything, the bridge, the new bridge.

The bridge dominated everything. You were always aware of it, of its bulk there, even when you could not see it in the dark like now. High up over the town, way out at the northern edge, where the single little business street became a gravel road out into the country, and where it soared above two little houses on its concrete bastions, it flung its spans across the river into Indiana and made everything else look small. You could not be outdoors anywhere in the town without being conscious of its mass there. Like a mountain. Or an ocean that you lived beside.

Dave drove slowly on downtown, just as aware of it a quarter of a mile away now as he had been right beside it, past the old rosebrick courthouse which did not have a square around it as in Parkman but was two blocks back off the single business street on the riverbluff, as if whoever had built it there in the old days had expected the town to grow up around it quickly and make its own square because obviously any town situated on the trade artery of the river like it was, was bound and declared to grow. It was a beautiful old building, simple and austere in its Revolutionary Period style like those courthouses you saw in Virginia and Pennsylvania, from which it had been copied. The second huge DAR sign out in front could not take away from it, nor could it destroy his feeling of having moved back in time.

Down closer to town the weathering old houses were smaller and much closer together, but they did not change the feeling of being in another world. Old saltbox clapboard houses, painted and repainted or left unpainted, white; God alone knew when they had been built. Every now and then you would see a new one, which looked out of place and shocked you in the same way seeing cars did, but there werent many. A lot of retired rich bottomland farmers lived here, Bob French had said, most of them ex-Kentuckians. Gradually they had formed a sort of colony, as Kentuckians will. But Israel was not called a rich town, as Parkman was, because these people didnt realize they were rich and hence didnt make a point of being wealthy. Basically country people, they held their constant family reunions, had fox drives, hunted coon in the bottoms with their dogs, hunted everything else in season, checked their crops their sons in law put out for them with tractors, fished the rest of the time, and in the evenings played cards at their own American Legion Post at which they were all devout staunch members without having any more idea of national Legion policy than did most Legionnaires, and then returned home to their wives in their old little houses or their old big houses, and did not realize—or if they did, paid no attention—that they were history, and were living on historic ground. Israel had been the first French furtraders' landing up river that the British had taken over and developed after the capture of Vincennes and Cahokia, and George Rogers Clark paused there just long enough to take it over on his way to Vincennes.

It was strange, Dave thought; he had been coming over here all the time when he was a kid, and he had never realized it was historic either. Until just now. Maybe it was because of the way Bob French had talked about it so, that night at Frank's, excitedly, lovingly. Or maybe it was just that you had to go away for a long time and then come back, in order to realize your home country had as many stories and romantic castles and ruined mansions as Hawthorne's Massachusetts or Faulkner's Mississippi. It was a strange mood he was in, and he couldnt shake it. He would have to, before he got to the Frenches. Funny, in all the times he had been over here in Israel, he had never once been inside the old courthouse museum. He would have to go. Sometime.

If they just had taste, he thought snobbishly, thinking of the huge DAR sign.

He turned left toward the black loom of the bridge when he reached the single business street. There were three or four blocks of little business houses side by side along it, mostly one storey, mostly clapboard. Bob French's house was right at the end of the business section on the river side of the street, separated from the last little business building by the cinder alley that deadened fifty yards back at the bluff. The driveway entrance was at the corner, and over it the old wrought iron gate to which Bob had had the local blacksmith add his name for it in twisted iron. *Last Retreat*. From back in among the trees downstairs lights shone out.

Dave remembered it all very clearly, now he saw it. The old brick house with its long narrow corniced windows, the steep tinned mansard roof with projecting dormered windows, and the little front porch with its small less-than-one-storey Ionic columns which always looked as though the builder had put this up last when he was running out of money. He remembered it well. This same cinder alley right here was one of the places out on the bluff where they had used to park with their homebrew beer, in high school. He had always thought very rich people must live there.

He turned in under the gate, the little Plymouth's wheels grinding in the crushed rock driveway. The trees were, as Bob described, very large and a number of them showed the mottled splotchy bark of sycamores in the light of his headlights. Before he could get stopped and cut the motor in the parking space up next to the house, a side door opened throwing light out across the yard.

"Right here!" Gwen French's voice called to him. "Come in this way!"

He turned off the ignition and pulled the key and followed along the little brick walk to where she stood in the doorway, wondering if this could be taken as a propitious sign—that she obviously had been watching for him; maybe even anxiously?

"Well, youre a sight for sore eyes!" Gwen smiled gaily, looking him over. "Come on in. You look all right." She led him inside. "I heard by the grapevine that you must have had yourself quite a time in Indianapolis with that gambler 'Bama. So I didnt know whether to expect you healthy and all in one piece or not," she said merrily.

"Hello, Gwen, how are you," he muttered selfeffacingly. Of a sudden, shyness had overtaken him again. He felt that she could see through him and his patently obvious designs upon her. They were on a landing of a staircase that went down into the high vaulted darkness of the cellar, he noticed, while thinking unhappily that she didnt sound very jealous. She led him up several steps into a room then, stepping aside for him to enter first, and what he saw had the effect of bringing him to a standstill in the doorway momentarily. He had to consciously make himself step on inside. Behind him Gwen followed him on in, smiling gaily.

"I was just cooking," she said merrily. "From the way you talked on the phone I didnt know when youd get here. Or Id have had it ready now." She went on past him to the stove.

They were in the kitchen. But what a kitchen! It was at least twenty five feet wide, and it must have been all of fifty or sixty feet long. It was enormous. Cupboards and cabinets—and at the near end, kitchen equipment—encroached upon its size only a little; a not unusually high ceiling added to the impression of immense length; five great support beams running crossways of the room added to it, too. Dave had the sudden impression he was staring down a huge hall in a medieval castle. And at the far end of this diminishing perspective of parallel walls was a big brick fireplace painted white, fully five feet high by seven or eight feet long, book shelves all around it, and in which a brightly blazing fire cheerfully ate its way into a huge backlog. Beside it, his head turned this way, looking as if he had carefully posed himself that way, sat Bob French grinning at him.

"Well, what do you think of our kitchen?" he said delightedly, like a child showing off a new bicycle. "Youre seeing it from the best place to see it," he added, getting up.

Dave couldnt help grinning; it was obvious old Bob had posed himself there deliberately, not vainly but thoughtfully, to give the perspective and size of a human figure in the room, and transmit the proper effect of the size. Bob, coming down toward him, returned his grin with a smile that was as understanding as the grin.

"Its beautiful," Dave said sincerely, "very beautiful." And it was, too. Exactly that. It was like a haven, like a haven on a snowy blowing freezing night. Like in one of those oldfashioned Christmas card pictures you always loved to look at but didnt much believe in places like that any more.

The far end had been arranged around the fireplace, in which still hung several old wroughtiron cranes. Two not expensive looking divans sat facing each other at right angles to the fireplace in front of it, the width of the fireplace apart, between them a low round coffeetable. Back of these with barely room to pass, a large dark heavy antique table with massive turned legs and ladderback chairs around it, set for dinner with heavy thick restaurant china, that oldfashioned olivegreen ware like you used to see in Chinese restaurants years ago. Under almost all of this furniture, with vivid blocks and angles of contrasting colors, was the biggest Indian rug Dave had ever seen. It stretched almost from wall to wall. On its edges were two reading chairs with floor lamps beside them. In one corner sat a big console radio-phonograph with shelves of records built around it. Bookcases stood along the sidewalls and over them near the ceiling were hung oldfashioned plate rails holding a motley collection of old pewter and German steins and handpainted plates painted with what Dave knew must be fat monks or drinking or hunting scenes. It was a room out of any artistic temperament's dream; he had used to dream of rooms like this himself, once. Only he had never expected to have one.

"Its not as expensive as you might think," Bob grinned at him, as if reading his mind. "We did most of the work on it ourselves. And we already had most of the furnishings, in the family you know. And of course we already had the room here to begin with."

"I told him he could not put books in the kitchen because the grease from the cooking would ruin them. But he went ahead and did it anyway," Gwen smiled dryly. "But I did get him to promise to keep them down at the other end." Standing at the kitchen counter, she was cutting lettuce, and some tomatoes from a long square cardboard container that said they came from Florida, into a big heavy bowl of the same olivegreen-with-white-insides ware that was on the table, her hands moving swiftly. On the stove was a single big pot, boiling.

"Whats a fireplace without books?" Bob grinned. He shook hands with Dave. "I did all the carpentry myself," he said proudly, "I built all these shelves and cupboards. Youll have a Martini I imagine, wont you, Dave?"

"Yes," Dave said. "Yes, thanks. Its a beautiful place," he said simply; there wasnt anything else to say, or any better way to say it.

"It really is you know," Bob said shyly. He went off to the bar, down at the other end of the long counter.

Dave watched him go, then looked back at the room hungrily. The bad mood he had had sitting in the crummy cheap hotelroom in Parkman, coupled to that strange feeling of having moved back in time when he drove down off the highway into Israel, and then feeling like that to walk into the beauty and romance and graciousness of this place, all of it together was almost too much to keep up with. He could not escape a sudden feeling that here suddenly for the first time in his life of thirty seven years he had walked into a place that was safe. And the more he looked at it, the stronger the feeling became. Just safe. That was the only word. Safe from what? He tried to analyze from what, but he could come up with only the vaguest of generalities. Safe from the savageries of frightened men. Safe from the witch burnings and destructions of people determined by their guilts to prove themselves unguilty. Safe from the frightful insanities of reason and honor and justice and happiness and—and love. Yes, love. Especially love. Safe and secure and beautiful and—and reasonable. He felt as though all his life until he walked in here he had been frightened, frightened and

afraid and full of terror, and hungry and thirsty and sleepy and itchy
and exhausted and—and—whatever else there was, he finished lamely.

"You seem surprised," Gwen said merrily, smiling at him over her
shoulder. "What did you expect? To find us living in some falling down
Southern mansion?"

"We were really only joking about the wind coming through the
walls you know," Bob said from the other end of the counter.

"No, but I certainly didnt expect anything like this," Dave said.
It was as if all those other things, those fears and terrors, had suddenly
relaxed allowing him to expand himself with these people, expand his
lungs, like a man coming in out of the weather into a warm house on a
freezing cold day. It wasnt only the place. It was them too. Both of
them. That they could have made it, he thought exuberantly. That
they could have *created* it, this place. In Parkman Illinois! That anyone
of their depth and sensitivity, which was so much like his own, he
thought, could even have had an *opportunity* to create this place in
Parkman Illinois. You didnt expect to find people like yourself in Parkman Illinois, he thought quite frankly.

He felt warm, and confident, and expanding, down in the very deep
bottom of his lungs as he filled his chest.

"Do you mind if I look around a little?" he said. Poor Villon, he
thought, poor Francois the conny-catcher, the doddipol Gnat-Snatcher,
in his Paris squalor, and his fear of the Patrol, and the gibbet of Mont-
faucon always touching him lightly on the shoulder—what he wouldnt
have given to be here. Him and his insane disease of love, love, love,
and his Katherine de Vausselles.

"Its almost medieval," he said.

"It is rather, in a way," Bob said, pleased, from down at the bar.

Dave had a ridiculous, almost tearful desire to please him, to make
him feel good. "Ive seen old kitchens in Nuremberg and Munich that
looked almost like this," he said thinking that it wasnt so false at that.

"Oh, say! I *am* flattered," Bob said. "You mention Nuremberg. A
great many of my things here came from Bavaria. I went to school over
there you know," he said almost apologetically.

"Yes, I knew," Dave said. He turned to look at Gwen. She had just
squatted down to get something out of a cupboard.

Her back was to him, as she bent forward, squatting. The fresh-
looking housedress she had on was tucked up under her knees, drawing
its skirt tight over the female width of her hips, outlining the swelling
twin roundnesses of her buttocks there, the slack of them full stretched
now inside the flowered material, and separated by the cleft between
them which ran on underneath, disappearing.

Like two desert hillocks in California outlined against the sky, he
thought staring,—separated by a steeply eroded, brushgrown arroyo wash.

She pushed things around inside the cupboard, looking for whatever it was she was searching for.

God, he thought exuberantly. It was strange, wasnt it, how when you got up very close to women they were much bigger all over than they looked from a distance.

Especially love; he thought. If a man could just live here in this place, just stay here alone and live here, he could be free of the insanity of love. Katherine de Vauselles. Love was only loneliness. Love was only fear. If he could just live here, alone, *all* alone, without anyone, he could be serene, could make his life serene. I could be sane, he thought. God! to find a place like this in Parkman Illinois.

God, to find hips like this in Parkman Illinois! he thought as she straightened up.

Gwen had turned around from the counter and was standing looking at him.

"Whats the matter?" he said.

"Nothing," she said, and turned back to the stove.

"Its really a beautiful place," he said hollowly.

"Thank you," Gwen said, not looking up from her work on the counter.

Dave turned quickly to look at something else. Sandwiched in amongst all the more modern kitchen fixtures was an oldfashioned brick cooking fireplace. He looked at this. On the inside wall, also painted white, its hearth crotch high, with a row of bricks laid end-to to make both the hearth and the arched crown, it was a beauty, and in it—or rather over it—the castiron door of an old old built in oven. On the white brick wall around it hung an ancient set of solid heavy gauge copper skillets crudely riveted onto some kind of lead alloy handles, eight in all, ranging in size from one that was almost three feet across and looked like a small table down to a little two-egg one. Near them hung a huge matching teakettle on an old iron hook in the wall. Bob French put a filled Martini glass in his hand from beside him.

"I got those at a logging camp in Wisconsin once, years ago," he said. "Our fishing party stopped there. They were actually using them. I had to go to town and buy a set of iron ones for them before theyd sell me these." He laughed; "then I had to draft my fishing friends to help me get them out."

"Theyre beautiful," Dave said. Again, like with everything else here, he thought, they fit.

"We *still* use them," Gwen said, almost angrily. "All except the big one. I dont believe in not using things," she said positively. She frowned at both of them as if she expected to argue, and there was a look of angry irritation, inarticulate and objectless, on her face. Dave thought he knew why, but then it was gone and she turned around to them cocking her head on one side.

"You know, some man made those," she said with a kind of wistful thoughtfulness. "Some lumberjack, up in Wisconsin probably, sitting out in the woods somewhere day after day by himself, working on them. He was probably big and hairy and ugly and awkward; and he probably put everything he ever felt about life and beauty and frustration into the making of them. Hes probably dead now, whoever he was." She moved, and started to go on with her work. "Isnt it strange? Here they still are, in our kitchen, and we use them." Her voice sounded sad, but her hands moved swiftly just the same, working. "We should use them."

Bob was smiling at her affectionately.

And perhaps a little quizzically, Dave thought.

"You see," Bob explained turning to him, "this room was their original kitchen here. They had house slaves you know of course to do the work. They did most of their cooking in the big fireplace down at the other end, and used this smaller one here for baking chiefly and for short orders you know, sort of I guess. The slaves of course ate all their meals here which is one reason the room is so big I imagine. How is your Martini?" he smiled. "I wasnt sure I made it dry enough for you."

Dave looked down at the glass in his hand and then took a sip from it. "Fine," he said. "Fine. Couldnt be better." This was true, too. But right now, here, he felt he would have liked it if it had been half Vermouth.

"Good," Bob said, rubbing his hands together and looking inordinately pleased, "good. I cant drink them much any more," he said ruefully. "Except when I go out somewhere. Then I am forced to. But Im having a Manhattan, and so is Gwen, so dont feel alone. —all right?" He strode off on his long legs back down to the counter bar, to mix the others.

"Ill have mine down there, Dad," Gwen said. "Dont you want to go down and sit by the fire, Dave?"

"Im fine," Dave said, and grinned at her fetchingly, and provocatively, to give it a double meaning. "Im fine right here."

She didnt answer, but stared at him from the stove noncommittally, and somberly.

Dave was a little amazed at his own audacity. All at once, for no reason, the old charm—the old engaging woman-charm—had begun to flow up through him. It was exactly what he needed, but he wasnt sure how long it would last. Sometimes it didnt last very long. Loin-fired, he could feel it flowing along his arteries and veins all through him like melted butter, and spilling out through his eyes and face and voice. It wasnt something he could control or call up at will whenever he wanted it; maybe some people could but he couldnt. It came or went in him according to its own private set of rules, paying absolutely no attention to him or his preferences, and usually those rules were based on confidence. So now he tried with his mind to keep it coming, and to put no stopgaps or stumbling blocks in its path before he got a chance to use it.

The old loin-heated, loin-melted charm and ability *to* charm. It came bursting out of you sometimes when you least expected it. It was composed of equal parts male cockiness and genuine warmth, mixed with sudden confidence, and it was a sort of basic tenet of the calculated conspiracy between men and women which both sides agreed to secretly and without speaking of and used as a basis of association, and without which no profitable understanding could be concluded. And when you had it—well, for a while you felt you could do anything. And women were affected by it. Because by the terms of the tacit conspiracy that no one ever talked about, it was what women had a right to demand of a man; to be charmed; if they were going to play. It wasnt what you said, or how, so much as it was whether the charm was genuine. Above all it had to be genuine. And it was notoriously prone to just capriciously decide to go away in the middle of a sentence, leaving you there. And no amount of superlative acting could fake it, then, and women always knew it was gone, because they were always suspiciously on the lookout for anything they could construe as the slightest sign of insincerity anyway.

In the first place you had to love women, generally and individually, love them strongly. Or maybe you just had to love yourself.

Dave took another sip from the glass in his hand and looked around, feeling the same selfwarmed selfconfident selfexpansion the house had made him feel. Probably that was what was responsible for the charm he was about to use. On the end wall long open shelves of canned goods and jarred spices added the bright gaiety of their colored labels to the effect. In the center of the floor space at this cooking end stood an old worn-dull aluminum cook's table that must have come out of some restaurant kitchen somewhere, with rows of utensils hanging from its double rack. Everything; everything seemed to fit. He noticed there was one of the brandnew just-on-the-market automatic dishwashers, too, set in beside the sink. It was the only piece of equipment in the whole place that *was* brand new. But even it seemed to fit. Gwen was no longer watching him in that way she had been, which was somewhat though not quite like a paralyzed animal watching a snake, but had turned back to her cooking.

If he could just keep the confidence, which meant the charm that came along with it. All you had to do was believe you were attractive. But that was the hardest thing to do. And for a man who was as ugly as he was . . . DONT THINK THAT! Come on now.

Holding his drink he leaned on his elbow on the counter, a little ways down from the stove, and let the melted butter bubble out, roll out, of him.

"Do you ever use that?" he asked, grinning the charm grin, and nodded at the brick oven. There were wood ashes in its firebox.

"Once in a while," Gwen said, looking up, and then looking right back down. "Its very good for Bostonbaked beans and big roasts and things like that. Barbecues. But its a lot of fuss and work to use it." She bent, long haired, competent, with that attractive sort of rawboned look she had that it seemed he had forgotten also until now, just as he had forgotten her voice, and opened the stove's oven to look inside.

Bent over that way as she was, this time she turned her back away from him, he noticed. Looking at her Dave had the same feeling hed had not long before observing Edith Barclay in Smitty's Bar and it reflected itself in the same thought, I could really love this woman!

Gwen straightened up obliviously. This time when she looked at him she smiled, sort of involuntarily, her eyes going out of focus with shyness that was not so much shyness as excited selfawareness, and when she moved it was with a conscious grace, selfknown, selfseen, as in a mirror.

It was working! Dave thought exuberantly, in spite of all her resolutions, and in spite of all her promises of disinterest; and even though she knew her way around plenty, this gal. A smell of rich meat and of some spice or other had flowed out of the oven into the room and this seemed too to belong there, to fit exactly like everything else. She likes for me to look at it, he thought, even if she does turn it the other way.

"Whatre you cooking?" he said intimately.

"Stuffed beef hearts. Do you like them?"

"I dont know. I never ate them."

"Youll like these," she promised smiling, and for a moment looked him fully and directly in the eyes. Then she looked down at her watch, and moved—gracefully, selfawarely—to turn off the burner under the single boiling pot that had been boiling away ever since he had come in. Holding the lid as a strainer, she poured the water off of what when she removed the lid was disclosed to be over a dozen huge potatoes, both Irish and sweet potatoes. Taking a big spoon she began to put some of both into the oven with the meat, bending again this time as before with her back away from him. Then, looking up and seeing the surprised look all those potatoes had brought to Dave's face, she laughed, tinklingly, merrily, selfheard, selflistened-to.

"You wont have to eat all these tonight," Gwen said gaily, getting another one on the spoon. "You dont know much about cooking, do you?"

"Oh, a little bit," Dave grinned. "Why?"

"You thought I was going to serve all of these, didnt you? But I always boil a big batch when I boil them," Gwen smiled up at him, her eyes squinted with that shyness that was not really shyness. "It saves me time, you see, and whats left over I keep in the icebox. The Idahoes become hashbrowns or I use them in soup or hash." For a moment, but just for a moment, her eyes changed; the shy squint disappeared, and they opened wide, looking up at him from the oven openly in a way that was intimate, and inviting, and made the smile still on her face below them suddenly flirtatious. "And the sweet potatoes I fry."

"Fried sweet potatoes?" Dave said softly, leaning on the countertop.

"Its Southern," Gwen laughed shyly. "Youve never tasted anything good until youve eaten cold sliced leftover sweet potatoes fried in butter and sprinkled all over with sugar." She had put four of the huge potatoes, two of each, into the oven. She straightened and shut the door.

"You always boil baked potatoes first?" Dave grinned softly, looking into her face.

Gwen nodded and grinned shyly. "Again, it saves me time. Im not one of these cooks who likes to spend hours and hours in the kitchen making a meal. And also, boiling them first makes them bake moist."

"Oh," Dave said. He straightened himself a little, languidly, and sipped at his drink, watching her over the rim of the glass openly. It was funny, the myriads of implications you could put into one word, a word that didnt say or mean anything.

Still with that squint of shyness looking at him that was not really shyness but embarrassed selfpleasure, Gwen turned and walked down to the other end of the counter by the door, not the one they had come in by but another one in the other corner, she walking rawboned and leggy with that almost masculine angularity, but with those definitely female hips. Hips she was aware of and enjoying now, obviously. She was having a flirtation as much as he was now. And she knew how to play it, he thought; perfectly. She wasnt beautiful, at least you never thought of her as beautiful when you were away from her, but when you were with her she was beautiful.

"Whatre you fixin now?" he said.

"Apples," Gwen said gaily and commandingly. "And now you go on down to the other end and talk to Dad and leave me alone until I get this food fixed. Or Ill never get it fixed," she laughed selfconsciously. "We will be ready to eat in just a very few minutes."

"Okay," Dave muttered selfeffacingly. It was all set. There was a note almost of promise in her voice and he reflected how easy it was, really, once your mood was right. But at the same time he was suddenly aware of Bob French, still standing down at the other end of the counter, still mixing on his Manhattans. It seemed to be *taking* him a very long time. He had completely forgotten he was here. He turned quickly, jabbed by the pin of memory, and started down the long room toward him.

"Guinevere, your drink is ready!" Bob called from the other end of the counter almost immediately.

"Put it on the coffeetable, and Ill get it in a little bit," she said from up at her end.

"It may get warm," he cautioned.

"All right," she said. "Ill get it in just a minute."

Dave walked on down the long length of the room to him where he stood beside the end of the inside counter which served as the bar, holding the two red tinged drinks with their Maraschino cherries in them.

"Lets sit down," Bob said. Then he grinned delightedly, childishly. "By the fire!" It was impossible to tell whether he had followed anything that had gone on up the counter or not. He didnt seem to have. But a man of his astuteness— Dave looked at his face to see if he could read it.

"Let me put some records on," Bob said gently, and went to the console where two large thick albums were set up neatly on its top. "Ive been listening to Bach's The Art of the Fugue a lot lately," he said, in that almost apologetic way he had whenever he spoke of anything that might be construed as culture, "and I have it out, here. Will that be all right with you?"

"Sure," Dave said quickly. "Sure, thats okay." He looked around the room again. Down at the other end Gwen was gracefully squatting down on one knee putting apples from a sack in a bin into a bowl, and he could see part of the inside of her bare thigh where the top of her stocking ended.

Suddenly, as if realizing exactly where he was looking, though she did not look up from her work, Gwen seized the skirt of her dress and jerking it convulsively tucked it up under her knee, covering the offending spot. Dave, confident now, did not bother to look away, and grinned at her openly.

"This is group III," Bob said, coming up behind him. Startled, Dave swung back around to him.

"My recording is transcribed for orchestra," Bob said. "I prefer that to piano only—for this, at least. Not always." He sat down beside Dave on the divan and picked up his glass unobtrusively, from where he had set it on the coffeetable, in the warmth radiating out to them from the huge fireplace.

Again, it was impossible to tell from his face whether he was following what was going on without comment, or was just missing it entirely. Then the music came out into the room to them—like also the warmth of the fire—low in volume, first one violin, then two, then other instruments, contrapuntal to the theme, exceedingly simple apparently and yet tremendously complex, slow and measured seemingly even in its faster parts, calm, cool, melodiously sweet, reasonable as only mathematics can be reasonable, and serene. To Dave, who knew next to nothing about classical music, it seemed as if this were the only music that had ever been written which could have been played here and now, and be such a perfect match and complement to all the rest of this place.

"Tell me," he said suddenly, feeling again that ridiculously emotional desire to please, to gratify, the older man and his host, "tell me, is it all like this?"

Bob grinned suddenly, coming up out of the music, the grin a little rueful. "No. No, as a matter of fact, it isnt. Its rather a good deal less so, as a matter of fact. Except here and there. But we hope to get it all done someday. Ill show you the rest of the house later, if you like."

"I would," Dave said. "I would very much."

"You see, we have so much stuff," Bob said apologetically, as if ashamed for having it. "Like that big table there. We have stuff like that sitting all over the house. That table is from my mother's family. It was carried overland in a covered wagon from New York State to Ohio, then carried overland again from Ohio to here. We have clothes chests, and sugar chests, and cedar chests," he said in a wearily enumerating tone, "and old beds, and corner cupboards, and chairs, and tables, sitting all over the house. Most of it comes down from one family or another. Although a few of the things my wife bought. She was an antiquer. But, you see, it rather got so we almost couldnt get into the house in Parkman, out by the school, and in order to get something from one chest we had to move another you know. Practically."

"That isnt true," Gwen said in that clear cold voice, coming down toward them from the stove with a bowl of apples. She sounded very positive, and very right, and almost prim. "I dont think you should persist in using the furniture as an excuse for buying this house just because youre ashamed of having a little money. I dont think thats fair to yourself or to anyone else. Its cheating, and its immoral."

Both of the men looked at her. In a very short time she seemed to have changed completely into another person; a person more like the coldly responsible schoolteacher Dave had met at Frank's, than the warmly—and perhaps overly—sympathetic woman he had ridden downtown with.

"You are quite right, dear Gwen," Bob said solemnly, looking at her quizzically. She did not look up, but went right on with her apples.

"Is that what you call Early American?" Dave said, looking away from her to the table.

"Well, if it is, it is rather a bastard type you know," Bob said in a pained voice that was very like his apology for culture.

"Its nothing of the sort," Gwen said without looking up, "and you know it."

"Early American is rather supposed to be quite plain, I understand,"

Bob went on to Dave. "Whereas you can see the legs of this table are not plain."

"Theyre not ornate, though," Dave said.

"Yes," Bob said, his voice still strangely, if a little whimsically, pained. "Theyre not ornate; quite so. You see I have rather an idea, as I said before, about eventually fixing up different rooms as different periods and styles, you know. For instance, we have enough Pennsylvania Dutch things to outfit a whole room. We have so much stuff, you know. And we have so many rooms. And its a project. And I like to potter around," he said apologetically.

Gwen said nothing, and went on with her apples. Then quite suddenly she reached out for her drink, which she had hardly touched, and drank it all down in two swallows abruptly, without saying anything or looking at anyone.

Bob looked over at her again, quizzically, his face not derisive so much, as kindly and understandingly humorous.

"What kind of wood is that?" Dave asked of the table.

"That?" Bob said, his voice still pained with the talk of furniture. "That is cherry and rosewood. The top is cherry. Thats unusual you know. Mostly they mixed mahogany and rosewood. The legs are solid rosewood. The thing that makes it good is the carving of the legs, however. Not the turnings themselves, but the hexagonal tapered panels between them, with those—sort of raised finger loaves on them," he said searching. "Ive never seen another quite like it actually."

"Its very beautiful," Dave said. "So are those chairs beautiful."

"Yes. Those chairs," Bob said. "They are quite good; for ladderbacks. You dont see that fine type of arching in the back slats too often. They came overland with the table," he said in that same deprecatory tone.

Dave nodded. He felt he had just about run out of anything else to say, or to comment on.

"We have a lot of antique furniture," Gwen said primly without looking up from her apples. "Really a lot. And in spite of the way he talks hes going to have a very unusual and beautiful thing when he gets the place finished."

"Yes, but it is coming along rather quite slowly," Bob said.

"I dont see how you can expect to complete a project like you have in mind in a few weeks or days," Gwen said crisply. "And Ive never seen anything that was worthwhile that didnt require a great deal of time and work and sweat." She got up with her apples, which she had finished cutting, having put each unpeeled slice in the pan and the neat cores back into the bowl, and took them down to the stove with her, walking in that mannish squareshouldered half belligerent stride of hers, as if there were nothing more to be said.

"Here!" Bob said heartily. "What about another drink, Dave. Your glass is empty." He got up, unfolding the long lean legs below the long lean torso, above which was that bright eyed, perpetually interested face.

"Yes," Dave said. "Yes, Ill have one. In fact, Ill have two!" He didnt understand about Gwen, what had happened to her, but Bob made him feel wanted, honestly wanted.

"A double?" Bob said, "fine! fine!" He went to the bar.

"Or a triple," Dave said extravagantly. A kind of wild exuberant emotion, reaction to all he had been feeling, all day and this evening, was spreading through him.

"Guinevere?" Bob said.

"Yes," Gwen said from the stove subduedly. "Yes, I believe I will have another."

"And so will I!" Bob said gallantly. "This is an occasion!"

"I had no idea you had any such place as this," Dave said, looking into the glowing, tinkling coals of the fire. He looked over at Bob, "I had no idea there was anyplace like this around. Anywhere. I thought nobody but the very rich owned things like these."

"Well of course we have a little family income," Bob said in that nearly apologetic tone, from the bar. "They are valuable. We are inclined to forget their value, I guess. But of course we didnt have to buy them you know. Most of them. If we had had to live off what we made as teachers and writers, Im afraid wed have become wards of the State some time ago."

"Oh now, I wouldnt say that," Dave said quickly.

"Dad," Gwen called primly, in that clear disapproving voice, "I wish you would stop castigating yourself this way. It isnt healthy, and you shouldnt be allowed to do it."

"But its a proven fact, dear Gwen," Bob said mildly. "Lets face it," he said, smiling at his use of the modern phrase. "Im passé. Im one of those oldfashioned poets. Im afraid the young people dont read me much any more," he smiled sadly to Dave. "And why shouldnt one admit the facts?" he said to Gwen. "One's vanity you know," he smiled. "It makes one rather want a little acknowledgment."

"The hardest thing in the world to get," Dave said.

"The least important," Gwen said, turning the stove burner on positively. She put a skillet on the burner, added butter and sugar, then dumped in half a small jar of oldfashioned redhots from one of the open shelves. Dave watched to see what she would do with the unpeeled apples. She dumped them from the pan into the skillet on top of the rest and began to stir.

"Here you are, Dave," Bob said, bending his long frame to set a larger glass on the coffeetable in front of him. He rubbed his hands together. "I believe theres just a little more there than a double," he grinned, hunching his spare shoulders and winking broadly. Once again, in the reddish light of the fire, Dave was struck by the strangeness of that long full mustache and the closeclipped crewcut hair, and between them those blue, bright all-engulfing eyes.

"Thanks, Bob," he said as the tall man went back to the bar.

"Pleasure!" Bob said heartily. "Pleasure!" He commenced mixing the new Manhattans.

Dave turned his head to look at Gwen again, who still stood by the stove, stirring. He couldnt figure out what had happened, what he had done wrong, and he was bothered by what she was going to do with those apples, which she had not peeled. The sweet fruit smell of them cooking had begun to drift down to him. Evidently she wasnt going to peel them at all.

"Your drink, Gwen dear!" Bob said gaily. "I assume you want it up there." And without waiting for answer, he carried it up to where she stood and set it down carefully beside her on the countertop alongside the stove. Gwen, still stirring the apples, glanced down at it briefly, saying nothing, and did not touch it. "Thanks," she said as he walked away.

"And my own!" Bob said grandly. He poured it out into his glass with a flourish and carried it to the coffeetable where Dave sat on one divan and sat himself down on the other. Behind them the serene precise music of Bach still played on on the loaded record changer.

"Gwen tells me youve been writing some poetry," Bob said in a tone that was delicately and carefully inflected to express both genuine interest and at the same time the knowledge that he need not talk about it if he didnt want to.

Dave looked over to where Gwen stood, her untouched drink still sitting beside her on the countertop. "Oh, just a little bit," he said looking back at Bob. "Now and then." He felt embarrassed. "Its not very good, and its not even poetry really." She shouldnt have told it. When he looked back at her again, he was surprised to note that her drink was gone. The glass sat where it had before, seemingly untouched, but nothing was in it now but the cherry. Apparently she had swallowed it off the same way she had the first one.

"Dont be too sure!" Bob cautioned, holding up a finger. "I wonder if I might have the privilege of reading some of it?"

"He didnt bring it," Gwen said from the stove in that clear, prim voice.

"How do you know I didnt bring it?" Dave said.

"I just know," Gwen said and turned to look him full in the face again, her eyes wide open, but withdrawn this time, instead of warm. "Well? You didnt, did you?" she said. Then before he could answer, "Gentlemen, we are ready to eat!" Using a hot pad she lifted the skillet and with a spoon scraped the apples into a dish of that same heavy olivegreen-and-white restaurant ware, and carried it to the table.

"No, I didnt," Dave muttered selfeffacingly. "I thought about it. But I didnt. I didnt think it was good enough."

"Perhaps some other time," Bob said cheerily, and apparently unperturbed by the action going on around him. "Come, lets sit." He got up. "Bring your drink. If you want another after you finish that one dont be afraid to holler at me."

"If I do, and I probly will, Ill mix it myself," Dave smiled at him.

"Good!" Bob said, nodding his crewcut head, "fine! Better yet! Do that! The things are all right there. —I hope I got that last one dry enough for you?"

"It was fine," Dave said. He still did not know what he had done wrong. He was beginning to feel the drinks a little now.

"You know," he said as he sat down, carrying his drink, "the thing that gets you about this place so much is that its so safe."

"So what?" Bob said, sitting.

"Safe!" Dave said, looking around the room. "You know. Safe!"

"Safe," Bob said. Looking surprised, taking up his napkin and spreading it, he looked around at it himself. "Yes, I guess it is that," he said courteously. "Although I had never thought about it in just that way you know."

"Naturally," Dave said. "You wouldnt. But its the safest place Ive ever seen in my life. Youre completely safe here! *I* feel safe here! Its *safe!*" he said, as if just extra emphasis on the word itself would convey what he meant.

Gwen had taken the beef hearts and the huge potatoes from the oven and put them on dishes and set them on the table. That was all there was. No bread, no little extras, no second vegetable dish. Now she brought the big salad bowl of lettuce and cut tomatoes and put it on the table, together with three salad bowls in a stack, and a small bottle of salad dressing which said *Girard's, San Francisco* on its label and which she shook vigorously for a moment and then set beside the bowls after removing its cap and putting it on the table.

"No," she said distinctly as she sat down. "Youre wrong, it isnt safe. It just seems that way to you. Actually, it isnt safe at all. Actually, it only removes danger to a more subtle level." She picked up her own napkin. Her eyes were just a little bit wavery from the liquor that she wasnt used to, and a wisp of her nondescript-colored hair had fallen over her forehead, her face still flushed a little from the heat of the stove.

"How is that?" Dave said warily, feeling very prudent. He still didnt know what it was he had done wrong, but he assumed he must have done something; that it must have been something he had done. Maybe it was the way he had looked at her leg, but that shouldnt have done it. Whatever it was, the confidence he had felt a while ago was fast going out of him, and along with it was going the charm. And in place of it, he was having difficulty in keeping from getting really angry now.

"Well, what kind of dangers are there?" Gwen said directly, with that positiveness of hers, as if answering a student's question. "There are only two. Financial danger and spiritual danger. Financial danger is the social danger from others, the outside danger. Spiritual danger is the danger from ourselves, from within. If weve removed the financial danger of day to day struggle for existence and shelter, we have only removed it to the more distant and more subtle danger of the bank and credit and economizing. Weve given up a lot of other things to have this place."

She stopped to catch her breath.

"Secondly, having all this," she said almost primly, "imposes an even greater responsibility on us. When you remove the struggle for basic necessities, you have to supplant will power in its place. Having no need to work, we could easily become drunkards, or jaded thrill seekers, degenerating into nothingness. All animals are lazy, like I once told you before. How do you think I know? Because of the potentialities of laziness in myself that I have to fight against all the time. Nothings *ever* safe, Dave, you know that. Youre only being sentimental." Her voice was shaking ever so slightly, and when she picked up her fork although there was nothing on her plate yet, it was trembling slightly, too.

Dave was puzzled. "Yes, of course youre right," he said selfeffacingly, and warily. "And Im wrong." His chest seemed to be constricting on him, and he drew in a great, deep sigh. "I think Ill mix myself another drink," he said, getting up.

"Fine!" Bob said to him cheerily, "fine, Dave! You go right ahead if you want. I dont believe I want another."

"Just imagine Marlowe or Nash or Robert Greene!" Gwen said after him, "trying to live here as quietly and as cheaply as we do! Tom Wolfe would run himself headon through that window and be lying out drunk on the lawn from frustration!" she said looking after him.

"Gwen, will you pass me those potatoes?" Bob said in a hearty, hungry voice.

"What?" she said. Then her voice changed. "Oh," she said. "Yes. Yes, of course." She reached for them.

"They look delicious," Bob said cheerfully. "I love potatoes. Dave," he called, "youd better come on and eat, fellow, or there wont be anything left. Im hungry as a bear."

CHAPTER 23

In spite of its rather inauspicious beginning, the dinner turned out pretty well. Gwen, after Bob asked her for the potatoes, changed again and suddenly became quiet and amenable. And by the time everybody had some food on their plates she was laughing and joking, her face still flushed and her eyes the least little bit wavery from her two cocktails. She kept up a steady stream of talk which displayed a sense of humor she had never shown before and which kept both men laughing. Gradually, as the meal progressed and the food she ate sobered her, she became less mercurial and more subdued but she didnt become again that way she had been.

The food also had a great deal to do with making the dinner turn out well. It was delicious. The beef hearts, which had come to the table from the oven wrapped in tinfoil that Gwen removed there, had been peppered with coarse-ground pepper and had partaken of the spicy flavor of the dressing which itself was fillingly fullbodied in texture and had been made, Gwen said, of leftover mush and stale bread and had been seasoned with—in addition to salt—sweet basil, oregano, chopped onion and celery. The cinnamon-flavored fried apples, which had turned mapleleaf red in the cooking, went deliciously with the rich heart. The boiled-then-baked potatoes filled out the meal to perfection. Dave, who rarely ate sweet potatoes and whose natural choice would have been the Irish, did however, at Bob's insistence, accept the other half of the huge sweet potato which Bob cut in two, and under Bob's instruction treated it with a large amount of butter only, and nothing else. No salt, no pepper. He discovered it was delicious and as good if not better than any baked Idaho he had ever eaten.

It was a strange meal. Informal was not so much the word for it as unceremonious. There was a sort of catch as catch can quality about it. The episode of the sweet potato showed it perfectly: Bob picked it up, put it on his own plate and cut it in two, and then handed half of it to Dave. If you wanted salad at this meal you grabbed a small bowl, served yourself out of the big bowl with however much you wanted, and then poured your own dressing on it out of the bottle. (The Girard's dressing, dark gray-brown in color, was one of the most delicious French dressings Dave had ever tasted. It turned out that Bob had eaten it once in a restaurant somewhere and asked about it, had been given the story of the oldtime Girard's French Restaurant in San Francisco, where it originated, off of the bottle with the address and they had been ordering it from Girard's Inc. by the case ever since. It was like that with everything—unusual, yes; but always with a very logical reason.) The meal was served by candlelight; reason: because Bob had refused to have any ceiling fixtures put in the room, as they would detract from the beamed ceiling and also would not make the kitchen look as old; thus the candlelight was needed, and therefore did not seem affected and hence was not treated so. The strange, heavy, green-and-white restaurant ware was what they always used; reason: because they both liked it and Bob thought it was rather medieval, and also they had made an excellent buy on two whole crates of it which were a wholesaler's remainder after it went out of style; and you could practically bounce it off the floor without breaking it, Gwen said, if you got drunk.

Dave was still puzzled. He still did not know what had gone wrong back there somewhere. He did not know what was happening now. Something was. But whatever it was, it wasnt flirtation. All the flirtation was gone. So completely gone that he couldnt help wondering if there had ever really been any, or if it had all been in his imagination. Yet he was sure she had given him an agreement in everything but words. Or if not agreement, at least the go-ahead sign to go on and try for an agreement, with reasonable expectation. But you certainly couldnt have told it from her actions now. Gay and laughing or not, her eyes were always subtly veiled whenever she looked at him. Well, if she had flirted, it was all gone now. And with it was gone his confidence. And when that was gone, his ability to be charming was gone also. Shyness, inarticulateness and sullenness replaced it, and he felt again that she must be able to see completely through him and his what must be patently obvious designs on her and this made him feel guilty. Why should he feel guilty? But he did, and frightened and panicky, too. And, worst of all, afraid that she might dislike him. Damn women, anyway. It was a good thing for him he had drunk as much as he had. The first stiff Martini he had mixed for himself had relieved the constriction he had begun to get in his chest. The second stiff one had set him up just fine, although this presented him with a new problem in that he got afraid he might get really drunk, and therefore ate a great deal more food than either his belly or body needed in order to sober himself, though this was not hard to do the food being what it was.

If Bob French was aware of any of all this he did not show it, but Dave could not help shrewdly suspecting again that he was on to all of it. Either way, Bob remained his same usual, affable self all through the meal. He did not eat nearly so much as he had at first proclaimed he intended to. When the meal was over, and the coffee which was served without dessert drunk, he pushed back his chair and announced that he was going downtown to the Grange meeting tonight.

Gwen appeared to be as startled as Dave himself was.

"Youre what?" she said guardedly. "To where?"

"To the Grange," Bob said affably. "You know they always meet on Thursday night."

"But I didnt know you were going," Gwen said.

"I always go," Bob said affably.

"But I thought with Dave here and all," Gwen began. "And Wally Dennis called, you know, and said he had some material for me to look at and he might bring Dawn and come over later."

"Wally doesnt mind if he doesnt see me," Bob said cheerily, "and he knows the Israel Grange meets Thursdays. Anyway, I rather doubt if Wally will make it you know."

"Why do you say that?" Gwen demanded.

Smiling cheerily, Bob raised his eyebrows and hunched his high shoulders, spreading his hands. "Well, you know how Wally is. Hes always more inclined to come when he hasnt thought to. Hes like that with everything."

"However," he said affably, "you are both invited to accompany me to the Grange if you would like."

"No thanks," Dave said quickly. "You two go and Ill go on home. I dont know the first thing about farming, or farming politics."

"It isnt really a farming or political organization any more," Bob said. "That was years ago. Today its only social."

"Yes," Gwen said almost sourly. "The women all get together on one side of the hall and talk about quilts and how to make pickles; and the men get together on the other side and talk about—what?" she asked, looking at her father.

"Mostly crops," Bob said affably. "And whether to draw to an inside straight."

"And whether to have another drink," Gwen said.

"It is true," Bob smiled cheerily, "that they sometimes discuss the virtues of homemade applejack over the boughten. Excuse me, I must get my coat."

"Look," Dave said, getting up from the table too. "Why dont you two go ahead and go to the Grange meeting and Ill go on home to Parkman. That would be better all the way around." Once again he had that feeling there was something going on here he was missing, wasnt getting, was not in on. Whatever it was, or wasnt, he had no intention of spending two or three selfeffacing hours here alone with Gwen, trying unsuccessfully and without confidence to make her. Or even spending two or three hours and not trying. It was all uphill work, tragic work, doomed from the start, the way *this* evening had gone. "Ive got some things Ive got to do for Frank tomorrow anyway," he said.

Another evening maybe, he thought, another evening might be a better one. After all, this was only the first time hed been here, he tried to remind himself.

"Nonsense!" Bob said. "I wont hear of it. If Guinevere wishes to go with me, theres no reason why you shouldnt stay here by yourself and enjoy the books and records and the fire until we return." He paused and looked back at them from the door, not one of the doors at the far end, but the single door up here in the sitting room end which led, he had said earlier, into the unfinished dining room which, as hed said, he didnt care if they ever finished because it gave them a good excuse not to have guests and he didnt like guests—present company excepted of course you know, he had added. Standing there, with that long spare frame above the long spare legs in that stooped slouch, and grayed crew-cut head and the long full mustache on the aging face, he looked so perfectly like the epitome of the professorial type, which of course in a way he was, that it didnt seem fair. All he needed was glasses.

"You know I never go to those things," Gwen said to him.

"Well then, you and Dave can stay here, and everything will have worked itself out just fine, and you will be here should young Wally come," Bob said affably, and opened the door and went through it.

Neither of the younger people said anything for a moment.

"Well . . ." Gwen said finally, and got up and began to collect the dishes in front of her. She moved on around the table, stacking the dirty plates and silverware and salad bowls. "Honestly!" she said, "sometimes he makes me so damned mad."

"Ill help you with the dishes," Dave said, moving to help her collect them. "Then Ill have to be going. Ive got a lot of things I have to do for Frank tomorrow." Reaching for a plate he thought with amused self-derision of his love poem which he had intended to get said to her hook or crook tonight, some way or other. Heh heh. Yeah, that would be great now, tonight, wouldnt it.

"No, no. You dont need to," Gwen said, intercepting him. "Its no trouble to do them. I have the dishwasher." She finished stacking them in the big salad bowl and the meat platter and carried them down the room to the sink. "You sit down and make yourself comfortable and relax."

"Well, Ill have a cigarette and another cup of coffee," Dave said. "But then Ill have to get going."

"You might as well stay a while," she said from the sink. "Ive got a couple of things I want to talk to you about." She went on about rinsing the dishes and fitting them into the automatic washer.

Dave poured himself another cup of coffee from the stove, without looking at her, and carried it back to the coffeetable in front of the fire. The fire was still eating its way into the huge backlog without any appreciable diminishment of it. He wondered how they had gotten that huge log in there. All he could think about now was getting away from here; from her, from Bob, from this place, from the whole thing. It was funny, how quick you got a yen to get gone once the sex issue went out of a thing. Loneliness ate at him.

Bob French came back in through the diningroom door then, wearing his topcoat and his dark slouch hat which Dave immediately recognized from high school, a very old, dim, almost forgotten memory. He wore it a trifle aslant, and with the brim turned down all along one side, Continental style. It always gave him a gay debonair dashing look, which was cute and lovable on him because he seemed at least, to be totally unaware of it. Dave remembered it well. It could even have been the same hat. He also carried a stick, an ivory headed one.

"I shall walk down to the hall!" Bob said, clutching his stick like a hammer and brandishing its knob in the air, "and I shall walk back from the hall! And I *will* not wear my rubbers!"

Gwen did not say anything.

Dave grinned at him. "Ill put some more wood on this fire for you, if you want, before I leave," he said.

"Thats fine," Bob said, "but theres quite a trick to laying a good fire in a fireplace you know. However, you go ahead and someday I will teach you how."

"How did you get that great big backlog on there?" Dave asked.

"There is a Negro man here in town who works some for me, amongst others," Bob said. "He does all my really heavy work for me. We have several Negro families here in Israel."

"I remember," Dave said. "I used to play football against some of them. They always ran circles around us. Why dont you hire me?" he said, looking around the room again.

"Im afraid I could not afford the wages you would demand," Bob said. "However, that reminds me. Why dont you plan to stay the night? We could talk some tonight when I return, if you like, and tomorrow I could show you our grounds which you havent seen yet."

"Id like to," Dave said. "Very much. But I cant. Have to get back to Parkman."

"Thats too bad," Bob said mock sorrowfully. "We dont really have many people come here who really appreciate our place. Your brother Frank, for one, doesnt think very much of it at all."

"Dad," Gwen said from the sink, but she was smiling affectionately. His airy mood had reached her, too. "You shouldnt say things like that!"

"But its the truth, dear Guinevere," Bob said affably. "I am not judging, Im merely stating a simple fact."

"The judgment is implied," Gwen said.

"Not so," Bob said cheerily. "Well, I must go. I hope we will have the pleasure of your presence again some time soon, Dave. And next time you come, bring some of that poetry, eh?" he said, winking jovially. He went to the side door, the one by which Dave had entered, and with a flourish of his stick let himself out. Gwen was looking after him, smiling affectionately. Then her face hardened and stiffened, and she turned back to the sink.

"I dont know what to do with him," she said, not without a real anguish, which Dave could recognize underlying the disapproval of her tone. "Hell come home drunk tonight now. Whenever he goes out when hes in this mood he always comes home drunk."

"Him?" Dave said. "Drunk?"

"Yes," Gwen said, "him. You didnt know he drank like that, did you? Neither do very many other people. Mama and I have covered up for him for years with the town, and the school. He was doing it when you and I were in high school, but you didnt know it. And neither did anyone else."

"You mean hes an alcoholic?" Dave said, astounded.

"No, I dont mean that at all," she said. "Hes not an alcoholic. He doesnt do it often, just every once in a while. Its mostly nervousness, and getting all screwed up. Thats why he doesnt like to have guests or go out and why I dont. Hes so softhearted, and he tries so hard to make everyone feel good, and hes so polite to everyone. He cant stand to see someone have a bad time. Just like this evening. I got upset, and you got upset, and poor Daddy tried and tried to smooth everything up and gloss it over and make it a pleasant evening. And for what? What difference did it make? In the end? And so he got terribly upset and all high and screwed up inside, and now he'll come home drunk.

"Thats what you get with people," Gwen said bitterly. She finished rinsing the dishes and put the last one into the washer and closed the lid and turned the timer to on. A low rushing roar filled the kitchen. She turned back and went to cleaning the sink. "You cant get two human beings together for more than five minutes at a time without something cropping up and some trouble of some kind starting, somebody's vanity or ego getting involved, some stupid petty little antagonism." She had to talk in a near shout now, above the roar.

"Well, like you told me at Frank's house, we are all of us still animals," Dave said from the couch, "primitive animals."

"Yes, but hes civilized," Gwen shouted. "One of the rare ones. Thats the tragedy. Hed be all right if it werent for people. So would the human race. If we could just live our lives without people."

"No one can live his life without other people," Dave said, mouthing the smug old platitude of governments pompously because instead of feeling sympathy for her he was irritated with her.

"You dont need to tell me that," Gwen shouted above the roar of the dishwasher. She had moved now from the sink and was cleaning off the countertop. "Ive known it some small while."

"Well, just between you and me," Dave said irritably, "I honestly fail to see why you give a damn. Hes not an alcoholic, is he? So what if he does get drunked up once in a while? Hes a poet. What do you care what people say? What difference would it make if somebody did find out about it?"

As she worked her way down the countertop toward him, she gradually lowered her voice. "Because he would have lost his job at the school," she said now, turning on him blazingly, "thats why. Its very easy to be a poet and ignore public opinion, when you have a couple of women at home to do it for you."

"Well, from the looks of this place," Dave said irritably, "he had enough money it wouldnt matter if he lost the job or not."

"I worry because of his health," Gwen said unconvincingly. "Hes not as young as he used to be." She came down from the sink, finished now, toward where he still sat on the divan before the fire and beside the low round coffeetable. "Oh, I know what youre thinking," she said. "You think Im moralistic and narrowminded. But thats not what it is." Instead of going on to the divan, or even to the other divan across the coffeetable, she sat down at the big antique table in one of the ladderbacks and rested her elbows on the table, an action so characteristic, with so much of at-homeness in it, that it showed she must have done it many times before, with just her father here. Or with no one here at all except herself.

"I cant help it," she said. "Hes so innocent and gullible. People take advantage of him all the time. Hes just naturally the kind of man people are always first to talk about, because hes different. And I dont want people to talk about him. They have no right to. And hes so *damned* cute. And sweet."

"He sure is that," Dave said.

For a moment they looked at each other across the distance separating them, then simultaneously both grinned, and then laughed a little, thinking of Bob and his flourishing exit. As if he had astutely succeeded in subtly outwitting both of them, the airy gay mood he apparently had created deliberately for them in his leaving came back into both of them again and back into the room, a tangible presence, as they thought about him.

"Hows your coffee?" Gwen smiled.

"Its empty," Dave said without turning to look at it. He had completely forgotten it.

"Ill make some more," she said, and got up suddenly from the ladderback, suddenly and flowingly, and walked back up the long room to the stove.

"I dont know what to do with him sometimes," she said conversationally and for a moment Dave didnt know who she meant. "He knows more about people and life than anyone Ive ever met. He sees completely through people as if they were windows. No one would ever know it, the way he acts, but he does. And he wont use it. Ive tried for years to get him to put what he knows into a novel, or at least a memoir. If I could just get him started I think he would. But he wont do it. He just says poets should not try to write novels."

"Maybe hes right."

"Perhaps for other poets, but hes not a poet. Or not *just* a poet. Hes much more."

"Theres nothing wrong with poets," Dave said defensively. "Ive always wanted to be one."

"Yes," Gwen smiled, "so did Tom Wolfe in his romantic foolish way." She came back down the room, the coffeemaker working now, and sat back down in the same ladderback. "After all, poetry is for children and young people," she said authoritatively. "And thats whom most of it is written by—no matter what their age. What is poetry? Its the evocation of an emotion. Fine. All very well and good. But novels not only evoke emotions in the reader, they also show what, and *why* they are *really* felt, by their people. They ex*plain*—or at least they should do." She was looking at him dead seriously. "Ive thought about it quite a lot.—"

"And evidently youve decided for the novel," Dave said.

"Naturally I have," Gwen said. "Oh, I love poetry. I still love it very much.—"

"You used to write it."

"Yes," she said indifferently. "Sometimes now," she went on, "I go on regular poetry binges. —But I know why Im doing it.— Basically, its several levels below the novel," she said positively, in that authoritative tone again. "Basically, poetry's at the level of adolescence, when it is sufficient to *feel* our emotions, without seriously wondering *why* we feel them." She looked at him expectantly.

"What about the memoir?" Dave said, clearing his throat guiltily. He was thinking about his own poem Hunger, and his proposed plans for it. Prospects didnt look so good.

"Oh, that," Gwen said. "He wont do that either. He just says that basically all memoirs are novels anyway."

Dave laughed delightedly. "Maybe he is right."

"Of course hes right," Gwen said impatiently.

"The coffee's ready." She got up—the same way again this time, suddenly and flowingly—and came around the table to where he sat by the coffeetable and bent to get his cup, and Dave found himself staring at the top of her small, delicate, well rounded, enormously affective head. Then she was gone, striding up the room again. In a moment she was back, with a tray, and on it the coffeemaker, two clean cups, sugar and creamer. She set it on the coffeetable and sat down on the other divan across from him and looked at him demandingly.

"When are you going to start writing again?" she demanded softly.

"Well, I dont know—" Dave began.

"Well, youd better start thinking about it," Gwen said crisply. "Its time you stopped all this silly nonsense about never writing any more. Youve never meant it, and you never will, and whats more you know it. Dont you?"

"Now just a—" Dave started irately.

"Dont you?" Gwen repeated crisply.

Dave sat and looked at her. Here was his chance. He had worked it all out how to tell her about the comic combat novel, how to bring it up, how to bring the conversation around to it, and then tell her all about it, and then ask for her help, all of it worked out before he even came over here. And now she had saved him the trouble and brought it up herself. All he had to do was take advantage of the opportunity; and he couldnt do it. It was like shooting fish in a barrel, he told himself, it wasnt fair. All was fair in love and war, but this was taking an unfair advantage even he couldnt take, he told himself. Then, looking into himself a little deeper, he admitted why it really was: It was very simple; he was afraid she wouldnt believe him. Would divine it was only a seduction effort.

Gwen sat looking back at him crisply, waiting for an answer.

"Youre making me mad," Dave said, trying a diversion.

"Im sorry," Gwen said authoritatively, "but it cant be helped. Youve got to face yourself and see yourself. All this selfpity and feeling sorry for yourself isnt going to help you one bit," she said crisply. "The raw cold truth is you just barely got started, you just merely served your apprenticeship with those two books, and then quit, just as you were getting ready to cash in and get in on the gravy. Now isnt that so?" she demanded.

Dave just looked at her.

"Sugar and cream?" she said, pouring into his cup.

"No sugar, just cream," he said.

"Much or little?"

"Medium."

"Here," she said, and handed him his cup.

Dave took it and set it down jerkily on the coffeetable, misjudging the distance and sloshing a little over the saucer and onto the table, in his irascible haste.

"All right, God damn it," he said angrily, "I *have* got an *idea* for a novel. Its—"

"I thought as much," Gwen smiled smugly.

"—Yes! Its a comic combat novel," he blurted. "You know what that is? And you wont believe me anyway. So the hell with it!"

"A what?" Gwen said.

"A comic combat novel," he said angrily. "A comic war novel." Then he saw he wasnt getting across, by the look of disappointment on her face. "No, no," he said. "A war novel. A war novel in which *death* is comic, in which *death,* and *mutilation,* and *war itself* are comic; instead of horrible."

Gwen's face began to change and look delighted as she got his point. "Oh, I thought you meant another *humorous* war novel," she said, "like the correspondents write." Then she laughed pealingly. "Oh, thats wonderful! Thats *marvelous!* And we need it so badly. After all these two-bit horror catalogs. Theyre all so smug and selfrighteous, these war writers, when they say so solemnly how they hate war. And all the time they can hardly wait till another one starts somewhere, so they can all go there in a body to 'hate' it." She caught herself up short, emphatically. "How long have you been working on it?" she demanded.

"I havent worked on it any," Dave said, his voice coming back down into what had apparently become his normal state anymore, sullenness. Sullenly, he reached out for his coffee and poured the sloshings sullenly from the saucer back into the cup.

"You ought to be ashamed!" Gwen said. "Why havent you?"

"Because I havent had time!" he said angrily. "I only got out of the Army a week ago! —What do you think I came over here for?" he said sullenly. "Youre a critic, aint you? I want you to help me."

Gwen didnt answer at once, and rubbed her cheek thoughtfully with her fingertips. "I suppose I could do correspondence work with you," she said thoughtfully. "You could mail me the chapters. I dont like correspondence work. But I could do it."

"But, you see," Dave said in a portentous voice, "Im not leaving Parkman."

"Youre not?" Gwen said looking at him with astonishment. "But you are! You said you were! So thats why you moved to the Douglas Hotel!!" Perhaps there was a little distress in her voice, also.

"I decided to stay," Dave said sullenly. "I put my $5000 in that taxi service with Frank and Im staying. I go to work for him as dispatcher as soon as we get the thing operating."

Gwen was looking at him disbelievingly. "Oh, not in that deal!"

"Sure."

"But why!"

"God damn it, because Im falling in love with you!" Dave cried angrily, and set his cup down again, spilling some more. He didnt really believe it, when he said it, and he knew it wasnt true; but at the same time the wrought up, actor's half of him felt it was true, and believed it, and that made it convincing. And, after he said it, suddenly he did believe it.

Momentarily Gwen did not say anything but merely looked at him as if he had spoken in Persian or Arabic. Then the expression of her eyes seemed to withdraw inward, leaving them veiled and blank.

"Oh you fool!" she said. "You real fool! You *must* be a writer, youre such a fool!"

"Im sorry I spilled the coffee," Dave said sullenly. "Wheres a rag? Ill wipe it up before it drips on your Indian rug."

"Ill do it," Gwen said efficiently, and was suddenly up and walking down the room to the sink where she snatched up the dishrag and came back and began sopping the coffee up off the coffeetable.

"Youve never been in love with anybody in your life except yourself," she said. "How would you know whether you were falling in love, or not? You 'fall in love' with whatever female happens to be nearest at any given time. Dont talk to me about love!"

Dave didnt say anything. He only wished he was gone, home, back in the miserably peaceful loneliness of that damned barren little squeegy hotelroom.

"You really like Daddy, dont you?" Gwen said suddenly without looking up.

"Yeah," he said. "Sure."

"And you have a friendly warm relationship with him. Already. Why the *hell*," she said, straightening up with the soppingwet rag carefully in her hands, her eyes blazing, "cant you have that kind of a relationship with a *wo*man, *too*?" Holding the sopping rag in both palms one under the other so it would not drip, she carried it down to the sink and dumped it, and then turned around to face him.

Dave, discovering himself to be almost totally without any kind of a rejoinder to that one, had stayed silent.

"I told you what I would do, Dave," she said reasonably, "And thats what I will do; and all I will do. Ill be glad to help you with this book, like you said, and criticize it for you, if you want. Not so much because Ill be of any help to you—in that way; but because if you dont have somebody around to keep pushing your nose to the grindstone youd never do any work. The only way youd ever do any work on your own would be if they put you in jail where you couldnt chase women and get drunk and were so bored youd have to work in selfdefense. Or else if you got old like Stendhal and got stuck off in some boring out of the way place," she said, pausing for breath. Despite the reasonableness of her tone, there was a sort of strange tautness on her vaguely rawboned face. But Dave did not notice.

"Thats not fair," he muttered selfeffacingly. "I need a drink," he said. "Do you mind if I have a drink?"

"Help yourself," she said. "And the reason Ill do it," she said as he went to the countertop bar where the gin and Vermouth were, —There was no ice in the mixer but he didnt give a damn.— "is because Id like to see that book get written. Its a book that ought to be written. We need it. And besides its a brilliant idea. But if I have to sleep with you to get you to write it," she said reasonably, but still with that strange taut-ness of face, "youd better get some other woman to help you with it."

Dave downed the stiff drink he had mixed, straight from the mixer, and began to mix another.

"You have to drive home yet, you know," Gwen said mildly.

"Whats wrong with me?" he said, without looking up.

"Whats what?" Gwen said. "*Wrong* with you."

"Sure. Whats so different from me than other men? Whats so wrong with me that aint wrong with them?"

"Nothing," Gwen said, the tautness even plainer on her face now. "Nothing at all. I told you before; its just that Im not interested in sex."

Dave swung around to look at her, holding the mixer in one hand the bar spoon in the other, his face contorted. He drank from the mixer. For a moment he felt he could not stand it, actually physically could not stand it, the thought of refusal. As if he would have to smash the glass mixer and slash his wrists, or something equally wild and stupid, just to get back in the lead again. That was what always happened with him. This was the way it always went. "But you slept with all those other guys?" he said contortedly.

"That was a long time ago," Gwen said, the strange tautness of her face growing even stronger. This time Dave noticed it. "And besides, there wasnt an en*tire* regiment of them. And I wasnt as smart then as I am now," she said, tautly. "I thought I could still find an answer there. In sex, and in love. But what do you have when you have it? Two people, fighting each other in bed and out, each trying to dominate the other in order to make him love him the most, each trying to hurt the other because if he hurts him and he *still* comes back to him, he knows he is *really* loved. Is that the purpose of life? To procreate more of us just like us? We are taught that it is," she said. "Youre thirty seven years old, Dave, you ought to have learned all that yourself by now. You talk like Wally Dennis. Wally's only twenty."

"You hate to hurt me," Dave said contortedly. "Well, thank you. Thank you for all the advice about life. Women always give me advice about life. —Look," he burst out, "they werent *all* handsome, were they?"

"What?" Gwen said uncomprehendingly.

"At least *one* of them was just ordinary looking maybe, wasnt he? maybe even ugly?" He drained off what was in the mixer and set it down hard on the countertop. For a moment, far away in the very back of his mind, he thought he might have broken it, then he forgot it. "Well, its not as if it was something that never happened before," he said con-tortedly. "I mean, its not as though its something that had never happened to me. Its just that sometimes youre inclined to forget about it, almost, for a while," he said, looking at her contortedly.

"Oh, Dave," Gwen said helplessly, shaking her head almost tearfully. "Dave, Dave."

"Oh I dont mind," he said, grinning selftormentedly. "Not really."

"Dave—" Gwen started.

"But I do want to tell you something," he said. The two stiff drinks were beginning to hit him, and would be he knew hitting him more later. Sort of instinctively, at the thought of "drink," he turned around to the unbroken mixer to start mixing himself another; but then he turned back instead and leaned against the countertop and folded his arms. "I want to tell you something," he said, contortedly, selfabusingly. "You know why I decided to stay in Parkman? You know why I put all my money into this damned taxistand deal with Frank? I dont give a damn about the taxistand. I did it on account of you.

"Yeah, thats right," he said, nodding. "You.

"You told me in the car that night that I wouldnt stay, that Id run away if I did stay. I wanted to show you. Thats why I put all my money in the taxistand. Thats why I decided to stay. I wanted to show you."

He turned around again toward the mixer, but quite suddenly, almost with surprise, he discovered there were tears in his eyes and he turned back to her again, and again leaned against the countertop and folded his arms.

"I wrote a poem to you tonight," he said contortedly. "Yeah. I have flashes of insight too. I know things too sometimes. I wrote it after I talked to you on the phone, before I came over here. I was going to bring it, with the others, but then I didnt. But that doesnt matter. I remember it. You want to hear it? You want me to recite it for you?"

"Yes," Gwen said simply, but meaning no.

"I call it Hunger," Dave said, looking at her through the tears in his eyes, the unbidden astonishing, almost completely unfelt, tears. "This is the way it goes," he said, looking at her.

> Once a young man, wandering beneath the bleary
> Streetlamps of a town that is all towns,
> Stopped at the door of a young unmarried woman.
> "I am hungry," the young man said.
> "For what do you hunger?" the woman smiled.
> "I do not know," he said.
> "Come," she smiled, "and I will feed you."
> And she took him to her bed where she poured ashes upon his head
> And laughed at his surprise.
> "Ashes are good for you," she said;
> "They are full of minerals."

There was a kind of second's pause, as he stopped, the amount of time it takes to get the punch line of a joke, and this made it seem both as if she were still waiting, and as if he were still going to go on. Then he didnt, and Gwen stood looking at him, those extraordinarily intelligent eyes of hers wide and still and receptive and still listening, if eyes could be said to listen, and then suddenly her face broke upward into humor and she laughed a hearty spontaneous peal of laughter that started low, broke upward, and then was suddenly cut off in the middle before it reached climax, leaving a startling silence.

Dave looked back at her, feeling the strangely, equally startling, emotionally unfounded tears in his eyes just as unexpectedly overflow his eyelids and trickle down his cheeks. They felt surprisingly cool on his skin, and he hadnt the slightest idea where they were coming from.

"Yeah. Its comical as hell, aint it?" he grinned, his voice cracking off into the upper register at the end. He turned back around to the countertop and picked up the gin bottle, and discovered just as suddenly and just as interestedly that he was no longer weeping the tears. They had gone away.

"I didnt mean to laugh," Gwen said from behind him.

"No, I wasnt bein sarcastic. I meant it," he said earnestly, his voice breaking again although he was no longer crying. "I think its comical as hell." He turned around holding the gin bottle and mixer and began to laugh uncontrollably, as if to prove it.

He didnt know what was getting into him, he thought, listening to himself laugh. It wasnt that funny. It must be the drinks.

"Stop laughing like that," Gwen demanded.

"I cant," he said. But he gulped air several times and swallowed it down and got himself stopped. But his diaphragm continued to heave with laughter inside, up against his lungs.

"Its very good," Gwen said, looking off and thinking. "I like it. Women are a lot like that too. Take your vitamins, George. Youre drinking too much, Henry. Eat your potatoes, John, theyre good for you."

"Theyre full of minerals," Dave said, allowing his diaphragm one extra snort. He turned back around and went on mixing the drink.

"And all the time all the men really want is to sleep with them," Gwen said thoughtfully. "—and make them admit that they really like it," she added. "—which of course they mustnt do," she added again. "But where would the men be if the women didnt act like they do? Besides, the men really want them to be that way. You really oughtnt to drink that much," she said, "since you still have to drive home."

"Im all right," Dave said thickly.

"The men really have it tough too dont they?" Gwen said softly and wonderingly, as if this were the very first time she had ever considered such an idea. "As bad as the women," she said softly.

Dave started to turn around and take her in his arms. It was really a purely spontaneous gesture, without calculation, and without what they used to call ulterior motives. A purely instinctive muscular hunger to give and receive comfort, that was all. Actually, all he did was to lay down the bar spoon in preparation for turning. He didnt move his feet or his body or anything else, just laid down the spoon. That was as far as he got.

"No," Gwen said positively. Just that. "No." She had either read his mind or the bar spoon. And he knew without seeing that her eyes had gone veiled and blank again. She turned and walked away down to the other end and leaned against the mantle above the fireplace.

"You must have had a very insecure childhood," she said thoughtfully, looking into the fire. "I bet your mother never loved you at all. Some mothers dont. In fact most mothers dont, really. Although they put on the big act in public. I guess the trouble is all in that they feel theyre not appreciated enough. I guess thats the trouble with the whole world. Everybody feels theyre not appreciated enough. I bet even Communists think theyre not appreciated enough."

"The Communists aint human," Dave said from the bar. "I seen them in Germany."

"Oh, but they must be," Gwen said; "biologically. They look human." She stopped, rather inconclusively, and continued to stare into the red, tinkling fire. "The men do have it tough too dont they?" she said again wonderingly, as if to herself.

Dave turned away from the countertop clutching the mixer glass, from which he drank, and looked at her, and continued to stare at her. It was what she had just said, that very last. Suddenly he understood it all; everything. He started down the long room toward her, but then, with the thought of not frightening her with perhaps the idea of an assault in his seemingly drunken state, he did not continue on to the fireplace or even to the divans close to her, but sat himself and the mixer glass down at the big table.

Suddenly out of a clear blue sky it had hit him what it was that had been wrong all evening, what it was he hadnt been able to put his finger on. And it really had nothing to do with him at all. Once you understood it, it was simple. It explained everything. This woman was a nympho. A real, archetypal, bona fide nymphomaniac: Driven forever to sexuality from which frigidity wouldnt let her get satisfaction; and at the same time driven forever back by her sense of guilt which made her try to keep "clean." Just like in the psych textbooks. She was the first one he had ever really met. He was astonished.

"Youre a nympho, arent you?" he said in an iron positive voice from the table.

Gwen turned to look at him uncomprehendingly. Then her face got that taut drawn look it had had before, the expression of the eyes actually withdrawing inward as he watched, leaving them veiled and troubled and blank, and guilty. Ha, he had got it!

He should have got it all along. It explained everything, why she had acted like she had, why Bob had been like he had been; it explained why she had flirted with him and then suddenly for no reason withdrawn. Her guilt. She wanted it but she was trying to abstain.

"Im not dumb! I know what it is!" he burst out excitedly and suddenly, without thinking, proud of his acuteness of perception. "Youre a nympho, Gwen! Arent you? Thats whats been wrong here all evening! Thats why you slept with all those men! Thats why you could never get any satisfaction!" After he had said it, he was sorry that he had.

Gwen looked at him strangely, out of that tautness of face, her face itself looking as if it were struggling to laugh, or else to cry, and she not letting it. "You are at liberty to think anything about me that you want," she said in a clear cold voice. "I neither affirm nor deny it." Then, like a stumbling afterthought, she added, "I never have and I never will."

"What the hell?" Dave said, embarrassed now. "Sex is nothing to be ashamed of, Gwen. You ought to know that."

Gwen looked back at him and then suddenly the tautness of her face broke and she laughed. But perhaps it was a little too airy, a little too carefree, he thought, a guilty laugh.

"I do know it," she said, her face relaxing and smiling at him very warmly and openly. "And Ill tell you one thing, Dave. Im no nymphomaniac whether you believe me or not. But you can think that if you want to. And, one other thing: you better give up the idea of being in love with me. Dont talk yourself into it. Because itll never do you any good. I dont suppose I can keep you from trying to make love to me every now and then; you can no more help trying to make love to every woman you meet than you can help breathing; you had a very insecure childhood. But I can tell you now, Ill ignore it and it wont do you any good."

Dave didnt say anything. He was still reveling in his discovery. He knew there had been something wrong. And if she wanted to think she could talk him out of it, that was all right. If that made her feel better, that was okay. Let her think it.

"If you want me to help you with that book," Gwen said, "Ill work with you on it just like I work with Wally Dennis. Ill be a friend and companion to you just like I am with Wally."

"Thanks," Dave said dryly. He could feel he was beginning to get pretty tight. It was a good thing he had figured it all out before he got tight.

"Because Id like to see it get written," Gwen said earnestly. "If you knew!" she said suddenly. "If you knew the number of people Ive had in my classes who wanted to be writers! I wish I had an actual count. And of all of these how many do you think had even the chance of becoming one? Two! Wally Dennis, and one other boy. Who went off to Chicago three years ago to live the artist's life and write. I havent heard a word about him since. Or from him. Two, out of all those people. If you knew how rare and valuable a thing it is that you have!" she said almost religiously.

"Yeah," Dave said. "Sure. Well, you and me'll work on it."

"—But thats all Ill do," Gwen said, the taut haunted look coming back in her face. "I wont do any more. I love literature, but— Well, dont expect anything else from me."

"Okay," Dave said. "We'll write it." He drank off the rest of what was in the mixer. He felt good. He was still mulling over his discovery. Hell, if that was all it was. If she was a nympho all he had to do was bide his time. Eventually he would catch her right. Be bound to. His investment was safe after all, and his selfrespect.

"Ive got to go," he said getting up. In getting up, he felt himself sway slightly.

Gwen looked surprised. "Arent you going to stay till Dad gets home?"

"No," he said. "Got work to do for Frank tomorrow. Ill be back." He looked around for his topcoat. It was lying across the back of one of the reading chairs, where Bob had put it—how long ago? A long time ago anyway. He started over toward it. He was drunker than hed thought. He had drunk more than he meant to, getting upset and all.

"Well at least wait till Wally comes," Gwen said.

"Cant," he said. "Anyway, I agree with your dad. I dont think hes comin." He reached the coat.

"Are you sure youre all right to drive?" Gwen said.

"Perfectly," he said. "Fine. Perfectly all right." He picked up the coat. He was drunk. Wow! In just that short walk from the table. But it didnt matter, everything was all right now. Just bide your time. He didnt feel upset any more.

"Here, Ill help you," Gwen said. She came over from the fireplace and helped him struggle into the topcoat and he could smell some bitter-sweet perfume radiating from her body, warm as it was from the fire. Dave set his hat on his head, the new hat, from Indianapolis, and looked at her.

"Thank you for a very pleasant evening," he said.

"Youre welcome to stay the night if you want to," Gwen said a little anxiously.

"Cant," he said. "Got to work for Frank tomorrow."

"Then come back tomorrow and spend the weekend," Gwen said.

"Maybe," Dave said. "Try. Anyway, thank you for a very pleasant evening," he said. He turned and started toward the door, which was at the far end from the reading chair.

"Youre very drunk," Gwen said.

"Sober as a judge," he said. He reached the door. He opened it and went down the three steps to the cellar landing.

"Please do come for the weekend," Gwen said from the doorway above.

"Maybe," he said. "Dont know. Try. Dont know if I can stand it, you know. Very sensitive person. Try not. Cant. Writer. Anyway, thank you for a very pleasant evening," he said. "Goodby."

"Be careful on the highway," Gwen said, "please."

"Perfectly." He put his hand on the knob, and then remembered he had forgot to fix the fire for Bob. He took his hand off the knob. "I forgot to fix the fire for Bob," he said.

"Thats all right," Gwen said. "Ill fix it."

"I promised him I would fix it," Dave said. He started for the steps.

"I know how to fix it," Gwen said. "Ill do it."

"But you dont understand. I promised him, you see," Dave said, putting his foot on the first step.

"Ill do it for you," Gwen said from above him. "Ive done it lots of times before. I know how."

"But I promised," Dave said.

"Thats all right," Gwen said. "He wont mind."

"Okay," he said, turning back to the door. "—But you tell him I remembered. Will you?" he said. "You will?"

"Ill tell him."

"You know, you are really quite a person," Dave said. "I like you."

"Thank you."

"I like you just as much. Perhaps I even like you better. Yes, I think I do," he said.

"Well thank you," Gwen said, unable to help grinning.

"Dont grin. I mean it. Seriously." He put his hand on the knob again, feeling a vague but definite impression that he should not talk so much. "I really shouldnt drink this much, you know," he said owlishly.

"Yes, I know," Gwen said. "Are you sure youre all right to drive?"

"But I sometimes do," he said gaily and debonairly, leaning on the door airily. He wanted to create the same impression in leaving that Bob had; but a tremendous hiccup, which was at least two thirds belch, suddenly burst out of him ruining the effect. "God!" he said in a startled voice. "That was loud!"

Gwen laughed outright from the doorway above.

"Excuse me," he said.

"Certainly," Gwen said. "Please be careful."

"Perfectly," he said. "And thank you for a very pleasant evening."

He opened the door carefully and let himself out, closed it carefully, started for his car and almost fell down. Gwen did not follow him out, and he was glad of that. He was just beginning to realize how drunk he was. He staggered seriously along the walk to where the car was parked, trying very hard to keep his balance, but each time he straightened himself from swaying one way he would push too far and sway the other, thinking intently only about getting home and to bed. At the car, after the consummate work of getting in and getting the door shut, he had trouble getting the key into the lock. His eyes would only focus for a second and then his insides would begin to whirl his head sickeningly and make him roll his eyes around to stop it.

Yes, he had drunk far too much. It was that getting upset and all. It was a damned good thing he had trained on Martinis and could hold his liquor or wow! As it was, he couldnt even see to drive. And there was still at least one big drink in him which had not even begun to hit him yet. He thought about the liquor somberly and objectively, and without feeling in the same way one thinks about an enemy who has battered and pummeled and outwitted and outfought one until even the loss of the game itself shrinks to a measure of complete indifference.

He backed the car and turned it carefully, intent upon focusing his eyes and not hitting anything. At the end of the crushed rock driveway he stopped, impregnated with a momentously sly idea. He was afraid to get up on the highway like this, with those big trucks and all. Why not drive home the back way? A splendid idea, old chap, old Dave! he told himself, mimicking Bob French.

At the end of the drive he turned right, onto the business street away from town and followed it out under the high loom of the bridge to where it became a graveled country road, and so it was that an hour later he found himself on a dirt lane which had continued on from the end of the gravel and which now ended in the winter cornfield before him, somewhere in the river bottoms. If there had been a road west to the left he had not seen it. Thinking that it was a good thing the ground was frozen or he would have long since got stuck in this bottomless mud, he turned off the lights and shut off the motor and lay down in the front seat to try and sleep, he was terribly sleepy, but he could not because every time he shut his eyes he started whirling and had to reopen them. The last thing he thought of with a kind of blissful peace of soul was that everything was all right now and his investment was safe because if she was a nympho all he had to do was bide his time and he would catch her right and working on the book was as good a way as any, and when he woke up that was the first thing he thought of, too.

It was three thirty. Frozen clean clear in to the bone, still drunk but able to see now, he got the car turned around in the deadstalked cornfield and, shivering and shaking convulsively so that he could hardly hold the wheel, he drove all the way back through Israel (there were no lights in the house as he passed it) and up onto the highway and back to Parkman thinking miserably, wow what an evening!

At the hotel he told the decrepit nightman to give strict orders he was still not in, crept up stairs exhaustedly, and after taking a huge shot of his remaining whiskey, slid his frozen body gratefully into bed under all the covers he could find, and tried fitfully to sleep.

CHAPTER 24

GWEN FRENCH had remained standing in the cellar doorway after Dave bowed himself out and closed the outside door. She leaned against the jamb, tall and almost masculinely angular, her hand resting above her on the wood, and listened worriedly to the low vague cursing and the pattern of uneven footsteps that receded out of hearing but she could not help grinning a little too in spite of her anxiety.

What she really wanted to do was follow him out there and stop him. She could take him home in her car and leave his here, if he still insisted on going, and for a moment she almost went. But she knew beforehand that his male vanity and pride would never stand for that, would never admit he was that drunk. So instead, she contained herself and merely stood in the doorway, listening alertly.

The immemorial status of the female, she thought irately, with a sudden fleeting violence. They also serve.

Eventually the car door slammed and then there was silence, silence for a long interval. Fumbling with the key, she thought. After a while though, when there was still no sound, unable to help herself, she tiptoed down the four steps to the landing and put her ear against the crack of the outside door. She stood that way, her hand on the knob, still half of a mind to go on out. But then finally the car started. She listened hard, holding her breath, while it backed up, stopped, turned. There were no bangs or crashes, it proceeded slowly and cautiously down the drive. Feeling only a little relieved Gwen went back up the steps and closed the inside door irritably.

Half of her no doubt, she thought, had been half hoping that he would hit something—something minor. So she would have an excuse to go out and stop him. Driving down the driveway safely was one thing. Getting up there on the highway where all those tractor trailer trucks came shooting through over the bridge was something else.

He might very easily get himself killed, she thought seriously, or have a serious crippling wreck.

—However she believed that he would not; and that nothing of the sort would happen to him. In fact, she knew it. She knew it because there had been too much of fate in all of this—in his coming back to Parkman, and in his meeting them—and things like that did not just happen through blind chance.

He had a tremendous driving animal vitality, that one. It filled almost to screaming any place he was in as long as he was there, and when he left, it left the place feeling physically empty. Well she had a flock of theme papers to read and grade before tomorrow, she reminded herself dutifully.

If something did happen, it was because it was supposed to happen, and couldnt have been avoided anyway, whether she made him stay here or not. Bob had taught her that principle long ago. If it did happen it was his Karma, and there was nothing she could do about that. If he died, he died. She walked down to the fireplace.

The fire itself was beautiful; of itself; an entity. Hands resting on the mantel, all her weight on one leg, she leaned at arm's length in the immemorial position of the inveterate fire watcher, her body bent just a little so that she could see beneath the lintel, her wide square shoulders supporting her weight. All of her was pervaded with that sense of sheer physical gratitude open fires always made her feel. They always kept the heat lower than normal in the house, so the fire would be more enticing. —Besides, she thought firmly, it was healthier.

She did not bother to fix the fire as she had promised Dave, and hardly even thought about it. In the first place the fire didnt need it. Any wood put on it now as hot as it was would simply burn right up and not last over an hour. He obviously didnt know anything at all about open fires.

In all the years—and that must be at least seventeen?—that she had been lying to people about her many lovers so that no one would suspect she was still a virgin, this was the first time she could ever remember having played her part so well that someone took her for a nymphomaniac.

Gwen laughed ruefully. That was one possibility she had not even remotely contemplated. She still did not know whether to feel complimented or insulted. But her tendency was all to feel insulted, and that was silly wasnt it? Because this was only the ultimate of the very effect she had been striving so hard to achieve. Nevertheless, she still felt it. She had worried so long about people not believing her that she had never considered the opposite, that of being believed too well.

Well, it was certainly a compliment to her acting ability, anyway. She really ought to get at those papers.

Tall, angular, selfcontained, competent, attractive, she stared into the red bell, tinkling incandescence of the fire as if sucking physical nourishment from it. Strange, the paths life took to make of people what they did become. It had burned down just enough from the last new wood to make a thick fat bed of coals, glowing and irradiant, from which little violet flames flickered. The big backlog, cracked and checked in perfect squares, split off little cherryred pieces of itself that dropped into the goldred of the coals with thin metallic sounds, as if somewhere within the cycle of chemical change from wood to ash there was a space where the wood was transmuted first directly into metal. Fire. No wonder the alchemists called it one of the four basic elements.

A virgin. A virgin at thirty five! What would he say, if she told him. Hoot in her face with disbelief. And run like a scared rabbit, probably, if she ever did convince him.

Raptly, she studied the pictures in the coals. They shifted and shimmered, formed and dissolved. Right now on the left she could see a gargoyle face from Notre Dame Cathedral. And to the right of it an old English castle on a hill. The gargoyle face slowly and imperceptibly changed into a dog's face for her. The castle gradually became a treaded tank with a long gun on its turret. It was live; alive—that was the only word for it, alive. The whole thing shimmered and pulsed with life.

Sometimes she imagined a fire was a window into the Fourth Dimension. Through which one might pass, and travel far, and then return. Sometimes, staring into a fire it was as if she herself came up out of herself, passing out through her own eyes, her windows, and on through the window of the fire into that other space. At other times it was as if the fire was healing, actually physically healing, its glows and rays passing inward through her eyes to circulate around her body healing whatever ailed. How frightening a house on fire was; the enemy; God the enemy; calling up all the old primitive racial fear and awed worship. And how opposite; how much a friend and succorer; when under control and contained within a fireplace. She continued to stand, nurturing herself on it hungrily. She ought to get at those theme papers.

What if it were really true! she thought suddenly, with a kind of half transported, minor wildness. What if a fire really were a window! When you looked closely, with the thought already in your mind, it did look like one, down in there, one which you could step down through and exit outside all the limiting confines of time—and space— and all the cherished human medievalisms. Exit, and returning, bring back with you all the knowledge that had ever been recorded on the time-pulse of the universe. And what if the fire should burn out before you returned? Would that mean you were trapped there, never to come back? Or would you be able to enter back through any fire? Gwen laughed; what havoc you could create if you stepped out through the fire in some stranger's livingroom! And with all the knowledge of the universe!!

—But always, whenever she seemed to go out of *her* self, When *she* returned, whatever knowledge, if it were there at all, always remained behind. Oh to live in the clean bright hard cold spirit of the mind alone. Without the dragging dullwitted body forever there to drag it back. The body that must eat meat and the leaves of plants to sustain itself. And then wear itself away in yearly depreciation trying to digest its fuel. Oh, if the fire only were a window!

Abruptly she turned away and sat down on one of the divans by the coffeetable. Okay, sure there was curiosity; she wouldnt be normal if there wasnt curiosity would she? The coffeecup he had used still sat there, a remaining bit of personality, enforcing remembrance. The mixer glass still sat on the other table. She felt like breaking both of them.

How many other times, when she had been telling people with the open frankness of a sophisticate about having had lovers, had they immediately jumped to the conclusion that she was a nympho? How many had thought it and never said it? My God! She blushed deeply and a terrible wave of embarrassment, almost physically cringing, passed over her. She shut her eyes wanting to crouch and hide somewhere. Momentarily she was helpless, completely crippled. Wave of it followed wave, hitting her like heavy seas crashing into a cliff in a high wind. Gradually it passed, though.

Gwen rose and picked up the cup and mixer and carried them down to the sink and rinsed them and then ran them full of water to soak so they would be easier to wash. She felt as though she had just walked over a subway grating somewhere and the sudden gust from a passing train had blown her skirt around her ears, exposing her completely, and revealing she had no panties on—a thing she was wont to do sometimes because it was more comfortable.

She turned back to the room indecisively. The thought—the very thought—of exposure had been enough to send another crushing, sick, degrading wave of embarrassment through her; in her time she had dreamed about such an event more than once. The theme papers still lay in a pile beside the one of the two reading chairs she used. She didnt feel like doing anything; there wasnt anything she felt was important enough to do. And yet she wanted to be doing something badly. Anything.

Sort of aimlessly, she wandered back down the room and sat down at the big table, the same place she always seemed to wander to. She rested her elbows on it and propped the sides of her long face between her hands and stared back cateyed at the offending fire.

A virgin. A virgin, at thirty five. Oh, how people would howl with laughter.

Did people see in beds of coals the things they wanted to see? Like in the ink blot tests? Psychological theory said you saw what you imposed there, what you were looking for. But what did they know? What did they *really* know? They were about as near to understanding minds as James Watt was to a turbo jet. Infancy. It was even different in *kind*. Hunh! The headshrinkers.

Psychiatrists! No wonder each one was having his own sittings with another one a little bit higher up. That was the way to insanity, through excessive symbolizing. She thought of some of the ones she had met in her year in New York. There were the artistic ones, who hung around with the writers and painters; and there were the business-minded ones, who commuted to Westchester and their expensive homes as if they were MDs. But never could quite believe they were as respectable as MDs. Just as the artistic ones could never feel quite as artistic as artists. All of them more neurotic than the patients they were trying to "help".

Her face still resting between her supporting palms, Gwen turned her head to look around the cleaned up table. The extinguished dinner candles still on it caught her eye and she looked at them, and at their drippings congealed into dead-white droplets down their rounded sides. You could see sex symbols in just about everything, if you looked for them.

The other thing was still there, back down there in the bottom of her mind. She tried to put it aside and think about Dave Hirsh instead.

Dave was one of the good ones, and she knew it. There was just something about them. You could tell. A sort of dumb innocence and a basic inherent sweetness of soul, combined with a ridiculously great vanity, and the bitchery and meanness of a fiend which cropped out every so often especially if they were drinking. Wally Dennis had the same quality. So did Mac Price, who had gone off to Chicago—and not been heard from since. She had learned about handling drunks from Mac. Mac had been in love with her, too. She suspected Wally Dennis was too, in a sort of a way off and on, although he had never mentioned it since that one time he had asked her to sleep with him. It was a little hard to tell about Wally, his reactions were somewhat hampered by the fact that he felt she was too old for him. They all fell in love, and out, and then back in, with such a confusing rapidity that it was hard to keep up with it. And they all had that other thing—that same quality so pronounced in Stendhal and Tolstoy—of desperately needing to indulge in selfexposure.

That didnt mean they had made the grade. Or ever would. But it did mean they had the qualities that could make it. But the more of those qualities they had, the more it seemed they would never make it. Look at Mac Price, running off to Chicago, to be an artist. Life beckons, he had said—seriously. I need love, he said. I need life; to live. He had

had a good novel well on the way, when he had left here. He was probably drinking and sexing himself into a state of stupor in Chicago.

They were all like runners, Gwen thought, runners with huge enormous feet. They were dependent upon their feet to run, and needed them. But those same feet were always tangling them up and tripping them. And if they ever did win a race it was both because of their feet and in spite of them, simultaneously.

But none of them knew this. All they knew was that they loved their big feet, for making them different, while they hated them bitterly for making them conspicuous. Such children.

—Nobody knew what drove them. All of them. As they were so obviously driven. Probably it was a need for love. But then everybody— anymore; in this world; today—had a need for more love. What made the difference with the Macs and Daves and Wallys? She didnt know. But she knew she could always pick them. She could always recognize them by reason of the fact that they were such absolute fools, in the first place, she thought smiling, if for nothing else.

Gwen got up from the table and strode on down to the fireplace again, but this time she avoided looking into the coals for pictures.

That Dave. He was probably still convinced the only reason he had stayed in Parkman and was embarking on this book was because he was in love with her and wanted to seduce her. He was really very sweet. She had noted how he carefully kept himself from getting physically close to her all evening. That was thoughtfulness. There was a quality of great gentleness about him, she thought lambently, which belied all the harsh bitter things he liked to say. He was astute, too. He had known there was something odd going on all evening. But he couldnt tell what, so he had gone ahead and made his deduction. His innocent deduction which, wouldnt you know it, was just almost diametrically opposite to what the truth was! Yet he had had legitimate reason to think that—given her own honesty. —which was of course where he slipped up: he ingenuously accepted her as honest. Nobody but a writer would ever do that, with a woman. He was such an ass, she thought almost lovingly, and so gullible. God, what a sucker he would be for any little flip who came along. The only reason he wasnt married right now was because up to now no female ever had considered him a worthwhile enough prospect. She really did like him a lot. Nobody but a writer would ever sit, and in a tone of elated discovery tell a woman to her face she was a nymphomaniac.

Gwen blushed again, and felt again the terrible embarrassment, so strong as to be almost unrational, traumatic, wash over her. It welled up blackly from the bottom of her mind like a flock of slave laborers released from a dungeon into the light. She remembered another time in New York once when she had felt like this; one of the rare ones.

She had been dating a boy, one of the bright young Yale men from TIME & LIFE, a genuine wit and a comic. They had had a number of dates. This time—they were going somewhere on the subway—the Eighth Ave it was—and below ground in the station waiting for the train he had maneuvered her before an ad panel where some child had scrawled the word fuck in huge letters across the face of the advertisement, and then he had talked her around, moving in front of her, until she was staring right at it, and as the surprised recognition crossed her face, had laughed delightedly. He had not said a thing, but he knew, understood: the point was, there were other people standing around, and her first thought had been to whether any of them had seen her looking. She had felt this same sick embarrassment then and wanted blindly to hide, followed by a fierce furious anger that was not at him, the fellow—or rather not only at him, but at everything. Everything existent in the world that could make such a stupidly embarrassing situation even possible of happening.

She could feel that same anger coming over her now, hot and searing, not anger at Dave so much, but at people, at life, and the stupidities of life, at society, at—at all the people who might ever have thought she was a nymphomaniac. There, in New York, she had covered it up as best she could and had laughed embarrassedly and turned away; there wasnt much else she could do. Here, as she felt it raging up in her, she felt like sweeping the mantel. Sweeping it of everything. The lovely brass candlesticks, the three steins, the ashtrays, everything, into a smashed welter on the floor. As if that would make her feel any better! she thought furiously.

Damn them all, and damn their primitive myths and superstitions about sanctity and chastity. In Africa if a man marries a girl and finds out she is not a virgin, he kills her; or, if he be more businessminded, makes her father add five more cows to the dowry. We were at least as primitive. For that matter, who was to say who was primitive?

In our country we took the females at an early age and began inculcating them with the mystical admonition that they had above all one priceless possession, their chastity, and that this must never be relinquished until legally and in the eyes of God they were united with one particular male, whose sole property this chastity became, and who would cherish it forever with fervent ardor. This union thus acquired a deep religious bliss in some occult way, and a powerful legal and social approval, and engendered a revered state known as The Family, in which the united male and female and their offspring continued to exist with an utter and complete mysterious happiness the rest of their entire lives, serving God, Country, society, and self with equal joy and spiritual greatness.

You didnt have much choice not to believe it. If you by some miraculous chance managed to survive the incantations of your *very* early childhood, as you emerged from the emotional hazards of puberty you were brought up against such a powerful force of propaganda that you scarcely could avoid succumbing. Your undiscriminating eyes were bombarded with such an array of movies and books full of love-ardor and the religious-worship of the empedestaled female vulva, such a collection of popular music love ballads crying the same—all just as you were discovering helplessly in adolescence that your life was going to be full of loneliness—that if your vanity did not cause you to acquiesce willingly, your fear would. Who wouldnt want all that adoration?

So you believed, as violently and pugnaciously as the rest, and shouted your claims to heaven just as loudly, and demanded your rights to be loved just as positively. Because your vanity informed you you were worth it, more than worth it—being loved; and because your fear told you you had damned well better be—or at least pretend you were; it was less frightening. Gwen swung around, tall, squareshouldered and suddenly dangerous in her anger and outrage, and glared around the room as if looking for enemies, or something inexpensive to break.

The truth the bald truth was, she was a very unhappy woman. Why not admit it? She was unhappy because she was a woman. Because she was a woman and had no talent nor desire for selfexposure, like Dave and Wally and Mac Price had. Or, if she did, she was afraid to use it. Afraid to expose, because she was a woman, and had been taught by a woman, like a woman, that women never never exposed themselves. It had taken her a long time to realize her mother was an ignorant stupid woman; she was still ashamed of it. How was she to have known? She was well educated, she was universally admired, she practically ran her church, her club friends loved her, she was considered a fine wife and mother, was said to be brilliant, was thought to be beautiful. How was she, a gangling knob-boned girl, to know these judgments and opinions were all wrong, were superficial, and were not even most of the time believed by the ones who said them; were merely part of the network of lies necessary to maintain the great human conspiracy of importance; the mass blackmarket of you-believe-me-Ill-believe-you. By the time she found out, it was too late. Her mind and opinions could be changed, yes, but you could never change the emotions that had been built into her brick upon mortared brick like a wall from the time she was old enough to have one. They were still there. And would stay there.

Men want to degrade you. That was the upshot of it. About as unoriginal a refrain as you could find anywhere in these 20th Century United States. But not to a frightened girl, who was already too proud for her own good anyway. Men want to dominate you and alter you, and then laugh at you. Men want to take the most precious thing you have, and destroy it, for their own selfish demands, and then throw you away like an old sack. Men want to make you big and ugly and fat with a baby. Men want to make you so you will never be beautiful any more. Men want to degrade you.

Before she even knew what it was all about she was hearing it. *That* was why she was still a virgin. A virgin, Gwen thought sourly. At thirty five. Oh, how they would laugh. *That* was why. It was one thing to understand yourself intellectually, and why you felt what you felt. It was quite another to change the feeling. The psychiatrists, the mighty psychiatrists, couldnt even do it for themselves. There was the measure of their success.

She had never talked about it with her father. She couldnt. She was too ashamed and too embarrassed; and she would feel too foolish. But she was sure he knew and understood it all. His own life must have been a veritable hell on earth, with her.

If she had been less innocent. More knowing. Other girls ignored parental "wisdom", and went ahead pursuing the horizon anyway. But not her: She believed.

No wonder she took it out in helping them, these bumbling ineffectual weakling male idiots, who did however have one thing, as Dave had said, this burning desire to unzip their soul's underwear and expose themselves in public.

Poor poor weak pittance. But she did it, because what they did was what she wanted most of all in this world to do. Expose. Her, a school teacher, a college English instructor, virgin.

It hammered at her in her head over and over again, carrying with it a deep blushing sense of shame, of ridiculousness, embarrassment, fear that someday someone might find out. She was a virgin. At thirty five! There were a lot of paradoxes in the quasi-religious American chastity superstition, and this was one of them. That she should be ashamed of being a virgin. But it followed. And thus it was, that so many librarians, secretaries, technicians and staff assistants (*and* school teachers!) gradually came to lead haunted lives, their ears constantly alert for any laugh behind them, any snicker, which might be directed at them. —Even those of them who in their time had had ample love affairs, forced by the primitive society they lived in to pretend theyd never had them by the very definition of their virtue, so that even that satisfaction was denied them.

And thus it also was, that she herself, Gwen French, college English teacher, but smarter than most, would do anything—anything—even be thought a nymphomaniac by everyone—rather than admit to anyone what she really was, a thirty five year old virgin college English teacher.

She sank down on the divan. Then she got up and went to put the pot on, for a cup of coffee.

It was really very funny. In a way. Like the man who took the stack of steel bars, tested them carefully for strength, fitted them meticulously and with exactness, welded them precisely and with accuracy, never realizing once all that time that what he was building was his own cage, his own cell for life.

There were times, in moments of wildness, when she thought to go out somewhere—anywhere, Chicago, Indianapolis, anywhere she was not known—and deliberately pick up some strange man and get him to sleep with her. Maybe then she could unlax, let down that constant watchfulness and fear of people finding out. Maybe then she could even selfexpose. Like Dave and Wally and Mac Price. At least it would be an act, an irrevocable act. —But she never did. For one thing, being a virgin at thirty five embarrassed her. What if the man, in sleeping with her, should find out she was a virgin? For another, she told herself she was wise enough to already know beforehand no such simple and artless thing would ever be able to uncage her.

It had been an easy cage to build. Oh, very easy. In fact, maybe all you had to do was be born a woman. So easy she had not even known she was building it. The first stage was back in high school, when she learned the easiest way to handle boys was to tell them you were in love with someone else.

That way they never got mad at you but instead acquired a great respect for you (as boys will for girls!) and wanted to be your best friend and confidant to whom you brought your woes—always hoping of course (you could see it in their face) that they could catch you right, and angry enough, some evening. But they never pushed you, and merely waited, passively. It made for nice relationships.

From there, for anyone with any brain at all, and any ability to use it, it was only a simple logical inference to the second stage at college, when all the girls began having affairs and talking about them: the sly smug look, the little smile, the possessiveness around the men. The look-at-me!-Ive-got-mine air. It was easy to convince the girls. All you had to do was look smug occasionally. She didnt know, now, how many had been really having affairs, and how many had been pretending like herself. But at the time she thought they all were having them. Except herself. All great love affairs, there was nothing a student in college admired quite so much as a tragic love affair in someone else. And, drawing from the girls, it was easy to know to tell the men you dated the same thing, and easy to discover they believed it even quicker than the boys in high school. The only difference was where in high school you said "in love" now you said "having an affair." Let them but think you were just getting over a heartbreakingly unhappy affair with the man you dated before you started dating them, and they became so tender and solicitous it was unbelievable; much moreso than if you had been a simple virgin; and you knew the poor things would have cut their tongues out, before they would have talked about you. And suddenly, although you didnt really know it yet, except very disquietingly vaguely, your cage was half built.

She could still have crawled out when she came back home from school. Maybe. But what could have been easier than to tell the men at home you were still violently in love with a boy from school? They believed it just as readily as college boys. Once you knew that, once you grasped the principle behind male guilt, it was just as easy when you finally took a sabbatical and went off to get your Master's, to use the same trick there, on the literary sophisticates you went out with. Except now of course it was a man back home—from The School. —from Francis Parkman College, Parkman's Own Liberal Arts College, Fully Accredited, Vitally Christian. The sign at the city limits said it well.

Only by then, Gwen thought, something had changed, and it was no longer a lark, it had become a huge black shameful secret, her virginity, to be hidden now at all costs. In essence, that was why she had become engaged to Casper Milquetoast as Dave called him who worked in the bank, after she came home with her Master's. They were engaged five years. She might even have married him, just to quell any suspicions, if it had not been she was afraid he might find out in bed that she was a virgin. And that would have ruined his romantic picture of her. Of course everyone in town knew very well right away that they were sleeping together, but of course that was all right, since they were engaged, and were going to be married. Only in this case they werent sleeping. When he was killed in a Japanese air raid upon a rear area Finance Corps encampment on some grubby little island in the Pacific, it was as if no one had died. That seemed to be his destiny. —But the last stage was set, for her. The cage was finished and she was in it. How could she ever marry any man now, even if she wanted, even if she loved him, in Parkman Illinois—or anywhere else she was known? Have him discover she was still a virgin? And all the stories only lies?

So she became the woman of the world who had had her share of love affairs and wasnt interested in sex anymore, sex bored her. Wally Dennis believed it. Mac Price believed it. The bright young Yale men of TIME & LIFE and the publishing world of New York believed it. Dave Hirsh believed it too, until he saw through it tonight, and realized she was a nymphomaniac.

She hadnt meant to flirt with him like that. At all. It hadnt started out to be that, and then suddenly it had slipped into it somehow without her knowing it. —And the truth was, her vanity liked it. But it wasnt fair to do that to a man when you never intended for it to go any further.

The coffee was ready now, but she didnt want any. She pulled the plug and turned it off. She didnt know what she wanted. The theme papers still lay in a jumbled pile beside her chair. Certainly she did not want them. And certainly it was not a man she wanted.

What law, moral or divine, said a woman *had* to have a man? Oh the myths and legends and superstitions we civilized people lived by. She stepped to the mirror that hung beside the dining room doorway and studied herself in it. She was *not* drying up. Her neck was *not* getting scrawny. She studied her face for signs of spinsterhood. She was just as attractive now as she had ever been—which, while it may not ever have been much, certainly was not getting any lesser. Evening at home, she thought. Miss French's evening at home.

Damn it all, why couldnt she be like Doris Fredric, whose father owned the bank, and who taught freshman English in the high school —who took all the men she wanted, and then claimed to be a virgin. That would be more normal.

A wild, halfcrazy, inflamed rebellion bubbled up in Gwen. Like the blood of a man machinegunned through the chest, she thought; theres an image for you. I should write. She knew what she would do. She would do what she did every time she got rebellious every six months or so. She would get out her father's pornography collection and look at it. Resolutely she went to the doorway at the other end, and up the back stairs to his bedroom.

She didnt know why she did it, why she ever did it. She only knew she wanted to do something horrible, and this was the most horrible thing she could think of.

The pictures themselves fascinated her anyway. They were horrible, sickening. They always made her think immediately of Suetonius' description of the orgies of Tiberius in his selfimposed retirement on Capri, while Rome lay slowly dying. You never realized what a really foul thing the human body was until you—She had studied them enough times—and with such pinpointed, almost unearthly concentration—that she practically knew each one by heart. That any woman —or any man—would do such things and allow themselves to be so degraded—and then allow pictures to be taken of it!—seemed unbelievable. Another thing was that there wasnt a single really sensitive face among them. Most of them were grossly animal, stupid, as if drunk or drugged. Now and then there was a face with a trace more, a hint only, of perception—but so rare among the others as to stand out starkly; but always where there was any hint of any deeper sensitivity than just animal, it came out manifested as pure hatred. Such pure, undiluted, utter and complete consuming hatred she had never seen on any human face, such smug degrading domination—as existed on these few slightly more selfsensitive faces. Never was there any trace of even a physical affection. It was a strange, dark comment on the real underlying pressures and motives and emotions of our sexual habits.

And this hatred was what fascinated her. After all, hatred was her forte, wasnt it? Pressures which we ourselves caused and imposed upon ourselves.

At the top of the stairs in the upstairs hall she went directly to Bob's bedroom and to the closet. High up at the very back on the very top shelf were three not large heavy-pasteboard boxes and one very small long box of 35 mm slides. She had to get a chair to reach them. Then she got Bob's little slide projector. Usually she took them to her own bedroom, but tonight with a wild flamboyant recklessness she took them back downstairs to the kitchen with her.

Why her father had them in his possession she had no idea, but she suspected that psychologically some way it had something to do with her mother. They werent the type of thing you would expect Bob to have. Where he had come by them she hadnt the least idea, and what he did with them she did not know. Evidently, he looked at them. He had had them a very long time; she had discovered them years ago, long before her mother died, in the house out by the school in Parkman, while rummaging through the back corners of a storage closet looking for something else. She had looked through them, her breath getting shorter in her chest, (she was past twenty five, and already knew—by hearsay anyway—everything they depicted), and then had put them back exactly as she found them (while she listened to her mother downstairs serving tea to one of her committees) and had said nothing. If Bob knew she found them, he never gave any sign. He did not move them to a new hiding place. It was hard to tell with Bob; you never knew what his motives were for anything, and he had a very devious subtle mind, really. After that she kept track of them, and noted that he took them out from time to time. When she herself, in moments of rebellion and sick fascination, took them out to look at them, she found that he often had added new ones to them. It was turning out to be quite a bulky collection. When they had moved out here to Israel it was as if she consciously divined beforehand just exactly where he would put them, and sure enough when she looked, he had.

In the kitchen Gwen spread the whole conglomeration out on the big dining table neatly. There were several of those little packs of playing cards with pictures on the faces, a great number of just simple photographs on glossy paper, a number of little printed books of stories with a few badly reproduced photographs which said they were made in France but which obviously were not since some of the photographs were the same as those printed on the paper. Anyway, the people in them didnt look like Frenchmen, they looked American.

All of this stuff she did not bother with, but instead set up the little projector (which she had seen Bob use a thousand times in the same way right here in this room, to show his own color snapshots and nature pictures) so it was focused on the wide white brickwall of the fireplace, the only blank wall in the room. Then she took the small long box of color transparencies and started running them through it.

She was well aware there was a strong element of danger in all of this, a possibility that she might be caught, but she welcomed it. Something wild and outraged and violated in her made her almost wish for it. It would make quite a nice little scene. It was only a little after nine, and Wally Dennis might still show up lugging along that chicken-headed little idiot Dawn, whom he was trying so hard to seduce. Or Bob himself might very easily come home a little early. Well, let them come; let them all come, damn them; damn them all. Let them catch her. Let them see her. She wished they would. Wouldnt they be surprised, and then she could tell them how she was a nymphomaniac.

There were a few pornographic scenes among the color transparencies but mostly they were only posed portraits of nude women, models apparently.

It was always a striking, startling thing to think of Bob being interested in such things. He was really such a dear sweet old thing. She could just see him, hiding his pictures away like a small boy and looking at them guiltily in his room. It would be funny if he did catch her, Gwen thought, and giggled nervously like a girl. Would his face be red! Who would ever have thought of him, Robert Ball French the poet, philosopher, thinker, recluse, collecting pornography?

Suddenly a wild idea came to her and she laughed outright as she began immediately to put it into action. She had wanted to do something wild, hadnt she? All evening she had dimly heard people going along the sidewalk outside the little fence, hadnt she? Laughing to herself with a kind of insane ribaldry, she selected one of the most garish, chorusgirl-looking nudes, put it into the projector. Then she went around turning all the lights off. When the room was dark she carried the little projector into the livingroom to the window edge and opened the window.

The cold air from the open window poured in over her. There were two slightly open spaces between the trees and bushes where you could see in a straight line to the street. Still laughing to herself nervously, Gwen switched the projector on and focused it through one of them, adjusting it till the picture of the nude, which she had put in sideways, appeared to be lying in the gutter beside the sidewalk. Then she switched it off and waited.

There was a streetlight at the corner whose feeble light, which reached this far, would help hide the beam of the projector through the air, while at the same time not being strong enough to kill the picture on the ground. The way the trees were situated before the house it would be next to impossible for anyone to see the beam. She waited patiently.

Pretty soon she could hear voices coming along the street from town, down the sidewalk on the other side across the street, a man's and a woman's. She couldnt recognize them. She waited until they were about a hundred feet away. Then laughing silently and nervously she switched the projector on.

"Whats that?" the man said, in a startled voice.

"Where?"

"There!"

The nude, which Gwen had switched on briefly and then off again so that it appeared only for a moment, looked to be lying down reclining in the gutter, the arms behind her head to arch her beautiful breasts, very nearly lifesize, perhaps a little over. She had recognized the voices now. It was the druggist and his wife, on their way home from closing up their store.

"It looked like a *naked* woman," the wife said faintly.

"That was what I thought it looked like," the druggist said.

Gwen switched the projector on again, and doubled up with silent laughter, trying to make no noise.

"There it is again!" the druggist said. They had stopped and were standing close together on the sidewalk.

"I see it! I see it!" his wife said nervously.

"It is a naked woman," the druggist said.

"But what would a naked woman be doing lying in the street?" the wife said unbelievingly. "On such a cold night. We must be seeing things."

"She might be dead?" he said. "She might be murdered?"

"Surely not," the wife said. "Not in Israel." Inside, Gwen switched it off.

"Now its gone!" the druggist said.

Inside the house, laughing silently and almost hysterically, her eyes beginning to brim with tears making it difficult to see, Gwen switched the projector on again, left it on a second, then shut it off and doubled over holding her nose and mouth.

"There it was again!" the druggist said nervously. They were still standing indecisively on the sidewalk.

"Maybe its some kind of a ghost," his wife said feebly.

"There arent any such things as ghosts, Mother," the druggist said without conviction. "Come on, Mother, I think we better get on home.

Its late," he said bravely. Through the trees Gwen watched him take her arm. They began to walk fast in the direction of the bridge, increasing their speed as they approached the spot where the nude had appeared to be lying, across the street from them on Gwen's side.

"Maybe somebody threw it there from a car passing over the bridge," the wife said faintly. "A gangster."

"From two blocks away?" the druggist said. "Anyway, theres nothing there now."

They were well past the spot now. And while their steps did not slacken, a sort of relief seemed to emanate from them.

"Maybe wed better call the police?" the druggist said.

"What? and have them find theres nothing there? Are you crazy?" his wife said. "We're going right straight home and go to bed."

Shaking silently, and doubled up with a pain in her stomach, Gwen kept her hand clamped over her nose and mouth and waited until they had gone on a little ways, then turned the projector on again, her diaphragm tickling her with frantic signals to erupt into a roar.

"There it is again!" the druggist said from down the block, his voice fainter.

"Stop looking back!" his wife said.

Gwen switched it off and shut the latticed window. Then she collapsed, sitting down weakly and letting out a very unladylike roar of laughter. Feeling some kind of strange release, she sat and laughed herself out until her diaphragm was relieved and her lungs were aching. Finally she got up and still shaking weakly with laughter carried the projector out to the kitchen and turned on the lights.

She did not even bother to look at any of the rest of the stuff, but began collecting it and putting it away back in the boxes. She was very careful to put it all back just exactly like she found it. Twice as she was putting it away she burst out suddenly with great deep throaty roars of laughter. Something had happened to her. She was no longer angry, no longer outraged, and she didnt feel violated anymore. In fact, she felt completely at peace with the world. Carefully she carried the stuff all back upstairs and put it all back very carefully on its shelf and replaced the chair exactly as it had been. Then she came back down to the kitchen and collected her theme papers she had to grade before tomorrow, and carried them up with her to do in bed. Then she remembered the fire and came back down and put another small log on it. While she was doing it she thought of the druggist and his wife and suddenly exploded into laughter.

In her bedroom she took a scalding hot shower in the cabinet shower Bob had had put in, and rubbed herself down vigorously and hard with a kind of narcissistic pleasure and masochistic enjoyment. Only when she was safely tucked in bed with the themes, the insides of her arms and thighs still quivering with the nervous tension she had been subject to, and the muscular exhaustion of the laughter, did the fear hit her. The fear that Wally might have come; the fear that Bob might have come home early; the fear that the druggist or his wife might have seen the beam from the projector. It would have been very easy for her to get caught. It was an insane thing to do. Any of them *could* have happened. But then the picture of them, the druggist and his little wife, scurrying along the sidewalk, made her burst out into another healthy indelicate roar of laughter.

—Anyway, half of her had known all along that nothing would happen, that she would *not* get caught. She had known Wally wasnt coming, she had known Bob would not come home early. It wasnt really dangerous at all. Just the same she promised herself resolutely not to ever do anything outlandish like that again. What on earth had ever made her do it? she thought with a sudden stab of fright, and embarrassment at herself made her flush.

She had to read late on the papers. It was after one o'clock before she finished them, and so she was still awake at twelve when Bob came in, tiptoeing a little unevenly up the stairs to his room.

Bob had been right about Wally after all, she thought briefly. He hadnt come. She wondered what had kept him from it? An attempted seduction of Dawn Hirsh, undoubtedly.

CHAPTER 25

WALLY DENNIS, Wally French Dennis, had fully intended to go over to Gwen's that night when he called her earlier. But it just hadnt worked out that way. It really didnt matter much anyway. It wasnt really important. And Gwen wouldnt mind.

Being as this was Thursday, he had had no classes under Gwen. And when just after noon he finished rewriting the last few pages of the two chapters she had marked for him, his first reaction was a feeling that he wanted her to read them and brag on them. And so he thought of calling her. But instead, he went downstairs in the big house and out to the kitchen and made himself a thick ham sandwich and got a bottle of beer out of the refrigerator. He had just recently scored a TD over his mom's team in the matter of keeping beer in the refrigerator. His mom's team consisted of his mom and Mrs Mertz the cleaning woman, who was a Holy Roller. Both were dead set against beer in the refrigerator. Finally, without bothering to argue and taking the bull by the horns so to speak, he had bought a dozen bottles of Schlitz and without saying anything just put them in the refrigerator, where his mom would later discover them.

"Wallace!" she had said. He had been sitting in the front room, reading. "Wallace, whats this beer doing in my icebox?"

"I put it there," he said coldly, and pretended to go on reading without looking around at her.

"In *my* icebox?"

"I cant afford to buy an icebox," he had said, turning the page ostentatiously.

Standing in the hall, behind him, she had hesitated—just a fraction —and he knew he had won. It was the coldness.

"But whatever for?" she had said.

"To keep it cold," he said. "What would you think?"

"Mrs Mertz will see it there," his mom said inconclusively.

"Shell probably see me drinking it, too," Wally said coldly.

"I dont like to think of my boy drinking beer," she said, but there wasnt much force in it.

"Im going to drink it anyway," he said and turned another page.

"Well . . ." she said, and let it dwindle off, thereby offering him a chance to say something else to her, something that would ease her defeat and his triumph. But he shrewdly had ignored it, and coldly gone on reading in silence, and after a moment she had gone on off. The beer stayed. Some time ago he had deduced empirically that whenever he showed pity or kindness to his mom, it invariably wound up losing him the victory he had already won.

Eating the ham sandwich and drinking the beer alone in the kitchen, Wally thought with satisfaction that he was beginning to learn how to handle her. He had scored some minor victories but this was the first real major triumph he had ever won over her. And it was all in the coldness, when you analyzed it. Somehow or other in the past year—since he had returned from Florida—the balance of power and authority had changed over from her to him, although he was still only twenty. It was all in the coldness, and because she did not want him to leave her. He had sensed the change, but up until the Battle of the Beers had not known how to take advantage of it. Being an only child had its advantages. Mrs Mertz's day was Tuesdays and the next time she had come he had made a point of drinking a beer openly at lunch when the three of them ate. The little wizenfaced old shrew hadnt dared to say anything about it. His mom had not said anything either.

She was gone now, off to some luncheon meeting somewhere. She and Dawn's mother were on some kind of committee together again, like the Red Cross—but no, the Red Cross Drive was always in the spring—or maybe the Xmas Baskets For The Poor committee. Probably that one was it. You never knew. They were on so damned many.

Wally reached into the center of the kitchen table where there was a lazy susan and pulled forth a narrow folder which he kept there and opened it up and began poring through it. He liked having the house to himself,—except that it was so damned big when there was only one person in it they seemed to echo. The folder was the catalog of W. D. Randall, Jr. of Orlando Florida, maker of Randall Made Knives. The thought of his Florida junket had made him think of it. Wally kept it there on the table where he could pore over it and look through it whenever he wanted,—usually in the mornings when he got up early by himself and made his own light breakfast before he went to work at his typewriter.

Wally had only seen one Randall knife in his lifetime, and this one was a constant source of chagrin to him. He had gone to Florida in the beginning with Steve Bennett from Parkman, who had been a year ahead of him in high school, to work on the piers and around the resort beaches of St Petersburg and Tampa. Steve had been there the year before and worked (when Wally was still a senior) and knew people and had come home and was going back. They had stayed five months the time Wally was with him and Steve had since gone back again. It was at the time before Wally had definitely decided to be a writer and was doing nothing but playing his trombone in some dance bands around home and was getting tired and bored with that. They had worked around the dirtiness and foreign Cubanness of Tampa The Cigar City until they ran into a guy who owned his own tarpon boat and was fitting out to go down to Venice-Nokomis in March for the tarpon season and had hired them both as hands but only for the duration of the tarpon-tourist season. It was at Venice—with the winter quarters of Kentucky Military Institute looming up across the big long central square that served as drillfield, and the grayblue clad platoons of little KMI boys and bigger KMI boys marching back and forth across the grass, when they were not in the drugstores eating icecream and playing pinball machines or helplessly ogling the young girls—that he first saw the knife. It was in a decrepit little drugstore where he and Steve had gone looking for sheath knives to use on the boat, and the owner had brought it out for them to look at with some other cheaper ones. The minute you held it in your hand, Wally thought again, you knew it was a real work of art. They could tell it even then, before either of them knew anything about knives. However, the old man at the drugstore asked seventeen dollars for it. He did not know where it had come from. It had been in the store when he acquired it. And he only knew vaguely that some man in Orlando named Randall made a few knives like this and sold them. The man who had had the store before him evidently had ordered it and then been unable to sell it because the price was too high, and had inventoried it on to him. That was why he couldnt afford to sell it for any less. Wally had wanted it so bad he could hardly stand it, but both of them were so short of money—and in addition were only getting paid on percentage, which meant no customers no money—that he knew they could not afford it. The sheath had darkened and dried out and begun to crack, and the blade had turned black lying in the store, but that didnt make any difference. Still, it would be insane to buy it. In the end, Steve bought it for fourteen, haggling the old man down that much, and Wally had bought a cheap one, and the next day they got a charter customer! After that Wally offered him twenty for it, but Steve wouldnt sell. Eventually, Steve the damned fool broke it in two at the hilt throwing it at a tree, after they came back home. Wally had bought the pieces and sheath off him for two dollars and still had them put away in his diddy drawer upstairs. It was only after getting home that he had seen a tiny ad in the back pages of a sporting magazine and written for the catalog.

Wally still could not think about Steve and the knife—and his own damned lack of courage that had kept *him* from buying it—without getting so frustrated and mad his spine twitched, and he thought about it every time he looked at the Randall catalog. There were nine or ten different models in the catalog and Wally had studied and re-studied them all, giving a great deal of careful thought to which one he would eventually buy. What he would have liked was to own one of each of them, but that was out of the question. Even one, with the way finances and money were here at home, was out of the question, now. But when he could afford the money, he knew which one he was going to buy. He had put a great deal of thought on it. The one he had decided on was the Randall #1 'All-Purpose Fighting Knife', with the double hilt, the 8″ blade, staghorn handle, and the buttcap drilled for a wrist thong.

This might not seem such a good selection at first glance, and might appear impractical. But actually it wasnt. The way he reasoned it was this: The #1, while basically a combat knife, could also be excellently used as a camping knife—and even as a general purpose boat knife, if you were extra careful with it around salt water. That was the reason for the stag handle, which would stand up much better around salt water than a laminated leather one; in case he ever went back to sea. Thus eliminating the extra expense of having three knives. And of course, this way, he would have a combat fighting knife if and when the Army ever got him. So far he had been let off the draft because of a bad ear and his mother, but he was too shrewd to expect to stay out of the Army forever.

Of course, the #1 was one of the most expensive models Randall made —twenty two dollars; twenty five, with the stag handle and the wrist thong—but Wally felt this was offset by the versatility of use he would have for it. And of course he would then have it if the Army ever got him, and should there be another war where he would need it. Just about everybody now accepted the fact that there would be another war, including himself, and it would come long before he would ever be near old enough to be safe from it. So really the #1 was the most practical choice.

He looked at the picture of the #1 in the catalog, as he downed the last of the ham sandwich. The way he had it planned—provided of course that he didnt finish his book first, naturally—when he was drafted, if he was, his mom would want to give him a going away present. But instead of letting her buy him something useless, he would ask her for $10 cash. With this as a down payment he would order the #1, and then pay the remainder out of his first Army paycheck; and the knife would then remain tied to his thigh the rest of the time he was in Service.

Swallowing the last of the beer, he studied the picture. It was a sort of a game he played with himself. Like getting out the Sears-Roebuck catalog when you were a kid. He had changed his mind and decided on different other Randall models several times, more as a study in comparision than in earnest, pretending he was going to buy one of them instead of the #1 so that he might compare their various merits and faults—faults for his use; they had no faults as knives—with the #1, but in the end he always came back to the #1 as being the most practical. For him. In his position.

He carried his dishes to the sink and ran water over them and then came back and closed the Randall catalog and put it back on the lazy susan. Then he poured himself a lukewarm cup of coffee he had made earlier and carried it into the living room with him to make his call to Gwen.

The big, old, ornate china clock which his mom kept sitting on the massive oak mantel to remind her of her once rich life, said it was ten minutes past one. On Thursdays Gwen had no one o'clock class, and could always be found in her little cubbyhole of an office in the English Department, working on that critical book of hers. She could usually be found there after school, too.

Sipping at the coffee Wally laid himself down in the big overstuffed main chair, draping a leg over one arm, and picked up the phone and dialed the number of the English Department phone at the college.

He still had this date with Dawn tonight—provided of course Dawn did not, in her accustomed and unpredictable way, decide to break this one too—but there wasnt much else to do with her anyway, except take her to the show or go pub crawling, so she might as well ride over to Gwen's with him.

Actually, and as usual, in the interim since quitting work he had got to feel more and more that the two rewritten chapters might not be as good as he had earlier thought they were, and because of this he wanted Gwen to read them and brag on them more than ever now, in order to reassure him. He saw no reason why he should not kill both birds, and take Dawn over there with him.

As he talked, Wally listened to his own voice putting forth into the phone an enthusiasm and exhilaration which he himself did not feel at all, and was not even intending to convey. After he hung up, he sat and stared thoughtfully at the horrible oak mantelpiece.

—It was so hard to be completely and wholly yourself, whenever you were in the presence of other people. —On the other hand it was practically impossible to know who or what yourself was, unless you *were* in the presence of other people.

This horrible old house, he thought vagrantly looking at the oak mantel. Sometimes he actually, actively hated it. But more than the house he hated all the other newer houses—none of them over ten years old—which had been built up all around them. In the heyday of his father, when he built this house in the 'Twenties, this place had very nearly been an estate, covering pretty near a whole damned city block. Gradually after he died, after first selling his oil company, his mom had during the Depression sold off pieces of the grounds to keep them going. In rigid tempo to the state of their finances, the new houses had risen around them, encroaching further and further, all nicer and more modern than this one really, though smaller, until now there were six of them, and the old house had left just barely enough ground for itself and its garage. Wally had no idea what had happened to all the money his father was supposed to have left; he knew next to nothing at all about business; but with a shrewdness considerably beyond his years he suspected old Judge Deacon who handled the estate for his mom was probably now in possesion of a good part of it; and with a cynicism at times approaching the shrewdness, if not equalling it, he was quite sure an investigation would show there was nothing illegal or untoward about how Judge had got hold of it.

But on the other hand, and at the same time, he found it both difficult and unpleasant to think people really did things like that—except in movies, or a novel—so most of the time he just put it aside and did not believe it. There wasnt anything he could do about it anyway. He was supposed to have an inheritance of his own of over $15,000, which he would come into when he was twenty seven. He could only hope the Judge hadnt got his fingers into that too.

He had talked to his mom—halfheartedly, it was true—a number of times about selling this house and buying or if they could afford it building a smaller, more modern one. Her answer was always that she could not get out of it what it was worth—which was, actually, true; if you were going by what it had cost—and she did not intend to give it away. But the truth was, she just couldnt stand the thought of giving it up. Her latest idea was to take in roomers—school-teachers, she said, young, single teachers, they were always nice girls, and Gwen could help her find some; reliable ones. He had managed up to now to talk her out of that one. The truth was, he did not want to move either. One of his fondest daydreams was to someday—when he was a rich famous writer; of course it was a fantastic idea, money-wise—buy up all the six houses and tear them down (or perhaps move them) and restore the old man's estate to its original lines. But at least he didnt make a goddamn symbol out of it, like his mom.

Wally did not remember his father. He had what he called 'second-hand memories'—stories about his father, and about him and his father, which had been told him so often by the family that they seemed to be things he remembered. But he had no real ones, and he was always careful to differentiate between the two. He had studied it, casting aside first this one and then that one as 'secondhand', until he was reasonably sure he had no real ones, in spite of what the child psychology people said about kids remembering things that happened when they were babies.

The old guy had died—suddenly, painlessly, and all at once—of a heart attack, when he himself was less than three. Just keeled over on the floor of his office, dead. A combination of too much work, too much good living, not enough exercise, and Bingo! the doctor had said later. He had died, Wally preferred to think, as coldbloodedly, and with the same unemotional dispatch, that he displayed in everything he did.

Resolutely, he pulled his mind back from its ramblings and put it upon the subject he had really been thinking about all the time:

He did not know what to do with Dawn.

In the beginning he had thought Dawn would make him an excellent mistress. He needed a mistress—increasingly badly—and Dawn Hirsh had seemed like an excellent bet. She liked the same things he did, and to talk about the same things. Everything had seemed in favor. They were both creative types, and both were intensely interested in the arts. She was pretty sophisticated for a high school girl, almost as sophisticated as he was; and they saw eye to eye on the dismal sorryness of Parkman Illinois. And in addition she was open and intelligently uninhibited when it came to discussing sex and sex relationships, like he was himself. —Also, she would be going away to school next year so he did not have to worry about marrying her. Then when she came home summers they could take up again. —Of course if she ran away to New York to act he would lose her and would have to find another. —But outside of that, (which he felt was more or less a sort of basic industrial hazard), and in fact, just about the only thing he could find wrong with the setup was that she lived at home and no place where they could go. But everything else had seemed fine.

But then, gradually, other things began to become apparent which had not been apparent at first. For one thing, Dawn was turning out to be very unstable. Not reasonable at all. She broke dates, she threw tantrums, she would deliberately try to make him jealous, at times she tried publicly to snob him, at others she refused to speak to him at all and he had learned for a fact that whenever she was not with him she talked about him disparagingly as though she thought him a child. And in spite of the fact that she was quite open—and even voluntarily frank—in discussing sex drives and desires and relationships, he had never been able yet—for one reason or for another—to get her to go to bed with him, to have sex with him. Obviously, she had an unhappy homelife; but then what the hell? so did he. For that matter, what kid didnt. There was apparently some other, some unknown quantity in this tentative equation he had not been able to isolate, and had failed to take account of. He had no idea what it could be, but it was making the equation insoluble, and he was getting damn tired and bored with it.

And the result was, he was not getting the sexual satisfaction he had expected and that a man of his age required, and which was one of the main reasons he had started this whole thing. He still had to make the same old run over to Terre Haute with Jack Beers or Tom Parker, to one of the whorehouses. And it took more money than he could afford. Especially when he was spending a good part of his funds on Dawn herself.

If he didnt know the driving power of her ambitions to act, he could almost have believed she was actually and deliberately trying to marry him. But he knew she wasnt. You might almost think she was a virgin? But he knew pretty positively, from several of the guys in school, that she wasnt.

Oh, the hell with it. Wally picked up the book he was currently reading. It was called *Decisive Battles Their Influence upon History and Civilization*, by J F C Fuller, a British Major General. Wally had finished Chapter IV, 'The Battle of Teutoburger Wald' on the defeat of Varus; and now he plunged into Chapter V, 'The Battle of Hadrianople', forgetting the by now cold coffee on the end table.

He had been reading quite a few books on military history lately, to prepare himself for when the Army got him, and he had become quite a student of war. But now he couldnt hold it. Irritating mind twitches and thought jumps kept him from concentrating. He put the book down and went across the hall into the 'Music Room', his mom called it. He looked at his trombone, sitting in one corner on its stand beside a music rack, then looked away. He looked at the not-expensive guitar, in another corner, which he had taken in on a trade—plus some boot—for his old bicycle. They were playing a dance next weekend in Terre Haute—for the goddamned squares at the goddamned Eagles Lodge, of all goddamned places—and he would be able to pick up a few bucks. This great big old house was so goddamned *deathly* quiet.

—If she didnt want to go with him over to Gwen's, she damned well didnt have to, he thought angrily. After all, it didnt make any difference to him, he told himself, more calmly, he wasnt getting anything out of it anyway.

Finally, he sat down at the baby grand his mom had never been quite able to bring herself to part with and leaning his left arm on the top and resting his forehead on his knuckles, began picking out multiple melodies in thirds and fifths, starting out with diminished triads and then shifting over to augmented triads and then to diminished sevenths, Kenton style. He was still at it, concentrating so raptly, that when the phone rang loudly in the hall where he had replaced it he was shocked and startled, and for a moment didnt know what had happened.

He went out in the hall and picked up the phone.

"Hello; Wally?" it said.

"Yes?" he said cautiously.

"Ed DeLancie, Wally."

"Oh, hi Ed!" he said; "I didnt know who it was." He tried to think of something more to say. "Hows the shop doing, Ed?"

"Okay, Wally," Ed DeLancie said indifferently. "Thats what I called you for, Wally. A woman brought her radio in to be fixed, and Im too busy to do it. It needs a good little bit of repair and adjustment. You want to do it for me?"

"Well; how much is in it?" Wally said.

"Oh, four or five bucks." In the background Wally could hear the little door-hung bell tinkle faintly in the shop. "Just a minute, Wally," Ed DeLancie said.

Wally smiled, seeing him in his mind's eye. Tall, slender, aristocratic already at thirty five, with those professor-ish rimless gold glasses with their shell-tipped earpieces, getting up from the battered work-bench where the phone was and stepping to the homemade counter he had made himself, in that little shop Wally knew so very well, every stick and wire and foot of it. Wally had worked for Ed from the sixth grade all through high school until he took off for Florida, in his little concrete block 'Tinker Shop' where he fixed radios and lawnmowers and just about any other mechanical equipment and held the local Harley-Davidson and Indian—and now Triumph—dealerships. It was Ed who had first got him started riding motorcycles.

"Excuse me, Wally," Ed's thin aristocratic voice came back on.

"Some lady with an electric fan she wants fixed for next summer. Well, how about it?"

"Okay. Sure, Ill do it," Wally said reluctantly. Ed put him onto little jobs like this from time to time. "I can sure use the money."

"How soon are you going to come over and eat dinner with us again?"

"Soon," Wally grinned into the phone. Then he said, "Maybe Ill stay tomorrow night." After he hung up, he stood looking down at the phone.

It was funny, Wally thought; Old Ed. Wally was still sort of 'Ed's boy'—just because he had worked for him all those years in grade school and high school, when Wally had been considered by everybody to be a boy radio genius. He grinned affectionately. Old Ed had taught him a lot. Ed always just went his own way, and never bothered anybody. Ed had known he was hard up, so he had gone out of his way to talk his 'cycle up to that Towns boy just on the strength that he might *want* to sell it. Just like he put him onto these jobs, which he always took for the money, even though he didnt enjoy doing them any more. Old Ed, he was probably the only man in town who had understood an inkling of his sudden ambition to be a writer. But even he doesnt *really* understand it, Wally thought, and amended: he just likes *me*.

Old Ed was a funny duck. The DeLancie family had owned and operated the single small bank in Israel for a hundred years. Ed's older brother Robert ran it now. And for a small bank it had a hell of a lot of capital, Wally thought. The DeLancie bank, Wally knew, was the only bank in this part of the country—the only one anywhere, for all he knew—that had not closed its doors during the big Bank Holiday in '32. They were solvent, Old Man DeLancie had said in his gentle way, so why should they close? So they stayed open. And there wasnt any run on them. Or anyway not enough of a one to bother them. Wally also knew that when The Holiday came, Judge Deacon had over $20,000 deposited there, in the DeLancie bank. Judge had apparently been withdrawing it from his own bank in smaller amounts for over a year and depositing it over there, in the DeLancie Bank in Israel.

Not many people knew any more that Israel had been named for a man, instead of the country in the Bible. Wally had learned it from Old Bob French. John Israel had been one of the first Anglo-American settlers there after the Revolution. It had always been a sort of gathering place, but Israel was one of the first homesteaders outside the compound, taking up land as a veteran. Then one day he had come home from hunting and found his entire homestead burned to the ground and his wife and four children and his two slaves all killed by the Indians. The Israel Massacre, they called it; and the story was that John Israel never tried to rebuild or anything, but spent the rest of his life hunting and killing Indians. Israel even was supposed to have practiced until he taught himself to load his rifle on the dead run, pouring in the powder and ramming home the ball as he ran, and the Indians called him 'The Man Whose Gun Is Always Loaded'. The Indians were deathly afraid of him. He would sneak up on a bunch of Indians and shoot one and then run, reloading while they chased him, and then turn and shoot and get another one. He was reputed, the story said, to have got eight or ten in a single day that way. Wally had read the same story in several histories of Kentucky and Virginia, about different men. Maybe it was only a legend, but if it was it was a good one. Such singlemindedness of purpose—and such efficiency— was what all men admired and hungered after. Anyway, they had named the town Israel after him.

Ed DeLancie could have been vice-president and cashier of the family bank; but instead, when he graduated from college, he moved to Parkman and in his mild quiet way opened his 'Tinker Shop' because he liked to work with motors and mechanical things. Ed's wife also came from one of Israel's most old and aristocratic families. They had three children. All of them lived quietly in this little house next to the shop, and once every week on Tuesdays Ed's brother Robert who still ran the bank, and his wife and kids, drove over from Israel to eat dinner with them. And whenever Ed's brother Robert had any repairs to be done to his radio or his lawnmower, he always drove clear to Parkman with them to have Ed do them.

Wally stopped in the doorway of the 'Music Room'. The big house sounded echoingly silent again. He didnt feel like going back to the piano. Something about Ed DeLancie's call distressed him. —loneliness, probably, he thought rationally. For a moment he thought of going down to his workbench in the basement and doing something. He had not been down there in over a year, except to do some job for Ed. And yet he used to spend almost all his time down there, doing one experiment or another, building something. Once he had built a Soapbox Derby car with special sealed Timken wheel bearings for the little boy next door which had put him clear up into the quarter finals of the Nationals at Columbus. He had built that workbench himself, years ago when he was still a kid, and had strung the wiring for the lights himself. That was back when he had decided his ambition was to be a radio technician. He still had all his old *Popular Mechanics* and *Popular Science* magazines (eight years of them without a break), together with his correspondence course papers from the course he took in radio, all filed neatly away down there. Whenever he thought about them and his old workbench he had such a painfully powerful affection for it, sitting down there by itself, that it was as if it were a real live person and somehow or other he had let it down. He had worked at it like a real son of a bitch for almost six years. By then his ambition had changed to being an inventor, like Thomas Edison. He remembered how he had laid himself out a rigid schedule, so much time for carpentry, so much for radio, so much for gasoline driven engines. God, but he had been young then.

And then suddenly it had been gone, it no longer interested him and left him bored. And with a dim half realized feeling of guilt and loss of confidence that was two thirds fright at his inability to be perfect, he had gradually dropped it and lost interest. It had been the same thing, the same cycle, with music later on in high school. It had been the same thing with motorcycles, too. He always found himself unequal to it, whatever it was, inadequate, imperfect. Somebody could always do it better than he could.

The thought of music suddenly sickened him, and he turned and went across the hall to the living room and back to the chair, but he did not try to read. Instead, he sat down in the chair and shut his eyes and tried to think himself outside of himself and away from his nervous bodily reactions which were upsetting him again.

At five thirty, feeling weary, he went up to his room and kicked off his moccasins and pulled on his best Western boots. (He had two pair.) They went on his feet like gloves going onto hands, and he experienced a momentary lift of spirits.

"Cowboy boots," he said aloud to the big Kachina doll that hung by the mirror and the P-38 which hung from the ceiling, "are the only really efficient footwear ever invented. With the raised heel and fitted instep your foot slides down till it molds the soft instep to it and keeps your toes from cramping up in the toe of the boot. For comfort there is nothing like it. Shoes do not even compare with them."

He stared at both of them, but neither of them answered. Then, shouldering into his Air Force surplus fleecelined jacket, he took his two chapters off the desk and went to pick up Dawn.

At the Hirshes he found Dawn already waiting for him with her coat and gloves on. "I just got home from school," she said, giving him her #3 or English Duchess smile. "Havent even had time to get my coat off." Knowing this was not the truth, Wally said nothing and led the way out to the car. As she slid into the front seat beside him Dawn looked down at the sheaf of papers lying in the seat.

"Whats this?" she said. "Some of your manuscript?"

"Yeah," Wally said. "Couple chapters. I was going to run them out to Gwen at the college this afternoon, but I never got the time," he lied. Quite suddenly, he had discovered he no longer wanted to go over to Gwen's. His mood had changed. He was no longer unsure, of himself or of the chapters, and he was no longer lonely. Instead, he wanted to do something exciting. It didnt have anything much to do with Dawn, really; it was just that it was evening, and some pressure had let down in him. It was evening, and the day's work was over everywhere, and he had a girl beside him just like normal people, and he wanted to be where there were lights and laughter and normal people who did not live in fear all the time, that was all it was.

"Ill just run out home and leave this," he said. "I wouldnt want to lose them." He put the little old Dodge in gear, and squealed its old tires a little, taking off.

"Great God no," Dawn said. "Not after the way youve sweated blood on it." She settled herself in the seat. "Well, what are we going to do tonight?"

"I thought wed run up to West Lancaster and do a little pub crawling," Wally said, driving. "Id take you over to a nice Terre Haute joint, but Im a little short on money."

"West Lancaster's fine with me," Dawn said. "As a matter of fact, I prefer it. Its so quaint. Nice Terre Haute places can be so damned boring."

"Its quaint, all right," Wally said. "Maybe well see a knife fight."

"Oh, do you suppose?" Dawn said eagerly. "No," she said. "This isnt Saturday." She laughed, and then suddenly she opened her coat and raised her arms and stretched and yawned, arching her back and her flat stomach in the sweater. Wally was aware of the large twin cones, pushing back the edges of the coat. "God! Its sure good to get away from home for a while where you can be yourself," she said luxuriously.

"Sure is," Wally said.

"Doesnt it take a load off you though?" Dawn said earnestly.

"Sure does," Wally said.

He drove up out in front of the house and parked under the big, young oaks on the parking and ran in with the chapters. His mom still was not home yet. He ran upstairs to his room and put them on the desk and laid a paperweight on them carefully. Then he took some more money out of the tin candy box in the lockdrawer of the little desk and relocked it. And then he paused, and looked down out the front window at the parked car. She seemed to be feeling especially good tonight. The pause became an intensely enjoyable moment of solo secrecy, and he kept prolonging it. Just standing. Just looking. Then he turned and ran back down the stairs pocketing the money.

"Ive had the most miserable time today," Dawn said when he got back in.

"The Drama Club?" Again he put the little Dodge in gear but this time he didnt bother to squeal the tires.

"Yes! What else? Were doing 'Mourning Becomes Electra' this time and I have the lead again. Its terrible. Really, terrible, Wally! Youd think even a high school Drama Club would have *some* people in it who were a little intelligent and sensitive."

"Not in this sorry town," Wally said.

"No, I guess thats right," Dawn said. "Thats *too* much to expect. Even the college Club doesnt have it when I work with them. But — . . ."

He let her ramble on. Anyway, the trip to West Lancaster wasnt far. You took State Highway Number One north about eight miles and then turned off east on a gravel road between two dinky filling stations. It was three miles from there to the river. Besides, he sort of enjoyed listening to her. He was using her—partially—for one of his characters, and anything he could get from her about the theater was very helpful.

Dawn talked on, getting it off her chest—(and what a chest! he thought), about the miserableness of the entire production and the people in it, and about her own part. It was hard enough anyway, to *really* get yourself into a part, without that too.

"Sometimes I think I have it," she said. "Have really *grasped* it. And then it will go away again, and I dont *really* have it, and its just like some stranger that you dont really know. Then when I think Im going to go com*plete*ly mad, it begins to come back a little. Its always that way."

"Its the same way with writing," Wally said. "You have to get *inside* of a character. You have to *become* them. And at the same time you have to be outside them, too—the author." He paused, inconclusively. "Its very hard to explain."

"Yes," Dawn agreed, and went on about herself. She talked hungrily, as if it had all been dammed up in her. By the time they had reached the turnoff, though, she had about run down.

"Hows the book coming?" she said.

"Oh, so-so," Wally said charily. "Its slow. But then its slow work, I guess." He didnt like to talk about it, as though that might cause him bad luck.

"I think you have the most wonderful title," Dawn said, and giggled.

"Yeah," Wally grinned proudly. "Its pretty good." He had taken the title—"The Scrawniest Monkey"—from an idiotic, funny story 'Bama Dillert had told him once with ironic relish and then howled over, slapping his leg. It was the story of the man in the jungle who came upon a band of monkeys. The monkeys all ran away, and the man was able to catch only one, which was a puny tiny weak little monkey who just couldnt run fast enough. The man picked him up and looked at him with disappointment and then said: "Well! You are without doubt the ugliest, scrawniest, puniest little monkey I ever saw in my life." And the monkey had answered him in a weak, puny little voice and said,

"Yes, I know. But Ive been sick." —That was all the story. Wally saw it as a vivid comment on the whole human race. He wondered if 'Bama had seen it as that, too; he must have seen it as something, from the ironic way he roared. Anyway, he intended to print the story opposite the title page. Gwen French thought it was a good title, too.

"You know," he said suddenly, making the turn onto the gravel between the still lighted filling stations, "if the band picks up a few more dance dates like it looks like theyre going to, Ill have a little money. Ive been thinking you and me might run up to Chicago for a weekend. How would you like that?" He didnt know why he said it. It was a ridiculous thing to say. He would never have that kind of money, not off of any dance dates.

"Like it!" Dawn said. "Id *love* it!"

"We could see all the shows," Wally said, going ahead with it anyway after his startle, "and hit some nightclubs. Have ourselves a real good time." It sounded good, even to him.

"So-and-so's playing there, I think, in . . ." Dawn went on delightedly, naming the plays that were playing in Chicago, and who was appearing in each one. She knew them all. "Oh, it would be wonderful!"

"Well, we just might be able to swing it," Wally said. "Wed probably have to sleep together in the same hotel room," he added, "to save money."

"God!" Dawn said fervently. "I wouldnt care. Itd be worth it!" She looked at Wally speculatively. "By the way," she said, "what have you been doing with yourself lately, anyway? I havent seen you in a week."

"Oh nothing much," Wally said elaborately without taking his eyes off the road. He had slowed down more on the gravel; they hadnt been in any hurry before, anyway. Then suddenly he thought of something. "Well," he said audaciously, feeling his heart begin to bulge up into his throat and pump behind his eyes, at his own audacity, "When are you going to sleep with me?"

"I dont know," Dawn said. "I didnt know you wanted me to."

"Are you crazy?"

"Well," Dawn said; "No." Her voice sounded both selfpleased and a little breathless: "Why didn't you ask me?"

"I have been," Wally said. "For four months now."

"But not very plainly," Dawn said.

"Well I am now."

". . . All right," she said. It was like a long-held sigh.

"When?"

"Oh, sometime. Not now. Not tonight."

"Name a date."

"All right, in May then."

"May! May!!" Wally exploded. "Why May? This is November! May's six months away!"

"May is such a beautiful month," Dawn said.

"What the hells that got to do with it?"

"I just happen to prefer May," she said, and paused. Her actress's timing made it a momentous pause. "You know Im a virgin, dont you?" she said.

"Well, no," Wally said, confused. "I didnt. I dont mean I didnt. I mean I never thought about it."

"Well, I am," Dawn said, watching him. "Do men really all want virgins?" she asked.

"Well, now, I dont know," Wally said academically, relieved to get back to the theoretical. Only later, thinking back over, would he feel he had been bested, in some way or other. "A lot of guys say they do. And none of them will admit the girl they married wasnt one. But all thats mostly vanity. I dont think it really matters, honestly. Now, personally, I prefer my women to not be virgins.

"On the other hand," he cautioned paternally, "I couldnt guarantee you all guys feel like me. So dont just take my word for it."

"I wont," Dawn said blithely.

Wally made himself nod. "Good." He was a little irritated, and still perplexed.

Ahead of him he could see the neon lights of the buildings now. West Lancaster. The gravel road ran straight down over the sloping ten-foot bank to the water's edge where they kept the ferry. Once a drunk had driven right on down it into the water—the ferry had just happened to be on the other side; though that wouldnt have mattered—but they had fished him out all right. There were five big two-storey frame buildings right down by the river, three on one side of the gravel, two on the other. Four of them were bars and the other was a sort of general store for the bars. Around behind these off the road, running along the river's edge among the trees so you couldnt even see them in the daytime, were several scattered houses; and that was West Lancaster.

"Now look," he said. "Glen and Gertrude's Place has got a new combo in from Terre Haute. I thought wed go there first and get something to eat. But Im kind of short on money, so go easy on what you order."

"Hamburgers and beer is fine with me," Dawn said happily.

"Okay; dont forget. This here little combo's pretty good," he said authoritatively. "Piano, vibes, guitar and bass. Four colored boys who live in Terre Haute. I know all of them so I thought I might introduce you later on, if you want."

"Oh, that would be wonderful!" Dawn said delightedly. She looked at him, a sideways glance. "You know quite a bit about Terre Haute, dont you?" she said softly.

"Yeah," Wally grunted. "The less ritzier places." He swung the car in under the huge neon sign that read: GLEN AND GERTRUDE'S in red and green. Several other cars were there already.

"Maybe you can sit in with them later," Dawn suggested.

"I might. On piano," Wally said. "I aint got my horn with me." Curiously, he watched himself slipping back into the formalized musiciantalk. "I aint much meat on piano though," he added.

Inside, Glen and Gertrude's was dimly lit and very dark and barnlike. A new looking bar with stools upholstered in red plastic on the right of the door ran a third of the way down the room. Behind it ran a row of half round booths upholstered in red plastic with red Formicatopped tables in them. Out on the floor stood round red tables, each with four red plastic upholstered chrome chairs around it. Down the whole left side of the wide, long single room supported with posts upholstered in red plastic in the center ran the dancefloor, and near the back on a little raised stand was the four man Negro combo, all of whom wore Mister B shirts with double Windsor ties, and three of whom—excepting only the bass player—wore dark glasses. They were playing dissident modern jazz in the style of Stan Kenton. The song was 'Willow, Weep For Me' which June Christie had made famous. One of the ones with dark glasses called "Hey, man!" to Wally and grinned flashingly.

"Hello, man!" Wally called back, and he and Dawn sat down at one of the open tables in the center and ordered hamburger sandwiches and beer.

Several other parties and couples were scattered around at tables or booths and one of whom, a petite dark-auburnhaired young woman of about twenty seven sitting with two men, both Dawn and Wally knew. She was Doris Fredric, the daughter of Paul Fredric the president of the Second National Bank in Parkman, backyard neighbor and ex-schoolchum of Dawn's father's office girl Edith Barclay. Dawn knew her as her former freshman English teacher; Wally had missed having her for English by three years, but had still been at the high school as a senior when she came there. From across the room she waved at both of them gaily and demurely.

They both waved back.

"Theres Doris," Dawn said. "But whos that with her?"

"Couple of out of towners?" Wally said.

"No, I recognize one of them. But I dont know his name. He works in the Sternutol offices."

Doris was talking to both men animatedly, turning first to one and then to the other, and smiling happily. Her loose hair, the color of old cherrywood, cut in bangs and combed close to her small head except where it fluffed loose at her shoulders, added to the effect of naiveté virginity, and innocence about her. An expensive off-the-shoulder day-dress did not detract from the effect, but only made her look more sweet and demure.

"Which one of them guys you reckon shes goin' out with tonight? Or both?" Wally asked conversationally.

"Wally!" Dawn said, scandalized. She looked back at Doris for a moment. "Ill tell you one thing," she said, turning back, "if I ever have to be a school teacher like Daddy wants me to be, I just hope Im the kind of school teacher Doris Fredric is. She goes her own way, and does as she pleases, and she doesnt give a damn what the moralists and the gossips say about her."

"You better wait till your daddy's president of a bank first then," Wally said. He was looking up at the raptly pleased faces and inscrutable dark glasses of the band. They had finished 'Willow' and were playing 'Safranski', the bass specialty which Eddie Safranski was so famous for in Kenton's band.

"Besides, I think shes a stunning girl," Dawn said. "A beautiful girl."

"Shes all right," Wally said, turning back. "She aint got any breasts."

"Some women just dont have," Dawn said magnanimously.

"True," Wally said, "true. You want another burger?" The band had wound up the 'Safranski' and started out on a sweet tune, for dancing. Wally knew how badly it must hurt them. "Or you want to dance?"

"Ill have another hamburger, *and* another beer," Dawn said excitedly. "Can we afford it?"

"Sure," Wally said. "I just didnt want to pay for no steak dinner, that was all, chick."

They ordered and ate their other hamburger, and after they finished it they danced some. Doris Fredric danced also, demurely with first one of her men and then with the other. She looked very sweetly and delightedly happy, Wally noticed. So did the two men. It was not, however, until after 'Bama Dillert came in that she came over to their table and spoke to them.

They had been dancing and drinking beer perhaps three quarters of an hour when 'Bama entered with Dewey Cole and two worn looking Terre Haute women. At least, to Wally they looked like some of 'Bama's Terre Haute women. 'Bama and Dewey both looked like they had got their heads caught in a whiskey barrel and had to drink their way out; but they both carried it well. Wally had noticed they always did. When 'Bama saw him, he made a beeline for their table, grinning, to say hello. Wally had introduced him to Dawn long before. He did not sit down. He stood, and talked a couple of minutes, kidding with Wally in that strange, very interested, very warm way he always affected around Wally; he could really be very charming, when he wanted.

"Yore out kind of late for a novelist, aint you?" he chided almost protectively. "How you goin to get up and work in the mornin with a clear head?"

"Yeh," Wally said, his face suddenly flashing guilt. "Matter fact, I was planning on leavin right away."

'Bama merely looked at him wisely and said something else.

"Well, I wont disturb yore happy party," he said finally, and winked: "We got to get these here pigs back home to Terre Haute tonight without they fall over and break a leg or something even more important." He left, and walked in that strange horselike gait of his over to the booth where the curly headed, sullen eyed, drunken Dewey sat with the two worn looking Terre Haute women. Both of the women looked a little the worse for wear, too.

Wally watched Dawn follow the departing 'Bama with her eyes interestedly, but silently. She did not offer to tell him her thoughts. But he could guess. There was something about 'Bama which always seemed to fascinate women, especially respectable women, and Wally suspected always that in some strange perverse way it had something to do with an instinctive desire to reform him, as if the respectable women found it not only acutely painful but also challenging, to see this sneer-faced man who just didnt give a damn about worshipping women, walking around loose. That was what he read on Dawn's face right now, sort of a look of steely but deeply interested speculation. It irritated him and made him about half peeved. It always did, the way they looked at 'Bama. No matter what kind of an act he put on, he could never make them look at him that way.

It was only a few minutes after 'Bama left that Doris Fredric excused herself from her booth and came over to them—walking in her straight backed, deliberately slow, small petite walk above which the small face floated demurely—at their table.

"Hello, my children!" she said, smiling her sweet, slow, virginal smile, and sat down with them. Wally knew he was being petty but he wished shed waited till she was asked.

"Havent seen my chicks in a *long* time," Doris said in her warm friendly way, and reached over and playfully rumpled the shoulder of Dawn's sweater. "It looks like youre out having yourselves a time."

"Hello, Doris," Dawn said almost worshipfully.

Wally resented the tone in Dawn's voice. Also, he did not like being called one of Doris's chicks since he had never gone to school to her.

As if she sensed this, Doris turned her demure child's face to him gaily. "How's our star author today?" she smiled. "How's that novel coming? Ive been hearing a lot about it lately."

Modestly with her eyes, she looked at him shyly. She had startlingly blue, baby blue, eyes—even bluer than Dewey Cole's, he thought. And the only way Wally could even attempt to describe them to himself was that deeper down, underneath all their various expressions, they always seemed to remain completely inexcitable.

Wally shrugged uncomfortably. "Not very good. Its slow work, Doris."

Doris shook her cherrywood colored head, smiling. "Oh, now youre spoofing me. Gwen was only just telling me about it the other day; and some of the fine things you have in it. She thinks its wonderful."

Wally *knew* this was a lie. He had asked Gwen not to say anything about it to anyone, and she had agreed with him that it was best not to talk about it at all. Also, he was wondering why, if Doris was going to come over and sit with them, she hadnt done it before 'Bama Dillert came in.

"Oh, its coming along, I guess," he said uncomfortably. "I think itll be good when its done. But its just hard work."

Doris smiled sweetly and shook her cherrywood colored hair again sympathetically. "All novels are," she said unnervously, as though she knew everything about novels. But Gwen had told him she didnt.

As if feeling shed put enough time on this, she turned back to Dawn. "How is the Drama Club coming, sweetie?" she said.

With eyes that were very near worshipful, Dawn wrinkled her nose distastefully. "Oh, Doris. Im having a terrible time."

Doris listened with an intent small girl's eagerness, as the younger girl laid out her troubles. She looks so absolutely demure, Wally thought. And so innocently childlike. And so completely virginal. Everything about her. The pert way she moved her head. It made you doubt all the stories. How any woman could look so com*pletely* virginal, and still sleep with all the men she was supposed to have slept with, was totally outside his knowledge. Unless it was that she herself really be*lieved* she had not slept with them. It might be that. Otherwise, the stories just had to be lies.

"Everything will work out all right," she said to Dawn, wrinkling up her eyes. "Youll see. Remember how it was last year. Thats a terrific new combo theyve got in, isnt it? Have you ever played with them, Wally?"

"No, but I know them all," he said. "Theyre all Terre Haute boys."

"They play my kind of music," Doris said. "For my money I would just as soon they didnt play dance music, and not dance, just listen."

"Thats about the way I feel, too," he said.

"Who was that tall man that stopped at your table?" Doris said.

"Thats 'Bama Dillert," Wally said, congratulating himself.

"Oh!" she said. "Is that the gambler?"

Wally nodded.

Smiling, Doris looked over at him in the booth with Dewey, her face demure. "I never knew who he was," she said, turning back. Then she laughed tinklingly. "Maybe I ought to get him to teach me to play poker? Daddy says Ill always be the world's worst poker player."

"I doubt if he gives lessons," Wally said, unable to resist. He got a warning glance from Dawn. Doris was unable to see her.

"Thats the most beautiful dress, Doris," Dawn said, reaching over to touch it. "Is it new? Its the most beautiful outfit Ive seen in a coon's age."

"Oh, this old thing?" Doris said, looking down at herself lovingly with a sort of modestly shy contempt. "No, its not new. What do you think, Dawn?" she said, looking up. "Should I meet the big bad gambler?" Before Dawn could answer, she said, "Well, maybe youd better introduce me to him anyway, Wally. Its worth a chance. I would dearly love to just quietly sit down some night—and take all of Daddy's money."

"Sure, Ill introduce you to him," Wally said, and grinned at her knowingly.

Doris looked back at him blandly and then smiled at him demurely. "If you were to get him back over here to your table, I could walk by a little later." She shook her cherrywood colored hair cutely. "Nobody knows how Id love to sit down some night and beat Daddy at poker," she grinned. It was an affective grin, completely innocent, and Wally found he still did not know.

"Ill see you later, kiddies," Doris said, and got up and went back to her own booth.

"Well, what do you think?" Wally said.

"You mean you think she wants to sleep with him!" Dawn said.

"Well, you gotta admit that might be a faint possibility," Wally grinned.

Dawn shook her head.

"No, I dont think so. Not with him. Anybody else maybe, but not him. I think she wants to learn to play poker. Just like she said. Shes an awful child, really."

"Yeah," Wally said cynically. And yet he still was not sure. "Well, I better go get hold of 'Bama." He started to get up.

"Dont do it yet!" Dawn said sharply. "Those two men would be sure to notice if you did it now. Wait a while."

He waited fifteen minutes,—until Dawn said it was all right. They danced twice more and had another beer. After he called 'Bama off and told him, the big man waited another five minutes. It was all beginning to smack more and more of a conspiracy.

"I think you like this playing matchmaker stuff," Wally grinned at Dawn after he came back.

"Well?" Dawn said, eyeing him excitedly. "Dont you?"

"Yeah, I guess I do."

'Bama came back and sat with them and in a minute Doris wandered by, ostensibly on her way to the ladies' room. She stopped for a moment to speak, whereupon Wally jumped up and made the introduction.

Standing, 'Bama looked the banker's daughter over speculatively. "Pleased to meet you," he said shortly. "Well, I better get back to my friends, Wally. Only trouble is," he added grinning, "they wont let me drink any. So every so often I have to go up to the bar to get myself a drink." He did not look at Doris, and Doris herself was looking at Dawn quite innocently. She had not sat, and in a moment she went on her way, to the ladies' room.

"Well, if that aint the damnedest weirdest thing I ever took part in," Wally said to Dawn after the others had both gone.

Dawn merely grinned at him excitedly. "When are you going up and sit in with the band?"

Wally made a face. "Not now. Theres too many people here. Waitll it thins out, later on. Then we'll go up and get in with them. Ill sit in on piano and have them take 'Willow' over. I know that one pretty good."

So they sat and drank some more beer, and danced, and gradually the majority of the customers left. When he did go up to the bandstand later on, he noted that Doris Fredric was standing up at the bar talking to 'Bama earnestly. He caught the word "poker". The small petite cherry-headed Doris was looking up at 'Bama with a demure child's expression. And 'Bama, with his semi-western hat, tall and with that tiny hanging belly, a reserved wry expression on his usually sneering face, suddenly looked a lot, Wally thought, like Gary Cooper. The two men—Wally looked to see—were still sitting in the booth.

Well, he thought happily, its things like this that make the world interesting and exciting. Puzzles.

He knew he ought to be getting home, and not stay so late, and not drink too much, or get emotionally involved with a jam session. So he would be able to get up fresh and clear headed and work tomorrow. It was a constant battle.

But he was still there, with Dawn, at nearly midnight when Doris Fredric left with her two men. Doris had had a number of drinks by then, and her eyes were a little glazed and puffy, but yet in spite of this she still looked girlish and innocent and virginal. He had wanted so damn bad to stay and see what happened. But apparently nothing had happened. 'Bama and Dewey and their Terre Haute broads were still there, and they did not get up and leave after Doris had.

Wally collected Dawn and went home; and 'Bama and Dewey and their women were still there when he left.

CHAPTER 26

THE weekend Dave Hirsh had made up his mind not to spend at the Frenches' when he went home Thursday night, turned out to be one of the pleasantest, most peaceful times he had ever had in his life after he changed his mind. He wouldnt have missed it for anything. Especially when looked back upon later. Because by then it appeared as the last brief respite before the storm of the taxi service,—that single short moment of happiness men seem to be given from time to time, a sort of ironic red herring, to trick them into false hope and not giving up, just at the time when Life or Fate, or Whoever it was, was secretly and gleefully preparing to lower the boom of misery on them.

He had lain in bed all day Friday at the hotel, trying to sleep and failing, and waiting miserably for his damned body to assimilate and throw off all the quantities of alcohol he had poured into it; three fourths sick, still chilled from the night in the cornfield, still drunk, and already hungover even before he was sober. It was one of those deep, bad hangovers in which a tight drawn dehydration and some subtle deterioration at the base of the skull combined to make everything unearthly and strange, including yourself. Finally in desperation he had gotten up and dressed and driven back over to Israel, dead for sleep, to accept their invitation. They had forced a couple of Martinis down him and then fed him richly, and then the three of them had sat up in front of the fire until after one, discussing his novel and trying to lay out a form for it; and he discovered with amazement that he was no longer tired or sleepy—and hardly even sick.

Everything seemed to smooth itself all out suddenly. There were no worries, and there were no fears. He seemed to have fallen accidentally into a state of complete desirelessness, and therefore of peace. Of course it was only a mood. But it was a damned good mood. And that was the way it stayed for the next two days.

A great deal of the weekend's success, he was quite sure, analyzing it, was due to the fact that he had discovered the hidden secret of Gwen's nymphomania. Knowing it, he was relieved of all pressure. The natural element of doubt, which you had with every woman, was gone. All he had to do was be patient, and wait, until one of her moods one of her spells—whatever they were, whatever caused them—hit her, and then he wouldnt have to seduce her, she would seduce him. It was unbelievable how much it put the mind at rest.

Actually, there had been damned few peaceful times in his life. When he thought about it. Without being more than only a little bit dishonest, he could say there were none. At least he could not remember any. He had always been running after some damned woman or other. Drive, drive, drive. Trying to engage in some damned love affair he could not engage in; or which—in one of the rarer instances— if he did, soon deteriorated so rapidly and left him right back where he started. But now all that was gone; for the time being anyway. He was momentarily at peace, and consequently his long weekend at *Last Retreat* was as though he had gone clear off the planet some- where, to Bacon's New Atlantis utopia or someplace.

He slept late. He drank little. He listened to music. He walked along the river bluff with Bob or with Gwen or both (breathing in the chill November air, looking out across the width of the river to the willow and sycamore thickets on the Indiana side, you never tired of it). He played chess with Bob in front of the fire, at which he was soundly and consistently beaten; or he played with Gwen, who was a good chess player in her own right and also beat him, making him re-swear an unkept resolution to himself that he would study up and really learn the game like they knew it. And he ate ravenously, of those strange delicious meals which Gwen seemed to throw together from practically nothing, during the middle of a chess game or while carrying on a heavy conversation. But mostly he talked, with one or both of them, and the constant subject was this novel of his. The con- versations ranged, widely, but always and inevitably they came back to the novel. They talked about it on their walks through the grounds, they talked about it during the chess games, they talked about it all through the meals.

Gwen had told Bob his idea—the comic combat novel—and Bob was enthused and excited about it. He agreed with Gwen that it was brilliant; and he agreed with Gwen that the thing to do now was to find a proper form for it, the right mold. Not a rigid plot-mold, you know; you understand? That would never do. But a channel, rather; some simple time-plan form which would give him a beginning and an end to work toward so he would not dissipate himself all over the place, while at the same time leaving him plenty of room to move around within it, you know. And he agreed with Gwen and Dave both that there should be no hero. No hero and no heroine and no love story. Leave out all the trash. Dont complexify it; this was not a big long character novel, with personal plots. The beauty of the idea was in its simplicity. And half of your striking power and smacking shock would be in the simplicity and shortness of it, in the simplicity of the story itself, and the simplicity of its presentation. Bob was very excited. When he would get to talking, he would stride his long-legged frame back and forth across the room slowly, forgetting the chess game, calm, and quiet, and the bright vital eyes snapping. But without per- sonal plot, what kind of form can you give it? It must have continuity, it must *progress*. What kind of form, then, to give it? If the people themselves are incidental? Oh, it is my move? Ah! you shouldnt have moved that bishop there, my dear Dave.

The three of them struggled with it all day Saturday, through two meals, three chess games, and four walks outside. In the end it was Gwen who came up with the idea of patterning it somewhat on the idea of George R Stewart's book, "Storm". There too, she said, the people were only incidental; the protagonist was the storm itself. Of course, it was not a deep book, wasnt even meant to be one. But nevertheless the plan was still valid. Did Dave know the book? There was a copy of it here someplace that he could take home with him to study. The main point was that the life of the storm, from its birth in the Pacific to its death across the mountains, formed the framework and the continuity.

Bob agreed excitedly. And so did Dave; he took it up and began at once to elaborate it. It was really ludicrously simple. All he had to do was take an organization, preferably a green one, and follow it through some campaign from its first combat to—Well, to the end: the end of the campaign, or the relief of the organization, or—perhaps—to the final replacement of the last man who had been with the original outfit. —But in this case, instead of the organization itself being the protagonist and hero, the main character would be the experience of combat itself—but controlled and dominated by that mood of the humorousness and comicality of death and war, as opposed to the usual solemn heroism and horribleness that everyone affected. And that would be what would make it shocking. Actually it was all really very simple.

It was strange, he thought, the labyrinthine complexities of thought people had to wander through and endure in order to come up with a simple idea. And the simpler the idea you wanted, the greater the complexities you seemed to have to go through to get it.

It had been a long time since Dave had felt in himself or seen in others that almost religious love of writing, and completely selfless abstract enthusiasm for it, that writing could sometimes give to people. He had had it once or twice, as a young man, but even then it had been all tied up with ego. But here today there was no ego; it did not matter—to any of them—whose name would be on the book, who would get the credit the money for it; it did not matter who contributed the best ideas, or who contributed the least; all that mattered was that the book existed—existed now as an idea, and was about to be created as a fact. That was *all* that mattered. It filled him with a wild, euphoric happiness that made him want to yell out loud and slap them both on the back out of sheer inexpressibility.

Here all that mattered was the work; and that was the essence of true creativity: just the work. No ego. The hell with the ego. Oh, how he wished he could take her to bed right now. He could show her what a lover *really* was. Shed never *had* a lover. He could really *love* her. High and enthusiastic and half drunk without a drink in him on just the awareness of his own creativity, he made notes and talked, talked and made notes, using Bob and Gwen as soundingboards and as a mirror to spread his ideas out before and throw his ideas against; and it was amazing what new ideas came to him, and poured out of him, pungent visions and pertinent correlations he had never seen at all all four years in the Army, all apparently just because they two were here to show them to. Right now he could hardly wait to get home and get started on the writing of it.

And yet in spite of all the exuberance—all the tons of emotion washing back and forth across the walls—there was still that calm feeling of a peaceful weekend, and it permeated everything. Naturally on Sunday everything tapered off. Sunday couldnt help but be an anticlimax. Nevertheless the ideas were there, the notes were down, the results existed.

As Bob said with a wry smile: "Now all youve got to do is write it."

But it was a very relaxed and peaceful anticlimax, Sunday. It was on Sunday that Dave accidentally made a discovery which puzzled him at first, but eventually convinced him more than ever that his basic theory about Gwen's nymphomania was correct.

Wandering around the house,—(they had shown him the rest of the house before, at which he had discovered, as he had expected, that it was not nearly in so bad a shape as they had led him to believe)— he had picked off a shelf a copy of Huneker's *Painted Veils*. It was the Liveright "Black and Gold" reprint edition, printed in '42. Beautifully made books. And cheap. He had seen them before, out on the Coast before he was drafted. They had also reprinted Stendhal's *Red and Black* and *Charterhouse of Parma*. But he hadnt expected to see Huneker's *Painted Veils* among such illustrious company. That was what had caught his eye.

It had been a long time since he had read the book. At the time he had read it mainly for the sex in it, but he could remember the rococo overly arty style, and it was interesting to look at it and speculate back. Dave leafed through the book, and that was when he made his discovery. And it shook him.

The book had Gwen's name written on the flyleaf, and on page 46 in the same hand was a margin note. Dave remembered the scene. It was the scene of the 'Holy Yowler' orgy of whiskey, religion and sex— a pretty heavily labored satire, today. Just before it, where the hero is being amused at the drunk whore Roarin' Nell, the writer (Gwen, it obviously was) had underlined the sentence, and in the margin written: "Horrible! Men always love to degrade women, dont they!" And on the margin of the next page—where the orgy itself was in progress—was written in large, no uncertain words: "EVIL! THIS MAN IS EVIL!"

For a moment Dave was shocked dead still. There was no way he could correlate this to the Gwen French he himself knew—or thought he knew? The woman who had had so many love affairs, the woman to whom sex itself was a familiar, ordinary, everyday occurrence when she felt like it, surely could not have written this. This sounded more like some virgin spinster. And if there was anything which Gwen French was not, which her very soul and personality showed she was not, it was a spinster.

He put the book back in its place and stood staring at the gold-filigreed spine with its red label, feeling guilty as if he had been caught window peeping, and at the same time casting around wildly for an explanation. But of course, it all did fit in, really. That sense of "EVIL!", which obviously came from inside the writer of the note herself, only went to prove his theory about Gwen's nymphomania. Just like how she would go for weeks, for months and months, even, without any sex at all; trying to dominate it, trying to be pure; and then, when the pressure got too much for her, would kick over wildly and throw a real blaster; and then crawl off to a corner, to gnaw her own guilts and sense of "EVIL!" It was the classic nymphomaniacal type, wasnt it?

Feeling considerably better, now hed worked it out, he turned to go back to the big kitchen, where Gwen and Bob were battling out a hard fought game of chess. Cherchez la mom! he thought, feeling as epigrammatical as Huneker. It was always the mother. If you ever found all the facts, you could always find that whatever it was the mother was behind it somewhere. Dear mom. Mothers might not lead happy lives, but they never let it hamper them from doing their job well, and installing that good old guilt that ruined everybody else's.

He supposed he would have to go up and see his own goddamned mother, sometime, eventually, now that he would be staying in town. Dear Frank would insist on it.

In the kitchen, which they had not yet brought the rest of the house up in keeping with, even though the rooms werent bad, and where Bob and Gwen sat at the chess table before the fireplace, he sat down to kibitz, still feeling more relaxed and rested and completely peaceful than he had felt in years and years. That "Black and Gold" edition had only been printed in 1942, he thought, looking at Gwen who smiled at him; that was only five years ago. Gwen was slowly but surely getting beaten at the chess. He sat back and let the afternoon slip lazily and luxuriously and pleasantly past him.

Monday morning, after a good sound night's sleep—his second in a row—and feeling like a different man from the Dave Hirsh of Friday, he called Frank at the store in Parkman.

"Where the hell have you been?" Frank wanted to know furiously as soon as he found out who it was.

"Been? Why?"

"Ive been tryin' to get hold of you for days, thats why!"

"Ive been over here in Israel visiting the Frenches."

There was a moment's pause. "Oh," Frank said. He sounded surprised. "No wonder I couldnt get hold of you. Ive called just about everyplace else in the county."

"What for? What do you want?"

"I wanted you to help me get the taxi service in shape to start operating, that was all," Frank said sarcastically.

"Well, Ill be over there in a half hour and help you," Dave said. It was like coming out from under the water and taking off your face mask and looking at a strangely, totally different world, and realizing this and not the other was the real one.

"I already done done it," Frank said disgustedly. "Its all ready to start operation—as soon as you can get here and start workin'."

"Then Ill meet you at the store," Dave said, "in half an hour."

"Okay," Frank said. "—Well, no," he added, from where he sat at his desk, looking at the pretty back of Edith Barclay's head. "Meet me at the taxi office instead. You know where it is? Its on Plum Street, right behind the Foyer poolroom. —No point in wastin' time in comin' here," he added.

"Okay, then Ill meet you there."

"The drivers probably already be there," Frank said. "I told them to report Monday morning. Before I found out I wasnt goin' to be able to get ahold of you."

His voice sounded disgruntled and accusative and Dave did not bother trying to answer him. He just said goodby and hung up. The phone conversation had brought Frank's personality back into existence vividly. You couldnt really blame Frank for being angry.

As he collected his belongings to leave—not a hard job, since they consisted only of the clothes on his back, a stack of notes on the novel, and a shaving kit—he wanted very badly not to leave. It was not that he had really forgotten Frank and the taxi service; but he had removed them to where they existed only in his mind, instead of as extraneous facts; and there his mind could control them. Now they were back full force, in their own right.

Gwen had already left for school and he had said goodby to her then, at which time she had sternly admonished him to get right to work on the book while it was all still fresh. (He intended to do just that.) Now he took his leave of Bob,—who was in old work clothes puttering around in his tool house out back with that blank faced look of a man about to write a poem—and for a moment he felt as if he actually, physically, could not leave. Bob must have understood how he felt, because he grinned wryly and invited him to come back any weekend, as he shook hands, or any other time he felt like coming, and to stay as long as he felt like staying. It was a very grand and very generous invitation, and what was more he knew Bob meant it. The secluded lovely yard with its big tall oaks and sycamores did not increase his pleasure at leaving a damned bit, either, as he walked to his car. He set out for Parkman in the little Plymouth with a feeling of going resolutely to meet his destiny, his miserable damned destiny.

As he drove out from under the loom of the bridge through Israel and up the side of the grade to the highway, something else was bothering him. He had discovered he wanted his money back, during this weekend. It was more important to him than he thought, in spite of his damned carefree gesture of grandly throwing it away for a chance at Gwen French. He liked the feeling of having enough of it in his pocket, and the double security of knowing there was more in the bank if he needed it. Apparently in a business you were still nominally the owner of your own money—in other words, you were still *worth* just as much—but you didnt have access to any of it, and therefore it was just the same as if you didnt have it; you were just as broke as if you were broke. Well if that was what business was like, the hell with business. He did not like to feel broke. It gave him the same uncanny, frightening feeling he had used to have on the bum: that you might be starving—you never were, though you were often hungry— but you *might* be, while all around you moved a world peopled with either strangers or acquaintances but no friends, who were too busy trying to assure themselves security to care about yours and if you fell down sick on the street would not be able to stop and pick you up, or sacrifice a fraction of one percent of their capital to put you in the best hospital in town. That was what most people used their families for, he guessed, only hed never had any. Except Francine. Nobody ever felt that way in the Army, by God; even a damned MP would take care of you. And you could spend all your pay. Hell, if he had known the truth about Gwen French, he neednt have turned his money over to Frank at all. But now, now the only thing he knew to do was to throw himself wholly and bodily into making this taxi service such enough of a damned big success that he could eventually get his money back and get out; and the nervousness made him eager.

However, it turned out to be more bodily throwing than he had bargained for. From the moment he got out of his car in front of the little ex-lunchstand Frank had leased with its parking space, he found himself submerged in a miserable, half-dead half-alive, hectic existence of work without rest that was so demanding he hardly even found time to sleep, let alone write anything, and which lasted—the worst part— for over two weeks, and then continued on only slightly better for over a month until he finally rebelled.

The main thing was they had not hired any relief for him; consequently, he had to work from seven in the morning until after eleven thirty at night, seven days a week, because even when he was not actually working at some damned paper work he still had to be there to answer the two telephones. He even had to have all his meals except breakfast sent in. The other thing was that Frank had not thought to provide any system of bookkeeping or accounts except for some readymade dispatcher's forms hed picked up somewhere and which in the end turned out to be so much more bother, red tape and time consumption than they were worth that they were discarded completely. As a result, he who had never done a damned bit of clerical work in his life, was left without any knowledge or system or records except some wildly scrawled junk in a spiral notebook that even he couldnt read. A third thing, which *no* one could have foreseen, was that the taxi service caught on tremendously almost from the first day. Whether Parkman actually needed a taxi service or not, Parkman believed it needed one; and the result was the same. Frank had advertised the opening date in both the Republican and Democrat papers, and calls started coming in right away the very first day. Apparently there was a large number of elderly women who could not, or did not like to drive, and an equal number of younger women whose husbands took their cars to work and left them no way to shop. These ladies provided an immediate backlog of business. Nobody knew how they had managed before "Frank's Taxi Service"—as the firm was immediately dubbed by the town, despite the red checkered band on the cars— came along to save them.

Eventually, Clark Hibbard even wrote one of his not infrequent back page editorial columns for the *Oregonian*, which were called "Observing the Hubbub with Hibbard", about the Hirsh taxi service and its important civic contribution; a column which incidentally— Parkman being a typical town composed mostly of practical political cynics—went largely unnoticed by everyone except Frank, who was proud of it.

Dave had neither time nor inclination to give a damn about the article. The ladies together with all the various other calls still did not cause what could strictly be called a land office rush, but it was a great deal more than enough for Dave to handle. Finally, in desperation, after a week of it, he called Frank. Frank had been making inspection trips every day in his odd moments—plus a trip every night at closing time to check the receipts—but the only things he was interested in were how much money they were taking in, and whether all the calls for cabs were being filled promptly. He had already decided to buy another car out of their capital and add it to the fleet of three.

He came right away when Dave called him, and while Dave laid out the situation and showed him the confusion of fouled up papers, stood in the grubby little office helplessly, repeatedly running his hand through his thinning hair with irritation.

"I dont give a damn what you do!" Dave bellowed frantically, his eyes wildly bright with his desperation, "but youve got to do something! Youve got to fix it. I cant handle it. At the rate we're going now we wont even have sufficient records to figure our taxes."

Frank must have been pretty desperate himself, because he immediately picked up one of the phones and called the store for Edith Barclay. Dave, who was aware that he himself was actually only half as desperate as he talked and acted, noted this with a sort of malicious pleasure. Not for anything less than a major calamity would Frank ever allow him to even get into the same room with his precious Edith. The truth was, Frank was as helpless as he. If Frank had ever done any bookkeeping, he apparently had forgotten it; and he knew for a fact that actually, in the beginning, back before Frank could afford himself an office girl, Agnes had done practically all his bookkeeping for him at the store. So he had to call in Edith. Dave could not help feeling vastly pleased.

Edith, when she arrived and looked at the mess, only shook her head disgustedly and hopelessly. There wasnt anything she could do with this mess. It needed a major revision.

"All right," Frank said balefully. "Do whatever you have to do to it. Ill pay you for the extra time. Get it fixed up, so theres a workable system. Then teach him to work it."

So for the next week, for an hour after the store closed and then again after supper, Dave worked side by side with Edith Barclay in an effort to straighten out the files and accounting of the "Red Checker Cab Company". He got to know her pretty well—that is, if you could even use that term in connection with knowing Edith. He had offered to have her supper sent in with his and to pay for it, but this she had flatly and unequivocally refused. She would go away somewhere by herself and eat, wherever it was she ate, he never knew if it was at home or a restaurant, and then she would come back after supper, cool distant and competent, and go back to work. Dave was uncomfortable and ill at ease with her because he could never get her to talk, or open up. She maintained toward him—in a way that was not insulting at all—an aloof reserve which puzzled him. Only twice did she ever say anything that was personal and not in line of duty: once when he

irately said that Frank should have thought of all of this before he
started—at which she flared up with hot loyalty and snapping eyes,
and gave him to understand that Frank had a lot of work and far too
many important irons in the fire to put his valuable time on a small-
change operation like this. The other time was when she herself,
sitting there working, suddenly asked him if he had served in Europe.
When he said yes, she asked if he had ever spent any time in France
or Paris. He said yes, some. Whereupon she stared at him candidly
and dispassionately for several moments as if trying to read something
in him, and said nothing further, and went back to work. When he
asked her why she had wanted to know, she said inconsistently—but
with complete selfassurance—that she had seen he was wearing his
uniform the night she met him and had therefore assumed he was a
veteran. The answer was so deliberately meaningless that it left him
irritated, as well as puzzled.

Just the same, in spite of all this other, Dave had to admire her
competence and the efficient dispatch with which she worked. It was
all really a very simple thing, when she had it all done. There wasnt
anything difficult or hard about it at all. He could have done it all
himself if he had known how. After she had it all set up, she went
over it again with him, explaining to him how to write down each entry
and why, showing him exactly how to do it. Then she came back for
a short while the next evening, carefully checked all his entries for
the day, said she thought he could handle it now, and left, saying she
would not be back. In a way, Dave kind of hated to see her go. He
could certainly see why Frank felt she was valuable.

She was really a very attractive girl, and he noted—without suspecting how Frank did the same identical thing—the way she bent
her slim pretty neck under the short haircut over her work. He had had
her pegged right, right from the start. She was a highly nubile female.
Although she kept this nubility under careful wraps obviously, when
she was around him, he thought ruefully. Frank must have warned
her that his kid brother was some kind of ogre.

So he found himself back alone again, in his seven AM to eleven
PM shift; after a week of helplessly watching a very sexually attractive
young woman, which only made it worse now. He had a good simple
bookkeeping system he could work easily now; but that didnt help a
damned bit toward lessening the hours he had to spend in this crummy
little hole, usually all by himself. Now and then one, two or all three
of the drivers (Frank did not have the fourth car ready yet) would
be sitting around in the office to talk to or play checkers with, but
that did not happen very often in any one day. During one day 'Bama
stopped in to see him a few minutes, just back from a week's highly
successful junket to Cincinnati, he said,—and left volubly disgusted

at the long hours his friend Dave was working; and another time Wally Dennis stopped by to talk writing, and beat him playing checkers. But that was all. He had written nothing at all since the Monday morning he had left the Frenches'. And obviously he had no prospect of doing any in the near future. Anyway, the high enthusiasm he had felt over there had already evaporated completely, leaving him empty. He was sleeping less than six hours a night. His bowels were off. And he had been nowhere since this damned thing started—except to his hotel.

Apparently, from what Frank said, they were making money. But of course, as he also said, it would be a long slow haul to replace their capital with quarters and thirty five centses and start paying a profit. Actually, he had to admit Frank had been pretty fair about the salary. He was paying him $50 a week; that was $200 a month. Hell, that was more than a buck sergeant made in the Army. The drivers were only getting $31.25, or $125 a month. Living as he was—which meant not going anywhere; not doing anything—he was even able to save a little bit every week. But then what was the point of saving up a little money if you had no way and no place to spend it? At least the drivers got two out of every three Sundays off.

Dave had gotten to know the three drivers pretty well, since theyd all started this thing. There wasnt much else for him to do. He studied them, and listened to them talk, and joined in the talk himself, whenever they were in the office; and when they were not, were out on calls, he speculated on them and on their lives. He found he had acquired a very deep warm spot for all three of them, and the more he learned about them the more he liked all three of them. All three were characters. They were all having the time of their lives, getting to drive cars all day long—and whats more, getting paid for it. Also, with a sort of startled sense of discovery, they were finding out that as the three taxi drivers they had become somewhat prominent figures in Parkman. This was a new experience for all of them, and they were relishing every minute of it. The lean, little, prominent-cheekboned, ferret-faced Ted Fitzjarrald—'Barry' he was to just about everyone in Parkman—was always good for a good laugh with one of his sour bitter pungent remarks. Tall, slow, blond Forrest Lee, who looked and acted like a Southerner, and should have been one but wasnt, good natured, easy going, the natural butt of everybody's jokes, had been taking life easy, the path of least resistance, for so long it had become a habit he couldnt have broken even if he had wanted to, which he obviously didnt. Both Lee and Fitzjarrald had been married and divorced before they were twenty three. Both had served reluctantly and unpatriotically in the Army during the war and seen considerable combat service, and both now remembered their Army time nostalgically and with the regret of loss. They had been classed as loafers, drinkers, women chasers, and generally town bums so long that they did not take their new found prestige very solemnly, even while they relished it.

But of them all Dave felt he liked Albie Shipe the best. Always laughing and saying something funny in his incredibly dumb and, actually, half-moronic way (this humorous bent was evidently something new that Albie had brought home from the Army) Albie Shipe was in the unique position of having everybody start to laugh at him immediately as soon as he grinned and opened his mouth before he could even say a word. Dave suspected that with some innate slyness— coupled with a strong desire to be liked—Albie had somehow or other, in the Army, learned by repeated and painful trial and error that with his obvious intellectual limitations this was the best way for him to get along with the world the most easily. Not tall, but with a tremendously muscular though narrow-shouldered build, guffawing confidently and cockily, Albie presented this sly perpetual role of oafish humor because it made everybody smile and laugh. Barely able to decipher a newspaper, he kept in the front seat of his taxi with him a huge stack of comic books, which he read slowly, laboriously and thoroughly, with avid concentration. He bought every ten- and fifteen-cent comic that came in at the newsstand, and when he finished them gave them out in bunches to the ten- and twelve-year-olds around town, who consequently—and also because he sometimes got out and played with them, although this disturbed their mothers—loved him. He loved movies with the same avidity he loved comics (and reasonably enough, Dave thought sardonically) and every third night, which he got off, could be found there. You could always tell when Albie was at the show, the other two told Dave, because his guffawing laugh would ring all over the theater at every slightest excuse for one. In spite of all this, he was a shrewd excellent checker player. All three of them were, although Fitzjarrald had a definite slight edge. All of them beat Dave.

But even knowing, and enjoying, and being friends with the drivers, wasnt enough to keep him in this wretched half alive existence for-goddamned-ever; and after miserably suffering it and its unfairness for over an entire month, in a fit of passionate love of freedom he worked himself up into, Dave decided he had had enough. Before rebelling, he decided upon who his successor—or his assistant, rather—was going to be: It was going to be Albie. Fired up with a flaming, passionate zeal for the rights of the individual, he called Frank at home at ten thirty in the evening.

"What is it now?" Frank wanted to know warily.

"Im quitting!" Dave cried fervently. He had already let the boys off early.

"What the hell? Whats gone wrong now?"

"Im not a slave!" Dave cried passionately into the phone. "I dont have to suffer this kind of treatment from anybody in the world! Im a man!—a human being! With a human being's rights and privileges! Nobody has the right to work a *mule* sixteen and seventeen hours a day—let alone a human being! The rights and dignity of Man are being destroyed all over the whole world! But as long as Im able, I intend to defend my selfrespect as a human being! Im through! I quit! Get yourself another slave!"

"Stay right there," Frank said wearily. "Dont go away. Ill be right down."

He looked haggard and tired and baggy-eyed, and also as if he had been drinking too much all evening, when he came into the office without his hat and his hair rumpled; but Dave, feeling flamboyantly righteous and wildly enslaved, was not going to be put down.

"All right," Frank said, irately running his fingers through his hair. "Now what is it?"

"Look at this place!" Dave bellowed. He swept his arm around the grubby little office. "How would *you* like to spend your entire life in here! I dont see *you* doing it! Its unjust! You call that *equality?* Every man has certain inalienable rights, by God! Even the lowest of the low! No man has a right to treat another like Im being treated! to force him against his will! and chain him to a desk! or a job! I wont stand for it! I dont have to! and I wont!"

"I told you it would be hard for a while until we got it going," Frank said tiredly. He sat down on the corner of the desk.

"If I wanted to be a slave laborer, I could go to Russia! What do you think we fought this war for! For freedom, thats what! But I aint got any freedom! Im a man! With a man's rights! You can kill me, but you cant force me to work seventeen hours a day!"

"All right," Frank said wearily. "We will get you an assistant. But we will have to pay him. And that means itll take just that much longer before we can start makin' any money."

"To hell with the money!" Dave bawled. "Im not going to live like a slave!"

"Okay," Frank sighed patiently. "Ill start lookin' for you for a guy tomorrow."

"Ive already got one," Dave said, his voice becoming normal. "Albie Shipe."

"Albie!" Frank exclaimed. "Hell, he cant even count!"

"Hes not smart, and hes too dumb to be dishonest," Dave said. "Hes the man I want."

"But he cant do that work," Frank protested.

"Yes he can. Your girlfriend set it up for us. The way she set it up, any ten year old child can do it."

"My who?" Frank said narrowly.

"Your secretary."

"Oh, her," Frank said, relieved.

"Ill work until five o'clock, but not a second later," Dave said. "And I want every other Sunday off. Sundays we can close at six and the guy on duty can work an extra hour."

"That means we will lose every Sunday evening's business," Frank said patiently.

"Hell with the business!" Dave bellowed. "Six or eight dollars business once a week aint worth a man's life!"

Frank sighed tiredly. "Okay. I might as well check the receipts with you while Im here. I take it you let the boys off."

Somehow or other, in some subtle way, Dave knew he had him buffaloed. Frank didnt want him to quit. By threatening *to* quit, he could make him do what he wanted. He filed it away for future reference, his chest swelling triumphantly; he felt he had accomplished a major victory for the rights of man in Parkman Illinois.

"Now I want to ask you somethin'," Frank said tiredly, while Dave got out his books to run the check. "Whatre the chances of these drivers cheatin' on us?"

"Cheating?" Dave said. "Oh, I see what you mean. Well, I dont see how they can, since I take all the calls and send the cabs out."

"Yes but what if they run somebody up town, say, and then another party hails them right there?" Frank said wearily. "We got no way of checkin' that, have we? Can you time them?"

Dave shook his head. "I cant time them. Sometimes they stop for a sandwich or a coke or to get a pack of cigarettes. Anyway, you cant tell how long a trip will take. No, I dont see any way you can control something like that, for sure, unless you buy meters and put them on the cars."

"I looked into that," Frank said wearily, and shook his head. "Too expensive. And it costs too much to have them put on."

"Then I dont see any way you can control it," Dave said.

Frank nodded. "Okay. But you keep an eye on them. And if one of them seems to be takin' a lot longer with his trips, see if you cant find some way to check him."

"All right. Ill see what I can do," Dave said, getting out the cash. He opened the book. He still had not lost his feeling of swelling triumph.

"You tell Albie about the change," Frank said when they had finished the check. "And Ill try to find another driver. I may not be able to find one tomorrow, though."

"Then we run short handed on two cabs tomorrow," Dave stated positively, "and until you do find one. Because Albie goes to work for me tomorrow."

"Okay," Frank said irritably. "Look: Ill see what I can do about a driver. If I can find one, I will. If you want to run short handed, run short handed, I dont give a damn. Now; is that all? You got any other problems you want to take up with me?"

"No," Dave said. "Thats all."

"Okay," Frank said. He got up off the desk corner. "Ill see you sometime tomorrow then," he said and went to the door. But before he got there he stopped and turned back around.

"You talk about freedom and the rights of men," he said irritably and wearily, but without anger. "I spent fifteen years doin' just what you been doin', before I got where I am. Youve spent one month at it. How would you like to spend fifteen years doin' it?"

"I wouldnt like it," Dave said certainly.

Frank opened the door. "Well, every man who ever gets to be a success in this world has to do it," he said as he went out. "He dont have any choice but do it."

"Yeah, and whats he got when he gets it?" Dave called after him.

Frank stuck his head back in the door. "He gets success, and admiration, and money, and fame, and love, and whatever else it is he wants bad enough to do it for," he said tiredly, and patiently, and with that baggy-eyed irritation that was not anger at all, or even disgust, but just weary impatience. He shut the door.

Dave leaned back in his chair and sat still looking at the door. Outside he heard Frank's car start up. He didnt have anything left to do but close down and lock up, since hed let the boys off early. He was a little surprised. He had expected Frank to be furiously angry and try to argue him out of it. Or else pull his slick businessman's act and try to sweettalk him out of it. But it had been ridiculously easy. Frank hadnt seemed to give much of a damn what they decided about it one way or the other, and that didnt seem like Frank.

CHAPTER 27

FRANK was having his own troubles. As he started up his Buick wearily, disgusted with his brother, he didnt give a damn whether Dave quit or whether they ran short handed or whether they closed the damn bitching place up completely. Frank had finally lost his mistress.

Finally and at long last.

As he had known he would.

It was after eleven and the display lights in the business houses were dark, the streets deserted, and sort of aimlessly—and because he did not want to go home—he drove along Plum Street to the end of the block and on up the hill and around the square. The square was nearly deserted too, and the only places still open and lighted were the two poolrooms and the single allnight restaurant. There was also a dimly reflected light from back in the office of his own store, and he knew without thinking about it that it would be Edith Barclay, working late on her monthly statement. Slowly and meanderingly he cruised the Buick completely around the square twice, and then, also without thinking about it, pulled it into one of the diagonal parking spaces in front of his store. It was the only car on this side of the square, and he looked out at the empty parking spaces. He had thought for a fleeting second of going in and talking to Edith a little while. But now that he was parked he didnt want to, could barely stand the thought of talking to anyone. He switched off the lights and motor and lit up a cigar and sat in the darkened interior smoking and staring out at his own darkened storefront, nursing his bruises.

That damned Dave! he thought irately, and was flooded again with the same feeling of weary, beleaguered irritation he had felt back at the taxi office, and which—now, as then—tapered off into the same residue of futile patience and angry impatience. He puffed hungrily on the big fat Ramon Allones 'Churchill' which he had switched to lately as if he might suck comfort from *it*, tasting its smoke rich and buttery in his mouth. He had been like this for over two weeks now. And there didnt seem to be any immediate prospect for sudden change in the near future.

Actually, of course, you couldnt blame Geneve. Not very well. She had to look out for her investment she had in Dotty Callter. He thought of how he had asked her that time in Chicago if there had been any women in on those parties she and Dotty had gone out on, and a great wave of sexual heat rose up through him making his heart change its tempo. Then he remembered other things. God damn it all!

No, you couldnt blame her. But he knew who you could blame. His damn wife Agnes; thats who. He didnt know exactly what she had done or how she must have gone about it—and he probably would never find out—but as sure as God made little green apples she was the one who was behind it. In some way known only to herself, without causing any scandal, she had brought enough gossip pressure to bear on Geneve that she didnt have any choice but to break it off.

My Christ! he thought, ire running up his back like a breeze rippling across a wheatfield, it wasnt as if he had been in love with Geneve! Or as if Agnes was in danger of losing him to her! If he had threatened her security, or thrown away more money than he could afford, or offered to throw her out of her home, he could have understood it! Futile protest filled him. He had provided for her every want, there wasnt a thing she asked for she didnt get—and he loved and respected her. He couldnt understand it. What difference did it make if he slept with some woman? She didnt like sex and never had. Was he to be held guiltily accountable the rest of his life because he did like it?

She had been so damned sweet and nice to him the past two weeks that it infuriated and sickened him. So damn thoughtful! She knew she had him beaten. And he was helpless to do anything; he couldnt get Geneve back if Geneve wouldnt come. Agnes could afford to be magnanimous. It had got so he could hardly stand to be in the house any more. He tried to wait until she was in bed asleep before he went home. And even then he didnt want to go. There had been times—several times—lately when in some subtle way, without ever doing or saying anything actually, she had indicated to him that if he needed sex it would be all right for him to sleep with her.

—just to relieve himself, of course, he thought bitterly, just because she was his wife and loved him and wanted to be of service to him.—

Well, he would be damned if he would! She could rot first. Anyway, he *couldnt* do it. He just simply couldnt *do* it. He didnt *want* to; he had no de*sire*. She probably couldnt understand that. But what did she expect?

The truth was,—the raw uncamouflaged truth was,—she had beat him. It had been a battle between them, and she had won it. That meant he had lost. She had dominated him, had forced him, by using tricks and unfair tactics, beyond his own free will as a human being to do something he had not wanted to do. Did she expect him to just shrug that off and forget it? and come running back to her? Well, he couldnt. Hed rather go to Terre Haute and take on a whore.

Damn you, anyway, Agnes! he thought plaintively. It wasnt as if he didnt love her. He just failed to understand it. It had all been such a nice set up. A better looking mistress than even Paul Fredric or Anton Wernz.

And the infuriating thing was, there wasnt a single damned thing he could do about it. He had already done all he could. He had called Geneve, and met her and talked to her, and it was just about the most humiliating experience of his life, and he could thank Agnes for that too.

In the dark car Frank puffed convulsively on the big 'Churchill', letting the thick smoke billow out around him, the red glow of the coal lighting his warped features.

Down at the end of the block he could see the night cop as he crossed the street going the other way. Well, to hell with him. He didnt care if he did see him sitting here, he thought, and suddenly to Frank it was as if there were two of him, two of himself, the one an abstract observer and personality-less person standing outside on the sidewalk watching the other in the car which was him, a short round-headed balding little man smoking a big fat expensive cigar and staring dead ahead with the hard cold eyes and a set face which held courageously contained an unapproachable agony, and meriting from the observer both sympathy and admiration.

——After getting home from Chicago, he had had no time to call her for the first two weeks because of the taxi service, and indeed, had not even thought about it. But that would have made no difference because it was immediately upon getting home from Chicago, he found out later, that Dotty had talked to her again and whatever it was Agnes had done began having its powerful effect. So actually it would have made no difference at all when he called. When he did call her the following Monday he had not even intended to then. Maybe it was the information she had told him in Chicago that had bothered him and made him want to get hold of her badly, while he still could. Usually as they had agreed she was to call him, but he did have a little out of town business that he thought he might as well do, and she herself could always get a day or two off from Dotty if she really wanted to. He had even been careful enough to go down to the Elks and call from a booth phone, and explained this to her at once, but he immediately sensed some change and not a good one had taken place from the cool, crisp tone of her voice. It had always been a completely and coldbloodedly merciless voice, anyway, even when she was being affectionate. Apparently someone had been standing right beside her, because she took the course of turning down an invitation to some kind of hen party; but it was more than that. No, she could not possibly attend. She had important business that day. She was sorry. Couldnt possibly. So in the end, but still coolly crisp: yes, she would love to meet at the Club for a cocktail tomorrow. —that was a prearranged gimmick between them that he would pick her up at dark on the street that led out to the Country Club. With dark and intense forebodings of disaster he had hung up. It was strange how *every*body could always make him feel guilty as if what*ever* it was, *wher*ever, *when* ever, it was his fault if it was bad.

Well, she had been there, walking, when he drove along by and he had picked her up, unable to help wondering what big awkward dumbassed Al Lowe was doing right about now to be so taken in. He circled back north and drove, slowly, out east of town toward Israel and over the new bridge and on north toward Terre Haute while Geneve coolly and calmly asked him about the taxi service. Was it making money? He was a pretty foxy one, wasnt he? He hadnt told her a word about it. She hadnt even heard it gossiped. She might have been willing to put a little of hers and Al's own money in it with him, if she had known about it. Feeling impatient, he nevertheless took the time to explain that it was really not an enterprise, but only something he had dreamed up to get his brother Dave off his back, and that was why he hadnt bothered to tell her. He hadnt done it, he said, to make money. She didnt bother to answer that, and let it go philosophically. Coolly, calmly, crisply, she told him what he wanted to hear about, how Dotty had talked to her again right after she had got back and this time, Dotty said, it was worse so this was her last warning.

"I cant blame Dotty. And I dont see how you can blame me," she said coolly. She was very beautiful with her cold, marble, mannequin's face like a Vogue model in which the eyes were brought out strikingly and with completely incongruous warmth by Maybelline or something. "I cant go out with you any more," she said decisively. "It isnt worth it to me."

"Well, I guess thats right," Frank said, trying to sound as indifferent and businesslike about it as she did, but not succeeding very well.

"Im sorry," she said crisply, looking at him—almost accusatively, he thought—with that marble face. "Someday perhaps, we may be able to run into each other at the Club now and then, and get away and have a little fun." Here she smiled. And the smooth, rouge-widened lips drew back moistly, looking (as he knew they were) as well trained in all their functions as a movie star's. She was the most beautiful—and the sexiest—woman he had ever laid, Frank thought wistfully. "But that will not be at any time soon that I can see. It certainly wont be until after all the big stink's blown over," she said.

"Yeah, I guess thats so," Frank said. "Well, I guess Ill miss you a little," he said, trying to make it casual.

"Its that damned wife of yours," Geneve said vindictively, but coldly. "Its a wonder to me youve ever succeeded as well as you have, with that millstone hanging around your neck. She dominates you completely," she said, very factually. "And you let her. You have nobody to blame but yourself in all this, Frankie."

"Well—" Frank said inconclusively, temporizing. He didnt think that was *strictly* true, but he didnt want to tell her that. Anyway, he didnt like to talk about Agnes with Geneve. In a way, she was right though.

"You cant blame me for not risking myself and my plans over something you cant handle," Geneve said coldly.

"No, I sure cant blame you for that," he said honestly; "anyway, its all water under the bridge now I guess, aint it?" He had seen the whitely gravelled mouth of a sideroad ahead, and braked the car to turn down it. They were still among the river bottoms, and it ran down off the steep highway grade into a little tree-lined lane.

"What are you turning down here for?" Geneve said in a cold voice, as he swung the Buick down into it.

"Well," he grinned, a little guiltily, "since this is the last time well be seein each other, I thought we might park down here a little bit. And have ourselves one more party."

Geneve swung around in the seat to stare at him coldly and pityingly. Up to then he had not noticed any more-than-usual coldness in her voice. And he did want to bed her down once more pretty badly— in fact, maddeningly. By the time he did notice, and felt the corresponding guilty start of surprise rise in him, it was already too late.

"I havent 'partied' in the back seats of cars since I was in high school," Geneve said with cold contempt. "And I am not about to start in again now. Not at my present age."

Stung deeply, feeling his neck stiffen, Frank did not answer right away. It took several seconds for the full humiliation of it to sink in. He had been made to feel infinitely small. Anger flowed up through him, like blood from a wound, to coagulate and form a protective scab around the hurt.

"Ill turn around," he said stiffly. There was a driveway over the road ditch into somebody's field just ahead. "Ive done a lot of things for you and Al," he said stiffly as he swung into it, staring straight ahead. "A lot of them things I havent even been asked to do."

"Youve been paid back in full for everything you did," Geneve said coolly. But there was a faint note of start in her voice. As if she hadnt been realizing fully what she was doing.

"Yes, but I wont be gettin' paid any more," Frank said coldly.

"No you wont," Geneve said. "Not in any parked cars. Im not a whore. —And if Im going to have any love affairs, Im going to have them in comfort."

"Thats your privilege," Frank said, still staring straight ahead. Still without looking at her, he turned his head back over his left shoulder and backed the car out into the lane, headed back the other way. Putting it in gear, he still didnt look at her. What he wanted to do, desperately and sanguinarily, was to tell her coldly and furiously that she could lay for him right here and right now like the whore she was, and they both knew she was, or else hed kick Al out tomorrow and to hell with what everybody would think. But instead, he said:

"But in spite of the fact I wont be gettin' paid, I hadnt intended to let Al go from the store." He pulled the car up the grade back onto the highway, and started back toward the river. "Hes not very bright. But hes learnin' what I want him to learn. And someday I intended to make him the manager of it. I might be a lot of other help to both of you. In a lot of other ways. —Whether I got 'paid' or not," he said. It wouldnt have worked anyway; the other. He knew her well enough to know she would have coldly and philosophically gotten out and walked home, or caught a ride. "That was what I had intended," he said coldly.

Geneve did not answer him. She did not say anything at all. He was beginning to feel pretty righteous. The scab of anger surrounding his wound softened a little. Still staring stiffly straight ahead, he drove along not hurrying, keeping it at fifty. Geneve still did not say anything. Not a word. They drove all the way back to the bridge in silence, and then across it.

"Well, are you going to let him go?" Geneve said coolly, as if the evening lights of Israel sweeping past below them were the code which unlocked her lips.—Those lips, he thought painfully, damn! They knew their business.

"No," he said. "No, Im not. At least I dont think so," he added virtuously.

Again Geneve had not answered him, and they drove on in silence.

"Incidentally," Geneve said coolly, but softly this time, "That was why I married Al. That dumbness."

"Well, that was your privilege, too," Frank said coldly, not looking at her.

After a moment she laughed a soft little laugh, heartily, if harshly. "But that didnt make a damned bit of difference—honestly," she said. "What if I had married a smart man? That didnt matter to me at all."

"I didnt figure it did," he said.

"You know, I like you," she said with her cold grin. "I guess, because youre a smart businessman. You make money. Dotty is a smart business-man. I admire anybody who makes money. I guess thats it."

Frank wondered sourly how much of this was flattery. "Im not goin' to fire Al," he said thinly.

Geneve smiled at the joke, but did not even bother to answer that as if she had known confidently all along that he wouldnt, that he would say that. Instead she paused a second, thinking something else, and then said:

"You and I may not have much—yet—but we both have enough income and make enough money, that we dont have to have sex in parked cars like the high school kids. We dont have to lower ourselves to that social level," she said, her voice chilly cold again; "ever again." It was evidently some point of honor with her.

This time it was Frank who did not answer. They were almost half way across the bottoms and he could see the Christmastree brightness of the night shift at the Sternutol, and the towering high gas flare. They drove on in silence.

"I just cant afford to take the chance any more, Frankie," Geneve said with cold rationality. "You cant either. We both have got too much at stake in this town."

Once again Frank had not answered. They were passing the old tree-grown cemetery that had been built out on the flat at the foot of the hill a mile outside of town. Just before they got to the outskirts she spoke again.

"Damn it, its all due to that damned wife of yours," she said irritably. "And because you let her dominate you. You ought to dominate her, Frankie."

"Like Al dominates you, you mean," Frank said thinly.

"Al and I understand each other," she said, out of that cold-marble face with its shockingly, incongruently, warmly made up eyes. "We have an understanding."

"You better be glad, then," Frank said. "Because if you do, youre the only married couple in the world who do."

They had driven the rest of the way on in silence.

——In the dark car, parked before his store, Frank leaned over and pulled a pint bottle out of the dash compartment and took a big drink that was less of an enjoyable drink than it was a wild expression of flagrant rebellion against his wife.

He still couldnt understand it. Why did she have to take such a damned dog in the mangerish attitude? As he came back slowly to himself from the painfulness of remembering, he noted that Edith's light was still on in the store, and quite suddenly he had to be where there were people, had to talk to somebody—if only about the weather— As powerfully and as frantically as just a few minutes before he was unable to stand the thought of people, now he couldnt stand the thought of being alone. Convulsively, like a reflex being tapped with a rubber hammer, he opened the door and jumped out into the street.

The cold air outside bumped him in the head noticeably, after the thick cigar smoke in the car. More calmly, he threw the chewed butt away and fished out his keys and went over to the door. It seemed like a haven, suddenly, in there; a dusty, quiet, utterly familiar haven; the one place in the world where he could go, he thought, turning the key, the one place left.

"Its me, Edith. Frank," he called as he opened the door, in case she might be frightened. Carefully he felt his way back through the darkened display room and across the storeroom to the office. He would sit a while, and maybe have a drink out of the desk, and smoke a cigar, and maybe then he could go home. Agnes would be in bed asleep by then.

Edith was sitting at her own desk, working. She looked up and grinned at him as he came in. She certainly didnt look frightenable.

"Well! What are you doing roaming around in the middle of the night? Hello, boss."

"Oh, just roamin' around," he said vaguely. "I sort of had the blues." He took off his topcoat and laid it on the desk and ran his fingers through his hair. "Dont let me bother you. You go right on with your work. I— I had a couple things I wanted to look at," he lied.

He sat down at his desk and unlocked it and opened the double drawer where the whiskey was and poured himself a little. Then he put some papers on the desk, to make it look like he really was hunting for something, but he did not look at them. Instead, he leaned back in his chair and cocked his feet up on the corner of the desk and sipping the whiskey, stared at the corner of the ceiling.

"Bout to get it finished up?" he said.

Edith wrinkled her nose. "Ill have it all done before very long. I dont mind doing it. I enjoy it."

"Well, you go right on with your work," Frank said. "Dont let me bother you."

"Whats the trouble?" Edith said gently, as she turned back to the desk. "Dave been giving you some more trouble?" She bent to her work. Like just about everybody else in town, Edith had heard the whole story, the Geneve Lowe story; and *knew* what was troubling him. She had already heard four differently garbled accounts of it.

"Who?" Frank said after a moment. "Dave? Oh, no more than usual. Tonight he wanted to quit."

"Quit!" Edith said without looking up. "What for?"

"Because his rights as a human being was bein' infringed on," Frank said. "In other words, he wanted more time off."

"Did you give it to him?" she asked quietly, working.

"Sure. Why not?" Frank said. "I didnt expect him to last this long and take it. You go on with your work," he said.

Taking him at his word, Edith did exactly that, without even bothering to answer. Pouring himself another small drink, Frank watched her from his desk. She was such a pretty girl, really. And that was strange, because she wasnt beautiful at all, like—like Geneve. And yet—such a pretty girl. She probably had a very satisfactory love life, he thought wistfully.

"How you gettin' along with that boyfriend of yours?" he asked her cheerfully.

"What boyfriend?" Edith said without looking up from the work.

"Didnt you get engaged to a fellow here a while back? A soldier?"

Edith's ears turned pink. "Oh, him. We broke it off quite a while ago." She dropped her head lower over her work. "He was transferred to Indianapolis later."

Frank felt chagrined, and at the same time very fatherly. "Oh, I didnt know that. Im sorry. What was the trouble?"

"We just didnt see eye to eye on a bunch of things," Edith said shortly.

"Well, I hope you got yourself another one right away, didnt you?" Frank said kiddingly.

Edith turned around and grinned at him puckishly. "I sure did. Four or five of them, in' fact."

Frank threw back his head and laughed. "Safety in numbers, hunh?"

"Thats it," Edith said, grinning wholesomely. "And there sure is."

"Well— You go ahead with your work," he said. "Dont let me disturb you."

"I dont mind," she smiled. "You dont disturb me. After all, you do own the store." But she turned back to her desk.

From his own, feeling warm inside and friendly and relaxed, Frank watched her again and then looked off at the corner of the ceiling. He could feel tears of warmth and affection come almost into his eyes. Great Christ! what was getting into him anyway? He wondered idly if she was sleeping with all four or five of them. But no; not Edith. She was too good a girl, and too level headed. Shed never have an affair with more than one man at a time. Not Edith. He was sure of that.

Feeling pleasantly old, and pleasantly fatherly, in a way he almost never seemed to feel with Dawn, he reached for his whiskey just as the door out front in the darkened store rattled loudly. He took his feet down off the desk.

"Ill answer it," he said. "Its probably just the night cop."

"He certainly earns his money," Edith said behind him as he left. "This is the second time hes been here."

Frank felt his way out to the front where the night cop's flashlight shone in at him through the glass of the door. He unlocked it.

"Its only me, Pete," he said.

"I saw your car out front, Mr Hirsh," the old man grinned. "But I thought I ought to stop and check anyway, you know."

Frank nodded. "Absolutely. I just came down to look at a couple things I wanted to check."

"Then Miss Barclay's gone?" the night cop said.

"Yes," Frank said. "Shes gone."

"She was down here workin' late on her monthly statement, you know," the oldster said conversationally.

"Yes, I know. I saw it on the desk. Well, Ill see you, Pete," he said.

"All right. Just thought Id better check. See you, Mr Hirsh," Pete said. He half touched his cap brim, a rather ridiculous gesture, in him, looking as if it were something hed seen in the movies once. He went on, ostentatiously flashing his flashlight against the buildings and windows, a thing he practically never did unless he knew he was being looked at. Frank locked the door and went on back to the office. Edith was still working.

He suddenly felt embarrassed. "I, uh— I told him you were gone," he said, leaning in the doorway. "I dont know why exactly. It just popped out. I guess I just thought itd look better if people didnt think we were down here at night together alone." He looked at her kind of worriedly.

"I dont think it would make any difference," Edith said efficiently. "But it doesnt matter. Ill be through here in just a minute. He wont see me leave. Hell be around the corner by then. There," she said. She stood up holding the sheaf of papers and smiled at him. "Would you like to look at these now?"

"Oh, no," Frank said.

"You want me to stay for anything and help you out?" Edith offered. "Id be glad to."

"Oh, no. God, no," Frank said. "Youve stayed long enough. Come on, Ill drive you home."

"You dont need to," she said. "Im used to walking." She put her papers away.

"Its no trouble. Id like to."

"I—" She stopped, and then shrugged and grinned boyishly. "Okay. Ride, it is." She got her coat.

From the corner of his desk, Frank watched her. Her coat on, she sat down at her desk again to put something away. Quite suddenly Frank imagined her sitting there stark naked, working. Absolutely, stark naked; and sitting there working! calmly typing at her typewriter, working her adding machine, bending over to make notes with a pencil. She got up from her desk with her coat on, and he imagined her getting up from it, mother naked, and turning toward him with a file of papers, and calmly walking in her high heels over to the filing cabinet and filing them. Great God in the morning! he thought desperately, what in the name of God is happening to me!

"Well," Edith said, "are you ready to go?"

"Ah, yes," he said. "Yes, Im ready." He got his topcoat.

Outside, after latching and checking the door, he held the car door open for her. The night cop was nowhere in evidence. He looked, a little nervously.

"Run you right out home," he said, getting in on his side. "Wont take a minute, and save you a long walk."

"Its awfully nice of you," Edith said.

"Nothing. Nothing at all. Not for all the work you do for me."

At the corner where the brick street ended and Roosevelt Drive turned south Edith gathered herself together.

"You can let me out right here," she said. "Itll save you having to run down Roosevelt."

"Run you right to the house," Frank said cheerfully. "No trouble."

"Id really rather get out here, Mr Hirsh!" Edith said incisively. "You see the folksll be asleep, and a car turning into the drive might wake them."

"Oh," Frank said. "Oh, okay."

After he let her out and turned around, he started back toward town along East Wernz Ave the mainstreet. When he happened to look back in the rearview mirror, he saw her, with a kind of frightened startled surprise, still standing there under the streetlight, looking after him ominously.

God, could she have read his mind? that silly damned thing hed imagined?

CHAPTER 28

EDITH was feeling sorry for her boss, not ominous. She was ashamed of herself for having gotten irritable with him in the car. —But she could just imagine what old Jane would say if she happened to be up, or woke up,—when the boss came bringing Edith home in his car at eleven thirty!

She had wanted to walk, anyway. She enjoyed her nightly walk home. Especially if it was after dark. She preferred to walk. But she couldnt very well have turned him down; not when he was in the shape he was in. He obviously did not want to go home, poor guy. —And so now she found herself in the ridiculous position of having to stand on the corner, waiting for him to get out of sight, so she could go ahead and take her walk anyway without him seeing her and getting his feelings hurt.

It made her irritable. He was really a very great source of annoyance and upset, a lot of the time, any more. —Especially lately, she thought trenchantly. In the past two weeks; since this Geneve Lowe affair broke up. He got his feelings hurt over practically nothing, over just anything. And she would rather do anything than hurt his feelings. It kept her constantly on edge whenever she was around him.

Edith mentally kicked herself in the tail for getting short tempered. She didnt give a damn about Geneve Lowe. He would be a lot better off without her. But it was doing something to him she didnt like. Something it ought not to be doing to him. He cared too much. He ought to not give a damn, she thought irritably.

He was such a nervous, miserable, lonely, unhappy little guy. And everybody caused him trouble. Everybody. His wife, his brother Dave, Judge Deacon, Geneve Lowe. Everybody he came in contact with seemed only to cause him more trouble. Sometimes you felt about him like you did your neighbor's baby, you wanted to cuddle him because he was so helpless, and pat him and tell him not to cry everything would be all right. That was the way he made you feel. And it wasnt pleasant.

—Itll be well before youre a man, she thought suddenly, the old phrase Jane had used to use on her popping into her head. —You wont even remember it, when youre a woman.

She waited until she could no longer see the taillights and then started walking back in the direction of town, past the big Fredric house with its dark tree-studded lawn.

She just walked along, not going anywhere in particular and looking at the big homes, and after a couple of blocks turned off on North Ash. The type of houses changed immediately. Her walk home from work in the evening was one of Edith's special pleasures. Especially if it was late at night and after dark. Then, with the streets deserted, and everybody else inside, it was as if it were her town; her private possession. She owned it. All the houses, the people in them, the streetlamps, the sidewalks, the grassed lawns, all. She allowed them all to continue to exist, and to live there,—as long as they kept her rules and did like they all should, and the people acted like people should act. She imagined she patrolled the streets, secretly unknown to all, keeping an eye on things and checking up on everyone, seeing that all was well. She never told anyone about it because it sounded so silly it would embarrass her. The week she had worked with Dave on the taxi stand's bookkeeping, she had walked home for supper every night, and then walked back, and then walked home again, and had enjoyed every moment of it. This time she walked, sauntering easily, along North Ash clear down to the I.N. tracks, then turned east a block and came back up to East Wernz the mainstreet on the next street over. Everything seemed to be well tonight, she thought to herself patricianly and affectionately, feeling a little ridiculous. At the corner of Wernz she turned back east the way she had come, toward home.

It was when repassing the Fredric house that she noticed the long black car parked on the drive. She was positive it hadnt been there before, and she recognized it instantly. It was 'Bama Dillert's car. Practically everyone in town knew the black 1937 Packard that the country gambler took such meticulous and oldmaidish care of, and drove like a God-protected demon with the hounds of hell after him.

The big old three storey Fredric house was set far back from the street with a big lawn, and just behind it to the east, set among big trees, was the expensive old livery house that was now their garage. It was right in front of this on the widened drive, where the trees over it shaded it from the streetlight on the corner and everything else, that the shining black Packard was parked. If she had not been walking, and even then if she hadnt been looking, she wouldnt have seen it.

The big house itself, she noticed,—because then she looked—was all dark except for the single night light they kept burning in the downstairs hall whenever Doris was still out, and which Doris always turned off when she came in.

For years Edith had had the run of the Fredric house. All through childhood, and all during the summers of Doris's college years, up until Doris came home from her year in the West to teach three years ago.

And she knew the layout of just about everything in it—as well as the rigidly held schedule of living the Fredrics followed and which had not varied in fifteen years. That light would not be on unless Doris was out.

—and, since Doris *was* out, and 'Bama Dillert's car was parked in their drive, it was pretty nearly patently obvious what was going on in the car! . . .

It might even have been there, she thought, when the boss brought her home; and even when she herself had walked past the first time. Parked way back there in the dark under the trees, almost nobody would ever see it. Especially this late at night. It was safe.

Filled with a sudden tickling excitement that made her want to giggle, and at the same time disguted her a little because she did want to giggle, Edith went on—very careful not to alter either the rhythm or the speed with which she was walking. If they were looking out and did see her, they wouldnt know she had seen them.

Well! Well! Some gleeful devil in her made her want to sneak up on the Packard from behind and snatch the back door open.

My God, would Doris be fit to be tied! Almost certainly she would be in a very embarrassing position. People didnt go out with that gambler 'Bama for hearts and flowers.

—But instead, she walked on, to the corner and the light, and then turned south on Roosevelt toward her own house.

During most of those years she had run around with Doris—(they had never run around together, actually, not to go out, and saw each other mostly at home, except for an occasional coke or soda downtown; Doris was older, and had more money, and ran with a different crowd)— during most of those years, she had been the confidant for all of Doris's love affairs; and they ran all the way from sophomore year of high school on up until Doris got out of college. They also ran all the way from football players, basketball players, wrestlers and trackmen on through the various horn rimmed intellectual brackets and the Business Administration types, depending upon what state of development Doris happened to be in at the time. Doris was always deeply and painfully in love with whichever one, when she would come to Edith to talk about it—or would call Edith up to come to her.

(through the back yard. the tangled old junky back yard. she remembered it emotionally with the remembered wonder that she the child had of it. creaky iron swing. one fair sized shade tree. the path led from the rusty fence off through the field, the bumpy grown-up bunchy-grassed field. which the Fredrics also owned. it led to the high immaculate hedge, with its own immaculate gate cut in it, and the lovely big back Fredric lawn. that was how they always went. it was so strange. everything strange. back then, the world was strange.)

She always went, when Doris called. They would sit upstairs in Doris's bedroom. Doris never talked about sex per se, it was never mentioned between them, and it was an understood assumption between them that it had nothing to do with these loves—any more than it had with Edith's own crushes; which they never talked about. Doris loved powerfully and desperately she learned gradually, really did and it was not an act, though you would never think it seeing the cool virgin calmness of her on the street. And almost always for some very legitimate reason, loved hopelessly. If it was the high school football captain who was only the son of a local truck driver— Edith remembered that one. Or if it was the horn rimmed glasses of a poet and psychology major who wanted to live in New York City instead of Parkman—that was another one she remembered. Sometimes Doris's desperation was such and so much that even Edith could hardly stand it.

Edith was past the corner and the cone of the light, where they could no longer see her, and she stopped.

—And after all that, she thought, and all that time, it was only now in the last three years since Doris had come home to teach, —and that largely through the auspices of Jane's inordinate talent—that she had heard all the recent stories, which somehow always seemed to stay under cover, about Doris's repeated and heavy (and this time, *sex per se*) love affairs.

Apparently, all this time, all through high school and through college, Doris had been giving her all for her love affairs, and thus proving them, and everybody had known it but Edith. Or rather, nobody had known it including Edith. Well, she thought correcting herself still again, with a grin, lets say everybody knew it but Edith, and almost nobody admitted it except Jane.

—Or, she thought, you might say everybody knew it while nobody believed it. You just couldnt look at the sweet shy demure modesty and calmness of Doris Fredric, and *keep* yourself from disbelieving it.

She went on. There were three houses between the corner and her own, and after each one she peered back between them at the distant Fredrics' driveway. The car was still there. If you knew it was there and where to look, you could see it. But hardly otherwise. She wondered suddenly, with a kind of dim but sure understanding, if perhaps Doris got an added pleasure out of her sex by having it there on their driveway, where—if it were daylight—it would be right out in front of God and everybody. Well, it wasnt her problem. The car was still there when she got to her own house.

As she approached the house, Edith saw with surprise and suddenly that there was a light on in the front room. It was sudden because she had been looking so hard the other way; and it was with surprise, because they never left a night light on. She got her keys out of her purse,—and then stopped:

—And yet, she told herself, you dont *know*. Nobody ever *knew* apparently, with Doris Fredric. Those stories might all be lies. And they might just be sitting out there, talking. (But what about? With 'Bama Dillert!) And all that other could all be in her own imagination. She couldnt be *sure;* because she didnt *know*. And yet she did know, too. She *knew*.—But then maybe she was wrong? Well—she separated the keys.

With the light still on in the front room of the little house, she let herself in quietly, wondering what Jane could be doing up at this time of night; because she knew it wouldnt be her father. John Barclay, when he came home from his boring, though tiring, relatively unimportant responsibilityless job in the Sternutol plant, read the paper, and then ate his huge supper, then read the rest of the paper, and then fell drugged with food and newsprint into his bed and slept like a dead man until the alarm went off in the morning to get him up to go back again; and nothing, absolutely nothing, woke him. Normally, Edith would have understood it about Jane, because usually this was about the time Jane got home from her 'dates'. But for the past few days she hadnt been going out nights at all and had been going to bed right after supper. Edith didnt understand it. —But she knew it was a damned good thing she hadnt let the boss bring her all the way to the house!

"Whats the matter, honey?" she said gently. "Whatre you doing up?" She had more or less surprised Jane standing barefooted in her nightgown in the living room.

"Aww, nothin'," her grandmother rasped in her gravelly throat. She looked both guilty and startled. "I just dont feel so good."

Edith took off her coat and unpinned her hat. There were dark circles under Jane's eyes. A wave of warmth and sympathy swept through her. "Your kidneys again?"

"Naww," Jane said reticently. "No moren usual, anyways." She looked away.

"Is it your heartburn? Youre not really sick?"

"I aint sick," Jane said, vaguely and inconclusively. "I just dont feel so good." There was a curious, and strong, reticence in her. In the long nightgown, without the confining armor of the huge brassiere and girdle, most of her just hung, resembling a collection of different sized ellipsoids fastened together at the center. Edith felt again her neverfailing sense of astonishment at the size of those breasts.

"You ought to have something on your feet," she said. "Thats a sure way to *get* sick, running around like that."

"Yeah," Jane said, looking at her hauntedly.

"Go and get your slippers," Edith said crisply, "and then come back"

—here she grinned—"and Ill tell you something that will tickle you and youll just love to hear."

Was it possible grandmother was falling madly in love again! It had all the symptoms. Oh, no! she thought, not again! She suddenly loved the old hulk desperately.

"Okay," Jane said, but without much enthusiasm. She ambled the few steps to her room and came back immediately wearing her taggedy runover slippers which must have been just inside the door for her to just thrust her feet in, and then sat down on a straight chair and placed her hands palm down on her knees in the nightgown attentively. The action resembled a prim little girl sitting up at school, and Edith wanted suddenly to get her arms clear around her and hug her.

"Well, I walked home from work," she started.

"You was out kind of late," Jane said reticently and without fire. "I thought you was in already."

"My monthly statement," Edith said. "Well, here was what I was going to tell you. —But first you must promise not to tell anyone or mention it to a living soul."

"I promise," Jane said solemnly. She crossed her heart.

"Well, when I passed the Fredrics' house, I saw a big black car parked back by the garage. In the dark, you know, under those trees. And the nightlight in the hall was still on. You know how Doris always turns it off when she comes in."

"What kind of car?" Jane said, crossing her arms over her chest.

Edith grinned a little. "A 1937 black Packard sedan."

"Haw!" Jane exploded raucously, showing her first sign of enthusiasm. She slapped herself hard on both thighs. "Well, Ill be damned! 'Bama Dillert!" She looked thoughtful for a moment and then said, "Well, Ill be a big blackhearted son of a bitch!" She shook her head solemnly. "That Doris is gettin' to the bottom of the barrel, aint she? Or else awful hard up for a man. To be goin' out with that cocky womanchasin' devil. I know him. I know him real good."

"I thought that would tickle you."

"Yes, sir!" Jane said relishingly. "Yes, sir! It sure does!"

"But you mustnt tell anybody about it, now," Edith cautioned.

"Oh, I wouldnt never," Jane said solemnly.

"No, I just bet you wouldnt," Edith said, already wishing now she hadnt told her.

"No sir I wouldnt," Jane said stoutly. "I crossed my heart, didnt I?"

"Anyway, we dont know for sure what was going on in the car," Edith said.

"Haw!" Jane said. "The hell we dont. Maybe you dont."

"We dont. They might just be sitting out there talking, for all we know."

"Yes, sir!" Jane said, cackling raucously. "Yes, sir! You bet! Especially that 'Bama. Hes a talker. He talks a average of about three words a hour; on his good days."

"Well, we dont *know*," Edith said primly. "Anyway, you promised you wouldnt tell anybody, and you mustnt."

"Tell anybody! Who, me?" Jane crossed her big arms again and sat back, like some huge rock. She grinned cynically at Edith. Then she said: "I been tellin' you about that Fredric girl for years and years now. But you wouldnt believe *me*. She was layin' all them boys she use to tell you about she was in love with, clear back in high school even."

"You dont *know* that," Edith said.

"Yes I do know. I know for a fact."

"You never *saw* them."

"No," Jane said, and grinned; "worse luck. But I do know people who has. And—"

"Who?" Edith said.

Jane waved her finger back and forth before her face. "I aint mentionin' no private names," she said slyly, and went on. "—And I do know what one of the boys said hisself one night, out to Smitty's Bar when he was drunk. He said that gal could even make *him* believe she was a virgin, and after hed just laid her lessn two days before."

"*Who* said that."

"Never you mind," Jane said. "Anyway, the boy denied it later. He said he was just drunk, and was lyin'. He said he made it up and never laid her at all. Tryin' to be a gentleman, you see."

"Then you dont have any proof," Edith countered.

"I got proof," Jane said happily. She tapped herself on the side of the head. "Theres all the proof I need. I been watchin' that girl for years and years and years. Ever since we lived right here. I been studyin' her, because shes interestin' to study and try to figure out. I dont know whether its because she was an only child and a rich girl, and her folks spoiled her so much. I aint quite got it figured clear out. But shes a funny one. Do you remember the time she bust your music box?"

"What music box?" Edith said. "No. I dont remember."

"You was both just little bitty tykes," Jane said, almost accusingly; "but you ought to remember your own music box. John bought you a Swiss music box in Chicago. He been up there lookin' for work. Back before your mother died this was. He come home luggin' this little Swiss music box for you. John must have been drunk"—Jane grinned raucously—"Or else feelin' awful guilty about somethin'. Anyways he paid $25 for this little Swiss music box. That was back when $25 was worth a lot of money. That was more money than we had to eat on. My, it was a pretty Swiss music box."

Jane's voice took on a wistful quality, under its thick rasp. "It was the prettiest Swiss music box I ever seen.—And Ive saw a lot of Swiss music boxes, in my time," she said. "It was made out of some kind of pretty red wood, and it had all little bits of white ivory-like and different kinds of other wood inlaid in the top and sides. You wound it up with a key like a clock underneath the bottom and it played three songs, London Bridge, The Banks of Lock Lomon, and Comin' Through the Rye. My I mean it was a scrumptious Swiss music box," Jane said wistfully.

"I remember it now," Edith said, feeling somehow or other a little awed by the phenomena of time and memory.

"You ought to remember it," Jane said reproachfully. "You were too little for a Swiss music box like that one. But here John come bringin' it. He must of had been awful drunk when he bought it. John sure never gave me nothin' like that ever. Nor your mom neither." She shook her head ruefully. "It was a beautiful Swiss music box. Well, when Doris Fredric seen it she looked like she had went crazy. There wasnt nothin' like it here nor in none of the stores in Terre Haute, and shed never saw one like that. Well, she grabbed it out of your hands and threwn it on the ground and bust it, just like that, without a single word. Then she jumped up and down on it, and run home cryin'. It was summer and you was out in our back yard with it when she come over. I jist happen to be standin' in the kitchen window watchin'."

"I remember now," Edith said, her voice a little awed. "Id forgotten all about it."

"After the little bitch jumped up and down on it," Jane said wistfully, "she looked at you so cold and mean I thought for a minute she was goin' to tie into you too. But she never. She just turned and run home cryin'."

"I remember," Edith said. "I came in the house cryin', scared. I was scared."

Jane nodded. "Thats right. I stood and held you."

"What ever happened to the music box?"

Jane moved her ponderous head, wistfully. "It was ruint. I tried to get John to take it over to the Fredrics' to show it to her folks what she had did. But he wouldnt do it. He just said he didnt want to go over there with it. So finally I took it over myself by God. I didnt give a damn if they was rich people. I figured theyd ought to by God pay for it anyways."

Again, Jane moved her head. "Mr Fredric was nice about it enough, I will say that. He paid me the money for it and said to just leave it there on the porch." Jane's dark circled eyes suddenly glinted dangerously. She hadnt got her reputation in Parkman undeservedly, or without earning it. "I told him I wouldnt leave it, by Christ. You see I wasnt aimin' to leave it there for that little redheaded devil to crow over. So he said all right, to keep it then. I took it out to the city dump and threwn it far away, where nobody could of ever found it."

"Isnt it strange?" Edith said slowly. "—And Id forgotten the whole affair."

"*I* never forgotten it," Jane said toughly. "I know all about that little miss priss bitch Doris. Shes one of them kind that has to have firsts on everything. They dont care if they keep it, as long as they got the firsts on it. If they get the firsts, theyll even give it away to somebody with a big sweet magnaminous smile, just to show you what fine people they are to them. But if they aint got it first, theyll smash it up."

"You loved it, didnt you, Janie?" Edith said softly. "You were the one who should have had it. Instead of me."

"Well," Jane said noncomittally. "You was really too young to have a Swiss music box like that. And especially with that little Doris bitch hangin' around here."

Edith smiled. "It sure looks that way," she said ruefully, "doesnt it?" She looked off toward the wall that was the direction of the Fredrics' driveway, where the black car was, and nodded toward it. "But maybe Doris has changed."

"She aint changed," Jane sniffed. "But shes barkin' up against a pretty tough apple when she ties into 'Bama Dillert. Nobodys got firsts on 'Bama Dillert. —unless its that sharecroppin' wife of his he never sees."

"Im still not *sure*," Edith said, half to herself. "Anyway, I guess its a good thing we dont see much of her any more, isnt it?"

"Haw!" Jane bawled derisively. "I guess so. You was her number one stooge for years and years."

Edith felt her back stiffen angrily. "Oh no I wasnt," she said crisply, "anything of the kind." But then she grinned. "Anyway, I took your mind off your troubles and got you over your blues, didnt I?"

Jane, who was in the process of lighting herself a cigarette, stopped the match in midair and stared at her, the haunted look slowly coming back into her dark circled eyes. "Yeah," she said slowly. "Yeah. You did."

As if conscientiously reminding herself she went on and lit the cigarette she no longer appeared to want.

"Whats the matter, Janie?" Edith said. "Whats the trouble? Youre not in love again?" Impulsively, she jumped up and rushed over to her to hug her. "Oh, I love you so much, Janie. Youre the best there is. Im so sorry for all the rotten things I say to you. As soon as I say them. If you want to use any of my jewelry—"

"Dont touch me!" Jane said, jumping up suddenly, before Edith could even reach her.

Edith recoiled. "Why! whats the matter!"

"Nothin'," Jane said reticently. "Nothin's the matter. My backs just a little sore, thats all. I was afraid you was goin' to squeeze me."

"Janie, are you sick?"

"Naww," Jane said irately, "damn it. I told you I aint sick. I just dont feel so good, thats all," she said, looking away. "Little under the weather. Little down in the dumps." She moved away. "Guess I better get on to bed."

"All right," Edith said lightly, watching her big bulk in that ridiculous nightgown. "Ill see you in the morning then, honey." My God! It *was* love! Again! Sure as hell. She turned away to her room.

"G'night, kiddo," Jane said, watching her grimly. She waited until Edith had closed her door and then turned to her own room, switching off the front room light.

Damn and blast! She would have given anything if Edith hadnt caught her moseying around the house like that; shed thought she was already home and in bed asleep. Jane could feel that haunted look spread there all over her face, but there wasnt a damned thing she could do about it. Always did have a damned open face; whatever she felt, it showed—automatically. She entered her room with a sick, frightened sadness.

Utter aloneness, with the stark knowledge of no help anywhere, engulfed her again as it had been earlier, and as it had not—up to six days ago—engulfed her since she was a young green kid. Shame scalded her, and guilt froze her; and both roared all through her like the winds released in an airplane tunnel.

Old whore! she raged at herself bitterly. She was right when she called you old whore. Just like you knew she was right then. And she did, too. With a very heavy hand she shut her door dejectedly. Then as an afterthought she locked it.

In her room the first thing Jane did was get a tissue from the box on the bureau, and standing barefooted on the floor (she had kicked off them damn slippers) thrust it up under her nightgown.

Well, I got it, she thought. I sure got it. I got the clap.

I surely do. —For perhaps the eleven thousandth time.

Oh. Damn, she thought bitterly, damn damn damn.

Horror and terror both slithered through her chest and stomach like a muscular spasm, at the thought of what to do. Edith and John. And here she was doing the cooking and all for them. Living in the same house and using the same bathroom. And all the people she worked for, too. —If she gave it to anyone of any of them, she would commit suicide. She had already made her mind up to that coldbloodedly and calmly. It would be the only way to prove her sorrow and her grief, and an old bat like her wouldnt be throwin' away too many years anyway. —She had made herself scrupulously and thoroughly clean, scrubbing and scrubbing her hands with lots of strong soap, before she ever went near the kitchen or went to one of her people's houses. Whenever she used a toilet, there or at home, she carefully scoured the seat and bowl both. It was costing her an hour to an hour and a half a day, scrubbing. —And even then it was no proof against possible infection for someone. My god, she thought with sick horror, what if she was to give it to Edith? A nice, pretty young girl like Edith? Or someone like Agnes Hirsh? The people she worked for trusted her.

Old whore, she thought viciously, guilt standing at her side like a black specter; towering over her. Thats what you are and thats all you ever been, all your whole life. Jane Staley. Her daughter, and her granddaughter, even her own mother use to know it, when she use to call her a baggage, didnt she?

She couldnt go to a doctor. She just couldnt. She would be too ashamed. Old Jane Staley. How would she be able to go up to Doc Mitchell or Doc Cost, and tell them she had the clap, and let them examine her? And she couldnt go out of town, either. She could sneak off to Terre Haute, sure, but what would Edith say to her, when Edith knew she hadnt been to Terre Haute or anywhere else out of town for moren ten years?

—And above all, above everything else, she mustnt let Edith find out. She just mustnt.

Horror and hatred of herself, and that old guilt she had lived with like a familiar toothache for almost fifty years now, welled up in her sickly and made life drag heavy at her shoulders.

She couldnt understand how she had got it. She knew none of her boyfriends had it. She knew that for a positive fact. She definitely *knew* it. Then how? And there wasnt any new ones among them. And she hadnt been out with nobody else.

—If only that damned oilworker son of a bitch husband of hers hadnt run off and left her when she was a green kid and six months pregnant. If only that. Then everything might of been different.

She might have got it off a toilet seat in one of the bars, Smitty's or Ciro's or one of them. She might have done that. But whod believe it. Old Jane Staley. A damned man could go to a doctor. It was just a big joke to wink at with a man. But not no woman. Maybe she was one of them carriers! People carried some diseases around with them all their life but they theirselves didnt get it, except just a little bit now and then. They just give it to others.

Oh my God, Jane thought in agony. If that was true she would of given it to all her boyfriends! And God knows how many other just plain people!

She knew that wasnt true.

Wearily, she climbed into bed and turned out the light, the springs creaking in weak protest under her weight, and then lay there, sleepless. What a horrible Thing I am. It had become a sick refrain.

There was one other thing, the worst, the most terrible of all, and lying wide-eyed and unblinking in the dark she thought about it now. Just a week ago she had been out with Old Man Herschmidt. Old Vic Herschmidt, Frank Hirsh's father. It was the first time she had ever had a date with him. And it was that same night that she had discovered she had the discharge. Even though it was her very first date with him, she couldnt of got it off him, she dismissed that, she knew enough to know it took six days. But if she had had it then—and she must have, if it showed up in her that very same night—then he had it now; would be comin' down with it yesterday or today.

And what would he be thinkin' about her!

Whore, thats what! Hed think she knew she had it all along.

Springs creaking, Jane rolled over with her face to the wall, presenting her broad back to the room, and huddling down behind it. From the room and from the world. In the dark she couldnt see the wall, but she knew it was there, and it made her feel better. Safer, and more hidden.

Oh, she wouldnt of done it for the world! If she had only knew, she wouldnt of gone out with him nor nobody else! That sick frightened guilty sadness of youth gripped her again, and she cried, tough old Janie cried.

CHAPTER 29

Old Man Herschmidt, about the same time Jane Staley was climbing into her bed, was feeling pretty chipper; and he did not have the clap.

Nor did he get it later. Whatever it was was wrong with Janie it evidently wasnt that, and in fact nothing could have been further from Old Vic Herschmidt's mind. In fact, his mind beamed with a sense of peace and well being. It werent too many men at his age who was still good lookin enough to attract the women, and he felt pretty cocky; and it werent too many of *them,* who still were men enough to satisfy them if they did, he thought smugly; though he hisself had never been bothered none in that way, he still had all he needed.

All in all he was pretty proud of himself and not only that, he thought balefully, he had finally got one up on Old Lady Rugel his goddamn landlady who run the pensioner's home where he lived you might say practically for nothing since she washed his clothes free and fed him and give him what little measly bits of money he could wangle out of her for beer—all because she wanted to marry him and reform him. Yes. But he was too smart for that, why should he marry her when he was already getting everything marriage offered without, and anyway he had never divorced (his mind froze coldly:) Elvira, and that cost money, though Old Lady Rugel had once offered to pay for it, he he, but he want about to, it would make Frank and them too god-damned happy. And now Old Lady Rugel was so jealous she could hardly stand it.

The very thought was enough to make Old Vic's crumpled sour bird-like face wreath itself in happy smiles. He he. Yes sir by God Old Lady Rugel could hardly stand it.

And if Frank! knew it Frank would crap his pants. His own cleaning woman and hired help. He wished (his mind froze:) Elvira would find out about it too sometime. Well, she probly would, eventually. So would Frank. He he.

Old Vic had been in this state of unqualified happiness for the entire week since he had happened into Smitty's Bar and picked old Jane Staley up and took her out and romped her—and on the very first time, too!

(Not so bad for an *old man*. Old Man Herschmidt! they could call him Old Man Herschmidt if they wanted, he thought balefully. He wouldnt have minded so much if they just called him Old Vic Her-schmidt; Old Vic wasnt so bad.)

Jane Staley was a pretty good looking girl too all and all. She had plenty of flesh anyway. He liked flesh. Women should have plenty of flesh. Hell, El-(his mind froze:)-vira never hardly had no flesh on her atall, he thought vindictively. But old Jane Staley did. He knew old Jane had plenty other boyfriends, but what the hell? whatd that matter? She had good taste. That was what mattered. She picked and chose. She didnt jist take on anybody.

Vic was out looking for her right now, to try her again. He had already walked all the way out to Smitty's Bar once, and would again, but she hadnt been there and she hadnt been at Ciro's either. He hadnt seen her around at all in the past week, but he expected she would show up before closing time. And right now he was on his way to the taxi-stand to see that boy Dave and get some more money.

That boy Dave was turnin out to be almost a human bein, Old Vic thought balefully. He seemed to almost understand what people felt. The son of a bitch. It was largely because of that boy Dave that he had got his chance at old Jane Staley any at all. It was that boy Dave who had bought him the fifth of whiskey hed had that night (and that certainly hadnt hurt him none, havin' that). And it was that boy Dave who had also give him enough money so he could go in the bar and sit and drink severl beers, instead of just having to drink one and git up and git out, like he usually had to do. He he. Old Lady Rugel didnt know where he was gettin' all his money all of a sudden. And it sure worried her. Up to now hed never had enough money at a time to do moren sit a few minutes and drink one beer, Old Lady Rugel seen to that, and if he went out nights at all, she wouldnt give him *any*. Yes sir, he sure had her worried. That boy Dave was turnin out to be damned near human, he thought malevolently. You might almost think he was a Herschmidt; instead of a Bales like (his mind froze:) Elvira.

He rounded the corner of Plum and West Wernz going down hill half trotting just in time to see the lights of the taxistand wink out.

What the hell. It want hardly no moren very much after eleven thirty. It was a damn good thing hed hurried.

"Hey!" he called anxiously, hurrying up the block. "Hey, you! Boy!"

Young Dave was standing just outside the door, locking it, holding something under one arm.

"What the hell?" Vic said. "Youre aleavin' early, aint you?"

"Yeah," Dave said. "Closed up early tonight, pop."

"Dont call me pop, goddam it," Vic said irately. "What of you got there? A book?"

"Yeah," the boy said. "I just been doing a little reading. Book about a small town. In the South; but that dont matter. By a guy named Faulkner."

"Never heard of him," Vic said. "Listen, boy, I need some more money."

"What the hell?" Dave said irritably. "I just gave you three dollars. What the hell did you do with that?"

"Now dont get mad. I spent it, damn it, whatd you think?" Vic said just as irritably. "On beer. I think I got me a date lined up, y'see. And I got to have it."

"A date?" Dave said.

"A heavy date," Vic said. He cackled. "In more waysn one."

"Aint you gettin about old enough to outgrow all that kind of crap?" Dave said.

"Gettin' old enough!" Vic said balefully. "Are you, damn you?"

The boy laughed, and Vic knew he was all right, that hed get the money. He really wasnt such a bad boy, he thought sneeringly, not compared to the rest of the sons of bitches who took after (his mind froze:) Elvira, damn them.

"How much do you need?" Young Dave said.

"Wall," Vic said beadily, carefully feeling his way, "I need enough for a fifth of whiskey, Ill need that; and then two or three for beer before the bars close. Say, six; plus two or three; ten dollars?"

"Jesus Christ!" Dave said. "I didnt take you to raise."

"No, and I didnt ast you to, you son of a bitch," Vic said balefully. "Ill give you seven."

"All right, if you want to be a tightass son of a bitch," Vic said coldly. The boy was looking in his pocket. "I aint got seven. All I gots a ten."

He passed it over. "Here, Ill give you that. But I want three dollars of it back tomorrow. What kind of a sap do you think I am? The bars close in fifteen minutes. You wont have time to drink more than one."

Old Vic folded the bill and put it in his pocket and kept his hand on it. "Well, Ill probly have to take a taxi to get out there, in time," he temporized craftily.

"The taxistand is closed. You forget. I run it."

"Thats right," Vic said. "Well then I better hustle. If I want to get there atall. Thanks for the money, boy." He turned and started back down the block toward Wernz, half trotting.

"Dont forget, I want that three dollars back tomorrow," the boy called after him.

Vic stopped and turned around. "Well you wont git it, you son of a bitch. Did you think you would? If youd of wanted it, youd of better gone some place and made change for it. If you thought youd get it back, youre dumber than even I thought you was."

"I wanted you to get out to the bar in time," Dave said.

"Go to hell," Vic said coldly. "That dont cut no ice. Dont try to use no sympathy on me. I dont owe you nothin' for *nothin'*. And you cant make me obligated to you by givin' me your lousy money." He turned and started off again.

Behind him he could hear the boy's thin laugh. He was beginning to learn how to handle him. The more you insulted him, the more it seemed to make him laugh and the better he apparently liked it. Probly thinks Im a tough old bastard, Vic thought craftily. Well, let him. Besides the ten, he had in his pocket four bucks left from the last two times hed hit him up for money. He he. Hed have to remember to hide it out in the yard before he went up to his room, he reminded himself. Or Old Lady Rugel'd find it suren hell and thatd be the last hed see of it.

He hurried along, half trotting, up the hill to the square and on across its corner to turn north out North Main and down the long hill toward the I.N. tracks and Smitty's Bar. Hed have to hurry. If he didnt get there before they closed old Jane Staley would be going off with one of them decrepit old sons of bitches she run around with. It was pert near five or six blocks out there, too. But it was all downhill. That was one thing. That boy Dave was a pistol. A real soft touch. The first time hed gone over there to that taxi building to hit him up, it had just been on a hunch, thinkin' he might be able to get a buck off of him maybe, because of that whiskey hed bought him in Ciro's that time. A buck hell! by playin' it careful, hed wound up with five! And it was part of that same five, plus what he got off of him the second time, that fixed it for him so he could get into old Jane Staley. Yes sir, a real sucker. Yes sir, he hoped that boy Dave stayed around this neck of the woods quite a while. Heh heh.

It was funny to think how he had made that boy hisself. And there he stood, like a regular person. Walkin' up and down, and eatin', and talkin', and lookin' just like any other *regular* person. Yes, it surely was funny. And yet he had made him, made him with (his mind froze stiffly:) old Elvira. He was the last one, the last of the six: Francine and Frank, Edward, Darrell, George, and Dave, a whole damn worthless bunch just like (his mind froze:) Elvira. And it didnt even seem the least bit sensible. Why them? Why not somebody else? Why anybody? And there they stood. Actin' just like they was people. Hollerin' and squallin' and yellin'. And eatin' their goddamn heads off every chance they got like a bunch of birds. No sir, by God, it didnt even make the least little particle of sense. And old (his mind froze sourly:) Elvira, who hadnt want to made them any moren he did, towin' 'em around and takin' 'em to her goddamned Sunday school so she could set back and let a bunch of dumb clowns brag on her and her stinkin' brats she cried and took on every time she found out she was goin' to have one of. And all strangers. Yes sir, no sense atall. He made every one of them and didnt know one from the other. He made that boy Dave and he didnt know him from Adam. Readin' books, and runnin' a taxi building, and everybody thought he was a people. Now what the hell sense was there in that? but he sure hoped he stayed around this neck of the woods a while, yes sir, heh heh.

Dog trotting anxiously down the long, slow hill toward Smitty's, Old Vic let himself dwell on the night he had made old Jane Staley. Yes, sir. Not bad for an *old man*. Old Man Herschmidt, he thought balefully. Yes sir by *God!* wouldnt that make young Frankie blow his head clean off and crap all over the floor when he found out! Heh heh. He he. It like to have killed Frank when he come back home that time and went to welding and wouldnt change his name, and this would even maybe kill him worse. Kill him even worse maybe than when he wouldnt take his damned money and move to Terre Haute. Trotting along, anxiously, and getting a little out of breath, Vic chuckled out loud and his beaked face wreathed itself in happy smiles. Yes sir, kill him.

Lovingly, and with more pleasure than hed felt over anything in quite a time, Vic ran his mind back lingeringly over the night of the seduction as he walked. It was really all just luck really, that was all. Hed just happened to go in there to Smitty's Bar, and hed had that boy Dave's money; and there by God old Jane Staley had been sittin' there, and there just happened not to be none of them old cruds of boyfriends of hers sittin' with her. Just pure luck, that was the only way you could explain it. But then hed always been lucky like that; all his life. Lucky Vic Herschmidt, theyd always called him that. Even when he was a punk green kid. Just like that thing with Doc Cost's wife Louise. Whod ever of thought of Louise Cost takin' up with a cheapassed welder, who old Doc had called out there to do a job? Hisself hed always figured it was because he was so horny and shed never seen no man like that before, certainly not in some Newport Rhode Island doctor son of a bitch. But then hed always been lucky like that. Lucky Vic Herschmidt. Theyd always called him that.

He had hid the fifth of whiskey before he went into Smitty's that night. Hid it across the tracks in the lumber yard, in a pile of stuck boards. He had bought it first with that boy Dave's money, figurin' to do just that. Hell, no use lettin' everbody know he had it, or cartin' it in there where some son of a bitch might lay hold of it when he wasnt lookin', no sir, heh heh. So he had set at the bar and ordered a beer, and laid his five dollar bill straight out on the bar so they could see it, damn them. That one armed boy from the Army had grinned at him and took his order and clicked them hooks at him.

"Who the hell you been robbin, Vic?" hed said.

"Never mind," hed said. "Not the govment, anyways, like you."

"By God, thats right! Its the State Goverment youre robbin. I wouldnt settle for nothin less than the Federal, myself," Eddie had laughed, and Vic watched him get the beer. He sure could use them hooks. There was more one armed and one eyed and one legged sons of bitches from that war anymore around this town than you could count whole ones almost. They must of been a bunch of regular amputatin' fools in that Army.

Eddie brought his beer back and he had took a great big satisfyin' slug and looked around. That was when he seen her settin' in the corner booth, all of her, she like to filled up one side of the whole damned booth, and all by herself. And hed knew right then that he was bein' lucky. But it was a while before he could get his nerve up to go over and say somethin' to her. He didnt want to look like no fool and be laughed at. But finally he done it. Shed been givin' him the eye anyway, hadnt she?

So he just took his beer and just walked right over.

"How do, Miz Staley," hed said. "Mind if I set down here with you a spell?"

"Christ, no, Mister Herschmidt!" old Jane bawled. "Please do!" Then shed lowered her voice; and her eyelashes. Vic had thought he was goin' to pop the buttons off his chest. "I seen you sittin' up there to the bar," she said, "and thought of astin' you to come sit over here where it was more comfterble, but I didnt know what you might think of me if I done that, Mister Herschmidt."

"Hell, I wouldnt of thought nothin'," Vic said. "Say, what do you say we cut out all this Mister and Miz stuff?" hed said, perhaps a mite too eagerly, and sidled over a little in the booth. "After all, weve knowed each other quite a while, aint we? Aint no use bein' so formal." His knee'd bumped hers underneath the table of the booth and accidentally rubbed against it a little. Heh heh. Hed felt hisself gettin' eager as some young pup.

"Well noww, why I think thatd be fine," shed said. "Ill call you Vic, and you call me Jane. —Long as there aint no sort of misunderstandin's comes of it, nor nothin' like that, you know." But hed noticed shed never moved her leg none.

"Why, course I understand!" hed said indignantly. Heh heh. "What kind of man you think I be?"

"Why Im sure you always been a perfect gentleman around me," old Jane said, "Vic," she added softly.

"You bet your life!" hed said, and let his leg rub against hers a little accidentally. "An I awys aim to be, Jane," he said, looking softly into her eyes—as soon as shed raised up her eyelids again.

But then shed moved it. "Excuse me, Mister Herschmidt! But youre gettin' just a little too close to me to be quite proper."

"It was a accident!" hed said. "A pure accident!" But hed wanted to cuss. Especially when he looked down at her chest. Jane Staley really had the bosoms.

"Im sure it was, Vic," shed said. "But Im afeard youre gettin' wrong ideas about me."

"Who, me? Not me!" hed said. "No sir! I dont never get no wrong ideas about nobody," hed said. He he. "Everybody's got a right to live his life, I awys say, and live it jist any how ever he wants to."

"Well, as long as you feel like that, Vic," shed smiled, "I guess its all all right. Dont you? But a lady has to be purty careful, you know. You understand that."

"Sure she does!" hed said.

"You know, youre quite a thinker, aint you?" old Jane said. "I like that there what you said about Life."

"Well, I do a mite of thinkin' about Life," hed said modestly.

"Yeah, I kin see you do," shed said. "I kin see youre deep. And youve seen a good bit of it too, I bet."

"Well, Id say I seen a bit more than the average, anyways," hed said modestly.

"Yeah, Ill bet you have," shed said, and slapped him gaily on the hand. Christ, for a minute hed thought she had done broke two of his fingers. "Yessir, Ill just bet you have. Say, whatta ya say we have a nother beer?"

"The best i-dea yet," he had said eagerly. —Eager! Chrisamighty, hed thought his eagerness was goin' to start his feet to twitchin' or burn off the soles of his shoes. Talk about hot feet. "Allow me to buy you one."

"Why, thank you, Vic," shed said.

"Hey there, Eddie!" hed hollered, startled at the force of his own bellow. "Two more beers over here!"

"Comin' right up, Mister Herschmidt!" Eddie'd hollered back.

"Now, where was we?" hed said, turnin' back and clearin' his throat. But one armed Eddie was already there.

"Right here you are, Mister Herschmidt, sir," Eddie'd grinned. "Thatll be forty cents."

"Here you are, Eddie," hed said, and tossed him a quarter and two dimes on the tray. "And keep the change there, Eddie!" hed said extravagantly. He he.

"Why, thank you, Mister Herschmidt!" Eddie'd grinned. "Thank you very much, sir!" Hed bowed and clicked his hooks at him.

"Now, where was we at?" hed said, just like he done this every day. "What was we talkin' about?"

"You was tellin' me how much of life youd seen," shed said.

"Ahhh, yes!" hed said. "All I said was I thought Id seen a mite more than the average. —Say," he said, "don't you think its gettin' a mite hot in here?"

"I hadnt noticed it none, Vic," old Jane'd said. "Do you feel warm?"

"Well, just a mite," hed said. "I was jist thinkin' we might get out and take a little walk for a breath of fresh air."

"Its purty cold out, Vic," shed said. "And I chill awful easy out." And shed dropped them eyelids again. Playin' coy. Old Devil. He hadnt knowed how to answer that. Ruther, hed knowed but he was a little afeard to say so soon he had a way to keep her warm. Maybe he should of said it. Maybe that was what she was wantin' him to say. But anyways he hadnt. So they had set there and drank beer for another half a hour. She drinked more beer than three grown men could in the same time. —Not that he minded the money. He never. It was just hard to believe, was all. Until finally he got up nerve enough to bring up the whiskey.

"Whats the use of us asettin' around here tankin' up on beer, Jane?" hed said. "When I got a fifth of whiskey hid out and put away?"

"Well, I never been much on whiskey, Vic," shed said. "Though I guess a snort or two wouldnt hurt me none, against the cold," shed giggled. "Where is it?"

"Never you mind," hed said, feelin' purty sly. Heh heh. "But it aint in here. Lets go git it."

"Okay," Jane'd said, lowering her eyelids again and smilin' at him shyly. "Lets do. Please help me with my coat, Vic?"

"Yessir! Yessir! I sure will, Jane," hed said. From the bar as they left, Eddie had give him a big long wink and clicked his hooks at him like he was playin' shamey-finger, but hed ignored him. Not that he want a nice boy, about the beers and all. But a man just couldnt—

"Now wheres this here whiskey?" Jane had said when they was outside. It *were* coldern hed remembered twas.

"It aint far," hed said with a chuckle just the same. "Jist folley me," and hed led her over across the tracks into the lumber yard where hed hid it.

"Well, aint you the foxy one!" shed purred. "Got it right here close where you can git it. And nobodyd ever find it in the world."

"Not unless I forgot it and some of the boys from the lumber yard come and unstuck this pile of wood," hed grinned. He hesitated then, though. "I dont know where we kin go to drink it."

"Well, whats the matter with right here?" shed said.

"You mean here? In the lumber yard!" hed said.

"No, silly!" shed said, lowering them big eyelids again. She nodded her head back across the tracks. "Right there. Look at all them cars."

"You mean one of them cars is yourn!"

"Hell, no!" Jane said. "I aint got no car!"

"Well you mean, go git in one of them other people's cars?"

"Sure," shed said. "Why not?"

"What if they come out?"

"They wont. They never have. Theyre all in there drinkin' and they wont come out now till old Smitty closes her up. I been—" Shed stopped.

So that was where she took all them old boyfriends of hers! hed thought. He he. Hed always wondered.

"I been sittin' in that bar night after night and I never seen nobody leave," shed went on. "Not this near to closin'. Come on," shed said.

"Hell; okay by me," hed said, and he had folleyed her back across the tracks into the cinder parkin' lot.

"Heres a likely lookin' one," Jane'd said. It was a new car, a Chevie. "Nice big roomy back seat, so we can be comfterble;—while we're drinkin'," shed said; shyly. "Might as well pick us out the best, hadnt we Vic? since we're pickin'? Come on, lets git in." She was a nervy one. Real nervy.

"Here, you want a drink?" hed said, when they was inside and had shut the door.

"No," shed said, like with a little giggle. "You go first. You aint tryin' to get me drunk, are you? Aint this cozy?"

"Sure is," hed said. Hed uncorked the bottle and took a little drink and then hed handed it to her, before hed risked puttin' his arm around her.

"Say, you got real muscle in that arm," shed said.

"I aint as thin as I look," hed said.

"No, I just bet you aint," shed said, feelin his arm with her hand. "I bet youre purty husky," shed said, puttin' her hand on his chest.

"Hows about a little kiss?" hed said.

"Well, I dont know if I should," Jane'd said, takin' a big healthy drink from the bottle.

"Why not?"

"Well, it aint very proper, is it? Out in a car like this." She giggled. "You might force me to walk home!"

"Nah," hed said. "Nah I wouldnt. Come on, just one."

"Well, all right." Shed had a nice soft mouth, he remembered. Itd surprised him. A real sweet mouth. "Ahhh!" shed said, when he left her go. Then hed corked the bottle and put both arms around her. Heh heh.

"Another one?" hed said.

"Well— . . . yes!" shed said.

When hed left go of her the second time hed been ready to come right out with it. Come right out with it, and to hell with it! Take the chance! Risk everything! "Come on!" hed said. "Lets do it!" Ah, hed been a terrier all right by God, hadnt he? a regular terrier, yes sir. He he.

"Do what?" shed said, playin' innercent.

"You know what damn it! It!" hed said.

"We shouldnt. What kind of a girl will you think I am?" old Jane'd said.

"Ill think youre a nice girl, a *damned* nice girl," hed said, about ready to explode. Yes sir, all ready to blow right up like a bomb he was, by God. He he.

"You wont think Im bad?" shed said.

"Hell, no!" hed exploded. "Hell, no! Hell no I wont think youre bad! Ill think youre good!"

"All right," shed said. "But youll have to never tell."

"Well, will we do it right here? in the car?" hed said.

"Hell, yes!" old Jane'd said. "You dont want to do it out in the cold on the cold ground, do you?"

"Well, but what if the people owns the car comes out?"

"Then we'll git out and git in another one!" shed said, "the hell with it!"

"Okay," hed said. "The hell with it!" He hadnt cared much anyways by then, hed found. He he.

She could really move around, that Jane, for such a big fleshy woman, and in a cramped car too. Hed wanted her to take the whiskey home with her afterwards. But she wouldnt take it.

"Its your whiskey, Vic," shed said. "I dont want it. I wont take it anyway. You keep it yourself." So he had hid it under the porch before he went up to his room.

"You sure got wonderful muscles in your back," shed said afterwards, runnin' them big hands across his back.

Gratitude, jist sheer gratefulness (and *damn* it), though he didnt know why, had been awellin' up in him all over—just as twas agin right now—though he didnt know why a man should be grateful to a damned woman, he thought balefully, they got as much out of it as him—and hed said gruffly to hide it: "Im still a pretty tough old bird."

"Yes, I bet you are," shed said. Shed run them big hands over his back once more. "We better git out of here. And I got to git on home."

She was a fine woman, Old Vic thought smugly, yessir, a fine woman, by God she was.—

Ahead of him the I.N. tracks and depot and the lights from Smitty's broke up his reverie, and Old Vic increased his pace a little, dog trotting anxiously. He was gettin' pretty winded. He sure did hope she was there by God. And none of them old devils of hern with her. He jist might have to set a couple of them down.

As he burst into Smitty's, the one armed boy Eddie was standin' just inside behind the cigar and cigarette counter.

"Gimme a fifth of that there whiskey I git, Eddie!" he said, and then turned to look at the corner booth, and discovered it was empty.

"Whats the matter, Vic?" Eddie grinned. "You look like you been to a fire."

"Wheres old Jane Staley?" he said. "I thought she was out here."

Eddie grinned. "She aint been here in severl days, Vic. Were you lookin for her?"

"Naw," Vic said. "I aint lookin' fer her. Shes just usually out here though, was all."

Eddie sacked the whiskey and set it on the counter in front of him. "I dont know whats happened to her," he offered anyway, still grinning. "She must be sick or something. She was just in here one time after that night you and her was talkin out here."

"Oh, you mean that night," Vic said. "Oh, is that right?"

"Maybe shes fell in love with you, Vic," Eddie grinned. "Maybe you got her goin."

"Who, that woman?" Old Vic said. "Nosiree. Not for me. Not for Old Vic Herschmidt. Im off of women. Women only cause a man trouble." He was looking at the whiskey. Hed have to take it, now, damn it. He was still breathin' a little hard. Even though he still had some left in that other bottle. Couldnt very well turn it down now, damn it.

"Maybe you got somethin there," Eddie grinned.

"Well, gimme my bottle," Vic said. "And Ill be moseyin' along home. Got to git home." He put the money on the counter.

Walking back across town to the pensioner's home, he drank a little of the whiskey; but it was small comfort. Now damn it all, what do you suppose could of happened to her? You reckon she did catched a chill and got sick from that night? Damn it all, anyways.

At the home he sneaked up and hid the bottle with the other under the front porch, and then went and hid his money. What was left of it, he thought ruefully. God damn the sons of bitches, anyway, all of them. Especially Frank. There was a light on inside, and he was especially careful to make no noise while he hid his stuff. Old Lady Rugel was obviously waitin' up for him inside, the old bitch.

When it was all hid, he walked loudly up the steps and across the porch. She was sittin' in her damned rocker before the fireplace gas logs, which she never burned just the same.

"Well!" she said, in her best chilly voice. "Where have you been to, Mister Herschmidt?"

"I been out, God damn it," he said balefully. "Where the hell do you think? And dont gimme that Mister Herschmidt stuff like you never went to bed with me. 'Miz Rugel'," he sneered. "And now Im agoin' to bed, 'Miz Rugel'."

"I see that you are drunk agin," Old Lady Rugel said coldly. "And please do not use that profanity and nasty talk in front of me. It wont do you no good. You cannot make me mad. Ill pray for you tonight."

"Aw, damn and hell and God and Jesus," Old Vic said balefully. "An why the hell dont you turn on them damned gas logs, if youre goin' to sit before 'em. Are you too tight to spend the gas?" He turned back to the stairs in the hall.

"Mister *Her*schmidt!" Old Lady Rugel cried chokedly behind him. "May God forgive you!" she whispered hollowly.

He went on up the stairs. He he. Let her stew, the old bat. The mealy mouth old bitch. Damn them all, the sons of bitches, anyway, all of them, he thought ruefully, everybody. Especially Frank.

CHAPTER 30

FRANK felt damned right enough, when he finally heard about it. He may or may not have been subconsciously aware of his old man's Benediction, but he was unalterably convinced that the old bastard had gone and done this thing deliberately and with malice aforethought, just to cause his eldest son embarrassment. Damned was exactly how he did feel. Damned to a life of being the perpetual laughingstock and punchingbag of Parkman. It was hard to imagine what terrible evil deed he must have committed in his life, to be cursed with the father he had had forced upon him. But whatever it was it must have been really something.

Frank could think of so many men, hundreds in fact, in Parkman who would have made him a decent father. And instead, what did he have? Not only the orneriest, meanest, most vicious, most irresponsible—but also apparently one of the longest-lived, who seemed destined to live forever. Youd think the very least the old son of a bitch could do was die. Now everybody in town would be laughing at him behind his back over this family escapade. And after hed just cleaned up Dave's.

Actually, Frank did not learn the news until a couple of weeks after the night Old Vic had tried unsuccessfully to get hold of Jane again. And he probably would not have learned it then, if he had not gone into Ciro's for a beer with Judge Deacon. It was late in the afternoon, just after work, and they had gone in there to have a beer and discuss some business, bank business, mainly because Judge wanted to go there and anyway he would never go to any of the clubs so there wasnt anywhere else to go. Judge had gotten over his pique about the taxi service and was apparently back on the best of terms again—if you could even use that phrase in connection with Judge, Frank thought sourly. Frank was still leary of him just the same. He knew better than to trust him. But on the surface at least, everything was all right again.

Well, there had been a bunch of those girls from the brassiere factory in there, that bunch which ran around with Dewey Cole and Hubie Murson, also having a beer after work. And he had just happened to overhear. They were talking about the Old Man and Jane Staley.

Actually, it wasnt scandal. It wasnt even gossip. The girls were just discussing and were a little amused. They thought it was cute. And probably no one else in town, except that bunch who hung around the bars, knew about it. But that didnt make it any more palatable to Frank. He would bet the whole town would hear about it eventually.

The Judge apparently read his face; because he grinned in that predatory, fatfaced malevolent way of his and said in his contemptuous sneering voice:

"You mean you aint heard about Jane and Old Vic, Frank? Why, thats the newest hottest love affair on 'The Strip'." —That was what Judge called the run from Ciro's to Smitty's. Judge read movie magazines in his spare time, and bought them by the dozens, although he had never been known to go to a movie.

"All the way from here to Smitty's, thats all theyre talkin' about," Judge grinned malignantly.

"Is that right?" Frank said, and passed it off. But later on he thought about it. He thought of mentioning it to Agnes when he got home that night, and discussing it with her. He was beginning to get over his serious loss, in Geneve, a little. But Agnes had been needling him about his family for years and comparing it to hers. Whenever she was mad at him. And anyway not only that but she was still being too damned solicitous and kind to him because of her triumph over Geneve. And that meant she would be sympathetic with him about the Old Man now. Although she sure wouldnt like it. Any more than he did. He didnt think he could endure her sympathy, so he decided not to mention it at all.

He had already decided not to tell his mother. It would only upset her needlessly and call forth that cold, silent, frightening anger which any mention of the Old Man always caused in her, and which always half-scared him with its iciness. He was still going up to see her once a week in the apartment he had leased for her at the Wernz Arms, and had been trying to get Dave to go up with him too. She was a strong old woman, he thought fondly, the kind that had made this country great; like the Pioneer Mother. She had raised a big family and worked hard all her life, and it was time she had the right to a little luxury and rest. She would almost certainly find out about the Old Man and Jane Staley from the members of her church anyway; but at least he would not be there to see it. He had tried and tried and Agnes had tried, to get her to quit The Church of Christ, Saved, and come into theirs. It would have looked a whole lot better for them all, if she only would. It was strange how The Church of Christ, Saved, always knew more about what went on in the bars in town than any other element in town except the bunch who hung out in them; —but it was only natural, since The Church of Christ, Saved, membership was made up mostly of the parents of the brassiere factory girls, and people like Dewey Cole's mother and Hubie Murson's, and in general the more or less aging parents of the rest of the low element which hung around the bars. Some of them would be sure to tell Mother about the Old Man and old Jane. But at least, he thought, he would not be the one to tell her about it.

From what he could find out—largely through his new spy Albie Shipe—the two old reprobates had only been out together once or twice apparently, and it was nothing serious and all this talk about a love affair was only amusement and joking on the part of the brassiere factory girls and Judge. But if it kept on, and got to be general knowledge in town, Frank didnt know what in hell he would do. Finally, for lack of anyone else, he talked about it to Edith Barclay at the store. There was just an off chance that she might be able to handle her grandmother. If anyone could handle her at all, Edith could.

"I hear my old man and your grandmother are steppin' out together now," he said, trying to make it sound like an easy laugh.

He must have failed, because Edith turned around and looked at him sympathetically. "Im sorry if its causing you any embarrassment, Mr Hirsh."

"Embarrassment! Who, me?" he said, confused. "Hell no. I think its amusing."

"Well, I know what a thorn in your side your dad is, boss," Edith said delicately.

"Hell, I dont care what the old bastard does," Frank said heartily.

"Well, I know its pretty hard on you sometimes on account of him," she said, still delicately. "What with trying to run a reputable business, and with the social position you have to keep up. Its different with me and Jane. I dont have any reputation to maintain."

"Yeah, I spose that does make a little difference in our viewpoints," Frank said.

"I guess Ive gotten used to her ways over the years," she said. "It used to worry me when I was younger and in school.— Are you planning to let Jane go?" Edith said.

"What?" he said, startled. —Christ, as if anything he would say on the subject would make any difference about whether Agnes ever let Jane go or not— "Hell, no," he said. "Shes the best cl— the best worker weve ever had at home. Been with us damn near since we were married. God no," he said. "—I just thought—you know—she might of said something about it to you."

"No, she hasnt." Edith pushed back her typing table and turned around to him, looking thoughtful. "—Jane hasnt been quite herself lately," she said honestly. She sort of grinned. "I suspected she was maybe falling in desperate love again; you know—she had all the symptoms. But she seems to be getting along over it, now, whatever it was.

"I couldnt say anything to her about it for you," Edith said, looking at him.

"Oh, no," he said hastily. "Oh no. Course not."

"Jane lives her own life," Edith said, still looking at him. "And I feel she has a right to," she said. "—Even though I might disagree with her on a lot of things." Here she flushed a little. "Anyway, she wouldnt listen to anything I said to her anyway. Not Jane."

"No, not Jane," Frank said. "In fact, shed be more inclined to do just the opposite, Id bet."

"Anyway, I like Jane!" Edith said defiantly. .

"Hell, of course you do!" Frank said. "Nobody said you shouldnt. I like her, too. Hell," he said, "the only reason I brought it up was because I find it so amusin'."

"Well, I wouldnt feel free to interfere in anything Jane did," Edith said more subduedly. "Although I hate to have her causing *you* embarrassment, Mr Hirsh. It dont bother me any more. —Its funny, theyve never run around together before," she said musingly. "Your dad never used to hang around the bars much, I guess thats probably why. I guess your dad never used to have the money to, did he?"

Frank stared at her incredulously. Suddenly he snapped his fingers. "Youve hit it, Edith! Youve hit it! By God, youve hit it!"

"Hit what?" Edith said, startled.

"Never mind," he said. "Forget it. Just let it go. Listen, if anyone wants me Ill be back in half an hour." He was up, had grabbed his topcoat and hat and was gone out the door before she could even answer.

Out in front he nodded distantly at Al Lowe and went on out the front door, headed for the taxistand.

Yes sir, that Edith was about the smartest, as well as the most understanding girl he had ever met or known! Certainly, she was the most under*standing* woman he'd ever met. Put her finger right on it. (He wondered who that date was with, that she had had? —Probly that jerk Harold Alberson who worked for Kentucky Oil. It was a shame. She ought to have a better chance than that jerk.)

At a half run he burst into the taxistand where Dave and Albie Shipe were both sitting reading, Dave at the desk near the phones, Albie over in the corner by himself.

"I want to talk to you, you son of a bitch!" Frank said. "Have you—" Then he saw Albie in the corner. "What the hell are you doing here?"

"I'm readin'," Albie said portentously, looking up with that selfaware comedian's look of his on his face. He held out his comic book as proof.

"You're supposed to be off today."

"I'm loafin'," Albie said with his comic's look. "I got nothin' better to do, y'see."

"Well look," Frank said. "Go up to the Foyer and get us all a coke and bring it back, will you?"

"Okay, boss," Albie said with his comic's look. "Okay. Ill go. Ill go right away. I'll run all the way." He shut his book and jumped up, landing on both feet, and the little building shuddered under his hundred and ninety pounds.

"Dont run. Take your time," Frank said.

"Okay," Albie said. He grinned slyly. "You want to give me the money first?"

"Oh," Frank said. "Oh, sure. Here." He reached in his pocket.

"Thanks, boss," Albie said, bugging out his eyes. He winked broadly, and left.

Frank could hardly wait. "Listen, have you been givin' the old man money?" he said furiously.

"What old man?" Dave said innocently. Dave had been watching him with Albie.

"What old man! Our old man, damn you."

"Oh, you mean Old Man Herschmidt."

"Yas, Old Man Herschmidt!" Frank shouted. "You smart son of a bitch."

"Why, no," Dave said. "Why? Should I have?"

"Dont lie to me! You have too," Frank shouted. "I know you have. There wasnt any other way he could get it!"

"Okay, so what if I have?"

"Well, youve got to stop it. You cant do it any more."

"I cant?" Dave said with infuriating innocence. "Why cant I?"

"Stop needling me!" Frank shouted. "This is serious! Because I say you cant, thats why! Youre gettin' him into trouble. Hes been out layin' old Jane Staley our cleaning woman with the money you been givin' him."

Dave's innocent look slowly crumpled up as if he could no longer hold it, into a broad grin and he laughed out loud. "Old Jane? No! Well, Ill be goddamned," he said relishingly.

Hes already got one old woman hes rompin', and thats enough. And besides thats all right," Frank said. "Because she doesnt give him much money to get around with. Hes got to stay at home. But if he gets to runnin' around with Jane, hes goin' to make me more of a laughing-stock in this town than he has already. And youve got to stop it. You keep on givin' him money to hit the bars," he warned, "and we will dissolve this damned partnership!"

"Go ahead and dissolve the son of a bitch," Dave said thinly. "Id just as soon you would anyway."

"Now listen," Frank said, more reasonably. "Be reasonable. Im willing to be reasonable. But you know the kind of reputation Ive got to maintain in this town as a businessman. And youve got to help me. If we ever want to do the things we plan to do, out of this."

"Well, dont come running in here yelling at me at the top of your voice like I was some of your hired help," Dave said. "Im sensitive."

"Im sorry if I offended you," Frank said carefully. "But I was upset."

"Well, *that* upsets *me*," Dave said. "—I dont know whether Ill stop or not."

"Why do you hate me?" Frank said.

"I dont hate you!"

"Yes you do," he said. "You both of you hate me. Why! Is it because Im gettin' to be successful? and neither one of you can stand it? Is it because Im gettin' to be too big of a man?"

"Damn it, I dont hate you," Dave said—almost guiltily. He looked away, and then scratched irritably at the back of his head. "I feel sorry for the old bastard," he said irately. "I dont like him any better than you do. But I dont think I can look him in the eyes and tell him no. You see? Not because hes our old man. But because I just cant do that to anybody. Im weak. Damn it all! I dont think I can thats all. I wont know what to tell him."

"Well, thats easy," Frank said, more coolly. "Just tell him you havent got it. Tell him youre broke and you havent got the money."

Dave looked surprised. "Yeah. I guess I could tell him that. I didnt think of that."

"And after a while, he will know he aint goin' to get any more and he will stop comin'," Frank said reasonably.

"But he'll know Im lying," Dave said miserably. "I wont be able to hide it. I never can."

"So what?" Frank said. "He wont be able to prove it, will he? He wont be able to throw you down on the ground and look in your pockets."

"No, thats right," Dave said, looking surprised again. "Thats true, aint it? He cant prove it. And if he does know, what the hell difference does it make?"

"Thats right," Frank nodded.

"Well, hell. Its really easy," Dave said, surprise in his voice; "aint it? Its really simple." He should have felt happy about his discovery, but apparently he didnt. Instead, he looked irritable. Irritable, and unhappy.

"Sure," Frank said smoothly, "thats all there is to it."

"—You know, the old guy kind of tickles me," Dave said hopefully with a big, wide grin at him. "Hes such a mercenary old devil."

"Well, he dont tickle me," Frank said emphatically.

"Frank," he said suddenly, "Im not happy in this business. I wish I had my money back. Im just not cut out to be a successful business-man like you are."

"I told you it would be rough for a while at the start," Frank said.

"I know it," Dave said, "I know it. I know you told me. Frank, do you know why I really gave you that money of mine and went into this thing with you like I did?"

"Why?" he said.

Dave opened his mouth, and was on the point of telling him some-thing—something that was the truth—but then he suddenly shut it again, apparently he couldnt, and instead in a moment he said lamely: "Because I thought Id be able to sit back and draw down some income, and spend my time writing. Ive got a book I want to write, Frank." It was obviously a substitute statement, even to Frank.

"You can do all that later, after we begin to make money," Frank said.

"Yeh," Dave said unhappily. "Yeh, I guess." Behind Frank the door opened and Dave turned his head to look, then moved his head at Frank warningly as Albie Shipe came back in with the three cokes.

"Here you are, boss!" Albie said in his bass voice, screwing up his face comically. "Three cokes. Three cokes like you ordered. Cokes for three." He set two on the desk and took the third back with him to his corner.

Frank picked his up, took a small sip out of it and set it back down. "You remember what I told you," he said to Dave, and went to the door.

"Hey! Aint you goin' to drink your coke, boss?" Albie said in his comic's voice.

"I guess not," Frank said. "I guess Ive had too many of them today."

"Then I will drink it for you," Albie said, raising his eyebrows and bugging his eyes. "I will drink it. Soons I finish this one."

Dave watched his brother angrily through the window as Frank went back up the uphill block to the square in his yellow camel'shair topcoat, and that damned Dobbs hat. Dave felt irritable and badly repressed. Somehow or other Frank had managed to put it over on him again. He didnt know how, but Frank had. He had not intended to promise he would stop giving the Old Man money. He had not intended to promise he would even *try* to stop. Why shouldnt the Old Man have a little money? And in fact, he *hadnt* promised. —And yet by God it had ended up that way tacitly just the same anyway. As if he had.

"What was he mad about?" Albie said from the corner in his portentous comic's voice.

"Maybe about life in general," Dave said irately, "I guess."

"Well now thats a good thing to be mad at," Albie said with comic hollowness. "I thought maybe it was he was mad because you been givin' Old Man Herschmidt the money to go chasin' around after old Jane Staley," he said without changing his hollow comic tone.

Dave swung the swivel chair around away from the window to look at him, unable to resist an irritated grin.

"—But I guess life in general is a lot better thing to be mad at," Albie said quickly and hollowly. "Theres so much more opratunity."

Dave had to laugh. You never knew how much that Albie knew, or didnt know. "Come on, Albie," he said. "Lets play a game of checkers."

"Id ruther read," Albie said, bugging his eyes and holding up his comic book. "Ive just got them to the place where the ape is about to tear her clothes off." He pointed to the huge-fanged drooling ape on the cover.

"Maybe he'll romp her," Dave said. "This time."

"He might," Albie said hopefully. "The hero's a long way off. But nawww. Theyd never 'llow that, I guess," he said wistfully. He buried his nose behind the dripping cover.

Just then one of the phones on the desk rang. Dave picked it up.

"606 South Beech," he said and wrote it down and turned back to the window.

"Old Lady Archey," Albie said hollowly from the corner. "Wantin' to go over to. Miz Burdieu's and gab a while." Albie sighed, and got up weightily to come over and get Frank's coke on the desk.

"Christ," Albie said, "I dont know if I can drink all three of them or not."

Dave didnt bother to answer, and merely sat, staring out the window at the December town. The view was dismal under the cold gray damp day. Christ! youd think at least it could snow a little, if it was going to be winter. This seemed to be three fourths of what this damned 'job' consisted of: staring out the window.

"But Ill try," Albie said hollowly, "Ill try my best," and carried both cokes back to his corner with him.

Dave kept on staring fixedly out the window. Since the rebellion of over two weeks ago Dave's dissatisfaction with his 'job' had been increasing steadily, instead of decreasing. So had his dissatisfaction with everything else. If he had thought more time off would help him, he couldnt have been more wrong. And now Frank had to come over here with that spiel and pull this on him!

Quite suddenly, Dave felt like throwing the phone—both phones— out through the pane and onto the public sidewalk. Albie, too;— except he probably wouldnt be big enough or tough enough to do it. Hunh. The 'Rebellion for the Rights of Man in the Hirsh Taxi Service of Parkman Illinois'. He could laugh about that now, yeah. My God no wonder Frank was inclined to think he was a screwball. He must have sounded pompous as hell. A regular idiot. Well—

Well, what? Well, hell.

The holidays would be coming up quick now. Frank was beating his brains out trying to get all stocked up, get everything displayed right. So were the other businessmen. Christmas. Christmas, hell, he thought sourly. It would be his first Christmas in the United States in four years, and what was it? Another damned day like any other. The hell with Christmas, Dave thought savagely, feeling sorry for himself. Nobody loved him. And Frank would probably want him to work anyway.

He still couldnt figure out how Frank had tricked him into that illusion of a promise about the Old Man!

—The sad thing was, it hadnt done him a damned bit of good; his Rebellion. Now he got every other Sunday off. And now he and Albie traded the day and evening shifts so that he got every other evening and daytime off. He got just as much money as he had got before. —And he still couldnt stand it. Just simply could not stand it; it was as simple as that.

There wasnt any problem to it. It was just simply that: A fact: He couldnt stand it.

And it was making him so he hated everything. And consequently, everything was going badly, everything: With some time off now to write he had started to work on the book, and found he could not write. He was rusty. His mind did not function. He could not concentrate. He could hardly string the words together, let alone give them meaning. Hell, even Wally Dennis was beating him.

—Also, he had had no appreciable success with Gwen. Didnt she know how much he needed her? And she needed him. She wouldnt have that guilt and that nymphomania if she had him. All she needed was a little real love. He could give her that. And he needed her. —Apparently, even he himself didnt even know how much he needed her. Or how much actual time he actually spent thinking about her every day. It must be hours. And the more she held him off at arm's length like this, the more it made him need her and think about her. Apparently, he was falling in love with her. My God, he must be crazy! really insane! he thought frightenedly.

Nevertheless, it was like a sudden revelation. A thought he had never entertained before. It burst upon him sanguinarily. He was falling in love with her. *Had* fallen in love with her.

Cocking his feet up on the windowsill, Dave continued to stare fixedly and concentratedly out through the window—as though he believed in some mystical way that if he did this long enough and strongly enough, everything would miraculously change, would become all right. Behind him Albie turned a page of his comic book.

Maybe she was doing it on purpose. Just for that very reason. Just to *make* him fall in love with her. It had been easy to tell her he was in love with her before that night when he wasnt—but now that he was he couldnt. Yes; he decided; he was in love with her. Yes; he was. And he had seen her three times in the past two weeks, and every time the consensus of everything she had to say to him was why wasnt he getting more work done on his book? On Sunday—his first Sunday; his first full day off—he had driven over there to spend the day. In fact, he had not even waited till Sunday but had gone over in the middle of Saturday night. He probably shouldnt have done that; but then how did he know they were going to act conventional?

After closing up Saturday night at eleven thirty, he had had several drinks by himself in the office and then had decided he would go over right now and not wait till tomorrow. They could all sit up and talk and have a good time like they did before. So he had gone over. He had had to pound on the door a long time before he raised anybody. Then they had come down, both of them, tousleheaded and in their pajamas and robes, to see what it was. Neither seemed very glad to see him. They did not sit up and talk. Bob showed him where to get a bottle of gin if he wanted it since he was not sleepy, and they both went back to bed. He sat up by himself and drank, in front of the fire they had already banked down with a fresh log over it to save the coals, until finally he got sleepy too and went up to his room to bed. And all day Sunday it was the same way. There was no rapport, no communion, no meeting of minds. He ate their food and took up their time, that was what it amounted to. He played Bob one poorly played game of chess. They did not talk about his book because Gwen said there wasnt anything she could talk about until he had something to show her. In the afternoon Wally Dennis had come over in his mother's car with part of a chapter he wanted Gwen to look at, and the two of them spent the afternoon huddled together in a corner. Bob read. Finally he himself left without even waiting for supper and came home. Nobody seemed especially perturbed to see him go. That night and the next he struggled with the first chapter of his book and tried to write, and he couldnt. The day after, which he had off, he couldnt write either. It was miserable; the writing, the trip, everything.

And the other two times he had seen them werent much different.

Dave took his feet down carefully off the windowsill. He was afraid if he did not he would convulsively kick them both out through the pane.—(and probably cut both his damned feet off probably)— Behind him Albie belched, a booming rippling sonorous sound which filled the office.

"God, Im full," he said hollowly. "I shouldnt of drank that third one."

Dave wrenched his mind back to his private miseries irritably. They hadnt even invited him to come over for Christmas! Well, to hell with them and their damned Christmas. He certainly wasnt going to *ask them* if he could come over Christmas. He would not mention it—if he did see them again. And if they did ask him now, he wouldnt go. Hed get drunk by himself Christmas and to hell with them. Maybe hed get drunk with 'Bama.

About the only damned bright spot left anywhere, Dave thought staring fixedly, was in 'Bama Dillert. And even that seemed to be bad for him, he added irritably. Twice during the last two weeks, when the complete hopelessness of ever again writing a decent line got too much for him, he had gone down to the Ath Club poolroom and looked 'Bama up. 'Bama never looked *him* up; just said he didnt want to bother him if he might be working good; yeah, damn him. But 'Bama did mean it seriously, you had to give him that, he really didnt want to disturb his writing. (In a fit of confidence he had told the gambler once, all about the new book; to which the big man had listened delightedly with interest, and then when he was all done had given his measured considered opinion that he thought it was a good idea!) So it was always him who had to do the looking up.

Both of these two times 'Bama had been on his way to some local lodge's poker game and had taken him with him; and both times both of them had made money. Also, both times both of them had got drunk. That was where the bad came in. He didnt see how 'Bama could stand it, day in and day out; Dave had always considered himself a pretty good drinker but—! Anyway, both times when he had had the next day off he had felt so bad he hadnt had the heart to try to write.

—But on the other hand there was still plenty of good in his going out with 'Bama too, though, he pointed out to himself. Mainly this good was in the money he had made. Both times he made more money than he got in a week at the taxistand. For some reason whenever he went out with 'Bama both of them seemed to be lucky. Nobody could seem to beat both of them. If 'Bama didnt win a pot, he would win it. Needless to say, this was highly exasperating to the other players. "I ought to hire *you*, just for a good luck piece," 'Bama had said jokingly across the green felt of the table. This was on the second night, when they had made the biggest money. But later on he had also broached it seriously. They had got an illegal afterhours bottle off the lodge bartender and taken it up to Dave's room at the Stephen A Douglas, after the game broke up at two.

"No kiddin," the tall gambler drawled, "you and me ought to form up some kind of a partnership in this poker playin." He was sprawled on his spine in the single armchair, the semi-Western hat over his eyes, holding a waterglass of straight whiskey. Dave was flopped on the bed. He had made over a hundred dollars. "We could work it out on some kind of a percentagewise basis some way. Pool our playin capital and then divide our total winnings. If I put in the most money, say, like I probably would have to at the start, wed make it sixty forty—or whatever the percentage was. Later on, if you put in a full half, wed change it to fifty fifty.

"We could make us a lot of money, I think," he said to the brim of his hat, pouring some whiskey in under it. "In gamblin theres certain periods where, for a bunch of reasons I never been able to quite figure out, you do real well—and know yore goin to do real well; and the smart guy takes advantage of it all he can when its there because he never knows when its liable to just up and leave him. Now somethin about you and me bein together makes that happen—right now, at least, anyway. We ought to take advantage of it.

"—Always provided, of course," he added conscientiously, "that it dont interfere with or disturb yore writin."

"My writing isnt doing worth a damn," Dave said from the bed savagely.

"Well, yore out of practice with it," 'Bama said moderately. "Thats understandable. Yore rusty. Thats only natural. You cant expect to start right out batting .400 when yore out of practice, can you? You just got to give it some time."

"Is that right? What the hell do you know about writing?"

With one careful thumb the tall ex-Southerner lifted his hat brim and grinned out from under it. "Just what Ive heard you and Wally talk about it, and what you two 've told me, thats all."

"Well, I dont think I could even do it anyway," Dave said more subduedly. "Ive got a contract with Frank, you know. Hes got me in a position so I have to work for him."

"Does it say that in the contract?"

"Well, no. At least, I dont think so. Ive never actually read it. But its got one of those partnership things in it. He told me about that. You know, that 'Give or Take' thing."

"Oh; yeah?" 'Bama said lazily. "Yeah, I think I know what them are. You mind if I take a look at it for you?"

Sitting in the taxi office, where one of the cabs had come back in and he had immediately dispatched it out to Old Lady Archey's, Dave remembered most vividly what had happened then. It was one of the few really bright spots in his present existence, was why. He had always assumed that Frank would be plenty shrewd enough, much more than shrewd enough, to take advantage of him in the contract and at the same time protect himself fully, which was one reason hed never bothered to read it: it would have depressed him.—And actually, to give the bastard full credit, that was apparently exactly what under all ordinary circumstances he had done. Only: there was an un-ordinary circumstance he had not thought about, apparently. Hunh hunh.

—What he would like to do, he thought relishingly, do right now, today, was go ahead and do it. Avail himself of it. Throw it right in his lap. And then let old Frank sit in it and sweat. Heh heh.

He had shown 'Bama his copy of the contract, which he had filed away in a pocket of the B-4 bag. The tall gambler had sat up, and with an intensity of concentration as great as that with which he played poker, had read it through from cover to cover, every word. It wasnt a very long contract. Then he had laid it on the table and picked up his whiskey, and sprawled back down and pulled his hat back down over his eyes. The upshot of what he had to say from under his hat after thinking a minute, was that indeed not only did Frank *not* have Dave by the throat, but Dave had Frank by the throat. There was absolutely nothing in the contract that required Dave to work for the taxi service. The 'Give or Take' clause was the standard one used around here, generally by the country people, he said, and which 'Bama seemed to know all about apparently. Talking from under his hat brim in a very lazy voice, he laid out what Dave could do if he wanted to. All Dave had to do was quit, if he wanted to. He would still own forty percent of the taxi business. Then it would be up to Frank to invoke the 'Give or Take' clause. If he wanted to. If Frank did not want to invoke it, Dave would still own his forty percent. If Frank did invoke the clause, Dave by the rules then had the right to name the price, and Frank then had the choice to 'Give or Take'. He could either buy Dave's share at the named price, or he could sell his own share at that price. In this case, since they were not fifty fifty partners, the price of each man's share would be arrived at on a mutual percentage basis. That was the

way the 'Give or Take' worked. He made it very clear, and it seemed
to Dave he knew an awful lot of legal language.

—Since such was the case, and here the gambler seemed to grin a
little, lazily, under his hat, all Dave had to do was name a price to
Frank that was too high, a little too high. The chances were, Frank
would then decide to sell. The chances were, that was why Frank had
had the clause put in in the first place: you see, if Frank decided
to sell, and Dave was unable to raise the money to meet the price (which
Dave himself had set), then Dave would be more or less honor bound
to sell his own share at just about whatever price Frank then decided
to give him. In that way, Frank could buy Dave's share at its original
face value of $5000, or perhaps even for a thousand or so less; Dave
would be in a squeeze and pretty much have to accept. The only other
alternative would be to go to court, in which case both men's assets
would be sold by the court. No doubt Frank could probably prevail
upon the judge, the chin beneath the hat grinned, to set a fairly low
value; then he would have a front guy to buy it—someone like Judge
Deacon, maybe—and then later he would buy it all back from Judge
and become sole owner, for less than the business was actually worth.
And Dave would be holding the short end of the stick.

"Then I dont see how the hell you can think I got Frank by the
throat," Dave had said irascibly, "by naming a high price."

"Because," 'Bama said lazily from under his hat, "in this case, you
would have the money to buy his share."

"I would?"

"Sure. I would give it to you."

Comprehension seemed to dawn. "Oh," Dave said thinly. "I see. Then
you would own the controlling share of the taxi service."

"Oh, no," 'Bama said. "I dont want to own it. I would loan you the
money to buy it. On a personal loan."

"Yeah?" Dave said thinly. "With how much interest?"

"None."

"No interest at all?" Dave said. "Well—Well then why would you
do it? What would you stand to make out of it?"

"Id make nothin."

"Then why do it?"

Underneath the hat 'Bama's chin moved in a grin. "I would just
like to do it," he said, in that lazy voice. "That way, you would be sole
owner of the taxi service, see? Huh huh huh. A profitable, respectable
business. Wouldnt Frank scream? —You could pay me back out of yore
gamblin winnings; or you could pay me out of the profits of the
business as they came in. Either way would be all right."

"Well, hell—" Dave said. "Frank's share would cost eight or nine
thousand. You aint got that much money."

"I got it," 'Bama said, raising his hatbrim and grinning at him charmingly.

"You mean to tell me you got that much cash stashed away in a bank in this town? I dont believe it."

"No," 'Bama said noncommittally. "I aint got it stashed away in a bank in this town. —But I got it. —And you can have it if you want it. Just let me know about a week ahead of time."

"But, why. Why would you be willing to do it."

'Bama grinned at him again, charmingly, intensely charmingly, in that way he had, and lazily. Then he let the hat drop back down. "Because it would tickle me," he said muffledly from under it. "In fact, it would tickle hell out of me." He laughed. And then he pushed the glass of straight whiskey up under his hat again. "—And I dont figure Id be takin no chance on losin the money. Because Im pretty sure yore honest enough to pay it back. Why the hell not do it?"

Dave had not answered. He was still trying to digest the whole thing.

"Well, I got to go," 'Bama said, gathering his long frame and getting up. "Got to get some shuteye. Its four o'clock. Thanks for the whiskey."

"You paid for it," Dave said.

"But either way," 'Bama said from the door, "you and me ought to get together on this gamblin deal. While its still hot for both of us. —Always providin it wouldnt hurt yore writin. We could sure make us a lot of money, while the luck lasted."

"Why the hell are you so damned interested in my writing?" Dave said irritably.

"I dont know," the tall man said amiably. "why do you like my gamblin? I guess, maybe its because yore the only writer I ever met, outside of Wally Dennis," he grinned. "Maybe I got intellectual pretensions. Maybe I want somebody to write a book about me. Who knows?" He laughed a little and shut the door. Then he opened it again, and stuck his face back in. "Or maybe its because Im interested in how you going to make out with that school teacher of Wally's, maybe? See you."

Feeling drunk, haggard-eyed, and too sleepless to sleep, Dave had gone right to bed and lain there thinking he had to get up and work tomorrow on the book, he *had* to, whether he felt like it or not. As an afterthought, he had got up again and drunk four large glasses of water, so much his belly sloshed when he walked, hoping that would help keep him from having a hangover tomorrow—or today, rather. He still could not understand why 'Bama would do such an outlandish thing. It wasnt even believable. Christ, he must have money to burn. The book: the damned book; it had become a point of personal honor with him now. Not only because of that damned Wally Dennis, and Frank and Agnes, but because of that son of a bitching 'Bama too, now. He *had* to write now. Or be a laughingstock. But could he? As he lay back down, the familiar loneliness of the Stephen A Douglas Hotel (it was much worse than The Parkman; why had he done it to himself deliberately? he neednt have come here;) had overwhelmed him depressingly, frighteningly. Oh, Gwen, Gwen. If you only knew how much I love you, how much I need you, how much Im falling for you, if you only knew. It was the next to last thought he had had before he slept. The last one had been that 'Bama apparently knew all about that, too.

Back in the taxi office, Dave was startled: Had he really thought that then? About Gwen? Or did he only think he had thought it, now. He couldnt have thought it, could he? If he didnt know he was in love with her? But he distinctly remembered thinking it. Maybe he was in love with her all the time? Yes, he must have been thinking it even then, without knowing it.

Outside the office window one of the cabs rolled slowly by on Plum and turned into their cinder parking lot beside the building, and his eyes registered it automatically, without its ever reaching the main part of his brain which still churned along about its love affair like a ship's propeller out of water. *Will* the crankshaft stand it? *Will* the seams all pop their rivets? *Tune* in next week.

The only bright spot. Out of all of it, 'Bama and his offer were the only bright spot. And that *one,* he thought sourly, a bright spot which he could not even understand and could make so little sense of that it frightened him to think of availing himself of it. Inertia was better. No wonder he was getting to hate everything.

If only a few of them would understand. If only *one* would! Well, write the book; make them understand. But understand *what?* Me! Thats what! Dave Hirsh! Me, Dave Hirsh, thats what! To understand Dave Hirsh is to love him. What great brain once said that? Was it Einstein? Must have been. In love. In love. And at his age, too. Was he a punk? Was he a child? Apparently. In love with a nymphomaniac. Well, that was about his speed.

Convulsively Dave flung the chair back from the window on its casters, riding it as it rolled, and swung around to the interior of the room. Albie did not even look up from his rapt trance with his comic book starring the clothes-tearing ape, and Dave stared at him.

My God! he told himself irately, look at Albie, youre a hell of a lot better off than Albie. And he stands it, dont he? You made over $150 last week gambling. And you own forty percent of the business. Youre getting $50 a week, and hes still only getting $31.25.

——But he wasnt Albie Shipe. He wasnt adjusting. They didnt have grade school and high school courses in Adjustment To Life yet when he was little. He had never had the opportunities; of reading Norman Vincent Peale; of studying Emerson (Fearless) Fosdick. His character had been neglected. And so he was getting so he hated everything. And that was bad. —In fact, it was terrible! he thought, suddenly frightened. Do you want to be *antisocial?* Do you want to be *bitter?* Do you want to *not love your own kind?* Do you want to be—whisper it—*Maladjusted!* You know what the moral code has happen to people in movies who do that: They die in the end, after a last minute change of heart to prove the moral. Thats what.

He wished Frank hadnt come over here today, damn it all. —Next to the telephones, he guessed he hated Frank the worst. Frank who had thought up this damned stupid taxi service idea in the first place.

Frank had hired a new driver to replace Albie, and Dave hated him too. Where Frank had got him, he didnt know. A tiny scrawny little punk of nineteen, with the sly face of an intent-eyed smiling toy size dog, who when he stood up *real* straight made a profile like a capital S from the side; and who was so damned intently obsequious that it not only irritated you but made your stomach flop over. Yes, Dave. No, Dave. Sure, Dave. You bet, Dave. Yes sir, Dave. No sir, Dave. All the time smiling intently and smugly as if he thought he was actually outsmarting you with flattery. Christ, he even made your own name sound to you yourself like a four letter word. Until even you were disgusted with your name yourself. *Well, he better stay away from me!* Rage and frustrated fury arced through him like the lightning from some General Electric machine, scattering sparks and searing his head. *Ill beat him to a goddamned pulp, by God!*

Wishing furiously that he had him here so he could do it right now, Dave pulled the swivel chair back up to the desk, and just then at the same time one of the phones rang. He grabbed for it sanguinarily.

It was another sickening sweet voiced woman wanting a cab, and after he hung up he suddenly felt much better. He had not blown up. He had not told her to go to hell. He had not even told her to walk, the exercise would do her good. In fact, he felt quite smug, thinking about his control, and suddenly he was confident again. He told the driver—Lee, it was; who had come inside and picked up one of Albie's comic books—where to go.

He still wished Frank hadnt come over here this afternoon, though.

Well, it was a fight to the finish. And he was not giving up. He was not going to let Frank be able to say he couldnt make it, didnt have what it took, he thought with blooming confidence. And wouldnt Frank just love to be able to say it!

If he wanted to go on giving the Old Man money, he would. Despite his promise. And he was not going to take advantage of the opportunity to work Frank that 'Bama offered, either. He didnt have to do it that way. And anyway he was above such dealings. They were against his principles. No, by God, he was going to prove he was a successful businessman. To Frank, and to all the rest of the Rotarian sons of bitches in this town.

—The way they all treated you so delicately, and patted you on the back so damned commendingly, as if they thought they were handling eggshells: "Youre really comin' along fine down there with that taxi service, arent you, Dave?" —"Youve really got quite a thing started down there with your taxi service, havent you, Dave boy?" —As if every Rotarian son of a bitch of them was still astounded he had stayed this long, and expected him to blow up and leave any minute, but were hoping sanctimoniously that he wouldnt.

Well, he would fool them all. Hed stay with her. Hed stay until hed made an incontrovertible success of her. And then when they thought they had him hooked, hed take his share and sell out and leave them holding the deflated balloon of their damned illusions. —And thanks to 'Bama he had the means of *making* Frank buy him out, now. All he had to do was tell him.

The state of euphoria stayed with him the rest of the afternoon till six o'clock. But then, in the time it took him to drive the little Plymouth home to the Douglas, the thought of sitting alone in that damned forsaken little room changed it just as suddenly back into an acute depression, a depression mingled with flaming overtones of ego left over from the euphoria. What he needed was a lay, a woman. He hadnt had one in over six weeks now.

And after shaving and changing his shirt he went back out, hurrying down the gloomy hall, to go to Smitty's and look up 'Bama.

The brassiere factory girls would be there, and if worst came to worst —and there was nothing better showed up—he could always take that Rosalie out again.

BOOK THREE

THE CRAFT

CHAPTER 31

'BAMA was not there, but practically everybody else was. The tension, vague fear, and that almost unbearable feeling that nobody on earth loved him, which had made him almost run down the threadbare corridor and stairs of the hotel, all left him weightlessly as he parked in the cinder lot under the dimly lit windows of the backbar high in the blank brick wall, and got out and went around front and in the door. He quite suddenly felt excited, and anticipatory, and in some way, vastly relieved.

As he let the door shut itself silently behind him, it was almost as if this were the same night he had been here before, and instead of having been away from here almost two months, had merely stepped outside a minute. Dewey and Hubie were here, and Raymond, and the same five girls were here, plus some others and their fellows he did not know. The same people, even, seemed to be sitting at the bar; and old Jane Staley was in the corner booth with two old men. For a moment he had a peculiar feeling that none of them had left the place, but had been here all that time, the perpetual hardcore nucleus of a neverending party, and only joined from time to time by others who drifted in and out.

Even Edith Barclay was in the same back booth with her boyfriend Harold. Harold Something. With a sort of caustic pride Dave was pleased to find he could not recall Harold's last name. Over the heads he caught Edith's eye and grinned and waved arrogantly at her. She merely nodded, film eyed, distantly.

Grinning back at her even more arrogantly, he walked on over to the booth where Dewey and Hubie sat crowded around the table with their own two girls, plus Rosalie, Mildred Pierce and the shapeless Ginnie, seven in all, and crowded so close together that it seemed actually physically impossible that they could do it.

"No. Im not goin out, I said," he heard old Janie say emphatically as he passed the corner booth. "I said Im not, and I aint."

"But why?" one of the old men whinnied eagerly.

"Because I dont feel like it. Thats why. I decided Id quit goin' out for a while. Thats a woman's perogative, aint it?"

"Aw, now, Janie," the other old man whinnied. They were not even competing with each other yet, apparently, but were standing together desperately to first convince her she should go out. The competition could come later. If any, Dave thought; because it didnt look like they were having much luck.

"Wall," Hubie drawled from where he sat squeezed between the

405

powerful shoulders of Rosalie and his own girl, Martha; "look whos here. If it aint God's gift to the V F W. I bet God's gift to the V F W kin tell us, Dewey."

"Tell you what?" Dave grinned. He suddenly felt fine now. "Can I sit down?"

"Sure. Get a chair from one of the back tables," Dewey Cole said happily from the end of the opposite seat where, as the fourth person, he had managed just enough space to perch one of his spare buttocks on the very end of the plywood. His other hung out in the air, where his leg was propped straight out to hold him up. His blue eyes shone happily. Next to him was his girl Lois with the lush body and long mane of hair and beyond her Mildred Pierce, and squeezed into the corner the vague-eyed dumpy Ginnie, who looked as though if she were to stand up suddenly all the excess flesh of her right side would remain molded into a definite right angle where the press had pushed her softness into the angle of the wall. The table was jammed with beer bottles in all stages of emptiness.

"Well— Will it be all right?" Dave said, glancing at Smitty behind the bar.

"Hell yes, itll be all right!" Dewey said happily. "They can throw us out if it aint, cant they?"

Dave went back past the bar to the wider back end to get a chair. From the next booth back, the occupants of which were evidently a part of Dewey's party and had been talking back and forth across the high boothback with them as he came in, a huskily built girl rared up and said something indistinct to Dewey across the head of Hubie, which Dave did not catch. Everybody laughed, and he instinctively wondered if they were laughing at him. Next to her in the booth he recognized the long horseface of Gus Nernst, erstwhile caretaker of Raymond Cole, and exchanged distant nods with him. At the rear, Raymond Cole himself sat at a table between two other men whom Dave did not know, but both of whom looked both as muscular and as dumb as Raymond himself. All three sat drinking and staring down into their beerglasses without looking at each other or speaking, almost as if each was sitting alone at a different table. At least, they did until Raymond looked up and saw Dave.

"Hello, there!" he said in a high friendly shout. "Hello, there! How are you?"

"Hello, Raymond. How are you."

"You looking for a chair?" Raymond shouted.

"Yes."

"Here, take this one!" Raymond shouted eagerly. His two friends, who had looked up, had already looked back down. "We dont need it. Theres only three of us. We will never use it. Take this one."

"Well, Ive already got one spotted over here," Dave said coming a little nearer, and feeling instinctively uneasy. He had meant to get one from the table nearest the booth of Edith Barclay.

"No. Now, by God, you take this one," Raymond insisted. "We wont never miss it. You *take* it, I say!"

"Well, all right," Dave said, feeling it was best to humor him. "If youre sure you wont miss it."

"That chair?" Raymond said, eyeing it contemptuously. "That chair wont never be missed. You take it."

"Well, okay," Dave said and came over to get it. His hands resting on its wire back, and in spite of his unease with Raymond, he looked up and across at Edith Barclay who was watching him, and grinned arrogantly.

"Hello, Edith," he grinned. "How are you?" It sounded arrogant and snotty and unpleasant, the way he said it, even to him. He did not know why she always affected him like that. He wasnt really that bad, really.

"Hello, Dave," she said back, levelly. "How are you." Her face, and her voice, were both carefully unexpressive.

"Oh," Raymond said in a lowered voice. "Gee. I didnt mess you up, did I? With the girl?" His two friends still had not looked up.

"Who? What?" Dave said bending down. "Oh, no. Hell no. I dont even hardly know that girl."

"Are you sure?" Raymond said, eyeing him narrowly. "Youre not just saying that."

"Positive."

"Well. Glad to be friendly, glad to be friendly," Raymond said, apparently appeased. "Take it away." He made as if to get up. "Want me to carry it for you?"

"Oh, no. But thanks," Dave said. He hoisted the light wire chair portentously and started off with it, relieved to get far away from Raymond, but still aware of Edith watching him, and because of this, feeling strong and powerful and tough and very dominating in a pleasing male way. To hell with these respectable women, he thought, with an inflamed mind. Hed take the barflies any time, even old Rosalie. Go ahead and watch me, Edith, he thought. Go ahead. Think about it.

——Edith, in her booth, was going on watching him. Both her face and her emotions were tightly closed against inspection, and her eyes were wide and level and carefully unreadable. But she wasnt thinking about Dave. He was, she had concluded often enough before, just about the biggest—most unprepossessing—ridiculously ludicrous—thoroughly distasteful single chunk of male vanity she had ever seen in her life still walking around on two legs. So often, it was not only unprofitable but boring to re-think it. What she was thinking was something else. Like a startling revelation, a sort of strikingly clear understanding, she had just realized why he fascinated her, and why she did feel drawn to watch him. It was because—although there was nothing alike in their characters at all—he looked so much like his brother. Edith had just realized she was in love with Frank.

With that sort of unbreathing, heartstopping mental shock in which everything seems to stand utterly still for a moment, Edith wondered how it could have happened? She certainly hadnt known anything about it, had she? It must have been going on for quite some time. In fact, now that she could see it, she could see where it had been. All those things she had thought and felt about him. Apparently, somewhere along the line, at some unnamed point in the near two years she had worked for him, she had stopped loving her job and started loving her boss, without knowing it.

It was obvious why she loved him. She loved him because he had all those fine and gentle traits of character in him which his brother Dave who looked so much like him, nevertheless obviously lacked. She loved him because he was shy, and pathetic, and lonely, and because he needed someone to cling to and depend on; in short, all the things his brother Dave was not, and was just the opposite of. But all this was hardly the point.

The point was that the whole thing was ridiculous. Ridiculous, and startling. It was not only startling, it was totally foreign; alien. It almost wasnt even her, even, she felt. Falling in love with a married man was not included in the list of probabilities, or even possibilities, that she had worked out for her life. It was not in her code of ethics, either. This was something that was going to require considerable thought and mental adjustment, and a great deal of careful appraisal—in private. Certainly, she couldnt do it here.

A married man almost old enough to be her father! Why, it wasnt even believable! A short, fat, plaintive little German man who ran a jewelry store, and worried. And who was so *un*stalwart, and *un*strong-willed, he couldnt even handle his own affairs adequately, let alone somebody else's. Who couldnt even keep his own wife from dominating him. He was just about the opposite of what she would have picked. And yet all those things were the very same things which wrenched her heart whenever she thought about him.

With slightly flattened, carefully unreadable eyes, Edith turned back to Harold Alberson sitting across from her in the booth and smiled flatteringly, attentively, and hunted for something to make conversation. What she wanted was to be taken home immediately, so she could think, but she knew better than to let that out. Harold would connect it with the way she had stared at Dave. —And probably draw the wrong conclusions! she added crisply.

For a moment, Edith looked up at Janie in her corner booth with her two old geezers. Whatever Janie's trouble—love, illness, depression, or fatigue—she was beginning to get over it now apparently and for the first time in her life Edith was actually glad to see her out with her decrepit boyfriends and not embarrassed by it. From here Edith could just barely make her out around the booth corner. Was that why Janie had kept on running Frank Hirsh down to her all this time? Janie knew as well as she did what a fine person he was. Was that why she did it? Had Janie foreseen ahead of time in some private fashion all her own that this was going to happen? and been trying to protect her? Oh, if she could only get home, and be alone, and think! What was she going to do?

She turned back to Harold, smiling warmly, and began to talk about how her grandmother embarrassed her running around with all these old guys like she did.—

—And to hell with her, Dave thought. There was plenty of other fish in the sea. The three women in that booth next to Dewey's all had men with them, he noted; but that still left Mildred Pierce apparently unattached, before he had to fall back on Rosalie. He set the chair down at the end of the crowded booth.

"Now!" he said profoundly, sitting in it. "Tell you what? My voluminous knowledge is at your command."

"Hey!" Hubie said. "Wow! Now you quit that swearin' in front of these ladies here."

Dave was looking at Dewey, but Dewey only made a shy grimace for an answer. Beside him Lois looked sullen.

"Wall, its like this, see?" Hubie drawled, answering for him. "Me and Dewey is seriously considerin' reenlistin' in the Army. Right now the way the setup is they want men bad, and we could both git back in with our old ratings instead of having to go back in as privates, see? And we want to get your professional V F W opinion of whether we ought to or not to."

"Yeah, thats about the size of it," Dewey grinned shyly, his eyes sparkling and his handsome face beaming mischievously. "We both gettin' sick of this damned town. Nothing ever happens around here exciting or romantic."

"Damn you, Dewey," Lois said gloweringly. "I want a home for my two kids. You know I do."

Dewey's happy face suddenly expressed a deep mock sympathy, everywhere except in his eyes which snapped with an almost bubbling good humor. "Well, honey, my advice to you is to find some nice fella that wants to get married and marry him," he said solicitously. "Thats my advice to you."

"You go to hell, Dewey," Lois said, "will you?"

"Well, now, honey," Dewey protested mildly; "honestly, honey, you cant expect me to marry you and take care of them kids just because your first old man got killed in the war, can you? They aint my kids. It aint my fault he got killed by the damn Japs." He winked at Dave relishingly. "By rights, them kids are the government's responsibility. But you cant blame me for it. If they was my kids, itd be different."

Hubie laughed whinnyingly and looked at Dave happily. It was plain that if the last time Dave had seen them all here the girls had had the upper hand, the tables were now turned and the boys were in control. Hubie's girl Martha, who rarely seemed ever to say anything, sat looking down glumly at her half empty beer glass. She still gave that same impression which Dave had noted in her the first time, that she had been born into a caste just a cut above these other girls in the social hierarchy of Parkman. She did not work at the brassiere factory like the rest, and she looked as though she might even have graduated from high school.

"Now, honestly," Dewey grinned, "can you?"

"Aw, you go to hell, Dewey," Lois said muffledly. "No. No, it wasnt your fault any. Youre an awful stinker Dewey, you know it?"

"He sure is," Rosalie said pugnaciously and brassily.

"Now, look at that!" Dewey protested amiably. "Aint that just like a bunch of women? You tell them the truth, the facts, and they call you a stinker."

"What about it, perfesser?" Hubie said in his nasal drawl. "What do you think? Give us your considered V F W opinion."

"Well, they do want men," Dave grinned, playing along with the game. "And if you had pretty good ratings, itd be a good way to get them back, right now. In another year they may change the ruling."

"Why the hell dont you keep out of this, fat boy?" Rosalie said in her brassy, perpetually incensed voice.

"Now you just shut up, fullback," Dewey said. "Or Ill tackle you." His eyes glinted happily.

Rosalie glowered at him, but subsided. Looking at her Dave got the impression that had it been anybody else but Dewey she might have offered to take him on. The fact that he had once been out with her did not titilate him at all now. He looked over at Mildred Pierce, who had so far not said anything, and remembered how he had wanted to take her on and try her out even back then, when he had heard her and 'Bama going to town in the next room. He guessed he *was* putting on a little weight, he thought; after all, two months sitting at a desk in that damned taxi office wasnt exactly a waist slimming operation.

"Sure," Dewey had just said to him; "thats what I say. Hubie was a buck sergeant and I was a staff. Itd be silly to throw away ratings like that, wouldnt it?"

"Well, its a lot of money," Dave grinned.

Dewey nodded solemnly. "Moren wed ever make in this jerkwater town."

"What about Germany, perfesser?" Hubie drawled. "Tell us about Germany. We never got to Europe. Is it as nice for a soldier to be in as Australia?"

"Well, its a mighty nice place to be stationed," Dave said, shaking his head wistfully and peering slyly at Rosalie. "Thats all Ill say; in front of the girls. Germany's a mighty nice place to serve in."

"What about all them German frauleins over there?" Hubie said.

"You go to hell, too," Martha said in a low voice from beside him, without looking up. She sounded as though the swearwords perhaps did not come as naturally to her as to the other girls.

"Is it true? what the guys say?" Hubie grinned. "I hear them frauleins over there will do everything for you. Move right in with you and wash your clothes for you and cook and turn their pay right over to you, and you dont even have to marry them at all."

"Thats right," Dave nodded. "They will if they like you. They dont care whether you marry them or not. But then those European women are different from our women over here. Over there the man's the lord and master."

Hubie nodded sagely. "Thats just what I heard." He turned to Dewey. "Thats what we ought to do, Dewey. Enlist for Germany. With out ratings back, and all that money—"

"You go to hell," Martha said again, in the same dead tone, still staring at her beer.

"There! How do you like that?" Hubie said. "I ask you. Is that fair or not? Her old man," he moved his head at Martha without looking at her, "—Old Man Garvey—he runs a big old fillin' station out in West End. He dont want his daughter runnin' around with no town bum and marryin' him. He wants her to marry a nice boy wholl run his fillin' station. And then just because I—"

"I said Id marry you," Martha said in that low dead voice, still staring at her glass, "except that Daddy and Momma wouldnt let me."

"There? You see?" Hubie said happily to Dave. "And yet shes of age, she aint a minor, she can do whatever she wants, cant she? No sir," he drawled, slyly relishing his own wry humor, "she just dont want to marry old Hubie, thats all. And then just because I want to go back in the Army and try a little of that German stuff . . ." He rattled on eagerly.

Dave had been looking at Martha while Hubie talked, and so had seen the one brief look that she had turned upward at him—at Hubie —while he rattled along. It was a look full of several things which Dave could hardly even name, and it filled him with a strange male exultation: It was a look full of frustrated possession, for one thing:

the hunger for ownership; it was a look full of guilty—but passionate
—desire, for another: the pure physical desire to feel sexually; and
then in addition, larding it all over—this look—like the grease that
holds several chemicals in solution in a face cream, was this indrawn
expression of guilt because she did feel these things, coupled with an
embarrassed look of shame because other people could obviously so
easily see—if only by her very actions in being here—just exactly
what she did feel. All these things were in the look and mirrored on
her face, exposed by the very muscular contractions with which she
tried to hide them. It was a short quick look, it didnt last long; he had
just happened to see it. And after directing it at Hubie she had turned
her eyes on to Dave, and seen him watching her, whereupon her face
became even more selfconscious than before, and then she looked
back down, and it passed back into that deadness, and was gone. But
it made Dave want to shout out loud with triumph. It was the kind
of look *he* would like to make that damned Edith Barclay feel, or
Missy Gwen French.

—Then however, suddenly, a new and deeper realism, a sudden
further penetration into understanding, dropped down over Dave's
sense of triumph, smothering it.

—It was like a sudden spiritual revelation to him, a warning almost;
one of those sudden deeper penetrations into things that go deeper
than you want to go. And that consequently you have to be alert for
because they only knock once, and lightly: This was what all men
wanted from all women. To make them like it, to make them like sex
and make them admit they liked it. To make them feel so good in sex
they would come back and ask for it some more. That was what men
wanted. But the very idea presupposed a woman who in the beginning
didnt like it, a 'respectable' woman; otherwise it would be impossible.
That was what intrigued him so about Edith Barclay, and about Gwen.
—*Why Gwen? Why her? a nympho? and yet he did include her.*—
But with a 'respectable' woman, it was impossible anyway: Even if
you managed to make her like it, and admit she liked it, the guilt and
the hate for you for making her go against her 'principles'—which you
would not have her without, and were the very thing which attracted
you!—would always be there, fighting you. She might like it—even *if*
she might like it, she still wouldnt *want* to like it. (And if she *did*
want to like it, wouldnt you think she was a whore?) And so he saw,
didnt he, the Revelation said to him implacably, that it was all impossible, it was a figment, a chimera, a vague nonexistent dream of an
illusion, and a snare and a delusion. A trap, a *self*-trap: and that was
where the warning part came in.

—But my God, the next thought came, what was left? What hope
was there? for love? complete love? full love? The answer was obvious,

wasnt it, the Revelation said implacably. None. Hastily, Dave picked up the full glass of beer from the bottle Dewey had ordered for him and drained it, staring straight ahead at the wall glassily. Then he poured another and drank it, and shut the door on the cold draft of the Revelation which said it was impossible and that everything else was lies, and only various acts played by various people. It had changed his entire mood. Obviously the only thing to do was not to think about it. I *need* love.

"—and so there you are!" Hubie finished up triumphantly. "I ask you. Is that fair or not?" He looked down at Martha unctuously. Dave had not heard a single word hed said.

"It sure is," he answered stoutly nevertheless, grinning wanly. "Its not fair at all. But then, who ever expected anything to be fair?"

Martha did not say anything this time, but continued to look down glumly into her half empty beer glass. Then, almost absentmindedly, in what appeared to be slow motion, she reached out and picked it up and drank what was in it and set it back down and continued to stare at it, empty now. Yes sir, Dave thought happily, yes sir, for once the Males sure had the Females going tonight. And it was seldom enough, he thought; seldom enough.

"Yes sir! I think thats what we ord to do, Dewey," Hubie drawled slyly. "Enlist for Germany. Ive always wanted to see Europe anyways.—

"—Dont you hit me, Rosalie!" he squealed suddenly, as the big Amazon turned to glare down at him. "You leave me alone, now! Or Ill sick Dewey on you!"

"I want a home for my kids!" Lois burst out. It was almost a wail, and there was a quality of desperation in it. She had begun to cry.

"You dont want a home," Dave said roughly, and with unexpected fury. "You got one. You aint out in the street, are you?"

"I live with my folks."

"Well, you see? All you want is some damned man, any damned man, to marry you. And take care of you and them kids and support you and be a damned father to them."

Lois looked up at him reproachfully, and not without puzzlement, tears still still dribbling from her eyes. "He would want to," she said still crying, "if he loved me." Her face seemed to be asking without rancor what he was doing trying to break up her love life for?

Dave suddenly felt ashamed of himself.

But the debonair Dewey had just set down his glass with savoir-faire. "Yes sir, it sure is rough," he said amiably. "People just shouldnt get married and *have* kids in this day and age, thats all. A person just cant *tell* whats liable to happen, anymore."

"Yes, by God, thats right!" Mildred Pierce suddenly said vehemently, her eyes swinging around the table as fiercely piercing as some hawk's. A small one, Dave thought, a sharp shin. "And thats about the only damn *true* thing thats been said here tonight!" It was the first word she had spoken since Dave had come in. Beside her, the sacklike dumpy, hump-necked Ginnie had so far not said anything. She had been occupying herself, he had noticed, by exchanging hopefully flirtatious glances with one of the various men at the bar, after which every so often, beneath those vague washed-out, apparently uninhabited eyes, she would smile coyly.

"Mildred, Mildred," Dewey murmured. "I didnt mean to go getting you all upset or nothing."

"Mildred," Dave said suddenly, aware of Rosalie extending out over the table beside him—"Mildred, how would you like to go out with me tonight?" Beside him, the extentions of Rosalie seemed to stiffen with injured beauty.

Mildred turned her head to look at him, her eyes relaxing back into their normal calmness. "Be all right. I wouldnt mind," she said, shaking her head slowly; "But Im just too tired. Ive been out the last two nights straight. And Ive just got to get a good night's sleep."

Dave felt his prospects plummet, and carry his optimism with them. He had staked it all on Mildred's usual willingness to go on a party. That and the fact that he was not 'going steady' with Rosalie. He had not considered a possible need for sleep. And beside him, little ripples of triumph seemed to emanate from Rosalie's heroic physique, as she settled herself to wait for him to ask her next; the brilliant predatory smile on her muscular face left no doubt as to what the answer would be, when he did.

"As a matter of fact, I think Ill go right now," Mildred said. "Before I wind up sitting here another hour. Let me out, you two," she said to Lois and Dewey. "Maybe some other time, Dave," she said after they had let her out, and patted him kindly on the big muscle beside his neck, and then went to looking for her coat among the loaded hooks on the upright post at the end of the booth.

Well, Dave thought ruefully, that was that. And ruefully he watched her pert little bottom, which was girdleless under that tight skirt, with a feeling very like a man who watches a bass which has thrown his hook swim slowly and safely down out of sight in the water: he was helpless. And beside him, the sanguinary Rosalie still waited. Nobody offered to help Mildred find her coat, nor did she seem to expect anyone to. When she finally found it, she put it on and turned back to the table.

"Well," she said, "how much do I owe on my share?" She extracted a man's folding wallet from her purse. She seemed to be talking to Lois more than anyone else.

"Ill get it," Dave said before anyone else could answer. "Just forget it. Ill take care of it."

"Okay," Mildred said. "Thanks." She put the wallet back in her purse. She patted him once more on his shoulder and left.

Dave sighed. "Well," he said, "what do you say we have another beer?"

"Well now I think thats the best idea yet anybody's had," Ginnie said in her toneless voice, smiling at him dully. It was the first she had spoken.

Dave studied her, seeing her for the first time, really—as an individual—since he had come in. Nobody else paid the slightest attention to her, or to her remark.

"Man," Dewey said. He and Lois had both sat back down. "It sure feels good to get both halves of my behind on this seat for a change."

She was, Dave reflected sadly, just about the poorest and most unprepossessing excuse for a human being that he had ever had occasion to witness. And yet: 'Bama had told him she was not only the best but also the least troublesome one of the bunch for a one night stand, hadnt he? He toyed with an idea. Well, why not? What did he care? He looked at her again. Ginnie was just about as shapeless as a human body could get, and still be recognizable as such. Where there was any definite shape to her at all, it was always the wrong shape, and in the wrong place. Like that hump of fat on the back of her neck that aging and poorly postured women acquired. And yet she wasnt an awful lot older than Wally Dennis: she had been in the sixth grade with him, hed said. Twenty three or four? My God, it was unbelievable! —And yet, after all, like they said in the Army, if you turned the lights out.

Still, there was Rosalie beside him, still waiting—with massive patience, and mountainous ill will, and with Amazonian combativeness —for him to ask her to go, so she could turn him down. In fact, the large pointed breasts of Rosalie seemed already to be quivering with anticipation, for a chance to turn him down. Like two muzzled hunting dogs held in by a leash strapped behind her back. Just waiting. Dewey had already ordered the new round from the one-armed Eddie.

"Ginnie," Dave said, "how would *you* like to go out with me tonight?"

For a moment he thought Rosalie was going to break him in two.

"Who?" Ginnie said vaguely. "Me?"

"Yes," he said. "Yeah. You."

"Why, that would be most nice," she said grandly. "Id love to." Surprise was spreading slowly over her round face. "As a matter of fact, I didnt have nothing doing tonight," she added coyly.

"Well thats fine," Dave said. "I didnt have nothing doing either."

"Well, I guess I better be getting home," the redheaded Rosalie said stiffly. "That makes me the extra at the party. And you know what thats like. That only dampers everybody. Good night, you all."

"Aw, stick around," Dave said. "Somebody else may show up yet."

"Yes," Lois, who had been missing all this byplay because of her own troubles, said glumly. "You dont want to leave so soon, Rosalie."

"I hate to," Rosalie said, "but Auntie Lou wants me to help her inventory the bar at West Lancaster tomorrow, so Id better. How much do I owe for my share?"

"Let it go," Dave said magnanimously. "Ill get it."

"Why, thank you, Dave," Rosalie said sweetly, and shouldered her muscular shoulders into her expensive coat. "Ill see you all."

"You made a wise choice," Dewey said, after she had left; "especially after asking Mildred first."

If Ginnie Moorehead heard this, she gave no sign. She still appeared to be getting over her surprise.

"She would have turned me down anyway," Dave grinned.

"You aint just crappin she would," Dewey said.

"Here, Dave," Hubie said. "You want to sit over here in front of Ginnie? Me and Martha'll move and let you in."

"No," Dave said. "This is all right. Ill just sit here on the end." He moved into the seat Rosalie had vacated.

"Yes," Ginnie said pleasantly. "Thats all right. He can sit right there."

"Well," Dave said, "heres to a pleasant evening."

"Ill sure drink to that," Ginnie said dully.

They all drank to it. But after that things sort of settled into an unexciting routine. They drank that round of beers and ordered another one. Then they drank that one, and ordered others. There wasnt much general conversation. Both of the other girls were glum, and Ginnie was just naturally not scintillating. Every now and then Dewey and Hubie, like a devilish man dropping periodic stones down on a pack of howling dogs whenever they quieted, would bring up anew the question of going back into the Army and discuss it thoughtfully. They were both having the times of their lives. It wasnt often they could get—and keep—such a strong upper hand over their girls, and they wanted to take full advantage of it. Perhaps it was because his mood had changed, but Dave no longer got much kick out of it. He seemed to see them through the same dark magnifying glass through which earlier he had seen himself, and love, and Martha Garvey. Eventually, Dave thought, they would wear it out and the girls would cease to be upset by it, and then they would either have to do it or shut up about it; but right now they were enjoying it to the full. But of course, they didnt mean to do it, and had no intention of even doing it. Dave himself tried desperately to think of something to talk to Ginnie about and felt upset and ill at ease because he couldnt, although in all fairness to Ginnie he had to admit it apparently made no difference to her whether she was talked to or not. Once, when Hubie and Dewey were discussing enlisting again, he mentioned 'Bama just to sort of be in on things.

"Why dont you ask 'Bama what he thinks about it?"

"That son of a bitch," Dewey snorted. "Theres no point askin him. Hes prejudiced. He thinks anybody's crazy who would have anything to do with the Army voluntarily. I know what hed say."

It was not long after this that, in the back of the room, Raymond Cole exploded again and blew up, like a bad bottle of beer going off and scattering foam and bits of glass all over the walls and ceiling. One moment all was quiet, the next Raymond had stood up bellowing, upsetting both his own chair and the little round table of beer bottles. The only understandable words were: "Ill beat the living hell out of all of them before Ill . . ." The rest was lost in the confusion as his two friends, both as broad as he was, grasped him each by an arm and hustled him, struggling, up front and out the door. "Be back pay you later," one of them said breathlessly to Smitty who was standing behind the bar as they passed.

"I dont know why I keep on serving Raymond," Smitty said mildly and reflectively to nobody, as he looked after them. "I guess Im just soft hearted. Someday Sherm Ruedy's going to catch him." Sherm Ruedy was Chief of Police in Parkman; Dave had already heard about him from 'Bama, almost none of it good.

"Glad it was them instead of me," Gus Nernst laughed to Dewey from across the back of the booth. "Tonight's my night off."

"Who were those two guys?" Dave asked Dewey.

Dewey had been looking after his brother disgustedly. "Couple friends of Raymond's. Old Army buddies. Served in the 132nd with him. Both farm down south of town."

The one armed Eddie had already gone back with a broom to clean up the debris. In a little while he came over to their booth grinning with another round Dewey had ordered.

"Raymond's not in very good form tonight, is he?" he grinned. "Didnt even hit one guy before they collared him."

"Aaanh," Dewey said contemptuously. He took some money out of Lois's purse and paid him.

"Look," Eddie grinned; "put a quarter down on the table."

Dewey looked up at him uncomprehendingly.

"A quarter," Eddie said. "Anywhere. Ill show you something."

Dewey shoved empty beer bottles aside to clear a space and did as he was asked.

"Now watch this," Eddie grinned. He lowered his hooks, carefully spread open, over the flat-lying quarter until their curved centers touched the table, then carefully brought them together on it. Slowly he lifted the quarter, holding it by its milled edges between the hooks, until he had it up in the air and then flipped it and caught it in his other hand.

"How about that," he grinned brilliantly. "Pretty good, hunh? Been practicing up on my tip collecting." He put the quarter back on the table.

"By God that is!" Dewey said admiringly. "Thats pretty damned good!"

Eddie moved his head deprecatingly. "Show you something else," he grinned. "Here," he said to Dave; "gimme a dollar bill and stand up. —No. Here. I got one myself." He pulled out a bill with his good hand. "Now turn around and put this in your hip pocket flatways. Slide it in flatways, see? Longways."

Dave did as he was requested.

"Now shut your eyes," Eddie grinned, "and see if you can feel me." While Dave shut his eyes and tried with the skin of his buttock to feel when he was touched, Eddie slid the slender hooks into the top of the hip pocket of his loose slacks, clasped the dollar bill with them and slid it out.

"Okay, open your eyes!" Eddie grinned. "Did you feel me?"

Dave turned around. "No," he said truthfully. "No, I didnt."

Eddie displayed the pilfered dollar bill triumphantly. "How about that, hunh?"

"Pretty good," Dave said. "I couldnt feel a thing."

Eddie crumpled the bill in his good hand happily and thrust it back in his pocket. "Bettern a damned hand anytime," he explained, waving his hooks, "for that kind of work. A hand's too damned *thick*." He picked up his tray. "Im going to start working on billfolds next, I think," he grinned.

"How about lettin me be your manager?" Dewey said. "We could go to Chicago and make us a fortune."

Eddie laughed happily. "Not a chance, pal. Why the hell should I cut you in on the gravy? Im the one with the talent. Ill go by myself." He tilted his tray rakishly on the plam of his good hand. He winked again at Dave, then dropped his hand out from under his tray, catching it by its edge as it fell, and went back to the bar.

Dave, who had remained standing—or rather, had forgotten he was standing—sat back down again, feeling lumpish and strange. He was hit again suddenly—to the accompaniment of Stravinski's 'Rite of Spring'—by that powerful, warning, depressive feeling of living in the last days of the Roman Empire, that he had felt here before and that Raymond Cole and the one armed Eddie seemed to have a peculiar power to evoke in him. These were the Plebs, he thought looking around the booth, the cynical Plebs. Maybe that was why. Here he was amongst the Plebs. The maimed veterans of the Legions, the shop-keepers without shops, the wives without husbands, the whores without cribs. The 'laboring element'. The teeming swarming life-loving lifedevouring antheap of the Forum, living their lives out in the taverns and the occasional circus given them for their vote. It was such an apt analogy. The almost unbearable twilight sadness. Of the cynical, the derisive, the sardonic Plebs, hooting at the false virtue of their leaders—but their willing prey none the less—and trying hard to forget the barbarian hordes gathering like a thunderhead in the horizons of the north.

And out at the Country Club tonight, the leaders. The vain energetic Caesars, the vain weakling Pompeys, the vain shrewd-politico Augustuses, their heads in a bottle (and why not?), and talking virtuously to each other about how virtuously to handle the people, for the people's own best virtuous good. We love the people virtuously. We serve the people virtuously. We virtuously ask nothing for ourselves—except the power, the virtuous power, to virtuously save the people from themselves. And with them all the woman-crazy Antonies and all the very rich, very pretty, pompously big-mouthed Ciceros; whose selfrevealing letters Octavian-Augustus shrewdly published, to help him become king.

—All of them, all, both here and there, all little bricks in the crumbling tumbling edifice of the unbearable twilight of the age; while the barbarian wind sweeps down chilling from the north.

Probably Frank was out there right now. Frank was a leader, he thought wanting to roar with unbearable twilight laughter, his brother Frank was a leader.

In a word: *decadence,* he thought, almost afraid to think the word. All of us. Everywhere. Decadence: that point of diminishing returns where impossible ideals which can not be kept, and never could be kept, finally obvert themselves and their own meanings and become their own reverse: where virtue turns into the appearance of virtue, which therefore becomes inordinately important, more important than the truth. Especially in politics, he thought, and love.

And all the time the barbarian hordes were making inroads in the north, and stamping their feet and whistling impatiently like horses, when they thought of the loot that still waited in the city.

Dave hated the Communists. He hated them bitterly. He knew why he hated them. He hated them because he feared them. ("If we can only just keep one atom bomb ahead of them.")

If there was only some way of finding out for sure that they were really human. All the ones he had seen in Germany personally, were not human. —But then those guys who had met them at the Elbe, they had thought they seemed all right, and human, then. Probably the truth was, it was not a barbarian horde. Probably it was only another empire, another crumbling empire, whose leaders also mouthed virtue. Two crumbling skyscrapers which, tumbling, would knock each other down. In the unbearably melancholy twilight of the world.

Now, this year, 1947, they had finally come out in the open and taken over Bulgaria, Rumania, and Hungary. And China! Would they now get China? Perhaps the only hope, the only real hope, lay in the possibility that they were not barbarians, the possibility that they were human, and as decadent and as virtue-mouthing as we Romans. Then both empires would go down together. In the twilight of the world. And we at least would not be conquered.

But if they took over China? Then, perhaps a whole new historical pattern might emerge, one that history had never seen before: in which that true barbarian horde—the mass of ignorant, illiterate, animal manpower of China—would be controlled dedicated fanatics for the decadent brains of a Caesar or Augustus, instead of an Alaric or Atilla.

Then! Then, by God, youd have something! . . .—And Gwen French was angry at him for not writing on a damned pointless novel. Why? Who would read it *then?*

He did not like to think about it. Any. At all. But he couldnt help it. It was in the room all around him; in the smoke filled, beery breathed, laughter riddled air; in the men, almost all of them veterans, drinking at the bar; in the booths of couples; in this booth; in the women, like Mildred Pierce who did not want to take on a husband for fear of losing him tomorrow. How could you help but think about it? here?

"Whats the matter, Davie boy?" a strange voice came in on him suddenly, cooing at him with dull coyness. He looked up startled. "You feel bad? You got the blues, Davie boy?" Ginnie Moorehead said with heavy caressingness.

"Damn it, dont call me Davie!" he exploded sharply. "Dont ever call me Davie! I hate that name!"

Ginnie's round face appeared to crumple into frightened chaos, from which her eyes peered forth like a hunted rabbit's. "Well, God, I was only tryin' to make—I didnt mean to—" she stammered guiltily, and then gave up and stopped and merely sat, peering at him defenselessly.

Everybody in the booth had turned to look at him with surprise, and the sort of dumb frightened guilt on Ginnie's face left him stricken.

"Im sorry," he mumbled. "I was thinkin."

"Thinkin about what?" Dewey said curiously.

"Thinkin about life, damn it!"

Dewey grinned with his handsome face. "Well; thats enough to make any one of us holler like we was jabbed with a pin."

"Its just that I dont like that name," Dave explained. "Everybody used to call me that when I was little, like I was some kind of a pet dog or mascot. Or their personal possession. I never have liked it."

"Oh, thats all right, Dave," Ginnie said pleasantly, smiling at him dully. —Whatever it was, the terror, that was the only word he could think of to describe it, pure terror, was beginning to recede from her eyes now.— "I didnt know. I wont call you that no more."

"I think we better get out of here," Dave said heavily, rubbing his hand hard over his face. "How about it, Ginnie? You ready to go?" He got out his wallet and put six ones on the table. "That should be enough."

"Any time you are, Dave," she said eagerly.

" 'Bama tells me youre workin on a book now," Dewey said to him suddenly.

"Yeah," Dave said reluctantly. "Yeah. Thats right."

"Was that what you were thinkin about a minute ago?" Dewey said.

Dave turned back to look at him. What the hell did you say? "Yeah," he said heavily. "I guess it was."

Dewey nodded. "I figured it was."

"Let me out of here, please, Lois and Dewey, will you?" Ginnie said in a stately voice. They got up.

"This book," Dewey said. "Is it about Parkman?"

Dave shook his head. "No."

"I thought maybe it was," Dewey said regretfully. "Well, somebody ought to write one about this damned town." He grinned that glitter-eyed rebellious grin of his.

"Lets you and me do it, Dewey," Hubie said. "We can write it in our spare time after we get back in the Army." Martha Garvey turned her head to scowl at him furiously, and he grinned happily.

"This is where I came in," Dave said. "Well, we will see you all."

"Yeah," Ginnie said in a queenly voice from beside him. "We'll see you all."

"Sure. Come back any time," Dewey grinned. "I reckon we'll be here. If Lois's money holds out, that is. —Sit down, damn it, Lois. Im gettin tard," he said. "Always provided we dont enlist, of course," he added.

Dave nodded at him, and made himself grin a little, to show he got the joke, as he escorted the short dumpy Ginnie to the door. He was aware of a sort of lull behind him in the place, as everyone more or less stopped what they were doing for a second and watched to see who was taking whom out, as he followed her. This made him inordinately happy, with a kind of wild, savage pleasure, a sort of deliciously enjoyed vulgarity, and he took the rotund Ginnie by the arm protectively so all could see. Ginnie positively beamed. He only hoped damned Edith Barclay was watching from her back booth with her Harold. Watching; and thinking about it. Make it harold, he amended complacently: lower case: from her back booth with her harold. This Harold was definitely a lower case harold.

Outside, he led the apparently very happy Ginnie to the Plymouth.

Sure didnt take much to make her happy, did it? One of the advantages of being dumb. In the car he drove her back uptown and to the hotel. The Douglas Hotel. It was the "Hotel Francis Parkman," but it was the "Douglas Hotel." Funny, what myriad minute forms our snobbisms took in permeating everything, he thought contemptuously.

"I thought wed go to my room at the Douglas," he said at length, as he rounded the square. "I dont know of anywhere else to go. I—I guess itll be all right to go there. Ive never taken anybody there before, though." He looked at her hesitantly.

"Oh, yes, itll be all right," Ginnie said reassuringly. "That old night man, he dont care," she said blandly. "Nor the day man neither, for that matter, honey."

CHAPTER 32

SHE was quite right. The night man merely looked up, once, with his country man's flattened eyes, then looked back down at his large format true detective magazine, thereby replacing his face with the pink top of his bald head which, eyeless, continued to stare at them.

As they walked across the lobby that was divided slightly (into Office and Lounge) by the old frame staircase which debouched out into it in the center of the back wall, Dave rather wistfully wished he had as much aplomb about it as Ginnie had. In the room, after first pulling the blind on his married friends across the way, Dave got out a fifth of whiskey and set it on the table. When he turned around, trying desperately to think of some adequate way to begin operations, Ginnie who had apparently been standing right behind him, put her fat arms around him and kissed him on the mouth.

They disrobed in silent unison and then just as silently went to bed. It was as simple as that, he thought with astonishment.

And for one night in his life, at least—well, perhaps not the *first* time; but certainly the first in a long time; and certainly a condition he had not experienced at all with Rosalie Sansome—Dave had his fill of sex. He was not only filled, he was runneth over; he was shucked out, saturated, and thoroughly bored with sex. He found, to his irritated surprise, it did not relieve him near as much as he had earlier thought it would.

Sitting exhaustedly in the single armchair after the first silent and ferocious session in the bed, her eyeballs red from fatigue and from liquor, Ginnie stared at him dully and with a look almost of anxiety on her fat face while she sipped repeatedly at her whiskey glass, suddenly began to talk about herself and her life with a speed and energy

Dave would not have up to now believed her capable of. She rattled off almost as if by rote a story whose sole interruptions nearly, were the other three times they went to bed, and which began with her earliest thoughts and childhood dreams and continued through her school years and right on up to the present, and she was still rattling it off with no apparent diminishment of speed or energy when Dave finally fell asleep, exhausted.

The upshot of what she had to say was that she liked sex. She began with this, and came back to it a number of times, and every time she said it a look that was sort of an anxious guilt came over her face as she peered at him observantly to see his reaction. She not only liked it, she said, she loved it, and as she said this she peered at his face acutely and observantly.

"Well," Dave said, momentarily at a loss, "theres no law that says women *shouldnt* like sex. That I know of."

"Maybe not," Ginnie said, still peering at him watchfully. "I dont know. I dont know what the law says. But everybody sure acts like theres one. Ill say that."

"Well," Dave qualified, "I guess—I suppose there is some kind of law about immorality. About adultery. Which means, I guess," he said gently, apologetically feeling she might need explanation of these terms, "sleeping with someone youre not married to. If you try to pin it down."

Ginnie nodded. "Thats the one." She continued to peer at him with her reddened eyeballs; it was not a frightened or nervous peering, merely an observing one.

"But just about everybody does that," Dave said. "At some time or other." He could not figure out what she was trying to get at. It wasnt that she was afraid of him turning her in to the police. She knew better than that. It must be something else.

"Sure," Ginnie said. "But some gets by with it and some doesnt," she added. "And, looks like, Im one of the ones nobody dont never want to get by with it."

"Thats probably due to the respectable women," Dave said didactically. "Who would probably all like to do what youre doin, but are afraid to take a chance on tryin it."

One corner of her small—almost prim, he thought—mouth in the round face lifted itself up in a sneer. "Sure. Thats who hates me. You think I dont know all the 'respectable' women in this town hates me? But whats wrong with a woman likin' sex, I ask you? That shouldnt be bad," she said, peering at him, again, observantly with those reddened eyeballs—(which did not seem even to have the ability to get angry)— as if studying him for some reaction she either hoped for or expected.

And yet in spite of that, she went on, she liked it. She loved sex. All her life she had, she said. Even her earliest thoughts and her dreams as a little kid, she said, had been all about sex. She knew that now, although then she had not known what they meant, that was even before she knew what sex was all about. She told him some of them, such as the daydreams she used to have even as a little tiny kid about how there had been a contest and she had won first prize for having the biggest titties in the county, while the judges cheered and the people all clapped their hands.

She told him other ones too; in fact, she talked on and on. Dave could see where they all could have had to do with sex per se; but he could also see where they might actually have had nothing to do with sex per se at all, but been only childish hungerings for attention and affection, and she herself only construed them as that, as sex, later. Whatever the fact, though, she was certainly convinced now they had been sex.

It was really very interesting. In her dull, almost mechanical voice Ginnie talked on, staring at him intently. Dave was interested in spite of himself. He would listen a while, and then shut off his ears and think about it a while when he got tired of listening (but still keeping his eyes on her attentively, of course). It was like being able for the first time to go completely inside a woman's head with the bars down, because Ginnie apparently had almost no selfconscious awareness. Not only did she have no outer defense structure, but she apparently had no inner guardblock either. In that she was totally animal. God, he wished he could get Edith Barclay to talk to him like this; or even Gwen.

They interrupted Ginnie's flood of dully intoned words long enough to go to bed the second time, after which Ginnie got up immediately, almost as if she begrudged the time spent, got herself more whiskey, sat down in the chair, and staring dully at him with her reddened eyeballs, began to talk again, going right on.

She had lost her virginity at twelve—that was when she was in the fifth grade—she told him, when her stepfather had made her do it with him in the barn. Wasnt that terrible? They were very poor, you see, and lived on a crummy little farm—truck patch really—just south of town, which her stepfather had owned and did no more work on than he positively had to, and he seduced her there in that barn there, and she had liked it even then. Actually, she did not say 'seduced'; but she did not say 'raped' either; she said, again, 'made her do it with him'; and her whole point was that she had liked it even then.

Well, when she was in the seventh grade—that was five years later, and she was almost seventeen—that was when the trouble came. Her and another girl had been sneakin' off to Terre Haute and goin' out with fellows over there, and one of them given her a dose of clap. She hadnt even of known she was sick. Well, her stepfather got her a date with a friend of his (He had a job by then. Working at the Sternutol. With this man.) and she not knowing nothing about it went out with him and give it to him. Her stepfather he hadnt got it. Well, he went to the doctor and he told on her, and the doctor told on her to the judge and they got the Truant Officer and the Health Officer and that son of a bitch Sherm Ruedy come down to the school and arrested her right in school and, well, in the end they sent her and the other girl away to a State Girls' School for a year."

"What did they do with the guy?" Dave asked. He had almost fallen asleep twice.

Ginnie's prim mouth twisted up in the round face. "Nothin'. He was married and had some kids and he worked at the Sternutol. The doctor and the judge and all kept his name quiet. And course, they never did find out about my stepfather."

"Hell!" Dave said, wide awake now, thoroughly incensed. "He was the guy something should of been done about."

Ginnie nodded somberly, and a pious expression slid over her face without ever quite reaching her red eyeballs. "If it hadnt of been for him I wouldnt never have got started in none of all them things."

"Youve had it pretty rough, havent you?" he said gently.

"Well, I guess I have," Ginnie said placidly. She looked vaguely pleased. Suddenly she got up from the chair, still holding her glass of whiskey, and began to walk around the room; but instead she went straight to the typewriter on the desk.

"You ought to have somebody to look after you," Dave said sympathetically from the bed.

"Yeah," Ginnie said. "But who?"

"Well, someday youll find somebody," he said sympathetically—if vaguely.

"Is that that book youre writin'?" she said.

"Leave that alone!" he said, and jumped up off the bed. There was an unfinished page in the typewriter, and he snatched it out and put it in a folder.

"I never looked at it," Ginnie protested anxiously. "Honest I didnt."

It was obvious she was lying from her face. But—in his new humanitarian mood—Dave decided he might as well overlook it. After all, she only lied because she was scared. Actually, he didnt care if she read it or not. It was just that it was so terrible he didnt want anybody to see it. An automatic reaction.

"Its all right," he said gently. "I didnt mean to yell at you. I just dont like for people to read what I write until its done."

Ginnie peered at him cautiously with her red eyeballs. "Whats it about?" she asked curiously.

"Oh, people," Dave said vaguely. "Just people."

"Am I in it?"

"What? No. Oh, no. See, its about the war."

"I thought maybe you might want to put me in it," Ginnie said, looking at him, dully but attentively, with her red eyeballs.

That was the reason she had been telling him this detailed story of her life, then, Dave decided. The same reason probably, he realized now, why Dewey had asked him all about it. And probably the reason for 'Bama's interest, too. The power of the pen.

"This is about the war," he said, "and theres no women in it."

"Youre not mad at me, are you?" Ginnie said. But before he had a chance to answer, she had turned in that strange abrupt way she had of doing it, and put her arms—still holding the whiskey glass—around him and kissed him on the mouth.

That was the third time they went to bed together.

It was during this that Ginnie did something which startled him half to death. Staring wildly and almost blindly at the ceiling, she cried out to herself in a loud, penetrating voice: "Oh, Ginnie, Ginnie, Ginnie!"

It was not only startling, it was also both disconcerting and a little embarrassing; almost in fact (he distinctly had that feeling) as if he were not even there. He was powerless to understand it, or what she meant by it. Nobody with as little selfconscious self-insight as Ginnie could be a bona-fide narcissist, could they? He did not mention it afterwards because it would have embarrassed him to, and also he was still a little piqued. Ginnie did not mention it either, and apparently did not even know she had done it.

The rest of her life story, which did not cover nearly so much ground as the first part, but nevertheless took her a long time to tell, she continued with afterwards, still rattling along almost—at least for her—hurriedly, as though she were afraid she might not get finished before he went to sleep, and with no visible diminishment of that sudden and unexpected speed and energy she had shown at the start. After the year at the girls' school she had come home a wiser and more educated person, she said.

She had hung around town for a year or two—until her stepfather died—and then gone to Indianapolis. The war was on then, and work was easy to get in the plants. It had been very unpleasant in Parkman after she got back. That son of a bitch Sherm Ruedy—she apparently never referred to the Police Chief in any other way: That son of a bitch Sherm Ruedy had watched her all the time and apparently took great pleasure in warning her about once a week that he would pick her up if she didnt walk the chalk line.

(He knew, didnt he, she said in an aside, that that son of a bitch Sherm had been appointed Police Chief just after the war started? to keep him out of the draft? He was just over thirty then, and was a distant third or fourth cousin of the Wernzes who owned the bank. He come from down in the country around the Dark Bend River. He had served a while once as a State Patrolman, she said, but had been let out. That was how they got him in as Police Chief: said he had had police experience. Sherm had right away hired a couple of his bosom buddies he run around with, and a couple of other guys, and got everything all set up for himself. There wasnt nothing nobody could do about it.

(Up to then, Ginnie said, he had just sit on his ass and lived on that farm of his uncle's, and lived off the Wernzes. She knew his family. He never was nothin' but a bum. Dave knew all that, didnt he? she said defensively.)

Dave, who had heard substantially the same story from both 'Bama and Dewey, nodded. There was no malice in Ginnie's voice, only a sort of plaintive wistfulness at the way life seemed to go. 'Bama had also told him, grinning, how as soon as Ruedy had got in he had the city buy them all new uniforms, exactly like the Servicemen wore, except for the cap. Sam Browne belts and all. Up to then the city cops had just worn caps and a badge. 'Bama said he held inspection every morning down at the city jail.

He would of, too, Ginnie said. Would of what? he said. Sent me back, she said; if he could ever of catched me. He made life unpleasant enough as it was, that son of a bitch Sherm, and so when her stepfather died and her mother kicked her out she had went to Indianapolis.

It was plain to see she was deathly afraid of Sherm Ruedy. Dave suddenly felt sorry for her. He got himself some more whiskey, and resolutely prepared himself to listen.

In Indianapolis she had worked for a while at the Allis-Chalmers plant, she said, looking at him plaintively with her red eyeballs, and then at some other plants, and then she had quit factory work altogether and had took up singing. The town was wide open back then because of the war, and there was a lot of young soldiers from Camp Atterbury and Fort Benjamin Harrison coming in on the town with lots of money to spend. They liked being able to go out with a professional entertainer who sang in a bar. She rarely had to buy anything at all for herself, she said not without wistful pride, and she made big tips into the bargain. She sang in several different bars out on West Washington. (Dave remembered them, dingy tacky little places.) She had not sung many populars, but instead mostly hillbillies. Hillbillies was always her type of music, she never cared much for populars and classicals, and the hillbillies was what most of the soldierboys wanted to hear anyway. So she had done real well and everything was fine— until she got mixed up with that soldierboy from Camp Atterbury who was over the hill. He told her he was on furlough; but the truth was he had broke into the home of a poor old lady who worked out at the Base and who, as she had apparently told just about everyone on the Base, kept all her money at home because she didnt trust banks. Evidently, or at least that was what the papers had wrote later, the boy had had to beat her up with a loose chair leg he found on her back-porch, and very nearly killed her, before she would tell him where the money was. It come to something over a thousand dollars. The poor old lady was still in the hospital, but beginning to recover, when the police picked him up at her's, Ginnie's, little one room apartment. She never did find out how they knew he was living with her, or how they even knew he had done it. Of course, she herself hadnt known none of any of this at the time. He seemed like a nice sweet boy to her, and was always kind and gentle, and he spent money on her like water. What girl wouldnt go for a boy like that? —Naturally, later on, she found out why he spent it so: He was trying to get it all spent before they caught him. He damn near did, too. —Well, after they had got him the police had turned her loose the very next day and said she was innocent of any crimes and knowledge. But of course it had made all the papers, and that was when she decided to come home to Parkman. Her landlady had ask her to move; the boss at the bar had told her not to come back; everything was ruint. When she got to Parkman she found it had made the paper there too, and it hadnt helped her reputation none. That son of a bitch Sherm Ruedy had come around and told her he didnt think she was innocent of all crimes and knowledge, and he better not ever catch her with more money than she was supposed to have·or he would send her away again so quick it would make her head swim, and she better get herself a job right away if she wanted to stay in this town.

Well, she had went to work at the brassiere factory, which was hiring all the help it could get just then after getting part of a contract for the WACs. And she had been here ever since. For a long time that son of a bitch Sherm had tried to catch her out with somebody. She had got to running around with Mildred and Rosalie and Lois and Martha Garvey and the rest of that bunch, after she got to know them well enough to see if she *wanted* to run around with them. They were all fine girls and she liked them. Of course, sometimes they were a little . . .— And after all . . .— Of course she didnt mean to say they werent . . .—

Dave was very nearly asleep. He hadnt meant to. But the dull unchanging monotone of her voice, hurrying plaintively on and on as if battling a time limit, had hypnotized him in spite of his interest. Her voice kept on fading in and out, the words still audible as sounds, but no longer having any meanings he could grasp, and he let himself go. The next thing he knew was when his heart leaped wildly and frantically in his chest, shutting off his air for a moment. Ginnie had begun to pummel him back awake with a sort of distraught playfulness, saying she wanted him to sleep with her.

"You went to sleep when I was talkin', didnt you," she said dully. "You bad boy."

"No," he said. "No, no. I was listening."

"You bad boy!" Ginnie said dully, pressing herself against him nervously. At close range her fatigue- and liquor-reddened eyeballs looked even redder; but even the redness could not disguise the hidden apprehension and almost panicky distraction that peered out from behind them.

And so that was the fourth, and last time they went to bed.

Afterwards, both Ginnie's sanity and his honor saved, but with his head pounding as if someone had thrust it in through the shell of a tympano playing Brahms' First Symphony which he had heard at Bob French's, he rolled away by himself, desperately seeking sleep and a diminution of heartbeats. The truth was, he felt he had had all the damned sex he would ever want in the rest of his whole life and if he never saw a woman again it would be too damned soon.

Ginnie, however, appeared to be reassured and much less apprehensive. "Dont go to sleep," she said placidly. "I got lots more to tell you."

"Okay," he mumbled. "I wont."

"I might as well stay all night," she said, "its so late?"

"Sure," he said, "sure." What the hell? He couldnt very well tell her not to.

"You know, I could really fall for you," Ginnie said dully. He distinctly heard that. The last thing he heard was Ginnie's voice, still rambling on eagerly and wistfully about something or other in her life. He wished suddenly it was Gwen lying there talking like that, instead of her. Or even Edith Barclay.

In that last lone second before sleep he was suddenly seized by panic himself. Why the hell did men do it anyway? He was just as lonely as if he had stayed in all night by himself. He suddenly remembered Harriet Bowman, his youthful unrequited love, and opened his eyes. But he was mature now, and he loved Gwen French more than he had ever loved Harriet Bowman. His typewriter mocked at him shamingly from the desk—how was he ever going to work tomorrow—and desperately he bored his way down through the agitated surface into quiet.

In the morning Ginnie had gotten up and dressed herself to go to work almost before the December sun had come up enough to make it daylight. Dave peered at her horrifiedly with one eye from under the covers. She had had less than three hours sleep. He did not see how she could do it. When she looked back at him from out of that round dull face with those bulging red eyeballs, which had been bad enough last night, but were worse now, he was suddenly made to think of a police car with two big red lights burning on its fenders and wanted to laugh.

Ginnie, as she finished dressing and went about primping herself out of her tasteless, worn purse, smiled at him anxiously and plaintively, and said something about having to be to work. The Company was getting ready to build on a new addition for wraparound girdles, she said, and some of the girls stood a good chance of getting promoted to foremen. She thought she might make it. But she had to be careful about absences. And anyway, she wanted to get out before that son of a bitch Sherm Ruedy was up and about. She was sorry, she said,— looking as though she were afraid she had made him mad; and this was apparently what she had been leading up to—that she couldnt stay long enough for a little morning 'party.'

Dave merely grunted and rolled back over. Personally, he was glad she couldnt, and only wished she would shut up and go away. It had nothing to do with that traditional morning-after thing of looking with disbelief at a harridan you had last-night found attractive; it was just that he was sickened out on sex, and would be for some time he felt. And also he was tired out. He was not really as young at thirty seven as he had previously thought he was, apparently.

"Well, I want to thank you for a nice time," Ginnie said dully in a stately way. She sounded like a properly mannerly, departing weekend guest. "I had a swell time, and I enjoyed it very much," she said.

Dave made himself roll over again, and sat up a little. In fact, and instead of that morning-after-distaste thing, the main thing he felt was a strong and almost psychopathic need to convince her that that morning-after thing was what he did *not* feel. He was sure she thought he did feel it.

"Well, thats all right, Ginnie," he said. "Thats fine. I had a nice time, too."

Ginnie was dully putting on her shabby coat. "Well, I better be goin'," she said, smiling anxiously.

"Hey, wait a minute," he said still leaning on his elbow. "Did you really mean what you said last night about you could really fall for me?"

Ginnie peered back at him wide- (and red-) eyed. She appeared to be thinking. "Oh, did I say that?" she said coyly after a moment.

"Yes."

"Well, I guess I did," she said placidly and complacently.

"Well if you did," he said kindly, and feeling very kindly, "I just wanted to warn you not to. Dont get hurt."

Ginnie looked a little startled. "Well," she said, "okay. I wont."

"You see," he said, "Im in love with another woman."

"Anybody I know?" Ginnie said curiously.

"No. No, no. Its nobody from here," Dave said. "Its a woman from far, far away." Then, a little dissatisfied with this, and in order to make it sound more convincing he added in a sad whisper: "A woman I knew in Germany. Ill probably never see her again," he said.

"Well," Ginnie said, "goodby, Dave. Ill see you down at Smitty's some time?

"—As a matter of fact," she added dully, "I got a boyfriend myself Im in love with, too. It makes my life very unhappy.

"—I guess thats why I drink so much," she added with an uneasy smile.

She went with dignity to the door, and then turned back. "Im sorry for your unhappiness, Dave," she said in a queenly way, and added: "I think Ill go down the back way."

"Goodby, Ginnie," he said sadly from the bed. "Goodby."

"Goodby, Dave," she said.

Whew! he thought, was he glad that was over! and lay back down. But after she was gone a minute or two he could not resist getting up and going to the window to watch her walk dumpily down the back street. His heart suddenly jumped with sympathy for her, as he watched her, and thought about her. Partly it was because the street was damp and wet, he guessed. Partly it was because she was going to Ciro's for her breakfast. It all added in together emotionally, was all part of the same thing. It was the pattern of her life. She didnt have very much, did she? and he felt he hadnt done much for her.

She was really a nice gal, when you thought about it. Sort of sweet, and good natured, and malleable. Even if she was dumb and not very bright. And ugly as a mud fence. At least there wasnt any meanness in her.

What she really needed, he thought, was some guy to take care of her. She wasnt smart enough to take care of herself. But some dumb farmer from down in the country; or some factory worker oaf who worked at Sternutol: shed make some guy like that a damned good wife. She wasnt a whore. She didnt take money.

Actually, there was probably a good deal of undeveloped intelligence in her, if somebody would just take the time to stimulate it, the patience to teach her. And he felt sorry for her because he was sure nobody ever would.

Well, at least he always knew where he could get a decent piece now, whenever he wanted it. —Always provided, of course, that he could stand the strain!— It was a comfort to him to know this, even though he was still, as he had been earlier, thoroughly sickened out on, and tired of, sex. Because he might not always be.

Wondering if Frank knew about that new addition to the brassiere factory she had mentioned, he went back and crawled back into bed, looking despairingly at his typewriter, which grinned back at him balefully, baring all its keys.

Well, by God, he thought spitefully, he was not going to go over to Gwen French's for Christmas, anyway. Especially after they hadnt asked him. He was still deeply hurt because they hadnt asked him. No, by God; hed get hold of old 'Bama and theyd go off and get drunk together somewhere Christmas. At least he had one real friend in this town.

CHAPTER 33

In Frank's home Christmas time was always one of the nicest times of the year, or so Frank always felt. Whatever arguments or disagreements or rambunctious fights there were current in the family at the time, they always seemed to dissipate themselves aound the 21st and dissolve into thin air until after New Year's. If, on January 2nd, they all suddenly un-dissolved themselves, and reappeared with a renewed vigor and vitality born of exhaustion, disillusion and emotional letdown— this still did not change the fact that from the 21st to the 1st, inclusive, there was this sort of No-man's-land of happiness and truce. If he did not go to church much, and had not read in the Bible since childhood when he was forced to, Frank was still nevertheless—especially around Christmas time—a strong believer in the Scriptures. His creed was: Sufficient unto the day is the argument thereof.

For two weeks before, there was always much secretive spiriting in of presents, much clandestine shopping, many private trips to Terre Haute or Indianapolis, on the part of everybody. Pre-Christmas shopping-time was one of the few times Agnes ever permitted Dawn to take the Ford out of town alone. Dawn did all her shopping by herself, would suffer no suggestions or advice from anyone. Dawn, with her artistic sense of color and line which she got from Agnes, always did all her own package wrapping herself. Therefore, there were usually three or four evenings when after dinner she would demand—and get —the dining room table to wrap on; and sheaves of various colored wrapping paper and ribbon—she went in for the more striking, vivid, deep solid-color backgrounds of the more modern types—could be found strewn around her upstairs, as if she had been holding them up together inspecting for the right combinations. Agnes had used to wrap all her own packages, too; but no longer did so, what with her heavy schedule of club work and all, and had them wrapped for her in the stores' wrapping departments. Frank had always had his wrapped for him at the stores; it was more expensive, but in the end it made a much prettier package.

Usually every year, they set their tree up on the 20th. It had become a family tradition. This was Frank's job. Usually what he did was to go over to Terre Haute even earlier (around the 12th or 15th) to the park where there were always tree salesmen with their trees set up on the grass, and contract for one of the best trees before they got picked over by the rush. He knew the height, complete with tip ornament, (a molded lighted Angel), almost to the inch. He always tried to get the biggest one around for the height the living room ceiling would allow. It would be cold, and by the time he got over there from the store after work, it would be dark; the grass of the park would be damp under foot; the few strings of lights the treemen had hung to see by would be on. He would shiver in his topcoat, watching the frosty steam of his breath in the dim light, and go around with the head treeman inspecting the trees. Sometimes there would be snow, and the head treeman's plaid mackinaw sprinkled with it. They would stamp their feet on the cold grass to warm them and blow their steamy breath at each other while they argued the price and discussed the various good trees. The head treemen were never the same twice, but they were always all alike; they would always try to sell him a little less good tree for the same price, and they never succeeded. Then he would pay for the best tree, make sure they tagged it as sold, and see it was put aside somewhere so it would not get bruised or bedraggled. The heater in the Buick was always luxurious on his stone-cold feet when he got back in the car, and on the drive home a tremendous feeling of accomplishment, as if he had really accomplished something, coupled with an indescribable and undefinable joy would always rise up in him and almost bring tears to Frank's eyes: Christmas! On the 20th, he would take off at noon and go over again and bring the tree home in the pickup from the store, and set it up in the living room, and they would decorate it. Agnes would drag out from the attic the dusty cardboard boxes with the lights and ornaments in them, and he would help her carry them down, and the three of them would set to work and spend the late afternoon and early evening decorating the tree. Agnes would serve them a buffet supper to eat while they decorated, or they would go out to the Country Club for dinner afterwards, leaving the house after a last lingering look at their tree, and inspect it from out in the yard through the window before they got in the car. It was at such times that Frank would think about the son he had always wanted but that Agnes had never been able to have—not that he would have wanted him in place of Dawn! No, sir! not at all!—and toy with the idea he had never broached to her of adopting one.

Somehow, after the tree was all set up and the strings of red and blue and green lights turned on for the first time, everything would change and the Holiday Truce would come subtly into effect. It was almost as if the colored lights in some way caused this. Strung out over the tree in the darkened living room, reflecting from the masses of tinsel

icicles and casting their variegated merging colored light on the walls
and floor—all red and green and blue and yellow and amber and white
—dimly, and almost shadowless—they seemed to create the same somber
beautiful patchwork as the sun shining through the stained glass windows of a cathedral—it was the only analogy he could think of—and
seemed to guarantee in a sober stately way, he would think sentimentally, that Peace On Earth and Goodwill To Men actually did
exist in the world.

Yes, sir, by God! he might not be a *good* Christian; but by God he
was a Christian; and he wanted to do better; and he believed in God!
And if we could only turn some of these irreligious foreigners and
heathen Asiatics into decent *Christ*ians, there wouldnt be all this goddamned trouble and misery and wars all the time in the world.

Since Dawn had gotten over Santa Claus and being little, they had
ceased getting up early Christmas morning and now opened their
presents on Christmas Eve. They would start early, opening, and after
cleaning out the paper and wrappings would get each one's presents
arranged in its own display pile so they could be seen tomorrow, and
then go out to the Country Club for dinner and the annual Christmas
Eve Dance. On Christmas Day Agnes always held open house and
served eggnog and breakfast or later on sandwiches, and one of them
would always stay home to host for their friends who came around to
view the presents—bringing presents or not themselves, according to
the understanding they had made beforehand—and serve the eggnog.
Usually Frank and Dawn would go around with the presents for the
various people who worked for them such as Edith Barclay and her
grandmother, and Al and Geneve Lowe; and Agnes would stay home
with the ladle. Then Frank would relieve her, while she and Dawn
went around to their various mutual friends such as Marg Dennis and
Wally, and the Frenches' over at Israel. Then Dawn would take over
for a while while Frank and Agnes drove around to the homes of their
own friends from the Elks or Country Club—carrying presents or not,
according to the understandings they had worked out with them beforehand—and drink some of their eggnog. And always there would be a
crowd at the house, and at everybody else's house, drinking the eggnog
and viewing the presents. Usually by noon the eggnog everywhere had
given out but that made no difference as almost everybody was by then
drinking Manhattans, Old Fashioneds or whiskey and water, while
they viewed the presents.

But in spite of the Good Fellowship, and the other numerous joys
of Christmas time notwithstanding, it was always—for Frank—the buying of the presents for his family which gave him his greatest fulfillment. He liked to buy presents for anybody, but those he bought for
his family always gave him his greatest pleasure and joy. To buy for

them gave him the same tremendous, captivating chokedup happiness that he got when he went to buy the tree for the 20th—only about a hundred times stronger. He never liked or appreciated himself quite so well, or found himself quite so easy to associate with, as when he was buying presents—especially Christmas presents—for Agnes and Dawn. Like he always said, that was what made Christmas Christmas. It always made him feel wonderful to be able to *give* people things, anyway. He was noted for his presents. But where it came to his family, well— Nothing was ever too good for his family, by God, like he always said, and Christmas only came once a year.

Frank never gave them presents out of his own store. He had made this an ironbound rule. He felt it was cheap; and anyway, it would almost certainly turn out to be something they had seen there, and consequently would be disappointed in. No, sir; he bought their presents at Marshall Field or Pogue's or Famous-Barr or someplace like that; and he paid the full retail price. Always away from his own store a good deal on last minute buying trips anyway, around Christmas time, he was able to search as long and as diligently—and as far away as Chicago or Cincinnati or St Louis—to find exactly what he wanted.

This year he was getting Agnes a new electric sewing machine to replace her old electric one; one of those Miracle Wheel jobs with all the attachments that did everything, in a full size mahogany cabinet. Also, a complete set of ultra-modern living room furniture—sort of on that new ranch-style line that was getting popular, and the best that money could buy—to replace the older, out of style stuff they had got just before the war. He had arranged to have one chair packaged and Christmas-wrapped to be set by the tree, so they could see what it was, and the rest would be delivered right after the Holidays. Also,—a more personal, a trivial, gift—he had gotten her a matched set—ring, large and small bracelets, brooch and necklace—of Mexican hand-wrought silver and amethyst import that he had just happened to run onto at Marshall Field's. As his *main* gift, he was giving her a mink cape-jacket. She had been wearing her mink stole quite a long while now, and he knew she was getting a little ashamed of it. And besides, he had been able to pick this piece up wholesale in Cincinnati for less than fifteen hundred, through a business acquaintance. (He felt that, in this case, with a gift of this magnitude, it would be all right to buy wholesale, although it still went against his grain, and he didnt really like to do it. But it would have cost him twenty-five hundred retail.)

He was getting Dawn a really snazzy, complete formal evening outfit, a Dior original, complete with shoes, lingerie, purse and wrap; she would want a new outfit to wear to Senior Prom. He had wanted to get her her own car, but Agnes had vetoed this because of her age; so instead he was having a sterling silver set of keys for his own car, the Buick, made for her. His other gifts—he didnt want her to feel slighted, compared to Agnes's—were several, the main one among them being a four piece set of ladies' luggage, the best he could find in Cincinnati; going away to college as she would be, she would need it. For a trivial present he had gone over to McMillan's in Terre Haute and got her the best damned tennis racket they had in the store.

(What Frank liked to do was give both his girls a small, trivial gift or two at first and make believe that this was all. Then, when they began to look disappointed, he would—under protest, sort of—bring out the bigger gifts—he always hid them, and didnt put them under the tree—one at a time, saving the biggest one till last.)

Frank didnt care a damn about getting presents himself—although sometimes they surprised him with something he really *did* want—and he would hardly have bothered to open his own presents, if he had not known it would hurt their feelings. But to be able to buy *them* things— To *give* them things— To be able to go into the best store, and order the very best they had for them— (Price was no object. For his family.) To be able to go into a *series* of the best stores, and keep hunting till he found the very best, of what he wanted— And then to watch their faces as they opened them— The surprised delight— The spreading smile— The quick excited glances at him, as they began to realize—

Well, he thought happily, his chest expanding within him, it gave him a real pleasure, and a real sense of virtue, and a powerful strong good feeling, and a happiness and peace it was just impossible to describe to anyone who had never had it. It showed him how much he loved them.

By God, no man ever had a better family!

It was on this same buying trip to Cincinnati, on which he got Agnes's mink and Dawn's luggage, and which occurred two weeks after his breakup with Geneve Lowe, that—immediately after he had bought the gifts, and consequently feeling relieved and released—and free of responsibility—he had got on the phone—he was staying at the Netherlands-Plaza—and got hold of a call-girl, whose number was known to most of his business associates in Cincie, who had given it to him—a really exquisite creature—and taken her out for the evening, and for a week after had worried and stewed and examined himself every time he went to the bathroom. Even if she did seem clean, and all his friends in Cincie did know her and recommend her, you still couldnt be sure what you might catch from a girl like that. Even if she was beautiful. And here he was with all these lovely, perfectly beautiful presents he had bought—and Christmas only a couple of weeks away! For a week he was in a perfect paroxysm of guilt and fear and selfhate—a remorse so strong it actually seemed that by the sheer power of his thinking will he could un-happen what had happened. Of course, nothing *did* happen; he didnt catch anything. God, the funny things a man's damned imagination could make him imagine!

On an earlier buying trip to St Louis, before the breakup with Geneve Lowe, he had bought Geneve a nice present, too—it was several pieces of that one-of-a-kind, 'famous-name' costume jewelry; really expensive, exquisite stuff—and now he had it and didnt know what to do with it. He had planned to give it to Geneve when he saw her alone—he couldnt very well give it to her when he and Dawn took hers and Al's presents over Christmas morning!—but he hadnt seen her alone, except that one time, and wouldnt now, anymore. He had thought about perhaps giving it to Edith Barclay—it was a shame to waste it; and a girl like Edith who had to work and didnt have much would really appreciate it—but if he did, Dawn would be sure to notice it when they took Edith's and Jane's presents out to them Christmas morning. And if she didnt, old Jane would! Of course, he could always give it to her when they were alone up at the store; but he had felt such a thing might not look too good, might make it appear as if he had ulterior motives; or something. She might take it the wrong way. And of course he didnt want that.

And anyway, Edith had been acting funny the last week or so. She had quit joking with him, had quit calling him 'Boss', and in fact hardly ever said anything at all anymore, unless it was business or she was spoken to first, and then it was always distant and formal, always 'Mister Hirsh.' He wondered if she was about to marry that young punk Harold Alberson and quit him, and it was her guilt making her act that way? Or maybe it was what he had said to her about old Jane that time? and she had taken it the wrong way and been hurt by it? Hell, he hadnt meant anything by that!

Whatever it was, Frank was considerably distressed by it. So the present—already gift wrapped in its little box—remained locked up in his private lock section of the safe for which he had the only key.

Damn it all, life was all screwed up! he thought with angry indignation. Why couldnt a man be friendly with a girl? People ought to be able to get together. But you couldnt do anything, or even say something friendly, without being afraid of somebody taking it the wrong way. A man might have the innocentest motives in the world, by God; but that didnt make a damn bit of difference. Somebody or other would be sure to take it wrong. Just because she was a girl and you were a man.

This year on the 20th—partly, he guessed, because of his great relief and genuine gratefulness to God for not having caught something off the Cincinnati call girl—he took off from the store earlier in the day than usual to go to Terre Haute after the tree. The three of them, he and his two girls Agnes and Dawn, decorated it earlier than usual amid much fun and gaiety that deeply touched Frank's heart, and after they had it done he took them out to the Country Club for the evening, instead of just for dinner.

All the Chamber of Commerce Christmas decorations were up on the square and along Wernz Ave the mainstreet and on North and South Main, including the big tree on the courthouse lawn. All the stores around the square had their own trees and decorations up. The very air, as if getting its current from the strings of lights, seemed charged with happy excitement and anticipation of pleasure. And Christmas time seemed, as it always did, to actually brighten up the gray wet dismal December weather. Or at least make it a lot more palatable. The Holidays Truce was suddenly on, not only in his own home, but everywhere. And in the car Frank covertly looked at his family warmly, and his eyes got moist.

There had been some discussion, previous to today—the 20th—about whether to invite Wally Dennis and his mother over Christmas Eve to open presents and share their tree; and also what to do about Brother Dave.

Dawn had suggested inviting Wally and his mom—because, she said, they wouldnt be having much of a Christmas. Of course, theyd have their own tree and presents, but she knew it wouldnt be very much as hard up as they were, even counting the presents from relatives out of town. Frank, who more or less liked both Wally and Marg (—and immediately made a mental note to pick up some presents for them at the store—), pointed out that the magnitude of their own Christmas and presents, of which there was going to be a good deal, might turn out to be embarrassing for everyone when compared with the Dennises', and make the Dennises feel much worse instead of better. Dawn, who had not thought of these things, agreed that that might be true.

As for the matter of Dave, Frank had already talked to Agnes some time ago about what they ought to do about Dave, whether they should invite him for Christmas or not. Agnes, personally, had been very much against inviting him; but she did not, on the other hand, see how they could very well get out of it. It was almost mandatory that they invite him, she thought. And that was how they had left it. But then later on, Agnes had seen Gwen at a tea one afternoon, and Gwen had told her that she and Bob were having Dave over there for Christmas and Christmas weekend. They were getting him a few little things, nothing much, books and things, to put under their tree. Provided, of course, that that was all right with Agnes and Frank. Agnes had told her it was. And this afternoon, while they were fixing the tree, she had explained all this to Frank, and pointed out that since such was the case, all they needed to do now was to invite Dave since they already knew beforehand he would not be able to come. Her answer had solved that whole problem. Frank had called Dave at the taxistand to invite him for Christmas, and Dave had said he already had another invitation and couldnt come, which settled that. Dave did not say where his invitation was *to*, Frank noted slyly; but then he already knew that.

As for the Dennises, they decided to invite them over on Christmas morning for an early breakfast, and without ever saying so, intimate they were invited to stay all day if they wanted. This would be left up to Agnes' discretion to handle. But since there would be lots of people around all day, and since Marg Dennis could not afford to hold open house herself, they could be reasonably certain there wouldnt be much trouble or question about both Marg and Wally being willing to stay around all day. Especially if, as Agnes immediately planned to do, she invited Marg as her closest friend to come to her aid, and pleaded that she desperately needed her help to help her play hostess and serve and help fix the food and look after the mob that could be expected. Marg would love that.

So everything had worked itself all out after all, Frank thought fondly as he drove them out to the Country Club. As it almost always seemed to do, at Christmas time. And he couldnt have felt better.

At the Country Club the big tree was already up, and had been for two weeks, in the corner of the big high-ceilinged main room which doubled as diningroom most of the time, dancefloor at dances, and reception room at weddings. A number of the little candlelit tables were occupied for dinner, a big fire blazed in the big fireplace at the other end, and everybody was hoping to each other that it would snow and make it a white Christmas this year. A lot of other people had also just got their tree up and decided to make it a minor occasion by coming out to the Club for dinner. This was becoming more and more of a thing, a regular yearly tradition almost on the 20th, and it lent a sort of gala festive air to everything. After saying hello all around to everyone, Frank and his two girls Agnes and Dawn ate a filet mignon with frenchfries succotash and green salad. Frank had several Manhattans from the bar, and Agnes had a couple, and Dawn had some cocktail sherry from the bottle Frank kept in his bar locker especially for that.

The Cray County Country Club was quite an old one, as country clubs went in the Middlewest, and it was both an expensive and impressive one. Anyone who was anyone in Parkman belonged to it. Everybody important and worth knowing in the county was a member —even Judge Deacon, as Frank often said, who wouldnt even go there. The current Governors of both Texas and Indiana, as well as Illinois' own Governor, had been guests there on different years, and had spoken, at Sternutol Chemical's annual 'Chem Men's Dinner.' More than one famous entertainer had done a one night stand there. Situated on an irregular sixty acre tract two miles southeast of town in the band of hilly country which scientists said had been caused by the snowplowing action of the last glacier which had melted there, it possessed a ten acre patch of woods for picnics, its own water system, a rough (and tough) nine hole par 37 course, the tallest flagpole between Indianapolis and St Louis, its own small lake, free quarters for its groundskeeper, a caddy shelter, a beautiful view, and a large clubhouse perched on a rolling knoll which took full advantage of it and from which play on six of the nine holes could be watched.

Founded, and built, in 1908 when the big oil boom was resounding all through Southern Illinois and money ran like water, its clubhouse was of that massive-bungalow style then enjoying popularity and considered to be the final evolution of Country Club architecture. Truncated pyramids of square red bricks, which jutted out in alternate courses along their corners, supported square white posts which held up the massive projecting eaves that ran out over the deep verandas. The verandas ran around three full sides and had steps at both ends and in the middle, and there were many French doors, always open in the summer, but inclined to lose a little too much heat in winter, so that the heating bill was often a little high. There were still extant a number of charter members who remembered serving on committees with Mrs Dorner and Mrs Toll when they picked the plans which, as they liked to recall, were styled after the originals brought back from Japan by Frank Lloyd Wright as a souvenir for California, and which spread out from there in a rash of country clubs across the country until there were about two billion of them.

But none was better, and few were bigger—certainly not in this part of the country—than the one at Parkman. And its flagpole, a service donated—and maintained—by Sternutol Chemical, was taller than any other *ground* level flagpole in the State, if you didnt count the ones on top of buildings. And the inside was decorated in keeping with the level of the rest. Dark walnut panelling supported one moose head and several elks', together with an expensive number of big stuffed marlin, sailfish and dolphins, personal trophies donated to the Club by various members whose wives would not let them keep them at home, each with its little brass plaque beneath it; and the hardwood parquet dancefloor in the main room would still be there after the rest of the building fell, while the kitchen was a model of tile floored cabineted efficiency. It was no wonder he was proud to be a member of the House Committee, was it?

All of this—clubhouse, site and course—was a memorial and a tribute to the success of the Eastern oilmen who came in from Pennsylvania with the boom, and also to the resourcefulness, energy and dogged determination of their wives. The men furnished the money and the wives used it. The men's names were on the cornerstone. They were: Dorner. Toll. Whitehead. Greenfield. Synder.—the list was long, and all dead now—together with other, familiar names: Wernz. Chandler. Madin. Crowder. Scott. Weger. Revell. The women's names were not on the cornerstone, but they were remembered just as well; so they probably did not mind. In fact, they were evidently used to that sort of thing, Frank thought, those oldtimers' wives.

It was Lucy Dorner who was the prime mover, which was why— together with the fact that he donated the most money—her husband Al Dorner was named main founder and elected the first president. Al Dorner was the head of Dorner Petroleum. Lucy Dorner had followed her husband west from Pennsylvania, where her father had been a Full Colonel in the Civil War, and had determinedly taken up her social life in the raw village of Parkman just as if shed never left Bradford. She dominated Parkman most of the rest of her life as if it were her personal property. If she wasnt a Main Line Pennsylvanian, as Agnes said, she had been just about the next best thing. As a young married woman, Agnes had made herself available to old Lucy, who was just beginning then to lose her power to younger hands, and served her as listener, driver, party arranger, refreshment handler, tea brewer, and confidante; which was why the Hirshes had gotten as far as quickly as they had. It was one of tough old Lucy's last official acts of power: to install the Hirshes formally into the hierarchy—at the bottom, it is true—and get them accepted for membership in the Club. They were slated as comers. It might have taken them another ten years, any other way, Frank thought, looking at his wife proudly. He had used to bitch like hell when Agnes made him pay for a baby sitter during the hard times of the Depression while she squired old Lucy Dorner all around.

It had been Lucy Dorner who had found the site, and had her husband sign the check to buy it —He was not averse to it; he was making plenty. He just wouldnt have thought of it.— and then donate it, as the first step. After that, it was easy to get all the others, who did not want to be outdone, to donate too. It was Lucy Dorner, together with Mrs Toll and the other ladies, who formed the committees and hired the golf course architect and the architect for the building, and handled just about every other, minor detail. Mrs Toll, Mrs Grace Toll, was the wife of Mr Rex T. Toll, and the mistress of Lucy Dorner's husband. Mr Rex T. Toll was Al Dorner's chief assistant in Dorner Petroleum, and became the second Club president. Later on Al Dorner also made him president of the Cray County Bank, which he owned and had founded; and there he stayed until he died, of overwork, it was said. Al Dorner did not die until some time later. Agnes, who knew the whole story on all of them from her association with old Lucy Dorner, said Rex

T. Toll did not die of overwork but from eating and drinking too damn much and living too rich of a life. After Rex T. died, Mrs Grace Toll continued to live on alone in the big house on East Wernz the mainstreet, supported by investments of her money made for her by Al Dorner and, after his death, on a substantial fund he had left her; and there she still lived to this day. Two blocks away further East from the woman who had been her chief lieutenant all her life in Parkman, Lucy Dorner also had continued to live on in her own slightly bigger house, also on a substantial fund left by her husband, after he died, and when she herself died, the house had been bought by old Anton Wernz III for his son in law Paul Fredric as an investment. Mrs Grace Toll almost never came out to the Club now any more, she was over eighty, but when she did it was a great occasion. And her first words were always how she wished Lucy were here to see it, now, today, and what a wonderful thing it had become. They had always been so close. Agnes, who knew them both well, said this evidently was so, she herself had never heard any but the nicest words by either for the other, but she suspected that in their hearts it was not true.

It was strange, Frank thought looking around the long main room which doubled as diningroom, dancefloor at dances and reception room at weddings as he finished his filet mignon frenchfries succotash and green salad, really very strange, how these people had come here as they had, and had made their money and spent it, and had left, or died, and the only thing that they really left behind them was the Club here. And what the Club stood for.

The Dorners and the Tolls had had no children. Their estates reverted to Pennsylvania relatives. All their real estate holdings had been sold. Mrs Grace Toll had had one boy, which did not look like Rex T. at all people said, but it had died in childhood. Mrs Grace Toll, the only one of the four of them left now, had no relatives except one female cousin, who had come here from Pennsylvania to live with her and take care of her and made no bones of saying she would sell everything and go back when Mrs Grace Toll died. And so it was with all the others, Frank thought, all those less familiar unnative names on the Clubhouse cornerstone: all were gone. The children of those who did stay either went back to Pennsylvania or followed the oil on to Tulsa. Out of all of them only two names had stayed, and had children who stayed, but these had degenerated back into being just ordinary people, instead of like their parents. So in the end, all was gone. Everything. Nothing. Except the Club itself, and what the Club stood for.

They knew how to live, those people, Frank thought sadly, with their White Steamers and linen dusters, their big hats and veils, driving out to their Club through muddy streets of roistering drunken roustabouts. They lived like sophisticated Europeans and Easterners. Like Al

Dorner, with his wife and mistress who were such good friends; and everybody else just closed their eyes to it and accepted it like reasonable people. Yes sir, they knew how to live. And they knew how to build, too, for their kind of living. Through the long row of French doors clear across the room you could look out across the veranda and the practice green and out over number one tee and down the long hill to the green at the creek, and the chill wet December night out there, glowing in the moonlight seeping through the winter overcast, made everything inside here seem that much more wonderful and cheery. Frank could almost imagine he could see them out there, walking back and forth. What difference did it make if the heating bill was a little high? And in the summer when the doors were open it was even prettier.

Why shouldnt a man's wife and mistress be good friends? That was the way civilized people did it. Frank was sure Agnes was wrong about that: about it not being true. Why shouldnt they be good friends? Agnes was letting her personal feelings influence her ability to be objective, wasnt she?—just a little bit?

But then, he thought, today wasnt like those good old days. Everybody had to pretend to be virtuous today—at least, they did if they wanted to stay in business. In a sort of melancholy mood of communion with the dead ghosts of an earlier, freer time, Frank ate his apple pie a la mode and drank his coffee, smiling fondly at his two best girlfriends, his wife and his daughter.

The big main room was beautiful, and it was swiftly filling up with people. With the big fire in the fireplace at one end and the huge well-lighted tree at the other, small groups of people drifted from one to other, down to look at the tree, and then back up to the fire where the lounge chairs and divans made a sort of loafing room around it. People who had not come out for dinner were arriving now, to spend the evening. They wandered around carrying their drinks and sat down with someone or other they knew for a while. There was no formality. Laughter sounded from here or there, above the hum of conversation. Big Doc Cost was there, a little tight as always, lingering over a long dinner with the latest of his series of out-of-town widows. This one was from Hammond, a pretty if pillowy woman, whom Agnes studied closely and then leaned over to Frank to comment acidly upon. Only at Doc's table did no one intrude, because of not wanting to interfere with his date.

Yes sir, it was a fine Club, a really fine Club, Frank thought complacently. They done us a real favor when they built it for us. And especially around Christmas time. The Holidays spirit of partying was already in the air. This was the way human beings was meant to live, the way everybody in America ought to have a chance to live.

After their meal, Frank went out to the men's bar in the lockerroom where the poker game was, Anges headed for the other lockerroom widows at the fire, and Dawn wandered off by herself, bored.

CHAPTER 34

DAWN did not wholly share her father's enthusiasm for the Cray County Country Club. Instead, she found it hopelessly middleclass and completely bourgeois. Nothing on earth bored her so much as when her mother and a group of her friends got together to discuss their committees; and she resented deeply the bourgeois institution of a private 'men's bar' in the men's lockerroom to which females were not admitted. A group of other bored teen-agers had formed their own little party in front of the Wurlitzer jukebox, where they were dancing in the tiny cleared space in front of it which was kept clear for that reason; but from her maturity as an actress for whom even the Parkman College Drama Club was small potatoes and whose ambition—and intention—it was to be supporting herself in New York before fall, Dawn found the thought of joining them insupportably depressing although she would have died before admitting this selfaware snobbery to anyone.

Luckily, she didnt have to join them. Before he left she had wheedled some slotmachine money out of her father. She hated having to wheedle like a child. This time however filled with the portending good spirits of Christmas, he had slipped her a ten dollar bill instead of the customary five, something Dawn instinctively knew better than to tell her mother about, and had winked at her. She took the bill in to the main bar—the 'mixed bar,' she thought contemptuously—to be changed, and on a sudden impulse asked for a drink.

The harassed pro, a wiry little Red-Irishman, who had all the moneymaking concessions for the Clubhouse as well as running the Pro Shop, was helping his equally harassed bartender behind the overcrowded bar. Dawn had been taking lessons from him the last two summers. She knew his life's ambition was to get to be pro at one of those big rich clubs in LA or Hollywood where the movie money hung out, but he plainly had about resigned himself to the fact that he never would. He was also the father of eight children, which did not decrease his resignation appreciably. His wife was probably one of those women who got pregnant at the drop of a hat, Dawn thought smugly. She was standing at the corner of the bar by herself, and the sweating pro turned to her and looked at her quizzically.

"A drink?" he said mildly. "Sure. What kinda drink you want?"

"Oh— A Manhattan," Dawn said airily. "Make it out of dad's bottle."

The pro grinned patiently. "Now, Dawnie, you know I cant make you a Manhattan unless its your dad who asks me for it. How about some of that cocktail sherry he keeps for you?"

"Why not?" she said. "Im of age."

"Thats got nothing to do with it, you know that. You want me to get your dad down on my neck? Hed light on me all spraddled out," he said patiently, and grinned at her again. "Anyway, youre not of age yet anyway, Dawnie. Now are you?"

Dawn grinned, and reluctantly shook her head. "No, but I can get drinks in Terre Haute, though." —He sure knew how to handle people; especially women. But then that was his business, wasnt it?

"Not if they knew how old you are," the pro said. "And not if you were with your dad. —And this aint Terre Haute. However, Ill keep your secret." He winked. "Now, how about some of that nice cocktail sherry?"

"Oh, that crap!" Dawn said explosively. "Im sick and tired of that crap." She stared at the pro imperiously, who wrinkled up his forehead at her ruefully. "Oh, you go to hell, Les!" She laughed out loud.

The pro grinned back sympathetically, but adamantly. "Well, now, if you want to go ask your dad—"

"Hes in the 'men's bar'," Dawn said, twisting it.

"Ill get him for you."

"Give me the sherry," Dawn said. "A big glass." The pro winked acquiescence. "And dont forget my slotmachine change!" she called after him. Everybody was so damned intent on protecting the morals of the young, and it outraged her.

She carried the glass of wine he brought, and the change, over to the slotmachine alcove across the bar, catching as she did so a glimpse of the smokefilled men's bar beyond the swinging door behind the bar as the other bartender passed through it. Men! she thought, the hell with men! The big pompous windbags. Youd almost think they really ran the world, like they pretended they did, the way they strutted around.

Dawn was aware of the system of bottle racks employed at the Country Club, and she thought it was ridiculous and a patent subterfuge, typical of men. Since both Parkman and the county were partly dry, only unbroken package goods and beer were allowed to go over the bar; hard liquor could not be sold by the drink. But at the Country Club, and in all the other clubs and lodges in this sorry town, this virtuous law was gotten deftly around by having the members—mostly made up of the same civic minded people who, for the good of the community she thought contemptuously, had backed the silly law in the first place— bring their own bottles to the club. The bartenders then tagged them and filed them, and sold the members only setups to go with their liquor. In that way their dumb law was complied with: no hard liquor was sold over the bar. This could not be done, of course, in a public bar—which as she knew, was the reason for the law. But to Dawn it was a sorry comment on the lying, virtuous bourgeoisness of the Middlewest, and was almost as ridiculous as having a separate "men's bar"—or as the moral preachments of Doctor Ed Revell who had been caught out on number one green in the trees on the creek last summer with the wife of his greatest competitor in the midst of a summer dance. And Doctor Ed Revell wasnt the only one either, she thought slyly. She knew of some others.

Dawn would much rather have been out with Wally right now, eating hamburgers and drinking beer and talking, somewhere like up at West Lancaster, than in this damned bourgeois place. At least with Wally you could talk honestly. But here—with these damned bourgeois men; in their damned silly lockerroom men's bar. Probably all they talked about was sex. Wally at least was the kind of man who was sensitive to a woman, and understood her intellectual needs.

Oh, well. Three of the ten slotmachines were not in use and she set the glass of wine, which she had not really wanted at all, down on the metal stand of a dime machine and commenced putting two dollars' worth of dimes into it, coming out with eighteen left after she had run them through. As she put them through again —this time she came out with twenty eight; she hit a three grapes; God, what a satisfaction it was, to see that third one come up!— she thought about that extra five dollars and began to feel very excited as she decided to take the whole five and put it in the half dollar machine. At least, she told herself wearily, it would keep her from being totally bored. And after all, it was extra money and if she did lose it it wouldnt matter because shed still have the other five left to play on like always.

Excited, she began to put the dimes through once more; whatever she made above her original two dollars capital she would throw in with the half dollar machine money.

Two machines away from her, the young wife of State Representative Clark Hibbard, Editor & Publisher, of the *Parkman Oregonian,* was playing one of the quarter machines concentratedly, her dark eyes snapping with suppressed excitement. Betty Lee was a Springfield girl, where Clark—Ye Olde Ed., Dawn thought contemptuously—had met her his first term in office. Her mother was a socialite, her father had made lots of money in Springfield off the State, and she herself was a beautiful bleached blonde with dark brows and lashes, openly conceded to be the most beautiful woman, and the most expensively dressed, at the Club, ever since Clark brought her home from Springfield four years ago. Right now, she grasped the handle of her slotmachine as if it were some kind of a weapon dear to her and slid her quarters in nervously with her other hand as though she could barely wait for the reels to stop turning, and whenever she got a pay she looked almost as if she would jump up and down and yell and have an orgasm. Betty Lee was one of the more noted addicts at the Club and could be found here almost every evening, Dawn knew, while Clark sat behind her at the bar indulgently, or else more usually, sat in the men's bar drinking heavily, she thought disrespectfully, and talking politics and his own re-election. She studied the beautiful blonde girl—she *was* truly beautiful; you had to admit it—for a moment, a little disdainfully, and then turned back to her own machine. Betty Lee was oblivious of everything.

What an edifying, educational way to spend an evening! Dawn thought, a little embarrassed for Betty Lee, and by association, disgusted with herself. She wondered if psychologically this thing of Betty Lee's mightnt be some sort of a sexual thing? After all, theyd never had any children. And the way she held that slotmachine handle. Passionately. Maybe a slotmachine handle was a phallic symbol to her. She would have to ask Wally about it the next time they talked.

She put another dime in the machine, and got two cherries, and was totally bored with it. *She* certainly had no slotmachine fetish. Herself, shed a whole lot rather be out with Wally right now.—if it wasnt for hurting the folks. That, she thought, and also the fact that Wally hadnt even called her for the past two weeks, the bastard. Shed be damned if she, a girl, was going to call him, a man.

It was just then that Jimmy Shotridge walked up behind her, carrying a highball glass.

Dawn did not need to look, to know who it was. She could tell it was Jimmy Shotridge from the way he breathed, standing there behind her. Jimmy Shotridge was a freshman at the University of Illinois, and was the only son and heir of Parkman's oldest and most stable, if not also the biggest, real estate office. Dawn had had a number of dates with him her junior year, when he was still a senior, and had dated him a good bit the following summer before he went off to school, at the same time she was going out with Wally Dennis. That was how she knew the way he breathed; she had allowed him to neck with her some after dates—after all, it was little enough for a girl to do for a man, after he spent money on her—and she would know that breathing anywhere. Also, he used a well known cologne—a particular scent which some girls seemed to like, but which she herself detested.

Because she had let him neck with her, Jimmy Shotridge apparently had decided she was seducible, and consequently had tried to seduce her all during the previous summer. This had caused her very little trouble, however. He went about it awkwardly in a thumb-handed unconversational way which was quite easy to handle. All you had to do was tell him to stop and he did. And there was never any trouble in anticipating when one of his attempts was coming on, because he would stop laughing and talking and kidding, and become as silent as a stone and get that nervous guilty shamefaced look and begin to maneuver for position, as it were.

It was almost laughable, how easy he was both to foresee and forestall. Or it would be, except that it got so damned irritatingly boring, having to do it over and over. With Shotridge it wasnt even exciting. All she had to do was sharpen her voice, when he tried to put his hand under her coat, and say something like, "Now you stop that, Jimmy Shotridge!" and he would recoil like a man who had inadvertently placed his hand on a hot stove burner, and then shamefacedly mumble something like, "Stop what? I aint doing nothing." To this, she need only not answer him at all, and compose her face into lines of indignation, and he would collapse back under the wheel in silence, and that attempt would be over for a while. She did not often let him off that hook.

He would really be almost pathetic, if he wasnt such a goofball. He was as square as a box. If sex meant as much to him as it seemed to, why did he have to act like a guilty peasant about it? Certainly, when she did give up her virginity, Dawn thought not without a certain smugness, it was going to be to a lover who was a hell of a lot more forceful and less shamefaced than Jimmy Shotridge. Apparently they just didnt make any Rhett Butlers anymore. There wasnt anything to be ashamed of in sex. Sex was beautiful.

Undeniably, there were times when she was not above deliberately holding off longer than usual, until he almost got there, before she sharpened her voice and told him to stop. And she really shouldnt do that to him— But if he wasnt such a goofball, and didnt ask for it so much, she probably wouldnt have and would have stopped him much sooner.

Though why it should give them so much pleasure, she couldnt imagine. Sometimes it seemed to Dawn that the whole country was suffering from a breast fetish, men and women alike. She knew girls, a lot of girls, who had regular traumatic fixations, she thought pityingly, just because they had no breasts. It was all so silly.

It had been along toward the end of the summer that—after another of her sharpvoiced rebuffs—that Shotridge, after his customary avowal, instead of sitting back in silence under the wheel, had suddenly begun to pour out a stream of more or less incoherent choked words the general sense of which, she finally figured out, was that she must not think bad of him and he really did not think she was not respectable and he was in love with her and wanted her to marry him. He had been in love with her for years, in fact, he said; ever since in the eighth grade. All that time he had loved her from a distance, he said. It dawned on her finally that he was proposing to her. He was proposing! It was Dawn's first proposal, and it both flattered and chagrined her. Of course, she was a good bit younger then in knowledge, and less sophisticated, but she had always thought of a proposal as being different from this; sort of more, well, more formalized. Since then however she had had two others, and neither of them from Wally Dennis, either, and had learned —if her sharpened actress' intuition was any judge—that proposals apparently almost always came at the most unexpected and unplanned-for moment, usually moments of strong emotion of some kind or other.

At the time, she had felt that Shotridge was merely using this proposal of his as a way of getting closer to her, and she immediately had refused it unequivocally. Anyway, there was no place in the life she planned in New York for a goofball husband such as Shotridge would make. He didnt know the first damn thing about acting or literature—and didnt want to, didnt care; he wasnt even good at sports. She had left no room for doubt in her answer. Nevertheless, and in spite of this, he had brought it up again, shortly before he went off to school at Illinois, and asked her to accept his Senior Class ring and be engaged. She had refused this too, though it had flattered her considerably after the strength of her first refusal, explaining kindly that her ambitions as an actress would probably never leave her time to marry, and that that was just one of the many many things she would have to give up and forego, and told him sadly how she intended to go to New York alone and break in onto the stage, —adding the qualifier, "after I finish college," because she did not trust him enough to be sure he would not go and immediately tell her parents, who liked him, about her intention to skip college; and also because she had told nobody except Wally Dennis who understood it, and more lately her uncle, Dave.

Of course, Shotridge already knew of her ambitions. All during her junior year, and the summer in between, and now during her senior year, he had dutifully come to every play production and musical and declamation contest she was in. He would drive clear down from Champagne and back the same night now, whenever she was appearing in anything—even to that small bit routine she had in the Parkman College Review: "Scandals of '47." He really was a sweet pathetic thing, and he was desperately in love with her apparently, poor thing, if only he just wasnt such a goofball!

And now—now, here he stood, behind her, breathing that peculiar slow, heated breathing of his and exuding the sharp-soft disagreeable smell of that cologne, and carrying that damned highball glass she had seen from the corner of her eye—which his damned father must have let him have—while she who was milleniums older than he, was forced to drink this weak crappy wine which wasnt fair and irritated her. She hadnt even known he was in town. He must have skipped some classes so he could start his Christmas vacation a couple of days early.

Standing before the dime machine, she put another dime in the slot and pulled the handle as if she did not know he was there, and concentratedly watched the reels spin.

"Hello, Dawnie," Jimmy Shotridge said hesitantly.

"Hello, Shotridge," she said without taking her eyes off the two last spinning reels. "How are you?"

"Oh, Im fine," he said. "I—"

"Oh! Three oranges!" Dawn, who a moment before had been bored, cried enthusiastically and bent to scoop out her winnings. It wasnt any three grapes or three bells, she thought excitedly, but it still would put her almost two bucks ahead when added to her other pays. That would make seven, instead of five bucks, for the half dollar machine. She suddenly felt very high and very lucky, and just knew she could hit the half dollar jackpot.

"I thought you all might be out here at the Club tonight," Jimmy Shotridge said with a conversational aimlessness from behind her.

Still holding her eleven new dimes (the Country Club machines always provided an extra dime to take it off pay) Dawn turned around to him, her faced composed. "Shotridge," she said calmly, "youre bothering my playing. I cant expect to make any money if I cant concentrate. —Now, what is it?" she said patiently. "All of us out here? Of course we're all out here. We always are on the 20th; for the past three years. After we get the tree put up." She looked at him expectantly, fingering the dimes, and trying not to show how deeply irritated he had made her feel by disturbing her.

"Well, gee," Jimmy said—(he had stopped swearing in front of her since he had proposed)— "I didnt mean to upset you. I just— You know—"

Dawn waited, composed and patient, for him to go ahead and get done.

Instead, he merely looked at her wordlessly, and then shrugged tortuously, self-effacingly. "You know what I mean," he explained and stood looking at her, his eyes large and wide in his head and looking like a guiltyfaced hounddog which had wet on the floor, Dawn thought acidly. "God, but you sure look lovely tonight, Dawnie," he said hollowly, looking shamefaced as if he were afraid she might guess what he was really thinking, she thought feeling amused—as if she didnt already know.

"You really think so?" Dawn said, looking down at herself with detached objectivity. This outfit did show her off fairly well. "Its just an old outfit Ive had for years," she said. "Youve seen it a thousand times before, Shotridge."

Looking tremendously relieved, Jimmy Shotridge's face broke into a broad grin. "Maybe so," he said, "but you never looked this da—durned beautiful in it."

"No, not really," Dawn said, with expert objectivity. "Not in this old thing. But guess what daddy's getting me for Christmas? A whole brand new formal outfit; complete. With everything. And guess what, Shot-ridge: Its a Dior original!"

Jimmy Shotridge looked as though he was not just sure what he was expected to say to this. "Well, gee! Thats swell, Dawnie!" he said anxiously.

"He doesnt know I know about it," Dawn said. "But I saw the bill on his desk at home. Just accidentally, you understand," she grinned.

Jimmy stared at her anxiously, as if deaf, and then grinned. "Well, gee, Dawnie! Thats swell!" he said again. Then as if with a sudden colossal inspiration, he abruptly wiggled the highball glass in his hand. "Do you want a drink, Dawnie?"

Dawn looked at the glass dubiously as though she hadnt seen it. "What are you drinking?"

"A whiskey highball," Jimmy Shotridge said happily. "Dad had old Les the pro fix it for me. Ill get you one if you want," he offered rushing on, suddenly bubbling over with talking now, after his inspiration. "This is my third. Dad said I might as well be doing my drinking at home, because Ill sure be doing it at school anyway. Dad told old Les the pro to let me have anything I wanted," he said jerking his head back toward the bar, "fix me anything I ask for. Ill just go and tell him I want another highball. Hell fix it for me. Its easy. I know how you hate that crappy old wine."

"I like this cocktail sherry," Dawn said fiercely—so fiercely that Jimmy Shotridge looked both startled and perturbed. "I wouldnt be drinking it if I didnt," she said.

"Oh, I didnt mean to run down your wine," he said hastily. "I like it myself, Dawnie."

Dawn looked around the crowded bar. "I couldnt drink it here any-way," she said.

"I know what," Jimmy said with another stupendous burst of in-spiration. "We can take them upstairs to the billiard room. Theres no-body up there. And Ill play you a game of pool.

"How about it?"

Dawn looked at him thoughtfully. Until only recently the billiard room upstairs at the Country Club had been a strictly male province; in the old days the men had retired up there after dinner with their cigars in accurate imitation of the English, instead of carrying their cigarettes to the lockerroom men's bar and the poker tables. But in the past few years it had been made coeducational. Even so, not many of the older women (like Agnes, Dawn thought) went there anyway; for them a vague odor of disrepute, composed of what young ladies were once taught about stale cigar smoke, dirty stories and the social taint of the public poolroom, still clung to it. But the younger women—from about the age of Betty Lee Hibbard on down—had taken to it with the unconcealed delight of invaders capturing a new country. And no small part of their enjoyment Dawn knew, because she felt it herself, was that same slightly risque, vaguely sexual quality (None of them, even the youngest, would be caught dead in a *pub*lic poolroom!) which made pool-playing disreputable to the older women—like Agnes, Dawn thought. It titillated them in some exciting but safe way, and a lot of them had got to be quite good players. There were three pool tables and one billiard table up there, and they held pool parties instead of bridge parties. And Dawn had been playing at these for over a year.

"Well, what do you say?" Jimmy Shotridge said eagerly.

Dawn, who had been practicing even more since he went off to school and knew she shot a pretty mean stick, studied him speculatively. "Ill play you for a dollar a game," she said.

Jimmy Shotridge looked both surprised, and a little shocked as if he thought this perhaps might not be quite proper. "Well, now," he temporized; "maybe we hadnt ought to do that. Im pretty good, you know. I dont want to take your money."

"All right," Dawn said. "Then Ill stay down here and play the half dollar machine like I was going to do all along." She turned back to the dime machine.

"Well, now. Now. Now wait a minute," Jimmy said. "Ill play you for a dollar a game. But dont moan if I take your money."

"All right, I wont," Dawn said, turning back again and putting her dimes in her purse. "We can play straight rotation or rotation slop. I vote for rotation slop; straight rotation takes too long to play."

Jimmy Shotridge looked a little taken aback. "All right," he said. He handed her his highball glass. "Here, you hold this while I get us a couple more."

Dawn looked after him, smiling happily to herself, as he went to the bar.

"You know," he said when he came back holding two more highballs, "I just meant this for a sort of a lark, you know. Just for kicks. I thought itd be exciting for you to play pool like a man, was all. I knew youd played a little bit."

"Itll be exciting," Dawn said grimly. As a matter of fact, a strange gripping excitement was bubbling and boiling up all through her: —To beat him; if she could only beat him!

"I su'gest," Jimmy said, saying it like an Englishman, without the first g—a bit of learning he had evidently picked up in his college English course— "I su'gest you carry your wine with you; and then if anybody comes up there, you can pretend to be drinking it instead of the highball."

"Oh, to hell with the wine, Shotridge," Dawn said potently, relishing the fleeting shocked look his face got, and also the look of nervous apology which replaced it.

"Well, I— Im sorry, Dawnie," he said anxiously. "I was only tryin to help you. Look after you a little."

"Okay, Shotridge; your apology is accepted," Dawn said. "Now drop it, will you?" But she took the wine. Carrying their four glasses, they threaded their way through the press in the bar. Several adults spoke to Jimmy Shotridge, and he smiled brilliantly and spoke back. On the other side of the press he turned back and waited for her.

Dawn studied him with a sort of amazed objectivity, and a feeling of firm and competent control which was about the only real pleasure she got out of Shotridge. That, and the fact she could marry him any time she chose. Shotridge would elope with her tomorrow. Sure, he would. And he was getting to be more of a goofball every day it seemed. The only reason she had ever started dating him was because he was the handsomest boy in the senior class, and consequently was quite a conquest for a junior girl to make; especially when everybody in school knew he never did anything at all unless his mother told him to. She had had to take him away from a senior girl, had taken him right out from under her nose,—and a girl who was considered one of the sexiest girls in the whole school, at that. And now Shotridge firmly believed he had been in love with her ever since they were in grade school. There he stood, with his slim crewcut figure like a tennis player,—although he never played tennis; or any other sport. My God, she thought, where were the Rhett Butlers of today! Well, at least he made a good perennial standby when she didnt have any other dates. As she approached, he gave her a bright, brilliant, if slightly nervous, smile. Together they went out toward the foyer and the stairs.

"You know, Dawnie," Jimmy Shotridge said, "I was wondering what you were doing Christmas? I thought we might get together and make us a day of it. The folks and me'll be comin over to your house anyway in the morning, for the eggnog."

"Well, Im sorry, Shotridge, but I cant," Dawn said piously. "Weve invited Wally Dennis and his mother over, you know? They wont be having much of a Christmas, you know? And Im expected to more or less look after Wally. Ill have to spend the day with him, you know?"

"Oh; well," Jimmy said solemnly, and nodded understandingly; "of course, if you have to do that. I didnt know that. Yes, its pretty tough not to have much Christmas," he said somberly. "Of course you have to."

"Yes, thats the way it is," Dawn said piously.

"Poor old Wally," Jimmy Shotridge said in the tone of a fraternity member speaking of a brother who has fallen upon evil days. "Hes sure had a rough go of it. It was an awful tough break, his old man popping off like that like he did."

"Yes, theyve had a pretty rough time of it," Dawn said.

"It was mighty sweet of you all to think of them like that like you did."

"Yes; well, Mother and Marg Dennis have always been good friends," Dawn said, looking at him piously. She was sure Shotridge had heard about her dating Wally; he must have. But youd never know it. She looked up at him slyly. She oughtnt to make fun of him like that. My God, you could make him believe anything!

"Dawnie—" he said, turning to her and stopping suddenly. They were in the deserted corridor along which the lockerroom opened. Setting one glass on the little table under the long string of portraits of the various Club presidents, he took her gently by the elbow and moved her back against the wall, then stood in front of her resolutely and leaned his hand on the wall beside her. "Dawnie, I want to tell you something."

"Yes, Shotridge?" she said. "What is it?"

"Dawnie," he said soberly, "I dont know hardly how to start. Dawnie, its like this. I know you think Im a jerk and a goofball. I know Im not very smart. But, Dawnie, the reason I stopped swearing in front of you is because I respect you. Thats why. I want to show you how much I respect you. I think youre a wonderful girl. Im sorry for all those terrible rotten things I did before— When I tried to get you— To let me— Well, you know what I mean. I didnt know what a wonderful sweet girl you were. Now I know. Thats why I love you so, Dawnie. Desperately, madly in love with you. I think I almost worship you almost. I want to make it up to you, what I did. And how I acted to you. Make it up to you the rest of my life. And thats the reason I quit swearing in front of you. I swear in front of other people."

He stopped and straightened up still holding the one glass and stepped back and looked at her as if he expected her to have become another person because of his speech.

"Well, thanks, Shotridge," Dawn said thinly. "I appreciate your sentiments." She didnt know what else to say. She smiled at him kindly, to sort of alleviate the slenderness of her reply, out of a ballooning and slightly smug portrait of herself as an alluring women which mingled with the excited anticipation of beating him badly at pool.

Apparently this was not the answer Shotridge expected and hoped for. He stood looking at her almost uncomprehendingly for a moment, then picked up the other highball from the table and said, "Well, I just wanted you to know. I love you, you see, and I believe youd make a wonderful respectable wife-and-mother-for-my-children." He said this last hastily and his face flushed guiltily as if he had said something unmentionable.

"Well, I cant, Shotridge," Dawn said. "Theres something here inside that keeps eating at me. I have to become a great actress."

"I understand," he said somberly. "Well, shall we go play pool?"

"Yes; for a dollar a game," Dawn reminded him.

"That is right," he said somberly, and set off for the foyer carrying the two highballs. Dawn followed him, carrying one highball and the wine and thinking God what she couldnt do to that boy if she wanted to, if she was the kind of a woman who did things like that. Why, she could drive him absolutely crazy. Or drive him to suicide. It was lucky for him she wasnt that kind. As they went up the stairs, she looked back down into the big foyer to see Bob French and Gwen entering the front door and called hello to them gaily, and paused long enough hoisting one arm—the one with the wine—to be sure they saw her. Bob, thought Dawn who knew a great deal more about Bob's habits than anyone figured she did —a great deal more about a lot of people's habits than anyone figured she did, she thought slyly— Bob was obviously pretty tight and as usual when he was tight obviously on his way to the poker game in the men's bar.

CHAPTER 35

FRANK was perched astride one of the four stools at the tiny little 'men's bar' in the lockerroom watching the poker game when he himself saw Bob French.

The oldster with his closecropped white head and incongruously heavy gray mustache came striding in through the door from the corridor in that longlegged footsnapping stride of his that ate up the ground like a racehorse, grinning from ear to ear and rubbing his hands together briskly with that extraordinary energy of his. Frank had once gone out for a walk with him when he and Gwen were down at the house, on a Sunday it was, but never again. After six blocks he had been forced to retire ignominiously and quit completely, totally worn out, and lean for a while against a phone pole and rest before he could even start home.

Frank grinned. Holding a cigar in one hand and a glass of whiskey and water in the other he was sitting placidly and in silence watching the hands as they fell to the stud players at the big table in front of him and leaning back on his elbows comfortably on that minuscule bar which had caused so many arguments and verbal battles between the husbands and wives of the Cray County Country Club. Ordinarily he would have been playing, but not tonight. When he had first entered the lockerroom he had seen the thin dark saturnine face of State Representative Clark Hibbard sitting at the other poker table which was not in use talking to Harry Shotridge, young Jimmy's dad. What those two might have their heads together about over their drinks he could not know. But he had been looking for a chance to talk to Clark about his secret plans for the highway bypass. Only up to now the opportunity had never seemed to come up. —Well, he admitted, maybe he had been a little scared to make it come up; it was an important deal. But now, seeing Clark here, and feeling as good about everything and Christmas and the party as he did, had decided him, suddenly and on the spur of the moment —and with a rising excitement that was at least fifty percent anxiety and made him think of the way he used to feel (he always had to pee) before a football game or basketball game in high school— that now was as good a time as any and he would talk to him tonight and if he didnt he would be a coward.

This was a pretty important deal. Maybe the most important deal he would ever have a chance at in his life. At least it could be if it turned out right. A readymade opportunity like this, for Expansion and Development and Investment, all readymade and on virgin ground like that. It was certainly too important to keep putting off. But hell, no wonder he was a little nervous.

So, having made up his mind he had settled back. Patiently, drinking and smoking placidly, apparently unexcitable, even dull, his face reflecting a loafing indifference he did not really feel but which he knew how to make himself believe he felt, inside, so it would show right on his face, he had continued to lean back against the bar watching the game while Clark and Harry Shotridge continued to talk. When he had first entered both men had looked up and spoken to him but neither had invited him to join them. From this he immediately figured they were talking some private business deal of their own and had kept his distance and got a drink and sat down at the bar. He didnt want to talk in front of Harry anyway himself. Hell, if this thing went through he might become Harry's biggest real estate competitor overnight. —Maybe hed even have to open up his own office!— He had been waiting nearly an hour when Bob French came in.

Grinning Frank watched him approach. He had always had a big soft spot for Old Bob. Probably because he was such a character probably. Neither Bob or Gwen had ever played a hole of golf in their life as far as he knew but both belonged to the Club and kept their dues paid up. They would not be seen for months and then would suddenly appear—either one of them alone or both together—at the most unexpected unlookedfor times and spend an evening, and then maybe not be seen again for months because neither of them ever came to any of the regular parties or dances. They were both that way in everything. Unconventional. Highly unconventional.

Gwen French herself was one of the few women around Parkman or the Club that Frank had never imagined himself having sex with. This in itself had a tendency to make him feel uncomfortable around her. Of course he couldnt exactly blame her for that. But somehow or other something about Gwen gave him the impression she was a sexless woman—an idea which he disliked intensely just on pure principle—and consequently always made him a little ill at ease around her. If he didnt know her better and in spite of all her frankness about her sex life—which he knew was a fact from allusions by certain men around town—he would almost say she was some kind of a religious fanatic or something so naturally he liked Old Bob the best.

"Hello, Robert," he grinned as the older man stopped before him.

"Frank," Bob said, grinning predatorily and rubbing his hands together eagerly.

Frank had only to look at him to tell he was pretty tight. He always got a curious added glint in his eye, when he was, which Frank was powerless to describe. It wasnt a wild glint, or an angry glint, and yet there were elements of both in it. Mostly it was a sort of hungry excited glint of eagerness. Extreme eagerness. Eagerness for anything. It was a glint of—of rebellious eagerness, if you could say such a thing. And that was the only way you could ever tell if Old Bob was tight. He never staggered, he never talked fuzzy, he never looked unfocused; just that glint, and you had to know him pretty well before you could learn to tell it. He just got higher and higher and more and more excited. And the more he drank the higher and more excited he got. For an old guy his age he could put away astonishing amounts of liquor. None of them ever mentioned this or talked about it and always treated him as if he practically did not drink at all, a sort of mutual agreement all around, and Bob himself with bland cheerfulness always kept repeating how little he could drink on account of his age and his health—looking you straight in the eye as he did as if he really thought you actually believed it—all the while helping himself to another and putting away quantities which would have killed a much younger ordinary man. And yet there were long periods when Frank knew for a fact he would go without drinking anything at all. When youd have thought it would have killed him, to quit. A very strange man. Frank had seen in Israel the private place he had rigged up for himself, to read in in the summertime; he had built himself a very comfortable chair in his shop and padded it himself and rigged it with an electric light, and then suspended it on two ropes hung on pulleys in the old disused well in his yard, by which he lowered himself half way down when he wanted to read, and pulled himself back up when he was finished; it was both very quiet and very cool, he said with intent seriousness. A *very* strange man. A poet. Well if he wanted to be a poet it was his own business, he could afford it. With his wife's money added to his own inheritance he could indulge himself in just about any outlandish hobby he wanted to. And Frank for one felt it was nobody's business but his own. But he knew a lot of people who didnt feel that way.

"What are you doin' out roamin' around tonight, Bob?" he said with a grin.

Bob French looked at him, grinning with that curious almost-angry glint in his eyes and rubbing his hands together briskly. Then he turned to the poker table. "Gentlemen! Gentlemen!" he leered blandly. "I see there is a game in progress! I wonder if I might perchance sit in?"

There was a droning bass rumble of assent from the table, but nobody seemed very happy about it and Frank knew why because he had played with Bob before when he was like this.

"Arent you indulging tonight, Frank?" Bob said grinning that grin at him.

Frank shook his head. "Not tonight, Bob. Too tired. Just sittin' here watchin' and havin' a drink relaxin'." He had in fact had four drinks here. And was getting ready to have some more. How long were those two bastards going to keep on talkin'?

"Well," Bob said. His eyes had almost the bright cruel eagerness of a hunting bird, and he seemed unable to keep from grinning. Frank decided the old boy was really quite tight.

"I think," Bob grinned, "I might just have one small drink myself now you mention it. I dont think one would hurt me."

The bartender was out as he usually was working the main bar beyond the passage door and Bob went around behind the counter. Keeping up a running and yet strangely laconic chatter all the time to Frank who had swung around on his stool to face him he mixed himself a highball glass two thirds full of Martini out of his own bottles on the rack. Leaving the ice cubes in it like a highball he carried it over to the poker table.

Frank swung himself back around to watch knowing what would happen. Bob French began to win almost at once. He played crazily, in a strange unorthodox way, betting and calling swiftly without even seeming to take time to think, and keeping up an incessant pointless—though witty—chatter all the time. This disconcerted the other five players who in contrast had been playing slowly and in almost dead silence; almost immediately all of them began to play badly and too fast—some irritably, some indulgently.

Frank watched grinning, and feeling his liquor a little. He had seen Bob do it before when he was tight like this. When he was sober he played just like anybody else and played well—except he didnt play often. It had taken Frank himself some time to get onto this style of playing of Bob's when drunk. Because under all the laughing chatter and apparently wild betting Bob was calculating everything just as coldly as any poker player. The trouble was, before long his laughing witty talk and seemingly recklessness had you laughing too—and letting down. If you didnt know what he was doing—hell, even if you did

know—you found yourself starting to play loosely and too wildly.
You found yourself doing the same thing he did—making wildly large
bets or ridiculously small ones—while a kind of reckless to-hell-with-it
attitude took hold of you. —Or else even worse you got mad, and started
playing foolishly in an angry effort to beat him.

About the only way you could play against him when he was like that
—and that was about the only times you got to play with him—was to
close off your ears to him completely and try to just play your cards.
But you couldnt even do that very well because you never knew what
he was doing; you couldnt tell when he was running a bluff and when
he wasnt. At stud he would raise and re-raise on the second or third
card, and then on the fourth just suddenly drop out, laughing; he
would open without looking, and then as often as not play the whole
damned hand that way. And win. At draw he would open and then
showing his openers drop clear out without drawing; or if he didnt
open he might draw a whole new hand and raise the opener without
even looking at them.

All Frank could figure out was that he must have been a hell of a
poker player in his day. But now whenever he played—at least when
he was tight—he appeared to delight in flaunting every convention of
poker playing, breaking every rule in the book, and disrupting everybody's game. He didnt seem to care so much about winning as he did
confusing everybody else and making them lose. It was almost as if
something drove him into deliberately trying to antagonize everybody
and make them mad, while some obscure form—or mood—or something
—of—of cruelty peered out of those rebelliously eager eyes of his as—
laughing at both you and himself—he reached out and swept in your
money.

Frank couldnt understand it. Usually Bob was the kindest politest
man there was in the world. A real old school gentleman. What got
into him, to make him act that way? What *could* get into a man, what
excuse was there, that would allow him to let himself be so rude and
uncivil, even when drunk? If there was anything Frank could not
tolerate it was bad manners.

It didnt make him like Old Bob any less. Not at all. But it sure did
make him disappointed in him. —Damn it, how long were those two
guys going to *talk*?

With neither his disapproval, nor anything else including his impatience showing on his face, Frank looked around the lockerroom lazily.
Clark and Harry Shotridge were still yaking away. Outside of them—
and the poker players—there was no one else around tonight. Except
for Tony Wernz IV of course at his customary table in the corner.

The tiny little four-stool bar at which Frank sat alone was built
against the lockerroom wall at an inside corner. The two poker tables

stood before it out in the center of the main floor space surrounded on three sides by lockers. Beyond it (it maintained one stool at the end and three across the front) the wall stepped back six or seven feet against the slotmachine alcove of the main bar on the other side. Here, between the corner and more rows of floor lockers were two other tables, battered dented secondhand round oak tables with chairs around them. Taken all together this constituted the 'Men's Bar'.

—which the damned women all resented so much, he thought, and ridiculed, and made such disparaging remarks about, as if they couldnt stand it that the men had one place left to get away from them, and had been trying almost frantically for years to get in there and re-decorate—with new furniture and decent taste, they said—as if, in some way, they could only leave their mark on it somehow, where the men would have to see it and remember them, then it would no longer be dangerous to them—a dodge which so far had been forestalled but the men had better do something, spend some money on it themselves someday soon, he thought, if we want to keep—

It was at the furthermost battered table, back in the corner by the lockers, that the figure in expensive sports clothes sprawled in the cornermost chair as if aware this was the farthest point to which he could retreat, one emptied whiskey bottle and one partly full one together with a pitcher of water and ice sitting on the table before him, and so drunk that he appeared in danger of falling off the chair at any moment, Frank thought disdainfully. This was Anton Wernz IV, father of little Anton V (and also two daughters), main stockholder—or would be—in the Second National Bank, and owner—or would be, when Old Anton III finally died—of the Wernz Investment Loan and the biggest single block-holding of real estate in Parkman and the County. Young Tony IV (who was a man of about forty and a few years younger than Frank) was such an eternal perennial at the back table of the men's bar that almost nobody took any notice of him any more, unless they just happened to be looking that way like Frank was now. Of course they all spoke to him when they came in, and went over and said a few polite words to him to which he would grunt thickly in return, and a couple of them would always be ready to pick him up and put him back on his chair if he should happen to fall off which he occasionally did, but outside of that he might as well not even have been here—either for the noise he made, or the notice he received. Usually, big Paul Fredric the Second National First Vice President (now President it was, since Tony had become Chairman of the Board) would be on hand to see that he got home when Les the pro closed up; although in the past few years since Paul had been moving up in the bank this privileged duty had been relegated to one of the brightest of the younger Vice Presidents. Or if his wife was with him—she was very prominent in the women's clubs circle—she would send someone back to collect him (he was always able to walk) and get him out to the car. On the few occasions when nobody from his hierarchy was there, Les the pro who owed his job to Tony and Marie, would always see that he got home. But almost always there was someone there, either Paul or the young Vice President or Tony's wife, who was president of the local W.C.T.U. because both she and Tony were leaders of the Prohibition and Anti-Liquor Leagues in Cray County.

Frank, at the bar, enjoyed looking over at him from time to time and feeling disgusted with his drunkenness and not a little bit superior, while he drank his own drinks and waited on Clark Hibbard. Tony's eyes were considerably dulled and he stared straight ahead slackfaced at the wall beyond the other, and empty, table. The only movement he made was to pour whiskey and water into the glass with his right hand and raise it to his mouth, which opened when the glass approached it. As a matter of fact, he looked like nothing, absolutely nothing, Frank thought enjoyably, he looked dead. Even so, Frank did not make the mistake of imagining that Tony IV was so dead that he could be taken on any kind of a business or real estate deal. He knew far better.

Eventually (damn, it seemed like one hell of a long time)— while Bob French continued to laugh and sparkle and win the poker hands—Clark Hibbard and Harry Shotridge concluded their talk and got up from the table. The tall Clark slapped the shorter Harry on the back, and followed him on up toward the bar after a polite word or two to Tony Wernz.

"Hows it going, Tony old man? Having a good time, boy?" Representative Hibbard said cheerfully in his crisply enunciated editor's voice.

The numb man might as well not have heard. "Unh," he said civilly, but indifferently, without blinking his eyes or moving.

For a moment Frank felt sorry for him. It must get pretty sickening to have everybody buttering you up all the time when you knew they didnt mean a word of it, and he for one was glad he wasnt in his shoes. If that was the result of power and prestige and money, Frank was glad he was only a common little man and content to remain so, by God.

"Fine, Tony, fine; thats fine," Hibbard said cheerfully. There may have been just a hint of sardonic edge in the precise intellectual's voice. But if there was Tony Wernz IV wouldnt notice it, Frank thought contemptuously. At the bar Clark slapped Harry Shotridge on the back again.

"Aint you playin' tonight, Frank?" Harry said. "You must be off your feed."

Frank smiled tiredly and shook his head. "Not tonight, Harry. Aint feelin' competitive enough."

"Youre probly right at that. Looks like Old Bob is on one of his rampages again," Harry grinned smugly, and moved to go. "Ill see you,

Clark," he said slyly, and added, "Got to find where that damn family of mine has all got scattered to—if I want to get out of here by the time old Les closes."

Clark Hibbard nodded solemnly. "Sure will, Harry," he said. He smiled. "And well talk about that other."

Harry Shotridge nodded back wisely, like a man who is proud of knowing a great deal more than he is telling, and then slapped Frank on the back condescendingly. "See you around, Frank," he said generously, as he started for the door.

"See you, Harry," Frank said benignantly, and looked after him. He was aware of Clark Hibbard watching him speculatively from just beyond his eye range. Could Clark have tumbled to his waiting? Well, it was never a good thing to bring things out in the open too damn quick. Lazily, he swung back around on the stool and cocked his elbows up on the bar behind him. Beside him, Clark Hibbard eased himself up lithely onto the stool next to him.

Frank was aware that Clark had always rather superciliously looked down on him, and had a low opinion of his mental equipment. But this did not bother him or hurt his feelings any since Clark was that way about pretty nearly everybody. This came of him having taken a PhD in English Literature, and one in Journalism. It had already occurred to Frank that Harry Shotridge might have been having the same idea about the bypass, and that that might be what he was talking to Clark about. But he was willing to dismiss that. Harry wasnt smart enough. He said nothing and waited for Clark.

"Well, hows my number one Cray County constituent?" Clark said easily. "Everything progressing smoothly?"

"Oh, pretty good, Clark. Cant complain. Wouldnt do any good if I did."

"Now wheres that damn bartender?" Clark said. "He hasnt been in here for half an hour."

"Pretty busy out the main bar I guess," Frank said noncommittally.

"I imagine so. I guess I shall have to mix my own damned drink," Clark said easily, but he did not get up off his stool. Instead he waited for several moments, watching Frank thoughtfully, which Frank ignored.

"Some poker game," he said absently without looking at Clark. No. Harry Shotridge was always having ideas, true; but they were always little ideas, not big ones like this one.

"It certainly is," Clark said cheerfully. He sighed. "Well, I shall never get my drink sitting here," he said and got up and went around behind the empty bar and his voice came from behind Frank. "Since it appears I must make mine, I might as well make you another, too. How about it? Like one?"

Frank pretended to shake himself and stretched and yawned before he turned around on his stool. He grinned openly. "Like to fell asleep, by God. Yes. Yeah, I would. Mine's about empty."

"Bourbon and branch water, I take it?" Clark said in his thin carefully enunciated nasal.

Frank grinned at his little joke and nodded. Clark had affected that precise semi-English accent of his ever since he had come home from Yale with that PhD of his in English Literature and it always irritated Frank. —It rather made Clark Hibbard look rather somewhat of an ass you know, old thing, he thought sardonically, imitating Clark's inflections inside his head while he smiled steadily at Clark across the bar.

But you didnt want to make the mistake of thinking he *was* an ass. Any more than Tony Wernz. No. No sir. As a matter of fact, when you considered it, Clark didnt even look like a good Republican; he looked more like one of those intellectual Democrats of Roosevelt's. Lately—in the last year or so—he had grown a thin little pencil line mustache that made him look even more so. But he wasnt. His family had been good Republicans since the days of Abe Lincoln. Before they founded the *Oregonian* even. And playing ball with all those Cook County Democrats up in Springfield on all the sugar bills didnt make a good Republican a Democrat; it was just the only way he could get along. —No matter what a lot of his constituents might think if they found it out. Frank had fiddled with politics and politicians too long to still believe there was any real difference between Republicans and Democrats, even to themselves. Especially to themselves. There was only the guys in office and the guys out. The Elected, and the Unelected. One side played up to the Labor Vote in the cities and the other played up to the Farm and Small Business Vote in the country, that was all. And all this talk about philosophy was so much bunk. Of course, they couldnt let the vote know that.

The trouble was—unfortunately—Clark Hibbard was too astute and well-trained a politician to ever take sides and lose one vote when he could compromise and gain two. If anybody else *had* been talking to him about the bypass he certainly wasnt going to take Frank Hirsh's side against theirs. He would play all sides. Frank had been one of his staunchest supporters ever since he first came out but he knew Clark and the facts of politics too well to think that would make any difference.

"There you are!" Clark said cheerfully, and set the two glasses up on the bar with a flourish. From behind them he looked at Frank speculatively.

Frank yawned elaborately. "Thanks," he smiled dryly. "I really need this."

Clark smiled his own thin, ascetic smile. "And so do I. That makes two of us."

"Yeah, I see youre out doin' a little early campaignin' already." So there would be no mistake what he meant he nodded his head vaguely sideways, behind him toward the door where Harry Shotridge had gone out.

Clark looked at him keenly from behind the bar. He had extraordinarily narrow eyes anyway. Then he pulled the corner of his mouth down and shrugged deprecatingly. "You know how it is. Someone's always wanting a favor of one—when one is in. A person does what he can, and hopes he gets a vote. —But probably they go right off and vote against you," he said wryly and they both laughed.

"Yeah, I imagine it does get pretty rank sometimes," Frank said with a grin.

"—Of course, you understand, I wasnt referring to old Harry there, when I said that."

"Harry?" Frank said. "Of course not."

"I was thinking more of all the ordinary run-of-the-mill. The peasants. The Dumbjohns" (Clark had been in the Navy a year in '42 and '3, as a full Lieutenant, before he had to come home and take over his ailing father's business, the newspaper; his record of service had helped a lot with his campaigns) "who think they own you body and soul just because youre elected to office. Someone with a boy in the pen whos up for parole; someone else with a son they want to get into West Point; somebody's daughter they want to get a job for in Springfield." He paused. "They never leave one alone," he said ruefully, "never give one a moment's peace."

Frank grinned at him blandly. "You ought to retire from it all, Clark."

"By God! You have no idea how really close I am to it!"

"What about all those Washington ambitions we used to talk about?"

Clark looked accurately guiltyfaced. "Well, thats the only thing that has stopped me, you know. Up to now. And I have rather about given that up."

Frank shook his head. "You might," he said.

"Might still make it? Well, that is what I keep on telling myself," Clark said looking attractively shamefaced. Under the heavy brows in his thin face the narrow eyes flickered at Frank astutely. He came around from behind the bar and got his drink and sat down on the stool again.

"Seriously, Frank, Ive about begun to wonder if all this helping-the-people business isnt more of a drain on us politicians than the good we do," he said confidingly and leaned forward on the bar looking attractively guiltyfaced and embarrassed. "Ive about begun to think its a total waste of time, trying to help the people. The people dont really want to be helped." His face looked a little sad, a little lugubrious, a little shamefaced as if he were confessing a secret sin.

"Well, thats somethin' every man must decide for himself, I guess," Frank said piously.

"Yes—" Clark said. "Yes— Yes, I suppose thats true."

"But for myself, Ill always believe in helping people," Frank said.

"Well, you always were that kind, Frank," Clark said. He shifted his buttocks on the stool and raised one elbow off the bar and took a sip of his drink. "Old Bob," he smiled in his thin way, and took another sip without looking around. "It does look like Bob is rather on another of his poker rampages. Doesnt it?" He was still waiting for whatever it was.

Frank grinned. "Sure does," he said. The slick bastard. He had no more intention of retiring from politics than he himself had of retiring from business, he thought with a grudgingly amused admiration. His wife's father had all kinds of influence up in Springfield and with the Chicago crowd, and Clark had right away moved upstairs into a different bracket the minute he married her. Of course, he still had to get the vote in his home counties; but he was handling that all right. With that kind of backing behind him it was easy, especially since Parkman itself was the biggest town and consequently held the biggest vote potential in the three counties. Yep, Clark was moving out and away from his old smalltime buddies. "When Bob's like that, he always wins," he grinned.

"Yes, I expect he does," Clark Hibbard smiled thinly. "He does it almost entirely by psychology, you know. It always appears to me as though in some pre-calculated deliberate way he is doing it only just to prove—perhaps I should say re-affirm—to himself just exactly how dumb most people really are."

"Thats just exactly the way Ive always felt about it," Frank grinned. "Though I never worded it just like that."

"No, probably not," Clark said thinly. From a case in his inside coat pocket he pulled a pair of heavy tinted dark-horned-rimmed glasses and put them on and stared at Frank, out of enlarged eyes, with all the sudden startlingness of a black bordered card of mourning pulled from a plain envelope. "Its very strange, you know. Here we have a really celebrated man—I mean really world famous—right here in our midst. The most celebrated man we of Parkman here shall probably ever have. And how do we treat him?"

"Oh but hes not really all that famous now is he," Frank protested.

"Oh, but he is! —There, you see? You yourself cant accept that Old Bob's that famous. The trouble is, we expect him to live up to his reputation, you see—if hes going to have one. We expect him to say profound things, and be magnificently brilliant, and dress like a rich man—in short we expect him to be different from us; and here he is, very common and very ordinary, no more brilliant than ourselves, the prey of his emotions apparently just like we are, as vain and egotistical as we are, and so we cannot accept that he is famous. He doesnt *act* famous, you see. So we are forced to assume that he is not. Is not, as they say, 'what hes cracked up to be.' And yet I know Europeans and Frenchmen who consider him one of the greatest philosophical poets of this era." Clark took another fastidious little sip from his glass, adjusted his glasses with his finger, and stared down at the bar broodingly.

"Well, whether hes famous or not, I like him," Frank said, feeling bored but patient. He had been through these things of Clark's before and had been expecting one tonight. It was just about a foregone conclusion that any conversation with Clark Hibbard would always include at least one of Clark's longwinded intellectual rigamaroles before it could get down to business. It was just one of those things you had to put up with. "Bob's a very nice fellow," he said, "and Im sure everybody in Parkman feels that and likes him."

—"You know, I wanted to be a poet once," Clark said mournfully; "I was going to take the literary world by storm, and hold forth to brilliant gatherings of artists." He paused and sipped fastidiously at his drink again. "Perhaps thats why Im not one," he said broodingly.

"Yes, I know," Frank said, very carefully without sarcasm. "I remember. Youve told me about it before."

"Yes; well," Clark said. The narrow eyes behind their glasses flickered just once sideways. He straightened up a little on his stool. "Hows everything with you, Frank?"

"Hows your wife?" Frank said.

"Ah. Betty Lee? Fine. Just fine. Shes having the time of her life since she moved down here. She really loves Parkman. . . .

"Right now I expect she is out in the bar beating the slotmachines to death," Clark smiled in his thin way. "Or at least the handles of them." The narrow eyes studied Frank speculatively, questioningly. "And how are Agnes and Dawn, Frank?"

"Oh, theyre fine," Frank said with a happy smile, and looked back down at the bar and his drink. "You know, Clark, whether you retire from politics or not you can always be proud of what youve done for your home counties up there in Springfield," he said virtuously.

Beneath the still-searching eyes, Clark gave him a brilliant smile. "Well, thanks, Frank," he said. "Thanks a lot."

"Youve done an awful lot of good for us home folks up there," Frank said. "Youve helped an awful lot of people. It ought to give you a real feelin' of satisfaction."

"Well, thanks," Clark said in his thin voice. "You know, it really does, really. Except when Ive got the blues. But it helps a lot sometimes, to know some of the people who voted for you feel like that."

"Well, a lot of them do," Frank said. "And I just wanted to let you know how *I* felt." With this, and with a big warm smile, he suddenly swung himself around on his stool until he was facing the room and the poker table. After a full minute of silence he said conversationally, "Say, that was a hell of a wreck out at the highway junction the other night, wasnt it?"

The highway junction out east of town was where the new road from the bridge at Israel stopped and turned back onto the old road that still ran through Parkman west and it was a dangerous spot, and would be one until the new road was extended and the bypass built. There was at least one wreck a month out there, but this last one had been an especially bad one.

"Yes it was," Clark said, eyeing him. "Yes it certainly was." He shook his head gravely.

"I wonder how the people are makin' out?" Frank said.

"Well, one of the three that were in the one car died this afternoon but the other two are going to be all right, I understand."

"Too bad," Frank said. "Sure too bad. All the people in the other car were killed, I guess, werent they?"

"Thats right, all four of them," Clark said soberly. "Killed outright. A man, his wife and two youngsters. They were from Montana."

"The others were from Pennsylvania, werent they?" Frank said.

"Thats right."

It was Frank's turn to shake his head. "I guess we'll all heave a sigh of relief when that bypass is built," he said.

"Yes, I expect we will," Clark said solemnly.

"I hate to see people get killed like that. Senselessly. For no good reason, you know?" Frank said.

Clark nodded, his narrow eyes still watching Frank speculatively. "Yes, its bad."

There was a sort of respectful silence and the two men looked at each other wordlessly for a moment, in a sort of commingled mutual brotherhood of gravity, while at the same time each one tried to figure out what the other was thinking and what his angle was, then both took a sort of decorous little drink, a kind of unspoken toast to the dead.

"I wonder when theyll get it built?" Frank said.

"Well, it probably wont be this summer, Frank. I dont imagine. Theyre only just beginning to buy up their right of ways now. Theres been some trouble about right of way, you know; a few of the people dont want to sell."

"Youd think they would have bought up all the right of way before they started the road at Israel," Frank said.

Clark shrugged. "Sometimes they do. Sometimes they figure to do it by sections, I guess . . . They might get it graded and the roadbed laid this summer, if they work late in the fall and the weather holds off, but they wouldnt be able to pour till the next summer." He smiled encouragingly.

"As I see it," Frank said, "theres only about three places where it can go."

Clark grinned. "Thats right. There isnt much room between the railroad and the college. Less than half a mile. —Of course," he said, his face sobering solemnly, "the State doesnt like to have to go through the procedure of condemning the land and forcing people to sell, unless they absolutely have to. It just makes bad feeling for whoever is in office you know." He took another fastidious little sip of his drink, the narrow eyes probing Frank curiously from above it.

"Of course, they always could run it around to the south."

Clark looked as if he was about to shake his head. "Yes, of course they could always do that," he said noncommittally, and took another tiny sip.

"Or build one of those new modern-style overpasses over the railroad," Frank said, "and run it north of there."

"They could."

"But itd be awful expensive. Theyd have to build another one to get back south of it again then."

"Yes, it certainly would be expensive. —You have a farm out there north of the railroad, dont you, Frank?"

Frank made a face. "Just a little one. Aint worth much. I took it in on a mortgage once. Its really more of a liability than an asset," he said.

"I dont think youll have to worry about the bypass cutting your farm in two," Clark said. "—If that is worrying you," he added.

"Well, thats good," Frank said. He took a deep drag on his cigar and then a swallow of his drink. "You have any idea just where it *will* run?" he said.

He suddenly wished he knew Clark Hibbard better. He wished they had been closer friends and had run around together more. But then he had never cared for that half-assed young-intellectual crowd in town the Hibbards ran around with. They only bored him; just like he bored them. "I was just curious," he said.

Clark eyed him with those narrow eyes of his. It was impossible to tell what the bastard thought from that face of his.

"Well, the plans," Clark drawled, "—the tentative plans, you understand—were originally drawn to run it right through the center of the strip between the college and the railroad, I understand. Im interested myself in it being as it was from my district you know. The plans, of course, were all drawn long before the road itself was ever started at State Line. But of course its a very flexible program and subject to change. Especially where it concerns the bypasses, which will be breaking virgin ground where no road ever ran before." He stopped and took another tiny sip of his drink and looked at Frank, having said exactly nothing.

Frank nodded at him and waited for him to go on but he didnt. "Of course someday theyll have to make it four lane," Frank said.

"Yes, of course, naturally, someday they will," Clark said and stopped again.

"You know, its surprising how little interest there has been in this bypass in town," Frank said.

Clark made a wry face. "Well, I wouldnt say there had been no interest," he said dryly. "I remember that the Jaycees and Chamber of Commerce and Rotary and all the rest of them got together and took *me* to task for letting the State build a bypass around Parkman."

"I didnt mean that. I know a lot of the local businessmen were against it, but I was never one of them."

"I know you werent," Clark said with his thin smile.

"I think that bypass could be a fine thing for Parkman," Frank said. "What I meant was that nobody seems to have any interest in any kind of development out there after it goes through."

He had touched on one of Clark's favorite sore spots. The editor shrugged sourly. "Thats the way people are for you. Most of them have no imagination at all. And the few that do are so scared and unsure they prefer to sit back and wait and see what everybody else does first rather than trust their own judgment. The herd instinct," he said pulling his mouth down sardonically.

"Well, that bypass is goin' to keep just about all the out-of-state tourist traffic out of town," Frank said.

"Well thats just something that cant be helped," Clark said defensively. "Its just one of those things. Nobody can do anything about that. Thats State and Federal."

"Thats what I told them at the meetings. Just the same, its goin' to be a hard thing on our little town, Clark. We businessmen get an awful lot of tourist trade off of havin' that highway run through town that we wont be gettin' after the bypass goes through."

"Well, I expect business will eventually build up out there around it."

"I reckon so but its a funny thing. I aint heard a single word about anybody buildin' up a place out there, Clark. Have you?" Frank was looking at the poker game, casually. (Bob French was still winning.) He felt Clark turn his head a little and eye him even more narrowly with those narrow eyes of his.

After a moment he said, "No. No, as a matter of fact I havent, Frank. But then as I said, that is the way people are, Frank. Isnt it."

"I imagine Harry Shotridge probly has some such idea. He usually does," Frank said still watching the poker game. He raised his finger-nails and inspected them. "But if he does I aint heard anything about it."

"I havent heard anything about it either," Clark said. "If he has, he hasnt said anything to me about it."

"Well?" Frank said; "well, I'spect theyll all get around to figurin' it out eventually," he said, watching Bob French uncover a winning holdcard. "But it seems a shame to do it that way," he added.

"I dont think Im following you," Clark said narrowly.

"Well, you know. When they do finally get the idea, therell be a great big rush out there; theyll all go about it all haphazard like, competin' with each other, each one on his own; and therell be a great big bunch of jerrybuilt tourist cabins and tacky fillin' stations all clustered up and down the road which will all be just one big eyesore and wont probly get much business anyway. Thats what I mean."

Clark snorted a mildly cynical laugh. "Yes, I imagine that is just about what will happen."

"It seems a real shame for it to happen like that, dont you think?" Frank said. "Somethin' ought to be done to stop it."

Clark did not answer for a moment, while he too watched the poker game. "Well," he said narrowly, "about the only way that that could ever be possible would be for one man or one organization to own all the land and control it."

"Well, I'spose it could be done like that," Frank said. "If it could be handled that way," he said. "—If such a thing was even possible," he added.

"Well, thats the only way possible that I can see it could be accomplished," Clark said narrowly. "Dont you?"

"Well, Id never thought of that, but its a good idea," Frank said. He took another long drag on his cigar and inspected it in his hand through the trickle of smoke as he exhaled it slowly through his nose. Then he rolled himself around on his stool until he was facing the other man and laid the cigar in the ashtray. He set his drink down firmly and looked the other in the eyes.

"Im goin' to level with you, Clark," he said. "Im goin' to be honest with you. I love this town. I love the town and the people in it and everything about it. Ive lived in it all my life up to now and I expect to live in it all the rest of it. Id be willin' to do just about anything, Clark, to help this town and make it a better place. For the people who live in it now. And for their kids. And for all the future generations to come. Id be willin' to do anything in my power to keep somethin' from happening like whats goin' to happen out there along that bypass someday."

"I love Parkman just as much as you do, Frank," Clark said narrowly.

"I know you do. Well; look here. Im goin' to be honest with you," Frank said. He raised his hand. "—Now I may be stickin' my neck out a mile— And gettin' it chopped clean off— Because theres not a thing in the world to keep you from tellin' this to anybody you want. But Im willin' to take that chance."

"Im sure you can depend on my discretion, Frank," Clark Hibbard said narrowly. "If its something for the good of Parkman."

Frank nodded soberly as if he actually believed that. "Well, Ive got an idea of what to do with all that out there, Clark, when that bypass goes through. An idea that will not only be a major asset and a credit to Parkman itself but will be—could be—one of the finest most talked about things in this part of the State."

"Well, Id certainly be glad to hear about it," Clark said narrowly. "But of course if you have the slightest feeling that—"

Frank raised his hand again. "No. No, Im goin' to tell you about it, Clark. I got to tell somebody or bust.—And anyway I would have to tell you anyway. Because Im goin' to need your help, if Im goin' to be able to do half of what Id like to do out there."

"Oh?" Clark said.

Frank nodded and went on, ticking off on the fingers of his hand all the items he had been mulling over for so long. The asset it would be to the community, the potentially perfect factory sites between the railroad and the highway—but that was for the future, the big modern shopping center where the bypass junctioned with Route 1.

"What I see is something like this," he said. "A big modern ranch-style place, built in a right angle—a regular shopping center with space for eight or ten or a dozen stores, and in the center of the angle lots of parkin' space, above all plenty of parkin' space, enough for at least two hundred cars, all marked off. Like those places you see pictures of out in Hollywood.

"All tied in with a beautiful big air-conditioned motel—maybe two of them—and a fine restaurant, and right next door a movie theater. Maybe even two movie theaters, a drive-in and a regular one, each showin' different pictures in the summer. And a big ritzy filling station and garage service next to that, all of it tied in together. Just exactly like them places you see pictures of in Hollywood.

"In short, a regular autonomous community, Clark. Completely autonomous," he said; he had asked the word of Dawn a month ago, and then looked it up to be sure of how to pronounce it, "a completely autonomous community, you see?" he said. "You know what I mean, Clark? A regular village in itself. You could even call it that: *Parkman Village*. Like they do them places out in Hollywood? *Parkman Village*," he said again, savoring the sound and astounded at his own creativity. "Yes sir, thatd make a fine name. *Parkman Village*."

Frank was looking off over the heads of the poker players, talking calmly, but he could feel his own eyes and face beginning to get pinched and narrow, not with the pinched narrowness of thoughtful caution of Clark but in an effort to keep his excited enthusiasm restrained inside. He breathed deeply through his nostrils, eyes narrowed.

He could see it right now, in his mind, as clear and as complete as if it already actually existed in the flesh and excitement threatened to possess him but he carefully smothered it down and moved his eyes back down to Clark's face.

He was pleased to see a look of surprised respect there.

"You can see what an opportunity for investment it would be," he said.

"Yes. Well. It would certainly be a wonderful thing for Parkman. Its strange no one has ever thought of it before. And like you Im in favor of anything that will benefit our town. But a place such as youre talking about," Clark said, his dark eyes narrowing thoughtfully behind their tinted glasses. "That would take a great deal of money to build."

"The money's the least of my worries," Frank said. "I can get the money."

"Where?" Clark said narrowly.

Frank shrugged. "I know more than one man already who wants to invest capital in it. Out-of-towners. Thats no problem. But youre forgettin' the third thing I mentioned."

"And what is that?"

"The factories. The factories, Clark. Cant you just see it. A string of them, all along that strip between the bypass and the railroad. Why, wed have to enlarge the whole damned town, by God. Add on a couple of new subdivisions. Think of all the labor that would flock in here— and each one of them would be a potential consumer of goods. For Parkman. You know yourself how many factory sites Parkman has lost in the last four or five years, just because they wasnt places conveniently enough located."

"Yes, I can see where it would be a wonderful thing. For Parkman," Clark said narrowly. He was looking at Frank as if he had never really seen him before, and was still surprised at what he saw. "Not only Parkman. Everyone in Parkman."

"Of course it would," Frank said, "and I knew youd see it. But the trouble is you cant have a bunch of uncoordinated individuals rushin' out there to put up cheap ass filling stations in competition with each other. No, my problem isnt the money," he said blandly. "Thats all taken care of. My trouble is that to build the kind of place for Parkman that Id like to build, that I dream about buildin' for Parkman, its got to be a one man operation, with one man in charge."

"Or a board," Clark said. "A board of directors."

Frank made a face and shook his head. "You know how boards and committees are, Clark. They never get anything done. While they were talkin' about it, the mob would be makin' its rush. By the time they got through discussin', the land out there would already be bought up and the shacks would be goin' up.

"No, not a board, or a corporation. One man.—Of course," he said, "that dont mean that other people couldnt be silent partners and have a share in helpin' to create such a grand benefit and fine service for our town, have a share of the honors. You know?"

Clark was eyeing him very narrowly now, his long thin eyes almost slits. He stared at him speculatively for several moments before he answered. "In just what way could a poor politician like myself be helpful in realizing this great benefit to Parkman?" he said. "I dont see how I could be of any service. Much as I might like to."

"Well, a person who was goin' to undertake doin' a big thing like this for his town would need to know just exactly where that bypass was goin' to run. Because even to consider startin' a thing this big for the town at all, this person would have to first buy up and control enough of that land that would be along the bypass."

Clark Hibbard rubbed his fingers back and forth across the lower half of his face below his glasses. "Well, in my opinion—which of course certainly is not infallible—that bypass," he drawled, "is going to run just about exactly where it was first planned. Now I understand all those people along there have been sounded out, and only three have said theyd refuse to sell the State right-of-way. I believe that the Highway people are just waiting, hoping to get them to change their minds without causing hard feelings, but if they dont I believe theyll go ahead and condemn the land for fair price and take it.

"—All this, of course, you understand," Clark drawled, "is public knowledge; at the disposal of anyone who wants to take the trouble to ask or write to Springfield."

"Of course," Frank said.

"Well now in my opinion that is what the State will do."

"But this person would have to know for sure," Frank said. "Because this person would have to buy up that land ahead of the rush. And that would be quite an outlay of funds you know."

Clark nodded. "Yes," he said. "Of course he would. That bypass is supposed to go—I understand—just north of the college grounds. I understand it is to curve up north to miss the college and then curve back south to the old right-of-way further west."

"I had never heard where it was supposed to go," Frank said.

"Well, thats it. Of course, now, I know very little about it, you understand. I havent followed it too closely. Only a little bit. And that just because it was in my district, you know," Clark said, adjusting his glasses again with his forefinger, and proceeded to marshal an imposing number of facts.

There were it seemed only eight land owners out there whose land the bypass would cross. It was all farming country. Of these eight only three had refused to sell the State right-of-way, but none of them liked the idea because in every case except one the new road would cut across fields which would make them if not impossible very impractical for planting. The one exception was the man who owned the land adjoining the college on the north, and the road would only take a strip off of his southern boundary. The college itself of course was out and not to be considered since its several land grants were all bound by conditions, which made it very difficult if not impossible for the trustees to sell off any land. One of the three dissenters was old Lloyd Monds the livestock dealer; one of his small feeding farms (he had five or six scattered around the edge of town) was situated on the west side of Route 1 where the bypass would cross and thus he would own two of the junction corners. Old Lloyd—who was a shrewd trader and a wealthy pennypincher and owned a number of more or less tenement houses which he rented without agreeing to pay upkeep, and for which he extracted rents as if they were teeth—had nevertheless apparently failed to realize the value of the corners he would own because he had insisted that if he sold at all the State would have to buy the northernmost lot (the part which would be cut off from his barn) for a fair price, in addition to the right-of-way, and old Lloyd was not even sure he would agree to sell then.

"Well, hes only tryin' to make money off the State," Frank put in.

"Of course," Clark nodded. "But the interesting thing is that he apparently doesnt see that the road going through his place will enhance its value as much as fifteen times." He gave his thin almost noiseless laugh. "A real case of what Sir Walter Scott or Charles Dickens would call penny wise and pound foolish."

"I guess so!" Frank said.

Clark sat up straighter excitedly. "You know, old Lloyd might be a good one for you to start in on, Frank."

Frank nodded. "If I could make him think I didnt know about the bypass. You know; so he could think he was takin' me."

"Always provided of course that I knew for sure the road would go across his place out there," he added.

There was a look of real respect—not liking perhaps, Frank thought, but still respect—on Clark Hibbard's face for a moment, before his expression and his eyes narrowed in again. "Of course as I say," he said narrowly, "you understand I really know very little about it. But I do know that old Lloyd has tried to use influence to get the road moved further north away from his place. Of course he hasnt any."

Frank could not resist shaking his head incredulously.

Clark eyed him narrowly. "Ill tell you what Ill do, Frank," he said finally. "The next time Im up in Springfield Ill look into it for you. Im sure I can find out definitely. And since after all it is public knowledge, in the public domain, theres no reason," he said narrowly, "why I shouldnt find out for you. Is there?"

"Of course not," Frank said. "And especially when it might turn out to be such a real benefit for Parkman. I was sure youd be willin' to help me out. But then I guess thats why we elect people like you to serve us. We know theyll help us when we need it."

"You know, Frank, if you start trying to buy up all that land out there, youre almost certain to run into trouble? Have you thought of that? About the second time you approach some one of those people wanting to buy their land, a lot of folks are going to start wondering and begin looking for your reasons."

"Yes, Ive thought of that," Frank said solemnly. He picked up his cold cigar and knocked the ash off it thoughtfully and then put it back down and looked up at Clark. "I thought maybe you might want to buy up some of that land out there yourself, Clark. I could buy some, and you could buy some."

"Oh no," Clark said at once and shook his head. "No. No, that wouldnt do at all. Not even for as beneficial a thing for Parkman as this may well turn out to be. People are always quick to suspect ulterior motives in a politician. Even when there are none. They would immediately suspect me of trying to make money off the project even when I wasnt."

"I guess thats true," Frank said suavely. "I would never of thought of that. Well, maybe we could—"

"However," Clark said, "I do know a man in Springfield who might handle it for you. This man would be willing as a favor to me to buy up what you didnt buy and then resell it to you. To us."

"But could you trust him?"

"Absolutely. Absolutely trustworthy. I can personally recommend him. This chap has a sort of loosely hung organization which includes men from just about every state in the union. He could send men in here from anywhere, if we wanted them. And if we wanted them to look and act like farmers, they would. Hes a friend of Betty Lee's father."

Here Frank nodded.

"I suggest we leave it like this, Frank: The next time Im up in Springfield, which will be in a few weeks, you can come up for a day or two as my guest. We will meet him and the three of us will get together on it, how about that? Because Im sure some way of corporate structure could be worked out without *anyone's* name having to appear on it if it wasnt wanted."

"All right then," Frank said. "Thats fine." He stubbed out the relighted cigar. "Because I really honestly think, Clark, that itd be a shame to have such a project as this that could do so much good for our town fall through, just because a bunch of greedy bastards without any organization all rushed out there to try and capitalize on it."

"Absolutely true," Clark said. "They could very easily make the whole community a terrible eyesore, give the whole town a black eye, so that *no* tourists would want to stop here. By the way, Frank, there is something else—which you may or may not know of, having had no experience with it—but there is a State law in Illinois to the effect that along a new stretch of highway such as our bypass here in Parkman will be, no new road entrances may be made. Only those roads which are already in existence may be used as entrances to the highway. Did you know that?"

"No," Frank said. "No, I sure didnt know that."

"This was done, of course, to prevent congestion, a rash of new buildings each with its own entrance to the freeway which would be a serious traffic hazard. And a very good law it is too, I think." Clark took a delicate little sip of his drink.

Frank nodded, thoughtfully. "Yes; yes it is," he said. "No, I sure didnt know that. But I see what you mean.

"If a person wanted a chance to do a nice thing like this for his community—like me, say; or you," he added—"if this person owned the land adjoinin' all the entrances to the freeway, he wouldnt need to worry about ownin' the rest of the land. Not really."

"Exactly," Clark Hibbard said.

"Well!" Frank said. "Well now I think thats a damn fine law. As I remember—if Im right—theres only three entrances to that bypass— provided it runs between the railroad and the college—and that includes the Route 1 Junction."

"I believe thats right," Clark said succinctly. He took another tiny sip of his drink—which was not that first drink, anymore, which he had mixed for them himself such a long time and one business deal ago, nor was it the second either, or even the third, any more than Frank's was. "By the way, Frank, have you decided on a college yet for Dawnie?"

"Western Reserve. She wants to be an actress," Frank said.

"Excellent school," Clark said. "Excellent choice."

"Youll let me know about comin' up to Springfield then?"

"I certainly will," Clark nodded. He took the drink which he had been sipping and tossed it all off. "Im always glad to help out any of my constituents when they need it—and if I can be of service," he said.

"—and especially when its something like this that will be such a real asset to the community," Frank said.

"Of course," Clark said.

Frank finished off his own drink. "Well, Parkman is goin' to owe you a real debt of gratitude for this someday, Clark. And I just want you to know it. Well," he said, "I guess I better get goin' along."

"Whats your rush? Stick around a while and join me in another drink," Clark said, suddenly expansive, but without real conviction.

"No— No, Id like to but I better not," Frank said responsibly. "I got to hunt up my family and find out where they are if I want to get out of here by the time old Les closes." He laughed heartily.

"Perhaps so. Yes, perhaps so. But I know where my family is," Clark said with his thin, intellectual's smile. "Betty Lee is always quite safe—and always in the same place—as long as she has money on her. And," he smiled blandly, "if she doesnt have, I always hear about it soon enough. Well, Ill see you."

At the door Frank turned to look back. Clark had already gone back around the bar to mix himself another drink, Bob French and the poker players were still huddled at their table, and Anton Wernz IV still sat like a stone in the corner. As Frank watched, he raised his right arm with his glass in it and as the glass approached his face his mouth opened. Frank grinned over them all and drew in a deep impulsive breath, in through his nose and deep down into the bottom of his lungs. Someday. Someday. This was going to be a day to remember, someday. He went out.

He was suddenly very tired. He hadnt done anything to be tired. All he had done was sit at the bar and talk. And drink. But he was still tired, bone-tired, exhausted. Well, who the hell cared? Also he was beginning to feel all those drinks. Not much. Just a little. That kind of waveriness inside, which did not quite reach the point of waveriness outside. And that tendency on your face to break into a silly grin. Well, who cared? He didnt. He liked it. He liked it, and he was going home and get drunker, really drunk. To celebrate.

In the corridor, where the pictures of all the presidents hung—hell he was liable to have his own picture up there someday now—thinking about Clark's last words about his wife that were still in his head, he looked around the corner into the still-crowded main bar and across it to the slotmachine alcove. Betty Lee was still there, still playing, cheeks flushed, eyes looking like they were in a trance. He didnt know what their trouble at home was, but whatever their situation Betty Lee wasnt happy with it. Any woman who played slotmachines like that was desperate and love-hungry and ready for some other man—whether she knew it or not—to step in and just kid her along a little bit and take her over. He would like to have a shot at it himself. But then, he was too old. She was quite a few years younger than Clark even. And he was five or six years older than Clark. Anyway, he couldnt afford to take the chance even if he had it. Not now since he was dealing with Clark. With one more long vacuum-cleaner-suction look, that he could feel the strength of in his eyes himself and that seemed by its own very force would actually suck the clothes off of her body for him to see—just to see! he shrugged it off of him and went to look for his wife and daughter. This deal was worth more than any woman in the world. And, in fact, he could already see it in his mind, as if it were already built and standing there, displacing air. The big angled ranch-style all done in brown and yellow out of concrete block and the blacktop parking lot all marked off in yellow, and over all of it the big cornice out of red brick spelling out HIRSH BLOCK out of yellow brick laid into it. But maybe HIRSH BLDG would be better? But no, it was a block wasnt it? Just like all the ones up town around the square. HIRSH BLOCK. And people would see it, and read it, and every time they did think of Frank Hirsh. Frank Hirsh, the man who built it. For a hundred years, maybe for two hundred years. By God it wasnt every man who would put himself out to this extent just to help his community.

It was funny, but he really did feel that he really had seen Edith Barclay naked, that time in the office, and not just imagined it. And he was convinced that should he ever actually see her nude—which, of course, he never would—he would find everything exactly as he had seen it first—he could not help calling it *first*—there in the office.

For a moment, on his way down the corridor past all the pictures of the club presidents, he thought with a coldwater shock of the money, and it shook him. That was his next problem. He had told Clark he already had it, or at least had it lined up. Well, he would get it. Clark himself would want to put up some, he was sure. As much as said so. And maybe that man of his in Springfield would want to put up some. He was sure he could count on Fred Benson in Indianapolis for some more. The rest he would get himself, if he had to hock everything he owned in the world. Everything. But it would have to be drawn up for him to run it. He would have to have sole control. He was sure he could trust old Clark. But he was not going to take any chances anyway. He was going to start work on old Lloyd Monds right away just in case. With old Lloyd's two corners in his own name he would have it by God, he thought, yes sir, and even the thought of having to go home could not puncture the fantastic sense of well-being that filled him and swelled out his lungs until they stretched his ribs and made them ache.

In the main lounge before the fire Agnes and Dawn were sitting talking to Gwen French and young Jimmy Shotridge Harry's boy was perched adoringly on the arm of Dawn's chair.

"Of course you could write; anybody can write," Gwen French was saying to Dawn in her peculiarly feverish way. "Always provided of course that you wanted to bad enough to work hard at it, and were willing to give up all the things a person has to give up."

"Im *sure* I could," Dawn said, her eyes bright, and apparently pleased with the answer she had gotten. "I think I have the qualities." She shrugged and stretched out her arms luxuriously. "Im just not sure that thats what I would want to do."

"Dawnie could do anything she made up her mind to," Jimmy Shotridge said fervently, looking at her worshipfully. Dawn gave him a warm smile.

Frank of course had no way of knowing that his daughter had

just won eighteen dollars off of Jimmy Shotridge playing rotation-slop upstairs in the billiard room. If he had he would have been distressed at her unladylikeness.

As it was, he was only thinking of what a fine young chap young Jimmy was—too good a son for Harry Shotridge that was for sure—as he approached them. He would like to have a son like that himself, in addition to Dawnie. —Well, maybe if this thing went through like it looked like it would and should, they would adopt a boy.

Then, as he came up to them, out of the corner of his eye he saw, just accidentally, far down at the other end sitting together at a table with some other young couple, Al Lowe and Geneve. His high spirits were strong enough—Thank God! he thought—to weather it, but for a moment he had a terrific twinge of pain in his belly. Carefully not looking or even glancing with his eyeballs in that direction and trying to look as though he had not seen them, because he knew Agnes would be watching him, he marched on up to his wife's chair and stood beside her and pretended to listen.

Gwen French was smiling back at Dawn. "As a matter of fact, just about anybody can write, honey. Without even working very hard at it. They dont even have to be very smart. Sometimes I think it may even be a hindrance. Look at all our writers today. How many are there? How many books? Thousands every year." She turned her head and grinned impishly at Agnes. "And Im not excepting Kenneth Roberts and Frank Yerby, either."

"Now you just lay off me," Agnes smiled. "Ive got your—darned list." She had obviously been going to say damned, but changed it. Dawn looked irritated. "Ive even read some of them."

"Oh, no!" Dawn burst in. "Oh, no! I mean really serious, really—philosophical writers. Who are trying to understand life. Like Wally Dennis is trying to be. A real artist."

"Well; there you have an entirely different matter," Gwen said quietly. "Entirely different. How many of those have we? Four, or five at the most. Perhaps two or three young ones. And of all of them, how many will wind up in the end as great? Perhaps one. Maybe two. Perhaps none. —And there is not one single woman in amongst them. Right now we have only one who has even a chance of making it: Faulkner. And we havent heard anything from him for almost eight years." She smiled. "Youre talking now about a profession that has a very, very high mortality rate.

"Trying to find the truth is hard enough, Dawnie," she smiled; "but finding it; and then having to admit to yourself what it is; thats even harder."

"Oh, but Im sure I could write!" Dawn said, her eyes bright. "It would be a tremendous sacrifice! But I could do it! For you cant live and work too as Wally says." She looked at Gwen. "He got that from you. But I could do it too." Then she stretched out her arms, fingers spread, and bent back her head. "But after all, acting is my first love. Oh, I feel—I feel as if I was making love to everybody in the world when I get up there on that stage. I feel as if every person in the audience is my personal lover!"

"Dawn!" Agnes said, scandalized, and then remembered where she was and smiled.

Gwen French turned to look at her, her face impassive. Then she looked back at Dawn.

"But its true, mother!" Dawn cried. "Its true! And I can be a great actress." She looked up at Jimmy Shotridge tremulously.

"She can!" Jimmy said inarticulately in a choked voice, looking at her with awe. "She can! Surely you can see that, Mrs Hirsh! Dont you think so, Miss French?"

Dawn smiled at him.

"I expect she can," Gwen smiled quietly, and Dawn turned to smile at her. But something apparently had made her lose interest in the conversation and she said no more, and without her leadership it languished, and then turned to other things as if everybody were embarrassed.

Frank had heard very little of any of it. He wasnt interested in art or writing anyway, and he was very much concerned with making his wife think he had not seen Geneve Lowe. To this end, he stood beside his wife's chair with his hand resting on its shoulder like in one of those old fashioned marriage portraits and carefully kept his rebellious eyeballs from rolling themselves down toward the other end as they wanted to and smilingly pretended to listen, and actually hearing a a random phrase now and then, while his belly muscles twinged and cramped with the pain of it.

He wanted his mistress back! There she sat, down at the other end of the room, decked out in her Vogue magazine clothes, and all he had to do was turn and walk down there—and he couldnt. Because his wife was here, and because her husband was here, and because she herself had coldly and remorselessly informed him she was no longer available to him. So there was that body, that woman's body, which he knew so well, and had seen so often, and availed himself of so many times, withheld from him. Withheld from him and encased in those clothes —those flimsy clothes—which as far as it mattered to him might as well have been locked steel or sealed concrete or bars, and he thought he was not going to be able to stand it.

But then, standing there clutching the shoulder of his wife's chair, quite suddenly and for no visible logical reason, something happened to him that could only be described as electrifying. His exceedingly high spirits over the forthcoming deal (which he still could hardly contain), and his pleased selfsatisfaction at it, together with the pain in his belly at seeing Geneve fully clothed, apparently had mingled and combined and fused together and shortcircuited, providing him with a sort of arc-lighted revelation of deep perception. He suddenly had the answer—without even having asked the question—to something that had been bothering him for weeks. Quite suddenly and for no reason he had just realized what it was that had made Edith Barclay act like she had been acting. It was because she was in love with him! He knew it. He knew it as clearly and surely as he knew his own name Frank Hirsh. Edith Barclay had fallen in love with *him!* She was not in love with that punk Alberson at all. It was such an intriguing idea that it made him forget everything, including Geneve.

Carefully hiding his excitement, which Agnes would be he knew sure to sense, he stood there mulling it over in his head with a sort of visceral amazement, until they were ready to go and Agnes got up.

"Arent you going to say hello to Al and Geneve?" she said after he had helped her on with her coat.

"What?" Frank said, "Who? Where?"

"Al and Geneve Lowe. Theyre sitting right down there," Agnes said sweetly. "Surely youre not going to leave without even speaking to them. Al works for you!"

"Oh," Frank said, looking all around. "Oh. No. No, of course not. I didnt see them down there."

"Well?" Agnes said, looking at him expectantly. "Go speak to them."

"Ill be right back," he said hollowly and walked down the long room seething furiously and hoping he was not blushing, aware of thousands of eyes watching although there were no more than fifteen pair of them present at most, but all of these *were* watching him. It was a very mean thing for her to do to him. He slapped Al on the back and spoke to both of them heartily and explained he had not seen them when he came back from the men's bar.

Then he made the long trek back up to the door. He had been caught completely off guard. "There wasnt any reason why I should have to say hello to them," he said gruffly. "They dont expect it."

Agnes infuriatingly said nothing, absolutely nothing, nothing at all, and they said goodby to Gwen and Jimmy. Jimmy, who thumb-handedly helped Dawn on with her coat and looked lingeringly after her. And Gwen, who seemed so quiet and calmly collected that none of them least of all Dawn had any suspicion of the bull-voiced temper tantrum and fit of rage she was going to throw as soon as she got safely home.

He had three reasons to get drunk, now, when he got home. The success (at least, of the first stage) of the bypass business deal; the new realization (which he had, so far, not contemplated nearly enough) that Edith Barclay was in love with *him;* and the fact that Agnes had deliberately embarrassed him publicly at the Club. He tried hopefully to make Agnes feel bad and think it was because of what she had done that he was getting drunk, and afterwards was able to feel that he had probably succeeded, though of course he could not be sure. Not with Agnes. With Agnes you never were sure. About nothin'.

He sat in the darkened front room after the two women—two *females,* he thought irascibly—had gone on to bed, and drank and thought about Edith Barclay being in love with *him.* It was, to be honest, an almost ungraspable idea. That anybody, anywhere, could be in love with *him.* Especially a goodlooking *young* woman like Edith. It was a pity she worked for him. But then that was his usual luck. Ever since he had been taken into the bank by Judge Deacon and voted onto the Board he had inflexibly made up his mind to a rule that he would never as became a successful and rising businessman sleep with any of his hired help again, and it was a rule he felt he could not break without damaging his integrity. Successful businessmen didnt *have* to do that. But he had not made any rule about thinking about it, had he? No, by God he hadnt. So he sat and got drunk, and thought about it.

He wanted something. He was hungry for something. Something definite. Very definite. But he did not know what it was and so he could not define it. It wasnt liquor. It wasnt Agnes. It wasnt eating or being eaten like Geneve. It wasnt even sex at all. It wasnt even the big bypass business deal, and he had a vague premonition that when he had that too it too would not satisfy. What he wanted, he guessed drunkenly, was some way of destroying and hurting himself that would not destroy or hurt him. Now how were you going to find that? It was funny, wasnt it? how the only times we could really be honest with ourselves was when we were drunk? No wonder the distilleries made money.

For no reason he suddenly thought of the time the Old Man had almost caught him playing with himself. He had been down the basement taking a shower and it was the soap that had done it and the Old Man had come down the steps to get something. The shower had been right at the foot of the stairs, and he had run back in under away from them. The Old Man had come on half way down and seen him and then turned around and gone back up without a word, but he had seen a curious glint in the Old Man's eye. A glint of what he could only call interested knowledge—interested knowledge and amusement. He had known. He had known and Frank had known he had known, and while at the time it scared and frightened him later on it had made him excited whenever he thought about it. Was that what he wanted? To be caught maybe? But he didnt want to be *caught.* He got up and went and got another drink and came back and drank it and went to sleep in the chair.

It was while he was doing this that Gwen French was throwing her tirade in Israel which, of course, he knew nothing about. Nor cared.

This time he had carefully kept himself from drinking so much that he would get the gastritis like he had that time in Chicago which had scared him so. But he nevertheless had a terrible, a ghastly hangover. He did not go down to the store until nearly noon. And so it was late afternoon before he weakly called the taxistand to find out how things were going and learned from Albie Shipe that Dave was gone. Dave's car was still out in front of the hotel, locked up, but Dave himself was apparently gone and had been gone since yesterday. Nobody, either there or at the hotel, knew where.

The only thing Frank knew to do was to call Gwen French in Israel after she got home from school and see if he was there, but Gwen —as cool and collected and calm and cold as she ever was—told him she had no idea where he had gone either. As he hung up, Frank could not help thinking that he had never seen *any*body who was such a cold fish *all* the time.

CHAPTER 36

SHE had not even waited until she had her coat off, but had let it loose the moment she was inside and had slammed the door. She couldnt have waited longer. If she had, she knew she couldnt be responsible. She had held it in all the way home in the car, which she had driven. (He refused to drive any time, except when circumstances absolutely demanded it.) And before that she had held it in for a full half hour after they had gone—while she waited in that damned lounge amongst that crowd of damned fools, for him to wear out his damned poker mania. To have held it any longer and she would not be responsible.

"The world is full of fools!" she demanded of his retreating back. "Did you know that? Did you? Simple, idiotic, ignorant, God damned fools! And does anyone *admit* it? No! Human beings! Fine, decent human beings! Pure ignor*a*muses! *A*nimals! *A*nimals, I tell you! Collections of arteries walking around with names attached to them! And thats all! And proud of it! *Thou*sands of them! *Mill*ions of them! And *proud* of it! Smugly going around calling each other human beings to their faces as if that were—not only a title of respect—but something significant and important in itself! With all the brains and rational intelligence of a frightened rattlesnake coiled to strike blindly in selfdefense! *Dignity!*" she cried, struggling to get her arms out of the sleeves of her coat, "*Dignity!* It *hurts* me! I cant stand it! Millions and billions of them! Simple—idiotic—ignorant—vain-foolish *clowns!* How do you account for that? How do you take account of that? in your philosophy? Answer me!"

Bob, who was no longer drunk at all and had not been since he had come out of the men's bar and the poker game, in spite of all the liquor she knew he had consumed in the last eighteen hours, calmly went on taking off his coat and then removed the rakish crush hat with its brim all down along one side and leaving them on the table went to stir up the big bed of coals in the fireplace and put on another log and from there, kneeling, looked up at her with those eyes she always felt knew so much, knew everything, but did not smile at her and for that she was grateful.

"Answer!" she demanded, finally getting her arms out of the coat and throwing it on the floor at her feet. "Answer me! How do you take that in account?"

"I accept it."

"You accept it!"

"Except when on occasion it gets too much to digest," he said, stirring the coals with the poker, "and then I act like youre acting now. Or else get drunk."

"You accept it!" she sneered. "*You* accept it! Im supposed to teach them! Im supposed to help them—*make* them—learn things! They dont *want* to learn things! It *hurts* them! The rational processes and mental sensitivity of a *frog!* They want *not* to learn things! How do you think I feel when I stand beside the sausage grinder and watch the big fat sausages rolling out of it day by day? All larded over and held together with the grease of their own fat smug minds and vanity? Fully accredited, vitally Christian—*sausages!* Meat and drink for Norman Vincent Peale! And *I* do it! Why do you think I do it?"

Bob had sat down in the big chair and, propping his elbows on the arms, was patting the tips of spatulate fingers together lightly while he gazed at her kindly over them. He rubbed his two index fingers against his lower lip thoughtfully.

"Answer me! Why? Why *should* I do it?"

"But thats elementary, isnt it?" he smiled sadly. "You do it because its easier and less frightening than doing something else."

"Something else!" she leered. "What else? Once in a thousand times, once in a thousand thousand, one comes along with that peculiar mental and emotional makeup that makes it possible to think, and leavened by that incorrigible, detestable, all-engulfing vanity which is so great it makes it more painful to be like everybody else than it does to go ahead and *think,* and then you have one with talent. Which you try to nurture. And so you watch while the vanity—that same vanity which in the beginning was the reason for the talent—balloons and corrodes and eats away until it destroys that which at the start it was the reason for the existence of. And once in a billion billion times it does not happen."

"It must have been a bad evening," Bob said kindly.

Momentarily Gwen put her face in her hands. "Oh—it doesnt matter," she said.

"Dawn Hirsh?" Bob said gently.

"Partly," she said. "Partly. Ive watched her for years you know."

"Yes," he said. "Well, women have a hard time you know. With sex, and all. Much harder than men do. It isnt important to men."

"I wonder," Gwen said.

"I mean not major," Bob said. He pressed his fingertips together again thoughtfully. "I only know three things, dear Gwen. One, we learn through pain—and *only* through pain. Therefore, two, to avoid pain is to embrace ignorance. Therefore, three, pain is not bad not Evil. Also, what is pain to one is not pain to another. *Dont* try to take away people's pain. Allow each one his own particular pain, even if its not your pain. What we learn sooner in one life, we wont have to learn later in another. But weve talked about all this. . . . I think its time we went to bed now," he said kindly, "dont you?"

"Yes, of course," she said. She bent and picked up her coat.

Bob came over and took it and then put his arms around her. She was a tall woman, but he was a tall man, and she leaned her head forward onto his shoulder.

"There there," he said, patting her on the head. "Come over by the fire and warm. Youre freezing cold. Your teeth are chattering."

"Liars!" she cried out. "All liars! Liars and cheats! And smug!"

"Of course," Bob said. "There there." She allowed him to lead her over to the fireplace where the new logs were blazing merrily, where it was warm.

When Frank called her next day about Dave being gone she did not think anything about it. She was still expecting him over for Christmas.

CHAPTER 37

WHEN Dave left Parkman heading south to Florida in 'Bama's Packard, he left as a non-resident. He felt he had nothing in this town and was leaving nothing. When he returned, finally, it was to discover he was returning as a resident: as a man who thought of himself as a resident of Parkman. What had made this change he did not know. Maybe it was just the simple fact of being gone so long without expecting to be. Altogether they were gone a little over four months.

He had of course had no idea of going to anywhere like Florida, when he looked 'Bama up. He had been thinking, actually, that they might go to Terre Haute. The night he had his wearing bout in bed with Ginnie Moorehead he had righteously made up his mind he was not going to spend Christmas with the Frenches, who had not even seen fit to ask him. The result of this decision was an acute depressive loneliness and a feeling of being totally unloved, especially after he had talked to Frank today, and lied, and told him he already had a date for Christmas. And after closing the taxistand at eleven in selfdefense he had started out to hunt the gambler down with the idea that they might do something together Christmas, go somewhere and get drunk together. He was hoping to get hold of him before he made other plans—this was the 20th—but even then he wasnt expecting much success because he had forgotten all about 'Bama's family down in the country and they would want him to spend Christmas at home with them, wouldnt they? He did not even know if 'Bama was in town. It had taken him over an hour of tracking him down to finally find him.

He started out with the two poolrooms, then moved on to the bars —Ciro's; Smitty's where he ran into Dewey and Hubie holding court; Maude's out in the very south end of town by the city park, a place known affectionately by the local drinking caste as Maude the Bawd's; and finally, the fourth and last, out at the West End business district, a place which was named The West End Serviceable Bar And Grille but was actually called Dinky Jack's because a tiny little man by the name of Jack something ran it. Then he started in on the clubs: the Moose, the Eagles, the Woodmen's, the new VFW lodge, any of which 'Bama might be at, playing cards. It was strange, what a definite visible dividing line there was in Parkman between the Respectable on the one hand, and the Disreputable and downright Unrespectable on the other, (he himself seemed to have drifted, quickly and automatically, almost entirely in with the latter two) and he did not bother to look at the Elks or the Country Club. Slowly he drove his crusty little Plymouth up and down the streets from one place to the next; it had reached the place with his car now where it had its own definite personality (Sturdy but Irascible) for Dave. Finally he found him, sitting in a stud game beneath his immaculate semiWestern hat, at the American Legion Hall.

"Well, look whos here," the tall man drawled from within the shadow of his hat brim which hid his entire face down to his lower lip, which grinned. "Its old pard. Hello, old pard."

"Come on, 'Bama, and play," one of the players growled. "Or you gonna sit and talk all night?"

"Just saying hello to my old pard," 'Bama said with amiable scorn. "Besides, Im studyin. —Ill see," he said and threw two blue chips out on the worn, threadbare felt that covered the table. "Come on and sit in," he said to Dave.

Dave did not want to, especially, but he did. It had been only lately that he had qualified for the right, when at 'Bama's insistence he had come by and paid in his two dollars for his membership. It was mostly dime and quarter poker; because most of the veterans of the first World War who hung out here had not been too successful in life. The ones who had been did not hang out here. All of the players at the table except himself and 'Bama were old vets, men of the First War of fast fading memory, all going a little too comfortably to fat and stooping shoulders and high complexions. Not old yet, but old enough to see their war, and their heroisms, all displaced. Dave wondered suddenly if Caesar's veterans might not have looked a lot like this in Augustus's time. He remembered every single one of them at the table from his childhood. They had all been hanging out here twenty five years ago. When the Old Man's younger brother Roland, now dead, who was a vet used to bring him down here. But they all looked smaller now and more narrow shouldered. Both death and success had made inroads on their numbers, but the rest remained. It seemed impossible now that some of them had once killed foreign men with bayonets and hand grenades. But the yellowing pictures still hung on the walls to prove it: the Rainbow Division; the 5th Marines; Sibley's Battalion; the 32nd Red Arrow Division. Dimly Dave could remember all the old names, like some kind of latterday roll call: Ching Cole (an uncle of Dewey's), and his brother Possum Cole (Dewey's father); Funny McAlister; Doc Ray Slade; Hurley Quinley, a house painter; Lab Walker, a concrete finisher; Karl F Wild, born a German, and his son Carl J, American born, both vets; the Barley brothers; his uncle Roland. Stubbornly the ones who were left, who were not dead or successful, clung onto their sanctuary.

The Parkman American Legion Post—Don J Zimmer Post No. 362—was located on South Main Street at the very end of the two blocks of business houses that trailed off down the hill from the square. The other half of the old brick building, now one of the more noticeable eyesores of the town, was occupied by the Western Union office which had been there ever since there was a Western Union office in Parkman and people no longer had to go out to the tower on the railroad to send their wires. For the Legion the storefront windows had been painted over, and when you went inside into the decrepit sitting room where nobody ever sat (but where all the yellowing pictures hung) you were met by a faint thickly comfortable smell of beer, ketchup, hamburgers and tobacco smoke; and when you went on through the swinging doors into the clubroom where women were never allowed, you knew where it came from. In there, among the slotmachines and beer cases, and the poker game always in progress, and the bar and griddle behind which stood the fat still crippled old vet known as the 'Custodian', you could cut it with a knife. These were not the men who made the chauvinistic National Legion policies and strove to get elected National Commander so they could later run for Governor; nor were they the city vets who loved their uniforms and a chance to swing their garrison belts. These were the small town vets, who went to the National Convention to get drunk, and wanted a place where they could drink on Sundays, and who looked absolutely sheepish—if not downright ludicrous—on Memorial Day and Armistice Day when they marched out to the cemetery in a body in their let-out uniforms. The Ladies of the Auxiliary (they met in the Hall upstairs), long since re-signed to only moderately successful husbands at best, had long ago given up trying to reform the Post; and the other ladies married to successful vets had all moved on, to the Country Club or Elks, and no longer had the problem. There had been some talk lately about the new highpowered younger vets of the Second War taking the place over and straightening it out and giving it some Respect and Social Conscience that would be more in keeping with our country's newly enhanced position in world affairs. But Dave did not believe that they could ever really do it, and the old vets hung grimly on.

Feeling as though he wanted to laugh or maybe cry, Dave concentrated his mind on the poker. He had never been a really *good* poker player; he got too excited, and then his imagination ran away with him and he overplayed. He knew what his trouble was, but he could not control it; the mere thought of playing always overwrought and excited him.

He played in their game about an hour, and in that time the strange alchemic thing that had happened with 'Bama and him before, happened again. They began to win. One or the other of them. They did not play together, or even try to. But gradually the percentage of the hands that either one or the other of them won began to rise, and kept on rising. Finally, after winning a big pot—big for this game anyway—on a King high hole card, Dave pushed back his chair.

"I guess Ive got enough. I didnt come down here to play poker anyway. I was just lookin for 'Bama."

Across the table the tall Alabaman grinned with his lower lip that protruded from beneath the shadow of his hatbrim. "Anything special?" he said. "Or just in general?"

"Oh, I thought we might go out and hit some joints, or something. Nothing special."

"Okay," 'Bama said without hesitation, "Im yore man. Hey, Elvie," he called to the 'Custodian'. "Fry us up six hamburgers to go. Come on play one more hand, our hamburgs be ready to go by then."

After the hand, they collected their six delicious-smelling hamburgers in a paper sack through which the hot grease had already begun to spot. 'Bama stuck his nose down in the sack and inhaled deeply. "Ahhh! Give us six cans of Greasy, too, Elvie," he decided. "Sanwiches like them needs beer."

With the beer and hamburgers, they left. The other players had already gone on with the game and were engrossed in it. None of them minded that the other two were leaving winners. They all played here every day just about, their faces seemed to say, and what they lost today they would win back from someone else the next day, or the next.

"Ill see all you gentlemen," 'Bama said from the swinging doors that led into the darkened never-used sitting room. He sneered it of course, by sheer force of habit, but it seemed to Dave there was a curious respectfulness, almost a gentleness, in his voice that he had never, up to now at least, noticed anywhere else.

"Well, where you want to go?" the gambler said when they were outside. They stood for a moment at the top of the concrete steps down to the damp street.

"Hell, I dont know," Dave said. "Anyplace, I guess. I dont even care."

'Bama chuckled. "I kind of had a hunch you just wanted more to talk. Well, lets take our sanwiches and beer on up to yore place at the Douglas. You got your car? You go ahead and Ill follow you."

When they were in his room, 'Bama broke out the hamburgers and pulling a beercan opener from his topcoat pocket opened two of the beers. "There you are, dig in." He himself drained off half his own beer in one long swig and then helped himself to the whiskey bottle on Dave's dresser and poured some into his can of beer. Then with the homemade boilermaker and his share of the sandwiches which he began to eat in two huge bites each, he sprawled himself out in the armchair as he had done the other times. "Well, how much you win?" he said, conversationally.

"About twenty bucks," Dave said. He helped himself to a sandwich and a beer. He had suddenly become acutely selfconscious. It had started when they stood outside the Legion and 'Bama had asked him where he wanted to go. He hadnt really wanted to go anywhere, he had wanted to ask him what he was going to be doing Christmas but he couldnt. Somehow or other he had put himself in a position of asking a favor of him, and he didnt want that, he wanted to approach him easily and from on a level. He had imposed on him by dragging him off from his game and for what, really? For nothing. He had not asked him what he would be doing Christmas there in the game because he did not want the other men to know that he himself had nothing to do on Christmas. Now he didnt want 'Bama to know he had nothing to do Christmas.

"I won about forty myself," 'Bama drawled. "Most of it after you come in. Its funny, you know it? Almost the minute you come into that game I could feel somethin change somewhere. I knew I was goin to start winnin. Did you feel that?"

"No," Dave said. "I didnt."

"Well by God I sure as hell did." 'Bama sighed around a mouthful of hamburger and laid his head back, the immaculate hat tipped over his eyes. "You know," he said philosophically, "gamblin's really a profession, a craft, just like anything else. A fellow gets into it he has to learn his trade, his craft. But beyond that hes got to have luck.

"Matter of fact," he said, "gamblin's an awful lot like farming. Ive done both. What does a farmer do? He gets everything ready, gets the best seed he can afford, gets his seed out, all that stuff. And what happens? In the end its all luck, whether he makes his crop or not. Its all the luck of the weather he gets. Its a *gamble*. He never knows if hes goin to make money or not, see?"

"Well, writing a book is just the same thing at that," Dave said. "Its a gamble."

'Bama looked over at him interestedly. "Well sure it is, aint it?" he said. "You never know whether yore goin to have a best seller or not."

"Thats right."

"That is right. Its a gamble too," 'Bama said, looking a little surprised. "Well, so is gamblin, see? Its all a gamble, and in the end it all hangs on luck. Which is something nobody understands the workings of." He seemed to be suddenly full of talking, almost a hunger to talk, as if he rarely got the chance. "Nobody knows anything about luck, except that it exists, and comes and goes, and that nobody can control it. Well now I actually honestly believe that luck's controlled by natural laws just like anything else, and that those laws are connected to a person's mind. I think luck's controlled by the mind. I dont mean by havin faith and all that religion crap;—I mean, you just cant make yoreself lucky just by *believin* youll win, no matter how hard you try; ever try it? —What I mean is, I think theres some actual *physical* part of the brain that controls luck. Some gland or nerve cell or something like that. The trouble is, we ourselves dont know how to control that gland or whatever it is. At least, not consciously. But I believe that when a man is hot and winning, hes got that part of his brain to going, and hes actually *physically* controllin them cards some way, with some part of his brain some way that he dont know hes doin. I mean actually *physically*, you see? Have you ever been hot and winning and you just *know* yore goin to win and yore goin to get the cards you want? and then you do get them? Shore you have. And have you ever felt that same identical way, and then *not* get them?"

"More times than I like to remember," Dave said.

'Bama nodded and picked up his last hamburger and took a half-a-hamburger bite out of it and pointed the rest of it at Dave speculatively.

"Well, I believe that that is because that part of yore brain whatever it is, that you cant control, is either workin or not workin," he said around the hamburger. "You see? Somethin sets it off and starts it workin, and somethin else shuts if off and stops it; and what you yoreself feel, or believe, dont really have nothin to do with it at all. Thats a different part of yore head entirely.

"But now if a man could isolate what it is that makes that special part of his brain work or not work, and why, then he could control it, see? And if he could do that hed *always* win. Or at least whenever he wanted to. He wouldnt want to all the time or everybodyd get suspicious."

"In other words, you dont really believe that chance exists at all?" Dave said, feeling a little surprised.

"Well, if you want an honest answer, no sir, I dont believe chance does exist. Let me put it this way: maybe chance seems to exist—to us, and in the actual effect, in actual practice, does exist for us; but only because we dont know and understand the rules and system it works by. If we did, wed see where its just as logical as everything else. I think its all right there in everybody's head. If a farmer could control that part of his brain, he could make the weather what he wanted it to be for his crop."

"What about other farmers?" Dave grinned, interested, "who wanted other weather?"

"Well, I dont know," 'Bama said seriously. "I havent got it all figured out yet. But why couldnt there be one kind of weather over one farm and right next to it a different weather over the next farm?"

"What about a writer? Makin his book a best seller?"

"Well, I dont see why he couldnt do it, do you? I mean, always provided of course that he could control that part of his head. But then if we could do that, we wouldnt even need any books, would we?" he grinned.

"I guess not," Dave said. "No, I guess not."

"And what if everybody could do it?" 'Bama said. "What would happen to a poker game then?" He shrugged. "Well, there just wouldnt be no more gambling. Whats more, there wouldnt even be any reason to gamble. Since there wouldnt be any good or bad luck to fascinate people. Wed all understand what luck was."

"Or any farmers either," Dave said. "They wouldnt have to make weather and plant crops. They could just make crops," he grinned.

"They wouldnt even have to do that," 'Bama said seriously. "They could just make food. Or better yet, just make themselves *nourished*. Without even havin to eat any food. You see what I mean? Its metaphysical—or at least what *we* call metaphysical," he said, "if you get right down to it and foller it all the way down. Ive got some books on it that I picked up when I was studyin luck. Maybe Ill show them to you sometime."

He looked straight at Dave, who was still astounded, and went on. "Ive done a lot of thinkin about it. Im convinced that that thing—that gland, or nerve cell, or whatever it is; maybe its a whole series of them— is right there in everybody's head, waitin to be used—and actually bein used, sometimes, although we dont know it—if we just knew how to control it. Maybe thats the next stage of life or evolution us human beins will evolve up to or something like that.

"People think gamblers are superstitious because theyre always wearin the same hat or carryin the same billfold or always keepin the same coin in their pocket and things like that." He pulled out a silver mounted rabbit's foot and held it up and grinned. "But the truth is, gamblers know that they got this gland in their brain—although they may not have any idea what it is—and they know that certain circumstances make it work. All theyre doin when they wear the same hat is trying to dupli- cate whatever circumstances it was that made it work for them the last time," he said, staring straight at Dave.

"I guess thats right," Dave said.

"You take you and me. Why is it when we both get together in a game somewhere, we both begin to win more? What causes it? I dont mean that we win them all, and sometimes maybe we will even lose; but the overall percentage of winning hands we have definitely goes up. Thats a fact. And so theres got to be some explanation for it. Some factor which we dont know about that would explain it reasonably if we just knew what it was.

"I shore wish you and me could form that gamblin pardnership we talked about," he said almost wistfully, "while we're still lucky for each other. We ought to take advantage of it while it lasts."

'Bama reached for his beercan and discovered it was empty, and then looked up, looking a little surprised. "Man, Ive sure been talkin a blue streak, aint I?" he said. He got up to open two more beers. "But you know, thats what fascinates a person about gamblin so much, you know? Its like death: We dont really know what it is, either: or understand it any more than we understand what luck is." He laughed—chillingly, Dave thought. "Well," he said, "what was it you was wantin to see me about anyway?"

"Oh," Dave said, suddenly selfconscious again, "nothing. Nothing special. I just thought Id look you up, you know? Hadnt seen you for a while. Say," he said, "what are you going to be doin Christmas?"

"Christmas?" 'Bama said looking startled. "Well, I dont know. Nothing. Why? —Whats today?" he said, "Wednesday the 20th?" He counted the days up on his fingers. "Thats Monday. Christmas is Monday. No, I aint doin nothing Monday that I know of. Why?"

"I thought we might celebrate," Dave said. "Go off somewhere and get on a good drunk together."

"Okay," 'Bama said. "But why Monday?" He was just handing Dave his beer. Then he stopped and slowly began to grin. "But aint you going to be spending Christmas over to yore little schoolteacher's in Israel?"

"Who? Me? Hell, no."

The grin widened. "You mean she didnt ask you."

"Look," Dave said. "What in hell are you talking about anyway? Whats all this schoolteacher kick youre on? Why the hell should she ask me for Christmas?"

"Aw now, come on, buddy," 'Bama said soothingly. "Everybody in town knows you and that schoolteacher of Wally's are hot for each other. Im yore old buddy."

"Now look!" Dave said irately. "All I did was come around and ask you to go someplace on Christmas. If you dont want to go, you dont have to. Just say so. But spare me your wit and homegrown psychology."

For a moment, just for a moment, 'Bama stared at him cold eyed, his face set like stone, as if debating whether he should openly take personal offence or not. Then he apparently decided not to. He moved, and rearranged his face.

"Okay," he grinned, "lets go to Florida."

Dave, who had only had time to think that everything was going wrong anymore, and had been for some time, could not believe he had heard right.

"To Florida!"

"Sure," 'Bama grinned, "why not? I aint been down there since I was at that Tankers' Vacation Home they sent me to in '45 when I come back from overseas. We can run down there for a couple weeks or so and have us both a *real* celebration. The winter seasonll just be startin and Hialeah and the dog tracksll be runnin. We might even make expenses."

"But what about your family? Dont you have to spend Christmas with them?"

"Hell, no," the tall slim Southerner said. "Ive done bought them all all the damned presents they want. All Im gonna buy anyway. So it dont matter whether Im there or not. My mom and my brother and all will be there. They always go down to the farm for Christmas. Hell, I never do."

"Well—when will we go?" Dave said.

"Go right now," 'Bama said simply. "Ill go back to the boarding house and pick up an extra suit and hat and you can be packin up whatever you want to take and Ill come back and pick you up here. Whatever we dont take we can buy when we get there."

"What about money?" Dave said.

'Bama sneered. That was all. Just merely sneered, with his mouth. He didnt say a word.

"Okay," Dave said. —"All right," he said, "lets go. Just one other thing first. Why dont we take a couple of women with us?"

"Women? What for?"

"Well, for the kicks, goddam it! and for the sex! what do you think. —I thought," he said, "I thought we might take a couple the brassiere factory girls? How about taking that Ginnie Moorehead, for me, and Mildred Pierce for you?"

'Bama looked at him with unconcealed astonishment. "Whoa!" he said. "Now wait a minute. Just because you romped old Ginnie last night dont mean you can push her off on me for a trip to Florida."

"How did you know I romped her?"

"Jesus Christ!" 'Bama sneered disgustedly, "whoever didnt see you take her out of Smitty's last night—and that aint many—knows all about it now because Ginnie herself's done told everybody in town about it at least once. Shes been tellin everybody she can buttonhole about it all day today and all night tonight.

"'My friend Dave Hirsh,'" he said, mimicking Ginnie's dully pole-axed voice devastatingly, "'you know my friend Dave Hirsh, yes we was out last night' then a giggle 'you know, Dave Hirsh the writer, my friend Dave's the brother of Frank Hirsh owns the jewelry store'.

"Look I know yore new around here," he said paternally, "and dont know the protocol, but you got to learn it. When you go out with old Ginnie, you dont take her out of Smitty's in front of everybody, you make the date and meet her outside later."

"Why?" Dave said. "You dont do that with the rest of them?"

"No, but you do with Ginnie. That way, when she tells people she was out with you and how good or bad you were, *you* can always deny it and nobodyll *know*, not for sure.

"And as for takin them to Florida, thats out," 'Bama said categorically. "And thats all. Why, hell, man! every secretary and nurse, and 'bachelor girl', " he sneered, "east of the Mississippi is going to be on vacation in Miami now lookin for some man. I mean *good* lookin girls. We should take them pigs *with* us?"

"All right," Dave said, "okay, okay. Youve convinced me. I just—you know," he said sheepishly, "I just felt sorry for her. You know. And thought the trip might be a nice thing for her."

"Shore!" 'Bama cried. "I feel sorry for a hawg strung up in a slaughter-house too but I dont put him in the back seat of my cahr and take him to Florida with me."

Dave said nothing. He still felt, though, that 'Bama was being a little too heartlessly cynical and coldblooded about another human being.

Even for 'Bama. After all, Ginnie Moorehead might not be much, but she was still a human being; and as a human being was entitled to certain rights, to a certain basic dignity and respect. He didnt care whether they took her or not, but a hog in a slaughterhouse was not the same thing as a human being, either.

"Dont you be listenin to nothin that that Ginnie tells you about *nothin*," 'Bama cautioned, peering at him with a certain sort of disbelieving astonishment, as if he could still not quite believe what he had seen. "I dont think you know enough about women yet, Hollywood or no. Now Ill go pick up my extra suit and hat and you pack whatever you want and Ill come right back and pick you up."

Then he was gone and Dave started to look around the room hopelessly to see what he would pack, at two o'clock in the morning. It did not seem five minutes—a five minutes of hacking and grabbing and stuffing and pulling out and shoving in to make one timeless suitcase do—that he was back and then they were on the road, heading east out of town, the two of them sitting silent in the front seat of the smoothly purring 1937 Packard, Dave's suitcase and junk in the back, and 'Bama driving and wearing those dark-green glasses he always wore when he drove which had partial correction for long distance. "My eyes just aint quite good enough for fast driving. When yore drivin 85 and 90 you got to be able to drive a quarter of a mile ahead at least." His topcoat collar was up around his ears, and the still-immaculate pearl hat low over his eyes, and his gloved hands rested lightly on the wheel. In the back only the one suit on a hanger with a toothbrush sticking up out of its breast pocket and the big square tan-and-brown Stetson hatbox on the seat attested to the fact that he was going someplace. Beside him sat Dave, still a little astonished to be on his way to Florida and looking out at the darkened houses as they wheeled past under the streetlights in the dead part of the night.

It was just about then, as he sat there looking out at the town, that Dave had his strong sudden feeling of non-residency. Of being a man who had no roots nor permanent contacts here, and who had no regrets at leaving, and who more than half way expected not ever to come back. He could not feel that (save for the simple, unavoidable accident of birth) he belonged here in any way at all. His car he was leaving parked and locked on the street. More than half of his clothes, and all his books, and most of the rest of his worldy possessions still reposed in that miserable little hotelroom—which, at 'Bama's suggestion, he had paid the night man a month's rent in advance for. And outside of that, outside of those things, nothing. Nothing at all. His interest in the taxi service he did not count; that was, so to speak, money under the bridge. If he never saw it again it did not matter; he had had it—and he had spent it. And if he never saw any of the rest of it again—the car: his poor faithful little old Plymouth, the clothes, the old B-4 bag, the books—what did that matter either? What did any of it matter? Emotion seized him. He was more than three fourths convinced that he would never come back here, and if he didnt what did it matter? Who would give a damn? He did not say anything about any of this to 'Bama.

Out of all of it, he had made sure of one thing: His typewriter was packed. His new portable typewriter. It sat on the floor of the back seat behind him, and inside the lid clipped to the big clip at the top all the manuscript he had done to date. It wasnt much, and it certainly wasnt good,—in fact it was terrible—but such as it was, it was his, by God. He was still a writer. 'Bama Dillert might be the best damn gambler in the world, but he was not a writer. Gwen French might be the greatest English teacher on earth, but she was not a writer. He was.

With a sort of spiritual start he realized he was back pressed firmly into the tight old mold, his nose pushed firmly against the moving grit of the same old turning grindstone. That damned Gwen French woman. She knew just how to hook you. She put her harpoon in your vanity. It was like getting a fishhook through your bag: you couldnt even move enough to try and get it out. You were a writer. And so every day's existence was governed by how well the writing went that day. If it went well, everything was wonderful; there was nothing bad enough could happen that it could upset your happiness and enjoyment. And if it went badly, everything was miserable. And if you didnt work at all—nothing on God's green earth could break through your wall of gloom and guilt. You didnt do it because you wanted to, because you enjoyed it, you did it because you couldnt help it, you had to do it, you had to do it because that was the only way you could justify to yourself all the weakness and pettiness and worthlessness of yourself that you hated;—and because your damned vanity was so inordinately strong that you had to prove that you *could* do it.

The heavy purring Packard passed smoothly off of the end of the brick pavement and out onto the concrete highway, and then the last of the houses were gone and left behind. Eyes a little moist with an emotion almost too powerful to contain, Dave wondered tragically if he would ever see this place again and doubted if he would, and said he did not care.

When they rode up onto the bridge approach at the river and heading for Terre Haute, Israel was all dark below them on the right, except for the few streetlights. Dave looked down at it broodingly with fiery eyes, from the bridge. If he ever did come back to this goddamned place, it would only be because he had not given up on that goddamned Gwen French woman yet. He was not defeated on Gwen French yet. He did not take to defeat as easily as a lot of people—especially Gwen French—thought, he thought, and stared down through the blackness of the bridge, trying to see the house, as if he hoped that by the very power of his outrage and indignation and his hurt he could penetrate with his eyes right through the walls of the house to where she lay, and cause her to turn uneasily in her sleep.

At the moment he had never loved anybody so much in his life.

Then they were across the bridge and following the big curve left along the river road, where Route 40 ran north to Terre Haute also on the river, and everything suddenly dropped away from Dave almost as if Parkman and Israel and Gwen never had existed and he had never stopped off there for a week on his way home to Hollywood from Chicago. All that was behind, spun out of existence by the spinning tires of 'Bama's Packard while at the same time they spun into existence new places and existences up ahead; ahead was a trip and, at the end of it, Florida.

They would, 'Bama had said, get on US 41 at Terre Haute and take it south through Vincennes and Evansville as far as Nashville, but after that he was not so sure; he had heard 41 wasnt in such good a shape now after the war; and they would probably be working on it now too, which would mean detours. At Terre Haute they waited on the stop light at the corner by the courthouse, and then made the turn south onto 41, the headlights lighting up the deserted streets and the flanks of the big semis rolling north, and as soon as he was past the other lights, 'Bama began that smooth solid acceleration that was like a gentle hand on your chest pushing you back into the seat and by the time they reached the last scattered outskirts he was already doing seventy. By the time dawn had seeped itself down through the leaden winter sky some three hours later, they were through Evansville and Henderson and had passed Madisonville Kentucky and were well on their way to Hopkinsville and Nashville, an average mileage of a little over sixty miles an hour. And all of it driven with no apparent strain or pushing.

To Dave, for whom driving had always been a sort of nerve racking chore, unpleasant but necessary in order to get to some given place, the kind of driving 'Bama did was almost unbelievable. After daylight, as if in some way the advancing light itself released him from some vow of silence, 'Bama began to talk more. In answer to an obviously admiring question of Dave's as to whether he had ever driven this road before, he admitted that he had driven it several times and began to expound on the art of highway-driving—as opposed to race-driving. During the rest of the trip he came back to it from time to time, whenever some incident on the road recalled it to him, and in the rest of the thirty hours it took them to get to Central Florida where they made their first real stop Dave learned more about driving than he had learned in the rest of his whole life all put together.

He had ('Bama said, talking easily and relaxedly, while the speedometer needle hovered between 80 and 90) driven this road—at least that part from Terre Haute to Nashville—three or four different times both ways since the war, in going back down to Birmingham. But that made no especial difference in how fast he drove the road, or any road, which was governed by several things, he explained: first, the natural terrain of the country—how flat or hilly it was; second, the age of the road itself—the older the road the sharper and less banked the curves; and third, the amount of traffic—heavy traffic naturally slowed you down. He would have driven this road, today, just as fast if he had never been on it. He was, Dave saw, obviously flattered by Dave's interest and admiration.

"Y'see, in the first place," he elaborated, "road-driving and race-driving are completely different because of two main things. One is that in road-driving there are cars coming the other way; that changes everything right there. The other thing is the relative speeds of the vehicles that are goin the *same* way: In road-driving you may be goin ninety and the car ahead of you thirty five; in race-drivin all the cars're going pretty much the same speed. Well, right there those two things changes all the problems a driver has to face. And consequently, the problem of passing—in road-drivin—becomes of much more importance. In road-drivin you have three objects moving, you and the car ahead of you yore goin to pass, and the third car moving toward you at some un-determined speed. Y'see? While now in race-drivin, you completely remove one of those three objects entirely; namely, the car comin toward you. Why my God, you must lower yore percentage of mishaps from just passin alone by—my God, I dont know how much—seventy five percent at least."

The further along he went, and the more he elaborated, the more he began to sound like some kind of a mathematician. It was obvious that he had made an almost scientific study of the subject for himself in his own mind.

"Y'see what I mean?" he demanded.

"I do now. Although I never quite thought of it quite like that before though."

"Well, yore main problem in road-drivin is passing. Thats where over two thirds yore accidents come from. You aint going to find many curves yore goin too fast to make—not if you know anything at all about drivin. But anytime yore across that black line in the other lane, yore in *danger,* see? Even if there aint a car in miles. I make it a rule never to come into no curve so fast that I need to pull over into the other lane to flatten the arc. But what do most of yore drivers do? They pull into some damn curve too fast, then brake while theyre *in* it—something you *never* should do, and then they cheat a little and slip over into the other lane to flatten the curve. And when they pass some car, the damned fools edge out real slow, then actually slow down when theyre goin around the bastard! and edge back in like they were scared to death. What they ought to do is get out there fast, get around him, and get back in. As long as yore on yore own side of the road yore not in too much danger, except from damfool drivers—which is nearly all of them. Now course in race-drivin you dont have none of that. And you dont have damfool drivers either, buddy, believe me. At least not for long."

"Did you ever do any race-driving?" Dave asked.

"Oh, no," 'Bama said. "No. Hunh-unh. When I was a kid in Birmingham we had a jalopy club—what the kids today call hot rods —old cars wed mill the heads down on and rebore the cylinders—and we used to hold regular races. But Ive never done no real race-driving." He grinned then. "Ive shore seen an awful lot of them though."

Dave had once again that feeling of what an almost mathematically scientific study and analysis of the subject of driving 'Bama had apparently made for himself. He had gone at it, apparently, in the same systematic organizational way he had gone at his gambling, cataloging everything, separating it all into categories, then approaching all of these with the coldblooded unemotional practical rationality of a trained logician. Apparently, he did that with just about everything—everything that interested him, anyway. Including people, Dave thought, not quite so admiringly, and thinking of poor dumb Ginnie. Then he remembered how he himself had jumped all over 'Bama when 'Bama had been kidding him about Gwen French.

"Listen," he said, "I want to tell you something."

"Whats that?" 'Bama said without taking his eyes from the road.

"Well," Dave said, "its this. I think I owe you an apology. For digging you and sort of—insultin you up there in the room before we left. I was pretty nasty, I guess."

"Oh, thats all right," 'Bama grinned cheerfully without looking away from the road. "I figured I had it comin. I thought about it, and I figured I had it comin. I didnt have no business stickin my nose in yore business. That was yore business, and if you wanted to keep it to yoreself, you should. I stuck my nose in."

"Well, it wasnt so much that," Dave said.

"I know. You was mad. But it still wasnt my business," 'Bama said cheerfully. After a moment, then, he suddenly let up on the gas and the Packard began to slow. "Now look there. Show you something. See that car up ahead?"

Dave looked, and saw a misshapen vehicle that did not look like a passenger car, at least a quarter of a mile away and more, ahead of them, just cresting a hill. "Yeah? Why?"

"You notice anything funny about it?" 'Bama said eagerly.

"Well, no. It didnt look like a car. A truck, maybe?"

"It was a tractor. Tractors travel anywhere from ten to twenty or twenty five miles an hour. Thats why Im startin to slow up now, soon as I see it. That tractor may be goin ten miles an hour. I dont want to run up on it, see?"

"Oh," Dave said, feeling witless, and then he watched as the slowing car began to run up more and more slowly on the slowly moving tractor; by the time they reached it they were doing slightly less than forty, and still moving up. The road ahead was clear for a mile at least. Two car lengths in back of it 'Bama swung out, gunned the Packard in that smooth solid acceleration, passed and swung back in, and had the big Packard back up to ninety before the tractor was out of sight as it dwindled away behind them.

"Y'see what I mean?" 'Bama said gently, sliding his gloved hands back and forth on the wheel. (He had kept the heat in the car turned almost off: ridin in a hot car heavily dressed would almost invariably give a guy a cold he said.) "Thats a principle you can always follow: Anytime you see something up ahead that dont look completely like another passenger car, start slowin as soon as you see it. It might be a tractor, or a wagon, or even an old fashioned make of car, or maybe only a truck. But until you know what it is and how fast its goin—you slow. If its only a truck, yore all right anyway; but even trucks're bad in some country where its hilly or curvy and they cant make any speed. See?"

Dave nodded. "Yeah. I see."

"You notice I never used my brake," 'Bama said gently. "Not a tall. A perfect driver never uses his brake. Never. Not for nothing. Except maybe like at stop lights after hes already slowed. He dont need to use it. That brake aint there to use. But we aint none of us perfect drivers and thats why that brake is there. Its there only so that when youve made a mistake—or the other guy has—it can be used to get you out of some jam. Thats all its for. See?"

"Ill remember," Dave said. He realized he was being taught.

'Bama gave him a quick grin. On his face behind the grin was a sort of shy apologetic but at the same time sardonic look as if—with that extraordinary and always unanticipated mental perceptiveness of his— he half expected Dave's comment might mean that he was being ribbed. When he saw no such ribbing was intended, he turned back to the road without saying anything. But after that, whenever some other similar situation occurred that caused him to use some fine point or little trick of driving, he would very carefully explain it, laying out just what he was doing and why, and more often than not then drew for Dave the general principle to be followed.

At one place, for instance, he passed a slow moving car up near the crest of a hill. There was no no-passing zone, so he was not breaking any law, but still to pass so was against all orthodox theory, and he explained very carefully why he did it. Ordinarily to pass in such a way was wrong, and dangerous, he said. But in this instance—and he pointed it out to Dave, who then but only then noticed it—he could see over the crest the top of the second car ahead. As long as he could see it and how far ahead it was, and also could see no on-coming car in the other lane, he knew it was safe to pass.

He was full of such little pointers, simple enough when called to your attention but things Dave would never have thought of himself. For instance, he went on, along that same vein about passing on hills, there were lots of ways of telling whether there was an on-coming car over the crest. At night, for instance, you could see the glow of their headlights over the crest before the lights themselves came into view. Another way in the daytime that often worked was a situation where you found yourself on top a crest that was higher than the next crest. If there was a car in the bottom of the hollow that you would want to pass on the next hill, you could often see the entire next hollow before you started down the first one and tell if there were any on-coming cars on it. If there were none, you were safe to pass going up the next hill; and if not, it was time to start slowing. —"Because y'always want to remember:" he said, "When yore driving eighty and ninety its goin to take you at least a quarter of a mile to get completely stopped, and you always got to allow for that."

The more of these little things he brought out, the more Dave was amazed at all the things about driving he had never seen. 'Bama also made other comments, from time to time as they went along, but these comments were on people, or the things and society of people that they saw. 'Bama had no more respect for people in general than Dave did—(and, Dave thought, a lot less for people in particular). These comments were not made with the eager enjoyment he had when he talked about driving; these comments were made with sardonic disgust and a caustic scorn that came close to flaying off the hide.

One time they were passing through a little town that sported the perennial signs that Eddie Cantor had made so famous in the 'Thirties and that now you saw everywhere: DRIVE SLOW. WE LOVE OUR CHILDREN. 'Bama merely snorted disgustedly. "Why dont they think up something new? Yas, they love the little bastards. Thats why they route the highway right past every school in town; to prove it. What theyre really hopin is that some son of a bitch *will* run over their damn kids so they wont have to feed em." He didnt say anything else for a minute, then he said: "Someday when Im rich Im gonna buy myself a whole town all my own and put up my own damned signs: DRIVE AS FAST AS YOU WANT TO. WE HATE OUR KIDS AS MUCH AS YOU DO." Dave could not help but laugh, especially as, when they drove on through, they sure enough passed two schools.

Still another time, when the gambler saw a State Patrol car bearing down on them from in front going the other way, he quickly hit his brake several times lightly with his foot, slowing the heavy Packard down to around sixty five, and snorted irreverently. "Bastards. It aint the expert drivers who causes their wrecks. Its them damn twenty mile an hour bastards. But its always the expert drivers who pay their damned fines. More people're killed by slow drivers than by fast, but cops wont admit it. A slow driver is a slow thinker." He grinned through the window at the State Troopers and waved friendlily as they passed.

"Sons of bitches. You know why the accident rate is goin up today? and keeps on goin up? Them! Everybody is so damned busy lookin out for cops they run right off the road or run into each other head on."

He apparently hated trucks, and once after finally shooting and getting by a solid string of four of them that were driving almost nose to tail, he delivered himself of a diatribe on them, too.

"Thats against the law," he said. "Theyre supposed to stay one car length apart. God damned trucks. Its got to be a damned custom in this country that everybody has to say what wonderful expert polite drivers truck drivers are. Christ, they even make movies about the wonderful truck drivers. Its got so damned bad that if you or me went out in public and said truck drivers were bums wed get accused of being un-American or Damcommunists. Thats how bad it is. While the damned truth is, only about one in a hundred truck drivers is a decent driver— and since the war that percentage has been goin down and down. Too damned many punk hotrod kids getting trucker jobs. And that aint the worst. Not only are they bad drivers," he drawled, "but their damn stinking trucks are whats ruinin our highways. The government cant hardly get a highway completed, before the truckers have already wore out the other end of it so that they have to start all over resurfacing. And you know who pays for it, dont you?" he said lazily. "We do. You and me. Every time you or me buy a gallon of gas, we're settin them up in business and payin their maintainance bills." This appeared to amuse him. "No wonder they runnin all the railroads out of business. More money's spent by trucking interests gettin bills passed than itd take to run our state government. What they ought to do is boost the cost of tractor-trailer and large truck licenses about a thousand percent, and raise the tax on gas for big corporation trucks about five hundred percent. Then wed have four lane all over the country. But they wont do it," he added answering himself, with a satanic grin. "Theres a big bunch of home-loving boys in every state capitol in the country who are gettin a big rakeoff not to do it, and they need that money to keep up them apartments they keep their chorus girls in.

"I wouldnt care so much," he said mildly after a moment, "myself. If theyd just hire some damned decent drivers."

As if to prove him right, it was not ten minutes later, in a patch of rough hilly country where they were driving less than sixty, that 'Bama suddenly exclaimed "Shit!" and let off on his accelerator and bore down on his brake harder than Dave had ever seen him do it. Even so, he did not slam it on, or press down hard enough to throw them into a skid. All this had happened before Dave had time to even see what was happening. Then he saw the truck ahead of them, apparently coming straight at them. 'Bama kept on braking coolly and edging over to the right as close as he could get without going off on the muddy shoulder, while at the same time with his left hand he was coolly rolling down his window, until finally he had come to a complete stop on the pavement.

What had happened was that at the top of a short hill in front of them, where there was a sharp lefthand turn onto a narrow bridge over a railroad cut, and where there was a warning sign of 20 M.P.H. —('Bama had already been slowing for this, luckily)—a big tractor-trailer job had swung out coming off the bridge around the turn to pass another, slow-moving car on the downgrade. 'Bama had seen him almost before he started and thrown on his brakes. By the time they were completely stopped the truck had almost made it, gunning desperately, and then whipping back in into his own lane in the scant space 'Bama had provided by stopping, while the man in the third car sat gripping his wheel looking wild-eyed back and forth from the truck to his own car and doing nothing. The truck appeared to miss the front of the Packard by inches. By the time Dave had grasped and understood all this it was all already over.

As the truck flashed by them 'Bama, grinning, waved his arm out the window he evidently had opened for just this purpose, and stuck his head out and yelled at the top of his lungs, *"Yore welcome!"* The driver, a boy of nineteen or twenty with a blond crewcut, had his window open an inch or two, but if he heard he gave no sign. He was jockeying the wheel of his truck desperately, his eyes huge and all whites, his face expanded all around with that look of unbelieving fear often seen on the faces of men killed in combat. Then he was past them, and they both turned to watch the big semi whipping back and forth as he ran on across the straight stretch behind them, until finally he got it straightened out.

"Well, he made it," 'Bama said coolly. "Well!" he said, turning to grin at Dave. "Its a good thing there wasnt anybody behind me, aint it?" Dave, whose own heart was thudding in his ears, could see the large artery in 'Bama's throat pulsing rhythmically. "That was a fairly close one," the tall man grinned. "He didnt miss us by much more than six feet. I could always of got clear off on the shoulder if Id of had to," he

said, "but I was afraid I might flip us and I thought he had enough room."
Across the road the middleaged fat man in the third car who had done
nothing—except as 'Bama said caustically drive along slowly and obey all
the laws and almost cause an accident—appeared about to stop to hold
a post mortem of the near calamity with them. "I dont want to have to
talk to that stupid son of a bitch," 'Bama said coldly. He put the Packard
in low gear and started smoothly off up the hill without so much as a
backward glance, just as the man opened his door. "That trucker probly
had been tryin to get around him for the last thirty miles. Well, at least
he didnt speed up any, did he? even if he didnt put on his brakes."

They rode up over the narrow rickety railroad bridge and down and
on along the other side of the valley. "This must be one of those bad
stretches they told me about back up the way," 'Bama said. Then he
chuckled. Whenever 'Bama chuckled, it always had that chilling effect
on you apparently. Though his laugh was different. "Its funny, aint it?
Just an inch or two, one way or the other. It makes all the difference.
Just that foot or two of space: —and nothing has happened; nothing at
all." And he was perfectly right, too. In four or five miles they had both
forgotten all about it. And in another thirty, it had never happened.

They were in Tennessee by now, and outside the car the rolling,
hilly Tennessee landscape swept back toward them on both sides, syn-
chronized with the highway itself which rolled back toward them and
beneath them. It was still early morning. Now and then cars came at
them out of the winter grayness, swelled, grew, then passed and receded.
Sometimes dwellings or a village appeared, rushed at them, then disappeared. Sometimes, too, human people were visible, moving. But none
of these things really had anything to do with them. They had reached
that stage of traveling on a long trip where, moving along a prescribed
restricted ribbon of area, touching the earth itself only on four points
of rubber, they had become insulated from everything. The world no
longer existed, and they themselves hung suspended between two points
on a map, in a suspended animation that would not cease until they
finally touched down. It was not hard to believe, looking out, that it was
they who were stationary and the rest of the world which moved.

And in a way, Dave thought, it might even be partly true—since they
were moving partly westward just now and if you took into account the
earth's eastward spinning, and added in as well its movement around
the sun and the solar system's drift through space, then it might very
possibly be that they were moving slower than the earth, that by getting
in the car and cutting off hotly down the road at ninety miles an hour
they were not actually moving themselves any faster at all but were in
fact slowing themselves down. That would be ironic, wouldnt it?
Wouldnt that be funny? Actually making themselves move slower, in

relation to the movement of the earth. Sometimes he wished he were a mathematician.

To look on beauty bare just for once; yes. To be a mathematician just for once. A mathematician without portfolio. Without portfolio, and without benefit of humanity. Just for once free of, and divorced from, human beings.

Yes, he wanted to be a mathematician. All he had to do, to do it, was to shuck off this body here he was sitting in; and then, probably, also shuck off whatever it was that was Dave Hirsh, too, after that. That was all.

For a moment a pointless, wholly object-less, confused anguish filled him unbearably. And almost like a revelation, which he seemed to see so clearly and so tantalizingly and still could not reach, he thought he could see that for a man to be himself, become himself, was really a very simple thing: The simplest thing in the world: All he had to do to become himself was to cease to be himself. All he, Dave Hirsh, had to do to become Dave Hirsh, was to not be Dave Hirsh at all.

And just how did you go about doing that? Outside of dying. Ha! yes, how? The whole thing, the whole laborious edifice he had erected to lead him to what he thought to be some portal, collapsed like a card house in a sneeze and descended into gibberish and unintelligibility leaving only the unbearable hungry anguish, which was so strong it made him want to squirm and twist and strain his belly muscles till they ruptured. Yes, it was simple all right; it was so very simple it became the most complex thing in the world. And nothing was left but paradoxes. Give up Pride and Vanity—(even if you could)? But Pride and Vanity were the only things that made men men, made anybody accomplish anything. They were not vices—at least, not solely vices; if they were it would be easy. Give up the love of life that made you love everything you saw, every hill, every tree, every woman—(even if you could)? And where would you be? Youd be nothing. Dead.

And so where were you? Nowhere. And the argument with yourself became perpetual.

Oh, if just once— Oh just once, to shuck off this gross slow ugly body that hampered and held and hemmed you in. But more than that, to sluff off and be rid of this personality. This personality which was you, and which restrained and hampered and locked you out from everything more than your body ever did, and which you detested.

Yes, he hungered to be a mathematician. In the same way and with the same intensity old Tom Wolfe hungered to be a poet. —Only, old Tom *was* a poet; and didnt know it? What was that line we used to say as kids? Hes a poet and dont know it? Well, D. HIRSH is a mathematician and cant do addition.

Oh Jesus! he thought. Jesus Jesus Jesus Christ!

Well, there was one thing he could do anyway. Never again would the name D. HIRSH appear on a story or novel or poem. He made himself a solemn oath. If he ever did publish anything again—and he knew he would, this book—he would use his name like it was and like it should be, without affectation: DAVID HIRSH. He could promise that. It would be a symbol; a symbol of the change in him, and in his viewpoint, personality, style, everything, by God! Like old Cabell did. Better yet, he thought hopefully with a burgeoning excitement, he would use it like it always was meant to be, and always should have been all along, all his life: It would be DAVID HERSCHMIDT! That was what it would be. A solemn oath. . . . —But then, after having done it, after having come to, and made, the decision, he found that nothing had really changed at all. It had made no difference, and everything was still just the same as before. *He*, the *him*, remained. A sort of terrified desperation gripped him.

Gradually, out of the welter, in a sort of filtered way, like quicksand oozing up through a sieve pressed down in it, the faint knowledge of what had upset him and put him onto this tirade swam up through his consciousness into his mind where he could grasp it and it was not a surprise so much as a memory: He never should have left Parkman. That was what it was. He never should have quit his book and come off on some crazy junket like this to Florida. Guilt riddled him: he had no right to do it. He owed it to the world, to the damned world that he was going to shoot off at the ankles, not to do it.

Beside him, the tall hollow-eyed 'Bama still drove easily, if tiredly, riding the big heavy Packard as if it were a horse. Dave stole a look at him, possessed by a hatred for him so strong he could have done him bodily injury. Implacably he hated 'Bama for deliberately talking him into making this lazy worthless pleasure trip to Florida, and Gwen French for putting him in a position where he had been forced to accept it because she hadnt invited him over Christmas when she knew how badly he wanted to come, and also Bob French for allowing her to do a thing like that and not stopping her. And he hated Frank for getting him to stay in Parkman in the first place. Implacably. All of them.

He was weak. They all knew he was weak. Why didnt they try to help him? If it wasnt for all of them, he could be out in Hollywood right now with Francine, living easily and peacefully, and working on this book without all this terror and anguish, and writing it easy.

Inwardly he drew himself up to his full five feet six inches coldly. Well, he would do it without them, any of them. He would become a mathematician. A mathematician of the human soul. God knew the world needed one. There never had been one, not really. There had been so much crap written about the greatness of humanity and love for the human race it like to turned your stomach. It was about time somebody did a little exposing.

It was a large ambition for a man who was thirty six years old and had never yet done anything toward achieving it. But he could do it. Perhaps he alone of all the world *could* do it, he thought valiantly. And *none* of them could stop him. None! And he thought of that magnificent line from Stevens's poem about *What Thomas an Buile Said in a Pub*: where God was about to destroy the Earth: and the one little man said: "Stay, you must not strike it, God; Im in the way; and I will never move from where I stand." And then finally, exhausted by no more than the turbulence and vitality of his own emotions, he went to sleep.

CHAPTER 38

In Nashville, 'Bama stopped long enough to gas up and to find out about the roads. Apparently the information he had been given further north was accurate, and Route 41 was not in too good a shape on south. Tall and squareshouldered in his topcoat and pearlgray semiWestern hat, and looking curiously stable for a man of his precarious habits, he leaned over a map out on the driveway with the station attendant while they discussed the routes. He might have been any young engineer or businessman off on some extended trip that would keep him away from home for over Christmas. After he got back in, still clutching the marked map, and got them started through the congested downtown area at which he cursed in a patient monotone, he explained what the attendant had said about the routes.

Dave, whom the stopping of the car had waked up in the station, had waked to find his previous mood all gone. Only a vaguely reasoned, but for that nonetheless definite, determination to change his writing name, and a stubborn intention to hold 'Bama and Bob and Gwen and Frank responsible for what happened to him and not to trust them, remained out of all that torrent of emotion. These; and an obscure indefinite feeling that he had had, or almost had, a sort of revelation about life that he could no longer put his finger on. More than once during that acute emotional upheaval, that he still did not know the beginning cause of, he had been at the point—if he could have trusted himself to talk at all—of telling 'Bama to turn around and go back except that it would have made him look so ridiculous. (That was something else that was so frightening: Because of your imagination, or some screwball logic you thought you had worked out reasonably, you started something moving— moving on the physical plane, that is, like packing and planning and with other people getting in the car and going; and then suddenly, when your mind had changed itself, you realized the imagination and logic were no longer accurate or right, but you were powerless to stop because you had already committed it to physical action with other people and to stop would mean you would have to go all that way back and change all those plans, not only of yours but theirs.) And anyway he had been afraid to speak, for fear the grinding hatred he felt for 'Bama would have communicated itself to him. But now he was glad he hadnt told him. And because he still felt that stubborn secret dislike that he was afraid for 'Bama to find out about, he was much nicer than he usually would have been.

The routes, 'Bama who knew nothing about any of this said cheer-fully,—according to the attendant—were none of them in any too good a shape. But 41 was the worst; from here to Chattanooga it was in bad shape almost all the way; and once you got on over into Georgia it was even worse. There were two other ways: One was to take Route 31 out of Nashville on down through Birmingham (this was the way he always went when he came home; the Bee-Line, they called it) right on down to Montgomery (Mongomry, he called it), then 231 to Dothan, and 84 on to Thomasville Georgia where you hit 19. The other was to take Alternate 41 to Shelbyville (that way you missed the jog to Murfrees-boro on 241), catch 241 there and follow it on through Guntersville and Gadsden on down to Columbus Georgia and from there take 280 and State routes 55 and 50 (new roads, he understood, and in good shape) on to Albany Georgia where you hit 19. He had, 'Bama said, driven all these roads—at least the parts in Alabama—and he was in favor of taking the second route.

They took the second route. Dave didnt care, and said so, it made no difference to him one way or the other, and when 'Bama came to the junction he decided it by turning them off toward Shelbyville. It was 113 miles to Huntsville Alabama, and they reached it before eleven. There they stopped for a sandwich and a bottle of beer, the first food they had eaten since the sandwiches in the hotel, and Dave noticed for the first time consciously something he had been aware of only vaguely in Nashville: They had entered, and were in, The South. Capital letters.

It was the result of a number of impressions, and the total overall effect of it upon him was to instill in him a feeling of nervous appre-hension. It had been noticeable in Nashville, this peculiarly Southern quality, but there it had been much less definite, had had its edges rubbed off somewhat against the North. But here in Huntsville it stuck out like a winter cardinal after a snowfall. For one thing, there was that look predominant among the men: tall, high shouldered, long waisted, with hard thin highcheekboned faces and narrow coldly suspicious eyes. There seemed a tremendous suppressed violence about them, in the in-tractible expressionless faces, even when they laughed. You could not

help but feel they all carried knives. Everybody seemed almost waiting
to get into some kind of a fight, solely to relieve the tension, and the aura
they emanated seemed to hang over the whole town like a dark cloudbank just above the courthouse.

Dave had had the feeling before, in the South, and he could only
think with relief of when they would get to Florida; but 'Bama seemed
to be totally at ease and in his element. Another thing, his semiWestern
style hat no longer looked out of place or like an idiosyncrasy because
almost all the men here wore them too. The same thing applied to his
clothes and square shouldered suit and topcoat. If he felt the cloudbank
of suppressed violence hanging over the town, he didnt show it. Apparently he knew Huntsville well, because he drove them right to a place
where they could get a beer and a sandwich; and inside he joked and
laughed and talked happily with everybody, even though apparently
they were strangers, and they did the same with him. From Nashville
on—after he had spoken with the station attendant—he had been talking
with a gradually more and more pronounced Southern accent and
enunciation, and in the lunchcounter it became even more noticeable.
He was obviously pleased and happy to be there; and yet as the accent
grew, the look of suppressed violence about him that he always had
about him even back up North in Parkman, grew more noticeable, too.
Dave felt an intense relief when they were back out on the road and
there had been no fights. No knifings.

'Bama had filled the tank up again in Huntsville; he always did that
whenever he stopped; cuts down on the condensation in the tank, he
said. And when they were out on the highway traveling fast again, he
let go of the wheel several times and watched it closely.

"What did you do that for?" Dave asked him.

"Checkin the tars to see'f one might be low. If one tar's low, itll pull
the cahr," he said. "Its a good thing to do ever now and thin."

Dave filed the information away. He had already learned more tricks
and fine points about driving than he would have learned in five years
of driving by himself. He did not say anything about what he had felt
back in Huntsville, at least not then.

But it was not too much later than that, that 'Bama—in an indirect
way—brought it up himself. They had passed Guntersville, and the big
TVA government dam there, and driven on down the bad stretch of old
road 'Bama had mentioned earlier, winding over hills and down long
narrow valleys beside the railroad, and were almost to Gadsden, when
'Bama with a sort of sparkling of enthusiasm suddenly began to talk
about, of all things, the Civil War.

Did Dave know who old Bedford Forrest was? he wanted to know.
Yes, Dave knew; a little bit; he had read a book about him once. Well
right here, at this town of Gadsden, 'Bama said, was where Forrest

chased Streight's Raiders through; did Dave remember about that? Dave
didnt. He had a vague memory of the term Streight's Raiders; and that
Forrest had chased them two or three days and nights, but that was all.
The single book on Forrest he had read had been years ago, out in LA
with Francine, when something he had read had set him off on a kick
of Civil War reading which lasted several weeks before he wore it out.

But before he could explain any of this, 'Bama with a kind of explosion of talking enthusiastically sketched out the story for him: how
Colonel Abel D Streight of the Fifty-first Indiana had taken a force of
two thousand picked men mounted on mules and marched them almost
clear across the State of Alabama from Tuscumbia—that was near
Florence—to Lawrence almost at the Georgia line, through the mountains and behind the Confederate lines, in an effort to reach Rome
Georgia and destroy the two important railroads into Chattanooga thus
forcing Bragg to abandon the city to Rosecrans—that was the strategy
of it—a daring plan, and Streight very nearly made it too. Except for old
Bedford Forrest. From Moulton, through Blountsville and Gadsden, to
Lawrence—a distance of a hundred and fifty miles—with almost no
rest for either side and damn little food, Forrest chased him four full
days and nights, fighting two pitched battles and keeping up a running
fight all the rest of the way. When Streight finally surrendered at Lawrence, five miles from the Georgia line, he had only about sixteen hundred of his men still on their feet and Forrest had only five hundred,
out of the thousand he started with. Streight's men were falling asleep
on their rifles and Forrest, who had wisely slept his men the night before,
bluffed him into thinking he had a lot more men than he really had—a
thing Forrest was often wont to do—and talked him into surrendering.
And not only all that, Streight had cleaned the country of horses and
mules as he passed, so that Forrest could get no fresh mounts. As 'Bama
recounted the story, it began to come back to Dave and he remembered it.

"Some of them probly rode through right along here where we're
drivin," 'Bama said excitedly. "That English general, that Lord Wol-
seley, said it was one of the greatest feats of cavalry there ever was and
read like a 'romance'." Then suddenly he pointed, off to the right, at
a blacktop road. "See! Theres the road to Blountsville there, on back in
the mountains." In another few minutes they were in the little town of
Atalla and had turned off onto the short four-lane into Gadsden. "Right
through here they went," he said. "Streight didnt even have time to
stop in Gadsden except to round up the horses and set a couple of store-
houses on fire, before Forrest was right on him."

'Bama, it turned out, was a considerable student of the Civil War.
Especially of the campaigns in the West, and of these particularly of
the campaigns of Nathan Bedford Forrest. His old granddaddy had been
a trooper under Forrest as a boy of fifteen and had been wounded seven

times, and after the war he had bought every book on the war and on Forrest that he could find, although he couldnt read himself and had to get his wife to read them to him. When he died he had left all his books to the youngest of all his grandsons; "That was me," 'Bama grinned. He could only remember his granddaddy as an old old man of nearly eighty who could hardly get around and talked in a quavery voice but was nevertheless still peppery enough to be always cussing everybody out, —"He was a mean old fart," 'Bama grinned— and who although he was only a pore old cropper used to save up enough money every two years to get in his old old uniform which was now too big for him and go to the 'Army meetins'. He had not been with Forrest on the ride after Streight but had been at Florence with Dibrill's regiment attacking Dodge, and it was one of the greatest regrets of his life. "But he still knew all about it," 'Bama grinned. When the old man died at eighty two, 'Bama had been fourteen and a freshman in high school in Birmingham. "I think thats why he give me the books," 'Bama grinned. "He made me promise him Id graduate from high school before hed leave me the books. I was the only one in the family who eveh did, and I guess he wanted to be sure I could read em myself. I still got all them books," 'Bama grinned. "Theyre all down at the farm up home."

Dave realized, suddenly, that he was probably hearing things about 'Bama Dillert that nobody else in Parkman had ever heard before. A long car trip was often favorable to such revelations. And what was more, he was suddenly intensely interested, in an almost feverish, perverse way; he was learning about the kind of Southerners he had seen back there in Huntsville and been afraid of, and he wanted more. When 'Bama stopped, he described for him the book he had read in the Los Angeles Public Library. He already had a hunch 'Bama might have it.

"It was sort of a grayish-brownish colored book; with big red letters on it sort of like italics: LIFE OF GENERAL NATHAN BEDFORD FORREST. Written by some doctor. Worth, or Wenth or something like that."

"Wyeth," 'Bama said. "Dr John A Wyeth. Yeah, I got that one. Published in 1899."

"Thats it! Why, hell, man, youve got a valuable book there! When I read it in L A, they wouldnt even let me take it outside the library it was so valuable."

"Yeah?" 'Bama said. "How much do you think its worth?"

"Why, it must be worth thirty or thirty five dollars anyway."

"Thirty or thirty five dollars!" 'Bama snorted. "Hell, that aint nothin. Thats peanuts."

"Youve got a distorted idea of whats valuable in a book."

"Valuable is valuable," 'Bama said. "And thirty or thirty five bucks aint very valuable."

"In a book it is."

"Well, its worth a lot more than that to me," 'Bama said. "I wouldnt sell mine for a couple hundred. Or any of the rest of them," he said finally. —"You know something?" he said after a minute, looking around at the country. They had left Gadsden behind some time ago. "Nobody today ever pays any attention to the Western Campaigns today. All they talk about is old Lee and the campaigns in Virginia. But the Civil War was won—and lost—in the West; not in Virginia. In Tennessee and Mississippi and Alabama and Georgia. But nobody ever pays any attention to that any more. Its all old Lee and Grant and Virginia. If youd of ever studied it, youd see."

"I dont know much about the Civil War," Dave said apologetically, "and what little I do know is all about Virginia." He could not escape a sort of embarrassed feeling, as if he personally had whipped 'Bama personally in a fight, and now didnt want him to be mad at him.

"Shore, thats the way everybody is," 'Bama said philosophically. "Well, the biggest mistake they ever made was puttin the capital in Richmond so close to the North. They should of left it in Mongomry. But everybody had a hero worship for the Virginia gentlemen. And the second biggest mistake they made, was ever lettin them get St Louis and then Memphis and Nawrlins and then Vicksburg and capture the Mississippi River. Yes sir, the war was won—and lost—in the West; not by old Lee in Virginia.

"And Ill tell you something else," he said; he was not speaking angrily, or wistfully, so much as in a purely academic way, and like a man who had studied his subject and was sure of his knowledge; "Ill tell you something else. There was a lot of good generals, and a few great ones, on both sides in the war; but the greatest general to come out of the war on both sides was old Bedford Forrest—and I dont say that just because my old granddaddy fought under him, either. Sherman said that himself. And so did old Joe Johnston and Beauregard. And it is a fact, that just about every time the South lost a decisive battle in the West or failed to capitalize on one they won, and Bedford Forrest was there, he had the right answer and couldnt get anybody to listen. At Fort Donelson he wanted to continue the attack, and if they had theyd have got the whole army out and maybe even have kept the fort; and even after they were ready to surrender he still got his whole command out without losing a man. At Shiloh when he found out Buell was landing he wanted to make a night attack before they could all get across and get in position, and he couldnt find anybody to give the orders. At Chickamauga he wanted Bragg to press on into the city after the battle and if they had they could have destroyed Rosecrans' whole army, but Bragg wouldnt and he lost the city permanently. And after that, Bragg tried to relieve him and Bedford Forrest told him to go to hell and got old Jeff Davis to transfer him, Forrest, back to Northern Mississippi.

"The whole thing was," 'Bama said, "he wasnt a West Pointer, like Lee and Jackson and Grant and Sherman, and the West Pointers ran the war. On both sides. I guess they just couldnt believe that a man who never went to West Point could be a great general until it was too late and the war was over. Even Forrest believed it himself, I think: 'He didnt have the advantages of education'. —But if theyd of promoted him up like they should have, given him the commands he ought to have had, he would have been way up there. Maybe even in command of the whole Army of Tennessee. And who knows what might have happened then at Murfreesboro, and Chickamauga? But West Pointers are just like any other class or profession. When it comes to their own special field, theyre snobs. Hell, even gamblers are snobs, when it comes to gambling," he grinned.

He shrugged and then paused a moment, the big black car shooting on down the road as he thought, driving it automatically. "I figure it was all sort of fate," 'Bama said. "Just fate," he said. "I dont think the United States was meant to be broken up into two little countries; where would we be today? against Russia? if we had? But you know," he said academically again, "there was only two real geniuses came out of the war, and thats Forrest and Jackson. There was a lot of great generals, but there was only those two real geniuses. Even old Lee wasnt a real genius I dont think. A great general, yes, but not a genius.

"You know," he said, "I dont know whether I read it someplace or somebody told me or I thought it up myself, but I think it would be a fine thing if someday—when the very last two survivin members of the Northern and Southern Armies finally died—they would plan to bury them together, in one grave at Arlington, and put one big monument over both of them. They could say something like: HERE, UNITED IN DEATH, LIE THE LAST TWO SURVIVIN MEMBERS OF THE NORTHERN AND SOUTHERN ARMIES IN THE WAR OF 1865."

Dave, who all this time had been making himself mental notes that he should read more about the Civil War and mentally kicking himself because he hadnt, and who was also still feeling the embarrassment and apologeticness of through no fault of his own having been born into the winning side, suddenly and in spite of his previously conceived resentful dislike of 'Bama, felt something touch him so strongly that it almost brought tears to his eyes. Simultaneously, he realized he could talk to 'Bama about the men in Huntsville if he wanted to; and also, that if he didnt do it now the opportunity might not ever come up again. At least, not so naturally.

"Yes," he said. "I think it would be a fine idea."

'Bama nodded. "Somethin simple like that," he said. "And not say on it THE WAR OF THE REBELLION, and not say THE WAR BETWEEN THE STATES. You know? Make everybody happy." He coughed apologetically. "Course, you could add to it. You could say: UNITED IN DEATH, AND COURAGE, AND BROTHERHOOD or UNITED IN DEATH AND SPIRIT AND THE HEARTS OF THEIR COUNTRYMEN. But I think all that would already be implied in that other. Dont you?"

"Yes," Dave said. "The first is better."

"Thats what I figured. The simpler you keep it the more dignified it is. I think it would really be a fine idea. In fact," 'Bama said, grinning suddenly with that penchant he often had for laughing at himself and his ideas, "in fact, I think it would be *so* fine that if I didnt have so much else to do, and so much business to take care of, I believe Id try to start an organization to get somethin done about it. But then, a twobit tinhorn gambler wouldnt carry much weight with the DAR or the American Historical Society," he grinned. "I aint respectable enough for somethin like that."

"We aint neither one of us," Dave said. "Listen, you know Ive been wanting to ask you something," he said tentatively.

"Yeah?"

"But I didnt know if I ought to."

"Shoot. Rattle em and roll."

"Well, when we stopped to eat back there in Huntsville I noticed something about—almost—all the men we saw. They looked—mean; like killers. Like theyd cut your heart out at the drop of a hat—and not only that but would be proud of it. And especially if it was a Northerner."

'Bama threw his head back and laughed. "Thats just because you dont know them and dont understand them. Yore strangers with them, and theyre strangers with you. But if you had lived with them a long time and got to know them—and they got to know you—youd find they wasnt any different from any other people. Little more closemouthed, is all."

"I dont mind admittin they made me nervous," Dave said. "I felt a definite sense of relief when we got back out on the road."

"Yeah? You really did?" 'Bama said, looking at him. "Well now, I never felt any of that. None atall. How much do you reckon of what you felt was all in your own mind?"

"Well, I dont know. Thats what I wanted to ask you."

"Well, Ill tell you something: When I first moved up North to Parkman I thought everbody was goin to hate me. I expected to be in fights and maybe even get run out of the town. But what actually happened was, everybody I met—within my limited social position, at least, that is," he grinned—"liked me just because I *was* from the South. I was a sort of a curiosity, you know? Well now, if you moved down there to Huntsville thats probly just about what would happen with you: Theyd probly make a mascot out of you. Their lives are no stranger to them than your life up North is to you. You see, I know the town and what the people are like."

"Maybe so," Dave said. "But theres still a difference. I can feel it."

"What Im tryin to say is that ever since you were a kid youve been taught to have a certain picture of the South, just like I was taught about the North. And everything you see in the South is colored by this picture you already got. But if you lived in the South, like I did in Parkman, then that picture you have would change.

"Shore, theres a difference. But not near as much as everybody thinks. The whole difference is that the South is more ignorant than the North. —No, thats not what I mean. What I mean is backward. Theyre more backward than the North."

"They all look like theyre still fightin the Civil War," Dave said.

"No, theyre not still fightin the war," 'Bama said; "I dont reckon youd find a single person in the South today who wouldnt want to be part of the United States," he grinned. "But they are still fightin the Reconstruction. Thats why theyre backward. The whole country and not just the South, is still payin for what the North done to the South after the war was all over. Old Thaddeus Stevens and a bunch of other sons of bitches like him sure fixed that up good. And thats why theyre backward. They aint recovered from it yet. And bein backward, theyre more simple, see? More primitive. Thats what scares you," he grinned. "Their emotions are closer to the surface— No, thats not what I mean. What I mean is theyre more ready to act on their emotions. Thats what I mean. If you insult them, they wont argue with you. Theyll fight you. And do it with a knife or a gun if its handy, and they think they can get by with it. Theyre more like the people use to be on the frontier, see? In a lot of ways I dont think theyve changed at all in the last hundred years. They havent got more sophisticated. *Thats* what you feel; aint it?" he grinned, "and what frightens you."

"Maybe so," Dave said thoughtfully. "I guess that is it."

"Course I aint like that any more myself," 'Bama said. "Im more sophisticated. But Ive lived with them and I know what theyre like, and theyre good people. If theyre yore friends, theyll give you anything they got; and you can count on them for friends a lot more than you can most people in the North. Well, thats natural, see? Because theyre more simple. They aint so sophisticated as we are.

"Now if you moved down in the South nobodyd bother you any unless maybe you said something out of the way, and even then they probly wouldnt do nothin to you unless they were drunk, but if they were drunk they might wind up in a fight with you and stick a knife in you. But it wouldnt just be for nothing. —And if afterwards it all turned out to be some kind of a misunderstanding, and you really hadnt

done nothin at all, theyd be the first ones to admit it and feel sorry—
and maybe even cry—because you were dead."

Dave thought he could feel a cold draft of air from the window on the
back of his neck. "Yea; but what good would that do the guy who was
dead?"

"I didnt say it would do him any good," 'Bama said. "I just said that
was the way they are. And, of course, theyre not all like that. Only the
less educated and more backward. And *they* wouldnt even do nothin to
nobody unless hed said something out of the way. Or done something
to have it coming."

"What about the Negroes, though?" Dave said.

"Well-l-l," 'Bama said, and scratched the back of his head carefully
below his hatbrim with one gloved hand. "I dont know if I can explain
to you how Southerners feel about niggers. I dont know if youd understand it. The truth is, most Southerners love niggers a lot more than any
white people in the North do. And most niggers love them more, too.
Now you may not believe that, but its true. Hell, they live with them; the
niggers fix their food for them and make their beds and take care of their
kids; they dont mind that. But at the same time they love them as individuals, they are scared of them as a group, see? Its sort of what you might
call an inbred fear, handed down from generation to generation, sort of
what a psychiatrist would call a trauma, because back durin the Reconstruction the Northerners who come down to get in on the gravy—not
ex-soldiers usually, but civilians, who never did none of the fighting—
they put a bunch of dumb no-count niggers, niggers without no education atall, into different offices and let them run things."

"Ive read about all that," Dave said.

"Yeah. Well, you probly still dont realize what a godawful mess it
made out of everything. And besides that, it hurt their pride in the
South. And they still remember that, see? Its a genu-ine fear. But that
dont mean they dont like niggers as individuals, see?—if theyre likeable
that is. And as for hurtin niggers they wouldnt do that unless the nigger
had done somethin to deserve it; just like I said a while ago about
stickin a knife into some white man. The whole trouble is, that where
you and me come from we wouldnt believe that the nigger or the white
man either, deserved to be hurt quite so bad as that for whatever it was
he said or did. But, like I said, thats because we're more sophisticated, see?

"Hell," 'Bama said, "it wasnt much moren fifty years ago that up in
Parkman a couple of farmers castrated some young town buck for
screwin one of the guys' daughter."

"A Negro, you mean!" Dave said.

"No, no; a white boy," 'Bama said. "Didnt you ever hear that story?
It all turned out to be a mistake, too, in the end. The boy—he was married—hadnt really screwed her atall; not that he hadnt tried; but the

girl was just scared of her old man because of gettin home so late, and
told him the boy had, to get him off her back.

"But my point is that nobody would even think of doin something
like that today in Parkman, now would they? Well, thats just because
theyre more sophisticated, see? But thanks to old Thad Stevens and his
boys a lot of people in the South just aint that sophisticated yet. They
still backward."

'Bama yawned, and after a moment said, "Lets stop up here ahead
and get another sanwich and a bottle of beer. Im gettin tard, and havin
a sanwich and bottle of beer always helps to keep me awake for a while."

After the stop—during which 'Bama had the gastank filled as he
always did whenever he stopped for any other reason—they went right
on, heading for Columbus Georgia now. Increasingly now as they went
on 'Bama was having to stop for a sandwich and a beer to keep himself
awake, and where hilly country did not slow his speed down he himself
deliberately slowed it down anyway. Dave, who had already had two
naps and wasnt sleepy, sat looking out at the wheeling Southern landscape and musing over the conversation about its people they had had.
His stubborn dislike of 'Bama—which he had clung to so strongly after
his violent emotional explosion of guilt and hatred above Nashville—
was all gone now, dispersed by the talk about the South. The whole
thing was so kind of astoundingly unbelieveable that for the first time
in his life he felt he had an understanding of Southerners and what they
were really like; and the conception was so exciting and opened up such
limitless prospects for thinking that he could hardly contain his enthusiasm. It was all really so simple, the way 'Bama explained it! The
modernday Northerner's popular conception of the Southerner as a
brutal, brooding, perverse, lawless killer was just exactly wrong—or was
only right from the Northerner's more sophisticated (and perhaps personally perverse?) viewpoint; the modernday Northerner would see the
men who settled the Far West the same way, if they lived with him
today. But since they didnt, he heroized in them the very virtues that
they decried as vices in the Southerner of today! Why, hell! it opened
up all kinds of— But how would you write it? how would you write
that and get it across? —Set it in some bar? and show two guys drunk?
and getting in some silly, vain, ridiculous fight? a fight that perhaps
killed or crippled one? and then show that both were sorry afterwards?
before the dying man finally dies? and yet at the same time neither one
really holds it against the other? Christ, what a story that would make
just in itself.

But then! Then, if you took that, and imposed upon it the modernday
Northerner's viewpoint, by putting it all down as seen through the eyes
of some Northern narrator—say some travelling Northerner like himself
who just happened to stop off at this bar—who not only was horrified

but had no understanding of what was happening at all? A kind of astonished pleased disbelief that he could think up such a story idea spread a glow all through Dave, but then something tugged at his mind and slowed him down, telling him it wasnt somehow quite the right vehicle yet. At least not quite. He looked back out at the country, excitement playing all over him like sparks of St-Elmo's-fire.

Beside him 'Bama yawned again, and then as if he in some way divined that Dave was still mulling over their talk, said, "You know, theres something else yore goin to have to take into account too; if you want to understand Southerners. And thats that in the South most all the men are dominated by their wives."

"Hell, thats true everywhere," Dave said. "Thats true in the North."

"Yas, but not as much; and in a different way," 'Bama drawled and shook his head. "In the South every married woman—and every unmarried woman, unless shes an out and out barfly or has had an illegitimate kid—is assumed to be respectable."

"Well, thats true in the North," Dave said.

"Yas, but in the South they really *believe* it," 'Bama grinned. "Course, you and me know it isnt true; why, just yore percentages alone is all against it. But in the South they been raised up on all this oldfashioned Bible stuff, and all that chivalry they used to teach them in the old days and that puts the women in the place of bein worshipped, as bein good and pure and gentle and sweet and wonderful. Naturally the result is that every man feels he aint really good enough for his wonderful little wife. Then besides, the women keep a pretty tight rein on the men, y'see, so that when they do break out for a little drinkin and hell-raisin theyre inclined to go hogwild; and then, added on the top of that, their guilty feeling makes them do even worse and go even farther than they ordinarily would."

'Bama yawned again, and then shook his head back and forth snappingly. "Im gonna have to stop for another sanwich and beer up here ahead. My eyes aint trackin." He had been without sleep—what, now? —at least twenty four hours, and possibly for as much as thirty six, Dave calculated.

"You want to stop somewhere?" he asked. "Or have me drive a while?"

"Not yet," 'Bama said. It was evidently some point of pride. He never ate or drank more than just the one sandwich and the one bottle of beer, when he stopped. No more and no less. He took nothing with him, either, in the car. They reached Columbus Georgia about an hour after dark. He held out that long before he had to give up.

"Guess Im gonna have to let you drive for a while," he said after they had pulled into the gas station, and rubbed his hands over his face. He sounded almost apologetic about it, as if he had let Dave down in some way by not driving all the way to Miami without rest.

"Would you rather stop someplace and sleep?" Dave said.

"Nah," he said.

They changed over in the station, and before Dave had got them out through Columbus and onto the stretch of beautiful four-lane that ran along in front of Fort Benning 'Bama was sound asleep, his hat tipped carefully over his eyes to avoid warping the back of the brim, apparently as comfortable and at ease as if he had been sleeping in a big inner-spring bed.

Dave drove slowly and very carefully, never going much over fifty, feeling a strong sense of responsibility for 'Bama's car. He had already fixed the two route changes he would have to make before they hit 19 at Albany in his mind, and had the marked map beside him in case he forgot, and he drove along letting his mind dwell on his story about Southerners. It was about time somebody came to the defense of the poor embattled Southerner a little; but that wasnt why he wanted to do it. He wanted to do it because it was a concept, a phenomenon, he had never seen before, and that somehow somewhere out of what 'Bama had said he had grasped for the first time, and not only that, had never seen handled anywhere in print before. It was something that *existed*. And it had not been seen before, and he wanted to describe it. More than that; depict it. Whenever he thought about it it filled him with a sparking excitement that was half vanity and half a humble fear that he wouldnt be able to do it justice, and on top of that a thin acidulous delight of happy iconoclasm at being able to shard some cherished belief to bits and fragments.

'Bama slept for slightly over an hour and then woke up as completely refreshed apparently as if hed had a full night's sleep and proceeded to straighten himself up a little in the seat, raising his hat brim just exactly enough to compensate for the change of position, and then folded his arms. He did not move again, and did not offer to take over the driving, and there then began one of those almost monosyllabic lessons in highway driving that Dave came to look to finally as almost an advanced course of professional instruction, and that in the end finally made him as expert a road driver as anyone who ever took to the highway in a car. 'Bama obviously dozed—from time to time you could actually see his head bobbing—and yet never did the opportunity to laconically and almost monosyllabically criticize an error get past him.

"Dim yore lights whenever you run up behind a car." . . .

"Always flick yore lights a couple times before you pass." . . .

"Dont slow down when you pass, get around him and get back in." . . .

"Yore runnin up on him too fast." . . .

"Always dim as soon as an oncomin car's in range of yore lights." . . .

"If he dont dim, flick him a couple times; but if he still dont dim, dont you put yores back on bright. Ever." . . .

"Let off on the gas, thats a truck. See the three lights?" . . .

And whenever another car passed them—which was much more often than when 'Bama himself was driving—and Dave did not immediately dim his lights, a thing he was not used to and had never even thought of doing before, 'Bama was always instantly there with his injunction as soon as the car was past them: "Dim yore lights whenever a car passes you. Youll blind him in his mirrors." He never missed.

Dave even took to making a little game with himself of it, just to see if just once the silent 'Bama wouldnt be caught near enough to sleep not to notice but 'Bama never was. Dave made a little less than forty miles in the first hour, passing through several small towns and hamlets. In the second hour he made a little more than forty; and in the third still less than in the first because he had to drive through Albany. In all he drove three hours, before they changed back over. Then 'Bama crawled back under the wheel and they were off again, in that steadily smooth accelerating that pushed you back gently in the seat. It was shortly after eight o'clock the next morning that they pulled up to gas in the little town of Dering in Central Florida in the lakes region, and Dave suddenly got the rest of his Southerner story just handed to him.

It all started with the man who serviced their car. He was a big man, maybe six foot two and weighing maybe two twenty and all of it meat, young, maybe thirty five, with the brooding dark eyes and heavy black brow and hair that marked him distinctly for a black-Irish Southerner with maybe some Indian blood, and he was leaning loafing against the gas pumps in dungarees and a T-shirt and Eisenhower jacket as they drove into the station. His name it turned out, was Jim Custis, and he could claim a direct relationship to the blood of Martha Custis Washington but that didnt mean much, the country was full of Custises, and he taught algebra at Dering College. He told 'Bama all this in a friendly way while he filled the tank and cleaned the windshield and looked at the oil. He did not, it turned out, work in the filling station at all, but was just loafing there today because it was run by a friend of his and there was no school as this was Christmas holidays and the week Dering College was celebrating its Centennial. He seemed strangely friendly, as did 'Bama to him, as if the two of them had been drawn together by some invisible spark which Dave was unable to sense or feel; but then when 'Bama went on to explain that he had Custis blood himself—and was able to trace his lineage back through his Granddaddy Dillert's mother to some branch of the Virginia Custises that Jim Custis was able to place and recognize—then the strange dark man really warmed up to them. Anything they wanted was theirs, by God. Anybody that had Custis blood was a buddy of his. He would even show them around the campus if they wanted and explain the Centennial to them. Had they seen the folk play yet? Did they want a drink? The county was dry of course, but he knew where he could get them some.

And that was the start of it. Before they left Dering Florida, where they had only stopped to get gas, they had consumed two fifths of whiskey between them (not counting what Jim Custis drank), had spent the rest of the day and the entire night—again without sleep—and had eaten four meals; and before they left Jim Custis, they had met most of his immediate family, including his uncle James Frye six or eight years his senior, and they had learned more about Dering Florida and its environs—which constituted, only and solely, Dering College—and met more of its people, than if they had come to Dering College for a year as exchange students.

Both of them knew about Dering College in Florida, of course: its history as a liberal school which admitted Negro students, and its renown as one of the very first co-operative schools where poor students could work out their tuition; all this was more or less nationally famous; but they both had failed to associate it with the town of Dering Florida when they stopped there for gas. Perhaps it would none of it have happened if 'Bama had not asked Jim Custis whether there were any antique shops in town. 'Bama was looking for an old eared three-legged iron pot and an iron teakettle, good ones, for his wife who collected all kinds of old kitchen stuff like they use to use years ago, and it was obviously that kind of a town. Were there any? There were, Jim said, there were at least three, and he personally would take them to them, by God; and he did. They found no iron pots but afterwards Jim Custis took them out to his house to look at an old brass pot which he owned and had been in his family a long time and he wanted 'Bama to tell him what it was worth, he himself knew next to nothing about antiques but his wife collected them. It turned out to be a brass jardiniere and was not worth very much and 'Bama told him so. Jim Custis looked disappointed, but while they were there, he said, he wanted them to meet his wife and kids. None of these had come into the front room while they were there, but now they did when Jim called them—the slender, pretty wife, and the two sons in grade school who were out of school today. The wife was plainly not very pleased and appeared to be perturbed at what was building up in Jim, whom she evidently knew well, but 'Bama with his experience of Southern women and with exquisite Southern manners (a surprise to Dave) charmed her completely out of it even if he did not take his hat off, although it was plain he did not reassure her. And all this while big Jim Custis stood sullenly and awkwardly by, trying to look like a host, but succeeding only in looking like a brooding wild bull, while some dark frustrated energy in him filled the whole room to bursting. He would just put on a shirt and coat and get out of these dungarees, he said, and he would be right with them. With a true cavalier's sensibilities 'Bama said they would be glad to wait in the car. No, no, he said, but then well, perhaps it would be just as well, since he would only be a minute.

"You want to meet some Southerners," 'Bama said as they sat in the car, "Ill show you some real Southerners. And you can figure them out for yoreself and make up yore own mind about them." Something wild had begun to burn in 'Bama too, some wild kind of pride, and when Jim Custis came back out of the house in a rumpled suit and white shirt with no tie, and looking more like a mad bull than ever, 'Bama grinned at Dave and then winked. That was when they bought their first three half pints of whiskey, which Jim Custis insisted on paying for,— bonded, government sealed whiskey, not no goddam Florida moonshine, he said. They bought it in a filling station—another one, not the one they had met Jim at—where they went in and Jim joked with the grease-smeared proprietor while he worked on a differential gear and gave him what was apparently a sort of required courtesy drink after he got it for them in the back. Then, drinking the whiskey but being careful not to be seen doing it, they drove around the town of Dering and parked a while at the deserted country club and a while on the campus and a while at the College's big outdoor theater, and mostly they just talked. They talked about the town, and about the College, and about the Centennial, and about the folk play, but mostly they talked about women. They must go to the folk play tonight, Jim Custis insisted belligerently, they couldnt leave without seeing the folk play, it was a big thing in Dering and besides there were all kinds of women out there just waiting to be had. And then, as if making some momentous decision that had to do with the big argument he had obviously had with his wife while they waited on him out in the car, he said that by God he would take them out to the damned folk play himself, by God, and they would all have themselves a time.

By now it was after noon and they ate a hamburger steak at a big truck stop on the edge of town where Jim Custis was well known. Then they went to get more whiskey. The more of it Jim Custis drank the more wild and dark his face became, and the more insultingly belligerent he got. Dave noticed the same thing in 'Bama, but in 'Bama it came out different; in 'Bama it only made him more deadly quiet and more hotly cold, until finally he said almost nothing at all and just grinned murderously while his eyes flickered all around under hooded lids like two living flames. Some wild emotional spark in him called to, and was complemented by, the same thing in Jim Custis. It was the first time Dave had ever seen 'Bama really display really powerful emotion. Dave could feel something of the same thing in himself. It was a wild desire to smash out—smash out at something he could not even have said what it was—and to hell with what the consequences were. He knew he must be getting it from the other two, because he never felt like that when he drank.

Jim Custis kept saying belligerently that they were both great guys and they were going to have to meet his uncle James Frye, yes sir, great guys, he said belligerently as if he hoped they would disagree with him about it so he could fight them for it. If they thought he Jim Custis was a character—and God knew he was one; God, *what* a character!— they should wait until they saw his uncle James Frye. He wouldnt tell them anything about him, he would wait and let them see for themselves. Except that he was the greatest slashhound in Lever County. The point was, James Frye was in the folk play. He played the part of a Confederate sergeant. See, the folk play had been done by some Playmakers Group from Cincinnati, and was being put on in conjunction with the College. It was all about the history of the College, how after Andy Jackson finally ran the Seminoles out in 1835 the town was founded and the College started, and then how when The War came the whole student body marched off in a body as a volunteer regiment for the Confederacy, and then after the war those that were left, the few there were, came back to make the College a place where everybody could go to school alike, Southerners, Northerners, niggers and Indians, and dedicated their lives to it. The villain was the old College president who got them all to go fight when they should have stayed and got their education. Of course, none of it had much to do with real life, but the point was, outside of the main leads the rest of the actors were local people—either students or just local citizens—and his uncle James Frye had been picked to play the Confederate sergeant. The point was, James Frye was the Confederate sergeant, and he could get them in back stage where all the women were. James Frye lived on his farm out in the slash pine with his wife and five kids but he would be coming in town soon to another niece's house, to get ready for the play. And, by God, he Jim Custis would take them down there. Wait till they met him. Wait till they *saw* him.

What they saw, when they barged into the little white clapboard house behind Jim Custis, was a slim rawboned highshouldered giant of a man six feet nine inches tall a few years older than Jim, with a pair of the most piercing eyes Dave had ever seen, and wearing long grizzled hair and a grizzled full beard. James Frye looked like a prototype of all the Confederates who had ever lived come back to earth, even without the uniform. He was standing leaning on a mantelpiece like an ordinary man would lean on a countertop, and holding forth in a tremendous voice to a nervous looking young man sitting on a couch who was obviously a college student. Frye was obviously not pleased to see his nephew, or the condition he was in, nor the two strangers with him, and he boomed out in that voice that matched the rest of him: "By God, Jim. Have you been drinkin again?" and proceeded to deliver to his nephew who was not much younger than himself a short nervously explosive lecture on over-indulgence in alcohol but at the end of it, to alleviate everything harsh he had said, the grizzled beard parted and white teeth flashed in an intensely vital grin and he said, "What're you drinkin?"

"Whiskey," Jim said violently. "None of yore rotgut. Want one?"

"No, no," James Frye boomed nervously. "You know Im on the wagon while the play is on."

"Heh heh," Jim said.

Again Frye grinned that incredibly intense grin that made him look as though he might at any moment explode outward in all directions. "Well, Im supposed to be." Then he turned his fiercely piercing eyes above the beard onto the two strangers. But when Jim introduced them Frye's eyes softened—toward all three of them, and looked at Dave unbelievingly. "Hirsh? Dave Hirsh? H-i-r-s-h?" The great piercing eyes narrowed; everything about him was great; his hand enfolded yours as if yours were a finger. "Now, yore not by any chance D. Hirsh? The writer, the novelist?"

Dave, who had long ago ceased to feel anything except acute embarrassment at the mention of his two abortive novels, nodded, unable to help wondering how this strange bearded giant in the backwoods of Florida would ever have heard of them.

As if reading his mind, James Frye's great high-cheekboned face above the grizzled beard took on a sly humorous look that was at the same time fierily indignant. "You think us crackers back here in the sand hills and slash pine and loblollies wouldnt know about yore writin, hunh? You think we're all ignorant Southerners; no education. Well, a few of us read a little bit even if we didnt go to school. Ive read both yore novels. The first one wasnt so much, but the second one—the one about the ball player—that was pretty good. Why aint you written any more?"

"Im workin on one now," Dave said.

"Yes?" James Frye said. "Okay." After that, there was not enough he could do for them. Yes, he would fix it for them to come backstage at the play; yes, he could fix them up with dates with some of the girls—of course, he said grinning that grin, he couldnt guarantee anything; that was always up to the man; but they could all get together and go out together on a big party somewhere afterwards; hed bring his own girl along, he grinned. He was obviously pleased that he was getting to take Dave out there and introduce him. 'Bama—who of course was not drunk and never had been, only emotionally involved, and who now had mellowed some and was sitting back basking because his sidekick and buddy had been recognized as a writer—James Frye only studied shrewdly and said very little to. His nephew Jim, whom it was plain he would rather not have had along, he was nevertheless scrupulously equitable to—except that he ordered him about like a patriach and was not above deliberately building up Jim's already obvious hero worship of him. He was not, as it turned out, actually Jim Custis's uncle; he was the uncle of Jim's wife—or more accurately, the husband of Jim's wife's aunt.

"Did Jim tell you he was related to Martha Custis Washington?" Frye boomed in his tremendous voice. "He is, you know. Well, Im related to the Carters. Who the hell were the Custises anyway? The Carters of Virginia were aristocrats when the Custises and Washingtons were pore folks.

"Well, what do you know," he boomed again. "And yore really 'D. Hirsh'. Hey, Jim, by God I b'lieve I will have one little drink.—Now, dont you tell on me, boy," he said dryly to the college boy on the couch. The boy grinned nervously.

Jim Custis passed his uncle his half pint bottle with a grin. Since coming into the house he had become—comparatively, at least—almost as quiet as a mouse. It was quite plain that he had a tremendous hero worship for James Frye. It was also apparent that everything had taken a turn Jim had not expected, with Dave's being a writer, and one that he did not like. He seemed to feel it put him out of his depth. And he apparently felt he had committed a bad faux pas by not recognizing Dave as a famous writer himself.

Taking the bottle, James Frye had a small drink and then leaned back on his elbow on the mantel and commenced to talk about the play. They were all nice kids out there, they all liked him and he liked them, most of them were young college dramatics teachers from different parts of the country come here to be in on the experience of the play, he said. It did not take long, watching him, for it to become apparent that James Frye was very vain of his great height and stature—and also of his beard and long hair. "It must be this damned beard Ive had to grow for my part," he said tugging it and giving that flashing violent grin of his, "that gets to them all so. I guess they never been kissed by a beard before. That and the fact that Im sort of a character to everybody out there," again he grinned, "theyre all civilized Northern city people, y'see." Yes, he could fix it up for all of them tonight, Frye boomed in his tremendous voice. He had another small drink. What would they need, four? four girls? Sure, he could fix that easy. Not only that, he knew a wonderful place where they could take them. He knew of an old deserted cabin back in the slashes where nobody lived anymore, where they wouldnt have to worry about the county law finding them. They could take a bunch of whiskey and some blankets and build a fire and have one hell of a party. The old cabin had a fireplace in it and a good stock of firewood; hed been out there before. This girl he had in mind for Dave, he said, slowly waggling his beard and grinning, hed had her out there. Shed be nuts to meet Dave; she wrote herself, and wanted to be a playwright. There was just one thing; he wouldnt have any way to get back out home tonight after the party; would they be willing to drive him back out to his farm? they would? then everything was fine. Matter of fact, his farm wasnt too far from the cabin. Yes sir, he boomed triumphantly, theyd have themselves one hell of a party, to remember the crackers of Dering Florida with.

But it did not turn out that way. After spending the rest of the afternoon drinking whiskey with Jim and then attending the play, which was very interesting, it turned out that James Frye could not get the girls after all. When they descended into the shouting cleaning-up pandemonium of the backstage afterwards, the lethal blood-thirsty looking giant met them still in his Confederate uniform that he was obviously reluctant to take off, Navy Colt still at his belt, his eyes screwed up almost in pain under the makeup, and took them off to one side and forced himself with great strength of character to admit that he hadnt been able to do any good. Something else had come up. The director of the play was giving a party at his place for some friends who had come down to visit him from Cincinnati and he had invited James Frye's own girl friend, and James Frye too, and Frye had not been able to talk his girl friend out of going. Of course, he himself wasnt going. The other two girls he had picked out for Jim and 'Bama also wouldnt go; of all the damned times in their lives they had had to pick tonight to have dates themselves. Only the girl he had picked out for Dave was available. And that was the way it was. And now he wanted to introduce them all around to everybody. If theyd just wait a minute. Before everybody left, y'see.

Nobody said anything except Jim Custis, who muttered: "Oh, great Jesus!" whereupon James Frye turned on him blazingly and said, "Now by God, shut up, Jim! Im not worried about you. Youve got me into enough trouble with yore wife my niece as it is. What Im worried about is these gentlemen. Theyre going to think we're pretty crappy pickins here in Dering Florida." But neither Dave nor 'Bama cared very much, any more. An afternoon of drinking with Jim—who as he drank more had waxed sentimental and taken them around to his old high school to show them his old football field he used to play on—and his peculiar brand of high-driving belligerent energy, plus so little sleep the night before, had finally worn both of them down into a state of dullness from which they viewed even women with apathy.

"Look, the truth is," 'Bama said equably, "we didnt either one of us have any sleep at all last night, we drove all night, and we wouldnt either one of us be any good anyway. The best thing is for us to just hightail it on out of here and go right on to Miami."

But now it was James Frye's turn to grow fierily belligerent. He absolutely would not hear of it. He had promised them a party, and he would by God see that they had one. And anyway, he still had to introduce them around yet; so theyd talk about it later. It was obvious that James Frye had been doing some pretty heavy drinking on his own, since he had had those first ones with them at the house. Not enough to unstabilize him, or hurt his acting of his role, but certainly enough to show. Meticulously, and even proudly, he led them around from group to group introducing them (it was plain everyone had a great affection for him) and then over to the lobby of the ladies' dressing room where when he introduced them to his own girl friend among the others he did it very coldly, and then took them outside to meet the director and the staff; (but it was plain that even Frye realized that he had overestimated the status of his guest celebrity, and Dave who by now was nearly hysterical from exhaustion could hardly keep from laughing out loud. Nevertheless, the giant Confederate carried it off, not only well, but with a great—if superimposed—dignity. Then he led them back to the men's dressing room where with obvious reluctance he began to get out of his uniform). The director had invited them all over to his place, he said, but he had declined; it would only be a bunch of intellectual conversation, and he knew they wouldnt want that. Now the girl—she was the very first one they had met—would be waiting outside in just a few minutes, if she wasnt there already. What he suggested was that Dave go on out with her and meet the rest of them later. (She taught up in Michigan somewhere and had driven down and had her own car, so they could take 'Bama's car and he could meet them in town later.) One of the restaurants. What did they think of that? he said, as lovingly he adjusted the gray uniform on its hangers and gently put it back in the locker and began to get back into his own clothes. The change did not really change him much, Dave thought ridiculously, just made him look to be on furlough.

Well, damn it, what did they think of it? Frye demanded. Dave had to flatly refuse to go, and finally take refuge in the fact that he would not leave his buddy 'Bama to go off with a girl when his buddy didnt have one, before the giant Confederate sergeant would finally give up on it. Even so, it was with a certain measure of reluctance that Dave turned it down; but his body was too exhausted by now to keep up with the wishes of his mind; besides, if he left 'Bama now he didnt know when he might catch up with him again. Everything was turning into one of those Walpurgis Nights.

"But damn it, man! You can make her!" James Frye protested violently, as if he couldnt believe his ears. "I know you can!"

"I wont leave my buddy," Dave said stoutly.

"Well," the giant Confederate grinned with that flashing vitality through his beard, "it looks like we all gonna have us a stag party then, dont it?"

"Lets go get some whiskey, for God's sake," Jim Custis said with furious misery. "My wife told me I couldnt come back home anyway."

"Youll have to wait till I go tell Arlene some story first," James Frye said.

And so it was that, some time after one o'clock in the morning (the play had finished at eleven thirty), with five half pints of the government sealed bootleg whiskey, the four of them were driving along back the way Dave and 'Bama had first come in some nineteen miles then out in the pine slashes on an old gravel road another ten miles to the old deserted cabin James Frye had told them about. The cabin was not on his land but on a neighbor's, but it was only a couple of miles from his place where they had promised to drive him, and they could let him off there on their way back. All during the ride Jim Custis had been alternately sniffling and cursing. They had not gone out of town very far before he had begun to blame his uncle James Frye vocally for getting him into the untenable position he now occupied, all for some slash he had promised but in the end was unable to procure.

"My wife told me not even to come home," Jim cried violently. "She told me if I went, not to bother to come back, goddam you, James."

"Now, God damn you, Jim," James Frye boomed out in his tremendous voice, "you lay off of me. I didnt drag you into a damned thing. You came down to Nell's house with these gentlemen expectin me to fix you all up with gals on short notice without even a day or so to prepare. I didnt even want to try it or take them out there till you forced me into it. Now damn it lay off of me and shut up your sniveling, or Ill beat you half to death."

"With what rock?" Jim taunted sneering.

"With no rock!" James Frye bellowed. "With these!" and he held up two fists that looked about as big as an ordinary man's head.

"You scare me, James," Jim sneered, and held up his own fists which were nearly as big.

"If yore a wise man, youll be scared," the giant retired-for-the-evening Confederate sergeant advised.

"Hah!" Jim Custis bawled. "When? Now?"

"Any time!" Frye said. "Now, or any other time!"

They did not fight in the car. Both were obviously too considerate of their guests to do anything that might damage 'Bama's car; and indeed, 'Bama did not even seem worried that they might, Dave noticed. Actually, they did not fight at the cabin until everything had been fixed up and the fire built and got to going good. The cabin contained only a table and two chairs by way of furniture, and these were already set up at one end, so they had practically the entire twenty by forty cabin for an arena. Two of the half pints of whiskey had disappeared during the ride, and another one and a half vanished at the cabin before combat finally came. They all sat on the floor by the fire and drank the whiskey for a while; and here, as back in the car on the ride, the two things James Frye could not get over and kept bringing up again were how Dave had turned down such a good thing in Arlene, and the defection of his own new girl friend in going to the party when he didnt want her to. "Damn you, Dave, you could have *made* her! I *know* you could! Didnt I make her myself? And shes a sweet girl, a very sweet girl. And you turned her down. Why, she was dyin to go out with you," he would say over and over again. And whenever he thought of his own girl, he would curse her stentoriously.

"God damn you, Jim Custis," he bellowed finally, "I never wanted to get into this damned mess tonight, but you urged me."

"*Me* urge *you!*" Jim cried. "*I* wanted to go *home,* James! Ive seen your damned play already. But you were so damned hot to get out there and show off your celebrity friends! You used to be a man, James. Before you took to running around with these damned play makers. Even if you did read books all a time out on that farm of my wife's aunt. You used to be a man!"

"And Im still a goddamned man!" Frye bellowed at the very top of his tremendous voice. "Man enough to beat you to death! If *you* had a little more gumption and brains and *read* a few more books, you might even turn into a human being!"

"Ill pull out yore beard, goddam you!" Jim roared.

They were both on their feet before the words had stopped ringing, and stood staring at each other insensibly in the red light of the fire. 'Bama, who with Dave had also gotten up, stepped in between them.

"You fellas give me yore knives," he said and stuck out his hand.

"Give you what knives?" Frye said.

"What do you mean knives?" Jim said.

"Give me yore knives," 'Bama said obdurately, still holding his hand out between them. Without taking their rage-dulled eyes off of each other both men reached a hand in their pockets and pulled out pocket knives and let them clatter into 'Bama's palm and 'Bama, taking them, retired to the table and two chairs at the end of the cabin with Dave where they sat down and 'Bama put the remaining whiskey carefully up on the window ledge where they could reach it, while the two men, the two Southerners, both of whom towered over 'Bama who was a tall man, advanced upon each other as irrevocably and as ominously as a black-ceilinged thunderstorm advancing over a town. Neither one made a sound, and did not, for the full twenty minutes the fight lasted, except a grunt now and then or some wordless exclamation. They merely stood, very nearly in the center of the cabin, and battered each other until both exhaustion and the blows they absorbed had rendered both of them near unconscious.

To Dave, sitting at the table drinking and almost light headed from fatigue and the whiskey, it was as if someone had turned the time back a hundred years, a full hundred years—to 1847—as he watched these two huge men, one of them with a full beard and long hair, silently beating each other insensate in this hewn-log cabin by the flickering red light of a blazing fire in the old mud fireplace. Every time one of them was knocked down, which was often, the whole cabin would boom and shudder and groan from the weight of it, and the whiskey bottles would tinkle up on the window ledge. Then the other would step back and wait for the downed one to scramble back to his feet again.

All in all it was a pretty fair fight; there were only two attempted head buttings, both of which ended in wrassles on the floor which 'Bama stopped by stepping in and grabbing hold of both of them and reminding them both to "Fight fair!", and one other time when first one and then immediately the other seized up split pieces of firewood which 'Bama made them put back down, and once Jim knocked Frye into the fire singeing his beard whereupon the Confederate uttered a stifled surprised shout and leaped back out to brush himself off and lovingly pat his beard while Jim waited on him, but that time was really an accident and not intentional. Neither attempted any defense at all or tried to evade any blows and at the end, after twenty minutes of it, both were still standing, wide legged and with clenched fists, glaring dully at each other and breathing stentoriously when 'Bama stepped in and said, "What do you say we all quit now and have a drink of whiskey?"

"Ill quit if he will," Jim said heavily.

"All right; so will I," Frye said dully.

"But that dont mean Im givin up," Jim said.

"Well, I aint giving up," Frye said.

"All right, if you both want to go ahead, go on," 'Bama said; "but I still say lets have a drink of whiskey."

"Okay," Frye said heavily.

"All right," Jim said dully.

"And nobody's quit," 'Bama pronounced. He did the honors and got the whiskey, and after they had had a drink tears began to trickle down Jim Custis's cheeks and he went to his uncle and put his arms around him and began to weep. "Im sorry, James," he said. "Damn it all. Im sorry. Im sorry, James. I wouldnt do nothing like that to you for the whole damned world," he sobbed.

"Thats all right, thats all right," the giant Confederate said, tears coming into his own eyes. "There, there. Its all my fault. Its not yours. I started it."

"I want to go home," Jim wept, the words torn out of him tortuously as if he could hardly say them. "I want to go home to my wife."

"I guess we all better go home," James Frye said. "And these gentlemen want to be gettin on down the road to Miami, anyway. Weve held them up long enough with our damned craziness."

"We're all right," 'Bama said mellowly. "We're fine. Heres you guys' knives back." Both of them thanked him profusely and apologetically, for having caused them all the trouble they had caused them, and when 'Bama got the car turned around they went out and got into it tiredly, Jim still weeping in the back alone, James Frye the Confederate in the front with 'Bama and Dave. Frye had a beautiful black eye that was gradually and inexorably closing and the skin was torn on the side of his cheekbone, and besides that his beard was shortened nearly half an inch all over from the singeing; and Jim in the back had an inch long cut in one eyebrow and one ear that was swollen nearly double and could not even be touched, and both of them had numerous knots and contusions all over them.

"You have to turn left up here," Frye sighed, feeling his beard. "Its only a mile or two." Actually it was more than seven. The depression Frye had felt after the fight was still with him and evidently there was nothing he wanted to do less than go home, and as they drove along he talked to them, more to relieve himself than to give them information. (The play would be closing soon, he said, right after the holidays, and he didnt know what he would do then. They would all be gone out there, the actors, all the makeup people, the girls. He would degenerate right back into the way he used to live, reading books from the college library and chasing the local pigs and his goddamned wife and farming. It was a hell of a prospect.)

"God knows what we'll do then," he said.

As if in answer, from the back seat, Jim Custis cried out, "Go home! Thats what! Just take me home to my wife," he said miserably. "You talk too much, James."

"I guess hes right at that," Frye said, and went on talking about The Play. It had been the most wonderful experience of his entire life. For the first time he had learned what art and creativeness really were. He had used to drive right along here with Arlene. Right there they had used to park, right under that big tree; and talk, about life and plays and books and poetry. God, but she was a sweet girl. He was too old to expect many more love affairs like that. God, but she was sweet. "And you turned her down!" he suddenly cried violently. "You could have had her easy, and you turned her down!" Well, Dave would never have a chance at a sweeter woman. She was a helluva lot better than that other traitorous bitch, he said viciously. And then suddenly he quoted several lines from Lanier's *The Marshes of Glyn,* fingering his beard sadly.

Beautiful glooms, soft dusks in the noon-day fire,—
Wildwood privacies, closets of lone desire,
Chamber from chamber parted with wavering arras of leaves,—
Cells for the passionate pleasure of prayer to the soul that grieves.

Yes sir, Dave'd never have a chance at a sweeter woman. She was—
God, James Frye said, wasnt it awful to have to go home? No matter
what we did, or didnt do, no matter how we tried to evade it, in the
end there always came that time when we had to go home.

It was a symbol of life, by God, he said. Slowly and gradually, but
perceptibly, as he talked, the confidence he had exhibited in the afternoon came back to him and with it the supreme vainness about himself
that went with it. "Damn, I like to ruined my beard," he laughed.
"I think when the play closes Ill just keep on wearin it.

"You know, the trouble with me was I was born just about a hundred
years too late. I should of been born before the Secession. Then I would
have died in the war, and Id have been all right, happy." He paused a
moment. "Im a goddamned Rebel, thats what I am! A diehard Confederate! You niggerlovers from the North, you cant tell me a nigger's
bettern a white man! I know better! A nigger's black and a white
man's white! Im a white man, and a goddamned Unreconstructed
Rebel! No damn nigger's as good as a goddamned white man! And you
cant tell me any different! Heres where I get out," he said. "Thats my
house right over there."

'Bama stopped the car. And Dave, who was dead for sleep but could
not sleep as long as he found himself around the tremendous violent
vitality of this man, and who had read in magazines for years about the
evil portents of such men who made such statements as Frye had just
made, found that he was smiling. There wasnt anything evil about it at
all, or even dangerous really. It was just a simple idea. James Frye
might, if forced, carry it to fire and sword, and if pressed, even his own
life, and he might kill other people over it, Negroes and whites alike.
But it was still just a simple idea; erroneous, sure; but no more erroneous
or evil than a lot of other simple ideas—such as the idea that a college
education automatically made a person more intelligent, or the idea that
the President of the United States has to be a great man. It was just—it
was just sort of—well, just simple. And instead of feeling his spine
chill and a sense of evil sweep over him, he only felt protective toward
this man.

"You dont hate Negroes, do you?" he said, grinning in spite of himself.

"Hate them?" James Frye said, looking mildly startled. "Hell, no.
Why should I hate them? That wasnt what I said."

"Did you ever think of tryin writing yourself?" Dave said.

From behind the singed beard came a sort of muffled wry smile. "Oh sure," James Frye the Confederate said. "Ive thought about it. But I dont think I could ever do it. Not well. I think Id be too inclined to make myself out too much of a hero. You know what I mean?" He opened the car door and unfolded, as it were, section by section his giant frame and got out. "Well, maybe Ill see you boys again some time," he said. "But I dont suppose so. Youll get old Jim here home all right, wont you?" he said tenderly.

"Just take me home to my wife," Jim Custis moaned from the back seat, "I want my wife," and commenced to weep again.

"We shore will," 'Bama said across Dave through the open door.

"Then Ill say no more," James Frye said sententiously, and shut the door. As they drove on off they could look back and see him standing in the moonlight in the road, all the long legged, high shouldered, six foot nine inch Confederate frame of him, the moonlight catching silver lights in his long hair and his beard. He waved once and turned toward his home.

He was the kind of people Dave had always had an affinity for. The kind of people, as old Van Loon had said once in his Life of Rembrandt, who would lie, and cheat and steal, and fight, and whine, and lie again, and die in the gutter, but who were always in the end just what they were and themselves. And Dave loved them just as much as old Van Loon did.

In the moonlight the white gravel road was very long and they wound in and out of the dark slashes of pine for what seemed forever. Nothing moved anywhere, and the Packard seemed to be out there totally alone in the wilderness of pine forest. James Frye had said they couldnt get off on the wrong road because there only *was* one and after they came to the highway they were to turn left, but now they began to wonder. Occasionally they passed houses, unlighted and dark, but these obviously housed only the dead, if they housed anything at all, not the living. A couple of times vicious dislikeable dogs, left behind when the owners had fled or died and now reverted to savagery, roared out bristling to bark at them for invading their domains. Once or twice in the back seat Jim cried out, "Please take me home to my wife!" and then burst into a fit of weeping. It really could not be called weeping; what he did, it was too violent and too full of harsh vitality. And it could hardly be called crying either, it was too emotionally turbulent. Finally, they reached the blacktop highway and turned left and began for the third time to cover the long straight wearing Florida road into Dering.

When they left Jim Custis out at his house, he hardly bothered to say goodby or even pause and made a bee line for the darkened front door, walking swiftly. 'Bama waited a minute to see if he was going to be locked out, but the door was not locked and he disappeared inside quickly.

"Well, what do you want to do now?" Dave said. "Go somewhere and bed down?"

"Christ, no," 'Bama said. "All I want is to get out of here and get back out on the road. Ive had all of this place I can stand for one session. Anyway," he said, as they drove through the now thoroughly sleeping town, "there aint anyplace here we can stop now."

"Arent you afraid youll fall asleep driving?"

"No; Im wore out all right, but I aint sleepy. I just want to get going."

"Thats just about the way I feel," Dave said. His heart was pounding in his chest, slowly and beatingly, in a sort of protest at the strain that had been put on it. He had had only two or three short snatches of sleep in forty eight hours and he was so totally exhausted that even to move his arm he felt might burst his heart and kill him, but he was not sleepy. His whole mind and intelligence was almost feverishly excited over his story "The Southerners", which he had tentatively titled it, and over what Jim Custis and James Frye between them and their characters had given him for it. They had filled out the missing link in it, which was a ridiculous thing but still the most important thing in it: he had had the story and the theme and even the plot—but he hadnt had any Southerners to go in it. He would use Jim Custis and James Frye. And somehow he would have to work some kind of a damned folk play into it, so he could use that beard and long hair Frye wore for his part as the Confederate sergeant. Without making it seem too outlandish. Then something clicked resoundingly in his head: the Confederate. "The Confederate"—there was your title! "The Confederate". The twentieth century Confederate, the Confederate of 1948! The very use of the word for a story set in the present gave it an added twist and power, and added all sorts of unsayable implications. "The Confederate"; the man who, as even he himself had said, should have been born a hundred years ago, but who had instead been picked up, beard, long hair and all, and set down here in a day of fast cars and airplanes, where everything he was and stood for was not only gone and outmoded and dead, but was looked at shamefully by a society that had moved on. "The Confederate". The very thought was enough to send a chill of creativeness rippling up Dave's spine and bring near tears to his eyes.

James Frye had a lot of things he could write about and should write about, but he would never do it himself. Well, he, DAVID HERSCHMIDT, would do it for him, and make people see it for him. The story would not be in a bar, it would be laid at the play; and the drinking would be done from half pint bottles; and the knife fight itself would be between James Frye and Jim, and they would kill one or the other—as they probably would almost surely have done anyway, if 'Bama hadnt been there; and himself the Northerner, transposed to the mild mannered little director of the play from Cincinnati, would be the uncomprehending and horrified narrator. Christ, what a story it would make. The dying Jim Custis weeping and calling for his wife. Dave sat and thought about it lovingly, his mind racing and excessively active from the same fatigue which chastized his body, as 'Bama drove on out the road that led to Polatka and De Land and finally to Daytona where they would hit Route One.

"You know, this damned road wasnt the best road we could of took," 'Bama said; "I dont know why I took it. Theres a jog back north from De Land to Daytona whichll take us twenty miles out of the way." He mused a moment. "Guess it was just fate, hunh?—Well, what do you think of yore Southerners now?"

"I wouldnt have missed it for anything," Dave said. "Ive got an idea for a short story out of it—out of what happened tonight, and what you and me talked about before—that I want to write as soon as we get to Miami."

He did not remember when he fell asleep, but it was after he had finished telling 'Bama about the story. But when he awoke it was to find the Packard parked in the driveway of a roadside park between the barbeque oven and a picnic table, and 'Bama sprawled back under the wheel with his hat over his eyes, asleep. The gambler had finally had to give it up. While he waited for him to wake he got out and sat at the picnic table and made notes on the story in pencil, pleased that none of the excitement about it had left him. It was already full daylight and cars and trucks whizzed past them through the moist spring air a few feet away on the road. He had no idea where they were but there was a Route One marker nearby so he assumed they were somewhere between Daytona and Miami. When 'Bama finally woke, he had already finished his notes and after a leak and a walk around the little park they got back in and started on, stopping at the first little town for some breakfast.

They reached Miami shortly before noon. Dave had never been there before, but 'Bama had, and knew his way around, and drove straight across the Venetian Causeway to the Beach. It was all very exciting and alive and vacation- and Florida-looking, with all the different kinds of palm trees and the Spanish-type buildings and you could smell the salt in the air and feel it on the open window ledges of the car. He drove straight up Collins Avenue to 41st Street and then to a little green and cream colored hotel a block off Collins near the canal where he had once stayed before, and where he engaged a corner suite of three rooms overlooking the canal. The same fat bald aging young Jewish man still ran it now who had run it back during the war, he said, and with the aid of half a bottle of whiskey drunk in the sitting room looking out between the palms to the boats moored in the canal they each went to bed and slept the rest of the day and all that night, and then Dave went to work.

It took him almost seven weeks to write the story. By that time it had ceased to be a short story and had become a sort of novelette, one of those long short stories or short long stories whose awkward length made them almost unsaleable to any magazine. But he couldnt have done it any shorter—not and got what he wanted to get—and anyway he didnt care. For the first time since—well, for years—he had done something he could really feel elated over, be proud of, something he knew was good. But this time there was some new added element in the pride and elation that had never been in it before and that he could not name but only sort of dimly feel. It wasnt sureness, and it wasnt confidence (hell, he never had that). He felt like a badly battered, much scarred, tough old veteran who had served in so many battles of the human ego, and had the wounds and missing parts to prove it, that one more didnt matter. If this battle was won, there would be another one next week; and if this war was won, there was sure to be another in five years. Maybe, instead of confidence, it was just merely lack of over-confidence that he felt. Anyway, whatever it was, he knew that "The Confederate" was good—perhaps the first really *good* thing he had ever written—but instead of feeling high and cocky he only felt relieved and grateful. After he finished it he copied it up in duplicate on his typewriter and put one copy away in his suitcase and the other in his typewriter case and went back to his novel.

They had set themselves up, or fallen into, an excellent routine. They would get up around eleven and 'Bama would take off almost immediately, sometimes without even having said a word, leaving him the whole apartment to work in. His breakfast he would eat out, so as not to bother Dave who worked better on an empty stomach. Then Dave would brew himself a barrel of coffee in the tiny kitchenette and have at it—anywhere from four to six hours before he quit, sitting at the little desk in the corner sitting room where, when stumped, he could look up and out through the open windows at the people and the dazzling white launches on the bluegreen of the canal. When he had finished the story, he let 'Bama read it before he put it away and was inordinately and deliberately pleased when the gambler gave it as his considered opinion that it was very good and gave a really accurate picture of Southerners.

When he got back onto the novel, he found that it had changed, too. For the first time since he had started it a couple of months ago in order to seduce Gwen French, he found himself approaching it with excitement and working on it with enjoyment every day. Anywhere from four thirty to six in the afternoon, worn out and sweating profusely from the armpits and crotch, he would quit and shower and dress and walk past the expensive facades of Collins Avenue and meet 'Bama at Winnie's Little Club for a drink, tense and keyed up and super-

selfconscious neurally from the working, where the bartender there after
a couple of weeks had got to know them and especially had taken a
shine to 'Bama with his strangely cut countrystyle suits and 'cowpoker'
hats, he called them. The 'tall drawl' as another habitue had dubbed
him, would always be there or if he wasnt, would arrive shortly. 'Bama
had become a great favorite with the Runyonesque lower level denizens
of the Beach and members of the professional gambling crowd that
hung out at the Little Club who had never seen anything like him and
largely spent their lives commuting between New York and Miami, and
there was always someone to come over and jaw with them and offer
to buy them a drink, a compliment which 'Bama albeit in a friendly
way invariably declined, although he would always happily buy anyone
else one, and which had become a sort of standing club joke and the
cause of constant small wagers 'to see if somebody could not get the
tall drawl to accept a drink', a kind of joshing 'Bama bore with goodnatured equanimity. He would have spent his afternoon—morning, it
was to them—at the track, playing the horses with that quite mathematical passion which Dave had never seen anything like; or, if for any
reason the horses werent running that day, he would go off somewhere in
the afternoon by himself. They would have two or three drinks at the
Little Club, 'Bama always anxious to know how the work had gone
that day, always ready with sympathy if it hadnt and pleased if it had,
and they would talk about how he himself had made out at the track,
and then they would go off to one of the better restaurants, where they
did not have a floor show and try to charge nightclub prices, usually with
a couple of vacationing bachelor girls they had made dates with. Sometimes they had dinner alone—for them, it was lunch—but very rarely.

'Bama had been absolutely right on the availability of women in
Miami Beach. There seemed almost to be a surfeit of them. They were
there from almost everywhere, New York, Cleveland, Chicago, Detroit,
St Louis, Birmingham, Memphis, Cincinnati; usually in pairs, sometimes in threes or fours, all of them secretaries or business girls come to
Miami Beach to spend their two or three week yearly vacations. The
threes and fours were much harder to break in with, but then there was
almost never a need to try them because there were always enough pairs
available. Many of them were obviously looking for temporary romance,
which they just as obviously hoped might become permanent,
and away from home where they were not known they could easily
afford to be much more seducible. Bill Jordan's Bar of Music any
time, and the Five O'Clock Club at cocktail time, were excellent places
to find them. Chic, well-dressed, well-groomed, obviously able to take
care of themselves—either with a man, or in other things—they were all
attractive although none of them ever had the beauty of face or the magnificent bodies of the more or less permanent chorus girls who drifted

around, in and out, everywhere; but, as 'Bama wisely suggested, it was a lot better to stick to the vacationing secretaries. They were a lot less mercenary, and it took a lot less money to entertain them; and besides, as 'Bama pointed out, they could have almost any of the chorus girls or models they wanted from anywhere from twenty to fifty bucks, depending on whose stable they were in, so why should they spend eighty bucks on taking them out for the evening?—and then they might have to do it two or three times before they could overcome their scruples?

No, the business girls were better. Here, too, Dave noticed, they either set themselves up—or else fell into—a pattern. Almost all of the bachelor girls could be made on the second date (if they couldnt, you didnt go back), and a great many could be made on the first date, depending upon how everything went. Then they would have themselves girls and be set up for anywhere from one to three weeks, depending on the length of the vacation and how much of it had already been spent when they met them. Then it would be back to the Bar of Music or the Five O'Clock Club at cocktail time to find another pair, and the process over again. That was another superiority of the bachelor girls, as 'Bama again pointed out, over the chorus girls; they never stayed around long enough to get any dangerous ideas about thinking they owned you, and you didnt either one get bored enough to fight. Or at least not too often. More romance.

After they were once made, it would be a sort of a semi-marital bliss for the rest of their stay. After taking them to dinner—lunch it would be, for 'Bama and Dave—it would be out to the track again or to the dog tracks, or perhaps to some play or show or the fights, then to a nightclub for a while, and then a big supper somewhere—dinner for Dave and 'Bama—and then home to whatever hotel the girls were staying in. Sometimes, if they happened to be very scrupulous bachelor girls and were also sharing the same room (usually each had her own room), Dave or 'Bama one would have to take his girl out somewhere and rent a room but this double combination didnt happen very often. But they never took them to their own apartment. 'Bama saw to that. He would always immediately veto anything which might interfere with Dave's work on the morrow, and having two women in the apartment was one of these, or allowing them to feel free enough to just barge in whenever they got the idea. He kept Dave almost as rigidly in training as an athlete. In fact, he kept him in a stricter training than most of the famous athletes they saw from time to time around the Beach—such as the famous miler they saw out drunk in a nightclub the night before he was to run over in Miami next day; and as for fighters, so many fighters due to fight soon were seen everywhere breaking training that nobody even thought anything about this. Obviously, a great deal of 'Bama's pleasure in this friendship and in Dave came from the fact that he was being on intimate terms with and was buddying with, a writer and artist; and was helpful to him in his work.

'Bama, who was an adept at the introduction and seduction routines with the bachelor girls, was not above using this selling point about Dave's being a writer on the more intelligent-looking ones of them, at first. But he soon stopped this. It was quite plain that all of them were much more interested, and intrigued, by the fact that they were meeting professional gamblers.

Dave himself said and did little, and let 'Bama handle all the seductions. 'Bama handled them so skillfully and adroitly, and Dave was wise enough to know that he himself for some reason or other could not do it. He apparently lacked some prerequisite and essential quality which 'Bama had in abundance. They discussed this once, over their afternoon drinks at the Little Club (to which they never invited any of the women). "A man has got to not care," 'Bama explained, "whether he makes them or not. —I mean, *really* not care. Hes got to convince himself in his own mind that he dont give a damn whether they put out or not; he'll just move on. Because an act isnt good enough; women are like any other animal, they know instinctively whether yore actin or not. They *call* it woman's intuition; but horses and dogs got it too. Did you ever try to convince some horse yore his master when you dont really believe it yoreself? Well, its the same thing with women; you got to convince them you dont give a damn if you make them, and the only way you can do it is really to believe it. Otherwise, they will know they can already handle you *without* giving in, and they wont *give* in.

"Now, I dont mean you have to insult them, and make them think you dont care for them a tall. You dont see me insultin them like that, do you? No, what you have to do is make them believe that if they dont put out yore goin to move on to one who will, but at the same time make them feel that if they *do* give in to you, you could—and probably will —fall madly in love with them. That way, you see, they feel they have somethin to gain. Because thats really all they want: to make you fall madly in love with them. Women dont get their pleasure out of sex much, the way men do. Thats all crap these two-bit marriage counciller books put out. A woman gets her pleasure out of givin a man pleasure, and feelin that he has to have that pleasure from her, and needs her, and has to have her, and that he would pine away and die if she was to leave him or not give him any more. And thats what they want to feel. It makes them feel powerful, and thats what love is, see? It all depends on who leaves who first. The one that leaves first wins; so the one thats most afraid of the other one leavin him is the one thats lost, see? Women are smart; theyre shrewd; and they have absolutely no ethics, nor morals, nor integrity, and thats why men dont understand them. And thats why, if you can really *convince* them that if they give it to you you will fall madly in love with them, and at the same time convince them that if they dont you wont, they most generally will give it to you. But you have to convince them. The reason I can handle them is I dont have any ethics or morals or integrity either, you see? I sort of meet them on their own ground, and they aint used to a man doin that."

Dave hated to believe that this theory of love was true, although he was forced to admit that at many places it coincided with what seemed to be the facts. But whether 'Bama's theory was accurate or not, his use of it in practice worked out admirably. Of course, all this was costing them a good deal of money. They were living well—off the fat of the land, in fact—and they were paying for it. And 'Bama always treated the bachelor girls royally. Whatever he might think of their ethics and integrity privately, he never stinted when it came to entertaining them. This, of course, helped to cut down their bankroll. 'Bama could occasionally shore it up with winnings at the track, but more often than not he lost although this did not bother or upset him in the slightest. But there was always a poker game handy somewhere, where when their funds showed danger signs of dropping below the margin of safety, they could repair and win themselves enough to carry them another two weeks. The strange occult winning streak at poker that seemed to be with them any time they got into a game together was still with them here, although it could not be made to work for anything else than poker. For that matter they did no other gambling, except the horses and the dogs. Casino crap games and blackjack were for suckers only, 'Bama maintained, the percentages were far too much with the house; and they only went to the casinos when one or another pair of their bachelor girls wanted to live the exciting life and gamble a little, and then they only risked but little. But at poker they won—so consistently so that they began to be enviously recognized up and down the joints of the lower Beach by all the denizens.

It was in many ways a very enviable life, and Dave could have just gone right on living it indefinitely. His novel was coming along well, so much so that for the first time he actually believed that someday he might finish it. He was for the first time since he could remember suffering no acute unnerving loneliness to drive him into Walpurgis Night escapades. In fact, the only thing wrong anywhere as far as he could see was the fact that he was putting on so much weight from so much good food and lack of exercise. With his Hirsh family build to start with he had begun to look like a barrel with a head. But even this didnt bother him. What the hell? Both Stendhal and Balzac were more or less barrel shaped, werent they?

'Bama, of course, who ate tremendously when he did eat but as often as not ate little or nothing, gained no weight at all. He still slept with his whiskey bottle and hat beside his bed and still got up in his underwear in the morning reaching for both. Perhaps his swaybacked hanging belly was a fraction bigger, but not noticeably so, and in fact four months of living the high life in Miami Beach had changed him little or none at all, either physically or mentally. He had bought himself three new summer suits, all made to order by an expensive tailor on Lincoln Road and cut to the style and cut of his old suits, all three of them made of a heavy pure raw silk with a Shantung weave, one powder blue, one a golden tan, one a pale aquamarine. It was exquisitely beautiful material and you could not help but grin a little when you saw them on him under that pearl gray Stetson. But outside of these, he had changed not at all—except that he had become a fanatically and passionately enthusiastic lover of jai alai. Whenever there was a program at the big jai alai court out on Thirty Sixth Street over in Miami, he was always there, betting avidly with other passionate spectators, and finally becoming so excited that he was actually shouting and cheering out loud amongst the long rhythm of the vicious crack of the ball against the back wall and the rustle and thump of the moving players. If ever any of their bachelor girls wanted to go somewhere else when the jai alai was on, they were out of luck; they either went to the jai alai or they got themselves other dates; and 'Bama even talked about him and Dave flying to Cuba to see the games there, which were supposed to be better, but he never actually did anything about it.

As far as Dave was concerned they could have gone right on, living this life for the rest of both of their own. But there never had been any question or doubt that 'Bama intended eventually for them to return to Parkman. That had been an accepted fact from the first day they had come and 'Bama mentioned it every so often, matter of factly and as a foregone conclusion, when discussing something. He was not the least bit flattered or impressed by the status they had acquired on the Beach among the denizens and the gambling fraternity, or by his reputation as the 'Tall Drawl', a genu-ine char-acter. He enjoyed looking at the incredibly expensive beauty and richness of the Beach and its big hotels and private estates, but reflected indifferently that they all of them probably owed three fourths to seven eights of what they had, either to the Government or to somebody. Once every week or two he would send a picture postcard home to his wife, which generally read 'Everything fine. Im fine. How is everybody there?', but always neglected or else never bothered, to put a return address on it; and finally at a ritzy antique shop called the Museum of Historical Arms on Alton Road he found the kind of pot-bellied iron pot and tea kettle he was looking for which cost him a little more than twenty dollars apiece and shipped them home to her via Express Collect because as he explained they took better care of things sent collect. As far as he was concerned apparently, Miami

Beach was not a damned bit different or more romantic than Parkman or Terre Haute Indiana and he was, Dave reflected, probably right.

Only once did they ever actually discuss Dave's more or less reluctance to go back to Parkman, and that was one afternoon sitting in the dimness of Winnie's Little Club over their drinks, Dave with a Martini and 'Bama with a straight whiskey. (He never drank anything else; but lately he had gotten onto drinking Jack Daniels Black Label sour mash, and reflected dourly that all this high living was shore givin him expensive tastes.) It was not any attempt on Dave's part to put pressure on him to stay, but Dave had had an exceptionally good day working on the novel and he suddenly burst out excitedly and explosively that he wished they never had to go back.

"Why not?" 'Bama countered immediately, eyeing him shrewdly, and Dave went on to try to explain why, floundering badly. Mostly, it was because he was doing so much more and better work here, though, he said; the way they were living. Back there, it would be the same thing over again it had been before. The miserable, cheap, terrifying little room at the Douglas; and the terrifying loneliness that went with it. Somehow loneliness was always much more terrifying when you were living cheaply and had no money, Dave thought, had 'Bama ever noticed that?

"No," 'Bama said, "cant say as I have." His look was no longer shrewd now but interested, and a little puzzled, as if he either did not know what loneliness was, or else accepted loneliness as such a foregone conclusion he could not see what it had to do with it—Dave did not know which. "But hell," the Southerner went on, "if you was to go into that poker pardnership with me like weve talked about, and quit that damned worthless job with Frank, youd have enough money. Wed make plenty. You could get you back that apartment in The Parkman and live as high off the hog as weve been livin here."

Perhaps so, Dave thought, perhaps so. But there was more to it than that. It had something to do with the way they were buddying around together here, living together like they were. They complemented each other. And more important, 'Bama kept him toned down, kept him from flying off the handle with his wild-ass crazy stunts he pulled in an effort to escape from that terrifying loneliness that always dogged him, and always hurt his work.

"Well, thats easy to fix," 'Bama said assuredly as if he couldnt see where there was any problem. "We'll just rent ourselves a house when we get back."

"Do what?"

"Shore," he said. "Theres plenty of houses around town we could rent or lease. Probly, wed better lease one. So they cant throw us out later if we happened to throw a wild party or two." He thought in silence

for a moment, his eyes squinted with that cold hard look of a mathematical calculator he sometimes got. "Old Judge Deacon could fix it for
us," he said at length. "Old Judge and me are old buddies. Lot of folks
might not want to lease to you and me, but he could fix it without
nobody knowing," he grinned. "Well, come on. If we're going to pick
them two broads up we better get to moving."

This conversation occurred almost two months before they left Miami
to go back, and after that 'Bama referred back to its decision a number
of times. Their leasing of a house had apparently become as much a
foregone conclusion to him as their going back, and once Dave got
acclimated to the idea it became the same for him. The thought of
it left him feeling heady and excited, not only because of the life they
would live, but also because of the work he thought he might be able to
get done. He had already begun to contemplate doing a novel about
Parkman.

And so Dave sat back and waited, working and living up the high
life in Miami Beach and getting fatter, and no longer feeling depressed
about going home. He knew 'Bama well enough by now to know that
when the tall Southerner—he seemed tall again, and Southern again,
now that James Frye had faded—had got a genu-ine bellyful he would
just get up some morning and say it was time to go.

And that was just the way it happened. One morning he got up and
put on his hat and socks and poured himself a small glass of Jack Daniels
Black Label and wandered out in his underwear into the sitting room
where Dave was already making coffee in the kitchenette and sat down
with the whiskey and said, "Well, I guess weve about wore this here
place out, dont you?"

They had left in December with the remnants of a dying snowfall
still on the ground before Christmas, and they were returning in May
when everything had been turned a fresh vivid green by the returning
warmth that had not yet had time to burn it up and you could no
longer see between the trees and it seemed like a different country. They
had left this country as two strangers more or less on friendly terms, but
they were returning as intimates whose common stock of shared experiences had welded them into this incongruous friendship that was so
taken for granted now that it was no longer even thought about or
mentioned. A friendship that had begun, and was to embrace, the most
productive period of Dave Hirsh's life.

Dave happened to be driving as they rounded the long curve east
of the river and the towers of the Israel bridge hove into sight and
beyond it, five miles away across the bottoms, the hill where Parkman
perched. Excitedly, he eased down on the accelerator delicately and
professionally, wanting to get there, and as they shot across the bridge

he knew that he no longer gave a damn what Frank and Agnes and the rest of this fossilized town thought or said or did.

And more important, he knew he no longer cared at all what Gwen French did or didnt do. This feeling lasted about two weeks—or to be precise, until the first time he saw her.

CHAPTER 39

IT HAD not been until Dave failed to show up for Christmas that Gwen had begun to think there was anything amiss about him not turning up for work at his brother's taxi service. One simply could not be negligent about a job of that sort; and in fact, she had been half angry about it ever since he had allowed Frank to talk him into taking it. She was hoping he had quit. It was ridiculous and foolish enough, if he was so idiotic as to let Frank talk him into putting all his money—that he could have lived on while he wrote his book—into some stupid business venture; but to throw good energy after bad and go to work in the damned place, that was even worse; it was impossible! All that really mattered was his book, and Gwen could not help but feel that the job at the taxi service was solely and purely an evasion of the issue on Dave's part because he was afraid he could not write the book. So she was really glad to hear he had not turned up for work.

But when he did not come over Christmas, and then as the holidays passed on into New Year's and were gone, and he still did not come, she began to worry and wonder if it were not something else that had happened. There was nothing in the world quite so emotionally dead and utterly useless as a still-decorated Christmas tree the day after New Year's; all you could think about when you looked at it was that you still had to take it down, and it was pretty much the same with the holidays themselves, when the December bills began to come in, and you thought about all the useless presents you had bought that you didnt really need to, and all the frenetic parties you had gone to and had given, all for some false emotional lift that was not really valid come January 2nd. Her own Christmas party she had given Christmas Night so as not to conflict with the party Agnes and Frank were giving that day. Wally and Dawn were there, and Doris Fredric and a date, and a couple of other young couples drawn from the more promising—or rather, from the least unintelligent—of her students, and a couple of Bob's old cronies, and she was expecting Dave. What she had expected was that Dave would come over Christmas Eve and, having noplace much else to go, stay the night. And later on Frank and Agnes had stopped by with Marg Dennis for a little while, on their way to the Country Club. They, it turned out, had had no word from Dave either.

She had already, earlier, when handing out the presents, quietly set Dave's back under the tree in a little pile where he could get them later, laughing about it as she did so. She and Bob had both bought him little presents, nothing of any real value really, just something to show him he was not outside, was liked and wanted, as had both Wally (and through him, Dawn), at her suggestion. Bob had gotten him a beautiful, and quite expensive, set of handmade cufflinks and tie tack of red agate set in silver; and she herself had bought him both a Roget's Thesaurus and an uncommonly good combination coat-wallet and note-book complete with gold pencil because she wanted to give him some-thing that would have to do with his writing. There was nothing to do but to put them all back for him. Then she threw herself into the gaiety of the party and into the role of hostess, which she knew how to do so well but rarely allowed herself to do much any more because of the energy it cost.

(It was a fascinating experience, to watch Dawn and Wally together here after having seen Dawn with Jimmy Shotridge so short a time ago. Where there it had been Jimmy Shotridge who had followed Dawn around adoringly, worshipping at her shrine and doting on her with his eyes and extolling her artistry and future greatness as an actress,— here the positions were reversed and it was Dawn who worshipped at the shrine of Wally. Dawn was not as obvious or as naively open about it as Jimmy had been, but the result was the same. And the effect, upon Wally, was the same as it had been on her with Jimmy. It seemed to thicken his whole head and mind, and even the ordinary muscular expressions of his face, expanding all of them outward several inches with smugness until he actually looked gross. He became very profound and delivered himself of aphorisms about life that would have choked even an academic. He was pompous as hell. Gwen had been noticing this same quality in his work for some time, flashes of it, and in fact it had been present in the last two chapters he had brought over to her a couple of weeks ago when Dave was here. But this was the first time she had ever seen it in physical action, or actually learned the reason for it. Wally was in love with Dawn—or, more accurately, Wally was becoming sure, confident, that Dawn was in love with *him*; just as Dawn was sure that Jimmy Shotridge was in love with her. Of course, none of this had transpired while their parents were there, only before and after. They could let themselves go, around her, because they felt she was their friend. Well, it was a hell of a position to be in. She, Gwen, had known for some time she was going to have to get on Wally about his work, and she dreaded it. It would mean a scene, a cutting, barbed, harpooning scene, in which she would have to puncture him. She could not, obviously—even if she would; and she wouldnt—talk to him about Dawn; so the only alternative was to get on him about his work, peeling his ego down layer by layer like an onion, while he sat looking at her out of hurt eyes, until she had frightened him enough to make him mad enough to pull his feet back down on the ground and set that bullheaded dogged mind of his to show her. She was, from watching them, pretty sure they were not sleeping together yet, but she was just as sure that eventually they would be; just as she was sure that, unless something she did not anticipate occurred, Dawn would also sleep with Jimmy Shotridge, if not for revenge, then in selfdefense. God, what a mess it was, life.)

They came back over, Wally and Dawn, for New Year's Eve. Bob was off somewhere celebrating with a couple of his cronies and she was alone. She had been taking advantage of the holidays and no school work to work on her critical book, and the three of them sat up and saw the New Year in and talked and drank a little. They were both such nice kids. Completely blind, completely unequipped, completely unprepared. What else could they be? Their parents had never taught them anything. How could they? They didnt know, hadnt been taught, anything themselves. Stumbling along blindly on stubbed painful toes and with the skinned knees and barked shins of a Boy Scout troop trying to hike through life with an inherited set of sophomoric rules to guide them and following a map that no more followed the terrain of the ground they had to cover than they themselves did. So these two rebelled, instinctively, knowing only the negative, that whatever their parents had done had been wrong, obviously, so perhaps the opposite had a chance of being right, just as whatever they did would also be wrong, and become the negative for their children to someday rebel against. Strophe and antistrophe. They still had not been to bed together yet, apparently. And Dave's presents still sat in their little pile under the tree.

After New Year's, when she finally got around to taking down the tree, and Dave still had not shown up, she removed the presents and stacked them neatly in a little pile behind the corner of the fireplace in the living room where they would not be obtrusive, and where he could get them when he finally did come. She was sure by now that this was more than just some drunken lapse and a binge, but the days ran on down toward the middle of January and the end of term and finals and all the work that that date implied, and she could not spend all her time thinking about one person. Nevertheless, at odd free moments she would discover herself thinking about him, briefly, with a kind of puzzled hurt that verged on anger, and wondering what had happened to him. Then she would plunge back into the papers and the work again. He was undoubtedly the most talented of all the potential writers she had had personal contact with—Wally was still too young to know yet—and that even included Mac Price who had run off to

Chicago and not been heard from since. Was Dave, now, doing the same damned thing? If her theory of the selfdestructiveness of talent, as propounded in the critical book on Dave's Los Angeles group, was actually true—and she could not but believe it was—then that meant that Dave was not only the most talented but would be, conversely, also the most selfdestructive. He might be lying dead somewhere right now, a suicide or from advanced alcoholism, unrecognized and unidentified because of the absence of the papers he would almost certainly neglect and forget to carry with him. Oh, the silly goddamned son of a bitching fool! she would think irately, and plunge back into the work again.

After the ridiculous —but necessary, because it was the only known way to make most students work—thus, as always, forcing the good to suffer with the bad— after the ridiculous but necessary fiasco of final exams was over, and the spectacle of frightened weary-faced students cramming themselves with dexedrine the dextrorotatory isomer of amphetamine and the knowledge they had neglected to learn all year, had passed, she had more time. Students rarely realized that finals, which were so hard on them, were also equally as hard on the teachers, especially if they had any human sympathy in them; but after the new term started and February came everybody, teachers and students both, slacked off and relaxed a little, and Gwen had more chances to speculate on Dave. She didnt do it all the time, but she did it often;—oftener than Dave in Florida would have guessed.

The thing that set her off was the fact that she had tried to remember whether she had actually invited him over for Christmas vocally, in so many words. And she was sure she had not. The more she thought about it, the more sure she was. Finally, she even went to the point of asking Bob about it: whether either of them had ever invited him over. Bob smiled his sad little, wise little smile at her and said he didnt remember but he was sure he had not, and unless she herself had asked Dave at some time when the two of them were alone together he was sure they had not. That, she thought, more or less proved it. She had not asked him. She had committed the unpardonable sin of assuming that he was an adult grown up human being. And she knew suddenly then, surely and as if with some divination, that this was the reason he had taken off, left, like he had, without so much as a word to them and without even notifying Frank and Agnes. Because she hadnt in so many words invited him over for Christmas! Oh the silly, vain, ignorant, foolish, colossally egocentric, something or other fool! she thought with a fierily bright anger at him. The worthless, son of a bitching fool, that he was!

This was in February, and she took the little stack of presents out of their inconspicuous corner behind the fireplace and put them away in a paper sack to protect them from dust on a shelf in the kitchen pantry.

Two weeks later she called up Agnes, on some pretext or other, to see if they had heard anything of him. She was no longer angry now, at least only fleetingly so at times in a way that never reached the surface of her mind, and more resigned, but it was like some mystery that never let you rest until youd solved it. The moment she mentioned Dave—when she finally did; offhandedly—she could hear Agnes's voice become cat-smug at the other end of the wire, and her instinct was to slam the phone down in her ear. But in spite of the smugness, Agnes was willing to give her all the news theyd had, all there was. No, they hadnt heard a word from Dave or about him and had no idea where— or with whom, Agnes said—he was. But two weeks ago the Chief of Police Sherm Ruedy—Gwen knew Sherm Ruedy!—had called Frank up about Dave's car. It was still sitting locked up on the street in front of the Douglas Hotel, had been since before Christmas, and it had to be moved. He was giving Frank a chance to do something about it if he wanted to; otherwise he would haul it off himself. So Frank had called the garage and they had got a key that fitted it, but the battery was down, so he had just had them haul it around to the taxistand and park it there. Then just a week ago, the man at the Douglas Hotel had called up. Dave had paid the nightman a month's rent in advance when he left, but now the rent was a month overdue and what did Frank want him to do about it? All of Dave's clothes and things were still in the room. Frank had told him he did not intend to pay the rent, since he did not know where Dave was or even if he was coming back, and as for the clothes and things he did not give a damn what he did with them; for all Frank cared he could package them up and sell them. For the rent. And as far as she was concerned, Agnes said, she was forced to agree with Frank. But the conscientious little man at the Douglas had packed them up and stored them away in the hotel and said he would keep them for him, for a while at least. And that, Agnes said, was all they knew or had heard. Had they, Agnes said sweetly, heard anything over there?

"Oh, no," Gwen said. "He wouldnt have written us. But he had such an excellent book started. I hate to see it go down the drain. I told you about it."

"Yes, I know," Agnes said sweetly, "I remember. Well, Dave never was very dependable," she said, and might have been saying, in so many words, "I told you so," except for that little added tone of sweet smugness which implied she knew a great deal more than she was saying she knew. "Well, dont worry about him, Gwen dear. Bad pennies, you know. Im sure nothing could have happened to him, not that one; if we do hear anything from him Ill let you know right away, dear."

"Thanks, Agnes honey." Gwen hung up, furious.

Agnes was really very likeable, and her friend—probably her best friend—in Parkman; but there had been several times over the phone when Gwen could have screamed violently at her into her ear like a fish-wife. When she started putting on that smugness of hers—which Gwen had always hated violently anyway, and which made her feel degraded— And then when she kept talking about Dave's car, left to sit out there on the lot and rust itself into a hulk— And his clothes, stuffed away somewhere where if he ever did get back to them the moths would have them ruined—.

And there wasnt a damned thing she could do about any of it. Well, there *was* something she could do about part of it. She couldnt do anything about the car; but she could send Bob over to the Douglas and have him pay the month's rent and get Dave's clothes so they could at least be taken care of. —and *piss* on what they thought, she thought convulsively.

Well, she had learned a couple of things from Agnes, anyway. She had learned that he had paid a month's rent ahead, which meant he must have in*tended* to come back, anyway, when he left. And she had learned that he had left at night, because it was the nightman to whom he paid the money. But all in all, it wasnt much. She still knew next to nothing. And it was not until the last week of March, more than a full month later, when Wally Dennis happened to mention—just happened to mention!—that Dave had gone off with 'Bama Dillert the gambler, that she learned any more. Wally, apparently, had known it all along, since January.

Gwen had only the vaguest idea who 'Bama Dillert was. She had had him pointed out to her in town once or twice. A tall man in a western style hat. He gambled. For a living. She also knew that Dave had been running around with him some. She had to pump Wally almost forcibly. "Well, damn it! sit back down and tell me about it."

Well, Wally said sitting back down and looking startled. He had been putting on his topcoat. It appeared that he had run into Dewey Cole and Hubie Murson, (Gwen knew of the Coles and Mursons), run into them several times, out at Smitty's Bar. He had discussed with them Dave's leaving. Anyway, they said that the evening of the 20th Dave had been in to Smitty's looking for 'Bama. When he didnt find him, he left right away. Next day he was gone. And so was 'Bama. Neither had been back since. Also, Dewey Cole had said his old man—his dad—you know, Possum Cole—(Gwen nodded impatiently) had been sitting in the poker game at the American Legion that same night when Dave had come in and found 'Bama. They had played about an hour and then left together. So it looked like, wherever they had gone, they had gone together, didnt it? he said grinning proudly. He was as totally dis-interested as he was completely pleased in his detective work.

Gwen found it hard to smother her irritation, but she managed it. "Where do you think they might have gone?" she said.

"Probably down to Birmingham. Thats where 'Bama comes from. But you never know. That 'Bama," he said admiringly. "Hes known for going off suddenly like that on gambling trips. They might just as easily be in Mexico City or California." He sounded almost a little wistful, as if he wished he might have gone with them.

"How long have you known all this, Wally?"

"Oh, in January. First or second week in January, I think it was. First time I ran into Dewey Cole anyway. We talked about it then. They know Dave, too." He got back up, and was putting on his topcoat again. "Anyway, it was just at the time when I was working on the last part of that chapter on the girdle factory," he said. He gathered up his new chapter.

Gwen watched him as he left, feeling once again that desire to laugh disgustedly and shake her head. Writers! They lived in sealed cells made of the hardened juices of their own exuded egos. What she would have liked to do was run blithely and lightly down the room, laughing and tripping merrily, and boot Wally in the tail so hard down the stairs that it would carry him on past the outside landing right on down into the cellar without touching a stair. God, would he be surprised!—and not have the vaguest idea what she did it for. At the landing he turned back to say goodby and thanks and waved at her over the stairs. She smiled and waved back tiredly. Damn the little snob, anyway! God damn him! she thought angrily. Lord, she was getting so she swore as badly and unthinkingly as a longshoreman or a soldier, associating with all these damned writers.

Well, that was that anyway. She felt considerably relieved. If Dave had gone off with this 'Bama the gambler character somewhere, at least he was probably in fairly competent hands. A man who makes his living gambling like that had to be fairly competent, and practical, if he makes a living at it. Also, this 'Bama apparently had a wife somewhere down in the country, and evidently owned property down there; and that meant he would come back. Of course, that did not necessarily mean Dave would come back with him; but still it appeared to increase the chances that he would, and she was somewhat relieved. But over her relief, growing in ratio as it grew, was a sudden outraged anger at him that grew and grew and grew until it sent shivers of fire along her nerves. He had so much talent. And then to be going off on some months' long junket with some bum of a gambler like that! Even if he did come back, and go back to work. All that time wasted.

Sometimes she wished she had never had anything to do with any of them. And by God someday she wouldnt! Wally, Dave Hirsh, Mac Price, or any of the other, lesser ones. None of them, by God! None of them appreciated what the hell you did to help them, anyway. How could they appreciate it when they were never even aware of it? Right now she had a boy in her one freshman comp class. He came from further down state and was studying for the ministry because he couldnt afford to pay his own way. But already he had begun to put out these feelers—toward writing. Only tentatively as yet, but every theme he turned in had that weird focused quality of being real, of happening, realer than life. Before long he would be turning in extra pieces of his own to her; already he had begun to look at her hungrily, and eye her body when he thought she wasnt watching; she knew the pattern. Then there was the crippled girl who was a sophomore in her English Lit class. Polio or something. Already she was writing brilliant, bitter, caustic pieces—so unlike her lovable personality—that she timidly brought to her. But just let one boy make a halfway decent pass at her, and ask her to marry him, and see how quick shed give up writing! Oh, they were all alike, all of them. Gluttons, thats what they were!— and not just for food, for everything! They wanted to make every woman in the world, and eat every meal, and drink every drink—and not just one of each, but all they could hold, until they fell over dead, or burst their gut, or fornicated themselves simple minded! And did they care? As soon as they could get back up on their feet they went right at it again. Even the homosexuals were no different. Their only difference was they wanted to make all the men instead of the women. Well, to hell with them! all of them! Someday shed be free of them all, by God! It was really pathetic in a way. All they wanted was to be loved. By everybody. And as far as they were concerned, for Love you had to read Sex; nothing else counted. Well, God damn them! she thought furiously. All of them! And WALLACE FRENCH DENNIS and D. HIRSH would be the first. And yet, in spite of all the fury of her anger, she had to admit she was still relieved. At least that 'Bama character would take care of him somewhat anyway. The stupid fool. The thought stayed with her.

And after a while she got up to go and look at an early chapter of Wally's that he was not satisfied with and had brought over for her to see if she could find what was wrong with it.

It was getting well on toward spring now, and as April came in it became more so. Day by day on the trees the bursting bud came further out in leaf. It was the prettiest time of the year on the campus—at least for her—April and May. Even the air seemed to change; car motors sounded different, airplanes flying past overhead had an entirely different tone. Walking along the walks on the campus and looking off through the ocean of air and amongst the spotting branches of the big trees at the new changed look of the courses of red brick in the buildings, Gwen wondered if fish ever became aware of the water they lived in when it changed its seasons.

This last year she had applied for a study in the library, of which there were some odd dozen, and had been assigned one with a girl who was in the history department. And now in the spring increasingly, as well as during the winter, she did most of her work here. It was a dingy little room, with the two big ugly desks in it and paneled with dark melancholy oak because the library was one of the oldest buildings of the College, and she loved it.

The truth was, Parkman College had had a pretty precarious history, even more so perhaps than most institutions of learning in the US. Founded in 1852, two years after the town itself, by a local Episcopalian widower, with the help of Bishop Philander Chase who also founded Kenyon, it was the last college the good Bishop had anything to do with before his death that same year, and it wasnt much. The Episcopalian widower (his wife had been a Quaker), whose name was Samuel Pliny Earle, was a farmer from eastern Ohio where he had been a fairly well off man, at least by the standards of the times. But then tragedy had struck him in his later years, and his Quaker wife and all four of his sons—two of them married—and their families had all died of smallpox in an epidemic. Alone, and unable to remain there where all of them had lived, he had just struck out and started West, walking. He walked across most of Ohio and all of Indiana until the National Trail led him to Parkman, which was then a very beautiful spot in a grove of oak and maple and beech so large it might have truthfully been called a forest, among the prairies, and there he stopped. And there he founded the College. Whether he knew about Kenyon and that Bishop Chase had since become Bishop of Illinois, nobody seemed to know. Probably he didnt. But it was clear that since the tragedy he had become very disturbed about the problems of the South and slavery—it was during that time—and the fate of the poor Negroes there, because his college was endowed by him in the charter as a theological seminary and school for missionaries to carry his faith of Episcopalianism to them there in that faroff dark land of slavery and its clanking chains. Apparently he had approached the local pastor, and through him Bishop Chase, with his idea and offer to sell off all his holdings in Ohio (which he had just walked off and left) to endow this school for twenty five students, which was all his holdings would be able to afford; and the good Bishop, who had been a missionary in the West himself, and who also, apparently, was a man who believed devoutly in education however humble and whatever the stipulations, accepted. And thus the school was founded as a denominational Episcopalian seminary. The Bishop suggested only one added proviso, and that was that regular college work also be allowed for. Samuel Pliny Earle lived long enough to see the original two small red brick buildings built on the pastureland he had bought up at the foot of the hill north of town, then over a mile from the town itself, and then died and was buried at his own request on the grounds. The last of his money was spent in having the bodies of his wife and all of his family removed there from Ohio to be buried with him. And now the tiny family graveyard, surrounded by a locked iron grillwork fence, lay in a secluded spot on the campus under some trees, off by itself, but still close to the buildings it had originated the first of, and not even this latterday generation of students ever seemed to have contemplated climbing the fence and painting the headstones with the school colors during Show Week in the football season; and a greater compliment than that not even Samuel Pliny Earle could have asked for. Gwen liked to go there sometimes and look at it because she felt that here—from back in those old days of very speedy and very frequent remarriage—lay one man who, whatever his other qualities, must really have loved his wife.

After him, The Parkman Seminary—for so Samuel Pliny Earle insisted that it be named—crippled along through twenty eight years of a considerably lean period, existing on its tiny endowment and with the help of its local church, sending its missionaries not to the faroff dark land of the South as Samuel Pliny Earle intended but to the West because not even the most ardent Episcopalian missionary could bring himself to believe it was honorable to descend into Virginia or Mississippi where there were already so many Episcopal churches and found new ones in apposition to them for darkies, and anyway by 1865 the reason had been removed. It managed to add its third building (a tiny chapel) and to raise its enrollment to nearly fifty, but more than that it could not do and it almost went under doing that, and would have if it had not been for its local church.

But then in 1880, when it seemed it must gradually dwindle away now and someday just die, politics saved it. It was reorganized and renamed Parkman College. It remained denominationally Episcopalian, and it kept its little divinity school, but now it offered a full college curriculum and dispensed Bachelor of Arts diplomas. More land was added to the original twenty acres and three new, and larger, red brick buildings began to go up around the two tiny ones and their tiny chapel, and the largest of these was the library. Three full floors it was, because now people wanted to look ahead for the school, and it was not until after the first World War that enough of its potential shelving space was filled to keep it from looking hollowly empty. This reformation was all the work of a local man named Judge Lysander Blaines. For the first time in its history one of Parkman's local sons had been elected to the State Senate, and this son was Lysander Blaines. He had been a poor boy who had studied at Parkman Seminary for the ministry and graduated there before he changed his mind and decided to enter the law because it paid better, but he had never forgotten his alma mater.

Now a weathered stone statue of him and his flowing mustache reposed on a pedestal in the campus yard.

For a time it looked as though Parkman College had reached the limit of its development, but then it got another dispensation. Another local man, who was also a politician, though not a lawyer, and who was also wealthy and who had also graduated from Parkman College, had a daughter whom he wanted to send to school there because he had no son, but Parkman College was a men's school. So in 1907 two new buildings began to go up, one of them dedicated to the new School of Science, and Parkman College became coeducational. It was a good trade for the school because not only did this other local man secure them more State funds but he also paid for a number of other things himself and in addition left the school a large personal bequest in his will. One of the two new buildings he secured was named Berry Hall, because his name was Berry. Needless to say, when Miss Berry graduated she graduated with honors.

And so there it stood now, concretely representing the various vague dreams of various men, its seven red brick buildings (none of them large, by university standards, but still imposing) sitting solidly at the foot of the hill from town in its fields that had once been pastureland sparsely covered with first growth timber right at the thinning edge of the arm of forest, and which now were very definitely campus and shaded invitingly by big trees. None of the original first growth trees had lived on, and when the last one died the great stump eight feet high had been preserved with a bronze plaque commemorating it as the last of its kind, and it was huge; immense. There was some talk now about taking it out, that it was an eyesore, but no one wanted to take the initiative, since 'The Stump' had now become a fixture; and anyway it was shaded by a newer younger tree which made it look less stark because other trees had been planted early and were now old trees in their own right. The whole place had acquired—through the simple process of just aging—a feeling and a look of beauty that it had not originally had, but that always seemed to come to originally ugly things that aged—or at least men thought and felt it did. What had once been pasture was now lawn dotted with concrete benches and stone benches and bronze sun dials on concrete pedestals and even a piece of marble or two, all gifts of various graduating classes, the whole surrounded by a number of brick gates and stone gates between which there were no fences, also gifts of graduating classes, and the town had grown out and down the hill until it met the grounds. Physically it was probably as large as it would ever get, even if it did get any more eccentric dispensations, and after the 1907 enlargement there remained only one more thing for it to acquire, and the influence of one more man for it to undergo, to become what it was to be now in 1948. The thing was academic stature and the academic attitude, and the man whose influence brought it about was Robert Ball French.

And naturally, Gwen thought, since it was Bob French who brought it about, it did not happen in any conventional or traditional way.

To have, in 1920, a man who had taken his PhD at Harvard and studied in Heidelberg teaching English literature in the high school of a town which also contained a college was embarrassing enough. And it piqued the prides and selfrespects not only of the College administration but of the Board of Trustees as well. But then, on top of that, to see the same man slowly sifting himself up to the top and to national prominence as a poet—it was not only embarrassing, it was ridiculous. And all the ridicule, they felt, pointed at Parkman College. Perhaps he did not have the popular fame of a bestselling novelist like Willa Cather, but he was well known among the scholastics. He could, they knew, probably have taught anywhere, at Harvard or any big university, except that he already had money. He had lived in Chicago with Sherwood Anderson's group, and he had known Harriet Monroe and Carl Sandburg; he was a personal friend of Van Wyck Brooks and John Hall Wheelock.

And yet, in 1915 he had returned home from all this kind of life, and married, and immediately had a daughter, and then for four years done nothing—except write criticism and poetry. And the only statement he had ever been known to make about it was that writers and academics were like chess masters; they were too vain and jealous a crew to ever live close together. Why in the end he had gone to the school board and asked to teach English in the high school, nobody knew, either. He was known to have said to someone that he was a born actor and that was why he liked to teach. But he had not even approached the College about teaching; and in this connection he was known to have said to someone else, quite simply, that he did not like their policies.

There were several opinions among the College administration and the Board of Trustees why Old Bob French—he was already becoming known as that—had done what he had done, and the prevailing one was that he had done it deliberately to spite Parkman College. Well, they knew they werent very academic, and they wanted nothing to do with him, either. The trouble was, he had money. He was wealthy—or if not actually wealthy, well off; what with his own money added to that of his wife. It allowed him to be eccentric. In all they had held out for eight years. Watching him blithely go his way while his poetry became more and more known. Then a new chairman of the Board asked if anyone had ever asked him to teach at the College? It turned out that no one had, so a small committee visited him.

Gwen remembered it well, she was about fourteen at the time. Bob had sat with them in the living room—and so had her mother, busting (she had to admit, remembering) to talk, but knowing better than to. For years her mother had been embarrassed and indignant because he taught in the high school; and Gwen had wondered since if she might not have dropped a few wellchosen remarks here and there which had helped to start the committee moving. They had made their offer, through the spokesman of the Board Chairman, asking him to take over the English Department of the College. Bob had sat and thought about it a while, while they sat and waited. "Youre sure you wont care?" he asked the head of the English Department. No, no, said the Department head, he was moving on to a better place in a bigger school anyway. "All right," Bob had said. "Then Ill take it. Ive got some ideas Id like to try out anyway."

(Gwen could not help grinning whenever she remembered the scene. None of them understood him at all, or what he was like. She herself was sure that he had never suspected that he was embarrassing the College by teaching in the high school, and was equally sure he was genuinely surprised when they offered him the English Department. He knew he was embarrassing his wife by teaching in the high school, and perhaps also his daughter—which he was—but it would never have occurred to him he was embarrassing the College.)

And so it was that, in 1928, (the very same year that Dave Hirsh had left high school for good, without graduating, Gwen thought, musing in her study), Robert Ball French had also left the high school and moved out to Parkman College as head of the English Department. He did not stop his periodic drinking and he carried with him his high school course in Shakespeare, transposed for college students, and still continued on occasion to act out the dueling scene from Hamlet, if he got excited enough. But what he did to the College excited other people.

Parkman College had always been adequate in its own way,—*four years of Liberal Arts, Gwen thought sourly, fully accredited, vitally Christian*—and nobody ever pretended it was anything than just what it was—a small teachers' college that was a teachers' college in everything but name. But with Bob French all this changed—at least, on the level of the faculty where the students did not exist. Bob French revamped the entire English Department almost as soon as he was there, and by the end of the first year began getting rid of all his English teachers who wanted only to teach what they had been told to teach. He did not want that kind of teachers. He wanted teachers who had very definite ideas about what they taught and worked up their own courses according to theories of their own and were willing to argue with him about them. He argued with all of them. And some he hired. It did not take long for the word to get around; and soon they began to come, a steady stream of them from here and there all over the country: that strange, thin race of young academics, and some not so young, hopeful, some even wistful, but every one belligerent as hell and dogged as an infantryman when it came to his theories. And it did not just stay in the English Department. A thing like that cant. Soon it had extended into the fields of history, and philosophy, and mathematics, and even somewhat to the physical sciences. And in his third year Bob French founded the Parkman Review Quarterly, and right away its literary level went up and stayed there. Gradually, inconspicuously, they infiltrated, the young academics, coming from here and from there, with the hungry eyes, and the pinched thin faces, and the set jaws, furiously argumentative at the drop of a doctoral thesis, or because one had not dropped, all those who wanted to escape the pawk and scratch of the Twentieth Century by theoretically building the Twenty-First, and soon it began reaching the level of the department heads, and Parkman College had become a brilliant school. And it also had become known, as had its quarterly review. And the sharp vinegary smell of intellectual ferment was everywhere, like the smell of burning perique, and the sizzling sound of the frying brains.

(Gwen could no more help being violently enthusiastic when she thought about it than she could help breathing. It was her life. And always had been. And probably always would be. She had been raised up on it.)

Superficially, on the surface, the College hadnt really changed much. It still remained denominationally Episcopalian, nominally—*four years of Liberal Arts, fully accredited, vitally Christian*—and the church still had some sayso about the running of it, and everyone gave it the necessary lip service. But underneath, of course, all that had changed; because underneath, naturally, all the young academics, and not so young academics, were wouldbe idolbreakers in their hearts—as was Bob French himself; and he encouraged them in it. Nothing must be too sacred to suffer close inspection. It was a basic principle with him.

But the church didnt care, they were broadminded, and neither did the townspeople, they were all too proud of what their little College had become, although they hadnt the slightest conception of what had actually happened to it; and anyway most of the money didnt come from the church now, or the townspeople, it came from the State and from the two dead politicians and even now there were still gifts, some outside funds; and in the end some of the new order even seeped over into the little divinity school a little. Somewhere in there—in 1941—her mother died and caused a momentary pause, and she herself gave up her apartment in town and moved back out on the campus to take care of him.

He could have been, she knew, President of the College, if he had wanted. When the last President had moved on up to better things, it had been offered to him in so many words. But he had turned it down, and so Dr Clarence Brock Pirtle had been imported. And Bob French, a man of nearly seventy with the vitality of a man of fifty still, had announced his retirement and bought the house on the river and moved there. "It bores me, dear Gwen," he told her confidentially, "if you want to know the truth, thats why. Its all vanity. Talk and theorize and speculate—all in the hope of someday becoming known as the discoverer of one new thing, you know. Another Whitehead, another Abrams, another Pepper. Im tired of it. It isnt living. Its more living than most. Because its keener. But its still not living enough. Not keen enough. At least, not for me. There must be a keener living yet. No, Im afraid my acting days are over," he had smiled. "Anyway," he added, "I think the level is beginning to go down. It always does, you know. Every new review, every new school. Its always the same. Too many cooks may not always spoil the broth, dear Gwen, but they almost certainly will always dilute it. Then there will be *noth*ing left but the vanity, you know. Im a poet. Thats where my keener living lies."

The Board of Trustees and the administration had tried to get him to reconsider; and obviously they did not understand him, or what he was doing. And it was plain that if he had explained, they still would not have understood it. But then he did not try to explain to them. He had merely smiled, and said—in that quiet gentlemanly and yet tremendously vital voice of his, and with those bright eager-for-life eyes: "Gentlemen, Im just too old for it any more. You need a younger man." Even the Trustees must have seen through that as something less than truth; certainly, Dr Clarence Brock Pirtle had. Bob, sitting there with that tremendous vitality of his and telling them he was too old. It was ridiculous.

In her study, Gwen sat up suddenly in her chair before the desk, staring straight ahead of her at the double row of multi-colored book spines above it. What in God's name had got her started off on all that old stuff? Oh. Yes. It had been the old oak paneling, hadnt it.

She lit herself another cigarette and turned back to her work.

Her own position with the College had been, of course,—and still was—profoundly affected by what her father had been to Parkman College. She was Robert Ball French's daughter, and there were very few moments around here when she could relax enough to allow herself to forget it. She had been watched closely—and still was being—to see if she was going to take advantage of her father. Every young academic on the campus watched her constantly and jealously, just waiting for that one opportunity to be able to say there! you see! living off her old man's reputation!

She stubbed out her cigarette, and laid aside the back issue periodical which contained a poem of Kenneth McKeean's, Dave Hirsh's buddy from Los Angeles, that she had been reading. A new bunch of them containing several of his poems and stories that the College librarian had ordered out for her had just come in from the State Library. She could only have them for three weeks, and so was going to have to copy off all of McKeean's things that were in them. Funny, she never thought of him as Kenneth any more—Kenneth McKeean—since talking to Dave about him, but as Kenny the way Dave called him—Kenny McKeean. A man shed never even seen, or spoken to, who had lived out his agonizing life out there, and now she was studying him. The poem itself was an excellent free verse love poem. She pushed the periodical further away from her across the desk, and lit another cigarette.

Bob himself had started a new, long poem recently, and she was getting excited about it. As much or more than he himself was. She had not seen any of it yet, and in fact did not even know if he had yet written any of it down, but he had told her something about it. Bob worked in a funny way and a way like nothing or nobody she had ever heard of, but he had always done it—or at least ever since she could remember. He would get an idea from something or other, and then he would mull over it, and would mull and mull over it developing it, sometimes for months even, before he ever began to write a line. And then, when he actually began to write, he would not sit down at a typewriter or with a pen and write it out line by line; he would write it in his head, carry it around in his head, in his *memory,* until—if it were a fairly short poem—he had the whole thing entire, finished, all in his head, and then he would just sit down and write it off all at once, from memory. If it was a long poem, a very long poem, he would sometimes do it by sections, writing and scratching out and revising and changing, all in his head, until he had one section done—what might amount to several single space pages of typed manuscript—so that it satisfied him; then he would write that one down on paper and go on to the next.

He had been doing an enormous amount of reading in connection with the new poem, all of it on chess. And on the history of chess. For a long time she had not known why, and of course he would never tell her until he was practically all through with the reading and had satisfied something in his mind. He was hunting for something, of course; she didnt know what. It was like being personally involved in a detective story. When he had exhausted their own meager supply of books on chess, Gwen had brought him home everything the College library had on it, which was pitifully little; and then still later had had the librarian write the State Library and take out everything they had on it, which was not much more.

For Gwen, as it always was whenever he got going like this on a poem, especially if there was a lot of research, the whole thing was a sort of exciting intellectual adventure. Just as if one had gone off somewhere, to the South Seas or to Asia, on a hunt for physical adventure. She knew better than to ask him what it was all about; she would only have gotten a shy smile and a wrinkled up forehead and a mumble of something incomprehensible; and he would continue to do that until he had worked something out for himself in his mind, solved or correlated something, and then he would finally tell about it.

There was, it seemed, not only pitifully little in the libraries about the history of chess (at least in Illinois), but actually pitifully little written about it, when compared to some subject like ballet. Bob had kept careful notes of any mention of other books in the books he had gone through, and in the end they had to do what they almost always did—they sent a list to their New York out-of-print rare book dealer to find for them. It included such choice items as Sir William Jones's "The Indian Game of Chess" in *Asiatic Researches* Volume 2 (London) 1790; Richard Lambe's "History of Chess" (J Wilkie, London) 1765; Duncan Forbe's "History of Chess" (William Allen, London) 1860; H J R Murray's "History of Chess" (Oxford. Clarendon Press, London) 1913. Whew! she thought; both the titles and the bills! And as they began to come in, Bob would leave off reading Through The Looking-Glass and pounce on them.

What he finally told her, when he had apparently worked it out to his satisfaction, was that the poem was going to be about chess (she had rather guessed that), and that it would use the metaphorical symbol of a chess game—and even the play by play, perhaps—in analyzing and expressing chess as a reflection of the relationships between humans— who of course had invented it—and the title of it would be THE KING IS HELPLESS. Basically of course, he smiled, it was really about the relationships between men and women;—what was not?

He had got the original idea one day last winter (she noted he did not say which day) when he was sitting by the chess table there, and it had struck him with one of those strange, sudden, newer insights looking at the board and men,—(almost, in a way, as though he had never seen a chessboard before, so that it looked entirely new and strange and changed)—that while the queen was the strongest piece on the board, the king was also the weakest—almost a liability, really, except on rare occasions or in the end game. And yet the object of the game was not to protect the queen, the strongest, but to protect the king, the weakest. Why had it been done that way? Why had whoever, whatever individuals or groups, who had invented modern chess not made the king the strongest piece, and the queen the weakest, and made the object of the game to protect the queen? That would have been any *man's* normal reaction, wouldnt it? Sheer male vanity would have demanded that. And yet whoever had invented it had done just the opposite. Had a woman invented the game?

Certainly, it was no new idea especially; but it had obsessed him. It was new to him, at least in the sudden new way he suddenly saw it. The title had come to him almost immediately THE KING IS HELP-LESS. He had begun to look into it. Especially about this thing of the strong queen and weak king. Was this fundamental? Had it always been part of the game? If so, was this a basic attribute of men and women? something in the race itself? And if not, just when *had* the strong queen come into the game, and *why?*

He had, he smiled, done a deal of thinking about men and women and sex in the past few years, as was perhaps the right of a once-fairly-sensual man of seventy two who could look back with chagrin and at least a small amount of pleasant memory, and had consequently taken to watching the manifestations of it in other people with some measure of objectivity. And the thing that struck him most was how often it seemed to assume the character of a competition, a battle. Then this thing of the chess queen had hit him, he smiled.

Well, what he had found out was—just about as he had expected—nothing. Nothing with any definite meaning, anyway. Let a bunch of *histor*ians get ahold of a wet dishrag, and they would wring all the water out and keep the rag every time. In the original Persian game *shatranj* which supposedly came from India where it was called *chaturanga,* meaning the four arms—four branches—of war, the queen had not been a queen at all but a minister or general, and she had not been nearly so powerful. The change had come about around the 15th Century in Europe supposedly in France. That would have been about the time of Villon then, when France was still medieval. Would it not have seemed more in keeping with the times—or at least what the times thought they were—if the king had been the powerful fighting piece, and the queen the protected weakling hiding in the castle?

The scholarly interpretation of how 'minister' got changed to 'queen' was simple homophony: the similarity of word-sounds. The Arabian word for 'counsellor' was *firz;* which became *fierge* in French—a meaningless word. But *vierge* in French meant 'virgin': 'female.' Thus the sudden switch of sex.

—Perhaps it was all an idle fancy, he grinned. And yet still, it had nevertheless taken possession of him. There was that astonishing foresight—in the roles of chess—of the power women would someday come to wield in modern society and over their men in all of our Western civilization. (There were no queens in Eastern chess, in Asia, you know: in the Chinese *tseungki,* the Japanese *shogi,* the Burmese *chitareen;* none.) And that gap from male 'counsellor' to female 'queen' was just too big to jump. Homophony might account for part of it, but not all.

Obviously, the only reasonable answer was that in Europe women were more important, even then, than they were anywhere else in the world. They were given more attention. Why? This was what had put him really thinking. If they were important, it could only be because they had more power and wielded it—and in the case of the nobility, real political power. Where did this power come from? It could only come from one place: Love! At that time, that was just about the only damned possession women were allowed to have, in fact.

A woman, or series of women, effect the changes in chess which turned 'counsellor' into 'queen'?—As he had previously thought? Nonsense! Certainly not! No woman ever existed who would be that willing to give her hand away!

On the other hand, during those several hundred years in medieval France that the change was taking place, how many petty knights with a gift for ironic punning—and whose wives were sleeping with the king or minister or cardinal, or even only the local count, and thus furthering both her husband's career and her own—which everybody at the court would know—how many such men had seen the humor of changing *fierge,* the French corruption of the Arabian *firz* for 'counsellor,' to *vierge*: 'virgin'? And, simultaneously, right along with them, how many fat henpecked tavernkeepers in whose places the game was played —and whose shrilling fishwives railed at them for getting drunk with the customers, while taking the Cut-Lipped Villons as their lovers on the side—how many of them must have noted the same similarity, and made their own little puns on *fierge* and *vierge*? A thousand of each? Two thousand? Ten? Each making his little joke, until finally the name just stuck—and none aware that he was foretelling history.

And so there, he grinned delightedly and happily, as though he were actually talking to some other man who would appreciate his theory, instead of to a woman, there was his poem! Whether it was provable historically or not, it would make a magnificent theme for a poem, wouldnt it? The research had changed his conception of it; he wouldnt try to use a play by play analogy, he said, but the history of the game itself and this extraordinary 'coincidence' of the growth of the power of the female piece and of modern woman. Today they dominated by using the same trick they had learned to use then—sexual morality plus its opposite attribute, physical attractiveness. A direct contradiction! Thus they made the men desire them, while also making them feel guilty for doing so; result: Love! And, also, the power to have their way—what*ever* it was they wanted. Because they held this power—this *moral* right to give, or to withhold, love. In a word: domination! *THE KING IS HELPLESS.* But certainly, he smiled, the queen is not. The medieval material itself would be wonderfully effective; he had always loved that age.

Gwen's very first thought—when he explained it all out to her —had been one of guilt. A vague indefinite guilt. And she had immediately thought that he had not, as he said, taken his theme from the chessboard itself first, but from watching her and Dave Hirsh here. She had tried to find out from him just what day he had first had the idea (she had noted at first that he had not said)—but here Bob hedged. He didnt remember just when, he said. Well, had it been before Christmas? she wanted to know. Yes, he thought it was perhaps before Christmas, though he had not really started thinking about it seriously until some time after the first of the year. And that was all she could get out of him. She was half convinced that he had gotten the idea from her and Dave—(perhaps he had been sitting there in the big chair by the chess table watching them, in that absentminded way of his; and had made the correlation then, immediately)—and that that was where his poem was coming from. Of course, other past observations, and his own experiences, came into it, too. He was really a very wise man, at seventy two.

Once again she stubbed out her cigarette—perhaps a little angrily this time—and pulled to her across the desk the stack of periodicals containing Kenny McKeean's work. My God! How much time! She looked at her watch. An hour?

—and just what the hell did he mean, if he *was* taking it from them; from her and Dave? That she was dominating Dave? She wasnt. That she was using love on him? in other words, the yea and nay, the come on and then push away, technique on Dave? To get work out of him? She wasnt doing that either. Any more than she had with Wally Dennis, or even Mac Price. It wasnt she who kept bringing the damned sex into it. It was them! Like Wally, a year ago, a kid of twenty, asking her if she wouldnt sleep with him! Damn them, all of them. They were all alike. Love! They wouldnt any of them know love if they met it in the middle of the street. Any more than any of the College's damned young academics, who nevertheless liked to spend all their off hours discussing it. Who the hell was Bob French to say that it was *women* who used love on *men!*—Gwen wondered, again, as she often had, if Bob had any inkling that she was still a virgin and not the woman of the world she claimed to be, as she opened the magazine with Kenny McKeean's love poem in it.

God! she hoped not!

Despite the really potential greatness of Bob's new work and her excitement and absorption with it, her own little book was coming along quite well—almost too well in fact. The closer she got to finishing it, the more she began to wonder whether she would ever be able to publish it at all or not. It was not as if they had all lived two or three hundred years ago and you were free to drag their private lives into it when you needed to. Three of the main ones—Dave and his sister Francine and George Blanca—were still alive, and might not relish such a thing—especially Blanca, who was now a very successful Hollywood scriptwriter. Not counting the widow of Herman Daniel; and God knew how many relatives of all of them! And yet the further she got into it the more she was unable to see how she could leave the private lives out of it, as she had once planned. Their private lives were what had made them—made them what they were, and controlled them, and in the end had broken them. And their private lives, like everybody else's, were largely their love affairs.

Only with one of them—George Blanca, the part Mexican—was it even remotely possible that he might have gone on and married his 'great love,' and still turned out to be what he must have once wanted to be—(what he obviously did once want to be, from reading his three early novels)—a real writer, as opposed to a professional Hollywood scriptwriter. But even that was apparently not possible either, it turned out, because from what Dave had told her, it was not Dave's sister Francine who was Blanca's 'great love' at all; she was merely his mistress. His 'great love' had been a young and very low mentality Japanese waitress down in the skidrow section of downtown Los Angeles! Good God, talk about selfdestructiveness of talent!

(She knew now—consequently—where Blanca had got that weird outlandish female character he used in the third, and worst, of his early novels. He had drawn her straight from his Japanese 'great love'! Japanese nationality and all. God! With what great selfconscious irony must he have had her marry a *Mexican,* in the book, and turn down the sensitive white boy—himself—who loved her! And with what great crocodile tears of sentimental selfpity must he have written the scene where the boy ritualistically goes through the rigamarole of burning his novel manuscript in the little fireplace in the bar where she worked! Little did Blanca know he was writing Blanca's own epitaph. Of them all, Gwen found she could not help but dislike Blanca the most.)

But of the three, Blanca was the only one who might have married his 'great love', or at least, gone on living with her—provided his 'great love' had remained Francine, as it was in his first two books. But the other two—Kenny with his dancer; Dave with his little girl-friend (about whom she still knew nothing, as yet; because he wouldnt talk about her)—could neither one have married their 'great loves'; not and still hoped to go on writing.

Herman Daniel of course, the fourth man, the one who was killed in the war, did not count. He had had someplace to return to. Whatever it was in the beginning that had driven him out of his environment, it was not the all-inclusive force that had worked on the other three. Herman Daniel had had a girl at home—and more important, had had a business at home. His father's business. Which he could return to. It was hard to believe that his 'great love' was his girl at home, but it must be true because he alone of all of them contracted no great loves in Los Angeles. He had his lovers of course, but no 'great love'; so it must be his girl at home. And in fact, in talking to Dave about them the several times she had, she had found out that this was the case. Dave said he talked about his girl at home at just about every opportunity.

Dave had given her a lot of important information, the two or three times they had talked about it—before he left—most of it about their private lives which in the end she might not be able to use. And most of what he had given her was about Kenny McKeean. She herself had known less about Kenny—she always thought of him now as Kenny, affectionately—than any of the others.

Kenny's girl—his 'great love'—had been an Armenian, or Syrian, nightclub dancer. He had met her in some cheap bar where she was working doing some exotic routine, and had kept going back to see it, and that was apparently what he had fallen in love with first, the exotic routine, but then later on after he had known her and they had been lovers, he told Dave he had also fallen in love with her comfortable commonality; her laziness, her sloppiness, her peasant wit and acquisitiveness—in short, all the things that made her human as everybody else. Knowing Kenny—or rather, Kenny's work—but then wasnt that Kenny?—Gwen could have anticipated that development. The girl had come out to the Coast from New York to make a break, either in the movies or in the big ritzy nightclub circuits, and spoke with a New York accent and rarely washed under her arms (which she left unshaved for her routine)—just put on more perfume. And she eventually made her break, although not in any big way and without becoming nationally famous, and married a moderately rich Hollywood Jew and from what Dave could gather later began washing under her arms and shaving them, a sort of concession to high society, as it were. She was about as animal, and amoral, as you could get and still be classed as human apparently, and would sleep with just about anyone, enjoyably, particularly and especially if they could do her any good in getting ahead, and frequently tried to get Kenny to go out with her and her other lovers, Dave told her (and apparently greatly enjoyed the telling of it to her, Gwen noticed; and looked as though he were hoping she would have to ask to have some of the terms explained). God, what a child! Kenny, Dave had gone on looking a little disappointed, had wanted to go, he said, and very nearly had several times, but in the end always backed out; something in his Eastern upbringing would not let him. And that made him a liar, Kenny maintained. The dancer had her own morality, he insisted; the morality of complete honesty. The thought of going both excited and hurt him, he told Dave, hurt him deeply, tormented him in fact—because he did not want her to go out with anyone else. And that was selfishness, he maintained, and truly immoral on his part. And yet he wanted to go. It attracted him.

Gwen could understand it intellectually at least—if not physically and emotionally. Physically and emotionally—in other words, where it would have concerned herself—it horrified her; but she could understand it in Kenny. It was the desire for unbridled license. The desire to roll in the gutter and smear the filth on your face and person and—in your imagination, at least—the bigger the audience the better. The desire to do bad things, and the badder the better, so that you could increase your feeling of horror and guilt and selfhate—so that, your mother (or someone) would take you in her arms and tell you it was all right: a thing which she obviously never had done, or you wouldnt be like that in the first place. It was the desire to expose, and self-incriminate, and it was as much a part of the artist as his head was. It was the desire to selfdestruction, because you had always been unloved, and must therefore be unlovable; and right along with it went its own opposite, this higher-than-normal, stronger-than-was-customary-in-humans sense of high integrity and great morality, forming that perpetually balanced and forever insoluable conflict within that made you the artist. Either the one or the other without its opposite there to perfectly balance it in conflict, and you had no artist. Without the morality you had the debauchee, the libertine, and all the professional drunks and fagots and fairies and dykes and fluffs. (oh, she knew the words; maybe more of them than Dave did; she had studied this) And without the *true immorality*—not *amorality*, my lads—you had the fool, *that* fool, the average human being. And sometimes, just once in a while, when you had the two together—plus that third and rarest of all qualities in humans, the virtue of honest self-study—you had a really *great* artist.

Kenny McKeean's life story was *so* archtypal, *so* hackneyed, that it would have been trite as hell—if he had not killed himself over it. It might be something out of the notebooks of Gauguin or Toulouse-Lautrec or Van Gogh. He had hung for four days in his little room apparently before anybody thought to miss him and go around since they often didnt see each other any of them for days, and then it had been Dave—poor old softhearted, sentimental, overly emotional, hungrily friendly Dave, she thought pityingly—who had gone. Sitting in her kitchen, he had cried unashamedly—or rather not so much unashamedly as unnoticingly, unawarely—when he told her. Kenny's head had swollen up and turned black already, of course. He had tied his feet together and then ingeniously managed to tie his hands together somehow behind his back, before he stuck his head through the slip noose in the clothesline tied to a ceiling spike and stepped off the chair. Apparently he wasnt taking any chances he might change his mind at the last moment. The wildly, and beautiful, poetic note he had left, Dave said, had left some doubt and was not quite clear whether he had done it because he could not stand to think of her sleeping with other men all the time and not marrying him, or because he felt he himself had totally failed morally, in *wanting* her to marry him and in *caring* if she went out with them, and in *not* going out on her parties himself.

He had been working on a novel Dave said for about a year before it happened, sporadically, in between the short stories and poems, but no one had ever seen any of it, and when they went through his effects none of it was found. The academic in Gwen had twinged greedily.

And so these were all that was left, the some six or seven stories and between twenty and thirty published poems, most of them printed in obscure hard-to-get little West Coast reviews. If Kenny's novel had shown the same organizational ability and objectiveness and this power to symbolize unobtrusively and without warping the material that his stories and poems showed, and there was no reason to assume it hadnt, he would probably have had one whale of a first novel. He had been twenty six when he died.

Over half of the poems were love poems, like the one she was looking at now. And so now she knew that they had been written to this hairy-armpitted Syrian pig as Dave had said (that *was* a new word for her, pig, the tone he gave it anyway) who was not even really a very good dancer. Well, it didnt matter. What mattered was that they were written, and you mustnt look a gift horse in the mouth. But the sheer ridiculousness of it all flamed up through her again with a wild anger and a sense of loss. They were all of them such fools! Such fools! Such abysmal and all-engulfing fools! Did it have to be that way? Apparently it did. But such a waste it was, such a criminal waste. Like with poor old Kenny McKeean. If they could only just learn at least to spread their selfdestruction out over a period of time and die like Greene of gout or Stendhal of apoplexy or Tolstoy of religion, at least then they would have more time left for their work.

But what she was trying to prove—if possible, conclusively—that the selfdestructiveness of talent had to do with Love. —or the lack of it. Even that point wasnt new. But what was new—she thought—was this almost mathematical clinical progression from the beginning sense of un-love up through the height (according to the individual) of talent to the Love climax—in which the individual either got, or did not get, his Love object—thence almost immediately into the decline of talent and on down to the inevitable destruction of talent, or the individual, one. And of course in the event of the destruction of the individual, that meant both. In some—apparently the more highly sensitized, (and therefore more talented)—decline and destruction was instantaneous, or nearly so. Like Kenny's suicide, and Dave's just suddenly *giving up* writing. In others, like Blanca, it was a longer period of gradually dwindling talent—of course, Blanca's real Love climax was Francine, not the Japanese girl which was only an attempt at repetition and therefore was false from the start; maybe he was even copying Kenny McKeean—and probably was—but he was unwilling to go all the way to the suicide, and that of course prostituted the whole thing and it became just an act; he just didnt really love his Japanese girl that much.

(But that symbolism of his—of Blanca's—of the white boy ritualistically burning his manuscript before the Japanese girl in the bar! What a symbolism it was of all of them!)

And that was the main point of her whole thesis: that the Love itself—or the illusion of it, for that was really what it was; an illusion of Love—was always and in every case *more important* than the talent, or the work that might come from it! It was a horrifying thought for Gwen to even contemplate; but it must be faced—it seemed to fit the facts. The talent was really only a *by-product!* A by-product of the neurotic—near-psychotic was better—a by-product of the near-psychotic love-hunger of the individual; and not only in a psychological theoretical way—but *in actual fact,* to the *individual himself,* consciously, or very nearly consciously. A by-product that the individual willingly gave up himself, when he reached the Love climax and either got or did not get the Love-object—after he had once first begun externalizing the Love-hunger onto some particular individual party.

Even Stendhal (than whom no human ever loved writing more) in his epitaph 'I lived, I loved, I wrote' put the 'I loved' before the 'I wrote'!

There were some who, by some quirk of fate or other that mingled propitiously with their personalities, managed to stay alive long enough to produce a fairly large volume of the best work before they got themselves destroyed, and these were the ones we called great. And then there were others—possessed of a stronger instinct of selfpreservation than most, or what was called 'cowardice'—who were able to live to a fairly ripe old age by simply refusing the problem in their minds in the same way a horse will refuse a jump, and who were therefore able to turn out a large volume of work themselves but the work was never much good because they were pompous, and who consequently had really succeeded in destroying themselves also and even earlier.

But for each of both these types, God how many Kenny McKeeans were there, God how many?

And how many Dave Hirshes?

Well, she had it anyway, she thought angrily, laying aside the first magazine whose poem of Kenny's she had copied and taking up the second in the stack. She had the material, and the facts, and the proofs, and the thesis, and when she was done marshaling it all there would be damned few loopholes.

But there were times when it was almost too painful for her to work on it at all. Especially when it was the work that had to do with Kenny. Sometimes she could hardly stand to look at it. And that was when the anger, and the outrage, came.

That they could have it all like that, the quality, the talent, the necessary plethora of emotion; and then spend their whole lives trying to get *rid* of it, trying to throw it away—for in effect, that was what it was, what they were trying to do. The very thing that she would have given her life to have!

She pushed the second periodical away from her and swung the chair to look out the window. Outside, spring had definitely come. In the brighter sunlight the grass was eye-shockingly green, and down through the limbs of new leaves she could see students moving along the walks and carrying books, the girls chic and attractive and tall looking in their bright colored coats and saddle shoes, the boys awkward and ungainly looking in dun topcoats or maroon letter-jackets and already carrying the air of apology around females that they would probably carry the rest of their lives.

There was a lot of truth in Bob's thesis of the powerful queen and weak king, a lot of truth. And you could see facets of it everywhere you looked. It wasnt that the girls were smarter or different, it was just that they were by nature more realistic. They *thought* they believed in Love but they didnt really, they just *believed* they did; whereas the men— eternal symbols of Infidelity—really *did* believe in it, and were in fact suckers for it. Which was why they were so consistently unfaithful.

She sat looking out at the beauty of the scene and at the beauty of the youngsters. Life was so very painful, and so very sweet.

Well, she would work on their damned novels for them, but she would be goddamned if she would handle their sex lives for them, too. And she wouldnt be working on their novels with them very damned long, she promised herself devoutly.

It was about three days after this that one of the young students who made extra money running errands and working for Administration knocked delicately on the door of her study and told Gwen that Dr Pirtle wanted to see her in his office. She stared at the boy's crewcut head, feeling irritable because after her eight o'clock class in American Lit she had her mornings free till eleven and that was when she worked and Dr Pirtle knew it, and then said all right, shed come. It was probably an invitation to some damned faculty cocktail party for the more ardent academics that Dr Pirtle and his wife were always giving and she would only have to refuse it anyway.

Dr Clarence Brock Pirtle was the College President who had been imported when Bob French had refused to take it and retired. He had been hired mainly to keep the Parkman Review Bob French had founded going, and to keep up the College's Renaissance in English and History, and he was just the man for it and was doing a good job of it. His field was early American Literature and he was a Modern Romantic, and he had already done two books on the Romantic influence in Hawthorne and Melville which were considered additions to the field and was now researching a third one on Henry James. He was a dyed in the wool academic, and looked the part. Everything about him was some tint of brown, his clothes, his hair, his eyes, his skin, his shoes, and his pipes. If there was any emotion in him at all, he never seemed to show it, but Gwen knew better because there was a certain really ferocious fierceness lurking behind his eyes which never showed itself except in argument and in the way he would lean deliberately forward and knock his pipe harshly against the edge of an ashtray, and whenever he got into a real political battle for the school. He could not probably have ever founded a Renaissance like Bob French had done in Parkman College, but he was much more capable of keeping one going once founded than Bob was, and he did not resent or hold it against Bob that Bob had been given first choice for the Presidency over him, and when she found that out to her own satisfaction was when Gwen first began to like him. He was sitting in the green leather chair behind his big brown desk blotter smoking one of his pipes when she came in and there were ashes on the lapels of his coat and on his vest.

"Miss French," he said in his crisp cold way and staring at her with his bulging ferocious brown eyes. "Do sit down, Miss French."

"Thank you, Dr Pirtle," Gwen said, and did.

She had begun to like him even more after the affair of the chapel bell tower, which had happened during his first year. The chapel was the third oldest of all the buildings and the chapel bell tower was in disrepair. The bell tower, which was not a tapered structure but a square tower seventy feet high which ran square up all the way to its crenelated top, was a landmark on the campus. Just below its battlements its top was supported by a series of open arches around all four sides within which the College's three bells could be seen hanging on their big pulley wheels, and there were stairs around the inside walls to get up there with. Chapel had long since ceased to be compulsory at the College, though it was still held and the bells were still rung, but for some time there had been a vague movement afoot to do something about the dangerous state of the bell tower. It came to a head during Dr Pirtle's first year. The idea was to remove the bell tower completely and then, in order to make the building present a harmonious whole, remodel the rest of the chapel into a more modern building. Most of the

Trustees were willing to go along, and the rest had been convinced so thoroughly that it was a good thing that they were ardently for it, but the Trustee who was most for it was a man who was also on the county school board and the high school board and a pious deacon at the church and who owned a brick kiln and the biggest lumber yard in town, and it was probably done because Dr Pirtle looked like an easy man to handle. But here they erred. Dr Clarence Brock Pirtle had gone coldly and crisply to work in his restrained ferocious way, and he used every principle of rhetoric in the Aristotelian sense. When he finished his speeches about the historic bell tower and the historic old school of which the townspeople should be proud, there were actually tears in almost every town eye. He organized his young academics into a phalanx which, armed with petitions, visited every woman's club business club civic club and church club in Parkman. He could find no reason or logic, he said, in tearing down a building that had been built in the days when America built well—just when it was acquiring the real beauty of age—and replacing it with some cheap modern raw brick monstrosity that would have to be replaced again in thirty years. General Electric may have spent two and a half millions on research to develop a lightbulb which would burn out quicker, he said, but as long as he was President of Parkman College the bell tower would remain, and if that smacked of Communism be damned to it.

As a matter of fact, after everything was over, he *was* investigated, on an anonymous tip; and it was not hard to guess where the tip came from. He received a deputation of two apologetic, selfconscious, and obviously oafish, young graduate lawyers from the FBI on behalf of his government, whom he crisply and precisely and with cold ferocity put in their place as uneducated men. This was something college people were becoming more or less used to, along with their meager salaries. Nevertheless, and needless to say, the bell tower remained. It was repaired and its old bricks repointed at less than one tenth of the cost of the proposed remodeling. It was, in fact, almost a foregone conclusion, since there was no pious civic leader in the world—even if he owned two brick yards—who could have matched ferocities with Dr Pirtle.

"Miss French," he said when Gwen had got herself seated, "I will be brief. Im sure you have work to do;" a hint of a smile touched his face fleetingly. "It has been decided by the Trustees to found a Parkman College Literary Fellowship for the novel, in conjunction with several generous-spirited local people and civic organizations, among which is the Parkman Tuesday Literary Club represented by Mrs Agnes Hirsh whom you know. The benefits of this fellowship will amount to one thousand dollars a year for one or two years. The only stipulation accompanying it are that the recipient be needful of it, that he or she be a student or graduate student of Parkman College, and that the work he or she is engaged upon be one of talent and consistent with—and an attempt at furthering—the Christian principles upon which Parkman College is founded and which are the foundations of American society." He took a small pull at his pipe, savoring the taste of the smoke, and stared at her fiercely with his bulging brown eyes from across his desk blotter without cracking a smile.

Gwen's mind had already started skipping and leaping around even before he had finished: How would she do it? *Could* she do it? There had been rumors of such a fellowship being in process around the campus for several months, but she had not put any stock in it—not much, anyway. "Yes, sir?" she said.

Dr Pirtle took another puff at his pipe, his face totally impassive, except for that always-near-ferocity that was always in those bulging brown eyes. "I myself have been working with the committee composed of two of the Trustees and the individual donors and representatives of the clubs, to form a small foundation which will finance the fellowship, and we have agreed that these are the stipulations which will accompany the bestowal of it." Another short pull at the pipe. "I have been delegated the authority of awarding the fellowship. But at my suggestion the committee had authorized you, Miss French, as the person to choose the recipient. You teach both of our creative writing courses, as I pointed out to them, and are therefore the logical person to make the choice. I am not. The committee agreed with me in this, and authorized me to tell you of their decision." Another little pull at the pipe, and Dr Pirtle continued to stare at her ferociously with fierce brown eyes.

"Yes?" Gwen said. There was no need to think or cast around now, either for a means or for a recipient, and her mind had begun to leap hopefully. If she could only get it for him, for Wally! "When is the award to be made, Dr Pirtle?"

"At any time henceforth," the President said succinctly.

"And will you thank the committee for me?" she added.

"I will," Dr Pirtle said. He took another puff at his pipe and continued to stare at her.

"Well," Gwen said, and tried hard not to sound triumphant; "is there any special way I am to go about making my choice?"

"You are to be the sole judge," Dr Pirtle said crisply. "You may go about it in any way you like. A committee, as I pointed out to these generous people, is hardly qualified to pass judgment upon the literary merit of an author, or upon the previous judgment of a qualified teacher and critic—especially when they themselves are not qualified. Such a thing would only lead to useless argument and indecision. After one year, myself or a single member of the committee will discuss with you the progress that has been made, if the novel remains unfinished, to see if it warrants a continuation for the second year, and will read the manuscript to see if the work is in keeping with the principles laid down by the fellowship. In the event the novel is published with the fellowship committee's approval, it will be requested that the title Parkman College Literary Fellowship be included on the title page in some form or other." A puff on the pipe. "But beyond that, Miss French," he said in his cold crisp way, "everything else is up to you. It would seem to me to be foolish to attempt to keep a month by month or chapter by chapter progress report upon so ephemeral and delicate a thing as a novel, or a novelist. And an outline would hardly be worth bothering with, dont you think?"

"Yes, I do," Gwen said; "absolutely." Well, at least she could get it for him for a year, anyway. They might raise a hell of a big stink after that, but there wouldnt be much they could do about it. Except get someone else to choose their next fellow. She had a distant impulse to laugh, thinking of Wally's girdle factory and the use he was making of it; and also of the very potent teenager love scenes he was writing in it. They were certainly not very much in keeping with the Daly Sisters teen-age charm books on innocent dating, or with the Youth Center theory of teen-agers. "Yes, I think youre absolutely right on that point, Dr Pirtle," she said.

"Then I believe that covers it, Miss French," the President said, staring at her fiercely. "You are entirely on your own. I expect you will want some time to think it over before you choose someone. You may even wish to have student manuscripts submitted to you. If so, that is up to you." He took another puff on his pipe and continued to stare at her with distant fierceness.

"Theres no need to think it over," Gwen said, staring back at him. "I already have the party chosen. Wallace Dennis."

"Ah, yes," Dr Pirtle said thinly, and leaned over to knock his pipe deliberately against his ashtray. "Young Dennis. Very well, Miss French. I know young Dennis, but only slightly."

"Hes the most outstanding creative writing student we have here at the College," Gwen said. "Or have ever had. And furthermore I feel he qualifies on all the points. He is certainly in need of the money. And while he is an unclassified student, he is nevertheless a student—in both of my creative writing courses, and in two Literature courses—so that does not disqualify him there. And as to whether his novel is an attempt to further Christian principles, I think I can honestly and in all sincerity say that it is," she said.

"Quite so, Miss French, quite so. Very well. As a matter of fact, I rather anticipated that you might pick young Dennis. I understand you have been working with him on a novel for some time now.

Very well. I need not remind you," Dr Pirtle said and looked up from his pipe which he was ferociously tamping down with the flat head of a four-barreled chrome pencil, raising his lids, and staring at her fiercely with the barely restrained ferocity of his bulging brown eyes, "I need not remind you, Miss French, that these generous people are endowing this fellowship largely for the purpose of furthering those Christian principles, as the fellowship itself says, which they devoutly believe in and wish to see perpetuated; and that it is your duty as well as my own in this matter to see that the spirit of their bequest is complied with."

"No," Gwen said clearly, opening her own eyes wide and staring back at him; "you do not need to remind me of that, Dr Pirtle."

"Very well, Miss French," he said. "Your choice will be communicated to the fellowship committee. A check in the amount of one thousand dollars will be forwarded to Mr Dennis as soon as the details can be arranged." He went back to tamping his pipe. "I think you may inform the lucky young man of his choice, should you so desire."

"It may be, Dr Pirtle," Gwen said distinctly, "it may be, that some discussion of my choice will come up at the committee meeting or elsewhere. Wallace Dennis is distantly related to me, and someone may choose to make mention of that fact."

"Miss French!" Dr Pirtle said ferociously and stopped tamping his pipe, his bulging brown eyes glaring. "I am quite sure that no one will question your integrity or intention, or mine, in this or any other matter having to do with Parkman College!"

"Im sure they wont, Dr Pirtle. But I felt I should mention it to you," Gwen said. "Naturally, no such considerations have anything to do with my choice."

"Naturally," Dr Pirtle said fiercely, looking ready to fight. "And I am sure no one will even mention such a possibility. Certainly, they will not in my presence! Now, if you will excuse me, Miss French. I have work to do, as Im sure you have." Again, a fleeting faint distant hint of a smile seemed to play around the corners of his eyes, without however in the least impairing their bulging brown ferocity. "I would not have disturbed you this morning, Miss French, had I not felt the matter at hand important enough to warrant such intrusion."

Gwen could not help but grin a little. "Im certainly glad you did, Dr Pirtle. And thank you."

When she got to the door, he stopped her. "Ah, Miss French. My wife and I are having a small cocktail party and buffet for a few of the faculty this coming Saturday night. We should like either you or your father or both of you to stop by and join us should you be free to do so without hardship."

"Im afraid we wont either one be able to, Dr Pirtle. Ive a tremendous lot of work to get done, and Dad's started working on a new poem lately."

The President nodded, not looking at her but working at his pipe. "Ah, quite so. Well, if youre unable to. Perfectly all right."

"But perhaps I might be able to get over for a little while," Gwen said, unable not to relent.

"If you can," Dr Pirtle murmured, looking for his lighter. "I would never impose, Miss French."

"I think I might," Gwen smiled.

Once more he stopped her, as she put her hand on the knob. "Miss French," he said pugnaciously. "Of course, I shouldnt like your father to know I did this, but I thought I might tell you. It was my suggestion at the last committee meeting that the fellowship be named the Robert Ball French Memorial Fellowship. But, alas, it was voted down by one vote—among the individual donors—I believe because they preferred that the name of the College, and hence of the town, be in the title somewhere."

Again Gwen smiled. "I honestly dont think he would even have known it if it had been voted. You know how he is when he gets to working on a new poem."

Dr Pirtle nodded. "Quite so," he said fiercely. "Well, perhaps the next fellowship. If we get another."

As she shut the door, he had already commenced the ritual of relighting his pipe.

Walking back to the library she tried hard to keep her mind down cold and control her wild feeling of elation, but it was hard to do. Wally Dennis needed that money. But more than that, he needed the prestige the fellowship would give him locally and in town for his morale. He had already begun to get a complex about being a bum around town who wouldnt work and lived off his poor widowed mother. And now he would have both, a little money and a little prestige too. And she had got it for him. By God, she had got it for him. The kind of wild, belligerent, tigerish elation made her eyes spark fire and threatened momentarily to carry her away. It didnt matter a damn what they did to her about it, she thought grimly, she had got it for him. And anyway, they couldnt do much; just give her hell—in private—and pick themselves another judge; and that would be a year from now. Hell, his book might even be done by then, and should be.

—Of course, she couldnt have done it if it hadnt been for Dr Clarence Brock Pirtle. Dr Pirtle must know; she was sure he knew, she knew he knew. She had tried every way she could to tell him. He was no fool. Maybe he even wanted Wally to have it himself; that would have been the way he would work it if he did. By turning it entirely over to her he could honorably free himself from taking the action his responsibility to the donors demanded; then he would have done his part, and it would not be up to him. And yet you never knew with Dr Clarence Brock Pirtle; you never knew what he was thinking for sure. Well, it didnt matter. He trusted her integrity, he had made that plain; even allowing that her integrity might be totally different from his own, he nevertheless still trusted it. That was all that mattered, that and the fact that Wally had got the fellowship.

She remained in a state of high elation the rest of the day, and that night as soon as she got home, called Wally up to come over so she could tell him the news. He arrived in his mother's old car, wearing his Army surplus Eisenhower jacket that in the spring replaced his Air Force surplus fleecelined one, and when she told him about the fellowship and that she and Dr Pirtle had awarded it to him, with a kind of stuttering tongueless surge of outrage that suffused his whole face and his bull neck Wally blew his top completely and swore he would not take it, he would refuse it, and he would write them a letter saying so tomorrow.

"Nobody's going to tell me what to write! Christian principles, indeed! Christian principles! They wouldnt any of them know a Christian principle if they—if they met it sitting on the next hole in an *out-house*!! Theyre not gonna tell *me* what to write. Ill write what I goddam please! And Ill tell them to their face that my whole goddam life is *dedicated* to showing *all* of them up for what they are and their goddamned Christian principles! No, sir! I refuse!"

"Wally. Wally! WALLY!!" Gwen said. "Shut up! Shut up a minute. Let me talk a minute."

"Theyre not gonna muzzle *me*, by God! No, sir! Not Wallace French Dennis. Anyway, I dont need their money. I get along. If they think they can buy me off, theyre mistaken! Let them keep their money." He would say a sentence, then stalk a few paces, then stop and say another sentence, and then he stopped suddenly and pointed his finger at Gwen as if it were a loaded pistol, so tensely his whole arm quivered. "Why, I wouldnt be surprised if that wasnt what the whole thing was cooked up for. An attempt to muzzle me and buy me off. They all know about my book. They dont want their secrets exposed! They dont want the truth told! Ill bet the whole damned deal was *planned*! And you, Gwen, you let them suck you into it! I thought you were my friend!" He jammed his fists down in his pockets and stood before her, thickly and unmovably. "Well, they wont get away with it. Ill write what I want to write! Ill write the truth! There never was a novelist in the world who was worth a damn if he let other people tell him what to write and what not to write!"

"Wally!" Gwen shouted. "Sit *down*!" But he wouldnt, and kept on pacing, and so she got up and placed herself in front of him, legs apart, her hands on her hips. When it looked as if he was going to run into her, he stopped. "Wally, sit down and listen to me!"

Grudgingly, he sat down at the big table in one of the ladderbacks and looked at her, furious, outraged, raped. "I know what theyre trying to do!" he started.

"Wally!" she said, and he stopped. "Wally, do you think I would ruin your book? Do you think I would even let *you* ruin it?"

"No," he said grudgingly; "no, but—"

"And I certainly would not let anyone else ruin it," Gwen interrupted. "Have I ever told you what to write?"

"No."

"Have I ever insisted that you write something you didnt believe in?"

"No."

"Have I ever made you change your mind about anything in your book?—except when it was something bad technically? or some damned ridiculous outlandish thing that would have ruined it?"

"No, but—"

"No buts, please!" she said. "Youve had your say. And said it quite well, running around here and flopping like a chicken with its head off. Now, I think you owe me an apology."

"Oh, *nuts!*" Wally said exasperatedly. "All right," he said grudgingly, "I apologize. But if you let them suck you in—"

"No *buts,* please! Youve had your say. Now you listen to mine. I went out on a limb to get you this damned fellowship. It might even cost me my job. If it doesnt, it certainly wont make me any friends in Parkman; when they see your manuscript. Dr Pirtle and I awarded you this fellowship. And we did it because you are the best student in the novel that we have. Nobody else had any sayso in it. The committee didnt even know who would get it. They dont even know right now, and wont until Dr Pirtle tells them. Nobody—and I repeat, nobody at all—neither the committee nor Dr Pirtle nor me—is going to tell you *what* to write. You and I will go right on with your book just like we always have."

"All right," Wally said grudgingly, "okay; but why all this damn Christian principles stuff then. Ive had Christian principles stuffed up my rear all my life since I was big enough to *crap!*" he said furiously. "I *hate* Christian principles!"

"Because the people who did it dont know any better, thats why."

"Then tell them to give their goddamned fellowship to Lloyd C. *Douglas!*"

"He already has enough money," Gwen said. "They meant well, and they mean well. They just dont know anything about literature. Theyre trying to formulate something that is good, and thats the only way they know to do it."

"They wont think so when they see my book," Wally said savagely, glowering at her. "At least I hope not."

"Perhaps not. But then again, perhaps they will. I like to think they will. But even if they dont, it wont matter. You will have had the fellowship, and you will have had the thousand dollars. So they will have done *some* good. Your book isnt bad. Theres nothing bad about it, its a very good and a very moral book. Whether it fits in with these people's idea of Christian principles or not. If it doesnt, thats their fault, not the book's."

"All right," Wally said grudgingly. "All right, I see that. But Im not going to take it anyway."

"And why not?"

"I dont know," he said, not looking at her. "Because its charity, thats why! Because its goddamned charity, and I dont need their charity. I get along."

"Oh, you fool!" Gwen said scathingly. "Oh, you poor, dumb, vain— ignorant—dumb—egotistical fool!"

"Okay," Wally said sullenly. "Maybe so. But I still aint going to take it."

"Im sorry I ever wasted my time with you!" Gwen said acidly. "I thought you were a *writer!* A writer takes everything he can get, from everybody and everything he can get it from, and he uses it and hes grateful for it. Its his right, as a writer, because he gives up everything else to be a writer. He gives up his possessions. And, Wally, the greatest of his possessions is his pride."

Wally sat glowering and said nothing.

"All right," she said. "You can either take the fellowship or Im through. I mean it. If you dont take it, Im through and you write the rest of your goddamned book yourself if youre so great and high and mighty."

Wally looked up startled, pain on his face and in his eyes. "You really mean that?" he croaked.

"I most certainly do. There it is. A thousand dollars, and the prestige of having the first fellowship Parkman College has ever offered. Take it. Take it and use it, in the best way you know how to use it, for the good of your work. Or else Im through."

"I wont take it," Wally said sullenly. "God *damn* them, I wont take it. The sons of bitches." But he was wavering.

Gwen could see that he was wavering, and in the end she went out to the workshop and called Bob in to her support, not so much because she needed him as because in that way she could save Wally a modicum of his pride in what had become a silly ridiculous battle of wills between them, and thus make it easier for him to accept, and after Bob gave his considered opinion that he should accept it, Wally did. He agreed that he would write no letter refusing the fellowship and gave his promise.

"I think you would be making the biggest mistake of your life, Wally,"

Bob said, "if you refused it." That was enough. He could take it, from a disinterested third party—and, Gwen thought bitterly, because it was a damned man.

"All right," Wally said finally, finally the words, the few single little important words. "Ill accept it."

Immediately everyone looked at each other, and everything seemed so strange and quiet, and all of them wondering what the hell all of the argument had been about, and Gwen heaved a profound inward sigh of relief, and after Wally left and Bob had gone back out to his workshop, had herself another mild case of hysterics, the first since the evening at the Country Club, and sat laughing and crying to herself, and finally put her head down on the table.

It was almost a month before all the details were arranged and Wally called her up elatedly to say hed got his check. One thousand dollars! he said. Man! Hot damn!

"By the way, have you heard the latest news?" he said after the congratulations. "Dave Hirsh is back."

"Yes, Id heard," Gwen said.

"Have you seen him?"

"No, I havent. He hasnt been over."

"I dont wonder," Wally said. "Waitll you hear the *latest* news! Him and 'Bama have leased themselves a house out in the west end of town.

"Looks like youve lost yourself a potential novelist," he said maliciously."

CHAPTER 40

IT TOOK them two full weeks of the most hectic kind of activity—first to get their house, and then to get it at least adequately furnished and get moved in; and that was the reason Dave had not been over to Israel to see Gwen sooner. At least, it was part of the reason. The other part was that he was so deliciously savoring his triumph—when he would descend upon her with the finished draft of "The Confederate" and, more or less claim his reward, so to speak—that he was almost reluctant to give up the savoring for the fact. The first thing he had learned when he got home—home it was now, oddly—and went to the hotel, was that Gwen had paid his bill and picked up his clothes and stored them for him. (The hotelman said Bob; but Dave knew it was Gwen, who had sent him, who had been behind it.) And just this one fact, and knowing it, had opened his eyes up to a great many things that he had not seen even before leaving for Florida. If he had, he might never have gone—(though he would have hated to have missed it). But he could see now where she had been in love with him all along. And he, damned fool that he was, hadnt seen it. The reason she hadnt slept with him wasnt because she found him less attractive than all those other guys shed had love affairs with, it was because she was trying to get him settled down and back to work and help him make something of himself. She probably wanted to as bad as he did. But she was making him do the work first. She hadnt been sleeping with all those other guys he imagined her sleeping with at all; lately. Probably she was saving herself for him all this time. Ah, Gwen. Gwen, Gwen. Triumph and gratitude seized him simultaneously, and he promised himself devoutly that he would never do anything to hurt her, or let her down, or make her regret her choice; and he cherished triumphantly their coming relationship—when he would show her "The Confederate"—with such savor that he was reluctant to see it move from the future into the present and back into the past and become a memory instead of anticipation. Also, he shrewdly felt it would do her good to let her sweat a little. And anyway, there was the house.

They had come home loaded. After 'Bama had made up his mind it was time to leave Miami, he had decided to spend two extra days collecting funds. There was, he said wisely, no point in leavin all that good money floatin around down here for somebody else to pick up when they could just as well take a big batch of it home with them to Parkman where it was more needed. They had played poker all night both nights, sleeping in the day, and drifting across both Miami and the Beach from one game to another whenever the action got slow or one game folded. And as always that strange, occult partnership of theirs worked, and they won consistently. It was hard, poker-playing work, not exciting or stimulating at all, but it paid well. Both of them carried large sheaves of bills in cash when they left, and more bills— properly divided and noted—reposed in the pocket of the cheap flimsy new suitcase 'Bama had picked up to carry his new suits in. The good thing about gambling, 'Bama said, was that it allowed you to cheat so much on your income tax. In fact, he went on after a moment, gambling was about the only profession left any more that had any individuality and freedom left at all and that was one reason he liked it. "Except for yore writin, of course," he added; "it has 'em." They were still dividing their winnings sixty-forty, but 'Bama had said that from now on after they got home he thought they ought to split fifty-fifty, Dave had learned enough about how to play poker now that he was earning it, the secret to playin poker was not so much to play yore cards when you had them as it was to throw them away when you didnt, to just keep on throwin them hands back even when you hated to; and Dave, his wallet fat with bills on his hip, felt that he had almost forgotten what it was like to live without money. They had not won *every* time they had gone out to play in Miami, but they had won damn *near* every time, and the very few times they had lost they hadnt lost much (that was where the good poker playing came in) and when they won they won considerable.

In the car going home 'Bama speculated a great deal upon what this strange quality was that was making them win so consistently— far beyond what the percentages prescribed for them to win. It was an abstract problem that fascinated him and that he apparently never ceased worrying around. Sometimes he even looked as though he half way wished it had never happened, so he would not have to account for it to himself. He had only had one comparable (compare-able, he pronounced it) run of luck like it in his life before, and that was back in the Army once outside the Huertgen and that only lasted for five days. What had made it come, and what had made it go, he hadnt known then and he still didnt know. It was the same way with this one. He was convinced it had something to do with belief; but the gimmick there was to know when you had real belief and werent just thinking you had it. Some element in there made the belief you felt real, but another time —when *you* might believe just as strongly—*it* was false. What made the difference? He thought it might have something to do maybe, he said leisurely, with some kind of mental electricity. They sparked each other; they made each other high somehow or other; they electrified each other;—but neither one of them knew it or felt any different. "You know, a guy can stand on rubber and all kinds of regular electricity can run through him and he wont feel any differnt at all as long as he aint grounded," he said. "And if nobody told him and he didnt already know what electricity was, he wouldnt *know* anything was happening, or that electricity was goin through him. He couldnt *feel* it."

He had read somewhere that there was this new theory that the human brain worked by electrical impulses, too tiny and too delicate to be measured by man. Well, maybe some of those same electrical impulses were what influenced luck. But then what influenced the electrical impulses? Your moods, probably. But when you started trying to analyze your own damned moods, you ran right out into thin air like a man running out from under his hat. Or his head. That was where he always wound up, by God, it seemed: out in thin air. And when he did, he would laugh his chilling saturnine laugh and say well they had better take advantage of it while they could, because it sure as hell wasnt going to last forever.

The first thing when they got home, he went to see his "ol' buddy" Judge Deacon about the house. Dave did not go along, and was in fact already occupied in doing his own chores and in discovering Bob French had picked up his clothes and that his car was gone, but 'Bama told him about it later. Since everything was gone from the Douglas, and he had plenty of money again, at 'Bama's suggestion he reoccupied his suite at the Hotel Francis Parkman—the same two rooms and bath on the corner that he had so very long ago come down from Chicago and taken for a week—and that was where they talked about it. It seemed strange, to have 'Bama sitting there (with his perennial waterglass of whiskey) where Frank had sat so very long ago when they had signed the contract for the taxi service. But then the whole town looked different now, newer, and at the same time older, different, to him.

'Bama had already been to see his ol' buddy the Judge. Ol' Judge was more than glad to help them out. In fact, he was delighted. He would start looking for them a house right away, he had said, and since they were back loaded and money was no object as 'Bama had said, he would see if he couldnt get them one of the best in town, maybe right on East Wernz Avenue the mainstreet, in the middle of the snobs. That ought to burn their tails. But here, 'Bama said explaining it to Dave, he had put his foot down. There was going to be talk enough and disturbance enough wherever they got a house probly, and there was no use asking for more. Rather reluctantly, ol' Judge had agreed with this; so he was only going to look for an ordinary, nice house. Comfort inside, 'Bama had insisted, and preferably a less inquisitive and less easily infringed upon bunch of neighbors.

"Hes a funny old duck," 'Bama drawled. "He hates this town worse than poison, even though he was born here. And yet he wouldnt leave it for nothin. Apart from the fact that hes got all his money tied up here. He wouldnt leave it if he didnt have any. I guess thats why he took a likin to me; I dont fit in nowhere with the 'respectable' elements."

It would take several days for Ol' Judge to find a suitable house and lease it, and it might even take a week. He himself was going to take a run down in the country to see his wife and kids and the farm and see how his cropper (who was from Alabama too, and a distant relative) was making out with his crops. Dave was welcome to come along with him if he wanted (this was the first time Dave had ever been invited down to his farm) but he really thought it would be better if Dave stayed in town and got his affairs straightened up, especially if they were going to go into this gambling partnership deal. He would want to see about getting his clothes and his car back. And hed want to see Frank about the taxi service. All of that would probably take him a couple of days, and by then 'Bama would be back from the country and they could start in on the house.

"Now, I dont know what you want to do about that taxi service," 'Bama said; "but Im assumin you dont want to go back to work there," he grinned.

"No!" Dave said vehemently.

"Well, theres nothin in that contract that says you have to work there.

Now, as to whether you want to buy it all or sell your share, thats something else again. If you want to buy it, Ill advance you the money. I can get it here in a week."

"What about you and me going into partnership with it?"

'Bama grinned. "That would shore scorch them, wouldnt it?" He shook his head. "But Id ruther not. I dont much go for ownin things. They just weight you down. My farm's differnt; I keep my family there. And anyway I kind of like farmin—as long as I dont have to do the work. But somethin like this, I guess I just aint interested in."

"Then I guess Ill sell," Dave said. "Thats about the way I feel about it, too."

'Bama nodded. "All right. Now heres what you want to do, then. You want to pretend like you want to buy it. See? And you want to get to name the price. Flash a little of that long green around you got on you; and let him know theres more where that come from. —Not in no obvious way, so he'll know thats what yore doin; but in a way thatll make him think hes figured it out. See? Now heres what you do," he said and carefully and very explicitly began to lay out for Dave just how he was to handle everything.

In the first place, according to the contract, Dave owned 42% and Frank 58%; actually, according to the amounts they each put in ($5000 and $7000 respectively, 'Bama said) Dave only owned five-twelfths or 41⅔% and Frank 58⅓%; but Frank had given Dave his one-third of a percent. As a magnanimous gesture, 'Bama said with his sneering grin, —and also as a matter of convenience in figuring.

"He did all that after I signed it," Dave said.

"*After* you signed it!" 'Bama said incredulously. "Boy, you shore trust people."

"Well, I— Oh, it doesnt matter," Dave said; "but I was supposed to put in more than that originally. $5500. So he had to change it."

'Bama shook his head dolefully. "Well, I just wanted you to understand the setup. Now heres what you do," he said carefully, as if speaking to a child. "You got to make him mad, see? Mad enough to ask to dissolve the pardnership. Because thats the only way youll get to name the price, see? According to the 'Give or Take' clause, one man has to ask to dissolve the pardnership; then the other man gets to name the price. Then the first man, who asked to dissolve, gets to choose—whether he'll sell his share at that price or buy the other man's share. So you got to get Frank to ask to dissolve, and then you get to name the price, and you make it a high one. *Then* you flash your money, see? and he'll decide to buy instead of sell, and youll get yore price. And thats why you have to make him mad enough to ask to dissolve."

"Frank's pretty hard to make mad," Dave said cautiously; "especially when it has anything to do with business."

"Well, thats yore job, see? You got to make him mad enough," 'Bama said. "But I dont think that thatll be so hard to do. Hes probly already mad enough at you now, for takin off and all. And he probly expects you to go back to work for him. If you just act even a little snotty, he'll probly blow his top off." He paused a moment, staring at Dave specula-tively, and almost unbelievingly. "Course you could go in and act cocky and ask to dissolve yoreself and *then* flash yore money around, and make him ask a high price, and then you sell. You see, the trick is all in makin him think you want to *buy*."

"I dont have much of a head for business," Dave said. "Why dont we just forget all this and let me go tell Frank I want out and that I want to sell him my share?"

"Christ-no!" 'Bama said flashingly. "Thats just what hed want! If you do that yore not even goin to get yore original five thousand out of it. He'll start talkin about how business is bad, and how much more youall've had to spend than you thought, and he guess it wasnt such a good idea as he use to think for a business. —Look," he said. "Business is no differnt than anything else, Dave. All you got to do is know people, and remember to read the fine print. Business is no differnt than playin poker. And yore a good poker player, Dave," he said almost pleadingly.

"Sure," Dave said. "I know what you mean."

'Bama looked at him, and then rubbed his hand and fingertips up and down his cheek thoughtfully. With his thumbnail he pushed his hat back a quarter of an inch. "I guess it is all pretty hard to explain in words, I guess. Unless you already know beforehand what it is Im talking about. —And you dont!" he said explosively. "Course, it would have been easier if you had wanted to buy instead of sell. That way it was all set up. And I must admit it would have tickled me to see you all set up as a respectable businessman in this town," he grinned. "—But I guess it wouldnt have been such a good idea. It would almost certainly hamper yore writin," he said, "and thats what we got to think about now."

"I think I understand it all right," Dave said. "All I have to do is make him think I want to buy when I really want to sell."

"Thats it! Thats it!" 'Bama said. "Now youve got it! Well, now do you think youve got clear everything I said?"

"I suppose so," Dave said. "I think so. But which way do you want me to do it?"

"Well, I—" 'Bama said and then broke off to stare at him. "Well, I dont know," he said. "I cant tell, you see. Id almost have to be there, dont you see? to see how things were goin at the time. I—" Again he broke off to stare at Dave incredulously, while Dave hopefully waited for him to go on. Then 'Bama rubbed his hand and fingers up and down the side of his cheek again and looked off at the corner of the ceiling thoughtfully. "Well, I reckon you better try makin him mad," he said finally. "Hes almost sure to be mad as hell at you anyway."

"Okay," Dave said loyally. "Thats the way Ill do her."

"I— Yeah," 'Bama said. "Yeah. Well!" he said, and slapped both hands down on his thighs, pushing himself up to his feet. "I better get to going. You get out of it whatever you can. It dont really matter much, anyway. What matters now is to get our house and get you back to writin on yore book," he said; "and also for us to make a little money gamblin while its still hot," he added grinning. "It might even be better if you didnt sell it at all, and just keep it and let him pay you yore share of the profits."

"No, I want to sell," Dave said. "I want to get out and get shut of it altogether."

"Well," 'Bama said. "Okay. Ill see you in two—three days at the latest. Then you can tell me all about how it turned out, and we'll see what ol' Judge has got for us in the way of a house."

He seemed a little glad to be getting away, Dave thought, and realizing what an oaf he was in anything to do with business, and what a trial he must have been in this specifically, he didnt blame him any. He just seemed to get a block whenever it was business. After 'Bama had gone, he mixed himself another whiskey and water and went to stand with it at the corner window and watched 'Bama come out below and cross Wernz Avenue the mainstreet in the bright fresh undusty May afternoon sunshine and get into the big black '37 Packard and drive off. He was a real friend, by God. And a man didnt get many friends like that in his lifetime. If he could count three—or even two—he was damned lucky. Nursing his drink he stood looking up Wernz Avenue (the mainstreet) at the square, and then turned around and looked at the long sitting room. What had it been? Six months and more; since he had occupied this place. And beyond the door into the little bedroom, the closet where the B-4 bag had used to hang. Only it wasnt there now, it was over at the Frenches with the rest of his stuff. He looked back out at the town, which still looked so totally different—not different outwardly so much, because of the spring; but different inwardly, because of the change in him. That was why really, of course. Damn! That 'Bama was sure a swell guy. A real friend.

This was one of those periods in a person's life when he was changing from one pattern over into another totally different pattern, and there was this sort of breathing space in there in between, in which you were no longer part of the old pattern, and yet you had not yet moved inside the new pattern, and so you didnt really belong to it either. Sort of a spiritual holiday, and also like a real holiday in that you had nothing you were required to do, and he was enjoying doing it, the nothing, to the fullest. Still holding the now half finished drink, he walked over to the phone to call up Frank. Might as well do it now and get it over with. Then, before he went to see him hed have another stiff drink and build his courage up to do it the way 'Bama had said. Christ, what a coward! But Frank had a sort of Indian sign over him and always had had. It came from Frank having played father to him for so long and being the one who gave the orders. It got to be a sort of psychological habit.

Standing with the phone in his hand, but not having dialed yet, he suddenly remembered his childhood—so vividly that he was actually back inside it for a moment—and how he had used to want to sleep with Agnes. When he was a little bitty kid. That was before Agnes had taken such a dislike to him and he used to let her play the mother to him and dress him and undress him and give him baths so she would see him naked, and later even after he got in high school—until he had started running around and drinking—she used to fondle him and rumple his hair and he tried to concoct ways of getting her to see him naked then, but never had nerve enough to carry any of them out. Thinking about it later, he had thought she had known—she used to have that kind of funny half amused, half embarrassed, half titillated look on her face—but she had never said anything about it. It had become a sort of delicious secret with him. He wondered if Agnes remembered any of that today. Probably not. And yet it might be one of the reasons she disliked him. Christ! he hadnt thought any of all that in years.

Frank turned out to be not in town when he called the store. He was up in Springfield on business, Edith Barclay said, but he was expected back at the store tomorrow. Dave recognized her voice. (She recognized his, too. He could tell.) So he told her who he was, as if he thought she hadnt recognized him, and asked her about his car. She knew nothing at all about it, Edith said distantly, but Mrs Hirsh would probably know if he wanted to call her. So he called Agnes up at home.

As soon as she heard him she recognized him, and he could hear that thin unpleasant edge come into her voice that she always got whenever she spoke to him unless she just happened to be feeling especially well. Well, to hell with them. He didnt have to worry or care about what they thought anymore. Yes, the keys were there, she said, at the house. The car was parked on the lot at the taxistand. Frank had taken care of it for him.

"Well," he said politely—especially politely, because of what he had just been thinking—"Ill send Albie or whoever's at the taxistand down for them. Will that be all right? Will you be there?"

Yes, it would be perfectly all right, Agnes said. And she would be there. He hung up and stood looking down at the phone for a moment, before he mixed himself another drink. Life was such a strange, elongated, complex, incomprehensible thing. —He noted that in spite of the fact he didnt care about what they thought any more, and didnt have to, it still bothered him to know that someone didnt like him. That was what the trouble would be with Frank, when he saw him, he thought; and he was supposed to make him madder.

Albie Shipe in his heavy-muscled narrow-shouldered wrestler's body was sitting behind the main desk in the taxi office, his feet cocked up on it possessively, smoking a big black cigar and reading a comic book to himself laboriously when Dave walked in. It might have been the same comic book, except the cover was one Dave did not remember having seen. The torn-clothed woman on it was delicious.

"Well, damn!" Albie said delightedly, bugging out his eyes like a comedian, and threw the comic book down on the desk and got up. "Look whos here, back from the dead! Where the hell ya been so long, boy?"

"I been in Florida," Dave said. "Hi, Albie." They shook hands.

"Florida, hunh?" Albie said in his hollow basso, letting his whole face sag and then lifting it up into a broad meaty grin. "Look at me! I been promoted since you left." He swept an arm as big as a leg around to include the desk. "I got your old job now. Take all the calls, and make out all the dispatches, and write up all the figures even. Course, Edith Barclay has to check them later. But I dont make many mistakes! What do you think of that, hunh? Im practicly an educated man practicly," he said and bugged out his eyes in his sly, comedian's look. "—So you been in Florida. I thought I heard somebody said they thought you and ol' 'Bama had went off tomcattin someplace together.

"Say! Youve put on a helluva lot of weight, aint you?"

Dave grimaced. "Ive been livin good."

Albie grinned. "So well whatta you know! Ol' Dave! Well, when are you gonna come back to work and do me out of my job?"

"I dont think Im comin back to work, Albie," Dave grinned. "Looks like youll get to keep the job."

"Aw, now," Albie said with portentous and comic earnestness, as though his role of the comic had become so ingrained he couldnt even turn it off himself when he wanted to be serious, "Aw, now. Come on, now. I wouldnt want this job if itd mean cuttin you out of it. You know that."

Dave shook his head. "I dont want it. I got a better deal. Me and 'Bama are goin into partnership gamblin. But dont tell anybody that. Its on the q t."

"Anything thats on the q t's on the q t," Albie said, narrowing his eyes slyly and putting his finger up beside his nose.

"Ill tell you what I came over for, Albie," Dave said, and told him about the call to Agnes and the keys.

"Sure!" Albie said. "Nobody's in right now; but Ill go down myself and get them for you myself," he said with obvious delight. "Ive bought me a car since you been gone! Ill go in my car and Ill get them keys. What do you think of that, hunh? Albie Shipe, Old Man Shipe's boy, with a car! Course, its only a jalopy. Not even as good as your old Plymouth. But its a car. —And it runs," he bellowed with portentous comedy, "it runs!" He hustled to the door, the footfalls of his heavy body making the little lunchroom building shudder. "And someday Ill get it all paid for! You watch them phones for me while Im gone, will ya? Oh. Uh— if you aint sure what to do if somebody calls up, I be glad to explain it to you?"

"Go to hell," Dave grinned.

Albie laughed and left, and from outside Dave could hear the chugging roar of what could only be Albie's jalopy, and sat down in the swivel chair at the desk where he had sat so many times before and looked out at the dingy uncivilized red brick backs of the square's business buildings that he had stared at so many times, feeling high and happy and free, and in a few minutes Albie was back with the keys.

When they went back outside and he saw the car, his happiness left him and he was infuriated. He hadnt bothered to go around back to look at it when he first came or while Albie was gone, and for a moment he wondered furiously if that wasnt why Albie had so slyly reminded him about watching the phones: just so he would get to be there and watch his face when he saw it.

To say it looked like the last rose of summer would have been putting it mildly. What had once looked like a pretty good 'used car' now looked like an 'old car'. An old wreck. A jalopy. It stood by itself in the very back corner of the cinder lot, looking as though it might at any moment roll backwards over the four foot wall down onto the buildings of the next street, and all the dirt and weather of four months of winter had assailed it unmercifully. He tried to tell himself that if it had stayed on the street where he had left it, it would have been the same; and it would have, and he knew it; but it was not the same. Frank had taken it, that was the difference. Frank had taken it, and with a hardheaded bullnecked sanctimonious righteousness deliberately put it out there and deliberately left it sit. Angry; sure, Frank was angry and mad at him; for leaving without notice like he did; and that was why he did it. But it was still a petty, sanctimonious, pompous dirty little trick to pull.

And once again—as always, apparently—right was on Frank's side. Apparent right, anyway. And Dave could already divine all the statements he would make to prove it. Well, he had left it out himself. Well, he didnt know whether he was ever coming back or not. Well, he shouldnt have left like that without notice, and then not sent any word. Well, what the hell *was* he supposed to do with the damned thing? After all, he ought to take care of his own damned car. Sure; he would say all those things. In all his life—and he had had some pretty big hates going for Frank, too, one time or another—Dave had never hated his brother, and what he saw as his brother's pompous sanctimonious righteousness, as he did right now.

"Itll look a lot better once you get it cleaned up," Albie said sympathetically from behind him. "Mostly its just dirt. The batt'ry's deadern a doornail—youll have to buy a new batt'ry—and the right rear tire's plumb flat, and all the tiresll probly drive pretty lumpy for a little while they been standin so long. But it aint really in near as bad a shape as it looks. Ill help you change that right rear tire if you want," he offered. "It should of been blocked up on blocks and had the batt'ry tooken out."

When they went closer for a better look, Dave found that Albie was right. It wasnt really *ruined*. But the knowledge did not make him feel any less hatred for Frank's just, upright, free from wrong, righteousness. The little door over the keyhole was stuck shut from disuse and he had to prize it open with the head of the key, and when they looked in the luggage compartment for the spare they found it was completely flat also.

"Slow leak," Albie said authoritatively.

"Youd better get back and watch your phones, hadnt you, Albie?"

"Screw the phones," Albie said, bugging out his eyes and opening his mouth to look comically startled, and rubbed his palm affectionately over the dirty fender, leaving a brighter streak. "I like cars," he said, as though he were speaking of people. "Anyway, there wont nobody die for lack of a taxi for a few minutes."

"Well, there aint much we can do here with it, anyway," Dave said, reaching in and slapping at the top of the seat. A thin film of dust had covered everything.

"No," Albie said, "an youll need to git a new batt'ry from the garage anyway."

Back inside the converted lunchcounter Dave called the Dodge-Plymouth service garage (which Frank had told him so long ago that he was a 'silent partner' of; probly owns it now the son of a bitch, he thought) and told them who he was and that he needed a battery and a tire fixed.

"Is that that '42 Plymouth thats been sittin down the taxi lot past two three months?" the lean, taciturn, strangely unhuman mechanic's voice said.

"Yeah."

"Youll need moren one battry to start 'er then," the clipped passionless voice said. "Ill bring along a booster'n hook 'em up parallel." It might have been speaking a totally alien language. And was, to Dave.

True to his voice, the mechanic who arrived in a few minutes in a red pickup truck was lean and dour, with flat passionless alien eyes, and very nearly unhuman except for the chaw of tobacco in his jaw.

"You jack 'er up, Harv, and run them two tars downt' the shop," he said to the other man just like him he had brought with him, after he had looked it over and raised the hood, and dragged two batteries out of the truck. "Bring first one back soon's you get it done, Harv."

Together they went to work, dragging the heavy jack out of the truck, then separated, Harv going to the rear with the jack, the other taking his two batteries to the front, while Dave could only stand and look on helplessly. Frank might own the business, but he didnt own these men. And in fact, he had no more to do with them than if he was on the moon—or they were. Nothing owned these men, nothing and no-body, including the cars they worked on with such cold swift alien impassiveness,—unless perhaps it might be the tools they worked on them with, and handled with such delicacy.

With his flat pitiless eyes the talkative one gave Dave an openly merciless appraisal as he worked on the batteries. "Be hard to start," he decided to say, passionlessly, tonelessly, and spat a tiny goblet of tobacco juice. "Gas run down out the pump. Oil's run down off the cylinder walls. Oxidization of the oil make it gummy. No lub. Take a while." As he worked, first under the hood with the batteries, then from behind the steering wheel staring passionlessly straight ahead through the windshield as he tried to start it, he cursed constantly in a low, heartless, guttering monotone—(like some wounded Civil War colonel, Dave thought, cursing his men he loved and who loved him and who were about to falter)—while behind him Harv worked on the tires in silence, or else cursed in the same way, making it sound as though they were holding some guttural alien extraterrestial conversation in some other-than-human tongue.

In half an hour the sluggish motor was chugging reluctantly, and Harv was back with the right rear wheel and had it on, and the talkative mechanic drove it silently and chuggingly and with no more interest in driving than he had in conchology, and Dave rode with him and spent the afternoon in that dim and oily half-world, or other-world, of the echoing-big garage peopled by these laconic, passionless, strangely un-human members of another and more passionate alien race, while they washed his car and greased it, and changed its oil, and fixed its other tire, and drained and flushed its gastank out, and changed its sparkplugs, and retuned its motor, and looked at him with polite flat eyes as if he actually *were* a visitor from another planet, while he himself felt like an interloper and intruder, and in the end it seemed like another car entirely. His bill was twenty dollars—not counting the new battery.

"Drive 'er around a bit," the talkative one advised him as he left. " 'll loosen 'er up. She be all right."

So he drove to Terre Haute and had dinner in the Marine Room of the Terre Haute House alone, hating Frank and his pompous rightness implacably, and afterwards feeling pleasantly a little tight on several martinis, had a taxi driver drive him to a pleasant, efficient whorehouse, before he went home and went to bed.

The next day he saw Frank.

"Where were you?" Frank said when he called the store. "I tried to call you last night. Ill come over to the hotel. You stay there."

"You still afraid to have me come into your store?" Dave said thinly.

"Hell, no," Frank said exasperatedly. "But I thought if we were gonna talk, wed want to talk in privacy. And there sure as hell aint none of that here."

"Ill be here," Dave said.

CHAPTER 41

FRANK hung up the telephone irritably and looked across the office at his mistress. She, however, did not look back, because she had her head down and her back to him typing something, some letter or something. So he winked experimentally, and as it were privately, at the back of her pretty neck. It was something he had taken to doing lately when he was upset because it soothed him. Sort of a private rebellion against the pronouncements, which Edith herself had suggested, and which he thoroughly agreed with, that they should never in any way at all even the tiniest look, let on that there was anything at all between them. Edith kept them admirably, and for that matter so did he himself, but she kept them almost too damned admirably, and sometimes he had an impulse to rebel a little, privately. As far as that went, what was half the good of having a mistress if nobody in the world but you and her knew about it? (Oh, of course, there was lots of *good!* Plenty!) But if *nobody* in the world but you and her knew it, then to all intents and purposes at least, at least as far as everybody in the world was concerned, you didnt have one!

Frank rubbed his hand angrily over his whole face to clear his head, pulling the skin under his eyes and cheeks down. That damned Dave. That damned Dave. And so now he was back and all ready to cause more trouble. Already *causing* it. Just when he was about ready to believe he was gone forever. He was worse by far than the Old Man. And what Frank Hirsh had ever done to be given such a torturous thorn in the side he could not imagine. Why did it have to be him who had a brother who wanted to be a writer and a crackpot artist? Nobody else in Parkman had a brother like that. Damn it, he had no sense of social responsibility at all! Other people had sane, reasonable, affectionate, normal brothers. Well, he would have to go over there now and see what kind of a hairbrained, trouble-causing scheme he had deliberately cooked up now. He rubbed his hand vigorously over his face again.

"Edith honey," he said to the back of his mistress's bent head, (she had her hair all cut off, cropped and curled in a roll about mid-ear in the latest style that had come in this year, and it showed the delicious dark whorls of fine close hair on the nape of her neck when she bent her head), "Edith honey, Im goin' to have to go over to The Parkman and see that damned brother of mine."

She raised her head and turned to look at him, no hint of anything in her eyes or on her face except the attentiveness of a good office girl and secretary. "Yes, sir, Mr Hirsh," she said crisply; if anything she was even less friendly now than she had used to be before—at least, when they were here in the store.

"If therere any calls of importance comes in for me, have them reach me over there," he said, looking into and at and all over, her face.

"Yes, sir, Ill do that, Mr Hirsh," she said impersonally and nodded, and there was nothing but complete impersonality on her face. It was kind of titillating in a way, but he disliked it nevertheless. There was such a thing as too much of a good thing. Christ, she almost never called him boss any more, or smiled—unless it was distantly. Sometimes he almost believed she actually disliked him, and became depressed and almost frantic. All this was only in the store, of course; when they were alone in bed, man she was passionate as hell. And of course, all this was necessary in the store, but sometimes he did think she overdid it a little, especially when they were in the office alone together like now. At least she could give him a lovin' look.

But just then, just as he was thinking this and just as she was finishing nodding, Al Lowe stuck his head in the door to ask about the account of a woman who wanted a Sunbeam coffeemaker from the new Sunbeam line they had put in recently and wanted to charge it, and Frank had to admit that this time for once Edith had been right. But still it was the rare occasion, rather than the rule.

"Sure, let her have it," he said to Al. "Shes good for it. It may take her a while to pay, but shell pay it."

"Well, she already owes us over fifty dollars," Al said.

"Let her have it!" Frank said irritably. "It doesnt matter. Shell pay. If it takes her a year. You got to remember, Al, that this business is based on good will and 'trust'. And refusin' to let somebody that you know is good charge something, is *not* a good way to build good will. Never do it unless you just have to."

"Okay, Frank," Al said admiringly, his open boyish face expressing admiration. "Just as you say."

Frank tossed his head a little. "I didnt mean to be irritable with you, Al. Dave's back in town. I got to go over to the hotel to see him."

"Oh, thats too bad," Al said funereally.

"It sure as hell is," Frank said disgustedly, looking at him waspishly.

He had begun to suspect Geneve had her cap set for Tony Wernz IV —if only anybody could ever get Tony sober enough to be interested in a woman. Youd sure never think Al had the Bronze Star, or Silver Star, whichever one it was, one of those medals like that, for bravery in action, he thought with a kind of irritable amazement.

Edith had already gone back to her work, and was ignoring both of them. Al's eyes flickered over toward her—or so Frank thought—just once, lightly, before he brought them back to Frank.

"Dont forget about those phone calls now, Edith," Frank said deliberately making his voice irritable at her.

"Yes, boss," Edith said, barely looking up, "Ill remember it."

"Was there anything else you wanted, Al?" he said irritably.

"No. No, Frank. I just—" he said, and then his voice dropped off into that funereal tone, "wanted to say how sorry I was about Dave." The voice lifted, "Ill go take care of Mrs Catlett. And Ill remember what you told me, Frank."

"Good," Frank said, "good," and got up. "Well, I guess I better get to goin' over there."

He got his spring hat, the gray (he had two) and then paused to uncap and slip out of its tube and light, a cigar, but Edith did not even look up from her desk at him. An aura almost of coldness seemed to push him away from her. Well, Christ, I hope she knows what I was doin', and what I did it for, and aint mad at her, he thought with a momentary uneasy twinge of panic, and looked back at her (but she still did not look up), and then walked out through the dim dusty storeroom where the crabbed old watchrepairman did not look up from his bench as if he already divined by the footfalls it was not a woman. In the contrastingly clean bright display room, puffing on the cigar, he nodded solemnly to Mrs Catlett as he passed. Al was already wrapping her coffee-maker for her.

"How de do, Mrs Catlett? Find what you wanted? Everything satisfactory, I hope?" The other clerk, a man now instead of the country girl who had finally married her soldier, was on the other side of the U of glass cases, polishing off the glass top. Americans, or so it seemed to Frank, had in the years since he was a boy acquired a strange new habit of whenever they were depressed or wretched or unhappy, running out somewhere and buying something—as if that would solve what was bothering them. And as a result they never got caught up. That was Mrs Catlett. He was glad to have her come in; it might just as easy have been a hat or pair of shoes someplace else. He had decided to brave the May weather without his spring topcoat and at the door pulled down his coat skirts and his hatbrim, took a final puff on the cigar and stepped outside into the coolish bright day, the big fat Churchill resting comfortably between his teeth. He had already decided to walk around to The Parkman, instead of taking the Buick.

That damned Dave. Always causing him *some* kind of inconvenience!

Well, under his tutelage—gradually—Al Lowe had practically taken over the management of the store, so that he did not even need to be there at all if he didnt want to. Al didnt know it yet, but he already *was* managing the store—in just about everything but name. Frank had been carefully grooming him toward that. As soon as he found it out, hed have the last thing he needed: the confidence. Then he would *be* the manager.

It could just as easily have been Dave, Frank thought with a kind of irritated sorrow. If he had settled down when he was young and worked hard and been a good citizen, like the rest of us.

Dave was going to be mad about his car. Well, that was just too bad. Frank still didnt feel he had done wrong about it. It had got just as good treatment from him as it would have had if it had stayed on the street where Dave left it. Sure, he could have put it inside somewhere, and blocked it up, and taken the battery out, and drained the gastank; it would have cost him a good bit, and he knew he would never have got paid back; but he still could have done it. But there was more to it than that, and what he had done he had done deliberately, to teach Dave a lesson. It was time he learned that he couldnt always go running along through life expecting everybody else to take care of him and what he owned all the time. People just didnt do that for you, and it was time he learned it; and time he learned to have a little responsibility, whether it made him mad at his brother Frank or not. Someday he would thank him for it.

Two things were disturbing him—not upsetting him; just making him thoughtful—about Dave. One was the rumor, pretty well conceded to be fact, that he had taken off with 'Bama Dillert the gambler, when he left. (Frank kept an ear or two to the ground, here and there.) He had nothing against 'Bama, and in fact, liked him, personally; he had played poker with him lots of times, and would again. But playing poker with 'Bama somewhere was one thing, and becoming his bosom friend was another. He had not said anything when Dave started running around with him some, and never would have; but when Dave took off with him for a four months' trip somewhere, it was time somebody woke him up and put him wise to just what kind of social status 'Bama had in Parkman. —The other thing was that Dave had moved back into his old rooms at The Parkman. That could only mean that he had some money again. He had probably picked up a thousand or so gambling while he was gone. He was going to have to be cautioned about what kind of a spectacle he made of himself when he spent it. Parkman wasnt big citified like Evansville or Nashville or Birmingham or Memphis or wherever they had gone. It was a small town and you had to live accordingly. He was going to have to get settled down and get back to work like he should. He should have been back to work today at the cabstand.

If he had just settled down when he was young, Frank thought again, and worked hard and been a good citizen, like other people had to do, he could have been just about anywhere by now. Managing the store, and lots of other things too. I would have been a good father to him. And he could have made me a fine son,—if hed only settled down.

But he wouldnt. And so instead, it was Al—Al Lowe—who would be running the store. As a matter of fact, he probably would have turned the store over to Al completely before now, if it had not been that when he did he would get to see Edith just that much less. It was hard enough meeting her as it was. They had arranged to get away together two nights a week pretty regular, staggering the nights within the different weeks, and sometimes working in an extra night when it seemed safe—but even on those nights they could only stay out safely till eleven or twelve, or at the very most one o'clock, and only once or twice had they even been able to stay all night.

It had been a strange thing, yes sir, very strange, he thought not without a certain vanity. Very strange. Here he had been, scouting all over, looking all around trying to find himself another mistress, and right there all that time under his very nose had been this young girl who was desperately in love with him. Working in his office, seeing him every day, kidding with him and calling him boss and talking to him, although actually they had said very few words to each other really, and all that time she was in love with him. It must have been very hard on her. He was even inclined to feel more magnanimous to Agnes now; because if Agnes hadnt seen fit to cause trouble between him and Geneve and force them to break it up, he might never have found out about Edith. And she would just have gone right on, cheerfully living her unhappy life, forced to work for and be around the man she loved and yet never have him, and he would never have known. She was a very brave girl, by God. And he really owed it all to Agnes— in a way.

How long all this had been going on, Frank had no idea. But there she was. And he hadnt even known. And then, suddenly,—back before Christmas it was; the 20th, in fact; the night he had taken Agnes and Dawn out to the Country Club for dinner after they decorated the tree, and he had been standing behind Agnes's chair, just shortly after he had (with such a painful hurt) seen Geneve sitting down at the other end with Al and some others,—when quite suddenly, out of nowhere, it had just hit him, just sort of come to him, the idea, that Edith Barclay was in love with him. You could have knocked him over with a feather. Hell, yes.

That was how it had started—with him, at least. With Edith, he didnt know. She wasnt a very talkative girl. Especially about herself. Except once in a while, like when shed had a few drinks, and then would suddenly start to talk, about herself and about everything, and would talk your leg off and appear as if she was never going to stop, but even then you couldnt make much out of it that would help you later, just scattered fragments.

He had been very careful. He had not done anything, or said anything, and had merely watched. He did not put much trust in these sudden intuitions and "ideas" that came to a person. They might come to you for all sorts of reasons, these "inspirations".

But the more he waited and the more he watched, the more he became convinced that this particular "inspiration" had been correct, she was in love with him, and yet there was never anything he could actually point to as proof. She never did anything and never said anything. There was never anything that might be construed as a sign she loved him. And yet in some funny odd way he had become more and more sure, more and more positive, that she did.

The trouble had been—he thought now, looking back with a sort of complacent amusement at the him of then—he might be wrong. Might *still* be wrong. Christ, he didnt want to look like one of these businessmen who were always lecherously trying to sleep with their female help. Or like old Judge Deacon and that secretary of his he had been sleeping with for years and years. Long ago, when he first began to get somewhere, he had promised himself he would never again sleep with his hired help. He didnt have to. Only the little guys had to do that; and it lowered them in *every*body's eyes. —But of course, if Edith Barclay was really in love with him, that made it different, and something else again and a horse of a different color. Only, how was he to know? For sure? In the end, still unsure, still on tenterhooks of uncertainty as it were, he had been forced to approach it in a way, of his own devising, that would make it look like he was not approaching it. If it wanted to be taken as an advance, it could, but if not, it would appear to be only fatherly friendliness on the part of the boss.

The system of inventorying Frank had instituted at the store and still always followed was one in which all the work was done after regular hours. He had seen too many potential customers come in a place and leave without buying because the clerks were all too busy inventorying to wait on them. It was harder work, and longer hours, and harder on the help this way, but he always gave everybody who helped a little bonus afterwards so that none of them would resent it. They would stay after closing and work an hour or so, and then come back after supper and work another couple of hours. Usually it took about two weeks. And this year, as they had last year—since the country girl had been practically useless—the three of them had done it, he and Edith and Al. Back in the early days, before they could afford help, Agnes had used to come down and help him with it; but as soon as they could afford it she had quit; and he did not have to worry about her coming down at inventory time because she still hated it.

As they had last year, which was Edith's first year there, they instituted a system in which Al did the climbing around and getting dirty, as was only fair since Frank was the owner, and called the items down to Frank who listed them on long sheets, which Edith in turn took and checked and corrected and copied up in quadruplicate on the typewriter (it was really a lot of fun, in some ways, just the three of them working there at night in the store; fun and friendly and warm and a lot of kidding; it was different; it was like a holiday; not like the regular day's grind; and every night about nine or nine thirty they would send Edith out for coffee down the street, and sandwiches or pie or whatever anyone wanted; he always footed the bill of course). And, also as they had done last year, they made an arrangement whereby Al drove Edith who had no car home one night, and he Frank drove her the next. And that was where his plan fitted in.

He had figured he would have just about exactly two weeks in which to work; or, six times of driving her. That was not an awful lot of time. On his evenings driving her he had concentrated on talking to her about her life and her future and her ambitions, and advising her about them. There was no reason she couldnt aim higher in life than her father had, or the status she had been born into. He himself had started even lower; what with a drunken welder for a father, and him running off with another man's wife. And he Frank would help her all he could. If there was anything she ever needed or wanted or any kind of boost he could give her along the way, all she had to do was ask. Any time. When people went to work for him, they became part of his family. They belonged to the team. At the store everybody was part of the same team. That was the only way a business could be run. Successfully. Or anything else for that matter. The government, the State, the Army, the Navy. They were all teams. Teamwork. You had to have teamwork. And as far as he was concerned Edith was on his team and he would help her any way he could.

Edith herself did not say much; in fact, she said almost nothing; she seemed to just sort of sit there. She agreed with him, and once in a while she said yes, and once in a while she nodded.

Sometimes he talked until he got afraid his jaws might lock on him, and what would he do then? What if he were suddenly to get tetanus? and couldnt talk? What could he do? Panic would strike him. And he still didnt know if she loved him. He was sure, but he couldnt prove it.

It seemed eons. And yet, by the end of the first week—that was three times of driving her; he drove her Mondays, Wednesdays and Fridays—everything was decided. Decided, if not consummated.

On Friday night when he drove her home, he stopped the car as usual under the Roosevelt Drive streetlight (she still always had him let her off at the corner streetlight, instead of driving her on down to the house) and prepared to let her out. He was still talking, when he stopped, admonishing her gently in a fatherly way about her future, and in the urgency of what he was saying he reached out—sort of subconsciously, in that it was a natural thing to do and he didnt really think or anticipate it; and yet with full consciousness of what he was doing, too—and put his hand on her knee over her coat, (it was very cold in January, with lots of snow; all that snow everybody had wanted for Christmas but hadnt got, of course), and in a friendly way squeezed it with his fingers to emphasize what he was saying, but ready to remove it instantly and deny that it was anything but fatherly, which it wasnt.

Edith did not do anything. She did not say anything, either. She neither moved closer nor further away. To all intents and purposes she was unaware his hand was on her knee at all. So he decided to leave it there and keep on talking. And that was what he had done, while Edith continued to stare out through the windshield, apparently listening to him, and apparently unaware his hand was there.

Then, just when he was afraid he was going to have to remove it because he had no more to say and was racking his brains furiously to think of something else he might add, she had turned to him and with a kind of terrifying groan which startled him and also scared him with its sort of grim desperate quality, had practically flung herself upon him and kissed him passionately on the mouth. He had barely had time to get his hand out of the way. He hadnt expected anything like that. Still startled, and with his ears still buzzing from the way his heart had leaped, and yet with a rising sense of tremendous triumph, he tried as best he could in his heavy topcoat to get his arms around her comfortingly and returned her kiss. For the moment he did not even care that they were parked under the streetlight.

At the time, he had had a strange, not-pleasant feeling that she had known what he was doing all the time, all along; that she had with her cool capable efficient way sort of, well—made her deductions so to speak, looked the situation over, and then made up her mind, and decided to go into it with her eyes open sort of, with full knowledge of what she was doing. But that was no way to go into a love affair, and afterwards he had decided that that startling, terrifying groan he had heard was the result of her passionate physical nature she had been trying to control. Later on, after he got to know her better, he was positive of it. Apparently there was something about him (he had no idea himself what it was) that excited her tremendously. And yet she never seemed to get excited when he himself wasnt. Apparently, it was only him who could bring it out in her.

It had been very uncomfortable in the car and awkward, both of them in heavy coats as they were, but he had held her to him as best he could and after the second long kiss had put his hand on her leg under her coat but on the outside of her dress. Edith had not done anything. But after another kiss, she had pulled her mouth off his and just breathed for a couple of moments and then said in a low quiet voice, "You better think what youre doing."

"I am," he said automatically, and reached for her mouth.

"Im in love with you," she said.

"Im in love with you too, Edith," he said.

She looked at him searchingly and then smiled, as tenderly as he could ever remember anybody smiling at him before, and then reached up her mouth to kiss him again.

"Even if I am old enough to be your father," he said. And it was true, he thought, he was in love with her.

"I think Ive been in love with you for a long time," he said. "And didnt know it." It was only then that he thought of the streetlight, and remembered they were under it. Someday when the bypass had gone through, this street—Wernz Avenue, the mainstreet—would become a sleepy backstreet; but right now it was the highway and the main road in and out of town. Even if it was late at night. Edith had apparently thought of it at the same time he did.

"We shouldnt be here like this," she said.

"No," he said. "Well, I guess I better let you get on home," he said chivalrously, but not meaning it at all.

"All right," Edith said simply and straightened her hat.

Frank had merely looked at her, sort of startled. He had not expected her to agree. What he had thought was that maybe they would drive on over to the Terre Haute road, and park; or get a motel. There were a lot of good new motels there; and if there was any question of them being recognized they could go on to the other side of Terre Haute where there were others. He had thought she would want to be with him —*have* him, have sex with him—and not just go on home. He had only said that to be properly selfeffacing.

"Well, what about your lipstick? and all?" he temporized craftily.

"I can fix it in the dark," Edith said efficiently. "Ill do it on the way home. Youd better get on back to town." She leaned over smiling to kiss him on the ear and then opened the door.

So he had sat empty-headed and watched her as she got out, and walked away out from under the cone of light, her head down replacing her lipstick that he would have to yet wipe off of him (and remember to throw the handkerchief away), her fleecelined overshoes with the little fleece collars zipped up over her high-heels moving swiftly over the packed path through the snow in the center of the walk. He was to learn later that whenever he said anything to her about doing something like that, she did it. That was all; no question, no argument; just did it. Even if she had seemed to be passionately hot a moment before. It made him have to be careful of what he said. But at the time he hadnt known that. So he just sat stupidly and watched her go, a little panicky that he might have hurt her feelings some way, and thinking that now it would mean he would have to wait at least three more days, till Monday. But he couldnt have hurt her feelings, could he? she had smiled and kissed him on the ear when she left, hadnt she? The weekend was going to be hell. Well, at least it had all been decided anyway. He did know that she was really in love with him like hed suspected, and apparently very violently in love with him too, he had thought triumphantly as he turned the car around. Monday. Monday.

—Frank in his progress toward the Hotel Parkman to see Dave could afford to smile back at himself with amusement now. He had reached the northeast corner of the square and he stopped there a moment, nodding pleasantly at people who passed and spoke to him, the breeze in the bright May sunshine whipping at the skirts of his suit coat, the cigar set comfortably between his teeth. In spite of Dave, he felt good. He wasnt even very mad at Agnes any more. Girls of twenty four did not very often fall in love with men of forty five—not unless the men had an awful lot more on the ball than usual and stood out pretty sharply from the people around them. It must have been when she saw the way he handled the business at the store and all the other deals he was engaged in. It had probably been a revelation to her. Hell, he didnt claim to be handsome, and never had, he wasnt going to try and kid himself it was that.

With his ballshaped head on his barrelshaped body Frank stepped off the curb and made his way slowly across Wernz Avenue the mainstreet to the north side of the square and turned west with a stately nod at a middleaged lady who spoke to him as she passed.

Monday had come soon enough, soon enough,—although he sure hadnt thought so at the time, he grinned to himself. It must have been the business, he decided as he made his way along the north side and down the hill. A fairly astute smalltown businessman can look an awful lot like a bigtime tycoon to a young girl, probably.

Monday night when he had driven her home he had not had to talk about her life and her future at all. But he didnt want it to look to her like that was all a put-on, and just an act, so he had talked about it a little anyway. Edith had sat beside him in the car quietly, not saying much of anything and staring straight ahead out the windshield after the one quick warm, sort of embarrassed smile she had given him when she first climbed in. He had had then a feeling that he was to have often again with her after that, and that was a sort of uneasy disquieting feeling of wondering what she was thinking so quietly. And if it had been Agnes, instead of Edith, it would have been a guilty feeling also—and maybe it was anyway, a little, though of course not as much. His reaction to it was to always think irritably, Damn women, anyway! And yet the atmosphere in the car was totally different and less charged than it had been Friday night, too. All of Friday night's heavy unpleasant suspense was gone now, and they were closer together, like sort of an unspoken but understood agreement between them, even if she was so quiet. He had waited until they were only about two blocks from the streetlight at Roosevelt Drive, but she still did not say anything, anything important anyway.

"Well, where are we goin' to go?" he was forced to say finally.

"Go?" Edith said immediately without turning her head. "I dont know. Where will we go?"

"I thought we might drive over on the Terre Haute road. Theres a lot of nice new motels over there," he said. "Nice ones."

"All right," she said. "A motel would be nice."

"Or we could just go over on the Terre Haute road and park someplace," he said. He started to say he knew a couple of places, but decided to refrain.

"All right," Edith said. "Whatever you prefer."

"Myself Id rather go to a motel," he said. "I dont think theres much possibility of either of us bein' recognized at any of these places," he said; "but theres a lot of nice motels over on the other side of Terre Haute, too. Of course, that would mean drivin' on through Terre Haute and thatll take a half hour longer—both ways—to get back." They had already passed the Roosevelt Drive streetlight now, he noted with a kind of relief. They were off the brick onto the concrete highway, running on out past the few remaining houses toward the bridge at Israel.

"I think wed better go on on the other side of Terre Haute," Edith said, still without turning her head. "The time's not so very important, is it?"

"Not so much," he said.

"And I suppose wed better be pretty careful about being recognized," Edith said. "Especially you."

"Well, we have to go somewhere!" Frank said.

"I suppose so," Edith said.

He had the feeling that she hadnt even thought what she was saying. But something was eating on him inside anyway. She seemed so very damned far away. He couldnt let it pass.

"Unless you dont love me any more," he said, feeling a little panicky to be saying it. "I can always turn around and take you home."

With that, she turned her head to him (for the first time) and smiled that warm quick sympathetic smile at him, and his touch of panic instantly faded and he felt relieved.

"Poor Frank," she said. It was the first time she had ever called him by his first name, or by anything but boss or Mr Hirsh. She didnt seem younger than him at all, he noticed.

"Oh, I make out pretty good," he said, feeling fussed but pleased, "all in all. Here. Come on over here. You dont have to sit way over there."

"All right," she had said gravely, and leaned over against him. It wasnt very comfortable, what with the heavy coats and all, but she had stayed there, and they had driven awkwardly on in silence until the Israel bridge loomed up in the lights and he had thought, Well, he had got her this far anyway. He had already realized that she was going to require some kind of obscure nursing along, in some way that he didnt understand.

When he went in to register at the motel, far out East on the other side of Terre Haute, almost to Seely, on the Indianapolis road, he had, suddenly, and without having thought about it at all, signed a fictitious name. He hadnt needed to really, and hadnt meant to especially, and in fact had not even contemplated signing a register at all one way or the other until it was right there before him. And he didnt know why he did it. Of course, he had had to give his own, correct license number.

Edith was waiting for him at the door and after he had parked the car they went inside where she took her coat off and laid it neatly out on a chair, and then said:

"Did you sign a fictitious name on the register?"

"Well, yes," Frank said, feeling a quick guilt; "yes, as a matter of fact, I did."

Edith nodded. "Good," she said. "I thought about it before and was going to mention it to you that you ought to, but I forgot it." She then took off her shoes and sat down in the other chair and sat looking at him expectantly—and yet not exactly expectantly, either—more, politely—her knees pressed together in her skirt, and occasionally wiggling her now unconfined toes up and down in the feet of her stockings.

Frank had thought to bring a bottle with them and had brought it in, and now he was glad. He took off his own coat and mixed them both drinks of whiskey and water, letting the tap water in the bath run until it was cold and talking back over his shoulder to her through the doorway, a constant stream of talking that he hardly heard and hardly even knew what it was he was saying. It was really a very nice modern little place, once the three lamps were on and the overhead light turned off, and he was glad of that. God! what stresses a man wouldnt go through! just for a little lovin' and sex.

"Im not used to drinking whiskey much," Edith called. "Dont give me very much. I dont want to get tight on you."

"All right," he said and put less in the second glass and brought them in.

"And you want to be careful about getting tight yourself," she said. "Remember, you have to drive back to Parkman."

"Yes," he said, "thats right." She was right, also, about the whiskey; after two—at least to him—not very strong drinks, Edith got a little giggly. "Im sure glad you brought that whiskey," she said at length, sighing and punching back her hair. He sat across the room from her on the bed and had not the vaguest idea of what they talked about or what he said or how many times the conversation languished. But finally after he finished downing his third stiff one he just simply got up and went over to her in her chair thinking everything was really so simple really if you just did it simply, why couldnt he ever remember that? Edith was still sitting with her knees together like a good secretary should and he got down on his knees by the chair and kissed both her knees in the textured stockings, and then raised up to kiss her on the mouth while she looked at him sort of helplessly.

He still had no idea how to go about or get through the awkwardness of getting their clothes off, no idea at all; and he was still in his suit coat. But finally, after a timeless period of kissing her—it was strange how all sense of time seemed to diminish and then stop, as sex drew near—he reached up with trembling fingers and awkwardly began unbuttoning the blouse of her tailored suit, trying to make it look playful.

"Wait," Edith had said tenderly—and almost sympathetically, he thought—and got up and went to the bath. "You wait there. Ill be right back."

Frank watched her go helplessly, voiceless, dim fear pictures rattling around in his head of her wanting to turn all the lights off or coming out in her slip or wearing a negligee he knew she had not brought or making him shut his eyes.

"But I want to *see* you!" he was able to cry out finally. "I want to *see* you!"

"Youll see me," she smiled and shut the door.

When she came out two or three nervous swallows of straight whiskey later, she came out nude, carrying all of her clothes neatly arranged together over one arm which she held away from her rather than using it as a cover, and wearing that odd helpless expression on her face that was not unlike a vaudevillian going out before an audience for the first time with a new act and wondering helplessly I hope theyll like me. At first, with the strong light of the bath behind her through the door, she was only a silhouette, but as she came out into the room the light from the three different lamps hit her and he could see her, the three lights creating flesh shadows and highlights on her body as she moved and lighting up the sculptured three-dimensionality of her, that was not like a painting at all but had real air behind it, and Frank gazed at her dumbstruck thinking once again that there was really nothing anywhere quite so beautiful in the world as a woman, a naked woman, and wondering also again why it was women never seemed to understand that. Or feel it, either; about men, or women. Still looking oddly helpless, Edith laid her stack of clothes neatly out across the back of the chair with her coat on it and then turned to him and smiled that oddly helpless almost embarrassed smile and walked over to him lightly through the three different lights that moved across her as she moved, to where he sat on the bed and knelt down on one knee and began untying one of his shoes.

As if burned with a hot iron Frank jumped up off the bed and away from her and began tearing off his clothes like a man tearing pages out of a magazine looking frantically for an address. Breathing heavily and glaring furiously he ripped them off and let them lay where they fell, pausing only to do the buttons. The strange thing was, her body looked exactly like it had when he used suddenly to see her walking stark naked around the store. Exactly. She did not have that bony and starved look of a *Vogue* model that Geneve Lowe had. Fractionally, for less than a second, he wondered about Clark Hibbard's wife Betty Lee again and what kind of body she had. Strange—if you ever got the chance to see—women's bodies were all as different and individual as their faces. Strange. But stranger yet was how Edith looked, in fact, so exactly like he had seemed to see her in the store those times. With a kind of awed momentary fear he wondered if there was anything supernatural in that, as with wild glaring haste he went on down through his clothes, layer after layer, flinging them off him.

"Frank! Frank!" Edith exclaimed softly. "You have. to wear those clothes back home. Dont do that!" and went round after him picking them up and straightening them out and folding them over the other chair back where his coat was. "Frank! You mustnt! Stop!"

But when he seized her—but not roughly—she suddenly became again, beside him, the almost wildly desperate woman who had kissed him so passionately Friday night, and emitted again that terrifying, almost-weeping cry which still startled him, and sounded as if she had lost her last friend and dignity on earth, as she turned to him.

There was something about when a man possessed a new woman that was like no other thing on earth, he thought triumphantly. It was a good thing women didnt know it, how men felt. But maybe they did know it? Sometimes, he thought maybe they did, and briefly, for a second or two, he felt vaguely but deeply frightened and could not say why.

—but Frank, standing at the northwest corner of the square now, having traversed its north side from the northeast corner, and looking down the two blocks down the hill to The Parkman where he had to go (that damned Dave!), was pretty confidently sure—and even a little bit smugly sure; he had to admit it to himself—that women did *not* know. If he was a woman and he knew, he would never let any man sleep with him ever. But then he wasnt a woman; he was a man. And women were not like men. They were different. They were women. And women hungered to be owned and dominated, their very nature made them hunger for it, he thought happily. They just werent like men. And Edith Barclay was a good example.

He had gotten her home all right that night, in spite of a couple more drinks he had afterwards, and had let her off there at the streetlight, and then gone on home to bed himself. And all the way home on the drive back, she had talked about what they were going to have to do to be careful, he thought, pleased. It had been obvious, even to him, that she was thinking more about him (and perhaps Agnes) than she was thinking about herself. They must not let on or ever show anything around the store that might be noticed, and if she even seemed a little colder to him than before he mustnt mind and must understand and not be hurt. She wasnt going to be *much* colder, that might be noticed too, but she was going to be very careful not to show anything that might be taken wrong, and he must, too. Also, she was not going to stop dating Harold Alberson, or any of the other young fellows she dated sometimes. She had thought quite a bit about that since Friday night, she said. It would look very funny if she suddenly stopped dating everybody. But she was telling him ahead of time and he was not to worry. Nothing would happen. And if he heard anything about her dating anyone, he would already know. She was not going to take any kind of chances of injuring him.

He had, he grinned to himself, had a very considerable twinge of rectum tightening pain run up his back at that; but she had already anticipated it and gone right on: There just wasnt any other way for them to do it, and he was just going to have to trust her that was all; and he neednt worry about a thing. And in spite of the twinge of strangely enjoyable pain, he was fussed and pleased at her solicitude; and he did trust her. As much as he trusted Agnes not to step out on him almost.

And that was the way it had been since January. That they had been able to pull it off so well, and keep it such a secret that nobody had found out about it, was sufficient proof of the wisdom of the policy. Even Agnes didnt know anything about it, and if anybody knew it so would Agnes; and in fact, he and Agnes had really been closer together and getting along together better the past five months than they had for years.

He and Edith had their night—evening, it was, really—or two a week, and a couple times had managed to stay all night together (during which Edith kept creeping and cuddling toward him in her sleep until he would wind up against the wall or on the very bed edge and practically sleepless, but he loved it); and as far as he was able to tell nobody anywhere was any bit the wiser. There were some joints up the river road north of Terre Haute around Clinton where nobody from Parkman ever went and where he took her several times for dinner and a few times they drove down to Sullivan and once drove clear to Linton Indiana, but usually it would just be a motel and maybe he would go out and get hamburger sandwiches for them afterwards, or even before, and they would sit and eat them and drink and talk, mostly about his deals, and he told her all about the bypass deal. It was really a wonderful love affair.

Usually, he would pick her up on some prearranged street where she had gone to walk (she had always walked a lot, and everybody knew it and would think nothing of it); but after the days got longer and it got to be spring they got so she would take the early evening bus that came through from St Louis to Terre Haute right after work, and he would meet her later at a little backstreet joint out in Twelve Points, the north end business district. And all the time she kept on dating that white-collar, bird-brained, idiot-headed jerk Harold Alberson and a few others; and he himself went on with his own life and business as if shed never even been his office girl even. And yet he trusted her. Completely. As much as Agnes almost. It looked as though he had finally found the mistress he had always dreamed about for years—not out of some chorus line in some city, or some sophisticated nightclub-chasing businessman-woman like Geneve Lowe,—but right in his own home town, a girl out of a lowclass laboring family (who had nevertheless grown beyond it), his own office girl and hired help.

Frank had given a great deal of thought to this thing of the office girl. And he had not forgotten his solemn promise to himself about sleeping with his hired help. He had never been the kind of man to just shuck off things like that and forget he made them, and he was not that kind now. If a man didnt stand by his own personal integrity and selfrespect, he was nothing, and he had nothing, and he was no good to anybody. But he could not honestly feel that in the case of Edith he had jeopardized either his integrity or his selfrespect. All that was cancelled out by the fact that she loved him as much as she did.

And that she loved him very much, there could be no doubt, he thought not without a certain pride. The whole point was, Edith was not of the material of which ordinary mistresses like Geneve Lowe were made. She was not particularly ambitious, she did not especially want money, she did not seem to give a damn about living the high life. She was just as content with hamburgers in a motel as she was with a ritzy dinner someplace.

When he tried to buy her gifts, she turned them down; even jewelry. She didnt want him to give her anything, she said, and she had no place to put them anyway, old Jane would be sure to run onto them—when she was cleaning, she explained—and wonder where they came from.

Once he had suggested her taking an apartment by herself, that he would finance it. Her answer had been that it would look very funny, wouldnt it? her suddenly moving to an apartment, and people would wonder where she got that extra money and start looking around to find out, no, she had better stay there at home. And she was always so cool and calm and collected about it. Apparently she wanted nothing from him except himself.

She was, in short, a—he didnt know quite how to say it—a re*spect*able woman. He would no more have dared to try any of the things with her that he did with Geneve Lowe than he would have thought of trying it with Agnes. That made a certain hardship in the relationship, he admitted, but it was the only one. And he yet had hopes of gradually and gently educating her. She was really very naive.

But other than that, he thought as he walked sedately down the hill, he had the perfect mistress. Once he had told her that if he made a real success on this bypass deal, he wanted to buy her a house. Deed it to her, and furnish it for her. —and he *did;* he wanted to *do* things for her; hell, it was the only way he had to show her he appreciated her— But she had merely smiled, that strange sad little smile she sometimes got for apparently no reason, and that looked so out of place on the face of a girl so young and always shocked him. She must have had some very unhappy experience, at some time in her life. A house, she said, would be worse than the apartment he had suggested, wouldnt it? and anyway she didnt want a house.

Hell! Frank growled to himself loyally as he progressed on down the hill toward The Parkman; hell, if this bypass deal went through like it showed every indication of doing, he ought to be rich. Hed take her over to Indianapolis and buy her a whole damned business of her own, a shoe shop or something, just for herself, and set her up in it, he thought pugnaciously. And *make* her take it. That would mean he wouldnt get to be near her as much, or see her as often, but by God hed be willing to accept that, hed suffer that. After all, she was a damned fine girl, and she deserved something.

The bypass deal was progressing admirably. He had been up to Springfield twice, once in February and once in April, at Clark Hibbard's invitation, not counting this last trip day before yesterday which he had just got back from. And all three trips had been nice ones. Clark had put him onto a friend of his who apparently knew everything, every joint and just about everybody, but Clark had not gone out with them himself. "Cant, you know," he apologized dryly; "Betty Lee's family." But Frank was not to let that stop him; and Frank hadnt. All the state offices were full of good looking competent girls come from all over the State to work as secretaries, typists, clerks of all kinds. It made Frank think of the bigger cities like Indianapolis and St Louis during the war. A man had no trouble getting a "date" for an evening if he was with someone like Clark's friend, who evidently knew them all. They went out every night he was there; and on one evening Clark had had him out to the house for a formal dinner, where flushed with cocktails he talked continuously to a large fat man beside him (he never did find out who the man was) in order to keep his eyes from being drawn like magnets to the body of Betty Lee in her evening gown at the end of the table. It was the same way on the April trip, and now this one. Each time, they spent a great deal of time with the man Clark had got hold of through his father in law, who was to buy the land up for them. And now after this last trip the actual dickering and buying was going forward. He didnt see how they could miss.

He himself had scraped together every penny he could get hold of just about, and had even mortgaged their house, their own home,—without telling Agnes. And Clark had been able to put together almost as much, in cash, without however having to touch the *Oregonian* or any of his business interests. Probably borrowed it from his father in law. And Betty Lee's father, who was evidently a quite wealthy man, had even offered to put some money into it himself if they wanted or needed any more, the voting power of which (and Clark agreed) he would put into Frank's hands, as Clark himself was doing.

He was not, the old man said, looking for something to run, he was a businessman; and a businessman's business was making money and when he saw something that looked like it would make money he would be smart to put some money into it if it was wanted. And he had personally congratulated Frank on his astuteness in working up the deal. He was not, he went on to say, so very interested in Frank's idea of getting factories in there and making it an industrial section— that was all a matter of conjecture; but apart from that it was an excellent investment, if only for the profit in buying the land and reselling it later on to businesses; and he hoped Frank would forgive his bluntness. Anyway, he was all for them; and he felt younger men should get into more things and developments like this.

He was a crusty old devil, tall and portly and white haired, and Frank thought he must be a lot like Old Anton Wernz II must have been, the real founder of the dynasty. And yet despite his crustiness there was a strange unusual feeling of gentlemanliness and trust about the whole dealing, Frank had noticed, which surprised him. This was not like dealing with people in Parkman, apparently, where nobody trusted anybody else. Like, say, dealing with old Judge Deacon. This was the real bigtime, and Clark because of his father in law was moving up into it too. Maybe he would get to be US Senator yet by God. Or anyway Governor. Sometimes Frank almost felt like he might be getting in over his head, playing out of his league. And yet he trusted them completely to do what they said theyd do. Especially the old man. And he knew they trusted him. It was a strange way to run a business.

The man whose organization was to handle the buying up of the land for them was a heavy, cold, fat Greek, with just a trace of a city accent, probably from Chicago—originally. He was, in fact, the more or less living picture of what Frank had always seen in his mind when he thought the words: Chicago gangster. And yet this man, however cold, was obviously not what you could call a gangster. And of course, he could never have been a gangster, not and associate with men like Clark's father in law, and whatever crude brutal beginnings he might have once had in Chicago—or somewhere—had long since all been rubbed off of him. He was what you might call a sort of a 'transformed gentleman.' And he was *such* a gentleman that he made all Frank's fingers turn into thumbs. He was as equally at home in Clark's father in law's huge dining room as he was in his own spacious office. He was charging them a great deal for his services—(and even so, as Clark had said, it was worth it)—and despite his price he had bluntly told them that he did not expect a one hundred percent success. It was very rare and next to the impossible, to ever be able to buy up anything like this entirely. His organization had just been working on a deal like this concerning some oil leases. Some people were invariably just not inclined to sell; and if you offered them more money than whatever it was worth, they got suspicious and became even less inclined, and frightened off others with their suspicions. This they must avoid. Still he would do the best for them he could, and would get what he did get as cheaply as he could. It was amazing to Frank how many of these people's business deals were conducted solely on trust. They ran their deals damn near like he ran his store, and an ordinary business or contractual deal by an ordinary businessman would never get completed if the participants had to depend on trust as much as these bigtime operators did.

Even now, right now, the big Greek's men might be infiltrating into town; or might even be here already, already dickering. Frank himself did not know, and wouldnt know. And neither would Clark. They might meet them face to face on the street, and they wouldnt know it. That had been decided early. It was, as Clark had said, better if they knew nothing at all about it. Then, they couldnt possibly do anything, or damage anything. The thought that even now one or two of the Greek's infiltrators might be dickering for some of the bypass land and him not know it even, excited Frank tremendously. It was like something out of a mystery story.

It certainly wasnt like Parkman, that was for damn sure. The only trouble either he or Clark had really had at all was in keeping Judge Deacon, their so-called business associate, from getting wise that something was taking place. Both of them had always gone to the Judge's Cray County Bank or Building & Loan to get their money, and this time they couldnt do that. Neither did they dare to go to Tony Wernz IV's Second National, or his Real Estate Loan. In the end, Clark had arranged to have them both taken care of in Springfield for whatever loans they wanted, through the bank of which his father in law was a director; and apparently they had succeeded fully, according to all indications anyway, because neither Judge Deacon nor Tony Wernz nor that fat bum Harry Shotridge seemed to have the slightest idea anything was going on. Nobody had even yet guessed apparently, just how valuable that bypass land would be after the road went through.

It was all a gamble. For him and Clark both—but more for him because Clark had not converted everything he had, while Frank had mortgaged everything he owned, the house, the business, and everything else. Everything except a few partnership deals like the taxi service and the Dodge agency which he was holding because he did not want people to know he was borrowing. He still didnt have enough capital to build his shopping center yet, Clark's and his together. But he still had hopes (he had never broached this yet; this he was keeping back) of getting Clark's father in law to put some money in that too. But if not, he would get it someplace else, from Fred Benson in Indianapolis, or from someplace. But hed get it. Hell, if he had another dime, or anything that he could sell, hed throw that in too. Throw it all in! everything! he thought with a kind of elated passionate conviction and recklessness. If youre gonna do it, go whole hog! and never look back! Thats the only way to do a thing!

It was all a gamble anyway. How many of those eight land owners would the Greek's men get to sell? Four? Five? Even six, maybe? Maybe one of them was walking around the square right now, and he had passed him without knowing who he was. They said they really looked the part, when they went in somewhere to buy. Wore down-at-the-heel shoes and socks with holes in them; sweat-stained hats. Hell, if it was a farm they were after, they might even be dressed in overalls, chaw of tobacco and all.

Hot damn! he thought suddenly, *Hot damn!* and a kind of intense excitement rolled and billowed up through him, which nevertheless the rest of him knew he was going to have to keep down under strict control. This was a long range deal, and it was going to take a while. The State itself was not going to start its actual buying until the end of the summer, Clark had told him with that small smile. Everything was working perfectly. It would be the biggest single service anyone had done for the town of Parkman in its history.

He had, on their evenings together, talked to Edith about the whole deal. (He *couldnt* talk to Agnes; or she would be sure to find out he had mortgaged the house, and the business, which was after all, or had been,—of course, it wasnt much, then—her father's business, which she had signed over to him.) So Edith was the only one he could talk to. Edith had agreed with him that he could trust them. "After all, they already have enough money, Clark and his father in law," she said. "Thats the difference. They dont *have* to cheat anybody to get it." He didnt know why he should especially value her opinion, but it reassured him.

There was one thing he didnt have to trust them on, anyway. He had, right after the February trip to Springfield,—and as Clark had already suggested he do, before—gone out and seen old Lloyd Monds and bought from him the small five acre feeding farm which when the road went through would be the two west corners of the Bypass-Route 1 junction, and that much was already in his own name. The whole thing had been ridiculously easy. All he had had to do was to use old Lloyd's country-acquisitiveness against him. He attempted to buy one of old Lloyd's *other* five feeder farms scattered around the edge of town, on the pretext that he was going to use it for feeding up his own beef that he was putting in on his farm north of town. Then he just sat back and let old Lloyd slyly put one over on him by selling him instead the one that would eventually be broken in two by the new bypass, which old Lloyd knew about, but which he himself, of course, did not.

It was amazing—absolutely astounding, in fact—to him, that with all the interest and talk and discussion going the rounds about the new bypass, nobody—absolutely nobody—had yet thought to look into it as a possible money-making venture.

Well, probably a lot of them—like him—had thought about it; and again like him —or almost— had just decided it was a wild dream and had not done anything about it. He had almost not done anything about it himself.

In front of The Parkman Frank stopped a moment and looked up at the brass-hinged, brass-push-railed swinging doors. Well, now he was going to have to take care of Dave. He still did not feel he had done wrong in the way he had handled the car. The boy was just going to have to learn that there were other people who existed in the world besides himself. The main thing now was to get him back on the job and back to work. Then theyd see. If he settled down and worked hard and assumed his responsibilities like a grownup adult was supposed to, there could be an important place for him in all this that was just getting started, and he could still turn out to be Frank's son. But he wasnt going to get it for nothing. Hed have to *earn* it.

Tossing the butt of the Churchill in the gutter, he walked in under the marquee and inside, nodding sedately to the fat one-eyed clerk behind the desk, and went upstairs.

CHAPTER 42

AT THE door of the suite they shook hands. There was open disapproval on Frank's face, as he came on in; and in spite of the enormity of hatred he had felt last night about his car—and still felt—there was a sort of puppyish eagerness to please on Dave's, as he led the way. Both of them smiled, too, each in his own style and fashion, Frank with a cold reserve and Dave almost painfully eagerly. It was curiously like one of those meetings of two amateur chess players who know each other well and are about to play again; the amenities are all there, the smiles, the handclasps, the warm looks, the gestures of friendliness, and back of each, in each man's own way, this same driving, fierce, predatory, actually carnivorous soul-hunger toward the mayhem of the other that can actually make the hands sweat and tremble, and nerves in the armpits twiddle, as both sit down to play a friendly game.

"I see youre back in the money again it looks like," Frank said.

"Not much, really," Dave smiled. "We made a little."

"Where were you?"

"Miami Beach."

"Miami Beach, *Florida?*"

Dave nodded. "Its a pretty nice town."

"Youve put on an awful lot of weight in four months."

"Ive been livin pretty good," Dave said, and gestured with his glass. "Would you like for me to fix you a drink?"

"No. Its too early in the morning for me to be drinkin'. And its too early for you, too."

"Well, you make up for it at night, y'see," Dave smiled. "I dont drink much at night. Sit down."

Frank did not answer this. He sat down in one of the chairs and leaned back and let his hands fall together in his lap. "Now, what did you want to see me about?"

"See you about? Well, the taxi service. I thought you wanted to see me," Dave said.

"I did. For four months now. What about the taxi service?"

"Well, I just wanted to tell you that Im not going to work there any more, thats all."

"Oh, youre not!" Frank said. "When did you decide that?"

"When I was in Florida."

"With 'Bama Dillert?"

"Thats right."

"And why not?"

"Because Ive had a better job offered me. One with better pay and better hours, both."

"Down in Florida?"

"No. In Parkman."

Once again, Frank could not entirely avoid looking surprised. "With who?" he said. "Doin' what?"

Dave grinned at him. "With 'Bama," he said. "Gambling."

"I see," Frank said thinly. For a moment he looked as if he were going to say more. Then he looked down at his hands still lying in his lap, thoughtfully, and rubbed his left thumb with his right. "I suppose you know what thatll do to me," he said without looking up.

"Ive thought some about it. If you mean it will ruin you I dont believe it."

"No. I dont spose it could actually ruin me. It certainly wont do me any good. And it will be embarrassing." He looked back up, at Dave.

"Well, Im sorry about that," Dave said. "I dont like to cause you trouble especially. But its just too good a thing to let go."

" 'Bama Dillert has a bad reputation in this town," Frank said flatly.

"So Ive heard," Dave said, "so Ive heard. But you know something?" He grinned a little and took a deep, almost convulsive breath. "Bad reputation or not, I trust him—and like him—more than I do the respectable people in this town. And that includes you," he said sharply. "If he was going to cheat you, at least he wouldnt do it in the name of God, or Business, or Social Responsibilities."

Frank did not look down but stared straight back at Dave, his face impassive, like a man standing open-eyed in a high wind or a rainstorm. He did not appear to be angry.

"And while we're on the subject of trust," Dave said. "Id just like to mention that I think that was one of the lousiest, pettiest, dirtiest, stinkingest tricks Ive ever heard of—even for you—what you did to my car."

"Nothing happened to your car that would not have happened where you yourself left it," Frank said.

"I know," Dave said. "Thats quite true."

"You yourself left it out on the street, and left no instructions to me of any kind about what to do with it."

"I know. Thats true, also."

"The city police called me up and told me about it. If I hadnt taken it, they would have hauled it off."

"True also."

"Nor did you leave me any forwarding address where I could reach you about it."

"True also."

"I fail to see that I did anything out of the way with your car at all. I think I did you a favor."

"Me, too," Dave grinned, "and I would just like to add that if I *had* intended to go back to work for you in that damn taxi service, I wouldnt now."

Frank nodded. "Thank you. On the subject of trust, I could mention a few things myself," he said. "However, I dont intend to do so."

"Well, thats damned magnanimous of you," Dave said. "You son of a bitch."

Without ceasing to look at him, Frank blinked his eyes once. It was not really a flinch. He continued to stare back at Dave, his face impassive, his eyes moving about over Dave's face thoughtfully. "You dont intend to come back to work at the stand, then," he said. Then he looked back down at his hands, rubbing his right thumb thoughtfully over his left, and Dave could not help but feel ashamed. "Then I expect youll be wantin' to buy me out altogether?" he said softly without looking up.

"Well, I—" Dave began, taken aback and feeling ashamed of himself. "Well, no. I mean not especially. I dont want to take your taxi service away from you. I—" He stopped.

"You mean youd rather sell your share out to me?" Frank said still not looking up.

"Well, I— Say, look here; I thought there was some kind of a clause in that contract we signed that was supposed to take care of all that?"

"You mean that 'Give or Take' clause?" Frank said still without looking up. He was obviously hurt; not angry, just hurt. "You mean youre wantin' to invoke the clause?"

"Well, I— No," Dave said. "No, I didnt mean that. But I thought that was what that clause was for, I mean, in case anybody wanted to break up the partnership, or anything like that."

Frank still would not look up at him. "No, thats just in there as a legal device, in case the partners cant agree any other way," he said softly. "As far as Im concerned, theres no disagreement. Im willin' to do anything you want thats fair. Do you want to buy? or sell your share? What do you want to do?"

"Well now wait a minute," Dave protested. "I never said anything about doing either yet, did I?"

"You mean you want to just leave it like it is?" Frank said, still not looking up from his thumbs.

"I didnt say that. I didnt say anything," Dave said. "You said all that. All I said was I didnt like what you did to my car, and I still dont. That, and that I dont mean to work in the damned place any more. That was all. Hell, Frank, I wouldnt do what you did to my car to my worst enemy's car."

Frank looked back up at him now, finally, impassive-faced, his eyes unreadable. "Well, now, just what *do* you want to do?" he said. "Im willin' to do anything you think is fair." That was all he would say. "I dont want to talk about your car," he said. "You know how I feel about it; and about your responsibilities. Theres no point in talkin' about it further for either one of us."

"Damn, if you just understood me a little," Dave said, his face troubled. "Im not a businessman. I never have been. I dont want to be one. I—" He stopped, looking hopeless and chagrined. "Well, I suppose if I was going to choose, Id rather sell my share than anything else. I dont want to own the damned thing."

"All right," Frank said. "How much?"

"Well, would six thousand be all right?"

"You think thats a fair price?"

"Well—yeah. I think so. Dont you?"

"Im not the one thats namin' it," Frank said coldly.

"I dont want to cheat you or anything."

"All right," Frank said unreadably. "If you think thats fair, its all right with me. You want me to send you a check for it?"

"Oh, nuts! Im gonna get myself another drink," Dave said agitatedly, and got up and went to the table where the liquor bottles were. Frank merely watched him stolidly, from his chair, neither reproving nor approving this time, his face closed, impassive, unreadable. Dave poured a strong one. "Look!" he said distressfully from the table. "I dont give a damn what we do with it. Im not tryin to cheat you, or beat you, or beat you out of anything. I figured six thousand was a fair price because the damned concern is making money. All Im tryin to do is protect my money. Now if you dont think thats fair, just say so."

"Im willin' to pay what youre askin'," Frank said impassively. "Now do you want me to send you a check today? I can mail it to you when I get back to the store, or I can send a boy over with it right away if youd rather."

"Look!" Dave said, turning to face him. "What do you think I ought to do?"

Frank shook his head. "Im not givin' any more advice to you."

"Oh, go to hell!" Dave said, and strode back to his own chair with his drink. "Look, Im willing to do anything thats fair. —Except I wont go back to work for you there. Thats out.— But anything else is fine. Ill sell to you, or buy your share, or let it ride just like it is. Anything you want to do. Ive got the money to buy your share, if you want to sell it," he said, and remembered to drag out his thickly packed wallet and show it. "So you just name it."

"Im not namin' anything," Frank said impassively. "All this is your idea and youll have to do your own decidin'."

"Look. I apologize for calling you a son of a bitch," Dave said. "I was mad."

Frank stolidly said nothing.

"Well, I wont go back to work there. Thats out!"

"All right," Frank said. "I gathered that. Now what else do you want to do?"

"Well, I dont know *what* to do!" Dave said. I dont know whats *right!*"

Frank looked across at him coldly, totally unreadable. "All right. Then I suggest you just let it ride until you do know what you want to do. When you finally do make up your mind, you can do whatever you want later."

"Will that be all right with you?"

"Anything'll be all right with me. This is not my party."

"All right; then thats what we'll do."

Frank got up from his chair.

"Wait! Just one more thing," Dave said. "I want my share of the profits sent to me. Every month. If any money goes back into the business, we can take that up separate. Okay?"

"All right," Frank said. "Thats all right with me. You wont mind if I put some of my own money back into it, will you?"

"Oh, quit acting hurt! Ive apologized to you for calling you a son of a bitch. I said I was mad. What more do you want me to do?"

Stolidly Frank again said nothing, exactly as though he were totally deaf, or else no words had been spoken, no question asked. He walked stolidly to the door.

"All right. Go ahead then. Act like a damned kid."

"At the risk of being told to keep my mouth shut, I *will* say just one thing," he said as he took hold of the knob. "I think you ought to go up and see your mother."

"Who?" Dave said, "oh. Oh, mother. Yeah, I spose I ought to, I guess," he said lamely.

"Youve been back home over six months now," Frank said impassively.

"Two of those months right here in town. It looks like youre going to be around a lot longer. Your mother asks me about you every time I see her. You ought to go see her at least once, dont you think? I know your mother would like to see you."

"Whats all this 'your mother', 'your mother'?" Dave snarled. "Shes your mother too."

"I *know* shes *my* mother," Frank said. "But, do you?"

"All right, all right, Ill go up and see her. Ill even take her a god-damned present. How do you like that?"

"I dont like it or dislike it," Frank said. "Your mother might like it."

"All right, okay, Ill go see her."

"Goodby," Frank said coldly, and went out and shut the door.

After he was gone, Dave carried his glass to the corner window and watched him march sedately back up the hill, a fresh cigar in his jaw, shoulders held back and his back as straight and stiff as a ramrod in that way he always walked, hat brim snapped down low over his ball-like Hirsh head, coat skirts blowing in the breeze around his barrel-like Hirsh body. It was like watching some foreign person, a Russian or somebody, about whose strange incomprehensible life you really knew absolutely nothing. He really *believed* all those damn sanctimonious things he spouted. Really be*lieved* them. The truth was, he was a fool. And yet he was smart as hell in business and things like that. But it was all rule-of-thumb knowledge. He really knew no more about life than he did about flying a jet airplane. He was a walking mass of other humans' ill-considered, un-thought-out opinions, which he had accepted, something hed read, something hed heard, something hed been told. And he believed he was *right*. Dave watched him sadly, hating him implacably still, and wishing now hed punched him in the head. He was already regretting that he had not gone ahead and accepted the six thousand. It was a fair price to both, and he wished now hed taken it. But he knew he wouldnt do anything about it now, unless he was just forced to. It was too unpleasant a thing to have to go through again, just to get the money. As far as he was concerned it could stay the way it was forever. Well, he would have to tell old 'Bama what had happened. Actually, nothing had. He took another drink from his glass that was not so much a drink as an expression of bitter feeling.

—While up the street treading his way back up the hill to the square, Frank chewed on his cigar and sucked in its rich buttery smoke complacently. Underneath his complacency was an additional feeling of sad but implacable pride. He didnt mind being called a son of a bitch. You could call just about anybody a son of a bitch, and not be wrong. And he probably had just as much of the son of a bitch in him as the next man. But *Dave* shouldnt have called him that. Even if it was true. Hed been like a father—more than a father—to that boy all his life. Still, it had all turned out all right, the way it worked out. It had been obvious from the start that no matter what he did, Dave was not going back to work at the stand like hed hoped. So hed given that up right away. But he couldnt have sent Dave a check for six thousand if Dave had decided to take it. He didnt have it now. Of course, he could have sold Dave his own interest, and put the money in with everything else hed put in on the bypass. But the taxistand was a pretty good little investment and he didnt want to let go of it, he thought complacently. So it had all worked out fine. But Dave shouldnt have called him a son of a bitch, he thought implacably. Maybe he was one. But he had never gone back on his word, and he had never cheated anybody, or played unfair with anyone. And *Dave* shouldnt have called him that.

Damn! hed sure had a lot of money in that wallet. Of course, it was probably all ones and fives. But it might be fifties and hundreds. And thousands. If it was he sure wished there was some way he could have got him to invest it in on the bypass!—

When Dave told 'Bama about the contest after the gambler got back to town, his car all dusty and spotted with mud-stuck gravels from the country roads, the tall man merely grinned. It was a good enough way to settle it as any. Dave would have the income off his share, and still would own it and it ought to be worth more all the time. For some reason or other Frank had not wanted to buy it right now, but he had no idea why that might be. Certainly it would not be hard for him to put his hands on six thousand dollars.

For the rest of the week it took Judge Deacon to find a suitable house for them, they spent their time loafing and did no work—that is, gambling—and hung out at Ciro's and at Smitty's Bar with Dewey and Hubie and the brassiere factory set. It was a very far cry from the high life they had lived up and down Miami Beach, although only Dave appeared to miss it; 'Bama certainly did not; and everybody was excited and very interested about the house they were going to get.

The house which the Judge finally secured for them was not on Wernz Avenue the mainstreet, but the Judge had come just as close as he could get, without actually violating 'Bama's instructions. It was located on West Lincoln, the first street south of Wernz, five blocks from the square in the west end, a big oldfashioned two storey clapboard house, different but still indistinguishable from its neighbors, with a wide front porch and a long back yard, and it was owned by Mr and Mrs Gene Alberson the parents of Harold Alberson, who now that their daughter Harold's younger sister was graduated from the State University and finally married, were retiring from Gene's office

job at the Sternutol and moving to St Petersburg Florida where so many
of their friends had also retired, while Harold was taking a couple of
rooms with friends of the family on the other side of town. The Judge
had leased it (for one year) in his own name for his clients, and the
Albersons did not know who was getting it.

Dewey and Hubie rode out in the back seat of the Packard with them
and the Judge the afternoon they went out to see it, making humorous
remarks about setting up housekeeping.

"Hell I never thought wed be bosom buddies to a couple of fagots setting up housekeeping did you, Hubie?" the handsome, blue-eyed Dewey
said, lolling back on the back of his neck in the backseat. "You guys
shore learned a lot down there in that big city of Miami, hunh, Hubie?"

"It just goes to show you," Hubie said philosophically, his elbow on
the armrest, his chin resting on his hand. "You caint be shore of nobody
no more, even your own friends. Hell, its li'ble to ruin our own reputations, you know it, Dewey?"

"You better scoot down in the seat, and not let anybody see you sittin
up there, Hubie," Dewey said.

"No wonder that Dave's put on so much weight," Hubie said, dutifully scooting himself down in the seat so his head no longer showed;
"I think hes pregnant."

"No, I think its 'Bama whos pregnant," Dewey disagreed. "Look at
his belly." They looked at each other solemnly and then both reached
for the opener and another can of beer from the box of them between
them on the floor.

"How'll we tell?" Hubie said. "Guess we'll just have to wait."

"Lets wait and see which one carries the other one over the thresh-
hold," Dewey said.

"You reckon we ord to throw rice or somethin' at them when they
go in?" Hubie said. "We aint got nothin' but beercans."

"Beercans'll be all right. In fact, I think they be very proper, Hubie."

"I aint had nothin' to do with fagots since I ran onto them Marines
in New Britain, and they was just ama-toors," Hubie called, "but if
ever one of you guys gets a mad on and decides to get a divorce,
you let me know. Im allus willin' to learn. Is that it?" he said, peeking
up over the windowledge as the car stopped.

"Why dont you bums shut up?" 'Bama said, "or Ahll cut off yore
beer. It looks all right to me, Judge," he said.

"It better," the Judge said. He had managed to squeeze in beside
Dave in the front seat. "Ive done already leased it. Now it aint furnished, you understand. Hand me one of them beers there, Dewey,"
he said.

"Well, lets go have a look," 'Bama said. "Open a couple more of them
beers, Dewey, and we'll go see."

"Hell, you guys're wearin my arm out," Dewey complained.

Over the front door, which was set off to one side and not in the center, was an oldfashioned fanshaped transom of stained glass pieces leaded in. "I like that window light," 'Bama said as they approached it. Inside, the empty house echoed to their footsteps. "They left it cleaned up pretty good," Dewey admitted reluctantly. From the front door the hallway with the stairs on the outside wall extended back half way and beyond it was a long narrow kitchen. To the right of the hall was the living room separated from it by an open arch of varnished oak spool turnings, and behind it was another room separated in the same way and behind this still another room the same, which opened into the kitchen and was evidently the dining room. Upstairs, opening off a central hall, half of which was bannistered and hung out over the right-angled stairs, were four bedrooms and a large bath.

"Christ, we're sure gonna have to buy a lot of furniture to furnish this place!" Dave said.

"Never you mind," 'Bama said. "We'll fix it. Now," he said when they were back down in the hall, and pointed to the oak spool turnings. "Can we yank all that junk out of there, Judge?"

"I dont know about that," the Judge said cautiously. "Ill have to write the Albersons about that, I guess."

"But we got the right to paper and repaint the insides, aint we?" 'Bama said.

"That was the agreement."

"Okay. Now you two halfwits think you can paint and paper this place in the next week?" he asked Dewey.

"Well, I dont know," Dewey said solemnly. "We're awful busy right now. We're very much in demand, you know."

"At least five houses waitin' on us right now," Hubie nodded vigorously. "All carpentry work, too."

"Hell with them," 'Bama snarled. "Let them wait."

"Will you furnish the beer?" Hubie said.

"All the beer you can drink—" 'Bama held up one finger, "—as long as it dont mess up your eye and ruin the paint job."

"We'll do it!" Hubie cried.

"And a half a case of whiskey apiece when its done," 'Bama added.

"We'll do it twice!" Hubie cried.

"Youll have to pick out your paints and papers first, you know," Dewey said more cautiously.

"Do that this afternoon," 'Bama said. "We'll all go down to Merritt's Paint Store."

"Well, we trade at Wolff's, me and Hubie," Dewey said.

"Okay. Then we'll go there."

"We might be able to get it done in a week," Dewey said.

"No mights!" 'Bama said. "Me and Dave'll come out and help on the crude work that dont take no master's touch like you guys got."

"Hell, anybody can hang paper," Dewey said.

"Not me," Dave protested. "Ive never even tried it."

"Hell, we'll show you," Dewey said.

They all stood in the hall and looked around at the place holding their beercans. The fat Judge ambled off toward the kitchen.

"Heres a good writin' room for Dave," he called; "right here." They walked back to where he stood at the end of the hall, and looked at a small ten by twelve room that jutted out from under the stairs and back into a corner of the kitchen. "Even got a window there," the Judge said, "and its on the quiet side," he pointed out, and they all looked outside through the small window at the vacant lot that extended clear to the corner.

'Bama looked at Dave. "Sure," Dave said. "Make me a hell of a fine writin room. Couldnt ask for anything better. A smaller room dont sound so empty."

"Good!" 'Bama said, and they all walked back down the hall, still carrying their now empty beercans. "Who's gonna go out and get some more beer?" 'Bama said.

"Me!" Hubie said. "I volunteer!" He set down his empty and went to the door.

"Judge, theres nothin in the rules that says we cant *paint* that damn stuff, is there?" 'Bama said, pointing again at the varnished oak spooling.

"No-o-o," the Judge said judiciously. "No, I guess not. The agreement says you got the right to re-paint and re-paper the interior."

"All right, good! We paint that crap a contrastin color it might not look bad. Might even look good. That dull finish paint, I mean. What do you think, Dave?"

"Sure. I bet it would look good," Dave said, and everybody stood and looked at the archway of spooling judiciously.

"Well, what do you say, Dewey?" 'Bama said.

"Well, I guess we can do it, if you guys're gonna help some. You wont want to do all them upstairs rooms and furnish them anyway, will you?"

"No, sir, by God!" 'Bama said. "Every room gets done. Done and furnished. If theres goin to be any damn parties around here, I want to be damn sure everybody has a room to take his woman to. There'll be no damn sleepin with in the living room. We're gonna be respectable around here."

"Well, we might be able to get it done anyway. I guess we can."

"Get it done!" Hubie cried, bursting in the door with the box of beer. "Hell, this wont be no job! This is a vacation! Thats what it is! And I been wantin' a vacation for three months!"

"All right," 'Bama said. "Now lets drink up this beer and get down to Wolff's and pick out that paper and stuff. Now, heres what Ive been figurin, Dewey. I thought we might paint the bottom half of the walls, see, and paper the top half? With some real good ritzy paper? gold lines and stuff? And then paint the ceilings the same colors as the wall bottoms."

"Wainscoting," Dewey said. "Yeah, that sounds real good."

"All right," 'Bama said. "Lets drink up and get to goin."

In a week it was done. Dewey was able to borrow, from a finishing carpenter he often worked with and who also owned his own truck farm, a medium sized Army surplus truck to use for the furniture. And Dave and 'Bama, dressed in oldfashioned bib-type overalls and railroaders' caps which 'Bama had bought expressly for the purpose, made run after run to Terre Haute to bring back the furniture. There had been more than a little worry on Dave's part about the buying of new furniture, and the expense it would cause, but 'Bama solved this in his characteristic way. A gambling buddy he knew from around the Terre Haute clubs who was also a traveling professional musician was selling his home in Terre Haute and moving to the West Coast permanently, and most of his furniture was already in storage. By a deal with him that was mutually advantageous, 'Bama purchased all the furniture he had for less than half what it would have cost them to furnish it new; and it was all practically new furniture,—and of that ultra-modern style of steel wire and metal and wood combined which 'Bama apparently had an especial hunger for—and was all in excellent condition. At 'Bama's instance, they did all the upstairs rooms first, and as soon as the paint was dry the two of them made the hauls to Terre Haute for the furniture that would go in the bedrooms, and were in fact moved into their own bedrooms upstairs before the paint smell was gone from the walls, or the downstairs finished. Here, as everywhere else, 'Bama's penchant for mathematical efficiency stood them all in good stead.

Long before it was even finished that week, it was all over town that they had taken the Albersons' house, and Wally Dennis—who appeared to take as big an interest in it as they themselves did, and was even more envious than Dewey and Hubie—came down to help too in the afternoons after he got through writing for the day.

"Men, you ought to hear my old mom go on about this here place to her club," he grinned, paint specks on his face from wielding a brush. "I sit up at the top of the stairs and listened. Accordin to the Diana Club ladies, its a sin and a shame and a regular den of iniquity and something ought to be done about it but dont worry, none of them ladies will. They all get their kicks talkin." He paused and painted a few strokes. "Christ! When I told her I was helpin you to decorate, she like to threw a bigger fit than she did when I first made her let me keep beer in the icebox."

The house itself was located in a pretty good section, and was in fact only about three blocks from Wally's. It itself stood on the south side of Lincoln among other ordinary houses, but directly across the street north were the better-than-ordinary houses whose backyards abutted against the big backyards of the big houses on West Wernz, and the north side of Lincoln was not to be sneered at. The whole thing, in an extraordinarily similar way, made Dave think of Hollywood and a successful producer friend of George Blanca's whom he had met several times and who after years of struggle owned a big home directly across the street—Sunset Boulevard—from the main gates of Bel Air but the poor man had died of a heart attack before he could make it across the street.

"Its a damn good thing Parkman's too backward to ever made any zoning laws," Wally chuckled, "or you guys would be unzoned." He was, quite clearly, jealous as hell of both of them, and he made no bones about admitting it. He would, he said, come live with them himself if he didnt have to take care of his mom, whether he was invited or not. Wally himself had garnered a good bit of publicity himself, when both papers printed that he had been awarded the thousand dollar fellowship of the College; but when he peered in through the door at Dave's writing room where a bespeckled Hubie was putting on the finish coat of light-absorbent light-green, he could not hide his envy.

When it was all done and all the furniture moved in, they gave a housewarming party with the smells of paint and wall paper paste still hanging in the air. 'Bama spent the afternoon before it going from room to room with a deodorizer, spraying diligently, but before he could get completely finished it was already ready to be done all over again and finally he said the hell with it disgustedly and quit. Everyone who was anyone in the lower echelons of Parkman was invited. Judge Deacon came (and took up happily with one of the brassiere factory girls named Marie). The pick of the brassiere factory's bunch were invited, and a number of the more habitual denizens of Smitty's like Gus Nernst and his girlfriend Lorelei Shaw from Terre Haute, whose family had money and who was studying to be a concert pianist but still loved pub-crawling; and Raymond Cole was there, on his best behavior with his hair combed and actually dressed up in a suit, an ancient one which he must have bought before the war because it no longer fit him. Dewey brought his girl Lois, and Hubie brought his girl Martha Garvey. Lois Wallup and Martha Garvey, as the girlfriends of the two sidekicks, had become practically inseparable, sort of like sisters in law. Mildred Pierce and Rosalie Sansome the statuesque were both there with a couple of the boys from Smitty's, and Ginnie Moorhead who of course had no date—though she wound up with two, at different times of the evening and for a short while, just long enough in fact to make quick trips upstairs to the bedrooms. There were even several younger members (war veterans all) of the Elks (and Country Club), who nevertheless liked to hang out at Smitty's in the afternoons after work with the boys, and who had prevailed upon their wives to come, but these did not stay long. Smitty himself was there, without his wife of course, but with several cases of cold beer. There had been much discussion at the house, while the work was still going on, about not forgetting to invite Smitty who, while he did not hang around with the gang much outside of working hours, and was trying to elevate the patronage of his bar, was nevertheless still goodhearted and would be sure to come and bring a lot of beer, and would certainly be hurt if he were not invited. One-armed Eddie the bartender was there with his young wife and a fistful of openers, which he used diligently.

Earlier in the afternoon when just the four of them—'Bama and Dave, and Dewey and Hubie—were there getting ready for the party, Hubie had come in the front room with a beer and being tired, more or less naturally stretched himself out full length on the ultramodern divan. 'Bama had immediately and without ceremony gone over to him and slapped his feet down off it. "When yore around here, keep yore crappy feet off the furniture," he had said in a chilling voice. "I dont give a damn what you do at home, but here you respect the furnishings. Or Ill personally throw yore ass out." There had been no question that he meant it and apparently it was a fetish with him.

Now, with the several roomfuls of guests chattering and holding glasses or beercans and standing around still unsettled after their recent arrivals, 'Bama slipped off his loafers and got up on a chair in the living-room and made a speech.

"Before the party gets goin Ah want to say that y'all of you are welcome and I hope y'all have a good time. Theres plenty to eat and drink, so help yoreselves. But the first one I see to set drinks down on the furniture or lay lit cigarettes on anything or drop butts on the floor, out he goes! Man or woman, it dont make me no difference. Theres plenty of Budweiser and Schlitz coasters stacked around, thanks to Smitty, and theres plenty of ashtrays. Use 'em. Because if you dont Ill shore as hell throw yore ass out."

There was a chorus of not-loud cheers, and several cries of "Hear, hear!"

"It aint a joke," 'Bama said icily, from the chair and holding up both arms for quiet. "Dewey and Hubie are appointed as bouncers. And if they cant handle somebody easy enough, me and Dave will help them. And if the four of us aint enough, I guess we can always call on Smitty and Eddie. With their experience, there oughtnt to be any question." This last got a good laugh and turned everyone's feeling into good nature, and he climbed down and slipped his loafers back on and picked up his drink.

It was remarkable what a well-mannered party it was. There was a buffet lunch that would have done justice to an oldtime saloon, and it disappeared at an astounding rate, along with the beer and the whiskey. But everyone was careful. Nobody got thrown out. Even Raymond Cole was exemplary. And Smitty was heard to remark that the next time he had a bunch of Elks and Country Club people to his house, he thought he would make the same damned kind of speech. The house was duly inspected and ohed and ahed over by the guests, but the thing that created the most interest and comment was Dave's little writing room under the stairs which he had fitted out with a typing table and standard machine, office desk, Artmetal filing cabinet, and a nest of Cole-Steel card files. Everybody was intrigued by this.

"I dont see how anybody can jist sit down there like that and write up things right out of their head," Hubie said proudly as he showed it to a group of them. "I caint do it. If I had to choose between that and dyin', I reckon Id just have to die. How about you?" There was a chorus of agreement from the group of guests and everybody had another drink.

Earlier in the day, before the party, Wally Dennis who had come by to help had got Dave and 'Bama off privately and explained to them that he would like to bring Dave's niece Dawn to the party. However, he was willing to forego this if they thought he should. On account of Frank and all.

"But Ill tell you one thing, men," Wally said earnestly. "You dont have to worry about little old Dawn. Shell never peep about nothin. You can count on her. Shes as close mouthed as hell when she wants to be."

"Its up to Dave," 'Bama said. "I dont hardly know her. Very well. Shes a pretty little thing."

"Shes a very sweet fine girl," Wally said, looking guiltily uneasy, and staring at Dave earnestly.

"Ah'm shore she is," 'Bama said solemnly.

"Sure, bring her along," Dave had said. "What the hell." And later, at the party, he had seen them come in, in the midst of all the other arrivals, when he was too busy to even say hello to them. But the change in both was, even from that glimpse, immediately apparent. Again, he thought Well what the hell. It wasnt any of his business. Theyd have to work out their own damned sex life. Still later, when everything had quieted down and the party was moving, Wally had brought her, breasty and muscular-hipped, over to him.

"Hello, honey," he said. "Havin a good time at our party?"

"Love it," Dawn said brilliant-eyed. She had a highball glass in her hand. "Just simply love it. I wouldnt have missed it for anything. Where have all these people been all my life?"

"Most of them dont exactly move in your circle," Dave said. "Come on, Ill show you my writin room."

"Id certainly one hell of a lot rather move in their circle than in mine," Dawn said. "God! Ive just been listening to Hubie tell how the Japanese officers carried their own fagots with them, and all the pornography he used to take off of them and sell to the Air Force."

"You can get my tail even further in a sling with your old man than it is already," Dave said as they wormed their way through the hall. "Very easily. If youre not careful."

Dawn grinned. "Dont worry. Daddy doesnt know anything mother and I dont want him to know."

"Your mother would be just as bad," Dave said, "from my viewpoint. If she ever found out you were here."

"*Mother* never knows anything *I* dont want her to know," Dawn said, grinning wider. "Dont worry, Dave," she said, consciously not prefixing it with Uncle like she used to.

"Call me Uncle," Dave said.

"Excuse me! Uncle," Dawn said, making a little bow—or as near as she could get to one in the crowded hall. "You shall be known as Uncle henceforth! Hear that, Wally?"

"Right," Wally said. "Hello, Uncle."

"Thats my boy," Dawn said. "God! youve sure put on an awful lot of weight, Uncle. Since I last saw you."

"Uncle's been living well," Dave said. "Here we are."

"Oh, its wonderful!" Dawn said, peering in through the door across which Dave had thoughtfully tacked a piece of clothesline rope. "Its magnificent! It ought to really be a wonderful place to work. You ought to do really good work here. And youd better, too. You know, youre going to have an awful lot of competition, Uncle, from our boy here when I get him to New York."

"Oh, are you two going to New York now?" Dave said.

"She is," Wally said, looking guiltily uneasy. "And I think its a good idea for her. And I suppose Ill wind up there, too, eventually."

"Oh. You mean youre not going together then?" Dave said.

"Oh, no!" Wally said. "Shes going right after school's out. I dont know when Ill get there."

"Ive got to get out of this damned town," Dawn said happily and luminously. "And so does Wally. Someday, that is, of course," she added carefully. "An artist cant live and work in a crappy place like this. —I dont mean you. Youre different. But youre not hemmed in and hampered and tied down by your parents like we are. Youre free," she said happily.

"I hope so, Niece," Dave said. "But sometimes Uncle doubts it." It was impossible not to be at least partially infected by her new-found pleasure with herself.

"God! You know who you sound like now, dont you?" Dawn grinned warningly, playing shamey-finger with the hand that held her glass. "Thats enough for me!" she said archly, and turned and started working her way back through the hall.

"You know, Gwen is wondering why you havent been over to see her, I think, since you got back, Dave," Wally said as he turned to follow Dawn.

"Im going over," Dave said. "As soon as we get settled in here."

"You ought to," Wally called back, and Dave watched him go—following Dawn—wondering at the strangeness that was people, and the changes that came in them—or at least, what they liked to believe were changes.

CHAPTER 43

WALLACE French Dennis, Holder of the Parkman College Fellowship for the Novel, was not unaware that there were changes. Furthermore, he was not totally foreign to the concept that what appeared to be changes might not be changes at all. In fact, as he walked away from Dave, he had been thinking about this a good bit lately. But so far he had not been able to isolate empirically just what the hell these changes —or un-changes—actually were, either in himself or Dawnie. Or anybody else.

The whole situation was very interesting to study, more so than he had expected. Or would be, rather, if it didnt make him so damned uneasy and half scare the living hell out of him half the time. He could never be quite sure what Dawnie would do, especially around other people. And he kept getting this feeling he had that something, if not actually *about* to happen, was nevertheless *liable* to happen. He had vague half-pictures—totally irrational, he chided himself, totally unconformed to the facts—of Frank Hirsh charging him with an oldfashioned bullwhip or a pistol to shoot him. And he was glad now he had bought that second-, or third- or fourth-hand Colt's Woodsman .22 off of Ed De Lancie (who, of course, gave him a good buy) two years ago during his Sportsman phase, and taught himself to shoot it to prepare himself for the Army. He was also glad he had bought those four Randall knives out of his Fellowship money, especially the #1 All-Purpose Fighting Knife. He had ordered them the same day he got his check, and they had just come in. It was amazing the sense of personal comfort they gave him. Especially the #1 All-Purpose Fighting Knife.

Of course it was all ridiculous, he told himself rationally. Frank

Hirsh was no more prone to physical violence than most men of his type. In fact, not nearly so much so as he, Wally, himself was. It was all old imaginative pictures out of the folklore. But by God hed kill him if he had to. If it was selfdefense they couldnt keep him in jail too very long. Though of course theyd take his Fellowship away from him. The trouble was, as Hemingway had so aptly written somewhere, a writer just had too damned much imagination. And had to have it.

And yet in spite of this part of it, it was still a very interesting thing to observe, and full of potential material. For instance, just about everybody seemed to know about it. Now, how? Gwen French had known about it the very first time hed gone over there afterwards, and he knew she did, though she didnt say anything——And this was without having read a word of his new stuff yet. (Gwen maintained she could tell accurately what was going on in a writer's life by what they wrote at the time, and he believed she could. Her theory was that only when there was *nothing,* nothing at all—at least, of any importance—going on in a writer's life, did he write his best and deepest and most truly alive work.)

Of course Gwen was smart; and Bob. Youd expect them to know. But other people seemed to know too and in fact, the only people who knew them both who didnt know were Dawn's own parents, and his mom. Now, obviously, this could only be because the three of them were deliberately subconsciously blinding themselves to it because they did not *want* to know. But Dave knew. And 'Bama had obviously known. And—here, at this party now—so did most of the others know, though none of them cared, or gave a damn. How had they all known?

In analyzing it, Wally decided that it was due to himself and Dawn. In a subtle way they were letting everybody know. Not that they were giving themselves away. That wasnt it, they were both too smart for that. But the truth was, at the same time while they were both being careful to keep it a secret, half of both of them *wanted* people to know it.

Now there was a *very* interesting development! While they were both doing everything in their power to conceal from people that there was anything more than usual between them, they were both of them doing whatever they had to do, and saying whatever they had to say, to achieve this end, all in such a way as to let the same people know in a *subtle* way that what they were saying and doing was not actually the truth at all and that, in fact, there was really a great deal more between them—a *great* deal—than they admitted.

When he himself talked to Dave and 'Bama about what a sweet, fine girl Dawnie was, he was actually letting them know that he was sleeping with her, and what was more he knew they would read it that way! and moreover, *wanted* them to! The same thing held true of Dawnie when she talked to Dave so possessively about taking him, Wally, off to New York with her.

And yet at the same time they both believed they were trying to hide it!

Wally had already figured out a way he could use this startling development in his book, and he understood that the really startling thing about it was the fact that both of them—both he and Dawnie—were really sincerely anxious to keep their sexual conjugality a secret. That was what he would have to show, or it wouldnt come off.

He had not talked about it with Gwen yet and discussed it, but he was sure now that—especially with all her experience in love—that she would agree with him completely. The truth was, no writer had ever really written accurately and truthfully about love before! None at all! —at least, not with the viewpoint he saw it from. Even Stendhal had not been *really* accurate. The simple truth was, love was a hoax, a mass hallucination! It was totally subjective. It had no more to do with material, objective reality than—than a novel by Faith Baldwin did. And conversely, you might almost say that people believed in love and fell in it—(by God, there was a good phrase! he thought, and made a mental note of it: people believed in love and fell in it, and came out smelling like a rose)—for the same reason they bought and read Faith Baldwin and made her a perennial bestseller. The eternal game of escape. They just simply all wanted to smell like roses.

Of course, Stendhal had seen some of that when he said: "As long as one has one illusion, one can love." But he didnt go any further. What caused the illusions? The hoax! And they werent even illusions really; they were hallucination. Totally subjective.

Very interesting. Hell, there were all kinds of damned things he had not seen, things he would never even have thought of, if he had not had the experience himself with Dawnie. And not the least of these, by any means, was the reaction upon Dawnie herself, he thought sitting beside her on the ultramodern divan, while she talked sparklingly to some of the more articulate denizens of Smitty's like Dewey and Hubie and Gus Nernst's girl Lorelei Shaw from Terre Haute about art and acting.

"And its contradistinctive!" she said excitedly. "Isnt that so, Wally?"

"What? Yes," he said positively. "Im sure it is."

The whole damn thing was amazing. She hadnt really changed at all. But she believed she had. She felt that not being a virgin any more made her a woman, so she started acting more like a woman. The same thing was true of him, too, though. He himself felt a very strong sense of responsibility for her, now. Something he hadnt wanted to feel or intended to feel, and in fact, had no reason to feel, actually. And actually, he *didnt* feel it. He just felt he ought to feel it. So he made himself. Although he didnt want to. Now; did he *really* feel it, or *not*?

Who could say? One thing was for sure, he had watched himself closely and observed that increasingly during the two weeks (they had been to bed together seven times, in that period, all told—and that part of it he loved) increasingly during those two weeks then, he had had to lie more and more to her. She evidently needed a great deal of affection, and she apparently felt that now she had the right to demand it of him. He had had to lie to her enough before, but after she became his mistress it was just about eight times that much, he calculated. It was not that he did not feel plenty of affection for her; he did; but he did not feel it at all the times, and in the sufficient quantities, she demanded. So he had to lie.

Now, the theory was, love was supposed to increase the spiritual intimacy between people. But obviously it did not work. Not when you had to lie more and more. Actually, and in fact, love appeared to *decrease* the real intimacy between people!

Apart from the general considerations, Dawn herself was intensely interesting to observe. There was that thing about her breasts, for instance. He had always known she was proud of her breasts. But, my God! he hadnt realized the extent of it apparently. There was something almost weird about it, as if she herself were standing back off somewhere outside of herself watching him, and pretending that it was not him loving them but she herself, as another person. So, obviously, she must love them a great deal. Now he would never have thought of putting that on one of his characters by himself, if he hadnt seen it.

She was really a very passionate girl, he guessed. And that in itself was another discrepancy. In all the books on sex he had read, a virgin was supposed to not like sex much and take a long long time to get around to where she enjoyed it.

"And you just cant create without it!" Dawn said sparklingly from beside him, and reached out her hand to touch him. "Isnt that right, Wally!"

"Yes," he said stoutly. "Absolutely!" and there he was lying again, in yet another way! He wasnt even listening to what she was saying. To his knowledge, nobody had ever written about just how much a part of love was made up of lying. Obviously, it was because the illusion did not coincide with the fact: you needed the lying to take up the slack.

Well, later on tonight, buddy, he told himself, later on tonight. He would have liked nothing better than to have talked to Dawnie and got her to go upstairs with him to one of the bedrooms, like so many of the others were obviously doing from time to time. But he knew it would be useless. Shed never consent to it. And shed probably get mad. Shed be insulted. And yet, at the same time, shed sit there and put out her hand to touch him and let everybody know that he was her lover. Very strange. Of course, he didnt give a damn if everybody knew he was her lover. In fact, he was all for it. He was proud of it.

Hell, hed been trying to work it around to that for six months, hadnt he?—Six months, hell; for a year!—Of course, she had promised him shed sleep with him in May, that night back in November, but hed never really believed that. He had thought she was just stalling him. And the truth was, he still thought so. The truth was, Wally had been pretty sure for some time—after carefully thinking back on it—that his getting of the Fellowship had had a lot to do with his making it with her. He would never have thought it would have been that important. But it had, it had, he thought, mentally slapping himself on the back. It had impressed her. In spite of what she thought about Parkman and Parkman College. The Fellowship, and one other thing, was what had done it.

The other thing was the way finding out about Dawn's virginity, that night back in November, had changed his viewpoint about having a love affair with her. In May or any other time. After that, he had decided to give up the project; hell, he didnt want to be the first one.

And that was where the irony had come in. When he had stopped trying to make her was when she started wanting him to. He had stopped hounding her, and had gradually (so as not to hurt her feelings) stopped calling her up for dates, and had quit talking about sex and sex relationships in general with her like they always had done—all on principle, you understand; not with any ulterior motives—and the result had been astounding. It upset her tremendously, she got more and more affectionate, she even began calling him up every now and then—something she had almost never done before. By Christmas and New Year's, when he took her over to Gwen's, she had been positively doting on him. He had not been able to understand it at the time. But as far back as February he had finally grasped the general principle behind it and begun for the first time, really, to use it consciously and deliberately.

Dawnie had obviously *wanted* him to make her. Otherwise, she would have let him go when he wanted to, wouldnt she? Whether she was using him as an experiment in sexual experience and her own sex education, of course, or was really in love with him, it was hard to say.

But in spite of the strategic victory, Wally did not believe that that would have really carried it, if it had not been for the Fellowship.

He had called her up at home the evening of the day he had got the check in the mail that morning and after he had already ordered his knives. Of course she already knew about it by then because her mom was on the committee. It was a school night, but they had let her go out anyway, since it was sort of an occasion. Looking at her beside him on the divan, he could not help remembering.

They had driven up toward West Lancaster, talking about the award. It was a beautiful warm May night, and Wally wished his mom's car was a convertible so he could put the top down. When he got to the two filling stations at the West Lancaster road, instead of turning over toward the river, he had turned west the other way onto the gravel that ran on back into the countrified interior of the county.

"What are you turning this way for?" Dawn had said.

"Oh, I dont know," he had answered. "I thought wed just go for a ride. I dont much feel like going to some pub where there are a lot of people."

"I guess I dont blame you," Dawn said. "Its a pretty momentous occasion. The first tangible proof of your talent; the first pay in cash for any of your writing. Well, youve finally made it, Wally. Youve finally made the grade."

"It isnt pay," he said. "Its only a Fellowship. A damned donation, charity. And I havent made the grade. The book isnt finished."

"Its still money," Dawn said. "And that makes it a proof of your talent. Its a hell of a lot more than Ive ever got."

"Gwen and Dr Pirtle got it for me. My book didnt get it. Thats not the same as selling your book and getting a check from a publisher."

"Its a proof that they believe in you. And its *tangible* proof. You can even spend it," Dawn said. "And its a lot more than I have ever got."

There was a curious kind of melancholy blues feeling about her tonight, and he felt very warm toward her. He debated telling her about ordering the Randall knives, she knew all about them from before.

"Ive already spent a part of it," he said. "I ordered my Randall knives this afternoon. In fact, I ordered four."

"Oh! Did you? Can I see them when they come?" Dawn said excitedly.

"Sure," Wally said. "Ill even teach you how to use them, if you want. Ive got a book on knifefighting and judo at home. A girl whos as pretty as you might need to know how to use one someday."

"I doubt it," Dawn said bitterly. "But Id like to learn it anyhow. If *youll* teach me."

"Ill teach you," he said. They had come, along the gravel road, to a patch of tall deserted woods into which an ungated little dirt road ran. The later May sun had only just gone down, and the last lingering red light of the evening banked up against the trees and sifted down through them. In the wood it was much darker than it was out on the road. Wally stopped the car to look at it. "Isnt it beautiful?" he said.

"It is," Dawn said, with melancholy. "It looks so safe and peaceful in there. Youd never think the world was in danger of blowing itself to pieces to look at that, would you?"

Without saying anything, Wally put his mom's old car in gear and pulled it in under the trees. It got immediately much darker. Old leaves and rotted hickory nuts crunched under the tires as he stopped it. Dawn did not say anything, either. He had not considered the idea of making her here, tonight, on this particular night of all nights, and it had not even been in his head at all when he turned west off the highway. Now it came in his head.

"God! Isnt it beautiful? So still!" Dawn said, swerving around to look back. "Look how much lighter it is out in the road! We could sit right here forever and no one in the world would ever see us or know we were here," she said. "Theyd drive right by and never see us. And we could sit here and watch them."

Wally tried to think of something to say that was pertinent to what he felt, but he could not think of anything appropriate, so instead he reached over and took Dawn by the shoulder and pulled her to him. It felt very good. And they had necked a lot before.

"Oh, Wally!" she said after he had kissed her. "Someday youll be famous! Just think about it!" She rubbed her forehead against the side of his chin, and he was simultaneously glad that he had shaved today and that he had a heavy beard. "Youll be famous, and rich, and probably have a winter home in Miami. And people everywhere will read your books and talk about you. And Ill probably be playing cheap bit roles in some summer stock and grubbing for a living somewhere. Will you remember Dawn then, Wally?"

"What do you think?" he said huskily.

"Im sure Ill remember you then," Dawn said.

"Listen," Wally said, putting his finger under her chin. "Here. Look here. Do you remember you told me last November youd sleep with me in May? Do you remember that?"

"Thats right, I did say that, didnt I?" she said.

"But I suppose you didnt mean it."

"I dont know if I meant it or not," Dawn said. "May was such a long time off then."

Wally did not know what to say to this. "Well, will you?" he said finally.

"Do you really want me?"

"You know I do," he said. He considered adding, for forcefulness, that he wouldnt be here if he didnt, but decided not to and said instead, "Dont you know I do?"

"And you really truly do want me?" Dawn said. "You really do?"

"Yes," he said.

"All right," she said, "you can have me;" and pulled away from him suddenly and just simply started to undress. Wally thought his head would burst.

"Lets get in the back seat," he said, but it was little more than a croak. When she got out on her side he simply followed her, as if hypnotized, without thinking rationally about getting out and back in on his own side, and he thought he had never seen anything as beautiful in his life—and never would again—as Dawn was, still in her skirt, standing in her saddle shoes on the old leaves and nut hulls of the nut trees, bare to the waist in the May air in that woods, the last dying light touching her torso and those magnificent breasts of hers with a rich red rose color.

"Kiss me," she said.

He did.

"Make violent love to me first," she said.

He did that too, or tried. And then her eyes changed and she looked up at him without seeing him, curiosity and surprised interest in her eyes and face, as she concentrated on feeling these things she had never felt before, but had heard and thought a lot about.

"Go ahead," she said impatiently. "Go on."

"Ah, Dawnie," Wally said.

................Lying beside him afterwards, in the minute or so before they moved to get up, Dawn was still rapt in and trying to sort out her impressions. She had more or less anticipated certain things, for instance, physical feelings, etcetera, and all that sort of stuff, but there were other things she had not anticipated. Her muscles were going to be sore but it wouldnt be any different or any worse than the same type of soreness you got after your first hard afternoon of tennis every season. And so this is what its like, she thought with a sort of satisfaction. Yes, she definitely liked it. But then it was all so natural. But over and above all that, over and above all the physical sensations, there was something else. Such a feeling of tremendous power! She had never felt such a sense of such great, tremendous power in her life before. Acting on the stage was as nothing to it; the audience loved you, yes; even worshipped you—if you were good enough; but the audience always went away after the show. It dissolved, and became part of other audiences, that went to other plays, and they forgot you. But even at the moment of acting to them, the power—great as it was—the love, was nothing as great as here. Here, she held almost complete power over this man. —this boy. And even the particular man didnt matter, not really—except of course this was Wally; her Wally. He needed her, and needed desperately. Needed, and had to have, what only she could give him. And she had the power to give it or take it away, as she chose. It was *such* a power, that she would have to be very careful and very wise not to abuse it, she thought warmly. "Old Wally," she said affectionately, "old Wally. Nice Wally," and reached over her hand to stroke the back of his head.

His lips moving against her cheek, Wally mumbled, "Thank you, Dawnie. I—Im sorry," he said in a choked, guilty voice in her ear, and Dawn wanted to laugh......................

Wally felt he could have lain there forever. But he knew they would have to get up sometime.

"Here," he croaked, suddenly attacked by large bunches of guilt. "Come on. Ill help you up."

"Thank you, sire," she grinned impishly, and he blushed red. When they were both back inside the car once more, Wally did not start the engine but sat looking out at the woods where it was almost nearly completely dark now. He wanted to remember it, just as it was, always, the woods, the leaves and the nut hulls underfoot, the fading light, the car, the scene, everything.

"What do you say we have a cigarette?" Dawn said cheerfully.

"Oh. Excuse me," he mumbled, "Im sorry," and fished out a pack and put two of them in his mouth and lit them, the ancient trite old gesture, that you saw in every movie to represent the moment of peace and closeness after sex, but that still made him feel good and very much the lover. He handed her hers.

"Its a beautiful woods, aint it?" he said.

"Yes! Yes it is," Dawn said. "And it will always be our woods now, wont it?"

"Youre not going to hate me, are you, Dawnie?" he said. "I dont want you to hate me."

"Well, what a ridiculous thing to say!" Dawn said. "Of course I dont hate you! I love you!"

"You really do love me, dont you?" Wally said.

"Of course I do, darling! Do you think Id even be here? and do what weve just done, my darling? if I didnt love you!"

"No of course not," Wally said, "that wasnt what I meant."

"Or if I didnt know you loved me?"

"Of course I love you. What I meant was that I didnt want you ever to have cause to hate me. Ever in your life. Youll never have cause to hate me, Dawnie, ever, I promise you that."

"I know that, silly," Dawn said tenderly, "Dont you think I know that?" She puffed on her cigarette. "God, Wally! Quit acting so damned guilty. Look at me; I dont care. Youre acting more worried about it than I am!"

"I just want you to know youll never have cause to regret your action," Wally said doggedly.

"Thank you, my darling," Dawn said, "I always knew that." She put her cigarette out in the tray. "Wed better be getting home, you know it? Its getting pretty late."

"Give us a kiss first."

They leaned together across the short space that separated them in the seat for a quick kiss that became a longer and longer kiss and turned into an even longer caress.

"Open your door a minute," Dawn said when they finally separated. "You reminded me. Ive got to put my lipstick back on."

Wally opened his door so the dome light would come on, and watched her lovingly as she carefully replaced her lipstick, another ancient, trite, but wholly memorable love gesture, which the movies did not use near as much, but ought to. That was pretty good, he thought, hed have to remember and use that. He could use it just like it was, and together with that about the cigarettes.

When she was finished, he shut the door and started the old car and switched on the lights, bringing to life the bottom ten feet of a number of shaggy-barked, gray hickories.

"Someday when we're famous from your novels," Dawn said softly, "we'll think back and remember our woods."

"And from your acting," Wally said.

"Yes, and from my acting," she said.

He backed the car out slowly until they were back on the gravel, and headed back toward the highway, driving slowly and leisurely, his muscles, his bones, everything about him relaxed and liquid.

"I just hope mother doesnt find out," Dawn said.

"Theres no way she can very well, is there?" he said.

"I dont think so. At least none that I can think of. Hell, even if Id forgotten my lipstick it wouldnt have occasioned any undue alarm. I just dont want her to find out. Until we're ready to tell her ourselves, you know?"

"Yes," Wally said. "Yeah." He felt a touch of irritated unease.

"My God!" Dawn said, turning to him and pecking him on the cheek. "Weve entirely forgotten all about your Fellowship! That was what we rode out here to be happy about!"

"Weve got other reasons for being happy, now," Wally said loyally.

"Yes, we have," Dawn said warmly. "Havent we?"

They drove on down the gravel, not hurrying, not in a mood for hurrying, not talking much, and looking out, both of them, each to his own side and through his own window, and in silent thought, at the spring night, and at the fat new leaves on the scrub in the ditch by the road in the light of the headlamps.

"Wally, I just want to tell you one thing," Dawn said in a clear resonant voice. "You and I can have a very powerful love affair. Or we can have a nice friendly little relationship, and have sex together, and let it go at that. Its up to you to decide."

"Well—you think we got any choice?" Wally said.

"But its only fair to warn you," Dawn said, "that I love very strongly. I know I do. Do you want me to let myself go and really love you as much as I am capable of?"

Wally found he could not help but fidget a little. Where a moment ago—when she had talked about telling her mother themselves—he had felt a slight touch of irritated unease, now he felt a much more than slight twinge of pained distress and a panicky sense of portending loss. "Well, I want you to love me. Of course," he said carefully.

"All the way?" Dawn demanded. "Because if you do, it has to work both ways. Otherwise, we'll just be good friends, and have sex. And Ill go out with other guys."

"Well, hell!" Wally said, in a kind of paroxysm of distress. "I dont want you to go out with other guys."

"Then it has to be all the way. Is that what you want?"

"Well, I guess it is," Wally said. "Hell yes it is. I love you, Dawnie!"

"All right then!" Dawn said happily. "Thats the way itll be," and as he turned his mom's car onto the highway she moved over to him and cuddled herself up against him.

"Somebody's liable to see us," he cautioned.

"Let them!" she said. "A fig for them! Anyway, that wont prove anything. They wont know anything."

They had driven the rest of the way back into town with his arm around her, her face pressed against his armpit.

"I can smell you," Dawn said deliciously. "You smell stronger than you did before, I think. Why?"

"They say some people secrete a musk, like," Wally said, flustered but pleased. "When they have sex. Maybe I do that. I never knew it before."

"I like it," Dawn said delightedly.

If they had not had to get her home because it was a school night, he thought, he would have turned the car right around and gone right back to the woods again. "Ill never hurt you, Dawnie," he said, "I promise you that."

And looking at her sitting beside him on the divan, as she leaned over raising her arm to pick up a smoked salmon canapé, he still wished they were up to their woods, right now. Godalmighty! it was amazing—amazing? almost frightening—how much sex there was in him apparently. He had never realized it, or been aware of it before. He actually believed he could just keep right on going, all night long. My God, no wonder older people didnt want you to find out about sex until you were married and it was too late! Because very few guys ever got a gal like Dawnie, probably.

Watching her proudly, and saying little, as she talked on and on sparklingly to Dewey and Hubie and Lorelei Shaw from Terre Haute, he was not sorry about the way he had decided that first night in the car. She had gotten very possessive—*very* possessive—of him since then; but it was funny about that. While half of you resented it and got edgy and irritable about it, he had noted, the other half of you loved it and ate it up and wouldnt have had it any other way, or given it up for anything. So it didnt really bother you enough.

Now, why had nobody ever written it just like that? That am-
bivalence?

It was funny about time and memories, too. They had been out up
to their woods seven times now in the past two weeks, an average of
every other day. And each time that they had gone, it had at least
doubled the remembered enjoyment of every time before, and been
itself at least quadrupled by them. Wally could see clearly for the first
time how, theoretically, the older a person got the more enjoyable his
life became. It snowballed. Each act enhanced and added to by all
those that had gone before, and each enhancing and adding to every
one that came after it. He had read about that phenomenon in Wieman's
The Source of Human Good that had come out in '46, and that Old
Bob French had loaned him, but then he had not understood it and
thought it smacked of Pollyannaism. But actually he could see now that
it was a mathematically provable proposition. Actually, the truth was,
he had used to feel that same kind of accumulative enjoyment, he could
see now, for his workbench downstairs in the basement at home,—each
time he used it being enhanced as it was by all the things he had made
on it before. And sex was the same.

He had rigidly and very carefully kept his promise to her, since she
had become his mistress, and had not even looked at another woman.
Dawnie had never, so far, said anything at all about marriage—at least,
not in so many words. And so he had not either. Time enough to worry
about that if and when the time came that she did mention it. Hell,
maybe hed even marry her. A writer could get a helluva lot worse wife,
probably, that was for sure. She would be going away to school at
Western Reserve in the fall, he thought suddenly, and it made a feeling
of befuddled hollow emptyness rise up in him.

—Because he didnt believe all this New York stuff she had been
spouting about going as soon as school was out. Wally wasnt worried
about the summer. He *knew* she wouldnt go. Somehow. And he himself
was not going to New York, either. With her or anybody. He didnt
have to go to New York, to break in in his career, like an actress did.
When *he* went to New York, *he* would go as an already big man in
his *own* right—as WALLACE FRENCH DENNIS, whose book was
already out, and whom people would want to meet as badly as he wanted
to meet them, by God! —No, he wasnt worried about the summer.

But the thought of her going away to school at Western Reserve in
the fall not only deboweled him but confused and addled his whole
head, like spinning on a gyro.

"—work of a novelist," Dawnie said eagerly beside him. "You know,
Ive about decided that acting is really pretty nearly a second class art.
After all, your actor is really not much more of an artist than a sym-
phony conductor. His job is not to create so much as it is to interpret

what someone else—the playwright or the composer—really created. And there is a moral question whether a personality like Stokowski is right in trying to relieve his own creative impulses by imposing his own interpretations upon the scores of other men who really composed the works. But of course one could be a great actress *and* a playwright, too. Dont you think so, Wally?" she said, turning to him demandingly.

"Well, I dont know," he said. "I dont think you can really confine creativity that much. It comes in its own way, you know, and on its own terms. Just like luck in gambling. Look at Toscanini, for example."

"Well, if I was writing a novel," Dewey said, "I know what Id do. Id make it all up. Id write it about the kind of life I wish Id had. Id make me the hero and the kind of person I wish Id been. Then Id put in all the kind of people I wish Id known—instead of the kind I do know. And theyd all be fine people. Theyd be honest and brave and strong and kindhearted. Instead of the chickenhearted slobs I really know."

"Thats because basically at heart youre a romantic," Dawnie smiled. "Instead of a realist."

"Sure," Dewey said. "Damn right."

"I dont know," Wally said, shaking his head. "Dont the realists do that too, though? Even the *realists* make people better than they *really* are. If they didnt, hell there wouldnt hardly be anything to read about. Hell, youd only be doing what every writer does, Dewey," Wally laughed a little drunkenly. "We all do that. Because if we wrote about people like they really are, there wouldnt be anything interesting enough to be worth reading even. So we all cheat and make them a little better than they actually are. The romantics cheat a lot, and the realists cheat a little less. But we all give them more character, or guts, or brains, or sensitivity than we really believe they have. Because if we didnt, we wouldnt have a book. I wonder if a guy could really write a book about people like they *really* are, and still make it interesting enough to read? I think, by God, Ill just try that on my second book."

They all laughed, and the conversation went on, and Wally drifted out of it again. He was thinking specifically about his mom. She was sort of his living proof. Now there was just about the world's worst mediocrity and most complete nonentity. She was like Kipling's poem about Tomlinson, whom God wouldnt let into Heaven and the Devil wouldnt let into Hell: he had never done anything good enough to go to Heaven, and he had never done anything bad enough to go to Hell. He loved his mom, sure—but why? Because he was *supposed* to love her. And because he had been *taught* he should so damn long, ever since he was born. But the truth was, she was just a dumb, and slyly acquisitive, slob. That was the truth. He just hated to admit it. She had lived just about as totally worthless a life as it was possible to imagine. And outside of giving birth to him, a potential genius,—which was more or less of an accident, because she couldnt *know* that; and also probably an accident physically as well—she had actually never done anything, anything at all, not a damn thing. Except to go to clubs to help the poor of which she would not admit she was one. And to marry his old man once. Her mind was filled with vague half-formed thoughts that just sort of drifted in and drifted out without any control or concentration, and were generally things which some other fool had told her about what was "right" and what was "wrong." Like going to Sunday School and keeping beer in the icebox. God! she was dumb. Her head was one big atrophied muscle. Just like the other day she had slyly approached him about Dawnie—thinking he was too dumb to see through her little schemes.

"I think its a very nice thing that you and Dawn are going around together as much as you are," she had said with her #2 (or Happy Motherly) smile, as distinct from her #1 (or Sad Motherly) (which she used the most) smile.

"Who? Dawn?" he had said, the sly acquisitiveness of Frank Hirsh's money down deep in the bottom of her eyes not lost on him. "Oh. Yeah. Shes awright. For a kid." And went on reading.

"Shes such a nice girl," his mom went on, after a minute. "I cant think of a nicer, sweeter, more decent girl that you could be going with. And your mother's pleased youve used your head like a real young man in making such a good choice for your girlfriend."

Still staring at his book, but no longer reading, Wally had said, "Yeah," and kept his eyes to his book.

"There are so many wild young people nowadays," his mom said. "Its not like when I was a girl. And so many of them are girls today, that a young man has to be thoughtful and very careful when he sets out to choose himself a girlfriend."

She thought she was so foxy smart. And she was actually so dumb. The acquisitiveness for Frank Hirsh's growing fortune was like two hot sparks in the very bottom of her eyes, and Wally had had enough.

"Mom," he said conversationally, "I have no intention of marrying Dawn Hirsh for her old man's money. Or for any other reason. I dont care if he makes a *million* dollars. I go out with her sometimes because theres no-goddam-body else around here with any brains to go out with."

"Why, Wallace!" his mom had said. "Wallace Dennis! I never had any such thought in my mind." She was obviously and deeply hurt, and it was plain she believed devoutly that she had been maligned. "And you ought not to talk to your mother in such a way. As a matter of fact," she said looking down and running her finger along the table edge, "youre far too young to marry. Youre not even of age yet."

"I will be in four more months," he said.

"But not till then. And Im not at all sure I would give my consent for you to marry," she said still looking down slyly, "anyone. And I certainly had no such idea in mind when I spoke of little Dawnie."

He wouldnt have cared half so much, if she just had the guts to be honest and admit it. If shed just come right out and say Wally why dont you marry Dawn for her money, he could at least respect her anyway. The thing was, she really *believed* what she was saying! And this trying to slyly outfox him.

"I know, mom," he said, "I know you didnt. But I dont intend to marry her anyway. And you cant work me into it even by pretending youre against it. If I did marry Dawn, then to get her old man's money Id have to go to work in his store. Just marrying her wouldnt be enough. And if I went to work in his damned store, then I wouldnt have any time to write. Hed see to that. And, mom, I intend to be a writer."

"Wallace, I wish you wouldnt swear like that, son," his mom said.

"Okay, mom," he said wearily.

"Wallace, Im shocked!" she said. "I think you owe your mother an apology."

"Well I *dont*," he had said, and that had ended it.

It was damn near unbelievable, he thought. Such dumbness. And then thinking she was smart! Such dumbness, and such lack of integrity, and of all the basically "good" human qualities—all coupled together in one person. It was incredible. How *would* you go about writing a novel about somebody like that? You just couldnt. There wasnt even anything there to write about.

And yet just about everybody he knew was just the same way. Or a very close variant of it. As Bob French was so fond of saying: they all run from pain. Run, hell! he thought, they protected themselves against it beforehand. With insulation. Well, thank God, he had never run from life and pain. The truth was, there just werent very many smart people in the world, that was all. Outside of himself, he only knew a few. Dawnie of course, and Old Bob and Gwen, and who else? Maybe 'Bama Dillert—in a way, but not really, only a limited way. But he couldnt really count Dave Hirsh as smart. They just aint many of us, he thought sickly.

The thought was so unpleasant and depressing that he pulled his mind away from it and began thinking about his knives. There was something a man could trust. And be proud of. —And *there* was a real honest-to-god artist; that Randall. Wally wondered what kind of a person he must be, a man who made his living just making knives— and yet who could make them such beautiful objects as these knives were. They were lethal, he thought, absolutely lethal, with the beauty of the absolutely lethal. Like sharks. And they had lines like sharks. That same streamlined lethal shape. Wally could suddenly hardly wait to get through with this damned party and get home so he could get his hands on them again. They had only come in yesterday, and after waiting to get them for so damned long—two? three years?—it was strange and almost unworldly to hold them, solid and weighty and three-dimensional, after seeing them so long as little pictures on a printed page. Naturally, they were much bigger than the pictures, and yet it seemed strange that they should be.

He had not really intended to order four of them until the day the check came in. —Until he sat down at the desk with the order blank, really. Then something had just taken hold of him. He supposed having all that money and knowing he could buy all of them if he wanted to, was what had done it. He had meant to order the #1 all along, from the moment Gwen had informed him of the Fellowship he had known what was going to be the first thing he would buy with it. But when he had sat down with the order blank on that day, the thousand dollar check lying beside him on his desk where he could look at it, he had been able to see where he really needed more than one knife, and that it was really a good investment in a way, getting more than the one, not a waste of money at all really, and besides, he had thought, what the hell? why not get all four of them? he had the money? live it up a little! to hell with it. Of course, afterwards, he had had an immediate attack of parsimony. But that of course was natural and now that they had finally come he was more than glad he had had the moral courage to do it. They were without doubt literally the most beautiful knives he had ever seen in his life.

What he had wound up getting, after his wild attack of profligacy, was the #1 'All-Purpose Fighting Knife' with the eight inch blade, stag handle, duralumin butt cap and wrist thong,—the same one he had always planned to get; and in addition, he had got the #5 'Camper and Yachtsman,' also with a stag handle and the butt cap (they would make it without the butt cap, if you wanted, but it was not so sturdy), but with a seven inch blade, instead of eight—this one for in case he ever went back to sea again and worked on boats any more (and what he wouldnt have given to have had it back then, when he was in Florida); and then the #7 'Fisherman-Hunter', five inch blade and standard laminated leather handle—for using around home here, hunting and fishing; and last the #8 'Trout and Bird Knife', a beautiful little four inch blade, with stag handle (it was only made with a stag handle, and without the butt cap)—to use for small game and birds, like squirrels. So he had a set of four, ranging in blade length from four inches to eight, and one of which would suit about every purpose; and on each of them (this service was a dollar and a half extra per knife) he had had his name WALLY DENNIS etched on the blade in block letters. All told, with the extras, the #1 cost him twenty eight fifty, the #5 twenty six fifty, the #7 eighteen fifty, and the #8 twenty dollars. Altogether that was $93.50. But he did not think it was a bad investment.

He loved them all, of course—but *of* them all, he loved that #1 the best. When you held that balanced, tempered blade in your hand you were touching hands, in a direct line, with Davy Crockett and Jim Bowie and Sam Houston, and all the men who had fought the Indians on the plains, or the Japs on Guadalcanal. As soon as the knives had come in he had got out his book on knife fighting and started practicing. Horizontal cuts, and vertical cuts, and the *in quartata* thrust, head cuts and hand cuts, all of it. (A guy had to be very careful with stuff like that, it was not information for civilian use.) And to sharpen up his eye and timing he had rigged up a soft pine two by four hung on a swinging rope in the basement which he practiced attacking, and which he had about already cut and slashed up enough that it looked like it had been through a machine-gunning. His right wrist and elbow and shoulder were still sore from it, but he was beginning to work the kinks out. It was a good thing he had taken a little fencing once, it not only helped the arm but helped you to understand the stance which, as he knew, was basically derived (by old Col. A J Drexel Biddle) from the sabre-fencing stance.

"Dawnie," he said suddenly, "you know we got to get going home, you know it? I got to get up early and work tomorrow."

"Yes, thats right," Dawn smiled at him warmly. "We do have to go. God! Ive been talking up a real fog, havent I? All evening."

"Its good for you," Wally said, getting up.

As they took their leave both Dave and 'Bama came over to shake hands and say goodby, and when they were outside in his mom's old car Wally leaned over to her for a quick kiss.

"Do you think we ought to go up to our woods this late?" she said. "When you have to get up and work tomorrow?"

"Youre probably right," he said. "I—I guess we better not, tonight. Tomorrow night we can go up early." He grinned at her. "And stay late."

So a block away from her house they stopped, instead, on a darker side street for a little necking, and then he took her on home.

"Wed better be careful," Dawnie whispered grinning, "about things like that. That son of a bitch Sherm Ruedy is liable to be mousing around tonight looking for lovers."

"Yeah," Wally said. "Did you see that new winter uniform he was wearing last winter? with the boots and Russian style fur cap?"

At her house he let her out, and beeped the horn lightly once at her as she went in. Then he drove on home. He was going to have a lot of work to do to make this changeover in the book.

He had not talked to Gwen about it yet, but he was going to have to. Major revisions of this sort he did not want to begin attempting until he had got her opinion on it. Besides, she might have some ideas of her own to add. She usually did. But he was pretty sure she would go along with the proposed change. In fact, he knew *she* would. He guessed the truth was he was just wanting her to brag on him a little.

Old Dave really ought to get over there and see her. And if he knew what was good for his novel, he would. She herself apparently didnt seem to care much, but he Wally knew she did. She always cared, about anything that had anything to do with writing. When he talked to her on the phone last week and told her about the house theyd leased, she hadnt seemed— And yet, he thought as he shut the garage door, that old writer's ear he had been steadily acquiring for inflections so much lately had noted something, some quality there.

The thought came to him out of nowhere suddenly and infuriatingly and with devastating force. And he stood and simply stared at the old garage door.

My God! she couldnt be falling in love with that bum Dave? Surely not? Why, hed gotten as fat as a damned hog, down there in Florida! He was a nothing! a bum! Good God! A bum who had once written two cheap, poor novels—which didnt sell. And had been living off his "reputation" ever since!! Surely not him!

The fury and scandalized outrage which shook him were completely devastating, and he simply stood, his hand against the door. But he put it down, out of his mind. It wasnt true. It couldnt be true! Hadnt she herself told him in so many words herself that love didnt interest her any more, love bored her? No, it wasnt true. Not Gwen. And not with that fat hog. He pushed himself away from the door. He refused to believe it.

When he got inside, he paused long enough to turn on the light in the kitchen and pick up the Randall #1 off the ~~lazy susan on the~~ kitchen table, where he kept all four of the knives, despite the protests of his mom.

When he got in his room he took off his coat first, and then unsnapped the sheath and drew the gleaming knife and stood in front of the mirror, weaving his forearm back and forth like a snake's head, keeping his wrist locked in the proper grip.

"All right, you son of a bitch!" he snarled, "come on!" and essayed a vertical hand cut to the knife hand.

Afterwards, after he quit his practicing, he was very careful to wipe the blade off clean with an oily handkerchief, before he put it away.

CHAPTER 44

WHEN Dave Hirsh woke the next morning at nearly noon, it was to a head like a pumpkin squash. For a while he just lay and stared at the ceiling. About the last thing he remembered was that, after about everybody else had gone, everybody except the old gang of Dewey and them, he too had taken the lumpish Ginnie Moorehead upstairs. What had he been? the third? or the fourth in the line. 'Bama had been upstairs in his own room at the time with one of the others, Rosalie, or Mildred Pierce, or one of them. It was amazing how that guy could keep them all coming back without making any of them jealous, Dave thought and rolled over in the bed while his head congested with blood alarmingly. El host! he thought with sour disgust, God! and was stricken with a kind of dull terror which rippled through him queasily at the knowledge that he would get no work done this day. Not the way he felt. When he finally struggled up and carried his head that felt too full of thickened blood downstairs, it was to find 'Bama in shoes and socks, underwear and hat, already at cleaning up the mess with a fresh glass of whiskey and water where he could reach it.

"We gonna have to get us a damn cleanin woman for this place, thats all," the Southerner drawled. He had already made considerable inroad on the mess.

Dave sank down in a chair dispiritedly. "Sure is a mess, aint it?"

"Well, it wont never be this bad again. And all in all, they done pretty well; after I made my little speech. Just the same, we got to get a cleanin woman. —Only trouble is, who the hell can we git? that would work for *us*?"

"What about Dewey's mother?" Dave said without enthusiasm. "She might."

"Yeah, I reckon. But shes such a squincheyed gossipy mean old broad."

"By God, I know who!" Dave said suddenly; "hell! Jane! Old Jane Staley!"

"Why, shore," 'Bama grinned. "Now why didnt I think of that? Hell, Old Jane would probly quit somebody else to work for us—if she didnt already have a day to give us. Well, we'll have to see her.

"Come on, give me a hand and we'll get this straightened out."

"I cant," Dave groaned disheartenedly, and put his head down in his hands. "Damn it, I just cant."

'Bama stopped what he was doing and looked at him narrowly. "Whats the matter?" he said cautiously. "Got a head?"

"Oh, the hell with it," Dave said miserably, and looked up with pain-tautened eyes. "Yeah. Yeah, I got one. But thats not what the matter. I— 'Bama, I havent done a lick of work—not a damned lick!—in over

645

a month now! You know it?" he cried, the terror he had felt upstairs suddenly exploding out of him. "Gettin ready to come home from down there, then two or three days to make the trip, then two weeks on this goddamned place, then that goddamned party last night. A month gone! Over a month!—And now I cant work today!"

'Bama set down the ashtrays he was holding and sat down on the divan cautiously, in his underwear and hat, cautiously holding his drink. His whole face was as alert and cautious as if he were in a big poker hand. "Ive kind of figured this was maybe comin," he said and took a drink from the glass.

How he could do it, Dave had no idea. Day after day, week after week, bottle after bottle. And it never seemed to show on him at all. It never made him sick, it never made his brain dull, it never seemed to affect him in any way at all.

"What am I gonna do?" he said almost hysterically. "My head's as dull as a bucket of mud. Over a month now! Gone! Ive *got* to get back to *work*! And I *cant*!! My head's like a rotten punkin!"

"Well now, lets just take it sensible," 'Bama said cautiously. "Yore sort of one of them tempermental type, Dave."

"Why do I get fat!" Dave cried.

"Well I reckon its probly because you eat too much," 'Bama said reasonably; "dont you think?"

"I eat too much, I drink too much, I hump too much, I *live* too much!" Dave said viciously. "I got no selfcontrol. None. You hear me? *None!* None at all. I do everything but work. But work, I never do."

"Well now, thats not *strickly* true," 'Bama said cautiously. He was watching him carefully and very closely. He seemed to be feeling his way along with this.

"Oh, but it is!" Dave said dispiritedly. "God damn it!" he burst out, "why do I get fat! Why dont you get fat!"

"I guess its just my inheritance," 'Bama said. "But then I guess I dont really eat quite as much as you do."

"But how can you drink so much! without it hurtin you? without makin you dull?"

'Bama nodded understandingly. "I dont know. Because Ive always have, I reckon. Hell, if I was to *stop* drinkin, Id probly fall over dead, already embalmed. They wouldnt have to do nothin to me. Just put me in the box."

"But I cant do that! It makes me dull!" Dave said frantically.

"Well, you use yore brains a lot more than me," 'Bama said. "You have to. But I dont really use my brains much atall, y'see."

"What the hell am I gonna do?" Dave said. The anguish of pain behind his eyes tautened them still more, until he looked as if he were about to cry. "God!" he said: "What am I gonna *do?*"

"Well now, lets just take it a little reasonable," 'Bama said carefully. "Lets look at it mathematically. Here we are; we're just about all set up in this place now. We knew it was goin to take us a while to get all fixed up in it. And it did. But we're just about all through with all that now, see? It aint like we was just startin it. Now we're ready to set back and enjoy the fruits of our labor. We got everything fixed up like we want it, and inside of a week we'll be back on a regular routine. Now, itd be silly to go and blow it all, just when we're about to get it fixed, wouldnt it?"

"I guess so," Dave said dismally. "I guess it would."

"Okay. Now what you want to do is just to take it easy for another day or two. Now aint that right?" he said soothingly. "We'll start cuttin you down on yore drinkin, just like we did in Miami. In a couple days more youll be right back into it, see?" He watched Dave carefully, apparently not sure he was doing right in starting to soothe him yet, quite this soon. "Now right now, you just go on back to bed and sleep. Just loaf around today, maybe tomorrow. Then yore head'll be clear and you can hit them a lick."

"I couldnt sleep!" Dave cried desperately. "I cant loaf!"

"All right then," 'Bama said, "we'll work. Come on and help me get this place cleaned up. Theres plenty other stuff we need to do around here, too, after we get this done. And no more heavy drinkin for *you*. And tonight we'll start makin the rounds of the lodges and start gettin back to work. But you dont want to get yoreself all worked up over an extra day or two *now*. That would just throw you, and keep you from gettin back to writin just that much longer. Now wouldnt it?" he said soothingly.

"I guess so," Dave said miserably. "I guess thats right. If I can just stand it that long. For a couple of days."

"Shore you can," 'Bama nodded. "Hell, maybe you be back to work tomorrow."

"Okay," Dave said. "Well, Ill go back up and get out of this robe and into some clothes, then. And then Ill come down and help you."

"All right," 'Bama nodded, slowly and calmly. "Ill be right here, ol' buddy. Ill go ahead with this here."

"What do you suppose makes me get like this?" Dave said.

"Well, I reckon its just because you feel guilty," the tall man said, "dont you reckon? Because you aint gettin yore book done."

"Thats what it is, of course," Dave said. "But—"

"Go on and get dressed," 'Bama said, grinning, with less caution now and more confidence, as though hed figured something out for himself. "And cut the crap."

It was, of course, exactly as hed said. Within a week everything had settled down into its own former normal routine, almost as it had been down in Miami. Dave was back hard at work on the combat novel and doing little heavy drinking, and the routine of nightly gambling at the different lodges and the pea-pool games at the Ath Club (Dave invariably lost at these; but he could feel he was beginning to get his stick back) had stabilized themselves into regularity, and what was more important that strange occult way of consistently winning more than they lost held firm and constant. Dewey and Hubie, and Wally Dennis, showed signs of beginning to hang out at the house regularly, and Dave and 'Bama went halves on buying a pingpong table at McMillan's Sporting Goods in Terre Haute for the basement. Their meals they ate either at Ciro's or the one uptown restaurant, or else out at The Nite Owl in the West End business district where most of the local denizens hung out after midnight and which was not too far from the house. The food was not as good as in Miami Beach, naturally, but it was probably a good thing, because Dave just as naturally began eating less. He did not, however, seem to lose any weight. Almost nobody—excepting Dewey and Hubie, and Wally, who all had the run of it—was invited to the house, neither from The Nite Owl nor from Smitty's, nor from anywhere else. The house was, and had immediately become, sort of their sanctuary—as soon as the housewarming party was over. Especially for Dave.

Only one thing, really, was very much different from the way everything had been for them down in Miami Beach, and this was the noticeable absence of vacationing bachelor girls. It became increasingly clear, even during the first week of their occupancy, that there were not going to be many—and in fact, *any*!—bachelor girls in Parkman, or for that matter in Terre Haute, who were going to be willing to go out with either 'Bama or with Dave. Any bachelor girls or career girls in Parkman—and in Terre Haute—were not on vacation now here at home; they went out of town for that. And what was more they were in towns where they were known, and lived, and where many had husbands, and they were obviously not going to be spending the night with any gamblers.

And perhaps, to do them full justice, Dave thought, it had to be admitted that a certain element of glamor was missing: a gambler in Miami Beach might be romantic; the same gambler in Terre Haute Indiana or Parkman Illinois wasnt. He was just unrespectable. He himself, Dave, found that he missed them keenly; but it didnt bother 'Bama. The tall Southerner seemed to be just as happy and satisfied with any of the brassiere factory girls or the drunken haggard Terre Haute barflys he had used to take around before he got his taste educated in Miami Beach. Once in the first week after they moved in they had made the rounds of all the lowclass Terre Haute joints, such as 'The Blazing Stump', and the old 'Toad Hop Inn' of prohibition days, and brought a couple of these home with them, and it appeared that this too would stabilize itself into routine.

It was ten days after the housewarming party, when Dave had worked himself back into feeling good about his book and was feeling confident again, that he finally made his first trip over to Israel to the Frenches. He had not forgotten Wally's comment the night of the party —Wally had said that he *thought* Gwen wanted to see him—and in fact, it had added considerably to Dave's savoring of his coming triumph. But he couldnt go over there in this mood of selfcastigation which was the residue of the near blowup 'Bama had worked him out of. That would ruin everything! And this trip to Israel, this time, he had become increasingly convinced, was going to be *the one*. D-Day, H-Hour, M-Minute. Everything was working for him. This time he was going to have everything playing on his side. The love affair— perhaps the only real love affair of his life; except for perhaps Harriet Bowman, which of course did not count, since it was never consummated —that he had been working for over six months to bring about, was going to be accomplished at last, this time, when he took "The Confederate", and the two hundred pages of his novel, over there to her. There was no reason why she, who had loved so many other men, would not love him too—and this time sincerely, and for keeps. She already did love him. He knew it. He could sense it. And when she saw the work he had done, and was doing—that would finish it. The last obstacle would be removed for her.

Naturally, then, it would be sheer foolishness to go over there until he was mentally ready. And the only way he could be mentally ready was to work, to *write* himself back into a confident, proper state for it.

The book itself, by the end of the first week in the house, was already back in that state where it had been during the last two months in Miami. It was alive. The people in it were real people for him, whom he knew as well as he knew 'Bama or Dewey and Hubie or Wally Dennis.

What he had done was really a very simple thing. He had taken a typical infantry company—(he had first decided on a platoon, and then later changed it because it didnt give enough variety of action, and personality; and you could only use just so many individual men anyway, why not spread them out over a company?)—a typical infantry company, then, of typical green men well trained. As well trained as any men can be who have never been in combat yet. And he had set them ashore on D-Day and followed them through the European campaign, and in fact had them up to around St Lô now. And would follow them on through.

It was a very simple structure, and a very hackneyed one. It was, in fact, the pattern for just about every damned combat novel that had been written about this war—or about the first war, for that matter. But it was right there that the similarity ended. And this was like no other combat novel that had ever been attempted. There were no heroes in this combat novel, and there were no bums. And there was no horror. At least, not in the book or the people. The horror would be in the readers—shocked horror. And there were no left-handed heroes either, in this combat novel, like Mauldin's Willy and Joe; no simple honest men who were good soldiers without being vain about it and really wanted only to get home. There was, in this combat novel, only a motley collection of human men, but men as human beings really were, and not as they liked to pretend they were in their literature they wrote—and like any such collection, when viewed honestly, they were wonderful material for satire and irony and ridicule and laughter. But the reader wouldnt laugh; because their life in combat was no more brave or fine, or possessed of any other human virtue, than their life at home would have been. Which, in short, meant none. Vain, foolish, pompous, egotistical, selfloving, these were the brave men who were fighting a war because their government and the other people in the country forced them too, and they had to, or else lose all their material possessions, which they wanted to keep, and worse yet, become unrespectable to their peers, and who would come home afterwards and become "veterans" and join the American Legion and all the other organizations and take care of a few orphans and tell the young men how to fight the next war, while in their hearts they were secretly glad the young men would have to do it and not them, they were too old. In short, laughable (but unpitiable) fools—and each one of them was DAVID HERSCHMIDT, who could look back on one of the most foolish lives of any of them, but who would no more admit it than they would, if accused of it.

One of the scenes he was especially proud of was one in which two of the characters are talking to another man who has been seriously wounded, and delicately trying to get him to let the two of them flip for an exceptionally fine combat knife he has, since he wont need it any more. (He had first got the idea from listening to Wally talk about the Randall knives hed ordered.) The third man, the wounded man, is already frightened—hes not sure he isnt going to die—and his feelings are hurt because he thinks they dont really care about him at all, only his knife. Which is only too obviously true—in spite of their sympathetic remarks. But he, the wounded man, is in a position where he cant say anything to chide them, not if he wants to appear a brave man instead of a sissy. So the argument finally resolves itself into the form of a moral argument. The two buddies point out to the wounded man that it is hardly right for him to be selfish and want to keep his knife, especially since he obviously can never use it in combat any more, and more especially since he might even die—of course, they dont think he will now, of course; but he might get infected or something—whereas one of them could really use it, and it might even save one of their lives. And if he did happen to die, it would make a nice parting gift to one of his pals. The wounded man has no real moral rebuttal for such an argument—except of course to say they are coldblooded, which would make him look un-brave—so he is forced to take refuge in the statement, which none of them believe, including himself, that he doesnt think he is so badly wounded that he wont get back into combat any more. Meanwhile the fire is getting heavier above and all around them, where they have drug him to a ditch. In the end, by clinging to his argument, the wounded man gets to keep his knife since they can hardly take it off him bodily, and after he gets back in the hospital it is stolen off him by a hospital Medical Corpsman, as Dave's own knife had been after he himself was wounded.

—There was, he remembered after he had written the scene, a similar incident in the 'boots scene' in *All Quiet on the Western Front*. So he got the copy from the city library and looked it up. But when he did, he saw that he need not have worried; Remarque used the scene strictly for pathos. Another thing, the scene in *All Quiet* took place in the hospital where the men were out of immediate danger; his own scene was in a road ditch under fire where the raising of your head was enough to get it machinegunned off, and the acquisitiveness of all three participants is still strong enough to stand it; and it was humorous, and funny; there was no pathos in it at all—except perhaps by implication, and even then only for himself alone.

Read today, he realized suddenly, the scene in *All Quiet* was bathos. And when Dave discovered this he was intrigued with the gestation of perhaps a *new* idea. Excitedly, he began to read through the rest of the book, beginning at the beginning; and everywhere it was the same—all bathos, false pathos, strained pathetic effects. The writing itself was accurate, and good; the characters were real and alive;—but everywhere the attitudes of the author Remarque and his purpose, and his beliefs about war shone through as antiquated. Total war had come to be such a normal and accepted part of our lives, today, that what he had written back then was no longer tragic, it was commonplace, even boring. Whats he making all this fuss about? you wanted to ask yourself. Why all this weeping? and gnashing of teeth? Hell, its only a war. And an inefficient, antiquated one at that!

Whats the matter with this bunch of young Germans? you kept wanting to ask yourself. Havent they ever been in a war before? But that was just it! They hadnt! Theirs was the first generation to serve in a really big, all out, total war. (And even then it wasnt very total!) And they, and the rest of their world, were still shocked by it, back then. It hadnt become normal yet.

Happily, enthusiastically, bubbling over with excitement, Dave laid the book aside and sat looking at its old original tweedy-type cover, which he remembered from his youth, and thinking how he could use this new idea. For one thing, it naturally meant the return of the professional warrior—not the West Point tactician professional, but the real fighting warrior like the Roman Legionary. Just like back in the Middle Ages, or during those days of the Roman Legion. The professional paid mercenary of his country, an honored man, and that was what his men in his book were. Or were becoming, at any rate;— those who survived. And at the end of the book that was what they would be, the ones who survived: the tough, wise, hardbitten, plunderhungry, battlescarred old legionaries. He had been wondering for some time what to do with the end of the book, and now he had it. The few, the very few, who survived to the end of the book (and of the war) would be what? naturally: theyd be the professional warriors, ready to go again when called, ready to drink and live it up amongst the conquered if not, the paid mercenaries of their country, just as they were today in every country. War was natural to them now; it was their craft, and their art, and their profession.

Why, hell! We're just *like* Rome, he thought. Look at all the valuable antiques and old steins and rare guns everybody shipped home, or brought home with them. The antique shops like those ones theyd gone to down in Miami Beach were already full of them.

And!—he thought sparklingly, his fingertips and extremities actually sparking, it seemed almost—and! the one tragedy in his book, the one real honest to God serious tragedy, would be the case of the veteran platoon sergeant who had survived through the whole mess, the whole war, only to be injured afterwards—lose a hand, or a leg, something like that—and be invalided out. Be forced to go back, in the end, to civilian life. To civilian life, which he no longer liked or wanted, and for which he was not fitted or needed, and sink down into the anonymity of its assemblyline factory worker lineup.

God! he thought smacking his fist down into his palm, God! what a scene he could do—when the guy, a former assemblyline factory worker, a management-union slave, finds out he is crippled and will have to be discharged and go back home and give up war and fighting and high living. Hell! Dave thought happily, maybe he even commits suicide! The Twilight of the Gods.

Damn, man! he thought galvanically. And that damned punk kid, Wally Dennis, he added triumphantly. Competition, Dawnie said? Competition, hell! That young kid was going to have to go a long way, and live a long time, to even be in the same league with this book! let alone competition! He could hardly wait to tell Gwen what he had worked out, and have her read what he had done and especially his prize scene.

And, hell! Not to mention "The Confederate"! Christ, he had completely forgotten all about it, thinking about the book.

And quite suddenly, he knew it was the time to go. He had been waiting for that, for it to be the right time, and now he knew it was suddenly. Everything was clicking, everything was moving along just right, and with all the volume of work he had here to show her, it couldnt go wrong this time. If he didnt make it with her this time, he was willing to admit that he never would. But there were no doubts, this time. He *knew* he would. Unable to sit still, he got up to go and gather all the stuff to take her.

But then, craftily, he made himself sit down and relax, and breathe deep a while. He didnt want to go over there in this electric state, screwed up like this. He knew he was too forceful, he pushed people too much, when he was like this. With consummate guile he decided he had better mix himself a couple of good stiff martinis first, before he went. That would let him down. And two would be just right, just the right amount. While he drank them, he gathered up the stuff: the original (not the carbon) of "The Confederate", already bound and neatly typed; the nearly two hundred pages of the novel, still rough draft and pencilled all over; and the sheaf of notes on how to develop and carry it on, all together in a manila folder. It made a rather bulky armload. And he was proud of it.

He left 'Bama a pencilled note on the hall table: "GONE OVER TO ISRAEL FOR A WHILE. BE BACK WHEN I GET BACK." Let him take from that what he wanted to! Dave wasnt worried about succeeding this time. With a last look around the house, he shut the door behind him and went out to the little Plymouth, still hating, in a way, in spite of his enthusiasm, to give up his anticipation he had been nurturing for so long.

It was almost dark when he approached the bridge and its long earthen ramp, and Dave thought again of what an important part memories and past emotions played in all our lives. The tall, high bridge loomed up high above him, catching the last light of the sunk sun. Down below the lights were on in the houses and the town was already in darkness. Both had strong emotional connotations for him, and which had nothing to do with the things themselves, either bridge or town, but were merely the emotional residue of past times he had seen them.

Actually, he saw two different bridges and towns. One was the bridge he crossed and town he passed on his way to Terre Haute. The other was the totally different bridge and town he approached whenever he came here to go down to Gwen's. And they were completely distinct and separate.

In fact, he saw a multitude of bridges and towns. The bridge he had crossed and town he had passed when he left for Florida with 'Bama, and looked down from, trying to pick out her house in the night, was a darkly unhappy bridge. And he remembered it so. But the bridge hed crossed and town hed passed when they had returned from Florida with him expertly driving 'Bama's Packard, that bridge had been a brightly confident and triumphant bridge. The bridge he crossed going to and from Terre Haute was a nothing, a means to get to an end. But this bridge now, and this town, that he approached on his way to Gwen's, was both a happy and an unhappy bridge, and a happy and unhappy town; and it could not help but influence his mood somewhat. Underneath his forcefulness, and confidence, a kind of gentle sad melancholy settled in him.

The trouble with memories was that, while they enhanced and extended all the happy acts connected with them, they also equally enhanced and extended the unhappy. But you never learned *that* until *after* youd been in love,—really deeply in love.

Probably nobody in the world would ever believe he was in love with her, he thought, if he told them. He guessed he didnt act like it. Not according to the guidebooks for the young, at any rate. He slept with other women. He did this and that. He kept her dangling over here for what?—almost three weeks? But what was love? Was it what Frank and Agnes—whom, he was suddenly sure, were very much in love—had? Was it what Wally and Dawn—whom, he was suddenly sure, were very much in love also—had? Was it what 'Bama and that wife of his—whom, he was also suddenly sure, were very much in love —had? Or perhaps even what Sherm Ruedy the cop and that thin sickly wife of his had?—though Dave could not possibly see what they could have? Or what all those other paired and mated couples in the world had? or thought they had? Love, he guessed, if you wanted to grasp at and wrassle a definition, was the insuperable desire to make another given party, chosen for one unreasonable reason or another, love you more than they wanted to make you love them. And more than that, make them *prove* it. And infatuation, then, conversely,— that trial horse phrase of all the selfhelp marriage counsellors—it would be the very same identical thing when the desire was not completely insuperable, and could be got over. And when it couldnt, we called it love. Well, he knew he could never get over his, never could, would never get over it, ever. Heavily, he shrugged it off of him, and turned down off the approach onto the cutoff down into Israel, glad he didnt have to look at that damned bridge any more anyway straight ahead through the windshield, and trying to get his supreme confidence back.

But he found he did keep on looking at it anyway, out and up through the open side window, to where it towered, catching the very last rays of the dying light above the green trees in the early June

evening. Apparently, he couldnt keep from looking at it. And it seemed
to tower so much higher, from down here. Christ, he hadnt meant
for those two martinis to let him drop this far, when they let him down.
But it wasnt the martinis. It was that damned bridge, that towering,
soaring bridge. He wished now he hadnt left that damned too-confident
note for 'Bama. That burned his bridges.

Well, there was one damned thing for sure. The stuff he was bringing her to show her was good. Damned good. And he knew it. And she
would know it. That helped to bring some of the lost confidence back.

Gwen met him at the ground-level side door after he knocked. Her
rawboned, masculinely feminine face was shockingly like it had always
looked, as she blinked. In six months of remembering it he had softened
its bone lines and slurred its detail.

"Oh!" she said, "Dave. Well, come on in," she smiled and stepped back.

"Hello, Gwen. How are you?" he heard his own voice say huskily.

"Fine! fine!" He followed her on up the three cellar steps from the
landing into that kitchen. The set of copper skillets still hung against
the brick oven. The steins and pewter still stood along the high plate
rails at the other end. There might have been just a suggestion of
restrained hurt feelings in her voice and on her face, but there was
that old native eager life-interest in her eyes, too. Thin, except for the
hips, high-square-shouldered, the long no-colored not very well cared
for hair in defiance of the styles. "Im just fine," she said. "And how are
you? Wont you come and sit down?"

"Hey," he said ruefully, "what the hell? Youre treating me like a
stranger."

She looked suddenly flustered. "Oh! am I? Well, I didnt mean to be.
Come on and sit down." Then she laughed, almost embarrassedly, and
shook her hair back. "Can I fix you some coffee?"

"Wheres Bob?"

"Out."

"Sure, Id love some coffee," he said and went on down to the massive
old table and its ladderbacks and sat down, displaying his armload of
manuscript on top of it prominently.

"Youve put on a lot of weight," Gwen said, from the stove.

"Christ! Everybody I see tells me that," Dave said irritably. "But
everybody. I guess Im going to turn out to be another Balzac or Stendhal.
I guess Ive just been living good."

"You enjoyed your trip to Florida, then?" she said.

"Oh, you know about that then?"

"Oh, yes," Gwen smiled. "And about the house you and your gambler
friend have taken. By the way, I suppose you know: I have your clothes
and things from the hotel all over here. Theyre all put away in moth-
proofs upstairs. Also," she said, with that almost-embarrassed little laugh,

and shook her hair back, "theres a few little Christmas presents that some of us got for you, lying around here someplace. I dont know just exactly where, but I can find them."

Dave felt such a sudden, sick twinge of pain in his stomach that perforce, like the explosive grunt of a man hit in the solar plexus, he muttered "Ahhh, Gwen!" before he could stop himself. He had had no idea that he had hurt her so terribly. If he had, he would never have gone. And yet, strangely, with that knowledge of her hurt—which was obvious, from her very restraint of it—all of his former forcefulness and confidence came flooding back in a wave of elation as if a dam had burst, and he felt both powerful and protective. If he had hurt her, she must love him; God! he wouldnt hurt her for the world.

She was standing and looking at him from the stove, just standing and looking, with that open little almost-embarrassed smile that was like the laugh, and he covered quickly for his grunted exclamation.

"Say!" he said cheerfully. "Arent you going to ask me what the hell it is Ive got here?"

"Why, yes!" Gwen smiled, "I was going to." And again she laughed and shook her hair back in that gesture. "I noticed it when you first came in. But I figured youd tell me. What is it? manuscript?" She was still reserved with him. But in her eyes was that natural eager interest that was as much a part of her as it was of Bob, and that she could no more reserve than she could her breathing.

"Manuscript!" Dave said triumphantly. "Of course, manuscript! Well? Hell, dont you want to see it?"

She had finished with preparing the coffee and had set the tall silvery electric coffeemaker off on the counter to perk, and was wiping her hands. "You want me to read it?"

"Why, hell yes! What the hell do you think I brought it over here for! Here," he said, and picked up the bound copy of "The Confederate", "come on here."

And, smiling strangely, almost shyly, Gwen came on down to him and sat down across the table.

"Here, this is what I want you to look at first," he said, and handed it to her, then riffled the pages of the rest with his thumb. "And this is all on the novel." He moved his hand to include it all. "All of its what Ive done since I last saw you. And all these," he said opening the folder of notes, "are on what to do and how to go ahead with the novel."

"Youve done quite a lot," she smiled. "The Confederate," she read, "whats this?"

"Its a story."

"Not a Civil War story?"

"No, no. Just a story."

"All right, Ill read it for you, Dave," she smiled. She opened the cover and scanned the first page. "I see youve changed your name?"

"I— Yes, I did. I— I suppose its silly. But I wanted to use another name. I wanted to get away from— Its a sort of a symbol to me, you see," he said. "You know what I mean? Like Cabell."

"You mean you wanted to get away from all the old associations of the old name D. HIRSH?" Gwen said kindly. "The associations of Hollywood, and of the first two books, and all of that."

"Thats it. And then I thought, what the hell? DAVID HER-SCHMIDT is really my *real* name, after all, really. You— I suppose it sounds silly."

"Not at all," Gwen smiled warmly. "I think its an excellent idea. A fine idea."

"Well, that was why I did it," he said, trying to pull himself back down to calmness, trying to stop pressing, what the hell? "But damn it, I want you to read it!"

"Ill read it, Dave. But I cant read it with you looking over my shoulder. Ill tell you what Ill do. Ill," she paused, and gave her almost-embarrassed little laugh and shook her hair back, "Ill go get those Christmas presents of yours that we all got—if I can *find* them anywhere!—and you can be opening them while I read the story. Otherwise, I might forget to give them to you."

"That would be fine," Dave said awkwardly.

"And I dont want to forget to give them to you!" Gwen said. "Theyre just lying around here taking up space. Ill go find them."

He watched her put the manuscript down carefully on the table and then stride long-leggedly beneath those wide hips, down the long kitchen to the pantry door. She was back with a flat paper sack almost before she had gone. No, he thought triumphantly, and powerfully and protectively, no, she had no idea where they were, did she?

"Now, you go ahead and open them or dont open them, just as you like," she said with a restrained smile, putting the package on the table. "Or else go get yourself a book. Theyre really not much, and you can just as well open them later at home." She picked up "The Confederate." "But youll have to leave me alone while I read this. Ill take it over here in the corner. I want to concentrate. Oh, and if you care for coffee, you help yourself when its done, wont you?" she said distantly. "I dont care for any."

He could see quite clearly that he wasnt going to get any biased reading. And he didnt. She sat down with it in the big chair by the fireplace —where a small fire burned now, instead of the wintertime big one— and from then on not a single flicker of expression crossed her face, or was displayed by any movement of her body. Her eyes glued staringly to the page, she read on, page after page, turning them swiftly but carefully so as not to smudge. And the restraint and strange, polite reserve —but not so strange, he thought, considering the circumstances; better than he deserved, really, in fact—that she had shown him since he arrived, lasted until she was done.

Or rather, until she was about half way done. Because it was then that Dave essayed to speak to her, to thank her for the present she had got him. He had, first, gotten himself a cup of coffee, finally, when it was finally done perking, and then had sneakily sat back down quietly on the near side of the table, so he could watch her face (fruitless pastime!). Then he had tried working the crossword in the daily paper (he got about half, he never had been good at crosswords; he did all right on the ordinary words, but had never learned the private little vocabulary of two- and three-letter words they used as fill-ins, like r-a, Ra, Egyptian sun god). And finally, there being nothing else, he had opened up the presents.

Inside the paper sack, they were still neat and clean in their Christmas wrappings and the colorful ornamental bows. That in itself touched him; but when he saw what Gwen had gotten him (the Roget's *Thesaurus* and the wallet-notebook across the front page of which was written in her large neat autograph, "Writers should keep notes! Gwen."), he had again the sudden sorrowful sick wrench of pain that was almost unbearable and simultaneously inflamed his ego. Only this time it was stronger, and it did not go away so quickly, and the nerves all over his back and shoulders seemed to ripple as before an attack of vomiting, and he felt he had to speak. If only to protect himself.

"Gwen!" he said. "Gwen? Listen, I want to thank you for—"

That was as far as he got, and it was doubtful whether she had even heard any of the words at all, just the sounds. Anyway, there was nothing restrained or reserved about her answer.

"Dave, please dont talk to me!" she said looking up, her eyes flashing. "How the hell do you expect me to concentrate? And please stop squirming and moving around! Or else go in the other room; or something." And before he could even nod, let alone answer, her eyes were back down, fastened almost physically it seemed to the typed page. His typed page.

So he shut up and sat, hunching up his shoulders, and opened the other presents, trying to do it stealthily and quietly. The other three presents touched him too, and only added to it. Bob's beautiful hand-made cufflinks and tie tack set; the humorous but thoughtful box of typewriter ribbons from Wally for his LC Smith Portable (which he had not even known Wally knew the make of); and the typical, to-be-expected copy of Joyce's *Ulysses* from Dawn. But more than these, and right along with them, the knowledge that it had been Gwen who had been behind it all, who had engineered it, and got them all to do it, so that Christmas he wouldnt have been left out and would have felt remembered. And all of that, too, just made it that much worse. Why in the name of God he had ever gone to Florida, or what he could ever have wanted there, he no longer had any idea at all. It seemed it must have been another person altogether. And when he pictured the happy bliss he could have been living here all the time, with her! With Gwen! Finally, in selfdefense, his shoulders hunched up tensely like a man in a storm, he went back to the crossword and racked his brain to think of a two-letter word for Hawaiian bird. It looked, if both his projected cross-words were anywhere near right, as if both letters would be vowels—or even both O's—and that couldnt be right.

When Gwen finally finished and closed the heavy paper binding, she sat for a time and stared tensely off across the room, her face totally and absolutely without expression. —Well, he had always known it wasnt any good, he thought sickly, and that he was only kidding himself.— as she got up from the chair and came over to him with it and laid it gently on the table.

—Well, here it comes, he thought wretchedly. It was almost a relief, in a way.

"Dave," she said, "its magnificent!"

"You really think so?" he said. "I thought it was pretty good."

Gwen picked the bound manuscript up and looked at it almost unbelievingly and then laid it back down. "Yes," she said; "yes, it is. And the title is magnificent, too. Mag*ni*ficent! *The Confederate*. Oh, how magnificent. And those two men . . ." It dwindled off, and she looked back down at the manuscript.

"Well, gee," Dave said. "Thats swell. I dont know what the hell Ill ever do with it. It took me six weeks to write it. Nobodyll ever buy it."

"Dont worry about it," Gwen said shortly. "This is the best thing youve ever written. Its one of the best things ever written by anybody of your generation. If not *the* best. Youve never written anything to even half way touch it. Its not even the same man. All that glib supersensitive arty stuff you used to write. Or the heavy portentous emotionalizing. This is *life*, Dave! *Life!*"

Dave felt for a moment as if he were going to cry, and swallowed.

Still standing by the table, Gwen reached out her hand and ran her fingers almost lovingly, and still as if she did not really believe it, over the cover. She appeared at last to be getting over the effect it had had on her, and looked up at him suddenly and grinned, and then sat down swiftly across the table from him.

"Its a very controversial subject," she said running her fingertips back along the hair of her temple thoughtfully, and looking off over his head —or rather, through his head— into the distance as if she didnt see him. Dave wished she would look *at* him. "Very controversial. The tendency today among all the literati and the intelligentsia is to join the NAACP and hate the cruel, brutal, sadistic Southerner. And itll get worse, before it finally levels off into reason. Of course, theyre oversimplifying. Thats the psychological need of the literati for a righteous cause, of course. Other people can always use them—especially when they think theyre being leaders. This ought to prove very healthful." She broke off, and slowly stroked her temple again lightly. "Im sure I can get it published for you."

"You can?" Dave said. "Where? No you cant," he said, "look at the length."

"Theres a new publishing firm called *New Living Literature*. Theyve gone into the field of paperback books exclusively, and are reprinting all the old classics of world literature in paperbacks. But in addition to that theyre going to bring out a semi-annual anthology of *new* writing. I know the publisher and several of the editors. The length of *The Confederate* wont matter to them, and neither will the controversial subject; in fact, that will help it. They publish a lot of arty crap in it, but as often as not thats because they cant get anything else. No, Im sure I can get them to publish it."

"Well, Jesus!" Dave said, brimmingly. "I never thought of anything like that when I brought it over. I just wanted you to read it, and get your opinion."

"Well, I think it might be done," Gwen said seriously. "Anyway Ill be willing to give it a try, for anything thats as good as this is." Excitedly, then, she sort of passed her hand across her face, fingertips against her forehead, and then looked up at him with that same almost-but-not-quite-embarrassed smile of earlier and made the same nervous gesture of shaking her hair back. "You know, I was so worried about you! I thought youd blown up. Just quit, and given it up. Just flown the coop. But then I found out at the hotel that youd taken your typewriter with you. But even so, its so easy to lie to yourself about working, you know? You can convince yourself of anything." Again she passed her hand across her face embarrassedly and ran her fingertips on back along the hair of her temple shyly.

Dave wished suddenly he had a switch at his hand and could turn all the different lights off and just step around the table and get down on his knees and put his arms around her, just envelop her in his arms.

"Tell me," Gwen said, "those two men. In the story. Is one of them drawn from your friend the gambler?"

" 'Bama? No, no. Those are just two guys we happened to run into on the way to Miami. At Dering Florida. But just the same, a lot of that story is due to 'Bama," Dave said. "It was him who showed me what Southerners are really like. I always belonged to the 'Sadistic School' of the literati, like you were talking about. Out in California that was the only attitude I ever saw anybody have. Until I got to know 'Bama."

"He sounds like a pretty remarkable person," Gwen smiled warmly. "You ought to bring him over some time."

"Well, as a matter of fact Id like to. I was going to ask you," he said. Then a sudden twinge made him add, grinning: "Youll want to watch out for him, though. Hes a great seducer of women."

Gwen laughed. "Then Im sure he wont be interested in me." With her left hand, which was the nearest to it, she reached out for the manuscript and pulled it to her and sat looking down at it, smiling. It was as if she still did not believe it had really happened, and did not want to let it get out of her sight, for fear it might simply evaporate.

"Im glad you changed your name," she said suddenly, reading the title label on the cover, and then looked up at him beaming, her eyes sparkling with pleasure and happiness. "A thing like that can be very important to you, as a symbol."

"It didnt change anything," Dave said. "Im still the same bum Ive always been."

"No, it can be very important—to *you*," she smiled. "It can give you a different—part to play. A different role to act, in life. Thats the whole secret, you see. We all act one part or another. So to change ourselves, all we have to do is envision a different role and start acting it. It soon becomes fact. We can thus make ourselves into anything we want to be. —Thats not original with me," she smiled parenthetically, "Bob taught it to me long ago.— And your changing of your writing name is only one step in that process. That 'D. HIRSH' you used to use was such a sort of literary affectation."

"But so is 'DAVID HERSCHMIDT' an affectation," Dave said. "Isnt it?"

"Of course! But the point is, is it not a better affectation? for you, and what you want to accomplish? Thats what you must judge it by! Not by some ephemeral, unattainable 'reality'. Now, isnt it better?"

"I suppose it is," Dave said, thinking about what he hoped to accomplish—had hoped to accomplish all along—still hoped to accomplish. "Yes, I guess it is," he grinned. "If you like it."

Excitedly, and still holding the manuscript, she got up and walked around the end of the table on the other side of which he sat and stopped and stood, looking at it. Then she folded it in against her breast in her arms, not lovingly so much, but more like a schoolchild carrying a batch of books, and yet still lovingly too, and looked down at him. "Oh, you dont know how Ive worried about you the last six months! Afraid youd just throw it all away! Or else start writing that same old trash again, just because it was easier—less painful—than the really good work. You dont know *how* Ive worried!" she exclaimed, and smiled. "But this!" she said, bringing it forth again and looking at it, "This is great! And I use that word advisedly! This is the kind of writing you ought to have been doing long ago!" she said excitedly, and leaned forward to kiss him on the cheek.

Dave, who had been enviously watching her hold his manuscript against her and looking at the part of that small right breast that swelled out around its edge—his manuscript!—suddenly—half instinctively, half deliberately—turned his head, and her lips, softened and pursed to touch his cheek, came against his mouth.

It seemed to him to last a very long time. But actually, of course, it didnt. Nevertheless, he made a number of seemingly slow, stable observations. There was that peculiar distinctive fragrance of hers, a sort of sweet-bitter-sweet aura composed partly of some perfume and partly of her own distinctive odor, that he remembered well from the time he had been drunk and she had helped him on with his coat before he slept in the cornfield. It was delicious. Then there was the warmth of her natural body heat, radiating out from her, and from her face against his own. And her lips, light and cool and pleasantly lipsticky, sealed against his mouth, her nose lightly touching his cheek. There was the light drift of that no-color hair—fall-honey colored, he thought, they would call it in the movies—against his face where it had fallen as she leaned forward, and that lovely Gwen-French-fragrance coming from it. He partook of all of these hungrily and thirstily, and filed them away. He had been wanting to kiss her for such a long time.

Then Gwen straightened up—almost, actually, in the same instant she had kissed him and had herself discovered her lips were touching him on the mouth instead of on the cheek—and stood looking at him helplessly and regretfully, as if she wouldnt have done it for the world, as if assuming immediately the mistake had been all her fault for not giving him some warning, and with a look of shocked wonder and wide-eyed embarrassment at how it could have happened. Then her face changed slightly and knowledge came into it, and the look of wonder changed into a sort of equally dismayed surprise at seeing in him something which in her excitement over the story she had entirely forgotten about—or else, after six months, no longer thought existed—and which changed everything. Namely, love—or at least, what he thought was love, and how in hell was she going to handle this, and she looked entirely helpless.

She started to put her hand up to the side of her face and then stopped it midway and just left it.

Dave said nothing. But he could feel his face displayed that he felt guilty and that hed pulled a cheap trick on her. —But it hadnt been a cheap trick; and he hadnt even meant to do it, really.

"Dave, Ive got to tell you something about myself," she said half desperately. Then abruptly she turned completely around and looked down at the far end of the kitchen as if someone had just called to her.

"Yeah?" he said with husky awkwardness. "What?"

But instead of answering she just continued to stare down the length of the kitchen, her long back to him, as if waiting for whoever it was who had called her to appear.

He did not understand. All right, so she had apparently completely forgotten he wanted to sleep with her, was in love with her. There was nothing so terrible about that. In fact, it spoke very well for his story. After all, you couldnt blame her for that—after six months, half a year. It was probably more his fault than hers, as far as that went. But even if it wasnt, there wasnt anything to be so terribly embarrassed about. Standing there, she looked totally helpless, completely female, and he thought she had never looked so lovely. He got up and went down toward her to put his arms around her.

But before he could, as if sensing the physical nearness of him, she turned back toward him and moved away. "Dont, Dave," she said. "Please. Dave, I have to tell you."

"Okay," he said, feeling awkward. He let his half-extended arms drop to his sides. "Tell me what? That you forgot? Okay, so you forgot. Hell, I dont care. I—"

"Forgot?" Gwen said. "Forgot what?"

"About us. About you and me. Okay, so what? Hell, its a compliment to the story. Hell, I dont care. Hell, I love you."

For a moment Gwen looked as if she were going to laugh desperately. But she didnt. "Dave, Dave," she said desperately. "Dont say any more. Please dont. Youve been embarrassed enough already. I didnt mean to embarrass you. My God, youll hate me!"

"I could never hate you," he said. "I love you."

"You really do? Do you really love me so much? Do you really want me so much?"

"Jesus Christ!" Dave said. "What do you think I did everything I did for? Why do you think I stayed in this town? and put all my money in that damned taxi service of Frank's? What do you think I did all this writing for? Why do you think Im staying here now? What do you think I went to Florida for?"

"I *know* why you went to Florida," Gwen said desperately.

"I thought you didnt want me," he said anyway. "What do you think Ive done *all* this for?"

"And you really did all of this for me?" she said wonderingly. "Just because you wanted *me?*"

"Why do you think? What else?"

"But you dont really love me. Not really. Youve just made a contest out of it in your mind. Its a sort of a game you have to win. You dont really love me, you just want to sleep with me. Isnt that so? You dont need me. Now, do you. Really. Your writing is all you need, Dave. And really all you want. I have the feeling you never even see me when you look at me. You see a—a character in a book, maybe. A character in your life. But you dont see *me*. You never have."

"Thats not true!"

"I never tried to make you fall in love with me," she said desperately.

Standing in the center of the floor and looking at her where she had backed up and leaned now against the countertop, Dave could only nod dumbly. "No, I guess you didnt," he said despairfully. He still could not understand what it was was going on.

"You just want to sleep with me. I know its important to you, but . . ." She stopped.

"Hell, yes!" he said, into the gap. "Of course I do! Isnt that a part of love?"

"It may be all of it," Gwen said.

"Well—All or not, its certainly a part of it," he said.

"My God, how youll hate me!"

"Hate you for what? I couldnt hate you!"

"For embarrassing you so. I never tried to make you fall in love with me," she said again.

"You never had to. Gwen, I love you. Thats all I know. All I know is, I love you, and I need you."

"You do. All right," she said despairfully. "Dave, go over and sit down in the chair. Theres something about myself I have to tell you. Go on. Sit down. No, dont look at me. If you look at me, Ill never be able to tell you. Look away. Look the other way."

He sat down in the ladderback at the table and, finally, at her insistence, pulled his eyes away from the tall high-square-shouldered figure and turned around in the chair and sat staring at the coals in the fireplace.

Behind him, there was silence.

"Oh, I cant!" Gwen said finally, and began to weep. "I cant! Its too much to ask! Its too much! I cant!"

He turned back around then, to see her leaning slumped against the countertop, her face buried in her hands and her shoulders shaking rendingly as she cried.

"You dont know what its like!" she said from between her hands. "Youve never been a woman! You dont know what its like to be a woman! Oh, I cant, I cant, I cant," she sobbed wretchedly.

"What is it, Gwen?" he said, alarmed. "What is it? Tell me. You can tell me. Nothing can be that terrible."

She looked up at him then, her face contorted terribly, wrenchingly, the fingers of both hands still across her mouth, her shoulders shaking wrackingly as she drew great sobs of breath, tears streaming freely from the eyes that watched him, and kept on watching him; and he sat awkwardly, not knowing what to do, wanting desperately to go over to her, and just as desperately afraid to, afraid he would be rebuffed again.

Then she took her hands away from her mouth that was still trembling and wiped them underneath her eyes. "Ill tell you," she said weakly. She looked both frightened and considerably shamefaced, like a person trying to lie who cannot carry it off. "Im a cripple, thats what!"

"A what!" Dave shouted, astounded, terrible images fleeing through his mind. "You mean youre a—a morphodite, or something?"

Gwen did not even hear him. "A cripple, just like you," she went on, guilty-faced. "Ive been in love with the same man all my life, just like you have been in love with that same girl out in Los Angeles. Ive been in love with the same boy ever since high school."

Dave had not understood what was happening all this time, had not been following, and moreover, had known he was not following, was missing out somewhere. Now for the first time it penetrated his own thick German skull that after all the histrionics were over she might not be going to sleep with him after all, and he wanted to pound his knuckles on it for being so thick. God, what an ass! what a thick skulled German ass! "Well," he said lamely. "Well— I dont believe it."

"I dont care whether you believe it or not." Gwen had stopped crying completely now, and was looking at him with bright, frightened eyes. "Its the truth."

"Who was it? Was it anyone I knew?"

"You probably knew him. He was in my class," Gwen said bright eyed. "His name was Milton Evans."

"Milton Evans?" Dave remembered the name, but as he sifted his brain he could not remember the boy. If he was right, Milton Evans had been a sort of a Milquetoast type; he had hardly known him. "Well, damn it, I still dont believe it," he said. "What happened to him?"

Gwen shrugged. "He grew up. He went away to school. He moved away. He got married."

"And he was the first one that ever—" he paused, "ever made love to you?"

"Yes," Gwen said.

"You dont mind if I mix myself a drink, do you?" Dave said heavily.

"No. No, of course not." She moved away from the countertop, and went back to the table, where the manuscript of *The Confederate* lay. She sat down and picked it up.

In silence Dave got the things out of the cupboard. There was still gin and vermouth. He walked down and got some ice cubes out of the refrigerator, looking at the bright set of copper skillets against the old brick as he passed. "Damn it, every time I come over here to see you I always seem to wind up having to get drunk," he said. He mixed himself a stiff martini.

Gwen did not say anything and continued to look down wistfully at the manuscript cover.

"What about all the other men?" he said finally. He took a big gulp of the drink. He had the feeling he ought not to get very far away from the mixer and the bottles.

"The other men," Gwen said. For a moment she did not say anything, and looked bright eyed and guiltyfaced.

"If it upsets you to talk about them," Dave said, "its all right. It doesnt matter."

"No. It doesnt upset me. Anyway," Gwen said, "I think you have the right to know. —I suppose you could say the other men were all just 'escapades'. Not any of them were ever real love affairs. I suppose you could say that I was just using them. I was—trying to find someone who would take his place. And I used them. But it never worked. And I hurt them all. But I never meant to hurt them, deliberately."

Dave looked down at the glass in his hand, which was empty, two big gulps had done it, and stepped quickly to the counter and the mixer. He poured out another double like the first.

"And thats why I didnt want it to happen to you," Gwen said. "I didnt want the same thing to happen to you, too. I dont think I could bear that."

"Why dont you let me be the judge of that?" Dave said as he stirred the drink. "If Im willing to risk it, and take that chance? Why should you worry?"

"I cant," Gwen said gently. "I know what would happen."

"Goddamn it, I still dont *believe* it!" Dave shouted straight at the upper cupboard above the countertop which was before his face. "Its not the *truth!* I *know* its not!"

Sadly, Gwen did not say anything.

"Is it?" he said violently, swinging around.

"I never led you on into falling in love with me," Gwen said earnestly; "and thats why," she said gently, guiltyfaced. "I never tried in any way to do anything that would make you fall in love with me."

"You didnt have to," Dave said darkly, and gulped off half of his second drink.

"Theres one thing I can offer you," Gwen said. "I can offer you love. I do love you, Dave. But not the kind of love that has sex in it. Because I respect you too much to hurt you. But I love your work, and love the talent you have, and what you might be able to do with it. And I love you, too. Just because of all of these things. I can give you encouragement with your work—and believe me, I know what lonely work it is—and perhaps I can even give a little help, sometimes, and we can have a love relationship, of a sort. If you want that."

"Yeah," Dave said, "sure."

"I wouldnt blame you if you didnt want it. But thats all I have to give, Dave. And one other thing," she said gently, "Dont worry about me going out and having sex with other men, Dave. I gave that up as a bad job a long time ago. That was what I really meant when I told you once that sex bored me."

"Yeah," Dave said, "sure. Well, thats one consolation. Anyway." He swung around on her, his face suddenly contorted, his eyes bright. "You know, I used to imagine you going out with all kinds of other guys, just for sex. And at the same time I knew you wouldnt go out with me."

"Oh, Dave!" Gwen said breathlessly, tormentedly.

"Will you just tell me one thing?" he said contortedly. "And really tell the truth? Just one thing?"

"Oh, Dave!" she said.

"Is the truth, the reason you wont go out with me, wont have an affair with me, is it because Im so fat?"

"Oh, Dave!" Gwen breathed again, her own eyes as bright with pain as his were, as hurt by him as he was hurt by her. "That I should ever hurt you so much! I have never ever meant to do that! Oh, no. No, no, no. A woman doesnt love a man because hes fat or slim or curly or bald or short or tall. She loves him because of what he *is*."

"And thats really the truth?" he urged. "Youre not just lying to me? to save my feelings?"

"Oh, no, Dave! No!" Gwen said painfully.

"Well, okay," he said. "All right. But I had to know. Damn it, I *cant* believe it!" he bellowed suddenly. "Milton *Evans!*"

"Its no more unreasonable than your own girl out in Hollywood, Dave," Gwen said. "Do you think *Im* not sorry it happened?"

"But I dont love *her* any more."

"Maybe you still do," Gwen said gently.

"Well, I dont," he said, and fell to mixing his third drink and it was then, while he was doing it, that the cellar-landing door opened and Bob came in.

Robert Ball French marched up the three steps from the landing and out into the center of the kitchen, his rakish old black slouch hat with the brim turned down all along its right side still on his head and smiling cheerily under his heavy thick moustache, and looked all around him and at both Dave and Gwen.

"Well, I see I have missed another dramatic installment," he said cheerfully, and not derisively. "I wish I had stayed home now. But if I had, it would not have happened probably.

"Hello, Dave, my boy," he said cheerily. "How have you been?" He was completely sober.

"Just fine, Bob."

"Dad," Gwen said, blandly ignoring what he had said, "Dave has brought over a long story hes done. I want you to read it. Its simply magnificent! Here, come look at it. I want us to send it to the *New Literature* people. You come here and look at it, and Ill make us all some coffee."

"Good!" Bob said enthusiastically. "Fine! But Im afraid I cannot read it tonight, dear Gwen. Tomorrow! Im late for my old bed, and I must get up and work in the morning. Good night, my dears," he said cheerfully, and took the hat off his close-cropped gray head and disappeared through the pantry door to the back stairs before anything else could be said.

"I must go, too, anyway," Dave said glumly, hoisting his third drink. "I have to work tomorrow, too."

"But arent you going to stay?" Gwen said anxiously. "Dont you want to stay the night?"

"No. I must go," he said.

"But— Youre not too drunk to drive, are you?" she said earnestly.

"Im not drunk at all," Dave said, and truthfully. He could hardly feel any of anything he had drunk. He also could hardly stand to stay in this house another minute. He took a long slow look at Gwen under lowered lashes, where she sat at the table erectly and leaning forward on it on both elbows.

"But I wish you would stay," Gwen said anxiously, her eyes bright and screwed up with anxiety and guilt. "Youre perfectly welcome. Id like for you to stay."

"No," he said with dignity. "I cant. Dont ask me to, Gwen."

"All right," she said understandingly. "I understand."

And with that, he turned to leave, quickly. At the door to the steps down to the landing, where she had come with him, but did not get close or offer to shake hands, he said,

"Ill just leave that stuff on the novel here. Maybe youll get a chance to read it."

"Ill read it tomorrow," she smiled nervously, "if I dont read it tonight. Then you want to go ahead with—with a kind of relationship like we talked about?"

"Yeah," he said, "sure. Why not? Only you musnt be mad at me if I break out once in a while. Im liable to try and break the rules," he said.

"Itll be perfectly all right," Gwen smiled. "Ill understand."

"Yeah?" Dave said. "Well, thats good." At the bottom of the three steps on the landing—where it seemed he had stood so many times before, in this same mood, and in these same frustrating circumstances— Gwen stopped him.

"Youre sure you wont change your mind and stay?" she said anxiously.

"No," he said. "I cant. Ive got to work tomorrow."

"Dave," she said, her eyes bright with pain, and her face still frightened and shamefaced looking, and perhaps—he thought—even with a little of some kind of a guilty sense of loss on it—but that was probably his *vanity*. "Dave, we all of us do what we can. What we must," she said almost beseechingly. "Not what we wished we could do. And not even what wed like to do sometimes."

"I know," he said. "Yeah, I guess thats right."

"And Dave," she said softly. "I dont think youre fat."

Not trusting himself to say anything to that, he winked at her, and left. From outside the door, before he closed it, he said, "You call me up when you get that read, and Ill come over."

When he had driven the five furious miles back to Parkman, he was astonished to discover the lights were still on in the poolrooms and restaurants and around the square. It was only nine thirty! and after starting on out to the house he turned around and came back and drove out to Smitty's, where he went in and picked up Ginnie Moorehouse, sitting at a table of brassiere factory girls. To hell with what they thought, with what they all thought. What the hell? The two fatties should stick together.

In the car going out to the house, Ginnie kept up her usual running conversation. She was, she said, very pleased to see him. "Have you been over t'Israel to see your teacher friend ever yet?" she asked in her dull-eyed way.

"What?" Dave said. "Who?"

"That teacher friend of yours. From the College."

"As a matter of fact, yes," he said. "Ive been over several times lately. Why?"

"I jist wondered," Ginnie said complacently. "Shes just such an awful bitch. Ive heard so many people talk about how awful many men and love affairs shes had."

"I dont know anything about any of that," Dave said.

"Course Ive never met her myself," Ginnie said. "But the thing that gets me is," she said wistfully, "they everybody let her git away with so awful much. Whereas me theyre always tryin to get into trouble. But you dont see that son of a bitch Sherm Ruedy ever goin around checkin on the like of her kind. Thats because shes rich and her old man use to run the whole College. I wonder what its like to be like that? To be rich, and have the pull, and be able to do anything you want to and git by with it."

"Everybody has problems," Dave said brusquely. "And Ill tell you something else," he said more sharply, "the less you worry about her and the more you look after yourself, the better off youll be all around."

"Well, Im sorry," Ginnie said wistfully. "I didnt mean to make you mad. Say, whats this here wrapped up package in the seat?"

"Its a present," Dave said savagely. "Its a present for my goddamn stupid mother."

"Yeah? What is it?"

"Its a pillow. And I bought it in Terre Haute. And I paid six fifty for it. Anything else?"

"Six fifty!" Ginnie said complacently. "Ill bet its purty!"

Dave took it, the package, and tossed it behind him into the back seat—and in the act of tossing suddenly remembered that he had forgotten to get his own presents, his six months old Christmas presents, off the table at Gwen's before he left. The thought sent a sudden twinge of anguish through him. He hoped she wouldnt think he didnt want them, he thought desperately. She herself had also forgotten them, too, hadnt she? in the upset they both had suffered?

Then, behind him, the package hit the seat and rustled to rest, and he brought his arm down. He had forgotten all about the damned pillow for days, and it had been lying in the seat for over two weeks. He would have to take it up there and see the old lady and get that over with.

"Come on," he said, pulling up into the driveway. "Here we are."

They got out. He figured he could get her gone and out of the house by midnight, long before 'Bama would ever be home to see her. Hed drive her back downtown himself.

BOOK FOUR

THE LOVE AFFAIR

CHAPTER 45

Mrs Elvira Hirsh, on the day that her youngest son finally visited her, was not expecting him. Mrs Hirsh was aware that David had been back in Parkman for over a month now because Franklin had told her he was back. That was back in May and here it was, the first of July. And David still had not come to see her. So she felt safe in assuming he would never come.

Mrs Hirsh did not hold this against David. She knew how young people were. And anyways, he was her youngest and she had always spoiled him a little, she guessed. Mothers always did that. And of course Franklin's wife had spoiled him a great lot more, Mrs Hirsh thought with a sudden vindictiveness, in spite of everything she herself had been able to say or do. But he was still a *good* boy. Just thoughtless, was all. Young people never really realized what their parents went through, bringing them into the world, and raising them, and caring for them— not until they grew up and had children of their own, and then it was often too late. But David was still a *good* boy. There wasnt nothing *bad* about him. Mrs Hirsh believed that and prayed to God for him and for his immortal soul. Such prayers were always answered. Maybe he was gambling and living an unChristian life right now, but she knew that someday he would settle down.

He had not had a very happy life, as a child. Thanks (Mrs Hirsh's mind froze stiffly:) to Victor. David had hardly knew his father, because (her mind froze stiffly:) Victor had left them all when he was hardly more than a baby. That was always hard on a child. But none of her children could ever be really *bad,* because she had raised them all to be decent Christians, and she did not hold it against David because he had not found time to come and see her. But when he did come, she was very pleased and glad.

He did not come until late in the afternoon, almost evening. She was about to cook her supper. And she had the radio on.

Mrs Hirsh had not risen early that day. She was not much of an early riser any more. There was no need. So, as usual, she had been awakened around seven in her little apartment on the second floor of the Wernz Arms, by the wife of the high-school football coach rummaging around to get her husband's breakfast in the apartment across the hall and get him off to school. He was teaching Social Studies this year in the summer school, his wife said. Mrs Hirsh lay, half-asleep, listening to them across the hall and listening to the birds singing outside her window in the already bright summer air, and half-thinking it was going to be another hot day today, until she heard the coach leave and lumber down the

673

stairs and his wife go back in and shut the door. After that, there were the faint sounds of her stacking the dishes in the sink and then going back to bed, and gradually Mrs Hirsh drifted back off to sleep, dozing a little, hearing the birds outside the open window, and finally sleeping completely.

They woke her almost every day like this. Except Sunday. But she didnt mind. Both of them, both the coach and his wife, were very nice to her because Franklin was President of the Alumni's Downtown Coaches Association and had a great lot to say about the highschool football and basketball squads. Both of them treated her very kindly, and the wife came over often just to sit and visit. The coach was a huge, big man, with a huge neck and shoulders, and almost more hair on his back (she had seen him several times working in the hall in his undershirt) than there was on his head. He had been a champion football player in college, and Franklin had been one of the main ones who got him on here. They had been here two years. In some ways, he made her think of (her mind froze stiffly:) Victor, when he was younger. Of course, (her mind held, stiff-frozen:) Victor had never been that big, but he had had that same kind of big neck and shoulders. But of course now, with the life hed led, he had lost all that strength and health and had become thin and scrawny. If a person led that kind of life and let their health go, they just naturally had to suffer the consequences, Mrs Hirsh thought with a vindictive frozenness. She had seen him—Victor—up town one day not long ago at the Kroger's, and he had looked as thin and frail as a bird. But once he had looked like the coach, though not that big of course. The coach and his wife had been married over ten years now and had never had any children, and she was convinced it was beginning to ruin their lives though of course neither one ever said anything about it. Mrs Hirsh was convinced it was the wife's fault, because anyone could look at the coach and those neck and shoulders and see that it could not be his.

Well, it was a tragedy, because they would never know the full joys and meaning of life until they had had children of their own and loved and raised them, she thought half-sleepily and sorrowing for them. From outside the birds sang sweetly in her ears. The still fresh summer-morning-air moved across her face. That poor coach. She slept again.

At nine o'clock she woke again and got up, and putting her wrapper on over her nightgown on her thin frame went into the little kitchen where she turned on the little table model radio Franklin had given her and put coffee on. Then she went across the big front room to the front door into the hall and reached out and got the morning paper, the Chicago Tribune which Franklin subscribed to for her, and took it to the kitchen and commenced to get her breakfast, her mouth watering with hunger. While she cut up leftover potatoes, she listened to the nine o'clock dramatic life story on WGN. She spooned bacon grease from the coffeecan beside the stove into the skillet and heated it till it was popping and put the potatoes on. While these cooked, she prepared a pot of hominy she was going to have for lunch and put a few strips of raw bacon in it for seasoning and set it on a back burner. Then she fried more bacon in the other skillet and after it was done fried herself three eggs in the rich-smelling sputtering grease. When the eggs were done she poured part of the fryings onto a piece of white bread because she did not feel like bothering with toast, and poured the rest into the hominy pot for seasoning. Then, when it was all ready, she ladled it all out onto a plate —eggs, bacon, the grease soaked bread, the fried hashbrowns—and sat down at the little table to eat it while she turned the radio to WLS for the nine thirty dramatic life story.

The morning paper, already unfolded, lay beside her on the table, but she did not read it while she ate. And she did not really listen to the WLS nine thirty dramatic life story. The rich yolky flavor of the eggs and the rich salt-smoke fry of the bacon and the solid mash of the crisped potatoes mingled deliciously in her mouth. Outside the little kitchen's window the summer mid-morning sun shown still and bright and the shadow of a tree branch moved delicately on the screen. Both sun and shadow impinged themselves upon her eyes, and the sounds of the birds and rustling of the trees assailed her ears, and the odor of fried food and coffee in the summer air made itself aware to her nose when she breathed.

After the meal, she took her three pills and then went in the bathroom and sat on the toilet placidly, but a little nervously and uneasily, while her bowels moved. She had started taking a new laxative a few days ago, but it did not really seem to add much help to what the other three were already doing for her. The other pills that were not laxatives that the doctor had given her did not seem to be doing her much good, or making her feel much better either; and for a moment she had a vague feeling of general uneasiness, but this passed. She did not really feel bad. And there was nothing really wrong with her, he said.

After that, after the unsatisfactory bowel movement, she went back out in the kitchen and had another cup of coffee and read the paper. The headlines this second day of July 1948 were all about the blockade of Berlin and the Air Lift and the campaign for President, and Mrs Hirsh read the stories slowly and carefully, getting a little more upset and nervous as she read them. Everything looked so bad that it gave her a sort of feeling of unpleasant happiness which she did not really enjoy feeling, and yet did enjoy too.

It was so easy to say to the world, I told you so! The trouble was, the world would not listen. It never had. The world no longer believed in God. It had turned its face away from Him. With frivolity and cynicism it had rejected and denied its Maker and its Savior. Little wonder it had fallen upon evil days! And until it mended its ways, and was willing to return to Him and pray to Him with humility and humbleness for His forgiveness, it would remain upon evil days. Only in Christ, Savior, was there hope of Eternal Salvation. But in their vanity and pride men had turned their backs on Him. They no longer worshipped in His House, and they no longer wanted His help, and they no longer prayed to Him.

The news was almost all bad and with her unenjoyable enjoyment Mrs Hirsh read on carefully, savoring painfully and storing away each new gloomier fact. The blockade of the Russians around Berlin was still being tightened. It was too soon to tell yet whether the Air Lift would work, whether it would be able to carry enough food and supplies. Or, indeed, whether the Russians would even allow it to go on through without shooting down the planes. If they shot down the planes, of course it would be war. An atomic war. Which would not only destroy civilization, but perhaps even the world itself.

The Russians were a Godless people, it was only all too clear, and Mrs Hirsh had read and followed the story of how their leaders had destroyed all the Churches, but even so she did not hold it against them. They were even worse than the Catholics and Papists, for whom she had no use whatsoever, but she did not hate them. The Russians were not responsible and were not their own masters. They had been sent as a visitation of God, a scourge to the world, because of its Godlessness, and so they could not be hated for what they did.

The only bright spot of light in the paper at all was the campaign for President. As the campaign got more and more under way, it was becoming increasingly clear that President Truman could never be re-elected and that Governor Dewey was going to beat him. Everything pointed that way, even his own party was not really behind him, and Mrs Hirsh was glad. What we needed was a really humble, God-fearing man in the White House, who would lead us out of the wastes of desolation and back upon the path of God's righteousness. And President Truman was obviously not that man. And after all, he was only Mr Roosevelt's Vice President anyway. Maybe Governor Dewey would be that kind of a man. Who would lead us back to God.

But she did not really think this would happen, she thought with a painfully gloomy happiness. Everything had already gone too far. The country was too far sunk in sin and sloth to ever elect a truly righteous and God-fearing man, and it would get what it deserved, and that, she thought vindictively, was as it should be. Only a few, only a very few, were saved.

Before she had completely finished the paper, the telephone rang in the front room and she went to answer it. It was Mrs Millar, another lady who was also a member of The Church of Christ, Saved, and often attended with her. But Mrs Hirsh did not think that Mrs Millar was really saved, not truly saved. But then, not many was, and she enjoyed her telephone conversations with her. Mrs Millar had been visiting down in Lawrenceville at her youngest son's where her eldest granddaughter was getting married, and she was full of news about the wedding. The girl had made a lovely bride, Mrs Millar said, just simply a lovely bride. And the boy seemed to love her very much. But she really did not think he appreciated what a wonderful bride Marjorie was. Mrs Hirsh agreed with her that this was probably true, and before the conversation ended they had both wound up feeling almost tearful that so few men appreciated the sterling wives they got or realized what those wives sacrificed for them and agreed to meet next Sunday and go to church together. They talked about all the hard times and harsh experiences that were ahead for Marjorie, agreeing it was a good thing the child didnt know what was ahead for her.

After she had hung up, Mrs Hirsh sat down and thought for a while about what they had talked about, her lashes damp. It was all of it only too true. She felt sorry for Marjorie. And yet it was life. That was the way men were. Victor (her mind froze stiffly:) Victor had treated her the same way.

Sitting there by the phone, which faced the front door, her eyes had come to rest on the framed painting that hung beside it, and finally it impinged itself upon her consciousness. It was an autumn scene along a country road. Franklin and Agnes had given it to her once for Christmas. It made her think of her daughter in law. It seemed that in this world, Mrs Hirsh thought vindictively, it was always the good men who got the poorest wives, while the really bad men like (her mind froze stiffly:) Victor always got the good wives. It seemed to be almost God's Will in a way; to cause us suffering. Mrs Hirsh was well aware that her daughter in law Agnes did not like her. She never invited her to her house to any of those parties she was always having. She almost never came to visit her, except once in a great while when she came with Franklin because he obviously made her. She never bought her anything or gave her any presents. But Mrs Hirsh was willing, and prepared, to accept all this and she prayed for Agnes just the same. But that Franklin should be saddled with such a wife when he had never done nothing to deserve it seemed to her at times almost too much of a burden for her to bear. It was Agnes's influence, she knew, which had got Franklin to leave The Church of Christ, Saved, and to join the Methodist. And it was Agnes who kept getting him to try and get her his mother to leave The Church of Christ, Saved, and go with them to the Methodist.

Mrs Hirsh did not have anything especially against the Methodists. It was a good enough church. At least it helped some in the fight against Papism and the Pope. But it did not take God very seriously, and was mostly a social church, where all of the snobs who were not Episcopalian went instead. Which of course was why Agnes wanted them to go there. Next thing, Agnes would be wanting them all to be Episcopalian, she thought vindictively. Once Franklin made enough money. And became important enough. As he was sure to do.

But The Church of Christ, Saved, was not that kind of a church. The Church of Christ, Saved, was a real church. It did not care for money or snobbery. It cared only for God and Christ, Savior, as it should do. Even (her mind froze stiffly:) even Victor had used to admit that. When he used to blaspheme God and His religion.

Her eyes still tendering her the impression of the picture which was still in front of them, Mrs Hirsh sighed heavily several times and coughed and cleared her throat rumblingly, placidly enjoying the moving whistle of air through her nasal passages and the vibration of her throat. It was sad that of all her sons Franklin should be the one to get that kind of a wife. It would have to be Franklin. Edward in Cleveland and Darrell in New York City and George in St Louis all had fine wives apparently. She had never met them because they had never been able to get back out home with their wives. But she was sure they were all fine girls. They looked fine in their pictures. They did not write her often because, as they said, they were all too busy making a living and raising their children and the boys were working. But when they did write they were always nice letters and every year at Christmas they always remembered to send her beautiful cards. And she herself always wrote them promptly every two weeks or so all the news from back home because she knew they would want to keep up with it. But poor Franklin.

Again, Mrs Hirsh sighed heavily several times, enjoying the movement of air through her nose and the muscular expansion of her chest. She had always had good lungs.

Of them all only David wasnt married. She wished he would find himself a nice woman, one who would not hate her mother in law she thought vindictively, and settle down with her. She would like to see him happily married before she passed on. And he was old enough now to stop being bitter about life and acting like an unresponsible child. Franklin was right about that, even if he was a little too hard on David.

With an effort, Mrs Hirsh took her eyes in hand and moved them away from the picture which called up such unpleasant thoughts and let them swing on around her living room. They stopped on her piano. It was an upright piano and stood against the end wall between the windows. Franklin had given it to her several years ago although she never played any more since she had given up being pianist at the church, but on it were all the mementos of her life. There were pictures of all five of her sons and their families—except David of course, who was in the uniform of his country. There, also, was the kewpie doll Franklin had brought her home from the carnival and had bought for her with his own money, once when he was eight. There, too, was the horseback statue of George Washington that David had painted in class when he was in the third grade. There, also, was her framed, colored picture of the Lord Jesus and His Mother that she had had ever since the early days in the old house before (her mind froze stiffly:) before Victor had deserted them. There was the old tintype picture of her parents, so stern looking and strong looking in their old fashioned clothes, there was a picture too of her brother Tom who had worked for the railroad in Chicago and become so successful and who had stood by her in her hour of need and sent her some money after (her mind froze again stiffly:) Victor had deserted them. There, too, was a smaller snapshot size picture of her daughter Francine.

There was no picture of her other brother, Dennis, who had died in an asylum taking the Keeley Cure. And the reason the picture of her daughter Francine was smaller than the others was because when Francine had run away and left them in their hour of trouble after (her mind froze:) Victor had deserted them, to teach school in Los Angeles, she had sworn before God that she would never have her daughter's picture in her house again and had taken all her high school pictures down. But then, during the war, when David had been overseas and Francine had come back home to visit them, Franklin had asked her to let bygones be bygones and to put up a picture of Francine so as not to hurt her feelings when she came, and she had relented, because it was Franklin, but she had purposely chosen a smaller picture, so that Francine would know she had not forgiven her completely. All the other pictures of Francine she had sent her over the years were stacked away on the shelf in the bedroom closet.

Sitting there and looking at the mementos and treasures of her life, Mrs Hirsh's eyes grew misty again and her lashes damp. There were not many who could point to such a honorable life, and she was humbly, before the Lord, proud of it. She had raised all six of her children to be decent God-fearing Christian citizens, and she had never forsaken God like (her mind froze stiffly:) Victor had done. She had never told a lie in her life, and she had never blasphemed, and she had never been unvirtuous. And when she passed on, she would leave the world a better place than when she found it. Six children. And who could tell? Perhaps someday, through her children and all that she had taught them and their children's children, as they spread out, carrying on the blood, her blood, the whole world might become a better place to live in, and nearer to our God.

Mrs Hirsh wiped her eyes with her fingers and sighed heavily, enjoying the passage of air through her nose and throat as she restricted them. Yes, it might very easily be. Except for (her mind froze stiffly:) Victor's blood that was in them, too. With one hand she pushed back her hair where it had come loose from the pins with which shed caught it back when she got up because she didnt feel like putting it up. She had never seen such beautful long white hair on an elderly lady, as that which grew upon herself. Though of course she would never admit that to a soul, she thought bashfully, and then turned to look at the electric clock Franklin had given her on the little desk which he had also given her, much earlier, and saw that it was going on eleven, while remembering that she had a beauty appointment day after tomorrow. My, how the time did fly. If it was eleven, that meant that the mail would probably be in.

Wiping her eyes again with her fingers and breathing heavily two or three times through her nose, Mrs Hirsh got a tissue out of the pocket of her wrapper and blew her nose and then walked down the flight of stairs from the second floor to the first floor entry where the pretty brass mailboxes were and got her mail and her copy of Lifemagazine which Franklin had subscribed to for her and which she knew would be in the box today. Then she went back up, and turned the big radio in the livingroom which Franklin had got her to WGN for the eleven o'clock dramatic life story, and for the next hour and a half she listened to the radio and slowly turned the pages of Lifemagazine looking at the pictures and reading the captions under them.

When she finished the magazine it was almost twelve thirty and, her mouth watering with hunger, she went out to the kitchen to get her lunch. The hominy was already done, and to go with it she got two pork chops out of the big beautiful new refrigerator Franklin had bought for her last year and fried them. After they were done she made a little gravy—there was nothing in the world made as good a gravy as pork; she just couldnt waste it—and poured it over her hominy and the chops. The kitchen radio was on as she ate but, entranced by the taste and feel of the food in her mouth, she did not even hear it. For supper she was going to have mashed potatoes and beefsteak and gravy, and if she felt up to it maybe she would make a pie. She would roll the beefsteak in flour, countrystyle, before she fried it, and she would cook some mustard greens. Enjoying her meal, she thought about supper hungrily. Maybe she would open up a can of peaches for some fruit, to go with all that other.

After lunch, she took a nap.

When the doorbell rang downstairs that evening, Mrs Hirsh had just finished talking to Mrs Ethel Weller on the telephone. She had not made the pie. She had received two phone calls from lady friends in The Church of Christ, Saved, and had made one call herself and listened to one radio program, and by then it was close to suppertime and too late to make the pie. My, how the time did seem to fly!

She could not imagine who would be calling on her. Not at this hour. Franklin always came around this hour, but he most usually came on Mondays. It must be Franklin though, she decided. It couldnt be any of the ladies from the church. Not at this hour. They most generally came in the morning, or else right after lunch. Like she herself when she visited. So it must be Franklin. If it was, she would have some real news for him. The phone call from Mrs Weller who was another member of The Church of Christ, Saved, had been about Doris Fredric the banker's daughter and the Dillert boy, the gambler who had become such a friend of David's. Doris Fredric, who went to the Episcopalian Church—and also taught English in the high school!—was having a hot and heavy love affair with the Dillert boy, who did not go to any church, but whose mother was a member of The Church of Christ, Saved, ever since she came up north from Alabama. Mrs Weller had never mentioned David, and Mrs Hirsh had not either although she knew that that was why Ethel Weller called her. Mrs Weller would not say exactly where she got her information but she said it was all over town. And that Dillert boy's poor wife, living down there by herself in the country. When she mentioned the house, which she said the Dillert boy had taken so he could meet with Doris Fredric, Mrs Weller again did not mention David, but said that Doris Fredric had been seen brazenly entering and leaving the house in broad daylight. Mrs Weller could not keep her pleasure out of her voice, but Mrs Hirsh did not mind because she was already thinking what a piece of news it would be to tell Franklin the next time he came, and now here he was!

But when she went to the voicebox on the wall by the door, and talked down below and found out who it was, she was so flustered and excited she didnt hardly know which way to turn.

"Why, David!" she said, into the voicebox. "Well now you just come right on in. Ill push the button. You just open the door. Come right on up. Its number two, second floor. The door'll be unlocked. You come right on in and make yourself at home. I want to fix up a little."

She hurried back into the bedroom, taking off her wrapper as she went and wishing now shed made the pie. She had been meaning to get dressed and put her hair up properly all day long, but there just never was enough time, and she wouldnt have enough time to get herself fixed up properly for him. In all, it took her fifteen minutes to get into her underwear and corselet and slip and dress and to put her hair up into its bun and make it look at least half way decent, and as she worked she smiled at what a piece of news she would have for Franklin and reminded herself that she must not mention it to David. Then, smoothing the print silk dress down over her hips and putting on just a little touch of lipstick, she came out through the little kitchen into the living room to see him there, sitting on the piano bench and holding a package on his knee.

"Well, thats no comfortable place to sit!" she protested with dismay.

But he got up when he saw her, and stood, awkwardly holding his package, and Mrs Hirsh stopped and stood looking at her son, her youngest son, and seeing him for the first time in nineteen years. Her lashes grew damp.

"Well, David!" she said, and then moved toward him. "Come and kiss mother."

He walked toward her, looking so awkward—he always was a shy one—and then bent over to kiss her on the cheek.

"Well! Is that any way to kiss your mother when you havent seen her for almost twenty years?" she said playfully, and shut her eyes and puckered up her mouth and turned her face up to him and he pecked her on the mouth while she put her arms around him. He always had been such an awkward, shy one.

"H'lo, mom," he said.

"My, my! I got lipstick on you, David!" she said bashfully. "Well! Let me look at you," she said, and held him off at arm's length. "My! Youve put on a lot of weight since those last pictures we had from you in Europe."

"Ive been eatin good since I got out of the Army," he said.

"Well! You surely have! Id say!" she said. "Whats that youve got there in your hand, David?" she added bashfully.

He raised his hand and looked at it as if hed forgotten he was holding it and then his face changed, looked less awkward, she couldnt say exactly what, but it didnt look awkward any more. "I brought you a present," he said.

"You did! A present!" she said. "For me!"

"Here," he said.

Mrs Hirsh opened it sitting in her chair by the roundtop table. It was a beautiful big pillow, maybe twenty four inches across, all gold and green and purple. On its silky cover was a big picture that covered nearly all of it, of a tall palm tree looking out over an ocean dyed purple into which a prickly-rayed golden sun was setting, and across the top circling around the sun rays in fine curly golden letters was the one word FLORIDA. Mrs Hirsh laid it in her lap and smoothed its silky cover with her hands and with misty eyes and damp lashes looked up at her youngest son, who was staring at her pillow fascinatedly.

"My!" she said. "My, my! Its scrumptious, David! Just simply scrumptious!"

"I got it for you in Florida," he said in a funny strange voice.

"You did! In Florida! Well, think of that!" she said bashfully. "And to think, you wanted to bring your old mother a present, when you came to visit her. Thats what makes me feel so good. Even more than this scrumptious present, son," she told him, her lashes growing damper. She clutched her pillow acquisitively.

"Yes," he said in that same funny odd voice, and Mrs Hirsh could tell he wanted to cry, too. She wiped her eyes with her fingers and blew her nose on a tissue. She was not going to give way to it. She was strong, too. Just as strong as he was.

"Well, I kind of thought you might like it," he said, staring at her pillow.

"I always like anything one of my children gives me," Mrs Hirsh said. "I know what Ill do with it," she said brightly, "Ill put it right here on the davenport, where it'll show," and got up and went over and placed it prominently in the corner of the divan and plumped it up. "There. Now hows that? Isnt that purty?

"Ill tell you," she said bashfully, and blinked her eyes at him, "Ill tell you. Im goin to be the envy of every lady from the church when they see it, you can just bet on that. When they see what my youngest son brought me from Florida."

Suddenly, he grinned—the first time really he had smiled since hed been here, really—and suddenly he made her think of (her mind froze stiffly:) Victor. Not as he was now, or as he was back then when (her mind held, stiff-frozen:) when he deserted all of them; but as he once had been, back in the very early days, when he had first married her, and promised to keep and care for her forever. He was heavier of course, she thought, than (and her mind froze:) Victor had been, back in the old days, but not too awful much really. She discovered that she was staring at David with her jaw set and that he was watching her closely, and she blinked her eyes at him several times and smiled.

"Youre goin to stay and eat supper with me, arent you?" she asked him bashfully, and once again his face took on that sort of embarrassed look.

"Im afraid not, mom," he said. "Im afraid I cant."

"Im havin mashed potatoes and beefsteak and gravy," she smiled coyly, to trap him. "Like I use to make when you were little."

"Im afraid I just cant, mom," he said in that awkward voice. "Ive got some business downtown Ive got to attend to."

This was her chance to ask him about his business, and speak to him about all that gambling with the Dillert boy, like Franklin wanted her to, and that he was always running around with that Franklin didnt like. But something about him stopped her and made her refrain. She did not know exactly what. Something about the way he looked, about his eyes, that made her stop, in spite of the fact that he still looked awkward. He had changed so much in the nearly twenty years since she had seen him. He had even changed from the last pictures she had seen. She just did not feel free to mention it to him.

It was the same way later on, when just before he left, she wanted to ask him to kneel down and pray with her. Franklin, although he wouldnt kneel and always just stood with his head bowed while she said the words, nevertheless always prayed with her, whenever he was here, before he left. Franklin never *said* he wouldnt kneel, he just made her feel not free to ask him to. But she did not feel free to ask any of it, of David. It was not that she thought anything unpleasant would happen, or that she was frightened of it, or anything. It was just—

He had stayed to supper, of course. She had been pretty sure he would. After hed first refused theyd sat around and talked—about the family, and about old times, and about when he was little, and all the good times the family used to have. And she had kept insisting that he stay and eat and finally he had agreed to. So she had taken him out in the kitchen with her and made him coffee and had him sit and talk to her while she got the meal. In a way it was almost like having the family back, like (her mind froze stiffly:) Victor almost. Except that of course it wasnt Victor or anything like Victor. Not really. Not (her mind froze coldly:) Victor. But it was like the family, and she enjoyed every little minute of it.

"I was plannin to make a pie today," she told him several times, "all day. But I never got the time. And anyway," she smiled, her lashes growing damp, "there wouldnt be nobody here but me to eat none of it. If youd of only let me know you were comin, Id of gone ahead and made it."

But perhaps it was just as well she hadnt, she thought vindictively after he was gone. Because he hardly ate anything, just picked a little at his plate. She had thought he seemed hungry, when she was cooking it. He must have already eaten his supper earlier, before he came, which was to say the very least thoughtless of him.

He would not pray with her, had indeed made it impossible for her to even ask, but after he was gone she knelt by herself and prayed for him anyway, alone. Because he had a closed mind to God was no need that she should have one toward him.

And after that, even though it was late and almost eight o'clock, she had called up Mrs Millar who had been so superior about her wedding— her *granddaughter's* wedding—and told her all about the visit and described in detail for her the beautiful pillow clear from Florida. And then she had gone to undress to go to bed. But before she undressed she stood for several moments in the print silk dress Franklin had bought for her not long ago, and looked at herself placidly in the bedroom mirror. When he had kissed her, she had gotten a tiny little of her lipstick— very very little, because she never wore more than just a little—on his mouth, and he had wiped it off and they had both laughed about it.

And unaccountably, she thought of poor Marjorie, Mrs Millar's granddaughter, and her marriage and what was ahead and in store for her. After seventeen years! she thought, after seventeen years of married life! When she had done everything she could for him, had borne his children, had made his home for him, and shared his skimpy life. Her mind froze stiffly, and closed down ice-hard. And he had seen fit to run off with another man's wife, who was a lewd woman, and leave them all, after seventeen years, his own flesh and blood and children. Left them in the lurch. And not only that, had then—when the woman threw him over—had the gall to come back and hang around town, without even so much as an apology or a single spoken word, hoping and expecting her to take him back. Oh, she knew what he wanted. Even today. Livin down there with that woman who ran that pension home. But hed come runnin back to her in a minute, if she would only say the word and let him, and move right in with her again. She knew he would. It was easy enough to see what he wanted, even though he never said a word.

But she was not just about to do it, Mrs Hirsh thought frozenly. She had never condoned his kind of sinfulness, or any other kind of sinfulness, in her life. She had not even spoken to him for over thirty years now. And she was not just about to start in to now. The Good Lord Himself alone knew what might have happened to all of them; David had been little more than a baby, and Franklin and Francine still in high school; if Franklin hadnt taken over for her and become the head of the house. She had thought when she had married him that she could save him. She had meant to reform him and make a good man of him. There had been so much good in him once. And she had wanted, when she went home to God's Heaven, for him to be there with her, together, in love and trust and faith, as it should be, and as God had ordained it. But now it was too late. She couldnt help him now. And she must go to Heaven alone.

She would not have had it that way. If there had ever been anything she could have done about it. But there wasnt. And never had been. Even now, he would not even now give up his sinful life. She knew all about his, (her mind froze stiffly at the next word:) Victor's, running around after that old Jane Staley woman and going out with her. Everyone in town knew about it. A common cleaning woman, she thought frozenly, who worked for his own son. There was nothing that could help him now. He had no more chance of going to Heaven now than a horse or dog or any other common animal. He never would pray; he never would read the Scriptures. The Holy Scriptures were not an ordinary book like the books of today that were written for amusement, They were the Holy Word of God handed down to His children. Jane Staley! she thought, outraged. Jane Staley who had never had any more morals than the lowest kind of a fish!

Well, it was upon his own head, Mrs Hirsh thought sadly and sorrowing for him, and turned away from her mirror and began to undo her clothes. When she had slipped her underwear off from under her nightgown and climbed into her bed, she breathed vigorously and deeply through her nose several times, deep heavy tension-relaxing sighs, drawing the air in and restricting her throat and forcing it out audibly, enjoying the movement of air through her nasal passages and throat and the expansion of her chest and lungs. Outside from the open window the sounds of the summer night impinged themselves upon her senses. There was a good many consolations in living a good, honest, virtuous life, and one of these was that the Good Lord looked after His own and saved you from suffering. Your very faith in Him protected you and lifted you up from the suffering that was the common lot of unredeemed mankind. And she could say in all honesty, she thought happily, that no matter how bad things might have ever been, she had never really suffered.

She had always loved God and tried to do His work. When He had seen fit to send her six tiny babies, she had accepted them cheerfully, and loved them, and cared for them, and taught them, and done everything in her power for them, these six new souls put in her care. And somebody had only to look at them to see, to tell.

Mrs Hirsh rolled over in her bed and shut her eyes. My! it had been a pleasant, fruitful, interesting day, she thought.

CHAPTER 46

WHEN Dave left his mother's he was thinking more than anything else about getting something to eat but first he wanted a drink. In spite of how hungry he was he couldnt eat her cooking; he had the feeling it was like putting pure poison into your system. Whether it was just old age or what had caused it, he didnt know. But she had used to be a good cook. Or at least he had used to think she was. But to have eaten the soggy grease-soaked floured beefsteak, and the mashed potatoes and gravy with pools of grease floating on it, that she had served up and called a meal, would have killed him. Or very nearly so. And he could not see why, if that was the kind of food she ate, it hadnt already killed her. She must have the constitution of a horse for it not to, and that must be where they had all gotten their tremendous physical vitality that all of them had. Except that the Old Man had had it too once, and still did for that matter. And for the first time since the episode of his car and what Frank had done to it he could really sincerely sympathize with Frank, if when he went to visit her every Monday like she said he also had to stay and eat her cooking.

Six little souls, she had said with tears starting in her eyes. My God! he thought. Six little souls! Six little souls God had given to her in His wisdom for her to cherish and take care of and to teach, she said. Dave had been actually horrified and honestly terrorstricken, thinking about it. And so this was the manner in which that ineffable and miraculous quantity we are so proud of and like to call the Human Soul got started in this world! Got started, and got taken care of, and got trained. A male like his Old Man and a female like his Old Lady met, competed, and mated. Each nursing a secret hunger and a secret vanity that the other was hardly even aware of. And then there were eight. (She had always been a beauty, everybody always said she had been a beauty, he had been lucky to catch her.) It was terrifying. It might be all right for dogs, but it was hardly proper for that ineffable and miraculous entity we call the Human Soul. Maybe the Chinese peasantry were better off after all; they were still animals and they didnt know any better. Didnt know the difference. My God! Vaguely but powerfully frightened, Dave ran on down the second floor stairs of the Wernz Arms as if something was after him.

His car, his little old Plymouth, was parked out in front and he went out through the entry and down the tall steps and walked across the sidewalk and the parking and around and got into it. Under the trees along the street in the first dark of the summer evening children played a game of flag-raid and people sat on their porches and down at the end of the block the overhead streetlight shot a cone of fuzzy light down on the street intersection. It was so much like his childhood, so little changed, after the passing of twenty five years, that for a moment he sat and stared at the scene a little shocked, mingled emotions rising in him, and wondering suddenly if a hypothetical Roman of the time of Tiberius could have felt this way about his own childhood under the early Augustus, could have found it so little changed. Perhaps if he had lived in a little country village. But still it just did not seem right. It should have changed more. He started the little Plymouth and headed home, where there was gin and vermouth to make himself a good stiff Martini, and some hamburger in the refrigerator he could fry.

He did not feel badly about taking the Florida pillow to his mother, or about lying to her about it. Moving along the streets in the Plymouth he grinned to himself a little sheepishly. Hell, it had been the only bright spot of the visit. And it had just been too good to resist, when he had seen them in Terre Haute there on a back counter in that department store while he was in there looking for something else. There were a lot of things you could tell yourself about it, really. You could say you did it for a joke. And you could say you were ashamed about it. You could even say you did it for her own good, because you knew it would make her happy and what she didnt know wouldnt hurt her. All of them would be partly the truth, but none of them would be the whole truth. The truth was, he didnt do it for a joke, and he wasnt ashamed of it, and he hadnt done it for her own good. He had done it really as a sort of cold-blooded experiment, just to see if he could actually get by with it and to see if she was really actually that bad, and he had enjoyed every minute of it, with a kind of unpleasantly painful enjoyment that she could actually be—and was—that bad, and that he was actually doing it. He wondered what Frank would think about it when he saw it there next Monday. Hell, he would probably believe the story too.

Still half-chuckling to himself, he pulled the Plymouth up into the double-pathed crushed rock driveway under the single big old oak tree in the yard. Inside, the house was immaculately clean and shining. Old Janie had only just been here yesterday and cleaned it up and they had not yet had time to dirty it again. She was a real pistol, he thought switching on the kitchen lights and went to the refrigerator and got out the big cardboard meat scoop of hamburger and made himself a big patty of it on the countertop. Or rather, two big patties pressed out thin and inbetween which he diced up half an onion—a cooking trick Gwen had shown him—and then molded the two patties into one with the onion in the middle. After he put it on to cook in the skillet—with very little butter, just enough to grease it—he got the things out and made himself that Martini.

They had taken to using the kitchen a great deal more now in the month Jane had been here. Partly that was due to old Janie who cleaned it up spick and span for them once a week and did up all the dishes that for the last day or two before she came they began to let go for her to do. But partly and even moreso, the increased use of the kitchen was due to 'Bama's new girlfriend Doris Fredric who of course could not go out and eat with them in public, at least not here in town anyway.

Old Janie, he thought affectionately and sat down with the drink at the kitchen table that was still almost crumbless and shining clean from her last visit yesterday. Ever since he was a kid she had been Frank and Agnes's cleaning woman when he lived with them, and now here he was back here grown up—grown up? middle-aged almost!—and she was his cleaning woman too. Janie was going to be one of his main characters when he did his novel on Parkman. It seemed to him actually and factually that she had not changed an iota since those days back then when he was a kid and living with Frank and Agnes, and that was at least twenty five years ago; but he knew that this was only a mental illusion of his own. He transposed his mental picture he had of her now back into the mental picture he had of then in which he was a child. How old was she? at least sixty. That would have made her thirty five back then, younger than he was now! Very strange.

Life was such an intriguing, fascinating, poignant, entrancing thing;

you felt you almost could never get enough of it, of being it and observing it, he thought happily. Life, I cannot get thee close enough, he thought paraphrasing the Millay. He had been like this for a month now, without a single letdown or fear to scare him into depression, and if he could have changed any of the circumstances of his life, he wouldnt—except for one, just one, just one single thing, he thought thinking of Gwen. But maybe he wouldnt even have changed that one. What the hell? he was happy as he was, wasnt he?

But then, of course, he would never know until he had changed it whether he ought to change it or not would he?

Janie, in the month she had worked for them, seemed to have lost some of that enormous weight of hers, and it made her look much healthier. She looked, in fact, better than he could ever remember having seen her look except for the deep dark-circles under her eyes which seemed to give her a sort of haunted darkeyed half-frightened look and was probably due to too much drinking and her kidneys she was always bitching about. Or too much work. But God! the vitality she had! When he was through working for the day which was usually around four he would be about through with the house and he would sit and drink a bottle of beer or two with her in the kitchen and, if she felt in the mood, listen to all the latest scoop she had picked up on her rounds in the last week and then he would drive her, either out to Smitty's Bar or else home to the little house on Roosevelt. Usually to Smitty's. When she came early in the morning John Barclay would bring her on his way to work, and when he and 'Bama got up around eleven she would always have his little writing room cleaned and the kitchen and most of the downstairs, and while he worked she would do the bedrooms upstairs, always being very quiet so as not to bother him.

She knew, it seemed, just about everything about everybody. She knew all about Wally and Dawn, which tickled her, and she knew all about 'Bama and Doris Fredric apparently, and which apparently did not tickle her, but she was always very careful not to say anything critical. She was, in fact, a living gold mine of material and at least half of this was due not so much to *what* she knew as to her judgment and her unique viewpoint of it. When he told her this she just laughed that great gravelly bosomshaking laugh of hers below the deep-circled haunted looking eyes and said that he might as well use it then because she doubted if she would ever have time before she died to write her life story and anyway if she did the sons of bitches would surely send her to jail, if they didn't take all her bankroll on libel suits.

Nevertheless it had apparently flattered her and after that she went out of her way to tell him things—"I got something for your book," she would say—about what went on in town. It was amazing what she knew about the private lives and loves of the citizenry of Parkman extending generations back. In forty years or so of cleaning other people's houses it had apparently become a sort of private hobby, an avocation, of hers.

When she had first come to work for them, the very first day, —after they had both gone out and looked her up at Smitty's and bought her a beer and talked to her about it, whereupon she had said immediately and unequivocally that she would love to work for them— Dave had caught her in the kitchen as she was going through and sat down and had a cup of coffee with her and had laughingly in the course of the conversation said that she had better watch out and not let Frank know she was working for him—for them, him and 'Bama—or she was liable to lose her job with Frank and Agnes.

He had only meant it as a joke, but old Janie's eyes had flashed dangerously, behind her deep dark-circles.

"If that son of a bitch, or any other son of a bitch, wants to fire me, honey," she boomed in her tremendous voice, "all they got to do is say the word. Theyll ony have to say it onct. And that goes for you too."

"Hey! Hey!" Dave said. "I was only jokin, just kidding you."

"I know you was, honey," Jane said soothingly and patted him ponderously on the hand. "I didnt mean to scare you. But theres plenty other jobs in this world. And any time anybody dont like my work, or what I charge, or dont like whoever else I work for or how I spend my own time, all they got to do is say so. They can get themselves somebody else five minutes later; and Ill even help them to find somebody. And that goes for your damned brother, honey, and you too," she said forcefully, and looked at him a little nervously as if fearing he might misunderstand and take it wrong, might take it as an insult to him rather than as the pride of her own personal code.

"Im right with you," Dave said grinning. "Thems my principles too. What do you think Im gamblin for a livin for, instead of workin in that damn taxistand of Frank's?"

"Honey," Jane bawled with a raucous laugh, "if I had the pardner you got, Id be tempted to turn to gamblin my own self. Youve got the best." Then her face sobered and she stared at him with her haunted looking dark-circled eyes. "But you dont need to worry none about that damn brother of yours. That damn brother of yours has got too damn many skeletons in his own damn closet to ever start tellin me about mine, the little son of a bitch," she said ominously and yet affectionately.

It was plain to Dave, in spite of her constant castigation of him, that Janie had a strong—if contemptuous—affection for Frank. He felt somewhat the same himself.

Jane seemed to debate for a moment, as if not sure whether it was ethical or not, then apparently decided that it was and commenced to tell him what she thought about Frank and Agnes. It looked like to her, she said, that Frank and Agnes were just about to get engaged in a hot

and heavy love affair again. Anyway the signs all seemed to point that
way.

"Youre kidding!" Dave said incredulously. "Theyve hated each other's
guts for years!"

"No I aint kidding," Jane said, "I dont kid about such things as that.
Heres the way I got it figured. Frank had this mistress, see, name of
Geneve Lowe. Her husband works for Frank. They was goin out before
you even come here. Back when Al Lowe was overseas in the war.
Everybody in town knew it. Then Agnes gets on her horse and takes
off and breaks it all up, in that way that only she knows how to do so
well, just about the time you came. After that theyd hardly speak to each
other and that went on for sevral months. Then suddenly Frank starts
bein nicer to her, nicer and nicer. Now how would you figure it?"

Dave shrugged. "He just got over bein mad, finally."

"No sir. Then you dont know Frank very good," Jane said. "No sir,"
she said stoutly. "Hes got another mistress. Thats what. And Agnes aint
found out about it. Thats the way I figure it. The result is, hes put one
over on Agnes and so he aint mad at her no more. And she aint mad at
him because she dont know about the new mistress. As long as he can
keep his new mistress without her findin out about it, they can be real
redhot lovers again."

Dave was astounded. He was not only astounded, he was also in some
obscure way deeply shocked. Even though it was all so reasonably logical.
But it didnt seem to bother Janie any. Instinctively, he felt a need to
keep her from finding out that she had shocked him; but he might as
well have whistled at the moon. "Well, shell find out about it sooner or
later, wont she?" he asked.

"Shocks you, dont it?" Jane said with a grin. "Well, thats life, honey.
Thats the way people are, and you might as well get used to it. Sure,
shell find out about it. At least she always has before."

Dave felt embarrassed because he had been shocked. And because
Janie had seen it. "Well," he said nonchalantly, trying to carry it off,
"whos the mistress?"

Janie looked at him with her deep dark-circled eyes and thoughtfully
rubbed her chin where there was a mole from which three black hairs
grew. "Well, I dont know," she said, looking him straight in the eyes.
"I aint been able to pick up nothing on it. It must be somebody from
out of town is all I can figure. Maybe some woman up in Springfield
where hes been goin so much lately," she said, and looked at him
hauntedly with those deeply circled eyes that were as unreadable as
two wells.

When she had first told him about it the first person that popped into
his mind had been her own granddaughter, Edith Barclay, probably
because he had once had a yen for her himself—but hell, Edith was only

twenty four or five; Frank was twenty years older than she was. And now he looked at Janie. It might be Edith, and she might know it. And then again it might not be, and even if it was she might not know it. Either way, Dave did not want to know, suddenly did not want to become involved in it, any of it. "Yeah, thats probably what it is," he said.

"Well, its the ony thing I can figure," Jane said, looking at him.

"Otherwise, somebodyd be sure to know about it."

"Yas. Youd think so, wouldnt you?" she said. Then she suddenly grinned. "But Ill be willin to bet you five bucks that Frank and Agnes are goin to be redhot lovers again before long, or Ive missed all the signs."

"I wouldnt bet with you on your own game, Janie," he grinned.

She had laughed suddenly, from behind those haunted looking deeply circled eyes. "That goddam 'Bama's taught you too goddam much," she said. "Well, I got to get back to work, or you guys liable to fire my big ass. And on my first day, too." And he had watched her trundle away out of the kitchen into the dining room, where she had been working. Losing part of that enormous weight had probably been good for her and helped her, as well as making her look better. Later, he had thought about what she had said about Frank and Agnes often, and laughed about it. It was really very funny, in a way, once you got over being shocked at the idea. The two-faced sanctimonious little bastard.

Sitting in the kitchen alone, savoring his drink and sniffing hungrily the smell of his frying hamburger and onions, Dave could not suppress a smile of affection. When she had come that first time, that first day, Jane had very carefully and professionally made a list of all the things she needed and that they would have to get for her, the various tools and equipment—different kinds of mops, brooms, polishes, waxes, glass cleaner, soaps, and that evening when 'Bama who had taken her home that time drove her, he had—rather helplessly—given her the money and sent her in to shop for them herself. She had come back out lugging a double armload of stuff, mop and broom and brush handles sticking out in all directions, and deposited them in the car and the next week had taken them out of the broom closet where they had stuffed them and rearranged them all to her satisfaction in the broom closet and the cabinet above it and declared that she was now ready to go to work in earnest. Every week she made it a point to clean one room thoroughly and completely. That way, she said, it never got too far ahead of you, and you didnt need no heavy big spring cleaning every year that way.

She had made a tremendous change in their house. With her coming there one day a week to clean, the house did not look the same and did not feel the same, and in fact it did not even seem to be the same house at all and its whole atmosphere was different. (But of course, he thought, a great deal of that feeling was probably due to his own change of mood in the past month, too.) She had, forcefully and unequivocally, given it to them as her considered opinion that they had done a great deal with this house in their redecorating, especially in painting that damned bastard oak spoolwork a contrasting color. She had, it seemed, worked here once before for someone else, back before those damn know-nothing Albersons whom she would not work for though they had asked her to stay on had bought it. Life was too damned short, she told Dave, to work for people who were so damned dumb and ignorant that they had no human feelings at all and bored you. "At least your damned brother and his wife got enough human feelings and emotions to fight a little," she said, "plenty of human feelings. Something's always happenin."

Jane herself, it appeared—from what Dave could gather from the gang at Smitty's, anyway—had almost entirely stopped her running around lately. He had never mentioned the Old Man to her; nor had she to him. She still held her court at the front corner booth at Smitty's, and all the old duffers still came sniffing around. He had seen the Old Man there once or twice and had slipped him a five or ten. But apparently she wasnt going out with any of them now, for some reason nobody understood. The Old Man included. "Christ! we gonna start havin a crime wave of octogenarian sex crimes in this town," Dewey had grinned, "if old Janie dont quit bein tempermental. You suppose shes turnin into a moralist on us?" Dewey had been picking up a lot of new words like octogenarian and moralist and even temperamental, since he and Hubie had been hanging out with Wally out here at the house. It was an interesting development.

Dave got up from the table, still grinning to himself over both Janie and Dewey, and slid his hamburger off onto a plate with a spatula and then mixed himself another martini and got two pieces of fresh white bread out of the bread drawer and sat down to eat thinking briefly, but only for a moment, of his mother and her cooking. The hamburger-and-onion steak was delicious.

Of course, it wasnt only the coming of Janie that had changed the house; there was something else too. The second thing was the advent of 'Bama's new girlfriend Doris Fredric onto the premises.

But neither of these things really had half as much to do with it as the change that had happened in himself. For the past month he had been happier than he had ever been in his life. Happier even than he had been during the Miami Beach junket, although he was not getting near as much sex. But somehow he didnt mind. He didnt understand it very clearly, but he nevertheless had to admit it. It appeared to be much simpler than it actually was. And something about it, about the situation, even seemed to actively attract him. He had Gwen, and his love for her, and his association with her—on the one hand; and on the other he had his 'sexual life.' If he got hard up for sex he could always find a piece around someplace, although it was never as nice as the vacationing bachelor girls he had had in Miami, but even that he didnt mind—and if he couldnt get it anyplace else, he could always go and pick up Ginnie Moorehead. Although this last had been happening less and less often.

But all that wasnt what was so strange, or what was puzzling him so. Dave had read somewhere once about the theory that a man should keep his 'Love', his wife, and his sexual satisfaction separate, and not sully the idealism of the first with the second—and had laughed at it at the time. It was such obviously biased, after-the-fact excuse in reasoning. But now something of the same thing seemed to be happening to him, and not only that, was making him happy! He was loving Gwen French—and loving her desperately—and was getting his sexual satisfaction elsewhere—from pigs like Ginnie, and it seemed to be actually good for him! It was making him happy, instead of frustrated, and it seemed to be helping his work. It made you think of Stendhal and those two years in Milan with the Countess Matilda whom he loved but could never make, except that Stendhal had remained celibate all that time—or was supposed to have.

But of course, a lot of his—his own, Dave's—happiness was also due to the fact that he knew for sure now that Gwen really loved him. If she didnt love him, she would never have refused to sleep with him like she had. She would have gone ahead and slept with him, tried him, like she had all those other men without caring if she hurt him. But with him, she couldnt do that.

In some ways it was a lot like that other time, back in May, when he had held off going over to see her after he got back from Florida and was savoring his anticipation. Only this was so much bigger, so much more inclusive. This was a real love affair. And there were times when, and increasingly so, he wished it would stay just like this always, without changing, forever.

When Gwen had first called him up about the book manuscript, which was only a couple of days after he had taken it over to her, he had gone over right away that same evening. Neither of them had mentioned what had happened the time before. Indeed, it might never have even happened, from the way both of them acted. And yet there was no constraint. They had sat down with the manuscript and a sheaf of notes Gwen had made on it, and while Bob sat back in the background by the record player playing records softly and reading, had gone over the whole thing together. They had been very close, warm friends—nay, he thought poetically, they had been lovers; lovers in that private silent language lovers have, that is mostly with the eyes and the expressions of the face, but that is just as valid and as valuable—perhaps more valuable—than the spoken word, at least to the lovers themselves. And yet not a word about love or anything of that sort was said. It had been a wonderful evening. And when he went home to bed celibate (for that night at least), he not only had not minded but had actually enjoyed doing it.

Since then he had been working with her closely, going over two and often three evenings a week for her to read what he had done, and in the little over a month that had passed since that first trip after getting back from Florida he had finished one chapter and part of another. It was hard, slow, boring, head-cracking work—not the kind of wild, quick rushing, excited work he had done when he wrote "The Confederate" in six weeks; but he was enjoying it. It was going to be a long pull.

He would take over what he had done for her to read, driving the by-now-so-familiar five miles through the twilight or after dark with a drink or two inside his belt, and then would amuse himself playing their records or reading their books while she took the never large number of pages off in the corner to go over them carefully, and then they would dissect them carefully and minutely and perhaps have a drink or eat something or talk to Bob or play a game of chess. Only rarely did she have a criticism, and she admitted to him rather happily that she had been pretty worried—though as it had turned out, needlessly—whether or not he would be able to do this kind of work. She had been afraid he would not. "This is fully conscious writing," she smiled, "you have a preconceived effect consciously in mind and are working deliberately toward it. Theres all the difference in the world between this and what I call unconscious writing—where you merely write out of the excess of your own emotions and what youve seen and felt. The unconscious writer doesnt really *know* what hes writing or its significance. As a result —if his emotions are valid—he often writes clear over his own head; but if his emotion isnt valid hes just as liable to stumble and lay an egg as big as a barrel. And he himself cant distinguish between them afterwards. He has no criterion of judgment except his own personal emotions. Thats the way your first two books were written, and "The Confederate" also, except that in "The Confederate" you showed a really firstclass overall organizational sense. But thats not the same as writing consciously." She sighed and ran the tips of her fingers back along her temple. "Wally is still in that stage of unconscious writing," she said perplexedly, in what was a sudden new intimacy with Dave, because she never talked to him about others' writing. "And I dread the stage coming when he will have to grow and change over into conscious writing. Its the worst period a writer can go through. And a lot of them never make it. Because once you become conscious of what you are doing you lose the validity of *innocent* emotion. Its no longer enough to just *feel* something, and then write it. You have to construct. And then you have a tendency to lose all the fresh originality of your emotions, which came out of your innocent unconsciousness of them, because now you know what they are. So most writers never make the change," Gwen said, "they simply avoid it, and live on and on into their old age, trying to imitate their old unconscious writing that they did when they were innocent and unaware—which of course they cant do. The emotion is fake then. God knows what will happen to Wally when he becomes sophisticated and begins to see himself."

Dave had seen Wally over at the house in Israel a couple of times when he had been there, and there had been nothing but the nicest of friendliness between them both times, they had played chess together (Wally always beat him), and had had a friendly drink of Bob's liquor, and yet he could not help but sense a new stiffness between them also, that had not been there until just recently. They were like two strange male dogs bristling, and he could feel it in himself just as much as Wally. It seemed to date from the housewarming party, when Dawn had made her comment about 'competition', and even when Wally came down to the house in Parkman to play pingpong it was still there, although Wally never stopped coming. (In pingpong too Wally, with his strongly intense competitive sense, always beat everybody—or else went away miserable.) Miss Dawnie, Dave thought sourly, Little Miss Dawnie. Hearing Gwen talk about Wally's work had somehow done away with his own competitive drive.

Bob French himself had not read any of the book, and said he did not want to until he could read it in more or less final draft. That way, he said, he could give them both a completely fresh viewpoint. But he had read "The Confederate" and was enthusiastic about it, and had already sent it off with letters from them both to the New Living Literature people. He expected an answer in a month or two, and he expected it in the affirmative. Unless of course something unforeseen should happen. They talked about this, and about all writing in general, and about people—personalities—, and about pretty nearly everything else, while Dave was over there. Twice he had upon invitation stayed over for the entire weekend, writing just the same every day, and doing it on one of their portable typewriters they loaned him in the, as Bob called it, unfinished—but which did not look at all unfinished to him, or even unfurnished—diningroom. He could not have enjoyed himself more. And he did not even mind sleeping two or three rooms away from her down the hall and knowing that she was lying in there so close, alone and undressed and practically within reach.

All this of course was taking a good deal of time away from his gambling junkets with 'Bama. But the tall man only grinned pleasantly, and was—in fact—all for it. After all, that was what theyd first taken the house for, wasnt it? so as to help him out with his writin? That was what they were tryin to do, wasnt it? to get this book done in as good a shape as possible. What the hell was he tryin to talk himself into worryin about, anyway? The thing was to stay with it, do whatever was necessary to get it done like it should be done.

The result was that they were now only spending three or at the most sometimes four evenings a week at poker. But, as 'Bama said, what the hell? They could afford it, couldnt they? On those evenings when he went to Israel 'Bama would sometimes go on out alone and play, though he almost never won as high a percentage in a game as just he alone did, not even counting Dave, when the two of them went together. Their almost phenomenal luck was, apparently, still holding. But more often than not 'Bama did not play on those nights Dave was gone, either. The truth was, 'Bama had a good deal to occupy himself also, because he was spending a lot of time now with Doris Fredric. He still made his more or less regular trips down in the country to the farm every week or two, but the rest of his spare time up in Parkman he spent with Doris.

Dave did not know exactly when all this had started. But it was not until some little time, a week or so, after the housewarming party (which she had not been at) that Doris Fredric had suddenly started showing up at the house at night with 'Bama. And it was obvious from the very first that they were already old friends, and that 'Bama had been going out with her—or at least, running around with her— for some time before they went to Florida. Just how long a time, Dave didnt know. Because 'Bama never talked about her, except for those vague pleasant inanities someone used about another person when they are being careful not to say anything about them.

It was clear that 'Bama was being a gentleman about her, a rare enough circumstance for 'Bama with a woman in its very self. And as to whether he was actually sleeping with her, Dave did not know and could not make up his mind; he had never seen any direct indications of it between them, no gestures and no spoken words that admitted it; but knowing 'Bama, he assumed that he was. And yet there was some quality about the girl that half-convinced you that they were not sleeping together and were in fact only just sort of intrigued and interested in each other, only just 'dating'. And yet she must obviously know he had a wife; everybody did.

Dave had spent a lot of time studying them,—and had had plenty of opportunity to do so. From coming to the house secretly at night with 'Bama (although neither of them ever alluded to or admitted it was secret, or even acted in any way as if it might be secret) it was only a short step for Doris to brazenly start coming by in the daytime— either with or without 'Bama—and in her own car. (She drove a bright yellow Ford convertible.) He used the word 'brazenly' advisedly, not because he himself thought her coming by in the daytime was brazen so much, as the fact that she herself seemed to think it was, and indeed did it for that reason. There was that quality about her—under her sweet, shy, modest virginity which she wore like some second suit of clothing. It was as if she were determinedly intent upon either calling fate down upon her pretty little cherrywood-colored head with her own destruction (which of course, she obviously believed, would be a great tragedy), or else proving that she could (because she was Doris Fredric, Paul Fredric's daughter) do any damned thing she wanted to in this damned town of Parkman and get by with it.

In another woman it might have made Dave admire her. But for some reason—which he could not formulate in words in any other way except to say he felt she was "false"—he had taken a strong dislike to her. And her more or less tempting of fate—or else her desire to be above it, whichever it was—just made him dislike her only that much the more. And Doris, who was obviously no fool, sensed it and disliked him equally, although she was always sweet and polite—and kind—to him and you could not have told she disliked him. And yet you could. Perhaps it was the kindness. It was condescending, almost. —and yet the moment you used that word, it became too strong for whatever it was you were using it for. It seemed to Dave that the longer he lived and saw, the more and more impossible it seemed to become that you—or anyone—could ever even remotely describe the nuances and niceties of the relationships between people. It made him think suddenly of Marcel Proust—whom Dawn had mentioned once when he first came back here, and whom he had not read since his early Hollywood literary days—and he decided to get a copy of *The Remembrance of Things Past* and reread and study him.

Another thing about Doris that made him dislike her was that she was so dumb. While a long *long* way from being a fool, and possessing (he was pretty sure) a great native shrewdness that was nevertheless without the slightest iota of selfconscious awareness, she was so dumb about everything except herself that it was actually irritating. For instance, she was a teacher of English in the high school—in itself a kind of lying pose, since with her money she didnt need to do anything; and yet she knew nothing at all—absolutely nothing—about English literature, or any other kind of literature, except just the barest rote necessities which she taught her classes. This had become apparent the first time she came to the house. 'Bama had—very carefully and laboriously—hauled all of his books up from the farm down in the country, after getting Dewey and Hubie to build and paint them some shelves, and had installed them in the house—(just as he was now in the process of building himself a workbench in the garage so he could work on his car; if yore gonna live in a house you might as well live in it, he said.) 'Bama's books were almost entirely on two subjects: the Civil War, and esoteric metaphysics; and while he openly and volubly did not consider himself an educated man, he had read all of them through at least twice. And in addition, there were all of Dave's books, literary ones, which he had been collecting ever since they had first gone to Florida and had kept on collecting after they got back. Doris Fredric had walked along past them in the 'middle living room' as they called it, which was between the dining room and living room and was where most of the books were, trailing her finger lightly along the shelves of book spines, as she inspected the house. "Oh, the Civil War," she said airily. And, "Oh, metaphysics." And, "Oh, *Thomas Wolfe's Letters to His Mother.*" All as if she knew everything about all of these, and had, ever since they were printed. But it turned out, upon questioning, that she knew nothing about any of them. She had never even heard of Nathan Bedford Forrest, and she had not even read one of Wolfe's novels, but none of this bothered her in the least. "Ill have to borrow some of your books and start reading up again," she said with her sweet demure little-girl's smile, and turning her eyes up intimately to 'Bama. But to date she had never borrowed a book, and it did not at present appear that she would ever be likely to.

'Bama himself did not appear to be at all violently in love with her. Indeed, he seemed merely to be amused by her. He would sit, listening to her talk—something she did a great deal of, for a person who gave the impression of being so quiet—a quiet half-humorous expression on his face and his eyes narrowed thoughtfully as he watched her. He himself said little, and said that in a half-sneering half-bantering way, and all of it was almost maliciously sardonic about the various Great American Myths which to Doris were—or at least appeared to be —deeply cherished beliefs. For example: her really deep love for her 'kiddies' (the high school freshmen and sophomores she taught) which she was always talking about. 'Bama would hoot at this derisively and take great delight in saying, "Kiddies? Little monsters, you mean. Little animals. Didnt you ever watch them? And you dont love them. Any more than you love anything else in this goddamned world, except yoreself." Doris would argue with him indignantly, while at the same time being highly flattered.

She would come by the house in the morning now that school was out, around eleven or just at noon, when they were just getting up, and park her yellow Ford convertible out in front on the street with the top down like a sore thumb, and march into the house wearing a long expensive terrycloth robe over a cute little one-piece bathing suit (usually cut like child's rompers) and take 'Bama off to go swimming with her, driving her yellow convertible through the back streets with the top down and 'Bama with that hat sitting beside her. Evidently she wanted people to know, while she herself kept up the appearances of not wanting them to. Dave could not believe that they went swimming. He just could not imagine the tall sallow-skinned 'Bama in a pair of brief trunks with that pendulous hanging belly of his and his horse-like swaybacked walk sitting on a sand beach somewhere at some lake resort around, or getting up and diving into the water and swimming around. More likely, and Dave *could* imagine this, the sardonic gambler would be sitting on a towel in the sand wearing his semiWestern hat to protect him from the sun and one of his Shantung silk boxback countrystyle suits, and his black shoes and conservative drab socks, holding a bottle of Jack Daniels Black Label in one hand and a glass of ice in the other, while all around him Doris and other people in bathing suits played and cavorted as became the happy, healthy, American-animal type of Coca-Cola advertisement. Dave not only could imagine it, he would sit and roar with laughter over it. 'Bama swimming!

This then was the woman—perhaps girl would be better; or even maiden—Dave still didnt know!—who, along with the coming of Jane Staley to keep them clean, had partially helped to change the house. She had brought out a collection of large fluffy expensive towels and distributed them around the bathrooms. She had brought a number of contour sheets for the beds. She had bought them a large expensive table lighter, like those advertised in the women's magazines, and installed it on the cocktail table in the living room. She even kept it filled. She had brought a number of bizarre brightly colored ashtrays and set them around. She had brought out some red and white checkered tablecloths for the kitchen table where they usually ate and some heavy medieval-looking candles which she liked to turn off all the lights and light and eat by the light of. And, perhaps the crowning and consummate gall Dave thought, she had brought out a number of her own books, complete with her own specially made bookplate and all of them third rate romantic historical novels, and with complete aplomb and total unawareness of any difference had placed them on the shelves with 'Bama's *Life of N. B. Forrest* and *Isis Unveiled* by Blavatsky and Dave's editions of Stendhal and Dostoievski and Conrad and Arnold Bennett. She had, in short, moved in and—and yet without ever any sense of encroachment or imposing—taken over.

Everything she brought out was from her 'hope chest', she told them laughingly; except of course the books. In a way it was almost sort of pathetic really, and Dave could see where it was—except for the colossal and unmitigated selfassurance and positiveness she displayed so openly. "Im going to teach you two good taste yet," she would tell them, smiling. And she actually believed it.

Also, she was learning to cook. They were teaching her.

His own selfcooked meal finished, Dave sat on, staring at Doris's red and white checkered tablecloth which Jane had put on fresh clean yesterday and at the two big brown monastery-looking candles, with which she had about turned their kitchen into a damned Italian restaurant. She had in the past month come more and more out in the open about coming out and had become more and more of an habitue, and had also become very friendly—in a sort of Queen Mother, or rather Crown Princess sort of a way—with Wally whom she already knew and with Dewey and Hubie and their girls. She played a good game of pingpong and was able to beat himself and everybody else except Wally who was really good and sometimes 'Bama who played just a fairly good game. She appeared to be an excellent loser. 'Bama had been talking seriously lately about buying a second hand billiard table from some poolroom that was closing up around the county (one almost always was) and setting it up in the basement too, and Doris was delighted and urged him to do it. She had learned to play when a bunch of the ladies had taken over the old billiard room out at the Country Club, and was anxious to try her hand at it again. Her pale blue eyes would light up delightedly like a child's when they talked about it, and she would shake her old-cherrywood-colored curls excitedly. She was really a very pretty girl. Dave didnt know what it was. He guessed he just didnt like her. It wasnt because he was jealous. He had no desire at all to romp her. Not in the present mental state he was existing in, anyway. The only way he could sum it up was that she was "false," was not what she seemed to be. But then which of us was? Still, he felt she was dangerous—although she certainly was not bamboozling 'Bama any, that much was clear. But he still felt she was somehow dangerous. Old Janie felt the same way, too, apparently, though she was careful not to say anything. Christ! if 'Bama thought Ginnie Moorehead was dangerous to him, to Dave—! At least Ginnie didnt impose herself and her personality on all of them all the time. Ginnie was just a big pathetic slob. But 'Bama's new mistress—!

Shaking it all out of his head as idle speculation anyway, and looking irately at the gay checkered tablecloth and big brown cloister-looking candles, he was just getting up to get himself a cup of coffee when he recognized the motor of 'Bama's Packard driving in on the driveway. Pouring the coffee, he listened, and heard behind him through the open screendoor across the summer night air the sounds of two doors slamming, and then the sounds of voices, male and female. That would mean that Doris was with him.

He poured cream in the coffee and took it back to the table and sat down and prepared himself, arranged his mind, to be pleasant. And just then something struck him, a whole new idea picture: Doris Fredric never talked of herself, or even thought of herself, apparently, as a rich girl. In fact, she went to the opposite extreme and was always looking for an opportunity to drag in some allusion—usually completely out of context—to the fact that she had little or no money. And yet in spite of that, all of them who hung out at the house always thought of her as a rich girl, which by Parkman's standards she was, and in fact she did not have to talk of or think of herself as a rich girl, because she always automatically and on a subconscious level acted like one, whether she herself knew it or not. But he suspected that she knew it. Certainly everybody else in Parkman knew that she was one of the wealthiest young people in town, her mother being Tony Wernz's sister and all, and whether she actually had money of her own or not and whether her folks actually gave her much money to spend or not, she still stood to inherit a large part of the Wernz family interests—as well as some farms up around Morris through her father's family the Fredrics who were Amish, old Janie had told him. And Doris must know all this. But of course she could just let herself not consider it, and actually blank her mind out to it.

Anyway, that wasnt the point. The point was she *was* a rich girl and they all of them knew it, and that had given him just now a sudden new insight into 'Bama. For the first time he thought he could see why 'Bama had always been so strangely warm and interested in Wally Dennis: Wally came from one of the older wealthier (or they once were) families of Parkman. And for the first time since he himself had met him Dave thought he could understand now that strange deference 'Bama had used to show him so noticeably, and that warm friendliness when they first met that was all out of proportion to the time theyd known each other: It was because he was Frank Hirsh's brother and Frank Hirsh was a big wheel in Parkman (old family or not) and a man whom just about everybody in town had picked as a comer. The fact that both of them, himself and Wally, were 'writers' only added to the gambler's sense of accomplishment at having them for friends. 'Bama was, it turned out after all, a snob—and not a rebel at all. But then, were not all rebels perhaps only inverted snobs who saw no way of getting the things they wanted and so eschewed them? That was all he himself had been, wasnt it? out in Hollywood?—and even after he came here, at first. And those very things—wealth, family, entrenched social prestige—the very things 'Bama himself did not have and sneered at and punctured with such devastating acumen—those were the very things about Doris that intrigued and fascinated and flattered him. Dave felt sad. And let down. As though he had lost another, one more, ideal. He remembered all the times he had tried to get the tall gambler to go over to the Frenches' big house in Israel. And how 'Bama had always refused, on some pretext or other, but the real reason of course was his feeling of inferiority.

It was a strange new picture of his old friend 'Bama, and Dave had barely time enough to adjust his mind to it, to the idea of it anyway, before the two of them were through the screendoor and in the room, the tiny, pert, but very well rounded Doris with her small auburn head hardly coming up to the tall Southerner's armpit, and the lanky, amused looking, cool eyed 'Bama with his hat on and wearing the gold one of his three country-cut exquisite silk summer suits he had had made in Miami.

"Well," Doris smiled prettily, "the brooding novelist, mulling over some deeply thoughtful sequence of events." Her print summer dress looked cool and cute and very becoming on her and as fresh as if shed only just this moment put it on.

"I was just looking at the candles," he said pleasantly. "Whered you get them, anyway?"

"Oh, those things," Doris said demurely, with a shy smile. "I just picked them up in some cheap store somewhere. Just saw them and happened to like them." Sedately, she walked on in. That seemed to take care of that.

Behind her 'Bama, wearing that look of communing with some private amusement that he always seemed to have around her, winked at Dave tiredly. "Hi, buddy." There was a strong affection in his voice.

Dave, sitting with one elbow on the table, winked back at him, a wink that like his, had nothing to do with Doris one way or the other but was only friendship, and grinned warmly. "Anybody feel like a game of pingpong?" he said pleasantly. Whether 'Bama was a snob of some obscure rebellious kind or not didnt matter. Neither did it matter whether or not he had first cultivated him, Dave, for obscure snobbish reasons of his own. If he was a snob, he was a better kind of snob than any other Dave had ever seen. And too many other things had happened since then, things that were important to a friendship and couldnt be cancelled out by anything.

"Whoo-o-o! not me," Doris said. "Im famished. Simply starved. And right now I badly need a drink," she smiled in a little-girl way and marched sedately on to the cabinet where they kept the bottles and pulled forth a Jack Daniels Black Label and set it up with Dave's Martini fixings. She had been drinking a great deal more lately he thought than when she had first started coming, and there were times when she came by in the morning that her eyes and cheeks would look puffy. "Whats in the refrigerator?" she said.

"Steak and hamburger," Dave said automatically. "And some lettuce, if you want a salad."

"Shall I fix us a steak?" Doris said, smiling archly back over her shoulder at 'Bama. She had already got two glasses out and now moved sedately with her small very straightbacked walk to the refrigerator and got icecubes for them. She poured approximately a double jigger in each of them and from the sink added water to one. Then, without even having to look where she was reaching, opened the cupboard door below and reached in and drew out a bottle of Seven-Up and opened it and filled the other glass to the brim with it. Then she turned around, holding the two glasses and smiling with what for lack of a better word Dave could only call coyness at 'Bama. She leaned the top of her rump—rounded out in the summer skirt—back against the countertop willowly. There was a sort of dramatic pause, and then smiling, she raised her own glass—the one with the Seven-Up—and drank, at the same time extending the other one out to 'Bama, while continuing to smile at him with her eyes over the top of her glass.

It was such a characteristic sequence of action from her, and at the same time pointedly deliberate 'big operation', that Dave watched it fascinated—fixed, hypnotized almost, in his own position without even breathing. It always made him cringe inwardly anyway, to see her pour Seven-Up into such excellent delicious whiskey.

'Bama, who had been watching her with a sort of appreciative amusement like an audience at a comedy of manners, came forward and got his glass. "Shore," he said; "I could shore eat a steak." He stepped to one side politely and reached behind her for the bottle and added more whiskey to his glass.

Doris took her glass down from her mouth and smiled at him. "Well, Ill get them right on," she said submissively.

In the end, however, it was 'Bama who had to come to the stove and tell her just exactly when the steaks were ready to turn, and when they were done enough. As she herself said, ruefully but at the same time sort of proudly, she had never learned to boil water until she started coming here.

Dave sat with them while they ate and had another cup of coffee by the light of the candles which Doris had lit and then turned the lights off, and finally, another drink after they had had several. Doris ate very slowly and primly, and very little, sitting very straight up in her chair, her sleek fluffy cherrywood colored hair that was cut like a child's hanging almost to her shoulders. She did not like her steak rare, but very well done. She ate only about half of it. When she had had several drinks like she had now, her eyes took on a strange smoky look and she would stare at you with them heavy-lidded and half-closed as if she were not seeing you. And the more she drank the more noticeable it became. Many people's eyes—Dave's own for instance, he knew—got brighter and more vivid and penetrating, but with Doris it was just the opposite, and if she kept on drinking they finally got until she actually looked like a blind person, smokier and smokier until her irises seemed to diffuse and merge with her eyeballs, or else as if her eyeballs themselves—attached to some kind of counterweights or other —had actually flipped back over, preferring to stare inside at the interior of her own lovely head rather than out. It was not sexy looking at all, it was just the opposite. It was not deadly looking either. All through the meal she kept talking a little, quietly and demurely, about what they had done that day, how they had gone over into Indiana for a "little ramble." She never did actually say where they had been or what they had actually done. But Dave figured if they had done any rambling they had done it in the car. He could just imagine 'Bama in his golden silk suit—or her in her print dress for that matter—climbing up and down fences and walking across plowed fields for a "ramble."

And yet in spite of it all, he could see where—sitting there so primly straight like a little girl (smoky eyes and all) with her small sleek cherrywood head—she might be immensely attractive sexually. There was some kind of obscure smoky hate in her, and in her eyes, that made you want to break her down, dominate her. And something about her that seemed to ask, even beg, for exactly that. Though she would still hate you still more for it.

After the meal, while Doris demurely did up the dishes in a tacitly feminine wifely way that was as near as you could come to acting wifely without actually coming out and saying so in so many words—an attitude which 'Bama ignored, incidentally, he—'Bama—pushed his hat down over his eyes and scratched the back of his head and slumped himself down in his chair and lit a cigarette.

"Howd the work go today?" he asked.

"So-so," Dave said charily. "Slow. But good, what Im getting." He was reluctant to talk about his work, or anything else personal, around Doris. And 'Bama of course knew it.

"Good," the tall man nodded and shifted himself in his chair. "You goin over to Israel tonight?" he asked.

Doris had, after finishing the few dishes, got herself another drink and come back and sat down with them and lit a cigarette herself.

"No," Dave said. "Not tonight."

"Well, we might as well go out and play a little poker then," 'Bama said.

"Youre not going to work tonight, are you?" Doris asked unplaintively, looking at him with her smoky eyes. She had picked up calling it, calling gambling, 'work' from them and used it all the time now.

"Shore," 'Bama said. "Why not? We got to keep you up in the style to which yore accustomed, dont we? Them goddamned Spencer rolls doan grow out of my ears, you know."

Ordinarily, Doris would have looked pained and hurt at the use of such insulting language, but this time she simply stared back at him expressionlessly, with those slow smoky eyes, while 'Bama himself stared back at her, coolly and amusedly. But then, breaking out of the stare abruptly like a walking man leaping into a dead run, when she found she couldnt outstare him, she threw back her head girlishly and shook her cherrywood colored hair childishly and laughed trillingly.

"I guess it doesnt really matter too much, does it?" she said with a sweet laughing smile. "Except that I thought you were already pretty well fixed for money, 'Bama."

"Nobodys ever well fixed for money," 'Bama said matter of factly and without anger. "Well, come on, David. Lets be a goin," he said and got up. "Just go ahead and make yoreself at home," he said to Doris. "You know where everything is. You can listen to the radio or read if you want. Maybe Wally or Dewey or somebodyll come by and play you some pingpong."

"I think Ill take a look at Dave's new copy of Doctor Kinsey's *Sexual Behavior in the Human Male*," Doris said with a slow smoky smile. "I saw it laying in the other room. And I want to find out what men are really like."

"Hell, I could tell you all that," 'Bama said. "See you."

They left her there, sitting smoky- and seemingly blind-eyed at the table with her drink, but before they even actually got outside the screendoor through which the summer night air circulated past the open door itself, she had got up and stretched herself luxuriously and insouciantly and, walking with little pert steps in her straightbacked marching way, her small fine head held as always stiffly above her long straight neck, gone on into the other room indifferent to them, and as much at home as she could ever be in her own house. She had obviously made the move deliberately.

"I hope they dont any of them romp her on the divan in the living room and ruin it," 'Bama said unexcitedly as they got in the Packard.

It was the first time Dave had ever heard him make any definite comment about her at all, sexually. Taking advantage of this, Dave asked him the question he had been wanting to ask him for quite a long time.

"Are you?" he asked pointblank.

'Bama started the car before he answered. "I dont know," he said, as he released the brake.

"You dont know!" Dave exclaimed. "What the hell do you mean, you dont know!"

"Just that," 'Bama said. "I dont know. I *think* I have. But on the other hand . . ." He let it trail off.

"Well, Jesus Christ!" Dave protested.

'Bama didnt say anything for a moment, and backed the car on out. Then he grinned. "But shes good at lots of other things. You know that old saying about school teachers: If you get them in a car theyll have their head in yore lap—or yore head in their lap—" he grinned, "before you can even get the door shut."

Dave could not help but grin back.

"Lets try the Moose tonight," 'Bama said unexcitedly. "They supposed to be playin pretty heavy there lately."

"Sure," Dave said. And so now, by God, he *still* didnt know!

CHAPTER 47

IT WAS in August that Frank finally learned the more or less final disposition of the various bypass lands. The Greek's men had come and gone so quietly and efficaciously that the supposedly up-and-coming—but actually sleepy—little town of Parkman (including the actual people they had talked to) did not even know that they had ever been there. In the end, it turned out almost exactly as the Greek himself had accurately anticipated. Out of the eight landowners along the stretch of the proposed bypass, his men had been able to buy out only three. Of the three, they had had to buy the entire farms of two, in order to get the bypass frontage; but the third—an incredibly lucky break—had been stupidly willing to sell, for a higher price than he anticipated getting from the state, that part of his land where the right-of-way would run plus a strip several hundred yards deep along both sides. In that way he would dispose of the whole end of his holding so that the road would not separate him. Together with Frank's own acreage he had got himself off of old Lloyd Monds, that meant they had been able to buy out four of the eight—fifty percent; which the Greek had told them would be a very good average. Actually, in acreage, they now owned somewhat less than fifty percent of the land along the bypass. But off-setting this was the fact that of the three entryways into the new highway, they controlled all except three of the twelve corners. Also, one of the purchases made by the Greek's men adjoined Frank's own two corners of the Route 1 junction, which meant that they would have plenty of land to build his shopping center and to keep on developing it, if they so desired. Of the three corners which they did not control, two were the key corners directly across the Route 1 junction from Frank's own two. These were owned by a dairyman named Allis whose house, when the road went through, would have to be moved back closer to his barns away from the right-of-way. Consequently his house itself would occupy the south-east corner of the junction. And Allis, whose property was only a rather narrow strip along the east side of Route 1 where the bypass would intersect it, and who was perturbed about the right-of-way cutting his small north-east plot off from the rest of his land, had insisted upon selling this whole north-east corner to the State when he sold them right-of-way. As a result, the State who had only just lately closed the deal now owned the north-

east corner of the junction and would make a small piece of parkland
out of it! Thus, two of the three corners which they did not control—
the most important two—were, thanks to Allis, out of action as far
as private enterprise was concerned. And from then on east to where
the cutoff ran into town on the old road, there was no other entry-road
so all of that land—none of which they owned—was useless anyway.
The other corner, the third, was far down to the west, the north-west
corner of the furthest entry-road to the west and could hardly cause them
serious damage. Other than that, only the four cutoff corners—two
on the west, two on the east, where the old road joined the bypass—
could ever be used in competition against them.

Frank, of course, was overjoyed when he learned the results. He had
been sweating it out for over three months now, waiting to find out,
never saying a word to anyone, while anxious all the time to talk about it
with somebody, and when the long distance call came from Clark's
father in law cheerfully asking him if he could come up to Springfield,
he had taken off right away.

He was sitting in the store office just watching Edith work, when the
call came in—(there wasnt really much of anything for him to do
around the store any more; Al and his new assistant were handling
everything), and he had said goodby to Edith and put Al officially in
charge, and gone home and packed a bag and said goodby to
Agnes, and taken off in the Buick for the long drive. It was mid-
morning when the call came in, and he got there late in the afternoon.
It was in many ways—except for his natural anxiety—one of the
pleasantest drives he had ever made in his life. Everything was going
well at home, he and Agnes were actually getting along better than
they had in years, Edith was still the same staunch old dependable
levelheaded Edith, the Buick was running beautifully smooth, and he
could not hardly help but believe that they would have at least some
luck for him up there with the land when he got there.

As soon as he got in, he and Clark's father in law and the Greek had
gotten together for a conference downtown in the Greek's big rich
office and they had told him the news. It was, of course, much better
than any of them had really expected. Clark himself was not there.
August was always a heavy campaigning month in an election year,
and he was out on an extended speaking junket making all the county
fairs and family reunions and speaking almost every day. (Frank himself was a Republican Committeeman and had been working with the
rest of them helping him out as much as they could in the home county.)
But Clark had left his interests and ideas in the hands of his father
in law to handle, so that his absence would not hold any of them up.
Whatever they all decided to do would, he had said, be all right with
him.

It turned out, when the Greek had finished laying everything out for them and explaining the deals he had made, that they all three of them—he, Clark, and Clark's father in law—each had a good deal more of his initial capital left than any of them had anticipated they would. Even after the Greek had been paid off his rather high price for his work. Partly this was due to the fact that they could not buy any more than what they could, of course; but partly it was due to the lucky stroke of being able to buy the one man's frontage without having to buy his whole farm, and also partly it was due to the excellent work done by the Greek's organization with their rundown shoes. As a result, both Frank and Clark would have considerably more money available to put back into the Parkman Village Shopping Center. They would not have enough to swing it, Frank saw immediately, but they would have a lot more to put in than he had anticipated. And between the three, they now had most of the best land for development along the bypass. All they had to do was just sit back and wait until the road was put through and people began to look around and want to buy spots for businesses out there, and they could all turn a very neat profit on the whole venture.

But Frank did not want to do this, and told them both so. Although the Greek of course was no longer in it, since his part was done and paid for. But Frank, encouraged by finding that he had quite a bit more money left than he had expected to have, began to lay out for them enthusiastically (just as he had once done for Clark) his whole scheme of development of the shopping center and along with it and allied to it the movies houses, motels, restaurants, etcetera. To his astonishment the Greek (it was Clark's father in law he had been trying to impress) suddenly and with his characteristic decisiveness decided pointblank that he himself would like to put some money into it. He thought, he said, if it was done properly it could be a tremendous money-making venture, and agreed with Frank that it was liable to take almost all the business away from uptown. He for one would like to invest in it. Clark's father in law, who was evidently as astonished as Frank at the Greek's decision, then decided cheerfully and humorously that if it was good enough for someone of the Greek's wellknown tightfisted acumen to throw in with it, he and Clark had better go along too.

And Frank, hardly able to believe in his own good luck, did not say anything at all about the factories he had used to dream of. Anyway they could not get that much of the land; but in his mind he still had not given up on it. There was always still the possibility that, by paying a stiffer price later on, he might be able to get at least enough of the rest of the land between the bypass and the railroad to swing it. And he knew it would be a perfect site for factories. But he did not tell them any of this right now. Better to wait, until all this other was settled and signed and in operation first. Some people just didnt have the ability to see that far, go that far ahead, all at once. But hed bring them around, eventually, he thought to himself.

What they decided to do, now that they were agreed upon going into it, was to leave all of the land in Frank's name. Clark, of course, being the local State Representative, could not afford to have his name on any of the land—not because there would be anything illegal about it, but because it would cause him too much local ill will: everybody would leap to say he had pulled a shady deal by using his office. And Clark's father in law was too well known in Parkman as his father in law for his name to appear on the land. The Greek didnt want his name on it in any case; it was his policy never to have his name appear in any deals he was in. So it would all go down under Frank's name. The Greek would see that the deeds were all made to him; it would appear that he was the sole purchaser. Then the four of them would form a development corporation, for the purpose of developing this land, each holding shares according to his capital, and Frank would sign an agreement with the corporation giving them first option on buying or any development. Then the corporation would in turn back Frank individually and finance him in building the Parkman Village Shopping Center, which would be a separate venture, by buying whatever share of it was necessary to fill out the needed capital. Clark's father in law would tear up Frank's mortgages on the store and the house in Parkman for an equal amount of shares in the venture. Frank would throw the Route 1 corner lot, the one where the Shopping Center would stand, in with the aggregate as part of his share in the capital—and, the Greek smiled, since it was all his idea in the first place anyway, he thought they ought to raise the value of the lot from what Frank had paid for it up to whatever it would be worth after the bypass went through. Smiling also, Clark's father in law agreed for himself and for Clark, and Frank once again found himself thinking with the same sense of astonishment that he had never run into such businessmen before, and remembered Judge Deacon. He could just imagine the Judge offering to do something like that!

The rest of the land, of course, would—actually and in effect—be under the control of the development corporation, though of course this would not appear so to anyone outside the immediate group. Then, depending on how the Shopping Center (Frank had already begun to think of it like that: with capitals) came along and developed, they would decide what and when to build next. Probably a good filling station, the Greek thought, and a motel next if everything went well. But the secret he said emphatically was to not count dollars; make everything as good a quality as they could, even if that meant holding off a while on further development, because only with the quality places could you get the quality clientele—and also, he smiled, the quality prices. Let the cheap tourists go someplace else. The Greek appeared to have almost a *phobia* about doing everything with quality. But then so did they all, Clark's father in law, Clark, and Frank himself. They were all agreed on that.

The State, Clark's father in law told them, was already in process of buying up their right-of-way now, just beginning it. As soon as the deeds in question could be made over to Frank, he could complete his own sales of right-of-way to them. Naturally, there would be no attempt whatever to make any money off the State; and whatever their price set, it would be accepted. The State expected to begin the grading work this fall, he had been told. With any luck on the weather during the winter they ought to be ready to pour the road next fall. That meant that sometime during the winter they ought to start to begin looking into plans and ideas and prices about the Shopping Center. He knew an excellent architect's firm in Chicago who could handle it for them. He could arrange for Frank to meet with them any time they were ready.

The Greek said that the deeds and right-of-way sales could all be accomplished easily tomorrow early, which would allow Frank to make it home tomorrow evening. He would take care of that part. Now, what else was there?

When they left the Greek's office in downtown Springfield it was after nine o'clock and already dark. Frank was staying at the Abraham Lincoln. Clark's father in law, in his oldfashioned *cavalier* way, had asked them both home with him to take "pot luck" dinner, as he smilingly called it. (Frank could imagine what his "pot luck" dinners would be like!) But the Greek had had another engagement already, and Frank—thinking about the beautiful breasts and blonde hair of Betty Lee—had cautiously declined also. He did not want to be taking any chances with anything now, and they always served an awful lot of drinks. So instead the old man—smiling craftily as though he understood—had called up from the Greek's office another "friend of Clark's" to look after him, and see he didnt have a boring evening as a stranger in town. (The other "friend of Clark's" Frank had known before was out of town with Clark, campaigning.) Frank was beginning to catch on a little. The first "friend of Clark's" was such a pleasant friendly man he had thought for a long time he actually was a friend of Clark's. In fact, until just now. He could not help wondering what all these "friends of Clark's" and of Clark's father in law did with the rest of their time when they were not looking after Clark's or Clark's father in law's out-of-town friends.

The man, who said his name was Eddie Berra, called him from downstairs in the hotel while he was dressing—putting on a clean shirt with French cuffs (Frank had been buying French cuffs lately, since hed started coming to Springfield) and a clean unwrinkled suit he had brought along just in case something like this came up—and Frank told him to come on up. This second friend of Clark's turned out to be a small wiry eager-faced young man with quick bright intelligent eyes. He was, he said, glad to meet any other friend of Clark's. Or the old man's. He thought he might line them up a couple dates, if of course Frank wanted one; but, he said, he was a little worried because it was on such short notice, and it was so late in the evening to be calling anyone.

While Frank was tying his tie and putting on his coat, this second friend of Clark's sat down by the telephone table and began calling. Long after Frank had finished dressing and had sat down himself, he was still calling. Only once did he get an answer, and it was a negative one. "Gal's roommate," he said. "Both got a date already." He must have made close to thirty phone calls for Frank. Finally he had to shrug ruefully and give it up. "These damn secretaries," he said. "I dont think any of them ever stay home."

It was decided they would go out together somewhere themselves and have some drinks and dinner and maybe they might run onto somebody. Somebody Clark's friend might know. "See, lots of the gals, if they dont have dates, they go out together someplace. Maybe they happen to meet fellows, you know?" he said. "Okay?"

It was all right with Frank. He did not really care, and yet he could not help but feel a little let down because he had been beginning to feel excited. But he tried to cover this up.

"But now if its only a girl you want," the wiry alert little man said solicitously, "I know plenty of places we can go."

"Oh, no," Frank said quickly. "I wasnt lookin' for a girl especially. Hell, Im an old married man. Its just that it gets kind of—you know— its always nicer to have somebody along when you go out."

The wiry little man nodded. "Sure," he said. "I know. Well now you just take your choice. Im just sorry its so late in the evening."

"Lets go eat," Frank said.

They went, at Eddie's suggestion, to another one of the big hotels first. Then they went on, to the clubs. They hit all of them, having several drinks in each, but they did not have any luck. Frank, after he had had a number of drinks—(Eddie did not drink much, it turned out; almost nothing, in fact), pointed out several likely looking prospects but Eddie always shook his head. "Ill try them for you, if you want," he said; "but I can tell you right now its no soap."

"But how the hell can you tell?"

Eddie grinned. "Hell, I know almost everybody in this town." He nursed his drink a moment. "Them gals all got guys, Frank."

"Then whatre they doin' out by themselves?"

"The guys are probly home with their wives," Eddie grinned. "Come on, lets try some other joint."

They hit a number of them, having a number of drinks in each—or rather, Frank had a number of drinks—while they looked around, and by then everything had changed and it had become a different evening entirely and not at all, for Frank at least, what it had been when they started out. He had been getting frustrateder and frustrateder and drunker and drunker. He wished now he had never started it. His mind was perfectly clear, but everything had turned into a continuous succession of rounds: drink followed drink, bar followed bar, prospect followed prospect—all unsuccessful, with no rest or break or time lag inbetween like the merrygoround. You rode it and rode it and the faces got blurred together and the lights ran together and always it kept passing and re-passing the brass ring, the one focusable spot, before you were prepared for it and before you were ever quite ready to reach. None of it seemed to bother wiry little Eddie, however. Nothing seemed to bother wiry little Eddie.

"Dont you think we better go somewhere and eat, Frank?" he said with cheerful solicitude several times.

But Frank did not want to go and eat. He wanted to get drunker and drunker, and go faster and faster, and eventually he would reach in time, and he would catch the brass ring. Did Eddie understand? Was Eddie able to grasp what that would mean?

"Sure," Eddie said soothingly. "Sure, Frank. The brass ring. Sure."

In one bar—by now it was after midnight and Frank no longer knew which one; in fact, they all really looked an awful lot alike, when you thought about it—he approached a woman sitting alone, against the advice of Eddie who said he knew her, and asked her if she would care to go out with him for dinner. He half-bowed politely, inclining his head, and was in fact preparing to widen his pleasant smile when her words, her answer, braked screechingly into sudden focus like the Lone Ranger's horse, as sharply clear as the brass ring itself, while everything else continued to flee blurringly on around the circle.

"Beat it, bum!" she said.

The words stood out in his mind as if etched in fire. Shocked, both in his pride and because he had not seen what kind of woman she was at first, he inclined his head stiffly and murmured in a vastly ironic voice Thank you, Madam and made his way sedately and with great dignity back to the table where Eddie sat. Later on, as they were leaving, he saw Eddie stop and speak briefly to the woman. Probably old Eddie was setting her straight on who she had been talking to. Telling her what he himself would not have deigned to.

In another place—the last place they went to, in fact—Frank became enamored of the waitress who waited on them. The more he saw her the more beautiful he could see that she was—it was astonishing to see such a beautiful girl working as a mere waitress; somebody ought to do something for her—and he had made up his mind he was going to have her tonight. It was more than clear that she was easy to make anyway. He was making out with her quite well, too, until he made her mad; but how was he to know she was some kind of a damned anti-feminist? He had given her several really lewd winks, and made several suggestive remarks, to all of which she had responded smilingly, and a couple of times when she brought him drinks had sort of leaned sideways against her leg as she set them down. Of course, she was a little shy. But then, hell, he liked them shy.

But then, as she was setting down still another drink for him, he had taken hold of her wrist with his hand in a manly way and gripped it a little to let her know he was really serious. It was the signal for a miniature explosion. His fingers went clear around her wrist, but in spite of that she had quietly—and indeed, with very little extra movement—got one of his fingers with her other hand and bent it back until he had to let go quickly and snatch his hand back or she would have sprained—or broken!—his damned finger.

For a moment he was half of a mind to just haul off and bust her in the jaw. These bums thought they could get away with anything, just because they were women. But then from the corner of his eye he saw old Eddie wink at him and shake his head, and he desisted. Old Eddie was right of course. After all, it was a public place. And by then she was gone of course anyway.

Frank was as sincerely shocked—and infuriated—by her change in attitude, and after giving him all that come-on too, as he had been with what the other woman had said to him when he had only politely asked her to go out to dinner with him.

"What the hell?" he protested. "What got into her?"

"Oh, you know how women are," Eddie said.

"You go over and talk to her, Eddie. Tell her hell I didnt mean nothing. I was just bein' friendly. Tell her we'll meet her after they close up."

He watched while Eddie went over to the serving table by the corner of the bar and talked to her. It was amazing how clear his mind was, with what hed drunk and all. He *thought* he saw Eddie hand her some money and so he congratulated himself that it was all fixed up, but he must have been mistaken because when Eddie came back, he said:

"I cant do a thing with her, Frank. You made her mad when you took hold of her."

"But, hell," Frank said. He was at a loss. "Well, maybe I better go over and talk to her myself. Explain it to her."

"No, I wouldnt do that, Frank, if I were you." Eddie's voice sounded authoritative. Then he grinned. "It wouldnt do any good. Shes too mad. And shes just a green kid. Shed be liable to call cops on you."

"Hell, I didnt know she was some kind of a anti-feminist," Frank protested. "How was I to know? I dont know what the hells gettin' into American women anymore. They dont want *men,* they all want *kids.* Babies. Or sissies. That they can handle."

"They all got it too easy, Frank," Eddie said, "thats what it is. Theyve all lived too good all their lives. They think they got everything coming to them on a silver platter."

"Well I for one got a bellyful of it," Frank said toughly. "Well, lets have another drink," he said.

"Lets have it at the hotel instead," Eddie said. "I want to blow this firetrap. That gal's got me disgusted."

"Okay, Eddie," Frank said, "if you say so. I guess shes got me disgusted too."

On the way back to the hotel in the cab they talked about the pennant races—which, it turned out, Eddie had been following as closely as Frank himself, if not even more so. They agreed that Billy Southworth's Braves about had it cinched for the National League, but what about that race in the American? The Indians, the Red Sox, the Yankees and the A's, all four of them only a few percentage points apart! There had never been anything like it, that either one of them could remember. Eddie, it turned out, was a Chisox fan and since Chicago was his hometown anyway rarely missed a game at Comiskey Park, unless he was out on some job. Frank himself of course had always been a St Louis man. Between them they laid out the ratings of the American clubs, deciding that the A's would fold first, and then Boston, and that the Yankees would beat out Boudreau's Indians. Frank felt fine.

But at the hotel, his stiff anger at the punk waitress gone now, Frank could not escape a deep sense of horror. Despite baseball, the shocks both women had given him had not dissipated, and he was filled with a mortifying, almost frightening embarrassment. It was all he could do to make himself walk publicly through the lobby to the elevators. And he could not get over this feeling he had that something was happening to American women anymore. Something bad. They werent even *women* anymore. They were *men.* —Or some kind of even worse sexless neuters of some kind. They all seemed to be turning into Geneve Lowes or Dotty Callters. They had no softness or sympathy or understanding or nothing anymore. And in fact it seemed to him that the only single person he had met all night who understood him at all was old Eddie. Eddie Berra, Clark's friend.

"You know, youre quite a guy, Eddie," he said when they were in his rooms and Eddie was mixing them both a drink. "Quite a guy, Eddie, quite a guy."

The wiry young man grinned. "We had us quite a time tonight, didnt we, Frank?" he said. He handed him his drink.

"We sure did, we sure did," Frank said. He took a gulp of his drink and it made his nose pinch up. "Christ!" he said. "You made this pretty strong. What the hell did you put in it?"

"Just whiskey," Eddie said. "And a little water. Dont you like it? You want another?"

"No, no. No. Its all right. Just sort of strong is all."

The wiry little Eddie laughed almost soundlessly, opening his mouth. "Good healthy nightcap, Frank old boy."

"You wouldnt be tryin' to knock me out, would you?" Frank grinned.

"Knock you out! This late at night? Hell its almost two o'clock," Eddie smiled. He sipped at his own drink while Frank drank his big one. "Come on," he said finally. "Help you get to bed if you want." He took off his suit coat—which did not appear to have suffered a single wrinkle all night long—and came over to help Frank and Frank saw a snub-nosed .38 in a shoulder holster hanging from his left armpit.

So that was his trouble! Poor little guy. He was so thin and small that he carried a gun around to protect himself with. Well, you couldnt blame him much, in a town like this Springfield. Probly he had a complex about his size.

"Come on," Eddie smiled, "Ill help you up."

Frank suffered himself to he helped up and out of his coat, and Eddie helped him get his tie and shirt and shoes off.

"You sure you all right now?" Eddie said. "You sure you can sleep? You want another drink?"

"No," Frank grinned sillily. "Hell, Ill sleep like a log. Though I wouldnt mind another drink."

"Ill mix you one if you want," Eddie grinned. "Man, you sure can put it away, Ill say that!"

"No, I dont want one I guess."

"Well, you go on and get in bed then." Eddie put his coat back on.

"Youre a great guy, Eddie, a great guy. Youre the only person I saw tonight who understands me, by God!"

"Anything for a friend of Clark's, or the old man's," Eddie grinned. "Anybody thats a friend of theirs is a friend of mine." He went to the door. "You go on and get in bed now."

"Right!" Frank said and dropped his pants and hung them on a chair and stepped across the double doorway into the bedroom and climbed into the bed. "There! You see? Good night, Eddie. And thanks again, old pal."

"I had a good time," Eddie said. "Well, good night, Frank. You sure youre all right now?"

"Im asleep already," Frank said.

"Okay. Good night. Ill see you," Eddie said and went out and shut the selflock door.

And as soon as he was gone Frank was back up on his feet, and went stealthily to the door in his sock feet and listened at it, grinning slyly to himself. They were not going to catch him napping by standing outside the door and listening to see if he went to sleep! What did they think they were trying to pull? Hed show them, he thought slyly, by God. All of them.

But then, standing there—hearing nothing, and gradually becoming convinced that he was really alone at last—he suddenly thought again of those two women, and the feeling of sick horror that he had had before on the way up to the rooms began to come back to him, seeping slowly from nerve to nerve like quicksand all through him. The conversation with Eddie after they got up here had stifled it, choked it off. He had even been able to forget it.

But now—alone—it slid back full force, and even stronger. Horror about women—American women—and horror about himself. He knew what a colossal, mortifying ass he had made of himself. They thought he didnt know. Drunk, partially befuddled, his mind that existed behind his brain—his *him*—was nevertheless clear as a bell and had been all evening. Detached, it had stood and watched, as horrified a spectator as any of the rest of them, at the spectacle he was making of himself. And now, leaning almost sickly against the silent door, he was gripped by an embarrassment so powerful it amounted to outright terror. Why, he could have fallen flat on his face!—and in the very best places in Springfield. And probably would have if it hadnt of been for Eddie.

Women!—American women. They just didnt play the game fair with you. They didnt act like women are supposed to act. How the hell could you handle them when they didnt give you the opportunity to? —But there was more to it than that; and in his spastic terror of embarrassment he faced the rest of it: Other men handled them. Other men know how to control women and mold them to their will, as men were supposed to do. But he couldnt. He just didnt have what it took, that was all. Wasnt that the truth? And never had had. He wasnt a man. He wasnt anything! Or he could have handled them too, like other men did. Women! Like a man was supposed to. But all his life—*all* his life—he had been under the thumb, handled and controlled, of some damned woman or other. First his mother. Then his wife. Who had never enjoyed sex with him; whom he was inadequate to make enjoy it. Even his mistresses werent the kind of mistresses other men had; he couldnt even handle *them*. Even they were stronger than he! He was a weakling. Because he couldnt handle them. Like an American man should. Women!—American women. They werent women. They were men or something. He was the woman.

Almost creeping, Frank hobbled sickly away from the door and over to the chair where the liquor was. He poured himself another drink, a stiff one—although not as stiff as the one old Eddie had tried to knock him out with—and sat down in the chair with it. The clear part of his mind knew he was liable to get sick again—that gastritis that Doc Cost said. And yet he wasnt drunk at all. Something had happened to him apparently, maybe the emotion. But he wasnt drunk. To prove it, he suddenly set the glass down and got up and putting his hands to his sides walked straight across the room along the line of the rug from one end to the other. He did not even waver. There, you see? He came back to the chair and sat down and clutched the glass again and drank from it greedily, as if it were salvation.

Gradually, after a while,—perhaps from just sitting there; because it wasnt the liquor, he couldnt even feel that—the sick horror and terrified embarrassment and hatred of himself left him. It seeped out of him as slowly and inexorably as it had come, leaving in its place something else: excitement. A kind of budding sudden secretive excitement. Which made him want to do something dangerous and selfdestructive. He began to feel better. Perhaps you could only feel an emotion that strong for just so long. Or perhaps it was because he was alone. Alone, and free, and unobserved, and—and his own master. In a way it made him think excitedly of when he was a kid and used to sneak off somewhere and hide, in spite of—and to spite—his mother. —(He guessed he *had* hated her, back then. Of course, he knew better now. You couldnt blame her. She was only doing what she thought was right, and what *was* right, for her kids. Now he understood it, and loved her for it.)— But he had the same excited feeling now that he used to get then, and he suddenly felt adventurous and daring and reckless and very powerful and very smart. They thought they could outsmart you all the time! Hah! And suddenly he knew what he was going to do. Still in his underwear and socks and feeling a high intense sexual arouse, he got up and went over to his clothes. He was going for a walk.

—A walk, at two thirty in the morning,—(was it only two thirty? had it only been half an hour since Eddie left him?)—and in a strange city, where he was practically unknown, a walk!

Who knew what strange things might happen to him, or that he might see, or become involved in? what adventures?

For a moment, picking up his shirt, he wondered what Eddie had wanted to knock him out for? He wasnt just an ordinary troublesome drunk, who wanted to get right back up and go out and cause trouble. Eddie should have known that.

Almost shaking with his burgeoning excitement, he got back into the rumpled suit he had worn—and given such a beating to—all evening. And then as a sudden afterthought, and for some reason he could not have named, he began emptying all his pockets, putting everything up on the dresser, all his identifications, his cards, his driver's license, even his name-engraved Zippo, everything that could have identified him or told somebody who he was, everything except some money. Then, feeling very light in his suddenly weightless clothing, he stood looking down at the jumbled mess feeling dangerous and destructive and tough. God, the things the crap we had to carry with us through our lives. Why?

Why did a man have to carry identification? They didnt carry identification back in the old days. Besides, if he should get picked up by the cops or somebody, all he would have to do would be to get ahold of Clark's father in law on the phone, here in Springfield. Feeling excited and adventurous and very much the lawbreaker, he turned and walked out of the room.

Frank nodded pleasantly to the elevator man who knew him when he got in, his heart beating loudly, and downstairs he made his way sedately and reputably across the half-dark deserted lobby where two elderly men were wielding mops and nothing else save the night force behind the registry desk moved. Leaving his roomkey—last vestige of any identification—on the desk, he marched on across toward the doors. If they found his body in the morning, he thought thrillingly, there would be no way at all to know who he was. Drunk, thick-tongued, partially befuddled, but with his mind functioning as clear as a bell and walking as straight as a string-line, he made his way outside to the street strangely aroused.

For the next two hours he walked up and down the late deserted streets of Springfield, his body thrillingly excited and alive to the night and silence and sense of adventure. In all that time he did not speak to a living soul. Once a night cop, leisurely walking his beat, met him and eyed him but went on. Once a cruising homosexual fell in step with him furtively and hopefully a few feet away on the sidewalk, but after several moments when Frank did not look around or speak or stop, turned off and sadly went away. A couple of times he passed tough-looking backstreet joints that were still lighted and serving drinks and into which people were still crowded, but he did not go in or even stop to look. He had no desire to, and drifted more and more toward the darker less-lighted more-deserted slum-type streets. Several times he passed other people, in groups or singly. Another time he saw a light in a third floor window over an alley above a fire escape, and though he went right on walking without even hesitating, he debated sneaking back and trying to find a way up to the fire escape's drop-ladder and climbing on up and looking in. Maybe it was a man and woman, or maybe two women, or two men. He could stand and watch them, without them ever knowing he was there. The thought excited him as he walked on. At four thirty he returned to the hotel and, calmly and placidly, picked up his key and went staidly upstairs to bed having seen nothing and done nothing and been in nothing and not spoken to a soul. He had not spent a cent.

Only when he was undressed again and in between the sheets did the fear and terror strike him, and he lay with his ear pressed down into the pillow safely while the nerve ends of his body quivered inwardly.

What if the policeman had stopped him and arrested him? Or if he had suddenly insulted him and made him arrest him? What if he had spoken to the homosexual and picked him up? And the man had beaten him up and rolled him? What if he had gone into one of those tough joints and picked a fight and been killed or crippled? What if he had climbed the fire escape and the man had shot him off of it and killed him? All of these terrified him and excited him and he lay thinking in terror and sexual arouse: *What if I had been caught?* The thought of being caught, as he lay contemplating it together with the triumphant knowledge that he had not been, so terrified and excited him that he was actually quivering. But he was too exhausted, both emotionally and physically, to do more. And clutching the pillow reassuringly, he went to sleep.

When the phone woke him at eight thirty he woke normally, but almost immediately the terror returned—without the sexual arousal— when he remembered all of last night. Was he going mad? To go out like that without identification! He might actually have *been* caught! He had difficulty keeping his voice from quivering when he answered the ringing phone.

It was the Greek, who had all the papers ready for him at his office. "Christ! arent you up yet? Everything's ready to sign." It was like a reassuring, sane and stable voice—and therefore even more terrifying— from a world of which he had only a dim faint memory.

"Ill be right there," he said. "Soon's I shave and shower."

"You boys must have had yourselves quite a time last night," the Greek said amiably.

"We did," Frank said, "we did. I got pretty drunk and Eddie put me to bed. Hes a good boy."

"Yes he is," the Greek said in his cultured voice that was so out of place with that self-made-man face of his. "Well, you hurry on down."

"I will," Frank said.

The terror—the sober, unsexual terror—did not leave him, even at the Greek's office when they signed the papers, although gradually it diminished. After all, he *hadnt* been caught. And anyway, he hadnt done anything. He hadnt done anything to be caught for. Hell, he hadnt even been untrue or unfaithful to his wife and his mistress, he thought with a feeling of relieved pride; he hadnt even done that. As soon as he was done at the Greek's he went back to the hotel and checked out and got his car and lit out for home without even stopping for lunch, and pausing only long enough to go in a book store where he wasnt known and buy a copy of that new book *The Kinsey Report*. Innocently wrapped, it lay in the front seat beside him. He would have to go by the store and lock it up in his desk, he reminded himself, before he went on home.

He had a terrible hangover to be driving, but he didnt mind. Frank wanted to get home to Agnes.

CHAPTER 48

WHEN her husband returned from Springfield Agnes Hirsh could tell the moment he came in the house, of course, that he had been doing some heavy drinking while he was gone. She could also tell, in some subtle fashion of her own that she herself could not actually delineate the exact processes of, that he had not had a woman while he was gone. Frank, when he had been out with some woman, had a way of acting coy and smugly cocky and flitting and flipping around the house as though he had gotten away with something. He acted "cute". It was almost always an accurate barometer to his "conquests". He acted somewhat that same little-boyish way after having been exposed to some criticism or other, too, flitting and flipping jauntily about the house, making jokes that were not funny but that he laughed at anyway, but there was a difference between the two although she could not say exactly what. Perhaps it was that after hed had a woman he was always a little more smugly cocky, a little more condescendingly "masculine", than the cute way he acted after being criticized.

Anyway, Agnes could tell he had not had a woman this trip to Springfield. The last time he had been up there he had had. And at least the two times before that.

This time, however, Frank came in the house carrying his suitcase and briefcase and deposited them in the bedroom wearing only that collapsed and sagging look under the eyes and down the cheekbones which came from that kind of driving, exhausting (especially to the people with him!), almost uncontrollable drinking-bouts that she had seen him get on and that Doc Cost had warned him about. It made him look as though all the muscles in the lower half of his face had suddenly given way and fallen; but this time there was nothing else there on his face. Except perhaps a kind of scared look, as though the drinking might have frightened him. But there was no flippishness, no smug little-boyishness, no cuteness. He was pleasant and subdued, and there was no cockiness about him at all, and his eyes were so totally and sincerely innocent that she knew—no matter how late he had stayed up, or how much he had drunk (which must have been considerable)—she knew there was absolutely nothing sexual in any of it. It would have shown, and there was just nothing there.

The knowledge—that this time he hadnt—filled Agnes with a sudden welling warmth of affection for him, as he kissed her and went on back to unpack, that was stronger even than the warmth she had been steadily growing for him these past three months. Perhaps he was actually finally growing up a little, she thought benignly, feeling almost maternal. Maybe those people up in Springfield were really good for him.

Agnes was not nearly as much in the dark about Frank's Springfield venture as she knew he thought she was. His very reticence about it had made her look into it closer. She knew, for one thing, that he was working on a deal about something that—for him at least—was immensely bigger than anything he had ever been involved in before. He had told her almost nothing about it, and he had deliberately minimized its importance to her; that much she had sensed, and that was how she knew how big it was. Because any ordinary deal—like that taxistand fiasco with Dave for instance—he always built up to astronomical proportions and made it sound far bigger than it was. So this deal must really be big.

She knew also, for another thing, that Clark Hibbard was involved in the deal some way. This she had had from Betty Lee the several times she had seen her at the Country Club and Elks and around, when she had been in town and when, standing talking to the vague dreamy-eyed strangely haunted looking girl, Betty Lee had always mentioned Frank and her having seen him this time or that in Springfield. Betty Lee had never mentioned anything about the "deal",—and indeed, Agnes was sure, she didnt know anything about it; none of them would have dared to tell her—but there was in her attitude toward Agnes this change, felt rather than ever said, which could only be described as the attitude of one wife toward another when both know their husbands have become partners in something. It was small wonder they hadnt told her. Betty Lee, who had never been especially famous for her mental powers, was almost incapable of mentioning anything—anything at all—that was not already there in the forefront of her mind. She was equally incapable of *not* mentioning it. In fact, it was reasonable to assume upon personal evidence that she didnt even have any other part to her mind except the forefront. Excepting, of course, with regard to slot machines.

And it was from this, plus the knowledge that the old man practically ran one of the banks in Springfield, that Agnes had deduced and finally become convinced that Frank had mortgaged the house and the store to him. It would be easy enough for him to do, even without her signature, up there in Springfield where the old man personally ran this bank. Moreover, Frank had been for some time converting just about everything he could into cash; so what would be more reasonable than to assume he would mortgage the house and store too? It was, if you looked at it, the only sensible thing for him to do.

The knowledge disturbed her somewhat, naturally; and she knew it had been disturbing Frank too; but she did not really care. When you went into something with men the caliber of Betty Lee's father, you should put into it every damned thing you could scrape together. Because those men didnt go into anything unless it made money. And everything you could put in would be just that much more profit coming back. And besides, you ought to carry your full share—or at least as much of it as you were capable of carrying among such big wheels—if you wanted to keep their respect.

She wished, a little wistfully, that Frank had asked her for her signature on it too, so she could have given it gladly and let him know that she was backing him, how much she trusted him. Whatever his other shortcomings, and he had plenty, Agnes knew he had an almost phenomenal business sense and was proud of both him and it. He had taken her own father's store, which had been only a cheap little novelty and notion store,—little more than a hole in the wall in fact—and built it into one of the very best businesses in Parkman. And Agnes was almost fiercely proud of this accomplishment.

She understood why he couldnt tell her about the house and store and take her into his confidence. It was almost some kind of a psychological fixation with him. The house itself with all the things and appliances he had bought for them and put in it was a sort of private symbol to him; it was his way of making up for—and freeing himself from—the guilt he felt for all his infidelities, and also his silent way of showing them that the inconstancies which he could not even bring himself to admit in words, even when confronted with them, did not really mean anything. Naturally, he could not bring himself to admit he had mortgaged it. While the store, which he had never actually bought, and which she had just signed over to him when her father died—although he more often than not told people he had bought it from her dad, depending upon who he was talking to, and how drunk they were—the store was an even stronger source of guilt since he did not really feel he had ever owned it, although he had paid her for it many times over, just in cash alone. Naturally, he could not bring himself to admit he had mortgaged it either. She understood it.

Still, she wished he had told her, had trusted her enough to know she would not throw a tantrum or be angry at him, and in another mood than the one she knew now it would have angered her that he hadnt, angered her terribly. But for the past three or four months Agnes had been steadily acquiring a warmth for her husband that she could not remember having had since they were first married—when they had both been green kids who hadnt even known any better, or what they were getting into. And now on top of all that other warmth there had suddenly come this. He had returned from Springfield this trip without having had a woman. She could only think of it as a sort of inevitable, foreordained culminating point: that time when he would someday return from some trip somewhere without having had a woman. She had always known it would happen. Someday. And it filled her with such a suddenly shy, brimming happiness and affection for him that she was doubly glad now she had never mentioned the mortgages and was proud she had kept her mouth shut, had shown her faith in him by letting him work it out himself.

When she had first broken him off from Geneve Lowe last year, she had known beforehand it was going to take him a long time to get over it. It always had before, and there was no reason to assume it wouldnt this time. In fact, this one was especially bad, just because she had dreaded doing it and had just let it go on for so long. So she had been prepared. He had hardly spoken a word to her for over two months, but that was to be expected and she had accepted it without a word. She had even suffered for him, and what he was going through. Then, as he began slowly—very slowly—to come around and she had seen no signs—either in his ego, or outwardly in other people—of any new alliance forming, hope had begun to grow in her. Maybe this time was the one.

It was that fear of another affair, more than anything else, which had worried her about his trips to Springfield. More than the mortgages, more than the business deal, more than anything. The last four or five times he had been up there he had had some woman or other. She was sure of that: the "cuteness". What had worried her was that it might be the same woman every time. A new mistress, up there in Springfield. She had even been almost willing to accept that; at least it would not be some woman she knew and saw almost every day, some woman here in Parkman who could lord it over her and feel she had put something over on her. —And then, when she had been about ready to accept it, here he was home from Springfield again without having had a girl-friend this time at all! Was it any wonder she felt warm and good toward him?

Obviously, it couldnt have been the same woman in Springfield all the time, but different women; either that or else he had broken it off all by himself.

Agnes did not really care if he had an occasional stray woman when he was out of town. —Or rather, if she did care, if it did hurt her— which of course it did, she thought—she knew enough to know there wasnt anything she could do about it. Of course, it cost him; it always cost him; just as it always cost every man; you just couldnt feel as warm toward a man when you knew he was having other women too; and if you could, you didnt let yourself. But all men picked up floozies. And at least a whore didnt feel she had put something over on you—like a Geneve Lowe, who got all her enjoyment out of taking other women's men. That was the way the girls had been in high school; they didnt even want a boy unless he was going steady with someone else. And anyway you never saw the whores and chorus girls. And besides that was just the way men were. The husbands of all her friends were the same way. Almost every one who spent any time out of town had at least one other mistress in another town. Not one was actually faithful to his wife—although of course they (and generally the wives too, at least in front of them) professed earnestly that they were. So she was willing—even at a considerable expense in pride—to accept this.

And yet here, all the time,—the thought burst in upon her again brimmingly, happily—here just as she was ready to accept it, steel herself to it, here he was home all by his little self and on his own hook without having had the woman—a woman—this time.

A long-held, waiting, growing love in her for him swelled ridiculously at the thought, and threatened to burst out through its bonds and the barriers she had imposed on it. At last he was growing into an adult. At last he was learning that sex wasnt really very important at all. At last she had managed to break it, to teach him. And maybe, as he matured, he was learning where real love lay. She had always hoped he would. She had prayed for it—actually, really prayed to God, at times—that he would give up this adolescent chasing after every bitch he saw like young men of twenty did and then attempted to carry with them over into later life as they turned into middle-aged roués. At last he was learning.

She didnt feel triumphant at all; she felt very humble. There was so much love for him in her—in her body and in her heart and in her mind —that it exuded over, out of her, as if there werent room to contain it all. Maybe that body was getting thick and heavy, and maybe that heart was getting old and flutterly, and maybe she wasnt a pert young thing any more. Like Geneve Lowe. Having a baby hardly helped you to stay young and pretty, and you couldnt be like them—like Geneve—and have Dawnie too she thought and it was a good bargain. But you didnt live and work and worry and sweat and trouble with a particular man for all those years without there being a tie between you that other people didnt have. And you didnt have that kind of love for him unless you *had* shared his life with him. Maybe at last he was learning it. And that it was all there for him. If he wanted it.

Almost unable, for a moment, to contain her feelings in silence without saying something about them, Agnes got up from where she was sitting at her secretary and went across the living room to the hall door, where she could see him across the hall through the bedroom door where he was still unpacking his bag. Her armpits in the sleeveless summer print damp with sweat in the hot still August air, and feeling the dampness of it on her legs and in the fringes of her hair on her forehead, she leaned against the living room doorjamb and stood looking at her husband. Frank looked up and gave her a wan smile. He looked very tired.

"Would you like for me to help you?" she said tenderly. She had been sitting at her secretary looking through Dawn's copy of *The Kinsey Report*, when she had heard the Buick drive in the driveway and recognized its motor. She had gone up earlier and borrowed it from Dawn's shelves upstairs when she had not known he was coming home this soon. Dawnie had announced it when she bought it two months ago but this was the first time she herself had looked at it. She had been hoping to find out something important or useful about infidelity and what causes men to do it, but this stuff was all junk; charts and graphs; and said nothing at all about what was right or wrong, or anything else about men that she hadnt already known all her life; and not only that, acted as though sex were important! She had barely had time to get it in the lock drawer of her secretary and lock it up before he had come in, carrying his bags, and now she would have to find some way to get it back upstairs before Dawnie got home tonight.

Frank was looking at her a little surprised from beside his bed where he had the bag and briefcase spread out just so, as he always did, unpacking them.

"You look so tired," she said, feeling such a warmth for him that she could hardly keep from speaking it. "And so worn out."

Frank continued to stare at her with surprise, uneasily, still standing half bent over above the bag, his head turned toward her. "Uh, no," he said in a strange voice after a moment, and smiled wanly. "I can manage it okay. Thanks though."

"You just looked so dog tired," Agnes said.

"Well, I—" he began and stared at her strangely. "Well if you really want to do it. If you feel up to it." He stopped and rubbed his fingertips across his forehead, still peering at her out from under them startledly.

"Of course I do," Agnes said, her voice threatening to quaver, and came on in. "You just sit down there on the other bed."

"Well," Frank said indecisively, "all right," and did as he was told. "A bunch of us fellows went out last night, you know?" he said wanly, as she went about putting the rest of his things away, "and hit some bars and did a lot of drinkin. You know how those parties are. Once they get started, you cant hardly stop 'em. Everybody wants to go home, but nobody wants to be the first and make the first move and admit it. And then suddenly everybody's drunk and all high and excited and it just goes on and on." He sighed tiredly.

"I certainly do know," Agnes said sympathetically. She finished with the bag and closed it up and put it on the floor of the closet. "I wont try to do anything with your briefcase," she said, "I dont know where anything in it goes."

"Theres nothing in there comes out except those two dirty shirts," Frank said, and she took them out, "all the rest of it, the papers, goes back down to the office. And then this morning when I got up—late, of course—I felt so rotten and was late for an appointment anyway so I didnt even try to get any breakfast. And then when we got the work all done around eleven I was so anxious to get out of there and get home I didnt even stop for lunch. I havent had a thing to eat all day."

"You mean nothing!" Agnes exclaimed. "Nothing at all?"

"Not a damn thing," Frank said, a little proudly. "Nothing."

"But you ought to eat!" she said. "Would you like for me to cook you a steak?"

Once again he looked a little surprised and startled. "Well, yes, sure. In fact, Id love it. Im famished. If you feel up to it?"

"Of course I do," she said, and then smiled, allowing a little of the tremendous warmth she had suppressed to seep out, tentatively, into the smile and into her voice. "Thats what Im here for, isnt it?" Someday he would know, would understand, would really realize, she thought. But maybe he did already; this time he had come home, hadnt he? She smiled again.

From the bed he looked up at her for a moment—strangely, almost unbelievingly, speculatively, unsure and insecure; and even a little bit embarrassed, she thought with amusement, such children they were— and then immediately his eyes widened emptily and he got blankfaced. "Okay. Fine," he said heartily in his Rotary Club voice. "But I got some news for you first. Good news."

"Come on out in the kitchen with me and tell it to me while I fix the food," she said. "I might eat something with you. I didnt eat much lunch."

"No, let me tell you first. Then we'll have a sort of a little celebration party."

"All right," she said, humoringly, and sat down on the other bed, his bed, where the briefcase still lay open, and listened with a growing astonishment and admiration the more she heard, while he told her the whole story of the bypass deal. How he had first conceived it, how he had taken it to Clark, how Clark had taken him to Springfield to the old man, about the big Greek, and the Greek's men, with their rundown shoes, how he himself had bought the Monds lots, what they had finally done with all of it and how it stood now. Agnes had known it must be a pretty fair-sized deal, but she had had no idea it was of this magnitude; and she had always thought it was oil or something like that, but she had never once thought of it being the highway bypass. Neither had anyone else apparently. All that time it had stood out there, everybody knowing all about it, no secret at all, and she had never even considered it or given it a thought, and nobody had even seen the possibilities in it. Except Frank. Her husband. She had done right after all to stay by him all these years, she thought admiringly, and excitedly. Why, they were going to make more money than they could even use, more money than any family in Parkman except the Wernzes and the Scotts, and as he told it she could already see where someday it would become a legend in Parkman. Well, she thought triumphantly, she had always known he had the talent.

When he came to the part about the mortgages of the house and the store, Frank hesitated almost guiltily, before he told her.

"Its all right," she smiled at him. "Ive known about them all along."

It was Frank's turn to be astonished. She enjoyed his surprise complacently.

"You have?"

"Ever since you first got them," she said.

"And all the rest of it? The whole deal?" He looked a little crestfallen.

"Oh, no! Just the mortgages. Not the bypass. I never would have guessed that!" she said.

"And you never said anything about it and didnt get mad?"

"Why should I have? I trusted you. I figured you knew what you were doing. It was what you should have done. It was the only thing you could have done. I would have done the same thing, if I had been you."

"You would?" Frank said, a little pained. "Our home? Well. —But how did you know about it?"

Agnes shrugged a little, winsomely, and smiled. She could not remember ever having loved him quite so much. "Oh, I just guessed it. Just figured it out. Wives always know things about their husbands, I guess."

"Well, you know theyre both cancelled now, dont you?" Frank said a little anxiously. "I didnt have them long. Clark's father in law gave them back to me—for an interest, of course. Not for nothing."

"I was never worried," Agnes smiled. "And now, if youre all through telling me about it," she smiled chidingly, "what do you say I get you out to the kitchen and feed you that steak? Before you faint."

"Sure," he said, staring at her strangely, but unsurely, "Id love that steak." He got up wanly off the bed. "Maybe we can have ourselves our own little private party. And have a couple drinks—I need one; bad—and a good meal. And talk?" he said, making it almost a question. "And just. Sort of. Generally celebrate."

"Fine!" she smiled, unleashing in her eyes and voice even more of the warmth in her than she had released before. "Id love to have a drink or two. To celebrate. Do you realize we stand to make more money out of what youve just accomplished than weve ever even thought of having? We ought to celebrate!" she said gaily. Such a child.

"I know," Frank said heartily in his Rotarian voice. "But somehow I always knew wed do it. Uh, but what about Dawnie?" he said suddenly. "Wont she be home soon? Its almost five."

"What would that matter?" Agnes could not resist saying; "she could celebrate with us. —But as a matter of fact Dawn wont be home at all all evening. She and Wally Dennis have gone to Terre Haute swimming and to see a show."

"Oh," Frank said. "Well." He still looked unsure; almost scared.

"And so we can have the whole house to ourselves," Agnes said gaily. "And Ill cook you the best and biggest steak you ever had."

"Well, I could sure eat a steak," he said, almost guiltily.

"I just bought some fine ones today," she smiled. "Theyre not even frozen yet."

"You know how I love steaks," Frank said.

"Ill pick you out the biggest one of the lot," Agnes smiled at him. "And cook it for you just exactly like you like it."

"Well, a good steak would sure fix me up," he said.

They were both standing now, between the beds.

"Theyre the best steaks Ive bought in I cant remember when," Agnes smiled.

"I love steaks," Frank said, almost desperately.

For a moment she wondered how much longer it could keep going on. She had said just about everything about the steaks that she could think of. Of course, it had been quite a while. On both their parts. Almost two years. But my God! youd think hed know! she thought irritably while still continuing to smile gaily.

But just then, as she was irritably about half ready to go on out to the kitchen, and into the silence that was like a long significant pause between them but was really not and not very long either, Frank uttered a strangled, muffled, desperate cry that sounded like "Oh, Agnes!", and took hold of her upper arms with his hands and then went on, as she just stood there and did not pull away, and put his arms around her. And there was real desperation in his grasp as he clung to her in silence. He positively clung to her.

His briefcase was still lying open on his bed, but there wasnt anything on hers, and she suffered him to pull her down there and stretched herself out across it beside him. Staring at the so-familiar ceiling quiescently as he pressed his shaven cheek against her own, she shut her eyes and concentrated on savoring it as he fondled her—enjoy-

ing not so much the touch upon her body as his enjoyment of the touch.
That was all she ever had enjoyed, really. All she had ever wanted in her
life, she thought almost tearfully and yet once again, was to be able to
give him pleasure. After a moment, she put her hand—the free one
that he had not pinned—up on the back of his neck tenderly and
maternally and got up from the bed and went to shut the bedroom door
and close the venetian blinds and then, in the appreciably deepened
dimness of the room she took off her clothes.

From the bed, Frank watched her, staring at her, his eyes seeming
to be great dark hollow pools in the dim light. A waft of breeze through
the open window in the hot August afternoon air breathed upon the
closed venetian blinds and moved them inward, then let them fall. And
still he stared at her. Then he too got up and began to take off his
clothes and the habit of long years standing took over, like some kind
of automatic pilot, moving and controlling both of them, almost without conscious thought.————

————And lying beside her afterwards, after all the storm-toss
and silent noise and soundless loud voices in his ears, already half
asleep and emotionally tattered, Frank could not help thinking peacefully what a really ridiculously trivial and unimportant molehill sex
was for everybody to make such a damned big mountain out of. And it
was a great relief to him to be able to feel that way, after yesterday.
After last night. After all, what the hell was it really? Take the imagination out of it, and the emotion, and what did you have? A very simple
thing, really. A simple, uncomplicated, commonplace and comfortable
physical act; and then you wondered what all the hullabaloo was about.
And that was the way it ought to be, too. No complications, no troubles,
no wild crazy ramming around, no looking for something that wasnt
there. You did it, and then you forgot about it. Half-sleeping, he flung
his arm out gently and laid it across the bosom of his wife. Maybe she
didnt care much for sex, and not even hardly know much about it
even, or even come close to understanding it, like he did; but that was
all right, and maybe it was even better. For both of them. What did it
matter if he couldnt give her pleasure. It was funny, he mused, how
habit had just sort of taken over and run things. And he was glad it
had. He had been so embarrassed and ashamed and full of guilt he did
not think he could have gone ahead and done it on his own. But old
habit, it had just took right over, and moved them both along. Idly,
he wondered how many times he had slept with his wife in all these
years? four thousand? five thousand? six thousand? Peaceful, relaxed,
comforted, letdown, feeling somehow safe, Frank realized suddenly that
this was the first time in a long time—the first time since the last time he
had slept with Agnes, in fact—that he had really had that peaceful, comfortable after-sex feeling without a driving restlessness of guilt gnawing

at him too, making him get up. But why had she suddenly wanted him back today of all days in the world, and after so long? He couldnt understand it. He knew her too well to imagine it was because of the bypass. Well, whatever it was, he was glad of it. He wasnt the one who had ever wanted them to be estranged, he thought sleepily; ever. Glad they were back together, relaxed, his arm resting on the full comforting bosom of his wife and all his former distress and emotional upset of a few minutes ago forgotten, he slept, glad to be back home.————

————She dozed a little while herself, aware of his arm resting across her and liking it there, some deep tension in her relieved and gone now. Then gently so as not to wake him she raised his arm and moved herself out from under it and went to the bath and came back and dressed. Then she stood looking down at him, smiling to herself. He looked so pudgy and round like a little boy sleeping. Whatever the tension was that was relieved in her, it wasnt sexual, she thought positively. She just didnt have any sexual tensions, and never had had. And she didnt believe that any woman did—unless there was something drastically wrong with her; or unless she lied about it. Or had read some of this modernistic stuff like that Kinsey Report, about drives and abnormality. According to those kind of people, everybody in the world was abnormal! They talked about sex as if it was one of the most important things in the world, instead of what it really was; and all they did was make people more aware of it all the time and make them think about it and dwell on it more. No, if there was a tension relaxed in her, it was the tension of love, not sex. She had loved him so long, and so hard. Whatever she lacked in sex, she more than made up in love. And he was finally learning it. It should have been obvious. A woman who liked sex—sex for itself—would like it just as well with any man as with any other. But he didnt want that. None of them wanted that. Smiling to herself, she stood looking down at her husband happily. No real woman, no honest to God good woman, ever really liked sex. She liked the man. Agnes had used to pretend, sometimes, just to make him feel better; and for a long time she had felt she failed him, completely; was inadequate. Now she knew the truth: He had never left her, had he? What he really wanted was the love. God! she smiled to herself, they were all such children.

As she turned to go out to the kitchen Frank, as if he were subconsciously aware that she was going out of the room, sat up suddenly on the bed and sat staring at her, staring almost wildly, his eyes wide dark pools in the dimness, and she smiled at him and blew a kiss to him.

"Did you like it?" he said suddenly. "Was it really good? for you?"

"Of course it was," she smiled down at him.

"Did you, uh— Did you—" he fumbled.

"Of course I did," she smiled. "Couldnt you tell? Im going out in the kitchen now and fix your steak."

Frank was biting his lip. "I shouldnt have asked you that," he said. "I shouldnt have asked you."

"Of course you should have," Agnes smiled, "why shouldnt you have? Now you lie back down and go back to sleep. When I get it done, Ill bring our meal in here and we'll eat it together in bed."

"No!" Frank said nervously. "No! No, Ill come out in the kitchen with you. Ill, uh— We'll uh— Ill mix us both a drink. Then, maybe, after we eat, and have a few drinks and all, we could, uh—"

"Again!" Agnes said, making a humorous mock gasp. "Do you think itd be good for you?"

Frank grinned. "Well, we'll see, hunh?" he grinned happily. "Lets wait and see."

So, wearing his new foulard robe she had got him for last Christmas, he followed her out to the kitchen and mixed them both Manhattans and sat down at the kitchen table. Agnes set her own drink on the countertop and sipped at it as she got the still unfrozen steaks out and put them on and then set about fixing up a salad, and as she fixed the meal they talked.

They had not talked together so much in a long long time, she thought, not in years, really. It was fun. At first they were both self-conscious. She didnt know why exactly, but she was aware that she herself was shy, and that he was too. But after he had mixed them both another drink, it went away, and both of them loosened up. And the talking—happy, released, gay, understanding—was for both of them like a dam being cut through, she thought, and all that pressure of water that had been backed up there for so long, came gushing out of both of them in a torrential stream of ideas and reminiscences and plans, and love. It all seemed so surprising and unreal to her, and yet at the same time it was the most natural thing and normal in the world. This was the way it should always have been between them. And it was all so simple, really. All they had to do was get together a little, just spend a little time together. Frank talked more than she did, mostly about the bypass deal that he had just concluded. And then, after the second drink, although still a little embarrassed to be doing it, he went on and told her his dreams about it. He wasnt just content to let it go now that they had got it started good, he said. No sir, by God. He wanted to do really big things with it. Last year he had driven through one of those little suburban towns outside Cleveland, on his way to a jewelers' show, and had seen a new 25 million dollar development going up there. New homes, big new shopping center, new plants and factories. And yet the town wasnt much bigger than Parkman.

"Well, why cant we do that here?" he demanded of her, warming to it as he talked, "by God. That strip of land runnin' between the bypass and the railroad, it would be a perfect spot for it. Not only new factories to take advantage of the transportation facilities, but new homes, new businesses, a whole new town almost. Now, why couldnt we do it? Will you tell me that?"

"No reason in the world," she smiled at him happily. "All you have to do is believe in it, and be willing to fight for it."

"Well, by God, we will do it," he said forcefully. "Ill do it. Myself." And he went on, talking about the details of it, the land, and the locations—things she hardly even paid any attention to, now, because she was so busy thinking how happy she was. She listened attentively, and admiringly, and even excitedly, as he spun out his dream to her while she cooked. A year ago she might have hooted at it, but not now.

It was only after they had both had several drinks, and were in fact in the midst of eating,—it was almost dark outside—both of them laughing and talking, that Frank got off that subject and dropped it, and brought up something else, his face sobering solemnly.

"You know, if you wont get mad, Id like to ask you something," he said haltingly. "Suggest something."

"Of course I wont get mad. What is it?"

"What do you say—what *would* you say—to us adoptin' a child?" he said embarrassedly. "A boy."

Agnes took another swallow of her drink and cut off a bit of steak and smiled. It was not as big a surprise to her as he was expecting it to be, or indeed even as big a surprise as she proceeded to let on. Perhaps it was the drinks, partly, but it was as if she were hearing something that she had known beforehand was going to be said. She had known for a long time that he had been toying with the idea, though he had never mentioned it specifically. Especially since the taxiservice when Dave had failed him.

"Adopt a child!" she said, managing to look embarrassed, but really giggling inside. "What on earth would we want to adopt a child for?"

"Well now wait a minute," Frank said, a little thickly, and stuffed his mouth with steak. "Let me explain my side of it," he said around it. Under the drinks he was acting a little bit lordly now,—not nastily, just enjoyably. Such children they all were, she thought.

They were going to have a good bit of money now, he explained, from now on. And they were going to have pretty big business interests by the time they kicked off. Why shouldnt there be a Hirsh to carry it on? As for the work part, they could hire themselves a full-time maid. And Agnes knew enough about handling children that that part wouldnt be any trouble.

"Hell," he said, "I can see it now. Frank Hirsh and Son Enterprises."

"What about Dawnie?" she said, still smiling to herself. "How would it affect her?"

"Hell, it wouldnt affect her at all. One way or the other. Shell be gone and in college. —Would it?" he said.

"No-o, I suppose not," Agnes said. She cut another bite of steak. "I dont know if I would be adequate to the task or not though," she said selfeffacingly.

"Hell, of course you would. Matter of fact, we're both of us only just now gettin' to be old enough and wise enough to raise a kid. We're only really mature enough, now, mentally. We really werent with Dawnie. —Not that she didnt turn out fine," he hastened to add.

"Thats true," she agreed. "But I dont know. The work, and all. And sometimes they are a lot of bother in a home. Maybe you wouldnt want to come home if it was noisy and got all cluttered up," she smiled. Sometimes—sometimes, he was so cute, really cute, not "cute", that she just couldnt resist deviling him a little.

"Nonsense!" he said. "Nonsense! You know better than that, Agnes. Hell, Id probably be here all the time. So much youd get sick of the sight of me, I bet."

"Yes, Im sure I would," she said, and then had to laugh.

"Now, we wouldnt have to get a regular little baby," Frank said. "We could get a slightly older one."

"A younger child, three or under, is supposed to be the best," Agnes said. "Then it wouldnt know it had been adopted. Or wouldnt care, by the time it grew older, say six or seven. Thats the current theory of what is best," she said smiling.

"Hell," Frank said vigorously, "even that dont matter. We could do like I read in the *Reader's Digest,* about this man and his wife who adopted an older kid. They told it that it was better off than other kids, because real parents had to take what they got; while they had got to pick theirs."

"By the time the child was ready to go to school, it would know it was adopted anyway," Agnes said. "The other children would make sure of that. So maybe that would be better."

"Sure," Frank said. "Sure it would. Well, what do you say?"

"Well, why not?" Agnes smiled. "It might be fun. I dont know. At least we can look into it, cant we?"

In the end that was the way they left it, when they went to bed. Frank would look into it. And they would wait and see. And Agnes would get some books on it and start reading up, in case they did do anything with it. That was the way they left it, but both of them already knew they were going to go ahead and do it.

"We'll have to talk to Dawnie about it, and get her reaction," Agnes said, happily. But she already knew what Dawn would say; Dawnie would be delighted. And what the hell? she thought, extravagantly, pushing a strand of hair back out of her eyes as she cleared up the dishes, why not? After all, how many of her friends did she know, whose second child was the result of a reconciliation after the parents had almost separated? She could literally count hundreds. Almost every one, in fact, who had a second child. Or a third, or fourth. Well, then, why shouldnt she have another child too? What difference did it make if it was adopted? If *their* reconciliations only lasted just about long enough to get the baby, that did not mean that hers would only last that long. Because she could already see ahead of her, down the line, down the years, how it was going to be. Their lives would be that happiness together that people were always hoping they would have, but never seemed to. She knew it as surely and as positively as she had ever known anything in her life, she thought vigorously. Because she would make it that! They both would.

When they went to bed, Frank of course did not want any more sex after all. He was too tired, and a little too drunk, and he never said a word about it. Neither did she. And after getting him in bed, she was able to get the copy of Dawn's sex book out of her secretary and back upstairs where it belonged. In a way, she was glad Dawnie had it. It wouldnt hurt her to know a little something about men—just so long as she didnt get to thinking that sex itself was important. She would have to talk to her, she reminded herself, about that.

CHAPTER 49

WHEN her mother finally told Dawn—rather hesitantly—about the prospective plans for adopting a "baby brother" for her, Wallace French Dennis' mistress was not very surprised. She had been aware for some time that there was a second honeymoon going on at home and it was quite obvious that her folks were sleeping together again; and in fact, she herself had been very careful lately so as not to disturb them, always making plenty of noise and treading heavily whenever she came downstairs or whistling jauntily and clumping loudly about the porch when she came home late at night. She did not view this new state of affairs as alarming or ridiculous, nor did she have any sense of adolescent moralistic distaste about it. In fact she thought it was rather cute of them, at their age. And it amused her that they should try so clumsily and shamefacedly to hide it from her. She knew, of course, all about the Geneve Lowe affair and she was glad to see that both their vanities were finally allowing them to get back together again. And she was not in the least upset by the prospect of them adopting a baby—

as she noted Agnes had obviously expected her to be. After all that was what happened to most married people who got back together after a big dry spell, wasnt it? they had another baby.

"Why, I think its a wonderful idea, mother!" she exclaimed happily. The two of them were sitting at the diningroom table in the heat with the big floor fan going. "After all, you and Daddy are going to need somebody around here to look after and be with, after Im gone. And it wont be too long until Im gone and away from here. I think it would be a splendid thing for both of you."

"You really do?" her mother said. It was she who was surprised.

"But of course! Its the most sensible thing the two of you could do! What did you expect? me to throw a big tantrum and be against it?"

"Its only tentative, you know," Agnes said. "We havent definitely decided to do it yet."

"Well, you should. And you should do it right away. The sooner the better."

"Well, we'll see," her mother said. "We'll see about it. But we both wanted to know how you felt about it first."

"Agnes, darling!" Dawnie said soothingly, and went over to her and put her hand on her damp shoulder in the strapless dress. "Do you think I dont know Daddy's always wanted a son? To carry on his business? Do you think I havent read any psych at all? Oh, dont look so shocked! Im only trying to say that I think its the most perfect thing the two of you could do. I mean, you dont think Id ever want to take over Daddy's business interests and run them, do you?"

"Youd still always be our own little girl," her mother said; "No, but you might have a husband someday who might want to."

"*If* I ever get married—and thats a big *if*—if I ever marry anyone at all, itll be to someone who wont need Daddy's business interests, Mother. Someone wholl be *so* succesful, and *so* busy with his own important work, that he wouldnt even have *time* for Daddy's business if he wanted it. And Ill certainly never want to run them myself! All Im trying to say is that Daddy needs a son. You both of you do."

"Well, we'll see," Agnes said. "Maybe we can get together with Daddy and all of us talk about it."

"Of course!" Dawn said, feeling very protective and old-motherly toward them both. "We're all of us adult grownup human people. We're not children. Lets get together and talk about it and act like it."

It was the last week in August when all this came up and Agnes had broached the subject of the adoption. And immediately after it— after the two of them had more or less (mostly less, Dawn thought wearily) thrashed that out—Agnes had launched into a nervous skittish high-voltage discussion about Sex. Dawn would be going off to college before very long and it was time she knew certain things, she said;

college boys were different from highschool boys. Not that they were different, really. They were all the same. But college boys were more experienced, with women, and therefore less awkward and harder to handle. Dawn understood that, didnt she? And then she proceeded to talk about sex, awkwardly and uncomfortably, very vaguely and only in the most hazy general way—(without ever once, not even once, being the least bit specific, Dawn thought tiredly and exasperatedly, about such things as were clearly and frankly explained in Kinsey)—all as if she thought she were giving her daughter valuable and necessary information. From the heights of her own field experiences Dawn could only look down at her pityingly, and pretend to listen attentively.

Dawn was already exhausted by the long misunderstanding and abortive discussion of the adoption, and one of the immediate exasperated vagaries that came in her head was the picture of what her mother's face would look like if she should suddenly just come out and tell her that she herself had been sleeping with Wally Dennis now for close onto four months. She and Wally, at seventeen and twenty respectively, apparently already knew more about sex than her parents had found out up to now in their whole lives—or were, apparently, ever likely to find out in the rest of them. Dawn could not help feeling sorry for them; they probably didnt either one get half out of their sexual enjoyment what they should. Probably it was just that, unlike herself and Wally, they came from an older less educated generation. But she knew that if she and Wally didnt get any more sexual satisfaction out of their own sex than *they* apparently did—well, she just couldnt imagine it!

For her mother's benefit, and also to protect herself, she pretended to be embarrassed by the subject—(which in fact was not hard to do, since she *was* embarrassed—not only by Agnes's gross ignorance, but also because it was just naturally embarrassing to try and talk to anyone as old as Agnes about sex at all)—and wished wearily that this fiasco would soon be over with. Finally with a sense of relief for both of them, she was sure, Agnes wound up the lecture by cautioning her to be very cautious with all boys, and Dawn agreed, heartily and embarrassedly. She had a date with Wally that afternoon to go swimming, and she left soon after. It was, she thought with a kind of enjoyable ruefulness as she went out to Wally's mom's old car, probably as close as she and Agnes had ever been to understanding each other or were ever likely to be.

But as far as them adopting the little boy went, she couldnt have been happier about it, and felt it was the perfect thing for them to do. It was not until almost a week later—when they had talked to Frank, and the folks had more or less decided to on ahead with it—that the real devastating force of it really hit her.

She was being replaced. She had grown up. She was on her own. And from now on, she would continue to be on her own. She was, in effect, a displaced person—a regular DP. With no one to turn to, and no one to depend on. Except herself. She was, actually and factually, being kicked out of the nest. It was what she had always wanted, really, and there was a kind of pleasant excited terror about it which made her heart beat and that she enjoyed at first. But as she thought about it more and more and dwelt and dwelt upon it the pleasant excitement and enjoyable terror, like a rising tone of sound that gets higher and higher until it finally squeaks out of hearing range altogether, raised its own pitch in her until it was no longer pleasant or enjoyable but really and truly terrifying. Longingly she began to look back to the time when, by her own sayso, she could have stopped and prevented it, but which now she no longer could. Now it was too late. Now she had nobody to turn to except Wally, nobody at all.

Probably it would not have been nearly so bad, would not have struck her nearly so forcibly, had it not been for the shopping expedition. Two days after they had talked to Daddy about the adoption— (she didnt want them *not* to adopt him, that wasnt it at all, she didnt want them to give him up)—Agnes had announced at breakfast that the two of them were going to Indianapolis to shop for her school things and outfit. They had driven over that morning and had spent three whole days, and a great deal of money—Dawn did not even actually know how much—and had driven home the last afternoon with a carload of stuff, both of them totally exhausted, and more things on the way being sent. She had not even had time to call and talk to Wally, who of course was working then, in the morning, but she had talked to his mother (whom, Dawn found, she was beginning to increasingly dislike: she was so mealy-mouth) and told her to tell him she would be gone.

More than any other single thing could have, that shopping trip to get the clothes for school had shocked her suddenly and with an electric jolt into the realization that summer was almost gone, and that here she was, suddenly, inexplicably, right smack into the first of September, without yet having done a single, solitary thing about running off and getting away to New York as she had planned to do. The papers and applications had all been sent in to Cleveland, and she was already accepted as a freshman at Western Reserve. Now, the clothes she was to take with her reposed, solid and real, in the back seat behind her, stacked up higher than the rear window of Agnes's Ford, and more of them on the way by mail. Driving home along the heat-shimmering nearly-curveless highway through the bright brassy gold of very late summer and September, filled with its own baking airless poignancy of the end of summer as it prepares itself to shade off into fall, Dawn was seized and gripped by a panicky terror so deep that it made her want to just open the car door and jump out—anything to stop it. She had put it off all summer—without ever having meant to—and time had run out and out, to the end of the string. Now it had reached the point where she either had to act—or else admit she was not going to; and that very fact, the very knowledge of it, caused terror and irresolution. If she had only acted before, when she still had choice—

She had never meant to let it get this far. That was what terrified her. She had meant originally to leave with Wally some time in June soon after graduation. But then they hadnt, and then she had kept putting it off a week, and then another week. It had been such a lovely, beautiful, wonderful summer she had just hated to end it. Swimming, and the long car rides through the country, the hot afternoons of tennis, golf at the Country Club where by a trick worked in conjunction with Frank who took out a junior membership for him she had got Wally in to play, horseback riding at the Stables, and then sex and love somewhere in the woods on the way back home in the cool red of evening; and all the time both of them baking and burning themselves into a deeper and deeper tan, darker and darker and browner and browner, until when they took their clothes off together on the old Army blanket of Wally's the white outlines of the brief suits showed startlingly dead-white flesh against the rest of them, and they had made a joke about their "little white suits". It had been the most wonderful summer of her entire life, this had. And she had not wanted to end it. She had never known it could be like this. Running around with the girls in the summer wasnt the same thing at all.

And now here it was ended anyway, almost, and nearly upon her, and she was forced back to a weakened untenable position where she no longer had the initiative, was being forced to act, in terror, where she wanted to act in joyousness and reckless gaiety. It wasnt fair!

Sitting tense and desperately tight-lipped and silent beside her mother as Agnes drove, Dawn stared hollow-eyed and tautly out, her lower lids damp with sweat in the hot air of the car, watching the almost limitless vistas of the flat rolling, and baking, Indiana countryside that the new-style highway offered them, and wishing they could get home to Wally. If Agnes would only get her home to Wally. All this, added to the top of them deciding to adopt the boy, had unnerved and broken her completely and all she could think about was Wally. Silently she pressed her feet against the angled floorboard of the Ford, as if the pressure she exerted would move them faster and get her home to Wally quicker. If only Agnes would drive a little! and not just amble! Wally, Wally.

She did not see him that evening when they finally got home. Completely done in and exhausted by both her wild flaming panic and the shopping, she only ate a little something and went straight to bed. But before she went to bed she called him to tell him she was home and asked to see him in the morning. More than that she could not do. Her brain was too worn out even to think.

"But you know I work in the mornings, Dawnie," he protested.

"I know," she said. It was reassuring just to hear his calm solid voice on the phone. "I know, but this wont wait. This is important. Terribly important."

"My God!" Wally said. "Youre not—? I mean, youre not—?"

"No, no!" Dawn said, listening to her own voice and fighting to keep it from going off up into hysterics. "This is important! *Really* important! I simply must see you! Id come over now, but Im too worn out to think. I know how you feel about your mornings, and I wouldnt ask you if it wasnt important. But this wont wait. Time! Time! Is very important."

"Well, all right," Wally said slowly. "Ill come over and pick you up around seven thirty."

"Goodby," she said, unwilling to call him darling over the phone, but trying to put into her voice all the love and relief she felt.

"Goodby," he answered, in the same way.

When she got up in the morning she was feeling some better, but every time she thought about herself and what she had to do—or equally bad, not do—she got a sick weightless feeling as if she were someplace where gravity no longer existed. The truth was, she was afraid. Terribly, deathly afraid. The truth was, she didnt want to go to New York. She didnt want to do anything. She only wanted this beautiful, lovely, wonderful summer to go on and on, like it had always been. But it was already over. Almost over. And if she didnt go to New York, if she didnt pluck up the courage from somewhere and go, she would not only be backing down—and publicly! before all her friends she had made her brags to—but she would be reneging on everything she had ever believed in and stood for. She simply had to go. And only Wally could help her. Only Wally, solid old Wally, had the necessary courage. They had talked about it a number of times, and he had never said he wouldnt go. She clung to that. A huge strange city, full of all kinds of hoods and criminals and—and white-slavers; no friends, no one she could even go to, except Daddy's brother Darrell, whom she couldnt go to anyway because of Daddy finding out; no job, almost no money, except the little bit in her savings account. But Wally would back her up. Wally would help her, Wally could fix it, and when he picked her up promptly at seven thirty she did not even wait but began pouring it all out to him as soon as she was in the old car, before they were even out of town. She looked lovely in the white and green print strapless summer dress which showed off her rich deep shoulders and the depth of her chest and breasts and the muscles of her back. She looked lovely, she knew she did. What they would have to do, she told him, was leave in the next two or three days. Plan it all right down to the last dollar, get everything packed up, and put it into execution. If there wasnt any chance that he could get his mother to let him take the car, they would have to take the train or bus from Terre Haute and leave the car there. But it had to be that soon, two or three days. Otherwise, it would be too late. Within a week she would be leaving for school, going up early for rush week and all that. Agnes was going to drive her up and see that she got settled in. It would have to be before then.

"Where are we going?" she said suddenly, looking around. "Where are we?"

"What? I dont know," Wally said, looking around himself. "I was just drivin."

He had, as if from instinct and having done it so many times before this summer, driven out southeast on the road to the Country Club in the so-called old glacier hills. Just this side of it and on the opposite side of the road, across from the number two fairway, was The Stables where they had come so many times to rent horses. They passed it in silence, both of them looking at it, and then looking warmly at each other. Then, beyond the Stables, he turned off left on the road that led to the Club, up the long hill beside the number one fairway to where the number one tee and the Clubhouse stood on top the hill, and then the miles and miles of woods beyond. He did not turn in at the Clubhouse but kept on toward the woods, his face showing her nothing much of anything really.

The sudden breathless burst of talking had quieted her down some now, and she was thinking hard, figuring on how they might pack and stow away all they would need and trying to balance this against the time theyd have.

"I dont suppose theres really much of any chance of you getting your mom to let you take the car, is there?" she said.

"No," Wally said. "Not any chance at all."

"I wish Agnes hadnt stopped Daddy from getting me that car for Christmas, instead of just giving me a set of keys to the Buick," she said. "Well, we'll just have to do without it then. That only means we'll have to take less stuff, thats all. We ought to be able to get by on two suitcases apiece, anyway. And your typewriter," she added.

"What'll we use for money?" Wally said.

"Well, I have a little over three hundred hoarded away that Ive been saving for it the past year. And we'll have whats left of your thousand dollars."

"I dont know if theyll let me keep it, if I leave."

"Why, of course they will!" Dawn said. "Its yours. You won it. Theres nothing in the scholarship that says you have to live in Parkman."

"No, theres nothing says I have to live in Parkman. But Im supposed to be a student at the College. I wont be a student any more if I leave."

"But wouldnt Gwen fix it for you so you could keep it?"

"I dont know if she would or not."

"Hmm," Dawn said, thinking. "Its complicated, isnt it? Well, then we'll just have to get along without it," she said blithely. It was strange how much stronger and confident she was, just being near him. But then he was so calm, and—and solid; just—just solid.

They had passed the Club's woods park and barbecue ovens now and were going on down into the glacier hills of woods on the winding, twisting gravel road that led on down into the other hills. A few of the better-off people were beginning to build ranch-style homes back here on it now, now that the war was over and there were materials again. The winding, twisting graveled road down itself led to nowhere except to a few very poor little tacky farms back in the wooded hills, where people clung as precariously to solvency as their shacks clung to the hillsides.

"We'll still have enough out of mine to get us there and keep us going until we can get jobs," Dawn said. "They say jobs are very easy to get in the Village."

"We'll have to get married right away then, hunh? before we leave," Wally said.

"No we wont. We can get married when we get there," she said. "Or any time. We dont even have to get married at all. Greenwich Village isnt Parkman," she smiled at him. "Anyway, I dont want to get married. I think I much prefer being your mistress. Its lots more romantic."

"Ahhh, Dawnie!" Wally groaned, and turned upon her a look of torment, pure torment.

She was still thinking hard, trying to work out the insoluble problem of what to take and what to leave and how she could possibly get the necessary outfits all into two suitcases, and it took a moment for the meaning of it to register on her. When it did, it froze her into a kind of startled, still, breathless shock. "Why, Wally!" she said.

He did not say anything but turned back to negotiate a sharp hairpin curve on the gravel road.

"Oh, Wally!" she said, feeling a kind of dismayed aimlessness. "Oh, my! Why, Wally! you dont even want to go, do you?"

For a moment he did not say anything. Then he took a deep breath "No. No, I dont. No, damn it, I dont."

Her mind still drawing a sort of breathless, aimless total blank, Dawn babbled the first thing that came into her head. "But of course. I never even thought. All your interests are here. Your work with

Gwen, your book, your scholarship. I never even thought. How silly of me. Of course. But of course."

Wally paid no attention to this, and quite rightly, part of her thought, and went on with his point. "It isnt even sensible, Dawnie," he said. "Dont you see that? It isnt even reasonable; at all. Youre just not clicking when you think it is."

"Of course. Of course youre right. I just wasnt thinking. You really are right. I was just thinking about—" She stopped. Well, what had she been thinking about?

"What would we live on?" Wally said in a kind of desperate voice. "Where would we live? How do you know we could even get jobs? If we did, whered we be? Living in some cheap top floor tenement or something; while you tried to break into acting and I tried to write and hold a job too. Honestly, Dawnie, it just wouldnt even be sensible."

"You couldnt write in New York?" she said.

"I— How do I know?" he said. "I dont know whether I could or not. For sure, I wouldnt have Gwen's help there. She helps me a lot. More than you know. Im— So how do I know whether I could or not? Certainly, trying to hold down a job would be sure to cut down on my time and energy I could give it."

"But you can write here?" Dawn said.

Wally snorted suddenly, a kind of nervous laugh. "Well—if you call what I do writing," he said bitterly. "Yes. Yes, I guess you could say." He had stopped the car, pulling it off in a wide spot on the road, and turned and slung his arm over the back of the seat to face her.

"But would you go?" Dawn said. She herself had not turned and was still facing front, through the windshield. "I mean, would you go anyway? I mean, because I asked you? You know; I mean because it was *me* who asked you?"

"No," he said slowly; "no, I dont think I would, Dawnie."

"Would you marry me though. If we stayed here," she said.

"I— Well—sure. Yes," he said. "I guess. Sure I would." He looked puzzled. "But you yourself just said—"

"But you wouldnt want to."

"No, thats not it; thats not it at all," he said earnestly. "But what would happen? Would you want to move in our house with me and my mom? Would you want us to move in with your folks? Your dad would want me to go to work for him in his damned store the minute we got hitched. Is that what you want?"

"Good God no!" Dawn said vehemently.

"Well, you see? You got to think of those things, before you can figure something out sensibly."

"Its just that its all rather hard for me to understand and digest, you see," she said thinly. "Then, the truth is—the real truth is—you never have really loved me at all, have you? Youve just been—uh— (its a silly word," she added apologetically)—"youve just been 'trifling' with me all the time, isnt that right?"

"Thats a pretty harsh thing to say to me," Wally said, unangrily, his face breaking upward into little curves of unhappiness.

"But its true though, isnt it?" she said coldly, surprised to find what a real icy coldness there was down inside of her someplace, to draw on. In fact, it seemed to be bottomless. A regular reservoir. She turned then, finally, to face him.

"Well—no," Wally said. "No, it isnt. Dawnie, you dont know how many times Ive sat and suffered and felt all empty inside, just because I knew youd be going off to school this fall."

"But not enough to go to New York with me. Or to keep me here with you. Oh, dont be hurt. Im just trying to understand it. Im just trying to figure it all out."

Wally did not say anything for a moment. Then he made a motion with his neck and shoulders that was like the beginning of a shrug, but never actually became one. "What can I say?" he said simply. "I guess not. If you insist on putting it that way. Thats obvious, ain't it?"

"And youve never really *loved* me at all. The way Ive loved you."

"Well, I dont know how youve loved me," he said. He seemed to be getting more and more selfconfident in some odd way, she noted, all the time. "If you mean have I worshipped you like a Goddess, and bowed my neck, and blindly and worshipfully done whatever you bid me to—then I guess I havent. Is that the way youve loved me? If so, I notice you havent mentioned anything about you just staying at home, and going on living with your folks, and staying in Parkman just so you could be my mistress."

"Thats true, isnt it?" Dawn said coldly. "Is that what you want me me to do?"

"Well—no; I didnt say that. I didnt mean I wanted you to do it for me. I just wanted to point out that you never even thought of that side of it. I—"

"—Thats just what youd like, wouldnt it be?" Dawn said. "Then you could have me right there under your thumb, at your beck and call any time. —The truth is, youve got yourself a soft deal and a real good setup there with your mom and you dont want to take any chances on anything busting it up for you. You can lead her around by the nose and sweettalk her and shell do any damned thing you want her to, for fear you might get mad at her and up and leave. You arent just about to go to New York, or do anything else, that might upset your little applecart.

"The only thing you really lacked in that setup is that you didnt have any regular sex that way," she added. "And that was to be where I came in, I guess." She knew it wasnt the truth, at least not all the truth, but it was near enough the truth to make him uncomfortable, which was what she wanted. It was a very unfair thing, consequently, to say to him.

"Well," Wally said thinly, in a kind of veiled magnanimous tone meant to display that he really did not believe himself what he was saying, "maybe thats right. I guess maybe thats right at that." She had never realized before, Dawn thought, what a really pompous person he was.

And she wanted to kick herself. She was giving him all the advantage. Just handing him all the cards and letting him play them, even playing them for him, playing right into his hand, right into his smug complacent hand.

"Maybe youd better take me home," she said abruptly.

"Okay," Wally said. "If thats what you say."

"Thats what I say."

In silence he started up the car and went on down a little way to where there was a field-turnoff and pulled into it and turned around, and they started on back up the long steep hairpin-curving gravel road to the big hilltop, neither of them saying anything. At the Club-house on the top several foursomes were arranging themselves and lining themselves up to go out, and young highschool kids and college kids— so young, Dawn thought bleakly, so young, and so innocent, and so childish—splashed and shouted in the pool; the same pool where they themselves had swum so many times this summer. She watched them, all of them, golfers and swimmers and the others who were just sitting, from the car, hardly even seeing them and thinking about the sense of power—such tremendous power—that she had had that first time they had slept together, and subsequently, all the other times. And how she had felt she must be so very careful and so very wise, not to abuse it and not to use it on him. Hell, it was nothing but an illusion, a pure huge selfconceited illusion she had perpetrated upon herself. And how guilty and grateful he always seemed at the time. She had had no power over him at all. Maybe she had had power at the moment, just for that moment, the simple power of Yes or No. But she hadnt understood men. When men had the hots for you, they promise anything, anything you asked or wanted,—and maybe they even meant it at the time. And would continue to mean it—up until such time as you reminded them of it. Or tried to claim the loyalty and integrity they had offered so freely. Yes, she thought brassily to herself, the poor tormented guilty creatures. So grateful, they were, and so guilty. Suddenly she began to talk.

"You know, I really depended on you a lot, Wally," she said coldly, carefully keeping her voice very calm now, unangry, matter-of-fact, a little wistful, as they drove on down the far side of the hill along the edge of the number one fairway toward the main road and the Stables. She had no idea where the words came from, or how she knew so surely they were the right ones. "I guess Id never really loved anybody in my life, until you. But then of course Id never slept with anybody else. I even used to believe I never would, except for you." His face screwed itself up painfully, at that, and she laughed a little, sorrowfully. "I really did, honestly. And I counted on you. You were like a rock, right there behind me all the time. I had given you my virginity," —again his face crumpled up painfully—"and I knew that no matter what happened, what bad thing or terrible thing, no matter what kind of trouble or anything like that that happened to me, I could always go to Wally. If I could just get to Wally, I would think. Wally'll fix it. Wally'll see to it; he'll make it right."

"Arghhh, Dawnie!" Wally said strangledly from his crumpled face.

"That was the way I felt when we were coming home from Indianapolis yesterday. All I could think of was to get home to Wally. I was terrified; wed bought all the clothes, school was suddenly upon me, and I hadnt done anything about getting out and going to New York. —I didnt have the courage, you see, really—I had failed myself. Id let myself down. But I knew Wally would save me. I kept pushing with my feet against the floorboard, as if that would get me home quicker, to Wally. Because I knew no matter how I might fail, or be weak, youd take care of me. Youd fix it."

"Unhhhh—!" Wally said in a kind of wrenched, exquisite, deep baritone nasal cry, his face scrouged up around his eyes. "Listen, Dawnie! If you want me to go, Ill go! It isnt sensible, it isnt even reasonable. But it doesnt matter. Ill go."

"No, it was just a wild idea," Dawn said coldly, but truthfully. "It doesnt even really matter. I dont think I really wanted to go. I was just panicky, and I got scared. I guess I was just looking for reassurance. Its funny; I think if you had agreed to go right off, and we had started planning on it, I dont think we would ever have really gone, in the end. I think I was just trying to test how much you really loved me." She gave a wistful little, sad little laugh. "So you see, if you had agreed to go, probably nothing would have ever happened anyway, and you wouldnt have had to go after all, and everything would have been all right after all."

"Oh, Dawnie!" he said almost pleadingly. "Please dont say things like that to me."

"I didnt mean to say anything to hurt you," she said, honestly and sincerely. "I was only just trying to explain how Ive always felt about you.—

"—Of course, nothing will ever really be the same again now," she said. "Even if we went. I suppose in her life every woman has one first lover that she heroizes, and who must naturally of course let her down some way. Its really just as well its happened like it has," she said earnestly. "Really it is."

"Oh, Dawnie!" Wally said, sort of hopelessly. It sounded as if he were meaning to go on and say more, but then—as if there wasnt any use— he didnt.

"You have your work," she said; "and I have mine. I suppose school is really what I really need anyway. I need more study, and more work experience—and more life experience, too—before I try to make a break. I know that."

Wally did not say anything to this, and they rode along a little way in silence, back toward town. Dawn thought again of those kids in the pool out there at the Club. So young they were, from her vantage point, so very young. And so inexperienced in their innocence; they didnt know what was ahead of them, did they? She had been like them, earlier in the summer. She thought about them bleakly. It seemed to put her in just the proper mood.

"Maybe in a year or two," Wally said suddenly with a kind of eager hopefulness, his face still contorted. "Maybe then when I got my book done, you see. Then we could go in together. I might even be able to help you along, if I had some pull. Then."

"Oh, sure," Dawn smiled sorrowfully, "Of course. Well, we can always talk about that later, cant we? But right now, Wally, I just want to go home. You dont mind, do you?"

"Oh!" he said. "No. No, no. Ill take you right there."

"And you just keep on thinking that," she said. She shrugged a little, "Ill be all right tomorrow."

Wally did not answer this. His face was still contorted, and now his mouth was drawn into a thin tight line across his face. Getting a little mad, was he?

"Dawnie, I never meant to let you down," he said after a minute.

"Oh, I know that," she said, "I know you didnt." She didnt hold it against him, she said. She understood what it was like. He had to think of himself and his work; if he didnt, nobody would. Women were just different than men. They had all been trained to think that when they gave themselves, they were giving something really important. Men just didnt feel that. Especially the first time, she added, if the woman happened still to be a virgin. —And the rest of the way on in she talked on to him (almost, in a way, as volubly as she had talked on the way out—except that now it was in a much more calm way, with a much more artistic sense) trying to explain factually what it was really like to be a woman instead of a man. Two or three times she mentioned her former virginity—not weepily, but matter-of-factly, objectively, in an effort to get at what she meant. Each time she mentioned it he winced visibly. But he did not say anything. His face got more and more contorted, and the thin line of his mouth got tighter and tighter. She watched his suffering coolly, wishing in a way that she could spare him, and tears welled up behind her eyes, tears of loss, and sympathy both for his suffering and her own.

"Will I get to see you again before you leave, Dawnie?" he said when he drove up in front of the house.

"Why, yes," she said; "if you want to. You call me up."

His face was still contorted, drawn up agonizingly and painfully around his eyes, and the thin hard rigid line of his mouth across his face under the old baseball cap was still as tight as ever, and as she stood on the porch and watched him drive slowly away she looked after him cold-eyed, a selfcognizant hollow shell of steel, aware again of that hard mind-gripping bottomless reservoir of coldness in her that she had never even known she had before. He would never marry anybody. He just wasnt that kind. Unless he happened to find one someday who played it exactly as he wanted, and never argued, and never fought, and never disagreed with him, some meek little mouse of a girl that he could order around like he did his mom—preferably an heiress— and otherwise he just by God wouldnt marry. He didnt have to. Nobody could make him. Hed sit in jail first by God. Because nobody was ever going to make him do anything. Opinionated, stubborn, selfwilled, phlegmatic, bullheaded, obstinate, totally immalleable. She knew all this standing there just as simply and as surely as if she had read an analysis of his character in a novel, and saw it just as clearly. Just as everything she had said to him—every hurt and scouring she had spoken to him, every sympathy she had made him feel for her—had not changed the thin hard resolution of his mouth one iota. Just as she knew, clearly and surely, that no matter how many hundred times he might agree to go to New York with her he would, in the end, back out on his promise, go back on his word, and turn around the other way and bullheadedly refuse to go. In short, he was not the stuff of which good husbands were made, Dawn thought coldly, and was a total waste of time. For any woman.

Only when he was out of sight—then—did the panic and terror hit her again. She turned around and went inside and went up to her room and lay down on her bed, as cold and rocklike as a statue, while inside of her every muscle and nerve inside her quivered and spasmed in sheer panic and terror. She was so afraid—of something—she could not even cry. It looked like it was school for her, and no other way out, and once again bourgeois society had triumphed. Coldly, while she quivered inside with a nameless fear, she accepted that. School it was. It seemed nobody in the world ever loved you enough to give up something for you. They loved you, of course, but not quite that much. And finally she found herself thinking unaccountably of Shotridge.

————Wally, on the other hand, felt only a vast sense of relief. His face was stiff and felt like plaster from the tension it had been subjected to and his jaws were sore, and every muscle in his belly was jumping uncontrollably. Panic and terror at his own spinelessness and lack of basic loyalty and integrity assailed him. But as soon as he got away from her and drove off from the house it began to wane, leaving him only with a great sense of relief as if the dentist had told him he was through with him for the day and he could go home. Limp, weak, sweating profusely from the armpits and the palms of his hands he drove slowly and shakily away, in a fog of emptiness.

She was right, of course. She was right in everything she had said to him. He had done everything she said. And she had not missed a single point or topic in telling him all of it, either. Still, all he felt was only a great sense of relief, relief to be alone, relief not to hear her plaguing voice in his ears any more. And that made him feel even more guilty. What the hell? He had never told her he would go to New York with her. Or that hed marry her either.—Though he would, of course, he supposed, if he had to; marry her, that is—not go to New York.

It was only ten or ten thirty. But he couldnt work any more today. —Any more? he hadnt worked any!—God damn women anyway, he thought and turned shakily north down the hill of town and out toward Smitty's Bar. What he needed was a drink, or several drinks.

God damn it all! he thought explosively, it was crazy! The whole damned thing was crazy. Insane. What did she know about New York? What did she know about living off of peanuts? Shed had everything she wanted all her damned life. The poor little rich girl! Shed last about two weeks working as a waitress in a drug store. And all them intellectual bums there, in New York, all sitting around drinking each other's liquor and talking Existentialism and how to be a Hipster while they tried to romp each other's wives. And patting each other on the back for being artists. What kind of crap was that? He had never been there; but he knew all about it. Hed read a little. The whole damned thing was crazy! he thought again violently, insane! the wild hysterical plotting of a damned teen-age ex-virgin! Completely irrational!

But he still could not escape a gnawing feeling that he had, in fact, as she said, let her down. And he could not get away, over and above his sense of relief at getting away from her, from a sick feeling in his stomach when he thought of their woods up by West Lancaster, and of those lovely breasts of hers, and that hard-soft mellow little body. And when he thought of her going off to school and maybe sleeping with some other guy as she had slept with him, it was unbearable.

Still nevertheless, he was God Damned if he would go to New York with her. He was sure that if he called her up, right now, and offered again to go, she would take him up. And he was equally sure that if he did not, that this was the end.

But if it was the end, then it was the end. Kismet! And down deep inside him some solid dependable rockhard something, that he knew he could always depend on, told him that it did not really matter anyway.

And after he had sat in the calm cool interior of Smitty's and cooled himself down a little, he was even more sure of it. In the end, all that mattered was a man's work, by God. What he produced. What he created. And not who the hell he was married to, or how many damned offspring he produced. Hell, any damned dog or cat could do that efficiently—and have more of them at one sitting than any damned human female.

With his third beer he fell to thinking about power, and power over women. He had just lately been reading Harold Lamb's *The March of the Barbarians* and his biography of Genghis Khan. Those old guys, those Mongols, they had power—over everybody. And power over their women. If they said "put out!" the women put out. If they said "Shut up and get out and leave me alone" the women did. The men had power over the women and the women therefore tried to please the men, because if they didnt those old Mongols they would cut their damned heads off and they knew it. They had physical power, and there were no humane laws to stop them, and so the women acted like they were supposed to act. And that was what it came down to. It was almost inconceivable to believe it, used to as we were to the way we lived today where there was no power, save in the State. It was just like with slavery. A thousand years ago slavery was common and accepted: it was the result of defeat in battle: if you lost the war you became the slave of the guy who beat you. But nowadays we always equated slavery with Negroes, we did and the Negroes did, but it didnt have anything to do with Negroes at all really. It just had to do with being weak and losing the war. Pink men, green men, white men, purple men—if you lost the battle you became the slave. But we today had forgotten all that, both us and the Negroes, so that when you thought of "slavery" today everybody thought of "Negroes." And it was the same with women.———

They saw each other twice more, after that, before Dawn left. And both times they went up to "their woods" up by West Lancaster. Dawn had made up her mind that she would not call him up, but finally—just four days before she and Agnes were to leave—he had called. And asked her if she wanted to go out that night. And then he had called again, the next night.

The first night she would not let him sleep with her, and she hadnt meant to any other time. Not that he had asked. He hadnt. But, without ever saying anything about it, he had made it plain when they were at GLEN AND GERTRUDE'S bar with its red plastic decor in West Lancaster, that he was available. She had chosen to ignore it.

But the second night, and she did not know just why, when he had again without ever actually saying anything made it plain that he was still available, she had made it equally plain without ever saying anything that she was amenable. And so, as they had the first night, they wound up driving on west to "their woods." But the first night they had only sat and talked.

Dawn did not really know why she changed her mind. Perhaps, in a way, it was because she felt that in a way it was farewell—as Wally apparently also saw it as a kind of farewell. Though the fact didnt seem to disturb him any.

But mostly, it was really a sort of experiment on her part. At least, that was the way she always saw it later. Certainly, she did not feel that she had lowered or degraded herself by consenting. What she really wanted to find out was whether she still liked sex. After all, he was still the only man she had ever been to bed with.

What she found out was that she still did like it. Like sex. But that she did not like it nearly so well. In fact, she didnt really like it at all; and she didnt dislike it. It just seemed to be sort of nothing, really. And in some way, what had once been in it before seemed now to have gone out of it entirely. Actually, it more or less bored her.

Of course, it still felt good physically, and all the various things. But that of course was after all purely physiological, and was to be expected. She still liked it—physiologically. She could not help wondering briefly, at the time, what it would be like sleeping with Shotridge also. Probably miserable, she thought bleakly. He was such an awkward fumbling guilty dumb jerk, Shotridge. He certainly would probably never be much like Wally, she thought looking up at him. Wally, she noted, had not had much to say.

Two days later she left driving with Agnes to Cleveland.

CHAPTER 50

DAVE suspected something of all this between his niece and Wally. Sitting as it were at his pinnacle of observation in the house—where it seemed that more and more everything connected with any of them seemed to center, writing hard every day and engrossed in his novel and his people to the point where he himself seemed hardly to live at all except in them, he was able to just sit back and watch what happened in everybody's lives with a detachment he had always envied, and without ever becoming involved or taking any part himself. And consequently, he was able to observe more accurately and with more objectivity than he had ever achieved in anything before. He did not even have to go out, it appeared; everything came to him, at the house. All he had to do was sit—and work—and eventually reel after spliced reel of everybody's life was delivered to him unasked-for and made to unroll its pictures for him. Naturally, for Dave, it was a very salubrious setup.

And in the case of Wally, it was more than clear that something had happened. It was impossible to know just what. Except that it must have been something to do with Dawnie. Not that Wally ever said anything about her. He didnt. But the mere fact that he never mentioned her indicated something; before, up until she had left for school, he had talked about her incessantly—always politely and in a gentlemanly big-brother way, of course. But from the first week of September on after she had left, he never spoke of her at all. He hung out at the house more and more, drinking more than he had ever drunk before and playing pingpong avidly and with wild pugnacity with everyone and anyone who would play with him, until he was spending practically all his time there. He still wrote in the mornings, of course. And he still attended his few classes at the College—as soon as school took up again. But all the rest of his time he was at the house until he became almost as much of a fixture there as the two owners themselves.

Dave knew from Gwen that at his own instigation Wally had come to her earlier in the summer with a fairly elaborate plan of his own for revising his book himself. A plan which, in essence at least, Gwen had agreed with; and had told him to go ahead with. It had to do with a new viewpoint about sex and love, Gwen had said without smiling in the least. That was all Dave knew about it. —All he wanted to know, since he agreed with Gwen that her writers should not talk to each other, and that she should not talk to any, about each other's books. At present she was engaged in getting some young ministerial student at the College started upon a novel about (and here she did grin) of all things, young ministerial students.

"Keep them writing," she smiled. "Just keep them writing. Time, the great healer—and peeler—takes care of everything else."

With Wally, it was clear that his new viewpoint about sex and love had come before whatever it was that had happened between him and Dawnie. By several months. And whether this more new—and evidently unpleasant—development had further changed and evolved his ideas about sex and love, Dave had not yet learned. But Wally was apparently learning—painfully; as what man did not?—something about the vagaries of women. And the more caustic and cynical his new knowledge made him, the more Dave found he liked him. He had lost none of his brash selfabsorbed confidence that was often a hard trait to get along with, so apparently Dawn had not clawed his soul too very deeply. Whether they wrote letters back and forth from Cleveland to Parkman, Dave didnt know but he suspected that they did not, or at least not very many. And by the end of October and first week of November—which celebrated Dave's first year of return to Parkman— Wally had done something which, since Dave had known him at least, he had never done before. He had taken to going out with the brassiere factory girls (bringing them down to their house, usually!) and finally had settled on, and formed a more or less half-way alliance with, the titian-haired Rosalie Sansome who towered at least three inches over him, but who nevertheless obviously did not tell him what to do, and whose own great pleasure in the relationship clearly had to do with the fact that she viewed Wally—a student at the College, and whose father had been rich—as one of the town's aristocracy.

Dave could not help thinking a little wistfully of Dawnie, whose lush woman's body moving magnetically about beneath her child's head and brain he had often looked at covetously, and—always provided he had not been her uncle and a member of the family, of course—would have so liked to seduce; and whatever their trouble, he could not only sympathize but fully empathize with Wally.

To have once had that rich young body, and then to have had it more or less forcibly removed for some reason or other by the owner— because he knew there was more to it than just her going away for a year to school—well, that was rough—

Anyway Dave was having his own minor troubles which more or less coincided, and was still wishing he could get Gwen to love him just enough to go to bed with him, instead of loving him so much she worried about what would happen to his soul if she did.

And in spite of the fact that he was more or less resigned to it, and even actively enjoyed their "platonic" relationship most of the time, there were still times when a full fury of frustration would rage through him at being apparently so near and yet at the same time so far, and make him want to do something desperate except that he could not think of anything desperate enough to do.

Why did women always have to be so damned "spiritual"? he wondered, wistfully desiring Dawn and Gwen both, simultaneously. Why did they always seem required to feel it was their duty to be "spiritual" and worry about a man's goddamned soul? They couldnt just sleep with you and love you, no. It had to be "spiritual". Why the hell couldnt there be women who thought like men thought?

On the anniversary of his first year in Parkman 'Bama, conspiring with Wally and Dewey and Hubie, threw a first year party for him. It was a surprise party—up until about the last three days before; but by then even Dave could tell there was something up somewhere. Nevertheless, he dutifully pretended to be deaf and blind; and when he came home to find the surprise party waiting on him, dutifully pretended to be surprised. Nearly all the gang from Smitty's were there, as well as other more or less indiscriminately invited guests asked by one or another of the organizers in a moment of enthusiasm. The house (as well as its occupants and hanger-outers) apparently was becoming quite celebrated in Parkman, and just about everybody—saving only Frank and the positively respectable element—wanted to get in on the act. Wally's two pals Jack Beers and Tom Parker were there with their girls; the owner of the Nite Owl Restaurant in West End came; Smitty and one-armed Eddie the bartender were there; so were Albie Shipe and the three drivers from the taxistand invited by 'Bama; as well as other people Dave only knew vaguely or not at all. And for the first time Doris Fredric attended one of the parties, moving brazenly and virginally about familiarly as if she had lived there since the place was leased. In fact, just about the only people Dave had had any associations with since he came to Parkman who were not there—saving only Frank and the positively respectable element, of course—were the Frenches, and Wally told him later that he had wanted to invite them but that 'Bama had demurred on the grounds that it would be too lowdown a brawl for highclass college people. Dave, thinking of Gwen and Bob, could only laugh. Both of them, he was quite sure, would have loved it.

Ginnie Moorehead, as it happened, was not at this party either. 'Bama, who was becoming increasingly suffocating and mother-henish about him and his writing, had seen to that. And Dave of course knew nothing about it until afterwards. On the surface it was perfectly fair and reasonable; 'Bama had just decided they would ask only guys, who could bring girls if they wanted. Then, he apparently figured, if anybody liked Ginnie well enough to bring her they were welcome to. That was fair. Of course, nobody did. Nobody was that willing to be seen with her, although someone or other brought almost all the other brassiere factory girls. The result was that this party was not a loose mixed party at all, but one made up of couples, and there were no stag girls—in itself a rarity at the house on Lincoln Street. And except for a few of the type of Albie Shipe and Raymond Cole, the two hosts—himself and 'Bama—were the only ones without dates. No; there was one other: Doris Fredric. Because if she was supposed to be 'Bama's date, no one would have ever known it. 'Bama paid no attention to her at all all evening, looking at her as if she were just one more strange party guest whom he hardly knew, and Doris herself moved familiarly and blandly through the house and about the party, apparently completely at ease, and at the same time ignoring both of them as if she had come with someone else and hardly knew them either. What she—or 'Bama either—hoped to gain by this Dave had no idea; almost everyone in town knew by now that she was 'Bama's mistress, and it was obvious that she could only be there as his or 'Bama's guest. But no one said anything, and everybody treated her as if her presence there were a natural and foregone conclusion, and she herself did not stay late and quietly got her things herself and left early. Although most of the gang who hung out at the house regularly stayed on late after the less familiar guests had gone.

As Clark Hibbard's society editor would have written for the *Oregonian*—had that lady chosen to write about this party; which she did not—a good time was had by all. Everybody got mellowly drunk, there was not one fight or argument, and after the more conventional elements had gone there was some bedding down upstairs by those who could talk their women into it. And as he sat drinking, a kind of spasmodic cramp of tear-starting sentiment seized on Dave and held him, as he looked around at all of them—his fellow citizens and Plebes, Romans all, he thought, the sturdy bricks of the empire-builders.

When he looked back over it, as he did that night after he finally got to bed, it seemed amazing and incredible to Dave how much his life had changed in the one year since he had come back to Parkman to stay one week only. It was as if—almost—the very cells of his body, as they gradually died off and replaced themselves with new ones, had not only replaced themselves but had altered each new cell they built until they had built a wholly new and totally different body and man. He just was not the same person who had come here a year ago. He did not think the same, he did not act the same, and he did not look the same. By virtue of having resolutely cut himself down on his eating he had leveled off at just over two hundred pounds now—as against a hundred and fifty five when he got out of the Army. Not too much difference, but far too much for a man only five feet six inches tall. (He had also resolutely tried calisthenics in the morning several times, but it rarely lasted over a week before hed give it up; and even when it did, he could not see it made him any difference.) But as his body had spread and softened, his mind had honed itself thinner and keener and much sharper. And as for the way he acted, belligerence was almost not ever in him any more, nor anger, coming only rarely and when it did come sweeping him with such a sudden blazing flame of rage and fury that for a moment he wouldnt even know what he was doing, or care, something totally foreign to anything that had ever existed in his nature before, and which was almost always gone almost before he felt it.

And as for thinking—and the way he thought—well, it was no longer even conceivable to him to think of living some kind of a life without writing in it. Day by day, hard, rigorous, craftsmanlike writing, saying all those things he felt, and thought, and wondered, and believed or did not believe—(but not saying them expressly or explicitly, but only by inference, through the craft of the work itself)—about people and their ways. It might not be the highest work in the Universe; but it was the highest ever attained to by sniveling creeping man, scrambling along holding onto and clutching his goldbag and his scrotum like some hairy tarantula dragging along its precious egg bag. It might not be the most immortal and powerful of occupations, but it beat being President, or Secretary of State, or Chairman of the Board of General Motors, or any of those other "great benefactor" positions so beloved by those who held them.

—And the sum, the upshot, the lump, of what he wanted to get said was that each man was a Sacred Universe in himself and at the same time, inextricably, a noisome garbage pail whose bottom had rotted out and was poisoning the garden air and needed to be got rid of posthaste, forthwith and forsooth. That these two were not only inextricable, but were actually one and the same. And that therefore there was no Evil; and probably no Good; only Growth;—or if there were, they were so inextricably involved, like man himself, that no man-brain or -system, no Philosophy of Meaning, would ever separate them without automatically perverting both. And that therefore there was only growth, only change, and the pain of change, and the ecstasies of that pain, to embrace; because that was all there was, to embrace. And all of which every single one each in his own way tried—from all four—so hard to shy away from. And most of all that people—people and their institutions—were not nearly so important, or so dominant, or so successful, in and to the Universe as people and their institutions— especially the institutions—tried so mightily to have believed.

That was all, really. All he wanted to say, get said. And at such times when he could come so close to verbalizing it, he could almost feel he knew the things he needed to know about himself to do it. But then the curtain would always fall. —No. No, he didnt think at all like he used to, like he thought a year ago.

And he owed it all, or most of it, to Gwen French, he told himself. Some to old 'Bama, and some also to Bob French, perhaps. But most to Gwen. Because he had once fallen in love with her, he thought looking back nostalgically, and had made up his mind to make her love him too. And she had. Finally. And not only that, had helped him; had worked with him patiently, and carefully, putting all her really large knowledge of literature at his disposal, making his aim her own. And he loved her very dearly for it. Cherishingly, as a man might love some fine rare piece of eggshell china, carefully, and warmly. Whatever her wild,

lurid past. And whatever her sexual predilections now. He had just about
made up his mind he was never going to be able to seduce her.

With a kind of start, Dave the artistic social rebel, Dave the hater of
convention, realized suddenly that he had—in some peculiar manner,
by some oddball twist—unconscionably worked himself into the position
of the typical damned husband with his little invalid wife at home whom
he couldnt sleep with but could cherish and love and look after and do
fine things for and his mistresses whom he did not love—at least not like
he worshipped his little wife—but could get his sex from. In many
ways—in a *lot* of ways—his situation with Gwen and with Ginnie
Moorehead (and of course, all the other women around that he slept
with too)—was just about the same damned thing. Of course he wasnt
actually married to Gwen. But that didnt change it. Well! he thought,
the wind gone out of him, feeling a little silly, and somehow deeply,
frighteningly embarrassed; Well, what do you know. And he hadnt even
seduced her yet.

It was just about this time, not very long after the party—and coming
almost inevitably, if one looked back on it (which of course he hadnt,
until afterward)—that Doris Fredric tried to seduce him.

The fall had come on slowly, this year, and had lasted long. This
year wasnt at all like last year. Last year at this same time in early
November, when Dave had arrived in Parkman, it had been raining
coldly and spitting snow, and then had developed into the winter's first
big snowfall—heavy enough to disrupt highway traffic and line the
big semis up along the side streets around the square until the highway
could be cleared for them on the big hill five miles west of town. That
was in fact the very night he had met Gwen, when the snow had begun.
When it all had begun.

But now this year was entirely different. So different, it might have
been entirely another planet. The heat of August and early September
had lingered on clear to the first of October, and then had come the
month of gradually chillier nights and bright blue warm days, and
the trees gradually turning, while the dry browned grass revived under
the rains and greened again below the vivid reds and yellows of the
maples and the russetbrown of the oaks until the landscape itself became a totally different one and did not even resemble its former self, and
now in November it was still Indian summer and people still went
safely around in shirtsleeves. The College was particularly beautiful
right now, and Dave had driven out down the hill from town past it
numerous times to look off across all the big old trees to where shoulder-
padded boys kicked booming punts on the practice fields and brown
legged girls in the awkward blousey shorts of the gym classes
squealed themselves through games of touch or softball. It was hard
to believe that any or all of them were actually laboring heavily along

under the weight of their own personal problems, looking at them, without making a conscious effort to go back and remember how you had been yourself in school, so that the result was a tendency to nostalgically remember the "golden days" of your "lost youth", if you didnt watch out. Frank had been an exceptional punter and placekicker, he remembered suddenly, the best the highschool had ever had. Which was the main reason he had been able to make the varsity, since he was too light for almost everything else except playing safety. The town was creeping back into Dave some way, powerfully, emotionally, inexorably, a powerful current carrying below its surface the jumbled slowly tumbling flotsam of dead uprooted memories. Watching the seasons change across its face had a great deal to do with causing it in him. He had never thought he would ever love this miserable, beautiful, backward-in-all-the-wrong-ways, progressive-in-all-the-wrong-ways, petty little Illinois town.

But he did.

Watching the seasons pass and change across Illinois did something else to him, too. It made him come gradually aware that he was running out his string, was not in fact getting at all younger. Each week that passed brought its change in the season, unavoidable, inexorable, relentless; whatever else happened the season advanced; making him poignantly aware that one more week of his life was gone, not to be recalled, or brought back, or used again. Each snowfall, each rain, each dry spell, each bright blue day, and where he had only been thirty six a year ago, now he was all of thirty seven. And soon he would be forty.

Forty!

Dave Hirsh, whom he had known and loved and lived with since he was six and ten and seventeen, forty!

There had been a time when he thought of forty as incredibly ancient, and of thirty as old age. And had wondered what people who were that old found to do with themselves. Now both seemed young. And it would drive him back to work with a slash and vengeance that it generally would take him three full hours working time to get over, before he could go back and re-do carefully and calmly what he had tossed out frenziedly any which way.

The summer that had passed now, gone, become a larger but already swiftly dwindling knot back somewhere in the perspective of the moving string, had been an excellent one. The house itself was fun to live in. Something was always going on through someone. And the strange, tall, sneering Southerner he lived with and had become so close to was always an increasing surprise to be around. Sometimes Dave felt that, in spite of all the time they had spent together now, he didnt know 'Bama at all. 'Bama, it turned out, was an ardent horticulturist—or rather, more accurately, turned into one after they got the

house. There did not seem to be anything he was not interested in.
—Excepting only people; people obviously bored the living hell out of
him.— But anything else, any new science or craft or technique, he
would sit and theorize over for hours, constructing in his thorough
mathematical way a careful system to follow in order to take all
inefficiency and haphazardness out of whatever it was, and then would
plunge into it enthusiastically, expending incredibly vast amounts of
physical and mental energy to see if his system would—or if he could
make it—work out.

The horticultural phase all started because of the vacant lot next to
the house. Early in the summer, almost before they had got comfortably
settled in, 'Bama had taken up the subject and the thorn of the
vacant lot. Already, still in May, it was grown up kneehigh in grasses
and weeds, and had evidently been let go that way for some years by
whoever owned it and the Albersons who owned the house, and 'Bama
didnt like it. It looked like hell, he said. The next thing Dave knew
the gambler was back from town bearing a brand new two hundred
dollar motorized rotary type mower and an armload of rakes and
scythes, and for a week they worked like dogs, sweating profusely in
the moist early summer heat, drafting Dewey and Hubie and even
Wally when they could, to cut and clean it up. (It looked like hell for
several weeks, all stubble, until the new grass blades began to come up.)
And from this 'Bama discovered lawning. He found a book on lawn
care at the local hardware dealer's who was the agent for Scott's Seeds
(most expensive of them all) and bought it and devoured it and then
went back and returned from town with an additional three hundred
dollars worth of equipment, a lawn spreader, fertilizers, weed killers,
and seed. And from there it was only a simple step to wanting to put
in some shrubs and trees and evergreens on both the vacant lot and
their own lot too, and the next step after that was of course flowers.
'Bama came in with armloads of nursery catalogs and sat up poring
over them until even Dave, who had never given a damn about flowers
or gardening or anything like that either, began to get the fever too.

It was an easy matter to get the permission of the owner of the vacant
lot to do all this, since it turned out that when they asked Judge Deacon
to find out the owner for them he informed them it was himself who
owned it, having bought it up once thinking to turn a dollar someday
on the resale for a home site. So they went to Terre Haute and bought
an easy five hundred dollars worth of flowering shrubs and evergreens
and young maples and flowers, three truckloads in all, which they began
putting out after 'Bama had placed it all off and drawn up to scale
on graph paper a plan of just where he wanted everything. If it was
extravagant spending (and 'Bama always spent extravagantly; he loved
it), it was all for pleasure and not profit. The Judge, after seeing it,

offered to sell the whole lot—which was about the size of half a football
field—to 'Bama for only a very little profit, hardly more than he had
paid for it, and—for the Judge—a very fair offer. But 'Bama would
have none of it. He didnt want to own it. Not any—none at all. He
only wanted to work on it and fiddle with it.

It was late in the season to be doing all of this, and just about everybody who had access to either of the budding gardeners was quick to tell
them this. Already it was too late for tulips and hyacinths which had
even stopped blooming a couple of weeks before. Everything would
surely die; the grass would come up and be burnt, the evergreens would
wither, the shrubs and flowers would not even come out. 'Bama—who
already knew a lot about farming and whose family had always planted
things in Alabama—ignored it all and went ahead with his plan in sneering arrogant disagreement, preparing the beds carefully, enriching the
soils, putting peat moss around all the new evergreens and trees to hold
the moisture, and rigorously and religiously watered everything carefully
and properly for the rest of the entire summer. Even Dewey and Hubie
got the fever and worked and sweated doggedly, digging holes for all
the myriad shrubs and evergreens and trees, while cursing 'Bama like
the ex-infantrymen they were for ever having got them in on this.
Almost nothing died; the evergreens and maples put out new growth,
the shrubs developed, the flowers came up on schedule and came up
beautifully, and by the end of summer what had been a weedgrown
vacant lot had developed into a beautifully laid out budding garden
which was the wonder of the neighborhood, and received a good deal
of talk all over town—as evidenced by the number of cars belonging
to the respectable elements which would drive slowly past,—without ever
stopping of course,—to take looks at it and see for themselves. This of
course heartily tickled Judge Deacon, and Dewey and Hubie would sit
in the house drinking whiskey and chortle with glee as the 'respectable'
people drove by to see *their* garden.

And then, just as suddenly as he had begun it,—although he
carefully kept up his watering regimen all summer—'Bama lost all
interest in it. His attitude was well displayed by what he said to Dave
one evening when they two were sitting out on the patio-porch looking
off across it.

This patio-porch was something they had built onto the house themselves, using Dewey's more or less expert help, after getting the Judge's
official opinion that it was all right to do so since he couldnt very well
see how such a nice addition to the house could be complained about.
It extended around the corner of the house from the back yard (where
'Bama the carpenter had built two trellises and planted honeysuckle
and morning glories) and ran along the east side to the kitchen door
where they could sit and look off across the vacantlot-garden, and

was really nothing more than a concrete floor with a lean-to roof over it attached to the house and screened in from floor to ceiling. It was while sitting out here with a drink one evening with Dave that 'Bama made his characteristic comment about all the time and energy and sweat and money they had expended on the lot they were sitting and looking at.

"Look at all that damned stuff out there," he said suddenly. "We went to work and planted it and fed it and took care of it and got it started, and now itll go right on growin and probly still be there when we're both dead.

"Kind of ridiculous, aint it?" he said softly with that sometimes chilling grin of his.

He apparently cared no more for it than he did for Miami Beach when he had been there, or for anything else once he had seen it and done it and was through with it. But he kept carefully to his water schedule just the same, and when the fall planting season came went to work replacing the few things that had died and could be seen out with a hand trowel planting tulip bulbs and hyacinths and jonquils in the spots where his master plan called for them, in preparation for next year.

His boredom with the garden did not keep him from doing other things, however. During the rest of the summer he worked off and on out in the little old two-car garage at building a workbench and wall cabinets for tools across the back so he would have a place to work on his Packard. He was quite capable—and often did it—of spending hours and hours of pure total concentration out there, working with his saw and square and hammer and nails; and more than once Dave coming to find him would find him so concentrated on some job or other that he could walk clear up behind him before 'Bama would even know anybody was there. And as the chillier nights of fall came on 'Bama bought an Army surplus space heater and got Dave and Dewey to help him set it up in the garage so it would be warm enough to work out there. —Also, he said, it would keep the car motors warm in the winter, which was very good for a delicately tuned car, and made it much easier to start.

About the time he got the work benches finished Wally brought his precious Randall knives down again for them all to look at and 'Bama got the idea of making a knife himself with Wally according to the instructions in the Randall catalog. This necessitated the buying of a good motor-driven grinding wheel and an anvil, which they duly set up in the back of the garage. And after that the two of them spent afternoon after afternoon out there, while Dave wrote, working on a stock of files they had bought at the hardware store to make knives out of them, grinding them on the wheel, beating them on the anvil and tempering them in the space heater though the weather was still far too warm to be firing it and overheated both of them. And eventually they got several pretty good ones, after ruining dozens of files, though of course nothing that could even compare with Wally's Randalls. Once they were made, 'Bama oiled them carefully and put them away in a drawer and forgot them.

It was then that Dave remembered one of his own lost arts, something he had not thought about since back during the war when he had learned it: knife-throwing. In the 3615th QM Gas Supply Company there had been an old carny man who had once had his own knife-throwing act and, finding Dave had spent some time with them himself, had taken to him and hung around with him and had eventually wound up teaching him knife-throwing. It was an almost mathematically exact science, gauging the distances and the number of turns the knife would make to strike point first, beginning at two feet and less when it didnt turn at all and you threw it flat, point-first, then moving back to six feet where you held it by the blade and threw it with one half-turn, and then still further back where you held it by the handle so it would make one full turn, and back further where you held it by the blade again to make one turn and a half, until finally back at twenty five or thirty feet you were throwing it by the handle to throw it making two full turns, and inching your fingers back along the blade or handle as you moved slowly back to slow up the speed of the turn, until finally the distance was too great and you had to reverse your grip. Wally and 'Bama, as well as Dewey and Hubie, took to it immediately. So he got them all out in the back yard and taught them, using the balanced knives that Wally and 'Bama had made. They had a croquet court set up out there which they had played on all summer, and at which especially Wally and Dewey had become particularly expert, winning good sized sums of money, and at the end of it they set up a broad wood target of soft pine which they had built and painted an outsized figure of a man on, and in the cool fall evenings they could be seen, standing in a group that moved slowly back further from the target, throwing the knives at it and betting who could come closest to the heart. It was in many ways the finest summer Dave could remember in his life.

But eventually, when he had more or less mastered that technique too and its principles, 'Bama suddenly became bored or tired or—at any rate, indifferent—to it too. And after he stopped, gradually so did the others. Apparently 'Bama was that way with just about everything—except gambling—and that included women.

The episode with Doris Fredric occurred a little less than a week after the anniversary party they threw for Dave—and at which Doris was so very much in evidence. It had that same strange, tangled, unbelievable quality about it that everything connected with Doris had, including the party and the strange odd way she had moved about so coolly and insouciantly as if there were nothing at all compromising or out of the way in her being there while at the same time her mere presence there obviously betrayed to everyone what her position was.

Dave had just quit work for the day about four thirty or five. Doris had been there since before four o'clock, coming there straight from the highschool in the afternoon as she often did. And 'Bama was gone, having taken the Packard and gone off somewhere alone after he got up at noon. When he quit work, Dave locked his little writing room (a thing he had taken to doing since Doris had been hanging out there so much) and went on through the living room to get the book he was reading—Ralph Roeder's *The Man of the Renaissance*; the Renaissance in Italy, and in England, always fascinated him: his own time seemed so similar—and went on out to the kitchen to mix a Martini and fix himself something to eat. Doris was sitting in the living room, coiled up in a chair in that deliciously and sweetly sexually attractive way of hers, her small delicate old-cherrywood-colored head bent above some weighty novel resting on her folded thigh whose pages she was languidly turning but obviously not reading, and the radio was turned on to some more or less poignant tinpanalley dance music, which was her favorite type. She was really very beautiful, and what was more was well aware of it and had obviously posed herself so as to bring out her best advantage—even though there was nobody else in the room. But then of course, somebody always might come in. Posing, always posing. And Dave went irritably on and said nothing.

After a minute or two Doris got up and followed him out to the kitchen bringing her book, and mixed herself a stiff drink of Jack Daniels Black Label and Seven-Up and sat down at the table with him. She did not say anything, not a word, and did not even look at him, and Dave did not say anything either; and so she continued to sit there, turning the pages of her book, perhaps even reading a little now and then, in snatches, while he went about fixing himself his regular five o'clock lunch on the stove—as if in some perhaps below the level of consciousness way all she wanted was the presence of someone near, to be near somebody, to make her feel better, more comfortable, less alone, less afraid or something. For a moment Dave felt a sharp powerful pity for her and for the first time came close to liking her a little. But then how can you like someone that you dont know who they are? that they themselves dont even know who or what they are? They both of them sat there for over half an hour, while Dave fixed and ate his hamburger-and-onion steak, both of them got up at least twice to fix themselves extra drinks, and not once did she even look up at him, and not once was a single word said. And it was then that they heard 'Bama drive in on the drive. In a moment he was in the house, dangling a half empty bottle of Jack Daniels Black Label from one of his basketball player's hands, and bringing a drunken blear-eyed harridan of a woman in with him.

The woman, Dave recognized at once, was one of those amateur-whore Terre Haute pigs which he and 'Bama were wont to pick up from time to time in the crummy joints down near the river and bring home for a big pure and simple sex bout. —Or, for that matter, pick up anywhere else, when they were in Indianapolis or Evansville; or in St Louis to see a ballgame—something they had done a good deal of all summer, since 'Bama was a hot baseball and St Louis fan. Why they both didnt get the full list of venereals off of some of them and begin rotting apart was a constant source of amazement to Dave, and could only be due to the new widespread use of that slash-hunter's miracle, penicillin. Here at home, after Doris had moved in and taken over, they had still continued to bring the bags home with them but they had had to be increasingly careful to bring them in when she wasnt around. And without anything ever having been said, because 'Bama never mentioned it once, Dave had sensed a growing dissatisfaction and irritation in him at having to do it that way. Now, apparently, he had just finally gotten a bellyful and decided to take the bull by the horns. Dave stole a quick glance at Doris, but her face showed nothing on it but her normal posed sweet serenity—at least not as yet.

"Hello, you all!" 'Bama said, friendlily enough,—without any belligerence at all—in his flat gambler's voice, and looked at them levelly and cheerfully out of those clear eyes, not a bit drunker than he ever was. "Hey there!" he called softly to the wreck; "Come on there, kid!" and the wreck who was—or at least definitely looked—old enough to be his mother followed him out of the kitchen and down the hall and upstairs.

'Bama plainly was not hurrying, and he just as obviously was not lagging. He was clearly just doing what he wanted to do, in his own sweet way and time, and making himself at home in his own house.

Dave stole another look at Doris without saying anything. He had not said a single word for some hours now,—except the one single startled "Hello" to 'Bama just now—and there was not much point in starting to say anything now. Doris's face still showed absolutely nothing, and she sat looking after them, her small dainty hand still lying flat out on her book, her whole face still covered with that aloof but angelic sweetness she habitually wore and which apparently nothing could wipe or shock off, her wide deep blue eyes still widely innocent, the same look in short that she always wore—except for a certain narrowing canary-swallowing-catlikeness about the eyes when she smiled—the same look and same smile which Dave had in the past seen on the faces of certain blonde and big shot actresses out in Hollywood who would have passed for sweet virgins anywhere but whom everyone in town knew to be the biggest and most prolific romps on the Boulevard though of course no one ever mentioned it except in private.

After a moment or two she turned back to her book, her cheek still childishly propped on one hand, and bent her small finely chiseled cherrywood-colored head to the print in silence. Only the unusual whiteness of her face showed there was any adrenalin of rage pumping through her or any faster beating of her heart or that she felt anything at all. Slowly as she read a faint flush spread over her face and then faded away again leaving it as white as before.

A couple of minutes later she got up and in her demure stately marching kind of walk, straight-backed and with the head and neck held high like they taught you in the Charm schools, went over to the countertop and mixed herself another drink and came back and sat down with it.

Dave did not know what to do. In fact, there wasnt anything much he could do. He was terribly upset. It wasnt that he felt sorry for her so much as it was just simply that he was embarrassed for her, and hated having been present as a witness. If he had been her, he would have preferred that nobody be present as a witness. Unable to do anything, he decided the best thing was just to ignore the whole thing completely as if it were a common everyday occurrence. He bent his own head back to his own book, which he had not been able to read and digest a full paragraph from for some time anyway, not since she had first come out in the kitchen, and pretended to read. Anyway, all he could see was the top of her small cherrywood-colored head anyway.

So they sat.

He did not know exactly how long. All he knew was that he read through one more page without grasping it either. Apparently Doris drank her new, fresh drink rather quickly. And then she got up again to go and make herself another. But this time, instead of going straight on around the table to her own seat on her way back, she suddenly turned off, toward his, put her glass down on the table where it and her finely boned little hand came into sight of his eye range beside his own glass, and then sat herself down on his leg, his thigh.

Dave was too startled to think or do anything for a moment. She was apparently quite a lot heavier than he ever would have thought, his mind noted. And the feel of her, the feel of the muscular backs of her thighs along the outside of his leg, all firm-soft solid female flesh, was heavily and deliciously sexual. Though he hardly had time to really savor or appreciate it. If she had kept her mouth shut and hadnt said anything, it might have worked.

But before he could think or do anything—either *de*fensive or *of*fensive—except straighten up, she leaned back against him, her eyes coming level just a little bit higher than his own—wide open, deep blue, childishly innocent—and said in a husky half-whimpering stage whisper,

"Nobody in the world has ever loved me. Nobody. Not ever really loved me. Ive always felt you could."

Probably it was pitifully true. He was not sure whether she was playing Rita Hayworth or Lana Turner, but the explicit movie tone of it was unmistakable. And pitifully true or not, she herself certainly did not believe it true. And that was why it didnt work. Such vanity—such totally un-selfaware and unjusti*f*iable vanity—was infuriating. If she had only kept her mouth shut . . . Dave continued to stare back at her, their eyes only inches apart, because to have looked away would in some obscure way have been admitting guilt.

"Ive always thought you were so pudgy and cute," she said in the same Rita Hayworth-Lana Turner whisper, and put her hand up and rolled a lock of Dave's swiftly thinning hair around her finger, and Dave had an impulse to bitterly and ridiculously laugh—to just simply let go and roar with sour, anguished laughter. "Youre sensitive," she smiled, "you have understanding."

"Get up," he said. "Get up before 'Bama comes back downstairs."

And that was the other part of why it didnt work. She was 'Bama's girl, and that made her 'Bama's problem. Whatever troubles they had was their business and between them, and he was damned if he was going to be turned into a pawn in a fight between them. If she wanted to get ahead of 'Bama she was not going to use him to do it. Shed have to find some other way.

Doris did not say anything for a moment. Then she got up off his leg and picked up her glass and stepped back around the table. And there, before she sat down, standing virginally and demurely straight, her small cherrywood-colored head held sweetly and girlishly high, she bent upon him such a potent look out of those blue eyes that he could actually hear in his ears the words those no-longer-childish but murderous snapping eyes shouted at him in silence.

"You Fat Slobby Sniveling Cowardly Gutless Son Of A Bitch."

The words, the actual words, left her eyes in a stream and entered his and passed on to his ears where he heard them loudly in the silence of the room. Dave's jaw tightened, and for the first time since he had first met her he opened up his own eyes and withdrew the curtain of politeness from them and through them shouted back his own opinion of her personality.

"You Dumb Ignorant Degenerated Whoring Pig of A Rich Girl Gash."

For several moments they stayed just that way, silently shouting absolutely murderous imprecations at each other, and finally it was Doris who dropped her eyes and Dave immediately felt embarrassed again for her, and selfashamed. But he could not help but marvel at her aplomb.

As virginal, and sweet, and innocently dewy eyed as she had ever been before, she sat sedately down in her chair and looked down at her book, took several healthy but very ladylike sips of her drink, and then looked back up at him with childlike china eyes and it was actually as if none of it had ever happened, ever been, and Dave felt his brain yaw around wildly like a man on a pitching deck, and wondered if he were going off his rocker. He knew it had happened.

"How long do you think theyll stay up there?" she said in a hurt helpless little girl voice.

Dave coughed selfeffacingly. "Well, when we bring gals home with us, they usually stay almost all night," he said embarrassedly, and found that now it was he who wanted to look away, and that his eyes had a tendency to keep wanting to drop away and look back at his book and he had difficulty keeping them up.

Doris did not answer right away, but swung her eyes and then her face away from him and looked haltingly all around the room, still wearing that hurt little girl expression. "Well, I suppose theres no point in my hanging around here waiting for him then, is there?" she said dolorously.

Once again, as it had just a few moments before when they were staring at each other, fury shuddered all through Dave. Not from what she said. A thought had suddenly come in his mind. It had entered his mind as he sat watching her as she looked haltingly all around the room, and he knew he had not thought it himself. It could only have come from her.

"No, I guess not," he said, struggling to keep his voice from quivering. "Unless of course you want to go on up there and crawl in with them. Thats what you were thinking, isnt it?"

He didnt give a damn what she did, or thought. That wasnt it. It was that damned uncrackable aura of respectability, and the way she so blandly denied everything.

Doris did not answer him at all, but stared back at him steadily, blankly, the hurt crushed expression still strongly on her face from before, as if he had not even spoken or she actually had not heard.

"Well, I guess I might as well go, then," she said. She got up from the table and collected her purse and coat and, walking in that very-straight-backed head-high demure and virginal Charm School way, went gravely to the door. From the door she smiled back at him tragically and in a hollow voice said "Good night, Dave" and went on out and left, leaving him with his book and his inability to read it.

The next day she was back again, right after school again.

'Bama was there this time (after having driven his horror back to Terre Haute some time in the very early morning) and she came right on in and mixed herself a drink of Jack Daniels and Seven-Up and sat down with them quietly. She did not say a word about the night before, neither of recrimination nor of reproach. But there was a hot clawing catlike smoky-eyed hate-filled passion about her for him—for 'Bama— that, to Dave's knowledge at least, she had never exhibited before. Dave tried not to see it, feeling very much in the way and somehow deeply embarrassed for her, but it was impossible not to see it. Doris couldnt keep her hands off 'Bama. And she practically ignored Dave. As if he did not even exist. Or—so Dave found himself guiltily thinking—as if he were beneath her comment or contempt for having tried to take advantage of her last night and seduce her when she was unhappy and not herself. —An action which, of course, she was too decent and too lady-like to mention to 'Bama. 'Bama himself sat back and watched her amusedly, like a biologist performing an experiment with some form of lower animal. But she herself could not see this, apparently; or if she did, did not care, or else thought confidently she could still defeat him, could still win whatever it was she was playing for. And that, too—if you knew 'Bama—made you embarrassed for her. Dave could not take it and finally got up and got out and went down to Smitty's. Watching two other people's lovelife was pretty nearly as embarrassing and as full of ridiculousness as watching two other people in bed together—no matter how important your own might be to you—and left you hoping you would not look as ridiculous to them. 'Bama only winked at him as he left, and said he would meet him later on at the Eagles' Lodge game.

He had already talked to 'Bama about it—about what had happened the night before—and in so doing had clarified for himself several things about 'Bama. It had been that morning, after 'Bama got back from Terre Haute, before Dave went to work.

"Well, you went ahead and romped her, didnt you, I hope," the tall man said.

"Hell, no!" Dave cried outragedly. "I wasnt going to romp your girl behind your back!"

"Well, God damn," 'Bama said disgustedly. "If you didnt, that makes you about the only guy around this camp who aint."

"You cant be sure of that."

"No," 'Bama said reluctantly; "no, you cant. I guess. But Ill tell you, if I was goin to bet on it I shore wouldnt bet the *other* way."

Dave had to laugh. "No," he said. "Neither would I."

"The next time you get yoreself a chance at her like that," 'Bama admonished, "you go ahead and take it. Cause it shore wont make me any difference."

"Ill probably never get another chance," Dave had said—and rightly, apparently—"but if I did, I still dont think Id take it. I just dont want to get involved with her. She bothers me. I dont like her, somehow. I guess—I guess its just because shes just—well, just dumb."

"Dumb?" 'Bama said. "Dumb like a fox. A fox dont read books, nor talk well, nor think rationally either, I guess. But dont never tie into him on his own ground where his instincts come into it. Youll take a whippin. And love and sex is women's home ground, see? and its where all their instincts are. Us men think we know a lot about sex and love, but there aint a man in the world who knows as much about sex and love as the dumbest fourteen year old virgin highschool freshman has known ever since she was born."

"I guess thats right," Dave said, though he didnt really believe it. "What did you do it for, anyway?"

"Do what?"

"Bring that pig home with you when you knew she was here."

"What the hell, its my house aint it? I got a right to bring anybody into it I want to. I dont owe Doris anything. But thats the way they are: they all work on you to make you feel you owe them something. But they owe you just as much as you owe them, dont they? After all, yore takin care of them too."

"Then you mean you really done it on purpose."

"No. I never done it on purpose, or not on purpose. I just done it. I didnt know if she would be here. But I shore didnt give a damn if she was. Ive just got tard of her tryin to run my damn life. Hell, since shes moved in here and took over you and mes had to sneak around like a couple gutless wonders the first year they married. I just figured it was about time I quit it and taught her a lesson. Just because Im rompin her dont mean Im goin to quit rompin other women."

"Do you think shell ever come back?" Dave had said. This was still the morning after she had left the night before.

"Well, the truth is, I dont give a damn," 'Bama said thinly. "If she dont want to come back she shore dont have to. There aint a thing forcin her to," he said. "But I expect she will come back," he added, "shes that type." And he was right. She had come back, and that same afternoon. "Look," he said. "Let me tell you something. —Let me tell you a story.

"When I was a kid in highschool," 'Bama said, "I played ball. Played first base. I played all through highschool and after that around on one of the plant teams there in town. Well, there was a guy played with me —he was a catcher—name of Jim Thurston. We called him Jimmer, for a nickname. And he was good. He played all through highschool with me, and afterwards on the same plant team. Now, I was never very good—I mean, I was good enough for there, you see; but I just wasnt never bigleague material. But Jimmer was. I mean he was *good*. He was a marvel of a catcher. Had an arm like a pistol shot to second base, and just as accurate. And glue fingers. And he was fast as hell. He developed this old trick of pretending to drop the ball and runnin back right around the umpire and fire to second. Suck a man on first into a steal time after time and throw them out at second. And he could hit. And run. I mean he was *really* good. He had *talent*. He *belonged* in the bigleagues.

"Well, even in highschool the scouts had their eye on him, and after he got out of school he got several offers to go on a farm club. But old Jimmer turned them all down, and you know why? Because he had a girl in town there, in Birmingham. And Jimmer didnt want to leave his girl. So—he took a job in this plant, and he played on the plant team. We worked together in the plant and we played on the same team like in highschool. We were good buddies. I tried to get him to go with a farm club when he got out of school, because he was *good*. I mean real bigleagues material. Everybody knew it. He would of made a great catcher. But he wouldnt, because he was rompin this gal regular, see, the first real regular romp hed ever had, and he didnt want to give it up; and she didnt want him to give it up either.

"Well, we played there on that plant team for two years. Back then there was more small team ball than there is today, you know? Every big plant had its own pro team it hired. We played all over around there. And Jimmer kept getting better and better. He got to be known everywhere around there.

"Well, finally a Cub scout made him an offer to go to Chicago and try out with the main club. Not a farm club, mind you; the main Cub club. If they liked him, and this scout assured Jimmer they would, they would give him a contract. That was back in the 'Thirties when the Cubs were really going great, you know? and he would be right in there with the main club. All hed have to do was show he had the stuff. Well, you just dont hardly ever get offers like that. The scout told him: It was the chance of a life time.

"Well, he come to me and talked about it. I told him to for God's sake take it. Well, he didnt know. Him and his girl were plannin on gettin married. I told him to marry her and take her with him. Well, she didnt want to go. She was scared to leave Birmingham where her family and all her friends was. Finally, he went and took the tryout. They hired him right on the spot. He was to go back and get things together and report at such and such a time.

"So he came home, and his girl threw a fit. She wouldnt leave Birmingham. If he wanted to go, hed have to go without her. So when it came time to go, he just never showed up. They sent a man down to talk to him. He had signed the contract; if he didnt report, the guy said, he would never get back into organized baseball again; theyd see to that.

"Well, Jimmer thought it over, and he decided he would stay in Birmingham with his girl. They got married, he went back to work in the plant, and kept on playin ball on the plant team. Thats the whole story. Hes still there."

'Bama stretched himself, suddenly, jerkily, as if trying to stretch some irritated disgusted tension out of his muscles. "All for a little regular slash." His usually cool eyes were snapping with suppressed outrage.

"Well, that taught me a lesson," he said, repressing his emotion and grinning, "a lesson I promised myself I would never ever forget. That gal was dumb. Just a dumb little country gal. And he let her wrap him around her finger and tell him what to do. All because it was his first regular lay, and he was afraid to let go of it. I made up my mind that no goddamned woman was ever goin to tell me what to do and ruin my damn life just because she was rompin me. —If you just could of seen that guy play ball!," he cried. "None of them. Just so they could make sure they could always handle me and control me."

It was the kind of a story that always angered Dave, too. Some dumb filly of a country girl. Who couldnt see any further than the end of her nose. With no imagination.

"Well, maybe hes happier as he is," he said after a moment.

"Happy!" 'Bama cried indignantly. "What the hell has 'happy' got to do with it? He had a *talent*. He should have used it. Would you be willin to give up yore writin, just so you could be *happy!*"

Dave could not help but grin. "Well, sometimes I sure as hell think I would."

"But you wouldnt!" 'Bama cried. "And you know it. And anyway what the hell is *happy,* anyway? Can you describe it to me? No, and neither can nobody else. But everybody's always bitchin and moanin about bein *happy.* Everybody should be *happy.* The purpose of civilization is to make more people *happy.* The Great American Middle Class Dream is to be *happy.* It makes me sick to my stomach!" He took a fresh breath:

"But a person who has a talent has a responsibility to it, by God. I dont care what kinda talent it is. Whether its bein a writer, or a great catcher, or an actress, or what. Talent is the only single damned thing that separates human beings from dogs or cats. And not very damned many people have any talent. Too damned few! All right, let them worry about *happy.* But when a person has a talent, it dont just belong to him. It belongs to everybody. And that gives him responsibilities to it."

"You really believe that?" Dave said.

"Yore damned right I do."

"Well, I guess I believe it too," Dave grinned. "But I guess it always embarrasses me to come right out and say it. But of all the people in the world yore the least one I ever expected to hear talking about the responsibilities of talent!"

"How so?" 'Bama said narrowly, bringing his voice back down out of its excitement.

"Well, you dont live like you believed in responsibilities."

"Thats because I dont have a talent," 'Bama said reasonably. "Maybe thats why Im able to appreciate talent. Because I dont have any myself."

"Baloney!" Dave derided. "You could do any damned thing you set your mind on. Youve certainly got a talent for gambling, thats for sure."

"Whats gambling?" 'Bama said thinly. "A way of makin money to spend like any other business. —And anyway, I dont even have that. You think Id be livin in this little old onehoss town on a few thousand peanuts if I *really* had a talent for *real* gambling?"

"No," he said seriously, "its true. I aint got any kind of talent, really. Not enough, anyway, to make it really something—uh—"

"Creative?" Dave said, smothering a grin.

"Yas. Creative," 'Bama said pugnaciously, "and dont laugh, you son of a bitch."

"Im not."

"Ive thought a lot about it. I just dont have no real talent. Im pretty good at a lot of things, but not *really* good at any of them."

"You could do any damned thing you wanted to do," Dave said categorically. "Anybody can. If they just want to do it bad enough."

"Well, then maybe I just dont want to do any one thing bad enough," 'Bama said thinly. "But I dont believe that. I believe a talent's born into a person. And I just wasnt born with any. But that dont mean I cant see it in other people and appreciate it."

"You know, Im going to have to take you over to the Frenches with me sometime," Dave said. "I want you to meet Gwen and Bob sometime. Youd like them, 'Bama. Youd like talking with them."

"Yeh," the tall man said shortly, and vaguely. "Sometime we'll have to go over there. But I just wanted to tell you the story of what happened to Jimmer Thurston so as to explain to you why I done what I done to Doris and why I dont intend to ever let no woman ever run me. I made up my mind a long, long time ago back then that if and when I ever got married it would be to a woman that I could run instead of her running me."

"And what kind of woman would that be?" Dave grinned. "Id sure like to know."

"Well, they got to be two things," 'Bama said seriously, although he had noted Dave's smile. "First, they got to be dumb. I mean really dumb. And second, they got to be very very respectable; and its better if theyre real religious too. Then theres another third thing: They got to be used to takin orders from the menfolks, so that they believe thats the right way of things and the way they ought to be. Then they dont get mean on you."

"Passive," Dave grinned. "True female passivity. And just where the hell do you find a woman like that today?"

"Well, theres not very many of them, Ill grant you that. In this day and age. There use to be a lot more of them."

"If you mean your Southern belles, your Confederate belles," Dave grinned, "Im afraid Im forced to disagree with you. Ive read too many histories and biographies to ever believe that."

"Youve only read about the rich ones," 'Bama said, "not the pore ones. They dont write about the pore ones. If you want an example, Ill give you one. Stonewall Jackson's wife was a good example of the kind I mean. She—"

"Lets dont get off on the Civil War," Dave grinned, "and all you know about it. Ive got to get to work sometime today."

"Well, thats the kind," 'Bama said. "And I guess you got to add one more qualification: They cant have been rich before you met them. Thats the only kind of woman any man with any brains would ever marry. And thats the kind I married, when I finally found one."

"What about her?" Dave said, emboldened a little by all the confidences that had been passing back and forth. He had never asked about her, and they had never again spoken of her, since that first day he had met the Southerner. "What about your wife?"

"What about her?" 'Bama said confidently. "Shes the type of woman I been describin to you, thats all."

"But dont she ever get mad at you? Or jealous? Dont she ever eat you out?"

"Why should she?" 'Bama said, with supreme confidence. "Shes got what she wants. I take good care of her; she dont never want for nothin. And shes got her religion, and her farm she runs and makes money on, and she got her kids. She knows Id never leave her for no broad. And my work—gamblin—which she dont approve of—but understands—because she knows thats just the way men are—keeps me away a lot, thats all. But I dont lie to her about it. And she knows it. She keeps whiskey down there for me—though she dont approve of that, either. And shes got her kids. When a woman has her kids, she dont really give a damn about the old man any more; because shes got from him, all right and proper, what she really wanted from him—long as he supports her. Ask any man whose wife has ever had some. Hell, I honestly think shes more relieved to see me go than she is to see me come." He grinned, blandly, confidently, supremely sure. "Her and me trust each other, and we're real good friends—though we dont neither one agree a damn with what the other believes or does."

"Its unbelievable," Dave said. "I just dont believe it. To hear you tell it, anyway, she sounds just about like the perfect wife."

"She is," 'Bama grinned. "Hell, I picked her myself. Very carefully. —Ill tell you what," he said. "Ill have to be goin down there sometime soon before long. Whynt you come on and go down with me.

"Look!" he said. "Armistice Day aint far off, and the hunting season opens. You come on and go down to the farm with me and meet her and judge for yoreself, and we'll stay a day or two and do some huntin. Theres some mighty good quail country down there in the farm. We'll take a couple my guns down," he said (he had brought all his guns— twelve in all—up to the house in Parkman and built a gun case for them), "and hunt it.

"—Then," he went on, expanding and elaborating it, "then we'll come on back up here and go on up north where I know where theres some good pheasant country and hunt pheasant a couple of days. What do you say? You can afford to take a few days off, cant you? Youve been workin pretty steady since we got moved in here. What do you say?"

"Sure," Dave said, "hell, yes! I havent done any hunting since back before the war. And then I never did too much."

"Well, we can go out here in town to the Skeet and Trap Club, of which I am a member," 'Bama grinned, "and practice up a little before we go. You ever shoot skeet?"

"Just a few times, out on the Coast."

"We can have ourselves a nice regular little huntin vacation," 'Bama said, suddenly enthusiastic; "and anyway," he grinned, "I would like to get yore opinion—yore professional, writer's opinion—of my wife."

"You got yourself a deal," Dave said. "But theres just one other thing, buddy," he said grinning, "that I want to mention: By God, dont you ever jump on me about bringing Ginnie Moorehead down here as long as that pig Doris of yours keeps on hanging around here!"

It was a touché. 'Bama grinned, suddenly, wryly. "Okay," he said wisely. "I wont. I was only tryin to keep you from losin yore reputation was all. And, to keep you from gettin yoreself in a position where none of the rest of the brassiere factory gals wont go out with you."

"Well, just stop worryin about it."

"Okay, I will," 'Bama said with that same wry, very wise grin, which seemed to see, and to say, that it would be silly to try to do anything else. "Just take one of the other ones out too once in a while to protect yoreself."

"I promise that," Dave grinned. "I will."

And he meant it, too. But sitting that evening in Smitty's, after he had left 'Bama and the wildly possessive, battling Doris in the house, and thinking back over all the two of them had said that morning, he decided it just wasnt worth the effort—not tonight anyway—and decided to put it off until another time. Ginnie was there tonight, together with some baker's half-dozen of the others scattered around the place, most all of whom he knew and including both Rosalie (who was Wally's girl now, though, more or less) and Mildred Pierce (whom he had never tried to go out with again yet)—and it was so much easier to just go get Ginnie, no buildup and no fuss nor feathers, when he needed anyone at all.

And tonight he needed somebody. Because now that he had turned her proposition down—and was still glad he had, in fact—he nevertheless found himself thinking about the cherrywood-headed Doris Fredric and reconstructing a sort of portrait of her in his mind pieced together from all the various times he had seen her in various bathing suits. And now that it was all over, he couldnt quit thinking about it and wishing now that he had taken her on, though he knew just as clearly that if the opportunity ever came up again he would still do the same as he had done before and still turn it down, just as he had the first time. —And then brood over it, he said to himself, grinning at himself wryly, God! —If she had only kept her damned mouth shut . . .

After sitting with Dewey and Lois Wallup (whom he also would like to try one time) and Hubie and Martha Garvey (who never had much interested him)—and with Ginnie and Mildred and some other one, who were all there with them—for a while, he went to the phone and called 'Bama at the house. 'Bama had said he would meet him later at the Eagles'.

"Is your friend and mine still there?" he said when 'Bama answered.

"Yeh," 'Bama said guardedly. "Why?"

"What do you say we just call off the game tonight, then? Im a little bit worked up myself, it appears like."

He heard a thin chuckle over the phone. "Preyin on yore mind a little bit now, hunh?"

"Oh, no. Not exactly. Well, what do you say?"

"Well—okay. If you dont want to play tonight, Dave. Its okay by me. Just as well, in fact." then he half muffled the phone and Dave heard dimly, in an amused tolerant tone: "Now damn it, let me alone for a minute, cant you?"

"Im bringin the fat one down with me," Dave said.

"Yeh? Well, okay," 'Bama said. "Its yore dong. We'll be in my room with the door shut."

"Right," Dave said. "See you in the morning then."

He hung up and went back to the table to get old Ginnie, whom he had not asked yet until he had checked with Bama that it would not be discommoding him any.

CHAPTER 51

HE REALLY had intended to take out more of the brassiere factory girls like he had promised 'Bama. He just kept putting it off, was all. He even went so far as to ask different ones of them out, a number of different times, but almost always they already had dates for that particular

night, or else didnt feel like going out at all, or worse, were in one of
those capricious moods where they clearly would demand a lot of convincing. And in point of fact, he did have a rather short-lived affair
with Mildred Pierce for a while in late November and early December.
But then Mildred got interested in another guy—one of the younger
laborers who worked in the Sternutol plant—and he himself was often
busy nights either gambling with 'Bama or going over to Gwen French's
for consultations, and the thing just kind of dwindled away and died
stillborn for lack of its own enthusiasm.

Then too, with regard to his affair with Mildred, it was obvious that
Mildred had always felt a little uneasy about going out with him on
account of Ginnie, and he learned later on that Ginnie had gone and
talked to her about it and had cried. That was shortly before Mildred
had started going out with the young guy from the Sternutol whom,
Dave was astonished to find, she soon married quite happily.

Most of the brassiere factory girls came from one of two sections in
town, either from the northeast corner back of Smitty's at the railroad
and which spread down the hill and east away from the college, or else
from the southeast corner which was clustered around the smoking
copper-tasting stacks of the Sternutol Chemical plant. The northeast
section was called "Hollywood" and had been so named back during the
Depression, with that wry wit that had named the Hollywood sections
in so many towns across the nation, either because of the effluvia of the
environs, or else because of the ironic contrast. The southeast section was
simply labeled "Down By The Plant" or "The Plant." Both corresponded
to the tenement sections of a city. The houses got progressively and
noticeably poorer the closer you approached the edge of town until when
you reached the very outskirts they were little better than just shacks,
and even many of those closer back to the better sections were pretty
decrepit looking, even though most of these actually had real furnaces in
them, instead of just stoves. Consequently, most of the brassiere factory
girls could only hope to marry someone who worked for the Sternutol or
one of the other two plants in Parkman—as Mildred had finally managed
to do. That was, in fact, Lois Wallup's trouble with Dewey Cole; while
Dewey was of the proper caste or class for her he was not, like most of
the young men, the marrying and breeding kind as he should be expected to be; but Lois could never quite assimilate or get used to this.
And as a result she remained his girl but unmarried.

One night when there had been a particularly unrestrained drinking
orgy at the house Dave had staggered out with an equally drunken
Ginnie onto the patio-porch in the chill night. Half drunk, and half
asleep, he had lain and listened dimly to Dewey and Lois quarreling
in the kitchen about this, (they had already been upstairs and had come
half-drunkenly back down for more drinks) and as he lay listening

Lois had begun to cry. She could not understand why Dewey, being who and what he was, persistently refused to marry her; and he—Dewey—was making it volubly plain to her that he did not intend to. And Lois, weeping—and never too bright, even when sober—could only say over and over "I want a home for my two kids!" to him accusingly. It was, for everybody, always a reminder of the war and her husband who had been killed in it. Lying where he was, drugged by liquor and sex into a sort of half-psychic somnambulant state, Dave's heart suddenly wrenched and went out to her—went out to both of them, her and Dewey both. And he suddenly had a strange weird feeling that there was something dangerous, and terrible, hanging over all of them there. Not just Dewey and Lois alone, but all of them. It was the first time he could ever remember having had that particular, so positive feeling, but he was to have it often enough again later on and when he did, he could always remember clearly with some strange kind of terror back to that clear-cut concise scene and moment when he had first had it. Although of course there were plenty of times—most of the time, in fact—when he did not have it at all or even think of it. He could never discover, either by deduction or divination, any psychological reason for it.

He never did know just exactly when he came to be regarded universally as Ginnie's "boyfriend". Probably there never was any actual exact point in time when it happened, and it happened to the observers the same way it did to him: he just suddenly woke up to the realization one day that he *was* so regarded, and had been for some time. Certainly, if there was any exact point, it must have come some time after the little affair he had with Mildred Pierce—which itself had come after the trip down to meet 'Bama's wife at the farm and the hunting. As far as he himself was concerned, he was *not* Ginnie's "boyfriend", and nothing anybody else thought or said made a damn bit of difference. He was simply a guy who was sleeping with her because he was either too shy, or else too lazy, to work up something else; and he did not intend to ever let it be any different—no matter what anybody thought. By that time Ginnie had already told him herself about having gone to Mildred Bell née Pierce and cried to her about him, and this amused and even flattered him a little. (She neednt have told him at all, you know, and for that he rather liked her.) She told him she did it because she loved him so and was afraid he was not going to ask her out any more, and this doubly amused him.

The trip down to 'Bama's farm was a delightful experience, if not very much of a revelation about 'Bama's wife. Apparently, to all intents and purposes as far as Dave could discover, she was just exactly what 'Bama had said she was and he was forced to tell 'Bama he had to agree with him entirely.

They started late one afternoon—November 11th it was, the day the season opened—throwing a bunch of old clothes and a game bag into the back seat of the Packard with a carefully gun-cased pair of 'Bama's guns, a twelve and a twenty, and just taking off. He had seen to it, a week or so before, that Dave got himself a pair of nice, good hunting boots—which according to him was the only special equipment needed, except for a gun. There was almost no fuss or preparation; one minute they were sitting in the kitchen having a drink and the next they had thrown the stuff in the back of the car and were on their way.

It was a fine day for it, bright blue and sunny, with a few high cumulus sailing slowly along like stately ships of the line, warm and winey in the sun, a little chill in the shade, all of it together making everything seem unexcitable and a little ambling, making the world itself seem as though it was actually truly secure. They drove along slowly, out of town, and then down the Route 1 highway south. The road to the Dark Bend River section in the south and southeast end of the county angled off to the left just outside the little village of New Lebanon to the south. A county road of graded gravel, it looked just like any other little county road and if you did not know it and where to look for it you could easily miss it. Forking acutely off from the highway, where there was always traffic, it led into a long straight stretch due southeast where there was no traffic at all (almost as if, in a way, you were turning off into an uninhabited region) and then, right-angling itself in and out among the farms and fields and boundary lines like some rheumatic snake, it continued jerkily on, past now nearly nameless hamlets where almost no one bought anything any more and which sat sleepily astride the road, on into the wooded hills and hollows that lay down there, deeper and deeper southeast into the very back country of the county, toward that very southeasternmost corner where the Dark Bend River flowed into the Wabash.

The Dark Bend River section had been, next to the old fur-trading post at Israel, the first part of the county to be settled. Coming up the Wabash in their canoes and flatboats, men got off there at the confluence they discovered, and spread gradually inland from the little town of Washington that the land-grant veterans founded there at the meeting of the arteries. Further west and north the Dark Bend—but there called by the different name of Mill Creek—flowed due south along the western edge of the county, before it made that great curve or bend back east to the Wabash which was the reason for its name. Or, rather, the reason for part of its name. The other part—the "Dark" part—came from those heavily, deeply forested hills and hollows and bottoms that the men struggled frantically and fearfully with, trying valiantly to let the sunlight into with their axes, and relieving themselves of their hatred and fear of trees—(which would live long after them in the children)—

with the great communal logburnings and the raw rum and whiskey of the frontier, in their primitive ritual dance of victory. Gradually, and as soon as they could manage it, they moved on west and north, out of the 'Dark' terrifying area and into the glades and prairies, leaving it behind them to grow back up again. And then, still later, "the civilization" moved on out into the bright sunlight sand prairies and great open glades—(which maniacally, with their insane fear of trees, they nevertheless triumphantly cut down just the same)—and centered itself in the newly founded hilltop town of Parkman. The Dark Bend became the hangout for all the horse thieves and killers and robbers and river rats who were not welcome in the towns, thus acquiring a new connotation of "Dark" Bend.

'Bama had acquired his own Dark Bend farm—(he explained to Dave as they drove along)—almost for a song, on a good deal two years before the war. Run-down, uncared-for, less than a third of it was level enough to be tillable and what was, was worn out by generations and generations of heavy corn farming that took everything out of the soil and put nothing back. In all he had 160 tillable acres out of a 480 acre farm, and for those two years before the war—before he had been God-damned-drafted—he had worked at building it back up, liming and phosphating, planting sweet clover in the wheat to be plowed under, planting inoculated beans, rotating the fields, putting out very little corn, and while he was gone in the Army his wife had carried on the work.

"Hell, I could have been let off as a farmer," he said with a thin-lipped grin, "let off honestly. Only I didnt happen to have any relatives or good personal friends on the draftboard—and I didnt belong to the same caste; which is important—like the important people's sons who got deferments. I know of several guys in Parkman, whose fathers set them up on farms they didnt even know how to run, as soon as the war got started."

"Why didnt you ask them?"

"Ask them?" 'Bama said witheringly with his most caustic sneer.

It was during the war, when he himself got drafted, that they had taken on the Alabama cropper, a one-eyed distant cousin of his wife's who had been farming down around Birmingham, (up till then 'Bama had always hired a local man), and he and his wife and family had been with them ever since.

"Hes a hell of a good banjo player," 'Bama grinned, "and there were two old houses on the place anyway."

The two houses were quite old, and had been there a very long time. But both of them were still in pretty fair shape, and gradually they had fixed them up a little bit, he said.

Dave did not know, from all of this, just what kind of a place he expected to see; but it was certainly nothing at all like what he actually did see, as first they drove down into a wide, dark-and-thickly-wooded hollow, crossed on an old wooden bridge the tumbling creek that ran through its bottom, and then came up out of it on the other side.

"There it is," 'Bama said.

About a hundred and fifty yards back off the road, up at the top along the same low ridge they occupied, was a large brightly white fresh-painted frame house three storeys high with a two storey Southern Colonial colonnade across the front, set in a thin grove of huge massive old bottom oaks four feet through across the bole and under which a ten- or twelve-year-old boy toiled manfully raking leaves on the well-kept grass. A quarter of a mile further on behind it on the same ridge stood another house almost exactly like it but smaller, its colonnade only one storey high. Between them, but at a low point in the ridge and then set still lower down on the rolling ridge's side was a large squat brightly red fresh-painted barn that dwarfed them both. And from the barn toward both the houses stretched other out-buildings, and pens, and corrals, all painted white.

Off in a field below the barn to the east a number of white-faced and black Angus beef cattle grazed together under a few big old cottonwoods that dropped to another creek; beyond the creek, from a series of steep parallel quartering hollows, rose the woods. On the other side of the big house, dropping down the gently falling ridge, was a big field where a corn crop had been harvested.

"Thats the second year," 'Bama said. "Now next year thatll be in beans." He had stopped the car when they came up over the ridge. "Inoculated beans. You see, you buy this inoculation and put it over the seed beans and that inoculates them before you plant them. Then these nodules form. Adds nitrogen to the soil. Then after you harvest it you plow that under and put it out in winter wheat. Then in February before it thaws you sow it in sweet clover or red."

"Why before it thaws?" Dave said.

"Hell, so you can git in the field," he said. "You wait till it thaws and you wont be able to get into it soon enough. Then after you harvest the wheat you plow the sweet clover under—or if its red for pasturage you cut it—and the next year yore ready to go back to corn again for two years.

"You cant see the rest of the cleared land from here," he said. "Its scattered out all over." He put the car in gear again and turned off the road into the lane up to the house. The twelve-year-old in the yard had already seen them and, putting his fan rake down carefully over the leaf pile to keep it from blowing, had started walking methodically and un-excitedly toward the house.

"Clint will probably go out with us," 'Bama said, referring to his wife's cousin the cropper, as he drove on in. "He loves to hunt, and works his ass off to have everything caught up so hes free for huntin season. Hes only got one eye but he can sure as hell shoot a shotgun. If we hadnt of come down, hed be out by himself."

Clint, it turned out from what 'Bama said as they drove on slowly toward the house, hadnt been off the place to town in over two years. And even before that had never gone any oftener than he absolutely had to. The families did all their necessary shopping in Israel on the river, which was only eight miles from the farm on another road, whereas Parkman was thirteen miles if you went by Israel, or eighteen miles if you took the long road through the bottoms the way 'Bama and Dave had come, but which 'Bama liked better and loved to drive. Consequently, nobody at the farm ever went to Parkman. And Clint would not even go to Israel. He loved the farm, and working on it, and hunting and fishing, and he read the baseball news in the paper that came by mail, and that was all he gave a damn about; and he always listened to the World Series on the radio. But other than that, Clint's wife had to buy everything for him from shaving soap to shotgun shells when she went to town on her weekly shopping trips in Israel in the pickup truck, and that even included his fertilizers and crop seeds and farm supplies, which she would have loaded for her by the men at the feed store and which Clint would unload at home.

"Or else sometimes I go over to Israel and get it and bring it down to him," 'Bama grinned. "But outside of that, Clint has no use for 'civilization'; and sometimes I think he resents havin that much. They do all their shoppin in Israel. I dont think my wife has been to Parkman more than twice since we first moved down here."

Clint was probably still out in the fields working somewhere with his oldest boy who was fourteen and always helped him after school. "But theyll be in soon as they know we're here to hunt," 'Bama grinned.

"It seems to be just about a perfect set up for you, dont it?" Dave said.

"Shore," 'Bama said, pulling the Packard up into the lot between the house and the little outbuildings, and getting out. "Thats the way I planned it to be."

The outbuildings, Dave noted, were all modern, all made of concrete block, all very neatly kept.

"We added all them ourselves," 'Bama said, following his gaze. "There was nothin here but the old barn and the two old houses when I bought it—and we had to fix them up. My wife raises chickens and sells the eggs and fryers," he said pointing to one of the white concrete-block buildings. "Matter of fact, theres quite a few people in Israel and some from Parkman who come down here from town to buy her stuff. Truck garden there, you see," he said pointing on behind the house. "Buys almost all the seeds by mail. She loves the pretty colored catalogs. Buys all the unusual items to try them out. New kinds of cantaloupes. Green peas. Biggest strawberries you ever saw. She likes that kind of thing. Even grows peanuts. Too bad I didnt bring you down in the summer. Churns her own butter, too, you see," he grinned. "Lots of people like country butter, and its pretty hard to get it any more. And fresh buttermilk.

"Yes," he said, referring back to Dave's original question. "It works out just fine. I told you they were all dumb, you know. And they are dumb, you see. —Only, dont make the mistake of thinking dumb means ignorant, if yore inclined.

"Come on, lets go on in."

The woman met them at the door, and held it for them. She was a long-muscled, heavy-boned, towheaded expressionless woman, not any taller than Dave but whose rawboned build made her look taller than she was, and she carried an almost-year-old baby with her left arm, propped on the jut of her hip as she moved about as if it were a five pound sack of flour or had grown there. Behind her stood two little solemn-faced towheaded boys of twelve and ten who looked exactly like her, towhead, boned frame, expressionless face and all, and as exactly alike as a smaller pea and a larger pea in the same pod. The baby was expressionless, too. (and Dave remembered suddenly that Dewey had told him last year—back before they had gone to Florida—that he thought 'Bama's wife was pregnant again) All four of them, including the baby stared at him—at Dave—woodenly and expressionlessly, as if they all thought him some kind of an enemy to be cautious of.

"Hello, Bill," the woman said woodenly as she ushered them in—and Dave also remembered suddenly, for the first time since he couldnt remember when, that 'Bama's name was really William Howard Taft Dillert.

"Hello, Ruth," 'Bama said with a curious mixture of gentleness and absolute authority. "I want you to meet Mister Hirsh."

Quite suddenly and immediately, the woman's face broke into a merry, bright-eyed smile, and the two little boys grinned in unison. Even the level-eyed little baby seemed to look relieved. And the peculiar narrow-eyed, high-cheekboned, almost Indian look evaporated from their faces.

"Well, howdy do," Ruth said, her eyes merry and pleased. "Im most very pleased to meet you, Mr Hirsh. Wont you step on in? Ive heard an awful lot about you. Here, set yoreselves down. Are youall hungry? Would you like somethin to eat? Theres coffee on the stove and Ive got some fresh homemade pumpkin pie. You, Johnny," she said without changing the tone of her voice, and the biggest towheaded boy moved his arm out from his side in front of the littler one and swept them both back from the table out of the way in the doorway to the next room, where they stood, silent, smiling beneath their high cheekbones, their young little eyes level and square and watching everything; and the woman, as she moved back to the big electric stove to look in the coffee pot and bent to get the pie out of the oven, continued to carry the baby expertly on the jut of her hip, where it rode, level-eyed and interested, like some miniature trick jockey who had been on a horse so much of his life he didnt even need reins or to use his hands.

Dave, not sure what he should do or what the protocol called for, sat down at the table and the woman slid an uncut pie in front of him on the worn blue-and-white oilcloth cover and almost in the same movement reached behind him to the oldfashioned kitchen cupboard for a knife and fork which she pinned to a plate with her thumb and sat in front of him, never once moving or letting go of the baby, who watched level-eyed and interestedly as if curious to see just what Dave would do.

"Just you help yoreself," 'Bama's wife smiled. "Cut yoreself a great big slab. Theres three more in the oven."

Dave looked at 'Bama, who had sat down in another chair and was now grinning at him, and picked up the knife.

"We come down to hunt, Ruth," 'Bama said in that curiously gentle and spare, absolutely authoritative voice. "Just a cup of coffee, thank you, for me," he said courteously.

"William never eats pie," Ruth said smiling merrily as she moved with the baby toward the stove and reached for cups. "Thats because he drinks so much. You, Ted," she said, again without pausing or changing her tone. "Run out and get Clint and Murray. Tell them yore daddy's here to hunt. People who drink a lot never eat sweets."

The smaller boy, Ted, walked—very slowly, and meticulously—to the door from which, as soon as he was outside, he took off in a wild, fleeing exuberant run, yelling.

"I drink a lot," Dave said, playing it along by ear so to speak, but unable not to feel astonished at her. "But I love pumpkin pie."

"Then dont be bashful," the woman said, smiling wisely back over her shoulder from the stove. "Cut yoreself a real piece. Not just that skinny little sliver. Ah'll be makin more anyways now. I like to see men who like to eat. I like stout men."

Dave, although a little taken aback by the allusion to his size, nevertheless took her at her word and cut another, larger piece and slid it on his plate with the small one. The pie was spicy and delicious.

"William ought to eat more," 'Bama's wife said. "He never eats enough. He just drinks his meals," she laughed merrily over her shoulder, pouring coffee into the cups. Deftly, she picked both cups up by their handles in one hand and set them on the table before the men while the baby watched from her hip. "There now," she said smiling, and put her fingers up beside her mouth and studied the table. "Ah'll get the cream." From the big modern, latest model refrigerator she took forth a small glass pitcher of pure rich thick cream and set it between them.

"Speakin of drinks," 'Bama said, "there ought to be some likker around here somewhere, aint there?"

"You, Johnny," Ruth said, nodding her head commandingly. "Go and get yore father's likker bottle."

The older boy disappeared silently into the next room, and came back just as quietly, carrying an already opened bottle of Jack Daniels Black Label.

"I took the one of them that wa'nt full," he said setting it before his father.

"Thats right," 'Bama said coldly in that curiously gentle yet supremely authoritative voice, and took the bottle and poured himself a drink into one of the glasses sitting in a bunch in the center of the table, and then handed the bottle on to Dave. The little boy stepped back in silence.

Holding the bottle, Dave hesitated. "Mrs Dillert?" he said politely. "Pour you one?"

"Oh, no. I never touch the filthy stuff," the woman smiled, amused at him even asking. "And never have. And never will!" The little boy, Johnny, was still standing staring silently at his father. "You, Johnny," she said. "Dont stand and watch people eat."

"Leave him be," 'Bama said. "Hes all right." He turned to look at the boy, expressionlessly. "What is it?" he said.

The twelve-year-old opened his eyes wider and took a great, deep breath. "Dad can I go huntin Dad can I go huntin," he cried out quietly.

"No," 'Bama said. "You dont know how to handle a gun yet."

"Ive been practicin with my .22," the boy said hopefully.

"A .22's not a shotgun. Its no good for birds, and therell be other men along all around you. You cant go."

"Yes, Sir," the boy said, his hopeful face settling into a high-cheek-boned stoic impassivity. He stepped back to the door.

'Bama watched him, staring at him coldly, expressionlessly.

"You get any squirrels?"

"I got two," the little boy said, coming forward. "And a rabbit. Settin."

"You do all yore chores this week?"

"Yes, sir."

"School work?"

"I got ninety-eight in g'ography."

A look almost of amusement seemed to flicker faintly over 'Bama's coldness, then was gone. "All right, Ill let you go. But you cant take a gun."

"Yes, Sir," the boy said stoically.

"You can take yore wooden gun and practice with it. But if I hear you yellin or gettin in the way—or if I see you lettin it point at anybody and not handlin it right—" he said ominously, "Ill send you right back home by yoreself. Youll be goin out with men."

"Yes, Sir," the boy said, "I will."

"Okay," 'Bama said, and turned back to his drink. For a moment, just for a fleeting second, his eyes flickered up at Dave and then back down. The little boy stepped stoically back to his place in the doorway, not entirely happy, but impassive with his disappointment.

"Mrs Dillert, this is the best pumpkin pie Ive ever eaten," Dave said, feeling a kind of awe for his sidekick, and a mixture of sympathy for, and pride in, the little boy. "And I mean bar none."

"I believe I did get a pretty good do on it," Ruth said shyly. "You dont need to call me Mrs Dillert. You just call me Ruth, Mr Hirsh."

"Then you must call me Dave," Dave grinned.

Ruth Dillert smiled tensely and inarticulately in a shy, pleased, incredibly bashful way and for a moment looked as though she were actually blushing. "Why, thank you very kindly, Im sure," she said, her eyes shining. Then, abruptly, for the first time she sat down at the table with them, gliding the baby around automatically off her hip so it sat on her thigh. Up till then she had remained standing by the stove. The baby, whose head just appeared above the table edge, stared at Dave gravely and intently, innocent of all conscious knowledge or ulterior thought, and Dave looking into those wide, deep grave eyes that appeared as though their new owner had not quite got completely used to using them yet, suddenly had the distinct impression that he was looking through two holes in the space warp into the deep, untraveled, untrammeled heart of the Universe. Two openings which had not been completely closed up yet by personality. He had the same feeling about the two older boys, too, several times, he noticed later,—when they looked at him openly, that is; and did not pull down their high-cheek-boned narrow-eyed stoic Indian masks. It seemed to him that almost none of the children he saw anywhere had that look any more, especially town children, but were instead little images graven of ulterior self-awareness, even when still babies. And he noted too that none of Clint's children, when they came over that evening, had that look either.

It was not long after that—after Ruth sat down with them—that they heard Clint coming. Clint and his boy Murray, led on by little Ted talking volubly, but who nevertheless when he entered the house became silent as a stone. Ruth had been asking them about the election just before, anxious to learn who had been elected to all the County offices. Dave, who had no idea even of who was running and couldnt have cared less, fumbled around trying to remember some of them, helped by 'Bama when he faltered. The County election had been predominantly Republican, of course, in spite of the fact that Truman had

been reelected; and Clark Hibbard and the rest of the ones who ran
again had been reelected, naturally.

"We all voted then went to Israel," Ruth said, talking excitedly about
what was obviously a thing of great importance to her, and a holiday.
"All except Clint, of course. And we followed the national returns over
the radio. But we hadnt heard about the County yet, its not in the St
Louis paper Clint gets." She was glad that Mr Truman had beaten that
Dewey. "It was very excitin. Nobody thought he ever would. Of course,
we're all Democrats here," she said in an apologetic tone which carefully,
and strictly, implied she was not trying to force her own opinions on
anybody else, "from Mother Dillert and William's brother Emmett right
on down to little Taylor here," she said, indicating the baby, who
looked at Dave satisfiedly as if he thoroughly agreed with her. The way
she said it made it sound almost as if they were a clan or tribe of settlers
set down in some alien landscape.

If they were a clan, there was no doubt whatever about who was the
leader of it. While 'Bama and Clint spoke to each other with that reserved restraint and authoritativeness of men who are equals and set
off from the others—from the women and the young—, it was plain that
Clint deferred to 'Bama's opinion, whenever opinions were necessary,
and 'Bama accepted this with the same quiet inflexibility and gentle but
absolute authority that was his attitude toward his wife and children. It
was almost like some sort of ritual-play that they engaged in, the way
they all acted. And if he seemed cold and unbending, he nevertheless
very carefully never imposed on any of the others' sense of their own
dignity—neither Clint's, nor Murray's, nor his wife's, nor the children's.
Dave watched and listened in silence, wondering if this was perhaps
not the quality that gave the children their look of peculiar strength:
an inflexible code they could depend on, as immutable as a law of life,
and as harsh, but which 'Bama would no more break himself than he
would allow them to, and which thus not only gave them a strong
authority but also security in it. And, almost as much, this applied to the
grownups, too.

Later on, after they were back in Parkman, Dave spoke to him about
it. 'Bama only grinned. "Its all an act. Like some kind of play script that
everybody has memorized their part in because their families been playin
it for generations. They expect it. And—it lets them all feel theyre important. That they mean something."

"Maybe they are important," Dave said softly.

"Maybe they are," 'Bama said, and then with that chilling grin of his,
"and then maybe theyre not. We dont any of us rightly know, do we?
We all just like to hope it. So we convince each other to believe it."

Dave could not help feeling a little shocked at such cold-bloodedness.

"Well, if I were you and had a place like that, Id move myself back down there and live there with them all the time."

"I would," 'Bama said, "but it bores me. I dont like to play the same act all the time. I like to switch them around a bit. And *you* are full of crap," he said unequivocally. "Yore a sentimental slob, and someday its liable to catch you up and tear off yore whole head. You wouldnt stay down there all the time no more than I would."

But whatever his later comments, he played his 'part' to perfection down there on the farm. Clint was a squat blocky man with a dusty black patch over one eye and tremendous arms and shoulders that elided down into a tremendous paunch that hung out over the belt of his work pants. His oldest boy, Murray, who was only an inch or so taller but looked much taller than he was because he was so slim, was a quiet, level-eyed, well-trained boy who said little and, at fourteen, wore that harassed haunted—and harshly triumphant—look of one who has just passed through puberty and feels he had discovered a secret no one in the world has ever learned before and while he is not sure he will ever be able to handle it, as least he means to give it one hell of a try. The two of them sat down at the table with them, were served coffee by Ruth, helped themselves at 'Bama's invitation to the whiskey, and talked about the hunting telling what they knew about the prospects.

Dave wondered how 'Bama was going to handle the matter, as regarded young Ted, about letting his older brother Johnny go along tomorrow. But he did not have to wonder long, because as soon as the three were inside the door 'Bama had taken it up.

"Im lettin Johnny go out with us tomorrow," he said to all three together in that inflexible decisive absolutely authoritative voice. "Hes too young to go, but hes not takin a gun. I told him he could take his wooden gun and practice. I told him he'll be goin out with men and he'll have to act like one, and if he dont Ill send him right back home."

"He'll do jes fhahn," Clint said, patting the tow head.

"Sure he will," Murray said solemnly.

Ted said nothing, but walked stolidly over to where his older brother stood at his place by the door and stood in his own place beside him. Dave had the same feeling of sympathy for, and pride in, him that he had had about Johnny a while before—a curious feeling that he wished fervently life didnt have to be like this; but that nevertheless it was, and —around here, at any rate—rightly so. Ted did not say—or show in his actions—anything that might be construed as envy or disappointment, or as anything else for that matter. And Johnny did not say or do anything that might be marked as triumphant over this slightly smaller edition of himself. The two of them stood stolidly and in silence by the door, their faces closed, like two small soldiers. Dave could not help feeling again the sort of awe he had before, both for 'Bama, and for

Ruth who kept her eyes down on the oilcloth tablecloth and effaced herself right out of the whole proposition.

After they had talked about the prospects, the males—all six of them —went down to the barn to look at the dogs; and here again Dave felt there was something of the played-out ritual. The two dogs, both good looking pointers, were kept in a run beside the barn to keep them true and from taking up the chasing of rabbits and other game. The men leaned their elbows in the wide mesh wire of the tall fence and put one foot up on the bottom wire. The two towheaded little boys in accurate imitation also leaned their elbows in the fence—at about the height of the crotches of the men—and placed one foot up on the wire. And the dogs, as if they had their own small calendar hung up in the ample neat-roofed doghouse and knew just exactly what was taking place, came humphing and whimpering to the fence and panted at the men pleadingly, while Ted and Johnny reached dignifiedly manlike through the fence and rubbed their ears and the redbone coonhounds in their own run came to their fence and barked enviously. Clint had said before that he had seen three, and possibly four, coveys around the place. Murray had said that he had seen two others his father hadnt seen in the south end. Now Clint said he had had the dogs out several times to run them and sharpen them up. After a while they all went back to the house.

That night they had a gala supper party. Clint's wife and other four children—two young girls of nine and ten, a smaller boy, and a baby— came over from the other house, each of them who were big enough which meant everyone but the baby carrying an armload of crocks or mason jars or boxes of food. Again there was that feeling of the played-out ritual. The men—whom Murray uncontestedly took his place among —sat out in the side yard on cane bottom chairs with the whiskey and got pleasantly and conversationally half-drunk, while the women and two girls worked themselves red-faced in the kitchen getting the huge meal. The three smaller boys, told off to mind the babies, sat quietly on the porch as close as they could get to the men for listening without being ordered to move off. When over the whiskey the talk turned to sex, as it inevitably must, Dave noted that young Murray's face got sharper and more dominating, even cruel, though not in any very unpleasant way. And in the kitchen, where the women worked hard but merrily, the talk was all about the prayer meeting they had been to two nights before at the Kirk Church, as they called it, Kirk being the little settlement two miles away where both the church and school were. Dave knew what the women were talking of, because once he had gotten up and gone in and offered to help. He did not do it again. When he offered to help the women with their meal, it embarrassed everybody. Though of course everyone looked down politely and did not say anything. Only 'Bama laughed.

"You aint in the city now, old sock, where the women have the men to do the dishes for them."

Once 'Bama had turned it into a joke the others were able to laugh, too, without feeling impolite. Ruefully, Dave laughed with them and acknowledged his breach of etiquette. He could not escape the feeling he had had once before in Florida that time: that he had been moved backward in time to another—would you say stronger?—America of a hundred years ago. And strangest of all was to see the cynical, sneering eminently sophisticated 'Bama sitting in the middle of it very much at home.

The meal itself was tremendous. There was fried chicken, and fried squirrel—which looked suspiciously fresh although the squirrel season had been over for some weeks and the farm was equipped with freezers —and mashed potatoes and chicken gravy, skillet fried cornbread, also biscuits, home-canned green beans, home-canned asparagus, and another dish of beans called 'shucky' beans which when Dave asked about it he was informed politely but a little amusedly by Ruth were fixed by stringing greenbeans on needle and thread and hanging them up to dry. "Oh, you mean shellouts," he said. "Oh, no," she said quickly and authoritatively. "These are dried greenbeans. The canned beans are shellouts. Shucky beans must be picked green and dried." There was also a dish of home-canned Southern squash. Then for dessert there was home-canned peaches, apple pie, and rhubarb served in a side dish with hot biscuits, and more pumpkin pie with home-whipped cream. As a fat man who was trying to lose weight, Dave was glad he did not eat down here very often. But the others had no such reservations. 'Bama himself ate nothing except some chicken, and presided at the head of the table with his never empty glass of whiskey and water. "Thats just the way some men are," Ruth said smiling at him tolerantly; "theyd rather drink than eat." But the rest of them, including the kids and women put away amounts of food that was astonishing; and young Murray, sitting between Dave and his father, chewed down such amounts of chicken, squirrel, potatoes, beans and everything else that it actually seemed there was not room enough in his thin young body to hold it all. In the morning they were up and already out by five.

Ruth fixed them a breakfast, too—and in fact was already up and had it all almost ready when she called them at four. Bacon and ham and her own sausage, stacks of thick light flannel cakes, eggs, lots of coffee, and hot biscuits. Clint and Murray who had been invited for the breakfast put away a lot of it, and even 'Bama ate a pretty good amount. But Dave who long since had gotten out of the habit of eating breakfast when he was writing ate almost nothing, and regretted it before the morning was half over. They ate in a kind of heated excitement, the guns and hunting coats stacked by the door, and Ruth watched them all from the stove where she was serving them with a flush of great pleasure on her face as they ate what she cooked for them.

The night before, after the boys had been put to bed, and after the men had lain around in a stupor for a while from the meal, 'Bama had shown Dave over the house with Clint and Murray trailing along, while the women cleaned up the kitchen. Down in the cellar he showed him the old twelve inch solid sleepers fastened with wood pins, and upstairs on the third floor where the ridge ran lengthways across the house from side to side and which was fully finished into two long rooms except for a closet space in the center he showed him with a flashlight the old bevel-halfflap handhewn woodpinned rafters, all the while telling him the history of the house itself, and of the other house and the barn, all of which had once been the main center of a huge old farm in the bottoms about a hundred years ago belonging to a quite wealthy family named Stoltz—which in fact had made their wealth on this very farm (much larger then than now, of course) before they wore it out and sold it and used the wealth to move to Springfield and become doctors and lawyers and influential in State politics. After that, of course, it had run down hill until he—'Bama—had bought it and begun to fix it up. At another place in the bottoms (now no longer part of the farm he owned) were the remains of a settlement where they had kept their field hands—slaves—who worked it for them. And back down the ridge, on the opposite side from the barn and between the houses, still remained the stone foundation of the building where the house niggers had lived. The North in looking down its nose at us Southerners, he said, seemed to forget there used to be a hell of a lot more slaves in the North itself back in those old days than anybody seemed to remember now. And so they fell to discussing slavery, back downstairs, while the women finished cleaning up in the kitchen. Should the Negroes have been left in Africa altogether? The point was, 'Bama said, that then they *needed* the *labor*; today machines did it, cheaper and better; but then they didnt have any machines, and so somebody had to suffer and it turned out to be the Negro savages of Africa. Certainly, anyway,—or so it was 'Bama's idea—the Negroes in the United States were better off than if they had stayed in Africa where they were suffering worse forced labor today than they had ever suffered here; instead of hating us—as very few niggers in the South did anyway—they ought to feel they owed us about as much as we owed them. And mightnt the Negroes, the smarter better-educated ones anyway, have a sort of a belligerence and a inferiority complex because they were so recently descended from savages and hated to be reminded of it? It was not an especially new argument, but Dave found he was more or less forced to agree with most of it. But that was not the point; the point was that when it came time to go to bed and all the rest were gone, it was Ruth who went up and spent a half hour fixing Dave's room up for him, making the bed up fresh for him, using one of her best comforters on it, fixing everything up to be just as nice as she could think to make it. She had not seen her husband for over three weeks, and yet she would take an extra half hour to appoint Dave's room for him. There even was, he felt—or perhaps it was only his own selfconscious imagination made him feel it?—an air almost of apology about her, as if she was pitying him because he was a bachelor. And so he had gone to bed, with that peculiarly painful, twisting loneliness of a man who sleeps alone in a guest bed while his host is ensconced with his lady. He had lain awake quite a while. And mostly he had thought about all he had observed today. Apparently there just wasnt any handle to pick it up by, no crack or chink in which to thrust a pry bar. Everything was apparently just exactly as 'Bama had described it to him beforehand. It seemed unbelievable. Christ, youd think a man who had it would stay right here with it the rest of his whole life! And he could not help remembering all of this next morning, when he watched Ruth who—after having first said a solemn grace, which indeed she always said before every meal, and which 'Bama never paid any attention to—stood at the big stove with her flushed bright excited face and cooked and ladled out the hunting breakfast for them. It was clear to him that Ruth had an instinctive understanding—or else, had been trained to have one—of what men were like and were expected to be like, and that that was the way they were; and if 'Bama drank whiskey and ran around and only smiled indulgently when she wanted to say grace, it did not upset her in the least or make her mad. The whole damned thing was, as far as he was concerned anyway, just about phenomenal.

They took the farm pickup, 'Bama driving—as was proper—and Dave the guest on the seat beside him, Clint and Murray and young Johnny in the back with the excited dogs. Not until they had reached (by an old sunken-road lane) the furthest limits of the farm to the south where Murray was sure he had seen two wholly different coveys hanging out, did they stop and get out and in the chill first light begin to tramp the stalk-bedraggled, harvested cornfields and the alfalfa fields and the fence-rows and the edges of the woods, the happy dogs ranging closely out before them.

"We really made a mistake," 'Bama said to Dave. "What we should of done was gone up north after pheasant first, and saved our own farm back until wed done all the huntin we wanted to do other places first. Thats the way to really do it."

Dave had not shot a shotgun since before the war, but the Sunday previous and several other days before they came down to the farm he and 'Bama had gone out to the Parkman Gun Club and practiced up on both skeet and trap. That made it almost six years since he had fired one, but out on the Coast he had done a little hunting and had spent one whole summer in an ecstasy of skeet shooting, burning up Francine's money like it was water. He was in for a rude awakening at the Gun Club. Shot after shot he would stare in warped painful disbelief as clay bird after clay bird would fly serenely on away from him untouched, apparently going right on through the cloud of shot. The truly satisfying relief of seeing one explode into smoke—or even only crack off a small piece, for that matter—was a great many more times in the minority. He was not doing anything wrong; he was not stopping his swing; he was not lifting his cheek off the stock; he was leading amply. He just could not shoot. Not having practiced, he could no longer shoot at all. It was intensely mortifying. He could not believe that just not having practiced in so long could make that much difference. Here was a man who while he had never amounted to much as a rifleman, and indeed had hardly even been trained as such—in the 3615th QM Gas Supply Company, had nevertheless accounted for eleven personal Germans in the Battle of the Bulge—and he couldnt even hit a clay bird with a shot column as wide as your arm! He reminded himself that rifleshooting and shot-gunshooting was as totally different skills as baking and frying were, but it did him little good. He felt totally ridiculous. 'Bama, who evidently did a *little* shooting every once in a while, was considerably better and that did not help the acute and painful embarrassment to Dave, either. It seemed incredible that the inability to hit a clay disc with a column of shot from a shotgun could actually cause so much miserable wretchedness.

Out in the field after the quail it was almost as bad. After they had flushed out and fired into the first covey (when he did not hit anything either) and were hunting down the groups and singles, he fired shot after shot hitting nothing. And all this time, of course, both Clint and Murray were knocking down bird after bird. Clint, with his one eye, had a curious way of warping his head across the gunstock so he could see to shoot because he shot right-handed and his left eye was his good one; but it did not hamper his shooting in the slightest. Nonchalantly, indifferently, phlegmatically, with his clean new white eye patch and his enormous belly, he would walk up and pick up his bird or take it from the dog—all as if the whole thing were such a simple, foregone matter of course—and stuff it behind him in his steadily thickening game bag. Murray was almost as bad, with his set close high-cheekboned face and gangling arms, shooting quickly with the superb coordination of youth, and accurately with the eye of an old hunter. They both had kept an eye out for the birds all year long as they worked the fields, and knew exactly where to go to look for them, and more often than not could guess just about where they would fly to as they scattered. It was the kind of hunting quail-shooters like to reminisce about afterwards—except that Dave was never the one who hit any of them; and the fact

that both Clint and Murray went about it in such a matter of fact inexcitable way as if it were an everyday commonplace. By noon when
they quit to eat, they both had their limit of twelve and had—at 'Bama's
suggestion (in which Dave hastened to heartily concur)—started working on his and Dave's. Consequently Dave found himself carrying eight
birds he had not shot in his new game bag, and viciously hating both
of them with such grinding murderous emerydust hatred that every tired
step he took was a pleasure—just to imagine mashing both of their indifferent faces into the ground. He had never hated any of the Germans
he had killed in the war one-twentieth so much, and he was so miserable
that he could not even enjoy the really beautiful day they had for it or
the truly magnificent scenery of the hills and hollows of the bottoms
woods which, wherever, however, anywhere they went, always seemed
to surround them completely and that before the week was out he would
look back on nostalgically, wishing ruefully he had remembered to study
and enjoy it. In addition, his feet were sore and his legs weary.

They ate their lunch at a strange little settlement in the bottoms
which was known as Castle Finn, although there wasnt a bluff or a
cave or even a real hill anywhere around. Three houses and two stores,
Castle Finn crouched dustily and dry-throated athwart a dusty gravel
road that came from nowhere and went to nowhere else, not a single
tree around it anywhere within a quarter of a mile though there were
woods visible on all sides. It had, 'Bama said, been settled by a bunch
of wild Irishmen long long ago, all of whom had either killed each other
off or else moved away. It had been bigger once, and it was reputed that
both Jesse James and one of the Younger boys (at different times, of
course) had hidden out here visiting some obscure relative while on the
run. Now, of the two stores one was a bar and a restaurant of sorts, and
the other was a general store. Sitting in the dingy tacky little bar, the
noon November sun hot and drowsy outside, they gorged themselves
ravenously on hot deliciously greasy smelling hamburgers and drank
beer interspersed with shots of whiskey and talked to the general store
owner who had come over from next door to see who it was and loaf, and
who because he was a country store operator apparently felt called upon
to live up to the reputation of all crackerbarrel philosophers. Most of
his philosophy had to do with the recent election. Murray, of course, was
not of age and it was illegal to serve him beer or whiskey; but this was
Castle Finn down in the Dark Bend River bottoms, the backwoods,
where the county law almost never came unless requested, and so
Murray was served beer and whiskey right along with the others and
nobody thought a damned thing about it, or worried about it (any
more than they really worried about keeping to their daily bag limit for
fear of seeing a game warden), or even mentioned it.

Sitting there with them, hungry, weak (he had had only coffee for breakfast), footsore, weary and birdless, Dave suddenly envied all of them again, as he had last night. They were together, and they had a pattern, and a place, and they were—*living*. He wasnt living, even when hunting with them. He was, at best, an outsider. He was a writer, and so he didnt—couldnt—live. He wasnt a hunter; because the pattern of his life did not offer him ample opportunity or association to be a hunter. For the same reason he wasnt a farmer either. He sat rootless, cut off, without foundation. Nowhere—but most especially in the great United States of America—was there any pattern or social framework for a writer to be a working part of. Even when they congregated together, like a covey of nervous peep-peeping birds, writers were not part of any unit or framework, but only a collection of outsiders being outside each other right along with being outside everything else. But it went even deeper than that. By its very nature, being a writer meant being an outsider, meant not living. Like these people lived. To live meant to act, and the very act of writing was itself an un-act—a putting of it down on paper instead of doing it. Bob French had a saying for it, which Gwen was always quoting so often: "You cant work and live, too." Every other man in the world, even a painter, could at least live while he worked. But not a writer. You had to be every-body, and every-thing, and hence you were no-body, and no-thing. An outsider, divorced from life and living by the very life and living you were trying to create. Doomed forever not to partake, only observe.

Even sports, even very dangerous sports, which a writer engaged in, could not give it to him. Could not give him a true sense of living. Because sports were, in the end, always situations entered into voluntarily, which living was not. And that one stipulation nullified all sports from the very start for everyone but a professional. Even writers who did other things, like farming, could not really live in them; or if they did they became, like Louis Bromfield, farmers who also wrote. But these men here, they were living; they were living because they didnt *know* they were living, or even think about it. They just did it. They acted, and hoped, and they took the consequences. That was the point. They took the consequences. Life made them. They couldnt tear the sheet out of the typewriter and rewrite the scene. Dave wanted suddenly, wildly, to start saving all his gambling money and buy a farm and run it—which would be to ruin it—and to take the consequences. But even that wouldnt work; what would happen would be that 'Bama would end up running it for him, or telling him correctly how to run it. And even if he didnt, it wouldnt work. Because he would be doing it consciously. Voluntarily.

Savagely, sitting there with them, he wished that goddamned bitch of a nymphomaniac Gwen French had never worked on him and gotten him into this. At least he would be living. —But even that was no help, no truth; because what had gotten him into this wasnt really Gwen. It was himself. His own nature, which had always been that of an outsider who could not live. Why else had he first gotten into writing in the first place, out in California? She couldnt be blamed for that. Christ! it was so *safe* to be able to *live*! He wanted to live! To do! To be safe in destruction! Loneliness and fright, and an odd objectless pointless terror that reminded him of that time he had lain by Ginnie and listened to Dewey and Lois arguing, assailed abrased and macerated him as, dead, he sat amongst the living as they drank their beer and talked about the election.

Not until late in the day did he finally get a bird. After the meal at the strange little lost settlement of Castle Finn, they drove back up to the north end of the farm where they had already started working on the four coveys Clint had spotted, before quitting to eat. Still terror-ridden and suffering that horrible aloneness in the midst of friends which is the worst kind, dejected, sore of foot, his arms and shoulders weary from carrying the damned unaccustomed gun, totally hopeless, Dave had just without thinking flung up the gun and fired as they flushed out three leftovers from a split covey. There was no doubt that it was his bird because he had fired first and the bird had fallen; it was the only one of the three that was hit. It was a moment of great triumph, and if he had stopped to think he would never have been able to have done it. But then, when he—carefully nonchalant—walked up and picked up the little feather-bedraggled lump with the gray membranes half closed over the tiny eyes and still warm, he could not help wondering at the ridiculousness of it, all of it, and wondering what the hell all the furor was about. He could not help feeling a sharp pity for the bird, and felt like some kind of huge monstrous foot-crashing oaf blundering and destroying through the woods. Still nevertheless there had been that crashing moment of triumph, and of breathtaking poignant tragic beauty that sent your heart up into your throat with emotion, as the shot column struck the whirring bit of feathers, arresting the flight with a jerk, and then the rumpled tumbling planing fall down to the ground to bounce lifelessly, dead. Sadly and not a little guiltily, he thrust the quail back into the game bag with the others that he had not shot and after being congratulated, went on with the others looking for more birds, his obscure but powerful terror not diminished or alleviated at all but actually stronger than before. All that preparation, the days of practice shooting, the getting up early, grown men walking themselves to death over the fields and hollows. It was all so silly, so ridiculously silly and without purpose, that shamefacedly he was half afraid hidden spectators standing behind the bushes might suddenly burst out laughing at him, as he straggled along after the others through the downed cornstalks, Clint and Murray happily and automatically knocking down more birds, and 'Bama too when he could, though he couldnt compare in shooting with

his cropper relatives. Home is the hunter, home from the hill. And the
cow's in the meadow and the sheep's in the corn. And what earthly use
or good to anybody any of it could be, Dave could only wonder dimly
and apologetically, wishing once again for perhaps the millionth time
in his life that he was like the others. Was like them, and had their
unselfconscious manhood that allowed them to shoot birds without
stewing about it or wondering why, instead of what he was. Whatever
it was he was.

He found out what earthly use or good it could be that night, when
Ruth and Clint's wife cooked the quail. Again they had a sort of communal gala supper. They had brought home a grand total of thirty-seven
birds, all but six of them (two of which were Dave's) shot by Clint and
Murray. Ruth cooked them all. And there were not any too many quail
either. Not a single bird was left on the platters when they were done.
However, Ruth said, at least there had been enough that she had not
had to eke them out with fried chicken. Murray alone ate six. Clint ate
five. Most of the kids ate three. And Dave, ravenous from thumping
around in the fields all day, stiff and tired and relaxed with several
whiskeys under his belt, almost terrorstricken now at the thought of ever
having to leave all this strange and wonderful security there was about
this place but still anxious to get back somewhere where he could have
a woman for himself again, ate five himself with several generous help-
ings of delicious slaw and the wonderful mashed potatoes. Certainly,
they had not shot any too many birds.

Next day they hunted all day again, and the whole same process was
repeated except that this time the grand total was not so high: Only
twenty six birds. But Ruth, as she had said, eked it out with two fried
chickens. Dave, beginning to get into the shooting a little now at last,
but still transfixed by that terrible sense of aloneness and separateness
that like some premonition seemed to disassociate his destiny utterly
from any connection with these people, even including 'Bama, which
was frightening, managed to kill four birds this time and in a melancholy
mournful way was quite pleased with himself. And so for the third
night, he went to bed very consciously alone with that especially painful
feeling of being the pitied bachelor friend of apologetic happy spouses.
It was, he felt, getting to be about all of it he could take, although half
of him wished fervently—for some strange reason; because such a
thought was foreign to him—that he might just continue to live right
here on this farm with its curiously strong sense of rockbed security that
it gave you, for the rest of his whole life, forever.

Of course, he could not say anything about any of this to 'Bama; or
felt he could not; but on the third day—without his having had to say
anything—they went up through Parkman north of Paris after pheasant,
just the four of them, and that night he and 'Bama spent at home. Clint

and Murray drove the farm pickup so they would have their own way back to the farm, and 'Bama did not invite them to stay at the house in Parkman. And so after a long day's hunting in which they did not get back to Parkman until late and some time after dark, they separated at the Route 40 junction and Clint and Murray drove the thirteen miles on back to the farm through Israel, after first promising to meet them early before dawn next day at the junction.

It had been a hard day's hunting, in which they got only two of the big ringnecks, and saw only four. That far south in Illinois the big birds were pretty scarce because for some reason of their own they would not live in any quantity south of an east-west line from Paris to Decatur to Springfield, though there were supposed to be lots of them in northern Illinois, and they tramped the fields all day long just to see the four. Everybody was dog tired when they finally got in.

"Why didnt you ask them to stay out at the house with us?" Dave asked as they drove on in from the junction, "if we're goin back out tomorrow?"

"Why should I?" 'Bama said mildly. "Theyd just clutter up the place and get in the way. Anyway they didnt expect me to ask them to stay."

"I know. I noticed that. But they didnt look like the kind of guys who would rat on you for having another woman around or anything like that."

"They aint. They wouldnt give a damn. That aint it. But that Murray's the biggest slash-hound in the Dark Bend. Anything he can get hold of. You know how a guy is at fourteen. And Clint's just as bad—when he can get hold of anything. I just dont want any precedents gettin started. If I did, theyd be up here all the time. And anyway I like to keep the farm and all them people separate from Parkman."

When they got back to the house, they found Doris Fredric firmly ensconced in the front room with a book and the radio playing popular love music.

"Well," she said with her slow confident smile. "Home are the hunters, home from the farm."

It was like another world. Truly, and actually, another, different world. And Dave, while he regretted the world of the farm and its astounding feel of security compared to this and suffered a nostalgic sense of loss, was nevertheless glad to be back in his own. Tired and sore and wornout though he was, he got out the little Plymouth and hustled down to Smitty's to see if he could locate Ginnie Moorehead and when he did, brought her back home and stayed up half the night in bed, before he sent her home.

Whether 'Bama slept with Doris that night or not Dave didnt know because they were still up when he and Ginnie went off upstairs, but somehow—in his own mind, in his deepest heart of hearts—(wow!)—

he was positive 'Bama hadnt. Even 'Bama, he was sure, couldnt be that cruel and hardhearted about his wife Ruth.

But whether they did or not, they stayed up late—very late, and the next day's hunting for pheasant, with both of them already pooped for lack of sleep, was even worse than the first. The second day they saw only three birds all day long and only one of these was even close enough for a shot, which happened to be Dave's, and which he missed.

Driving out to the junction before dawn in the morning, they found Clint and Murray waiting patiently in the pickup parked just on the town side of the raw dirt grade of the new bypass which the big cats and earth movers and sheepsfoot rollers, all looming silent and dead now in the predawn, had been working at as industriously as huge ants all fall since back in September. Neither of them seemed to think anything at all out of the way about not having been invited to spend the night at the house, or having to get up at three and drive the thirteen miles back up from the farm. As far as Dave could judge it was perfectly proper and understandable to both of them; and once again he had this strange feeling about the odd Southern clan that inhabited the hills and woods of the Dark Bend down there on 'Bama's farm, and of which 'Bama was the openly acknowledged leader. They all of them really knew more about life he felt sometimes—life as it was really lived—and understood it better, knew better how to live it and cope with its apparent inconsistencies in their simple uncomplicated way of just accepting them, than any of the more highly 'educated' people—such as Frank, say; or Agnes—whom he knew in Parkman. In the Packard followed by the roaring pickup, after a good warming shot of whiskey all around standing beside the road ('Bama announced that this was to be the last day, as far as he was concerned; and Dave heartily agreed with him, though he never would have said so first) they took off to the North.

Dave's one shot—the only shot any of them had all day—came just shortly after lunch. Coming down a great long field of downed cornstalks with an unplowed water-coursing running across its middle, they had seen a big cock pheasant get up—too far ahead of them to get a shot—and bear off to the left and finally settle in the water-coursing. They had not brought their dogs which were not trained to pheasant and wouldnt trail, and were counting on driving the birds to the ends of the fields, although there were only the four of them. It was a kind of half-hopeless foredoomed hunting any way you looked at it, especially when the birds were so scarce and none of them really knew the country well. When the bird went down, still in that same big field, the four of them swung their line about and went over that way down the water-coursing after him. Dave was the left end of the line and it was him the cock chose to be near when he went up again. Nobody else had a chance for a shot. They had walked down the unplowed water-coursing that was calf high in grass and weeds past the point where the bird had landed, figuring they were driving him ahead of them though of course there wasnt a sign of movement in the grass. That was when Dave heard the furious panicky neurotic cak-cak-cackle and the bombshell explosion of the beating wings as the big cock flushed again—only, it came from behind him! The bird had run about twenty five yards from where he had landed across the water-coursing, then had either settled down in the grass or else slipped through between them until they were clear past him. Why he chose to break then, when they were past him and moving away, nobody would ever know except that it was the unreasonable unpredictable way of ringneck pheasants. Dave, unable not to be startled by the furious explosion of the noise in spite of the fact that he was expecting it at any moment, swung around in midstride that way, to his right. The bird had gone up about ten or fifteen feet behind him and to his right, headed away to the left, away from all of them. Dave was between him and the others who would have been shooting directly over his head. He was carrying a .12 gauge Winchester doublebarrel 'Bama had loaned him, ready and alert to swing it up, his thumb carefully on the safety so he wouldnt forget it. The pheasant was still towering: going straight up to get height before leveling out. He had all the time in the world. His feet were planted properly, he was on balance, not a thing was wrong. Taking his time, he thumbed the safety, swung the gun up, got it on the bird, pulled it on out in front of him, just as the bird leveled out and started to streak away from him. He even remembered to hold a little high because the pheasant would be imperceptibly rising, before he fired. The gun butt slammed his shoulder, and he watched over the gunbarrels in cramped warped painful disbelief and startled wonder as the big bird continued to fly right on away from him, his mind shouting a panicky frantic "No! . No! . No!" to him over and over again. For a moment he was so disbelieving that he didnt do anything, then he swung the gun on and fired the other, the full-choked barrel, knowing he was not on the bird and having no idea whether he was leading him or not. The bird flew on and came down in another field a quarter of a mile away. That was the last cock pheasant any of them saw that day, although they did scare up a couple of lethargic impudent hens who seemed to know quite well they were safe.

To have hunted them two whole days like that, walking over the damned rough cornfields all day long, stubbing and tripping over the perverse downed stalks that caught your feet, not even getting close enough to one to fire a single shot even in vain hope; and then to miss a shot like that. It was almost physically unbearable, and Dave—like 'Bama had said earlier before they started in the car—had had enough; it was the last day for him, too. When he got home that night, he felt he had been mercifully released from some sadistic selfimposed prison where they forced you to take guns and walk through the fields all day and shoot at birds. Once again Doris Fredric was sitting there waiting for them, and once again he got out the little Plymouth and went to town to pick up old Ginnie and bring her back and prod her in a kind of paroxysm of selfrelief, balm to his bruised and lacerated ego, before he sent her home at midnight.

He had been down to the farm, and he had hunted four days, each single day of which had been a single separate private misery of sore feet, tired muscles, and mental anguish; if there were men who enjoyed doing that, let them—if they were that big of a masochist. And yet—it could only be due to his own particular masochism, he guessed— he was glad he had done it, and as he massaged his blistered feet and stiff sore legs felt proud and as if he had accomplished something by having deliberately and needlessly caused himself such pain and mental torment. Maybe all hunters felt like that. —As for the farm itself, he had discovered exactly nothing; 'Bama's wife Ruth was apparently just exactly what 'Bama had always maintained she was; and all he had come away from there with was a strong envy of 'Bama for his wife and a sense of wonder that 'Bama didnt stay there all the time; these, and that kind of haunting sense of loss for the overwhelming security they all seemed to have down there. And perhaps for the first time in his life he found himself with a sorrowful—and carefully unexpressed— wish that he had married a woman like that Ruth himself, years ago, back when he was young enough to have got one. Right now, it appeared that the only kind of woman he would ever be able to get to to marry him—if he wanted that kind; which he didnt—would be a Ginnie. Certainly, he would never be able to get Gwen French to— even if he did succeed in making her.

Doris and Ginnie had taken quite a shine to each other in the past few weeks that he had been bringing Ginnie to the house. Apparently, they had become quite close, although they never saw each other anywhere except there at the house. They would sit and drink together and sit and play cards together and sit and listen to popular love ballads on the radio together, while he and 'Bama went out on their night rounds to gamble, for all the world like two wives or two mistresses—which last, perhaps they possibly were, in a way, though not in any usual or expected way—whose husbands or lovers had to go away on business trips together. For her part, Doris enjoyed having a satellite who worshipped her, and it amused her to have somebody around she could teach and instruct. Twice she took Ginnie to Terre Haute and bought her some half-way stylish dresses and a presentable coat, and had her get her hair done in a new way designed to minimize her round fat face. Even new dresses couldnt do very much for Ginnie's waistless middle and lumpish figure, but she informed both Dave and 'Bama in her dull-eyed poleaxed-looking way that she had gone on a diet and had lost four pounds in the last two weeks. Doris even got her started reading some books—by books, meaning the romantic big-breasted period piece historical novels that Doris favored.

And for her part, Ginnie adored and worshipped Doris as a sophisti-cated lady, and with dull adoring infatuated eyes would do just about anything Doris told her. She would probably have jumped off a bridge in front of a roaring freight train if Doris had told her it was the thing to do. She even went so far as to start drinking her whiskey—(which formerly she swallowed straight or with a beer chaser)—with Seven-Up in it like Doris did, because it was more ladylike. And every so often, and increasingly, she would simper fatly in a grotesque imitation of Doris's cool staid virginal smile.

The whole situation was amusing to all of them, even to 'Bama. And it was plain that Ginnie amused Doris immensely, as she amused Dave himself.

It was just about that time—after the hunt—that Dave had his short-winded, lukewarm, lackadaisical, three weeks affair with Mildred Pierce.

CHAPTER 52

IT WAS in January that Mildred Pierce's marriage took place, and it was only shortly after that that Raymond Cole Dewey's older brother was killed—or rather, just simply died. Looking back on all of it much later, Dave could never decide which of these two events it was that seemed to be the signal for everything to start going to pot—or even whether it was either of them. But from the time that Mildred Pierce married and Raymond died it seemed that everything began to slide off—at first only slowly, and not dangerous at all—like the start of an ava-lanche fall under the feet of a party of climbers in the Himalayas, the great mass slipping away so gradually and quietly, at first, that nobody is frightened at all and still all believe they can get back out of it. Dave, both then and later, could not help remembering that strange somnambu-lant premonition of disaster, of something horribly and terribly danger-ous to all of them, that he had had as he sprawled drunk beside Ginnie that time and listened to Lois Wallup weeping.

There was a time lag of several weeks in there, before the first week in December when he and Mildred mutually agreed to quit, and the second week in January when Mildred married her Sternutol laborer, and almost all of it Dave spent with Gwen, in Israel. He still worked at home in Parkman, of course, and he and 'Bama still made their poker rounds to make their living money; but every evening that they didnt gamble, and almost every weekend, found him at the big brick house in Israel on the river. He was, although he didnt know it at the time, making his last desperate effort to reach Gwen.

They spent a great deal of time together during that month. He was not seeing Ginnie at all, had not started in seeing her again after Mildred, and Mildred herself was fully occupied with her young man from the Sternutol. When it came her time to marry, Mildred Pierce went about it just in the same way that all the rest of the brassiere factory girls got married. She and her Sternutol man (who had been going together, and frankly sleeping together, just over a month) went up to the County Clerk's office in the courthouse and made their application, took their medicals, got their license, paid their two dollars, went down to the JP's office in the basement for their ceremony, and started living together. That was all there was to it. No weddings, no receptions, no parties, no nothing. The new union was recorded without comment in the daily *Oregonian* along with some four or five others, and that was all. To Dave it was astonishing. They seemed to be quite happy.

But before any of that happened, there was that month he spent with Gwen. It was all of it in the dead of winter, because the beautiful fall that had held on all through November, after the first of December gave place to winter with a vengeance. Repeated snowstorms, brittle cold weather, and gloomy sunless days. And yet in spite of that, afterwards, after Raymond had died and the avalanche had slid on down and buried all of them, he always had the impression that it had been summer, that month they spent together.

There was no doubt that she was truly and honestly and wholly in love with him, and she looked magnificent and deeply tanned in her shorts and halter although she was wearing a fur coat and galoshes. And he was equally just as much in love with her and felt powerful and slim in his trunks although he was fat and had to keep his head huddled down into the fur collar of his down jacket. They walked along the bank of the summer river on the paths behind the big house with the river-bottoms scrub brush at the foot of the bluff and across on the other side making two impenetrable masses of green although there were no leaves on anything and chunks of ice floated in the river. Leisurely cool-hot summer walks, from which they would have to return to the house quickly sometimes to warm their fingers and feet and ears and numb faces before the huge fire roaring in the big old fireplace. She drove him along the hot dusty roads, being very careful not to skid on the stretches of ice, to a number of all her secret places where when full of anguish and dismay years ago she used to go alone for solace, places to which she had never taken another living soul. One of them was a summer cornfield out the road north out of town and under the looming sun-baked bridge, near where he had got drunk that time and slept all night in the Plymouth. It was, she said, a place that was almost impassable except in summer—except that you could probably also get in in the winter when it was frozen. It was a typical bottoms cornfield, and they pushed their way through the hot humid forest of green leaves high above their heads, with their sharp edges that you had to be very careful so as not to get cut by, to where they could see the fragrant grass of the levee and where Dave tripped and nearly fell over one of the downed, dried, harvested stalks. And beyond the levee where they sat in the cool shade of tall sycamores and willows—at this place where Gwen had used to come—ran the lazy summer river and they sat and watched it although they had to hurry back to the car in which they had wisely left the motor and the heater running.

The other place he especially remembered afterwards that she took him to that summer, was a big bluff on the river; higher even than the bluff at Israel. They drove out south along the hot dusty summer gravel road that the community-owned snowplow of Israel had already cleared, out five or six miles along this road, which was also—ultimately —the other road down to 'Bama's farm. The bluff itself, a high whale-shaped green oasis in the fields of rippling ripe wheat and young corn and beans, was set back from the river, so that the road ran tortuously along between it and the high bank that did not need a levee here. This was where she drove him, through this tunnel of live summer green made by the tall trees arching high over the road, cool and easeful after the white molten heat of the open prairie that made you squinch your eyes. Half way through it there was a road up the bluff but Gwen did not go up it; instead, she pulled off there in the wide mouth of its opening and stopped and got out and led him a little way up the hill to her other place, where they brushed the snow off the big flat rock and sat down—as she had used to sit, alone—and looked out through the thick foliage of the trees down between the columnar trunks growing on the riverbank at the smoothly flowing summer-cool Wabash River, Terre Haute-corrupted, and rolling on down to Vincennes.

"It used to ease me," Gwen smiled; "Of something. Of life. Or myself. Of myself mostly, I expect. I only come in the summer. I wouldnt want to come in the winter. I hate the winter. It would be horrible in winter." This time, too, they sat so long they had to almost run back to the car to get warm.

She took him to other private places of hers too, all places she had used to drive to all the way from Parkman, long before they bought the house in Israel, but mostly they spent the evenings—and the days—hugging the huge roaring fire in the big old fireplace and looking out at the never unfrozen weather which hovered perpetually just above or just below the zero, talking interminably of literature, and the art and craft of literature, and of life, and how you could never quite seem to pin it down to a reasonability and understanding that you could write about with faith, and how the moment you thought you had it it was gone and that moment was when you had it least. They worked over his steadily accumulating manuscripts with care and dogged perseverance, or ate the strange peculiar unheardof delicious meals Gwen concocted so automatically. It was the worst cold spell for that time of year, everybody said, that Illinois had had in years. There were no places to ski in the flat fenced-in expanses of Illinois, but Dave suddenly wished there were, so that he might have had and kept that too.

He never spoke to her of sex, at least not at first; and not for a considerable time. He was content just to be with her and to see that light, that ever-increasing light of personal, explicit love, that shone out of her face and was directed at him—at DAVID HERSCHMIDT— in that unbelievably warm intimate way.

It was just about this time—the middle of December—that the news came from Gwen's female editor friend at *New Living Literature* in New York that *N. L. L.* (as the lady always referred to it in her letters) was accepting Dave's story "The Confederate" for publication— both in her own anthology of 'novellas' and in the *N. L. L.* bi-annual collection of current writing. There was a check for $500 from the *N. L. L.* bi-annual collection, and one for $250 from the 'novella' anthology.

And so it was that the first time sex did rear its ugly head, so to speak, it was a mistake—a mistake due to an excess of triumphant exuberance and of warm grateful love. When he left that evening Dave took the money with him and deposited it in the savings account where he had been keeping the monthly checks from his share of the taxi service ever since they started to come in—but not before he had made his exulting proposition to Gwen of what he thought they ought to do with the money; and been refused.

The letter from Gwen's lady editor friend was not an especially long one, and most of it was taken up with technical details. The *N. L. L.* bi-annual collection would be out some time in February; the anthology of 'novellas' would not be brought out until some time next summer. Consequently, they might expect the page proofs for the *N. L. L.* bi-annual collection to arrive sometime soon. She hoped they would, the lady editor friend went on to say, go through these and return immediately upon arrival, without fail, as this would not leave too much time for the printers to make changes or corrections. And both Bob and Gwen, she was sure, would realize the extreme importance of not throwing the printers off schedule for their deadline. The lady editor friend went on to say, in part, that "*we believe David Herschmidt possesses a considerable and provocative, if rather macabre, talent which, if it continues to develop, shows fine promise for the future. It might even be that someday David Herschmidt will develop into a writer of real stature. In spite of a number of technical flaws, including one rather disturbing (for the reader) change of viewpoint for a moment in mid-stream, the story shows an unusual grasp of social and character formulae. And we are pleased to be able to publish this story of his which shows such penetrating, if rather bizarre, insight.*" The rest of the body of the letter went on to inquire after the welfare of Bob and Gwen.

"What the hell does all that gibberish mean?" Dave said irritably.

"It means," Bob smiled, "that she thinks you are a good writer—but does not at all grasp what you are about, and so takes refuge in techniques. You puzzle her. And so she probably also resents you positively and intensely. But not enough to keep from wanting to publish anything else you might write. Which is the nicest compliment any writer ever gets from a New York literary person."

Bob had been much in evidence—during those times they spent at the house—and yet never did he seem to be obtrusive. He ate with them, and talked with them, and drank with Dave, and yet with that exquisite sensitivity of his he always seemed to be absent at those closer, warmer times when it was better for him not to be there. That was the way it was this time. He was there when the letter (addressed to both him and Gwen) was opened in anxiety and read with exultation, and moments later—in the flush of victory and the elation of success—he was gone, off somewhere.

So they two were alone, that peculiar lovers' light on their faces and making magnetic contacts back and forth between them. They were sitting at the big table in the kitchen, the fire in the fireplace blazing, the letter lying there between them on the table. It was then that in the excess of his triumphant exultation Dave made his elated proposition.

"Look!" he said, waving the two checks under Gwen's nose happily. "Seven hundred and fifty bucks. Lets you and me take this money and make us a trip somewhere. To Indianapolis. Or Chicago. Or Memphis. Or maybe even New Orleans. It would be nice in New Orleans now. We'll blow the whole thing and have ourselves a real wonderful time. Its as much your money as it is mine, anyway. Id like to spend it on you."

Gwen was smiling at him lambently and did not answer.

"Well, come on!" he said enthusiastically. "What do you say?"

"Its wonderful of you to ask me," Gwen said softly. "It would be a wonderful trip." She paused, reluctantly. "But I couldnt possibly go, Dave. It just isnt possible."

"Why not? Why isnt it?"

"Because, for one thing, I cant leave my classes. You know that. I couldnt possibly just take off from school in midterm like that and go off someplace."

"Yes, but Christmas vacation will start in a week or so. We can go then. You wont have any classes till after New Year's."

Gwen shook her head slowly, still smiling at him with a sad, sweet, shy, intensely bright lovers' light shining at him from her eyes. "I couldnt leave Bob like that, just to fend for himself? Especially over Christmas and the holidays."

"Oh, hell! Of course you could. He wouldnt care. Besides he can take care of himself probly better than you can."

Again she shook her head. "I couldnt possibly. I just couldnt do it."

"Dont you *want* to go?" Dave said. "Is that it?"

"I—Id love to go," she said smiling sadly.

"Well, dont look so miserable about it," he grinned. "All right then, let me ask Bob. If he says its all right with him, that he'll be able to manage all right by himself, then will you go?"

"No!" Gwen said, her smile changing to a straightened mouth; and two little pinched lines appeared on her forehead between her eyes. "No, you mustnt say anything to Bob. You must promise me you wont."

"Okay, I promise." And once again she was smiling. "But he must know all about us, Gwen. About how we feel. He couldnt sit around the house like he has and watch us looking at each other, a man of his sensitivity, without knowing."

"If you asked him, he would naturally say he didnt care, even if he did. No, Dave, I couldnt leave him alone. Not over Christmas. —Besides," she added, "what is there for him to know?"

"What is there for him to know!" Dave said. "Gwen, you love me. You know you do. Youre in love with me. You know you are. It sticks out all over your face, just like it sticks out all over mine that I love you. Even a blind man could see it."

Gwen did not say anything and lowered her eyes. After a second she reached out hesitantly for the letter between them.

"You are in love with me," Dave insisted. "You do love me. Dont you?"

She looked up for a moment, straightly, almost piercingly, then dropped her lashes back down again. "Yes—I love you," she said hesitantly, with such a shy, helpless, bashful, almost frightened look of self-exposure on her averted face that it brought Dave's heart leaping and pounding up into his throat with both sympathy and triumph.

"Why?" he demanded, wanting to hear a detailed, comprehensive list of all the fine things she saw in him that made her love him.

She looked up at him again, straightly, with no shiftiness, but with a drawn-in incredibly selfconscious look in her eyes as though it took all her force of will to keep from looking away. "I guess," she said; "I suppose—I guess because youve had such a miserable unhappy time of it in your life. And because youre such a horrible Goddamned *fool*." She toyed with the corner of the letter nervously.

"Well," Dave said, feeling his smile of encouragement stiffening a little. "Well—"

"I suppose thats why all women love all men," Gwen said, a little hastily, "dont you? Because theyre such idiotic fools they need taking care of." She looked up at him with a shy analyticality.

"Im not lookin no gift horses in the mouth," Dave said valiantly. "I love you because youre all the things Id like to be, but am not: good, kind, honest, truthful, sensitive, selfsacrificing. —Look; lets go away for just two or three days, and be *back* for Christmas. We could have a wonderful time in Chicago on this," he said, waving the checks.

"Oh; you really are a fool!" she said suddenly.

"But why? You could go. School gets out next week. Youll have over a week till Christmas. We could take the train up for two or three days and be back in plenty of time."

"I dont want to! You dont understand! I cant!" Gwen cried almost frantically. Momentarily she put her face in her hands but then immediately took them away again. "I have to stay with Dad," she said reasonably.

"Do you hate sex?" Dave said suddenly.

"I—I dont know," she said hesitantly. Then she amended herself quickly. "No. No, I dont hate it. But I dont like it. Sex destroys love; look around you and see if it doesnt," she said suddenly, and with a sudden curious hopefulness. "Look at the lovers you know who have sex together. How long do they stay true lovers?" she said, a light beginning to grow in her eyes and on her face, such a light, such a sudden and blindingly intense light, of love, and something else: that curious hopefulness, that it actually made Dave's head go dizzy and his eyeballs want to roll around.

"Listen:" she said, almost as if mentally grasping at something, some straw. " '*It is Anguish I long conceal from you to let you leave me, hungry, but you ask the divine Crust and that would doom the Bread . . .*' " It sounded like some quote from something. " '. . . *I was reading a little Book—because it broke my heart I want it to break yours. Will you think that fair? I often have read it, but not before since loving you. I find that makes a difference—it makes a difference with all . . . The withdrawal of the Fuel of Rapture does not withdraw the Rapture itself.*' " It was a long quote, if it was a quote, and if it was, she must have read it many times, because she did not hesitate over a single word.

"No," she said, her eyes almost luminous with that light, that light of love and curious hopefulness; "It does not withdraw the Rapture; it enhances it. Dont you see? You and I are both too old to make a major recasting of our lives now, Dave. Lets keep what we have. Lets not destroy it. Sex kills love."

"What kind of silly damned books have you been reading?" Dave said.

"Oh, but its true! Sex does kill love. It weakens it, dilutes it. Millay said it: 'Let me lie down lean, with my thirst and my hunger.' And I love you too much to kill our love. I couldnt bear it!" And then, as if she had just remembered something, some of the passion went out of her voice, and out of her face, and she said: "Because you see, I know. Ive had the sex, you know. More than enough of it. And thats why I dont like it, and dont want it. Always, always, it destroys the love."

"Thats an awful lot to ask of a man," Dave said heavily.

"Oh, you *are* a fool!" Gwen said softly. "Well; is it too much?" she said, her face lighting up again with such a warm, deep, luminous love for him that in his own emotion Dave felt that *nothing* would be too much.

"I dont know," he said heavily. "I dont know. —No," he added, quickly. "No, no. No, its *not* too much."

"Look at us," Gwen said softly, almost pleadingly. "We're both nearly forty. Weve led two different kinds of lives too long. Its too late for either of us to change and remold ourselves now. Youre a gambler, with your friend 'Bama. Im a schoolteacher, an academic English teacher. What could we make of that together? Nothing! You know we couldnt. The only thing that draws us together at all is our mutual concern for writing. —And our love," she said softly. "We couldnt make a life of that. —But oh!" she said ecstatically, "oh, what a wonderful life we could have together the other way, without complicating it all with sex. I could promise you such a life, and such a love, as you had never dreamed of. The things we could do! The work we could accomplish! The fun and joy we could have!" She peered at him brighteyed, ecstatically, love for him so filling her that it must perforce run over, out of her eyes and face.

"Yeh," Dave said heavily. "Yes."

"You take your money home with you, my darling," Gwen smiled lovingly. "Put it in the bank and save it. Or spend it on something else. Spend it on yourself. And it will be just as if wed had our trip to Chicago anyway.

"Dont forget youre invited over for Christmas now," she smiled at him as he left. "Just in case you get any wild ideas in your head. I wanted to be doubly sure you knew, beforehand." And—although he did not know it, of course—after he was gone she went back and put her head down on the table and wept. They were all such fools, all of them. What was wrong with them? Didnt they ever see anything? Why couldnt they be forceful? Why couldnt they be positive?

Dave brooded over his new problem for several days. He did not stop going over to see her, and he did not say anything further to her about it. But it was something entirely new in his experience. Here was a woman who loved him, deeply, even passionately; he had even gotten her to admit it in so many words, had gotten her to say the point-blank phrase "I love you"; and still he could not make her, could not get her to sleep with him. It wasnt even a matter of personal pride and vanity and triumph any more, like it had been at first. He loved her. He himself was as much in love with her now as she was with him, and he desired her, physically, mentally, spiritually, as every lover desires his beloved. Hell, was that wrong? Was that abnormal? Sometimes he hungered for and desired her so much it was just plain unbearable, almost. He had never believed such brain-shaking powerful emotions lurked and existed below the surface of himself. Finally, he went to Bob about it.

There were only two or three days left until Christmas vacation at the College and after that she would be home all the time herself, so he had to go before then or he might not get a chance to see Bob alone. He drove over early one afternoon before school was out for the day and accosted Bob out in his heated workshop, working at his lathe turning out more chair legs. Since the topic was Bob's own daughter and her love and desire for him as well as his desire and love for her, about which he could not very well be explicit under the circumstances, he had to adopt a sort of general philosophical approach and the whole conversation wound up as an abstract discussion of life and writing, and incidentally of love and desire. It might have been laughable, even to him, if he had not been in such deadly earnest.

Bob, who with that keen exquisite sensibility of his was always quick to sense those things that were below the surface, indicated a tall plain unfinished white-pine stool and sat down on another one himself, and hooking their heels over the rungs this was where they sat, and talked, surrounded by sawdust and shavings and workbenches and Bob's power tools.

"I just thought Id come over and talk a while," Dave said apologetically. "Ive got a problem—a technical one—I cant solve."

"Yes?" Bob said with that curiously youthful life-eagerness in his old life-ravaged eyes. "Well, perhaps I might be of some help to you. Though I doubt it. What is it?"

"Well, for one thing, you always seem so happy," Dave said awkwardly. "Nothing ever seems to bother you. Why is that?"

"Ah! but you only think that," Bob smiled. "Things do bother me. In fact, with—I hope—pardonable pride, I might say *every*thing bothers me. After all, thats my profession, you know."

"Sure, but in spite of that you have some quality of—of, I dont know —of serenity, or something, an acceptance, that I dont have." He had not meant to start out this way, but he labored on. "In any given situation you seem to have the ability to accept it, and the facts of it. I cant do that."

Bob smiled sadly. "Im afraid you are romanticizing me. You mustnt do that, you know. Youve seen me drunk here, when things—just things, you know,—seemed so bad I couldnt stand them any other way."

"I know that," Dave said doggedly. "But still, that other thing is there too; and you know it as well as I do. What is it?"

Bob shrugged gently. "The advancement of age, and the running down of vital energy, I expect. When you get so old, you can accept many things you could not before."

"No; not true. I know lots of older people who arent that way—most of them, in fact. In fact, thats just what I mean. Look at me: Im thirty seven; and already Im worrying and brooding about the time coming when I will have to die, cease to exist. But that doesnt ever seem to worry you, at over seventy."

"Well," Bob smiled gently, "a discussion of that would take a long time and cover many things, all of my life and everything Ive read, in fact,—and there is no assurance at all that it would help you anyway, and given the data you might not come up with the same answer at all as I have. Surely," he smiled even more gently, "that doesnt have anything to do with the technical problem you mentioned. Or does it? If it does, we can take it up; or try to."

"No," Dave said. "No, no, it doesnt. No, heres what I wanted to ask you about. See, Ive been toying with the idea of introducing a love affair in the novel—my novel—between one of the GIs and a French girl it would be—and—"

"Do you think that wise?" Bob interposed, shaking his head gently. "At this stage? Youre almost half finished, arent you?"

"Just about half."

"A love affair?" Again Bob shook his head doubtfully. "A love affair —a *real* love affair—(I dont mean in the movie sense, of course)— would require an entire novel to do it justice, to even come close to doing it justice. And then Im not at all sure it could be handled adequately. A real love affair is probably the most inclusive, most all-enveloping subject there is." Again he shook his head, gently, dubiously.

"Well, I may not even do it," Dave said awkwardly. "Ive only been toying with it." He could not be sure just how far below the surface Bob could see. "But thats what happened to me. I got thinking about it, you see, and the more I thought about it the more I thought I couldnt do it. *Because,* you see, I couldnt for the life of me make it believable to myself. I couldnt see any reason why this particular GI and this particular French girl should fall in love with each other. Or, for that matter, any other particular male and female. And that led me to the general. I cant see any honest-to-God reason why any two given people might fall in love. In writing I dont think I could ever make it reasonable or believable. And yet they do, they do. But why? What causes it? Just what is love anyway? My God, no wonder the movies depend on the tried and true old mishmash they use. It would be impossible to show a *real* love affair in a two hour movie. I tell you," he said, with a carefully heavy earnestness, "its beginning to bother me so much Im afraid itll throw me off my work."

"Ah!" Bob said, "you really do have a problem there." He peered at Dave wisely, smiling sadly, and once again Dave wondered just how far below the surface he could see. After a moment Bob said, "Well, suppose we attack it at the highest level—the highest *philosophical* level— and ask Socrates' question 'Why?' Why is this so? *Why* does one fall in love?"

Dave shrugged helplessly. "Because one *needs* to, I suppose."

"Quite so. There is a definite need. But why does one *need* to fall in love?"

Again Dave was forced to shrug abortively. "Nature? Instinct? The animal in us?"

"Yes, of course theres that. The animal man. But youre not taking into account the other levels in man. I think we may assume—for our discussion, at least—that there are three levels of man, dont you? The animal man, the mental man, and the spiritual man. Agreed?"

Dave made a helpless gesture. "Yes." He had always intensely disliked the word spiritual because it made him think of his mother's primitive religion, and indeed the primitiveness of all religion, but with Bob he more or less had to allow it.

"Well then," Bob smiled gently. "When you say Nature, and Instinct, you are only taking into account the one level, the animal man. Im sure this is at least a partial factor, as it is in all animal forms; but if that were all, then a man 'in love' would be thoroughly satisfied with any female he might mount. And as long as he had available some female, any female, to mount, then he must of necessity be happy and satisfied. Now would you say that such a state approximates love in man, and the situation of being in love?"

"Certainly not," Dave said, almost indignantly.

Bob smiled, and shrugged apologetically, ever so slightly. "Then we must go on to another level to find the cause of love. On the mental level—which we humans assume man alone of all the animal forms possesses; rightly or wrongly—man has the added facet of selfconscious awareness, and the ability to anticipate—to imagine—and to take forethought. Because of this—within individual limitations, of course— he is able to anticipate, to imagine, an ideal female that suits his particular desires. Agreed?"

"Yes?"

"Consequently, by this selfconscious anticipation, he eventually settles his desires upon one particular female —generally, we must add, I think, because of physical proximity; availability— which seems to fit closest to his ideal female. (This of course applies to all individuals, of course—male or female, as the case may be—you understand.) He —or she—then transfers, by his imagination, his ability to anticipate, upon this other individual of the opposite sex all of those qualities which he has always imagined his particular, personal ideal to have. This of course varies with the individual man or woman. He may then be said to be 'in love', may he not?"

"Yes," Dave said, a little irritably. "But you make it sound awful cut and dried, awful mechanical."

Bob moved his head slightly and smiled, as if to say his triumphant "Ah!", but instead he said: "Lets leave that for now. We can come back to it. —Now; we have our individual 'in love', by virtue of his having idealized—and I use that word in its simple factual sense— another given individual. Now, what would you say our individual— man or woman, as the case may be—desires of this other individual he or she?"

"Why, to be loved in return," Dave said.

"Quite so. Even so. And why does he, or she, desire to be loved in return?"

"Well—" Dave said. "Because—" He did not finish.

"Would you not say it was because he wanted to be appreciated?"

Dave struggled mightily, without ever moving his feet on the stool rung. He felt he was being trapped in some vague net. "Yes," he said finally. "I suppose."

"Yes or no," Bob said gently. "Yes?" he said. "Or no?"

"Yes."

"And why does he wish to be appreciated?"

"Well, hell. Thats easy enough," Dave said irritably. "I can see your answers ahead of you, too. Obviously its because he feels he is worthy of appreciation."

"Quite so," Bob smiled.

"Damn it, youre pulling a Socratic dialogue on me," Dave said irritably. "Youre making a sort of Alcibiades out of me."

"Not at all," Bob said smiling. "Im only asking you questions, only helping you to figure it out for yourself. Otherwise, when you find the answer you might disagree with me."

"Well, thats Socratic, aint it?" Dave said, unable not to grin.

Bob merely smiled. "And why does he feel he is worthy of appreciation?"

"Because he thinks he is a nice person, of course."

"Would you not say he loved himself?"

"No! I wouldnt say that," Dave said quickly. "Maybe he hates himself."

"If he thinks he is a nice person?"

"Maybe he both loves *and* hates himself. Thats possible. Maybe he hates himself because he does love himself."

"Very good," Bob smiled, his eyes twinkling with pleasure. "And quite true. Nevertheless, he *does* love himself? Even if he hates himself for it?"

"All right. Yes," Dave said.

"You have no other choice," Bob smiled gently. "Very well; with that peculiar selfawareness of the mental level man, he does love himself. Now: Why does a person fall in love?"

Dave shrugged irritably. "Because he wants someone else to love him as much as he loves himself." He had, in fact, known it all his life. Lived with it all his life. But it was a different thing to be forced to admit it to an innocent bystander though.

"And why does he want someone to love him as much as he loves himself? Why is he not content with merely loving himself by himself as much as he knows he is worthy of?"

"Reassurance?" Dave said. "Vanity? Ego? Anyway, because he needs for somebody else to believe it, too."

"Of course. And why does he need for someone else to believe it? Why isnt it enough to simply love himself?"

Dave shrugged again, unhappily. "Obviously, because he wants to prove to himself his love for himself is valid."

Bob nodded, smiling gently. "So that," he added on, "as you said, he will not have to hate himself any more for loving himself."

"Maybe so," Dave said irritably, "maybe so."

"Yes?" Bob smiled. "Or no?"

"Yes."

"Well? You have your answer, dont you? Why does man fall in love? What is the prime motivating factor that causes man to fall in love?"

"Selflove," Dave said defeatedly. "Because he loves himself."

"And because he hopes to make someone else love him as much as he loves himself."

"Id hate to believe that," Dave said vehemently.

"Why so? Its true, isnt it?" Bob smiled paternally. "You just proved it yourself, didnt you? Why not believe it?"

"Because I dont like to think people are that bad."

"Bad? Bad? Who said anything about bad? Not I," Bob smiled.

"I want to believe people are *good*!" Dave cried. "I *do* believe people are good!"

"It is you who are making the distinction between good and bad, not I, dear Dave," Bob smiled sadly. "I dont remember having said anything about this selflove, which we have proved, as being bad. You did. You, of all people, who in your own book are exposing the hearts of people as it is only rarely done, you who are exposing the human condition of war and combat for what it really is—you dare to make a distinction between good and bad?"

"But what about all the people who died? You said the mental level; what about the spiritual level? What about all those other people: the Resistance leaders, and the simple unpolitical people who wouldnt knuckle under, what about the innocent Jews and Germans who died under torture by the Nazis? What about them?"

"You put this on the *spiritual* level?" Bob said. "I think it belongs on the *mental* level, dont you?"

"How so? No, sir! Youre caught there. Youve defeated your own argument there. Youve trapped yourself!"

Bob smiled again. He had never yet raised his voice; though Dave had been almost shouting several times. "Very well. You ask me about all those who died under torture at the hands of the Nazis? Then I must ask you about all the Nazis who died under torture at the hands of the Russians; what of them?"

"But they were wrong!"

"Are the Russians not wrong?"

"Yes," Dave said, collapsing inwardly. "Yes; they are wrong."

"And I must ask you also about all the Americans who died under torture at the hands of other Americans—at our own Redeployment Centers? Are they not also wrong?"

"Yes," Dave said quietly. "Yes, they are."

"But have we punished them? If you ask these things, I must go even further, you see; and must ask you about all those Christians who died under torture at the hands of the Romans; and then go on and ask you further about all the non-Christians and Reformists who died under torture at the hands of Mother Church during the Inquisition; what of them? But the Church still exists, does it not? We have not destroyed the Church, have we? We have not punished Christianity." He paused a moment and shook his head gently. "I fear you are not thinking straight, dear Dave. I fear you are letting your emotions get the better of your judgment."

"Yes," Dave said. "Yes, of course youre quite right."

"And as for all these people who have died under torture—or died not under torture; or for that matter not died at all—are they *good* simply because they believed as they did? Of course not. Or are they *good* simply because they were tortured? If so, then all any of us need to do in order to be *good* is to be tortured by someone else. We could hire professional torturers to wrack us all, who in turn could be tortured by others so that they might be good too. No, I think you must put all this back down on the mental level; and if so, we come back to our original proposition: *Why?* Why did these people do as they did? Why were they heroic?—

"Let me ask you? why did the soldiers, the men you fought with, why did they fight as heroically as they did? Can you answer?"

"I—" Dave said, and then paused. "Yes, I guess I can."

"Truthfully? Out of your own experience only? Why, then?"

Dave shook his head defeatedly. "As you said," he said: "selflove. They wanted to be admired, and respected—"

"—even loved?—"

"—even loved, by the other humans they lived with."

Bob shook his head gently. "Then, there is your answer to the others— the Resistance leaders, the Russians, the Nazis, the Americans, the Christian martyrs, the non-Christian martyrs. They all did what they did for the very same reason. Selflove, the separate, separated, selfconscious self-sealed-off, selfawareness of selflove that man exists in on the mental plane; the mental level."

"All right," Dave said defeatedly; "I agree. But what is the spiritual level? How does it operate? Where does it come in?"

But before Bob could answer, he interrupted himself. "You know, if I were a logician," he grinned heavily, "I could tear your argument to shreds."

"Of course," Bob smiled; "but you and I are not logicians. We are intuitionists, you and I. We are—I hope—creative men. A poet and a novelist. Where would we be if we tried to work by pure logic. I would not have posed you a logician's argument, even if I were capable of it—which I am not."

"All right," Dave said subduedly, feeling unaccountably depressed. "All right. What about the spiritual level? Where does it fit into this? *Why*—I say *Why*, you see—*Why* does man fall in love on the spiritual level?—Or rather: *Why* on the spiritual level does man fall in love?"

Bob smiled at him gently and shook his head. "I can give you a simple answer. But you already know that yourself. And to attempt to do any more than that would be to enter upon such an incredible complexity that we would literally be talking for weeks. Without, Im sure, ever deciding anything at all. Youre asking me about a wholly different field, a subject Ive spent years reading and musing about—and still know practically next to nothing of. We would have to leave our so-called philosophy and enter into metaphysics, a subject where two minds who do not already agree could argue and speculate forever. I should have to take you back and ask you whether Christ Himself taught reincarnation—metempsychosis—or not. I believe that He did, and that all of this—or all but the most veiled allusions to it—were excised from the Bible and from His teachings over a period of time. First by St Paul, who deliberately changed his Master's teachings to suit his own ideas;

and then at the First Council of Nicaea and later; and also by Augustine and others. And if you accepted that, which Im sure you would not, we would only be at the barest beginning of it all."

"Youre referring to some kind of Theosophy now?" Dave said.

Bob smiled. "No, not exactly. But somewhat, too. The great Theosophists like Madame Blavatski—like the great Christians; or the great anything else—were not Theosophists—or Christians—they were seekers; only later, when these words acquired popularity and became creeds, were there professional 'Theosophists' and professional 'Christians'— who thereby, in direct proportion as new members of the creed were added, diluted and weakened and vitiated the power and truth of their own teachings. The same can be said of Emerson and the Transcendentalists. The more adherents any Great Teaching acquires the more primitivized it of necessity becomes."

"I can buy that," Dave said, thinking of his mother.

"But as I say, we would still only be at the barest beginnings," Bob said gently. "I have no way of telling you how incredibly complex the subject is. And it is impossible to convey the even greater complexity of the system of true spirituality which the subject purports to describe. Suffice it to say," Bob smiled in his gentle way, "that there appears to be—from what small bit I have been able to assimilate, at any rate—a whole entire world of bodyless souls, spirits, complete with its own body politic, its own hierarchy of Leaders and Lords and Masters and Teachers—minor Gods; Demi-Gods, if you will—surrounding the material world we inhabit; in—in another dimension, so to speak; and which is infinitely more complex and complicated than the world we ourselves live in. And you know how complex that is! It would be foolish to attempt to explain any more. Except to add, that this is only a very small part of the inhabited Universe—Truly, worlds within worlds. —and that these people are apparently in constant contact with some parts of our minds, without our knowledge of course, guiding us, directing us; beneficently, not malignantly."

"Thats pretty hard to believe," Dave said, a little breathlessly.

"Naturally," Bob smiled. "I find it rather hard to believe myself, at times. In fact, Im not at all sure I believe it at all. Im only telling you what Ive garnered out of a number of years of reading on the subject."

"Have you ever had any contacts with this—other world?" Dave said.

"None at all. Absolutely none. Never. Never once in my life have I even had what might even remotely be called an 'occult' experience. — Though I have often wished," he smiled sadly, "that I might have had; at least it would be a proof to me. But you must understand that so-called 'occult' experiences are a very, very low level manifestation of these spiritual phenomena. Its comparable to taking a very low ignoramus brute of a man off suddenly to Mars and asking him to describe Earth. Thats what almost all of your so-called 'mediumistic' accounts—if they are sincere, and not hoaxes—and the common reincarnation experiences consist of. It is a mistake to believe that just because a person dies and enters the astral world, he becomes transfigured and has a greater intelligence or a deeper soul than he had when alive. Actually, he is very little different from what he was when alive—and probably wont be, for a number of other lives."

"Then—then it truly is complex," Dave said, unable not to feel awed.

"Infinitely," Bob said sadly.

"And you really believe in all this?" Dave said.

Bob stared at him a moment, smiling, perhaps a little apologetically, a little stiffly, as a man will who does not care to talk about certain things but feels for one reason or another that he must, then after a second gave his almost imperceptible shrug. "That is what all of these books teach. I dont *know*. Most of the books disagree between themselves in the minor details—which," he added, "is certainly understandable considering the incredible complexity of it all. All I do know is that I believe in metempsychosis—in reincarnation, rather—as the evolution of individual souls. I do not believe that human souls incarnate in the bodies of animals as some types of metempsychosis teach. That is only a superstitious primitivization of reincarnation. Yes," he said, spreading his palms, and smiling. "Yes, I believe in reincarnation; but I cannot even prove that to you."

"Well—" Dave said. "Well—" This was getting a long way, a very long way, away from the subject of "falling in love" that they had started out on. "Well, what about that simple answer you said I already knew? Maybe I dont know it after all?"

"Let me say this first: Man is, apparently, in a state of evolutionary development. Man—or rather these souls which use man. And each soul, apparently, carries out its own private, selfcontained evolution— a small world in itself. But mankind itself—the physical, material race of man—is also in a state of evolutionary development on another, quite much lower level; and actually, we really have no slightest idea of what unimaginable physical—or non-physical—forms we may someday come to be. (That these two such different phenomena could coincide so neatly, incidentally, is one of the miracles of the system. And also, this miracle of coincidence is responsible for a great deal of the mistaken understanding and misconception about the process, since it is such a common idea with Christians to take the soul-man and the body-man—the envelope-man—as being inextricably locked and one and the same forever, whereas actually they are two totally different phenomena, almost completely unrelated. Except insofar as they temporarily use each other.)

"Well. If man—both his soul and his body, though separately, and on different planes—is in a state of evolutionary development, this means that he is growing, is learning. The 'organic metaphor'—the 'growing plant'—of the modern romantics comes very close to understanding this in the 'occult' way. However, what your romantic—who accepts blindly the materialistic Darwinian type of evolution (which is all right, as far as it goes) as the last word—does not realize, is that evolution was not always the case. First, before there could be *evolution*, of necessity there had to be *involution*—the going outward from God; which, unfortunately, has become the *supposedly* Evil, and totally erroneous, symbol of the Jews of Satan and his Dark Angels being kicked out of Heaven. In fact, the *involution* can no more be Evil than the *evolution*; since without the one the other would be impossible. Now, if you take the whole process and look at it in the shape of the letter V, with God at both ends at the top and man here on Earth at the bottom, the point, you have the whole situation. We souls here on Earth, which actually *involved* down from God to meet our gross— and by gross I only mean dense; no derogatory connotations—material bodies as they *evolved* up to meet us and be used by us, are actually right now at the very lowest point of the V and preparing, and only just now beginning in fact, to evolve back upward whence we came. Now—"

Bob, whose voice had been growing more and more excited as he talked, suddenly stopped himself. In silence he raised one corded-veined hand and ran it vigorously once back and forth over his close cropped crewcut head, and then brought it down and smoothed back his big mustache, first to the right then to the left, and stared at Dave quizzically for a moment, smiling gently, out of his wise old face.

"Well—" he said. "There are so many things," he said apologetically. "The principle of Karma; the *unevil* concept of Shiva the Destroyer; the Seven Sacred Rays. I could go on and on, you know.

"About your simple answer: which I am quite sure you already know: If one can assume that man *is* evolving—which I think we may more or less safely assume, for our purpose at least;—though of course one could even argue that point practically forever without ever really proving it;—if we do, for the sake of brevity, assume that point for the present: that man is evolving; is growing; then let us ask *how* he grows."

"How?" Dave asked obtusely.

Bob nodded. "What is the one cardinal phenomenon by which he grows? Which *forces* him to grow?"

"Im lost," Dave said. "Youve lost me. With all that other."

Bob smiled. "A hint, then: The classic worn example: The child who although he has been told not to, puts his hand on the hot stove."

Dave stared at him, feeling totally ridiculous now, and also for some reason a little scared. "Pain," he said. "Suffering."

"Even so. Pain. Physical pain, mental anguish, spiritual suffering. There never has been, and never will be,—contrary to what we humans would devoutly like to believe—any growth or any learning, without pain. Pain the great Destroyer, and the great Healer. Pain the fertilizer, pain the grower." Bob smiled. "I think if we 'humans' should give thanks to God for any single thing at all, we should do so first for our God-given ability to suffer pain."

"That sounds like some sort of new cult of masochism," Dave said, still feeling a little bit uneasy.

Bob grinned delightedly. "Perhaps it should be! A new Beatitude!" he smiled: "Blessed are the Masochists for they shall be the heirs of the Sadists.

"Well, there you have your *simple* answer: Which, as I said, you already know in your heart: You asked why on the spiritual level does man fall in love: I should say that because only there, or mostly there, in the selfsealed selflove that man lives in on the mental plans of existence, can the really greatest—the only truly shell-breaking, crust-dissolving pain be found."

"But thats a plain paradox," Dave protested.

Bob smiled and spread his corded-veined hands. "Of course? What is not? Is it not also a paradox that in our efforts to escape pain we all run immediately for salvation to human love where we find the greatest pain of all? Perhaps old Plato was not so factually wrong after all, with his idea that male and female once inhabited the same body, and have ever since spent their lives frantically trying to find their Other Self. Today we prefer to look on this statement of his as an amusing, rather sly, symbolism; but perhaps we are wrong; it may be—it may be," he smiled, "that he was actually, factually correct."

Dave was rubbing his hand over his jaw, which he had neglected to shave today. "Well, youve solved my technical problem, anyway, Bob. In order to make my love affair believable—if I decided to write it in, of course; which I havent decided yet—all I have to do is show that both of them—both my GI and my French girl; or any other two lovers in the world—are just simply both plain blind fools."

"Of course," Bob smiled. "Handle it just the same way you would handle your heroes, and your soldiers, and your warfare. I have a book inside in the house that explains it all very well. *Quite* well. Its written by a man—a Master—who calls himself simply 'the Tibetan,' and who purportedly used this English woman to set it down for him. The way he explains it is that its all a problem of *Glamours*. —A very apt choice of a word, I think, dont you?— Everything, everything in the world, is a *Glamour*. Because, after all, the world doesnt really exist. War is a *Glamour*. As you know. Politics is another *Glamour*. Religion, as man knows it, is another *Glamour*. So the problem really resolves itself into one of simply getting rid of all one's *Glamours*. And love—love is probably the greatest *Glamour* of them all.

"Its really all very simple," he smiled.

"Yeh," Dave said. He got up off the stool. For some reason he could not exactly have said, he wanted, or needed, or anyway felt required to—felt it was proper to—shake hands with Bob, and he held out his hand. Bob French grasped it warmly and firmly with his aging corded-veined hand, smiling.

"Ill go in and get it for you if youd like," he offered.

"No," Dave said quickly. "No, not now. Right now Ive got a whole hell of a lot more than I can digest or assimilate. Perhaps some other time."

Bob smiled happily. "You know," he added, "I have a little theory of my own that Ive been sort of developing over the last few years, in connection with reincarnation. I have about come to the conclusion that the true artist, the great artist—whose work I have always held to be the greatest endeavor of man—is really only the last evolutionary stage the individual soul goes through, before it becomes that lowest of all the Initiates—as the 'occult' books call them: the beginning Disciple, working consciously and specifically with some Great Master; and that all the anguish and suffering artists like you and I go through—all our great vanity (which causes us so much pain) and our oversexualization (which also causes us much pain)—all these are both a sort of testing-ground for us and also the very means by which we learn to sluff off those *Glamours* which we must get rid of in order to become a lowly Disciple.

"Its rather a comforting thought—at times," he smiled; "and also a very humbling one. I figure it will take me about three to ten lives—depending on my various Karma—to become a truly great enough artist to be able to make the crossover." He smiled at Dave kindly, his eyes twinkling with a curiously high good humor.

"You think so, hunh?" Dave said with a weak grin. "Jesus Christ! then where does that put me?" he said hollowly.

"Ah! but one never knows," Bob smiled. "You may be far ahead of me. In fact, considering the work youre doing lately, I suspect that you are."

"Say, you know," Dave said suddenly, "Ive got a friend Id like for you to meet. He thinks a very great deal like you do, in many ways. Though of course he cant say it as well. Its 'Bama Dillert; the gambler, you know. The guy I buddy around with. What youve been saying about Glamours made me think of him."

"Well, by all means bring him over," Bob said delightedly.

"Well, its not that simple. Ive been trying to get him to come over with me for six months. But hes shy. He wont come."

"Good Heavens!" Bob exclaimed; "surely hes not shy of someone like Gwen and myself."

"Well, he thinks youre both intellectuals, you know?"

"Great Scott!" Bob grinned. "What have I ever done to him that he should want to insult me so?"

Dave laughed. "Well, maybe I can drag him over sometime. He really does think an awful lot like you do. In fact, he reads a number of occult books himself."

"I should very much like to meet him," Bob said in his exquisitely polite, wholly old-world gracious way.

"Well, we'll see," Dave said. "Ill see you, Bob."

"Dave," Bob said gently. The younger man stopped at the door of the shop. "Why dont you just go on in the house and wait? Gwen should be home at any moment—if she isnt here already. Go ahead," he smiled. "Go right on in. Make yourself at home, if she isnt here yet."

"Well," Dave said. "All right. All right, I will."

And so that was what he did. He crossed the snow covered yard, with no idea at all that Bob might be exhausted by their conversation, and in the house he put some of Bob's classical records on the player and got himself a can of beer out of the icebox and just wandered around looking at some of the books on the walls, as he had done so many times before. He still could not tell just how far below the surface of all this Bob French could see. Had Bob merely invited him to go on in this time, in that curious way he had done, out of innocence? Or had he done it because he was aware of everything, and just didnt care? Maybe he had done it to deliberately show Dave that he *was* aware, and that he *didnt* care? All the other things, all that occultism stuff, was on Dave's mind too. Evidently Bob did really seriously believe in metempsychosis— in the reincarnation of souls into an ever evolving series of personalities; and the fact that he did shook Dave. A man like that, with the real mind he had. For him to believe that stuff— When Gwen came home from school in a little while, he had already drunk three cans of beer, and they went for another ride in Bob's little coupe out through the forbidding hard-frozen, really dangerous winter Illinois landscape. If a man got caught out here, away off in these fields that stretched away literally for miles under the glowering sky, without a car and a heater, and couldnt find a farmhouse anywhere— As they drove along, he told her about the discussion with Bob, and asked her about it.

"Does he really believe in that? In reincarnation?"

"Oh, yes. Yes, Im sure he really does," Gwen said. "Weve had a lot of discussions about it."

"Do you believe in it too?"

"Yes. Yes, I think I do," she said. "Let me put it this way: I dont know of course that its a fact; but of all the different systems of religion,

and so-called life after death, and retribution and punishment and reward and all that, reincarnation seems to me the only really logical
answer to the problems of the soul."

"Logical!" Dave exclaimed.

"Yes. Logical. After all, what could be more illogical than what the
various forms of Christianity teach: That an individual soul is created
every time a child is born; and that then, when it dies after a span of
sixty or seventy years, it is judged for all eternity by what it did or did
not do during those few years. Either to eternal Heaven or eternal Hell-
fire. To me thats simply ridiculous. Its unjust on the part of God in the
first place, and in the second place its simply wasteful. Think how many
new souls that takes every day! Heavens, God would be so busy making
new human souls that He wouldnt have time to create new galaxies or
solar systems or other life forms or anything else. In fact, the whole idea
flagrantly violates the law of the conservation of energy. If everything
else is subject to the law of the conservation of energy, why should we
insignificant little humans so arrogantly assume that our precious human
souls are sacrosanct and above it? Think of the trillions and trillions of
souls that would be, with all the borning and dying thats gone on for
millions and millions of years; where would they all go? And all just so
they could live some sixty or seventy years in order to be judged. No;
I think its all just our incredible human vanity, which makes it impossible for us to believe that our 'I', our 'me', could ever be used again
by some other personality.

"Its just that to me it seems to be the most logical hypothesis. Why
should souls not also evolve? since everything else does? And if I am
to believe in God at all, I must be able to believe He is just."

"Sure," Dave said; "me too. But thats no proof. God may very easily
be unjust, for all we know; and from our viewpoint. Maybe God's idea of
justice and ours dont necessarily coincide."

"Probably they dont," Gwen said. "I didnt mean that God must be
just by human terms. I meant He must be just by His own terms; since
those are the only terms there are, He therefore must be."

"That doesnt necessarily follow," Dave said irritably.

"I didnt say it did. All I said was, thats how I feel. What I was trying
to say was: If Whoever or Whatever it was that created everything,
did create it—and I think we can assume Something or Someone did
create it; that there was a Beginning somewhere—then everything He
did create must be just in an abstract sense because it is all a part of
Him and is all there is. So it must be just, according to His concept of
just—whatever that is. It has to be just, simply because its all there is.
There isnt anything else."

"Oh," Dave said cogitatingly; "oh. I think I see what you mean, now.
But its a hard thing to try to say. But I think I get what you mean.

Just simply because of the fact its all there is, it *is* all there is. So it has to be accepted as just."

"Yes." Gwen turned to smile at him, that incredibly warm, lambent lovers' look, that she had been giving him so much now these past few weeks, and he smiled back at her—their two pairs of eyes saying many silent things; all sorts of things—and wanting desperately to take her in his arms here in her car and love her, make love to her. A little chill went over him when he remembered that so short a time ago Bob had so concisely and devastatingly held up for him the whys and wherefores of 'love'. Had, in effect, proved almost conclusively that there wasnt any such a thing as 'love,' except insofar as it was love of self. But, damn it, if you *felt* things they existed didnt they? If you *felt* them, they *must* exist. If he could only figure out what it was that was wrong, with her. Something, somewhere, was wrong; he could feel it; he could sense it. But he couldnt find out what it was. If he could only reach her, find out what this thing was. . . .

Gwen's Christmas vacation started three days later. Dave said no more to her about making the trip to Chicago. It was obvious she wasnt going to go anyway. Once the College had let out he started spending more and more time over at their house in Israel. He still worked some in the mornings; but not nearly as much as he had been, and he began spending most of the nights over there too, in that same bedroom he had occupied before but which now had been fixed up into practically a private, personal room for him. He had a razor and shaving things and toilet articles he kept there, and a number of his clothes hung perpetually in the closet whether he was there or not. It was, in fact, *his* room now; "Dave's room" was what they all called it; and he felt free to come and go any time he took the notion.

More than once, as he lay in the bed in "his" room—sometimes half-drunk; sometimes wholly sober—he was more than half a mind to just simply slip out of bed and go down there and accost her, where she lay in her own bed only two doors away, so secure, and so near he could almost imagine he could hear her breathing, and yet at the same time seemingly solar systems away; just accost her, and force her to sleep with him, make her, take it away from her. He was sure, somehow, that if he did, if once she slept with him, everything would somehow all be all right then. If he succeeded. But always in the end the thought that he might not succeed stopped him. She had made it plain she didnt want to sleep with him, had no intention of sleeping with him. And if he did *not* succeed, if he tried and failed, everything would come down, everything, tumble down like a shack in a hurricane, about his ears, and there wouldnt be *any*thing left. And after all, he was a guest in her house. So he did nothing, and would simply lie, running his hands up and down miserably over the fat of his chest and belly, hating himself for being so unlovely and unattractive, and for being so gutless, until he finally went to sleep.

Christmas in 1948 was not like Christmas in 1947. This year it was a real white Christmas—all through the month of December—and Dave was over there in Israel almost all of that time; he helped decorate the house and fix the tree and plan the party they would have; he was consulted on what presents to buy for the various ones, including Gwen's young ministerial student and the crippled polio girl from the College who were invited this year and hence were not going home for Christmas but were staying in town to work on their novels; and he went to Terre Haute by himself to buy his own gifts for all of them. He came home drunk and exhausted. It was all of it ridiculous; childish; he detested it; but once the shopping part was done, it was nevertheless fun to do, to have done. It was, in short, Christmas. The radio and newspapers, as always, made much of it. They also made much of other things.

'Bama had decided since Dave was going to be in Israel, to go down to the farm for Christmas this year. So the house in Parkman was locked up, and a key given only to Dewey and Hubie. Doris Fredric wouldnt need a key anyway, since she was going to be home Christmas with her family.

Wally and Dawn—who was home for Christmas from Western Reserve—were very much in evidence in Israel during the preparations for Christmas. Dawn, or so it seemed to Dave, didnt seem to have changed much—except that maybe she was a little less openly displayful of her sophistication now, as if she had gotten a little more used to it as a fact; and also she seemed a little more reserved, more cold. Whatever warmth there had been between her and Wally last summer the times they had come to the house in Parkman, had apparently either gone underground or else gone away entirely;—although they were together all the time, just the same.

Wally himself, on the other hand, appeared just as reserved and cold as Dawnie did—although he had apparently given up Rosalie Sansome for the Holidays while Dawn was home. And for the first time since early last summer he was being distant again with Dave, and had been for two or three weeks. The only reason Dave had been able to figure out for it was the acceptance of his story by Gwen's lady editor friend with *New Living Literature*. But during the Holidays, when they were all over at Israel so much, and were all thrown together in a body so much, he discovered there was more to it than that. Wally was jealous of him with Gwen. He obviously thought they were sleeping together and were lovers, Dave deduced wryly.

On Christmas day Frank and Agnes, according to tradition, came over for their eggnog and to see the presents. It was the first time Dave had seen either of them face to face since Frank had come up to the hotel after he got back from Florida. He and Frank eyed each other constrainedly, and said hello politely.

"How're you making out, Frank?"

"Oh, pretty good. Im doing pretty good," Frank said, distantly, cold-eyed. "I guess. I guess Im making out all right. And you?"

"Fine, Frank, fine," he said. "I couldnt be doing better. My book's over half done."

"Well, thats good," Frank said. He did not sniff, actually, but he looked as if he wanted to. And when they left, moved by some obscure impulse, some vague feeling of warmth and all the things that he truly owed his brother in the past, Dave went up and said goodbye and held out his hand to him. For a moment it looked as if Frank was not even going to take it, but then —half full, and half tight, from the eggnogs he had been drinking all morning all over town; and probably with some dim obscure feeling about Christmas Cheer and Good Will to Men— he took Dave's hand and shook it, though of course they both knew— from the very moment he hesitated, on—that it really meant nothing.

Well, to hell with it, Dave thought, a little tight himself. To hell with it. He didnt care. He didnt care any more than Frank cared.

The rest of the Holidays—or almost entirely all—he spent in Israel with Bob and Gwen. On January 3rd Gwen started back to her classes; and Dave moved back to Parkman.

But he knew, even before that, even before she started back to school, that it wasnt going to work—wasnt going to be any good. He knew, all during that week between Christmas and New Year's, although he never let on and never said anything to her, or anyone, about it. It just wouldnt work. If she wanted a 'platonic' love affair, if that was all she had stomach for any more, after all the rest of her unhappy sex experience, if that was what she wanted, she would have to find another man to have it with. It just wasnt part of his makeup. In his makeup, you couldnt divorce love from sex. He just wasnt built that way. It was too painful. He had thought for a while, had hoped, that he might even be able to live like that. But he couldnt. And it was just too much to ask. And after that week of the Holidays he could see clearly that she wasnt going to make any change. He could have sex with a woman without loving her; but he could not love her, and go on loving her forever, without having sex with her. He had given up hope. Without saying anything about it, and leaving all of his things still there in "his" room, he went home to the house in Parkman carrying a sick hollowness and a loneliness which, he was quite sure, was greater than any of the other lonelinesses he had ever felt in his life, all lumped together.

A week after that Mildred Pierce married her Sternutol laborer. And just a few days after that, Raymond Cole died.

CHAPTER 53

During the month he had spent so much time with Gwen, Dave had nevertheless a number of different times gone out to Smitty's Bar with 'Bama and the boys and sometimes Wally; so he had seen Raymond several times.

Some nights Raymond would not be there at all, and on other nights he would show up with one companion or another—all of them, invariably, men who if they were not as completely uninhibited as Raymond, were nevertheless that same general type of man: men who wore the heavy florid faces, or lean florid faces, of hard drinkers and the big-muscled bodies of shovel-laborers, while they moved about with wild, haunted animal-like eyes, looking as if they were always just missing something, something important to them that they were seeking to grasp, but never could quite, forever checked and frustrated by their own baffled bewilderment, their own dull inarticulate unanalytical minds, just as they were about to reach out and grasp it; men who, Dave always felt, like Raymond would have made wonderful durable beefy frontiersmen a hundred years ago, but who now had been completely by-passed and left marooned, unuseful and indeed unwanted; war casualties of a totally different sort, by virtue of the fact that just as they had found themselves in their element, and had begun to enjoy it with that wild, animal joy of which they were capable, even the war had cheated them by stopping and being over, thus leaving them doubly lost, doubly marooned, with a hungry memory of a success and happiness they had never had before, and probably would never get to feel again. All of them—like Raymond—intensely vital, intensely strong, intensely awkward (among well-dressed "civilized" people), and intensely outcast. It was, to Dave, as if a sort of latterday roster of the men who died in the Alamo had been in some miraculous way rejuvenated and forced to roam around the nation they had helped to make: Bowie, Travis, Crockett: they would have been at least as embarrassed, and as shocking, as Raymond and his friends. The mere fact that Raymond and the others could continue to live the wild, virtually homeless, dimly drunken lives they lived without just keeling over and dying, attested superbly to their endurance and tremendous physical vitality, which nevertheless always had the effect of putting everybody else ill at ease, since it was so powerfully strong it frightened the more civilized.

At other times Raymond would appear alone, and then would sit by himself in one of the old-fashioned-drugstore wirebacked chairs, at one of the old-fashioned-drugstore tables in the back, drinking up a forest of empty beer bottles and slyly sneaking swallows of whiskey from the pint bottle he hid inside his worn old leather jacket. He would sit so for an hour, hardly speaking to anyone and talking to himself under his breath, and ogling lavishly and hungrily all the women in the place with what he fondly believed to be his irresistible masculine appeal, unaware that none of them would even be caught dead with him,—even if they were alone without boyfriends (which they never were; and to which he attributed his lack of success with them), and then after an hour or so he would charge up—as often as not knocking over the chair he was sitting in, just out of sheer animal vitality—and stalk confidently out in his rolling punchdrunk fighter's gait and climb into his decrepit old Dodge and go chugging laboriously off into the night no one knew where—probably to a whorehouse in Terre Haute.

Raymond still spent very little time at home with his wife and one kid, apparently—from what Dave gathered from the boys—only going there whenever he was out of money, and hanging around until his wife, who worked, would—probably more to get rid of him than for any other reason—give him a little money. Winter was the hardest time of the year for Raymond, since he could get almost none of those laboring jobs (at which he rarely lasted longer than two weeks and one paycheck) that he lived off of in the summer.

Dave, whenever he saw him there, in Smitty's, could not help seeing him as a casualty of Empire like the plebes of Rome; and, whenever he saw him so, could not help musing sorrowfully over our Victorian moralisms which would not allow us to have gladiators and a circus where they could perform upon each other, as Rome had so wisely done, to take up the slack of surplus. Raymond might have been happy as a gladiator.

Raymond apparently had some dim feeling that Dave carried some sort of affection for him, because whenever Dave was there and he came in, he would roll up and insist on buying Dave a drink and then with his massive shoulders and back, pull up a chair and shoulder his way in on the party, talking to Dave all the while in a loud voice about Life and The Sorrows Of Living and offering happily to beat the living hell out of anybody for him that Dave did not like, to prove his friendship.

Whenever he did all this, he would invariably irritate and embarrass his brother Dewey, who was usually in the party, to the point of fury. And it was one of these times, just about the middle of December, that he irritated him beyond the point of where anybody could calm him down or hold him back, and they had another of their locally famous fights. The last one, as it turned out.

Dewey had been spending a great deal of time at the Lincoln Street house with Dave and Wally, and that probably had a great deal to do with it. Ever since last summer, when Dawn had used to come down to the house with Wally, Dewey had been discussing art and music and literature with all of them. It was as if a whole new field to challenge had opened up for him. He was becoming "educated"; and a great deal of all their ideas could not help but rub off on him. He had read all of Wally's manuscript and later—at his own suggestion—had then read Dave's. And from this it was only one short step to the idea of writing a book about his own life. He talked about it with both Dave and Wally. Dewey thought it would make a real good story. "Im a rebel," he would say; "just like you guys. Only I aint got any cause. I aint even got anything to rebel *against,* even. What could I rebel against? your brother Frank and Clark Hibbard and the Country Club? That 'Lost Generation' of the 'Twenties, they loved it; they never had it so good. But my generation, we cant even be lost—because we never been found. What was I ever taught? What was I ever shown? Nothing! thats what. I never even learned to brush my teeth and make up my bed till I got in the Army. My folks was always too busy fighting. What do they give my generation to believe in: A happy home, a union to increase my wage, a new car, and an automatic washing machine. We're not even a *lost* generation, my generation. We're an *unfound* generation. The 'Unfound Generation' of the 'Forties."

He talked a good deal about this, and Dave listened and made mental notes and unblushingly stole everything of it that he could use. He did not feel guilty about it, because while Dewey talked about writing a book about his own life he never actually did anything about it. He only talked about it. He talked about it a lot, and grinning with his boyishly handsome, blue-eyed face, said that some day he was going to start in on it. Dave told him (not entirely truthfully) that all he had to do was sit down and start, that there was a novel in every man's life, that all you had to do was sit down and write it. But (truthful or not) Dewey never did. And Hubie only hooted derisively when he would start talking about his book, and about literature. "Im gonna write a book," Hubie howled into the conversation one day, in his twanging country voice, kicking up his legs in the big armchair. "Im gonna write a book. Itll be a soulful hist'ry of the human race. I even already got the title for it. Im gonna call it *No Forehead.* Thats from a poem. Im gonna print the poem right behind the title, see? like all them regular writers do," he said in his twanging drawl. "You remember that limrick about *The Young Man from Dundee?*" and proceeded to quote it.

"There!" he yelled, as they all shouted with laughter, and looked at them smugly. "What do you think of that? Aint that some title! *No Forehead.* Soulful hist'ry of the human race."

It broke the literary discussion up into a general paroxysm of laughter, in which Dewey—if a little ruefully—joined as much as anybody, and from that time on Hubie's "book" had acquired its permanent title, repeatedly referred to by somebody. But in spite of Hubie, and in spite of the fact that he only talked (to inflate his ego, as Dave told him), Dewey nevertheless was becoming "educated"—tremendously so, compared to what he used to be.

Consequently, it would infuriate and embarrass him almost beyond reason whenever his brother Raymond would come horning in and lugubriously begin to talk to Dave about Life and The Sorrows Of Living in his loud-voiced strongly positive and totally ignorant, ingenuous way. This, with his new-found depth of educated subtlety, Dewey simply could not stand. As 'Bama said of him, grinning sardonically: "Like they say, theres no Catholic as rabid as a converted Catholic."

This particular time, while they all sat around a drugstore table in Smitty's, Raymond had said something about what a sad, sorrowful thing it was that people who didnt really hate each other had to go to war and kill each other; war was a great tragedy, he thought, didnt Dave?

"Jesus Christ, Raymond," Dewey said with a cold, steel contempt, his beautiful blue eyes searing, "can you not ever shut up even? Must you always open that big fat yap of yours and expose what an ass you are?" Dewey's grammar, as well as his vocabulary, had been steadily getting better since summer. "I know you are dumb," he said with bitter-cold devastation; "but I didnt think even anybody as dumb as you are could open their mouths and make themselves look that much dumber."

"Now, what the hell did I say?" Raymond demanded. "All I said was I think war is sad, thats all. It is, aint it? And anyway, I was talkin to my friend Dave here, and not to you. So why dont you keep your nose out?"

"Raymond, Jesus Christ," Dewey said, with insulting patience as if counting blocks to a child. "I think if you went back to school for ten years you might, you just might, if you were lucky, come out of it about as smart as a nine year old Mongolian idiot. Look: You never had it so good as you did during the war. You never were as happy and successful in your life and neither was I and Hubie. For the first and only time in our life, the three of us, we belonged to something, to a society, where we had a definite place and an important job. We fit. What we did was right, and what people wanted us to do. We had regular definite things we could do, for somebody, responsibilities, definite—and important— jobs to perform. All three of us were squad sergeants. And we were needed; the men needed us, and the Company Commander needed us, too. We filled a place. And you loved it, and I and Hubie loved it. Now what the hell is all this crap that war is sad, hunh? Just what the hell are you yapping about?"

"Well, sure," Raymond said belligerently; "I guess I liked the Army. In some ways. But I still say war is sad; sad for them that got kilt; and Ill stick to it."

"Well, I say it isnt sad," Dewey said icily. "I say its happy. I say the ones that got it are better off dead. Look at us: We're all three bums—as far as this town is concerned. This town would be happy if all three of us left it; for good; and never came back. Theres not a living soul in this town gives a damn whether any of the three of us lives or dies. And that includes the Old Lady; Mom. And the Old Man, too. Right? All right, I say *peacetime* is sad; *not* war. Now how about that?"

"Well," Raymond said perplexedly, caught short and wrinkling up his brow with a prodigious effort to think. "Well—Maybe peacetime is sad, too. I guess it is I guess. But I still say war is sad. Now, damn it, Dewey, you *know* war is sad. You *know* it. When your buddies get killed and all. Now what kind of crap are you tryin to hand me anyway?"

"I say, I maintain, theyre better off dead," Dewey said thinly, his eyes icy and hard; if there was any sardonic humor in him over all this, it was well hidden. "Theyre better off dead than they would be to come home and live the kind of life youre living. Or I and Hubie are living. Now isnt that right? So I say it isnt sad theyre dead; I say its happy. Just like you would have been better off and happier if you had got killed before the war ended and not come back home and lived the kind of miserable crappy life youre living now."

"Well," Raymond said, "no. I dont live a bad life. Hell, I live a good life. I have lots of fun."

"Fun! You wouldnt know fun if it came up to you and punched you in the mouth, you dumb bastard," Dewey said icily.

"Hey," Hubie said. "Come on. Take it easy, Dewey."

"Ah, the dumb son of a bitch," Dewey said disgustedly.

"All right, maybe Im dumb," Raymond said. "Maybe I aint no smart son of a bitch like you. But, by God, I still say war is sad. I still say it; you hear? In spite of what everything you say."

"Well, *I* say war is happy," Dewey countered.

"I say it aint," Raymond said.

"I say it is," Dewey said; "you miserable ignorant dumb animal son of a bitch."

"Dont call me none of your family names," Raymond said, opening his mouth and laughing loudly and looking around the table for applause at his quip.

"Lay off," 'Bama said from across the table. "Let him alone for Christ's sake."

"Go to hell," Dewey said furiously. "You let *me* alone. —No," he said to Raymond, "I wouldnt call you any of my family names. Because I wouldnt want anybody to know you were my family."

"Now damn you, Dewey!" Raymond said warningly. "You cant talk to me like that, now. Maybe I aint much, I know I aint, but after all I am your brother."

"Youre no brother of mine," Dewey said, "you dumb slobhead, you."

"War is sad," Raymond said stubbornly.

"War is happy," Dewey said, mimicking him.

"All right, damn you!" Raymond bawled. "You son of a bitch! You come outside and Ill show you whether war is sad or not and who's the dumb slobhead!" He jumped up, once more knocking over his chair as usual.

"Fine," Dewey said. "Fine. I wondered how long it was going to take you to get around to it." He got up himself, slim and wiry-muscled beside Raymond who towered thickly at least a head over him. "Come on, lets go." Drunk—as was Raymond; and for that matter, all the rest of them—he stood with his slender chin pulled in bullishly, his blue eyes flashing gravely with a kind of happy excitement.

'Bama and Hubie had jumped up and taken hold of Raymond. "Come on, you guys," 'Bama said. "Lay off. Sit down and drink your drink."

"No," Raymond said, jerking his arms loose. "Leave us alone. We aint mad. We know what we're doin. You ready, Dewey?" he said.

"Sure, you fat bastard," Dewey said. "Lets go."

Around them, all around the walls in the booths, the low din of conversation had ceased now and all the parties of males and females were watching them intently. This was what they all came here for, hopefully; and maybe now they were going to get to see it. It wasnt, Dave thought suddenly, really so very much different from the Roman arena after all; less homicidal, was all. That, and of course, the fact that they did not have to pay their gladiators anything.

They moved in a body to the door up front, 'Bama (who had shrugged and given up) and Hubie leading, then Raymond with Dewey behind him, and Dave bringing up the rear; and behind, the crowd began to form, mostly men with a few tittering girls in it—the whole making Dave think of some kind of strange religious parade in which everybody trooped to the temple to genuflect and do worship before the Great God of American Sportsmanship and His cardinal Commandments: Thou shalt not fight inside the bar: Thou shalt wait until both sides are squared off and ready: Thou shalt not hit the other guy when he is down: Thou shalt not kick: Thou shalt not bite: And above all, Thou shalt not hit below the belt. Well, he thought seriously, there were a lot of worse Gods. But that was not the way it happened after all:

When Dave, who was fifth in line, got to the door he saw that it was snowing again. Oh no, he thought, his stomach sinking. Ever since the war he had hated snow. But he didnt have any more time to think about it then. 'Bama and Hubie, who were first, were already standing down the foot-high step on the sidewalk in the fresh snow; Raymond and Dewey up on the indented little stoop; himself in the doorway. Then Raymond turned to his brother and started to say something, shucking back his old leather jacket down over his arms. That was when Dewey hit him. Unbelievably fast, quick as a streak of greased lightning, Dewey hauled off and swinging around on the ball of his foot, belted Raymond with a tremendous punch, his ice-blue eyes dancing fierily and excitedly. Raymond, heavy as he was, flew off of the step; he lit on his butt on the sidewalk in the snow and skidded across it straight between 'Bama and Hubie like a carom ball that had eyes and came up crashing into the door of a parked car, his arms still in the sleeves of his jacket.

"God damn you, Dewey!" he bellowed, a knot rising swiftly on the side of his jaw. "You foxed me." He struggled back up and shucked his jacket on off and flung it from him. "You cheated!" he bellowed and charged across the sidewalk for Dewey still on the stoop. Hubie picked up Raymond's jacket, and Dewey—grinning strangely and excitedly, obviously no longer angry at all—came to meet him, diving headfirst straight at him off the stoop. They met with a shock in midair and went down in a welter of arms and legs in the snow, square in the middle of the sidewalk, as the crowd behind Dave surged through the door anxiously, moving him out onto the sidewalk with no effort at all on his part.

"Get back! Get back!" 'Bama hollered, trying to widen the circle.

"Get back! Get back! Give 'em room!" Hubie yelled, waving Raymond's jacket at the closing crowd.

"Come on, get up," 'Bama said, trying to grab each of them by the arm. "You want to get jailed? Come on around the side."

Grasping and grabbing and punching, and trying to hook each other's legs with their own, the two brothers rolled around and struggled in the inch-deep snow on the sidewalk, muttering muffled curses. Dave saw Raymond's big right hand, aimed straight down, strike the concrete sidewalk where Dewey's head had been a moment before. A moment later they had rolled and Dewey, grinning happily and making a strange high whining noise in the back of his throat, was on top and trying to bang Raymond's head up and down on the sidewalk.

"Come on, come on, get up," 'Bama said. "Help me, Hubie. Dave?"

Between them they got them separated and led both of them, jerking and pulling to get loose, around the side of the building into the parking lot between the bar and railroad, under the one high single night light. They were like two fighting cocks, struggling frantically to get away from their handlers and at each other in the pit, and when the men released them they both charged at a dead run, met chest on and rebounded, neither getting in a punch that landed or a grip that would hold, and then charged again. But this time there was a change, and Dewey instead of charging on in met Raymond with a very professional left jab that snapped his head back and stopped the charge; and from then on the pattern of the fight was set. Raymond would rush and

Dewey would jab. No longer carried away by the initial strangely joyous excitement that seemed to sunbeam out of him, playing it cool, Dewey did not try to meet Raymond and fight him on the ground where Raymond's strength was such an advantage. He did not back away; he would stand his ground and jab his brother as he rushed, stopping him, then driving him back with more jabs and sometimes a crossing right, and then Raymond would charge again. Raymond really had no choice. He was not awkward, and his punches were straight, not wild flailings, but Dewey was just too fast for him; he could start a jab at the same time Raymond did and beat him to the punch every time. Back and forth across the lot through the snow Raymond charged, Dewey jolting him with the jab and sometimes giving ground when the rush was too powerful for his jab to stop, then coming back in again and driving Raymond back. As the fight progressed, Raymond got madder and madder, while Dewey got happier and happier. It was a strange weird thing to watch his face as, grinning happily, his blue eyes flashing excitedly, he would talk to Raymond affectionately, almost lovingly, telling him to come on, come on Raymond, look out Raymond, watch that one Raymond, you got me a good one then Raymond, all the time in a high-pitched almost wailing musical inflection of intense excitation which sounded almost crooning. And all the time dipping and bobbing and jabbing and crossing with whooshing rocketlike punches that looked as though he actually hoped to tear his brother's head from his body. That was the pattern. Dewey was the rapier, the whiplike darting probing rapier; and Raymond was the sledgehammer, swinging and swinging in its own arc, tireless, its twenty pound head whistling through the air with incredible leverage and power, which if it ever hit the rapier solidly on its hilt would smash blade, handle, hilt and all to shatters, but which never did.

Dewey did not have the fight all his way by any means. More than once when the jab was insufficient to stop Raymond's charge, the bigger man was able to get a bearlike hug on his lighter brother and throw him, himself landing on him thumpingly and heavily, and then would begin punching him sickeningly and resoundingly to the body, and punching his hands down into the cinders that were under the snow while he tried to catch Dewey's darting rolling ever-moving head—and Dewey, laughing happily and ecstatically while his brother beat him in the ribs, would punch viciously back up at Raymond (who merely growled) and bob and duck until, catlike, he was able to roll the heavier man and get back up. At least twice Raymond was able to catch him with a wide right hook to the side of the head that knocked him completely off his feet in what appeared to be a side-somersault, Dewey's feet rotating up out from under him as his head rotated down until he lit heavily on his side, his feet still in the air, and looking like some kind of happy, laughing, professional tumbling clown in a circus. Then Raymond would fall on him. But gradually the snapping, whipping left jab began to tell on Raymond, landing repeatedly on his nose and face until his cheekbones began to swell, squeezing up against his eyes until they made him look like some kind of fat-faced chubby Oriental. Dewey knocked Raymond down more than once, too; and whenever he did he would cheerfully charge in and dive on him lightheartedly, giving away pounds of weight and strength, in an effort to beat his head up and down on the cinders and hard-packed snow, until Raymond like some enraged bear would shuck him off through the air and get back to his feet.

And so that was how they fought, their clothes gradually wettening from contact with the snow, their knuckles beaten raw from punches that went awry into the cinders and dripping thick droplets of blood into the white snow from time to time which made Dave's stomach squeamish with memories of blood on the snow at the Bulge.

In the falling snow which steadily thickened, whitening the tops and hoods of the parked cars in the little lot between the brick building and the threadlike railroad tracks, under the highup gooseneck of the single big bulb of the nightlight beneath its inverted platter of a reflector, through whose light the thick feathery bunches of flakes could be seen in all the snowstorm's real thickness drifting straight down silently, the two brothers fought on, Dewey laughing and crooning crazily, Raymond merely growling stubbornly. Already there was an inch and a half of silent fresh snow compounded on top of the hard compact layer that the car wheels had packed down on the cinders; the brothers slid and rolled and scrambled through it, wet practically to the skin now, and clusters of white flakes lit on their dark heads and clung there, sparkling as the men moved under the light, until they melted. Here and there tiny little droplets of red marked the white field vividly from the barked knuckles, and at other places brown masses of the churned up cinders marked it too. And the cold spectators ringed them, shivering with chill in the iron cold but unwilling to go back inside and leave the show— although several of the women did go back in for their coats, bringing other people, mostly women now, back out with them. That was the way it went, time itself lost in the quiet sinister falling snow, so that no one even was aware of how long it went on. And then finally Raymond broke Dewey's nose.

It was the first totally solid punch that Raymond landed on the bobbing ducking laughing Dewey, and even then it did not knock him down as some other, less solid punches had done. Dewey was just throwing one of his whipping left jabs when Raymond, his eyes more slitted above his swollen cheekbones now and half closed and looking like a Chinese, threw a hard right hand at precisely the same moment. It landed flush on the bobbing Dewey's handsome nose, and you could hear the pop of the busted cartilage. The sledgehammer had finally landed. The blow stunned Dewey completely, although it did not put him down, and he backed off slowly, taking five or six other hard punches to the head in his befuddlement, before he could even think enough to turn away. Blood had begun to flow in a rushing stream from his nose and down his shirt, and he stood for a moment half-blinded by the stunning and then turned and walked woozily over to the brick wall of the building and leaned his hands against it above his head and leaned over and let the blood run on the ground.

That was when Dave got sick, and that was what it was that made him sick. Not brutality, or mental nausea, or anything else, except the simple factual physical sight of the widening spot of red blood—such a redness—on the white snow. Like at the Bulge. He had not thought it would stay with him so long, in fact he was as surprised as anybody. With the gorge rising, and the snowflakes silently tickling his nose and face with such a long-ago but powerful memory, he quietly and with dignity walked over to the wall himself further down and off by himself, and vomited in a running choking stream everything he had drunk that night and just about practically everything he had eaten that day. He had thought he was over all that; but it was like a signal key re-action, triggering an automatic counterreaction. He looked down the wall at Dewey and the widening red stain between his feet—oh, so very red—on the white snow and turned back to the wall and retched again.

"What is it?" 'Bama said, coming over and putting his hand on Dave's shoulder. "What the hells the matter with you?"

"Nothing," Dave said chokingly. "Im all right. Be all right in a minute. Its just the blood on the snow, thats all."

"Oh," 'Bama said gruffly. "Yeah. Sure." He continued to keep his hand there, on the shoulder, firmly, steadyingly.

Hubie had gone over to Dewey and given him a handkerchief, which he pressed up against his nose; and Raymond had walked over up behind him.

"Well, you give up?" he said growlingly.

"Hell no, you big ox," Dewey said muffledly from behind his hand-kerchief. It was already soaked and dripping. Hubie handed him another. In all he used up four of them, before he was done. "That was a beauty of a punch," he said; "but you was just lucky. You couldnt do it again in a hundred years."

"Well, I guess I showed you war *is* sad," Raymond said triumphantly. "I guess I proved it to you."

"Go screw," Dewey said muffledly. Then he laughed to himself under his handkerchief. "War is *happy*."

"Well, are you gonna fight some more or aint you?" Raymond growled.

"Sure," Dewey said. "In a minute. Wait a minute or two. Are you in a big hurry?" He dropped the second soaked handkerchief down with the first, and took a fresh one from Hubie who had collected some from the spectators.

"Well, I aint got all night," Raymond said. "I got things to do."

"Horse shit," Dewey said muffledly. "You aint had nothing to do since you got out of the damned Army. Thats whats the matter with you."

"Dont worry about whats the matter with me," Raymond growled. "Worry about yourself. Worry about your damned nose."

Dewey did not answer and accepted the fourth handkerchief from Hubie and pressed it against the base of his nose.

"Christ!" Hubie said. "I didnt know you had that damned much blood in you even, Dewey."

"Go screw yourself," Dewey said muffledly. By the time the fourth handkerchief was just about soaked up, the bleeding had subsided to a thin but persistent trickle. "Well, I guess it aint going to quit entirely," Dewey said, standing up and leaning his head back. He dropped the fourth handkerchief down with the others. "Well, come on, Raymond. Are you ready, you big oaf?" he said, moving out into the area.

"You damned right," Raymond said, and charged. "Ill hit you on your damned nose again, damn you."

"How much you want to bet?" Dewey laughed. He met the charge with a stinging left jab to Raymond's right cheekbone and followed it up with a right to Raymond's left cheekbone. "I bet you dont hit me on the nose before I shut up both your eyes," he said, and that was what he proceeded to do. Jabbing and crossing, he battered Raymond's face in an almost infinite series of identical combinations: left jab and right cross; and Raymond's puffing cheekbones continued to swell up tightly against his eyes while the lumps on his forehead swelled down. The persistent trickle continued to run slowly down over Dewey's lip onto his chin and he would blow it out with his mouth so it wouldnt get in his throat, spattering Raymond with red droplets, until Raymond finally complained about it.

"What the hell're you tryin to do?" he growled. "Blind me with blood so you can whip me?"

Dewey did not fight as ecstatically and jauntily now as he had before, but more seriously and earnestly. But if he did not laugh and croon to Raymond as much as he had done, he was nevertheless grinning happily. Methodically, he worked on Raymond's eyes to close them, while Raymond—bull-like, angry, getting desperate now—rushed and rerushed him trying to land another hard punch on the swollen throbbing pulsating lump of macerated flesh that was Dewey's nose.

"My God," Dave said to Hubie; "do they always fight like this?" He had come back to the intently interested ring of spectators, carefully keeping his back to the big stain of blood and handkerchiefs against the wall that the fresh falling snow was speckling with white. He was beginning to get his old Walpurgis Night feeling again, although this time he was sober.

"Hell!" Hubie said. "You ought to seen some of the fights they had when they was both younger. Sure they always fight like this. Thats why they only do it two or three times a year. They couldnt stand it any oftener."

Dewey was steadily closing Raymond's eyes now, and could hit him anytime he wanted now, almost at will. He would dart in and punch his brother heavily, while Raymond whose eyes were no more than mere slits of gummed lashes now, would strike out wildly trying to hit where he thought Dewey was.

"I could whip you, goddam you," he growled, "if I could only see where you was."

"Pretty soon you wont be able to see at all," Dewey laughed merrily. "You better give up."

"No, by God. I wont. Just dont let me get hold of you," Raymond said. "War *is* sad," he added thickly, as if this were the only thought left in his mind now, a sort of catechism he was clinging to in some vague dim belief that right must always triumph.

"You better give up," Dewey said again, and skipped in and threw a whooshing right hook which landed wallopingly on the side of Raymond's head and staggered him.

"You cant knock me out," Raymond said through his thick lips. "You never could knock me out. Not with just your fists."

"You better give up?" Dewey laughed, and staggered him again and skipped back away. They went through several more sequences like this, Dewey slipping in and rocking him, only one of them actually strong enough to knock him down. It was apparent that Raymond was right when he said Dewey couldnt knock him out; and yet nobody, neither 'Bama nor Hubie, nor any of the spectators seemed to have any thought of stopping it—as if everybody knew beforehand that neither Raymond nor Dewey, any more than Dewey would have if he had been losing, would want or allow them to. Finally, after his younger brother staggered him again, Raymond came to a stop in the center of the area, glaring around wildly through what to him must have appeared as a wet rainforest of eyelashes—if it appeared as anything at all.

"All right, I give up," he said heavily, and with a great reluctance. "There aint no point in tryin to go on fightin you when I cant see you, damn you. So I give up. You son of a bitch."

"Fair enough," Dewey said, "fair enough;" and went over to him, not angry, not triumphant, not anything. He slapped his brother on the back and put his arm around him. Raymond put his own arm around Dewey, in his big bearlike hug—and then suddenly, measuring him by the arm he had around him, raised his right arm, its barked fist clamped tight shut into a hammerhead, to smash him again on the broken nose. But 'Bama, who knew the ways of Raymond well, was already there and grabbed his arm from behind.

"Come on now, Raymond," he said soothingly. "The fight's over."

"Okay," Raymond said, and laughed a loud laugh out of his battered up face. "Just a joke." He put his other arm around his brother. "No hard feelins, hunh, Dewey?"

"Hell no, Raymond," Dewey said. "Hell no. No hard feelings. You know that."

And suddenly everything seemed to have stopped. The snow (which actually did not stop), and the single big light over the parking lot (which did not stop either), and the blood which still trickled down from Dewey's nose, and the two brothers stood in the center of the churned-up snowfield, crystals of it gleaming from their hair, each with an arm around the other and grinning, like two professional prizefighters posing for some phantom photographer an after-the-fight picture, which —or so Dave thought—might someday be bought by some new symbolic photo magazine and used as a symbol of the history of the whole human race. The ring of spectators began to break up and go back inside, looking sheepish and ashamed for having watched and enjoyed the mayhem.

"We're both of us a mess," Dewey said cheerfully. "Lets go down to Dave's and 'Bama's and get ourselves cleaned up."

"Okay; fine," Raymond said heavily. "Hubie, wheres my jacket? You show me the way to the car," he said to Dewey.

But before they could even get started, the single Parkman City-Police Car rolled up slowly to a stop before the driveway into the parking lot alongside the railroad.

"Oh-oh," 'Bama said.

The door with the big gold and black star painted on it, opened up and out of it climbed a slow methodical chunky man in a uniform. And such a uniform. On his head the slow methodical chunky man wore a dark blue Russian-winter-type cap with a light blue fur earpiece and bill turned up all around. His dark blue mackinaw, which he wore with its collar turned down very properly although it was cold, had light blue lapels and collar and light blue bone buttons. His leather gloves were black. And below the mackinaw, beautiful light blue breeches with a dark blue stripe down their sides flared out widely as he walked and tapered into black leather puttees and black para-trooper boots, laced in the same intricate chainlike lacing paratroopers affected. A wide black leather Sam Browne belt went around the slow methodical chunky man's waist over the mackinaw, and on it, running from his right to his left around him were: a gleaming black holster containing a big Smith & Wesson .357 Magnum; a gleaming black cartridge holder; a gleaming black handcuff holster; another gleaming black handcuff holster; and a gleaming black holster for a sap. On the mackinaw's breast, of course, was the bright gold star of the Chief of Parkman Police. He walked over to them slowly and methodically.

That Smitty would have called him out was unthinkable. Smitty never called the police unless he absolutely had to, even if the fights took place inside his bar. And none of the spectators would have gone and called him, certainly not from inside Smitty's bar. There were no houses nearby, so the fight could not have waked anybody. All the other businesses in the little business section had long been closed; and across the railroad the lumber yards were dark. The only answer was obviously that he had been out cruising. There was nobody else with him in the car. The five men stood and waited for him.

"Hello, Sherm," 'Bama said.

"Hello, 'Bama," Sherm Ruedy said slowly and methodically and levelly, but it was obvious he did not relish being called by his first name. "Looks like you boys might have been having a fight," he said, looking slowly and methodically around at the evidence. That it might, under the circumstances, have been a funny remark apparently did not occur to him.

"Just a friendly little altercation," 'Bama said pleasantly.

"What about?"

"As a matter of fact, it was an argument about whether war is sad or happy, Sherm," 'Bama said.

Slowly and methodically and levelly the Police Chief turned his head slightly to look at 'Bama as though he might be being made fun of. "Sounds like an awful little argument for such a lot of fight," he said looking over at the handkerchiefs and blood stain against the wall. He was only about a year or two older than 'Bama or Dave.

"As a matter of fact, everything's all over," 'Bama said. "We were just going home when you drove up." Instinctively, the others had all looked to him as the spokesman from the first.

"Afraid thats impossible," Sherm Ruedy said, looking at the battered brothers. He took a few steps out into the center of the arena, then over to the blood stain by the wall, then came back. He also did not miss Dave's vomit stain.

All of them had watched him make his tour, and when Dave's gaze hit the blood stain on the snow, turning black now,—oh, so black— he retched, automatically, instinctively, and turned away.

"Whats the matter with you, Dave?" Sherm said slowly and levelly. "Drunk?"

"No," Dave said. "Just an upset stomach, Sherm."

"Are you sure?"

"Blood on snow makes him sick," 'Bama said pleasantly. "The war, you know. He was in the Battle of the Bulge."

Once again, slowly, methodically, levelly, the Police Chief turned his head slightly to look at 'Bama as though he might be being made fun of. He had not been in the war; and in fact, had become Police Chief only just about then. "You were in the Battle of the Bulge, too, werent you, 'Bama?" he said.

"Yes," 'Bama said. "But I was in a tank. He wasnt."

Sherm turned his head back to look at the others. "You two boys better get your coats," he said slowly and methodically. "Afraid Ill have to take you down."

"Has there been a complaint made, Sherm?" 'Bama said pleasantly.

"Theres been a law broken," Sherm countered slowly and methodically, turning his head to look at 'Bama. "Theres a law against fist fighting. Disorderly conduct. Theres a law against drunkenness, too, 'Bama."

"Thats true," 'Bama said. "But we're not any of us drunk. And the fight's all over. Like I said, we were just goin home. You dont suppose you might give us a break, Sherm?"

"Afraid not," Sherm said, and then slowly nodded his head. "But I tell you what Ill do. Ill give you other three boys a break. I wont ask you to go down to the doctor's and take a blood test. But Im afraid Dewey and Raymond will have to come down with me. Ill have to take them to the doctor and get them patched up anyway."

"Okay," 'Bama smiled; "Yore the boss, Sherm. We could fix them up just as easy at home though."

"Afraid not," Sherm said slowly and methodically.

'Bama shrugged. "Okay. Like I said, Sherm, yore the boss. Raymond cant see very good, and his jacket's here. Is it all right if Hubie goes in and gets Dewey's coat for him?"

"I guess so," the Police Chief said.

"Go get his coat," 'Bama said to Hubie, who turned and took off without a word. "Havent seen you around lately, Sherm," he said conversationally while they waited. "I understand you just got back from that new FBI school for police, in Washington?"

"Thats right," Sherm said slowly, methodically, levelly.

"Pretty good school?" 'Bama said pleasantly. "Teach you quite a bit?"

"A good bit," Sherm said.

"Any judo?"

"Some."

"Must be a pretty good school," 'Bama said pleasantly. "Criminals aint got much of a chance anymore, in this day and age, to get away with anything, have they?"

"Not much," Sherm said slowly, levelly.

"And a good thing too," 'Bama said. "Us respectable citizens need all the protection we can get from law inforcement officers. They *should* be trained."

Behind him Hubie came up quietly with Dewey's old Army mackinaw. "Heres your coat, Dewey," he said. He helped him put it on.

"You boys both ready?" Sherm said.

"I guess so," Dewey said with a happy laugh, now that there was no chance left. "I guess we are, Sherm. Raymond, it looks like we're goin back to jail for another good night's sleep again." He flung his arm around his brother.

"I just hope they give me my same old cell back," Raymond said with his loud guffaw.

They went ahead of Sherm to the car, the officer following them slowly and methodically, and climbed in the back seat.

"Im taking you up to the doctor's first," Sherm said in through the window. "Though I hate to wake him up for the likes of you." They all knew who he meant. The doctor was a new man, young—under forty, with strange, sadistic eyes, who had come to town from the East with a lot of money and bought out one of the five local 'sanitariums'— privately owned hospitals—and was now making a lot more off the better class of people with his really exquisite bedside manner. A thin, tiny little man, unmarried, who played no sports or did much of anything else, except make money; and be very social. Sherm Ruedy took all his own and his family's, as well as all his City Police business, there.

" 'Bama," he said, turning back after he had closed the door on them, "how are you boys making out with that house of yours down there?" Slowly, methodically he leaned his gloved hand against the top of the car a moment.

"Just fine, Sherm," 'Bama said pleasantly. "Just fine. Why?"

"I just wanted to tell you," Sherm said slowly "that you better be careful about what goes on down there. Ive got my eye out on it."

"Has somebody made a complaint?" 'Bama said pleasantly.

"No. If anybody had, Id have been down there."

"Well, you come down when you get a complaint, will you, Sherm?" 'Bama said pleasantly.

"You bet I will," the Police Chief said. Slowly, methodically, levelly, he stared across the intervening space at the tall Southerner for a moment, as if deliberately waiting for it—for his warning—to sink in, then slowly and methodically he took his gloved hand down off the car and went around to the other side and got in.

"See you guys tomorrow after court," Dewey called.

After they had gone—the black Police car with its big gold star moving off with the same slow, quiet, methodical, consciously dangerous way that Sherm Ruedy himself moved—'Bama began to curse, quietly, potently, savagely. "Well, we better get on home, I guess," he said after a minute. "You want to come on down to the house with us, Hubie?"

"I might as well," Hubie drawled in his deliberately comic way. "I aint very sleepy now anyway."

They all got in 'Bama's Packard and started home. Dave, who had deliberately and carefully kept himself inconspicuous and back out of all of it, found he had in him somewhat the same feeling Hubie must have been referring to. There had been—all during the time that Sherm Ruedy had been present—an uncomfortable, deadly, almost devastating, tension—in the air, on the ground, in each of them, everywhere. As soon as he was gone, so was that tension; but its flavor and the overtones of it lingered on. You couldnt get completely rid of it—not until later, when you forgot Sherm Ruedy. It was the same thing with Dave whenever he met Sherm uptown, on the street, as he frequently did. He would be walking one way and Sherm with his slow methodical chunky walk the other, and they would look at each other across the width of the sidewalk and that tension would be there, pass between them. Sherm would nod at him, gravely, slowly and methodically and levelly, and say "Hello, Dave"; and he would nod at Sherm, tensely and gravely and reservedly himself, and say "Hello, Sherm"; and that would be all there was to it. How could you say it? there wasnt anything you could point to; or put your finger on. He could understand why poor old Ginnie so hated and feared him. He hated and feared him himself. And the stark raw hatred that had passed between Sherm and 'Bama so pleasantly on the one side, and so gravely and slowly and methodically on the other, was actually a livid living flame of a thing. Once again Dave thought that he would not ever want to have 'Bama mad at him.

"You know, he doesnt do anything," he said out loud in the car; "he doesnt do anything wrong, I mean. You know?"

"He never does," 'Bama said. "He never crosses the line; and he makes it his code, as rigid as a brick wall."

"I mean, he could have took them down and thrown them in without actually *having* to take them to the doctor," Dave said. "They didnt either one really need to go to the doctor anyway."

"Oh, he would never do that," 'Bama said. "Hes always fair. Always scrupulously fair. He leans over backwards to be scrupulously fair. Always."

"We use to have a good Police Chief in this town," Hubie said. "Old Max Thompson. Remember him, 'Bama? He kept me from gettin' sent to reform school once for stealing cartons of cigarettes and sellin' them. Got the guy to drop the complaint, if Id promise to pay it all back out of my paper route." He laughed. "Took me a year." He sighed sadly: "But old Max—he wasnt really old; about Sherm's age—got a better job as a trouble shooter with some big company in Chicago. And then we got Sherm."

"I dont know what it is," Dave said. "Or rather, I know what it is; only I cant say it. You get the feeling that hes set himself up as a sort of overseer of everybody's *morals*—personal and private, as well as public. Not just their *acts*, you see; but their *thoughts*. Their *morals*."

'Bama turned to look at him momentarily with a sort of wondering thoughtfulness. "By God, I think youve hit it. Thats right. Hes not only gonna make them *do* good; hes gonna make them *be* good. Make them *think* good. I never been able to quite say it before. But thats it."

He did not say anything for a moment. "I never been quite able to say it before," he said half to himself.

Again he did not say anything for a little while. And then he suddenly broke out into savage, furious tirade. "—And all the time drivin that fat funny little oddball daughter of his to school. He drives her out to the highschool every morning in the Police Car; and every afternoon drives back out and picks her up again. That funny ugly fat daughter of his."

"Its her glands," Hubie said. "I heard somebody say it was her glands, made her like that."

'Bama raged on, as if he had not even heard. "Him and that new doctor are always gettin together. And hes got this old buddy of his from the Dark Bend, that hes always goin fishin and huntin and everywhere with. Always together, when hes off duty. Guy never does anything; doesnt work; never earns any money; just lives with his mom and dad down there on their farm; doesnt even work on the farm; just drives around town here in his beatup old coupe; and runs around with Sherm. Who supports him? His folks?"

"Maybe Sherm supports him," Hubie grinned.

"Maybe he does," 'Bama said savagely. "Or maybe hes got a still down there somewhere." He was raging. "And that washed-out oddball of a wife of Sherm's, and that oddball fat daughter. And that odd duck of a mother of his who goes around preachin at meetings down in the Dark Bend."

"Look, what the hell's eatin' you all of a sudden?" Hubie said.

"Nothing!" 'Bama said savagely. "Not a damn thing. Heres this whole bunch of crazy people from down there in the Bend. Heres this guy who is going to stick up for law and order to the point of insanity, just so he can make himself like himself a little better (and at the same time fool everybody else) about him being smart.

"Why should anything be eatin me? You slob! Sure, Sherm believes in 'Law and Order'; hes got to. Hes afraid *not* to. Because that way he can keep one half of his mind totally divorced from the other half, and not think about it. You think Sherm would have kept you out

of reform school when you were a kid like Max Thompson did? Hah!
Hed have made damn sure you *went*; hed have *recommended* it; and
then hed have made damned sure you *got* there safe and sound.
And you would probably be some petty safe artist and second storey
man somewheres in Chicago or Hammond, today, from what you
learned there. People talk about juvenile delinquents—is it any wonder
we got juvenile delinquents? Sure we got 'em; and we'll probably have
a lot more of them. Theyre not fools enough to believe the mishmash
of crap we try to feed them about justice and 'Law and Order'." He
raged on.

"But you dont know Sherm's that bad," Dave said.

"I dont, hunh?" 'Bama said furiously. "And let me tell you something. Yore an ass. Yore a sentimental slob. You like to believe the
best in people. You got a streak of sentimentality a yard wide in you,
Dave, and someday its goin to get you into a situation you wont be
able to bull yore way out of, and yore liable to get yore head tore clean
off of you, because of yore sentimentality. You remember what I said."

Dave, feeling both flustered and embarrassed, and a cold little chill
of the possibility of truth in it, in this sudden attack, said nothing.

"Oh, lots of people know about Sherm, Dave," Hubie said easily, not
upset at all as 'Bama was. "What the hell you gettin' so worked up
for?" he said to the tall man.

'Bama took a deep breath and snorted it out explosively, as if to relax
himself. "Ill tell you why," he said more calmly. "Because its all a lie,
thats why. Here, we got a guy who (like Dave said) is attempting to
set himself up as a policeman of everybody's morals; their *thoughts*
yet, even; and who for some reason is allowed to more or less get away
with it. And yet this guy himself is a sadist—and yet nobody says or
does a damn thing about it. Now, I say thats a damning comment on
our whole American civilization. Dave here's always talkin and talkin
about Rome, and the decadence of Rome. Well, how much more decadent can you get than this? That we set up this character to administer
our laws to us and keep us in line, and all the time the guy himself is
a real sadist, and gets his kicks that way.

"And you think the people in this town dont know about that? Hell,
you talk about the decadence of Rome! Anytime you got laws—a moral
code—that people give lip service to in public and dont believe in
and ignore and break in private, you got decadence. Rome!"

"Hell, I agree with you," Dave said.

"Rome, Schmome!" Hubie said. "The whole world's like that. And
always has been. And probably always will be."

"Well, if you want to know one reason why Im a gambler and wont
'work' and why I sneer at our so-called 'American society' and thumb
my nose at it and aint got any use for it," 'Bama said caustically, "right

theres a good one for you to remember: Sherm Ruedy. One, I may add, of many," he said sarcastically.

"—And Ill tell you something else," he said. "While we're on the subject. You want to know why theres so many neurotics and 'juvenile delinquents' and sadists in this country today? I can tell you. Ive done a lot of thinkin and watchin about it. Its the simple fact we dont give our children *physical* affection like we use to. *Physical* affection: Holdin them, and pattin them, and rubbin them; and lettin them pat and rub against us. And do you know *why* we dont? Its because in the kind of society we live in where sex is the most important thing in the back of everybody's mind we're *ashamed* to, *thats* why. Theres a certain sexual pleasure in it, for both parties, and we're embarrassed and afraid of that. Afraid of what the neighbors might think. Afraid maybe our kids will turn into some kind of sexual oddball, or that people might think us ourselves are peculiar. —Well, by God, none of my kids will ever turn into neurotics! If they want to come up and put their arms around my legs and push their face against me, I let them; and if they want to sit on my lap and rub their bare back against me and run their hands up and down my chest, I let them! and I run my hands up and down their chest too. Just like my daddy done to me; and my Grandaddy done to him. They wasnt neither one of them afraid their neighbors might think they was neurotics because they done it, either. Ruth carts them kids around on her hip all the time till theyre old enough to walk; and if after that they come and rub against her she dont push them off and look embarrassed or ashamed. —Of course, she dont know what shes doin consciously, she just does it by instinct; but by God I know; and I know its right. When kids are little they need that kind of touch. They get something out of it. A confidence. They get a certain *physical* reassurance. And they *dont* turn into Sherm Ruedys.

"You can give a kid all the damned "love" and "mental affection" you want to; but unless you give them that feel of touch and that *physical* affection, it dont mean a damn thing to them when theyre little, because they cant understand anything but physical affection; and it dont do them a damn bit of good. You can baby them, and spoil them, and let them have their damned way all the time, and never make them mind or do anything they dont want to, and all the rest of that crap; and it wont do them a damned bit of good if you dont give them *physical* affection. In fact, itll do more harm. I make them mind me, but I give them physical affection. If more people would forget their own goddam sexual fears and worries and horrors about somebody thinkin they might be strange, wed have a whole lot less trouble with the kids. I hold that Sherm Ruedy's crazy preachin mother is responsible for Sherm.

"Hell," he said seriously, "the guy's actually crazy. That Sherm Ruedy. Look at what he does with all the parkin meters. Hell, last fall when Clark Hibbard was campaigning here—(and he had one of the State Highways men drivin him; a guy I know; thats how I come to hear about it)—Clark and this State man were parked uptown on the street, both of them sittin in their car, waitin for Clark to get ready to make a speech; and Sherm comes over to them and gives them a parking ticket; right there, by God! Their meter had run out. And they were both in the car with the motor runnin. So the Highways man, who told me about it, takes the ticket down to the City Hall and he says to the clerk: 'Look, do I really have to pay this ticket Sherm Ruedy gave me?' and the clerk says to him: 'Well sir, Ill tell you. The other day I just happened to be lookin out the window, and I saw Sherm come down the street and go right up to his own car, the Police Car, and give himself a ticket; the meter had run out, and he wrote himself out a ticket, and he came in here to me and he turned it in and he paid me the fifty cents.' So the State man said: 'Well, I guess I better pay it then, hadnt I?'

—"Talk about *immoral*," 'Bama said savagely; "thats the most completely *immoral* thing I ever heard of. Give me an honest thief anytime; because whenever you got a guy who is so scrupulously honest and virtuous he'll do a thing like that—then hes either acting, or else hes crazy. You can be pretty damned sure hes *really* cheating some other way, and only tryin to cover it up—either to the world or to himself."

"Thats a pretty shrewd remark," Dave said.

"Well, Im a shrewd guy," 'Bama said savagely. "Too shrewd for the likes of that oaf, anyway. Unless he should happen to kick over the traces someday and go berserk and break his own code and just shoot me down in cold blood like hed like to do. But I think Id even be prepared for that eventuality," he grinned coldly. "Cant you imagine how horrible it makes him feel to imagine us livin down here and gettin by with something? Hed love to stick us. Only," 'Bama grinned coldly, "he never will."

As he climbed out of the Packard, he slammed the cardoor savagely, loudly, behind him, swinging it with his whole leverage, something Dave had never seen him do to the Packard since he had known 'Bama.

He turned toward the house, breathing the cold air deeply as the others climbed out. "You watch," he grinned; "in another three quarters of an hour or so, he'll be cruisin down by here."

They did watch, through the venetian blinds carefully after they had turned off all the lights and after they had all got themselves another drink, and sure enough in less than an hour, the black gold-starred City Police car came creeping down Lincoln Street—slowly and methodically and quietly, as it only could look when Sherm was driving it—and passed by the house; and then went on around several blocks and came back and passed by again, patient, waiting, self-contained, unflagging, never-tiring, before it went away.

"What did I tell you!" 'Bama hooted raucously. "The bastard."

CHAPTER 54

THE next morning Raymond and Dewey were hauled into court and tried and each fined $50 and costs. 'Bama was there with the cash to make up any deficits, and between them he and Dewey paid both his fine and Raymond's; and shortly thereafter Dewey appeared down at the house, grinning from behind his grotesquely bruised and swollen broken nose which from time to time he fingered very gingerly, his blue eyes looking very peaceful now and relieved of some obscure tension. Both he and Raymond had submitted voluntarily to blood tests by the doctor and had been judged drunk. The charges against them were drunkenness and disorderly conduct; and except for an affidavit from the doctor about their drunkenness, the only witness to appear against them was Sherm Ruedy. That night the *Parkman Oregonian & Evening News* carried mention of the event, in amongst other news of the day in court, much in the same style in which it had mentioned Mildred Pierce's marriage. As for the nose, the thin little doctor had said there was nothing much to do about it, just keep it packed with cotton until it mended and the swelling went down. When it did go down two weeks later, what had been a clean straight boyishly handsome nose had changed into a grotesque, hooked, off-center monstrosity of a nose with a big knot on it and pushed over to one side of Dewey's face. It changed the whole look of his face and gave him a curiously mean, Satanic, Mephistophelian look, which he grinned out from behind sourly. He wasnt handsome any more.

Raymond did not come down to the house with him after the fines were paid but, able to at least see somewhat out of his swollen eyes now, picked up his old battered Dodge at Smitty's and chugged wheezingly off out of town somewhere, alone,—after first promising in his loud too-hearty way to repay 'Bama soon for the fine. He never did repay it, of course, but then nobody had ever expected that he would. And of course, less than a month after that he was dead.

But the thing that struck—or impressed itself upon—Dave so much about the whole affair was the reaction that Doris Fredric had to the whole story. She was at the house later that same afternoon when Dewey came back from the court with his hugely swollen nose; and she flew into a veritable fit of fury and outrage. Dave had never seen her—not once; not even the night she tried to seduce him himself—when she was not under that icily sweet, virginal control of hers. Nothing, as far as he knew, could ever upset it. But this time, when her distant cousin Chief of Police Sherm Ruedy was mentioned, she threw caution and propriety both to the winds. The things she said were not so very different from what 'Bama had said, but the tone and implication were entirely different; and it was obvious this was not something she had heard from him. It was clearly something she had thought quite a bit about before.

"Hes nothing but a dirty little sadist," she said with icy fury of her distant relative. "A useless, worthless, dirty, nasty little sadist. Ugh! Ive never seen a human being who was so completely and totally despicable. Chief of Police! That son of a bitch! That the likes of that filth should ever be allowed on the police force at all!"

"Well, it was you Wernzes who put him in there," 'Bama drawled amusedly, no longer upset at all now, himself.

"The Wernzes dont act as a body," Doris said furiously. "And what Tony—or my mother or father or any of the rest of them do doesnt mean that I agree with them. Is it any wonder every kid in town breaks his neck to leave this dump as soon as he can? Who wants to live in their crappy little filthy town? I certainly dont. Nobody does."

"Then why dont you just up and move out of it?" 'Bama grinned.

"I may just do that," Doris said fierily, her blue eyes flashing. "I may just do exactly that someday!" She was sitting at the kitchen table with them, holding her drink: a big glass of Jack Daniels Black Label and Seven-Up. Her chair was back from the table a little, and so she was holding her drink in front of her in both hands, as she spoke she threw it—not across the room, or at anyone or anything, but straight down, between her feet, suddenly and convulsively, the crash of the broken glass punctuating what she had just said, the liquid wetting her expensive shoes.

They did not any of them see Raymond again very much after that. Only once did he come back into Smitty's when they were there. It was shortly before Christmas, and he was alone; and on that one time he did not stay, or try to barge into the party and sit with them. He was drunk, of course—but he did not have a drink while he was there, though Dewey and all of them offered to buy him one. He came in, walked around, grinned and waved a hello at them with his too-loud, too-hearty voice out of his big face from which almost all the swelling had disappeared now, refused the drink they offered to buy him, and left. That was the last time any of them saw him until his funeral. Two weeks later he was found dead in his old Dodge in an out-of-the-way backwoods cornfield down in the Riverbottoms not far from the old Rivertown ferry landing, frozen to death.

Apparently, he had got down in there, drunk, down in those almost perpetually deserted bottoms, and had got lost and gone to sleep. The decrepit old Dodge, which did not have a very good heater anyway, was out of gas when they found him and in neutral gear and with the hand brake set, as if he had left the motor running when he went to sleep. What he had been doing down in that God- and man-forsaken place where there were almost no roads and which consisted only of strings of cornfields with little openings through from one field to the next, nobody could figure out. The Rivertown ferry had been inoperative for years, and Rivertown itself across the River on the Indiana side had ceased to be anything but a name long before that. Almost nobody ever went down in there except the farmers who worked the fields on their tractors, and they went as seldom as possible, and what Raymond could have been doing or looking for down in there, especially in the dead of winter, nobody had the vaguest idea.

All of them there at the house felt a sort of shocked dismay when they heard the news, a sort of unalleviable sorrow that they could not do anything about, potent, stomach-wrenching, but unassuageable, mingled with a kind of shocked horror that anything like that should happen to Raymond, and a curious guilty feeling too, which all of them seemed to feel. Raymond had never actually spent much time at the house; he had never really run around with their little clique; but after the fight, there had seemed to be a deeper closeness to him than before, even though—for Dave, at least—they only saw him that one other time. But if all of these feelings were strong in them when they heard the news, and afterwards at his funeral,—it would have been a great deal stronger, and a great deal more perplexing, and puzzling, and disquietingly unintelligible, if any of them had been able to be with him in some occult way, right there inside of his own head, that night when he—all unknowingly—took his last ride.

——————He left the American Legion early with two fifths of Imperial, Raymond did, and roared his Dodge out of town north on Route 1, heading for the West Lancaster road. But as soon as he was outside the city limits and across the new bypass grade they were building but had had to stop on because of the weather, he stopped long enough to open one of the bottles and had himself a good stiff bellyburning drink and then put the open bottle between his knees. He could do that out here, where Sherm Ruedy had no jurisdiction. The two fifths had been a lucky windfall from running into the Old Man at the Legion and making a loan of a few bucks. The Old Man was all right; he was a good guy, even if he was a town bum. If he had ten, he would always give his boys five of it. But Raymond hadnt expected to see him. Raymond had been hanging out at the Legion more, lately, since he had had the fight with Dewey, and had not been going to Smitty's where they hung out. He knew he upset them when he came around, especially Dewey, and he didnt want to do that to them. And Christ it would be six months before he was ready for a fight like that again. He still had sore spots all over him. But boy that was sure some fight. It was the best fight they would see around Smitty's for some time, by God. In the car, heading for the West Lancaster road, Raymond chuckled to himself happily and took another drink. When they wanted better fights by God, Possum Cole's boys Raymond and Dewey would give them to them. But there wasnt any use going back around to Smitty's this soon, when he only bothered them. Raymond knew he bothered them. It was because he was so dumb. He didnt mean to do it, but he couldnt help it. He couldnt help it if he was just born dumb and everything he said rubbed Dewey the wrong way. Dewey always was the smart one, and he could have made good grades in school if he had only worked at it a little. He took after the Old Man; Raymond, he took after the Old Lady. She always had been dumb. So the best thing was just to stay away from them until they were both healed up and ready for another fight. And that was why he had taken to hanging out at the Legion more, when he was in town. Raymond liked the Legion. He liked the old guys from the first war, like the Old Man. Raymond liked to sit around with them and get them to talking, and then listen to them, about their war and not say anything about his war. They had had a good war, the old guys, just as good as ours. It just didnt last as long. But it was a good one. And they never got to talk about it much any more. They liked to talk about it, but they were shy. So he liked to sit around the outside of the poker game with his drink and get them started and then just let them talk and listen to them. The old guys enjoyed it, and it gave them pleasure, and they knew he could appreciate the combat stories because he had seen a lot of combat himself. Hell, yes! Guadalcanal, New Georgia, Bougainville, the Bismarcks. They knew he could appreciate it. But then some of the new guys had come in and spoiled it. They just wouldnt talk around any of the new guys but him. So he had just got his two fifths and left quietly. The high-powered new guys didnt like him, Raymond, any better than they liked the old guys, and he knew it. It always made him uncomfortable and he didnt like to be around them.

Raymond drove on up Route 1, drinking and singing some of the old Army songs to himself as he went, and turned off toward the river at the West Lancaster road. But he did not go on into West Lancaster to any of the neon-lighted joints. He could see their lights, all colors and happy looking, but just before you got to the buildings was a road right, back south, and Raymond turned off on it. This road led to the River-bottoms, and this was Raymond's secret. He laughed as he slowed down on the gravel and took another drink.

They always wondered where he went when he went roaring out of town in his hot old Dodge. They thought he was going to Terre Haute to the whorehouses. So he just let them think it. They really thought he was the gash-hound all right. So he just let them. But he didnt go to the whorehouses; he went to the Riverbottoms. And not a soul knew it. Hell, yes! Raymond laughed to himself and had another drink.

So he just fooled them all. He came over to the Riverbottoms. It was his secret. Every man ought to have one secret. And the Riverbottoms and the River, they did something to a man. They opened you all up. Maybe a smart man couldnt do it; hed get to thinking too much. But a dumb man like him could. He could sit and look at that River by the hour. Hours and hours. It was never the same two minutes in a row. It just flowed on and on, so smooth. Treetrunks and old branches and cans and bottles sometimes and once in a while a piece of an old boat. They just came floating along into sight, and then they went floating along out of sight. You could almost think there was something down underneath swimming along pulling them along so fast. And you just sat and watched and watched them. Until you couldnt see them any more. Knowing that down below Evansville they would hit the Ohio and turn west and float on down until they hit the old Mississippi at Cairo and then they would float south. Finally they would hit old New Orleans. Then they would float right on out into the old Gulf of Mexico, these same chunks and bottles you saw right here at Cray County. Maybe they would even float from there on out into the whole Atlantic Ocean. It was wonderful.

Raymond laughed out loud happily and looked out at the white snow-covered fields. He decided he would go down to the old Rivertown ferry tonight; he hadnt been there for a long time. Shed be iced up tonight. Maybe shed even be frozen clean over. Ahead of him the road from West Lancaster deadended into another gravel road east and west and he turned back east again toward the River. These roads over in here were the roads old Abe Lincoln and them old pioneers traveled, not Route 1. But then, they called just about every damned road in Southern Illinois "The Lincoln Memorial Highway", anyway.

Hell, he knew this country like the back of his hand, Raymond thought. He had been coming over here in the Bottoms ever since he was a kid and learned to drive and to sneak the Old Man's car out. In just about a mile now he would hit the shelf. The shelf was the ledge between the High Bottoms and the Low Bottoms, a thirty foot high dropoff that ran along side by side with the River, as straight as a string, almost all the way from Israel clear up to West Lancaster. It stretched off to the south and to the north as far as you could see and right on its lip the road forked, and below it the Low Bottoms, as flat as a table, ran on down to the River; and above it the High Bottoms, as flat as another table, ran on back to where they tapered off into the higher ground of the prairies. When he reached it Raymond stopped the car and had another good drink and sat for a while at the fork, looking in the moonlight out across the brush and uneven little fields of the Low Bottoms to the heavy tree line of the River. It never failed to astonish him how far you could see, clear over into Indiana, from the shelf. When he reached for the bottle, he was surprised to find it was almost empty, so he killed it and threw it out and opened up the other one. Then he started down the incline, on the left fork, toward the old Rivertown ferry.

Almost at once the gravel petered out from under him and Raymond laughed to himself softly. He was really getting down in here now. The other fork, the one that ran south along the lip of the shelf, was the main used one. It ran on down south, would take you all the way to Israel if you follered it, and along this road—up there at the top of the shelf—was where all the farmhouses were, where they were safe when the River overflowed the bottoms. Old Joe Kilburt's fine old place was one of them, an old old house, made out of brick and with a big chimney at each end. Maybe a hundred years old maybe. Maybe even more, Raymond didnt know. Somebody had built it up there long ago, so as to have that beautiful view of across the River.

But this fork; this fork was dirt, almost as soon as you got down the sloping shelf. Nobody ever come down here, except the farmers when they come to plow their Low Bottoms fields. Raymond laughed happily and took another drink out of the new bottle and guided the Dodge skiddingly and jouncingly along the frozen ruts. Sure as hell was cold out. Sure was. Yes sir, he was really getting down in here now. Nobody. Not since they stopped the Rivertown ferry, anyway. There was a place along here where you had to ford a little creek on the shale rock, then you had to bear left right after that at a dirt fork.

When he reached the riverbank, he slowed the car almost to a crawl. The road, which was little more than a sandy track now, curved around behind some trees; it had used to go right down the bank then to the ferry, but now the River had washed away the landing and the road, and there was a ten foot bank straight down to the water. You could drive right off of it if you didnt know about it or werent careful. Down in around here a fellow had to be *real* careful.

Taking the bottle with him, Raymond climbed out and stood on the sandy frozen ground looking out over the bank at the River. It was frozen clear over all right, or at least it was as far as he could see it: lumpy and uneven, a long expanse of snow covered ice which had broken and heaved up and pushed against itself into a long stretch of frozen desolation like some wintertime no-man's-land. He took another big drink and stood and looked at it some more, but finally the cold drove him back to the car. Clutching the open bottle between his knees tightly, he turned the car around by simply backing it off into the field that was ditchless on either side of the sandy track, and a sense of awe and wonder gripped him at the thought of all those hundreds and hundreds, maybe even thousands, of people who had crossed the old-time River on that old Rivertown ferry, as he drove off back the way he had come. But instead of going on back west to the shelf, he turned off left—south—again on another little track through the fields. If he followed this track down along the river it would bring him back to the shelf road further down about five miles in a big circle.

Yes, sir. All those people. Hell, he knew this country like the back of his hand, he thought, and Raymond laughed happily. He listened to him, listened to Raymond laughing happily. That Raymond. He was a bum. He sure was a bum all right. And dumb. But he liked him. He liked Raymond. Him and Raymond had been coming over here together ever since Raymond was a kid. He bet there wasnt a man in the country knew the Riverbottoms between Israel and West Lancaster as well as Raymond did. And he had shown him all of it. Use to steal Raymond's Old Man's car out when Dewey wanted it for some woman he was taking out, him and Raymond did. And drive it over here.

That Dewey, Raymond thought thinking about the Legion and the old guys and the new guys and their wars. He laughed and took another drink as the car bounced along the track. That Dewey sure was a rough one. By God, he had sure broken his goddamned nose for him, by God! And he was just as smart as he was rough. He had been right about the war, too. Of course, Raymond was right too: the war *was* sad. When guys got killed and all. But it was more happier than it was sad. Of course you were scared all the time, and there was always the chance of getting killed, and you hated to see your buddies get it; but you were shooting Japs all the time, and you were living out in the open, under the sky, with your gun and your C-rations. Raymond had never been healthier in his life than he had during the war. And that wasnt all of it,—because in between campaigns you got to go back to New Zealand or Australia where everything was wide open and there was plenty of women and liquor, plenty for everybody, even Raymond, and then off youd go to a new campaign again. Hell, yes! War wasnt sad at all. Old Dewey was right all right. He always was. He was a smart one all right. Raymond laughed softly to himself and took another drink. By God, he sure broke his damned old nose for him, though, good old Dewey. Hell, yes!

Suddenly he slammed on the brakes of the Dodge. Now how the hell did that tree get there? He must have got off the track and into some damned field. Now what do you think of that? Oh, Raymond took the low road, and almost hit a tree. Oh, you take the high road, and Ill take the low road. Hell, yes! Carefully he looked all around the field and could not see any exit. But there must be one, or how else did he get in here? Laughing softly to himself, happily, he corked the bottle carefully and what little was left in it and lay down in the front seat, thinking about Dewey and how he had broke his damned nose for him, and laughing happily for himself and Dewey. Hed get out of this old field tomorrow. Ill be free of this damned old field tomorrow. Suddenly he wished Dewey was here with him and they were getting drunk together, then they could talk about all the things they used to do and play together when they were kids. That Dewey. He sure had one hell of a fine left jab, that Dewey did. Hell, yes! A hell of a left jab. Closed his eyes up tightern a drum. He couldnt see a thing.——————

It was Hubie who phoned them up the news, from downtown at Ciro's, where he had just heard it. The farmer who had found him had been out running a trap line and had called the sheriff, and the sheriff had gone out and had just now brought the body in. Everybody uptown was talking about it.

"Wheres Dewey?" he said. "I got to find Dewey before he hears about it. I got to find him before somebody else tells him."

Neither Dave nor 'Bama had the slightest idea where he was, but it was not long after that that the two of them came walking in from town, their faces red with the cold. It was clear from the look on Dewey's face that Hubie had already told him.

"I never should have made him give up," Dewey said, staring at them disconsolately out of his mean, malevolent, no longer handsome face behind that crooked nose, his blue eyes bright with pain. "I never should have made him say he had enough. I should have quit, when he couldnt see any more."

"I keep tellin him that that didnt have nothin to do with it," Hubie said. "Hell, Ive seen Raymond make Dewey give up two dozen times; and Ive seen Dewey make him give up at least that many. I keep tellin him, but he wont listen to me. You guys tell him," he appealed to them.

"Hubie's right," 'Bama said. "Ive seen both of you make the other one give up. That didnt have a damn thing to do with it."

Dewey would only shake his head disconsolately. "I should never have made him admit hed had enough."

The four of them sat around the kitchen table drinking coffee, since nobody—excepting only Dewey—much felt like having a drink, talking about Raymond and telling things they remembered about him, holding a sort of private wake as it were, interspersed with long periods of silence. Into these silences Dewey would every so often say his one single disconsolate, painful sentence, shaking his head, "I never should have made him give up." There was no point in trying to tell him any different.

And equally often, at other moments, he would put his hands on the table and start up, and say vaguely, "I think Ill have a drink." But one or another of them would always talk him out of it. By some sure instinct, which none of them could have described in words, they managed to keep him from drinking anything for almost two hours. But finally he simply told them all to go to hell and would not be brooked any longer.

"God damn it, Im going to have a drink!" he insisted, his blue eyes blazing furiously behind that new, malevolent-nosed face. "I *need* a drink!" And so, when nobody refused him flatly, he got himself a bottle and set it on the table in front of him and proceeded to get blind staggering drunk. By now Wally Dennis—his young writer's face alert and interested and making mental notes at this first real tragedy he had ever had a part in—had heard the news and come down to join them, and the four of them sat up with Dewey while he drank. Finally, when he had got himself drunk enough, he took his bottle and went off alone with it into the front room and lay down on the couch, saying almost nothing except his one flat, declarative, haunted sentence over and over again: "I never should have made him give up."

Later on in the day some of the women began to arrive: Doris Fredric, Lois, Hubie's girl Martha. Lois went in alone and tried to reason with him and soothe him, but Dewey only cursed her savagely and told her to get the hell out and leave him alone. Finally, between all of them, they got him upstairs into one of the bedrooms, still hugging his bottle —a new one, now—that he would not let them take from him. He did not weep, or cry, or show any other emotion, except to drink savagely and curse them when they tried to make him stop, and tell them over and over that he should never have made Raymond admit he was whipped. He stayed drunk for two whole days until the funeral, unshaven, unbathed, disheveled, not even taking off his clothing he dozed in, wandering around the house savagely and disconsolately. But when it came time for his brother's funeral he came out into the kitchen, a gaunt spectral broken-nosed and red-eyed shape, and announced that he was ready to go.

"My God! You cant go lookin like that!" Hubie pleaded with him. "Why dont you stay here? Ill stay with you. Or Lois will."

"Sure; I will," Lois said.

"Im going!" Dewey said.

"Well, at least let us get you cleaned up," 'Bama said. "Let us shave you, and get yore clothes changed, and fix you up a little. You look like the wrath of God now."

"No!" Dewey said. "Im going! And Im going like I am! To hell with it! What does all that damned crap matter anyway?" He paused, and peered at them drunkenly, his blue eyes savagely, hauntedly pleading. "I never should have made him give up," he said heartbrokenly.

All of them tried to reason with him, but Dewey was indomitable. He was going to his brother's funeral, and nobody was going to stop him. And he was going just like he was, there wasnt time enough to get cleaned up properly anyway, he had no change of clothes here, and he didnt give a damn anyway. It was almost in a way as if it were some sort of penance. So in the end they bundled him up into one of Dave's topcoats which fit him as to length fairly well and, drunk, disheveled, gaunt faced, red eyed and unshaven, they half-carried him in a body to Raymond's funeral, arriving en masse and sitting down at the back, a loyal delegation of the town undesirables, so to speak, the town bums, true to their own.

"Raymond would have liked it better this way anyway," Dewey hiccupped brokenly. And who was to dispute his word?

The funeral was in the dinky little Church of Christ, Saved, out in the East end which Dewey's mother staunchly belonged to, and their entrance there and Dewey's appearance made a lot less of a furor than it would have at, say, the Episcopal or the Methodist churches. These were people the majority of whose husbands and sons were pretty heavy drunkards anyway, whenever they werent actually working; and they were not unused to the idea of a man getting wildly drunk to relieve his pain at a funeral. The sermon was preached by the thin elderly Church of Christ, Saved, pastor; and it was terse and not very long. Mostly the pastor dwelt upon Raymond's war record. There wasnt very much else for him to dwell upon. Afterwards, after almost everybody else had filed past, Dave and 'Bama supported Dewey to go up for the traditional last look at the corpse. Dewey stared down at it for a moment quietly, his blue eyes wild and stretched wide with a cloudy-faced fury and rage of disconsolation, then he walked on quietly. He insisted on going out to the cemetery, too, and stood hatless and bareheaded in the cold between Dave and 'Bama in Dave's topcoat, and when that was all over he shook hands politely with the pastor, and then they took him home. After a couple of more days of drinking 'Bama's whiskey, during which somebody—usually Hubie—was with him most of the time, he allowed himself to be gradually sobered up.

His eyes red-rimmed and bloodshot but clear, he came out into the kitchen and ate the first food he had eaten in almost five days. "What the hell," he croaked in a voice hoarse from so much whiskey, his new, malevolent face snarling at them from behind the sideways, knotted nose. "What the hell. There aint nothing left in this town anymore, anyway. There never was much. Who gives a damn for this town anyway? Lets you and me go back and join the Army again, Hubie," he said, turning to snarl the question at his sidekick. "What do you say? Thats where we belong anyway. Thats where weve always belonged. The damned Army's the only home we ever had."

Hubie, who was sitting solicitously across the table from him, merely laughed. "The goddam Army was never no home to me," he said, positively and unequivocally. But six months later, after taking that long to definitely make up their minds about it and hashing and rehashing it over and over again endlessly and arguing and cursing each other, out of their new bitterness, which largely came out of Dewey's sheer forcefulness, as they worked less and less and drank and talked more and more and went swiftly downhill,—finally, that was what they did;—leaving their two girlfriends callously to their own devices, with no other going away present than the three years' wasted time and effort that might have been applied toward marrying other men. But before that happened, a lot of other things had happened, too.

Dave, who had watched the whole sequence of events concerning Raymond from the position of sort of an innocent bystander as it were, inbetween his more and more numerous visits over to see Gwen which were his main concern at the time, found he could not overcome a vague disquieting feeling—which he was sure all the others dimly felt, also— that somehow or other they were all of them responsible for Raymond, and had somehow failed him. Certainly, he knew that Dewey felt it,— although Dewey never mentioned his brother again after he sobered up after the funeral. Certainly, too, from that time on was when everything began to go bad: From the time that Mildred Pierce married, and Raymond Cole died, which was of course also the time that he himself had given up definitely and finally on Gwen, the centrifugal force that seemed to hold them all together as a mass, a homogeneous group, in this particular era of their lives, had begun to dissipate and fail. And a long time afterwards he came to believe positively that if Dewey and Hubie had never gone back to the Army, had *not* reenlisted, he himself would never have married Ginnie Moorehead.

Because after all, Dave thought, all that time, Wally was still running around with and sleeping with the Junoesque Rosalie Sansome, wasnt he? and he hadnt married her, had he?

CHAPTER 55

WALLY FRENCH DENNIS had no intention of marrying Rosalie Sansome. He had no intention of marrying anybody. The Christmas vacation with Dawnie had proved that to him, finally and conclusively. Whatever heartburnings and qualms he may once have had over her and her going away to school, he had been completely absolved of them during her Christmas vacation home from Western Reserve.

He did not know what exactly had happened to her,—to Dawn. It was not something he could delineate empirically and rationally and point to with his finger and say. This is it; this is what she is doing to me. It wasnt like that at all. If it had been, he would have felt a lot easier about it—about all of it—and would have had a much surer sense of control. But instead, this way,—the way it was in fact,—he was not even sure he was not imagining all of it; and (by analyzing himself shrewdly) he came to the conclusion that because of this—because he could not be sure he was *not* imagining it—there existed in him this certain uneasy guilt caused by a reasonable doubt. That, of course, placed him in an untenable position: Maybe he was wrong about her, he would find himself thinking, maybe he was unfair. The result was, he would repeatedly find himself trying desperately to reach her, to break through that invisible wall;—while she, aloof, distant, uninvolved (quite unlike himself) merely remained far off; indifferent, and untouched.

And yet he was not imagining it. He knew he wasnt, and he was pretty sure Dawnie knew it. Take sex, for instance. Last year, last summer, in the first throes of their truly ecstatic—(that might be overwriting it; but it was the only word he could find that really accurately fit)— ecstatic love affair, Dawnie had been as keen on thinking up new places to go as he had been. And she had loved it, and been just as keen on all of it, as he had.

But now—now it was entirely different, and all that was gone. He had slept with her just exactly three times during Christmas vacation; and each time it was the same: In a word: she submitted. Each time, she would lie back and *allow* him to sleep with her, and if she enjoyed it any herself she gave no signs. He suspected that, in fact, she did enjoy it; physically, at least;—perhaps that was male vanity; he wasnt sure of anything any more—and that she deliberately held it in and did not let on, because she knew how much it would have meant to him. But he could not even prove that.

Wally was well aware that all of this had started back in September, when he had refused to take off to New York with her, and he was more or less convinced that this was her own private secret way of making him pay for it. After all, it had started right away immediately after that had happened. It bespoke a tremendous compliment to the depth of acumen of her female instincts, of which she appeared to have a full complement. How else could she have known that that was the best and most efficient way to handle a man?

But what a way to live! Now that he had had it occur in his own personal experience, Wally could penetrate through the screens to the hearts of a number of marriages and love affairs he knew about and had followed but had never been quite able to understand what was wrong with them. Great God! Women who, when they could not get you to do exactly every particular thing they demanded of you, simply clammed up and went cold on you in bed, deliberately and calculatedly, their instincts telling them what to do so accurately and thoroughly that they never even had to think about it consciously and so were able to keep their virtuous integrity and purity of motive intact and secure, serene and proud. Until such time as you gave in and humbly and obsequiously accepted your defeat, when they would probably suddenly become warm and close again—until some other disputed ground arose. He had learned a very very great deal—a whole hell of a lot—about women since this had happened, and was already planning how he could incorporate it into the main love affair and ending of his book. But as for living that way with some damned woman or other, the hell with it! Just imagine! living with some woman that way all your *life!*

My God! The very thought of what she had done infuriated him beyond saying. It would never have occurred to him, he would never even have believed it possible, if it hadnt happened to him. That a woman, a live, breathing, warm, sexy woman, would coldbloodedly and maliciously do that to a guy! Go cold on him! Just to get even with him over some pique! The very concept was horrid, inhuman. Why, it put men completely at their mercy. —Or would; if the men allowed it to.

Obviously, the only recourse, the only defense he had, was to go cold on her in return himself. And after the first time she pulled it after coming home for Christmas, that was what he had done. He had acted just as cold and indifferent as she did. It had not, however, seemed to do much good. She was just as far away and distant as ever. And so you had the spectacle of two people, two humans male and female, going to bed together in this most intimate and close relationship two humans male and female could have, and doing it as if they were two total strangers who did not even know each other's souls, and what was more didnt care. It was not only ridiculous, it was boring, and actually almost unpleasant as well.

Finally, on the third occasion,—which for other, totally different reasons was sexually exciting for Wally; though it probably wasnt for Dawnie at all—he had blown up, blew his lid completely, and told her off. It made one of the pleasantest experiences of his life.

They were down at his house, that third time, when it happened. His mom had decided right after Christmas to go up to Chicago and visit her sister there and stay till over New Year's. She had wanted Wally to go with her, of course; but—partly because of Dawnie, partly because his writing was going good and he didnt want to leave it, and partly because his mom's sister in Chicago and her whole damned family bored the living hell out of him—he had declined and said he would stay home alone. So, with her gone and out of the way, he had had the house to himself; and two days after she was gone, after first going up to West Lancaster and dancing and having a few beers on his swiftly dwindling fellowship money, he had brought Dawnie back down to the house.

They had made themselves right at home, and fixed coffee and sandwiches in the kitchen and had a couple more beers while Dawnie talked on and on about her Playhouse-Workshop stuff at Reserve, and then they had gone—after a little lukewarm necking and some insistence on his part—upstairs to his room to go to bed. That: the fact that he had her there in the house and had the run of it: was not what made this last time so sexually exciting for him. Or maybe it was, partly. Yes, it partly was, probably: seeing her nude there in his mom's kitchen with him and watching her walk through his mom's hall and up his mom's stairs to his own room, himself following behind her: just having the free run of the place and knowing they could do anything they wanted: Yes, that probably was it, partly. But, nevertheless, this was not the main thing. The main thing that excited him was that he was sleeping with her in his own bed in his own room, where twice before he had slept with Rosalie Sansome, and thus was getting even with her (without her knowing it, of course) for what she had done to him. Twice before on separate occasions, when his mom had gone off somewhere for a day or two to visit some damn fool friend of hers, he had sneaked old Rosalie down to the house for a party in his own bed. And now he was doing the same thing to Dawnie and in the same place, and in so doing was putting himself one up on her, was getting revenge, for all the mean cruel things she had been doing to him, and her coldness ever since he had refused to take her off to New York. He had not started off to do that, he hadnt brought her down here deliberately for that purpose, but now that the thought had occurred to him, he was glad. And it was both strange and startling how excited it made him.

And after it was over, and they had gone sort of straggling back downstairs with that curiously ridiculous feeling a person always had after sex when he asks himself why all the fuss and what in hell had he been so ridiculously excited about, and had dressed themselves again, he decided to just come out with it, to lay it on the line and get it over with; —not because he had finally revenged himself and had gotten one back up on her; it wasnt that at all;—but just simply because he didnt want to go on this way with her any longer; that was what it was, quite simply; he had just gotten a bellyful.

Sitting in his mom's kitchen over another beer, Dawnie sitting staring down into her glass silently and pensively, her soft hair against her cheek, himself thinking back sourly to all that crap he had read in Weiman's *Source of Human Good* and (Sucker!) had actually believed: all that crap about how good was cumulative and made itself better and better in Time so that each act was better than and enhanced by the previous times,—Phooey!—and also wondering how he was going to go about it, bring it up, finally, he just came right out with it and blurted it out.

"You dont like to go to bed with me any more, do you, Dawnie?" he asked.

She looked up at him, coolly, distantly, totally untouchable, not the same girl—not the same *woman*—he had known last summer at all. "Do you feel that?" she said coldly.

"What the hell else is there *to* feel? Its obvious, aint it?" he said. "Dont you feel anything? Dont you enjoy it at all?"

She shrugged a little, almost imperceptibly, staring at him coolly. "I suppose I enjoy it about as much as any woman does. Women arent made the same as men, I dont think. They dont just like sex for sex sake. Women like to be loved a little bit with their sex."

"And you dont think I love you enough?" Wally said.

Again she shrugged.

"Or love you at all?" he said; "is that it?"

"I suppose you love me as much as you are capable of."

"But thats not enough, you mean?"

Dawn eyed him distantly, almost disinterestedly. "I give you what you want, dont I?"

"No!" Wally said. "No, you dont. I want your*self*. You dont give your*self*. Hell, I can get sex anywhere. I can buy that. I want you to love me."

Dawn smiled at him a little, pityingly, a sad little smile. Then suddenly she flung her head back and shook her hair back and stared at the ceiling, a sad convulsive movement, before she looked back down at him, straight in the eye. "Maybe there isnt any self of me left to give any more," she said distantly.

"Then maybe we just better call the whole damned thing off!" Wally said, louder, and angrier, than he meant to.

"I suppose that would be the wisest thing," Dawn said coolly, unruffledly, staring him straight into the eyes.

"All we seem to do is cause each other misery and trouble and unhappiness any more," he said; "we dont give each other any happiness at all, any more."

"I expect that would be the best," she said disinterestedly. "For both of us."

"Its a good thing we didnt go on and get married, aint it?" Wally said. "Why didnt you answer my letters?"

Dawn shrugged. "I was busy," she said, in that same untouched, untouchable tone. "As a matter of fact, I did answer all of them, didnt I? eventually?"

This was not strictly the truth; but it was the truth as far as it went. A week or so after she was gone, caught up in a hunger and loneliness of missing her, he had written her a very passionate loveletter up to

Cleveland. He had gotten an answer right back; but it was a cool, distant, indifferent little short letter that was so unlike his own that it was like a bucket of cold water in the face. After an answer like that he had waited several weeks before he wrote again, just to let her know he wasnt actually dying for her, and then there was a long wait before she answered again—the same cool, short, distant little letter like the first. After that, he had waited longer and longer, before answering the other letters, all of which he answered in kind, and that was when he looked up Rosalie. And all because he wouldnt run off to New York on some crazy junket which they would have been back from in six weeks. It was ridiculous.

"I suppose you mean because you had some man on the string up there," he said disgustedly. "Is that what youre implying?"

"As a matter of fact, there was an actor I met at the Playhouse," Dawn said indifferently; "a very nice gentle kind sort of a chap."

"You mean, not at all like me," Wally said.

"No, not very much," she smiled.

"Then he'll never be a great actor," Wally said darkly.

"Probably not," Dawn said disinterestedly. "However, he might make some girl a nice husband someday. —Not me, of course," she added. "As I said, I guess there just isnt any self of me left to give."

"Now dont start trying to get on my back about me taking your virginity away from you," Wally said.

"Not at all. I didnt mean that at all," Dawn said coolly. "You dont owe me anything at all. In fact, I feel in some ways that its I who owe you a great deal. You did me a favor. And youve taught me a great deal about men, Wally," she smiled, that cool pitying smile.

"Yeah," Wally said; "yeah." He could not touch her at all; any way at all. He could not even make her angry. "Well, youve taught me a hell of a lot about women."

"Well, Im glad you feel that way, Wally. I really am," Dawnie said, still in that same cool, distant, cold, unreachable way. "Was there anything else you wanted to ask me?"

"No. Come on and Ill take you home," he said flatly, putting finality in his voice.

Without a word Dawn got up from the table, leaving her still unfinished beer, and looking suddenly tall and regal walked into the hall and got her coat and put it on, and then turned and looked at him, waiting, expectant, cool, ready to go.

He got his fleecelined jacket and clapped his old baseball cap on his head, and he took her home. And as he watched her go up the steps onto the Hirsh porch—as he had watched her so many times before; only now it was for the last time, the last time he would watch her climb them late at night like that—he was glad. If there was a little hollow feeling in him that he had perhaps not done right by her—(not about going to New York, he had been right on that; but about taking her virginity)—and perhaps there was a little such feeling, he put it down. After all, she had wanted it as much as he had; that was the truth. And she was not the same girl—same woman; same female; because she was a woman now; a goddamned female—that he had known last summer. Not the same at all. She went straight up the steps, still looking tall and regal—which was odd for one as short as she was, and straight on in the house without saying goodby or looking back. Wally watched her, thinking Well, it was back to old Rosalie for him. He put his mom's car in gear gently and carefully and drove away without any roaring of the motor or skidding of the tires, so as to let her know he wasnt angry and did not care either.

A couple of days later—New Year's Eve day, it was—he was uptown and saw her riding around in the Shotridge's big family Cadillac with young Jimmy. It hadnt taken her long, he thought grinning to himself. Well, if she wanted to trade him in on a square oaf like Jimmy Shotridge, it was all right with him. Shotridge, who was only nineteen and only a sophomore at UI. In Business Administration, yet! Wally was pretty damned confident *that* wouldnt last long. Not that he wanted her back; he didnt. He was through. And he was glad (and felt he was pretty lucky) to be out of it as easily as he was. That Shotridge; he always was the kind of an oaf who took somebody else's leavings.

Sooooo, it was time to start redistributing life and interests again. That night he got hold of old Rosalie Sansome and brought her back out to the house again. He might as well take advantage of his mom's absence while he had the chance.

Rosalie had never been very satisfying to him. Whenever he slept with her it left him feeling just as empty and as itchily, irritably lonely as he had felt before. But then he felt the same damned way with Dawnie too, any more. Rosalie wasnt very bright, but she was hard as nails and she amused him. The first time he had sneaked her into the house when his mom was off visiting overnight, she had walked all around the house, looked at everything airily and intently and said:

"Why dont you marry me, Wally?"

He had laughed outright, while she continued to stare at him, and she kept on staring at him, obdurately, questioningly, silently demanding an answer.

"Why the hell should I want to marry you?" he grinned.

Rosalie swung her arms out away from her, around at the music room and the hall and his mom's heavily over—and-he-did-mean-over—stuffed furniture in the living room. "Oh; Id make you a good wife," she said categorically. "I could live here with your mother and cook for you and take care of you and lay for you and help you with your writin' and give you material for books out of my life. Youd like me for a wife. Id make you a goddamned good wife."

"I dont want a good wife," he smiled. "Or any other kind of a wife, for that matter. Im happy like I am." This wasnt exactly the whole truth (though it *was* some of it); but it was certainly all of it he would ever tell Rosalie.

"Every man needs a wife," Rosalie said unequivocally. "Thats nature. Besides, I like this place," she said. "Your mother really has wonderful taste."

"Yeah," he said, masking a grin.

"This place is even nicer than my aunt's place up at West Lancaster," Rosalie said. "You know, my aunt's really worth a lot of money—what with that bar she has at West Lancaster and them whorehouses she use to run years ago. Its not like I was one of them brassiere factory girls. I dont have to work. My aunt supports me. And I help her out some once in a while. Shes really quite well off."

"Yeah, but Id never see any of it," Wally grinned.

"Dont be too sure," Rosalie said, pointing her finger at him like a dominant sword. "I think Im in her will. Im the only close relative shes got, you know."

"Well, I aint about to marry you anyway," Wally grinned. "You nor no other woman. Whether theyre rich or not. I like living by myself and I mean to keep it that way."

"You wouldnt say that if your mother was dead and wasnt here to wait on you," Rosalie said. "Anyway it was just an idea."

"Thats all itll ever be," Wally said, "I can assure you." Jesus! She was a whole head taller than him—and bigger: she probably outweighed him ten pounds, though there certainly wasnt any fat on her. He looked her over covetously, his breath short and his palms damp at the prospect of her and of them both, being here, three-dimensional and solid and with air all around them, standing on the carpets and moving from room to room in his mom's house where the Diana Club met, their two nude figures showing strangely and weirdly and almost impossibly unbelievable against the shifting back-drops of the room-walls with their pictures and hangings all of which he knew so well.

No, there wasnt any fat on her; but she was just too big, for him. And not only that she was just about as low class—was from just about the lowest strata of society—as you could get. In Parkman Illinois anyway. And not only that, she was older than him. Marry her! Yeah. He could just see his mom's face.

He had had her a number of times before this of course, down at 'Bama and Dave's house; but it was not like having her here in his own house, his mom's house, in his own room and his own bed; not at all. And it had been the same thing again only better, on New Year's Eve night, when he had brought her home again, after seeing Dawnie up-town with Jim Shotridge.

"I sure do like this place," Rosalie had said again candidly. "I sure would like to live here. You better marry me, Wally, before its too late. I might hook some other man."

Who the hell was Dawnie? he thought. Who is Syl-vya? What is she-ee? Yeah; what *was* she?

The only trouble was, of course, that his mom did not go away visiting overnight often enough. Not for a man of his propensities and abilities, and needs. As Rosalie had said New Year's Eve night: "You sure are a horny bastard, Wally;" and patted him on the leg; "That flatters a girl." Of course, he did not tell her about that empty, itchy, irritable loneliness that came right back afterwards.

But that was why—because his mom wouldnt go away often enough—that he had to rely on 'Bama and Dave's house most of the time. He had been keeping his hand in, going down there often, just to make sure it would remain all right. 'Bama of course was always the same: one hell of a good, and smart, guy; but Wally had been more or less off of Dave for the past month or so. Getting that damned Southerner story of his (which was an *ex*cellent story) accepted had made Dave get a little big-headed and pompous, Wally felt. Probably it was natural enough of course, but he did not feel that he would have been as pretentious and inflated about it as Dave obviously was. After all, it was only a story; a piece of finished work; good as it was. Forget it; go on. —And of course there was always Gwen. Damn her.

It was a very strange thing about Dave, Wally had noted. When he saw Dave over at Gwen's house, and when he saw him at his own house or out at Smitty's with the boys, it was as if he were actually seeing two different people. It was as if Dave actually *was* two different people; two people who more or less resembled each other, closely, physically—superficially—and who when you saw them apart, separately, you might easily mistake one for the other but who when you saw them both to-gether you instantly could tell them apart. The Dave who appeared to be spending almost all his spare time over at Gwen's was totally dif-ferent in kind and texture from the Dave who hung out with 'Bama and the guys at Smitty's.

Wally had been down there the night of the fight between Raymond and Dewey himself, (That was before Dawnie was home, and he had been sitting in the very next booth with Rosalie.) and Dave's suddenly getting sick at his stomach and throwing up had surprised and interested him. He had never thought of Dave as that sensitive a type before. Also, the idea that a *physical* memory: the sight of blood on snow like that out of a man's combat experience in war, could just sort of come back of itself out of its own volition, suddenly and unexpectedly after so long a time, was fascinating. He would never have believed it. But obviously Dave was not acting. So Wally had had to more or less accept it as a valid thing. It was astonishing what quirks the human mind could work up and impose on itself.

What amazed him most about the whole thing was Dewey's insuperable and unrelievable guilt in feeling he was to blame for Raymond's death, when there were absolutely no facts at all to substantiate such a hypothesis. It seemed to Wally at times that guilt —individual guilt; eating, acid guilts— was the cause of all the evil in the world. If people could only shuck off their guilts, or better yet, not even assume them in the first place, they would cause themselves a great deal less pain and bloodshed. And just from looking at himself, and his own life and experience, he could not see or understand why they did it.

He didnt do it. He never had; and he never intended to start, either. It wasnt rational or reasonable, and it was totally unobjective. It was just plain damned foolishness, to let your emotions get the upper hand over you like that. He could have been just like Dewey, and let himself go all to pieces with guilt over Dawnie—if he allowed himself to. But he wasnt going to allow himself.

But then, of course, it wasnt really Dawnie that he had ever really loved. It was Gwen. It had always been Gwen, and it probably always would be Gwen. He realized that now. He had loved her really, really been deeply in love with her, ever since she had got him started on this goddamned writing business. The only thing that had attracted him to Dawnie in the first place was all those many qualities about her that made him think so much of Gwen: her sensitivity, her interest in the arts, her honesty about society, that square shy look in her eyes.

But it was just that very thing that could have torn him apart with guilt about Dawnie: He had really cheated her, in a way; because he had never really been free to really love her. His heart, and his soul, and all the love there was in him, already belonged to Gwen French.

He hadnt meant to do that to her. He hadnt done it deliberately, and had not even known it at the time. He had really honestly believed that what he felt for Dawnie was really love,—and not just infatuation. And it had taken Dawnie, and the terrible hurt he had had to give her (which he sincerely regretted), to show him what the truth really was: that he was in love with Gwen, and had been all along.

Distant cousin or not, relative or not, years older than him or not, Wally had realized finally and at last whom he really loved and wanted. The years' difference in their ages didnt matter a damn to him. He had only just recently seen a movie in which a young guy—in the face of his friends, and parents, and everybody else—had married a lovely woman so cool and beautifully detached who was ten years older. Joan Fontaine played the woman. Gwen had always had that lovely, cool, serene detachment—until only lately around Dave. The years' difference in their ages, their distant relationship, none of it mattered a damn to him; he didnt care about any of that. But of course, Gwen did. She had let society and its primitive tabus catch and blind her: she still thought of him as a kid. That one time two years ago when he had approached her, had asked her pointblank to sleep with him (he still blushed with a scringing bellygrinding painful embarrassment whenever he thought about it), she had smilingly turned it aside without even the decency to refuse him openly. He had carefully couched it in sophisticated terms and made it appear like a worldly proposition, never letting on or saying anything about the real love and adoration he had for her;—and she had not seen through it, had not even tried to look below the surface facade to what was really there. And now she was sleeping with Dave Hirsh!

Hell, anybody could see it. A blind man could. He had suspected it last summer, but hadnt been willing to believe his own intuition. But you only had to see them once together over there at the house in Israel, and watch all the loverlike smiles and looks and peregrinations, to know it and know it positively. It was not only painful to Wally to see, it was both embarrassing and disgusting. He was embarrassed for Gwen.

Wally knew the whole story on Ginnie and all about her going out with Dave. He had seen them together down at 'Bama and Dave's house time after time. Dave didnt even make any attempt to hide it from him. And if he had not seen them together again lately, that did not mean that they werent. What he would have liked to do was slip over to Israel on the q t and put Gwen wise to just what kind of a guy she was giving herself to.

But of course, damn the son of a bitch, he couldnt do that. However much he might like to. It went against everything he believed, everything he held to be his integrity. To have done that. Against the ingrained code he had so carefully and laboriously built up and taught himself to adhere to, when it came to other people's sex life. To have done a thing like that would have been to put himself in the same class with Dave Hirsh. And he would not do that.

So all he could do was stand and wait, and hope, watching the woman he loved and adored more than anyone else in the world being taken in, until someday she would wake up and find out for herself just what had been done to her. Then, and only then, he could come forward and offer himself and what he had to give, at that time when she would probably need it most.

It was all he *could* do. And at times the sheer anguish of it—especially when he had to be around Dave down at the house on Lincoln Street, after his mom had come home from Chicago and Dawnie had gone back to school—seemed almost more than he could take in silence. Thank God he was lucky enough to have the sexual release of Rosalie handy.

But as for Dawnie, that was through. Finished. He had made up his mind, back on that night he had taken her home, and he had not changed it. There would be no more damned Christmas parties at the Hirshes' for him, where he and his mom were treated so sympathetically like poor relations. If his mom wanted to swallow crapped-up charity like that, that was up to her. He would not. And there would be no more tricky damned 'Junior Memberships' at the Country Club that Frank Hirsh had got for him—and paid for. No more damned expensive dinners; and no more damned charitable gifts; and no more damned being a "member" of Frank Hirsh's family—and letting Frank pay for things for him he himself could not afford. Dawnie had made her choice, when she let him take her home like that when he asked her to. Well, he, Wally, had made his, too.

And if her damned father Frank didnt like it, he could lump it, or shove it, or do any other damned thing he wanted to do with it. And to hell with Dawnie and her cocky smugly superior ways. Next thing you knew she would be believing she had been a Rich Girl all her life—instead of just the last two years.

And so, probably, would her damn old man.

CHAPTER 56

IF FRANK HIRSH had any suspicions, even in his subconscious mind, of the maledictions Wally Dennis was hurling at him and at his daughter, none of them ever got as far up as his conscious mind where he could think about them, and in truth, Wally Dennis was the least of his worries. For one thing, Frank had no idea at all of the really personal interest Wally had been taking in his family lately; nor of the extent to which that interest had been carried, either. With the sharp eye of the worldly man, Frank had watched little Dawnie very closely when she came home for Christmas after her first semester at Western Reserve, and after thoughtful deliberation, was convinced that his daughter had come home just as much of a virgin as when she went away. That satisfied him.

And as for Wally, there had been a time when Frank had looked on him rather fondly as possibly a prospective son in law. While the Dennises had no money any more, they were still a fine old family—a family which, in turn, came of the merging of two fine old families; and they had once been pretty high up there,—until The Crash came and old Jess Dennis died. Wally, Frank had once thought, would make him a fine son, and an excellent boy to manage the store for him—after working his way up from the bottom and learning the business—and perhaps even someday to take over his other business interests for Dawnie. But that had been before this adoption business; and also, before he had consummated this bypass deal. Now, Dawnie could have just about any young man in town she wanted and set her heart on; or for that matter, any young man outside of town that she set her heart on. Chicago; New York; Detroit; Cleveland; they would any of them be glad to marry into the Hirsh family about a year from now. If Dawnie wanted to continue to carry on her childhood friendship with Wally, that was all right as far as Frank was concerned. But he was glad to see that there appeared to be no signs of anything stronger. Let Wally continue to write novels for Gwen French.

It was not, as Wally had secretly accused him, that Frank was hastening to be rich and forget where he had started from. It wasnt that at all. And if Frank had even guessed what Wally thought about him, he would have been shocked and hurt; and probably angry. Because Frank had no intention of ever forgetting his antecedents and where he came from. Or of ever letting his children or grandchildren forget it, either. He had come from nothing and from nowhere, that was where; and as he got richer—if he did; and it looked like he might—he intended to remind himself and everybody else more and more just exactly where he did come from: He was a selfmade man, that was what: He was the same man who all his life, from his early teens on, had used to walk around the square and look up at the crowns of the buildings that read: PARKER BLOCK - 1907 and McGEE BLOCK - 1904 and WERNZ BLOCK - 1900 and MADIN BLOCK - 1923, and dream of the day when he would buy one of them and renovate or rebuild it and name it HIRSH BLOCK - 1940 or HIRSH BLOCK - 1950: He was the same man who only a year ago had told his brother (who had, incidentally, laughed at him) that he intended to acquire those things which made people admire you, and love you, and respect you: namely, money and property: all that admiration and love and respect and prestige that none of them in their family had ever had—thanks to the Old Man; but *he* would have them: And would use them to the good of charity and humanity until everybody would love and respect him: That was him: He was all of that: He was that man. And he wasnt ashamed of it. Maybe he wouldnt actually tear one of them down and rebuild it, but he would be having the next best thing,—or perhaps a better one: When the Parkman Village Shopping Center was done and built, right up there on the very top, on the crown, would be the legend in yellow brick on black and four feet high: HIRSH BLOCK - 1950 or 1951. Dave would have done a lot better, and been a lot wiser, if he had stuck with him. And if Wally had asked him, he would have told him the same damned thing, just like he would tell everybody else. But of course, Wally would not ask him. And anyway, Frank wasnt thinking of Wally at all any more. In the first place, he was far too busy—what with running his own affairs and running the store, and trying to handle this adoption thing too. And in the second place, he was far too happy enjoying and being in the midst of the new love affair that had developed with his wife.

Frank could not remember a time when Agnes had been as wonderful, and sweet, and loving, as she had been the past six or seven months. Even when they were first married they had not been as warm and close to each other; there had always been that tight reserve and holding back part of herself in some odd way in Agnes, even when they were first married. But that was all gone, now. Now, everything was fine. In October, after getting little Dawnie off to school and all settled in, they had taken themselves a month's vacation and spent it in Miami Beach. They had stayed at the Lord Tarleton with its private beach and private pool and cabanas, and had gone deepsea fishing and hit all the clubs and nightspots and shows, and done the races and the dog tracks, and seen a jai alai game. It had been wonderful, and had been practically a second honeymoon, and they spent money like water. And to hell with it, he'd thought proudly. He had never been happier in his life. In Florida everything was set up for serving the visitor and they treated you like kings and he and Agnes had never been so close or happy. They spent several days in Key West and saw the Little White House that the poor damned Republican taxpayers were paying for and went fishing again for sailfish out of Marathon on the Overseas Highway. Both of them were brown as berries when they got back home in November and Agnes had made a talk on the trip and shown the slides at the Country Club. And from now on they were going to do the same damned thing every year, and maybe even better; maybe next year they'd stay at the damn Versailles itself.

Before he left for Florida Frank had, finally, and at long last, turned the management of the store officially over to Al Lowe and had officially made him Manager. He had even had Clark's reporter (Clark himself was still away campaigning at the time) put an item on it in the *Oregonian*; and Al had been almost tearful in his pride and appreciation. (God, what an ass!) That meant that now, finally, he Frank was at last giving up personally running the store for his other 'business interests'; and it also meant that now Al would move officially into the office in the back. But Frank was already prepared for that: He would, he told them, all, everybody, still keep his own business office at the store; he had no other offices, and saw no reason for taking some. And so instead of moving out, he just had his own desk and personal files moved over into the corner and moved a new desk in for Al. That way he could be near Edith whenever he wanted, and be there legitimately; and he could also keep a check on Al and the store, too. It meant, of course, that Al would be in and out of the office much more than formerly, but that did not really matter since Al spent most of his time out front anyway. And anyway they were always careful never to do or say anything in the office that might look suspicious.

He was still seeing Edith once and sometimes twice a week, of course, when he left for Florida; and in some ways he half way hated to go, mostly because he felt sorry for Edith. He wished there were some way that he could take her on a vacation too, like he had Agnes, but of course that was impossible. But Edith understood. And anyway, she always asked very little of him. When she went on her vacation she would have to go alone;—but he saw to it that she had an extra large bonus when she went (in December; she went to Miami, too), and he boosted her vacation from the two weeks she had had formerly (in the summer) to a full month. It meant, naturally, that he would have to boost Al's vacation to a month, too; and that he would have to hire another girl to take her place, when she would be gone that long; but he was more than glad to do that much. To do at least that much.

He was, in fact, without any doubt or question, happier than he had ever been in his life: a devoted wife and a devoted mistress, two women who both loved him deeply and unselfishly; a good solid paying business in the store; and prospects just up ahead for a real killing. He might even wind up a millionaire. What the hell more could a man ask for?

From the time that the actual grading work on the bypass had started, Frank had kept his eye on it closely. During the good weather before it turned off bad in December he had driven out there almost every day to watch the progress, except for the one month he and Agnes spent in Florida. And one of the first things he did when they got home was to run out there and see how much progress had been made while he was gone. It was probably—his trip out there, was probably—the highest point of every single day for him. Before the weather turned off bad he would drive the Buick out Route 1 to the new junction—or what would be the new junction—every afternoon after lunch, so that he could watch them working, instead of going after the store closed when they would be through work for the day. He would pull off and park the car—not far from the old barn of Lloyd Monds's feeder farm, which he himself now owned—and sit and watch them work, and watch also his own two corner lots which he owned and which they were raising and grading the right of way between. Already, by the end of September —little more than a month after they had started—they had changed the whole face of the landscape. What had before been just fields with scattered trees across them, was now one long sweeping graded right of way, flowing in an easy curve around the town with the massive un-stoppableness of a glacier or a river, wide and level, rising imperceptibly from where it met the end of the new road east of Parkman to where it met and joined the Route 1 junction and then flowed on to the west, its wide wide, shallow drainage ditches, wider than the road itself, clean and untreed, making a long vista view both ways that the old fields themselves never could have provided. Right now it was all raw yellow clay dirt, already cut here and there by erosion runnels, but in his mind Frank could already see it finished: the long wide white ribbon of the highway with its line of black bisecting it and the long green expanse of the shallow drainage after it was grassed. And right there at the Route 1 junction, where he understood there was to be a four way stop and go light, would be the massive ultramodern expanse of The Parkman Village Shopping Center in green and cream, and on its raised crown in black and yellow the builtin device proclaiming its legend: HIRSH BLOCK - 1950 or 1951. It made his stomach squinch up so with excitement and anticipation that sometimes he was afraid he would get half sick.

He had already been up to Springfield twice now to see the architects. He had originally intended to go to a firm he knew himself in Indianapolis, for the plans. But the old man, Clark's father in law, knew of and was apparently obscurely associated with another firm in Chicago whom he wanted to have it and give a break to; and since they were a good highclass firm Frank had agreed to them immediately. What the hell difference did it make who built it? Their man met with him, and with the Greek and Clark's father in law, in Springfield. Already, with two visits, most of the plans were drawn and approved. All that remained was to wait until the bypass itself was done and open.

Already, by the time the weather broke the first week in December, the huge cats and earth movers and sheepsfoot rollers had finished most all of the really heavy work; and all that remained was the final grading before the concrete could be laid. And in late January and early February, when the bad weather broke and turned off good for several weeks, they were right back at work on the final grading. By March or April, or as soon as the weather turned good in the spring, they would be ready to move the huge roller driven concrete laying machines in and lay the road itself. And then it would only be a matter of picking their own time, to begin the Parkman Shopping Center, HIRSH BLOCK - 1950. Or 1951. It all depended on how the contracting and the work went, which year it would be; it was that close to the materialization.

Happy! Hell yes, he was happy. There were times when, remembering the various anguishes with both his women and his businesses (that old bastard Judge Deacon!), Frank felt almost like pinching himself hard and painfully, just to make damned sure he was not asleep and dreaming all of this. That Judge Deacon: the old devil: he knew there was something in the wind: he could smell it: but he was lying low because he couldnt figure out what it was: he had been properly fooled. He had no idea at all Frank was in on it, whatever it was. And when he did find out, it would be too damned late to do him any good. Happy? Yes, he was happy all right! And then, just when it seemed that no further happinesses could be given him, he was given two more: the adoption papers were approved; and he completed and consummated the sexual education and sophistication of his mistress Edith Barclay, which he had been hungering and hoping for so long. Hell, everything seemed to be going his way.

It was, Frank thought in his happiness, almost as if God Himself was Personally intent upon seeing that for his unselfish service to Humanity every blessing he asked for was to be heaped upon him. "Ask and it shall be given unto you," his Mother had so often used to quote to him. So many times. How many many times? And by God, it looked like she was right.

The adoption of course was pretty much a foregone conclusion. There had never really been any question about it. There wasnt a Welfare man in the world, Frank was smugly positive, who would turn thumbs down on placing a child in a home like this one. All they had to do was look at it; and as for the character and financial references, all they had to do was just ask any damned body in the town. Which was, of course, just exactly what they did. Still and all, it was good to know the whole think was okayed and that the coast was clear. They were being given the child this month, in February. They had begun the thing back in September, shortly before they left for Florida. Of course, there would be another six months of "probation" after February before the legal adoption could go through,—at least that was what the law said. But Frank had already looked into that and found that there were cases in which the County Judge, if he had good reports from the Welfare people, could go ahead and make it a fully legal adoption before that time. There wouldnt be any trouble there: The County Judge, like Clark Hibbard, was a good Republican and a good friend of Frank's. He would be more than willing to do that for one of his Committeemen.

When they had decided, back in September—after talking it over with little Dawn, to go ahead with it,—he and Agnes had decided to just do it all right through the State Welfare people. They didnt want to get involved with any tacky, fly-by-night outfit, like some of the orphanages were, and the Welfare people were all of them highly trained and very specialized operators. Most of them had their Master's or Doctor's from college on it. And all the medical and family histories of each child were thoroughly checked and looked into by a careful staff. You could always be sure of the validity and aboveboard-ness and suitability of any adoption that came from them. And when you were getting a child—and an heir!—you were going to live with the rest of your life, you wanted to be *damned* sure.

The chubby, pleasant little Welfare man who visited them in their home was obviously impressed with it, and with both of them. It was customary to check their people very carefully, he explained; Welfare was always very meticulous about checking their prospective parents very very carefully; consequently if he asked them some rather personal questions, they would understand, wouldnt they? Then he went on to ask the questions: their ages? their homelife? their compatibility? their drinking habits? their religious affiliations? their financial status, of course; no police records or anything of that sort, of course; no extra-marital affairs or anything like that on either side? They both smiled at him benignly and let their attitudes answer for themselves. Their religious affiliation was Methodist of course; and as for their drinking habits, Frank said, they both drank a little, a cocktail before dinner now and then; perhaps they might even just get a little bit tipsy, on holidays, once in a while. And as for the financial status, he waved his arm around the room and commenced to go into intricate details; but the chubby pleasant little man smiled and shoo-shooed him off of that apologetically and made some notes in his notebook; it was really their compatibility, and their drinking habits, and the depth of their religious beliefs, that Welfare was most interested in. It was easy to see that they were the kind of people who assumed responsibilities well, though. Of course, he would check all this with their friends and neighbors and business associates anyhow, also; that was part of the procedure, they understood of course. Now, why did they want to adopt a child? Frank and Agnes smiled at each other tenderly. After all, they already had a child, a daughter, of almost eighteen, the Welfare man smiled. And they were both of an age at which adopting a child was rather unusual and—in the majority of cases, of course; not theirs especially—was rather frowned upon. What did the eighteen year old daughter think of the adoption?

Agnes turned to look at Frank as the spokesman, and Frank had patted her gently on the hand. Well, his wife loved children; that was one thing. And—this was rather difficult and embarrassing to talk about— they had always hoped there would be others, after the first child came. For a moment tears threatened to come in his eyes. Of course, as the Welfare man knew, none ever had. Frank himself had always wanted a son; that was another thing. A son who could carry on his name, someone to whom he could leave his businesses and investments to be carried on for the family name. And, he spread his hands again, now that they had reached the place where they were—well, at least comfortably well off, he smiled—they had decided that the best thing they could do would be to adopt a boy who otherwise might never have an opportunity at these advantages. What could be nicer? Or more reasonable? As far as their daughter, Dawnie, went, she was away at her first year in Western Reserve now, but if the Welfare man wanted her address to write to her, he Frank would gladly give it to him. She had absolutely no sense of insecurity about the adoption, and was in fact all for it. They had discussed it with her frankly and openly at some length, before arriving at their decision. She had told them herself that she would not want the business and other interests, and would only liquidate them if they were left to her; and she herself told them in so many words that she thought they ought to adopt a boy. She was a very mature girl for her age. And naturally, of course, she would be well provided for in any future wills that might be made—she knew that, of course.

The Welfare man nodded smiling as Frank talked, and made more notes. And he did, in fact, take Dawn's address with him when he left. Someone probably would, in all probability, write to her, he said; although confidentially he himself did not deem it at all necessary. He did not believe he had ever seen a home, or a family or a situation, he told them before he left and after he had inspected the boy's future room, where he would rather have placed a child, and some little boy was in all probability going to be a very lucky young man with them. Of course, all this would take time; so they must not be too impatient. There was all the other checking to do of course, and Welfare was almost always literally besieged with requests for adoptions which kept them working overtime and made them slower than they would have liked; and of course there was the problem of first finding a suitable child. But the fact that Frank had decided he wanted a boy of six or seven would expedite matters considerably; most people preferred new-born babies and did not want to take the older children. He would begin his other checking as soon as possible. Also, he would probably drop in on them again between now and the time they got the boy, and also of course someone would be dropping in during the probation period before the adoption became legal in the courts.

The next time he returned, which was after they returned from Florida, he was even more full and higher in his praise of their home and "situation", as he called it. No one he had talked to in Parkman but what had had the highest regard and praise for the Hirshes, Frank and Agnes.

Frank knew beforehand that that would be the case, of course. The only thing that had really worried him any at all was the existence of the Old Man, and of Dave, in Parkman where the Welfare man might run onto mention of them. But he had mentioned them both himself during that first meeting there at the house, and had explained about his father running off in his youth and about him living up there in that pension home, and why, and about his younger brother who had gotten into trouble while still in high school and had turned out to be rather a ne'er-do-well. And so that had taken care of that. The Welfare man had nodded and smiled sympathetically and made some notes and explained that that sort of thing really had no effect at all upon a decision; things like that happened in just about every family, the very best of them, in one generation or another.

And so, in late January, he had received word that they could pick him up, probably the first week in February. Frank could hardly wait to see the little bugger. He was blond, and seven years old, and of German extraction like their own family, the Welfare man wrote; more than that, anything about his background or situation, it was against their policy to discuss. But he was satisfied that both of them would be immensely pleased with the boy and would love him dearly. Of course, if they ever wished they could at any time return him, if it did not work out during the "probation" period; and the Welfare people themselves had the right to remove the child if they thought that best; up until the final adoption was effected, of course.

The first thing they did immediately, of course, was to write Dawnie the news at school; to which they got back a high, happy, enthusiastic reply from her. And the first thing they planned to do as soon as he arrived was for Agnes to take him on a shopping spree in Indianapolis to get him more clothes and school things, and a flock of some sort of toys that he might want to pick out himself. He would go right into the second grade at school, the Welfare man wrote, in mid class, since he had already been going to school where he was; and in fact, had been doing exceptionally well.

Frank, of course,—something which Agnes knew nothing about—was going to have to break the news to Edith. He wanted to do it himself before the boy got here and she heard it somewhere else. If she had not already. But it was amazing, in view of the investigations the Welfare man had carried on in town apparently, how little the news of the impending adoption had got noised around. Perhaps he had asked his informants (several of whom had told him, or had told Agnes, that they had been approached) for secrecy.

Quite honestly, he was not too worried about how Edith would take it; but just the same he felt a little nervous about it. He was sure, by some instinct or other, that it would hurt her deeply. And he hated to have to do that. But Edith was a pretty solid girl; if she was hurt, she would keep it to herself. And he knew she would get over it before long.

He decided that he would do it, would definitely tell her, the next time they went out together. He had decided the same thing twice before, but both times when it came down to it, he had lost his nerve and been unable to tell her. He didnt know why he should be so worried about it. She probably wouldnt even care. But some sure, exact instinct in him warned him that he better *had* worry. Maybe it was only a sort of fatherly guilt, that he felt for her. Whatever it was, it had cost him a lot of sweat and anguish. The trouble was, he could not seem to find any natural, normal, simple way to bring the subject up—without just up and blurting it out. And if he did that, just blurted it out, it would show her that he felt he *had* to tell her, which in turn would make it look as though he himself thought there was something wrong with it, when in fact he didnt.

In fact, in a lot of ways, Frank thought suddenly—and with that crystal-sharp clarity suddenness sometimes brings—transfixed with a sort of shocked surprise, he seemed to be in the same identical state of sweat and anguish and anxiety with this about the adoption, as he had once been a few weeks earlier with sex.

Only now it was worse, because in addition to all that other, there was added that sharply poignant sense of warmth and affection and gratitude he had had for her ever since he had fully and unqualifiedly consummated—that was the way he always thought of it—their love affair. That had only been two weeks ago, and the newness had not even worn off yet. He would hate to lose that now. But then, he had been deathly scared of that too: afraid she might take it wrong and be horrified. But then that had worked out all right, hadnt it? At least it appeared to have. So then, why shouldnt this? It was just that he would hate to lose her now.

When he picked her up at the little bar out at Twelve Points in Terre Haute where they always met, after the letter from the Welfare man had come only two days before, he had definitely made up his mind to tell her. In truth, he had no other choice; she would find it out soon enough anyway, now. And if she found it out that way, instead of him telling her himself, it might be even worse. She might even quit him. They had a couple of drinks in the little bar, and then drove up toward Clinton, this time. To a little out-of-the-way place they sometimes went for dinner. And Frank, seeing a group of children walking along the street, had a desperate inspiration. Children: that was the answer! He could say something about the children, and from that lead into it naturally. But by the time he had thought of it, the group of children was already past. Well, the next bunch of kids he saw; that would do it. And he could explain to her how badly he had always wanted a son to carry on the business.

So the rest of the way to Clinton—about ten miles—he kept his weather eye out anxiously for children. He saw exactly none. All the way to Clinton, driving through Clinton out to the dinner place, at the dinner place itself where they had more drinks and ate, he saw not one child. Normally there would be at least two or three eating with their parents in the dinner place. But tonight, no. It was as if in an accurately timed conspiracy against him the entire world had suddenly become bereft of children, deliberately to deprive him of his opening wedge for what he had to say. Only when they finally reached the motel where they were going to spend their two or three hours of secret, illicit, dearly bought companionship, did he see a child: The motel manager's two young sons were sitting in plain view from the car in their father's office, raptly reading comic books.

Son of a damned bitch! Frank thought despairingly; because by then he had given up. Hell, he couldnt do it now. He could not. To tell her now while they were getting ready to go in and get their motelroom and go to it alone together and make love, he just simply could not do it. What if there was a scene? What if she blew up and cried and got mad at him and made him take her home? What if she quit him for good? right here and now, just when he was all ready and primed to go to bed? No! He couldnt do it. If this was going to be the last time he would ever get to make love to her, he was not going to sacrifice it right at the last minute; he would have to find some other way to tell her, afterwards, after they had *been* to bed. Then, at least, if she quit him, he would still have that last time to remember. Did that make him a cheater? Well, if it did, to hell with it. So he was a cheater.

But, luckily, when they got inside and settled in and Edith had begun to undress for him (she no longer had to betake herself shyly to the bathroom, now, to get undressed), Frank saw on the wall just beside the bureau where he set the whiskey bottle a framed full length painting of a child, a nine or ten year old boy. There was his excuse, as if God after deliberately mocking him all this time and proving to him his own lack of integrity, had suddenly relented and given him an out. And afterwards —what a soothing, peaceful, fully satisfied word—Afterwards, after they had talked, and drunk (Edith was much more used to drinking now than she had used to be), and had petted, and finally had gone ahead, and had made their love, he made himself get up when all he wanted to do was lie there peacefully and savor, and went over to the bureau to pour himself a drink and looked at the picture and commented to her on it and then came back, with the drink, and sat down on the bed and told her. He laid special stress on how he had always wanted a son to carry on the business, and his name.

Edith, lying back with her arms behind her head merely stared at him mutely and said nothing, did not answer. There were no tears in her eyes exactly, or anything like that, but there was pain in them as he had instinctively known there would be and he wanted to smash his fists deliberately bloody into the pastel-painted concrete-block wall, because she simply lay there and looked at him in that funny way as if he had suddenly and for no reason slapped her stingingly in the face.

Gradually he stumbled and faltered into silence. "I suppose it must be sort of a shock," he mumbled. "I dont suppose you had any idea about it."

"Oh, yes," she said faintly without moving. "Id heard about it."

"You did? Who told you?"

"Jane. She told me all about it."

"Jane! Well, God damn her! How did she find out?"

Edith smiled, faintly, weakly, without moving. "Who knows? Who knows how she ever finds out all she knows about everybody? I think sometimes she just divines about half of it. Ive been wondering when you were going to tell me."

"Well, Ill be damned," Frank said. Then he paused. "I hope it doesnt make you feel unhappy," he said.

Edith merely smiled, weakly, that same sad faint smile, looking at him out of her slapped-looking eyes that were not crying, and said nothing.

Frank waited, hoping she would say something, hoping she would say No, it didnt hurt her; but she still did not answer.

"I think I need a drink," he said, getting up and heading for the bureau.

"Bring me one too, will you?" Edith said.

He turned around and looked at her, searchingly, questingly, from the middle of the floor, and she smiled back at him.

"A good, big one!" she said cheerfully.

Frank stood, looking at her, looking silently and disconsolately at that small lithe big-muscled big-boned body, so different from the thinness of Geneve Lowe that he had also known, thinking back to—and about— that Wednesday night two weeks ago, when he also had not known, when he had not been sure either,—(She might yet still tonight say something, do something.)—then he went on to the bureau and the bottle, suffering, and wondering with a dim awe how here on God's earth the human race, anybody, everybody, could continue to suffer so: so silently, and so hopefully, so batteredly and stumpwornly: all those fears and hates and horrors and hurts and guilts, that had, for some Unknowable Unreasonable reason, been placed in them.

. . . . It was only another of their regular ordinary Wednesday (or Thursday or Tuesday or Friday) nights, except that he was a little drunker than usual. At least, it started out to be one. But it did not wind up one.

Another thing, of course, was that he had been doing an awful lot of reading in the past few months about this thing. Everything and anything he could get hold of about the subject, which was surprisingly damned little. Kinsey's book (which he still kept locked and hidden in his desk in a plain wrapper he had made for it; though he was ashamed and angry to have to do it like that; but what else could he do?) Kinsey's book was his greatest help and source of knowledge, largely because there was so damned little else even written about it. The information had all been suppressed, *almost everywhere*, as if some huge conspiracy were in action to keep him—and everybody else—in ignorance; as if that way, just by publicly denying its existence, it could be made in actual fact to not exist. A lie, of course; a false and also useless idea in the first

place. Because it did exist. And existed with surprising commonness, as
Kinsey's book showed with its chart of incidences and frequencies. But
as for— Well, he couldnt even conceive of even discussing it with his
wife. And of course, everyone felt like that, too, probably. And so what
did you tell your son? Or your daughter? You told them nothing, that
was what. You couldnt afford to. It was too dangerous. You just let them
find it all out like you had done: the hard way; on their own; sneaking
around guiltily, looking shamefacedly in hidden books; painfully,
anguishedly, frightened horrified and 'morally' terrorstruck; feeling sinful and evil and on the more terrified occasions thinking scaredly of
suicide. Some even went ahead. But of course that was never published
in the papers along with the suicide accounts.

But even without the reading, he probably would not have dared to
chance it with Edith if he had not been so drunk. But drunk as he was,
coupled to all the heavy reading on it he had been doing, he was at just
that mental state where he didnt give a damn. To hell with it! he thought
savagely. What if he did lose her? There were lots of others around,
werent there? They were lying together petting, and when the idea
struck him and he embraced it savagely, he got up and went and mixed
them both another drink, a really stiff one. —Might as well have everything on your side you can get: Every businessman knew that. Businessman! Businessman! Bastard! Bastard! And after they had drunk the
drink, he said: "Lay back. I want to show you something."

———————— Edith Barclay, feeling shock and alarm as he touched
her, shut her eyes. Fear and selfhorror rolled down over her diluting her
tenderness, but which nevertheless did not go away. She thought of
the soldier who had served in Paris, that she had almost married. Except
for this; and things like this. And then she thought of all those things
that she had always dreamed of having: even dreamed of *wanting*: The
home, the children, the security of a man who loved you, adored you
even, and for yourself, for the You of you. Those were the things she
had dreamed of having. And these were what shed got: the mistress of a
married man with a grown daughter—(And now a son; oh, she knew;
an *adopted* son); and more: mistress of a married man who *loved* his
wife; and more yet: a little piddling job of working for him, just to be
his lover. Like any chippy. Was there no limit to how low Love must
make you sink? No limit at all? Completely bottomless? Oh, it would
be easy to know what to do, if the tenderness had gone away. Oh, it
would be easy. But the tenderness had not gone. It was still there. Still
there, and perhaps even stronger than before: the poor guy. The poor,
haunted, painfilled, anguished guy. Oh, she knew hatred; she knew
it well; she knew it when she thought of that woman, that big fat beefy
loudvoiced dominating woman. Agnes. And he *loved* her: Agnes. From
the Greek that was: meant chaste, pure. She had even looked it up in

the Webster's Intercollegiate. That was how far gone she was. That was how low she had fallen. From the Edith Barclay she had someday meant to be. And now this too. And yet he loved her, loved her too also. In his way. And she clung to that. It wasnt much. Oh, it would be easy to know what to do, if she didnt love him. Oh, it would be easy. Edith submitted.——————

"Thats enough," Frank heard her say. "No more."

"Oh, God, I love you, Edith," he said tormentedly. "Oh, God." He kissed her on the neck and put his face against hers.

Edith patted him on his head, and as she did so, made up her mind—or, rather, found her mind was already made up for her. If she was going to stay—if she was going to be involved—she ought to be involved entirely; all the way involved. It was only fair.

"Now you lie back and relax," she said. ....

With the bottle in his hand Frank stood looking over at her, in this other, different, but somehow just the same motelroom that was not like the other, that was not like any of the others, or any of the other others, that they had been to, and yet was just exactly like them all. Then, starting inwardly and looking down at his hand that held it and coming back from a long long way away, he poured the drinks and carried them back to her in silence. What words were there to say? What words were there in existence anywhere that would say what he would have liked to say?

"That damned Jane," he said, sitting beside her on the bed. "She seems to know just about everything about *every*thing."

Edith lowered her glass, from which she had been drinking greedily like someone sucking in solace desperately. "Yes," she said cheerfully. "She does."

A thought struck Frank suddenly which, even in his wildest most hopeless moments, he had never considered before: "Do you suppose she knows about—about us—too?"

"If she did," Edith said, "I dont think she would ever tell that to anyone, do you?"

"No, I suppose not," he said without much belief. "You bein' her granddaughter and all." He took himself a drink.

"Yes," Edith said faintly. "I think she does know about us, as a matter of fact. She has never said anything to me about it; but I think she knows."

Frank nodded disconsolately, staring into his glass. Well? Well? There wasnt a whole hell of a lot you could do about it? Except just wait and hope she didnt talk? "Shes always hated my guts," he said gloomily.

"If shes hated you, shes also loved you a lot too, I think," Edith said. "Dont forget that."

Frank looked up at her. "You think she really has?" he said shyly. "Ive always liked her." He gulped a swallow of his drink and then stared down into his glass. "You know, Ive been meanin' to ask you about Janie for some time now. She dont look well to me. She dont look well at all."

"I know," Edith said faintly, in that peculiar almost soundless voice she got when she had to talk about something she would have perferred not to. "Ive tried to get her to go to a doctor about it, but she wont. She just laughs and says theres nothing wrong with her a good drunk wont cure."

"Shes lost an awful awful lot of weight. Ive noticed it lately."

"I know. She just says its good for her. But Im worried, and I dont like it. You know shes given up all her other jobs except at your house. Did you know that?"

"No," Frank said. "No, I didnt. She never mentioned it."

"Shes even given up working for your brother Dave and his gambler friend, 'Bama.—

("Those bastards!" Frank interjected.)

"—And I know she liked working there. But she says shes tired of all these other jobs, says its time she started to retire. But I know she liked working for Dave and 'Bama. She says shes been at your place the longest and so as long as she keeps on working anywhere thats where she should keep on working—and then laughs in a funny way and says: Unless she should get fired. You know Janie." She paused. "I dont know whats the matter," she said, "but I know she wouldnt quit any of her jobs if she was able to keep on doing them."

Frank was getting a little tired of Edith's grandmother. "Well, she aint as young as she used to be. She probably just drinks too much, I guess," he said moodily, staring at his own glass and then raised it up and took a long deep draught.

"No, no, I know it isnt that," Edith said; "she doesnt drink half as much as she used to." And suddenly, launching out from mid-leap as it were, she was off on one of those strange quick fast desperate strings of talking of hers, which were the only times she ever really talked much at all, this time about her grandmother. She had called her a whore once, she said anguishedly, called her a whore to her face. Once when she was mad. Her, of all people. To call Jane a whore. She went on and on, talking about when she was a little girl and Janie had took care of her, and about the time when Doris Fredric had broken her music box, the words tumbling out faster and faster until Frank could hardly follow their meaning.

He waited, hardly listening, until there came a pause and the beginning of a tapering off. "Well, you know, Ive always thought it would be good for you to get out and away from there," he said, once again for perhaps the hundredth time; "why dont you let me buy you that house for yourself like weve talked about? Hell, I could buy it tomorrow, with the credit Ive got up in Springfield now. Buy it through a Springfield agent, and nobody would ever know I had anything to do with it. Wouldnt have to be a big place, but you could furnish it like you wanted, and—"

"No, Frank," she said. "It wouldnt work. You know it wouldnt. Nobody would ever believe Id ever gotten enough money together to buy a house. And right away theyd start looking for the reason. Anyway," she said, "I dont want to leave Janie now."

Frank looked at her not knowing what else to say. Theyd been all over it many times before. It would make him feel so much better, if he could only just *give* her something, *buy* her something. Anything. But she never would take anything. If she just knew how much better it would make him feel—

He thought for a brief moment about saying something else about the adoption that might perhaps make her feel better, but quickly decided against it. It was better not to even bring it up again. He had told her; and that was what hed had to do. At least, he had told her, he told himself. At least he had done that. Nobody could ever say he hadnt told her.

"Well, I guess we better get on back home," he said wanly, wornly, and then for a moment sat watching her as she got up to dress. Never in his life again, he realized suddenly with a kind of miserable, desperate, murky anguish, would he ever enter a motelroom—or see one—or even drive past a damned motel, even—without thinking of Edith Barclay. What a chain that was to impose upon yourself.

God! he called silently, God! God?: what miseries, and guilts, and horrors, and terrors we all bind upon ourselves.

But of course, as soon as he let her out at the corner of Roosevelt and Wernz Avenue the mainstreet and drove on home, his happiness—all his happinesses—returned; and he could sit back and think of all of it with pleasure and satisfaction and comfort and release. Never in his life had he been so really truly happy.

CHAPTER 57

IF EITHER Dave or Wally—or for that matter, his own sophisticated daughter Dawn—had in some way known about Frank's moral anguishes and desperate fears concerning his sex life, they would have laughed out loud;—or else felt an adult's consummate but uncommunicable sympathy for him as a child. All of them had solved that problem for themselves long ago; Dave, a long long time ago; and Wally and Dawn, a younger generation still, had solved theirs last summer in the midst of their spirited love affair even before they had read any Kinsey.—

Although Dawn of course, perhaps, might have a different attitude now: now that she was engaged in that great and infinitely popular American preoccupation of changing lovers. It wouldnt have bothered Dave, though.

But what did bother Dave was the matter of old Janie Staley. When she came to them and quit, almost with tears in her eyes (he would have sworn it), it appeared to Dave as only one more manifestation of the downhill change which for some unknown reason had seemed to begin with the death of Raymond Cole.

Not only were Dewey and Hubie more troublesome and harder to handle, drunk almost all the time, but something had happened at Smitty's too. The oldtime sparkle and enjoyment their bunch had used to have there wasnt there any more; the life had gone out of it. And not only that, he and 'Bama had begun to lose at gambling. And now, on top of that, Janie had to quit them!

The change in the gambling wasnt really very noticeable. They were not losing dangerously. But there was still enough of a change for both of them to note it. For over a year now, ever since they had started it out in Florida last Christmastime, they had been winning consistently a far higher percentage of poker hands and money than could ever be explained away rationally or mathematically or logically. And now that percentage had started to go down. 'Bama sat up around the kitchen filling sheet after sheet with calculations by which he figured out averages and percentages of both the hands they won and the amounts of money, working at it delightedly and sparkling-eyed and interestedly, trying to formulate for himself some theory about winning and losing which he could prove positively, enchanted by and enjoying all of it with the dispassionate interest and elation of a research scientist, apparently feeling none of the sense of possible impending doom which Dave felt—or if he did feel it, not caring before this possibility of working out some theory on the percentages of winning, and proving it. They were, he said, looking up from his calculations, definitely losing more. It was very slight—as yet—, but there was a definite change, he said excitedly; he wanted to see if it kept on. And if so, why?

Dave knew as well as he did that if they *did* continue to lose more, if the percentages *did* keep on dropping, they would not be able to go on living like they were. The house, that new garden, all the things they were continually buying for both, the immensity of their liquor bill, the trips here and there, the freedom that comes only of having a more than adequate income; they would lose them all. And Dave wanted to keep them. He did not want to lose them; and that sense of deep impending doom settled over him lower and lower. But if it bothered him, it did not bother the happily calculating 'Bama at all.

What *could* be the cause? Dave wondered darkly. *Could* it be that in some strange way Raymond Cole was, after all, sort of their luckypiece? a living talisman? But how *could* that be? when they had started they had hardly ever seen Raymond; and they really started in Miami, not in Parkman—at least as a definite operation; and Raymond hadnt been there. Surely it *could* not be the act of Mildred Pierce getting married; that hadnt broken up the gang; it hadnt affected anything; one way or the other. It *couldnt* be that. The only other thing he could point to was his own having given up and withdrawn from the race for Gwen French, (if you could pardonably call it that); but how *could* that have affected anything? His relationship with Gwen didnt touch any of them, or have any visible—or invisible—effect on *their* lives. How *could* it be that?

But what else *could* it be? except one—or all—of those three? He didnt know of anything else it *could* be? When Jane Staley quit her job cleaning for them, he chalked up one more in a suspiciously growing list of mishaps, and continued to wonder murkily.

Could they have, he and 'Bama, together or separately, committed some great—great— . . . sin or other (it was the only word he could give it; the only word that fit, even though it embarrassed him: Great God! shades of Elvira Herschmidt, he thought distastefully)—some great sin, then, that they did not even know about? some sin of omission, or of commission, that neither of them was aware of? so that whatever power or force it was that had protected them had suddenly been withdrawn? He had, gloomily and despondently, been thinking more and more about the strange talk he had had with Bob—and after that with Gwen—and what they had said about reincarnation and about the Group of Masters or Spirits or whatever you wanted to call them Who were supposed to be in charge of everything and governing everything. Could there really be such a thing like that? Could They really exist like that? like Bob had said? And if so, even supposing they did, what would they ever have wanted to give luck to him and 'Bama for in the first place? He and 'Bama went against just about every moral law that everybody taught was right; hell, they went against just about every damned thing the Bible taught you you should do. Hell, even the damned Communists wouldnt want him and 'Bama, would think they were immoral. Why should these Masters or Spirits or whatever They were even be interested in two such "sinners" as him and 'Bama were? Why should They have given them this consistent luck—if that was what it was; was where it came from? And then why take it away? What had they ever done either to deserve it or to lose it?

And most of all, with a speechless voiceless almost unbelieving awe, he wondered about what Bob had said about artists, about writers, possibly being below—the very *greatest* of them just one step below—the lowest, lowliest Seeker or Disciple or whatever they called them. Jesus Christ! if that was so, that was *nowhere!* He him*self* was nowhere, but *nowhere!* Hell, he might as well be *dead!* *He* wasnt even a *great* writer! As the house settled immediately and inexorably into deterioration and muss and uncleanliness just one week after Jane was gone, he wondered gloomily and darkly, and tried to work on his book.

It had been a touching scene, that day she left. In the first place he knew there was something wrong with her; she wasnt well. He had tried to ask her about it several times before, but she only hooted raucously and gave a hollow laugh and denied it. He had been sitting in the front room reading in Gibbon's *Decline and Fall of the Roman Empire* (he had started in on that again lately, with renewed and heightened insight, now) that afternoon when she had come in to get her pay, and told him she was leaving them.

"My God, Janie! What for?" he said. "Have we done something? me and 'Bama?"

"Naw, it aint nothin like that, Dave," she said in her gravelly voice, staring at him out from behind those dark hollows around her eyes. "Hell, I like workin here better'n any other place I got. I really hate to leave. But I figured, by Christ, its about time I started in retirin a little bit, What the hell, Im sixty three now."

"Sure, but dont leave us. Hell, we need you. Leave somebody else. Are you leaving all your other people?"

"All but Frank and Agnes. Ive been with them the longest—so long I really got to stay there; as long as they want me. I had druther work here, but I feel I owe them that. But Im quittin all the rest." She grinned, wanly, tiredly. "The old hoss just aint what it used to be."

It wasnt, either. She had lost an enormous amount of weight and folds of skin hung from her like draped curtains. The big dark-circles around her large dark eyes had steadily gotten bigger and bigger and darker and darker and deeper and deeper, making her eyes seem even larger and more dark. Dave looked her over thoughtfully, while she grinned back at him independently. But her heart really wasnt in it.

"Lets go out in the kitchen and have a bottle of beer and talk it over," he said.

"No," she said; "it wouldnt do no good, Dave. And anyway Ive about quit drinkin beer and whiskey. Its hard enough leavin anyway and stringin it outll only make it worser."

"Janie, are you sick?" he said.

For a moment Jane looked startled. "Sick? Sick? What do you mean, sick?"

"Well, you know. Youve lost an awful lot of weight lately and all."

"Oh. Naw, I aint sick," she said, looking vaguely relieved. "Hell, no. Healthier'n I ever been in my life. I just been on a diet, and Ive bout quit drinkin. Dont you go worryin about me, honey. If you was half as healthy as I am, youd be fine."

"Well, we sure do wish youd stay," he said, and looked back up at her, hopefully, questioningly. But she only shook her head, silently. That was when he would have sworn he saw tears in the large dark deep-circled eyes; or, if the tears werent actually there, they were very close to being there. "Do you know of anybody else we could get to take your place?"

"Naw, honey," Jane said, and a trifle of her old truculent vitality came back into her raucous grin. "I dont know a soul. I dont hang around with none of the other cleanin women in this town, and they dont hang around with me. I aint quite respectable enough for them, you know." She hooted out a raucous gravelly laugh. "And they aint respectable enough for *me*."

"Well, come on," Dave said. He got up and slapped her on her still-thick broad back. "Come on, Ill take you home. I guess we'll be able to find somebody eventually."

When she got laboriously out of the car in front of the little non-descript house on Roosevelt Drive, she stopped and turned back and smiled at him. "Well, so long, Dave honey. Ill see you sometime."

"Maybe down at Smitty's," Dave said.

"Sure. Maybe there," Jane said. He watched her into the house and then beeped the Plymouth's horn, and when he drove on around the circle and came back out on Hull he was choked up himself and there were tears in his own eyes. He didnt know why exactly. But something was wrong; she was sick, or something; anyway something was wrong somewhere. Why did he seem to have this damned feeling of impending doom all the time? And of course, he thought as he shook it off, he had always been sentimental about old Janie, all his life. Ever since he was a kid and she used to babysit him.

It was Gwen French who got them another cleaning woman finally. He had continued going over there once or twice a week after the College had reconvened on January 3rd; even though he had more or less given up on the love affair, she was still helping him with his book—and helping him immensely. It was the 25th of January when Janie worked her last day and left them, and the house was bad enough after the first week; but after the second week it went from bad to worse. He and 'Bama tried to slick it up a little, but they could only awkwardly scut the surface dirt without making any inroad on the deepdown real dirt, and ashtrays that were emptied and washed one day were already filled and overflowing and smelling stale the next; too many people were hanging out there too indifferently, and drinking and smoking far too much. Probably it wouldnt have bothered them eight months or a year ago, but they had had it too good—with Janie's consummate slick cleaning and polishing; they had gotten too used to that, and now without it it was horrible. Dave could only sit in his little writing room, which was not clean either, and stagnate on his novel. When Gwen finally commented gently on how his work had fallen off in volume, he told her what was causing it: (about Janie, that is; he did not tell her the rest of it about the bad poker luck and the growing list of mishaps); and she had said she would see if she couldnt get her own cleaning lady to work for them. That was the middle of February, and he had been sleeping with Ginnie Moorehead again for almost a month—since a week before Janie left, in fact.

Gwen's cleaning lady was a Negro woman and a devout Methodist. She and her husband had worked for Bob and his wife, and later for Gwen, for years and years. There were three Negro families in Israel (There were none in Parkman.) and all three of them had been there for generations, going almost as far back as the Civil War, in fact; and all of them belonged to the Israel Methodist Church. Most of the children, when they grew up, moved away—to Terre Haute, or to Chicago, or to Indianapolis; but out of every generation one son or daughter invariably married and stayed in Israel, and the three families (their names changing once in a while, when it was a daughter who stayed) continued to live there. They worked as caretakers and cleaning ladies for the ex-Kentuckians who mostly populated Israel, and their sons were a constant thorn in the side and the perpetual bane of Parkman High School, who could never beat Israel High School in football or basketball or track whenever one or more of the Leesbeck, Wilson or Totter boys were playing. One of the Wilson boys, a bachelor, whose nickname was for some reason "Squab" and who had been a magnificent baseball player in his youth and might have been another Jackie Robinson had he been born twenty years later, had stayed and set up as a barber and cut the hair of all the ex-Kentuckians of Israel because the ex-Kentuckians wouldnt go anywhere else or let anybody else cut their hair. Gwen's cleaning lady's name was Shardine; Shardine Jones. She had been one of the Leesbecks but had married a man named Jones from Terre Haute. Dave had met her many times over at the house in Israel. She was to come and clean for them in Parkman one day a week on Thursday, at Gwen's suggestion, for a dollar an hour. Her husband was to drive her over from Israel in the morning and pick her up that evening. She came and worked one day—and left and refused to come back. And Dave murkily chalked up one more item in his swiftly growing list of mishaps.

It was, actually, more or less Ginnie Moorehead's fault about the new cleaning lady quitting. It wasnt that Ginnie really did anything, or said anything. This was truly a Sin of Omission—or more accurately, if there was such a term, a Sin of Appearance: All Ginnie did was come in the house in the late afternoon after she got off work at the brassiere factory and sit down at the kitchen table while Shardine Jones was still there. She did not even mix herself a drink, just sat down. But it was enough.

Shardine Jones was a good-looking Negro woman of thirty six or eight;

she certainly did not look as though she had six small children at home. She had been more or less skittish and jittery all day. 'Bama, of course, had got up and got out as was his custom, and Shardine had only had a brief glimpse of him, but it was enough—as Dave who happened to be near noticed—to widen the whites of her great dark beautiful eyes. Dave himself of course was around all day (trying to work) and that probably did not ease her any. Also, he made the mistake of inviting her to eat with him because he was trying to show he was friendly and did not believe in race segregation. Shardine merely stared at him, almost contemptuously, as if she had never truly seen him before when she saw him over at the Frenches, and declined politely. Neither would she eat at all while he was in the kitchen. Finally, by peeking clandestinely around the door of his writing room and down the hall (his work was all shot to hell for the day anyway), he was able to see that she actually did rather gingerly get herself a tiny little something out of the icebox and eat it. Ginnie coming in was evidently the last straw.

Shardine did not say anything; or do anything either. She went right ahead and finished up her work carefully and meticulously, (she was an excellent cleaner), still looking skittish and jittery, infinitely polite, and when her husband arrived promptly on time came to Dave for her money. He paid her, and she thanked him very politely, and did not say anything—not a single word—about the fact that she was not coming back. In fact, it was only a few days later when he was over at the house in Israel that he even found out at all that she was *not* coming back, when Gwen solemnly—(but unable to keep from laughing a little)—told him the story.

Naturally of course, he did not know that Gwen, because she was so delicately sensitive of his feelings concerning her and her mythical love life, did not tell him the whole story which was the reason for her laughing. How could he have known that?

————————Shardine Jones had had her husband drive her directly to Gwen's house when she left the house in Parkman. She and her husband did not even go home first, and they did not stop—or for that matter, even slow down—on the way.

Gwen was already home from the College and was sitting before the big fire (which Shardine's husband took excellent care of) grading some papers, when Shardine burst nervously and indignantly upon her through the back door. Her husband had apparently been ordered to remain out in the car.

"Miss Gwen, I not going to work at that place," she said, jitterishly, but furiously. "What kind of a place you trying to send me to, Miss Gwen?" She was quivering with rage, and outrage, all over.

SOME CAME RUNNING

"Why, Shardine!" Gwen said, genuinely alarmed. "What happened? Did somebody do something to you?"

"No; and they never going to!" Shardine said furiously. "What kind of a place you trying to send me to, Miss Gwen? You never told me that gambler 'Bama Dillert lived there. Im a respectable married woman. I got six children at home. You dont think I going to work at a place like that, do you?"

"Well, I never thought about it," Gwen said, startled. "Whats the matter with it?"

"What the *matter* with it!" Shardine cried, setting her jaw, her great dark eyes snapping. "Why, its the worse house of sin I was ever in in my life! Its a regular den of iniquity. Those people theyre the spawn of the Devil, the worst lowlife bums and white trash in this part of the country. That Dewey Cole fum Parkman and that Hubie Murson they both hangs out there with them chippies of theirs from the brassiere factory. There a whole *cabinet* full of liquor bottles in the kitchen. They aint hardly got room for no food for the liquor bottles. They dont work, neither do they sow nor reap. All they do is sit around that place and smoke cigarettes and drink and *gamble*. Why, they the worst lowlife scum in this county. You think I going to work for people like that?"

"Well, I never thought," Gwen said helplessly.

"And then when I finishing up the work, what you think comes walkin in? That Ginnie Moorehead from the brassiere factory. Shes the worst hore in Parkman! Just comes walkin in and sits right down as nice as you please! I dont know which one of all of them *shes* sleepin with. Maybe with all of them. No, sir, Miss Gwen; I not working for any people like that. I dont think you knew where you was sending me."

"Well, youve met Dave over here before; lots of times. I always thought you liked him."

"I never knew the kind of people he run around with. Why there aint a decent respectable person in Parkman who will even talk to those people. If that Dave's a writer, hes shore a immoral one."

And Gwen, thinking of her lover warmly, had to grin at that one. "Most writers are, Shardine."

"Well, thats fine," Shardine said, setting her jaw stolidly. "Thats fine. But I aint a writer. Im a respectable married woman. And I mean to stay that way. I go to church, and I got a good reputation. Everybody knows me knows I have. Those people aint got *no* reputation. Theyre trash and scum and bums and gamblers and just plain immoral. The ony thing I will have to do with people like that is to pray for them at church. But I shore wont work for them. And thats all."

"Well, you certainly dont have to, Shardine, certainly," Gwen said, "if you dont want to. I had no idea youd feel like that."

"Well, thats how I feel," Shardine said. "I love you, Miss Gwen. And

I love your father and I loved your mother. I worked for your father and
your mother most of my life even when they lived in Parkman and Ive
worked for you. Youre a fine lady and a sweet girl. If you want to associate with that kind of trash, thats your business. But I aint just about to.
What would become of my reputation if I worked over there? Even if
nobody did try to do anything to me? Why, you dont know what maybe
goes on in that place! No, sir, Miss Gwen. I wouldnt never work for no
people like that. If you want to associate with them, you go right ahead
and Ill pray for you at church, too. But I aint about to."

And that was the end of it. Even if she knew it meant not working
for Gwen any more, Shardine said, she would not work for Parkman's
house of sin. Why, everybody in town knew about it. She just hadnt
known where she was going. Gwen, working hard to conceal her tendency to grin, assured her that she certainly didnt have to work there if
she didnt want to, and that it made no difference at all about her working
here for her.

And as she watched her leave,—(realizing now why she had prudenti-
ally made her husband Jim stay out in the car)—, Shardine's back still
stiff with righteous outrage, she could not help but laugh a little. What
made her laugh was thinking about her own lurid if mythical reputation.
Shardine must know about that, too; she must; everybody else did. Gag
at a gnat and swallow a camel. But then of course she was 'Miss Gwen':
Mister Bob and Miss Nelle's girl. That made a difference, she thought
laughing, and thinking warmly of Dave and of all the remarkable things
about his friend 'Bama that he had told them.

This, of course, was what she could not tell Dave, when she told him
the story. In the first place she couldnt talk about her reputation with
Dave at all; certainly she could not tell him the truth. And in the second
place she was too delicately aware of how it might hurt and upset him
if she pretended that the reputation was the truth. He was walking a
very thin, finely balanced line as it was, on account of her, she knew.
He was having a hard enough time swallowing her foibles and stipulations without reminding him of all the lovers she was supposed to have
had. But he was making a valiant effort, that she knew too. And someday,
she thought warmly—Someday—But it wouldnt do to tell him any of
that now.————

Dave, when she told him the story, was as righteously indignant—as
Gwen herself told him—and as furiously angry, as Shardine had been.
The fact that he could detect the laughter which Gwen was trying so
hard to hide did not help his outrage any, either.

"What the hell?" he said savagely. "Who the hell is that damned
bitch to pass judgment on my morals? You think I liked having her in
the house? She jittered around all day like she thought any minute some-

body was going to throw her down and rape her. I got no work done at all, for her jittering around, always making me aware of her being there. I want a damned cleaning woman who goes her own way and does her work and dont make me aware of her personality all the time."

"So does everyone else in the world," Gwen grinned. "If you ever find out how to train them like that, you could make a fortune. In the East they may have servants like that. Not in the great independent Middle West."

"If you ask me," Dave said savagely, "the reason shes so damned teed off is that nobody *did* throw her down and rape her."

Gwen laughed, a rippling little trill that she choked off immediately, and that sounded like a rill of water finally trickling out of an overfilled receptacle. "Thats the history of all cleaning ladies, isnt it?" she said. "For that matter, its the history of all *women*, isnt it?" she added gently.

"Yeah? What the hell are you laughing at so for," Dave said furiously. He was thinking concentratedly and one-mindedly of Shardine.

"Im laughing because you look and sound just exactly as furiously indignant and righteously outraged as Shardine did when she came in to tell me she wouldnt go back."

That stopped him. And he tried to recover his equanimity. He had to grin ruefully. "Youre pretty damned smart, arent you?"

"No smarter than I should be," Gwen said sadly. "I can assure you."

"Well, it isnt the woman Im mad at. She probably cant help it. Its the principle of the thing. Its the damned dumb moralists like her who are ruining the damned world. And dont think theyre not dangerous!"

"Dont start philosophizing about your principles to me," Gwen smiled. "Ive heard it all before. You were just plain mad."

Dave could only shake his head, dismayed that she did not understand, perturbed because he had not made clear what a very strong force for harm this moralism in the world was.

Finally, after another week of muss without a cleaning lady, the two of them—he and 'Bama—held a desperate conference and decided upon an equally desperate decision. They hired Dewey Cole's mother, aware that she would be willing to work for them forever. In addition to being a member in good standing of the Church of Christ, Saved, Mrs 'Possum' Cole (whose name was Vona) was the biggest and perhaps the most potent gossip in Parkman. A tiny roly-poly woman with a shoe-button nose in a round face, she was not half the cleaner that either Shardine Jones or old Janie were, but she was more than willing to work for them just so that—along with her money—she could carry away any choice gleanings of gossip she might be able to uncover there in that obviously fertile field. While doing this she made it plain to them that she did not ordinarily engage in cleaning work and in fact would not be working for them at all if it were not that her son Dewey was such a good friend of theirs. Because of this she was willing to do them this favor, she said;— although both of them knew for a fact, as did everyone else in town of course, that she cleaned elsewhere and made most of hers, and Possum's, living at it. Also, she loved to talk. It soon became apparent that in her eyes at least her son Dewey could do nothing wrong. She was positive that Dewey did not drink at all; if at times he appeared to be dizzy, it was because of his headaches; he had had these terrible headaches ever since he was a small boy, Vona said. Besides, no son of hers could ever be a drunkard. She never mentioned her other son Raymond at all, and to all intents and purposes as she went merrily and whistling about her work while keeping her beady eyes open to see what she could see and carry away to tell, she was not in the least disturbed because he was dead. Dewey—naturally—flatly refused to come to the house on the days his mom was there which was Tuesday; he had no use for her at all, and would only look disgusted whenever she was mentioned—although he would never say anything about her neither good *nor* bad. Doris Fredric, also, never appeared at the house on Tuesdays when Vona came, at her own suggestion. The sum result, then, was that every week Tuesday became a big operation and an ordeal. Monday night Dave and 'Bama— and whoever else was there—would go carefully through the house searching for and removing any evidences that might in any way be construed by Vona as remainders from some previous orgy, (lipsticked cigarette butts, for instance), and all liquor bottles would be locked up in their cabinet. Stray bobby pins were another hard-to-locate item; they never seemed to find them all. Vona did, though; and always laid them carefully on the countertop next the lavatory in the bathroom in a neat little very conspicuous pile. Tuesday morning 'Bama, who invariably slept until ten thirty or eleven would have his alarm set for six thirty and would be up and gone and out of the house by the time Vona came. He couldnt stand her either. Dave, whose profession forced him to stay home and who was not that lucky, would lock himself in his little writing room where he spent most of the day running his fingers frantically through his hair while he stared at his unused typewriter and listened to Vona whistle as she worked. He would not eat lunch with her in the kitchen because she talked all the time and would even forget to go back to work. And while he had once loved to listen to old Janie's gossip, which had behind it the hand of a native master psychologist, Vona's gossip had a peculiarly unpleasant and malicious salaciousness about it which upset him. At five thirty he would come out and pay her and she would leave and he would hurry to the kitchen and unlock the liquor cabinet and mix himself a stiff double Martini. Consequently, Tuesday became more and more of an ordeal every week—just in order to get the house cleaned. It was nervewracking. It got so finally that almost as soon as one Tuesday was over and the sigh of relief heaved, the next Tuesday had already begun to haunt them and hang ominously over their heads. All just to get the damned house cleaned. Dave brooded over it, and in the end was forced once again to once more gloomily and darkly chalk up another item in that steadily growing list of mishaps and bad luck that had begun to dog them: One of them had been *not* having the house cleaned. Now *having* the house cleaned was another.

God! he wondered somberly. Was it going to keep going on like this indefinitely? further and further? worse and worse? Hell, percentages alone would make it change some time, wouldnt they? —Or would they? Percentages hadnt made the *good* luck change, had they? Also—as the eagerly interested 'Bama kept him informed—they were still continuing to lose more at poker, and their percentages were still—slowly it was true, but apparently also inexorably—spiraling down.

He could not free himself of this inexplicable sense of an impending portentous Doom with a capital D hanging over them, of something out of tune somewhere, of something slightly off balance. But what was it? What *could* it be?

More and more he found himself darkly and unpleasantly remembering that chill night last fall—when drunk, exhausted and somnambulant (or could you almost call it clairvoyant?) he had lain beside Ginnie on the patio-porch and listened to Lois crying inside the kitchen to Dewey who only laughed, and had had that ominous doomed feeling of something infinitely dangerous to all of them crouching over them in the dark and only waiting its time to pounce.

It was probably all this: this brooding over their Fate, so to speak— that made him blow up and throw a tirade and viciously and deliberately insult the ubiquitous Ginnie Moorehead one night. She had been hanging around more and more, making herself more and more perpetually present, more and more at home, not unlike an overly affectionate dog who in the excess of his affection keeps getting underfoot and tripping you up while getting stepped on himself. In this instance, Ginnie got stepped on good. It happened one evening just a few days after his story "The Confederate" had come out in mid-February and made its appearance at the local newsstand—(the bus station, he thought bitterly and almost frightenedly; the bus station, remember?)—in the paperback *New Living Literature* semi-annual anthology of *New American Writing*.

Dave had not known just exactly what to expect from Parkman when his story should appear on the stands. (Maybe itll win the Ig-Nobel Prize, he told himself laughing.) There was no real bookstore in Parkman, but both the drugstores as well as the newsstand-bus station sold a few books along with their myriad newspapers and magazines and comic-books; a very few of the books were hard-cover volumes, but most of them were the paperback pocketbooks which were becoming such a big thing. So a few copies of *NLL's New American Writing* ought to filter down to Parkman. Even so, he did not delude himself with the illusion that there would be a big night of public fireworks, or that the town would declare a legal holiday, or perhaps vote him in as Man Of The Year. He had been all through all that long ago out in Hollywood when his first novel came out. He did not haunt the newsstand looking for it; he would not let himself do that; he would not give them that much pleasure. The lady-editor at *NLL* sent him four gratis copies of the little volume which he looked over, showed off at the house, then filed away and forgot about. The truth was, "The Confederate" no longer really interested him at all now that all the work with it was done. He was through with it and it bored him.

But still, just the same, he had thought there would perhaps be some little comment on it by someone or other. What in fact happened was nothing. Abso*lute*ly nothing. A few of the denizens from Smitty's such as Gus Nernst and one-armed Eddie the bartender, and even Smitty himself, approached him smiling shamefacedly and clearing their throats told him they had read it and enjoyed it, especially that knife fight scene. About three weeks later he learned from 'Bama, who had none of his compunctions and was as always still the same old loyal proud partisan whenever it came to Dave's writing, and who had discussed it with the man at the newsstand, that in fact he as well as the drugstores had sold an unusually large number of copies and had had to reorder three or four times. Nevertheless, when Dave himself was uptown or at the grocery or shopping somewhere, not a single one of the respectable citizenry of Parkman ever let on that the story had even been written or ever mentioned it to him. Except for one, that is: Two days after the anthology first appeared at the newsstand his brother Frank called him up at the house in a fury of choked outrage (the first time Frank had ever called the number of the house since they had taken it), and asked him—hardly able to do more than whisper in his anger—secretively to meet him out in the north end of town near the College on a side street. He would be driving his new Cadillac, he said.

"Park your car and get in," Frank said coldly, when he had driven out there and pulled up beside the pale blue Cadillac which sparkled like a jewel in a dust bin amongst the poorer low class houses, none of which probably cost as much as it did. "Bring your keys," he commanded. "I want to talk to you."

"Okay, what is it?" Dave said after he had slipped into the seat beside his brother. He had no idea what could be the matter. He did not even know the anthology had appeared in town as yet. "Why all the secrecy? The FBI after you?"

Frank did not bother to answer the joke but slid the Cadillac in gear and moved smoothly off. The car had that fresh-leather, brand-new smell, rich and expensive. Frank did not say anything for several moments but took several deep quivering breaths, his face set like a block of stone.

"What the hell are you tryin' to do to me?" he growled finally. "Why are you always tryin' to damage me and hurt me?"

"First maybe youd better tell me what Ive done?" Dave said.

"This!" Frank snarled savagely. "As if you didnt know." He pulled a copy of the *NLL* anthology out of his topcoat pocket and dropped it on the seat. "Thats what youve done!"

"Oh, the story," Dave said, pleased. "Have you read it?"

"Read it? Hell no, I havent read it! What the hell would I want to read it for? I aint interested in Confederates."

"I thought maybe you might want to read it because I wrote it."

"I dont need to read it. All I needed to do was read the damned name you stuck on it!"

"Oh. The 'Herschmidt'. Sure." If Dave had ever once thought of what effect his name change might have on Frank, he had forgotten it so long ago and become so used to it as his penname in his thinking that it had never recurred to him.

"Yas the Herschmidt sure!" Frank said furiously, "damn you. If you wanted to make a laughingstock out of me in this town, youve sure as hell succeeded." He looked down savagely at the book, then snatched it back up and stuck it back in his pocket as if he physically could not stand the sight of it. "These damned things are everywhere in town. Both the drugstores and the newsstand are selling them."

"Well, to *hell* with you!" Dave said incandescently, "so what about it?" As he spoke Frank's face jerked sideways at him, suddenly, eyeingly, almost as if he were expecting to be hit. "Dont worry," Dave snorted malevolently; "I aint going to hit you."

"You damn right youre not," Frank said coldly. "If you did Id have you in jail so damned quick it would make your damned head swim."

"Yes, I bet you would too," Dave said bleakly. Rage was building up in him to a pressure that equaled Frank's. The pompous son of a bitch: he didnt even *read* the damned story!

"Youre damned right I would," Frank said. He was still driving the Cadillac, cruising slowly around the north end of town, until they were now at the College grounds. It was cold and patches of snow still lay on the ground in the shade and no one was in evidence outdoors. Inside, electric lights burned in all the rooms. Taking a deep quivering breath of anger, Frank turned in onto the curving blacktop road that wound across the grounds.

"Arent you afraid somebody might look out a window and see you with me?" Dave said sarcastically.

"They couldnt see us from that far away," Frank said automatically, as if he had already considered it. "All my life Ive been tryin' to live that damned name down in this town. First the Old Man and then you. Right now everybody in this stinkin' town is laughin' up their sleeve at me. Well, if you wanted to pick a good way to hurt me, you sure as hell succeeded this time."

"Look. Lets get something straight. I dont give a damn about you one way or the other. I used the name because its my name. My legal name. Im not ashamed of having it."

"No!" Frank said explosively. "No, it isnt your legal name, either. When I changed our name to Hirsh, you were my ward. Legally. That changed your name to Hirsh too. Legally. Legally your name is Hirsh, not Herschmidt."

"Legal or not, it was the name I was born with," Dave said, "and like I said I aint ashamed of it—like you are. Maybe I better go up to the County Judge and get my name changed back to what it ought to be."

Frank did not say anything for a moment. "Yes, why dont you?" he said thinly; "you could make it a lot worse by doin' that than it already is. Yes, why dont you do that. Thats what you ought to do. You could hurt me even more that way."

"Maybe Ill just do that," Dave said coldly.

"Why dont you?" Frank continued to drive them on around the curving roads of the campus, past the deserted tennis courts, the deserted football fields, the deserted baseball diamond. "What did you want to do that to me for?" he said finally. It sounded almost pleading.

"I—" Dave said and stopped. Inwardly he blanched at ever attempting to explain to someone like Frank the value he had felt it would be to him as a writer to change his writing name. "I did it because my other two novels were published under the name of Hirsh and they were both poor. I wanted a different name, thats all."

"Then why didnt you pick Jones? or Smith? or Epstein? or Gordon or Wernz or Slobowski? Why did you have to pick *Herschmidt*?"

"Because it was my real name. I thought it might bring me—bring me luck. Or something."

"Luck!" Frank almost yelled. "Yes, it sure ought to bring you luck! Thats a lucky name all right, Herschmidt is. A very lucky name."

"Well, Ive used it; and I mean to go right on using it. On everything I publish. Any more stories I write, and my novel when I get it done. And I dont see that theres a whole hell of a lot you can do about it," Dave said coldly.

"Why dont you get out of this town and stay out of it?" Frank said, almost hopefully. "What the hell do you want to live here for, anyway? A hick town like this. You dont like it. You never did. Why not just leave? If its money you need, I can help you out with some money."

"Because Im not ready to leave. When I do leave, Ill leave because *I* want to go, and *Ive* decided. Not because anybody else tells me to."

Frank shook his head and turned the car around and started back toward the tall brick fenceless gate. "What do you hate me so much for?" he said. "Seriously: What have I ever done to you to make you hate me as much as you do and always be tryin' to hurt me and make a laughingstock out of me? What have I ever done to you?" He turned right at the gate, then left back down the sidestreet where they had left Dave's car.

"Just run me off from home," Dave said. "At the tender age of seventeen, and before I could even finish highschool. —And with five dollars in my pocket. *Five dollars.*"

"That was for your own good," Frank said. "As for the five dollars, I didnt have much money at the time, then."

"You had enough you could have given me more than that. And there wasnt any need to run me off at all."

"Would you rather have stayed and married that farm girl?" Frank said caustically. "Have you ever seen her since you got back? Big fat sloppy farm wife, with eight or nine kids some of them grown? Would you rather done that?"

"We could have got me out of marrying her without having to run me off."

Frank stopped beside Dave's little Plymouth and rubbed his hand over his face a moment. "Well, maybe I made a mistake. Okay: I *made* a mistake. I was thinkin' of the fam'ly at the time, and of the fam'ly's reputation. That was right at the time when the Old Man had just got back, and the scandal was at its height again. But maybe I made a mistake. Okay. Is there any reason to hold that against me the rest of my life and hate me for it and try to hurt me and get me laughed at? Is it?"

"Damn you, I dont hate you!" Dave almost shouted. "I dont try to hurt you! I told you why I changed my name back and you didnt even listen. You were so damned full of your own worries about your reputation that you didnt ever hear me. Hell, I dont hate you! I just think youre so full of self-pity that it runs out of your ears, thats all! Youre so goddamned worried about your goddamned reputation alla time that you cant see nobody else ina world but you!"

"Well, it looks like somebody's got to worry about it," Frank said thinly. "You sure dont. And the Old Man dont." He rubbed his hand over his face again. "Go on, get out," he said from under his hand. "Get out and go on back and see if you cant think up somethin' else to cause me trouble."

"Why you miserable dumb son of a bitch!" Dave yelled. "Sure. Sure Ill get out. And Ill be careful not to tell anybody you drove up here on the side streets to meet me, you sniveling bastard. So it wont hurt your reputation any."

"Thanks," Frank said thinly. "Just do me one favor, will you?" he said hollowly. "Just forget you ever had a brother named Frank Hirsh who raised you and took care of you and fed you and put you through school, will you? Just try and forget you got a brother named Frank. Will you do that for me? Maybe then youll stop tryin' to think up new ways of causin' me trouble and embarrassment."

"Sure I will, you respectable son of a bitch!" Dave cried. "Oh, boy, are you respectable! Youre so *damned* respectable you cant even *think* something unless the damn board at the Country Club tells you its all right to think it! Sure I will! And you just forget what a hard time you had trying to raise your younger brother to be like you. *You* forget *you* got a younger brother."

He got out and slammed the door. Frank sat behind the wheel looking across and through the closed window glass at him for a moment, and he stood staring back. Then Frank and the new pale blue Cadillac with its beautiful fishtail taillights pulled away from in front of him slowly, leaving him still staring, but at his own little Plymouth now. And as he walked across the street and climbed into it, he could not escape the feeling that just there, as they had stared at each other in silence for one timeless infinite second through the window glass, four eyes staring, without anger, without warmth, without sadness, without anything, and without all the garbage of personality and emotions, or the extraneousness of physical bodies, just four eyes staring at each other through a window glass, that just there two meager souls of two meager men had met and recognized each other as both had always tried to do and failed, had recognized and understood, or at least sensed, each other for what they both were, with all the meager pity that was at their command at least, even if it was not much. And once again Dave had that strange dark feeling of impending Doom and foreboding that had been engulfing him so much lately. The thought struck him, unreasonably, that he might not ever see his brother again and what a leavetaking. It was unreasonable because he would surely see him, if only on the street. Furiously, he slammed in the clutch and started the motor and threw the little Plymouth into gear and drove away.

Perhaps his run-in with Frank had a lot to do with his jumping onto Ginnie. Certainly his brooding over this feeling of impending Doom did, and all the bad luck they had been having.

It started when he was driving her home to the house from Smitty's the next night after he had seen Frank. He was still brooding about his "interview" with Frank, and continued to for some time. Ginnie was excited about the appearance of "The Confederate" too, but not exactly in the same way Frank was: Ginnie was proud of it. She had evidently in her slow dull way discovered that in a small way at least she was basking in reflected glory from it because she was—at least, among the brassiere factory set—Dave's "girlfriend".

"Everybody's been congratulatin me about your story," she said complacently, as he cut over from North Main to Plum to avoid the square. Behind them North Main the crossstreet stretched away down the hill between the rows of big trees, bare now, and the slush-covered curbs, to the railroad and Smitty's just beyond it.

"Congratulating *you!*" Dave said.

"Yes," Ginnie said. She had taken to saying Yes quite a bit lately, instead of Yeah; that was the Doris Fredric influence. "You know. Because Im sort of a friend of yours like."

"Yeh?" Dave said. "Who?" He had made the stop for Wernz Avenue the mainstreet now, and then crossed it on Plum heading south toward Lincoln the next street.

"Oh, all of the girls. Theyve all told me how much they liked it," Ginnie said complacently. "And a lot of the fellows, too," she added hastily.

"Well, its the first Ive heard about it. Nobody's said anything to me," Dave said, a little irascibly. They were just passing the Hirsh Bros. Taxi Service on Plum, which was not closed yet. It was only ten o'clock. And he could look in and see Albie Shipe sitting at the old desk laboriously writing up his reports. He ought to stop in and see old Albie; he had been meaning to for months. The emotion of the taxi service during those early months when he had worked there leaped into him fullblown with all its many nuances, total, complete, exactly as he had felt it then, making him feel sad and even angrier. It had really been fun, and nice, in a lot of ways. He ought to write something about that some day; maybe he could get rid of it that way. "Have you read it yet?" he said.

"Well, no. I aint," Ginnie said. "I want to be able to sit down with it all alone so I can really concentrate on it good. But I bought a copy. In fact I bought nine copies."

"*Nine* copies!" Dave said. He had reached the City Hall at the end of the block,—Sherm Ruedy's stamping ground, he thought—,and he turned west on Lincoln. "Why *nine?*"

"Well," Ginnie said complacently, "I brought one for myself you see. The other eight I autographed and give to some of the girls out the factory."

"You did what!!" Dave cried.

Ginnie's complacent look faded, and was replaced by that dull-faced, nervous, eye-darting look she got whenever anybody shouted at her or took her to task for anything. "Well, yeh," she said nervously; "what was wrong with that? I just wrote their names in them and put: 'I hope you like it' and then signed them. Just to a few of the girls, you know; like Mildred Pierce—I mean Bell—and Lois and girls like that. I thought it would be good publicity for you," she added placatingly.

Dave groaned. "Look!" he said. "You just dont go around autographing somebody else's story to anybody you want to. You just dont do it. If theres any goddamned autographing to be done the goddamned author himself does it. See? Understand? Can you get that through your thick head?"

Ginnie put her hand up to her mouth and rubbed the corner of her lip with her fingertips nervously.

"And dont do that, either!" Dave cried. "My goddamned idiot mother used to do that; when she was thinking—or thought she was thinking! Friends of authors just dont go around autographing the author's book to people."

"Well, I didnt mean to do nothing wrong," Ginnie said, snatching her hand down. "I was just—and besides we use to sign books to people for Christmas. When we didnt even know the author."

"Thats different. That was a Christmas gift, and you didnt know the author. Everybody does that. But when youre a friend of an author and go around autographing his books or stories to people, you make yourself and him and everybody else look like a damned ass."

"I dont see whats so different," Ginnie said, less nervously and more angrily.

"Maybe not. Maybe youre not bright enough to see it. So just take my word for it. Its my story: I wrote it: You didnt write it: And if I want copies of it autographed to anybody, *Ill* do it. And I dont need any goddamned help from *you,* dumkopf!" For a moment Dave thought his head would burst, with frustrated anger and frustrated inability to explain it. It was an imposition, a profound personal liberty she had taken, but she was too damned dumb to even know it! "Of all the damned gall!" he said. "Who the hell do you think you are? You got no right to just go around appropriating *my* story and autographing it to your stupid friends. Who the hell do you think you are?"

"Im your girlfriend," Ginnie said smolderingly.

"Yeah? Well, thats something else we better get straight. Youre not my girlfriend. Youre a pig that I happen to be sleeping with, for a while. And if you dont like that, you can take it or leave it. Youre not my girlfriend."

"Well, everybody thinks I am," Ginnie said.

"I dont give a damn what they think. Im telling *you* youre not. See? And if I ever even *hear* of you buying any more copies of that damned story and *signing* them to people, Ill kick you out so quick itll make your thick head ring like a goddamned bell. Got it?"

Ginnie did not answer, did not say *any*thing, and merely sat, lumpishly pulling her chin in—her chins, rather. She had lost ten pounds by the scales in the last month, but nobody would know it to look at her. Gradually, with dull slowness, but with all the unstopableness of some force of nature like an avalanche or a waterfall, her back stiffened angrily and furiously. Dave watched her, suddenly almost beside himself with rage.

"Of all the damned ignorant dumb stupid sons of bitches in the whole damned world that I ever heard of, you take the cake. A fat pig of a one-nighter with just barely enough brains to come in out of the rain, if somebody leads you. And then you got to go and get *literary* pretensions! Autographing *stories!* *My* story! And you havent even got enough damned brains or will power either one to even sit down and read the thing! But youll buy a bunch of them and *autograph* them to your idiot friends! The biggest; fattest; dumbest; laziest; most useless; most worthless most ignorant most *stupid* whore in Parkman! Didnt even complete the seventh grade! Autographing *stories!* Go to bed with anything; everything; everything coming and going! And *autographing stories!* Jesus," he said disgustedly, at a loss for any further words. "Jesus Christ!"

"You cant talk to me like that," Ginnie said strangledly. It was as if her neck, stiff as a board with rage now, had stiffened so much it had choked off her air.

"I cant, hunh? Im doing it, aint I?" Dave said. "And what are you going to do about it?" In his sudden, blinding, infinite outrage, he had driven almost past the darkened house. He slammed on the brakes savagely and threw the complaining little Plymouth into reverse and screeched back to the driveway to turn in.

"You got no right to talk to me like that," Ginnie said in a low choked voice from somewhere deep in her broad fat stiffened back. "You got no right."

"I dont, hunh? Well, you got no right to go around assuming possession of things that belong to me." He rammed the car up the drive between the trees and stopped it jerkingly before the garage. "And, if you dont like it you know what the hell you can do, dont you?" he said, and got out and slammed the door shudderingly. He went on in the house.

'Bama was not there, of course—in the darkened house—was off somewhere on some junket of his own. And neither was there anybody else there: no Dewey or Hubie, no Doris Fredric, no Wally Dennis, nobody. He turned on the lights in the kitchen and flounced across it to the bar, the nerves in the inside of his elbows and knees quivering vibratingly, got out ice slamming the refrigerator door, and rattlingly mixed himself a half a pitcher of Martinis. Still swearing savagely, though at the moment he was so furiously mad he could not have said why and the rage had become an end in itself, he took the pitcher and a glass to the table and sat down and commenced to drink his way through them. The house was very quiet except for the outraged noises he himself made. Before he had drunk one cocktail glass of Martini, he had begun to feel sick inside and ashamed of himself.

Perhaps if 'Bama had been there—or Dewey and Hubie—or even that bitch Doris Fredric—

Well, what the hell was she doing out there? He hadnt heard any door slam. For a moment he had a blind unreasonable, and unexplainable, panic when he thought she might have slipped out quietly and gone back to town. Guilt, it was more, instead of panic. He hadnt meant to hurt poor old Ginnie. He looked down at himself: at his own fat belly; and felt of his own double chin. He was damn near as fat as she was, as far as that went. Poor damned thing, he thought sickly. Poor damned, dumb, unwanted, unloved, damn thing. Ordinarily, her dumbness only amused him; he got a kick out of it. Actually, she hadnt really meant to appropriate and move herself in, hadnt really meant to assume possession of anything; it was just that she was dumb. And she wasnt really so dumb, at that, exactly; she was just uneducated. How could you expect her to know what kind of a huge crashing faux pas she had committed? How could you expect her to be any brainier than she was? no more education or training than shed had? In a way, she was sort of a female symbol of the failure of all of us, just as Raymond Cole was a male symbol of the failure of all of us. What the hell else could you expect her to be, except just what she was? With a background like that and a life like that what else could be expected of her? A sudden warmth and pity and a willingness to overlook, bred of guilt and shame at the things hed said to her, and coupled with a vague unspecific desire to teach her some of the civilized things somebody should have taught her long ago—as Sister Francine, luckily, had taught him; else he wouldnt have had them either—rose up in Dave. Hell, who knew what she might turn into eventually, if somebody would only teach her a few things? Well, what the hell *was* she doing out there? Or had she slipped out of the car and gone on back to town? God! he hoped not that; at least he wanted a chance to apologize.

Dave gulped off the rest of his second glass of Martini and feeling very ashamed of himself for the way hed treated her, (He had been rough; and after all if you were sleeping with somebody, even a pig, you at least ought to treat them as human.), he went to the back door and walked out into the freezing cold night and over to the car. Ginnie was still in it, still sitting just as he had left her when he slammed the door and went inside, except that her back was not as stiff as it had been then, although it was very nearly so. He put his face up against the steamed up window glass and stared in at her, and Ginnie slowly turned her head to look at him. What the hell? it was way below freezing, only 8 or 10 degrees above, and colder than hell. And here she was just sitting out here. He opened the door.

"What the hell are you doing out here?" he said.

Ginnie continued to stare at him, her features almost indistinguishable in the darkness and her eyes only two dark pools of accusation in the shadow. "I aint doing nothing," she said with great reserve. "Im just sittin."

"Well come on in the house," he said. "Do you want to freeze?" He almost added irritably: you damned fool. Not as an insult but only as a natural phrase; but he carefully filtered it out and refrained.

"You sure you want me to come in?" Ginnie said with great dignity.

"Hell, yes. You cant just sit out here, can you?"

He stepped back from the door, still holding it open, and without a word Ginnie climbed out and walked in her squat lumpish way to the house.

"You want a drink?" he said after they were inside.

"I guess," she said distantly. "Jack Daniels and Seven-Up, I guess." The Doris Fredric influence again. He mixed her one and set it down before her and sat back down with his pitcher of Martini. Ginnie curled her hand around the glass but did not raise it and stared back at him, her eyes large and round and bright with a fierce pinpoint focus like the unblinking eyes of some proud unapproachable hawk, her eyebrows arched and quivering like the eyebrow feathers of the bird.

"Look," he said; "Im sorry for what I said to you. I apologize."

"You got no right to talk to me like that," Ginnie said. "Nobody does. To nobody. You got no right to treat me like you did."

"Youre quite right," Dave said.

"Im human," Ginnie said. "I got just as much rights and feelings as anybody else. Im a human bein. Nobody's got the right to talk to me like that. I may not be much, and I know I aint; maybe Im dumb, and igerant, and uneducated, and maybe I dont look like much. Maybe Ive done a lot of wrong things. But Im a human bein. Maybe I dont look like I got no feelins, but I do. Im human, and I got just as much rights as anybody. Nobody's got the right to treat me like that."

"Youre absolutely right," Dave said, feeling deeply and humiliatingly ashamed before her dignity, a little sick at his stomach to look at himself in this mirror. He could not help but remember that time when he and 'Bama had sat in his room at the old Douglas Hotel and he had suggested taking her and one of the other brassiere factory girls with them to Florida, and what 'Bama had said in return: about her being a pig, and about feeling sorry for 'hawgs' too without wanting to carry them around in his car. He himself, he Dave, had been outraged at 'Bama's callousness and cynical cold bloodedness at the time. And now here he was, looking at the unflattering mirror of himself in Ginnie's eyes after having done the same damned thing. Not only did it make him sick with shame and dislike of himself, but it threatened to choke him up with tears of regret and sorrow for what he had—all unwittingly —done. Ego! Dave thought; ego! Every human being had certain rights:

to life, and limb, and dignity and respect; but how easily our ego could sometimes make us forget it. "Youre absolutely right," he said again. "And I apologize."

"Its all right," Ginnie said awkwardly. "I guess I dont really care. But I wanted you to know how it was I feel."

"I know how," Dave said. "And youre completely, absolutely right. All I can say is Im sorry and that I apologize. Ive been upset about a lot of other things that have nothing to do with you, lately. Thats the only reason I can give, and its not very good."

"Im a human bein and I got my rights," Ginnie said. Gradually she let down a little and relaxed, the stiffness went out of her back and her eyes lost their bright pinpoint hawk look and returned to their former dullness. She picked up her glass like a lady, holding her little finger carefully out away from it, and took a drink of the Jack Daniels Black Label and Seven-Up.

" 'Bama dont like me much, does he?" she said in her dull way after a moment.

"What?" Dave said, startled. "Oh, I wouldnt say that."

"Hes never tried to make me again," Ginnie said, "except that once a long time ago."

"Well, maybe your type just dont especially appeal to him."

"No; I know he dont like me. And he dont like for you to run around with me, either."

"Oh, I wouldnt go as far as to say that," Dave said helplessly. He looked all around, not meeting her once more placid eyes, and then got up to make himself more Martinis. He needed them.

"You dont have to kid me," Ginnie said. "He druther you went out with that English teacher Gwen French over in Israel."

"Look," Dave said, stirring the pitcher rapidly. "Lets leave Gwen French out of this, what do you say? She has nothing to do with what we're talking about. As for 'Bama: no; its true he doesnt like you. But then thats his privilege, isnt it? To like and dislike whom he pleases. Just as its yours or mine."

"I knew it," Ginnie said in a low dull voice; "I knew he didnt like me. I knew it all the time. I could tell. You dont have to kid me: I know you been sleepin with that Gwen French. For more than a year now. Why, last Christmastime there was moren a whole month when I didnt even see you. You was over there in Israel all the time."

"Look," Dave said, bringing the pitcher back and pouring himself a big one. "I said leave Gwen French out of this. She has nothing to do with you and me. So leave her out." He took a big swallow of his drink. "Ill tell you one thing, truthfully: Ive never slept with Gwen French in my life. So lets just drop her. Lets leave her out."

"You mean you never really screwed her?" Ginnie said, "honest?"

"No I never have. Honest," Dave said irritably. "Now lets leave it, I said!"

"Then what do you go over there all the time for?"

"Because she helps me with my work. With my writing. She teaches writing. At the College. And she helps me with my book. She helps Wally Dennis, too; and a lot of other people."

"Then you aint in love with her?" Ginnie said.

Dave hesitated—a pause that, in her dull way, he could tell Ginnie did not fail to notice—but he couldnt help it. "No," he said. "Im not in love with her. Nor anybody else. Im not in love with anybody."

Suddenly, abruptly, startlingly, Ginnie got up and left her glass and in her lumpish way, dull-eyed, came around the table. Forcibly, he was reminded of that first time he had slept with her at the Douglas Hotel: she had done that same sort of thing then. While he sat, she twined her arms around him and blew her whiskey breath in his face. "Oh, I love you so much, Dave," she said painfully. "You dont know how much I love you. Youre kind and honest and smart and aboveboard and in- tell'gent—all the things I aint." Tears welled up in her dull eyes incon- gruously, and then commenced to run out of them, carrying with them in solution along black streaks down her round cheeks the mascara Doris Fredric had bought her and taught her how to use. "I aint never met nobody like you nowhere ever. Oh, I love you so awful much."

Dave, irritated, but full of pity and of sickishness at what he had done to her before, patted her on her broad fatty back. "There, there," he said. "There, there. Dont cry. Im sorry for what I did to you. I didnt mean to hurt you." He stood up and Ginnie released him and stepped back. "Come on, Ill take you home," he said gently.

Ginnie snuffled up through her nose and looked at him dully. "I dont mind stayin a while if you want to sleep with me," she said.

At the moment he most emphatically did not want to; but what was he going to say? without hurting her feelings? For a moment he con- templated going ahead to bed with her anyway; but it was just too much. He couldnt do it.

"Ginnie, Im just too worn out," he said. "Not tonight. Ive worked hard all day, and then weve had this big upset. All I want to do is get about half tight and go to sleep."

She stood looking at him dully and its was impossible to say, from her face, whether this made her unhappy or not. She did not say anything one way or the other, and he finished off his drink and took her out to the car to take her home.

After they had driven almost back to town in silence, Ginnie said suddenly out of a clear sky: "And you never really slept with her?"

"I never have; really," Dave said. "Honestly."

"Whenll I see you again?" she said after a moment's thought.

"I dont know," he said. "You come down. Anytime. Just as long as you dont come in the morning. Or in the afternoon when Im working. Other than that come down any time you want."

"Well— Okay, Dave," she said. "I wish you knew how much I love you."

"I do," he said, "I do." He watched her get out and make her lumpish way across the yard of the house where she had a room. It was out in the East End, on the fringes of "Hollywood," amongst the slightly better houses nearer in to town. Even so, it wasnt much of a house. A great pity and sadness and sorrow for everything—for every*body*—filled him up. And he turned around and started back toward town.

Probably it was that, more than any other separate thing, that gave him the idea for the second story. Of course, his run-in with Frank and his damned pompous Cadillac had something to do with it too. But he could—on the way back home, driving across town—suddenly see her, and see all of them, all of that gang: Dewey and Hubie, and Lois and Martha, and Gus Nernst and Eddie the bartender and all of the brassiere factory girls—all of them—see all of them in a sudden new sad pitying—and blinding—light of insight. All their lives, and all that they had lived here in this town—always the bums, always the lower classes, always the ones just on the fringes—see that together with all of their own weaknesses (so like his own) and vices (which of course the respectables never had, did they?) and all of their violent physical emotions so close to the surface because they never had been trained or raised (I wasnt raised; I was jerked up) to repress, and which so shocked all the respectables who had been trained out of them completely, or else taught to conceal them. Perhaps it was that very thing: that closeness to the surface of the expression of their violence and frustrations: which had drawn him to them all from the very first. As he had not been to the respectables like Frank, his brother. Anyway, the story seemed suddenly—in just the time it took him to drive back to the house from the East End—to leap fullblown into his head, the same way "The Confederate" had done down there in Florida. Perhaps even the publishing of "The Confederate," as it had been, and so recently, had something to do with inspiring him to the new one. Perhaps also his guilt over the way he had treated Ginnie, too. Anyway, whatever it was, and whatever combinations of perhaps all of these things that went into it, he had it; he had it fullgrown, complete, plotted, the characters complete, everything but writing it. When he got home, he sat up alone in the kitchen ('Bama was still gone) with another pitcher of Martinis and made notes on it, voluminous notes, writing them so fast his hand would hardly scribble fast enough to keep up with his surging, frantically insisting head. He did not know what to call it. He wanted to call it "The Plebeians"; or "The Plebes." But the connotations of both words, which had become a part of English language over the intervening two thousand years, and in doing so had been almost completely divorced from the original Roman feelings and meanings—both words were too ambiguous, too double meaning. 'Plebe' connoted West Point; 'Plebeian' connoted hick or commonplace. And he wanted the old Roman usage, the meaning that had once existed in the Empire of Augustus amid the squalor, and the circus, and the put-on synthetic 'Triumphs'. Finally he decided to call it "The Peons."

They would all of them be in it; 'Bama and Dewey, Rosalie and Ginnie, Raymond and Lois Wallup; and the story of it, the plot of it, was the fight between Dewey and Raymond and then the death of Raymond and how in some strange guilt-ridden, life-haunted way it— the death of Raymond—affected all their lives. When he went to bed, he had it all, whole, complete, and finished, in his drunken mind.

The next day, getting up without a hangover in spite of the fact that he had gone to bed drunk, he began to work on it. He worked all day that day and late into the night, and fell in bed asleep without a drink. He worked on it the same way all the next day, and the next. 'Bama came and went, and—with his peculiarly subtle sensitivity— realized his pal was up to something and, apparently remembering the writing of "The Confederate" in Miami, left him entirely alone. And when anybody came to the house, 'Bama ran them off. Even Dewey and Hubie, and young Wally Dennis, and Doris and the rest of the women. He carefully and almost tenderly allowed nothing to bother Dave; and in a week it was done. Dave copied it up in duplicate and sat down and read it through with tears of disbelief, and almost of awe, in his eyes and then proceeded to get wall-eyed drunk.

As soon as he sobered up, he took the original over to Israel to show it to Bob and Gwen—only to discover that in the week since he had seen them a very different change toward him had come over both of them, but especially over Gwen. She was no longer warm like she had been—although she was, of course, being Gwen, always pleasant and gentle, like always. Both of them thought it was a powerful, excellent story; even a great one. But they both said it so strangely, and with such reserve. Bob sent it in to the *New Living Literature* people for him (since it was even longer than "The Confederate," and also too outspoken to be sold to any magazine) and not Gwen, like the last time. Gwen said she was too busy at school just now to be able to do it for him. Also, she informed him that she was already making plans to go away next summer and go back to school herself as soon as the College let out. Well, how long would she be gone? She really didnt know; perhaps only for the summer, perhaps for much longer. She couldnt be sure. She had been seriously thinking of taking a teaching job in a larger school. In any case, he was far enough along with his novel now that he wouldnt need her help by then and could finish it himself. Yes, she would be glad to work with him on it up until she left. Dave had never seen such a tremendous reserve and distance in her since he had known her, not even that first night he had met her there at Frank's at dinner.

He couldnt understand it. No matter what he did he couldnt reach her. If he looked at her warmly and tried to smile his love at her, she looked back—but her eyes were guarded, her smile very carefully only friendly. Naturally, it frightened him.

And he never did, of course, ever find out just exactly why.

CHAPTER 58

GWEN had been sitting by the fire in the kitchen grading papers, when she heard the knock on the side door. It seemed to her sometimes that she was always sitting grading papers; either by the fire, or not by the fire—but always grading papers. She had been home from school for nearly an hour, and already the gray overcast day showed signs of sliding gradually off into night. Bob was out, either in his workshop, or else gone somewhere, as he almost always was at that time of day. And she had already figured out what she was going to serve for supper: sweet-sour cabbage stuffed with her mother's old recipe for Spanish rice—except that her mother never served it stuffed in sweet-sour cabbage, and that Gwen herself was using the very last remains of a former garlic flavored beef roast instead of hamburger. All of which of course made it an entirely different dish, not her mother's Spanish rice at all. It was one of Dave's favorite dishes and since she had not seen him for almost a week, she had thought he might turn up tonight. She had cooked the beef roast, another of his favorites, two nights ago and he had not shown up then either and the next day she had used most of what was left of it to make beef stroganoff, still another of his favorite dishes, but he had not shown then either. Five days or a week had gotten to be in the past year a pretty long time without his coming over. She could only conclude he had gotten hot on his book and was going to town on it, or else had gotten off onto something else, perhaps a story. He had been talking to her a lot lately about the death of Dewey Cole's brother Raymond who had frozen to death in his car drunk out in the riverbottoms; apparently, in some obscure way that he either could not or would not say directly, it had disturbed Dave greatly; and she would not be surprised to see him turn up with something written about it. It was strange how, when you had started working closely with a person on their writing, how intimately you became involved with their thoughts and lives—especially if you happened also to be in love with them. She had the same intimate involvement with Wally and his book, though not of course to the extent she felt it with Dave, and more lately she had been feeling it somewhat with the young ministerial student and the polio girl. It was as if she somehow knew the thoughts and emotions and mechanics of their minds even better than they themselves did, know not only what they *were* thinking but also what they were *going to be* thinking; but then of course she had an objectivity about them which they themselves naturally lacked. For instance, Wally's writing had changed its whole tone and texture recently about love, and had become mocking and blasé and cynical about it. Prior to Christmas he had been deeply disturbed about love, and the writing had been highly electric and emotional with a deep powerful sadness and sense of loneliness; but after Christmas when Dawn Hirsh had been home on vacation something had happened between them, Gwen was sure, and the writing had changed to this sardonicism. It was not really inconsistent with the progress of the book at all, if a little work was done on it; and she could see where it would fit right in, and even be a very great enhancement of it. And the fact that Wally's cynicism was as selfconscious and unreal as his former emotionalism really had no effect upon the book at all; whether Wally was acting or not—and it was clear that he was—the book remained: a sort of record of progress toward—toward maturity?—toward himself?—at any rate, toward that coming time when his emotion would become total and real and no longer simply a role, and therefore personally devastating to him, which it was not now. But the book would remain: all that was left of an unrecallable personal pilgrimage of youth toward reality. With Dave of course, she thought smiling warmly, it was different. There wasnt any love in Dave's novel, and indeed should not be; to drag in a love affair would merely ruin it. And he knew that himself. Or to drag in some series of events approximating the powerful emotional experience and personal symbolism Dave felt about Raymond Cole. That was a different structure entirely; and Dave of course knew that too. But—and this was partly why—she was willing to bet that for the last five days or week he had been off the novel, working on a new story that involved Raymond Cole, just simply in order to get rid of it and go back to the book.

With all of this running haphazardly and without continuity through her mind, Gwen laid down the paper she was reading without finishing it and slammed a B– on it and got up, feeling a powerful sense of relief which she nevertheless knew was only an illusion because finally, in the end, she would have to come back and do the rest of them if only later in bed, and went to answer the door.

She had no idea who it could be. Everybody who came to the "Last Retreat" in Israel used the side door on the cellar stair landing exclusively, just as she and Bob did, but none of them ever knocked. They just came on in. And tradesmen and salesmen, depending upon whether they sold insurance and vacuum cleaners and wore white collars, or sold groceries and produce and did not wear one, went either to the front door or clear around to the back door that opened into the big kitchen pantry. So she had no idea at all who this could be.

It certainly wasnt Dave or Wally, she thought smiling, or any of the rest of her brood: They always charged right in and headed straight for the bar, and that included the young ministerial student who was changing his ideas with incredible rapidity; included all, in fact, except the polio girl who with her crutches had to be helped to navigate the three steps up and who very primly did not drink.

She went down the steps and opened the door and saw a dumpy young woman with bland dull eyes and several chins in a nice new-looking winter coat which nevertheless had already begun to show its wearer's personal sloppiness. Behind her on the drive stood a battered weather-beaten sun-faded black Ford coupe (with an Illinois plate) that Gwen did not recognize.

"Yes?" she said. "What is it?"

"Are you Miss French?" the dumpy girl said in a voice that matched her dull eyes. She could have been twenty, or forty. "Gwen French? The English teacher out the College?"

"Yes?"

The dumpy girl looked her up and down. "I thought you was. Youre awful purty," she said. "Purtier than I thought you was."

"Well, thank you," Gwen said; "but—"

"My name's Ginnie Moorehead," the dumpy girl interposed, "you probly dont know me. But I know you. Least I know about you. I wanted to talk to you."

Gwen looked her over again, more carefully. So this was—to quote Shardine—"the biggest hore in Parkman"; the same who had sent Shardine running stiff-backed out of the house on Lincoln Street, simply by her presence, simply by having come in and sat silently down. There was about her, in addition to her natural lumpishness and naturally dull eyes, the sort of held-in quality of a distrustful and watchful animal—a horse that stands quietly but rolls its eyes, or a parakeet that sits its perch and expressionlessly and without moving alertly and carefully watches you walk around its cage. Gwen had had a parakeet once. And over and above this quality, faintly, almost unnoticeable, there was also something else: a sort of waspish, irascible, nervous hawklike quality which showed nowhere except in a tiny brilliant pin-point in the very deepest bottom of the dull eyes, and in the arched quivering angry eyebrows that were the only parts of the masked face that moved. Well, if this was "the biggest hore in Parkman", it certainly did not speak very highly of the taste and discrimination of the men, Gwen thought harshly, and immediately put this typically feminine reaction down.

"Well, wont you come on in, Miss Moorehead?" she said pleasantly, and stepped back courteously. The girl went ahead of her, dully, lumpishly, up the steps and into the kitchen without a word. Gwen followed, suddenly feeling sorry for the poor drab thing.

"My! this sure is a purty place!" Ginnie Moorehead said.

"Thank you."

"But can we talk private here?" the girl said knowingly, looking ostentatiously about.

"Surely. Theres no one here but me. Come on over here and sit down," Gwen said smiling at her, and led the way to the big table with the ladderbacks around it. The girl sat down without taking off her coat. "Will you let me take your coat?"

"No," Ginnie Moorehead said decisively. She rolled her eyes under those apparently perpetually angry brows around at Gwen edgily, nervously.

Gwen smiled warmly, reassuringly. "Well? What was it you wanted to talk to me about?"

"Miss French," Ginnie Moorehead said, trying—apparently—to achieve Gwen's formal tone of address, but succeeding only in sounding like a child addressing a teacher at school: "Miss French, are you goin to marry Dave Hirsh?"

"Am I what!?" Gwen said sharply, stiffening.

"Are you and Dave Hirsh goin to get married," she repeated, looking at Gwen dully, but steadily, from beneath the arched quivering waspish brows.

"Certainly not!" Gwen said almost automatically, stiffly, feeling infringed upon. "Whatever gave you such an idea!"

Ginnie Moorehead put a forlorn expression on her face. "I just thought it. You see, hes in love with you."

"I think you must be mistaken," Gwen said stiffly. "However, if he were, and if he and I were getting married—which, I can assure you, we are not planning—I dont think it would be any of your business, would it? Why do you ask?"

"Well, it is sort of my business in a way, Miss French," Ginnie Moorehead said forlornly. "You see, Dave's been sleepin with me for over a year. Ever since almost the first when he came to this town." The forlorn expression slid slowly across her face with the arched predatory brows, and she looked at Gwen mournfully. "Course that was before he met you, I guess. I knew him real well, back then. He wanted to marry me, then. Before he met you." She smiled sadly.

Gwen stared at her, torn between this invasion of her privacy which made her stiff, and a strong sense of revulsion and horror at finding herself—in essence, at least—placed in the same category as this creature: that was the worst of all and in contrast to the stiffness of her pride, made her want to go entirely limp. And, over both, faintly and growing steadily stronger, a sense of shame at her own snobbery for thinking of Ginnie as "a creature" like she did.

"I know I dont look like much," the girl said, as if reading her mind, and so woebegone; "and I aint got a good reputation especially like a fine lady like you. But he never use to let that bother him none before. When he use to hold me. And tell me all the things wed do, and places wed go, someday, when he got his book done. When he use to kiss me and make love to me. He never let my looks nor reputation bother him none then."

"Really, Miss Moorehead!" Gwen protested faintly.

"Oh, I know," Ginnie Moorehead said. "I know. But now hes comin over here so much the time, I dont hardly never see him. After hes been over here, that night he dont want to touch me nor even want me around. So it aint too hard to see. Oh, I know," she said again, "I know. I know you could take him away from me if you wanted. I aint no fine lady like you, and rich like you are. But Im a human bein too. I got some rights too. I know I dont stand a chance with you. But dont forget, he use to love *me*, too; before he met you. He use to hold *me* in his arms; and whisper things to *me*; and make passionate love to *me*, too. He use to love *me*, too."

"You certainly do have rights," Gwen said abruptly; "you certainly do have. Miss Moorehead," she said faintly, "you dont need to—"

"Why dont you just call me Ginnie?" the girl said helpfully.

"What?"

"Well, we're sort of friends, or ac-quaintances, in a sort of a way, you know."

"Oh," Gwen said. "Yes. Well. —Well, what I was about to say, Ginnie, was that you dont need to catalog all of your intimacies with Dave for me. I perfectly understand your position."

"Dont take him away from me, Miss French!" Ginnie Moorehead cried out abruptly and forlornly. "Hes all I got!"

"Im not going to try to take him away from you," Gwen said stiffly. "You have my assurance of that. Please dont cry."

"Ill try not to, Gwen," Ginnie said, peering at her over the handkerchief pressed against her mouth.

"What Im trying to tell you," Gwen said faintly, "is that—whatever you may have thought, or imagined, or whatever Dave himself may have told you, or inadvertently caused you to think at some time or other, there is absolutely nothing between myself and Dave, and never has been. Consequently, Im not your rival at all. Youve made a mistake."

"You got lots of other men!" the girl cried out again, abruptly. "Dont take *him!*"

Gwen could not think of anything else at the moment except getting her out of the house. Out of the house, out of her sight, out of her dully ringing ears, out of her mind. Just out. Away. Anywhere. Besides, what if Bob should come home and find her here?—and thus find out the whole farcical wretched story? If he was out in his workshop, he might come in at any moment. *That* must never happen; she got up and went over to her and put one arm around her tenderly, and with the other raised her to her feet. Ginnie Moorehead was dully sniffling, with her head down, and at the same time peering up at her through those arched quivering hawklike eyebrows.

"Now you must go on home, and dont worry," Gwen said gently. "Everything will be all right. You have no competition to fear from me," she said positively, "believe me. Dave and I have never been lovers, and are not about to be. I have only helped him with his writing some, thats all. Youve made a mistake."

"I was so scared, Miss French," Ginnie Moorehead said weakly, looking at her carefully. Apparently she was not yet entirely convinced.

"Well, there was no need to be," Gwen said. "There never has been anything but friendship between Dave and me. Now you just go on home and dont worry. I was just getting ready to leave when you came, and I have to go out."

"All right, Miss French," Ginnie Moorehead said; but she still made no move to go. She continued to stare at Gwen, her dull face a twisted mask of forlornness—or at least of what Ginnie Moorehead apparently interpreted as forlornness, the very dullness of it—of the face—a sufficient disguise in itself to hide those target-round hawk-predator's eyes encased in red veins and the quivering hungry eyebrow feathers. And there was that set stolidness about her, which Gwen could feel through both her arms touching her, that told emphatically that if she did not want to move there was nothing in God's world that was going to move her. Oh, God! if Bob came in!

"If there ever had been any possibility of anything between Dave and me," Gwen said, searching desperately, "which there never was, it would be gone now after what youve told me."

Apparently that was what Ginnie Moorehead wanted to hear, because without her even moving any at all, the stolidness in her relaxed and she allowed herself to be led. "Come on, now," Gwen said gently. "Dont be unhappy any more." She walked with her down to the stairs at the other end of the kitchen, one arm still around her broad thick back, the other hand grasping her arm. It was sickening. It was physically sickening. There at the stairs she released her and took her other arm from around her shoulders, the skin of both of them burning dully within her, and watched her go on down to the landing.

"Hes a very fine man in a lot of ways," Gwen said to her, forced herself to say—fairly—to her, "as most men go. And he has a chance to be a very rich and very famous writer someday, if he is handled properly. Dont forget that."

At the last sentence, Ginnie Moorehead had stopped dead, and was listening carefully, one hand still on the knob.

"You aint goin to quit helpin him now, are you Miss French?" she said.

"No. Of course not," Gwen said. "Why should I? Theres no reason why I should."

"Thank you," Ginnie Moorehead said. "Thank you so awful much, Miss French. For ever'thing. Youve done set my heart at ease," she said before she closed the door. "I really do got to go," she said affectedly, looking out through the door. "I got to get my girlfriend's car back. I borryed it to come over here."

"Goodby," Gwen said gently. As the door closed, she turned back to the kitchen—the same kitchen, it was; the same kitchen he had stood in so many times, had stood in, and drunk in, and worked with her in, and laughed in with that bullthroated laugh that washed such tremendous vitality against the walls in waves and threatened to vibrate the steins right off their shelves; she had walked with him down the length of it to the door too, as she had just done now; and had stood at the head of the stairs looking down at him on the landing, as she had done now; the first time he had ever been here she had done that, him so drunk he could hardly stagger and she had worried about him having an accident, and he had (he told her later) wound up going to sleep in a cornfield out north of town; the same kitchen; the same kitchen, it was—and she stood looking at it desperately and frantically because it was not the same kitchen. It was not the same kitchen and nothing in it was the same, not the copper skillets on the old brick wall nor Bob's steins on their platerails nor the big fireplace with its fire nor nothing else. All the familiar things looked suddenly strange and new and different; not the familiar things she knew at all. And it never would be the same kitchen, that same kitchen, again; to her. Not now. She had an almost irresistible impulse to call up Shardine right now, this late in the evening, and start her to scrubbing; she herself would help her and they would scrub it all with strong naphtha soap and biting bristle brushes, from top to bottom, walls ceiling floor and every item in it. She had the same feeling about her two arms, which still burned dully at her sides; she wanted to scrub them the same way, with the same soap and brushes, till the very hide of them rolled up like dirt. Or take a paring knife and scrape them, scrape them clean, like you scraped a crisp raw carrot. Convulsively, Gwen raised both her arms and grasped each one with the hand of the other and rubbed them hard, hurtingly. But it was not enough and she dug her fingernails into them painfully. Well; well; well, at least Bob didnt come home and find her here and find out all about it. That was something, she thought, sickening at the very thought of it. At least that was something.

Almost dazedly, she inspected her forearms and the red-purple crescent marks of her fingernails in them. Childish, childish. Yes. Childish. But what she wanted to do was rip them off, tear them out by the sockets, and throw them away on some trash heap somewhere. It was easy to know why Cranmer had thrust his own hand down into the fire at the stake. In crisis she had not acted properly either. She had not acted in the crisis like the Gwen French she liked to think she was should have acted. She had pretended, and had lied, and had acted, and had been wishy-washy. She had been "genteel". God! and she had put her arms around her—around that thing! God! Dropping her arms, she went back down to the table where the theme papers, graded and un-graded, still lay and sat down staring blankly at the red pencil B– she had made just before answering the door.

Even it did not look the same. The very lines of it, written in her own hand, looked strange and new and different as if it were not her hand that had written them but a stranger's.

Dully, blankly, she picked it up and put it on the graded pile and picked up the red pencil. Mechanically, she noted the name of the student on the next one and read the first paragraph and marked the paper C and put it with the others. That made not quite half of them that were finished, which would leave about fifteen still to be done, and they had to be done. Tonight. Methodically and mechanically and swiftly, wanting only to get done, she went on through the others the same way. For the first five she read the first paragraph before she graded them, but after that she only read the student's name and marked the grade beside it. There was no point in reading them anyway—although usually she religiously made herself do it—and she had only to glance at the student's name and recall the face and she could tell automatically what grade he or she deserved and would in fact earn, if she read the whole theme through. She did not give any As. She gave three or four A–s to students who invariably got As or A–s, and with a kind of mali-cious vicious pleasure she docked each paper one grade below what she knew in her mind it should have had. The little sons of bitches. They would all look at their papers tomorrow and say to each other that Miss French must have had a rough evening last night. Well, let them. Miss French had. But at least Bob had not come home and found her here and found out all about it.

When she finished them, she stacked them neatly and slid them into

her briefcase and zipped it shut and laid it down on the end of the
table where she always kept it. That done, she sat down again and
stared at it, not knowing what to do next and wishing she had not
finished them so quickly. Her mind no longer mechanically in use, the
pain and sheer stomach-turning physical sickness of it all began to rise
up again, like fumes from a brandy barrel, dizzying, choking. —An
age old, soured, liquor soaked, alcohol permeated brandy barrel. Gwen
French, the Tun of Heidelberg. She fought to keep from retching as it
filled her nose and mouth and made her eyes water sharply. God!
O God, God! Well at least, the constant refrain ran through her mind
again, at least Bob had not come home and found her here and found
out all about it.

So that was what they were like!? What *all* men were like apparently:
Anything: Anything at all: No matter how horrible. Just *any*thing!
Any old thing, as long as it was female, and walked on two legs.

And her: with all those foolish romantic dreams and illusions:
thinking all the time he was giving something *up* for *her*: was deliberately holding himself back to help *her*: was gentling *her*, and helping
her, adjusting himself to her fears and foibles, patiently, lovingly, until
she could find her own way clear with *him*: and all the time, all that
time, he was actually sleeping with that—that—that—She could find
no word sick enough. An animal. A female animal. No mind, no brains.
Why, she probably couldnt even read the *words* in his stories, in his
novel, let alone the *sense* of them; and least of all *help* him with them!
God! God! if he got her, he would be getting just exactly what he
deserved! It sickened her.

Unable to sit still, wishing now that Bob would come home as hard
or harder than she had wished before that he would not, she got up
convulsively and walked across to the small mirror on the kitchen wall.
All around the big room, wherever she had looked, she had seen a dozen
Dave Hirshes, two dozen, like some montage or composite photograph:
standing, sitting, lying on one of the couches, drinking, laughing, talking, putting records on the player, all the thousand and one positions
and attitudes and actions she had seen him make or take since he had
first come here to this room; all of them; they had swelled and shrunk
and swelled again, looming in on her dizzily, squeezing her out,
crushing her, then receding swiftly small again while she ballooned and
her viscera yawed inside her and the hollow booming clinking drinking
tones reverberating in her head. She had seen and heard them all.
Now she looked at herself in the mirror, as if desperately seeking the
one point left of solid ground: Mirror mirror on the wall: Whos the
dumbest of us all:

Gwen French, the old maid: *Miss* Gwen French: Miss *Guinevere*
French, the dried up virgin old maid: Elaine the Fair, Elaine the

Square, Elaine the *Lily* of Shalott: and Sir Lancelot came riding, riding, riding, up to the old inn door: where Bess the landlord's daughter, Bess the landlord's black-eyed daughter, stood plaiting a dark red love-knot into her long black hair: his pistol butts a-twinkle, his rapier hilt a-twinkle, under the jeweled sky: Look for me by moonlight, Watch for me by moonlight, Ill come to thee by moonlight, though hell should bar the way! *Ah yes, by moonlight!* and Go down to Kew in lilac-time (it isnt far from London!) And you shall wander hand in hand with love in summer's wonderland go down to Kew in lilac-time (it isnt far from London!). Gwen the landlord's old-maid daughter, Gwen the landlord's virgin daughter, Gwen the landlord's dried-up daughter, the pining Lily of Shalott, lying robed in snowy white that loosely flew to left and right, as she floated down to Camelot.

Ah, yes: God in His mercy gave her grace, the Lady of Shalott.

She put her hands up over her face and blotted out the sight that was not the solid ground either. Not even competition for a fat, sloppy, slimy pig of a female animal! Not even that. Not with this lined haggard haunted face that got bonier and bonier and drier and drier every year that passed, this *old maid's* face. She pulled her hands down compulsively, until her fingertips pressed against her mouth and stared into herself that stared back into her from the mirror. As she looked, all of them began coming back to her again: as they did more and more often and so many times, now, anymore: all of those old-maid jokes she had heard so many of in her lifetime: there must be thousands and thousands: like the one about the old maid on the train: that was stopped and robbed: the robber came into the car and announced he was going to rob the men and rape the women: and a reverend preacher stood up and said gallantly Take our money but spare the women: and the old maid who was sitting up in front stood up and said: *Sit down! Who the hell's robbing this train?*

or the one about the old maid who had been saving her money to bury her with: but since prices were going down and everything was cheaper she told her neighbor she would like to have just one man before she died: she would give five hundred dollars half of all she had for one night: so the neighbor lady who could use the money sent her husband over that night: next day when she went to get him back the old maid was cooking breakfast for him: she stuck her head out the window and said cheerfully: *Just go on back home Mrs Brown: Ive decided to keep him another night and let the county bury me!*

Have you heard the one about the old maid who ran up an ice bill? the iceman said if she didnt pay, he would bang her: she refused: so he screwed her and marked the bill paid: the old maid said: *Oh, no you dont! You brought that ice in here ten cents at a time and youre going to take it out the same way!*

Or how about the one about the old maid whose house was being burgled? The burglar brandished his gun at her and said Ive come here to rob you and rape you Mam so prepare yourself: the old maid said: *There isnt a cent of cash or anything worth stealing in the house: But go ahead, son: Ill write you a check!*

Have you heard the one about the old maid who took a tramp in the woods and had a fine time?

Is there anything happier in the world than two old maids playing squat tag in an asparagus patch?

or how about the one about this

and how about the one about that

Oh, yes! she knew them all. Or almost all. Her fingertips had slid on down from her mouth to her chin, where they now were pressing themselves defensively against her jawbone, as open-mouthed, tears running from her eyes, Gwen stood looking at herself, laughing hysterically.

Well, at least there was one thing, she thought again: at least Bob had not come home and found her here and found out all about it. At least there *was* that. At least she *did* have that. (No competition even for a sloppy fat town whore!) —It was, she felt, about the only consolation left her.

But when Bob came home, to find her sitting dry-eyed at the table, cool and calm and with a drink before her that she had made herself but had not touched, the first thing she did was tell him all about it, herself. As perhaps she had known she would all along. She had to talk to somebody. And after all, Bob was just about the only one there was.

"I had a visitor while you were gone," she said lightly when he had shucked off his heavy overcoat and his debonair old hat and, tall and spare in his conservative tweed jacket and brown slacks with his closecropped head and heavy mustache and those bright, always interested, always sympathetic eyes, came down toward her. If she could ever just be half the man her father was, she thought again for perhaps the ten thousandth time.

"Oh, yes?" he smiled. "Who?" His bright, kind eyes studied her.

"A girl from Parkman," Gwen said lightly. "Name of Ginnie Moorehead."

"Ah? And who is that?" Bob said. "Is that someone I should know?"

"I rather doubt if youve ever met her," Gwen said lightly and smiled brightly. "She works in the brassiere factory. Shes Dave Hirsh's mistress."

"Oh?" Bob said, surprised; and then his eyes clouded. "Ahhh," he said, sadly, sympathetically.

Gwen continued to smile lightly at him, feeling for a moment that she must break and crumple, afraid for a moment that she might, that her face itself might, of its own volition.

"And what was she doing here?" Bob smiled. "Did Dave bring her?"

"No. She came herself," Gwen said. "On her own hook. She came to ask me if I please wouldnt help her to keep Dave."

"I see. And what did you tell her?"

"I told her," Gwen said clearly, "that she had nothing to fear from me."

"I see," Bob said.

"Oh, Dad!" Gwen said desperately, fighting to keep that wail which she wanted to put in her voice, out of it, and not succeeding entirely. "Oh, Dad! What am I going to do?"

"Well," Bob said thoughtfully. He came on down to where she still sat still clutching the untouched drink glass, and made as though to put his hand on her shoulder, then refrained, as if he thought perhaps she might prefer him not to. Instead he sat down in the ladderback beside her and leaned it back on its rear legs judiciously. "I take it she was not a very prepossessing person?"

"No," Gwen said. "No, she was not."

"Hmm," Bob said, "well," and eased the front legs of the chair back down. "Well, dear Gwen, its not entirely uncommon you know, to find one man carrying on love affairs with two—or for that matter, more—women at the same time. It is, in fact, I believe, only slightly less uncommon than finding one woman carrying on love affairs with two or more men. I rather expect its an experience that happens to nearly all of us, at some time or other. All of us seem to have two sides to our natures. The oldest bronze in existence is Janus, you know."

"But, oh Dad, if you could only have seen her!" Gwen said helplessly.

Bob smiled gently. "I must say, Im rather glad I didnt," he said. He stroked his mustache back on both sides with two fingers, a gesture he sometimes had when he was nervous and upset. "It does make Dave out rather a cad," he said reluctantly. "Doesnt it?"

"Cad!" Gwen said. "Cad?" It was, from her viewpoint, just about the greatest masterpiece of understatement she had ever heard. Her eyes suddenly brimmed with tears that threatened to overflow; in spite of herself.

"See here, you mustnt let this upset you so, dear Gwen," Bob said painfully. He leaned over and patted her gingerly on the knee. "We must try and look at it objectively, so we may decide what you should do. Try to imagine it as if it were two other people, strangers, whom you dont even know."

"Oh, Dad!" Gwen said despairfully.

"Yes, I suppose it is rather hard to do," Bob said unhappily. "In your case. When one gets as old as I am, dear Gwen—" It petered off, and he smiled, unsurely. Then he raised the chair up on its hind legs again and teetered it musingly for a moment, his lips pursed beneath the mustache, looking off at the ceiling. "You know, Ive rather followed—ah—your love affair—yours and Dave's. Followed it rather closely, dear Gwen. Since it began. Back last year. I must say, I was quite extremely pleased by the whole thing." He paused, and cleared his throat cautiously. "I—ah— Its rather hard to say, dear Gwen, what it is that makes men do as they do. When two people are in love and sleeping together and also are in a nearly complete accord on things, on life, such as you and Dave were—(an experience, I might add, which I have only had twice in my life," he said sadly; "and, as you probably know, neither of them was your mother)—well: when two people have such a relationship, its rather difficult to explain what makes one of them, usually the man, desire additional sexual relations with another—or even more than one—woman."

Gwen listened, horrified: Bob, too, thought she had been sleeping with Dave: like Agnes and Frank—and, Ginnie Moorehead: and probably everybody else: had, in fact, believed it all this time: a whole year, and over: and more than that, actually *condoned* it! Her own father! —Well, she thought, catching hold of her mind and drawing it back firmly, and desperately; well, that was reasonable—since, like everybody else, he did not know the truth. The truth that she was still a virgin. Well, that answered one problem for her, anyway: She had always wondered, both fearfully and anxiously hoping that he did not, whether Bob had seen through her act. Her "woman of the world" act. Now, when she discovered that he in fact did not, she found herself feeling both resentful and a little disappointed in him: she had always thought Bob was smarter than that; she had always felt that if there was anyone in the world who understood her fully and completely, it was Bob. Now, obviously, it was clear not even he did. Even Bob had been fooled by the Act, the Role, the: ha-ha: Great Impersonation; the *Cage,* she thought bitterly: the home-made, do-it-yourself-kit Cage, that she had built so sturdily and solidly for herself. Oh God, wasnt there anybody! Wasnt there anybody anywhere! It was a fearfully appalling prospect to have to face, and to look ahead at down the dim bad-lighted corridor of your life ahead of you. Gwen fixed her eyes and her mind on Bob and tried to listen to him rationally. At least, she was going to have to appear to listen to him rationally. Because she could not tell even Bob. He must never know. She would be too ashamed. So she composed her face. All of this had slid through her mind, in a kind of revelatory instantaneous flash, sliding on the greased skids of momentary panic, in just the split second it had taken him to draw a breath to go on; her expression had not even had time to change, before she mastered and controlled it; and so she sat, still listening to him concentratedly.

"But speaking as a man myself," Bob was going on gently, "I can assure you that it really means very little. To the man. I know youll find that rather hard to believe," he said awkwardly. Then suddenly he broke off, staring at her penetratingly—but gently—as though he had sensed the change in her. Some change, of which he was not sure of the meaning. "Did I upset you by what I said about your mother?" he said gently.

"No," Gwen said. "No, Ive known it a long time of course."

Bob nodded. "I assumed that you had," he said, and laced his fingers together and stared down at them. "Your mother was a peculiarly sexless woman," he said to them; "I never did understand just why." Again, he cleared his throat. "But that is neither here nor there. Well, what I was trying to say about men was that only when *pity* and *sympathy*— and *guilt*—enter into this other—ah—extracurricular sexual relation, only then is there any danger to the previous love, I think. And this of course is what all women strive to activate in men: It is not really *desire* so much, as it is the desire to be *fair*—to be unguilty—that causes men to leave their wives and marry their secretaries, dear Gwen. I—ah—" Again he broke off and stared at her perplexedly. "I—ah—Im not really saying anything, am I?" he smiled sadly. "I mean, Im not really saying anything to you that reaches you, helps you, am I? Nothing that does you any good. I know Im not reaching you."

Gwen tried to smile back at him, and suddenly tears came in her eyes again: she loved him so much: and he was trying so hard: and she herself, in effect, was lying to him. And after all, he was the only one, the only one anywhere, to turn to, who understood at all.

"Let me try and put it this way," Bob said. "In men of a high degree of spirituality, like Dave—"

"Spirituality!" Gwen cried.

"Yes," Bob said gently, but positively; "after all, he is a writer. And a very fine one. He may, even, become a great one. With some little help from you and me."

"From you," Gwen said bitterly. "Not from me."

"As I said," Bob went on; "in these men, then, who have a high degree of what I can only call spirituality, there seems in some strange way to be, also, this inordinately high degree of sexuality.—"

Gwen sniffed.

But Bob shook his head. "Youve studied the writers, dear Gwen," he said. "Tolstoy, Stendhal, Byron, and the rest. It isnt so much that they have more or different or greater desires than other people; its just that their desires are more intense. Everything is more intense. And as the degree of spirituality is higher and more intense, so also is the sexuality; and this is what they must fight against, this is what they must work to conquer. If only to keep from being physically destroyed by it, if for no other reason. Probably none of them ever fully do so in any one life," he smiled. "But that appears to be their task. And of course their art, their creations, are only the residue, the inconsequential byproduct if I may use such a term, of the strife and suffering they undergo: the ash created by the fire, as it were." He shook his head again, sadly. "But of course you know all this; it is the theme of your own book, dear Gwen."

Gwen merely nodded.

"Would you expect Dave, who in fact formed part of the group youre studying, actually to be exempt from your own theory?" Bob said gently.

"Well, what do you want me to do?" Gwen cried.

Bob shook his head gently and spread his hands. "You must, of course, do what you *have* to do, dear Gwen."

"Oh, Dad!" Gwen said despairingly, on the verge of tears again. She had been on the verge of tears continuously for such a long time now, she thought tiredly. "Its easy for you," she said. "Youre not in love with him."

"Are you?" Bob said gently.

Gwen stopped, brought up short. "Am I?" she said, almost in a comedian's double-take. "No," she said abruptly. "Im not. Not any more. Oh, Dad! If you only could have *seen* her! She was horrible!"

"As I said, Im glad that I did not," Bob said. "As I also said, hes really quite a bit of a cad. A real rotter. Im not trying to negate that. Well, what are you going to do, my dear Gwen?"

"Do? What *can* I do?"

"Do you intend to go on working with Dave?"

"No," she said. "Im not. Yes. Yes, I am. Oh, I dont know! I dont know what Im going to do."

"I suspect there is a very strong possibility that Dave may never finish this novel," Bob said gently, "unless you do go on working with him. It purports to be a fine novel. It might even turn out to be a great one."

"Its far enough along now that he doesnt need me," Gwen disagreed. "Its more than two thirds done, right now. I dont think anything could stop him from finishing it."

"Dont be too sure."

"But I am sure. No. Yes, Im not sure. Oh, *I dont know!* I dont know anything. About anything. What do you ex*pect* of me! Just how much am I expected to suffer and accept? Im just not equal to such responsibilities! Why me?"

"None of us are," Bob said sadly.

"Oh, Dad! I just cant!" Gwen wailed, letting it loose, all that she had been so tightly holding back. She slipped suddenly from her chair to her knees and laid her head in her father's lap and wrapped her arms around his legs, like a little girl, like she herself had done so often, as a little girl.

"Im going away," she wept. "Ill finish out the term at school. But after that Im going away. Ill work with him till then—if he needs it. I suppose I cant get out of doing that. But after that Im going away, as far away as I can get. And to hell with all of them! Let them all write their own damned books! They dont any of them, not a damned single one of them, appreciate the help I give them anyway. The work Ive put on them."

She clutched her father's legs and burrowed her head against him. And Bob patted her gently on the head.

"Im no good," Gwen wept against him. "You dont know me. Im no good at all. Im a liar, and a cheat, Im a coward, Im not even honest, I havent even any guts either I guess. You dont know me. You dont know me. You dont know me at all."

"Which of us knows the other, dear Gwen?" Bob said sadly. "Which of us knows the other's suffering? I know that youre a fine woman, and that Im proud you are my daughter."

Gwen only wept louder, and burrowed her head against him convulsively.

It was just two days after that that Dave, after having been gone over a week, appeared with his new story.

CHAPTER 59

HE DID not know exactly what he expected from both of them, when he carried the new story over to them at Israel. Certainly he had expected praise. And he had gotten praise. Of course, he *knew* what he had *really* expected: he had expected them to brag on him, and be proud of him, and to be happy with and for him. And, in a way, they were all of these things. He supposed you could say that. But with what reserve!

Bob, in his own admirable way, was pretty much his old warm, enthusiastic, friendly, helpful, kindly self. But even he was awkward and disturbed. And Gwen: Gwen was so far away it was as if he was talking to her through a thick glass wall—beyond which he could still read her lips and now and then see her facial expressions, and just faintly hear her voice. It was terrifying. Though, of course, being Gwen, she was kind and sweet and pleasant all the time—but that just made it all just that much more frightening, made her seem just that much farther off. And when—while Bob was still there, and only shortly after he himself had come—she came out with her announcement about leaving the College and leaving town after the current term, Dave felt the bottom drop out of his stomach completely with a kind of terrified unrational panic.

He stayed over there six hours that night, over twice as long as he had had any intention of staying, and it was after one o'clock when he left. And when he left, he knew no more about what had happened than when he came. Bob himself stayed up valiantly with them until after eleven, playing Dave two full games of chess and bravely filling in with cheerful talk the gaping holes that appeared in the conversation, before he finally gave up and went to bed. But even then Dave could not bring himself to leave: he had to find out what had happened. So he stayed, resolutely playing out chess moves on the board from one of Bob's books, resolutely playing records on the player, resolutely helping himself to more and more Martinis, while he tried desperately to find something to talk to Gwen about that would last longer than one minute and thirty seconds, and while the panic grew in him by leaps and bounds.

For one thing, he had belatedly realized he was still in love with her—hopelessly, miserably, unfortunately in love with her. Finding her so distant, so withdrawnly pleasant, made him abruptly aware of that. And for another thing, he was suddenly shockingly aware of how much he depended upon both her and Bob. In the past year the warmth and closeness he had had with them, the understanding, had become so much a part—and so important a part—of his life that he had ceased to even be aware of it. Until something like this happened. They gave him confidence in himself he sorely needed, faith in himself and belief, they perhaps of all people really understood what he was trying to do, they gave him hope that he might even accomplish part of it. They were necessary to him. All he could do was stare at her beseechingly and try desperately to find something of mutual interest to talk about, while in the back of his mind once again as it had so often lately appeared that damnable picture that had engraved itself upon his brain last fall when in that somnambulant drunken almost clairvoyant trance he had lain beside Ginnie and listened to Lois Wallup weeping and wanting a husband and a home for her two kids, and had felt that sense of impending danger to them all.

Why the hell did that always keep coming up? What the hell was it supposed to mean? Christ, it was only a mood, wasnt it? He could only stare at Gwen anxiously and rack his brain to try and find out what he had done wrong. What could he *possibly* have done to them, to make them act like this? While at the same time, before this immensity of reserve of hers, he did not dare to ask.

Finally, when Gwen announced at nearly one that it was late and she had to go to bed because she had to work tomorrow, he did ask. Just blurted it out. He had had several more drinks by then, and was also in a state of almost totally unnerved panic.

"Whats the matter, Gwen?" he said, as she got up, and he got up himself. He had been up, and down, and up, and down, and up again, almost all evening. "Whats wrong, anyway? Whats happened over here?"

"Happened?" Gwen said courteously, pleasantly, smiling almost shyly. "Wrong? Why, nothing. Nothing that I have noticed anyway." She looked at him embarrassedly, almost warmly—as warm, in fact, as she had looked at him all evening. The smile, pleasant, courteous, affable, was a little strained—by embarrassment or something. She carried all the coffee cups to the sink.

"But there is!" Dave insisted desperately, and followed her. "There is too something wrong. Youre— Youre not— Youre not warm to me any more. Youre— But, hell, I dont have to tell you! You know it yourself."

Gwen did not say anything, and ran water in the cups, appearing to be almost blushing. "Theres nothing wrong that I know of."

"Why did you suddenly decide to go away? After school's out? To leave the College? Last week you werent planning anything like that; when I saw you last."

"There doesnt have to be something wrong just because I decide to leave the College for a while," she said blushingly. "Please, Dave."

"But why?!"

Gwen was still staring down into the sink, and peering, she leaned forward and picked up one of the cups that evidently did not satisfy her and dumped the water out and filled it up again. "I go away every so often to study somewhere. Ive been here almost five years this time, without a break. Its about time I went again. Thats all. Everybody needs a break, a change."

Dave was still staring at her, trying to get her to look back at him, but she wouldnt. He did not say anything for a moment. "Are you trying to tell me youre not in love with me anymore?" he said finally. "Is that it?"

"I suppose so," Gwen said embarrassedly. "Yes. Yes, it is. I was hoping you would understand without our having to go into all of that and embarrassing both of us." She leaned forward and ran her index finger along the rim of one of the cups, washing the coffee stains off its lip with the water. "Without our having to talk about it."

"But why? What have I done wrong?" he said. "Is it because of something in this new story? Or because I didnt come over for a week? You know I was working on the—"

"Good heavens, no!" Gwen said, "of course not. Its none of those things."

"Then *what?* What have I *done?*"

Gwen raised her finger up and dried it meticulously on the dishtowel; then she turned to face him, her own face shy, embarrassed. "Is it necessary for someone to do something wrong for another person to fall out of love with them?" she said embarrassedly.

"Oh!" Dave said, flabbergasted momentarily into breathlessness. "Oh. No. No, I guess not. No of course not. I guess I hadnt thought of that. You mean youve found yourself another new guy already." If she had been a heavyweight, and had hit him in the pit of his soft fat stomach with her fist, she could not have paralyzed him more.

Gwen was still staring at him embarrassedly, her face incredibly shy and blushing and embarrassed, girlish almost, he thought, and for a moment he really felt sincerely sorry for her. It must, after all, be hell on somebody: to be like that: a nympho.

"As a matter of fact," she said embarrassedly, "yes. At least, I think so." She didnt say anything for a moment. "Im sorry, Dave."

"Well," he said. "I— Well. Is it any of my friends?" he said coldly. "Anybody *I* know?"

For a moment, Gwen's eyes flashed, almost painfully he thought. "That really isnt any of your business, is it, Dave?" she said, not angrily but softly, shyly. "After all, you and I have never actually *been* anything to each other, have we?" She looked at him apologetically. The implication was clear.

"Well, if we havent it was only because you wouldnt even—" then he stopped himself. "Well, no," he said icily. "No, I guess it isnt, really. Is it. And thats why you never would sleep with me, isnt it?"

"I told you once," Gwen said embarrassedly, running her finger along the edge of the set-in sink in the countertop, "I told you once that I wanted never to hurt you."

"Well," Dave said, still paralyzed, and angry, still breathless. "Well. Yes. Yes, you did. Yes, you did tell me that, didnt you? Yes, I distinctly remember you did tell me exactly that." Not hurt him! Not hurt him!! God and Jesus! He pulled a rigidly held mask down over his face, and felt it there, stiffly. Not hurt him! "Well, I guess there isnt anything else to be said, is there?"

"No," Gwen said embarrassedly, and again for a moment—even then—he felt desperately sorry for her; as sorry as for himself. "No, I guess there isnt."

"Okay," he said. "But theres one more thing: Will you continue to help me with my book?"

Gwen made an embarrassed shoulder movement. "I will as long as Im here," she said; "if you need it. —However long that may be."

"Well, thatll be till the end of the school term, wont it?" he said.

Gwen merely nodded, looking at him honestly, incredibly and unbelievably shy and girlish and blushing looking, for a woman who got around as much as she did. Well, maybe that was what made nymphos: that shyness, and that girlishness: they just never grew up.

"Then thatll give me until June to finish it, wont it?" he said stiffly. "Well, I think I can make it. I only ask this, you understand, because I need your help with it. I have no pride when it comes to my work. The work is the only important thing, really; isnt it. And Im willing to do just about anything to help it."

"Ill be glad to help you all I can," Gwen said embarrassedly, "till then."

"Thank you," he said dignifiedly. "Well, I guess I better go." From the door on the landing he left a parting shot: "I think Ill be able to get it done by then."

Of course, a lot of it was pride—backhanded pride, inverted pride—but just the same he did mean what he said about the work: Nothing, in the end, was as important as the work; that was what lived after you were dead. And, of course, he had had no way of knowing at the time that he wouldnt be able to work at all, that it would just dry up.

He found out: immediately: the next day. When he woke up, feeling fine, he remembered what had happened with her the night before, and plummeted—even before he was out of the bed. While he drank his three cups of coffee he brooded about it. When he went into his little writing room to go to work, he couldnt think of anything, not a sentence, and the scene he had been working on seemed sheer gibberish, he could not even remember what the purpose of it had been, nothing, nothing except Gwen. Gwen, Gwen, Gwen. That strange way she had looked: so embarrassed. And the odd sense of total mental confusion he himself had had. What had he done wrong? Where had he failed with her? He knew, knew positively, that she had loved him, and loved him deeply. All he had had to do was— And he couldnt do it, hadnt done it. Hell, he couldnt even name it. What had he done *wrong*? Why *hadnt* she wanted him? God! God and Jesus! Probably the only man, the only one, who had ever lived in the history of the world who had been in love with a nymphomaniac—and had her equally in love with him—and then been unable to get her to sleep with him! Undoubtedly, the only one in the entire history of the world—and it would be Dave Hirsh. Probably right now she was out with this other guy, whoever he was. Probably some guy from Terre Haute or Indianapolis. Or some young punk instructor out at the college. Right now they might be off somewhere—him making love to her! God oh God oh God! Gwen, Gwen, Gwen! Where had he failed with her? Where oh where? Finally, in sheer selfdefense, he quit without having written a word and got rotten blind drunk. And the next day, with the worst hangover he could remember since before the war, he dragged himself resolutely and hopelessly to the typewriter and the same thing happened. In five days he did no work at all, each day getting a little drunker a little earlier, each day getting up with a little bigger hangover to drag to the typewriter with him. Everything was gone. He couldnt concentrate. All he could think about was Gwen. Gwen Gwen Gwen and how much he had loved her and what he could have done to make her quit him and withdraw like this. He could not even remember what his novel was about, what had gone before, what was supposed to come after, what the original purpose of it had been. He saw nobody, excepting only 'Bama, of course—and one day Dewey's mother Vona when she came to clean. 'Bama kept him more or less supplied with liquor, and what little food he ate, but he couldnt even talk to 'Bama. How could he talk to 'Bama? How could he tell that iron man that it was a woman who was causing this?! It would have embarrassed him too much. Dewey and Hubie, drunk almost all the time now anymore, (Even as you and I, 'ey?), had practically taken over the kitchen of the house—on those days when Vona wasnt there to clean, of course. Dave would not go near them, and in his present state detested both of them. He sat upstairs alone in his bedroom most of the time, staring out the window at the grim winter trees and sky and the dingy sooty houses, now and then coming out from under the heavy sheets and layers of drunkenness and perpetual brooding to a vague awareness of where and who he was. And those moments were the most painful of all, almost unbearable. The worst was, he could not even write any more. At all. It was all gone. He no longer even attempted to go to the typewriter. Finally, in sheer desperation and not knowing anything else to do, he went back over to Israel to talk to Bob. He had gotten himself on that round of misery that forever turns back in upon itself, feeding itself with itself to grow larger and more healthy, more unbreakable, speeding itself faster and faster, until to break the chain becomes impossible. Over and over and over again, faster and faster and faster. What had he done? What *could* he have done. Gwen Gwen. What had he done wrong to her? He went meticulously and carefully over every single event of his life that had happened to him in the year and three months since he had met her: every trip he had made, every drunk he had had, every pig and whore he had laid, every page he had written: he could find nothing, nothing anywhere, in any of it, that would have made her just suddenly up and quit loving him, withdraw from him. My God! least of all could she, *her,* care about the *broads* he laid. And anyway how would she even know.

Bob, when he saw him in Israel, was not much help either. What is the use to deliver to a drowning man a treatise on the chemical properties and density of water? Whats the use to present a starving man a lecture on the various recipes for breadmaking? Bob gave him sympathy—

honest sympathy (even as dull-drunk as he was, Dave could see that)—
lots of sympathy, a great deal of philosophy, and no facts.

He found him, as usual, out in his workshop. Languidly and dreamily
turning chair legs and fixing a strained ladderback, his mind very obviously star galaxies away from what he was doing. It was, Dave thought
dismally, hopeful just to see him. As if he were the one really real and
solid and unchangeable thing in a swiftly shattering world. There was
always the off chance that you yourself, with some luck, might live long
enough and acquire enough serenity to be like him. He went on in, out
of breath, puffing, bleary eyed, puffy faced and mentally dead, and sat
down on one of the tall smooth unfinished new-wood stools.

"Ive got to have some help," he said, "Bob."

Bob could not, however, tell him anything about what might have
made Gwen get off of him.

"Is it that you dont know?" Dave said heavily; "or just that you wont
tell me?"

"Id rather not try to answer that, either," Bob said gently.

"Then you do know."

"Let me put it this way," Bob said kindly. "Im not at all sure that I
do know, entirely. And if I did know, Im not even at all sure that it
would be at all right, entirely. And lastly, Dave," he smiled apologetically, "this is something which I very strongly feel I must not interfere
with."

"That dont help me a whole hell of a lot," Dave said puffily, and
heavily.

"Im sorry. But I simply cannot say any more. Please dont ask me, dear
Dave."

"I guess you know Im in love with her," Dave said.

"Yes— Yes, I rather suspected as much," Bob smiled sympathetically.

"I thought she was in love with me?" Dave said heavily.

Bob said nothing.

"Ive even been wanting to marry her," Dave said, looking at him
anxiously. "But I just didnt dare ever quite say anything about it for
fear of being laughed out of the place." He paused, but Bob did not
offer to say anything. "Shes such a strange person," he add heavily.

"Yes, I suppose she is," Bob said kindly, his bright, eager, interested
eyes taking Dave in sympathetically. "I expect she is rather. But then
we all are, dear Dave."

"Well, it doesnt help me very much," Dave said, heavily, and then
shuddered convulsively with a burst of frustrate fiery energy. "If I just
knew what it—" The sentence tapered off, and fell away, and he got
up to go.

"Stay a moment more, Dave," Bob said apologetically. "Sit down a
moment. I really am sorry that I cant help you. I love both you and

Gwen a very great deal. Of course, Gwen is my daughter. But I feel as great, or nearly as great—perhaps in some ways even greater, being a man too—an affinity for you. As if you *were* my son. Or perhaps even myself, when I was younger. And I have a profound respect for your talent."

"I aint written nothin since I left here," Dave said dully.

Bob smiled sadly, sympathetically. "I suspected as much," he said. "But in spite of that, in spite of all of that, even in spite of your not writing, I simply *cannot* interfere in this matter. Not only because it is a personal matter between you and Gwen. I wish I could convey to you what a *very strong* feeling I have against taking any part in this. I feel that to do so would be almost tampering with Fate in some unholy way. It would be attempting to tamper with your Karma, both of you. Not to mention the Karmic seeds, the Karmic attachments, I would be making for myself in doing so." He smiled apologetically and shrugged, almost with embarrassment: "The only phrase I can think of is *Divine Will*." Again he shrugged, "One has to accept that, to believe in cosmic forces. Naturally I have some Karma to work out with both you and Gwen—or I obviously wouldnt be here; but as I see it, (and I dont see it at all clearly, or surely, dear Dave), my Karmic attachments to both of you are relatively minor. I dont want to incur more. But apart from that, there is a tremendously strong Karmic attachment between you and Gwen in some way. An absolutely tremendously powerful Fate of some kind. Maybe youve both been building toward some ultimate decision that may not come to flower for say ten lives yet ahead. So what right have I to take charge and direct what is perhaps being directed by someone who obviously knows more about the overall purpose than I do? I wouldnt attempt to intervene. In spite of how much I would like to help you both, I feel it would be the most absolutely *unholy* thing I could possibly do. I simply could not. Do you understand, dear Dave?" he asked.

"You really believe all that Kismet stuff, dont you," Dave said dully. "I mean, really believe it: believe in it strong enough to actually *act* by it, run your life on it?"

Bob smiled, gently, although his eyes were still pained, still anxious for Dave. "I would like to be able to say I run my life by it," he said; "but Im afraid I cant, honestly. But in the instance of you and Gwen, I do feel it, feel it most strongly."

"Say, you still got some of those books around you were telling me about?" Dave said dully. Abruptly, unexpectedly, he hiccupped loudly.

"Yes," Bob said. "Yes, I have them. Would you like to borrow some of them?"

"Yes," Dave said. "Yes, I would."

"Come on in the house. Ill pick some out for you."

"Wait!" Dave said, and put out his hand. "Wait!" He paused awkwardly. "Is *she* in there?"

"No," Bob smiled gently. "No, Gwen's not here. Its only a little after noon, Dave."

"Oh. Yeah," Dave said. "Thats right, aint it?" And he rubbed his hand over his face.

"Come on," Bob smiled.

In the house, he said, "You go on down and stand by the fire, dear Dave, you look chilled. While I hunt something up for you. Mix yourself a drink if you want it."

Dave walked on down to the fire, wanting a drink but too worn to make one, and spread his hands before it and tears suddenly welled up in his eyes, blinding him. That fire, that big fire, that they kept going all winter long. While Bob was out of the room in the diningroom, that was also lined with bookshelves, he took advantage of it to wipe them dry and suck in his trembling lip to get control of it, and turned around his back to the fire and put his hands behind him. If you could only go up to people, and say to them: Look at me! Please look at me! Please see how horribly Im suffering! —But of course you couldnt. And anyway if you did theyd probably be so busy with their own suffering which you didnt see that they would only stare at you blindly and pass on. All but old Bob, anyway, who had apparently taught himself how not to suffer. Bob came back in the room and from the fire he smiled at him tremulously.

"Ill put these on the counter down by the door, where you wont forget them," Bob smiled, and as he walked down with them all, commenced to talk again. "I dont know if you understand the principle of Karma. Of course, its all very enormously complicated and intercrossing and involved. But—while this is actually a very gross oversimplification —the way I like to think of it is that whenever we meet people and create *desires* in them: whenever we cause them to love us or to hate us,—or perhaps both, which are the very strongest of *desires*: in so doing we are making Karmic attachments between them and us, all of which must be worked out in future lives, the power of the Karma depending of course upon how strong the desire we create in them. Of course, its vastly more complicated than *that*. Their original desires toward us come into it too; and almost always our meetings with people in our lives are holdovers and in one way or another the working out of meetings in past lives. And that doesnt even halfway explain it. The purpose always being, of course, to eventually free ourselves of all Karma—both good *and* bad—which we must first do before we can move on to another plane of existence.

"But its rather eerie at times, when one is aware of this theory, to stand back and watch how people run and strain to make others love them, trying so very hard to become loved, when they may be binding themselves to those very people for untold generations of lives. Its almost terrifying to stand and watch them." He laid the books down on the corner of the countertop beside the doorway down to the landing and turned around and smiled, a quick sad smile. "Perhaps if they knew what it is they may be doing, they wouldnt all be so anxious to be loved." He started back toward Dave. "Anyway I, personally, am convinced you and Gwen have that type of a Karmic attachment; and a very powerful one."

Dave merely stood, dully, feeling the fire warm on the backs of his legs and buttocks and his hands, trying to contain his still trembling lip, and casting his eyes about the room: the bright brass skillets hanging against their weathered brick: the signature-covered German regimental steins on their plate rails around the ceiling: the books: the recordplayer: the big old table. He did not know how long he could stand it, seeing them, being here, but he knew it would not be for very long. Bob came on down toward him, still talking, talking almost compulsively, his kind eyes crinkled anxiously, and Dave realized belatedly for the first time that it was his own new poem Bob had switched to and was talking to him about. It was the first time, to Dave's knowledge at least, that he had ever heard or known of Bob discussing his new poem with anyone; and the result was to make the tears want to come back in his eyes again: old Bob: trying to help— without helping.

"So you can see the astonishing symbolism, dear Dave," Bob was saying. "Which is why, of course, I call it *The King Is Helpless.*"

Dave could not resist a sad, wry, sardonic snort of laughter at that one. It certainly fit in his case anyway.

"I just happened to be sitting at the chess board and noticed it," Bob said, still coming down toward him. "Im about convinced that it is a definite evolutionary development: with a definite evolutionary purpose: namely, to make the men more *sensitive.* Women almost completely dominate today in our Western civilization. But it must, like everything, do at least equally as much good as bad. When the Germanic tribes broke the civilization of the Empire and set up the Dark Ages of Christianity in Europe, they brought with them a tremendously pompous paternalism and lord-and-master-ism. Today its finally being broken. And while it may be bad for all the fat domineering middle-aged bridge-playing wives and widows, it may be their lives are all sacrifices in an *inverse* way. At any rate, its certainly good for the insensitiveness and pompousness of the men. And Im convinced its going to spread over the entire world before its done. Look at the changes in Japan already, since the war. The world really owes Queen Victoria a great debt, after all." He stopped in front of Dave and smiled, and then reached out his hand and laid it on Dave's shoulder. "We just happen to live in a time when the race is becoming totally dominated by the females, dear Dave."

"Youre not," Dave said thickly. "Youre not dominated."

"Im not in love with anyone," Bob said simply.

"I have to go," Dave said, pulling down the corner of his mouth to hold the trembling, and blinking his eyes quickly, "I have to go. I have to get out of here. I have to."

"Of course," Bob smiled, his eyes crinkled up painfully.

But Dave was already moving, even before he got it said. If he stayed a moment longer—here—in this place— At the cellar door he looked down vaguely at the books, remembered them and picked them up.

"It didnt any of it help me any," he said dully from the landing. "Nothing helped me." His eyes—as if reluctant to do what he was forcing them to do: namely, leave—scanned the room once quickly, hungrily, the long room with the big fireplace and its roaring fire, and Dave ran outside. Bob was still standing before the fire. He waved. "You didnt help me," Dave said to himself.

And it was true. None of it, none of anything Bob had said or done, had helped him in the slightest. The one thing he needed to know Bob could not or would not give him; so instead he lectured. Give a drowning man a lecture on the sea. And when he got home the books did not help him any either. There were several by the English woman Bob had mentioned that time before: Alice A. Bailey. *Discipleship in the New Age; A Treatise on Cosmic Fire; From Bethlehem to Calvary;* and *Glamour: A World Problem,* the book Bob had mentioned to him specifically. Also, a two volume work of Madame Blavatski's *Isis Unveiled,* which 'Bama already had, and which Joyce had been so interested in when he was writing *Ulysses.* Dave knew that much from the commentaries.

Dewey and Hubie were having themselves a rowdy, pugnacious ball in the kitchen with their two girls. 'Bama was gone somewhere. Wally Dennis and Rosalie and Ginnie Moorehead were all sitting up with them, although it was still only mid-afternoon. He mixed himself a quick pitcher of Martini and took it and the books upstairs to his bedroom with him, and when Ginnie Moorehead tried to follow him he told her from the stairs to get the hell out and leave him alone. Ginnie merely smiled at him sadly, forlornly, and returned to the kitchen. He really oughtnt to treat her so nasty, Dave reflected; she really wasnt such a bad kid. But at the present he just didnt give a damn. And besides, there were the books: he wanted to get into them.

But the books did not help him. In his bedroom, he locked the door and sat down with them and the pitcher and began pouring through them, looking for something that would tell him something, give him an inkling, a hope, an understanding, some little awareness of what it was that was happening to him.

How could they make these incredible outlandish statements about reincarnation and Hierarchies and all that stuff? They acted like they *knew!* In fact, they baldly *said* they knew! How the hell could they *know?* Who the hell were *they*, to just declare they knew? Was he supposed to take *their* word for it? He read on, skipping here and there whenever he could no longer follow, finding nothing really specific and factual at all, nothing that helped him, until finally he was only reading words. Just words. One word after the other word. He closed the books and put them on the bed-table, and then just sat, staring out the window at the gray dismal dirty winter day. It looked just like the inside of his own damned soul must, he felt. He had had a ridiculous feeling over at Bob's that he might have learned something from them. He had also had a feeling equally ridiculous that Bob was treating him as he himself might treat a nervous parakeet, sitting skittishly on his perch, unable to get it through his dumb little head what it was you were trying to teach him, unable to realize you werent going to hurt him: such a low-level mind that it might almost be called no mind at all: and that was the way Bob was treating him. It hurt Dave's vanity terribly. But compared to all the other misery and anguish and pain he was suffering, that one little added pain was almost nothing. Downstairs he could hear them laughing and talking, and the phrase *No help anywhere* kept going through his mind over and over: *No help anywhere No help anywhere.* Most of all, he had to get back to work and *No help anywhere.*

In the end, it was only anger that helped him. Just pure outraged furious hate-filled anger. Black stormy anger and black hate. Anger at everybody. Anger at the world and everything in it. Anger at Wally Dennis for being so smugly selfsatisfied, and anger at Rosalie for sleeping with Wally when she had once slept with him. Anger at Dewey and Hubie for getting as drunk as often as he himself was, and anger at Lois and Martha for sitting like two toads. Anger at 'Bama for studying him and sympathizing with him. Anger at Ginnie Moorehead for being so dumb. Anger at Doris Fredric for being a whore when she was so rich. But most of all anger at Bob and Gwen French, for treating him like they had, for taking his affection and bruising and abusing it like they had and then dropping him. He had never hated so many people with so much pure black hatred in his life, and he sat back in it and reveled and savored and loved it. It got him sobered up and back on his feet and, finally, after two weeks of laying drunk and not writing a line, it got him back to work. Furiously, his jaws and buttocks taut tight with cold dark stone iron bullheaded-German resolve, he read through everything he had finished up to date and made notes on how to continue and determinedly set to work again, pure hate exuding from his pores and dripping down to form a greasy slippery invisible carpet over the floor. Gallons of adrenalin must have pumped through his head. The truth was,—except for 'Bama, of course—the only one who really sympathized with him and cared about him at all was poor damned, dumb Ginnie Moorehead, the town whore. There was a laugh for you! He punched the typewriter savagely. It was not the kind of cool, calm writing he had done before: careful and dogged and meticulous and slow and infinitely worked out. This was fast writing: hard and fast and slashing, ripped out page after page, in an ecstasy of savage excitement. Every now and then the slow sick feeling in the pit of his stomach would creep back into him, with its feeling of terrified bottomlessness, but always the black anger and black hate came to his defense and saved him.

And then,—just then,—just as he was getting back to work and beginning to hit his stride, 'Bama had to go and get himself shot.

Actually, it was not the shooting itself so much as the aftereffects of it, which caused the bad trouble. And the aftereffects, of course, Dave did not know of, at the time. The first he heard of any of it at all, for that matter, was when 'Bama called him long distance from St. Vincent's Catholic Hospital in Indianapolis at six o'clock in the morning. He had been away for several days, and Dave had not heard from him; but that in itself was nothing unusual, since he had taken some money and gone over to Indianapolis to play the horses. He was often away several days like that without word, when he was off playing the horses somewhere.

"What the hell are you doing in a *Catholic Hospital*?" Dave wanted to know.

"Anhhhh," 'Bama's voice came back over the phone irately. "These damn fools. When the damn cops asked me what my religion was, I was teed off anyway; so I told 'em I was a Greek Orthodox. And I guess they figured a Catholic hospital was as near as they could come in Indianapolis." He muttered some low indistinguishable oaths under his breath.

Dave could not help but laugh, since the tall man sounded like he was in good health anyway. "All right; that explains the Catholic," he said. "But what about the *hospital*? What are you doing in a hospital?"

"I got shot," 'Bama said pleasantly.

"Shot! Who shot you?"

"Some damned second story man decided to go big time and tried to hold me up."

"And he shot you?!"

"We shot each other," 'Bama said. "Yeah, he shot me; after I shot him first." There was a dry pause. "I guess it made him mad," 'Bama said wryly. "Hell, I had moren two thousand bucks on me. I wasnt goin to just give it to him."

"You must have won," Dave said.

"Won?" 'Bama said innocently. "Won what? That was my last fall's corn crop money I was bringin it over here to invest."

"Oh," Dave said. "Sure. Well, what do you want me to do? You want me to come over there?"

"Yes. I wish you would. Thats why I called. I know yore back at work, and I hate to disturb that. But these damn fools wont let me out of here. They say I aint fit to drive. I want you to come over and pick me up. Christ! this is worsen bein back in the damned Army!"

"Sure, Ill come over and get you. Where did he shoot you?"

"In the hip," 'Bama said. "It aint nothin serious. But these bums shot me full of tetanus shots, and penicillin shots, and Christ I dont know what all. And now they wont let me out of the stinking joint."

"Will they let you out if I come get you?"

"You damned right. If they dont, Ill walk out in this night-gown." He paused again, dryly. "As a matter of fact, I think theyll be damn glad to see me go. Now, look. You get Dewey or somebody to come with you and drive your car back. Then you can drive me back in the Packard."

"Okay," Dave said. "Ill be there as soon as I can."

"Well, just dont take your damn time, thats all," 'Bama said. "Im so sick of this place that Im actually startin to teach these nuns to shoot crap and play poker." Again there was that dry pause. "It wouldnt be so bad, but Im afraid theyll take me. —Aint that right, Sister?" he said to someone beside him.

Dave laughed again. Evidently the nun had been there all during the conversation. "Okay," he said, "Im on my way," and hung up happily. Only 'Bama seemed to be able to do that to him any more: make him laugh and for a moment at least, feel happy. Then he thought of Gwen again and got that sick feeling in his stomach. For a moment, there at the very first of the call, still half asleep, he had had a flash of momentary panic until he had heard the obvious healthiness of 'Bama's voice. My God! what he would do without the omnipotent, very nearly omniscient 'Bama he didnt know. It brought it home to him.

When he got there, he got the whole story off of 'Bama. 'Bama had called him at six in the morning and it was ten when they got there. Dave had rounded Dewey up down at Ciro's and Hubie, who was with him, wanted to go too, so they all went. He released them with the Plymouth outside the hospital before he even went in. "Now dont get drunk," he cautioned them, "for God's sake. Be careful." Dewey stared at him coldly from behind the wheel, his blue eyes piercing in his no-longer-handsome face behind that sardonically twisted nose. "Dont worry about me," he grinned snarlingly. "I wont hurt your damn cheap car. You just get 'Bama out of this cheap firetrap. We need somebody around who can make money." He took off in a grinding clash of gears—from within Dave's car.

St Vincent's Hospital was a big pile out on Fall Creek Boulevard which ran alongside the creek itself amongst parklike lawns and trees, the Boulevard itself an endless stream of traffic, all drab and glistening wet now in early March. Inside, after a considerable argument because it wasnt visiting hours and which he only solved by the excuse that he was from out of town, a Catholic Sister took him up in an elevator and then down a long gleaming hall to where 'Bama had seen fit to hire himself a private room. "Here you are," the Sister said, smiling at him sweetly with her disembodied face entirely surrounded by cloth. "Now, you mustnt stay long, you know." She left him.

Inside, after he had knocked and another sweet woman's voice told him to come in, he found 'Bama. The Southerner was sitting up in the bed in one of those long flimsy short-sleeved ridiculous-looking hospital nightgowns, and he had his hat on. The pearl gray Stetson, its nap glistening softly in the mixture of artificial and rainy outdoor light and slanted low over his eyes and for which the bedlamp behind his head had been pushed aside to make room, rode there on his head as much a part of him—to Dave's eyes, at least; if not to the hospital's—as his face or his hands. Beside the bed in a chair sat a bright—and eager-eyed laughing-faced Catholic Sister of an indeterminate age, the lines of humor and amusement in her face tautened in an effort not to grin, but unable in that ingenuous face to hide her enjoyment.

"Well, so you finally got here," 'Bama said. "What the hell took you so long?"

"Howre you feeling?" Dave countered.

"Im feeling fine. Did you bring my clothes?"

"Was I supposed to?" Dave said.

"Shore you were!" 'Bama cried. He turned and winked at the Sister, whom he had obviously enchanted. "How else am I goin to get out of this joint? You expect me to expose my bare bottom to the elements in this rag?"

"As you can see," the Sister said, still trying not to grin, "Mr Dillert has made a singularly uncooperative patient."

"You bet yore life," 'Bama said firmly. "And I aim to keep right on bein one until I get out of here. These places give me claustrophobia. Its like bein in jail or in the Army.

"They got my clothes," he grinned at Dave, "but they didnt get my hat. The Sister here's been tryin to talk me out of it ever since I met her."

"Well, you must admit, its rather unusual to wear your hat in bed," the Sister said. Suddenly she giggled, a high shrill stifled little giggle. She must have been forty or forty five. "What I cant figure out is how you manage to sleep in it without mussing it up."

"Someday Ill tell you," 'Bama said. He grinned at Dave. But underneath his laughter there was a drawn look around his eyes. "And while he Sister's been tryin to talk me out of my hat, Ive been teaching her now to deal second top card and first and second bottom card, and the rudiments of poker."

"Please, Mr Dillert," the Sister said; "not teaching me. Showing me."

"Well, you gals play bridge, dont you?" 'Bama said irreverently. "Second bottom card would come in mighty handy at bridge. You could win everybody else's allowance."

"I must admit, the gambler's manual dexterity does fascinate me," the Sister smiled, looking childlike. "What was that one where you make them go up and down?" She moved her hands like an accordion.

"The gambler's ladder," 'Bama said. He reached over to the table and picked up a deck of the large size poker cards, two or three of which he always carried with him, and riffled the cards out in a long line and brought them back together. "Here," he said. "Want to try it again?"

"No thank you," the Sister said, looking at Dave embarrassedly.

"Well," 'Bama said, "then how about you goin and gettin my clothes? My friend's here to drive me home. And Im ready to leave right now."

"Mr Dillert, you know I cant do that," the Sister said, repressing another grin. "Not unless Doctor approves it first."

"Then go and get 'Doctor'," 'Bama said, mimicking her usage.

"Hes making his rounds now," the Sister said.

"Then get some other doctor," 'Bama said grimly. "Because Im leavin here in fifteen minutes. Doctor or no doctor. Bare bottom or no bare bottom." Then suddenly he grinned at her and winked. "And I might just take you with me, too." Dave had seen him do it at least a million times before—and with almost that many women, he thought;—he could no more resist playing his act for them than he could resist breathing.

The Sister, who obviously did not believe this either, nevertheless looked a little flustered and suppressed another grin. "Cant you wait till he finishes rounds?"

"No," 'Bama said. "I cant. Will he wait for me to pay my bill?" He made as if to get up out of bed.

The Sister got up hastily. "All right," she said anxiously. "Ill go and see what I can do. Of course, I cant promise anything. Now you know youre not supposed to get out of bed."

"Ill wait fifteen minutes," 'Bama said with finality. "And as for gettin out of bed, Ill be out of this place in less than an hour and on my way home, so how can gettin out of bed hurt me?"

"Will you see that he stays in bed?" the Sister said to Dave.

"He cant keep me in bed any more than you can," 'Bama said, "I told her," he said to Dave, "I told her I never was no bedpan and duck man. In the Army they could courtmartial me for it, but they cant do it here."

"Please stay in bed," the Sister said from the door.

"Get 'Doctor'," 'Bama countered. As soon as she was gone he looked at Dave and shook his head disgustedly. "Jesus!" he said out of the corner of his mouth, and shook his head again. "Jesus H Christ! If I had back half the energy Ive spent sweettalkin that old biddy along so as to help me out of this crappy dump, Id already be well already." He put his hands down on the mattress and shifted his buttocks in the bed and groaned out loud. "Christ, Im stiff as a board," he said, and turned to look out the window with its diamond-mesh of heavy screen wire. Outside the dreary day was drizzling again, and 'Bama stared at it churlishly for a long moment. Dave had never seen him so grouchy and crabbed and flighty before. "These damn places give me the willies," he growled after a moment. "I cant stand them. Id rather be locked up for real. At least there you know what the real score is: yore locked up for definite and you cant get out. But hospitals are like the Army: they give you just enough rope to make it look like yore free, only you aint. Christ, Id rather be in a cage than on a leash anytime." That was evidently as much the cause of his bearishness as the pain in his hip, and when the doctor came, his churlishness gave place to definite pugnacity. "Wait till you see this rich bum of a doctor," he had snarled to Dave earlier.

But before the Sister came back with the doctor in tow, he told Dave the full story of the shooting.

He had been playing the horses, of course—which was what he had come over for. This particular night—two nights ago, that was; God! he had been in this foul dump of a hospital almost two whole days!— this particular night he had stayed late at the bookie's to get the results of some California night races and it had been almost one o'clock when he left. He had driven the Packard downtown to a little restaurant near the Claypool where he sometimes ate late. The streets were very nearly dark by then, with so many of the lights off, and were almost deserted. As he braked to pull in to the curb, a car that was behind him pulled out and went around him and stopped ahead of him down at the end of the block, the only other parked car visible. A man was out of it and walking back toward him before he himself was even completely stopped. He had not thought anything about it at the time: he himself was parked squarely in front of the lighted restaurant: and the man could be going there just like he was.

He never did know, 'Bama said, whether the man had just picked him out at random as a likely prospect for a holdup; or whether perhaps the man had seen him earlier at the bookie joint and had seen how much

hed won. He himself certainly did not recognize the man from anywhere. Anyway, just as the man was abreast of him, he swerved and
came over to the Packard toward the open window. (As Dave knew, he
more often drove with the two front windows open than not; and
whether the man noted this, and changed his mind from some other
plan he had in mind, 'Bama didnt know.) It was, actually, the first time
'Bama had more than merely noticed the man; and by the time he was to
the car he already has his gun out, a snubnosed .38 Police Special. The
gun came through the window first, the butt resting on the window slot,
and the man's face appeared—outside—above it.

By that time, of course, he had known what was up. But it was too
late to do anything. He very carefully kept both hands on the steering
wheel where they had been, and didnt move them. "I want your money,"
the man said in a tough voice.

"You sound like you mean business," 'Bama had said cheerfully. He
was still trying to figure some way out. He had over two thousand dollars
on him in cold cash, and he was not about to give it to some hopped up
punk of a hood, gun or no damned gun. If the car had been running,
and in gear, he might have been able to goose it and let out the clutch
and run out from under him. Only, it wasnt running.

"I do, pal," the man had said toughly, and earnestly.

"Well, my wallets in my inside coat pocket," 'Bama had said cheerfully. Actually, it wasnt. It was a folding wallet and it was in his left
hip pocket—buttoned down. The only thing inside his coat was the little
.32 Smith & Wesson in its springclip holster; and it looked like there
was nothing else for it: he was not about to turn over two thousand
bucks.

"Reach in and get it," the man had snarled, "and throw it out on the
seat."

"Yes, sir," 'Bama had said cheerfully, and elevated his left arm keeping
the hand still on the .wheel. He reached slowly with his right inside the
coat, keeping on talking cheerfully as he did so: it was a pretty slim
squeeze any way you turned it and you might as well give yoreself every
advantage you could get: "I never did see the sense of gettin killed over
a few lousy bucks, mister. But my driver's license and car registration and
cards and stuff in there too. Dont take them, will you? They wont do
you no good." The last two sentences were pretty well drowned out in
the roar of both guns inside the car. (Christ! I thought I been deefened
for life!)

The little .32 had slipped easily out of its springclip without having to
raise it and he had flipped it out, straightening his arm only just enough
so he could turn the gun far enough to bear, and fired. The man, looking
startled and dismayed, had clamped down on his .38 snubnose convulsively and fired almost simultaneously. The .38 slug struck 'Bama

in the hip, slamming him back against the car door. He never did know for sure whether he actually got those last two sentences said or not. But he had made up his mind beforehand to go on and at least try to say them, because he didnt want any time lag when he pulled. The man, outside the car, dropped his gun into the car and disappeared from view, his face looking surprised and rather hurt and offended as if he had been tricked and cheated unfairly. The bullet from the .32, 'Bama had learned later, had struck him squarely, high in the right chest, nicking the top of his lung. If he had only straightened his arm out just a hair more before letting go, he would have got him straight in his heart and killed him like he meant to. He just had been a little too hurried.

(But the look on that man's face still made him want to laugh, 'Bama said; every time he thought about it. Here he was: tryin to hold me up, and take my money, and even willin to shoot me if he didnt get it: and he looks resentful because I pull a gun. As his face had slid from view below the window, he had looked as if he would have liked to say: "Hey! You got no right to do that to me! Im holdin *you* up! And then you pull a gun on me—and without even givin me fairwarning!" 'Bama threw back his head and laughed, and then groaned—at having moved his hip.)

Inside the car, feeling nothing of course, no pain, just numbness, 'Bama had held onto his gun and waited to see if the man got back up, or—something he had been considering—if someone else got out of the other car up ahead. It was possible and even highly probable that the man had somebody with him. His hip was dead feeling, but what he was afraid of was that the bullet, considering the angle and the place of entry, had gone into his lower abdomen and of course that would mean peritonitis. Actually, as he found out later, because of the angle of entry, the lead slug had been deflected by his pelvis and gone on around outside the abdomen toward his back and lodged there. What he had hoped, of course, was that the surprise would make the other man miss him altogether. But at the moment of course all that was neither here nor there. When the man did not get back up, and when nobody else appeared from the other car up the block (as it turned out the man had been alone), he had laid the gun carefully in the seat where he could get it easily and had shucked out of his coat sleeves and got the little shoulder holster off and leaned over and stuffed it in the dash compartment and put his coat back on. By that time people had begun to come out of the restaurant, when they saw there wasnt going to be any more shooting.

The police, of course, and an ambulance had already been called from inside. They were not long getting there. The man outside on the sidewalk had either knocked his head when he went down or had fainted; anyway, he was unconscious. He himself had suspected, from the way the man had dropped the gun inside the car instead of hanging onto it, that the man was not a professional stickup man; and as it turned out this was right. The man had a burglary record, but up to now had never been involved in anything liked armed robbery. 'Bama himself had stayed in the car until the police came, even though the ambulance got there first, because he wanted the police to see everything just like it was. They arrived only a minute or so later, and he had turned the gun over to them and told them the whole story. Then he let them put him in the ambulance, being careful not to let anybody get hold of, or muss up, his hat. The police of course had found the shoulder holster in the dash compartment—which was perfectly all right with him— and he had shown them his lapsed Sheriff's permit from Illinois and explained that over there he sometimes wore the gun when he was carrying large amounts of cash, and of course always took it off when he came over into Indiana. The gun, he had told them, had been lying beside him in the seat of the car, because he was carrying so much money. Whether they believed it or not, he didnt know and anyway it didnt matter much; he was obviously the attacked party. And anyway, he knew a number of the cops in Indianapolis, who knew him and knew he was not only just an Illinois farmer. He was clean. He did not intend to press any charges. The state could do that if they wanted to, and probably would. He might have to come back later on as a witness, and they would have to pick up his gun down at the station on their way out of town. That was the whole story.

Dave listened to it all, fascinated, mainly by the coldblooded coolheadedness 'Bama had displayed all through the whole thing, from the stickup itself to his handling of the police part, all just as if it were a common everyday occurrence and not dangerous at all. He felt a strong sense of inadequacy at ever being able to do anything like that himself. He had absolutely no doubt that 'Bama had intended to kill the man (who it turned out was here in this same hospital under lock), and would in fact have done so if he had been able to. It was also obvious that he had no compunction about doing so. But what fascinated him most was the way 'Bama—completely caught short; the drop on him; carrying the short end all the way around—had just simply bullheadedly locked up his mind and decided he was not going to give up two thousand in cash. Whether it got him killed or not. And that was the kind of thing, Dave felt, that he himself could never have done.

However, if 'Bama was proud of it, he certainly showed no signs. He finished up his story several minutes before the doctor came, eased himself into another position in the bed while he groaned and swore, and then stared out of the window at the drizzly March weather. "And all I got to do now," he said irately, "is get myself out of this damned. miserable. bastardly. frump of a hole!" Dave had never seen him so edgy and irritable. But if he was edgy and irritable with himself alone and with Dave, his irritation changed to sheer pugnacity when the doctor arrived.

The doctor was a tall, heavyboned, selfsatisfied looking man with cool commanding eyes, fiftyish with distinguished looking gray hair, and obviously used to a great deal of respect. Perhaps this was what 'Bama didnt like about him, Dave thought studying him. But he didnt appear to look so bad to Dave. He came in striding slowly and dignifiedly behind the Sister who held the door for him, carrying a clipboard chart and wearing a sort of stern-father smile. He was not wearing his white coat but was dressed in an expensive and conservative business suit, a diamond stickpin conspicuous in his tie, a large diamond ring equally conspicuous on the little finger of his left hand.

"Well, Mr Dillert," he smiled paternally. "Giving us more argument today?"

"Hi, Doc," 'Bama said insolently. "Givin me more medicine today?" His ingrained sneer that was always on his face anyway, deepened appreciably.

The doctor didnt like it, but he had admirable selfcontrol to go with his commanding presence. "As a matter of fact, I expect we will be," he smiled. "I have some things here I want to discuss with you," he said, raising the clipboard. "Sister Theresa tells me youve been asking to leave again today."

"'Ats right, Doc," 'Bama said with the same insolence. "My friend here come to drive me home like you said, although I still think I could of done it myself. And I aint *askin* to leave, Doc. I *am* leavin."

"Im afraid thats impossible," the doctor said crisply.

"Whatta you mean, impossible?" 'Bama snarled. "As I understand it, theres no law that says you can keep me in your dump if I want to leave it." The commanding presence obviously did not work with 'Bama. Dave thought he could see why it rubbed him the wrong way: The man was so completely sure of himself, of his knowledge and of his authority, that it disturbed you. You felt as if you were only a small boy while he was a big grownup adult. Dave himself felt a little afraid of him in some vague undefinable way. But 'Bama was making an insolent ass out of himself.

"Quite so, Mr Dillert," the doctor smiled. "Thats quite so. All I could do would be to insist that you sign a release to myself and the hospital absolving us of any responsibility."

"Gladly," 'Bama snarled.

"However, if you were in a critical condition," the doctor said thinly, "I might be able to insist that you not be moved from here, even against your will. But—"

"We could always put that to a legal test," 'Bama said.

"We certainly could," the doctor said. "—But, as I started to say, you are not in that condition. No one wants to keep you here against your will."

"Then why dont you give me my clothes and let me go and quit yappin about it? If I have to, Doc," he said insolently. "Ill go without the clothes. Believe me."

The doctor smiled officially, but his face was a little stiff. "As I said, Mr Dillert, there are some things here I want to discuss with you." He raised the clipboard and leafed through its several sheets a little portentously. He plainly did not like to be called "Doc", and with his authoritative air was equally plainly used to being treated with considerably more respect. The look on his face showed both, and 'Bama's cold eyes narrowed and seemed to glint flame.

"Then lets have it, Doc," he said. "I want to get goin."

"Youre rather a sick man, Mr Dillert," the doctor said, underplaying it, but nevertheless bluntly. "You definitely have a rather advanced case of diabetes, and your condition is complicated by a definite cirrhosis of the liver."

"I got what?" 'Bama said, his eyes narrowing.

"Diabetes mellitus," the doctor said. He smiled gravely. "Sugar diabetes. We ran the usual tests on you that we run on all in-patients, and discovered sugar in your urine. Finding that, we ran a blood-sugar test on you also—not one of the usual in-patient tests—and discovered a fairly high blood-sugar content. I note you are from Alabama, Mr Dillert, and that your father is no longer living. May I ask what he died of?"

"Gangrene of the legs," 'Bama said immediately, staring at him narrow-eyed. Dave, who had tried to keep himself in the background as much as possible, was listening unbelievingly.

"A fairly common cause of death in cases of neglected diabetes, Mr Dillert," the doctor smiled. He looked as if he had just won the poker hand. "Diabetes is inherited. Or rather, let me say a tendency toward diabetes is *often* inherited. This tendency is aggravated, usually, by overeating and overdrinking until it becomes definite diabetes. That is what you have. Inherited from your father evidently." He paused, and smiled again. 'Bama was still staring at him narrow-eyed, evidently imperturbable.

"Do you," the doctor said, "often feel listless and weak and tired?"

"Yeah," 'Bama said insolently. "I been feelin that ever since I was big enough to stay out at night."

The doctor did not smile. "Do you," he said, a little thinly, "have to get up often at night to pass water?"

"Yeah."

"Have you noticed itching of the skin, particularly around the genitals?"

"Yeah," 'Bama said. He grinned narrowly. "But I always thought that was just another dose of crabs, Doc."

The doctor did not answer this. He did not actually wrinkle his nose, but it was evident he thought the remark was in poor taste, especially in front of Sister Theresa. "These are all symptoms of diabetes, Mr Dillert," he said. "The best test is of course the blood-sugar. It definitely confirms my diagnosis."

"So what am I supposed to do? Weep?"

The doctor did not answer this either, and instead turned a page on the clipboard, his face set rather stiffly. "When I noted considerable alcohol in your system, also, Mr Dillert, (we always run an alcohol test on gunshot wounds), I decided to check for cirrhosis. I shall want an X-ray, of course, also. But what you have is undoubtedly Laennec's cirrhosis; a type formerly thought to be due to excessive use of alcohol; now known to be due to the associated nutritional disturbances. The liver is slightly nodular, with fibrosis especially in the portal spaces; characterized by degeneration and regeneration of the hepatic parenchymal cells, often accompanied by ascites, esophageal varices, and ultimately icterus."

"Whats ascites?" 'Bama said.

"An abnormal accumulation of serous fluid in the abdominal cavity," the doctor said.

"Whats icterus?"

"Acute jaundice," the doctor said.

'Bama stared at him narrow-eyed, silently, asking no other questions; and the doctor stared back at him, stony-faced, authoritative, disapproving. For almost half a minute they simply stared.

It was the doctor who finally spoke. "How much whiskey do you drink a day, Mr Dillert?" he said.

"Oh, I dont rightly know, Doc," 'Bama said insolently. "A fifth. Maybe more. Maybe less."

"You will, of course, have to stop drinking entirely, and immediately. Alcohol puts enormous sugar in the blood."

"I will?" 'Bama drawled.

"Also, the rather advanced diabetes," the doctor said, "coupled as this is with the cirrhosis, requires immediate treatment, Mr Dillert. That much is imperative, and immediate."

"You mean Im liable to die?" 'Bama said bluntly, his eyes completely flat, completely expressionless.

"No, Mr Dillert," the doctor said sternly, "not immediately at any rate. I would say you have five—maybe even ten—years of life ahead of you at the rate youre going now. But your condition should have immediate treatment. Any further complications, such as an infection or a virus pneumonia or something of that sort, could be very serious and might easily kill you sooner. Those are the facts, Mr Dillert." He looked at 'Bama with a certain satisfaction.

'Bama merely stared at him narrowly and did not say anything.

"I recommend," the doctor said authoritatively, "I recommend that you stay here in the hospital until we can run further tests and set up your individual insulin allowance and your diet and teach you how to use the syringe and all the other knowledge and information needed by diabetics, by confirmed diabetics."

"Thats what you suggest, Doc?" 'Bama said. "Okay. Now will you have Sister Theresa go down and get my clothes for me?" He stared at the doctor, flat-eyed.

For the first time since he had entered the room, the doctor lost his complete aplomb and poise. He opened his mouth as if to say something further, and then shut it again; and then he looked down at the charts in his hand as if to make sure they were still there, were correct. Then he looked back up at 'Bama stonily.

'Bama merely stared back at him, narrow-eyed.

"Sister Theresa," the doctor said, "go downstairs and get Mr Dillert's clothes and his other articles. Bring a release form with you for him to sign."

The Sister, who had been watching all of this, first from one of them then to the other, anxiously and almost unbelievingly, went to the door without a word. 'Bama shifted himself a little in the bed again, painfully, but Dave noticed he did not groan this time. He and the doctor continued to stare at each other.

"Hows this hip wound, Doc?" 'Bama said after a moment.

"I probed for and removed the bullet and opened up the puncture wound," the doctor said stonily, "but I thought it best to put gauze drains in it. There are drainage wicks in it now."

'Bama merely nodded and continued to stare back at the doctor. "Doc," he said after a moment; "were you ever in the Army?"

"Yes," the doctor said. "I was."

"What were you? A Colonel?"

"I was a Lieutenant Colonel," the doctor said.

"In the Medical Corps." It was a statement, not a question.

"Thats correct," the doctor said stonily.

"I figured you were," 'Bama said. "I was a sergeant, Doc." He paused a moment, staring at the doctor. "A tank sergeant. You know, I was wounded twice in that war, Doc. Both times they put me in the hospital. And you know something, Doc? I actually preferred bein shot at up the front to bein in those hospitals because both of them were full of doctors like you. Can you feature that? In the Army, Doc, you could have made me stay in the hospital, if you decided you wanted me to. And Id of had to stay. Or get courtmartialed." He stopped, the words seeming to hang on in the air, apparently unfinished, but actually not unfinished at all, and stared at the doctor with eyes as flat, and as expressionless, as two wind-less ponds.

"It would be better for you if I could do so now, Mr Dillert," the doctor said stonily.

"Maybe. Whats 'better', Doc?" 'Bama said, flatly. "Doc, do you believe in adultery?"

The doctor's face stiffened. "Mr Dillert, I dont think—"

'Bama raised his hand and waved it. "Or in excessive alcohol drinkin?"

"No, Mr Dillert," the doctor said; "I do not."

'Bama grinned. "Well, you see? theres the difference. I believe in both adultery and excessive alcoholism for the human race, Doc. In fact, I dont see how they could get along at all without 'em. You and me just dont see life alike at all. You believe its yore *duty* to live like you do," he said insolently; "well, I believe its *my* duty *not* to live like yore duty tells you to *do*," and he grinned again. "You see, Doc?" he said easily; "we just aint alike atall." And once again they stared at each other in that strange antagonistic way, the doctor's face as stony as 'Bama's eyes were flat.

"Well, Mr Dillert, perhaps so," the doctor said finally, in a flat stony voice. "At any rate, I feel it is my 'duty' to try to impress upon you the seriousness of your condition."

"You done did, Doc," 'Bama said.

"Then my 'duty' is done, Mr Dillert," the doctor said. "If you will excuse me, I have other important 'duties' to perform. Please sign the release which Sister Theresa brings."

"Sure thing, Doc," 'Bama said with insolent cheerfulness as the doctor went to the door; and after he had gone on out, he sat motionless staring at the door, his eyes and face flat and cold—(flatter and colder than Dave could ever remember having seen them; and once again Dave had that chilling feeling about his friend)—until gradually he became aware of Dave and his face gradually softened. He turned to look at him and suddenly he winked, and then grinned, and then laughed out loud.

Dave moved, realizing suddenly from his stiffness that it was the first time hed moved since the conversation started. "I guess that last was about the best statement of the credo of the artist Ive ever heard," he said with a grin.

"Shore," 'Bama grinned. "Im a real artist." He moved himself gingerly and painfully again in the bed and this time he groaned. He looked back out the window at the drizzly weather. "I hate hospitals. And I aint got much use for most of the medical profession, either. The pompous bastards. Always insistin on savin some poor bastard's life.

It never occurs to them that its *his* life. Maybe he dont want the son of a bitch saved. But, by God, theyre gonna save it *anyway*."

"What are you going to do about the diabetes?" Dave said.

The Southerner shrugged. "Ill worry about that when I get out of this dump. I got a doctor at home I go to. Ill see what he says."

"You dont think this guy was lying, do you?"

"Hell, no! He would never do that! And hes a damned good doctor, I 'magine. Hes right, all right. I just cant stomach him, thats all. Hes just a little too happy over all he found wrong with me. Come on, help me get up out of this sack. I got to piss."

When the Sister returned with his clothes and the release form, he was standing by the window in the knee length gown. ("It aint so bad when Im standin up," he had told Dave, and laughed. "Boy, I really got racked up this time, didnt I?") He signed the release form and returned it to her, and looked at the pile of clothes on the bed, the suit pants and the coat still both torn and bloodstained. "Sister, what about my money?" he grinned at her. "Thats what I got into all this mess over in the first place."

"Theres a slip there," Sister Theresa said. "You can draw it at the desk when you go down. Mr Dillert, you werent supposed to get out of bed!"

"Sister, Im gonna be out of this place and walkin in five minutes," 'Bama grinned. "Cool off."

"Just the same, you should have rested all you could before you left," the Sister said scoldingly. "The trip is going to be quite an ordeal for you, you know that." Frowningly, she started to fluster and bustle around trying to help him. It was obvious she was going to miss him when he left.

"Sister," 'Bama grinned, "you just go on out and let us get me dressed. We can manage it all right; and you know how bashful I am."

"Yes! I certainly can see *that*, Mr Dillert!" But reluctantly, she went outside. When they had him dressed and ready to go, amid much groaning and cursing and gasping, she came back.

"God bless you, Mr Dillert," she said simply, her round little face encased in its cloth staring at him earnestly. "God be with you."

"Sister," 'Bama grinned, "Im shore he is. I left that deck of cards there for you on the table. Dont forget to practice."

They left her then, standing in the doorway, still looking embarrassed over the card playing.

The trip home was every bit of the ordeal she had said it would be. 'Bama, silent and tightlipped while Dave drove the heavy Packard for the first time since they had come back from Florida, tried to sit on his left buttock and favor his right. A hard thing to do in a moving car. Only twice did he speak at all. Once it was to tell Dave, grinning stiffly at him, that his own wound was actually very similar—almost weirdly so—to the wound received by Bedford Forrest at Columbia Tennesseee from the hands of the young Confederate officer who shot —and tried to kill—him because Forrest had transferred him from his command for incompetency. Tightlipped and speaking through clenched teeth, he went on and told Dave the story, how the young lieutenant had come to Forrest to ask to be taken back, how when Forrest who happened to be twirling a closed penknife in his fingers had refused he drew his pistol and shot Forrest, how Forrest had grabbed the gun and got the penknife open with his teeth and stabbed the lieutenant in the belly, a wound he later died of, how the lieutenant had then run from the building and Forrest had then walked to a doctor and being told the wound was probably mortal had seized a pistol and started after the lieutenant to make sure he killed him too, how in the end when he was assured the lieutenant who was by now lying in the street would also die he had desisted. Forrest's wound was in the left hip whereas his own was in the right, and Forrest's bullet had passed clear through him while his own had lodged inside; but in both cases the bullets had struck the pelvic bone and been deflected outward so that it did not enter the intestines. Finally, in the end, Forrest had had himself carried later to the room where the lieutenant lay dying so the lieutenant could apologize, and they had wept together over it.

"In a lot of ways it was like yore story," 'Bama said grinning tightly. " 'The Confederate.' It might even be a sort of history of all Southerners. They were great fighters. They just spent too much time fightin with each other."

The only other time he spoke was some time later, when he suddenly began to talk about the diabetes and told Dave he had half way suspected it for some time. He just hadnt had himself checked or done anything about it because he didnt want to know for sure. Well, now he knew. He hadnt known it was diabetes, of course, and hadnt connected it with his father's gangrene, but he had known something wasnt right with him. After that he spoke no more until they had got home.

It was something like seventy five miles from Indianapolis to Parkman and long before they got there the trip had turned into a nightmare for Dave. Everything seemed totally unreal and as if it wasnt happening and yet seemed to promise to go on endlessly. After a while he did not believe they would ever get there. The man beside him, his friend, tightlipped, teeth clenched, obviously in constant pain and yet not saying a word about it; himself, driving, pushing hard, trying to get them there, and yet at the same time trying to drive as smoothly as he could, nervous and edgy and upset. The wound had opened up again from all the moving around and was bleeding steadily, if not heavily. It was an experience Dave did not soon forget, and seemed somehow to set the mood for everything that followed.

"Dont say anything about this diabetes stuff to anyone," 'Bama said tersely when they finally pulled into the drive and sat looking dumbly and unbelievingly at the house, and Dave only nodded.

As soon as he had got him inside and helped him upstairs to bed, he called Doc Mitchell the doctor 'Bama said he went to. Dr Earl Mitchell was a roly-poly little man with a big fleshy nose and kindly eyes and an air of sad, sympathetic understanding. He was, Dave already knew, one of the few successful doctors in Parkman who had made money and not used it to open up a "clinic" or a "sanitarium." He came right out when Dave called, and Dave sat upstairs with them while he dressed the wound and they discussed the diabetes.

"Well, if theyre right and it is diabetes," Doc Mitchell said in his mild sad way, "and Im sure they are in a big place like that, the best thing to do is to get you into a hospital and have them check you out."

"I wont go into any hospital," 'Bama said. "Thats out. Ive had enough hospitals today to last me forever." His lips were still drawn tight across his face from the changing of the drainage wicks in the wound. "Cant you do it all for me and fix it up without me havin to go in?"

"Well, I guess I can, 'Bama," the little doctor said. "Itll be a little harder. But yes, I can do it all right. Ill just take the blood for the test myself and have one of the labs here in town do it. Ill get the syringe and all the stuff and show you how to use it. Its simple enough, if you have any intelligence at all." He smiled, his small mouth moving with a curious sadness under that fleshy nose. "When I have the blood-sugar test from the lab, Ill know how many units to start you out on."

"What about this drinkin business?" 'Bama said.

Doc Mitchell spread his hands, almost helplessly. He was as kind and selfeffacing a man as the doctor at the hospital had been commanding. "Hes quite right about that, of course, 'Bama," he said sadly. "You should quit drinking entirely. The diet itself isnt so tough, or complicated. They make a lot more out of it than they need to. All you really need to do is cut out the carbohydrates and eat lots of leafy vegetables. They have regular diabetic diet sheets. Ive got them down at the office. Ill bring you one. But you should quit drinking."

"Ive been drinkin whiskey all my life," 'Bama said, his voice flat. Then he grinned. "In fact, I could use a drink right now, after the way you tore me up, Doc."

Doc Mitchell laughed, ruefully, the humor in his eyes curiously tinged with that sadness.

"No, I been drinkin all of my damned life," 'Bama said flatly, "and I dont reckon I aim to stop now."

Again, the little doctor spread his hands, helplessly. There was a curious look of sad understanding on his face. "Well, try to cut it down all you can," he said.

"What about this dying business?" 'Bama said.

"Its hard to say," Doc Mitchell said evasively. "But he was probably right about that, too. And then again you might live on damned near forever. Its just hard to say," he said sadly.

"Well, to hell with it," 'Bama said. "Five or ten years is quite a while anyway. Dave, go down and get me a bottle of Jack Daniels, will you?"

And that was the way they left it. 'Bama kept on drinking whiskey. Doc Mitchell fixed him up with everything else he needed, brought him out the syringe and equipment, showed him how to use it, even brought him a couple of books on diabetes. 'Bama studied them carefully with that meticulous mathematical attitude of his and learned all about the insulin injections and the mechanics of the disease itself easily and quickly; he started right in giving himself the injections, but he did not stop the drinking.

"The thing I hate about most doctors," he said to Dave, "is that they always want to force you to live, to *dominate* you into living. Now Doc Mitchell's not like that, and thats why I like him: he understands. But what do they want to do it for? Just to keep the business? Or to prove how damned important they are? And then after theyve *domin*ated you into living, and you do go on living, all the damn fun's gone out of living anyway. So what have you got?"

In three weeks, nearly the end of March, he was up and around again, still limping but able to navigate and to sit up and play poker all night at the Moose or Eagles. The wound had healed well and quickly, and every day he faithfully gave himself his shot of insulin. Dave would see him sometimes, late in the morning when he had got up and Dave himself was on the way to the bathroom past his door, sitting by the light of the bedroom window, his pants down around his ankles, the little glass and metal insulin syringe in his hands against the light. 'Bama would look up and laugh, and make a gesture as if to goose him with the syringe. All of his diabetic equipment and the insulin and the books he kept locked up in a little cabinet in his room meticulously and carefully. Neither of them ever mentioned anything about it ever, to anyone.

'Bama had digested the books on diabetes immediately, while he was still laid up with the hip. He also went through all of Dave's books on reincarnation and metaphysics that Bob had given him, although neither of them ever talked about them, and Dave did not know if he had gotten any more out of them than he himself had. As soon as he was back up on his feet again and the limp had nearly subsided, he packed his little diabetes cabinet in the Packard and went down to the farm and stayed for several days, almost a whole week, the longest Dave had ever seen him stay down there.

Apparently, to all intents and purposes, he was the same old 'Bama. But he had changed.

CHAPTER 60

IT was strange to live with him and watch the change take place, grow more pronounced,—especially for Dave: Dave who, he realized now, had always had this almost worshipful hero worship for him. It was not so much that he changed physically. He didnt. If anything, he looked to be even healthier; after he started taking the insulin. That sallow, hollow-eyed look that he had had ever since Dave had first known him faded away somewhat, and more color came into his face. The strange protruding paunch that he had also had since Dave met him melted away a little too, probably from the diet and from keeping his bowels open with plain water enemas as Doc Mitchell had advised him. It was eerie, almost unbelieveable, to Dave, to think that even back then, a year, almost a year and a half ago now, when he had first met him there in Ciro's with Dewey and Hubie, even then the tall gambler was probably already suffering from this disease which only now had been brought out into the open. The change wasnt physical, it was something inside himself, inside 'Bama. The old cool, collected, objective, powerful, always-in-command-of-the-situation 'Bama was being sucked out of him, eaten away, slowly and before your very eyes. In its place was a flighty, irascible, often petulant man whose judgment was no longer dependable and whose grin, when he grinned at all, was bitter as gall and worm-wood. It even showed up in his gambling: from the cold methodical poker player, patient as a steel trap waiting for an advantage to present itself, he became an irritable greedy player, always more anxious for the *next* hand than for the one being played now; he was even on occasion given to wild fits of wild unreasonable betting on hands which even he knew werent worth it, but unlike Bob French in his sporadic poker jaunts he could not dominate the hand and push his bluffing through. And then, he—'Bama the hard, 'Bama the silent—would actually complain almost querulously about losing! It was as if,—or so Dave analyzed it—it was as if, knowing that he was sick, and even more than that knowing that he was *dependent*—upon insulin, upon diet, upon *help*—took away all his old selfconfidence and sureness of himself and left him no longer powerful, no longer positive—exposed. Only when he was thinking—Dave never knew about what—or when he was reading some of his metaphysical books on luck, or working at his calculations of percentages of their still dwindling wins, did he seem at all to be the old calm mathematical systematic 'Bama. Only then, and when he was driving the big black car.

The change took place in an astonishingly short space of time, actually—from the time he got out of bed which was the last week in March, to Easter which fell on April 17th in that year of 1949: about three weeks. In that time he had become an entirely different man, and even Dewey and Hubie and Wally and the others noticed it, although of course none of them knew the reason for it. Most of the time he didnt talk at all. And the diabetes and cirrhosis was never mentioned except between Dave and himself. Like all diabetics, he had taken to carrying two or three cubes of sugar in his pocket all the time, upon Doc Mitchell's advice, as insurance against insulin reaction. And also, there was always the possibility of diabetic coma should his insulin allowance fall too low, or should he eat and drink too much and forget to take his insulin. None of the others knew anything about any of this at all; all they knew about was the shooting; but the change in him was apparent to everyone, and the last vestige of the old unity and sort of gay rebelliousness in the house disappeared. 'Bama took to spending more and more time down at the farm with Ruth and his kids and Clint and his family, and Dave as well as all the others were thrown more and more upon their own devices, their own amusements and associations. For Dave this gradually came to consist of Ginnie Moorehead who was always around except when she was working. But mostly, it seemed, for all of them, it consisted of the liquor: whatever else, there was always plenty of liquor at the house; 'Bama saw to that. He himself was drinking even more now than he had been before the shooting; it was almost as if he were deathly afraid of being caught sometime without a bottle at hand.

"Whats the matter with him?" Wally Dennis asked Dave once; after 'Bama had come in and gone up to his own room without a word to anyone. "Whats happened to him since he got mixed up in that shooting scrape? Has he lost his nerve? Did it scare him out or something?"

Dave, who knew what it was but was bound to silence, could only glare at him. "Ill tell you one thing," he said tensely. "Ill tell you one thing, kid. And dont forget it: Whatever it is thats happened to him— and its none of your business; and its none of mine—but whatever it is thats happened to him, he hasnt lost his nerve." He said it loud enough and for the benefit of all of them, scattered around the kitchen, and no one of them would meet his eye and offer to take exception or argue with him, even the sanguinary Dewey. But it appeared that nevertheless, the opinion voiced by Wally was the general consensus of opinion. "Youll all of you sit around here and practically live off of him, drink his damned liquor by the caseful, and then sit around and talk—over the whiskey he bought for you!—about him bein a coward and losing his nerve. Well, I wouldnt wipe my feet on the whole damned bunch of you!" He glared at all of them, fat and wind-less as he was, all ready to go to the mat with any one or even all of them. But, for the moment at least, his fury was too strong for any of them, even Dewey, and nobody would meet his eye.

"And Ill tell you something, kid!" he said to Wally sarcastically. "You better learn something about nerve, kid; before you go shootin your mouth off about it. Maybe someday youll learn what nerve is."

Wally merely looked at him in a peculiar way, and did not say anything. He did not like being called 'kid' at all, it showed plainly on his face, but he only looked down at his glass—filled with 'Bama's whiskey—and then took a big drink of it. Wally had been having his own bad troubles lately, Dave had sensed it, although he did not know what it was.

"Im sorry, Wally," he said awkwardly.

"Its all right," Wally said without looking up from the glass. "I guess I had it coming."

Dave looked around at all of them. He had said his little piece. But it plainly hadnt changed anybody's opinion. It was all he could do. He got his own Martini and took it upstairs to sit with 'Bama in his room a while. It was a futile gesture. They really talked very little together any more, except for just perfunctory superficial things. But he sat down anyway, holding his glass. There was a half full bottle of Jack Daniels on the bedside table. And so he just sat, in silence. It was all he could do.

'Bama was reading one of the Alice A. Bailey occult books, *Discipleship in the New Age* it was, and he only glanced up in acknowledgement of Dave's arrival and went back to the book. After a moment Dave cleared his throat. "You like that stuff?"

"What?" 'Bama said and looked over at him. Then he turned the book around and looked at the cover. "Yeah," he said. "Very interesting." Then he grinned that bitter, wormwood grin. "I guess Id like to believe its true."

"Thats the way I feel," Dave said awkwardly. "Id like to believe its true, too. I guess thats why I distrust it. Its always so easy to just believe something you want to believe. I distrust *myself*."

"Yeah, I guess thats how I feel," 'Bama nodded, his head with the hat on it already back in the book.

"Why dont you come over to Israel with me sometime soon," Dave said, "and meet them: Bob and Gwen." Then his stomach sank away from under him again, leaving him with that sick bottomless feeling, at the thought of her. He hadnt seen them since 'Bama had been shot.

'Bama dropped the book again, and grinned that grin like gall. "What for?"

"Oh, you could meet them," Dave said awkwardly, "and talk to Bob maybe. He has a lot more of that stuff; and knows a lot more besides that. Hed be glad to talk to you about it." But inside, the sick empty feeling in his stomach, he was hoping desperately now that 'Bama would not accept, and wishing now he had never mentioned it.

"No thanks," 'Bama said, raising the book again. "I dont want to."

"Well, it was just an idea," Dave said, feeling relieved, but wishing now, a little guiltily, after 'Bama had refused, that he had accepted, for his own good. The sick bottomlessness in his stomach did not go away. "Well, I guess Ill go on back downstairs," he said lamely.

"See you," 'Bama said, head still in the book.

Dave nodded helplessly from the door and then went on slowly down the stairs, and in the darkened hallway Ginnie Moorehead met him, talking soothingly to him, and he put his arms around her.

And that was the way it went. One time 'Bama would be icily, totally unapproachable; and the next time as flighty as a virgin on stilts, resentful, petulant, even querulous.

Dave, who still remembered that weird night he had heard Lois Wallup weeping, could only watch and helplessly do nothing. It was only one more of that steadily increasing series of mishaps that had come to them since the first of the year. Only this time it was something more than just a minor mishap. It was a major calamity. Not only to 'Bama himself, but to the house, to all of them. But why had it happened to come, or had to come, just now? It had been in progress back almost a year and a half ago when he met them, the seeds had already been planted then; perhaps 'Bama had actually already had the diabetes then. But why had it happened just now? after January of 1949? Why hadnt it happened last summer? or a year before that? or two years after January 1949? Why right after Raymond Cole had died? after Mildred Pierce had got married? after he himself had quit with Gwen? Was all this only superstition in his own mind? Only a reaction to his own guilt? He could not escape a feeling that it was all connected, that in some way it all tied in together some way: the three incidents, the series of mishaps, and now this. And yet, he knew for a fact 'Bama had had the disease prior to January. He had to have had. And yet why was it only discovered now? and if it had *not* been discovered now, had not been discovered at all—*would it still have been there?* He had a weird crazy feeling that it might not have been; he almost believed that if 'Bama had not been shot and learned about the diabetes in the hospital, the diabetes which he already had, 'Bama would actually not have the diabetes now. That only the discovery of it had brought it into existence. And that was insane. He must be going off his rocker.

The old life—the life that he had so unconcernedly and so unconsciously moved into when he first met 'Bama and Dewey and Hubie that first day he was in Parkman, that life he loved and that had existed a year and a half since he entered it, and perhaps a year or two before he came—that old life, that niche, that pattern, was breaking up, and he was watching it. In fact it was already broken up, was already gone. All that remained was for the people to move on into new spheres, away from each other, and for the house to rot and fall down, and the garden they had made in the vacant lot to grow back up in weeds, then it would all be gone. But where would it have gone? Where, in fact, was it now? where had it ever been? Change. Inexorable change. What had caused it? what prenatal, preexistent elements, lying there dormant and unknown in darkness, had grown and fused and caused Change? What was the answer? *Was* there any answer? He had stood and watched it disintegrate all about him, and inside him too. All that remained was the disposal of the ashes, the remains: the interment. He had never in his life, despite all the whiskey the tall gambler drank, seen 'Bama actually drunk. Now he began to see him drunk increasingly. Eyes glazed, his steps and movements and speech slow and thick, but always able to walk without staggering, 'Bama turned up dead drunk more and more often. He even played poker that way, something he would never have done before.

Was he himself, Dave, somehow personally responsible for all of this? Was it somehow all his fault? Had he, by entering into the life of this group, caused it in some way to fall all apart? What if he had never come back to Parkman at all? Perhaps 'Bama would never have contracted the diabetes at all? Was he, Dave, in some obscure unknown way responsible for that too? —Or was all this only the haunted imaginings of some unnamed guilt in him? All his life, it seemed, he had been just an onlooker. Back out in Hollywood, even in the Army too, and now here. Always a sort of outsider. He had never participated; he had never *acted*. Just a sort of a nonentity, wandering around the fringes of life. Only when he was violently in love with some woman or other, did he ever really *act*;—and even then his actions never extended far enough beyond his immediate vicinity to reach and affect any other person, so that even those actions were not actions at all even either, not in the true sense. Bob French had said a writer *should* be an onlooker, a nonparticipant, *should* be a nonentity: a sort of physical and emotional recording machine, without personality, without opinions: so that, if need be, he could write both from the viewpoint of a Democrat and a Republican as if he believed both, as if both were right; or could write both from the viewpoint of the Murderer and the Murderee, as Bob called it. But was Bob right? Would not such a man be just a sort of emotional and spiritual octopus, sucking the vital energy out of everyone he came in contact with? —Or again, was this just his own obscure guilt? that guilt that everyone, every human in the world today, seemed to suffer from? It was that same guilt that the Russians and the Chinese used in their brainwashing techniques—like with Cardinal

Mindszenty—using this powerful but unspecific unobjectified guilt to get their victims to confess to any crimes they deemed suitable to the occasion. Where did it come from, this new guilt in everyone? It didnt use to be in people a hundred years ago. And what did it mean? What was its purpose? If there was really a definite evolution, as Bob claimed, where did this great vague guilt fit into it and what was its use? —Or was it just that it came from your mother beating you when you were a kid when she caught you? just mechanically came from that, augmented by all the toilet-training of civilization which instilled such a horror and feeling of filth that you wound up constipated, mentally and emotionally constipated as well as physically? Perhaps that was all it was? Well there was one thing about him anyway: he certainly wasnt emotionally constipated. If anything, he had diarrhea of the emotions. And all he could do was sit, feeling somehow vaguely that it was his fault, and watch old 'Bama fall apart.

Dave himself —in spite of his protracted furies of work interspersed with shorter lean spaces: that new way he had been working the past six or seven weeks: as contrasted with his former slow methodical routine— had only come up with about twenty five pages of finished manuscript in all that time. That was something less than a half a page a day. Most of what he had written in his extended furies he had gone back over later and in a fit of despair decided to throw out. What was left wasnt very much. And he wasnt even sure it was any good. He had not been over to see Gwen with any of it, and when he tried to pull himself back into the old slow methodical routine he failed miserably. Only when he worked himself up into an emotional frenzied fury of attacking it could he work at all, burning out of him by sheer weight of energy his worries and fears; otherwise his mind was too full of both Gwen and 'Bama to concentrate at all. And the work done this way, in these frenzied attacks, was not nearly as good at all. It plainly lacked discrimination. And yet he could not work the other way, the old way. And even his furies of energetic hate and anger, that drove him to the typewriter to bat out ten and fifteen pages at a crack, were now diminished and weakened by what had happened to 'Bama.

Only once during that six or seven weeks from the end of February when he had last seen Gwen, to Easter on April 17th, did he take anything over to Israel to show her; and that one time was just the same as the time before: she was just as embarrassed and vaguely upset and distant as she had been before. She read the manuscript—as did Bob— she thought it was good, and said it seemed like a very little for so long a time. He did not say anything. What could he say? That he couldnt write because he was so in love with her? Hell, if she didnt know that already, she never would. Bob had had an answer from the new story "The Peons" that he had sent in; the lady-editor at NLL had bought it for the same price as "The Confederate"; $500; and was going to use it in the fall collection. She thought it was good, even better than "The Confederate", though she did wish he would try sometime to write about more *normal* people. Bob gave him the check and he took it and put it in his pocket. It meant so little to him that he carried it around in his pants a week before he discovered it again and deposited it in the bank with the other. And he did not go back to Israel after that; it was just too painful, too enervating. All he did was just hang around the Parkman house, in painful helpless silence, and watch what was happening to 'Bama. The increasing change in 'Bama was utterly unbelievable.

One day when just the two of them were sitting alone together in the kitchen, talking over how their poker percentages were still dropping, 'Bama suddenly began to talk about himself. Most probably it was talking about the money that did it. —(They were at the place now, 'Bama had said after making some private cabalistic calculations of his own, where it was nearly fifty-fifty: they were only winning slightly more than they were losing.)— And it was perhaps this that started him to talking about his own finances. Anyway, he suddenly launched into this description of how he was going to leave everything after his death. At first he was very cool and mathematical about it.

"The farm's all in Ruth's name anyway, you see," 'Bama said in that cold precise voice that was always him at his best. "And has been ever since I got back from the Army. Shes practically had the full runnin of it ever since then. I only advise her a little now and then. Shell have the four hundred acres, and both houses, and all the stock; and whats more shell know how to take care of it. Thats what she likes. So her and the kids, and Clint and Murray and the others as long as theyre willin to work with her, will all be more than adequately taken care of. In addition to that," he said coolly, "theres a good bit of cash there already, already in her name. About thirty five percent of everything Ive won in the last three years since I got out of Service, Ahve turned over to her; every time Id win Id give her thirty five percent of it. Shell—" his voice wavered a moment, almost quavered, and he paused, "shell be a really wealthy widow. For around these parts, anyway. Shell be able to marry again, and just about pick her own choice, with all that." Again, suddenly, his voice almost quavered, and he drew a long deep breath. And Dave sat painfully and helplessly and watched him bat his eyes. 'Bama, iron 'Bama, was actually blinking tears back out of his eyes! and it embarrassed Dave. "Shell—" he said, "shell—be worth sixty or seventy thousand, all told." Momentarily his voice steadied: "Therell be enough to send all three kids to college if they want to go. And, whats more important, all thats in her name. No matter what happens to me, or how much I might happen to lose or throw away, I would never be able to touch that. No matter— No matter how I—" This time he could not blink fast enough, and the tears glistened brightly from his eyes and threatened to overflow. "No matter how I fall apart. No matter how goofed off I get. No matter how I crap up or what happens to me." 'Bama blinked his eyes and swallowed heavily and his lower lip was trembling. He was not looking at Dave but off over his head at the wall. "So—thats—all taken care of," he said, his voice quavering and going off up to a higher pitch on the last word. And two big wet tears ran out of his two eyes and down his face, slowly, keeping exact pace with each other, almost hesitantly, as if—Dave thought—they were strangers here and were breaking new ground where no trail had ever gone before.

Dave did not know what to say, or to do. Painfully and embarrassedly, he merely sat, his buttocks held taut on the chair seat, trying desperately to keep his face from screwing itself up with what he felt.

"I dont know whats gettin into me," 'Bama said absently, more calmly; "Im skitterish as a damn heifer any more." He wiped his face off with his hand. "Now," he said and cleared his throat. "About you. I can let you have three, four, even five thousand anytime you want it, Dave."

"What the hell would I want your money for?" Dave cried painfully. "You aint going to die tomorrow! Or even next month! That doctor said five or *ten* years, for Christ's sake! And Doc Mitchell said maybe even longer!"

"Well, you may wind up needin it," 'Bama said, and again his voice quavered. "And anytime—anytime—you want to break up housekeepin here, its perfectly all right with me. Ill understand." Selfpity had again attacked him, leaving great gaping holes in his defenses.

"What the hell would I want to do that for!" Dave cried painfully.

"Well, you probly will, before long," 'Bama said. "And I just want you to know its okay with me." He sounded as if he was going to go on, but then he didnt, and he stopped. Kind of vaguely, he looked down to where his glass of whiskey sat as if for a moment he didnt know what it was. Then, suddenly, he picked it up and drained off what was in it and holding the glass drew his arm back savagely like a pitcher about to uncork his fast ball.

Dont do it! Dave wanted to shout: Dont do it, 'Bama! Youll regret it! youll be ashamed you did afterwards! —It was almost as if he already knew, could already see it and hear the words, what the gambler was going to do and then to say, and Dont do it! he wanted to yell: youll be embarrassed afterwards! But he couldnt say anything, he could only sit and look. How could he say anything? What *right* had he to say anything?

There was that seemingly long, timeless pause, but which was really only a split moment, and then 'Bama threw and the glass struck the wall above the sink and shattered tinkling down into it and 'Bama put his head down on the table in his arms, the hat, the pearl semiWestern hat, pushed back to expose that widow's peak of his, coming up level in Dave's gaze as the gambler bent forward.

"Why?" he said brokenly—saying the very words that Dave had already heard in his mind, had somehow known he was going to use: "Why? Why does it have to be me? Why *me!* Why did it have to happen to *me!*"

Dave did not know what to say. Embarrassed for him, ashamed for him, aware with an almost physical pain of how much 'Bama would detest himself later for it, he could only sit and look. The iron man was broken, and he did not want the iron man to be broken. Out of everything, that was the one thing Dave had hung onto: hung onto for so long now that it seemed it had been there all his life: whatever weakness, whatever cheap petty ignorances, whatever cowardlinesses he himself had always been subject to, and he was chock full of them, that was the one thing he could always depend on: 'Bama the iron man would remain as solid as the iron he was made out of: And now the iron man was broken, too.

"Why *me?*" 'Bama said, weepingly, muffledly, rolling his head back and forth on his arms. "Why *me?* Why *me?*"

Dave got up quietly and went and began to pick the glass up out of the sink. He was ashamed and embarrassed inside himself to look at him, and he knew 'Bama would be ashamed later on that he Dave had been there. He wished somehow he could just shrink down into the floor, and just not be there. Not be there for 'Bama to see when he looked back up.

But when he turned back from the sink after dumping the broken glass into the wastebasket beneath it, 'Bama had already raised his head. He had pulled the hat forward until it slanted so low Dave could not see his eyes, and under the brim he was wiping them with his hand.

"Im goin down to the farm," 'Bama said muffledly, "for a few days," and pushed himself up from the table.

Dave did not know what to say to him, and for a moment did not say anything. "Why dont you give up the drinking?" he said softly, embarrassedly.

"No!" 'Bama said from the door into the hall. "I dont want to! Theres little enough damned pleasure in a man's life as it is!" He turned and went on upstairs.

"Its not too late to stop," Dave said after him.

'Bama did not answer him, but when he came back down, carrying his little diabetes cabinet that he kept always locked, he stopped by the back door out to the garage. His hat was still pulled down low over his eyes shamefacedly, and beneath its shadow he wore that wormwood-bitter grin. "Sure," he sneered, "I could give up drinkin, and give up smokin, and go down to the farm and live and keep regular hours and a regular diet and not stay up late. I might live for twenty, thirty years like that. And what would I be? Id be bored to death, and Id be Ruth Dillert's invalid husband. Thats what Id be," he said sneeringly.

"Ruth wouldnt mind," Dave said.

"Mind! Yore damn right she wouldnt mind! Shed love it," 'Bama sneered. "My life aint never been like that, and it aint never going to be."

"Thats only pride," Dave said quietly.

"Well, if its pride, its all I got," 'Bama said. "Its all Ive ever had. By God Im goin to keep it."

Dave did not answer, and embarrassedly still did not look up, but still the big man lingered by the door. "Listen—" he said hesitantly.

"I wont tell anybody," Dave said, and shook his head.

"Thanks," 'Bama said awkwardly. He went on outside to the Packard.

Dave listened to him from the table as he got in the car and slammed the door and started the motor and raced it viciously. The 'Bama he had known a year ago would never ever have done that: raced his motor. And the 'Bama he had known a year ago would never have descended to asking him, even hesitantly, not to say anything; he would have known automatically that he wouldnt say anything, and even if he should have said anything, 'Bama wouldnt have cared. Outside the car drove off, and Dave had another drink and went to bed.

But perhaps the biggest evidence of the change in 'Bama was what happened with Doris Fredric on Easter Day. Doris was still coming down to the house, and still trying in her strange icy-on-the-inside virginal-on-the-outside way to hold and dominate and bind to her—bind to her by ties of love, he thought, heh heh—the house and everyone who came to it. She was not succeeding nearly so well since 'Bama had set her down that time with the Terre Haute woman, and other times, later; but she was still trying although not as obviously or openly. It seemed that—to Dave's imagination, at any rate—there was some psychological fascination for her in the place and all of them in it and the task, the challenge, she had set herself of dominating all of them. Ginnie as well as all of the other girls including Rosalie, were already her willing slaves. And Dave was convinced, from the half-resentful half-smug way they treated her, that she had already slept with both Dewey and Hubie. Wally he was not sure about: she probably considered him too young. But as things began to go bad for everybody at the house, for Dewey and Hubie after Raymond's death, for Dave himself after his scene with Gwen, for 'Bama too now after the shooting, Doris Fredric seemed to bloom and blossom and grow more beautiful and virginal and desirable every day. She had nothing to do with any of the troubles, of course, but it was as if in some secret way she was nevertheless taking to herself with her smug sedate smile all the credit for them anyway. She did not know, of course, anything about 'Bama's diabetes, but she knew just as everybody else had sensed it that something had happened to 'Bama after the shooting scrape in Indianapolis. It was almost, Dave thought maliciously, as if she had singlehandedly both nominated and elected herself to the honor of the responsibility for that tragedy also—sweetly, and demurely, and sedately, and proudly, in her virginal way. She was, apparently, seeing herself more and more in the role of the *femme fatale*.

'Bama had gone down to the farm for Easter. The Saturday night before Dave and he had played poker very late—until after three—at the Woodmen's Lodge, and when they got home he had unloaded Dave and loaded up his little diabetic's cabinet and started right then for the farm. He might stay a week, he said. He had been doing that more and more lately: going off at odd hours and in the middle of the night and going down there to the farm. This time, however, he came right back the same day. Sunday evening, Easter Day, he came storming into the house with his face black and lowering with rage.

Almost everybody was at the house, celebrating Easter in appropriate fashion, i.e., getting drunk. Doris, however, did not happen to be there. 'Bama looked around for her and then drew Dave off by himself and took him upstairs. Doris had been down to the farm. She had been down there seeing Ruth.

"My God," Dave said, "did she—"

No, no. Nothing like that. She was too smart for that. And she would never admit that about herself anyway. But he, 'Bama, was onto her game and he knew how she worked. She was one of those broads who couldnt stand prosperity; always had to have a fight going. What had happened, apparently, was that she had gone down there Saturday morning to buy some eggs. She had told Ruth she was going to have a big egg-hunt party for her freshman English class, and she bought every fresh egg Ruth had on the place, some six dozen. She and her "kiddies" were going to color them and then hide them and have a party Sunday morning, after dawn Services. She had made a wonderful impression on Ruth. Ruth thought she was just simply wonderful. Such a sweet girl. Doris had spent half the afternoon sitting talking with her and Clint's wife. Drank coffee with them and they all sat around the kitchen table and had a wonderful gabfest. She was going to come back next week for some chickens, and she was going to start buying all her butter and cream and buttermilk and fresh vegetables for herself and her folks at home from Ruth because she thought she had a simply wonderful place down there. Apparently, it had turned into a regular mutual admiration society. Wonderful eggs. Wonderful chickens. Blah, blah, blah. And now get this: Didnt she have any turkeys? She didnt? Well, hadnt she ever thought of getting in some turkeys and raising them? Ruth was high as a kite over both her and the idea of starting a turkey farm. Maybe she could even raise domestic pheasants, too, Doris had suggested. And she would come down next week and spend the afternoon with her and they could look into it and discuss it. She might even be willing to put some money in herself, in such a real paying proposition. Ruth had told him all about it this morning, as excited as could be over it.

"Well, what did you tell her?" Dave said.

He had told Ruth that Doris Fredric was probably the biggest whore in Parkman, and that she had better look out for her and stay away from her. But you know Ruth; shes not very bright; not to that kind of an operation anyway. Ruth hadnt believed him, and had been shocked at him.

"What do you think her game is?" Dave said. "Doris's?"

"How the hell do I know what her game is?" 'Bama said blackly. "I just know shes out for trouble. Maybe shes just doin it to upset *me*. Or maybe she wants to cause trouble between me and Ruth—which she couldnt do anyway; but she might think she could. Or maybe theres something in her in that bitchy selfsatisfied way of hers that makes her think it would be amusing to be the best friend and business associate to the wife of the man shes rompin, behind the wife's back. Ive seen that happen plenty of times. I dont know what she has in mind. But whatever it is, its trouble. And I mean to stop it. The smug little bitch."

"Howre you going to stop her going down there just to buy produce?"

"Ill stop her," 'Bama promised blackly. He raged pantherishly, nervously back and forth across the room, pounding one fist into the palm of the other. "That no good whorish smug rich little bitch. I always knew she was a bum." He turned and stared at Dave menacingly, narrow-eyed. "Come on, lets go on back downstairs and have a drink. I want to be there when she comes."

"Maybe she wont show up? After going down there?"

"Shell show up," 'Bama said. "She wouldnt miss it for anything."

The party was at its full height when she did show up; the wit and liquor were flowing freely, in the kitchen and in the living room, everybody was laughing drunkenly and hysterically at mots and jokes they not only would be bored with but would be ashamed to tell, if they were sober. Everybody, that is, except 'Bama. 'Bama sat by himself, scowling blackly and drinking drink after drink, or he paced back and forth and from one room to another skittishly, nervously, jitterishly.

"That farm is the only damned thing Ive got left in the world any more," he told Dave once blackly. "The only damned thing, now. The only place to go. And nobody is goin to crap that up for me. Nobody. Not even if I have to kill them." He was certainly not the cool, cold, mathematical, methodical 'Bama who would have handled the problem of old.

Doris came in—through the kitchen door; as everyone always did, there—looking her usual calm, sedate, beautiful self: small, petite, beautifully and expensively dressed, her small head with its old-cherrywood-colored hair held high and straight above the long slender neck, beautifully—though not ostentatiously—fixed up, and oh so very virginal looking. Tonight she was wearing a black ribbon choker to show off the neck. Dave happened to be standing against the kitchen sink when she came in without knocking, without hesitating, very much at home, and so had a ringside seat for everything. Looking at her as she came in —(she went straight to one of the kitchen chairs and laid her beautiful expensive red coat across its back herself familiarly; she was not that type who would wait for some "gentleman" to help her with her coat)— he had to admit ruefully that she was really beautiful. If you did not count that slight puffiness under the eyes—which in certain lights only made her look more smolderingly sexy—she was really exquisite. She had—he was absolutely sure of it—really actually become increasingly more beautiful lately, as things at the house had gone from bad to worse.

Dewey was in the kitchen also, standing at the bar where he had just fixed himself another drink, alongside Dave leaning against the sink; the two of them had been talking about—of all things—the Army. There was on Dewey's face, Dave noted once again, that curiously sly, pleased, smug look—which was also half-resentful—as from behind that warped ugly nose he looked out at Doris.

Doris herself looked happier than Dave could ever remember having seen her look. As she turned from meticulously and delicately laying down her coat she smiled at both of them benignly, almost maternally. But that was as far as she got. And Dave never did get to probe, to find out just how happy she was, and why.

Because that was when 'Bama came storming in through the dining-room door from the other side of the house, his face black and ominous. It was as if he knew by some sixth sense that she had finally come in, or else had kept an ear peeled through all the radio music and talk and other sounds for the sound of the back door opening and closing.

"Hello, sweetiepie," Doris said, smiling her magnanimous assured smile.

"Sweetie pie, hell!" 'Bama said loudly. And with the loud words everything became still in the other part of the house—excepting only the oblivious radio, which droned its music on into the vacuum—and everybody began to come out immediately to the kitchen to see what was going on and whether it was a fight. Almost all the gang was there—all, everybody, including even Rosalie, except for Wally Dennis who had not shown up tonight, and they came in cautiously at both doors, quietly, almost before 'Bama could even get his next sentence out: "What were you doin down at my farm?"

Doris looked surprised, and pleased, as if she had not expected this violent—and quick—a reaction to her gambit, and her baby blue eyes widened a little: innocently, but at the same time with almost greedy little glints in them.

"Why, darling!" she smiled benignly. "I only went down there to get some eggs for my kiddies' Easter Egg hunt this morning. Was there something wrong with that?" To Dave, it was incredible how selfassured and confident she could remain in the face of 'Bama's anger. He certainly couldnt have.

"Yore damn right there was!" the tall man cried frenetically, almost bending over her. "And you know it!"

Doris beamed at him, looking up at him demurely. "Why, 'Bama! Youre upset! Did I do that to you? I had no idea I would upset you like that, just by going down to your farm to buy some eggs." To Dave, it was clear she thought she had him; and she plainly didnt mean to turn loose of the screw. Never before had 'Bama ever lost his poise with her, or his cool control of everything.

"Yore not to go down there any more," 'Bama said peremptorily.

Doris's smile was still virginally demure, but there was just a trace of stiffness, of a set jaw, in it now. "Well, I really dont see how you can stop me. As long as your—farm sells produce; and I want to *buy* produce. Why arent I to go down?" she smiled, magnanimously, pityingly, demurely virginal. Dave, still standing by the sink glass in hand, could have punched her in the head himself.

"Ill *tell* you why," 'Bama said through clenched teeth, his whole face black and ominous as a tornado cloud. "Because if you do, Ill kill you. If I ever find out that youve gone down there again, or even hear youve been down there, Ill kill you. Believe me."

Doris looked startled and disbelieving as if she had not heard right. Probably nobody had ever said those words to her before. She looked up at 'Bama wide-eyed, almost amazed, tried for a moment to control her face back into its benignity, and then for the first time since he had met her, anyway, Dave saw her role break down. Open fear came onto her face. She was scared. She believed him. (And Dave himself had no doubt but what he meant it, either.) In any case, Doris believed him; and before this reality—or at least what she believed to be this reality—her whole facade broke down. And she suddenly looked like a little girl, a little tiny girl, of eight or nine, who has done something she was specifically told not to do, just to prove she could, and has been caught, found out, caught in the very act, her red-stained finger still deep inside the illicit jam jar, scared and guilty, already looking for an excuse in her mind even before a word's been said, but who knows already therell not be an excuse good enough.

And while she stood, looking at him like that, 'Bama, his eyes narrowed furiously and murderously, reached out a big hand and slapped her in the face.

It very nearly knocked her down. Her head snapping around to the side and her spine perforce following it, she only kept her balance and saved herself from falling by wildly flailing her arms around in the beautiful expensive dress. For Doris Fredric is was a most undignified action, movement, and Dave was forced to admit he enjoyed it exceedingly.

"You didnt have to hit her," Dewey said, almost mildly for him, and 'Bama swung around on him, his eyes blazing.

"You want a fight?" he snarled. "You want a real fight, Dewey?"

"No," Dewey said softly, and dropped his eyes. "No, I dont want to fight with you, 'Bama." Then he raised his eyes. "But I think I could whip you," his pride made him add.

"Then keep yore nose out," 'Bama said, ignoring the last, and swung back around on Doris, who was standing with her hand on her face, kind of feeling it gingerly, disbelievingly. "As for you, you get out. And dont come back around here any more. Not while Ahm livin here. If you do, Ill boot you right out through the screendoor and down the steps. —And dont you ever go back down to my farm. Because if you do, Ill kill you sure as theres a living God. It dont make me no difference. I aint got very much to lose anyway. So you remembeh what Ah said.

"Now git!"

Keeping her widened blue eyes on him, Doris walked around him, giving him a wide berth, to where her coat was. She picked it up and came back around him, walking backwards, and backed to the door. At the door, feeling it behind her, she paused, still looking at him, just for a moment, then she backed on out. If she had thought for a moment of making some parting shot to restore her dignity, she had also thought better of it.

And so another "loveaffair" was ended, Dave thought wryly; and another ant carried out another grain of wheat.

'Bama swung around on the others when the door closed, his eyes wide now, not narrowed, and burning with an almost maniacal murderousness. His eyes slashed around at them, at Dewey who was unafraid, at Dave who was scared to death, at the others standing in both doorways. From outside they heard the yellow convertible roar away. Then, still looking at them in utter silence, holding them bound as it were, by his eyes, 'Bama raised his big fist up slowly without a sound, staring at all of them challengingly, and brought it down full force on the kitchen table. Three glasses bounded to the floor and smashed, and the one whiskey bottle fell off and rolled across the floor, its liquor gurgling out, and the two table legs nearest him spread dangerously, one of them cracking where it was screwed to the top. Still silently, without a sound, his eyes wild, 'Bama looked down at it and then stepped back and kicked it full force, full leg, just as if he were punting a football. The table up-ended in the broken glass and skidded across against the refrigerator, the two legs on the opposite side bent inward now beyond repair. Then, looking around at all of them almost daringly, daring all of them, still in silence, 'Bama stepped to the countertop bar and caught a bottle of Jack Daniels by the neck and walked through the broken glass to the hall door where the people there faded out of his way, and tramped heavily up the stairs to his room.

It was half an hour later, after things had quieted down, and they had cleaned up the liquor and broken glass and set the now very rickety table back up on its damaged legs, and Dave was sitting at it musingly with a drink while the others made love, or talked, or drank, or listened to the music in the front room,—it was then that Wally Dennis came in, his heavy almost-Slavic face almost as black with anger and rage as 'Bama's had been earlier.

Dave had been sitting musing sadly over how ironic it would be if 'Bama did die: then Doris Fredric could go down to his farm and buy produce anyway: and she would undoubtedly do it too. Five years, ten years, it wouldnt make any difference: not to her: and in the end she would probably become his wife's best friend after all. His widow's, rather. Doris would see to that, by God. That was what he was sitting by himself musing about, and the sight of Wally and his black-angry face surprised him. Wally had already had several drinks and his hair was rumpled, and it turned out he had got them at the wedding recep-tion: Dawn's, Dave's niece's, wedding reception. After proceeding to get himself eye-glazingly drunk, he told Dave about it. That was where Doris had been; she had been at the wedding and reception, too. Dawn had married Jimmy Shotridge; that was Harry Shotridge's boy, did Dave know him? Dave knew Harry Shotridge, by sight and to speak to, but he did not know his son Jimmy; and he had not even known about the wedding, had not even sent a present or for that matter even had an invitation. But Wally had had one, and he had gone. But he had left the reception early and gone on home because the drinks had made him mad and he was afraid of making a fool of himself. Doris, though, had still been there when he left. So she must have come straight here from there.

That was all he said. After he had said that he shut up like a clam. He sat at the table with Dave, too rickety for either one of them to lean on, and drank swiftly and ferociously, looking at Dave occasionally with a black sullen angry look from the depths of which every so often sheer utter blind helpless panic would flash out at Dave blindingly.

And so, Dave thought drunkenly, still another ant had carried out still another grain of wheat.

Unable to say anything that might help him, since he himself would not even talk to him about it, Dave in turn told Wally about the scene with Doris Fredric in detail while Wally stared at him and listened hard and nodded his head and heard nothing. Once Rosalie Sansome came out into the kitchen to discover her boyfriend there, and Wally insulted her savagely—always a rather easy thing to do—and she left in a huff. Dave watched sadly wanting to tell Wally that he was making a mistake: he should always hang onto one gal if he was losing another; but, as seemed to be his only role anymore, he merely sat sadly and said nothing. Gradually all the others left, too, and finally Dave too left him there, still drinking, and drunkenly took his old plug Ginnie Moorehead upstairs to bed.

Well, so Dawnie had got married. To old Harry Shotridge's boy. And he hadnt even known a thing about it. Hadnt even heard about it. But of course they didnt run in the same circles anymore, he and Frank. And it was obviously Frank's doing, this marriage, and this wedding—Frank's and Agnes's both—and also that he had not received an invitation. Dawnie—he was quite sure—Dawnie would have sent him one.

BOOK FIVE

THE MARRIAGE

CHAPTER 61

IT WAS quite true that it was Frank's and Agnes's doing that Dave did not receive an invitation, but it was not true that the wedding, and the marriage, were their doing. The marriage, and for that matter most of the wedding, were all Dawn's doing.

It was her campaign, and after she had versed herself in the strategic situation and the tactical exigencies, she had planned it; and she herself had executed it, swiftly, and admirably, and with dispatch. When she came home from school the last weekend in March and informed her parents that she and Shotridge were going to be married Easter Day, her parents were as surprised as Shotridge's parents and everybody else. At first they both bridled and were all against it: Agnes tearfully thought she was too young, and too inexperienced; and Frank wanted her to wait—once his bypass deal was through with she could have her pick of any of the eligible wealthy young men in the Middlewest, he said. But Dawn, after having conducted the triumphant major campaign she had just executed, was not about to be outmaneuvered by either one of them in a *minor* campaign, good generals as they both were. She left school Friday afternoon cutting one class, and arrived home early Saturday; by Sunday morning that smaller, swifter campaign was over too; and both of them had given in. They both had always liked Shotridge anyway, better than Wally Dennis; and once the battle was over and decided, Frank said that by God they were going to have the best damned wedding Parkman had ever seen. Having won the war on both fronts, as it were, Dawn turned over to her mother the handling of the victory triumph and went on back to school, after making only one stipulation: she wanted to be sure that her old pal and childhood friend Wally Dennis was invited, along with his mother whom Agnes would invite anyway. She told Agnes what kind of clothes she intended to wear, who her bridesmaids and the maid of honor would be, and left the rest of it up to her. As that was Sunday March the 27th, Agnes had exactly twenty one days to get everything done; because she was not going to wait till June, she was going to do it Easter Sunday when she and Shotridge were both home for Easter vacation. Agnes, who both sentimentally and practically wanted her to wait till June, bowed before this new forcefulness plus tactical genius in her daughter. While the menfolks, Frank and seven-year-old Walter (whose name they had finally decided not to change to Franklin Jr; and whom Dawnie had met only for the first time this very weekend), relegated themselves to the kitchen and tried to be scarce, the two women sat down in the living room at Agnes's secretary and worked it out for Easter. Once again that new forcefulness which Dawn had only so recently found waiting to be used in the depths of herself, had triumphed.

She supposed, really, it was only the quality of growing up: of getting over a lot of childish romantic ideas you had as a kid in highschool, like all kids had: of at last realizing that as an adult you had responsibilities to the adult world you were going to live in. Once you came to face that, the forcefulness just naturally came to you. And she had put it to its first real acid test Christmas vacation, those few times she had seen him. Actually, of course, it had first come to her—she had first begun to feel it—back early last fall, when she had stood on the porch and watched him drive away with his old baseball cap jammed down over his eyes. But it had been such a totally new feeling, then, that not only had she not trusted it, she had not even known what it was. At first she had thought it was just the result of anger and fright. But then, as it had grown in her steadily all during the first semester up to Christmas vacation, when he had been writing all those letters: the first one so lachrymose and full of guilt and reeking with selfpity, and then all the others, gradually getting cooler and cooler: and she could see for the first time really down deep into the depths of him: then, she began to see what that new feeling of forcefulness really signified in her. But she was not willing to accept it blindly, even then. Objectively, coolly, she determined to put it to a real test Christmas when she saw him again. The result was that it not only reenforced her opinions, it doubly reenforced her faith in both the strength—and the efficacy—of her new forcefulness:

When they had sat in his kitchen, that last time, and had talked for so very long, she had realized at last and for sure what a really ungrown-up person he was. He was a perpetual adolescent who, when the time to mature came along, just had not met the challenge, had just refused to mature. A sex-crazy adolescent. And, vain, arrogant, jealous, never thinking of anyone but himself, he remained just exactly that: a sex-crazed child. Sex was all he could talk about. Sex was all he could think about. And when she hadnt wanted to keep on talking sex with him forever, the only thing he could think of was that she had another man. So she had just let him think it.

Actually, her first semester in Cleveland had been the most lonely and most terrifying experience in her life. The school itself was all right, it was fine, and she had made straight As (although of course she hadnt known that till the January exams). But the people she had met and fallen in with in her acting Workshop outside the school frightened her, if not actually horrified her. And the young actor (whom she had let *him* think she was going out with) had turned out to be almost as equally susceptible to the charms of men as he was to those of women. She had only had half a dozen dates with him before she lost him to another man. Dawn had only slept with him twice, and so she did not think of that as a love affair, she did not think of it as anything. In fact, she did not think of it at all, any; but she had not bargained for that kind of a life when she started out intending to be a great actress. Those were not the kind of people she had intended spending the rest of her life among. And in addition, they were all so snide, so highly *highly* "sophisticated", so very *very* "chi-chi", that the few very small roles she did get while being so insignificant as to mean almost nothing, were nevertheless very volubly and loudly criticized by all of them in their snide way, everyone. You could only take just so much of that, either.

All that, coupled to what she found out for sure when she came home Christmas, was what decided her. And once she had made up her mind, with that new forcefulness that had been growing steadily in her since September, and which reached its full maturity with *him* Christmas, she sat down and carefully thought out her campaign, and put it into action immediately.

Dawn had only seen Shotridge just a very few times, just to speak to, since the previous Christmas when she had run onto him out at the Country Club that time and had beat him playing pool. Several times after that, during the rest of her senior year, he had driven down from Champaign to see her in Drama Club productions, and after one of these she had gone out to the Country Club with him for a few drinks. But after that, after school was over and graduation, she had been spending so much time with—with *him*—all that summer, so very many dates they had had, movies, going swimming, tennis, horseback riding, all those very usual and normal things young highschool daters do, that she had hardly even seen Shotridge at all except just to speak to. Of course, he had seen them, around, and they had seen him. At the Country Club, or The Stables, or over in Terre Haute at the pool. But after all it was only the kind of *normal* dating that all highschool kids do; some girls dated, and "went with", the same boy for two or three years in high school, before they finally outgrew them and matured into real women. Some of them even pinned or ringed each other. She had never been pinned or ringed.

She knew of course where to find him. He would be out at the Country Club every evening he was home. And it had been an easy thing to get Frank and Agnes to take her out to the Club for dinner; they went almost every night during the Holidays, anyway. And the next night after being down in *his* kitchen, she had got them to take her. Shotridge, of course, was there; with his own folks; as she had known he would be. All she had to do was take some money in to the slot machines and after a while he appeared, at her elbow, breathing in that heavy way and exuding that despicable cologne. She had been very careful not to treat him too nice, and to act disdainful—an acting job never too hard to get into the part of, with Shotridge; and before the evening was over they were dancing with the rest of the college kids home on vacation to the music of the jukebox in the diningroom, and when she had finally allowed herself to loosen up a little and even laugh a little with him, poor old Shotridge had looked supremely happy. It sure didnt take very much—to make some men happy. The next day was New Year's Eve Day, and they had spent the whole afternoon and evening together, with a date for dinner at the Club, and during the afternoon after the matinee when they were driving around uptown for a coke at Bennett's Drug Store she had seen Wally Dennis walking uptown: It was strange: She had hardly recognized him: Her old childhood pal and good friend had grown up to be almost a total stranger to her, in all the ensuing years since they had used to play together when they were kids. Life was strange.

They had spent the next two days together, she and Shotridge, and before both she and Shotridge left to go back to school, Shotridge had asked and she had invited him to visit her at Cleveland to see one of the productions she would be appearing in. That would be in mid-January, right after exams, and he could drive to Chicago, she thought, from Champaign and leave his car at the airport and fly to Cleveland and she was to meet him at the Limousine Service terminal. That was what he decided to do: he only had one Friday afternoon class, which was a snap course, and he was all set up in it anyway, so he could leave Champaign at noon: by taking the late afternoon flight (he called and checked on it) he could be in Cleveland in time for dinner Friday evening. Dawn had never realized what a really forceful individual Shotridge really was; she had always known Shotridge was sweet, but underneath that surface shyness of his was a really forceful personality she had never known about.

That first time they had had a quick dinner at the Playhouse Restaurant next to the Cleveland Play House, and then had taken a taxi over to the out of school Workshop Theater where she was appearing, and after the show had ridden back downtown and walked through downtown Cleveland to the Hollenden where Shotridge was staying, for a drink, before she took the Euclid Avenue bus on back out to her sorority. The next two days Shotridge rented a U-Drive and they drove the Memorial Shoreway along the Lake and back up Liberty Row from the Lake to Wade Park and walked for a while in the cold air beside the Lagoon, and Saturday night ate at the Playhouse Restaurant again and took in the show at the Play House. Late Sunday Shotridge took the late evening flight back to Chicago in order to drive back down to Champaign in time for Monday classes. It was a truly lovely weekend Dawn thought.

And so began a series of similar weekends that lasted for the better part of three months. In February and March there was scarcely a single weekend that Shotridge did not drive to Chicago and fly to Cleveland to see her. Shotridge's father had increased his allowance (always liberal) during his sophomore year because he had passed in all his freshman subjects, and Shotridge used it to come to Cleveland to see her; and he gallantly spent money on her like a millionaire. Only rarely did he run so short because of the plane fare that she would have to give him money from her own allowance from Frank, and they saw a side of Cleveland Dawn had never seen before—since young actors were seldom attached to large allowances; and she had never been just about to spend any of her own money on *them*. Shotridge stayed at the Hollenden because he remembered his father had once stayed there on a business deal, and sometimes they would have cocktails and dinner there. Then they would take in a show, or a movie, or go to the Alpine Village for the floorshow, or if they wanted to spend a really intimate evening, a tête-à-tête, theyd go to the Sky Bar Inn out in the East End near the Park Plaza Hotel. They ate sea food at Fisher Rohr's downtown, or steaks at the Playhouse Restaurant. A couple of times, just for kicks, they went slumming to the 49er's where the strippers did their business on a stage built inside the bar. They took in the old Stadium Hotel on St Clair, the Dunham Tavern Museum, the Terminal Tower, the Garfield Memorial, and the Zoo in Brookside Park. They drove out to Shaker Heights, and Garfield Heights, and Brooklyn Heights, and out Lake Avenue to Lakewood and drove through Metropolitan Park. They drove out Euclid and past old Severance Hall at Euclid and East Boulevard and through the University, then took in the Museum of Art. It was a gay, money-spending, safe way to live, entirely different from the somehow frightened, cheap, pennypinching way she had lived last semester: there was safety somehow in spending money. And if Shotridge, after taking five whole weeks to screw his courage up to it finally, tried to put his hand on her when they were parked at a viewing point at Lake Front Park looking out over the Lake, or at some other place, she let him —after a suitable period of demurrage—when he kissed her. She did not, however, let him do any more than that. And when two weeks later, after finally getting up his nerve enough to ask her up to his room for a last drink after all the bars were closed, Shotridge actually did so ask her in a hollow voice, she went. But she was careful to do no more than that.

It was a strange, cold, desperate, frightened game she played, as laughing gaily she went everywhere with him. Not so much a race against time—because time wasnt important—as a race to find, and keep, perfect timing. It did not matter really how long a time—or how short—it was; just as long as the timing was right, was perfect. And she worked at it coolly and carefully; she had to. Most of the time she was completely and wholly, even desperately,—(he was really *very* sweet)—in love with Shotridge; and loneliness and an odd vague indefinite fright drew her to him for comfort. But then, at other times, as if someone had run a stream of water down over the front of the movie camera, or dropped a pebble in the pool, the picture would waver streamily like a funhouse mirror, and then clear, and she would be looking at a totally different picture: She had learned a lot about men from *him*. The main thing was that she had given *It* up too easily. Too easily, and too painlessly. She had done that, simply and ingenuously, because that was the way it had been, not knowing any better. And of course, *he* was not as tractable, as malleable, as Shotridge. Some women it was really painful for, apparently; so apparently she was just lucky. One last point was that she should never *never* have let on that she liked it, even though she did. Then the movie screen, the mirror, would shimmer and waver again in front of her eyes, and she would be looking at the first picture again. Horrible loneliness for Shotridge would assail her. If it was the middle of the week, she would be so sickly lonely, miss Shotridge so damned much, that she would go out alone after her last class and go to movies, one, two, sometimes even three in an evening, just to take her mind off how much she loved and missed him.

She was prepared. The next weekend after she had been up to his room for the nightcap drink he asked her up again, on Friday night, and again she went. That was the third weekend in March. And this time she allowed herself to be talked into having a second drink, and then a third. Everything seemed to be right. At least she thought it was. Of course she couldnt be abso*lute*ly sure. The funny thing was she wasnt drunk at all, or even half drunk. She believed she could have drunk a whole *bottle* of whiskey, without even feeling it at all. When Shotridge fumblingly unbuttoned a middle button of her blouse she only protested feebly, not positively, and made her voice sound a little breathless. It was a very delicate thing: to protest too positively would have made him jerk away with that hangdog look, but yet it could not be too feeble to sound convincing, either. She thought she achieved the proper tone.

From the look on his face it was plainly a moment of great triumph for Shotridge. Of course, the triumph didnt last long. But there wasnt any way he could get inside the slip, not without undressing her, and after a bit dissatisfaction made him withdraw his hand and try to try the other route. But Dawn's sense of timing came to her aid there: It was too soon yet, some instinct told her; and she stopped that.

Foiled there, looking plainly nonplussed for a moment, Shotridge finally came back to the blouse hesitantly, obviously expecting to be halted at any moment. But Dawn did not stop him; instead, she kissed him back lovingly, giving the impression she was unaware of what he was doing. After the blouse was unbuttoned, Shotridge paused perplexedly for several moments: He was no nearer than he had been before: But finally inspiration came to his aid and he reached around behind her. Dawn waited patiently.

Finally he made it, and Dawn's sense of timing which she was listening to carefully told her it was time to speak: "Oh, Shotridge! Please dont!" she whispered.

Of course he ignored her. Just putting the "please" in it assured that.

"Please, Shotridge!" she said again, and once again he was perplexed and foiled.

Shotridge stared at her gloomily and hopelessly. "Dawnie—?" he said miserably. "Dawnie, I—" The words, whatever he was going to say, trailed off into unhappy perplexed silence.

Dawnie ran her fingers along the back of his head and through his hair and smiled at him tremulously. "Turn off the lights," she said lovingly.

"Dawnie!" Shotridge said, his large eyes seeming to bulge. "You mean—? You mean you *will*? Will you?"

"No. I dont want to, Shotridge," Dawn said, lowering her eyes. But before she could say more he had leaped off the couch and run to the light switch by the door, as if he had suddenly realized his mistake—his blunder—in ever asking her any questions she could say no to. A breathlessness at her own audacity, and at what she was going to have to do next, and do very carefully and accurately, suddenly assailed her. It was, in some ways, probably the greatest role she would ever play.

In the dark she stood up and took off the rest of her clothes that Shotridge had figured out no unnoticeable way to rid her of, and went and lay down on the bed. In the dark, somewhere near the couch she could hear his shoes hit the floor.

"Dawnie! Dawnie, where are you?!" he cried suddenly, his voice high with near panic, from the vicinity of the couch. He apparently hadnt realized she had left it.

"Here. Here I am, Shotridge," she said, making her voice low and embarrassed.

"Oh," he said, with tremendous relief. Then there was a long silence.

What happened then was in some ways almost weird. It was as if she were standing outside of herself looking back down at her there on the bed, as she fought and cried out and tried to jerk herself away. And yet away down deep inside of her, part of her—no, more than part; all of her—meant those things: wanted to cry out and weep and get away. Wanted nothing to do with him, or with any man. And yet all the time she was also coolly standing off watching herself and analyzing it as if she were critically watching a third person stranger do a role.

It very nearly frightened Shotridge off entirely. But then, apparently, some ancient old male instinct, of cruelty, or of forcefulness, an instinct that had been forced underground in him, beaten down, oppressed, driven back, outlawed, first by his mother and then by his father and then by just about everybody else who knew him—nay, driven back, even, in generations of his ancestors before he was even born, and so pushed back in him to the very deepest labyrinthine bottoms of his soul, came to his aid.

"I cant help it, Dawnie!" he cried miserably. "I got to!"

"I know you do," Dawn whimpered softly. "I know you do. Its all right."

And in a way it was true for both of them. In an odd new way Dawn had never felt before.

Afterwards, bathed in both physical and emotional exhaustion, the two parts of her stared at each other closely, and almost unrecognizably, through the plate glass running down the center of her head: Both knew that one of them would be saying goodby forever to the other one, in just a little while. "You go on to the bathroom," she whispered. Silent with an almost tangible guilt, Shotridge got up and paddled to the bathroom in his bare feet and shut the door. This part had been planned before, a long time before. Dawn raised up and reached for her purse which she had been careful to see was lying on the bedside table and opened it and took out some tissues and a bottle of mercurochrome. Shotridge was still in the bathroom with the door shut, as if reluctant to come out. Dawn slipped to the bathroom door and opened it slightly, said: "May I come on in?", and went inside. Shotridge, his thin frame bent forward, was staring at his face anguishedly in the mirror above the lavatory. He started.

"Gee, Dawnie!" he said miserably. "You should of told me. Id of dressed."

Dawn smiled at him gently, a feeling of great love welling up in her. "Its all right, Shotridge. After whats happened between us, I guess something like that doesnt matter. I just had to come in," she said. She turned toward the waste basket with the tissues, and smiled at Shotridge brimmingly.

"Oh, *Dawnie!*" Shotridge cried anguishedly, and made as if to rush upon her and throw his arms around her; but then, belatedly, he stopped. "Oh, *Dawnie!* Im sorry! I am sorry!" He stared at her miserably.

"Dont be sorry," Dawn said softly, and meant it, "dont ever be sorry. I guess its as much my fault as it is yours. Its always as much the girl's fault as the fellow's. Ill be all right in a while.

"You get out of here now and let me have this place for a minute," she said embarrassedly. "Ill be all right in a little while. —And dont ever be sorry!" she said softly.

Shotridge stared at her dumbly, his face filled with sorrow and regret, and yet not without a certain triumph, underneath the look of love.

"Now you go on," Dawn said shyly. "Now get." And without a word he went out and closed the door.

She stayed in the bath quite a while and took a boiling hot shower and when she came out he had the big light on and was fully dressed and had lit a cigarette and was sitting staring at it without smoking it, kneading his knuckles together miserably.

"Im sorry I did it to you, Dawnie," he said anxiously as soon as she came through the door. "I didnt mean to do it. I—I dont know what came over me. It must have been the liquor. I guess. I just want you to know that I would never have done something like that to you. I love and respect you."

"Dont be sorry," Dawn said tenderly. "Im not sorry, Shotridge. I guess in a way Im even—glad."

"You are?" Shotridge said, his large eyes appearing to bulge outward with surprise.

"Well, now we—we belong to each other," Dawn said, and could actually feel herself blushing. She smiled at him lovingly.

"Thats true," Shotridge said wonderingly, his eyes wide with thought. "Well, I just want you to know I . . ." He went on talking hurriedly, a long breathless stream of talking, and Dawn sat down across from him in a chair noting that even as he talked so anguishedly, his eyes—as if they had uncontrollable ideas of their own—were ogling her. Finally he ran down and stopped, and just stared at her pleadingly, guiltily.

"When are we going to be married?" Dawn said bashfully.

"When? Whenever you want!" Shotridge said, his face lighting up eagerly. "Gee, you mean youll really marry me, Dawnie? Gee, we'll tie the old knot whenever you say the word, Dawnie."

"Well," she said, "let me think about it a minute." She got up, arching her back in the thin slip. "Gee, but Im stiff and sore! You must be a pretty virile man, Shotridge. Now you turn your back, Shotridge, while I get dressed. Dont look at me; please!" she said, and went over to her clothes.

Dutifully, he turned his back; and while she dressed Dawn noted that, as she had expected it beforehand, one of those two of her was gone. There was no plate glass down the center of her head anymore, and where the two of her had stared at each other so intently, one was gone now. The other gradually and slowly moved across and took over the whole area. A tremendous, swelling, powerful, poignant love for Shotridge welled up inside of her until she thought she could not stand it and might have to cry. When she was dressed, she sat down in the chair again.

"You can look now," she said softly.

Shotridge swung back around, his long thin large-eyed face anxious. "Gee, youre beautiful, Dawnie. Dawnie," he said, and took a deep breath, "Dawnie, you dont hate me, do you? I mean, not really. You dont *hate* me, do you?" he said anxiously.

"You couldnt help what you did," Dawn smiled warmly. "I understand about men. I know what its like with them. I know you couldnt help it. I understand."

"Do you?" Shotridge said miserably. "Do you really?"

She nodded, smiling maternally. "Thats why its the woman's place to—to put on the brakes. But I was afraid youd think I was—"

"No!" Shotridge said quickly. "Oh, no! No, no! I know you better than that. Why, what just happened with us proves it. —Listen," he said anguishedly; "I have a confession to make to you."

"Whats that?"

"Ive been out with other women before."

"You have? Where?"

"Over at the whorehouses in Terre Haute," Shotridge said guiltily, and stared at her anxiously.

Dawn smiled, sadly. "Well, I suppose thats just like most men," she said. "Its kind of a shock. But I guess I dont really care. I love you anyway."

"You do? And you dont care? You really dont care?" Shotridge said miserably.

Dawn smiled, sadly, and shook her head. "I guess I really dont care about much of anything, Shotridge, wherever *youre* concerned."

"Listen," Shotridge said. "What were you going to say about getting married."

"Well, I was thinking about it while I dressed," Dawn said. "I think we should get married Easter."

"So soon?!" Shotridge said, his eyes bulging. "Thats an awful short engagement!"

"Well, Im a little afraid of something happening; you know?" She looked at him shyly, and she was not acting; she felt shyly. "If not this time, maybe later on when you come back. They say you never can be sure, even with those—those things you use. And thats why I say Easter; I think it would be safer. Its only a month away. And wed be safe then."

"Gee, I never thought of that," Shotridge said, his eyes widening. "Well, its okay with me. But what about school? We cant drop out of school."

"Well, here was what I figured," Dawn said. "We get married Easter, at home, on Easter vacation. I think its even nicer than being a June bride. Everybody will know we're married then and it will be all right then. Then we'll both go back to school, you to Illinois and me to Reserve, until after June finals. Then next year Ill transfer to Illinois so we can be together, and we'll set up housekeeping there someplace. Lots of kids are doing that anymore: getting married and living together while they finish school. Its not like it used to be before the war: when you had to wait till you were out of school for it to be proper. Why, theyre even having—" here she almost blushed—"babies, and still going on to school."

"Gee!" Shotridge said, awed at the thought. "You suppose we'll ever have any babies, Dawnie?"

"I want lots of babies," Dawn said softly. "Lots and lots of babies."

"Well, by God, we'll have them then!" Shotridge said stoutheartedly. "Gee, Dawnie! You dont know what you mean to me. You dont know how much I love you. Ive loved you all my life."

"After the wedding you can still keep on coming over here weekends whenever you want," Dawn smiled shyly. "Only then itll be all right. Because we'll be man and wife. We wont have to worry then."

"Gee, Dawnie! Well, that sounds fine with me," Shotridge said eagerly. "Gee, Dawnie!"

"Of course," she added blushing, "You can keep on coming over before the marriage too. If you want to, that is."

"If I want to!" Shotridge cried. "If I want to! Gee, Dawnie, you dont know how much I want to. And it—it feels—it *feels* so good," he confessed embarrassedly. Suddenly he got up and came over to her and put his arms around her tenderly, and Dawn put her arms around him too, and it was substantially this same story and this same plan that she told her parents when she went home the next weekend, the last weekend in March.

"I love you so much, Dawnie," Shotridge whispered, holding her. "You dont know. Ill always cherish you. *Cher*ish you."

"I love you too, Shotridge," Dawn whispered back, and pressed his head against her and ran her fingers through his hair. "Dear Shotridge. Dear *dear* Shotridge."

After this tender scene of such powerful emotion that it brought tears to her eyes and very nearly made her weep, very nearly made them both weep, they sat back up and discussed the wedding and marriage plans some more. This was on Friday, and the next day instead of going out pub-crawling after dinner and a show, they went straight up to his room in the Hollenden to have several drinks and make love and afterwards talk about the marriage. By the time he left Sunday evening, they had everything pretty well worked out. Dawn would go home the next weekend to tell her folks. Shotridge was not going home himself; he had too much studying to catch up on. Instead, he was going to call his folks from Champaign and tell them the news. Dawn, in her turn, would have her mother call his parents from Parkman.

Which was exactly what she did. After she and Agnes had sat at the secretary that Sunday morning in the last week of March working out a rough sketch of plans for over an hour, she had her call up Eleanor Shot-

ridge. They, Eleanor and Harry, had already heard from Shotridge late
last night, it turned out. At first they hadnt known whether to believe it
or not, it was so sudden, Eleanor said; not that they werent pleased.
Then she feared to call Agnes about it, for fear she had not heard about
it from Dawn yet; and she thought she ought to hear about it first from
Dawn.

"Shes right here," Agnes said. "Yes; weve been sitting here all morning trying to work out some kind of plan. She only got home late last
night," she lied.

Dawn, sitting beside her, nodded vigorously.

"And weve been talking wedding plans ever since, until my head is
whirling," Agnes said, without mentioning the arguments. "What? Yes,
it is. Awfully short. But then times have changed since we were girls,
Eleanor. I wanted them to wait till June, too. But then I guess theyve
been going steady ever since Christmas Holidays, and thats almost four
months. Even so, it seems like a very short engagement. But I guess
nowadays, since the war, they do things differently than when you and I
were young. They dont want to wait. I was only reading in *Life* magazine the other day about the newer generation of young married college
students. Yes. Oh, did you read it too?"

There was a pause while she listened a moment.

"What?" she said. "A party?"

Dawn, who had one ear practically touching the phone, moved back
and shook her head "no" vigorously.

"No, Im afraid we cant. She has to be leaving right away to get back
to school in time," Agnes said loyally. "She says Jimmy didnt come home
because he has so much studying to catch up on. Hes been flying to
Cleveland from Chicago almost every weekend for the past two months.
Yes; imagine that? No, they didnt court us like that when I was in
school, either!" She laughed heartily into the phone. "Yes; Ill bet you
did wonder where his allowance was all going. Well, now you know.
—No," she said wistfully, "it looks like we'll have to do without a party
entirely. But you and Harry and Frank and I will have our own
little party. Youre hereby invited for tomorrow night. We'll all go out to
the Club and drown our sorrows and try to forget how old we are.
And tomorrow I want you to come down here and spend the day with
me, Eleanor. Weve both got a lot to do, and only twenty one days to do
it in; do you know that! Yes. Yes, we'll really have to jump. And Frank
says theyre going to have the best *damned* wedding Parkman's ever
seen; you know Frank!

"Yes.

"All right.

"Tomorrow then. Goodby, Eleanor."

She hung up and Dawn, forgetting her newly acquired adult status, grabbed her around the neck and hugged her. There obviously was not any need for her to worry about the wedding as long as Agnes was handling it. All she had to do was leave it up to old Agnes. Suddenly everything in the world seemed so safe now, all of a sudden. This was the way a person's life ought to be lived: reasonably, and safely, without suffering, without breaking the rules and having to worry about it. A husband, and a home, and your own sweet darling little children, and a solid safe well-off family behind you you could always depend on.

From the phone, after she had been hugged, Agnes looked at her, speculatively, and a thin film of censorship slid slowly down over Dawn's mind, silent and liquidly smooth like a moist transparent membrane. It kept nothing back she did not want kept back, and it allowed everything to come through. It did not change her expression either, and she went on grinning at her mother happily while Agnes looked at her. For a moment Agnes appeared to be about to say something. Then she thought better of it and turned back to the secretary, and Dawn knew —suddenly, and as well as she knew her own name—that from the date of the wedding on Agnes, in privacy and in silence, would be checking the calendar. To satisfy her own curiosity more than anything else, because Dawn also knew—instinctively—she would never say anything if she did discover something, even to Dawn herself. Well, that was all right. Let her check. Because there wasnt anything *to* check.

They turned back to the desk, both of them, suddenly close in their very apartness, their very separateness and reserve—closer by far, Dawn thought suddenly, than they had ever been before when they were trying so hard to reach each other—and went over for a last time the list of notes Agnes had made. Of the six bridesmaids, all from Dawn's class in highschool, only one had stayed in Parkman to attend Parkman College; of the other five, one was in Champaign at Illinois, one in Chicago at Northwestern, two at Michigan in Ann Arbor, one at Lindenwood in Missouri. Agnes would call them all for her long distance, to make sure they got them quick enough, and Dawn herself would write them from school. The maid of honor would be Shotridge's older sister Susan, a senior at Illinois and in Champaign also. Agnes would call her, too. It had been Agnes's thought ("Since we're going to *have* a big wedding, we might as well do it up brown")—that while all the bridesmaids would of course wear matching outfits, it would be a good touch to make them different colors, to which Dawn agreed; and they decided upon: Sky Blue, Mint Green, Coral Pink, Lemon Yellow, Rose Lavender, and Pale Grape. The maid of honor, Sue Shotridge, would wear Aquamarine.

"Your father wants a memorable wedding," Agnes said, "so we're going to give him one. Ive already talked to him, and the bride's father is going to buy all the bridesmaids' outfits. That way we'll be sure they all can afford to come."

"Ohhh, Mother!" Dawn said, and clasped her hands and brought them up between her breasts.

Agnes smiled, her eyes still questioning, still speculative as they looked at her, and laid down her pencil. "I just wish you could have waited till June. Youd have given me a lot more time," she said tiredly. "And I just wish you could have picked somebody a little more in keeping with your own social status."

"Theres nothing wrong with the Shotridges' social status!" Dawn said fiercely. "They own the oldest and biggest real estate firm in Parkman."

Agnes smiled slowly. "Well, it doesnt matter, I guess, as long as you really love him. And apparently you do." She picked up her pencil and bit the eraser. "I guess Ill have to get out my Emily Post," she said smiling tiredly. "And check up on details."

As for the bridal dress, Dawn had specified that she wanted a high neck, long sleeves with a point over the wrist, and a fitted bodice, preferably with yards and yards of French tulle and with plenty of *point d'Alençon* or Chantilly. When she came to this item, Agnes checked it and said, "Why dont you just wait until I see what I can find. Your father and I talked about the wedding a long time last night, and Im going to be flying to New York for the dresses." She would, she said, have to be careful to get all the bridesmaids' sizes exactly when she called them; and just to doubly check, would also call all their mothers about it too.

Once again, Dawn was both surprised and thrilled and clasped her hands and brought them up against her breasts. —and immediately afterwards was once again, as she had been the first time she slept with Shotridge, struck with a kind of dumb awe at her own sheer audacity. The talk of flying to New York brought home the reality of what she had done—and was doing—more than anything had done before: It was all in action now, started; its own momentum would keep it going to the inevitable conclusion. It was no longer in her hands. For a moment she thought she might cry, but underneath all that other and its sudden sense of fright was still that sure sense of safety, and of control, with Shotridge; safety *because* of control; control that she knew positively she held the reins and keys to, as long as it was Shotridge; and this sustained her. And a deep sense of love for Shotridge, and of responsibility for her power—her woman's power—over him, gave her an almost holy feeling of responsibility at the same time that it gave her sureness.

"Being in love certainly has changed you a lot," Agnes said narrowly, eyeing her. "A very great deal of a lot."

"I suppose being in love changes everyone a lot," Dawn said mellowly, and made a mental note not to clasp her hands up against her breasts any more.

After they finished with their lists, they went back out to the kitchen where Frank and young Walter were playing checkers on the white enamel table, Frank boisterously and with a pre-lunch drink beside him, young Walter gravely and in silence, speaking only when spoken to. He was a strange, reserved, selfcontained youngster, and Dawn had not got to know him at all the last two days. Looking at them and watching Walter as he began to win again—fair and square, and without any help from Frank—Dawn had again the feeling that she had had a number of times yesterday: that Frank might be the child and Walter the aged parent. He was like a quiet, mature, little old man. Agnes had written her back in February that less than a week after they had gotten him, even though there was a six months probation period and Agnes had advised against doing it so soon, Frank had had all the signs at the store—including the big expensive neon one out over the side-walk—changed to read FRANK HIRSH & SON, JEWELRY instead of FRANK HIRSH, JEWELER. Looking at him now, from her own vantage point of maturity and forcefulness and her new security, Dawn felt she could forgive him for always having wanted a son so badly. She looked down at her father, who would be spending this fabulous sum on her wedding, and smiled at him. Quite suddenly, for the first time in her life, looking at him, but thinking of Shotridge, she realized all at once (something she had never understood before; although she loved her father) why her mother had married him.

Frank winked back at her and got up, conceding the checker game happily, and announced that they—*the family*—were going to drive her to Indianapolis this afternoon to catch a plane for Cleveland. If Jim Shotridge could fly to Cleveland all the time to see her, there wasnt any reason why she couldnt fly herself. And another thing, he announced: for a wedding gift, he himself was going to give them a car; when you were grown up and married, you needed a car; it wouldnt be a brand new one, but it would be a good one; he would see to that: he already had one in mind and picked out, down at the Dodge-Plymouth Sales where he was a silent partner: a last year's model Dodge sedan. Just one more thing, he added, and his little speech would be through: Since Dawnie was a grown up woman now and getting married, she might as well have a couple drinks with them before lunch like any other grown up married woman.

So saying, and smiling happily with his round face, he strode over to the cocktail stirrer while young Walter carefully and meticulously, and silently, picked up the checkers and the board and put them away neatly in the drawer where they were kept.

So, while Agnes apologized for not being able to fix a regular dinner because of the wedding plans and got them all out some inch-and-a-half-thick deepfreeze steaks, "pot luck," she said, and had her own drinks while she cooked them, Dawn had two Manhattans with her parents in a kind of private little ceremony. Feeling the two drinks very definitely, (something she had not felt at all that night with Shotridge, on a lot more drinks than this), and amidst all the laughter and talk and high spirits that tended to allay natural caution, Dawn felt once again that liquid smooth moist transparent membrane of censorship slide silently and secretly down over her mind, carefully filtering everything she said, or might say. Laughing, happy, gay, the very picture of what a blushing eager very-much-in-love young bride should be, she could carefreely and safely say anything that popped into her mind without worry, because the membranous filter would not let anything else, anything dangerous, appear there.

In the new Cadillac on the way to Indianapolis, sitting in the back seat with young Walter while Frank and Agnes sat in front, she tried to get acquainted with her new foster brother, who had—all unwittingly, of course—ousted her from her family. He was so damned quiet. And Dawnie wanted to know what made him tick, what he was really like.

It was, as she discovered, a hard job to take on. Walter sat quietly and inconspicuously in his corner and watched the drizzly March countryside interestedly. When she would ask him a question he would turn and gaze at her gravely with his little old man's face and answer it and then, unless she asked further questions, go back to his careful, interested perusal of the landscape. He volunteered nothing himself.

Agnes had told her what a wonderful little housekeeper he was, and she could well believe it. She had never been one. But he was, Agnes said: a really great help to both her and to old Janie Staley whenever he was home. He made his own bed every morning, cleaned and polished his own shoes long before he had to be told to, kept his own clothes hung up neatly in his closet, and always very carefully put away afterwards any of his toys that he got out to play with. His room was always immaculate. And in addition to that he cleaned up the dishes and the table after every meal all by himself, and had learned how to operate the automatic dishwasher. He did it after every meal unless Agnes specifically and forcibly ordered him not to. And the first thing he did every evening when he got home from school before he went outside to play was to empty and wash all the ashtrays in the house.

Suddenly Dawn was struck by the really odd strangeness of it all: Here was this little boy, this small individual personality, whom she knew almost nothing of, not his background, not his ambitions, nothing, and who was just entering the household just as she was leaving it and whom consequently she would probably never get to know. And yet he was officially, and legally, her little brother—or soon would be. In a way, sort of, though of course he couldnt know it, he was partly responsible for her leaving, and getting married, and everything else.

"How do you like it at school, Walter?" she asked, smiling at him pleasantly.

One hand still resting on the window ledge, where he had been intently looking out, he turned and gazed at her gravely. "I like it fine," he said. "We have a real fine second grade teacher. Shes a very nice lady." He waited, politely, and when she did not say anything more, started to turn back to the window.

"Well, I guess youre not much used to going off on long rides like this on the spur of the moment," Dawn smiled, a little hastily.

"No, Im not," Walter said, turning back to face her.

"Well, its lots of fun, to live like we live," Dawn smiled reassuringly.

"Yes, it is," Walter said, looking at her gravely.

"Mother says youre a wonderful housekeeper," Dawn said.

"Yes, Mam," Walter said. "They taught us at the orphanage to do things for ourselves, and they told us to always be as little trouble and concern to our new parents as possible." He looked her straight in the eye, gravely, seriously, politely.

Dawn was embarrassed. "Well, this is beautiful country, isnt it?"

"Yes, it is," Walter said.

"I dont suppose youve seen rolling country like this up north?"

"We drove me over to Indianapolis to get some new clothes when I first came to your house," Walter said politely, "and I saw it then. But I cant remember all of it. Only some of it."

"Well, I guess I cant remember all of it myself," Dawn said, a little startled. "And Ive driven it lots of times. Its beautiful country in the summer and in the fall when the trees are all red and yellow."

"Yes, I bet it is," Walter said. He continued to gaze at her, gravely, politely.

"Well, you go ahead and watch the country," Dawn said embarrassedly, unable to think of anything else to say—anything, that is, that did not concern his orphanage. And she couldnt mention that.

"Thank you, Mam," Walter said and turned back to his window.

"You come from around Chicago," Dawn said politely, after a minute, "dont you?"

"Yes, Mam," Walter said turning to look at her politely. "When I was little I lived in Lake Forest. With my *old* parents."

"Oh!" Dawn said. "Thats a fine, rich, expensive town."

"Yes, Mam," Walter said; "but my parents wasnt rich."

"Oh," Dawn said, embarrassed again.

Walter gazed at her gravely, thoughtfully, for a moment, as if debating carefully whether she wanted to hear more, then decided that apparently she did, and began to talk. "My old father worked in a garage," he explained. "Him and my mother was divorced and he left. Then when my mother died they could not find him, and I did not have any other relatives. So they sent me to the orphanage. They didn't call it an orphanage, they called it something else, but that was what it was. I was there for a year before I was adopted." He stopped, finished.

"I see," Dawn said, somehow nonplussed.

"Whats going on back there?" Frank said jovially from the front. "Dont you let that big sister of yours give you any guff, Walter. You doing all right, bub?" Dawn listened, thinking it was strange how none of them even Frank ever seemed to call him Walt, or—her mind froze, suddenly, stiffly: or-Wally-or-something-like-that.

"Yes sir, Dad, thank you," Walter said. "We were just talking about the country and about me before I was adopted."

"Well," Frank said jovially. "Well, thats fine."

"Do you like it at college?" Walter asked her suddenly, turning to gaze at her gravely, almost—she thought—as if he had figured it out that he should be interested and ask some questions himself to be polite.

"Yes. I guess," Dawn smiled. "Its a lot of fun. Ill be transferring though, to Illinois, once Im married."

"Id like to go to college," Walter said gravely. "I want to be an engineer."

"A train engineer?" Dawn smiled.

"No, Mam," Walter said. "An electrical engineer. Id like to build big dams."

"Oh," Dawn said.

As if he had done his duty, Walter turned back to his window. And after that Dawn did not try to question him any more and watched the country herself.

They were a wonderful family, she thought suddenly, warmly. All of them. And they were doing so much for her. So *damned* much. She missed her Shotridge. At the airport, after she had kissed them all, including Walter, the last thing she did before getting on the plane was to remind them not to forget to invite her old chum and childhood playmate Wally Dennis to the wedding along with his mother whom Agnes would be inviting.

CHAPTER 62

WALLY DENNIS received his formal engraved wedding invitation on Monday just exactly a week and six days before the wedding on Easter Sunday. His mom received hers at the same time, in the same mail on the same day. Wally had long ago formed a habit of taking a break from his

work to look over the mail when the mailman came, and on this particular day as soon as he heard the mailman's heavy feet hit the porch resoundingly down below his room, he switched off the light beside his
typewriter—feeling pretty good, he was; his stuff was going real good—
and went downstairs.

His mom already had the mail as usual, and as she always did was
sorting it out on the little hall table, one pile for his and one pile for hers.
She always got the most mail; because she spent so much time writing
letters to people and relatives. Wally himself rarely got much. But even
so he did not like to leave her down there with it, because he suspected
that if he did not come down right away and get his, his mom would
always be inspecting it, turning it over and over and looking at the return
address and the postmark and even holding it up to the light to see what
she could see through the envelope. This time there was only a couple of
mailing list items for him about camping equipment and a new camping
magazine—(Hell, he was on more damned mailing lists any more than
John D Rockefeller Jr, he bet)—and this one pure white square envelope
postmarked Parkman with no return address. He took it all out with him
to the kitchen to get a cup of coffee and open it.

All his Randall knives—except the #1 of course, which he kept upstairs—were still lying on the lazy susan (despite his mom's repeated
protest) and he picked up the #8 "Trout and Bird" knife and unsheathed it and opened the three envelopes. He always used the #8 to
open mail because he had noticed repeated cutting of paper dulled the
really keen *shaving* edge surprisingly, and the #8 was the knife he used
around *here*, around home, the most anyway when he went hunting for
quail or went fishing, so that it rarely had a real *shaving* edge like the
others.

As soon as he saw the inner envelope of the Parkman letter he knew it
was some kind of damned invitation or announcement or something, and
he looked at his own name "Mr Wally Dennis" written in ink by some
vaguely familiar hand (he realized later it was Agnes's) and slit that
envelope too. When he slid out the contents and opened the single
folded double sheet and shook the tissue paper and two cards off it, he
forgot entirely about the other mail, the mailing list ads, and sat down at
the table. The script-engraved invitation read:

> *Mr. and Mrs. Franklin L. Hirsh*
> *request the honor of your presence*
> *at the marriage of their daughter*
> *Dawn Anne*
>
> *to*
>
> *Mr. James Harry Shotridge*
> *on Sunday, the seventeenth of April*

One thousand nine hundred and forty-nine
at four o'clock
Parkman Methodist Church
Parkman, Illinois

Wally read it—or rather, did not read it but took it all in at one fell glance, as it were, his eyes focused on those two words there: DAWN ANNE—his heart suddenly beating strangely and frighteningly and his eyes narrowing instinctively on the beautifully printed lines of script at which he was staring so hard that they seemed to get bigger and bigger and smaller and smaller and then bigger and bigger again. The whole sheet seemed to swell and recede and swell and recede in time with the beating of his heart in the backs of his eyes. He laid it down carefully and picked up the tissue paper and fished the two cards out of it. One, the bigger one, said:

Reception
immediately following the ceremony
The Cray County Country Club

The favor of a reply is requested
608 North Bancroft Street

The other, a personal greeting card, read:

Mrs. Agnes Towns Hirsh
608 North Bancroft Street

And in the lower left hand corner:

Within the ribbon

was written by hand, and below it, also written by hand:

We want you both to be with us.

Wally laid them down alongside the invitation and spread all three of them out and looked at them. But it was the invitation that seized his eye, and would not let it go. The rectangular sheet with its beautifully centered, neatly spaced beautiful lines of script across it. And that was where the words DAWN ANNE were. DAWN ANNE — DAWN ANNE — Wally picked it up, his hands trembling almost imperceptibly with some unknown unnameable fear like nothing he had ever felt before, as if the ground had dropped away suddenly from beneath his feet, and his heart continued to pound remorselessly in his ears. DAWN ANNE—REQUEST THE HONOR OF YOUR PRESENCE—MR. JAMES HARRY SHOTRIDGE—AT THE MARRIAGE OF THEIR DAUGHTER—It was all so *complete*; and so *official*. That was the most disturbing, most frightening thing of all. So already *done* and *accomplished*. This was *official*. This was *legal*. And only last Christmas they had both of them sat right here, at this very same table, both nude, and then they had— Wally heard his mother's steps coming down the hall, and quickly laid the invitation down; but he could not stop staring at its neatly printed lines.

From the look on his mom's face when she marched into the kitchen, he could tell she had had one too. Her mouth with all those vertical wrinkles running up and down from it was warped and twisted around like she had just bitten into a green persimmon. Her eyes were screwed up almost shut. She had always wanted him to marry Dawnie—for Frank's money, of course. He forced himself to stop staring at the invitation and grinned at her.

Her own invitation and cards were in her hands and she had made as if to lay them down in front of him, but then she saw his own and so continued to hold hers.

"Well, there you are," she said vindictively.

Wally grinned. "Yeah, looks like a big deal, dont it? We'll have to think of some kind of presents to send."

His mom's mouth tightened up even more so. It was so tight now it looked like she couldnt even get the words out. "I told you—" she said, pushing the words out forcibly past the drawn lips.

"You told me what, Mom?" Wally cried out angrily. "That you wanted me to marry Dawnie for Frank's money? Yes, you told me! And what did I tell you? I told you I wouldnt marry her and work in that damned son of a bitching store for anything in the world! Didnt I? Didnt I tell you that?"

His mom's face relaxed a little before the vehemence of his reply, and her eyes widened.

"Now for God's sake leave me alone!" Wally yelled. "And think up some kind of damned presents to send!"

His mom took a step backwards and blinked, then her face gradually tightened up again. She held out the personal 'admission' card, with the *"within the ribbon"* and the: *"We want you both to be with us."* on it; identical to his own.

"Yes!" she said viciously. "Shell send me that! And send you one! And you know what it means, dont you?"

"Sure I know!" Wally cried. "It means we'll be dear friends of the family, and sit with all of them, and itll show that all that time and them dates me and Dawnie spent together last summer was all only good friendship, and everybodyll see it; thats what it means! Okay, so what? I dont blame her. Nothing ever happened between me and Dawnie anyway," he said loyally.

"It also means," his mom said, her mouth screwing up tighter again, "that its a nice polite way of getting rid of me. And you. We sit with the honored guests at the wedding, and after that—" She let it trail off, her eyes like gimlets, her mouth drawn up persimmonishly.

"Well, what the hell did you expect!" Wally yelled furiously. "For her to go on being 'best friends' with you? Shell be best friends with Eleanor Shotridge now, from now on.

"Jesus! but you make me *sick* at my *stom*mick sometimes, Mom," he said thickly, sickly. "Now shut up! and leave me alone." He seized his own invitation and cards and envelopes and tissue paper, and jumped up from the table and ran upstairs to his room, leaving her still standing there.

In his room he looked all around wildly and then went back and shut the door, then looked at his typewriter sickly and laid the invitation and cards out on his desk and sat down and looked at them. All so *official*. And so *legal*. So *Documentary Evidence*. So *final*. MR. JAMES HARRY SHOTRIDGE. Was that the Jimmy Shotridge that he knew who was a sophomore at U of I? the same one that Dawnie never referred to by any other name but just plain "Shotridge"? Surely it couldnt be. It must be somebody else, from out of town. Somebody she had met in Cleveland at Reserve. Yes, that must be it. —Only, of course, it wasnt, he thought sickly. He picked up the invitation again and brought it up close to his eyes and stared at it closely. DAWN ANNE—DAWN ANNE—Was that Dawnie Hirsh? What a lovely name: DAWN ANNE. Gee, he never would have thought *she* could do this to him, after as close—and as intimate—as they had been to each other. He put the sheet back down. Then he picked it up and put the tissue paper and the two cards back inside of it, just like it had come, and slid it all into the inner envelope and put that back inside the outer envelope and laid it all on the desk and stared at his own name and address on the front. It had been posted Saturday. He sat and looked at it sickly, trying to imagine that it had not been opened and had not come, and that what was inside it was not what was inside it. Then he took it and pulled it all back out again and spread it out again on the desk. But it had not any of it changed. He stared at it sickly, to make sure. He wanted to beat his fists up and down on the desk. But he couldnt, his mom would hear him. He wanted to beat his fists into the plaster wall, and bite and kick and tear, and throw his head back and gnash his teeth and howl. Just howl. Like a dog. Howl out in a long quavering scream his misery and anguish and disbelief and pain. But he couldnt, his mom would hear it. He had never had anything in his life to hurt him so, like this. Why, she had been a virgin when he first slept with her. Shed told him so herself. And besides he knew it anyway. He could tell. She had given her virginity to him. Shed stood there in the red light of the woods, at dusk, bare to the waist in her skirt and bobby sox and saddle shoes; he could still see it; as clearly and photographically as if it was happening now; and then they had climbed into the back seat. Ahhhhhhhhhhhhhhhhhhhhhhhhhhhhhhhhhhhhhhh-hhhhhhhhhhhh!—He held it in, holding his belly muscles tight, so it would make no sound, the pressure forcing blood up into his head until his eyeballs started, the only sound a high faint thin keening in the back of his throat that reached no further than his own ears, until finally he had to gasp for breath. His head was charged with choked-off blood. That was dangerous: You could break a blood vessel in your head and have a stroke and die like that. All right then, he thought wildly, then die! Then go ahead and die! And he did it again: Ahhhhhhhhhhhhhhhh-hhhhhhhhhhhhhhhhhhhhhhhhhhhhhhhhhhhh! long, silently, held in. He looked down again at the invitation, the white paper appearing to be speckled with flecks of red in his eyes, his eyes focusing themselves again upon those same two words, those same two lovely words, as they always did:

> *at the marriage of their daughter*
> DAWN ANNE!
> *DAWN ANNE!*

DAWN ANNE—This time he could not hold it in. Sitting at his desk, the white knuckles of his clenched fists lying on it, his mind blank, empty, his face blank, his eyes blank, staring blindly at the wall in front of him, he opened up his mouth and from lungs full of selfcompressed air the long high drawn-out quavering howl poured out of him and filled the room, trickled out through the half open window and down the quiet street in the warm sunny April day.

"Ahhhhhhhhhhhhhhhhhhhhhhhhhhhhhhhhhhhhhhh!" only this time it was out loud, and he didnt care who heard, didnt a damn.

Almost immediately, he snapped back to full awareness, horrified by what he had done.

From downstairs he heard his mother's terrified voice: "Wallace! Wallace! Whats happened! Whats wrong!"

His mind clicking swiftly and alertly, Wally jumped up and went to the low dresser under the mirror and grabbed his Randall #1 "All-Purpose Fighting Knife" which he kept there so he could practice with it before the mirror, unsheathed it, and slashed it down across his doubled up index finger. The eight inch blade was shaving sharp, he kept it that way, and in his hurry he slashed it much harder than he meant to. With almost no sense of pulling or of cutting the knife cut his finger clean to the bone, and blood began to pour out of it. Staring at it only momentarily, surprised, Wally put the knife down on the dresser and grabbed his handkerchief and wrapped it around the cut. Blood began to soak through it immediately.

Behind him, his mother had run up the stairs and was already at the door crying "Wallace! Wallace!" Wally met her there as she opened it and thrust the bloodstained handkerchief and finger at her.

"Its nothing," he said calmly. "I just cut my finger."

"But the way you yelled!" his mother said, her face still terrified, breathless from the stairs.

"Aw, it just made me mad," Wally said. "Thats all. Damn fool thing to do! It aint cut bad."

The terror from that long-drawn quavering howl had begun to seep out of her face. It was as white as a sheet. "I thought you were dying!" she said.

Wally merely stared at her grimly. Yes, and I was, he thought.

His mom shook her head. "I do wish youd quit playing with those horrible knives," she said fearfully, looking at him anxiously. "Is it cut bad?"

"I wasnt playing with it," he said disgustedly, "I was sharpening it; and the damn thing slipped. No, I told you it wasnt cut bad. Now, for God's sake, Mom, go away and leave me alone. I got to doctor this."

"Do you want me to do it?" she offered.

"No, damn it! Ill do it myself."

Reluctantly, still looking at him anxiously, his mom turned away to go back downstairs. "Please dont play with those sharp knives any more, Wallace," she said.

"Damn it, I told you I was sharpening it!" Wally said angrily. "And I dont play with them. I *practice* with them. Please, Mom! Im irritable because I cut myself. Go away and just let me be."

When she had gone, he shut the door and went back to the dresser where the knife was. It was stained with blood a quarter of an inch up both sides of the edge, and he got out another handkerchief from the drawer and awkwardly because of his wrapped finger, carefully wiped it clean. Then he carried the knife into the bathroom and let cold water run on it from the tap and then wiped it carefully dry and sheathed it. Nothing in the world would rust and stain a knife worse than blood. Only after he had done that did he take another look at his finger. The cut was between the knuckle and second joint, running across the back and down the thumb side of the finger. Blood still ran from it in a thick dripping stream and he held the handkerchief under it so it would not drip on the floor. In a way he was really kind of proud of it. Anyway, at least it had fooled his mom. Christ! but that had been a near thing; if he hadnt cut it she would have known what was wrong for sure. And it would make him a good scar. Yeah; a good souvenir, he thought sardonically, a nice scar, to remember the day he got the invitation to Dawnie Hirsh's wedding by.

But now that the crisis was all over, and he was safe with his misery again and alone, and had nothing more to do like cleaning the knife to occupy his mind, the sick feeling, the sense of disbelief, the unwilling-ness to accept it, came back over him with a rush, making his stomach drop away from under him. Wrapping a clean handkerchief around the cut, he went back to the desk and sat down and looked at the invitation and the cards, almost physically sick at his stomach with the effort— the necessity—not to believe it. Dawnie—DAWN ANNE—DAWN ANNE—He could still see her clearly as she had looked, bare to the waist, that first time up in the woods, and he thought he could not stand it.

He dropped his forehead down on the desk, his work forgotten for the day, sick, beaten, empty. And so much in love with what he had lost that it was like a physical hunger for food when there is no food. Dawnie— Dawnie—

Maybe it wasnt true. Maybe she had only done this to devil him. Maybe she had gone to a printer and had this one copy printed up just to send to him, and then she and her mom got together and concocted this. Maybe it wasnt true at all.

Is this the Wallace French Dennis who drove her home so positively and implacably that night? who sat in the car so expressionlessly and emotionlessly and watched her go inside? Is this the Wally Dennis who quit her cold?

Yes. Yes, yes, but he had never thought she would do something like this to him.

In the end, only anger and outrage came to his aid. Anger at her that she could callously do this to him, obviously and deliberately,—because it was obvious she had done it deliberately, just to spite him—after all the things he had done for her, after all that they had been and meant to each other, after all he *knew about her*. And hell, she loved it. Why hell, she was a regular damned *wanton*! And how in hell Jim Shot-ridge could ever keep her satisfied in bed he couldnt figure. Wait till he married her and found out!

—But in this direction lay danger, too; and as all the old memories flooded back through his mind in *proof* that she was just a damned *wanton*, the sick hungry bottomless feeling began to come back in him at the hungry remembrance of them. So he put this thought down, away, too; and concentrated merely on sheer anger—anger and outrage at her deliberate spiteful attempt to hurt him by marrying another man.

Angrily, outragedly, in the next few days, he prepared himself. He would show them. Show them all. He took his mom's old car to Terre Haute and spent a hundred dollars of his dwindling (almost nonexistent, anymore!) fellowship money on a silver service for a present, and on the back of the platter he had engraved *in script*—just like that damned in-vitation—the legend: *"To Dawnie and Jim   Many happy days!*

Wally"; and if it was bad form to engrave a personal message on a wedding gift, to hell with it! For a moment he seriously contemplated having them engrave it to read: *"To Dawnie and Shotridge"*; like she always called him; but finally he decided not to: he was afraid it might be a little too much, and he did not want Shotridge getting wise. That would only ruin it. What he wanted was to remind *her*: to fix it so that whenever she used that tea service, or even looked at it, if she didnt use it, she would remember. Remember Lake Audubon, and remember the woods at dusk out west of West Lancaster, and remember all the *other* times and places. And then lets see how goddamned sanctimonious and proper she could pretend to be!

He had it sent out from Terre Haute, so his mom would not see it.

During the two weeks before the wedding he did not go anywhere. Except to classes at the College. He did not go down to Dave's and 'Bama's, he did not look up Rosalie, he did not go to Smitty's. Some instinct of some fright, some fear of some embarrassment, some powerful though vague suspicion that everyone might be laughing at him, kept him away. And anyway, he just simply did not feel like going anywhere, didnt have the stomach for it. Thank God he had never talked to anyone about his love affair! Not even to Dave and 'Bama. Nobody really knew there really had ever been a love affair. Love affair—Oh, God! Dawnie— DAWN ANNE—DAWN ANNE—*request the honor of your presence*—

Only when he was working, in the mornings, was he anyways near free of it. He would get up early, after a night of bad dreams and nightmares (*Once he dreamed they were on a vast plain, he and Dawnie, a huge unending plain at the one end of which where they were, were beautiful high mountains, and it was against these mountains where Dawnie had built her house, a beautiful modernistic house—only there was a high wire fence around it, with barbed wire strands at the top jutting out over the fence like you saw at Army camps. He was outside of it. And he came up to the fence, and inside on the patio he could see her, standing there nude, with those beautiful breasts of hers. And the gate, beside him, it was locked. With a big thick chain, padlocked together. He grabbed the wire. He called out to her. She had locked him out. She had locked him out. He could not get in. He called, and pleaded, and finally he got down on his knees and begged and wept. She only looked at him and put on a robe, a beautiful silk robe, covering up her body so he might no longer see it, and then she went back inside the house without a word, in silence.* He woke up calling, calling for forgiveness, weeping and crying. And then he had that vast sense of great relief that comes when you realize it is only a dream. And then, his heart beating fearfully in his ears, he realized that it was *not* a dream. Not a

dream at all.) and after nights like these, he would get up early, sometimes at dawn, and plunge furiously and frantically into his work on
his book, writing pages and pages, all morning long, sometimes not
even sure what it was he had written, that morning or the day before.
He did not have the heart to try and go back over it and read it, let
alone try to work on it. He just kept it, filing it carefully away, more
pages per day than he had ever written in his life before. And plunged
on ahead. Because only then could he be even momentarily free of it,
forget it.

Shotridge! he would think outragedly, Shotridge! Of all people,
Shotridge! MR JAMES HARRY SHOTRIDGE—*at the marriage of
their daughter*—and of all people, Shotridge! Why, anybody! anybody
else would have been better. But Shotridge! If it had just been anybody! anybody else! it wouldnt have been so bad. He wouldnt have
minded somebody, anybody! else, near so much, so bad.

But the rest of the time, when he wasnt working, he could only sit
around and brood. In the afternoons. Because he couldnt concentrate
to read any more. He tried to go on with his reading plan: (he was
working on the Harvard Classics now, Dr Eliot's Five Foot Shelf,
sandwiched in between the military histories, and he had reached
Volume 27: English Essays, Sidney to Macaulay): but he could not.
When he would quit work exhausted at noon and come down for
lunch, he would have to be pleasant and engaging—above all, non-
caring—in front of his mom for forty five minutes or an hour. That
was even more exhausting. And when after lunch he would sit down
with a book, he would read a few lines and agony would strike him:
he would remember. It would smite him like a halberd or a medieval
mace. If he tried to go on reading, the words would lose all sense. *at
the marriage of their daughter*—DAWN ANNE—DAWN ANNE
—If his mom was home he would shut himself up in his room. To fool
her, and to fool himself, he took a small table up there and some tools
and started working on model airplanes again and his old radio sets.
If his mom was not home, he would simply sit, one leg up over a chair
in the venetian-blind-shaded living room, staring at the horrible ugly
once-expensive furnishings; or go into the music room and play chords
on the piano.

This pain was not the kind of pain he had always imagined went
with a lost love affair. He had had love affairs before, sort of, everyone
did; crushes on teachers, the hots for some girl or other in school. He
had even slept with a couple of them. And always afterwards there had
been that tremendously melancholy, sad, pleasant pain of loss; those
had always been enjoyable pains. But then he had not slept with
any of those people regularly. Had not *really* loved them. Consequently,
he did not have any specific memories about them. Oh, he could

analyze it. He could analyze it all right. But that didnt get him free
of it. Why, he knew the body of this girl who was marrying Shotridge! knew it as well as he knew his own! It was not the kind of pain
he had bargained for.

Once the wedding was over—Once he showed them at the wedding—

Once that miserable, horrible, spiteful, deliberate, mean, hateful wedding was over—

Once that was over—(they would go off together then; they would be
living together then)—Once the wedding was over, he was sure he
would be all right. He would show them at the wedding.

Ahh, Dawnie, he would think with a convulsion of agony—Ahh,
Dawnie— If you only knew— If you only realized—

But that was just what he must never let her do. Or anybody else. He
got back a little handwritten note from her, thanking him for the gift.
His mom got one too, for hers.

He got his good suit, his *one* suit—a really good royal blue gabardine,
that he had bought in St Pete with his money he had made fishing in
Florida, together with gray flannel slacks and a light blue jacket so that
he could interchange them—he got his suit all cleaned and pressed and
spruced up at the cleaners, had them press his best navy-blue tie, sorted
out his best white spread-roll-collar shirt with French cuffs, and blacked
and polished his best wing-tip black dress shoes himself—the same shoes
he used to wear playing dances with the band. All of it fixed, all of it
ready, so there would be no slip up.

Easter Sunday he spent the morning lounging around in his room
while his mom went to church, unable to write today, feeling nervous
and somehow breathless—and, before the prospect of the afternoon, less
agonizingly unhappy than he had been in the two whole weeks. It
seemed to him that three o'clock and the time when he could begin getting dressed would never come.

Once the damned wedding was over, and out of the way—

Wally had only been to two or possibly three weddings in his life,
none of them especially exceptional, so he was not at all prepared for the
sight that opened up before his eyes as he and his mom arrived and went
inside. First of all, when he drove up with his mom in his mom's old
car, he found that there were cars parked on both sides of the street for
almost two full blocks in *every* direction from the Methodist Church,
and that included the side streets. It looked like a homecoming football
game. Or a funeral for the President of the United States. At the three
corners nearest the church cops were out in the center of the intersections, directing traffic; and at the corner before the church itself stood
Chief of Police Sherm Ruedy, looking very handsome and square-jawed
in his new spring uniform. By the time Wally found a place to park
they were almost three blocks from the Methodist Church. They might

as well have left the car at home and walked down, it wouldnt have been much further. And the sidewalks, as he walked back to the church sedately beside his mom who had splurged herself and bought a whole new outfit for this wedding, were actually crowded with people, or appeared to be, all heading for the two main doors of the big ivy-grown stone church around the street-corner from each other. He could not help feeling a little stunned, and somewhat awed.

But the picture that met them inside as they entered and he handed the two "admission" cards (as his mom had carefully instructed him) to one of the ushers who was a boy Wally remembered from high school as a friend of Shotridge, that picture *over*awed him, even more: The entire church was banked with ferns and masses of white flowers, branches and garlands and sheaves and bunches, around every wall of the place, all the green in the world and masses of more white lilies than he would have believed even could be *found* in Parkman. Although they had arrived twenty minutes before the ceremony, the whole entire church was already filled with people. Looking out over it from the door Wally judged there must be at least a thousand persons there. (Actually, he found out later, there were only some six hundred. Yeah; only six hundred!) But he didnt have time for more inspection then. The usher, who was wearing a dark blue jacket, gray pants, a white carnation boutonnière, blue and white bow tie, had accepted the cards, secretly consulted his list, and now smiling and chatting to her quietly offered his *right* arm to Wally's mom and escorted her down the right one of the two main aisles. Still numb, still stunned, Wally followed, his good suit sinking into a royal blue obscurity beside the outfit of the usher. At the white satin ribbon separating off the first twelve pews, already well-filled, the usher lifted off the ribbon, led them through, replaced it, and then escorted them to the second pew on the left or center section, where there were two seats vacant on the end. They sat down.

Just for a moment, out of the corner of his eye, Wally gave his mom a sharp quick glance and she, smiling pleasantly and dignifiedly, looked back at him the same way. Then he faced front and sitting on one hip in the uncomfortable wooden pew, folded his arms in the blue gabardine suit and stared straight ahead studying the lavishly and beautifully flower-decorated chancel. He had known he was out of his depth the moment he saw the outfit of the usher, and that *right* arm;—and all these people. He had sort of suspected it before that, when he saw all the cars and how far they had to walk. He just hoped he hadnt done anything conspicuous. He knew next to nothing about weddings. He knew enough to know they were sitting on the bride's side, but that was about all. Directly in front of him, on the end of the first pew, was a wide open space where nobody was sitting which he did not know the purpose of. Suddenly, belatedly, he realized he ought to be talking and smiling and not sitting like a lump, and he turned to his mom. Smiling at her and trying to look at ease, although at the moment he hated her guts, he bent over to her and, conversational looking, asked about the empty space in front of him and learned that this was reserved for the bride's parents, and also found out that the bride's mother did not appear until just a moment or two before the procession started. So they would be sitting right behind Frank and Agnes. His mom was smiling at him very pleasantly and happily, and then turned to say something to the person on her left; and after a moment or two, feeling a little more at ease, Wally allowed himself to turn his head and look around a little.

When he did, his heart sank down in him awedly, stunnedly. They were sitting amongst scads of Hirshes. He recognized Frank's three brothers from New York and Chicago and St. Louis by their faces. All three were there with their wives and all their children. And he recognized Frank's twin sister Francine from Hollywood, with her husband and her children. Beside her was sitting old Mrs Hirsh, Frank's mother. Dawnie's grandmother, he thought sickly. Apparently, every Hirsh in the world was here. He had had no idea of the magnitude of all of it. Also sitting all around them, inside the ribbons, "within the ribbon", were numberless other people whom he did not know or recognize; but by questioning his mom—who knew every damned one of every one of them, of course—he learned that these were numerous cousins and distant relatives of both the Hirshes and Agnes's family the Townses, some of the Townses—his mom said—even coming from as far away as Kansas City. Wally's heart sank even further. Farther away in the church, both within and without the ribbon, he could recognize just about every dignitary and person of consequence in Parkman and in Cray County. And for that matter—his mom whispered to him—there were even a number of important people here from Springfield. Clark Hibbard and his wife were here, within the ribbon of course, and right next to them Clark's wife's father and mother, (very rich, his mom said), and next to them a big dark Greek man by himself whom even Wally's mother didnt know, but who definitely had a very commanding presence. If Wally's heart could have sunk in him any further, it would have; but it had sunk about as far as it could go. He had had no idea. No idea at all. And the magnitude of it all overwhelmed him in the same way, but even more so, than had the sense of Officiality, of Stern Legality, of finality, he had got from looking at the invitation. He suddenly felt lost; totally lost and drowning in a sea of people, all of them more important than he was; and about as significant and of as much consequence as a grain of sand upon a beach.

Further off yet—just barely "within the ribbon" in fact—he saw Edith Barclay, Frank's office girl, and her grandmother Old Janie Staley, and just for a moment a note of surprised kindness rose up out of the depths of his resentment: At least Frank and Agnes werent snobs, if theyd put Old Janie and Edith Barclay "within the ribbon". Then, closer in from them, and still "within the ribbon" he saw Gwen and Bob French, and with a sudden start realized for the first time that he had not seen Dave. Dave was not here! To make sure he looked closely all through the relatives again, but neither Dave nor Old Man Herschmidt, Frank's father, were among them. There were Hirshes by the score—by the hundreds and the thousands, damn near—but no Dave, and no Old Man Herschmidt. Old Man Herschmidt he would have expected to be absent; Frank's father and Frank and their feud had been a joke in Parkman for twenty years. But to not invite Dave! A sudden wild blazing fury of hatred and disgust flamed up in Wally scaldingly, not only at Frank and Agnes, but at all of it, at all of *them*, Clark Hibbard and his father in law and that selfcontained-looking Greek man, at everybody here. Not to invite Dave! Dave, the best—best—*brain*, and best—*sensitivity*, the best mind and best intelligence, and the *only* real thinker, in their whole damned family, the only *real* artist. Wally was actually horrified, and a sense of warm protective affection for Dave slid over him. Hell, he didnt care about himself. So he was insignificant. So nobody noticed him at all. So he was a nothing, a town bum. But to do that to Dave! Dave, who had already published one story this year, and had sold another! Dave, who was his greatest competition! Well! he thought stiffly. Well. If that was the way they were, the hell with them, with all of them. He would sit here at their damned wedding, and be bored, and be polite, and wait it out; he was here, he had to do that; but that was all and to hell with all of them.

But it didnt work. As soon as the flaming anger—which he had carefully not allowed to reach his smiling face—as soon as it diminished and died away for lack of new fuel, his heart which had been lifted back up by rage at the injustice to Dave, sank down in him again. He did not know what he had expected when he came. He certainly had not expected everyone to get up and stare at him when he came in; and he had not expected anybody to say anything to him about Dawnie. No, he didnt know what he had expected. But he hadnt expected to be a complete nonentity, a complete nothing, just another grain of sand on the beach. But that was what he was. That was what he and his mom both were. And there was no getting around it, any way you tried to look at it. Just a couple of unnoticed, inconspicuous grains. A couple of "also-sats". Two of the least noticeable, and least important, guests. Sickly, he wished he hadnt come. And suddenly he became aware that he had been listening to music for some time without even having been aware of it. Music from the organ and some singer he didnt know who was standing alone in the choir loft. And had been hearing it, ever since they first came in. Sitting with his arms folded, his face a mask of that slow heavy Slavic look which he had always hated but which stood him in good stead today, hoping desperately to look happy and pleased, and wanting only to get up and get out, which of course he could not do, Wally stole a peek at his watch on his wrist and saw that it was nearly four o'clock.

> at four o'clock
> request the honor of your presence
> —DAWN ANNE—
> at the marriage of their daughter—DAWN ANNE—

Here, arrayed all about him, closing him in, closing him in completely, were all the forces and powers and usages of society, of public opinion. All the blank-faced expressionless forces, all the blank-eyed not-seeing usages, all the expressionless not-caring-to-see powers, of human society. Which if they did not see the truth, which whether they saw the truth or not, did not see the truth. Did not care to see the truth. And which therefore carried on, indomitable as a mountain, forcing by sheer weight of mass the truth to be what had beforehand been decided the truth ought to be, according to the traditional usage. He had never really come up against it before, never really seen its power in action. Now he was. For the first time in his life, really. It was not any one of them, not even any group of them, but the whole mass, the whole faceless mass of many faces. And here he sat, he Wally Dennis, who had been this girl's lover for the best part of a year, this girl who was being married, and he had not been this girl's lover, because he just simply could not have been. He just simply had never been this girl's lover, and here he sat behind her mother and father to prove it. It was not only agonizing to him, it was actually terrifying. He wanted to get up and run. Run anywhere. Anywhere where there werent faces. Faceless human faces, faceless dignitaries lending their moral support, faceless important people lending their presence, to this mass of opinion and belief that was forcing him by sheer weight of will to not ever have been this girl's lover. My God! he wanted to cry out, at least let me keep *that!*

On the other aisle across the center section there was a little stir. One of the ushers was escorting Eleanor Shotridge down the groom's aisle, dumpy little Harry Shotridge following them. Then when the usher had returned to the back, Wally could hear the stir, the same quiet little stir, on his own side; and finally into his eyesight—straining sideways toward his right—came the same usher escorting Agnes Hirsh as if she were very fragile and might break or had been involved in a tragedy. The music had stopped. Agnes was wearing a beautiful taupe outfit with matching hat and gloves, and some kind of lavender flowers. She looked neither to the right nor left, with great dignity. The usher seated her directly in front of Wally and went off, and right behind him came two other ushers, stringing white satin ribbons along the outsides of the pews and fencing everybody in. Hell! he couldnt even have got up and seized Dawnie if he had wanted to; what would he do, jump over the ribbon? They thought of everything.

In front of him Agnes had turned around, ever so slightly, after first speaking to her mother in law and Francine on her left, and smiled warmly at him and his mom and murmured something he couldnt hear. He smiled back and made his mouth murmur an equally meaningless sound. Agnes was already beginning to cry. And after she turned back around, his mom—his Wally's mom!—leaned forward and just touched her lightly, sympathetically, on the shoulder. Oh, she was a master, his mom! A real master! Agnes raised her own hand and touched his mom's hand and turned her head a little and smiled tremulously. Then the measured strains familiar to every American movie-goer of Wagner's 'Wedding March' began and the preacher came out of the vestry room and right behind him came the groom Shotridge—MR JAMES HARRY SHOTRIDGE—and his best man who was some guy Wally didnt know.

Behind him he heard stirrings as people turned to look, so he decided it was all right for him to turn and look too. Down the aisle came the procession, first the ushers, then the six bridesmaids all in different colors, all friends of Dawnie's whom he recognized, then Shotridge's sister Sue alone, then two little girls as flower girls, then a little boy all in white carrying a cushion, ring-bearer he must be, and Wally recognized him suddenly as the new little boy Walter they had adopted whom he had never seen before, and then came Dawnie on the right arm of Frank.

They paced slowly and stately to the music, Frank's round head flushed with excitement (and probably a few drinks) but very solemn, and Dawnie was an apparition of loveliness. Clouds of white stuff Wally didnt even know was tulle enveloped her. The high-necked dress was cut perfectly to show off those beautiful upthrust breasts, and the whole top half of it was some kind of lace over some other cloth. A tiny little veil in front hung almost to her eyes. She was absolutely beautiful, and Wally stared at them numbly. They didnt see him. They didnt see anybody. They walked, pacing perfectly to the music, with their eyes straight ahead looking at nothing, at nobody.

Through this, and through most of all that followed, Wally watched it with somewhat the same feeling of a man watching a movie film reel by, when the man knows nervously that the spools are a little too far apart and that the tension might snap the film. He had a feeling that at any moment the picture he was seeing might crack and split, and then crumble into nothing but white wall—or just nothing; nothing at all, not even white; just nothingness. The feeling was so strong in him that he kept expecting it, waiting for it, and every time he blinked—gratingly, loudly—he was afraid that that might do it. He heard almost none of the words that were said. And when Frank, after giving her away, came back and sat down in front of him, it startled him. Gradually, both during the ceremony and afterwards when they all began to leave, the ushers conducting the ladies up pew by pew, and Frank before he left turned around and gave him, Wally, a happy wink although he had been crying too,—gradually during all of this Wally felt like he was shrinking, shrinking up smaller and smaller and smaller until he was about the size of a mouse, into the most utterly devastating inconsequence and triviality, the most total uselessness and unimportance, of his life. So much did he feel it that when he got up to follow his mom and the usher up the aisle, he was startled to find out he was still as tall as she was.

Outside, he escorted her to their old car. The bridal party had all already left, of course. He walked his mom to the car without saying a word, without trusting himself to say any word, helped her in it, then went around and got in himself and started up the motor. He had been her lover, he was thinking, he had been her lover. He kept saying it to himself desperately. But he had never been her lover. And he knew it. He was convinced. And besides that, he knew now that he had failed. When he sent her that engraved silver plate, he had failed utterly to achieve his purpose: which was to keep reminding her. Because he knew now, finally and at long last, he didnt know how he knew it but he did, that Dawnie herself no longer believed that she had ever slept with him. And so consequently, when she looked at his hundred dollar silver plate, the only thing she would remember—the only thing she *could* remember—would be a kind of warm affection for her old childhood pal and playmate, Wally Dennis.

"Now, Wallace," his mom said, as he drove them off, "listen carefully. I have to go to the reception, but Im not going to stay. As soon as we get through the receiving line, Ill head for the refreshment tables and get a glass of champagne or whatever theyre serving, then speak to several people I know, and then Ill be ready to go. So you keep an eye on me. Youll have to drive me home. If you want to come back, you can; thats perfectly all right."

His mom's mouth had taken on that twisted, warped persimmonish look. "Im not going to hang around and be an extra third-party wallflower," she said. "Agnes and Eleanor are going to be the closest of best friends, and I intend to bow out gracefully and quickly, before I become conspicuous. And anyway," she said wailfully "I dont feel well." She ran her fingertips delicately across her forehead under her new hat. "Dont feel well at all." She was getting herself worked up into her role.

"Mom!" Wally said balefully, much louder and angrier than he had really intended. "Ill drive you home! I dont know if Ill come back or not! Now shut up, damn it!"

Taken a little aback by the force of his tone, she did, and said no more, concentrating on working herself into her role of not feeling well so she could leave early. They were out south of town now on the road to the Country Club. On their right they passed The Stables, and while he did not glance over at it, Wally was sickly aware of it. How many times they had ridden there together!—DAWN ANNE—He turned the car and started on up the long slope to the club house.

The receiving line would be the main thing. The ordeal; or un-ordeal, as the case might be. There he would meet her face to face, touch her, shake her hand he knew so well. What would she say? What would she do? Oh, God! he thought, sickly, anguishedly: And there wasnt a damned thing he could do.

Not. a. single. solitary. thing. Oh, God!

"Now remember," his mom said, as he parked. "You con*grat*ulate the groom; but you wish the *bride* happiness. Its a breach of good manners to congratulate the bride on having secured a husband."

Wally nodded, and did not say anything.

Agnes met them at the door of the big combination lounging-and-diningroom just inside the foyer. Right behind her was Eleanor Shotridge. They had really done it up brown. Almost all the furniture had been removed, and around behind the two women on the north wall was a long table with a huge punch bowl and a myriad of little cups. Along the west wall, before a big bank of flowers and ferns, stood Shotridge, Dawnie, then Sue Shotridge and the six bridesmaids. And all along the long south wall with its french doors that looked off down the hill stood tables of just about every kind of food and drink imaginable, and waiters in white jackets behind them stood almost shoulder-to-shoulder along the entire length of the wall. Out in the center of the room, looking like they had been posted there and told exactly how far they could walk, stood Frank and Harry Shotridge, two curiously similar short figures, pacing first four steps one way, then four steps the other, and talking. Already a number of people had got there and gone through the gauntlet and hit the serving tables and were walking around, although how the hell they could have got there so quick Wally had no idea since he and his mom were among the first to leave.

While they waited in the line, Wally noticed there wasnt any waiter behind the big punch bowl on the north wall yet. Evidently that was for later, a sort of spare, or else to avoid a traffic jam in the line.

When they got to the head of the line, the hired announcer standing on the other side of the big double doors from Agnes asked their names and announced them:

"Mrs Margaret French Dennis."

"Mr Wallace Dennis."

His mom and Agnes shook hands and put their other arms around each other tremulously, but joyously, and his mom said: joyously, but with just a trace of that wailfulness that would later be her excuse for leaving: "Agnes, darling! Such an exquisitely lovely wedding!"

"Marg darling!" Agnes said. She was still a little weepy; but bearing up bravely. "I was glad to know you were there behind me." And his mom went on to shake hands warmly and happily with Eleanor.

When it came his turn, Wally stuck out his hand, smiling happily, the words coming up from some deep place in him he had not known was there: "Mrs Hirsh," he said. "A beautiful wedding, and a beautiful bride." He thought it sounded rather good.

"Wally dear," Agnes said and bent forward and touched her cheek lightly against his own and he got a whiff of her perfume. "We're glad you came. It wouldnt have been right without you and Marg."

Just for a moment, for one fleeting but sharply focused moment, as she touched her soft cheek against his, Wally was positive that she knew—knew the whole story, everything, from start to end, and had known for some little time. Since Christmas maybe? Not that Dawnie would ever have told her, but that she had somehow figured it all out for herself in silence. He went on and shook hands with Eleanor. "Mrs Shotridge," he said, warmly, dignifiedly, like he had been doing this stuff all his life.

Then he was walking across the long expanse of floor past the punch bowl toward the banked flowers of the west wall. In a way, he was prepared for what happened; and that was good. Very good. The singular revelation he had had walking from the church with his mom had prepared him, so there was a lot less of a shock when he looked into her eyes.

But first, of course, there was Shotridge. Shotridge with his thin frame, and his thin face, and his thin nose, and his thin voice. He certainly took after his mother, that was for sure; he didnt take after roly-poly Harry. "Jim," he said, making his voice deep with sincerity. "My heartiest congratulations. Youre a very lucky man." Shotridge thanked him, and then he was standing in front of her. In front of Dawnie.—DAWN ANNE—*immediately following the ceremony*—

From somewhere deep within him, in that place he had not known was there, and from whence had come the lying, totally sincere happiness for Agnes, now rose up something else: a sudden, equally lying, and equally totally sincere, kind of debonair gaiety. He was astounded, himself, as he spoke.

"Dawnie!" he said, grinning. "Ah, Dawnie! The most beautiful bride these jaded old eyes have ever seen!" He took her hand, tenderly. "It was a magnificently beautiful wedding! I wish you happiness."

All the time he spoke she was looking at him, bloomingly, smiling happily, the look in her face—and deep down in her eyes as well—expressing nothing except the sincere affection of a happy bride for an old childhood friend and playmate. This was what he had known walking to the car. And having known, having anticipated it, made him able to digest it now.

"Wally darling!" Dawnie said, in the voice of a happy bride speaking to the best male friend of her now-nostalgic youth. "Dear Wally!" She put her other arm up on his shoulder. The long points of lace at the ends of her sleeves reaching to her knuckles showing off her lovely hands beautifully, and in the so-tightly fitted bodice those lovely upthrust breasts. "Its so good to see you, old Wally!" she said with all the warm, smiling, sexless friendliness in the world. And it wasnt an act. She meant it.

"Do I get to kiss the bride?" Wally said gallantly and debonairly.

"You certainly do!" she said delightedly. "If anybody does!" And just for a moment her lips brushed his own, cool, relaxed, distant, the perfect kiss of friendliness for an old childhood pal now grown up. Then he went on, through Sue Shotridge, on down through the rest of the bridesmaids, not seeing any of them, really, not hearing what they said, not knowing exactly what he said, except that he was sure both his face and voice were under control, and when he reached the end of the line he looked around vaguely, the memory of those cool lips that just brushed his own, not quite sure where the tables or any of the other things were, and misery and anguish descended upon him again like a cloak, powerfully, blastingly. He could feel the big trunk artery in his back beating thuddingly against his kidneys, and once again his heart sunk down in him so low that he was reasonably sure it was now a hemorrhoid. Then numbness that was painless engulfed him.

His mom was over at the tables, getting a glass of champagne, and as he moved over there she moved off. She did not drink the champagne, she only held it; and moved off talking pleasantly, smiling gaily, to some of the hoard of relatives, all of whom she knew. He supposed you had to give her credit in a way; but God! she sickened him. He got a glass of champagne himself, but he drank his. There were cases and cases of it, cases and cases, all imported, overflowing out through the french doors behind the table onto the porch. This thing must be costing Frank a regular fortune. With his glass he moved over to the center of the room to talk to Frank and Harry Shotridge, looking so curiously alike, himself numb, totally painless.

Frank, already a little tight, threw his arm around Wally and drew him affectionately in with them. Wally was suddenly just as equally sure, as he had been with Agnes, that Frank did *not* know. Probably Agnes had only carefully instructed him to be especially nice to Wally;

maybe she had told him she suspected Wally had been a little in love with Dawnie. Anyway, Frank was wonderful to him, and even offered him one of his big Churchills, which Wally took and stuck in his jacket pocket.

While he talked, and moved around, and got another glass of champagne, he kept an eye out on his mom. Finally, when there was a lull in the line at the door, she gave him the nod and he drained off the rest of the glass and went over to her. She made her wailful excuses to the two unoccupied mothers at the door, and he followed her out.

"Youre coming back, arent you, Wally?" Agnes asked him, taking his hand again. "Im sorry about Marg. Do come back."

"Yes," he said. "Ill be back."

And after he had driven her home (a chore which very nearly suffocated him in the doing of it, he was so anxious to get out of sight of her) he did go back. More just to be away from his mom than anything else. Anyway, what the hell, he thought a little bit tight himself, there was all that damned imported champagne still there to be drunk, wasnt there? He might as well get all he could of that.

As the reception lingered along, and more and more guests kept coming in, until finally they began to trickle off and then finally stopped altogether, he drank more and more champagne and wandered around talking to this one and that, accentuating that deep heavy rather portentous Slavicness in him that there had been several occasions now lately that he was glad he had. He was amazed at how totally painless he felt. He got one of the first pieces of the cake, and washed it down with champagne. Once or twice he even spoke to Dawnie and to Shotridge, a word or two, when they happened to appear somewhere in front of him. It was nothing much, just a pleasant word or two. He had had his little moment, in the receiving line. Even if nobody noticed it but himself. That was all he could really ask for, expect. Wasnt it? He talked to more people, and drank more champagne, playing the role of the happy best-male-childhood-friend of the bride. Finally, when he realized he was getting a little tight, he decided he had better go. But it was amazing, how really totally painless he felt.

And it was then, just then, while he was thinking that amazed thought once again, that a sudden black bubble of fury burbled up through him and burst, like a blown up wad of bubblegum, drenching the inside of his head—the inside of all of him—with a wash of black inky burning acid. He stood for a moment by himself, looking all around, imagining the scene he *could* create if he wanted to, if he would let himself, let himself go. Then, wisely, he turned and left, slipping out quietly by himself.

The pain, which he had been waiting and waiting for, started the moment he was outside the foyer door in the fresh cool spring air. That was when he went down to Dave's and 'Bama's. He drove his mom's old car down there and parked it and went on in. It was the only place he knew to go. But nothing there helped him, either.

When he woke up the next morning, lying on the couch in their living room, he remembered vaguely that he had been told about 'Bama running Doris Fredric off, that he had remembered seeing her at the wedding and reception, that he and Dave had sat up and drank, that he had insulted Rosalie and she had left, that he had sat up alone and drank after Dave had gone off to bed. Nothing had changed. The pain inside him burned and scalded until he wanted to convulse himself and fall down on the floor and writhe and twist.

Dave and 'Bama were sitting in the kitchen drinking coffee when he went out there, but they were not real. Nothing seemed to be real. He sat down and tried to talk with them, and tried to listen to what they said, and drank a cup of coffee, and the pain inside him seared and burned. He could feel that his face was sort of blank. He had never felt anything like this. The cup of coffee was not real. Finally he got up and left and shaky and hungover drove his mom's old car, which was not real, up Route 1 which was not real to the West Lancaster road, which was not real. But before he had gone on down the gravel road to the west, which was not real, more than a mile or so, he lost his nerve and turned around in a farm lot and went back before he ever got to the woods. Where would they be now? Hadnt somebody said they were going to Chicago for a week's honeymoon before going back to school? Theyd be on their way to Chicago then. Or maybe they were already there, by now. He had talked with her once about going to Chicago, long ago. But they never had.

This was not the kind of pain he imagined a lost love affair gave. This was not the kind of pain he had seen in any movies or read in any books. This was, in short, not the kind of pain he had bargained for.

He drove the car home and put it away in the garage and went upstairs to his room. Luckily, he did not have to see his mom. His suit was rumpled and mussed from last night and he had spilled whiskey on it down at Dave's. He took it off and got it ready to send to the cleaners. When he did see his mom later he told her he had been out celebrating with a bunch of the boys from the wedding. She did not argue with him, and he knew why. And also, in addition, she was not real anyway. And all the time this pain seared and burned and scalded inside of him, as if he had swallowed live acid, until he wanted to throw a convulsion and fall down on the floor and twist and writhe and bite and claw until he made it stop.

Well, if that was what she wanted, if that was what she had intended, if that was what she hoped to cause, she had succeeded. Admirably. Fully.

Of course, he could not write. How could one write with a typewriter that was not real upon paper that was not real words that were not real? Ridiculous. And it went right on and day followed day and it did not abate. He lay around his room that was not real and ate his meals that were not real, and his mom who was not real carefully left him alone. He did not get drunk any more. What was the use? Up until now, during those two weeks before the wedding, he had not gone anywhere but he had at least kept on attending his few classes at the College, and he had at least kept on writing. Now he did neither. At the end of two weeks when it had not abated, indeed had not even shown any signs of lessening, this scalding burning searing pain all through the inside of him, he began to get frightened and panicky. What would he do, if he could never write again? Finally, he went to Gwen.

CHAPTER 63

GWEN had seen Wally at the wedding, and also later on at the reception at the Country Club, so she was not entirely unprepared for his visit. She remembered, at the wedding, that she had not seen him at all for two weeks, and after the wedding she had noted quietly that he stopped attending the two English classes he took under her, and had inquired around casually and found that he had stopped attending the other two, non-literary classes he was taking. Of course, there had been a week's vacation in there, after Easter. But when he still did not show up, either in Israel or for his classes after they reconvened, she thought she could pretty well guess what he was going through. She was not, however, at all prepared for the vehemence with which he was going through it, or the power of its effect on him. It didnt take long though, as soon as she saw him with that blank slack haggard face in which the dark eyes darted frantically about as if both were looking in concert for some means of escaping out of this body which held them, for her to realize how far she had underestimated his unhappiness. Even before he spoke a word.

Partly, she guessed, this was due to the way he had conducted himself at the wedding; and at the reception. She thought he had conducted himself admirably. Much better than his mother had, with that fake hearty happiness of hers that—for Gwen at least—was so obviously false, and failed to cover up her thwarted ambitions of having her son there, in Shotridge's place. Of course, it probably played well enough, for everyone except herself and Bob. But as for Wally, she thought he had done marvelously, and she was proud of him. Because she knew, of course,—or rather if she did not *know*: factually: she was nevertheless positive in her own mind—that Wally and Dawnie had been sleeping together since the beginning of last summer. And if he could overcome his first major love affair like that, so easily and so well, she had great hopes of him—of his work—in the future.

Also, partly why probably she had so grossly underestimated Wally's unhappiness, was that she was still having a lot of trouble—and a lot of unhappiness—of her own, over her own first major love affair. Well, if not her *first* major one, she amended to herself quickly, at least her first major one of any real consequence. Of any real authority. She had been rather in love several times before, in her extreme youth.

The most horrible thing about it was that while she could not forgive Dave for what he had done she still loved him. Only when he came to the house (He had only been three times now, since that last scene when he tried to get her to tell him what was wrong.) only when he came to the house did she become cold and distant and reserved with the horribly deep hurt to her soul that he had given her. The rest of the time, when he was not there, she did not feel that way at all. She thought of him warmly and affectionately, almost lovingly, even when it hurt her to do so. He had been drinking a great deal more lately; it showed in the puffiness of his face and the circles under his eyes; and she worried about him considerably. She worried about his work, too, which had fallen way off. And yet when he came to the house, she could not help acting distant. No wonder he did not come more often!

If only he had not done what he had done to her. If only he had been willing to wait a little, put up with her foibles for a little while. She knew she was grossly neurotic, she knew she exhausted everyone's patience. But if only— But most of all, if only he had chosen some other woman to have his mordant love affair with! Any other woman; any half way human, half way sensitive woman! Instead of that fat sloppy *ignorant* woman! A regular town whore! And *he* had a love affair with her! Not just a one night's entertainment, but a *love affair*! Ginnie Moorehead! God, how could she herself feel any other way than what she did? The very act, itself, and the very person of her, placed her herself, she Gwen French, down in the same pigsty category with her. It degraded the very real love they might have had into an animal relationship, the pantings of a male dog after a bitch dog. A bitch in heat. Ugh!

But the really worst thing, worse even than the fact that she still loved him, was the real guilt she felt—when he was not there—for treating him the way she did when he was. Each time, all three times, after he had been there she had wept and upbraided herself roundly for having treated him as she did. And yet as soon as she saw him, she would freeze up into a cold ball inside. She could not help it: she would imagine him in the arms of that fat pig of a woman, whispering love words in her ear, kissing her, making love to her. And when she did she would freeze tight as a drum, no matter how much—when he was not there—she wanted not to. But the guilt went deeper than that. Because Gwen could not escape a deep conviction that it was basically all her fault. If she had given herself to him, back then before all this other had got started— If she had not been so damned reluctant, so afraid of him finding out that she was a virgin— If she had not been afraid of being laughed at— Maybe he wouldnt have minded at all; maybe he wouldnt even have laughed, either outwardly *or* inwardly. The thought tormented her. And the way his work was falling off, both in volume and in excellence, tormented her also. That was also her fault. If Bob was right, in his guess, and Dave could *not* finish the book without her— What then? That would be the most horrible of all.

Oh, Sex! Sex sex sex. Men and sex. God, would they never any of them ever grow up to where sex did not dominate their lives? Before their work, before their health, before their nourishment, before their education—SEX came first; SEX controlled and governed their whole lives. It was her theory. She had evolved it, from studying Stendhal and the others, from studying the moderns like Faulkner and Hemingway and Fitzgerald and the rest. It was her theory, and she had applied it to her own study of Dave's old Los Angeles group and made it into an almost ironbound, irrefutable treatise. It was her theory, and now it was impinging upon and threatening to ruin her own life. Men and sex. Sex and men.

Already the young ministerial student had finally got around to asking her to sleep with him. This one was much quicker than most of the others. Maybe she was beginning to look easier? She had turned him down, kindly and smilingly, and he had gone away and brooded, and *his* work fell off. At the same time, and even before, she had noted him looking speculatively at the polio girl when they were here together. Braces on her legs and all. And the polio girl, of course, had returned the look aloofly and coldly and distantly—but of course, as she told Gwen, she admired him deeply as an artist, and respected his talent, even envied it: in other words, she was still waiting for the approach! And the polio girl herself! While waiting for the approach from this one, she had already taken to running around with another young ministerial student—a really bona fide one, studying fanatically to become a preacher—and now instead of writing those caustic bitter penetrating funny pieces she had been writing, she was turning to drippy sanctimonious little things about how God had helped her through her misfortune, how she had finally found God through having suffered polio, and though she was crippled she would not have traded the experience for healthy limbs because of the Faith and the nearness to God it had given her. She never did say just exactly what or who God was, or what He looked like, or what He said to her. She never described her Faith either, in anything except the vaguest of terms; though apparently this did not in the least lessen its power any. Her bona fide ministerial student, her second bowstring as it were, undoubtedly read all her new stuff and helped her with it while their Souls communed in God; and at present it was a toss up whether she would wind up writing for the Christian magazines, or as an avant garde Dorothy Parker, all depending upon which bowstring first strung the bow. Well, her bona fide ministerial student might read her new stuff and express great joy over it. Gwen could not. And didnt. And told her so, in no uncertain terms. At which she was naturally deeply shocked. Sex and men, men and sex. Sex and women, women and sex. Sex and sex.

Then she would think how Dave had not even waited, but had taken up with his fat whore almost as soon as he had met Gwen herself. The girl—Ginnie Moorehead—had as much as told her so, albeit unwittingly. That in itself was proof that no matter what she herself had done, or not done, she could never have prevented it or helped it. But then the guilt would return just the same, and torment her. If she had been honest with him from the beginning— And so she went, backward and forward, pulled nearly completely in twain by the insolubility, the not knowing, the not having even of enough fact to be sure, one way or the other. She was even getting so she was screaming at Bob when he was late for meals, while the poor dear said nothing. And nowhere was there anyone to turn to for answer, not even Bob—unless she were willing to tell him the whole truth, and about how she was yet a virgin, and she could not.

Of them all, only Wally seemed to show any signs of real stability, real maturity, she had thought. Wally was becoming more and more her main hope. He was young, and green, and he had never really suffered yet. But perhaps maybe, just maybe, he was not the type who suffered from sex. God hope it were true.

Then she would think of Dave again—when he was not there—and a sad melancholy poignant love for him, whatever he had done he was sweet and thoughtful and kind, he was sensitive, would fill her up and bring tears to her eyes. Tears both of love and of guilt.

She could forgive almost anything in Dave—or so she thought until he showed up. Then the ball of ice inside her would freeze her up again.

When she got the news of Dawnie's wedding and then later the invitations came, she did not really intend to go. She would send a present of course, a nice one, but she did not want to go. She didnt have the heart for it, just now, with all her own troubles and the misery she was going through. What she wanted to do was to spend the whole of Easter vacation, from Good Friday right on through to the end of the next week when school reconvened, working on her own book. It was getting well along now. Two to three months of good hard work would see it finished. And only when she was working—long, hard, arduous, methodical hours of slow meticulous research and careful reconstruction—could she be free of thinking about herself. But when she saw Agnes's card marked "within the ribbon", she knew they would have to go anyway. Bob of course was amenable, one way or the other; he didnt care if they went or didnt go. And, in another way, Gwen thought it was fitting that they go: it would be a fitting way of saying farewell to Dawnie. Dawnie had always been one of the ones she had had such high hopes of. So few women ever seemed to turn into writers, real writers. They lied to themselves too much. And Dawnie had had talent—not only in her acting, but in her writing too; the few things she did. It seemed that all of them were falling by the wayside, or preparing to, except Wally.

And so when she saw Wally at the wedding and later at the reception, and the way he conducted himself, she had been very pleased. Of course it was hurting him—but *not* enough to throw him. Maybe here at last was *one* writer who put his writing first, before sex. Maybe, after all, that was where the really *great* ones came from. And to hell with her own theory! If it was true, she was willing to stick it out till the end of the school term—and longer—if it would help him. She would even be willing to stay on here the rest of the summer—in spite of Dave and her own unhappiness—if it would help Wally to get finished up. He only had six more months' work at the most, to finish it. And in May his fellowship—"The Parkman College Fellowship for the furtherance of Christian Principles"—would be up for its allowable second year renewals.

It did bother her some, when he did not show up the last week of April for classes, after the week's Easter vacation; but still, she had thought hopefully, maybe he was going good on the book, and maybe that was why he was cutting school: to work on it and take advantage of the high. But when in the first week of May she saw him come in through the side door and drag himself up the steps and across the kitchen to where she stood getting supper, she realized immediately and at once how wrong she had been in her estimate of how unhappy Dawnie's marriage had actually in fact made him. At once and immediately, before he even spoke a word, she steeled herself and her mind to argue with him, and to try and figure out how best to get him straightened out. Her own troubles and unhappiness were forgotten.

Wally did not make any bones about it. He came right to the point. When she smiled at him and said, "Well! Come right in, stranger. Ill put another can of beans in the pot;" he did not bother to answer, but only went straight on across and flopped himself down in one of the ladderbacks, while she feared for its fragile structure.

"I cant work anymore," he said brokenly, in a hoarse voice. "I havent written anything, not a word, for two weeks. And for two weeks before that I dont think I wrote anything that was any good."

"Oh?" Gwen said, and carefully turned the burners on the stove off so she would not burn anything, then turned to him. It might be some time before she got back to cooking supper. She had never seen him looking so bad, so beaten down. His face stared at her slackly, blankly, while his two eyes darted here and there frantically like two frightened animals. He looked ready to come all apart at the seams. "And why might that be?" she said, laying down the spoon in her hand.

"Dont you know?!" Wally cried. "Dont you know?! You were at the wedding! Dawnie got married. She married Shotridge!"

Gwen did not say anything for a moment, then came over to the big table and sat down at the end. Wally flung his ladderback around to face her without getting up out of it, and Gwen winced inwardly for the antique chair. There would be another one for Bob to fix, probably, like the one Dave had strained apart without ever knowing he had done it. With his heavy, muscled body and broad Slavic face Wally had in him much the same torrential energy and tremendous physical vitality that Dave had so noticeably, and her heart contracted in her thinking of it. Even in despair and wretchedness they both poured it forth like dynamos. "Were you really that much in love with her?" she said quietly.

Wally stared at her anguishedly, his eyes roving over her face desperately and at the same time hopefully. "I cant sleep!" he cried suddenly. "I cant eat! I cant even concentrate to read!" Abruptly he paused, and ran his hand over his face and shook his head, as if to clear it. "Nothing seems *real*, any more," he said more calmly. "You dont seem real. Nobody seems real. Its like Im dreaming and cant wake up."

"You seemed in such good shape at the wedding," Gwen said quietly.

"An act!" he cried. "All an act!" Again he made that abrupt pause. "You know, its funny," he said almost in an analyzing way. "I didnt really hurt much at the wedding. Not really. Or at the reception. It was only afterwards that it really began to hit me; when I really began to realize it. The moment I left the reception, the moment I got outside the door, that was when it hit me. It fell down on me like a ton of— of—wheat," he finished lamely. "Now I cant think of anything but *her*!" he cried. "No control over my own mind at all. Think of *her*. And—" he stopped abruptly, and momentarily his eyes cleared, stopped their frantic darting, and he looked at Gwen straightly. "Look," he said, "what Im telling you is strictly secret. We never told anybody about our love affair, and I dont think hardly anybody knows about it. But we were—were sleeping together; all last summer. And we were very much in love. Now do you see why?!" he cried suddenly.

"Well, of course, I never suspected anything like that," Gwen lied calmly. "I only knew you were running around together. But if it was that strong, why didnt you marry her yourself?"

"Well, I wanted to," Wally said hoarsely. "But I couldnt. I mean, I knew if I did Frank would have me working in that damned store for him, you know? And I couldnt do that. Dawnie, on her side, wanted us to run off to New York and live there. But I couldnt do that, either. I had my fellowship, and I had to stay here. Anyway, we didnt have any money. And then—then she just started to draw away from me. And then she left me," he said brokenly. "For *Shotridge!*" he cried.

"Well, I dont know what to tell you to do," Gwen said. "What do you want me to do?"

"Help me!" Wally cried. "Youve got to *help* me! Hell I cant read any more! Hell, I cant write! All I can do is sit around and think about *her*, and about all the— Youve *got* to help me!"

"How can *I* help you?" Gwen said. "Youve just got to get over it." Guilt assailed her: God! Help him? How could she help him! She couldnt even handle her own love problems; and her heart squeezed in her again, at the thought of Dave.

"Well, what do *you* do?" Wally cried. "To get over a love affair? You must have been in love a hundred times. How do *you* get over feeling like I feel now?"

"Oh, Wally!" Gwen said faintly.

"Well, what *do* you do?!"

Gwen gazed at him a moment, her heart sinking guiltily at the deception, at the very ridiculousness of it: of him asking her, of anybody ever even considering asking her: Gwen French the worldly-wise. She tried desperately to think over all of the advice to the lovelorn, all the "remedies" for love affairs, that she had ever read about. There didnt seem to be many. And of those there were, they were all suspiciously slim, all of a suspicious sameness. "You just have to let time take care of it," she said lamely. "Let it wear itself out. After a while, it will. Though you may not believe it now. —Or," she said, lamely, "one of the best ways to get over a love affair is to go right into another one. Fall in love with somebody else." They sounded stupid, even to her. And she thought of Dave again, painfully.

"But I *cant* let time take care of it!" Wally cried. "Itll kill me before that much time *passes*! I honestly think itll kill me, if I dont do something! And anyway, I aint *got* that much time; I got to get back to my work! And as for fallin in love with somebody else, thats ridiculous; I dont think Ill ever be able to fall in love with anybody else again!" He paused abruptly again, in that way, and made a herculean effort to get control of his facial muscles, stopped his eyes from their wild darting, and stared at her. "Will you have a love affair with me? To help me get over it?"

"Oh, Wally!" Gwen said, faintly. "*I* wouldnt help you, not like that. That wouldnt help you. It might even make it worse, comparing me to her." Dave, Dave! She got hold of herself. "No," she said. "No, I wont.

I cant and I wont. Ive told you I was tired of sex and love. Well, thats my reason: Because I dont ever want to have to go through again that agony youre going through right now." God help me, she thought; God have mercy on me for the liar I am.

Wally let his gaze drop, and looked down at the floor. "Well, I suppose it wouldnt have worked anyway," he said gloomily, miserably. "I guess it was just a wild gasp. You know, I used to think I was in love with you, once. Hah!" he said bitterly. "How green was my valley? How green was my *head*! I didnt even know what love was! Even when I *had* it, with Dawnie, I didnt even know what it was. Thats the *worst* thing!" he cried tormentedly.

"Believe me, Wally," Gwen said, tiredly, "time *will* take care of it. In time, it wont hurt you any more at all. Its an awful struggle at first. A real battle . . ." It trailed off, and Gwen didnt even feel like trying to finish it. God! God oh God.

"Time!" Wally bellowed. "You dont under*stand*!" he cried. "I think of her all the time! I cant get her out of my mind! I keep remembering her how she looked up in the woods that first time— —See, we took my mom's car up to a woods," he explained, as if under an unquenchable necessity to talk about it, "on a gravel road out west of West Lancaster. It was just at dusk, and— In early summer, it was. There were old nut hulls on the ground. She took off her sweater and bra and stood out in the woods bare to the waist, and wearing bobby sox and saddle shoes. That was the first time we ever made love together." He paused and took a quick gasp for breath, then went on. "But I think of her other places, too. I cant hardly stand to sit in the house at home or my own room, because I took her down there a couple times, when my mom was gone away visiting. Everyplace, anywhere I go, its always someplace where I was with Dawnie, and reminds me of her. If I go up town, if I go out by the Country Club, or The Stables. Even when I come over here. Or out to the high school; even out at the College: we used to go to the football games together. We played *ten*nis out there! *Tennis!*"

Gwen listened painfully as he went on talking about himself and Dawnie and all the places they had gone, more exquisitely painful than she could ever remember having felt before. Everything he said was not himself and Dawnie, but herself and Dave—except that the things they had done, things he and Dawnie had done, were things she and Dave had not even got to do. They had not even got to do those things. They didnt even have those things to remember. Probably, she thought, the pain bright, exquisite in her, probably those were the things he did with *her*, with Ginnie Moorehead. As unobtrusively as possible, she brushed her hand across her forehead and shook back her hair and smoothed it back and shut her eyes and let her hands lie lax in her lap, and listened.

"There isnt anything!" Wally cried in fine, "not a single damned *thing*! in this town, that dont remind me of her. I ought to get out of this damned town entirely!" He stopped, and a kind of silence fell, and Gwen opened her eyes.

"Aww, Gwen!" Wally said, selfgrindingly, selfcastigatingly. "Gee, Gwen, I didnt mean to make you *cry*." Suddenly he pulled his legs together and warped them around sideways writhingly, drawing his feet up, as if he could not stand it, physically could not stand it, what was happening, to him, or to her either. "I *had* to talk to somebody. I *got* to do something," he said justifyingly.

"Thats all right," she said calmly, "Im not crying. Its just that I felt so sorry for you. For everybody. You know," she said, even more calmly, "I think it *would* be a good thing if you got entirely out of town for a while. Look; why dont we do this. Why dont you go away for six months, to New York say, and let us finance you, Bob and myself. Wed both be more than willing to do that. We can give you enough money to keep you going that long, and in six months you ought to have your book done. Im quite sure I can get you the second year's renewal on your fellowship, and if you need more money than that let us give it to you. It would get you away from here and all the bad memories, and—and maybe youd find yourself a new girl, there. In time."

Wally stared at her slack-faced, his eyes wide with thought for a moment. Then he shook his head. "Thanks a lot, Gwen. Thats nice of you. But I couldnt do it."

"Why not?"

"Well, I just cant take money off of you and Bob like that."

"Well then, lets say we're loaning it to you. You can pay it back later, out of the royalties of your book."

Wally shook his head again, stubbornly. "What about the fellowship?"

"Im pretty sure I can get it renewed for you, even if you do go away to New York for a while. I think Dr Pirtle will work with me. Even so, if we dont get it renewed, what does it matter? if Bob and I loan you the money youll need?"

"Cities scare me. I dont like them," Wally said. "To go somewhere like that where nobody knows you. New York most of all. Why, you could fall down on the street and die there, and nobody would even stop to look at you."

"I know lots of people in New York. I can give you letters to all kinds of people. It might even help you to get your book published later."

Wally stared at her, narrow-eyed. "No," he said, and shook his head. "I cant do that. But youve given me an idea. I know what I am going to do." His eyes, so dull and darting up to now, flashed suddenly with a high frenetic enthusiasm. "Im going to join the Army."

"Youre what?!" Gwen was flabbergasted.

"Sure! Join the Army and see the world. Think of the material Ill get."

"But Wally," she protested. "Wally, thats ridiculous. You dont imagine youll be able to write and finish your book in the Army?"

"No!" Wally said eagerly. "Hell, no! Ill just put it aside while Im gone. Then when I get out Ill be able to finish it, and Ill also have a novel about the Army I can write, too."

For the first time since he had arrived, he sat up suddenly in his chair, creaking it dangerously, no longer depressed, his eyes bright with a kind of frantic enthusiasm, and leaned his arms on the table and flexed his fingers potently. "A couple years in the Army like thatll give me more maturity. I aint seen very much of life you know. Just that one winter in Florida."

"Its three years," Gwen said, "if you enlist. Isnt it?"

Wally shrugged the extra year away enthusiastically. "Okay. So three years. Ill just be that much more mature. Maybe Ill sign up for Hawaii or someplace like that."

Gwen was caught completely short, did not know what to say. She tried desperately to think of every deterrent that she could. "Well—But you were turned down for the draft, werent you?"

"A bad ear," Wally said enthusiastically, his eyes bright as the idea took deeper hold on him. "All I got to do is get it cleaned out before I go up for examination and theyll never notice it. I let it run before," he said, a little guiltily, "on purpose." He smacked his fist into his palm energetically, suddenly transformed from the unhappy boy who had entered earlier. "Gwen, you dont know how youve helped me. Yes, sir; I think Ive had the idea in the back of my mind for quite a while, only I just didnt recognize it. I was talking to Dewey Cole and Hubie Murson not too long ago about the Army. Theyre both thinking of going back in. Maybe Ill go with them."

"Wally, be sensible," Gwen said, fearfully, her heart beating with a kind of desperate foreknowledge. "You dont belong in the Army. Youre a writer. Your job is writing. Dewey Cole and Hubie Murson may belong in the Army. Maybe it would be fine for them. It wouldnt be for you. Youre just making an excuse to escape away from your work."

"But I cant work anyway, any more," Wally said enthusiastically. "Anyway," he said, "Ive taken a lot of guff in this damned town, because I was turned down for Service. Guys dig me about it all the time. Hell, most of the guys I was in school with are all in Service. Why shouldnt I do my stint? Its not like there was a war on. Its not even dangerous. Not that Id care. No sir, by God!" he said with finality. "Thats what Im going to do. Then when I come back Ill have forgotten all about Dawnie Hirsh. Dawnie *Shotridge*," he said caustically. Like a drowning man grasping at any straw that might save his life, he clenched his fist, then raised it, and then smacked it down into his palm again with enthusiasm. "Gwen, you dont know how youve helped me!"

Gwen looked at him, at the frenetic enthusiasm on his face, her heart sinking in her desperately. The last one, the last one left, and the Army! She tried a ruse. "But what will all the people in Parkman say, when you go in the Army so soon after Dawnie's marriage?"

"To hell with them and what they say! I wont be here!" Wally said triumphantly.

Once more, as she had done at least twice before since he had come in here with his troubles, Gwen pulled herself together firmly and disregarded her own misery. "Well, youre not going to do it," she said positively. "I wont let you. Ive put God knows how much energy and work and time and thought and belief in on you, and Im not going to let you just throw it all away for some damned wild excuse to get over a twiddling little love affair. Ive got some rights, too. You didnt marry Dawnie last summer when you had the chance because you wanted to write. Well, *want to write now*. Stop feeling sorry for yourself. You sound like a ridiculous child.

"This is something I have learned from Bob. First you have to have a job and work. *Make* yourself do it. Because if you dont your mind will gallop from one idea to another all your life. Your job is writing, not saving your country. And when you deny it, youre denying yourself.

"What if it had been you who quit Dawnie last Christmas, instead of her quitting you? Would you be so upset and miserable now?"

"I did quit her," Wally said, dismally.

"Ahh, yes! But then she turned the tables on you by not caring. She married someone else. And left you holding the short end. Thats the truth of it. She outsmarted you. Thats what *hurts* you. Thats why youre so miserable. She *dominated* you. When all the time you thought *you* were dominating her. Thats why youre unhappy. Your ego, your vanity, cant stand it.

"Stop pitying yourself, Wally. Of course you cant work. Youre too damned busy feeling sorry for yourself because Dawnie bested you.

"Pity," she said; "if only we understood the word Pity. I think all the chains, and limitations, and prisons we build around ourselves resolve themselves into that one word Pity. Pity reduces everything to futility, Pity involves us in the problem, whatever it is, Pity holds us caught by the thoughts our Pity builds in our minds. Weve learned to make derogatory the words Ego, and Vanity; but we still hold Pity up to view as a virtue. Well, Pity for yourself or for another person is only the same identical thing. Its the opposite way from Freedom. Just as much as Ego, and Vanity. And it doesnt matter a damn whether you Pity yourself or Pity someone else, Pity always binds you closer to the imperfection you see—that you *hunger* after—and that has caught your emotions."

Her voice had suddenly gone off higher, become nearly hysterical, and her ears were listening to it carefully, trying to make her stop, to pull her voice back down.

"Stop pitying yourself, Wally," she said screechingly. "Of course you cant work. Your entire emotional strength, your entire time and energy, your whole existence is limited to this little state that you have built up in your mind. Love! A mountain out of a molehill! Stop it!" she cried, almost hysterically; because she herself could hear her own mind screeching her own words at herself.

Wally was staring at her, wide-eyed, startled. And at the same time, all during her long-winded diatribe, that thick heavy Slavic bullheaded stubbornness had been growing more and more powerfully pronounced in his face. She couldnt change him. She would never change him. Her words would not change, or affect, his mind any more than they would change or affect her own.

She got herself stopped, and then sat looking at him, her heart sinking down in her defeatedly. She wanted suddenly to slap his face, back and forth, with both hands, until his ears rang and his eyes fell out.

"Go on and join the Army," she said defeatedly. "Go ahead and go. I dont give a damn. I dont care whether you go or not."

"Ive looked at everything," Wally said sincerely. "Ive *thought* of everything. Its the only thing for me to do."

"Just remember one thing," Gwen said dully; "I wont be here when you come back. Youre the last one," she said, obscurely. He obviously didnt understand that; but she did not feel like elucidating. "You can get somebody else to help you with your damned writing, because I never will."

Wally smiled at her, warmly, affectionately, magnanimously, then got up. "Youve helped me a lot, Gwen. Youve helped me a lot today, too, even."

"Yes," she said bitterly. "Yes, Ive helped you a *lot*."

"Youll feel differently when I come back," Wally said magnanimously. "Youll realize it was all for the best, the best thing I could do." For a moment he put his arm around her, where she sat slumped in the chair, then patted her tenderly on the shoulder. From the door on the cellar landing, just before he went out, he smiled and said: "Just remember one thing. No matter what happens. No matter what. Just remember how much Ill always owe you, and how grateful I am to you for all youve done for me."

For a long time after he left she did not move. It seemed somehow that whenever the crises came, Bob was never here. It was as if none of them even wanted Bob to be there. If Bob was there, they all just marked time and waited, until he was gone, before they brought their crises up to her. Bob, the only wise man of the lot. Dumbly, Gwen shook her head. Maybe Bob could have helped it; maybe Bob could have convinced him.

Join the Army! The last one, the very last one left. And she had failed again, as she had failed with all of them. Guilt clawed at her vitals, and her heart lay sunk down in her as far as it could go, defeatedly. She didnt know where Bob was, and she simply sat, waiting for him. She knew what she was going to do. She was going to do, in defeat, what she had once hoped to do in triumph. She was going to take her own book and go far away and to hell with them, and she was not even going to wait till the school term ended. She was going now. Somewhere where there would be peace, and where she could work, where she would not be required to love a bunch of oafs who could not stand to live unless they were in hot water all the time and burning up emotion; where she would not, either, be required to be "in love" with another oaf who did not even know it, did not even care, when someone was in love with him, and only wanted to rut in the gutter with some fat piggish whore. You could save the whole world and lose your own soul. Where was Bob? Where was Bob? Where oh where oh where was Bob?

He sat and heard her out while she told him. He did not even offer any objections or dissuaders. Sitting around the corner from the end of the table where she still sat, and had been sitting without moving since Wally left, he leaned his chin on the crotch of his hand and listened kindly.

"I might," Gwen said bitterly in finishing, "I just might, by staying on till the end of term, be able to get the young ministerial student married to the polio girl. But thats the only job left now," she said acidly. "That would be the only reason for staying."

Bob smiled sadly. "Im sure theyll be able to manage it somehow by themselves without you," he said. He leaned over and patted her gently on the hand. "Dear Gwen," he smiled gently, "if that is how you feel, I think that is exactly what you should do. Go. One can only take just so much in any one period of one's life. The—ahh—ability to absorb punishment differs in different individuals, mentally as well as physically, and one must realize one's own limits."

"You always agree with everything I say," Gwen said, disheartenedly.

Bob shrugged slowly, looking at her questioningly, then smiled, sadly.

"The only thing I worry about is leaving you here alone," Gwen said dispiritedly. "I dont know if I should do that or not."

"Dear Gwen. Dont give it a moment's thought. Shardine and Jim can take excellent care of me. Ill hire Shardine full time as cook and house-keeper. Youve gone away before like this, you know."

"Never like this," Gwen said. "I dont know if Ill ever come back or not. Always before I just went away to school for a while, knowing Id be back."

Bob shook his head in gentle disagreement. "That doesnt matter. You must do what you feel like doing. If you dont come back, you just simply dont come back. However," he smiled, "I expect someday you will. If only for a visit. Where do you think youll go?"

"Ive been thinking about Tucson. Cousin Wilson Ball is still out there, still running his Florsheim shoe store. I could stay with them until I got settled. I dont feel up to trying to go to school anywhere this summer. And the country out there is beautiful: the long vistas, and the colors. Mt Lemmon in the Catalinas is right there close at hand. There might even still be some snow on it in May. I could ski. And I expect Cousin Wilson Ball still has horses. I feel like maybe it might be—be healing. But most of all I want to take my book with me and get it finished up and sent in to a publisher. And I think I could work there."

"It sounds fine. It sounds like a splendid idea, dear Gwen," Bob smiled. He paused, and hesitated. "And dear Gwen," he added awkwardly, "dont be shocked if your old father says this to you—but—find yourself another man. Its often one of the best ways." He smiled apologetically.

Gwen stared at him a moment, then suddenly began to laugh out loud hysterically. She could not stop. She did not even want to stop. Wildly, ribaldly, it rose up out of her in waves, great roaring waves, and she threw back her head and let it come. Poor Bob, poor dear old Bob. He was as about as inept at giving her advice as she had been with Wally. Apart from all the other: that he did not know: Gwen French the worldly-wise!

Bob got up quickly and came over to her solicitously, and standing, held her head against his lean tweed-jacketed stomach. "Dear Gwen!" he said apologetically. "I didnt mean to upset you. I didnt mean to remind you."

"Oh, Daddy!" Gwen gasped, laying her head against the once-so-safe, tobacco-smelling tweed. "Daddy, Daddy! No, no— It isnt that. Its just— Daddy, I said the same identical thing to Wally! Oh, Daddy— Daddy— Oh, Daddy! arent we all so ri*dic*ulous!"

"And so sad," Bob said.

Once it was all decided, it did not take long to put it into action. She did not even go back to the College at all. She didnt want to go back there. All her manuscript and most all of her research, all that she would need to finish, was already here at home. Bob called Dr Pirtle himself personally that same night, to arrange about a substitute teacher. It was the work, he said; trying to do all the research and the writing on her own first really major work and handle all her classes too. No, she wouldnt even be able to come tomorrow. Very nearly a complete breakdown, yes. He hated giving such short notice, but he really feared for her health. No, she wasnt seeing anyone. As soon as she was able, she should go away for the summer. Probably to Tucson, yes; they had relatives there. Dr Pirtle, as always, was very understanding. He would arrange for the substitute. If need be, he would teach the major upperclass courses himself; he had worked with her on them, and knew her plan and materials. As for the undergrad subjects anyone could handle them. Three days later she was packed and gone. Because Bob did not like to drive, nor liked long goodbys either, any more than she did, she said goodby to him at the side door, the cellar landing door, that everyone used, that all of them had used so much. Bob would explain to the young ministerial student, and the polio girl, and to Dave, and anyone else who came. Shardine's husband Jim drove her in her own car to Indianapolis to catch the plane.

As for Wally, he left that same day that he had talked to Gwen. He didnt see any reason for hanging around, once he had made up his mind. High and enthusiastic, glad at last to be doing something that kept him occupied without having to think, frenetically excited, he stood and looked around his room and realized there wasnt very much to put away. The table and tools he had imported from the basement during the two weeks before the wedding, and the rest of the junk, he would let his mom worry about. She could do anything with it she wanted. His manuscript he packed carefully in typing paper boxes and locked it up securely in a bureau drawer. The key he hid carefully down amongst the mechanism of his typewriter, then slipped the leatherette cover over it. He didnt want his mom looking at his manuscript. If the house burned down while he was gone, the hell with it; hed write the whole damned thing over. Hed probably have to anyway, when he was maturer. Hell, maybe hed throw that whole damned book out entirely—he had learned on it—and start a wholly new one. And for the first time in a long time he felt really free, with no guilts worrying him about getting up early and working. His three Randall knives—the #3 Hunter, #5 Yachtsman, and the #8 'Trout and Bird'—he locked up in the bureau with his manuscript. The #1 'All-Purpose Fighting Knife' he packed carefully in his bag, of course. That was why hed bought it: for the Army. He only packed one small bag; he wasnt going to need many civilian clothes where he was going; and after he packed it, he hid it in the closet where his mom would not see it, and went to make his goodbys.

He had a couple of buddies still in town, fellows from the old band, and he went to say goodby to them first. Then he went down to Dave's and 'Bama's, hoping to find Dewey and Hubie there too, which he did. Of them all, only Dave tried to persuade him not to enlist. He did not, of course, tell them of his talk with Gwen. Dewey and Hubie, raising their heads up from their glasses, gave the considered opinion that a hitch in the Army was good for every young man; it grew them up; besides, it was a great experience, nobody should miss it. 'Bama didnt seem to have an opinion, didnt care one way or the other, and shook hands with him stolidly after he had had one happy farewell drink with them.

At the last moment, after he left them, when he was already on his way home, Wally got the idea of going by and saying goodby to Frank and Agnes Hirsh. After all they had been very nice to him in the past. And besides, they would probably mention it to Dawnie in their next letter, about him enlisting. He didnt hold a grudge against her any more. Not really. She probably couldnt help what she did. No, he didnt really hold it against her any more, but he could not help wondering with a little thrill what she would think when she heard the news. Would she, maybe, feel just a little sad?

He found, when he stopped by the house, as he should have expected but in his excitement had not thought about, that Frank was not there. Only Agnes was home. Frank, of course, was down at the store. Hell, he should have known. That meant he would have to go down there, too, like Agnes suggested he do. Anxious to get moving and get going, he nevertheless sat down and talked with her a few minutes. He felt he had to do that much, since he had come by. Happily, enthusiastically, he told her about his plans. Being on the selection committee Agnes naturally asked him about his book, and he explained how he was laying it aside until he got his service in. They would get him sooner or later anyway. Then when he came home he would finish it up, and in addition have a novel on the Army too. What the Army was *really* like. He might, he said happily, even find that he might be able to do some work on the first book while he was still in Service. She seemed very understanding, he thought, and when he left she kissed him.

At the store he shook hands with Frank, and with Al Lowe, who as a combat veteran of War II gave it as his sober opinion that it was a fine thing he was doing by enlisting, but Frank's officegirl Edith Barclay was also in the office quietly and efficiently going about her work, and Wally suddenly felt constrained by her presence. There really didnt seem to be too much to talk about, unless he talked about himself, and he didnt want to do that in front of the girl. When he left, he accepted another of Frank's big Churchills and stuck it in his pocket.

Back home, he got his bag from the closet where he had hidden it because he did not want to have to put up with his mom's sniveling and crying for an hour and a half, and came downstairs with it to say goodby to her. Five and one-half minutes later he was on his way walking out of town to hitchhike to Indianapolis where he intended to enlist, feeling freer and more happy and excited than he thought he had ever felt in the bright, warm, windy May spring day.

That Edith Barclay, he thought suddenly, as he thumbed the first two trucks that passed. She really had a body. Now there was a woman who, he bet, would really let go and love a man once she knew she loved him, love him all the way, and for as long as he wanted her. Hell, she might even still be around town when he got home.

CHAPTER 64

IF FRANK HIRSH had been able to guess that Wally Dennis was thinking covetously of his mistress Edith Barclay, he would have been pleased and smug. And if he had known Wally was imagining having designs on her three years from now, he would have laughed. —Or, at least, he would have laughed a month ago. He had never been so sure of Edith's real love for him as he had been a month ago. Now, however, he was not quite so sure.

But of course, Frank did not guess what Wally Dennis was thinking, because it would have been hard for Frank to realize that a boy like that, a mere child, would ever even think of sex. Hell, he was no more than just barely out of high school. True, kids were growing up a little quicker nowadays—witness little Dawnie's getting married —but they still werent growing up all that quick. Besides, he had known Wally ever since he was a baby. Anyway, getting married— just the simple fact of *being* married—grew a person up almost overnight. The added, new responsibilities; the necessity for engaging in a meeting of minds; the need to realize that life after all was not just a one-way proposition, but a give-and-take relationship; all of these and the sudden awareness of them, turned a youngster into an adult all at once. Suddenly they werent kids any longer, and consequently they were *ready* to learn something about sex. The odd thing was you didnt even need to talk to them about it, about sex and all that stuff. They just picked it up themselves, once they married. And all this hullabaloo about sex was just so much hogwash. They learned it themselves, when it was time for them to learn it. Frank had never seen anything as amazing as the sudden change into adulthood that had come over Dawnie, when she at last made up her mind and realized and faced the fact that she was getting married. She had become a mature, thoughtful, forceful person overnight.

But all that did not apply to young Wally, who had never married, and what was more, had no plans for getting married. Instead of going into the Army, he should have found a nice girl and married her and settled down. Frank was all for marriage. It was the great grower-upper. And he himself had never been so married, so very much married, all the way up, as he had been with Agnes the past year. And he had never been so happy in his life.

Of course, he knew why the boy was going into the Army. He had tried to treat him nicely, when he came by the store to say goodby, and he thought he had. He felt kind of sorry for him ever since Agnes had told him she suspected maybe he had had a boyish school-kiddish crush on Dawnie. Probably going into the Army was the best thing for him.

That damned wedding! Frank thought a little smugly. It had cost him a young fortune; but it had been more than worth it. When you only had one daughter, and she only got married once in her life, you ought to give her a real sendoff. It had been his idea to get all the relatives in from out of town. And he himself had called them all long distance and offered to help pay whatever expenses they incurred by coming. No one accepted of course, except Francine in Hollywood. With her husband and herself both school teachers, they wouldnt have been able to come if he hadnt helped them out. There had been a devil's own time, getting all of them put up, and in the end they had even had to resort to the hotel, for which he footed the bill. It was, he reflected happily, a damn good thing that he had almost unlimited credit in Springfield with Clark's father in law and the Greek. He wished his own damned motel out on the bypass had already been built! He could have really done it up brown then: just put them all in it and turned it over to them. But then with a wife like he had, a wife like Agnes, who could handle everything perfectly, it had not been a problem anyway. He had just turned it over to her. And, as always, Agnes had handled it all superbly. She had done a magnificent job, flying to New York and all. Frank had never been as proudly, and as happily, and as *sat*isfiedly, married as he had been those three weeks before the wedding, and the big week of parties after it.

He had just let Agnes handle everything, and in only two things concerning the wedding did he have anything to do with it. One was that it was him who suggested putting Edith Barclay and her grandmother "within the ribbons"; and the other was that it was him who handled the Old Man.

Both he and Agnes had agreed right away against the advisability of inviting either the Old Man or Dave. The Old Man of course was out from the start. He probably didnt even have a suit of clothes any more he could wear to a wedding; and if you went out and bought him a brand new one, he would be just as liable to show up in it without having shaved for six days and dead drunk. And as for Dave, since he had taken to living in that damned house with 'Bama Dillert and sleeping with that horrible low-life bum of a whore he was sleeping with—(everybody in town knew about it; and was laughing at it)—they had decided that it was best not to invite him either. He had only seen Dawnie a couple of times since he had been back in Parkman anyway, both of them times when he had eaten dinner at their house and just happened to see her there. And in the last year he had turned into being almost as big a thorn in both their sides as the Old Man.

With Dave there was no problem. They just would not send him an invitation and, moving in the circles that he did, he would probably not even hear about the wedding until it was over. Unless of course, some of the relatives wanted to visit him beforehand; but that could be easily taken care of by simply explaining the situation to them and asking them, if they wanted to see Dave, to wait until *after* the wedding. And as a matter of fact, the way it turned out, Francine was the only one who put up much of a beef. All the others, once they had had it explained to them what he was doing and how he was living, not only agreed that it was better not to invite him, but wound up not even going to see him *after* the wedding. Francine, however, had seen that story of his in the *New Living Literature* pocket edition out in Hollywood—(Agnes had a copy of it, too, there at home; kept it out on the coffee table, so that people would not think they were bitter about Dave)—and while Francine thought it was a fine story—(as did Agnes!)—Francine was not in the least upset or perturbed about Dave's going back and using the old family name Herschmidt that they had all been trying to live down for so long. It didnt matter a damn to her, Frank thought, whether it disturbed the rest of the family or not. And so, with her wild scatterbrain "artistic" ideas about Art and Freedom, Francine had insisted that Dave be invited to the wedding and treated like the rest of the family. However, with her three fairly young children (the oldest was eight or nine) to take care of, her protest was pretty half-hearted; and anyway Frank had always been able to handle Francine. And when the rest of the family, including her own husband, sided against her Francine gave up; although she insisted that after the wedding she was going down to see Dave. And in fact did go to see him.

But so all of that was worked out and taken care of pretty easily, with Dave; but the Old Man was a different thing entirely. Even if Dave heard about the wedding, Frank knew he wouldnt come unless he was invited. But the Old Man was a different horse. He was just as liable to take it into his head when he was half drunk—or cold sober for that matter!—that it was his granddaughter that was getting married and by God he was going to go, and then show up at the church in his overalls and old mackinaw and that wornout railroader's cap he affected, and just plump himself down in a seat. The older he got, the more cracked and crotchety, and just plain mean, he became. So it was delegated to Frank to see him and talk to him and fix it some way so he would not come. He had gone and looked him up, and tried to talk to him as kindly as he could without actually coming right out and asking him not to come. But that was not, of course, the way to try to talk to him; and he should have known it. There was no known way—or at least, Frank had never discovered one—of being kind to Old Vic Herschmidt.

The house, the pension home, where he lived, was just across the street north on North Main Street the crossstreet from the end of the business district, so that Frank did not actually have to drive up and park in front of it conspicuously. He could park, diagonally, in front of the last of the business houses and not make it look like he was going there. Frank did not like Mrs Rugel who ràn the pension home, and with whom the Old Man had been having a "love affair" for the past three or four years; and he did not want to go to her place. So what he did was park in front of the business houses—being there at the end of the business district, they were naturally among the poorest and least patronized businesses—and wait; until the Old Man came out of Mrs Rugel's along in the middle of the morning. When he did come out, and started up North Main toward town, Frank opened the right-side door of the Cadillac and leaned over and called to him.

"Hey! Come on and get in. I want to talk to you."

Whereupon the Old Man, instead of doing as he was told, naturally, merely stopped and put his scrawny fists on his hips and stood and grinned at him evilly. "Well, hello, boy!" he said.

Frank waited patiently, still holding the door open, and finally the old devil came hopping along in his crablike way over to the car. He stood in front of the door for a while without saying anything, still grinning maliciously, and then finally he got in.

"Well, how have you been?" Frank said heartily. "Been a long time since Ive seen you."

The Old Man merely grinned more contrarily. "Scared Ill come to yore girl's weddin week after next and fox it up for you, 'ey?" he said.

Frank, after having made up his mind to be circuitous and kind, was rather taken aback. "Well, that *is* one of the things I wanted to talk to you about," he said awkwardly. "Along with finding out how youve been and all."

"Cut the crap," the Old Man said raucously, and then cackled maliciously, grinning evilly. "How much is it worth to you if I dont?"

"How much?" Frank said, taken still further aback. "What do you mean how much?"

"What do you think I mean when I say how much? How much cash. How much money. You think I mean eggs?"

"Well, how much do you want?" Frank said.

"I aint made up my mind exacly yet," the Old Man grinned. "But I been a-thinkin on it. Make me an offer."

"Well, I dont know what you have in mind," Frank said. He still had not recovered his aplomb from the suddenness with which they had got to the subject of money. "You want me to buy you a couple bottles of whiskey?"

The Old Man cackled. "More than that! I want a lot more than that!"

"Well, just what do you want?" Frank said, a little irritably.

Obviously enjoying himself thoroughly, the Old Man leaned back in the sumptuous seat of the Cadillac and opened up his frayed mackinaw. "Sure is a nice car you got here, boy," he grinned. "How much she cost you?"

"Great God!" Frank exclaimed disgustedly. "Dont try to tell me you want my car now!"

"No," the Old Man grinned. "No, I dont want yore damned car. But Ill tell you what I do want."

"Okay. Damn it, tell me and quit beatin around," Frank said heatedly. "And we'll discuss it."

"No discussin," the Old Man said, and shook his birdlike head vigorously. "I aint comin down none in my price."

"All right, damn it! Lets find out what it *is*!"

"Ill git to it," the Old Man grinned. "Ill git to it. Dont try to rush me none, boy." He leaned back in the seat contentedly, grinning, and thought a while. "Well, I want two things," Frank's father said finally. "First, I want fifty dollars. In cash. Right now, this morning. —No, seventy five dollars; Im changin that to seventy five dollars." He peered at Frank beadily, and grinned.

Frank stared back at him, saying nothing, giving no motion of either assent or dissent.

"And the other thing I want," Old Man Herschmidt said expansively, "is somethin I been thinkin about fer some time now. I want a trip to Wisconsin."

"To Wisconsin!" Frank said. "What the hell for?"

"Fer fishin," the Old Man grinned. "I want to go up to Wisconsin fishin. Once more before I die. To a place I used to go to up there. —That was before I knew you, boy," he added parenthetically— "Yes, sir; thats what I want." He slipped his mackinaw lapels back expansively and hooked his thumbs through his overalls bib. "I figure," he said happily, "itll cost you three, four hundred dollars. To do it the way I want to do her. Do it up real right. Well, what do you say?"

"Fishing! Well for Christ's sake!" Frank said. Then quite suddenly he was irritated, angry. "Hell, I would have given you money for something like *that*. Long before. You dont have to trade me out of it like Im a tightwad. If youd of just come to me and asked me, Id of been glad to finance you for a fishing trip to Wisconsin."

"Like hell you would," the Old Man said shortly, positively.

"The hell I wouldnt!" Frank said angrily. "What do you think I am?"

"I know what you are," the Old Man said promptly.

"You do, hunh? Its your damned layin' around drunk all the time and makin a spectacle of yourself and embarrassin' the family that I dont like. Id be glad to finance you to go on a fishing trip."

"No you wouldnt," the Old Man said, promptly. "Youd of told me to go screw, if Id a come and ask you that. Anyways, I wouldnt never of ask you, you son of a bitch. —But," he said expansively, "this way we got a trade. I got somethin you want, and yore willin to pay for her. Even-steven."

"Okay, its a deal," Frank said, struggling inwardly to keep from losing his temper and blowing up. He reached in his coat and pulled out his wallet and slid out a fifty and three twenties from a thick sheaf of cash.

"Small bills, please," the Old Man said, "small bills, please. I aint got yore credit nor reputation."

"All right," Frank said irritably, and exchanged the large bills for tens and fives and counted them out for him. "Now how soon can you leave for Wisconsin?"

"Not now, not now," the Old Man said, and shook his birdlike head. "Late June, or July or August's, the time to go. But Ill tell you what I want. I want you to deposit four hundred dollars in a savin's account for me at the bank. Ill pick the book up myself. Soons I got that book in my possession, Ill see to it that I dont show up at yore girl's weddin."

"Four hundred dollars is a lot of money for a fishing trip," Frank said.

"Four hundred's my price. Take it or leave it," the Old Man said, and grinned at him evilly. "If Im a-goin on this fishin trip, I aint goin cheap. I aim to do it up brown and enjoy it."

"All right, like I said, its a deal," Frank said. "But how do I know you wont go back on me? Ive given you money before to do something, and then you reneged on me. What guarantee have I got?"

"Heh heh," the Old Man said. "I reckon youll just have to take my word for it, you son of a bitch." He cackled happily.

"Ill give you the four hundred *after* the wedding," Frank said.

"Nope," the Old Man said promptly. "Now. Today. I dont trust you either."

"Ill give you my word," Frank said.

"I wont take yore word," the Old Man grinned. "Just yore money."

"All right," Frank said irritably; "but by God you better not try and show up at the wedding and ruin it. Christ, it would ruin it completely for you to show up there drunk. We're plannin' on havin a big wedding for Dawnie."

"Yair. Ive heared about it," his father grinned.

"Okay. You just remember that," Frank said threateningly, to which the Old Man merely grinned contentedly. "Do you want this savings account? or do you want me to give you a personal check for the four hundred? I can write you out a check right now."

The Old Man looked at him slyly for a moment, then nodded. "All right; Ill take a check. But you just better not try and stop payment on it," he grinned warningly.

"Dont worry about that," Frank said angrily. "You just remember your side of the bargain. Youll have to give me time to get back to the store and call the bank and tell them, so theyll accept the check without any question from you." He got his checkbook out, and wrote off the check, his hand trembling a little with anger, and with hurt feelings that the Old Man would ever think he wouldnt have helped him out for a fishing trip.

"All right, Ill do that," Old Man Herschmidt said magnanimously. "Just you dont try and stop payment on it. Because Ill take it right up there today and that weddin is still two weeks off." He accepted the check and folded it carefully and stuck it down in his overalls bib pocket. Then suddenly he cackled slyly. "Now, Ill tell you somethin, boy! I wouldnt of give a damn whether I went to yore damned weddin or not. But I knew youd be around. Hell, I aint seen that girl of yourn moren three times, I dont reckon. I wouldnt even reco'nize her on the street. What would I give a damn whether I went to her weddin or not?"

He slapped Frank on the knee and cackled as if he had just put over a big fox of a deal, and opened the door of the Cadillac and got out. "Just you dont try to stop payment, though, you son of a bitch," he said narrowly, and grinned. "Or by God sure as God made little green apples Ill go to yore damned weddin anyways." He opened his mouth and tilted back his head and peered down the length of his beaklike nose wisely at Frank inside the car. Slowly the open mouth grinned, and he shut the door and walked away. "Goodby, boy!" he called back, and cackled smugly.

Frank sat in the seat, heatedly, angrily, irritated and edgy, and cursed under his breath as his father walked away, up toward town. As it turned out, later on, it was to be the last time that Frank was ever to see him, because in July of that year—on the Fourth of July, that very day, it was: Independence Day—he was to die without ever having got to make his fishing trip to Wisconsin. He would die in the night in his room at Mrs Rugel's of a stroke brought on by drinking all day (and probably several days before that; and God knew how many years before *that*) in celebration of the Glorious Fourth. Frank would, of course, give him a nice funeral. A funeral to which, however, very few people would come, except for Mrs Rugel his "mistress," and Frank and Agnes. His wife of course, naturally, would not come. The four hundred dollars would still be in the bank, and would be very helpful in paying the funeral expenses. But of course, Frank did not know any of all this then, as he sat in the car; and for that matter, did not know it later, in May, when he was thinking back over all of these things. And as far as that went, if he had known, he wouldnt have cared. He had been hoping the old son of a bitch would die for fifteen years now. Anyway, he did not come to the wedding.

The one other thing Frank had anything to do with, concerning the wedding, which was getting Edith Barclay and her grandmother seated "within the ribbons," had been his own idea. When the invitations were being sent out and Agnes was deciding just who to put just where, he had gone to her with his suggestion. His sole suggestion, actually, concerning the invitations—except to add the Greek's name in along with Clark Hibbard's father in law and mother in law. When he told her, he put it all on Old Janie, just to be careful: It would, he thought, be a nice gesture to have Old Janie sit inside the ribbons, since she had been working for them so long. Hell, she was practically one of the family; had practically raised Dawnie; and it would please her tremendously. And especially since she so obviously had not been in good health lately. And of course, if they asked Edith, which they would have to do, he said, since he was asking everybody else who worked at the store, they ought to have her sit with Janie.

He did not really know what made him do it, but it elated him to think of his mistress sitting among the honored guests at his daughter's wedding. It was the kind of thing the Anton Wernzes, grandfather father and son, and the Scotts and the Crowders, or those old oil magnates who had founded the Country Club, might have done. Or Clark's father in law up in Springfield; or the Greek, if he had ever married. They were all pretty sophisticated people. Being wealthy like those people made you sophisticated. Anyway, it pleased him immensely to think of it; and besides that, he felt he owed it to Edith, after all she had been to and done for him. But of course he could not tell or explain any of this to Agnes, with her old-fashioned ideas. And indeed, had to be damned cautious in even approaching her with it. Agnes could smell a "clandestine affair" about four times as far away as she could see one. And in fact,—up until the last year, at least; when they had got back together—had accused him of having affairs with lots more women than he had had, accused him of going out with women whom he had not only not been out with but whom he had hardly ever even considered *going* out with. But of course all that had stopped in the last year since they had been back together and so happily married.

It was really amazing, when you thought of it, that she had never yet tumbled to Edith, and indeed, had never even suspected such a thing apparently. Frank himself could only attribute it to Edith herself, and the extreme caution she always insisted upon so insistently.

When he approached Agnes with the idea, she had looked up from the lists she was working on that evening and looked at him thoughtfully, chewed on her eraser a moment, and then said that she thought it would be a fine idea and she wondered why she hadnt thought of it herself. Poor old Janie had been going downhill rapidly the last couple of months.

For a moment, just for a split second, Frank thought she might have guessed—even from this tiny bit of evidence. It was not even a thought, really, hardly more than a fleeting momentary feeling. An old habit pattern, probably. Then she smiled at him, and he knew everything was all right, that he had put it over.

When he told Edith about it later, the next time he saw her, she was angry and did not think he should have done it, but underneath he could see she was pleased just the same. Pleased that he thought enough of her that he was willing to take that kind of a chance for her. However, she still thought it was a silly thing to have done, and that having her there at the wedding was not that important, for the risk he had taken. But finally he convinced her that he had really put it across, and that Agnes suspected nothing.

The truth was, Frank did not need Agnes to tell him how badly Old Janie had been going downhill the last couple of months. He knew a lot more about it than Agnes did; because he got it from Edith. It was, in fact, about all Edith could talk to him about any more when they were together. Agnes had told him that Janie was practically worthless around the house to work anymore. She still came every Friday, and she still did a little bit, and Agnes would never have said anything about it to her for the world, but it was little more than a token gesture any more, her Friday cleanings; Agnes herself, together with little Walter's help— which proved to be invaluable—was doing almost all the real house work now on the days Jane wasnt there. He and Agnes both knew by now that Janie had quit all her other jobs, including the one with Dave, in order to keep on working for them; and he agreed with Agnes that they could not say anything to her, or let her go. Hell, she had been with them ever since the first year they were married. And yet, Agnes said, whenever she tried to talk to her about her health Janie only clammed up and changed the subject, or else grinned and said she was dieting.

But he learned a lot more about her from Edith, the times they were out together. Almost too much, in fact. Because that was damned near all Edith could talk about any more when they were together. Jane this and Jane that. She almost never talked about them, herself and Frank, any more. Jane was just about as worthless and ill at her own house as she was at his. She made a kind of token gesture of cleaning it up, but if any real cleaning was ever done it was Edith who did it. Janie would fix supper for herself and John in the evening, and not do too good of a job at doing that, and the rest of the time she just lay around the house, weak, always tired, always worn out. She seemed to eat almost nothing any more, Edith said. But then she would take spells of eating like a regular horse. It was no wonder she lost so enormously much weight. And yet, Edith said, she steadfastly refused to go to any doctor, and just as stubbornly maintained there wasnt anything wrong with her, and said she was just dieting to lose weight. Oh, Ill go sometime, she would say, just for a general checkup, although I dont need it. Edith could not understand it.

"I dont know what to do," Edith would say to him in her distress. "Ill say something about her health, and shell just look at me with that old gravelly grin out of that thin face and say theres nothing wrong with her."

She did not even go out any more at nights to Smitty's, Edith said; and Edith, who had once been embarrassed by her always sitting there in the corner booth every night with the old men and had wished something would happen to make her stop doing it, now wished only that she could see her sitting there again and damn the embarrassment, because it would mean she was feeling all right again. Once, Edith told him— and often retold him—once she had got Doc Cost to come out to the house and take her by surprise to look her over; but Jane had refused to be examined. She had allowed him to peer down her throat and thump her chest, but she would not go out to his hospital. Doc Cost had tried to josh her into coming in with him then and let him give her a full thorough examination, but she had refused. She had agreed she might come in some time later and let him look her over, though it would be a waste of time she said, but then she had never gone. Doc had told Edith privately that she ought to get her down there and let him examine her. But Edith could not get her to go. Edith, out with Frank, must have told him this same story at least a dozen times in a couple of months, or if not that many, anyway every time they were out together almost. Jane did not even drink beer any more, or only a bottle now and then once in a while. It was frightening, she would say, to see this woman who had once been so big and hefty and strong as a bull, looking so fragile and thin that the first strong wind might blow her completely away. Sometimes Frank got almost more than he could take, about Jane. It seemed sometimes that that was the only thing he heard from Edith any more. And anyway, he did not like to talk about sick people and death. It disturbed him. It disturbed him because it made him think about himself dying someday, and also because it made him feel so helpless because he couldnt do anything for them or help them any.

But as if that were not enough, it had gotten to the place now, in May, after the wedding, that Edith was getting more and more reluctant to go out with him. She was afraid that something might happen to Janie while she was gone. Maybe she might collapse, or even die, and there would be nobody there to help her or be with her. Maybe John would come to get her to help and find she wasnt there! John would be totally helpless, himself.

"I simply dont know what Id do," Edith would say, "if she died in the night when I wasnt there to maybe help her." She would be almost weeping, and there was nothing Frank could do to comfort her. "Ive treated her so terribly so many times," shed say. "Without ever having any idea maybe of how scared and lonely she might be."

"Oh, come on now," he would say, trying not to sound irritable. "Shes not that bad now. Shes not going to die. Not for a long time anyway."

"I dont know," Edith would say. "Nobody knows. How can they know, when she wont even go to a doctor? All I know is that she looks bad, horribly bad. I just wish I knew why she refuses to go to a doctor."

And so it came about that Edith started breaking dates with him. Not breaking them exactly; by that he meant she did not actually stand him up. She would just simply come to him when nobody was around at the store and tell him that she could not go out tonight. And no amount of persuasion would change her mind. That had been going on since before Dawnie's wedding, and was still going on when Wally Dennis came by the store to say goodby on his way to the Army, and it kept on going on after that right on into May. And a month and more of that was almost more than *any* guy could stand. She didnt break all their dates, but she broke nearly all of them. And even when she did go out, she was reluctant.

But there was more besides that to disturb Frank. Ever since that night back in January when he had first educated her into the subtle arts of lovemaking, it seemed to him that Edith had been drawing more and more away from him in the sex they had together. It wasnt exactly anything he could put his finger on with surety. It was more just a sort of feeling. She always went to bed with him when they did go out, but it was as if—as if—well, the only way he could say it was that she didnt *like* it. She did it—sex, and everything,—but she didnt *like* it. And well, hell, what was the point in having sex with somebody if they didnt like it? and just did it to please you? Hell, the whole point of sex was to get them to *like* it, to like it and want it as much as you liked and wanted it. Otherwise, what the hell did you have? Somebody *submitting*.

And it was this—as much or even more than the way she was acting about Jane—that had made Frank not quite as sure of Edith's love as he had once been, that day when Wally Dennis had come into the store to say goodby.

And it didnt seem to be getting a damn bit better after that, either.

But if he was inclined to be a little unhappy over Edith at times, he could easily forget it in the development of the bypass, and in the development of young Walter. The two of them, between them, not only kept him happy, they kept him occupied most of the time, too.

The bypass itself was fast approaching completion. The whole look of the land, out there, at the junction, was changed now and it was hard to even remember what it had once looked like: old Lloyd Monds's feeder farm with its two old barns under the big trees along one side of Route One and the little dairy farm along the other, and beyond both of them nothing but farm fields running straight on off to the distant woods of the hollows. It didnt look like that now. The long raw-clay ribbon of the bypass grade swept up in a massive curve to the junction from the east, then curved on off beyond it to the west, making a distinct and very definite dividing line between the town-side on the south and the country-side on the north. The stretch of good weather back in January and February had lasted long enough to complete all the major grading work. March and most of April had been rainy and bad. But now in May the weather had turned off good, and the minor grading and smoothing up work was being rushed to completion. Already nameless men with tractors were out along the right-of-way sowing ryegrass on the raw dirt, and in the one or two steeper places gangs of men were filling the winter washes and sacking them over with gunnysacking to prevent more washing until the grass could take hold. On the east side of the junction the steel forms to contain the concrete were already up and in place nearly all the way to Route 1, and on the west side they were laying more of them in every day, approaching the junction from the west. If the weather held good till the end of May, they said, they would begin pouring around the last week in May. Already the big concrete pouring machines had been moved in on low-boys, one at either end of the bypass. These machines, moving backwards, would lay down a single ribbon of concrete the entire width of the highway inside the forms at one swath. They would pour the whole thing in less than a week. And since they would be using that new fast-setting concrete that did not need to be seasoned out, a week or so after it was poured the road would be ready to use. All that would be left to do would be to paint the black line down the center and grade dirt up against the raw edges of the concrete after the forms were removed. Almost certainly by the middle of June, if not before, the new bypass around Parkman would be open.

And suddenly, as if seeing for the first time in the as-yet-empty concrete forms curving away in two parallel lines the form of the road that would be laid down between them, as though it required this definite sight-picture of the road's skeleton to make them realize it, the town began to wake up to the fact that it was going to have a bypass; and inquiries, from real estate dealers and would-be speculators, men like Tony Wernz IV and Harry Shotridge and Judge Deacon, began to be circulated about as to such and such a business site or this or that piece of ground. Most of the inquiries wound up at, and ended with, Frank Hirsh. It was gradually discovered, by a few of the more up-and-coming, imaginative, far-sighted wheeler-dealers of Parkman, that Frank Hirsh had title to a good three-fourths of the potential business sites along the bypass; and had, in fact, had title to them for some time before their imaginations started working. Frank himself, of course, could not have been happier. From the moment this bit of knowledge got bruited about among the "insiders" Frank had more telephone calls and requests for business appointments than he could possibly handle and was spending less time at the store than he had ever done. It was a damned good thing that he had had the foresight to make Al Lowe manager of it. About the only time he spent at the store now was to pick up lists of his phone calls, decide which ones he wanted to answer, make the calls, and then beat it out to another bunch of appointments. Since there was not room enough in the store's little office which he shared with Al to have any privacy and private talks, he made all his appointments to be in the other people's offices—or else in the afternoon or at lunch, in the Elks Grille or out at the Country Club—and he was on the go all the time. At the very first, a long time ago, he had contemplated taking offices somewhere around the square, knowing that the store's office would be inadequate; but now, some odd quirk of pride and amusement made him decide against this: It looked so strange to everyone, to all of them, to find that the man who held the real key to any business to be done on the bypass did not even have offices to do it in. He could read it in their faces. And it tickled Frank's fancy to continue.

A few of them, notably Harry Shotridge (who was now his daughter's father in law), and Tony Wernz (who could not conceive of anyone in Parkman not leaping at the chance to make a deal with Tony Wernz), approached him about going in with him and putting up capital to develop his holdings. Frank could only tell them, politely and indifferently, what he told everybody else: He already had partners, very wealthy ones in fact; he did not need any capital. Frank's stock in Parkman rose even higher, immediately; and he merely sat back and watched it complacently. It was very noticeable in the personal invitations both he and Agnes began to get almost immediately, to dinners, to parties, to private dances, to the Club, all of them from people and to homes which they had both seen very little of heretofore.

The scene with old Judge Deacon was a particularly pleasing one, for Frank. Frank had learned an awful lot about politeness and dignity and aplomb up in Springfield from the Greek and the old man, Clark's father in law; and he had been putting it to good use and practice the last couple of weeks since the calls started. Judge Deacon, as a matter of fact, had called him three times before Frank was able to call him back; and after that he called three more times before Frank was able to even find time to have an appointment with him. And it wasnt entirely a put-on, either; it was the truth. When he finally did get over to the Judge's office, he could only stay a short while because he had another appointment—with Elias Crowder, of Crowder & Scott, this one happened to be.

The Judge took it in pretty good grace, he had to say that for him. Better, much better, than Frank had thought he would. He was clearly puzzled. He had been caught completely short, completely flat-footed, and he knew it. Not very hopefully, but more as a sort of gesture of covering all possibilities, he too offered to put up capital if Frank needed it. And Frank explained to him, politely, just as he had the others, about his wealthy partners. The Judge did not try to pump him about his partners, but it was plain he would have liked to know who they were. Which was natural enough, since he had been caught flat-footed here too. All he said was, thinly, that he assumed they were from out of town—to which Frank merely said nothing, neither yea nor nay. Frank did not try to rub it in on him; he didnt have to, since the Judge was taking it in such good grace. When he had envisioned this scene a long time ago, Frank had imagined it as a verbal knock-down-and-drag-out, a no-holds-barred double barrage of insults, like the Judge was so prone to when he had the upper hand, only this time it would be going both ways, with the Judge getting as good as he gave. But there was, in fact, very little insulting this time on the Judge's part—no more than he was just naturally addicted to by his nature. But compared to the way he had used to insult Frank, he was very soft with him.

Just before he left—to meet Elias Crowder, of Crowder & Scott—the Judge asked him dryly if he still intended to stay on with them at the Cray County Bank, now; or did he want to sell out those holdings he had and put them on his new business.

"Well, I might as well stay in the Bank," Frank said. "Its all of it good solid investments. But of course," he added softly, "I wont be able to devote all the time to it that I used to, you know."

"No, I suppose not," the Judge said dryly. Then he grinned his fat evil beady-eyed grin. "Well, you really pulled one off, Frankie boy."

It was a minor triumph, to have such a remark as that from Judge Deacon. And it seemed to Frank that his cup had finally come clear full and even had runneth over. "Why, thanks, Judge," he said with a selfdeprecating smile. "I didnt really do much. I guess I just happened to think of it before anybody else did, is all."

The Judge merely stared at him out of his greedy little eyes wedged in in the midst of all those chins, and said nothing more except goodby.

It was strange, and it was clearly evident almost every place he went, what a sought-after person he had become in Parkman, Frank thought, in the past couple of weeks. At least among the town's elite. The lower elements, the ordinary oafs with their ordinary businesses, hadnt even waked up to the fact of what had gone on with the bypass yet. But they would, eventually. He told nobody anything about any plans he had for the bypass land, and did not breathe a word to anyone about the Parkman Village Shopping Center. Time enough when it started going up. Then, by God, everybody would be aware of what had been, and still was, going on with the bypass.

But in spite of all the sudden new interest in him and all the new claims upon his attention and his time, Frank did not let them interfere with his time with Walter. He kept that carefully and meticulously apart, and nothing encroached on it. Back in February, when they had first got him, Frank had started taking him to all the Parkman High and Parkman College home basketball games. All during the winter they had not missed a single home game of either the high school or the College; and of the Parkman High games away from home, they missed only one. They would drive forty, and fifty, and even sixty miles sometimes, to see them play up and down the Wabash Valley League. The College's games away from home, played by necessity at even greater distances, they did not get to see all of; but they saw more than half of them. And anyway, as Frank figured, it would be the high school where Walter would be going to school first—and as far as that went, probably would never attend Parkman College at all—and it was more important for him to see the Parkman High games than those of the College. Next fall he planned to take him up to Champaign to see the Illinois home football games, because it would probably be there that he would be going to school someday. And then later, as the spring came on and the basketball season faded, Frank started taking him to the track meets. Every Saturday afternoon he and Walter would drive to wherever either Parkman High or Parkman College were competing, if it was out of town, and if it was at home Saturday afternoon would find them out either at the high school or the College track.

Walter liked basketball all right, and thought he would like to play, but it soon became apparent that he liked track much better. He would, he stated, much prefer being a runner to anything. Preferably a long distance runner, like the mile. Frank, who was mostly a football and basketball fan as far as high school went, had no idea why long distance running would appeal to Walter so much, but it was clearly evident that it did. Whenever the mile was run at a meet they attended, Walter would sit forward tensely in his seat in the stand and grip the rail if there was one in front of him or his program if there was not, and his quick bright eyes would widen in fascination, and he would remain that way until the mile was run, when he would sit back looking emotionally exhausted. He could not explain very clearly just what it was that fascinated him so, and all he could say was that it must be very satisfying just to get out and run and run and run. Frank didnt know what to make of it, but if Walter wanted to be a runner, by God a runner he would be; and Frank began to read up on cross-country and its rules and its season which came in the fall.

Walter liked baseball, too, though not as well as running. And while Parkman College did not have a very good team (the high school had none), Frank and he nevertheless went religiously to all the home games as the spring came on, and Frank planned on taking him to see several big league games during the summer in St Louis or Chicago.

But probably most of all, more even than the sports, the thing that thrilled Frank most about Walter was the first time he took him out to see the bypass, and explained it to him and showed him the land they owned, he and his partners. It was good weather and just at the time when they were finishing putting in the steel forms for the pouring of the concrete, and Frank drove him all around and up and down and showed him the various places. Walter sat quietly and watched attentively, while Frank pointed out the two corners which he and his partners owned and why they were more valuable than the other places. As soon as Frank was done explaining, Walter had pointed his small hand at the two opposite corners, the bare one and the one where the house of the dairy farmer Allis now stood, and asked who owned those two, and would not someone be able to build filling stations on them too that would take business away from Frank's side. He had grasped the whole principle of the whole deal immediately! Frank could not remember when he had felt so positively thrilled. So he had had to go ahead and explain about that part of the deal, too: how Allis had insisted on selling his north plot to the State because that would cut his land in two.

"But that was silly!" Walter said disgustedly.

"It sure was," Frank grinned delightedly; and then he had explained that as for the fourth corner, the one where Allis's house now stood, it would probably never be any competition to them mainly because

Allis would probably never want to sell his dairy farm; however, he conceded, it might happen that at some time in the future, for one reason or another, Allis might sell, and that someone might build there to compete with them.

"Then the thing to do would be to buy it first, before anybody else got it," Walter said.

"Yes; dependin' of course on whether you could get it first, and whether it would cost you more money than buyin' it would be worth." Walter listened and nodded solemnly.

But the thing that fascinated him the most about the bypass was all the big road-building equipment. He could sit by the hour in utter silence and watch them work. He was so plainly attracted to them that one evening after the road men had quit work Frank took him to get a closer look at them. They walked up and down the highway apron and along the wide shallow drainage and inspected the sheepsfoot rollers and the huge cats and the heavy graders and earth movers, and looked at all of them for over an hour and a half and were late getting home for supper. Frank had never looked at them closely before, himself. Walter did not want to climb up on the seats and sit and hold the steering wheel and pretend he was driving, like youd think a small boy would, he wanted to look at the workings and the motors. He wanted to find out what each mechanism was, and what it did, which lever did what, and how did you work that. Frank could only tell him a very little about them. But after that, whenever Walter asked for something —which was very, very rarely indeed ("They told us at the orphanage never to ask our new parents for things," he said.)—that was what he asked for: to go out to the bypass and look at the graders.

Frank, remembering he had seen some of them somewhere, scouted around in Terre Haute until he found a place which sold the miniature scale models of the LeTourneau road-building equipment, and bought Walter a full set of them. Walter would play with them by the hour. Frank, thinking he would tickle him and make a big treat for him, laboriously got out hammer and nails and boards for the first time in years and built him a sandpile in the back yard to play with them in and had clean fine gravelpit sand hauled in and put in it; but after Walter played in it a few times, he came to Frank—rather hesitantly —and explained that it did not work good. As soon as the wet sand dried out, it would crumble apart and ruin the roads he had built, and it was his suggestion that most of the sand be removed and replaced with regular dirt which could be mixed with the remaining sand. So Frank had this done; this time he hired a man to do it. After that, Walter would play with his LeTourneau models in the sand- or rather dirt-pile, making roads up and over and down and around, grading them with his graders, rolling them with his sheepsfoot rollers, until they hardened into reasonably solid structures, and then would run his small cars and the road-building equipment on them until he tired of that particular road layout, and would tear it up and construct himself another. And whenever he was not in evidence, that was where he might be found. He was going to be a model-railroad-man sure as hell, Frank could tell.

And Frank himself liked to sit out there with him in the evenings now that it was warm, with a good stiff drink and the evening paper. Sometimes when he did so, tears would actually almost come in his eyes, and he would have to hide them behind the paper. This was something he had dreamed of almost all his life, it seemed. His own son, playing in the yard, himself sitting there with him, protectively, ready to help, ready to be called on if needed, but not intruding himself if he wasnt. He had always wanted this. A daughter was all right, a daughter was fine, but your own son, who would carry on your own name— Well, there just wasnt anything like it. He still half-way wished they had changed his name to Franklin. He would have got used to it soon enough.

All that guff about giving him a complex was pure crap. Hell, he knew he had a happy home here with them; and he knew they loved him. But it was too late now, he guessed. And anyway he didnt want to bring it up to Agnes and have an argument.

But in spite of that small regret, it seemed to Frank that finally at long last his life had really opened up into being what he had always wanted it to be. By dint of much perseverance, and hard work, and shrewd business planning. He had earned it. It hadnt just been given to him, by God. And if he had earned it, by God he had the right to enjoy it, didnt he? And in fact, if there was anything he could have wished for at all now any more, today, it was that his mistress would be just a little more loving to him, like his wife was.

But as for Walter, he was a sane, normal, healthy kid—a little brighter than most. And when he could, when he was not actually working, Frank took him everywhere with him that he could, because that was the way a father ought to be with his son. If he had to run down to the grocery in the evening for Agnes, he would take Walter with him. And he had already given him the run of the store, and shown him all around it, and shown him also the signs he had had changed to read FRANK HIRSH & SON. In fact, just about the only place he did not take him was when he went out with his mistress, Edith.

They were going out together a lot less often now, as May and spring progressed toward June and summer, and that of course was due to Old Janie being sick. And Edith, the rare time when she did go out with him, seemed to be receding further and further away from him. Into some blank distracted silent place of distress and worry all her own. He didnt like it worth a damn. But there wasnt a whole hell of a lot he could do about it. Hell, he loved Old Janie himself; but sometimes he wished she would either hurry up and die or else get well and get it over with, one way or the other.

He oughtnt to think something like that, but sometimes, irritably, he did. If Janie should die—which, eventually, she must anyway; whether she got over this illness or not—he still had hopes of Edith allowing him to buy her a house and set her up in it, like Tony Wernz had done for his mistress and like the old time oilmen had done for all their mistresses: like Al Dorner who had founded the Country Club had done for Mrs Grace Toll after her husband Rex T. died. Edith and John Barclay had never been very close anyway and John could get himself a housekeeper after Janie died. If Janie died, he amended. Frank had already been scouting around a little and had found a nice little house a couple of blocks off North Main the crossstreet out north toward the railroad that would make a nice place for her with a little fixing up.

Only once in the last couple of months had he mentioned it to Edith, and that one time—mostly because she was upset over Janie—she had not only refused again but had gotten angry. It was funny with Edith, when she got mad; she didnt say much but her eyes flashed fire. After that he had not brought it up again; but he had not given up on it. He still had hopes someday of getting her to see it his way. Her argument, which of course was true, was always that it would give away their relationship because she didnt have enough money to buy a house. But Frank was sure that, given time, he could find some way to make it look legitimate. But he had not mentioned it any more that night.

One other night during those two months was notable, in that— because Edith was seeing him so seldom, and when she did see him was so worried about her grandmother—he had gotten pretty tight and had had another attack of that gastritis. He had been drinking rather heavily the last few days before, because of seeing so many people. (It was strange, how much business and drinking seem to go together; even if you didnt want to drink, you had to if you were seeing someone at the Elks for lunch, or meeting them at the Country Club.) And when he had hit the bottle pretty heavy that night with Edith, the gastritis had hit *him*. It was several hours before between them Edith could get him straightened out enough to get him able to drive home, and they did not get home until after two. Usually they were home before midnight. At the time it had rather frightened him, but when he got home Agnes was sleeping soundly and next day apparently thought nothing of his being out late. And once that fright was over, Frank was rather glad it had happened. It was the first gastritis attack he had had with Edith. And he had never had anybody work over him so tenderly and take such tender care of him, as Edith did. Not even his wife, Agnes.

He only wished that there was some way he could get her to stop stewing and being afraid for Old Janie—at least to the point where she would start going out with him again regular. Then everything in his life would be about perfect. But he couldnt think of anything to do.

However, that problem solved itself before the end of May. One morning Edith called Al Lowe at the store early, weeping and sobbing almost inarticulately, and told him that she would not be to work that day because Old Janie had died in the night. It was early when she called and Frank was still at home, and Al called him from the store. Al had not been able to make too much out of what she said, but apparently the thing she feared most—or, at least, part of it, Frank thought secretly—had come to pass. Janie had died in the night, and no one had known a thing about it. Edith and John her father had both slept through it, only to discover it the next day when, finding that she had not gotten up, Edith had gone to her room to wake her. Janie had not died easily. Apparently she had been both awake and conscious. And as Janie always would have done, she had fought dying hard; as hard as she had always fought her other enemies. But, whether purposely or not, she had not made much noise. Not enough to wake anyone at least. Edith had called the doctor to come out and they were getting the coroner. And that was about the story, Al said. They didnt know yet what had killed her.

Frank thanked him, and then as an afterthought told him to close up the store altogether until after the funeral as a gesture of respect. When he hung up, Frank was shaken. Maybe at times, when he was feeling irritable and teed off, he had wished Old Jane would hurry up and die and get it over with; but he had not really meant it. He had not really wanted her to die. He went and told Agnes immediately. From what Al had said on the phone, John Barclay had felt that he ought to go to work on his job at the Sternutol anyway, and Edith was there alone. So he and Agnes drove out there right away, to try and be all the help to her they could.

And it was while they were driving out east on Wernz Avenue the mainstreet to Roosevelt Drive that the idea of how to get Edith her house, now, without Agnes or anyone suspecting it, hit Frank suddenly. He must remember to ask Edith later on whether Janie had any insurance or not. Whether she did or not, they could say she did. And the house for Edith could be bought with Old Janie's "insurance money."

But when he finally did see Edith again, afterwards, after the funeral and after everything was taken care of, he forgot all about asking her. Because he had never seen a person so much changed in so short a time. He was too astounded to even remember to ask her. Edith, who had always been so inwardly confident and selfcontained, clung to him in the motelroom like a lost child. She broke down, of course, and cried to him about Jane, but it was more than that. She was completely changed, and she seemed to cling to him—him, Frank Hirsh—and hang onto him hungrily and desperately as if he were the last solid thing left in the whole world. He was, naturally, very pleased. It was very flattering. But what a surprise: to see anyone so changed.

CHAPTER 65

IT WAS not her grandmother's death, so much, which broke Edith, and broke her completely—or rather, it was not *alone*, not *entirely*, her grandmother's death that broke her. It was what she learned about it afterwards.

After they had found her—it was she herself, Edith, who first found her and then called John—after they had found her and she herself had called the doctor, and at his suggestion then called the coroner, Edith had stayed in the room with her until they came. She could have gone out in the other room, but it seemed little enough, pathetically little enough, to do. It was a thin sad pathetic futile gesture, but it was all she could do, all there was left to do, so while she would rather have not, she forced herself to stay there with her. She did not examine her closely, or touch her again, after that first time when she had tried to raise her up and seen that it was useless; she did not even look at her very closely; she preferred not to, as if in some way she felt it might have embarrassed Janie, to be seen like that. But nevertheless there was one thing Edith could not help noticing: it was plainly apparent through Janie's thin old pathetic nightgown: Janie was wearing her frayed worn old sanitary belt, underneath it. Afterwards, after the doctor and the coroner had been there, Edith talked with Doc Cost, and between them they figured out pretty well what had happened.

It had been a bad, a horribly bad, six months for all of them. There was no question about the fact, by then, that Janie was ill, seriously ill. Even John, in his dumb slow way, had finally realized it and given up making his foolish flattering remarks about her losing weight and what a figure she was getting, which he made only to be pleasant, but which instead merely devastated everybody without him knowing it. But even John had known there was something wrong, that she was ill, for the past six months. Janie herself knew it too, Edith was quite sure, although she would never admit it. It made for an unpleasant, strained, tense relationship for all of them around the house; and as a result there were more fights and spats and arguments than ever. But there were also—and later on Edith was to think back to this hungrily, desperately, and remember it hopefully—there was also more tender making-ups and warm scenes of really tender love between them, too. She could only hope, desperately, that Jane remembered that too.

Edith could think back to the night when she had come home late and caught Janie wandering around the house barefooted —the same night it was, when she had first seen 'Bama Dillert's car parked under the trees on the Fredric drive, and she and Jane had sat up and talked about it— and wondered if it had all been going on then, too. The sickness. Perhaps it had been starting then? They had been so very warm and close, she and Jane, that night, talking about the Swiss music box of her childhood. She herself hadnt known about the illness then, that far back. But for the past six months she had known; they had all known. And Janie had known too, Edith was quite sure.

And yet there she was, her, Janie, who ever since Edith could remember had spent almost as much of her cleaning money on doctoring as she had on beer and her old duffers,—there she was, refusing to see any doctor about anything. God! Edith thought, bitter tears of total helplessness coming into her eyes at the thought, oh God! there was an irony for you! Jane and her kidneys! Jane and her "gravels"! And then with this horrible thing in her, she wouldnt be examined. And Edith knew why. That was the worst, most horrible thing of all! After she had talked with Doc Cost, she knew why. If she had only known at the time, before it was too late! She could have gone and talked to her. She could have reasoned her out of it.

But then, nobody ever knew anything much about Jane really. Did they? Not the real Jane. Not really. Oh, great God! Edith thought wretchedly, Oh, great God! But Jane always knew everything about everybody else, didnt she? Yes, sir. Yes, she sure did.

Almost from the very first time it happened—back a year ago January, it was; a year ago during January inventory—Edith was about three-fourths sure that Janie knew she was sleeping with Frank Hirsh; had, in fact, become his "mistress." She never said anything about it, never anything that could make Edith be sure, and maybe after all it was only a certain guilt in her herself, that made her imagine it, but Janie would sit and look at her with those big eyes (which seemed to get larger and larger and larger, as she lost more and more weight and went downhill), and it was as if Jane knew. She did not look at her accusingly, or pityingly, or angrily, or any other way. She just looked at her. And Edith was sure she knew.

They only talked about it once. And then they did not talk about it. They talked around it. And, in fact, did not even talk around it. Because everything they said could be taken one way, or taken another way, and actually said nothing except what you yourself chose to interpret it as saying.

It happened one night late when John had already fallen, drugged by food and newsprint, into his bed and the two of them were sitting up out in the kitchen with a cup of coffee. This was about four months before she died, when Janie—after already having lost an enormous amount of weight—had suddenly started to go downhill fast; swiftly, with startling suddenness. Jane had stopped going out to Smitty's Bar at this same time: (up until after Christmas she had kept on going out to Smitty's, even after she had quit all her cleaning jobs except Frank's, although she wasnt going out with any of her old duffers any more); and so Edith had stopped going out as often herself, in order to be home with her, and had stopped having all her "cover-up" dates with Harold Alberson and the one or two others she went out with. Although she had not yet started cutting down on going out with Frank himself.

It was not only sad in a helpless way, but actually terrifying, to watch daily and weekly the old tremendous vitality and zest seeping silently out of this body of her grandmother along with the weight she lost. And it changed Janie herself completely. She no longer laughed and swore and bulldozed her way through her life, but instead slipped gradually and swiftly into a child-eyed, sort of wonder, a quiet way, withdrawing more and more from everything sort of. —And looking back, with the benefit of hindsight, Edith thought she could see, or at least seemed to see, that it was as if Janie's gnarled tough old hands were gradually relaxing their throttlehold on life, loosening slowly and tiredly from around the throat of life which she had used to shake back and forth like a rat, dominating it; as if slowly but surely in a sort of preparation, she was withdrawing from life. But Edith only saw that later.

They had been sitting talking, and Edith had been—almost angrily; irritably—trying once again to get her to go and see a doctor. Withdrawing from life or not, quiet or not, Janie could still be as stubborn as a mountain or an elephant or a whale.

"Honey," the old woman said, almost placidly, her dark eyes large in the thinning face, and already with the first touches of—in Jane— that unbelievable fragility she would soon acquire, "honey, everybody's got to live their own life." And she looked at her, then, in that way that for some time had made Edith think she knew. About Frank.

"I suppose," Edith said, and dropped her eyes; not because of Frank, so much, as because of the Death she seemed to see staring at her out of her grandmother's eyes.

"An we all do," Janie said. "You and me. And John. And everybody. I dont understand it. An I aint never claimed to. But I know its right. You and me, we dont agree on lots of things. And never have. Well, thats all right. An we both goes our own ways just the same, dont we? We go right on and do what we aimed to do. Well, thats the way it should be. And dont you never forget it."

"Well, thats easy enough to say," Edith said. The remarks did seem as though they could have a double meaning. "But when youre sick—"

"I aint sick," Jane said, immediately, stubbornly. "I just been dietin and you know it."

"Oh, God!" Edith cried angrily.

"Hush!" Jane said, with something of her old bawling vigor. "Im talkin. And I started to say that no matter what you do, if its what *you* got to do, then its all right for you to do it. And nothing nobody else ever says to you—no matter what *they* believe you should do—makes no damn difference, see? Now, you always remember that, will you?"

This seemed to have even more of a double meaning, or so it seemed to Edith. Was she referring to the "scandal" of her being Frank Hirsh's mistress? or perhaps just to her own unwillingness to go see a doctor. "My God, Janie," she said. "You say youre not sick, and then you go talking as if you werent even going to be here long. Or something," she said lamely, embarrassed at having made even this roundabout allusion to Death.

"Not at all," Janie said, not angrily at all. "Nonsense! Ill be around here a hell of a lot longer than anybody thinks. Im a tough old son of a bitch. A hell of a lot longer than anybodyll *want* me around, I reckon. Probably Ill outstay my welcome."

"Oh, Janie!" Edith said, near tears. "Thatll never be true as long as Im here."

And Janie had smiled at her sweetly. So very incredibly sweetly. Not at all like that tough old gravelly smile she once had had. It was as if, in a way, she knew; and yet at the same time, did not know. Or perhaps did not *want* to know. *Refused* to know. And yet again, Edith thought, and was to think again so very many times, maybe she did know and was just trying to make it easier for her, Edith, and for everyone concerned?

"What is it?! Whats wrong?! Whats the matter?!" How many times, on how many occasions, had she cried those words at her: Sometimes tearfully, sometimes frightenedly, sometimes furiously angry. And all the time, if she had only known, she could easily have fixed it up! All she would have had to do was just simply *talk* to her! And when she had learned it, from her talk with Doc Cost, after both of them together figured it out, it had been too late. *All too late!*

But whether Janie had been alluding to her own affair with Frank that time, and other times, she never did find out for sure. Positively. Yet Edith suspected that she knew.

Her own feelings about her affair with Frank had undergone a number of subtle changes in the year or so it had been going on. And some changes not so subtle, too. For one thing, she found she had a great deal more sympathy for Agnes Hirsh than she had ever had before. Not that she liked her any better; or that she ever completely lost the very real, very devastating hatred of her that sometimes rived her like lightning riving a tree. But she could nevertheless certainly sympathize with her a lot more. And this was because she understood her, Agnes's, husband better.

She had thought once, a long time ago—a long long time ago it seemed, that she understood him when she was only his officegirl working for him in his store, when she had saved his goose more than a number of times, both from his wife and his former mistress, and had watched him with all his troubles. Well, she understood him better now. He was about as petty, and jealous, and totally selfcentered a man as probably existed anywhere. The truth was, he had the mind of a child. And always had had. And probably always would have. Nothing really concerned him except himself and whether he could indulge one of his various pleasures, sexual or otherwise, and if he could he was totally happy; and if he couldnt he was totally miserable. She had watched him all through this troubled time with Jane, and had watched him get more and more edgy and more and more irritable because she could not go out with him every time *he* wanted her to. He had no conception at all of what she herself was going through or what Janie was going through, and no real sympathy at all for either of them. Oh, he talked sympathetically enough—at times; when he wasnt too irritated—and he probably did feel some little sort of rudimentary sympathy for them; but only when it did not impinge upon something that he wanted for himself, such as sleeping with her or his other things.

Apparently he was congenitally incapable of ever *really* loving anybody, and at the same time had this psychological need of having as many women in love with him as he could cluster around him—a need which he was willing, at great sacrifice, to cut down to two: one wife, and one mistress; in order not to have trouble at home. Consequently, this placed herself, she felt, somewhat in the position of being his personal whore. And yet there was more to it than that: Because he did really have this strong need to have more than one woman in love with him—at the very least two; but preferably more, except for the trouble it might cause him.

And yet in spite of all of these things about Frank that she had come to see pretty clearly in the last year or so, she still loved him, and was in love with him. She didnt know exactly why. Probably a lot of it was that old thing she had thought out for herself once before during a love affair—and had, however, conveniently managed to forget when she wanted to enter into another one—which was that any woman seemed, once she had given herself and her love to a man, almost totally unable to let go of him, unable to admit that she had been wrong, that she had given herself to someone who not only was unworthy of the gift, but also did not even appreciate it. Women, apparently, were both willing and capable of going through an awful lot, an awful hell of a lot, before they would ever admit a love affair, once entered, could have failed. But more than just that, it was that that very same childish quality about him which made him so totally selfish—so totally self-centered—was also the quality about him which made him so completely vulnerable. And because he was so vulnerable, he was extremely pitiable. And perhaps pity for him and his childish ways, an amused sad indulgent pity—when he did not make her mad, was what made her still love him. She liked to hold his head and soothe him, which was a kind of superiority, she supposed, in a way. And she knew for sure, positively, that should she ever leave him—leave him completely; quit her job, and leave town—that he would be broken up and in a terrible, and real, panic over it. He did need her. —Or rather, lets say, he needed her as long as he did not have her. When he had her, and was sure of her, he didnt need her at all.

It wasnt a very pretty picture, or pretty situation either, and it was a long far cry from the love life she had once imagined herself as having someday; but she did still love him. The poor selfinflated, selfconfused dope. And he was really very lovable at times. He would be so small and petty as to get petulant with her because she didnt spend enough time with him, when she herself was worried to death about her own grandmother sickening and dying; and yet at the same time, he would then do something like going out of his way to do some ridiculous foolish incredible childishly-romantic thing like risking everything he had, and had built up for himself, to get her a seat "within the ribbon" at his daughter's wedding. So apparently in his way he did love her as much as he was capable of. Edith had been very touched by that at the time, even though she knew it was foolish of him. The truth was— the whole, entire, bitter truth was—he was a Rotarian. A child. He *belonged* in the Rotary. He *loved* the Rotary; he really did; and he belonged there. With all the other Rotarians-and-children, singing their silly sentimental songs, and playing their silly games, and whatever else it was they did. He loved the Rotary passionately, and he went to every meeting, and that was just exactly where he should be.

And as a matter of fact, by God, Edith thought suddenly, he was probably never happier, probably never *as* happy, as he was when he was there, on Thursday, at a Rotary Club meeting, singing and laughing and talking and eating with all the other grown up children, all the other Rotarians. And Kiwanians. And Lions. And Chamber of Commerces. The truth was, Edith didnt feel like his mistress, she felt like his mother. Was that how Agnes also felt about him?

She had been aware for some time, Edith had, that Frank was back sleeping with Agnes again, and had been since some time in the summer or fall last year. And with a kind of penetratingly acute, acidulous acumen which had been growing in her steadily in the last year or so, Edith understood clearly that it was herself whom she—and Frank —and Agnes—had to thank for this development: There was your really classic irony: Almost two years ago, after his wife had broken him loose from Geneve Lowe, he had been petulant and peeved and sore and hurt and panicky. His pride was too injured to allow him to go back and sleep with his wife after she had done that to him; and probably, Edith suspected, they had not been sleeping together for a year before that: ever since Agnes knew about the Geneve Lowe affair; or before. But—BUT—and here was where she herself came in—as soon as he had started a love affair with her, with Edith, which his wife knew nothing about, he felt he had avenged himself, had got one up on her, on Agnes, felt he had *restored his dignity as a man,* in other, words; and because of that he had been magnanimously willing to begin sleeping with his wife again. So, not only in effect, but in actual fact, Frank and Agnes Hirsh owed their "second honeymoon", their new closeness and warmth, to her: Edith Barclay.

Acidly, Edith laughed out loud, and was suddenly startled to realize that she sounded almost like Jane's old harsh raucous gravelly laugh she had used to hear so much. And then, immediately, being reminded of Jane, she wanted to weep.

But probably the thing that hurt her the worst, *really* hurt her, down deep where she could not even laugh about it, really *hurt* her, exquisitely, was when he had adopted the seven-year-old boy Walter. She herself could have really *borne* him children. *Real* children. His own and hers. Only—she was prevented; by everything social, and private, and public, about their relationship. And so instead, he and Agnes had *adopted* a child. Janie, during her last months there, had talked about the little boy a lot. Jane had liked him, he was really very bright apparently, and no trouble at all. And because Jane liked him, Edith had found herself liking him. And because Jane *could* talk about him, was in a position where she could see him and could do so, Edith found herself urging Jane on to talk about him, as if in some way that she did not understand she had a need to prod and poke this sore spot deep inside her in order to make it hurt her even worse, in the same way that it was almost impossible for you to stop biting down upon an aching tooth so that the sharper greater pain might relieve the lesser. So, in the end, she wound up knowing almost as much about the little boy as Frank and Agnes themselves knew. Agnes would tell everything about him, every cute or smart thing he did, to Jane; and Jane would relay it on to Edith. In a way, he was almost her little boy. After all, it was she who was really responsible for him, wasnt it? They would never have got back together and adopted him if it had not been for her, would they?

The boy himself Edith had seen a number of times uptown at the store. And he was a cute little codger, so solemn and like a tiny little old man. But she did not want anything to do with him. And did not even want, or like, to be around him. So she had been very distant— even cold—with him. And as if he sensed immediately that she did not like him, or at least did not want to be around him, after the first time he never talked to her again, except when required to by some politeness, and kept away from her. Which was exactly the way Edith wanted it. And she admired him for his depth of acumen.

He was a smart little devil, and in truth Edith did not think she had ever seen so mature a youngster. He was the most polite, most well-trained, most unobtrusive little boy she had ever seen. He very obviously did not intend to let anything break up his new windfall, or cost him his happy home, if he could help it, and for that Edith doubly admired him, although she did not want to associate with him.

But if she herself did not want to associate with him, Janie had had no such compunctions. On Fridays when she cleaned at Frank's (she couldnt have been doing much work, Edith thought, the past few months, in her condition) she had played with little Walter, and he had helped her with her work. They got to be great pals.

Oh, Janie! Edith thought despairfully. Janie, Janie! If only she had known! If only Janie had been willing to confide in her! And, making it bite into her soul that much deeper, Edith knew why Janie hadnt.

The night it happened did not seem to be a bit different from any other night. There was no forewarning, no imminent collapse, no nothing any different from any other night. How was anyone to know, have any idea, that this was the night she was going to die? Janie was her same fragile, worn, large-eyed self as she had been every other night the past few months. She was no thinner this night than she had been last night. No more sick. No more tired. Though she was more thin, more sick, more tired, than she had been a month ago. Edith had cooked the supper. She had been doing that for some time, had unobtrusively but deftly and without calling attention to it, taken over almost all the cooking. Not only so that Janie would not *have* to do it, but also because Janie *could* not do it: could not do a good job of it. They had all three eaten sitting at the kitchen table. John, as was his dull wont, had immediately taken himself off to bed where he fell into his customary coma. Janie had gone to bed almost as immediately herself. Edith had sat up a little while in the little living room, reading a magazine, the current issue of *Life* it was, all about the suicide of James V Forrestal, and the Chinese Communists entering Shanghai, and some stuff on the new State of Israel being admitted to the UN, and then she had sewed on a skirt she was altering. And finally had gone to bed herself. How could she have known? How, in any possible, earthly way, could she have guessed that Janie would not be there in the morning? Edith had paused at her door before she went to her own room, and everything had been quiet.

Jane, in her room, had heard her pause at the door, and she smiled tiredly to herself. She was a good kid, Edith was. A real good kid. And as she thought it, fear rose up in her throat again: Thank God she had never given the kid anything. Thank God the kid hadnt caught it from her. Nor nobody else, yet. But especially the kid. Janie waited until she heard her go on, so she was sure she would not hear, and then rolled herself over wearily in the bed, her face to the wall again. She had got to know that damned wall real good in the last few months or so, by God. She wanted to go to the bathroom and wash her hands, but she knew she would have to wait until the kid was asleep before she could. Good kid, she thought softly, such a good kid.

God damn that son of a bitching Frank Hirsh, she thought fierily again, for perhaps the ten millionth time in the past year and a half. God damn that son of a bitching Jew bastard. She knew he was a Jew. She just knew it. That ornery bastard. That ornery slippery dirty bastard. You might know he would pull some damned trick like that. Christ, he would have tried to make her herself, Jane, years ago if she hadnt been so strong and hefty he was scared she might hurt him if she ever did get in bed with him. Damn him, she thought half-affectionately, the fire subsiding in her for lack of fuel energy, damn the little bastard. Well, it was the kid's problem. Shed have to solve it for herself. Im too old to try to do anything about it; and John's too dumb. And anyway, nobody oughtnt to nose into affairs of the heart like that, especially when its somebody else's heart, by God.

She rolled back over on her back again and stared upward in the dark, tired, and worn out, and yet not sleepy. Damn it all.

If she only just knew where she could of got it. That was the damned thing. Just where? Back then, over a year ago it was, when she had first thought she got it—the time she had been so scared she had give it to old Vic Herschmidt—it had gone away of itself and she had thought she was all right. And besides that, she found out she hadnt give it to Old Vic after all. After that, she decided it just must of been a strain. Men got strains and had a running; could women get them too?

But then—then, just when she was beginnin to feel fine and all right and git her confidence back, beginnin to lose a little weight and look good too and feel better, then the son of a bitch had started up again. What was it, six, eight months that she hadnt had it atall. And then it had to start up again. She was only sleepin with two guys at the time, and she knew it couldnt of come from either one of them. So she had decided it had to just of been from that other time, and that she hadnt really got cured up after all. And yet, she hadnt give it to either one of them. Well—

At least she hadnt give it to nobody, she thought with relief again, neither in bed nor off a toilet nor any other way. That little boy Walter; she had to be so awful careful around him. It would be awful if she was to give it to a little kid like that, and she still scrubbed herself religiously. Well—she thought tiredly.

It was probably that that was makin her lose all this damned weight, probably. But she had never heard of the clap doin anything like that to nobody. But then different things affected different people different ways. She really ought to go down and see Doc Cost about it, Jane thought miserably. But she just couldnt. She just couldnt have nobody find out about it, find out she had the clap. She just couldnt. People laughed at her enough as it was, by God. Just because she was big and hefty—used to be, anyway—and talked in a voice like a rockcrusher, people thought she didnt have no feelins. But she did. She had feelins just like everybody, by God. And she just couldnt have nobody find out. But most expecially the kid. Expecially Edith. It would shame the kid to death. Hell, it would shame herself to death. She just couldnt.

Old whore, she said once again to herself bitterly. That was what she was all right. Just couldnt leave a man alone. Anybody. Even them old whiskery bastards. Just couldnt. Old whore. And everybody knew it. Everybody in town knew it, and laughed about it. No wonder the kid use to get mad about it. Old whore, she cursed herself grindingly, wanting to weep. She was sure right when she called you that, all right. Just an old whore. The biggest old whore in town. She really ought to go down and see Doc. But she just couldnt. To have the kid find out. She just couldnt.

So damned wore out and tired all the damned time, she thought wearily, and moved her legs lazily again. She really ought to git up and go wash, but Edith might not be asleep yet, and she was so damned tired. And thinking this, she finally dozed off and fell asleep.

She woke up suddenly and wildly, her heart beating in her ears and no idea of what time it was, to a terrible pain in her groin. She had never had no pain like that before, ever. It almost made her grunt out loud and wake somebody. Well, it sure wouldnt be John shed wake; it would be Edith. She lay feeling it, hard and snapping and bright there in her belly, for a moment; and then, just when she thought she was going to have to yell, it stopped and went away to only a little tiny dull ache. Janie relaxed, when it stopped, and took a deep breath. Now what the hell was that? She had never felt nothin like that before, by God. Right down in the pit of her belly. She relaxed herself down into the bed with the relief of the cessation of the pain and lay looking up into the dark. Wow! She hoped she didnt have no more pains like that, by

Christ! But in a few moments, as she lay still relaxing from it, she began to feel the pressure in her belly. It didnt hurt much, just uncomfortable. She lay back and shut her eyes as it kept on growing stronger. Now, what the hell? She suddenly felt woozy, and then she began to feel cold, and then she found she couldnt get her breath. She was gasping for breath, and the uncomfortable pressure in her belly kept on growing stronger, and it was then that she realized she was dying.

She lay for a moment, finding it hard to believe. It was like something had bust loose inside her. Was she maybe bleedin? Was she maybe bleedin to death inside? They would find her in the morning. And when they found her, theyd find her old belt on her. No, they mustnt find that. Was she really *dying*?

No, sir, by God! By God, Ill show them! Ill show the sons of bitches! And powerfully, using the arms that even now, thin and weak as she was, still had the rockhard muscles of a man, she surged up in the bed. Ill show all the sons of bitches! They cant kill me! and yet at the same time, dimly now, was still the same thought in her mind that she mustnt make no noise that might wake Edith, because if they were going to find her with her old sanitary belt on, if they did find her, then she didnt want to be here, let them find her dead. Powerfully, with those strong, man's arms, but quietly, she grasped the top of the headboard and pulled herself, almost all dead weight now, up into a sitting position. Sons of bitches! All of you! Think you can kill Old Jane Staley? Then she fell over sideways on her face, and everything faded out.

And that was how Edith found her in the morning: lying sideways on her face, one arm bent under her, the top of her gray head toward the door.

She had gotten up early to fix the breakfast. She had been doing that lately. She had waked John so he wouldnt be late for work, and then had cooked the platter of bacon and eggs, and made the sandwiches and filled the thermos for his dinner pail. She had been glad Janie was sleeping late for once. But after John had finished eating and was getting ready to leave, and Janie still had not appeared, she had thought shed better call her, and went to her room.

The moment she opened the door and saw her in that strained odd wrenched position, she had known nothing would really be any use. But she had made herself walk forward and lift the strong, muscled arm and try to raise her. The arm fell back down slackly. There was something—something obscene, about touching another person's dead body. Instinctively, you knew they wouldnt have liked it. It had never happened to Edith before. You felt kind of embarrassed for them, some way. She stepped back to the door and stood looking at her for a dull moment.

Clearly, Janie had fought hard. And neither one of them had waked up and come to her. Maybe they could have helped her. At least they could have *been* there. Edith called for John, not even crying yet, but her voice nevertheless high and squawky.

"Daddy! Daddy! Come here quick!"

With his slow dull walk, John appeared behind her, carrying his work jacket over one arm and his dinner pail in his hand, his cap already on his head. Even the tone of her voice did not make him move faster. Not John. Edith put her hands up over her nose and mouth and turned to him, tears—as she realized the magnitude of it, the finality of it, the irrevocableness—beginning to spurt from her eyes and make John appear to shimmer and distort wavily. He looked placidly past her through the door.

"Well, I guess there aint nothin we can do," he said slowly. "I guess shes gone."

Edith wanted suddenly to slap his face, stingingly. Damn him! Damn him! Didnt he ever feel anything?

"I guess you better call the doctor, hadnt you?" John said, after a moment of laborious thought.

Edith got control of herself. Still crying, tears streaming silently from her eyes so that she could hardly see the numbers in the phone book, she called Doc Cost. Then, at his suggestion, also called the coroner.

She hung up the phone, weeping uncontrollably. They hadnt even waked up and gone to her. John came and put his heavy calloused hand awkwardly on her shoulder.

"Dont cry, Edith honey," he said. "Dont cry. It had to happen some time." Edith put her own hand up on his and he patted her shoulder awkwardly. "Shes been purty sick for a long time," he said, evidently trying to find some note of consolation.

"Oh, God," Edith said, thinking of Jane, old Janie, lying in there all alone and dying all alone, while they slept on around her, not even anybody there to hold her hand, or anything. "What are we going to do?" she said.

"Well," John said slowly, misunderstanding what she meant. "I reckon I better go on to work, or Ill be late. There aint nothing much I can do here. But I dont think you better try to go to the store today, upset like you are, Edith honey. Why dont you call the store and tell them?"

"Yes," Edith said. "Yes. All right. I will."

"You sure you be all right here alone? till the doctor comes?" John said solicitously.

"Yes," Edith said. "You go on. Im all right."

After he left, his slow dull steps passing across the porch and down onto the walk, Edith stared after him almost calmly; then suddenly, abruptly, like a sneeze, was struck by another fit of uncontrollable weeping. She gave herself up to it. Then she called the store. And that was the way it went: she would be all right, almost dry-eyed in fact, and go about whatever it was she had to do, whatever had to be done; then, suddenly, she would remember something about Janie or something about her death, and tears would spurt suddenly from her eyes as if they were water jets, and another sudden uncontrollable seizure of weeping would take her like a sudden gust of wind shaking a tree.

It was while she was sitting with her in the room waiting for the doctor and the coroner to arrive, that she noticed for the first time the worn old sanitary belt Jane was still wearing, under the sheet, and did not understand it or what or why. Later on, after the undertaker and his men came and took her away—(Edith went out to the kitchen while they removed her; she could not bear the thought of seeing her arms flop around maybe, or her head lolling)—she and Doc Cost talked about it.

Doc Cost, so big, so inarticulate, and so incredibly sensitive that it seemed impossible that he could continue to live amongst all the human suffering he worked with, took her out in the kitchen and sat down with her. He had only made a brief examination of her when he first came, and had told Edith then: "It looks like it was an internal hemorrhage."

"But theres no blood!" she had said.

"There was some," Doc Cost said gently. Later, after he and the coroner had examined her together, and then the undertaker's men had taken her away, sitting at the kitchen table, awkwardly, gently, with all of the sympathy and understanding that Edith had wanted John to have but which John hadnt, Doc Cost reconstructed for her what he thought had happened.

"I rather expect we'll find its a diverticulosis of the lower bowel," he said.

"Whats a diverticulosis?" Edith said. She was dry-eyed now, and coolly and coldly in possession of herself.

"Well, its a kind of a pocket," Doc said awkwardly. "A fistula. Shes probably had it for several years, and finally it ruptured and caused an internal hemorrhage."

"Fistula!" Edith said, unbelievably. "Janie?"—And then: "Thats whats caused her to lose all that weight and go downhill like she did?"

Doc Cost nodded, gently. "Diverticulitis is a false pouch, a pocket, in the large intestine. In the lower portion. Fecal matter lodges in this pocket and causes an abscess. Sometimes, if it doesnt heal by itself, it breaks through and adheres to the bladder or the uterus, and forms a fistula—or fistulous tract to the other organ. Fecal matter goes through the fistula into the bladder—if it is the bladder, and we'll probably find that it is—and infects it. It causes a low grade fever, and— Look, Edith," he said awkwardly. "Do you want to know all about this stuff? Theres no need to go into all of the details of it with you."

"I want to know everything about it," Edith said firmly.

Doc Cost nodded, slowly. "Well, its been my experience with rectal-vesical fistula like this—especially if its in women, and if it adheres to the bladder—that it is often mistaken by the patient for a venereal disease." He paused, painfully.

"Oh, *no!*" Edith said, her eyes widening. She put her hand up to her mouth.

Doc Cost nodded again, reluctantly, as if he wished he did not have to. "I expect thats what happened here," he said. "Of course, if its caught soon enough, diverticulitis can usually be remedied by surgery."

"But why wouldnt she ever go to a doctor with it? She knew she was *sick!* Why!"

"Well, Ive known Janie for a number of years," Doc Cost said, sadly, awkwardly, as if embarrassed by the pain he caused her. "She used to doctor with me a lot. And I think I know her pretty well. Did you notice that—ahh—she was wearing a sanitary belt?"

"Yes," Edith said. "I wondered about it at the time."

"Well," Doc said, almost inarticulately, painfully, "well, with diverticulitis of this type there is a certain amount of vaginal discharge in the later stages. Particularly if the fistula has adhered to the bladder, there is frequency of urination, burning, and a pus discharge." He paused, then shrugged helplessly. "In short, all the usual symptoms connected with gonorrhea. Of course, you know Janie probably better than anyone else, Edith," he said apologetically. "But I know her pretty well. Ive joked and kidded with her a lot. She was a very sensitive woman, although a stranger wouldnt have thought it, just to look at her. And now I—ahh—well, I expect she thought maybe she had contracted gonorrhea, or some other social disease like that, and that was why she wouldnt go to a doctor. She was too embarrassed." He looked Edith sadly in the eyes, apologetically, awkwardly, hating to have to say what he had to say.

Edith, as the implication dawned on her, put her hands up to her face, her eyes widening above them. "Oh, *no!*" she whispered. "Oh, no! Oh, no!"

Doc Cost nodded sadly. "I expect thats what we'll find," he said gently.

"Oh, *no!*" Edith said again.

"She was very sensitive about her reputation in town," Doc Cost said with a sad smile. "She kidded about it. But it bothered her, too, just the same, I expect."

"Doc—" Edith said haltingly, "Doctor— Then— then it was *me!* I caused it! You dont know! I— I called her an old whore once, when I was mad at her over something. More than once, probably. And I used to try to shame her out of going out with those old duffers—just because—just because it embarrassed *me!*"

"Well," Doc Cost said awkwardly, "I doubt very much if that had anything to do with it, Edith. I really do. There was a lot more to it than that. There was the whole town. You mustnt blame yourself for it. Dont recriminate with yourself. There was a lot more to it than just that."

"Oh, but—but I did," Edith said. "Doc, I did. And I caused it." Suddenly she broke off, and dropped her head down on her arms on the table, wanting only to shrink up and die, sobbing uncontrollably, convulsively. Doc Cost reached across the table and took her hand, and then when she did not stop got up and came around the table and put his arm around her shoulder and held her.

Finally, she got control of herself again. After she did, Doc Cost tried to reassure her again that it was not her fault. To which Edith said nothing. There wasnt really anything more to say. What was the use of weeping and wailing over your guilt? That didnt, and wouldnt, change it any. It was just something you would have to live with, that was all. And you would live with it, too, she thought; all your life. She faced him then, red-eyed from weeping, but clear-eyed too. And when he saw the look on her face, as if he had seen it many times before and recognized it, Doc Cost stopped expostulating with her, as if he knew it was no longer any use. Quietly, he got his hat and bag and left.

At the door, where Edith had escorted him, he stopped and turned back. "You know, if youd like, Edith," he said awkwardly, "we can have a post-mortem performed on Janie. Then you would know exactly the cause of death, and well—everything about it. Im reasonably sure my diagnosis is correct. And Im *positive* theres no—ahh—external vaginal infection. But, taking into account the way you yourself feel, I would suggest that you have a post-mortem done."

"You mean, an—autopsy?" Edith said faintly.

He nodded, his face awkward and embarrassed and pained for her.

"No," Edith said, faintly. "No, Doc. I dont think I could stand that. To cut her all up, and handle her bowels and organs, and everything like that. I just dont think I could stand it. The thought of it. Its—its somehow an—an indignity to Janie, Doc; do you see what I mean?" she said anxiously. "I dont mean anything against you, you understand. But to cut her up like that, its—its obscene. I know Janie wouldnt like it. Lets just let her be. Lets let her rest in peace." She stood, looking at him faintly, holding onto the door with her hand. The very idea of it made her feel sick all through.

"Well," Doc Cost said, "I know there are people who feel that way, Edith. Of course, to a doctor its purely a professional matter. It has to be, you know; or we couldnt do it. I—ahh—" he paused awkwardly. "I—ahh—wouldnt make any charge for it, Edith, if you wanted it done. I suggested it because I thought it might help put your mind at rest."

"No," Edith said. "No, Doc. I wont let them do that to Janie. I just cant. It would embarrass her. Shes had a rough enough time as it is. And I just wont let somebody do that to her."

"Well, all right," Doc Cost said in his awkward painful way. "We'll just let it go then. Ill ahh— Ill see you, Edith." He tipped his hat and smiled, painfully, and Edith watched him walk down off the porch to his funny little MG. How could he stand it? she thought wonderingly; all the pain and agony he had to wade through in his profession of helping people? Did he know what he was getting into when he started to medical school as a young boy? God! she thought; no wonder he drank as much as he did when he got home from work in the evening. He must go home an exhausted wreck every night of the world. She shut the door and went back into the house and sat down and began to weep again.

And, suddenly, she knew something else that she was not going to let them do to Janie, she thought. When it came time for the funeral, she was going to insist the casket be left closed. She was not going to allow them to open up the casket and let all those people parade past and stare at poor old dead Janie. It was barbaric, that was what it was. It was barbaric enough at the other funerals she had been to; but it was not going to happen to Janie. Staring at your dead body, that you yourself no longer had control over, it would make any one feel ashamed; it was embarrassing, and naked, and obscene, and it was barbaric. All funerals were barbaric. And she didnt give a damn what the custom was, they were not going to do that to Janie. John probably would be puzzled and wouldnt understand, but she didnt care. They had to take her to an undertaker, and expose her poor old body there, and that was bad enough. Edith wished they didnt even have to do that, that they could have buried her just like she was. But they were not going to do any more than that, they were not going to expose her in her casket.

She had done enough harm to Janie in her life, Edith thought, sickly, and with a sudden forcefulness that was spine-stiffening and unbrookable she made up her mind that that was the least she could do for her. She was going to see that Janie had dignity in death.

Edith snuffled up her tears and blew her nose and wiped her eyes, and got up to go about doing the things she was going to have to do to get Janie finally away in the ground.

It was just then, as she was walking to the phone to call the under-taker's, that Frank and Agnes Hirsh drove up, to see what help they could be. From them Edith learned that Frank had had the store closed up as a gesture of respect, and she appreciated that, deeply; and she also appreciated them coming out to help. But she did not want them there, and she did not want to be around them, either one of them, but espe-cially Agnes. She talked with them a little while, and then she politely got them to leave. She did not cry while they were there.

Frank and Agnes were only the first, however. While they were still there, Agnes went to the door and admitted two neighbor ladies. They were women Edith hardly knew, just to see and speak to, both wives of men who worked for the Sternutol like John. They had seen the doc-tor's car, and the ambulance from the undertaker's, and the other cars, and they had come to see what they could do. After they had expressed almost perfunctory regrets to Edith, they went immediately to the kitchen and began cleaning it up from the breakfast cooking.

And they were only the first. As if wafted aloft on the same wind that carried the copper-penny taste of Sternutol Chemical across town, the news spread swiftly, wildly, and others came. Some from the neighbor-hood, and some from other parts of town. All of the people whom Janie had worked for for so many years came to pay their respects. And of those who stayed, mostly neighbors, neighbors Edith hardly knew in fact, one or another of them took over doing everything that needed to be done, such as the cleaning and evacuating of Janie's room from which the presence of Death, detestable to everyone, needed to be swept. Some brought food already cooked, others took over the kitchen and cooked more food there. And not long afterward John came home from work, still carrying the dinner pail which she had fixed for him that morning, and which he had not touched, since it was not yet noon. They had sent him home from work and told him not to come back until he felt like it and everything was done. John looked perplexed to find his house so full of people, and turned his dinner pail over to the ladies in the kitchen who cleaned it out and washed it as it had probably never been washed in its life before; and then, upon Edith's instruction, went to take a bath and put on his *good* clothes, as contrasted with his *work* clothes. Social usage had taken over.

Edith detested all of them, and wished only that they would all go away and leave her alone and let her be. They were not doing it for her, anyway; or for Janie. They were, she sensed, doing it for them-selves. As if in some way, by helping here, they were all cocking the snook at the Death who would someday be the master and the lover of them all. She wished only that they would go away; she could have done everything herself that they were doing; she was not incapacitated; and yet she was also glad that they were there. Because, she gradually realized with surprise, the mere presence of social usage: the mere simple fact of greeting people and accepting from them the regrets which some fierce pride in her made her want to *not* accept: all this was keeping her mind occupied and away from her own pain.

Shortly after Frank and Agnes left, Geneve Lowe drove up and came inside with her husband Al who only stood awkwardly, and Geneve wanted to know if there was anything, anything at all, she could do. Al had called her from the store right away; he had been terribly upset; and she had gone and picked him up. Now: what could she do? Edith could not think of anything she could do, but then she thought of something and said yes, there was something she could do: she wanted to buy Janie a whole new outfit, complete, from lingerie and shoes right on up and outward to a fine expensive dignified dress. Would Geneve see to that for her? Geneve would. Geneve would see to it personally; she would see to it that she had the finest, most tasteful outfit in the store.

"And one other thing," Edith said, having another idea. "Wait a minute." And she went into her own bedroom and shut the door. In the bedroom, with all the noises of people moving and talking outside in the house, she got out her jewelry box. From it she took her most prized pieces—the most prized possessions of everything she owned, in fact: the matched set of Mexican amethyst and roped silver, bracelet, ring, earrings, and the pin made in the shape of an owl with big amethyst eyes; and the other pair of apple green jade earrings for which she had paid thirty dollars: the same ones Janie had used to sneak in and try on so often in front of the mirror: the same ones they had fought over: Edith stood looking down at them for a moment: if she had only done it before, if she had only done it when it would really have meant something: instead of being an idle, futile gesture: Well, maybe Janie would know, somehow, maybe she was watching, somewhere: Edith felt a little silly, but it did not dilute her determination: She took the jewelry back out and handed it to Geneve Lowe, and asked her if she would leave it with the undertaker? The amethyst pieces were all to be put on her; the jade earrings could be slipped in with her somewhere, under the pillow maybe, or beneath her head. They were things Janie had always liked, she said, and she wanted to have them with her. Then, afraid for a moment that she might break down and cry again, she turned away. Geneve did not bother her, merely touched her on the shoulder, and collected Al and left—with the jewelry, and to see about the outfit.

And no sooner had Geneve gone, than Doris Fredric drove up in her yellow convertible. She knew Edith did not have a car, she said, and she wanted to place her car at Edith's disposal. She would drive her anywhere she wanted to go, and help her with anything she wanted to do. She meant to stay right with her, from now on, until the funeral was over, and everything was done, and until she had gotten hold of herself again. Edith had not seen Doris for quite a long time—not since before she had seen 'Bama Dillert's car parked on the Fredric drive, in fact. And for a moment she was deeply touched. The two girls put their arms around each other and laid their heads on each other's shoulders. But it soon became apparent that Doris meant just exactly what she said: She appointed herself as sort of major-domo and aide-de-camp to Edith, and nobody could even get near her without first going through her representative, Doris. She did everything, and took over everything, that Edith herself might have done; but there really wasnt much Edith could do, or could have done. Someone, somebody, was doing everything. From the fixing of meals, to the washing of dishes, to the making of the beds, to the cleaning up of the house after so many people had poured through it. So there really wasnt much for Doris to do. But just the same, Edith was glad to have her there with her. She drove Edith everywhere she went, and went in with her, and waited for her and drove her back. She even slept with her there in the house in her own bed, the two nights before the funeral. She had, she said, told them at the school that they would just have to get someone to replace her until the funeral was over. No one had ever loved Janie as much as she had, Doris said, and almost commenced to weep. If Edith was a little irritated at her at times, she was nevertheless glad to have her there. And it was the perfect kind of a show for Doris Fredric. Which did not, however, make Edith feel any the less grateful.

The next two days passed in a kind of wild, unreal dream for Edith. She had decided to leave Janie to lie in state in the undertaker's chapel, rather than move her out home. Then there was the funeral itself. It was to be at the Baptist church, a member of which Janie's mother had once made her when she was a little girl, but which none of them in the family had been inside of since Edith was small enough to be forced to go to Sunday School. So there was the minister to talk to. Then there was the problem of Edith's decision to keep the casket closed. She had already talked of this to both the ever-present Doris and to John. Doris thought it was entirely up to her, if that was what she wanted to do; but old John, old fuddly-duddly John, was a little perturbed by the idea in his perplexed amiable way. A lot of people might feel bad about it, he thought; after all, they done a lot for them, the neighbors and all, and they might want to look at Janie in her casket. The very words, as he spoke them, chilled Edith. And of course, it was impossible for her to get through John's thick head just exactly how great of an—an indignity it would be to Janie to expose her to the curious eyes of people. What was the use of buyin all them pretty expensive clothes, John wanted to know, if nobody was goin to be able to see her? They did not actually argue about it; and John, as he always did, acquiesced in Edith's decision, finally, when she positively and forcefully refused to have it any other way.

Edith was glad that Geneve had taken care of the clothes. Whatever else one said about Geneve, she did have exquisite taste. Maybe it was silly, to go and buy her a whole new outfit and a fine expensive dress, when nobody was going to see her; but whether anyone was going to see her or not, by God Edith meant to see she looked good. It was all kind of ridiculous, anyway, in a way: what did it matter what you did with the person's dead body once the person themselves no longer inhabited it? —And yet, counteracting that feeling, was the other: the only way Edith could articulate it was that she intended to give Janie the best send-off she could give her.

It was funny, she thought: we dont really do all we do in funerals to help the dead, we do it to relieve ourselves. We do it to atone: atone for the guilty fact that we ourselves are still living: atone for all the kindly things we might have done for them, if we had only known they were going to die, but which because we *didnt* know, hadnt known, —How could we have known?—we had neglected to do.

They went down to the undertaker's twice, she and John and the ubiquitous Doris, in Doris' yellow convertible, once to pick out a casket (for which Edith picked a very good one, much better than they could afford; but which she herself intended to pay off), and a second time to see how everything looked. She had instructed the undertaker on the first trip that she wanted the casket kept closed, at which the undertaker looked a little nonplussed as if he felt she did not trust his work. But he did as she told him, and when they went back the second time, everything was fixed up and Janie—in the closed casket—lay in state in the undertaker's chapel. As if hoping friendlily and wistfully that she would change her mind once she saw her, the undertaker asked hopefully if they would not like to see her. The jewelry had been put on her, he smiled, just as Edith had requested, and the apple green jade earrings had been placed just beneath the side of her neck where they would not show; he would show them to her. Edith stared at him, feeling faintly sick, and the spine-stiffening resolution rising in her powerfully, but despairing of ever explaining how she felt about keeping the casket closed. (What could she do? Tell the undertaker that she thought all funerals were barbaric?) But looking at him, she was suddenly startled to realize that his feelings were actually hurt because they would not look at his handiwork. Yes. Sure. He had probably worked hard on her. Oh, God. But she knew then that someone was going to have to go look at her, if they did not want to injure the undertaker's professional pride in his work. So she sent John in to look, explaining that she herself simply could not, that she wanted to remember Janie as she had been alive, and stayed outside with Doris Fredric. John, dull old John, wouldnt mind anyway. It wouldnt bother him.

And in fact, he didnt. He came shambling out hat in hand, his *good* clothes looking as ridiculous on him as they always did, snuffled a little and wiped his eyes. He was glad to have seen her.

"She looked real purty," he said in his dull voice. "Real purty, Edith honey. Your jewlry looks nice on her; and he put them other earrings under her head just like he said."

"Yes," Edith said; and thought further: yes, and how can anyone look lifelike when theyre dead? How can all the cosmetics, and preparations, and chemicals put back in them the look of the life that was in them once? It was impossible.

"Are you sure you wouldnt like to leave the casket open?" the undertaker asked anxiously, and hopefully. "Theres been lots of people here already, Miss Edith, who came to see her. And lots of flowers."

"Im quite sure," Edith said. "Its all right for the family, like that. But I must insist you close it back up now and keep it that way."

"Very well," the undertaker said ruefully. "If you wish."

After he had reclosed the casket, Edith herself went in, with Doris and John, to look at the chapel. There really were a great many flowers, from all kinds of people, both high and low estate. She was glad of that. She complimented the undertaker on how he had arranged everything, complimented him excessively, because she had had to hurt his feelings so over closing the casket. Then, as politely as she could, she announced that they had better go. She felt she could not get out of there quick enough. Janie? Jane Staley? What did all of this have to do with Jane Staley? Foreverafter, the smell of many banked flowers would haunt her painfully.

But by the time the funeral came, the funeral itself, Edith was in such a state that she just merely sat. She felt nothing. She had ceased to feel. It was surprising how many friends Janie had had in Parkman. There were really an awful lot of flowers. And a lot more people came than she had ever expected. But she didnt care. It was an ordeal, that had to be got through; not for her own sake, but for Janie's. And that was why she had done it all: not for herself, but for Janie. It would probably take her and John together half a year to pay off all the expenses; but she didnt care: It was a good send-off for Janie. And Edith could not help but feel that Janie in her closed casket, if she were aware, would be chuckling happily and cockily to herself. And so she sat, flanked by John and by Doris Fredric—who was weeping—her own eyes bonedry and cold and distant: Edith had never been one of those who could share her grief with large groups of people. Almost all of Janie's friends had come by the house before; and almost all of the people she had worked for—excepting only 'Bama Dillert and Dave Hirsh, who did not come by—had come by the house, too. And at the funeral almost all of them were there, also. She even saw Dave Hirsh, sitting slack-faced and looking half-drunk and hungover by himself at the back, although 'Bama Dillert was not with him.

And so, Edith sat through it all, feeling nothing. And it was only after it was all over, after the trip to the cemetery and the interment, after all the people had given the house one final cleaning and had gone, after Doris Fredric who had not left her side for a single minute the last three days and had only gone back home late that evening after the funeral that afternoon,—it was only after all of this, that her conversation with Doc came back to haunt her and the guilt and utterly total helplessness she felt then assaulted her. It had been she herself who was really responsible. It was she who had called her an old whore to her face. It was she who had deviled and ridden her so viciously about going out with her old duffers. It was she whom Janie had really been trying to hide it from. And if it hadnt been for all these things, Janie would have been willing to have gone to a doctor with her trouble. If it hadnt been for these things, Janie would not have been ashamed to talk to her, Edith, about it. And they would have been able to catch it, catch that horrible thing growing inside of her, before it killed her. And Edith sat alone in the house—(John had already gone to bed, worn out with the confusion and excitement)—and faced it: faced this horror: this horrible horror: that would live with her the rest of her life: *If it had not been for her, it could have been prevented.* And it was this that broke her. And the Edith Barclay there had once been, the Edith Barclay who had once been sole owner and proprietor of Parkman Illinois because it was by her sufferance its people were allowed to continue to exist, that Edith Barclay was no more. That Edith Barclay was broken, and was no longer a contender. And it was this that made her turn to Frank so desperately, and hopelessly, and frightenedly like a little child, and cling to him, the next time he saw her.

Doris, before she had gone home that night after the funeral, had insisted that Edith have a couple of drinks with her, to ease her. She had come prepared, and went out to the yellow convertible and came back with a bottle, and they had mixed the whiskey with Seven-Up and sat at the kitchen table and drunk them. But the drinks had not helped Edith, and had not eased her. And after Doris had finally gone, she lay in her bed dry-eyed and staring at the ceiling, while John snored away in his own room, and she did not sleep. But next day she was back at work at the store anyway, and it was then she discovered that only when she was working could she forget it, and forget Janie, and what she had done to Janie. Only when she was working, or when she was with Frank.

It was not the first time that she went out with him after Janie's funeral that he suggested the buying of the little house for her, but the second time. And then he went on to explain how they could say she had bought it with Janie's insurance money. The "insurance money," he said, would also take care of all the debts she had incurred with the funeral. Edith did not hesitate at all. She accepted.

In actual point of fact, Janie had had a little insurance. A pitifully little. A $500 life insurance policy with some cheap company, which, when all the small print deductions were taken out of it, left a little over half the total face value to be paid. This had already been paid to her and John (and would not cover even half the cost of the funeral) but it meant that John would know she was lying when she told him about the new "insurance money." So Edith did not even try to lie to him about it. She came right out bluntly, and told him the whole truth, and did it almost enjoyably.

Doris Fredric, who had taken to coming over often now after Janie's funeral, might enjoy talking—and weeping—about her love affair with 'Bama Dillert; and in fact did so, to Edith. Time after time, now, she would come over and tell her the whole story, and weep and bewail her fate at having lost him. She loved him so very much; with all of her whole soul. And he had thrown her over. It wasnt him, it was that bunch of bums and drunkards he hung around with—Dave Hirsh, and Dewey Cole, and Hubie Murson, and all those brassiere factory girls, just whores—who had caused it. He, 'Bama had been going to leave his wife and marry her, Doris; and she would have married him gladly and to hell with what the town of Parkman or her parents and relatives thought. But they had talked him out of it; had stifled it. And then she would cry heartbreakingly. Doris might talk about all of this, to her, Edith. But Edith was not the type who liked to talk about her love affairs. She could listen to Doris, and indeed more or less had to, after all that Doris had done for her after Janie's death, but she would not talk about herself and Frank; and actually, Doris appeared not to know a single thing about it.

But when it came to telling John, Edith found she had no such reserve. With an almost cruel, nearly breathless, enjoyable, pleasurable, selfcastigating eagerness, she told him everything: just exactly what the situation was, how long it had been going on, and just exactly what she meant to do. She even dwelt upon it, eagerly, at some great length. Much more than she even needed to. Breathlessly, needfully, she told how they were going to buy the house for her on Janie's fake "insurance money," and he John could do, or say, any damned thing about it to any damned body, that he pleased. But of course, she knew he would never say anything.

John, of course, was flabbergasted. He had had no idea at all such a thing was going on, of course.

"Well, Edith honey," he said, trying to be kindly, but wrinkling up his brow with shocked pain, "I never thought you would ever do nothing like that. Never."

"Ahhh, well, but I have," Edith said eagerly. "I have; and I intend to keep right *on* doing it. Maybe the rest of my whole life. Im Frank Hirsh's mistress. Frank Hirsh's *whore*, you might say.—"

"Oh, Edith honey!" John said, shocked. "Edith honey, dont say that! You could never be a—one of those, Edith honey."

"—Oh? couldnt I?" she went right on, eagerly, not even hearing what he said. "But I am. Frank Hirsh's *whore*. His mistress. I sleep with him. I go to bed with him," she said, relishing feverishly the look of deep moral shock on old John's face. "Thats exactly what I am. He keeps me. And has been keeping me. And now hes going to buy me a house, and Im going to live in it."

"But what will *people* say?" John said feebly, perplexedly, his brow furrowed with the pain of facing a moral situation he had never faced, had not even suspected. Edith, his face seemed to say, Edith was his baby. "What will the people in Parkman say?"

"Theyll probably never know about it. But I dont care!" Edith said eagerly. "Do you understand? I dont *care* what they say! I hope they say *every*thing, if they find out about it. *Every*thing!" Shakily, she got hold of herself. "You can get yourself a housekeeper," she said. "Or you can batch." Then the eagerness seized her: "I can help you," she said; "with the money Frank Hirsh gives me. I can hire you a housekeeper. Keep you in style. Do you want it? Do you want me to?"

"Well, Edith honey," John said perplexedly, "I dont think—"

"Ill do it anyway," she said. "Ill send it to you. He keeps me. So Ill keep you. Whats wrong with that? Those are the facts. Thats the truth. Isnt it?"

"Well, Edith honey—" John said befuddledly.

"Im going out with him tomorrow night again," Edith said. "We always go to motelrooms. Im getting tired of motel rooms. When I have my house, he can come there. Ill receive him there. And tomorrow Ill tell him its all fixed up. Now, if you want to go and tell everybody how your daughter is Frank Hirsh's whore, go ahead."

"Ahhh, no, Edith honey," John said anguishedly. "I wouldnt never do nothing like that to you, Edith honey."

"I dont care if you do," Edith said eagerly. "Dont you understand? I dont care if you *do!* I dont give a damn. —Oh, go on to bed," she said. "Go on to bed, Daddy, and leave me alone."

So on the next night, when she went out with Frank again, she told him everything was fixed. She was much colder, much more level-headed, less feverish, with Frank. John, of course, knew, she said; but he would never say anything. And Frank said he would be glad to pay for a housekeeper for him. And Edith, desperately, frightenedly, filled with a nameless panic that had become her constant companion in the weeks since Janie's death, clung to him fiercely when they went to bed; clung to the only love she had ever found in the world that she herself had not already killed. And Frank said that he would set about seeing how to get the house. Right away. He could work through Springfield. And she could do all the decorating herself, if she wanted to. On the house that Janie's funeral had bought.

CHAPTER 66

DAVE managed to make Old Janie's funeral. Just barely. He did not make his own father's funeral two months later, but he did make Janie's. He didnt make the Old Man's partly because he did not even know about it— How would he have known? since by that time he was going nowhere and seeing no one?—but even if he had known about it, by that time—six weeks later—he was in no condition to go and couldnt have gone anyway. He had learned about Gwen's leaving just a few days before Old Janie died, and already its effect on him was prodigious; but by the time the Old Man's funeral came six weeks later it had reached really astronomical proportions. In that short six weeks of time—short; but so very, very long—he had fallen completely apart.

But he did make Janie's funeral. It was considerable of a struggle, it was true, but he did get there. He felt he ought to go—since Old Jane had practically raised him; and he managed to rouse himself out of his drunken stupor enough to shave (three cuts on his face) and wash enough of the mushy drunkard smell off him to be reasonably presentable, and put on decent clothes, so that he would not be too much of a spectacle. It took a number of extra drinks to get him that far, but he made it. He learned about her death—where else?—at Smitty's, where he had been, at the moment, doing his drinking. He had not had guts enough to go out to the Barclay house to pay his respects, not in his drunken, mentally pole-axed condition, and when he went to the funeral at the Baptist church he slipped in alone at the back and tried to be as inconspicuous as possible. He saw Frank and Agnes sitting down front near Edith and her father John who were accompanied by a weeping Doris Fredric. He did not go out to the cemetery for the interment, because he did not want to get close enough to anyone to breathe on them. Anyway, he didnt have the heart for any more.

He had tried to get 'Bama to dress and go with him; after all, Janie had worked for them; but the big gambler only sneered sourly and said funerals were the last thing he wanted to think about and he would not have gone to anybody's, even if it was his own damned mother. So when Dave got out of the church, not feeling that he had accomplished anything at all in going, really, he chugged his little Plymouth slowly and brain-numbedly back home where 'Bama was sitting up with a bottle, and joined him. It seemed to be all either one of them was doing anymore; and in fact, or so 'Bama said—not without a certain bitter grinding enjoyment—they had reached the point in their gambling together where they were now losing distinctly more than they were winning, which meant of course that now they were living off their capital, 'Bama said grinning with sour pleasure. *His* capital, 'Bama's capital, Dave added to himself silently when 'Bama told him.

He had been doing all right, doing pretty well, Dave had thought; until he learned about Gwen. He might not be turning out as much work, and not doing the smooth enjoyable day-by-day work routine he had once had; but he was still at least turning out *some* work. In spite of 'Bama's illness and breakup; and in spite of the gnawing difficulty with Gwen which bothered him all the time, and which he could not figure out the reason for. After that time he had taken the new story "The Peons" over to them and found her changed, and the ensuing blowup he had, when he had talked to Bob, he had settled down into an abortive unhappy but at least somewhat productive routine. And in fact, he had been working quite hard, in spite of the heavier drinking he was doing, for over a month before he went to Israel again—because he wanted to take a decent batch of manuscript over there. And then, just a few days before Janie's death, he had driven over there with the manuscript—and found out from Bob that she was gone! And had been gone for nearly a month. Had not even finished out the school year! And all that time he had been working hard to have some decent stuff to show her! All that time! And her already gone! It threw him completely.

If it had not been that he had heard Gwen snort so derisively and so often over old George Blanca's novel where he had the young writer burn his manuscript in the fire in front of his Japanese B-girl love, he would actually have torn his batch of manuscript to shreds and scattered it over the lawn of Bob French's *Last Retreat*. And he had thought he was doing so good! the last month and a half.

It was during that month and a half, when he was settled down into this at least somewhat productive, if abortive routine, in spite of the heavier drinking and worrying he was doing, that his sister Francine visited him. It was just a day or two after young Dawnie's wedding, that he had not been invited to. When he saw her standing there on the porch, he recognized her and at the same time, simultaneously, did not recognize her. Everything about her looked enough like her, like Francine, to convince him that it was her; but at the same time nothing about her looked like the Francine he had known on the Coast before the war. Her face, always rather sharp in contrast to the ballheaded, blocky Hirshes, was even sharper now. And her slim figure that she had always kept did not look so much slim now as bony. Her breasts, never too out-standing, as it were, had fallen even more so with the three quick babies she had had, only one of whom, the oldest, Dave had ever seen.

"Well, arent you going to ask me in?" she grinned.

Dave did, and the very next thing she said was, and would be, naturally, damn it, that he had put on an awful lot of weight since she had last seen him. "Youre turning into a regular butterball," she smiled. And then, after she had flung her arms around him and kissed him, she stepped back and exclaimed: "God! You smell like a regular brewery. Youre not trying to write drunk, are you?"

"No," Dave said, smiling, if perhaps ruefully. "Thats from last night. I never could write drunk; nor nobody else, I dont think."

"Well, I should hope not," Francine smiled happily. "Well, now show me all around your place here. I want to see everything. I want to know what kind of life youre living. God, its been a long time, Davie, hasnt it?"

He showed her all around the house, explaining how he and 'Bama had taken it together, then offered her a drink which she refused on the grounds that it was still morning and not yet noon, and then they sat down with a cup of coffee in the kitchen at the kitchen table. 'Bama was gone, out, probably down to the farm, so he could not introduce her to him, although Francine asked to be.

"I read your story in the *New Living Literature* semi-annual," Francine beamed at him; "I always buy them. The story was magnificent. Just simply magnificent. Where did you ever get the idea for it?"

"Well, a part of it happened, sort of," Dave said awkwardly, "on a trip me and 'Bama made to Florida."

"Well, its just simply splendid!" Francine said and sat and beamed at him. Dave, who had entirely forgot about "The Confederate" in the press of more recent writing and more recent worries, was at a total loss as to what to say.

"I always knew," Francine grinned happily, "that you were the one who had the real talent. If only it could be got out of you. You had more talent than the rest of the bunch all put together."

It was strange to him, to suddenly be thinking again after all this time of all the places, and all the people, that had congregated around this woman who was his sister back out there in Hollywood so long ago. Harriet Bowman! he thought suddenly, and wanted to laugh. Who married a lawyer! And Kenny McKeean, and old George Blanca

Francine's lover, and big old Herman Daniel, dead now in the war. Naturally, now, the two of them, near strangers and sitting here after having gone such diverse ways the last seven years and a war apart, naturally they fell at once and immediately to talking about the old times, and the old people, and the old places. The swimming parties and how they used to drive down to the public beach below Malibu. And then build a fire and roast hot dogs and buns in the dark afterwards. It seemed to Dave as though all this had happened to another person named Dave Hirsh, not himself. He wondered if Francine felt that way too? Apparently she did not.

She wanted to know all about the new book he was working on, and he told her about the new story "The Peons" which NLL had also bought, and she promised she would watch for it. She had changed; changed very much. But he could not quite put his finger upon just how. Until finally he rather inadvertently, if not actually thoughtlessly, mentioned the fact that Gwen French was writing a critical book about their group they had had out there. But that was later.

First, Francine told him all about the wedding, and about how Frank had asked all the relatives not to go and see Dave until after it. Frank was really terribly incensed about Dave's having gone back to using the old family name: Herschmidt: on his story.

"Yeah, he told me," Dave said shortly.

"Well, I told *him*," Francine said sharply. "He really has an almost rabid phobia about it, since Dad ran off with Doc Cost's first wife. And by God I told him it was a petty filthy little trick not to invite you to the wedding."

"I didnt care whether I went anyway or not," Dave said.

"But of course it didnt do any good," Francine went right on. "But by God I got him told. They keep a copy of the NLL anthology out on their coffeetable, you know; with your story in it. Thats to show they have no hard feelings toward you."

Dave grinned, but wished they could get off of this and onto something else.

"I dont see how you can stand to live in this crappy little town," Francine said crisply. "If you really want to write, you ought to get out of it and get into the fresh air, go someplace where people are tolerant. This little jerkwater town is too inbred. Everybody knows too much about everybody else. Art simply cant flourish in that kind of an atmosphere," she said decisively.

"Well, you know, Ive kind of got so I like the old town," Dave said. "So many memories attached to it, you know. Id like to do a novel about my childhood next, while Im still living here. And I have my own group of friends, you know." He grinned. "Sort of the lower elements, you might say. You know? The town undesirables."

"Yes, Frank spoke about that, too," Francine said, nodding vigorously. "Told all of us about how you run around with the town bums. And some fat whore youre sleeping with: he was especially upset over that."

Dave flushed; could not help flushing, both from anger and from a vivid picture memory of Ginnie Moorehead. "Well, its none of his business who I sleep with."

"Exactly what I told him," Francine said. "Told all of them. Writers are eccentric people, all artists are, and perhaps sometimes they prefer to sleep with fat whores. Thats really why," she said, "thats really why none of the other relatives came to see you while they were in town. What Frank said to all of us. But, by God, I told him I was coming. And he could take it or lump it. So I just left Charley there with the kids, and I came down myself. We'll be leaving for the Coast tomorrow. And Id never have forgiven myself if I hadnt got to see you."

Dave nodded, feeling awkward and embarrassed, wanting only to get off the subject. Where was all the closeness, all the "spiritual rapport" he and Francine had used to have so long ago?

"Do you ever see old George? George Blanca? anymore?" he asked, to get onto another topic, more than anything else.

The effect upon Francine was instantaneous, and amazing. She preened. "Well, no," she said, smiling perhaps a little smugly. "Not often, anyway. We dont run in the same crowds any more, you know. Charley and I have our own activities, you know. More, actually, than we can possibly take care of. What with both of us teaching, you know. And Charley's principal of the whole high school now. Which makes it just that much worse. That much harder on both of us. Meetings, and fund raisings, the PTA, all that sort of stuff. And of course, George is a bigshot writer now—bigshot *screen*writer, that is—" Once again she seemed to preen, just a little, as she said: "I wonder what has happened to all of those great literary ambitions he used to talk about so much?" She shook her head, sadly. "—Well, anyway, I have seen him once or twice, since the war. At cocktail parties out in Beverly Hills, that Charley and I just happened to get invited to. All thats really far over our heads, you know: we're just simple poor school teachers: but we do have a few artistic friends here and there. And of course, George is married to that rich blonde wife of his, you know," she said, and preened again. "And he is quite a bigshot in The Industry, you know. Though of course hes no real writer any more."

It was then that Dave told her about Gwen French and the critical book she was doing on the old group. Perhaps it was Francie's remark about George being no real writer any more. That fit right in with Gwen's so ingenious, and so almost mathematical, theory about the sex part of it. He only really mentioned it in passing, and explained a little of Gwen's theory, and was intending to go on to something else.

But the effect upon Francine was as instantaneous, and as startling, as the mention of George Blanca had been; but in an entirely different way. Francine's eyes narrowed dangerously, and her face got stiff, and she sat up stiffly and straighter in her chair.

"Whats this?" she said. "Whats all this?"

Dave went back, a little startled, and told her more about it. How she was using Kenny McKeean and his Syrian dancer and his suicide, and Herman Daniel and how he went home to marry his high school sweetheart and quit, and himself and—hunh hunh—Harriet Bowman. She had not known about Harriet Bowman, of course, but she surmised her existence, and in fact had pegged her down almost exactly without ever having seen her, amazingly; he himself had told her all about it so she could use it. And of course George Blanca, and his love affairs: the Japanese waitress downtown in the skidrow section, and the rich blonde girl he finally married. Francine knew about all of them. The whole thing, Gwen's whole theory, which was its very ingeniousness, lay in the love affairs, of course.

"And whos doing all of this?" Francine said narrowly. "Who did you say was doing this?"

"Gwen French," Dave said (and his heart contracted: Ahhh, Gwen, Gwen!). "Guinevere French. She teaches English at Parkman College here in town. You probably never knew her. But you must have known her father, Bob French: Professor French. The poet."

"Yes, I knew Professor French," Francine said narrowly. "I took English under him in high school. Ive always thought he was a fine poet. And you say this is his daughter? And shes writing all this up? For a *book?*"

"Yeah," Dave said, "you know. Its one of those scholarly treatises English professors and students do. You know."

"And am I in it?"

"Well, yeah. Sure. I told her all about you and George."

"Then," Francine said crisply; "then, she had better never print it. Ill sue the life out of her. What do you mean!" she cried angrily; "what do you mean, telling her all of those things about me? About me and George? My God! What do you think would happen to me? if a book like that got out, and got passed around where I live?"

"Well, I never thought about it," Dave said hesitantly. "One way or the other. I was just interested in her theory. Anyway, its all the truth."

"Well, you better think again!" Francine said coldly, her eyes narrow, her face set stiffly. "Truth or not, what the hell does that matter? Truth or not, shell have to prove it in a court of libel; and George would back me up. You and her better both think again. What do you think would happen to Charley's job if all that old stuff got out

—got *published,* in a *book!* Or to my job? It would ruin both of us. I was young then, we all were. And we didnt any of us have any reputations to look out for, even. Im a respectable married woman. With three children. What would my children think if all of this stuff came out? Well!" she said, and stared at Dave dangerously, narrowly.

"Well, I didnt think youd feel that way about it, Francie," Dave said, almost apologetically. "I thought youd be proud of it. Of your association with the group. Her theory is that if George had stayed with you, he might have turned into a real writer. Hell, it—"

"I dont give a damn what her theory is!" Francine said coldly. "I know my rights. We were all young then, and it was during the Depression. Everybody was living wild out there. But Im not going to have all that old stuff dragged up to ruin me. We were all young."

"*You* werent so young," Dave said.

"Well, I was younger than I am now. And I was in an entirely different position! And a different environment! I have my reputation to think of, today. And my children's. And my husband's job. And Charley: what about Charley: he doesnt know anything about all of this."

"You mean you never told him?"

"Hell, no! Of course I never told him! Are you a fool? Well!" she said. "Well, you just tell them for me, both of them, that the minute a book with anything about me in it hits the stands, theyre going to have a big fat libel suit on their hands! You just tell them!"

"Okay, okay. Ill tell them," Dave said irritably. "Man, man, you sure have changed, Francie, from the gal I used to know!"

"Of course Ive changed," Francine said narrowly. "Ive got responsibilities now. You just dont forget to tell them!"

She did not stay long after that. And Dave was just as glad. She *was* changed. Yes, she certainly *was* changed. And not for the better, as far as he was concerned. She did manage to become warm again, and smiling, friendly to her kid brother the writer, before she left. But she did not attempt to talk about the old times in Hollywood any more, he noticed. Just before she left, she went back once again to how stifling a town like Parkman was upon an artist's work, and told him that any time he wanted to get out of it he could come and stay with them back in North Hollywood.

"Everything's on fire out there now," she smiled. "The whole town's ablaze with creativity and creative activity now, since the war. You really ought to get out of this crappy place and into the free air of real tolerance that a real city has. Dont forget, if you ever want to come: You dont even have to write a letter. Just come."

"All right, I will," Dave said. What else was there to say? He had already stated his position; which she had chosen not even to hear.

After she left—it was almost noon—he mixed himself a drink and sat down with it sadly. Yes, she had changed. And he guessed he had changed, too. And old George Blanca had changed. Everybody had changed, it seemed. It made him feel very sad, and not a little panicky and frightened. Where had it all gone? The old talk, the old rapport, the old ambitions they had all had, the old fire and energy. Francine had become an opinionated, petty, pompous dilettante: a chaser after the arts. God! It was, of course, out of the question that he could ever *ever* go back out there again now.

There were times—during the six weeks between old Jane Staley's funeral and the Old Man's—that he nevertheless contemplated doing just that: just packing up and going and descending on Francine and Charley in North Hollywood. It would have been an out. —Or rather, might have been, had he not seen Francine here in Parkman. If Francine had not visited him in Parkman, he might have actually gone out there. But after the talk they had had, that avenue was closed to him forever now. All avenues were closed to him forever, it looked like. And anyway, in the dull torpid stupor of constant semi-drunkenness that he existed in after he found out Gwen was gone, he would not have had the energy or the mental presence to even pack and go. He simply stagnated.

He had waited, waited quite a long time in fact, so that he might have a good-sized important-looking batch of manuscript to take with him to Israel. —And all that time, she had already been gone. When he drove up into the crushed rock drive under the big old trees of the *Last Retreat,* and got out, and went in, and found only Bob there to greet him and learned why, it stunned and enervated him in a way that he had never felt in his life before. This was the finish. This was the end. The *real* end. At least, there had been hope, *hope,* slim as it was, as long as she was still there. But when Bob told him that she was gone, and perhaps for good, that she had in fact not even made arrangements to teach at the College again next year,—well, it just simply floored him; it put him down for the whole count. Hell, she hadnt even let him *know* she was leaving; hadnt even left him a note or anything.

She had, Bob said, painfully and kindly, as if he knew the pain he was causing him, she had been gone since right after the first of May. Just shortly after Wally Dennis left to join the Army, in fact.

"But *why!*" Dave said. "*Why!*"

Bob shrugged sadly, awkwardly, embarrassedly. "I expect just because she was worn out. Shed had quite a heavy time of it, you know, the past year and a half or so. Working with all of you, and trying to carry her classes also."

Dave searched his mind, rummaging through it desperately. "Well," he said haltingly—"well—did Wally's leaving for the Army have anything to do with it maybe? You said she left soon after he did."

Bob pursed his lips and pulled them sideways. "Yes, I expect it did," he said gently. "Shed been working with him for, well, nearly three years now, you know. And then to have him just throw it all up, and decide to go into the Army. That was pretty discouraging, you know. She judged that six more months, at the *very* longest, would see his book done and in printable shape: acceptable to a publisher. Yes, I expect that did have a good deal to do with it. And then, her young ministerial student and the polio girl werent working out too well, either, you know."

"But gee," Dave said hopelessly, "gee, she didnt even let me know she was going, gee."

"Well I rather think she rather felt it best to just slip off, Dave, without telling anyone. She doesnt like farewells any more than I. Youre the last one of them to know, because you were so long coming over. The ministerial student and the polio girl were both here weeks ago. And then, of course, they knew it through the College."

"And I brought all this manuscript over to show her," Dave said lamely. "Thats why I waited so long: so Id have a lot."

Bob smiled at him, painfully, almost as if he could hardly bear this interview. "Well," he offered, "dear Dave, I can read it myself if you like. Im not as much up on your book as Gwen was, but I am rather up on it somewhat. Enough to follow."

"Sure," Dave said hopelessly; "you might as well, I guess. Why not?" and made as if to hand the manila folder over; but then suddenly he drew it back. "No," he said indifferently, "I guess not. I guess Ill keep it. What difference does it make, anyway?" he said apathetically. "What difference does it make who reads it? What difference does it make whether I *finish* it?" He stuck it laxly under his arm and made as if to turn away, then suddenly he swung back around on Bob, suddenly full of fiery energy, the energy of anger. "But Bob!" he cried; "Bob, *you* know—"

In a quick gesture, Bob held up his hand and stopped him, still smiling at him nevertheless, if sadly.

Shardine Jones, the negro lady, had been at the stove fixing supper when Dave first came in. But under the impact of the news Dave had hardly even noticed her till now. Shardine had looked at Dave when he first came in, and had sniffed audibly to herself, her dark thick face closing down tight like a snail clamping itself back into its shell. She plainly wanted nothing to do with the likes of this man, and she equally plainly could not understand why Mr Bob and Miss Gwen did, either. But just as equally plainly, written on her sensitive dark face, was the conviction that it, after all, was not any of her business; and she did not intend to make it so. She had gone ahead stolidly with her work of fixing Bob's supper, her ears and mind as closed up as her dark face that she kept sullenly averted.

But nevertheless Bob turned to her now, his hand still up to stop Dave. "Shardine," he said politely, "I wonder if you could let those things go for a while. Id rather like to get my room straightened up, before I retire tonight."

"Yas, sir," Shardine said sullenly. "I kin fix it. Ill just turn the food off." She kept her face still averted away from Dave.

"Also," Bob said politely, "please fix up a guest room upstairs. Mr Hirsh may be staying."

"Yas, sir," Shardine said, and left.

"I aint staying," Dave said dully.

"Maybe youll change your mind," Bob said. "Lets have a drink, Dave."

"I dont care," Dave said, dully; then he suddenly cried it out, loudly: "I dont *care!* I dont care if I have a drink or *not!* I dont *care!*" But he followed Bob over to the countertop where he got out the mixing things.

"I think Ill have a Martini with you," Bob said soothingly.

Dave hardly heard him. Pacing back and forth behind him while Bob got ice and mixed the drinks, suddenly transfixed with energy again where a moment before he had been apathetic, it all came spouting out of Dave in a regular torrent of words.

"Bob, you know we were in love with each other! You *know* it! I *know* she was in love with me! She even told me so once! And *you* know it, too! Now, dont you?"

Bob hesitated a moment, then spoke without turning his head from the gin he was pouring, "Yes, I know it," he said. "I suppose theres no harm in saying that much, now. Yes, I know she was in love with you, dear Dave. And still is, I expect, at the moment. If thats any consolation to you. Although I expect its just the reverse. Yes, Ive rather followed yours and Gwen's love affair with considerable interest, Dave, right almost from its very inception."

"And is that why you got her to go away from me?" Dave said accusingly.

"Dear Dave," Bob said, almost crisply, for him, and stopped stirring the drinks in the glass before the rather momentous implication of Dave's remark. "Dear Dave, I had nothing whatever to do with Gwen's going. She made her own decision. And she made it entirely by herself. As a matter of fact, if I had any inclination at all toward any opinion, it would have been to have had her stay. But as I told you once, I feel very strongly that I must not interfere in any way at all in this matter between you and Gwen." He had gone back to stirring now, and his voice had gentled. "I told you this, and I have continued to do it. Gwen made up her own mind to go away."

"But *why!*" Dave cried. "She loved *me!* Why!"

Bob steadily poured the drinks out into two little round glasses and turned around with them. Offering one of them, he stared steadily into Dave's eyes, and then smiled, gently, "Here, take one of these and lets go sit down at the table, Dave."

Dave took the glass and stared at it, hardly knowing what it was, and then followed him limply to the big table.

"But *why!*" he cried, as soon as he was seated, as if this act released him from silence. "Youve got to tell my *why!*"

"Im afraid I cant do that, Dave," Bob said steadily. "In the first place, Im not sure I know. Not for sure. Because I think it was a combination of a lot of things, not the least of which was Wally's leaving. Then, too, Ive come to suspect that theres some element in all of this that Im missing somehow; that I dont know. But I cant tell you any more than that. Anything else I know is in the strictest of confidence, and I cannot divulge confidences. —And," he added more gently, "as Ive told you so many times before, I feel very strongly that I, as an individual, as an outside third force, must not interfere Karmically— thats the only word I have for it—in something that is solely between yourself and Gwen."

"More of that damned Yogi stuff," Dave snarled viciously.

"Dear Dave," Bob said smiling gently, "dont try to take out on me your grief over Gwen's leaving. That wont do you any good. Or me any good. Or anyone else any good."

Dave rubbed his hand roughly over his face and took a swallow of his drink. "Of course," he said. "Youre right, of course. Im sorry. I apologize."

"And it isnt *Yogi*," Bob smiled, conversationally. "Its *Yoga*. Pronounced *Yog-h*. *Yoga* is the system, the general noun form. *Yogi* is an individual practitioner of it, of the *Yoga* system."

For a moment Dave so far forgot himself, and his distress, that he was able to grin. Old Bob! "I apologize," he said solemnly. "Yoga." But then it hit him again, a spine-riving, stomach-shuddering, tooth-grinding force, that he had no more control over than he did over his heart's beating. He took another swallow of his drink, and discovered that the glass was now empty.

"If you want another, help yourself," Bob smiled. "Better yet, Ill fix it for you. But Im going to nurse this one," he said apologetically. "If I have more than one, I often find Ive gotten started. And if I have the third, Im gone. Especially when Im emotionally disturbed."

"No; no thanks," Dave said. "Look, Bob," he said leaning forward eagerly. "Where is she? Where did she go? Maybe I could write to her. Do you know where she went?"

Bob hesitated for a moment, as if—and Dave could almost read this in his mind—as if he were going to say: No, he did not know where she was. But then instead, he said: "Yes, I do know where she is." He said it sadly. "But Im afraid I cant tell you that, either, dear Dave."

"But if I just knew where she was," Dave said, eagerly. "If I could just *talk* to her, you know? Bob, you dont know how much we— And do you know, Bob, we never—" He was just on the verge of telling him that they had never slept together, even; but then he could not: it was too much of an intimate revelation, not because of his own pride, but because of his feeling for Gwen. So he did not say it. "Well, what if I wrote a letter? and left it here with you? to forward on? Would you do that."

Slowly, almost painfully, Bob shook his head. "No, Im afraid I cant do that," he said, sadly, but his eyes while sad were positive and steady and unchangable as any eyes Dave had ever seen. "You see," he said, "she left instructions that no one was to know where she was; and she did not want to hear from anyone, Dave. Anyone. Im bound to the instructions she left. Im not even writing her myself, in fact."

Bitterness rose up in Dave acidly. "Well, tell me this: Has she got another man, or two, with her?" he asked caustically.

Bob did not like this, at all, and his face and eyes grew cold; but he did not say anything about it, or recriminate. All he said was, gently: "No, she has no other lover with her. I think I can assure you of that."

"Im sorry," Dave said, and rubbed his hand over his face again. "I shouldnt have said that, Bob."

"No, you shouldnt have," Bob said gently.

"But you dont know how much I *love* her!" Dave said. "You just have no conception of how very much I love her."

"Dear Dave," Bob said gently, suddenly looking like a scholarly elder advising the young, "I have found that human love between two persons very rarely varies in intensity—only in articulation. Even the lowest brute of a man can suffer consummate agonies when he feels human love for his brute of a female." He smiled. "I have been in love. Youre no exception, Dave. And in fact, though it may seem cruel to you to say this, I rather think youre playing just about par for the course."

"Well, but whats she going to do?" Dave said eagerly. "Wherever she is. Whats she going to *do*? If she has no lovers, like you say (and which I believe; I cant help but believe she was in love with me when she left), and if she has no writers around. So whats she going to do?"

"Well, she said she intended to work on her own book. And in fact, I believes she intends to send it on off to a publisher even before ever coming home. If she does come home, which was still undecided by her when she left."

Like a sudden dousing of cold water, Dave forgot himself entirely, momentarily, remembering Francine. "Listen, theres something she should know about," he said. "This isnt any subterfuge, or anything like that. See— Well, do you know the structure of her book?"

Bob nodded. "Yes."

"Well, see, my sister Francine was home for my niece Dawnie's wedding; and she came to see me. Well, I inadvertently told her about Gwen's book—but now I guess it was a good thing I did—and Francine figures pretty prominently in the book, you know. She was George Blanca's lover. Well, she says if Gwen prints anything about her, shell sue. Gwen ought to know about this before she sends the book in."

"Yes," Bob said right away, "she should. And Ill see that she gets the knowledge, Dave. And thank you. Even if I have to break 'radio silence' with her. This is important enough she should know. Shes been rather worried about the possibility of suits over the book for some time, ever since she really began to delve down into the real truth of all of it."

"I always did tell her it ought to be a novel, that it was a novel she had there," Dave said, and his eyes suddenly filled with tears. For a moment he choked and turned away. "Ive got to go, Bob," he said after a moment. "Ive got to go. Thanks for inviting me, but I cant stay. —And Bob, I dont hold anything against you. I know youre only doing what she asked you to; and also what you yourself feel you should do. Im not mad at you or anything. Its just that— Gee, Bob, I really did — But Jesus!" he said, "if I only knew *why!*" Again, he choked and turned away.

Bob's face was lit up with a bright sorrowful pain, when Dave turned back to him. "Dear Dave," he said; "I know very little about life. Its purpose, or its reason—its rationality—if there even is any rationality. But in my life I have learned just one thing: and its the most painful thing Ive ever learned:

"Every man must find his own salvation. Its not to be found outside. In another person. Not in friendship; but most particularly not in love. Thats where our American culture—our whole *Western* culture—has fallen down. Its tried to teach us that salvation can be found there: in love. But it is our culture, and being our culture, we're both bound by and limited to it. Listen to a love song on the radio and see how it affects you, emotionally, even while your mind may be laughing at it."

"I know," Dave said.

"The simple avoidance of loneliness is not enough. The simple avoidance of pain, of discomfort,—physical pain and discomfort, and mental pain and discomfort—is not enough. That way we stagnate. We become vegetables again. Thats regression. We depend too much on creature comforts, in our culture; and love is one of these. One of the main ones of these. Did you ever notice how disgusting, how really idiotic—how *dumb*—requited lovers are? Only when their love finally wears out do they really become human again, suffer again.

"It was the hardest, most painful lesson I ever had to learn," Bob said sadly.

"Your philosophy does me very little good," Dave said wryly, and then an old quote from the Bible, from what section he did not even know, came into his mind: *"I asked for bread and you gave me a stone,"* he said.

"Its all I have to give, Dave," Bob said sadly.

"Well, I must go," Dave said and got up.

"What are you going to do about your book?" Bob said, getting up with him.

"Hell, I dont know. Maybe Ill finish it. Maybe I wont. I dont know. What difference does it make?"

"Well, that is something only you can decide for yourself," Bob said.

"Hell, I only started writing the damned thing because I wanted to make Gwen love me," Dave said apathetically. "Who cares?"

"Ill read your manuscript, if youd like to leave it," Bob offered again.

"No. No, I think Ill take it on back home with me."

"Well, are you coming back over any more? now that Gwen is gone?"

"I dont know," Dave said. He had reached the landing, the old cellar landing, by the side door. "Yeah, I guess I will. But I dont know."

"Thats also something you must decide for yourself," Bob said, smiling sadly.

"We'll see," Dave said. "Ill probably be back over to see you sometime. So long," he said.

"So long, Dave," Bob said.

Apathetically, outside in the little Plymouth, he dropped the manila folder of manuscript in the seat, and apathetically he started the little car up. Apathetically he drove it out through the gate of Bob French's *Last Retreat.*

Empty was really the word, he thought. More than apathetic. He just felt empty. He didnt care whether he ever worked on the damned book any more or not. Apathy was what he felt for *it,* all right. And as far as that went, if he never worked on it again, if he never finished it, maybe it might be a good thing. Maybe it would show her someday what she had done to him; and to the book itself. Maybe that was what he ought to do, just put the damned thing away and forget it.

It was a long drive back to Parkman, that five miles. He shuttled himself into the seemingly never-ending stream of great trucks coming off the bridge at the cutoff below it, and then he sandwiched himself in between two of them and just stayed there. He was too empty, and too apathetic, to even try to pass one of them. He just rode along.

Harriet Bowman and Guinevere French. The two unrequited loves. It seemed to be his destiny. Maybe there was something in his basic character which caused it? Maybe that was the only kind of loves he was capable of being drawn to? Well, if it was, it was a hell of a poor kind of a basic character to be saddled with, by God, that was all he could say. He had thought that one was rough: out there in Hollywood: back before the war: Harriet Bowman. Harriet Bowman! Who married a god-damned lawyer! But that one was nothing compared to this one. *Nothing!* And this time he wasnt even a vigorous young man any more. This time he was an old man. Nearly Forty. And fat as a butterball. No wind, no stamina, no looks, no prospects, no nothing. And yet she had loved him. She had really loved him. Harriet Bowman never had. But *she* had. *She* had loved him. How would he ever again, in the tag-end rest of his life that remained, how would he ever again get, find, induce, a woman to fall in love with him again? Him, the him he was, today. Hell, even the thought was ridiculous. And he found he was staring ahead into the bare nude face of loneliness, which stared back. Two friendly old enemies, who have fought each other for so long they not only knew each other better, but cared for each other more, than either of them did for their friends.

What woman on earth would he ever find who would marry him? *him?* Fat and forty and broke and prospectless.

By the time he got back to Parkman, tamely and apathetically following his truck, the emptiness and loneliness in him had been replaced by anger and sheer burning rage at Gwen, at Gwen French, for what she had done to him. Not even a word. Anger and outrage at her because he *still* didnt even know *why*, did not under*stand* what could have made her, loving him as he knew she did, do what she had done. Well, he would get hold of old slobby Ginnie Moorehead and have a royal drunken romping party tonight, and to hell with *her*.

Maybe he would write the damned book anyway, just to show *her* what she had missed. —But then when he looked down at the manilla folder in the seat, emptiness and apathy for it rose up all over him. He wasnt even interested in it any more. But by God maybe hed write it anyway; force himself to write it. Anyway, he would sure get hold of slobby old Ginnie tonight.

I have been faithful to thee, Cynara, in my fashion. Yeah: what other fashion did they give you a choice of? what other choice did they even allow you? At least slobby old Ginnie didnt just up and cut you dead for no reason, and then take off from town without letting you know where or even leaving you a word.

But when he did get back into town, and did get hold of slobby old Ginnie, he did the very same damned thing that he had warned Wally Dennis against doing when Wally insulted Rosalie back Easter night:

He antagonized her; the anger and hurt and outrage in him made him take it out on her; and then they argued; until finally they had a fight, their second real fight, and Ginnie left in a huff and he did not even get to sleep with her.

It started in the car on the way home after he had picked her up at Smitty's, when he jumped on her for picking her nose.

Ginnie looked hurt, and embarrassed, and furtively wiped her finger on the tissue she had in her other hand. "Well, I seen you pick your nose an awful lot of times," she said defensively. "A lot of times."

"I dont give a damn what youve seen," Dave said savagely. "Anyway, I dont do it out in public."

"We aint out in public."

"All right then: Lets say I dont do it when Im drivin home with somebody to go to bed with them," Dave said. "It certainly dont make you any more attractive."

"Now you just lay off of me," Ginnie said fiercely, rising to her own defense. "I aint done nothing to you. Whatre you gettin on me for?"

"Because I dont like to see you picking your goddamned nose when Im getting ready to take you home and go to bed with you," Dave said savagely. "I must admit, it somewhat dampens my ardor. I thought you wanted to learn to be a lady."

"Now, damn it!" Ginnie said irately. "I didnt come and pick you up. You came and picked me up. And you can just lay off of me!"

"Maybe I aint no lady," she said guiltily. "Maybe not. But I notice whenever you want a party, you always come around to me."

"Only because youre so goddamned easy," Dave said, not even knowing why he was doing it now.

"You aint got no right to talk to me like that," Ginnie said stoutly. "Maybe I aint none of your high-toned ladies, but I aint been out with a single soul in the last three months but you. You can ask anybody. Ask anybody down at Smitty's. Theyll tell you. I aint been out with nobody but you for—well, for almost three months. And you aint got no right to talk to me like that. I know you think Im a dog. Well, I dont care what you think."

"Jesus but youre gettin awful high-minded lately," Dave said viciously.

"Well, if you want to sleep with me you can at least treat me decent like a human bein," Ginnie said. "I aint slept with another soul but you for three months; and I done it a-purpose. 'Cause Ive had chances. Ive had plenty chances. But I was tryin to show you how much I cared for you, and I turned them all down. All of them. It aint like I didnt have chances."

"What kind of chances?" Dave said. "Some of them whiskery old bastards that use to go out with old Janie Staley?"

"You just go to hell!" Ginnie rejoined. "There was a guy today, who tried to pick me up. A one-armed Marine he was, from out of town, arm off right up at the shoulder. And a nice boy. I was in at Ciro's after work, and he was there. And all I did was have a beer or two with him and sit and talk with him a while. And when he propositioned me, I turned him down. You got no right to talk to me like Im one of your Terre Haute dogs. Im a human bein. And I got some rights."

And so they were back off on her 'I got some rights' kick again. She elaborated on it angrily. And in his soul Dave knew she was right, she *was* a human being, and she *did* have some rights, and she *did* at least deserve respect, and he felt guilty about it. But he could not stop it. He kept on deriding her the rest of the way home.

"Say now? Just whats eatin you?" Ginnie demanded finally, after he had pulled up in the drive. "I dont like this a little bit."

"You want to know? You really want to know?" Dave said suddenly, viciously. "Ill tell you then. Shes left me, thats what. Gwen. Gwen French has left me. Shes left town and I dont even know where she is. Didnt even wait to finish out the school year. And Im in love with her."

"Oh?" Ginnie said. "Well, thats too bad, aint it? But that dont give you no right to take it out on me. —Evi-dently she aint so much in love with you, though, is she?" she said.

"Oh? and what would you know about love?" he said savagely. "You fat whore you. Just tell me, what would you know about love?"

"Dave, you cant talk to me like that," Ginnie said warningly. "I dont have to take it offen you. Just because some broad youve been sleepin with takes off and leaves you in the lurch dont mean you can take it out on me and insult me."

Rage, fury, misery, outrage, hate,—everything that had been seething in him all evening, suddenly came boiling up out of him like alcohol fumes in his head. That she would have the gall to call Gwen French a "broad"! Suddenly he began beating the bottoms of his fists up and down softly on the steering wheel. "Whore," he said. "Whore, whore, whore. Fat pig of a whore whore whore."

"All right sir," Ginnie said stiffly, and resolutely. "Ill show ya. Ill show ya, damn ya. Ill go back downtown and get the feller. I turned him down all day on account of you, and *been* turnin *ever*body down. Ill just show ya, boy. Ill show ya. I been in love with you, and what do you care? And I been true to you. And then you treat me like some kind of old dog. Well, I got some rights. I dont have to take it. Ill just show ya." Resolutely, she got out of the car and started walking stiff-backed right back toward town the way theyd come.

"Go ahead!" Dave called after her; "go ahead and see if I give a damn!"

"And I aint comin back till you apologize to me," Ginnie said reso-lutely from the walk. "Not never."

"Dont hold your breath," Dave said. "Oh, go to hell." And he turned and went on in the house, and proceeded to get drunk, stinking slobbering drunk and remained so for three days. And, in fact, he stayed that way until the day of Janie's funeral; and he did not entirely sober up on that day either.

And true to her word, he saw no more of Ginnie. He did not even see her at Ciro's or at Smitty's, later on, when he ambled dully and torpidly into those places for a drink. Later on, he found out the entire story about her, and about why he didnt even see her. But that was not for some little time. And when he did find out, he didnt care. The listless, leaden stupor and apathy of constant three-quarters-drunkenness kept him from caring about that, or caring about anything.

'Bama was not home that night, probably down at the farm, when he came in after running Ginnie off, and he sat down with a bottle of gin and drank himself to sleep. And when he did get up the next day, finally, he got another bottle and started right in again. Selfhate and selfviciousness rode him like two roweling spurs. He did manage to rouse himself sufficiently to shave and clean up enough to go to Old Jane's funeral, but that was all he did. When 'Bama did come back, and although he had refused to go to the funeral with him, they sat and got drunk together. Night after night. Sometimes, nearly dead-drunk, they would go out and play poker somewhere and lose; lose even more than they had been losing normally, before. But the rest of the time, they merely sat in the house and got drunk, and talked. They talked about everything, about life, about death, about afterlife, about Republicans, about Democrats, about Russia, about the Chinese Communists who were hitting it up so strong on the Asia mainland, about everything, talk, talk, talk. They would talk and drink until they were both so drunk they didnt even know themselves what they were saying, and could not make out what each other was saying, and still they talked. And got drunk.

And then 'Bama would go away to the farm and leave him alone and then he would get drunk by himself. Sometimes Dewey and Hubie sort of appeared, drank a while, and then sort of disappeared. And that was the way it went that six weeks between Old Jane's funeral and his Old Man's funeral, later, which he did not even know about until after it was over. And it went on longer than that, longer than that six weeks, on into July.

It was somewhere along in here that he learned, from Dewey and Hubie, about what had happened to Ginnie that night he ran her off, and since then.

He was very drunk when they told it to him, but later he remembered it dimly. He was very drunk almost all the time now, as a matter of fact. But later on, when he happened to be not quite so drunk, he questioned them about it again, a little more clearly, and got all the details. It was a very funny story, and they all three sat and howled over it. ('Bama was gone somewhere, to the farm probably.)

The night he had run her off—or, to be more accurate, had antagonized her into running off herself—well anyway, that night, Dewey and Hubie told him, they had been sitting up at Ciro's with Martha and Lois. Doing a little beer drinking. So they had been present when Ginnie came in. The one-armed ex-Marine was still there, and Ginnie had sat down with him and right away they became engaged in a deep absorbing conversation.

Dewey and Hubie had been drifting in and out and around all day, they said, so they knew about the one-armed ex-Marine and had seen him earlier. They did not, in fact know he was an ex-Marine then, they just knew he was one-armed and so hence concluded, in this year of Our Lord 1949, that he was an ex-something: soldier, sailor, Marine, or something. They were so many one-armed, or one-legged, or one-eared, or one-eyed ones floating around any more; and you could pretty near be sure they were ex-Servicemen of some kind or other. Just why this one-armed ex-Marine had decided to get off the bus in Parkman no one seemed to know. He was headed east. Probably he had gotten hard up for a drink. (Maybe it was *Fate,* Hubie giggled with drunken sarcasm; it just must have been "Fate".) Anyway, he had gotten off the bus—a great deal like Dave had two years ago—and had headed straight for the nearest bar which was, of course, Ciro's. He had bought himself a half pint, which he concealed very skillfully, as if he was used to a town where only beer was sold over the bar, and had started drinking beer at Ciro's, lacing it occasionally, and eyeing speculatively whatever women happened to be around, which was very few at that time of day. Dewey and Hubie had seen him then and had a drink or two with him, and found out he was an ex-Marine; but he seemed like a fairly reasonable soul, in spite of this. But later, after the brassiere factory girls got out from work, there were a lot more women. And that was when he met Ginnie. (With that sort of unerring instinct, Hubie giggled, that all ex-Servicemen have for immediately picking out the quickest and easiest.) Well, anyway, they had seen Ginnie talking to him a lot, earlier, —before Dave came and picked her up. And then she had come back, alone; and started talking absorbedly to him again.

So, just for kicks, after a while Dewey and Hubie (with Martha and Lois of course) had slipped over into the booth right next to them, taking their beers with them, naturally.

Well, what they heard, Dewey and Hubie grinned at him, what they heard, had them all four laughing so hard they were in stitches and in fact had difficulty in keeping silent and not giving the show away. Ginnie and this one-armed ex-Marine were having such a deep absorbing conversation they did not even notice Dewey and Hubie and the girls slip into the next booth. They were really at it. So they all four just sat and stifled their laughter and listened. Ginnie was snowing this ex-Marine. Man, but really *snowing* him. The story of her life. And he was eating it up: all about how she, Ginnie, was the local banker's daughter; or rather, had been; and had been born to the purple. But then alas (she told this sadly) the Depression came along and her old man had lost everything, and then to top it off, had died before he could make it back (Oh, he was a shrewd cookie, she told the ex-Marine, her old man was); and this of course left her and her mom holding the sack. The empty sack. Well, her and her mom had never got along so good, so as soon as she graduated from high school (There was no possibility of college now, of course.) as soon as she graduated from high school, she had went out on her own. Yes, her mom still lived here; but they didnt hardly never see each other no more. That was because, not only because of the bad feeling that had always been between them, but also because Ginnie had chosen to throw in her lot with the common people, and decided to work in the local brassiere factory. Oh, her mom was an awful snob; awful. She herself, of course, Ginnie, had —having had such a rich father and all— never been trained to no kind of work. No, sir, she was supposed to be a lady. Consequently, when she did cut loose from her mom and go out on her own, the only kind of work she was able to do was take a common factory worker's job in the brassiere factory. But, she said, she felt she could hold her head up: she was earning her own way, and paying her own way, and she was proud of that. That was a better more selfrespecting way to live than to just sit around and let someone else support you and dominate you at the same time. She was, at least, a free individual.

She had, Dewey and Hubie grinned, gone on at some length in this fashion. And the one-armed ex-Marine—whether he was just drunk by now; or whether he had got hit on the head in the war—believed every word of it. And inbetween times when Ginnie was talking, he told her his own life history: He come from a rich family of wheat farmers in Kansas. And in fact, he wasnt just sure how many acres his old man did own. But his trouble was a lot similar to hers: Him and his old man never did see eye-to-eye. And of course, he admitted, he *had* been a little bit wild when he was younger. Then the war had come along and he had joined the Marines, of course: the only really worthwhile outfit the United States forces have. And it was in the Marines that he had found himself: that he had become a *man*. He loved the Corps: they were *men,* by God. And if it hadnt been for him losing this arm at Iwo, he would have stayed in the Corps and made it his career. But of course, after losing this arm, he was through as far as the Marine Corps was concerned. Yes, he had lost it at Iwo; oh sure, he had got a flock of medals: Silver Star one time, Distinguished Service Cross another, Congressional Medal of Honor another—that was in the little fight he lost his arm in—and probably half a dozen damned Purple Hearts, he grinned. But what was a flock of medals to him? when it meant he could no longer stay in the Corps? He loved the Corps.

(If he lost his arm at Iwo, the cynical Hubie said parenthetically to Dave, it was probly when he stuck it out to make a left turn signal and some truck took it off: heh heh.)

And so, with the Corps no longer possible as a career for him, the ex-Marine finished telling Ginnie tragically, he was back with the old man wheat farming. Only, he couldnt take it for very long at a time. He was, in a way, like herself, he said: He was on his own: Right now he was just off on a trip, hoping maybe something would turn up for him. What the hell did he care if his old man was rich? He didnt want his damned money;—but he would probably wind up going back, anyway. A one-armed man didnt have much chance of breaking into a new racket. And, after all, his old man did have the acres, and the bucks.

(And if his old man's a rich wheat farmer, Hubie giggled, so is mine.)

Anyway, there had been a great deal of this kind of talk between them, and Dewey and Hubie had sat and listened to it, with their girls, all four of them stifling their laughter—especially when Ginnie got to her part about throwing her lot in with the common man. Also: when the ex-Marine told all about his rugged combat experience with "The Corps", and then went on to say that what he really needed, he guessed, was a woman's gentle hand to guide him, a woman like her, like Ginnie.

Finally, Dewey and Hubie said, the two of them: the ex-Marine and Ginnie, got up and left Ciro's. Where they went for their romp, Dewey and Hubie didnt know. Anyway, they called a taxi. The ex-Marine was spending money, all right—whether his pension money, or his father's wheat money, he was throwing it around. Dewey and Hubie had heard Ginnie mention to him something about another, nicer bar named Smitty's out north by the railroad; so after the two of them left, Dewey and Hubie had collected their gals and gone on out there. And sure enough, about half an hour later, here came Ginnie and the ex-Marine, looking a little rumpled, and perhaps a little drunker, but still in fine fettle. Ginnie introduced him to all of them carefully (they had all already met him anyway), but she was very careful to keep him pretty much away from them. Probably, Dewey grinned, she didnt want them to say anything that might show up any discrepancies in her story.

Which was all right with them, Hubie grinned, because later on they all slipped into the next booth to them again, and listened to more of this talk. It was great. Really terrific. And it went on like that all evening: Ginnie appropriated just about every illustrious ancestor the town of Parkman possessed, even including old Anton Wernz II, and in fact retold the story of the railroad depot and the Madin Block where Smitty's resided, changing it a little however so that her ancestor Old Anton II came out the victor rather than Frank Madin. Hell, it was a great evening. And by the end of the evening, both pretty drunk, Ginnie and the ex-Marine were drunkenly holding hands in Smitty's and discussing how strange it was that Fate had had them meet.

To make a long story short, this drunken courtship went on for three more days—four days in all, that the ex-Marine stayed in town. He really did have money on him; wherever it came from. Because he really did throw it around, lavishly. And at the end of the four days, when he left, Ginnie had left with him—and get this, now!—to be married: She was returning with him to his father's rich wheat farm in Kansas to become his bride. She came around and, in her simpering smug way she had picked up since she took to sucking after Doris Fredric, had made sure that everybody knew about it. Several times, in fact. That night they left on the westbound bus for Kansas.

"Hell, maybe he really has got a rich old man who's a wheat farmer," Dewey said. "I dont know."

"Nope," Hubie said, categorically, "Ill stake my reputation on it that that guy was snowin her as much as she was snowin him. Pretty near as much, anyway." And he began to laugh again. "But did you get that? Banker's daughter! *Banker's* daughter, yet! God!"

Dave laughed with them, drunkenly, thinking about slobby old Ginnie the banker's daughter. He laughed with them both the first time they told it to him when he was very drunk, and also the second time they told it when he was not quite so drunk. It was, in fact, funnier than hell. Howlingly funny: The whirlwind four-day courtship: and plenty of beer.

But then, later on, after they had left with their drunken laughter, after telling it the second time, he got to thinking about it—alone in the house with 'Bama gone off somewhere—and it did not seem nearly so funny. Hell, now he didnt even have old Ginnie any more. First Gwen gone; then Ginnie, too. No: First Harriet Bowman: who married a lawyer. *Then* Gwen; *then* Ginnie. It seemed to be the story of his life. He couldnt even hold onto a poor slob like old Ginnie.

And what would he do for a woman, now, poor guy? —And what will Cock Robin do then, poor thing?— Yeah. There wasnt even one of the brassiere factory girls who would go out with him, now, any more. Even with Ginnie *gone*. Old man: fat and forty and broke and prospectless. Hell, they werent even winning their usual gambling money, any more.

But it did not really bother him. Not really. He had his drinking to think about. Nothing really bothered him, in fact. And to hell with everything. To hell with you, Gwen French! And he would go and get another drink. Slack, lax, apathetic with the perpetual three-quarter-drunkenness he remained in any more, all he had to do was go and get another drink. If panic struck him over Gwen, he would get another drink. If double-panic struck him over Ginnie Moorehead, he would get another drink. If triple-panic struck him over being fat and forty and broke and prospectless, he could always go and get two more drinks. If he could never get another woman again, well what the hell? As long as you stayed drunk, you didnt need a woman, didnt need the reassurance,—and in fact couldnt even do a woman any good, anyway, probably. So what the hell?

And yet, underneath it all, underneath the gin-bravado, the panic still lurked like some kind of spiritual indigestion, ready to rise up the first moment he let the alcohol level in his system get a bit too low. And not the least of its causes was that manuscript lying in there in that little writing room, gathering dust in there from week to week because he would never let Dewey's mother Vona clean the writing room: that manuscript: whenever he looked in at it and saw it, no matter how drunk he was, he had to go quick and have another drink. And have it right away.

And that was why he could not stop. That Gwen; that damned Gwen: She had made a writer out of him again, when he hadnt wanted to be a writer any more again, and now he was one, help it or not: and he was letting the manuscript lie there and rot because he was too drunk to work on it. That was why he couldnt stop: If he stopped, he would have to face the fact that he had wasted over two precious months of a nearly-forty-year-old life and on what? on being drunk and sorry for himself: two months, and more, that could never be regained. And that was why he couldnt stop. He could not face that; not without help.

Love. Love, love, love. Where was love? Where was love that would help, that would aid, that would save? Gwen?—Yes, and not even a word, not even a single word, when she left. Hell, even Ginnie was better than that: at least old Ginnie had warned him what she was going to do. He brooded more and more on that odd, somehow frightening night when he had lain beside old Ginnie out on the patio-porch and listened to Lois Wallup weeping in the kitchen, with its sudden sense of presentiment that had hit him so chillingly. Weeping for a home for her two kids. Home! Where was home? Where was home for anyone? Were we all to be forever homeless? Was this what old Bob French meant when he said each man must find his own salvation for himself, alone, and that it was a painful experience to learn? Forever homeless, except for whatever poor shack of a home you could build up inside yourself, without help, without aid, without succor from outside. Every man had to find his own salvation: and he, Dave Hirsh—DAVID HERSCHMIDT—just didnt have guts enough to look for his. Scalding his soul worse than any of the rest of it, than all of it put together, this would *always* drive him back to find another drink. And the manuscript continued to lie and gather dust.

He had meant to go back over to Israel to see Old Bob. But lethargy and apathy made him even incapable of that. He kept telling himself he would go, but he never did. Anyway what good could Bob do him? Hadnt he said himself no man could *really* help another? And anyway, he could not stand the thought of going there inside that house with so many myriad memories of Gwen, everywhere he looked. Hell, even Ginnie Moorehead, slobbish as she was, was more honest than Gwen. At least she told you. Gwen! Gwen!

Dewey and Hubie, at least, were a great help to him, anyway. They had been coming around more and more now, and without their girls. Whenever they were there, he could laugh with them, howl with laughter with them, over anything: sour, caustic, bitter, like the mean-looking broken-nosed no-longer-handsome Dewey had been laughing ever since his brother Raymond's death. At least there was that much release from pain.

But then Dewey and Hubie left. And there was nobody left but 'Bama.

They came around one day, both three-fourths drunk, to make their farewells and announce that finally they had at last decided to go back in the Army. After struggling with this momentous decision for six full months, they had at last made up their minds: They had weighed both sides, and had decided in favor of the Army: After all, what was there here for them, they said? A couple women that wanted to marry them and tie them down? A cheap job in some plant somewhere, where they could work away the rest of their lives and possibly, just possibly but not at all definitely, wind up like somebody like John Barclay with a little house they would still be paying on when they died? The unfound generation, Dewey had said; and now said again: What do we know but the Army? Whatever other training did we ever have? Well then, why not use it? We're both good soldiers; well-trained soldiers; why not go back to our trade, 'ey? Why not ply our trade we were apprenticed to for six years? —They were, in fact, acting out in their lives the very principle Dave had evolved for his novel and developed there: the modernday professional Roman legionary—though of course they were not aware of this.

(But Dave was; and wanted to weep, while they talked, thinking about that manuscript in there still gathering its dust.)

And besides, they added, the gov'mint's offerin to take back the World War II vets at the old ratings they had when they were discharged: offerin all kind of added inducements: and, by using a little pull here and there like an old soldier knew how to do, they ought to be able to fix it so they could stay together, in the same outfit.

They were the block the modernday prosperity was founded on, werent they: the old Army pros? and the defense industries? Why shouldnt they get in on as much gravy as they could? Theyd never get in on the rich living any other way.

And so, after one more heavily drunken party with Dave and 'Bama, they left, going to Chicago to reenlist.

And right away, without the comfort of that illusory companionship, everything started going from bad to worse. With them gone, and no longer around to laugh—however wrongly, Dave could no longer see himself and 'Bama and their situation as adventurous. Which only drove him back for more drinks, quicker.

He did not ever remember just exactly when they left. It was sometime in July, he was pretty sure; but in his benumbed, apathetic, befuddled state at the time, he could never be just sure afterwards when it was. He remembered distinctly—he thought—that it was Dewey and Hubie who had told him about his Old Man's death and funeral a week or so after it had happened. Or had that been 'Bama? Anyway, the Old Man had, he learned later, died on the Fourth of July; so that meant that Dewey and Hubie must have still been there around the middle of July. —If it was actually them who told him.— But whether they left then, or in early August, he never did know for sure. He had been too drunk too long to place events properly in their time sequence for nearly that entire summer, and he never could do so afterwards.

Finally, he got so bad off that even 'Bama got on him about it.

"Hell, at least I sober up a little bit anyways sometimes, when Ahm down at the farhm," he said drunkenly. "But you dont never sober up at all."

"So what?" Dave said lethargically, and equally drunkenly.

"Well, Ah just hate to see it, thas all," 'Bama said drunkenly. They were both sitting at the kitchen table, drinking. 'Bama's Southern accent got much stronger when he was drunker. "You got a talent, Dave. Thats why. And if you got a talent, you got yoreself an inborn duty to it. You aint done no writin on that book of yores for what—almost three months now. Hell, what do you think Ah tied up with you in the first place for?"

"Because I was bigshot Frank Hirsh's brother."

"Mebbe so; at the very first. But that aint why Ah went to Florida with you, and then taken this heah house with you. Ah admired you, and Ah admired yore talent. Hell, I used to respect you."

"I used to respect you, too," Dave said slackly.

"—And now—" 'Bama said drunkenly, and grinning bitterly, "—and now—we dont neither one of us respect the other."

It sounded like an epitaph, and was in fact a rather momentous statement, and Dave recognized it as such, drunk as he was. But it could not impinge upon his drunken apathy.

"Thats about the size of it, I guess," he said.

"Well, its yore life," 'Bama grinned. "And its yore book. I caint git you out of it."

"You want me to leave?" Dave said thickly. "After all, its you thats spendin all the money, and payin all the bills." Which was true. Dave had some time back run through all the money in his savings account: the money from the two stories, the accumulated money from his share of the taxi service, which was still paid to him; and now he was throwing his share of the taxi money, which wasnt very much, into the kitty every month. "Just you say the word," he said.

"Did Ah say that?" 'Bama said. "No. Yore welcome to stay here as long as you want. As long as we keep this place, anyway. It dont matter about me. Hell with me. But, man, you got a talent. You oughtnt to jus' throw it away."

"Why not?" Dave said drunkenly. "Its my talent."

After that, 'Bama said no more to him about it. But the acid accusation —at himself as well as at Dave; and Dave understood this—was often in his eyes. As a matter of fact, they had not in fact renewed the one-year lease on the house, which had fallen due in May—any more than they had, this year, worked any on their vacant-lot garden they had all expended so much energy and money to create last summer, and which was now growing back up in weeds, although the outlines of what they had done and the larger shrubs still remained. But Judge Deacon had arranged to sort of carry them along on a month-to-month basis with the house, handling it both for them and for the Albersons in Florida (who were not so particular about the social caste of their tenants, now they were away from town, as long as they got the money). Judge Deacon was doing this for them, until they could definitely make up their mind about it. Which, by the end of July they had not done. Neither of them was in any condition to do so, and what with the old life that had existed here for a year being totally gone now, neither one of them was sure of just which way the log would fall. And now they were both engaged in this protracted jag, which not only took all their time, but also sapped their energy.

What had made it change? Dave wondered, wonderingly. What had made it all change, from what it was a year ago? He had seen it coming, had felt it, almost, in his bones, that it was coming. Was it really true that Raymond Cole's death back in January had actually had something to do with it? Or was it that, back then, at about that same time, he had fatuously convinced himself he was no longer in love with Gwen French and that he had given up on her? Or was it the simple fact of Lois Wallup weeping bitter tears in the kitchen while he listened and pleading for a home for her two kids that somehow had caused it? had started that inexorable avalanche of mishaps sliding? He didnt know. Probably he never would know. He went back to get another drink.

It was not until some time in August that an event—any event; any event important enough to him personally—happened to cause him to start coming out of it. By that time, between them, he and 'Bama,—not counting Dewey and Hubie and the others, when they were still there—had consumed untold gallons of whiskey and gin, and probably never would entirely get over it, either one of them, physically. Especially 'Bama. But then, as Wally Dennis had once told him rather profoundly, as if he had just personally discovered this fact for the first time in history: The human body can stand an amazing amount of punishment and absorb it and still get over it, still recover. Old Wally, Dave thought dimly and affectionately (now that the kid was gone), wonder how hes likin the Army now?

The event that happened which started bringing him, at least somewhat out of it, was that he got a letter from Ginnie Moorehead, in Kansas. Delivered at the house where they got all the regular mail—almost none of which either of them received, any more; and Dave was receiving none—it lay for several days stuck in the mail holder of the mailbox on the porch, before Dave happened to see something white there one day as he was driving his little Plymouth carefully and drunkenly in from having been out at Smitty's. When he got it, and saw in the crabbed cramped almost illegible handwriting on the envelope who it was from, he wanted to laugh. When he took it inside and opened it, it read:

Dear Dave

I guiss you will be suprized to hear from me after this such longe time. Will you remember old Ginnie Moorehead that you use to date. Well I am living out hear in Kanzas and I aint happy. He lied to me Dave. His fathor dont have no big wheet farm atall. His fathor has a littel tiny shack of a plase where he grow a few littel akers and some truck patch. It is a horibel shack and I am the only woman. I hav to cook for both of them on a old wood range. It is teribel. Theres not no trees no plase for miles around. And the hot sun beat downe. When I cry he beats me up. I am very unhappy. He held a gun on me onct which he brung home from the Marynes and threaten to shoot me. If I ever trid to run away. Pleaze help me, Dave. I dont know nobody else to rite a letter to. I am afrad I will git killd. I am riting this leter secret. Pleaze help me. Pleaze send fiffty dolars to Gen'l Delivry. It is the only way I can git away. I relize now it was you I lovd all the time. But I did not know it. Pleaze help me. Pleaze send the mony. You the only one I can tern to. You are so kind and good. But I want you to know even if you do not send the mony I will always lov you anyways all my lif for

*ever and ever. But pleaze help me. Pleaze send the mony. Yore loving
frend*   *Ginnie Moorehead*

He did not know whether to laugh or cry over it, after he read it.
Mostly he just felt amazement at the spelling. Poor old Ginnie. And so
"Fate" had finally caught up to her too, just like the rest of us. That she
did indeed love him, Dave suddenly realized for perhaps the first time.
How did he look, he wondered, seen through her eyes? He was not naive
enough to think that all the protestations of love were not without
ulterior motive: i.e., getting away from that hellhole; but you couldnt
blame her for that. And in spite of that, some quality of real agony
seemed to reach him through the scrambled crabbed handwriting. Christ,
it was probably enough of an effort for her, to even write a letter, that
it would require a major cataclysm of some sort to even drive her to
such desperation. Suddenly, half drunk as he still was, and had been
for so long, he felt genuine pity for her. Everybody treated her like a
bum. And apparently he was the only one anywhere to whom she could
turn.

He showed the letter to 'Bama, when the big gambler came home, and
they both laughed—a little shamefacedly—over it; and yet there was
that same quality of—of pity; or of surprise; on 'Bama's face too.

"Well, yore goin to send her the money, aint you?" he asked. "Might
as well go ahead. I guess there aint no need for everybody to suffer as
much as you and me do. Not, anyway, when it can be prevented for
just fifty bucks. And I guess she wont be no worse off here than she was
before." Suddenly, he swore savagely. "Christ, now we'll have that slobby
bitch hangin around the place again like before."

Dave sent the money. He had to cash a check, and then get a money
order at the Post Office with the cash, so he had to shave and at least
clean himself up a little before going down into town proper. That
started it.

And then, quite suddenly, he began to sober himself up and to think
—for the first time in months—without fear about his book again. At
least there was somebody in the world who needed his help, a little bit,
anyway.

That day, after he had mailed her the money order according to her
instructions, he drove out North Main the crossstreet to the new bypass,
which had been opened up in June. He had never even seen it before;
or if he had, he had been too drunk to remember it. But then 'Bama had
told him about the tremendously huge new building that was going up
at the junction, and that Frank Hirsh was building it. It was supposed to
be some kind of a new-fangled "shopping center." So Dave drove out
to look at it.

It was indeed going up: almost all of the external brick and tile work had been completed and they were beginning to put the roof, the flat Western-style roof, on; and after he had parked his car off the pavement, without getting out however, and sat in it to look it over, he saw at the center of the right angle it was laid out in, the high facade rising up over all the rest of it upon which was spelled out in letters of green and yellow tile the legend: HIRSH BLOCK.

Old Frankie boy was really getting up there, and he remembered how once—so very long ago, it was; when he first returned to Parkman— Frank had wanted him to go in with him permanently. After a while, he turned around and drove back home.

CHAPTER 67

FRANK was out at the Shopping Center, as it happened, when Dave drove out to look at it; but he did not see his brother's car. He was far too busy. But if he had seen it, he would not have done anything. Except perhaps look at it a moment, and feel a little bit superior, and say to himself those most delicious of all words: "I told you so; but you wouldnt listen to *me;*" and then go back to the plans he was discussing with the architect. He had offered Dave a chance, once, to go in with him; and Dave had turned it down because he just didnt have the faith, just didnt be*lieve,*—that his brother would ever accomplish all the things he said he would. Now, he was being shown: just like everybody was being shown.

Success had dropped its mantle upon Frank Hirsh like a large tent (or like a large rock, he thought) and while its material was of beautiful texture, complete with gold thread and encrusted designs, and he loved it, it nevertheless came damned close to suffocating him sometimes. If Frank had thought he was busy back in May, when the bypass was being poured and all the too-late speculators were scrambling for sites, he just, by God, didnt know nothin'. Back in May was as nothing compared to what happened to him after the Parkman Village started to go up, and the news got bruited about as to just what it was, and that he was building it. He had never rushed around so much, or met with so many people so much, or talked so damned much, in his life before.

The Greek and the old man, Clark's father in law, were doing it up brown—true to their strictly-adhered-to principle of quality before everything. But in this case there was quantity as well as quality. Quantities of quality. They were spending the money. Having decided to go into it, they were—as they both did in everything else they invested in—practically pulling the stopper clean out of the bottle. There were to be twelve places of business in the unit, five along the short side of the L and seven along the long side, and space for nearly three hundred cars in the parking lot inside the angle. And Frank was handling the whole thing. It was not his money, but he had the spending of it; and to all intents and purposes that made it the same thing as if it was his money. —Of course, part of it was his money: a small percentage: all, in fact, that he could beg, borrow and steal and scrape together to put into it: just a little over a hundred thousand dollars: which was a little less than one-fifth of the total since the whole Shopping Center operation alone without counting any filling stations or anything else was going to run close to seven hundred thousand to build. And that one-fifth was everything he could put his fingers on, with the liberal credit they were giving him in Springfield. But his share figured to pay itself out entirely in six months or less, which would bring him entirely out of debt—and therefore give him just that much more to pour back in.

So some of it was his money. But most of it was not, and he knew it. But, since he had the spending of it, it was just the same as if it was his; because everybody had to come to him: contractors, architects, salesmen, everybody. And he reveled in it.

But all this was only a small portion of his time that was being taken up so fully: He was making innumerable trips to Springfield; he was consulting constantly with the architect firm (one of whom was on the spot at all times; had, in fact, just moved himself down from Chicago for the duration; oh, they were sparing nothing, the Greek and the old man); he was also constantly consulting with the contractors, too; he was constantly consulting with salesmen of all the plumbing appliances and other appliances. But this was only a small part of his time.

Because, once it became known in town just what this place was going to be, every businessman in the county was on his back. He had to talk to one right after another of them, all day long, and then go right on back to talking to the same ones over again all day long the next day. They were, all of them, placed in damned near an untenable position by the Parkman Village Shopping Center. They were placed in the position of either having to open a branch store themselves in the Shopping Center, or be faced with the fact that they were going to be facing new competitors—all housed in a bright shining modern beautiful new store. Almost without exception, this meant—temporarily, at least—overextending themselves, to open a branch store. The only other choice was losing a large volume of business to a new competitor in a brand new store. So naturally, most of them were a little worried.

And Frank Hirsh was the man they all had to come to.

And Frank talked to all of them. Both singly, and in groups, at meetings. Because there were innumerable meetings. He talked to just about every businessman's club in town: the Chamber of Commerce, the Junior Chamber of Commerce, the Rotary (his old pals), the Kiwanis, the Lions, everybody. He made speeches to them all. And invariably his speeches were the same: he took the line that the new Shopping Center was intended mainly to be based on tourist business. This would mean, of course, that it would not actually take business away from town; at least not too much, anyway. And as added assurance, he always pointed out that the motel and the theater were the priority items of the next things he intended to build.

All this was not, of course, the truth. And what was more, everybody knew it was not the truth—though they all pretended that they thought it was. But there was nothing anybody could do about it. They either had to come in, and go along, or else get out and risk losing a lot of business to a new place. The result was that, with one or two exceptions, all the leases for business places that were gradually built up in his files were for branch stores to be opened by already established hometown merchants. Only the very top business houses in town were even being considered: Frank had discussed this with the Greek and the old man, and both agreed with him emphatically that he should keep the level—and the price—up just as high as they could possibly make it. Consequently, all the second rate competitors were out from the start, and just had to sit and suffer in it. And of the top-rate ones, that were being considered, it was made quite plain to them the high level of the stores they were expected to maintain, and this was written into the leases. The leases themselves, naturally, since everybody was scrambling for one of them, came very high.

Together with the Greek and the old man, Frank had planned it so that once it was completed and in operation, the Parkman Village would be as nearly completely an autonomous business section as it was possible to make it with only twelve business sites. In other words, there would not be two hardware stores, for instance; or two drugstores; or two jewelry stores. (Frank himself, of course, was taking the lease for the jewelry store; and intended to move Al Lowe out there as manager and let someone else run the old store in town.) But take hardware stores, for example. In Parkman there were actually already three hardware stores. Two of these were pretty good; the third a poor one. The poor one was out—although Frank had to talk to the owner at least eight times, to convince him, in a kindly way of course—but the other two, the better stores, both badly wanted the lease in the Shopping Center. Consequently, Frank was able to play one off against the other. And, in the end, the hardware store lease brought as much as any other lease in the unit. And it was the same way with the other businesses they decided they would let in. In short, the Parkman Village Shopping Center Corporation consisting of the Greek and the old man and Frank Hirsh, and Clark himself as a silent partner, was in a very enviable position.

And Frank himself, at least from Frank's viewpoint, was in the most enviable position of all. There were times, when he would stand out on the dirt within the angle of the L where the blacktopped parking lot would eventually be, and look up at that beautiful green and yellow facade with its attractive legend: HIRSH BLOCK, that Frank could hardly believe it had all really happened. He even felt like pinching himself to prove he wasnt dreaming, a number of times, but of course he never did for fear someone might be watching. But HIRSH BLOCK! and he would look up again. The dream he had held for so very, very long in his secret heart was at last a reality: HIRSH BLOCK. 1949. Just like MADIN BLOCK or WERNZ BLOCK or PARKER BLOCK. HIRSH BLOCK. He could not get enough of saying it, or of seeing it.

He had had, in the end, to take out offices after all. Trying to work at the store, and spend the other times in the offices of the people he was seeing, just did not work out once the local business owners began to descend on him. Also, there were the conferences necessary with the architect and the contractors; the little office at the store would not even hold all the blueprints that had to be spread out, and read, and studied; let alone get them all onto his own desk in the corner. So finally he had wisely succumbed to the increasing pressure. The offices he took— with the notice painted immediately on the glass door for him, at his order: FRANK HIRSH & SON ENTERPRISES—were upstairs over the drug store on the west side of the square directly opposite from his own store on the east side. When he first moved in, he seriously debated moving Edith Barclay in right along with him as secretary and clerk; but at the last minute he decided, with some wary instinct, not to do so. He could always move her in later on; and in fact, she was badly needed at the store, was almost irreplaceable, now that he himself was having to take his hands off of the running of it entirely. So instead he hired a new girl, a pretty little thing, just out of Business College, but green as a gourd.

One of his reasons for doing so, was that he had become increasingly nervous about Agnes, lately. She just didnt seem to be as warm as she had been early this year, and last year. He didnt see where there was any reason for her not to be, and maybe it was only an old habit pattern; but some instinct kept telling him to be careful; be careful.

Of course, a lot of it might be—and probably was—due to how hard he was having to work now that the Parkman Village was going up. He was forced to spend a great many more evenings out and away from home and Agnes and young Walter, and away from Edith too. Hell, it seemed he hardly ever got to see Walter any more. He did get to take him to three big league games in St Louis; Frank saw to that. Even though it meant throwing up his work schedule entirely on each of the days they went, and having to work like hell to catch up after they got back. But he intended to see that Walter got to see some big league games, by God; come hell or high water. But outside of those days, he really got to see his new son very little any more. Almost every night, it seemed, there was some damned meeting he had to go to. Some deputation of salesmen of appliances who could not be squeezed in during the course of the day; some group of damned businessmen who wanted to be reassured about the Parkman Village Shopping Center; some sudden emergency with the architect or the contractors that had to be taken care of immediately.

Sometimes, when these things happened, as they did increasingly after June, Frank wished he had never gotten started in on this damned thing. It was at those times that he felt he might very well be suffocated by the cloth of gold of success. But then, a look at the big facade out at the Parkman Village and those beautiful green and yellow tile reading HIRSH BLOCK always reassured him.

And of course, all these busy evenings meant that he had to spend much less time with Edith than he would have liked. And damn it all, especially now—when they had got her house for her. He loved to go there, and sprawl around on the couch in the tasteful living room and look at all of it, have a flock of drinks, and then go to bed with her in their own bed.

He had been especially careful in the handling of Edith's house. The Greek, in Springfield, had gladly and cheerfully handled it for him. His boys, the Greek's boys, could do just about anything. Frank had gone to him, to the Greek, in preference to going to Clark's father in law because Clark's father in law knew Agnes well, whereas the Greek only knew her slightly. Anyway, the old man was so damned sedate and kind of austere; although Frank knew for a fact the old boy had at least two mistresses himself. But the Greek understood things like this, Frank felt instinctively.

The Greek had handled it all very shrewdly and cannily for him. The money had been paid to Edith in a lump sum check drawn on a Springfield bank, and using the official name of one of the Greek's business fronts, which name—reading as it did—might very easily be taken for the name of some obscure insurance company. Edith had deposited it personally in the bank in Parkman. Nobody seemed to think a thing about it; it all went off just beautifully. And she had begun the fixing up, and buying for, and redecorating of her house. Frank, of course, could not be with her; but on the nights when they still met in some motelroom somewhere, she would discuss it with him and tell him all about what she was doing and planned to do. He wished he could have gone with her and helped her select things. But, when it was all finally done, and she had moved in, and Frank himself went there for the first time (he always parked the Cadillac up town and walked the three blocks to the house), all that discomfort faded away in his enjoyment of his mistress and his mistress's house.

Damn it all, he didnt see why Agnes had to be so damned ornery and old-fashioned about these things. He would have liked for them to be friends, Agnes and Edith, close friends. He would have liked to go places with them together. Hell, here they were, just about to make more damned money than they could even spend, just about to move up into the very highest rank in Parkman; why the hell couldnt they be sophisticated about it like other people and do like they did. Hell, if they were going to be rich, they ought to act rich. They ought to be sophisticated like the rich people they would live among. But not Agnes.

Edith herself, he was quite sure, wouldnt have minded about being known as his mistress—not any more, at any rate; not since old Janie Staley's death. Frank had never seen a person change so much, as Edith had changed since Janie died. He did not know what had caused it, but he was certainly all for it.

There was still that strange turbulence about Edith—that strange sort of double-naturedness, sort of, was the only way he could describe it—that had been in her, back when he had first seduced her: that whatever-it-was that had made her seem so cold, outwardly, and most of the time, but when sex itself came up changed suddenly into a sort of heated franticness. Frank remembered still, how she had groaned so strangely and suddenly that first time he had kissed her in the car. Well, these things were still in her as before—but now, somehow or other they had changed their quality: She was, if anything, more cold and far away and selfcontained, outwardly; but then on the other hand when they went to bed now there was an almost hungry wild rapaciousness about her now, was the only way he could describe it. And she would not let go of him until long afterwards. Long after their "party" was over, she would continue to cling to him, rub her face against him, and sort of nurse herself on the skin of his shoulder with her lips. And as far as the sex itself went, she was wildly the leader of it—in everything. Frank was, naturally, pleased. He had never known anything like it. It was as if she could not get enough of him. He had never thought he was that attractive. Naturally, he did not intend to lose this kind of love for anything, not for anything in God's earth.

By contrast, Agnes had been getting cooler and cooler when they went to bed together. He had noticed it for some time now, and it bothered him. It was almost something like the way she had acted before she broke him off from Geneve Lowe, and he wondered if she could possibly have found out about Edith? But how could she have? Everything had gone off as smooth as silk, about the house. It had been a brilliant idea to handle it as though it was old Jane's insurance money that Edith bought it with; if he did say so himself. And it had gone off smooth as glass. So how could Agnes possibly know? Nevertheless, he worried about it.

He wanted his wife to love him. Love him as she had been the past year or so that they had been so very happy together. Love him as his mistress was loving him. She still went to bed with him, of course, Agnes did. Whenever he asked her. But there still was, he felt, this noticeable cooling of her ardor.

Frank wished he could talk to her about it; but he was afraid to. He was afraid she might be insulted, and get her feelings hurt in thinking he didnt find her desirable any more. But that wasnt it, at all. He just wanted her to desire *him* more. If he could only talk to her about it, maybe he could find out what it was that was bothering her. But he was scared to try to, because then she would know that he had recognized this cooling of the ardor between them. So he just pretended that he did not notice it at all. And as long as he did that, he could not, of course, bring it up and talk about it.

He wished he could talk to her about other things, too, for that matter. He wished he could just sit down calmly with her and explain to her what it was to have a mistress. How it didnt really mean anything at all: hell, lots of men had mistresses and they and their wives got along all right, and clearly deeply loved each other. Frank was sure of that. Why did she have to be so damned old-fashioned about it? Here they were, with the whole world by the tail, just preparing to make more money, more good cash money, than they had ever dreamed it would be their good fortune to possess. Here they were, all set up in an operation that within two or three years could very easily make them— he almost breathed the magic word, not even really daring to say it, hardly daring to think it—make them Millionaires. Yes, by God, Millionaires.

What did it matter if he had himself a mistress, like other—other— Millionaires? He would still be her husband, he would still buy her everything under the sun, he would still take care of her, give her all the money she ever wanted, and look after and live with her and Walter. He would still love her, and be her lover. Her own dear sweetheart husband lover.

If he could only dare talk to her, reasonably and rationally, and explain it. But the very thought was unthinkable. It panicked him down to the very depths of his soul to even think of daring to talk to her about it.

Once again, for the first time since that wild strange night in Springfield not quite a year ago when he had walked the ratty backstreets of the city all night long, Frank began to have vague stirrings to get up at night and walk the streets. Not for any special reason. Just to see. Just to look. Just to feel the strange nervous excitement as he looked at houses and lights and wondered what their occupants might be doing?

Just to be out there, alone and unknown, out there where there might be adventure. Where there might be—danger. And as June and July slipped on into August, he took to getting up and going out at night. He would get himself real drunk beforehand, there at home, real three-quarters drunk, knowing excitedly what he was going to do later; then he would lie in bed staring at the ceiling sleeplessly and tinglingly excited, until he knew Agnes was sound asleep; then get up quietly out of bed and dress and go out and walk up and down the streets of Parkman. If they knew he was out here, looking at their houses, they would be disturbed. This was his hometown. He had been born here. This was his hometown, and he bet there must be an awful lot of stuff went on in this little old town. He never did anything. He never approached any houses. He just walked. And when he was up in Springfield on his frequent trips, he took to going out at night like that again up there. Gee, if he could only talk to Agnes about Edith.

Well, he knew one thing for sure: Whether she ever found out about it or not, he was not giving up Edith Barclay: He was not going to give up the kind of loving he was getting from Edith Barclay for *any*thing, for anything in God's apple green world.

But still, Frank thought hopefully, maybe it was all his imagination. Maybe it was all the work he was having to do now and that was keeping him away from home so much. Maybe she didnt really suspect anything about Edith at all. Fervently, Frank hoped not.

Gee, if he could only talk to her about it, he thought plaintively, and explain what having a mistress really meant, and was. It meant being a rich man, for one thing; a rich sophisticated man. And as to what it *was*—it was only one of the basic rights a man who worked as hard as he did had earned, and deserved, and ought to have. And it didnt mean a damn thing about how he felt about his wife. If he could only talk to her.

As it turned out, Frank was to talk to her about it much sooner than he knew.

CHAPTER 68

AGNES Hirsh found out definitely that her husband was having an affair with his office girl Edith Barclay just a few days after the day Dave drove out to look at the bypass and new Shopping Center in early August.

She had been waiting for the news almost a month—and hoping desperately that what she suspected was the truth would not turn out to be so. And in fact, when she initiated her investigation and started the machinery rolling that would either prove or disprove what she suspected, she could not help but believe fervently that it would prove her wrong. It was nearly unthinkable for her to believe anything else. They, she and Frank, had been so very fully and completely happy the last year or so, that she *couldnt* believe anything else. She just simply could not believe that he would take up with another woman, not while that had been going on, and when they were so happy together. And as a matter of fact, she had started her investigation more to allay her own fears, and prove to herself what a meanly suspicious woman she was, than for any other reason. If she proved herself and her suspicious mind wrong, it would put her mind at rest, and she could begin her act of contrition. But, it had not proved her wrong. It had proved her suspicious mind was right. And the proof just very nearly tore her apart.

There were times when, devoutly, despairfully, painfully, Agnes wished fervently that she were not so smart;—or else that Frank was not so dumb. If she could only be, could only have *been*, a dumb trusting ignorant housewife, just some country housewife, who went along her dumb ignorant trusting way, without ever realizing how her smart husband was hoodwinking her. But she was not that. And Frank was not that smart husband.

—Although she had to admit, painfully and unhappily, that he was pretty smart; this time. The trouble was, he just wasnt smart enough. Damn it. She could almost wish he were.

It seemed to Agnes that the more rich and influential they got, the more this kind of a thing receded to other, more impersonal levels: For instance, in the affair of Geneve Lowe: Agnes had done all her field work herself: buying the glassware, going down to Dotty Callter's, etc. But this time, contrasting with that so strongly, she merely sat back, did her figuring and planning, and then simply wrote a couple of letters. She supposed it must be the same way with wars or politics: The higher up you got, the more removed you were from the actual field operations, and the more theoretical it became. Of course, she didnt know, but she suspected this.

It had all started, of course, with Frank asking to have old Janie Staley and her granddaughter Edith seated "within the ribbon" at Dawn's wedding. He never should have done that. That was really incredibly dumb of him. He had handled it shrewdly, but it was nonetheless dumb. She had thought nothing of it at the time, what with old Jane being sick and all. And in fact, she had not thought of it at the wedding either when she saw them sitting there together; she had been far too upset and busy with everything else she had to do, and with making her own entrances and exits. And yet, looking back later, it was as if in some automatic calculator way, it had all registered with her then, right then, to be filed away and digested later. Mostly, it was

Edith's face: when she saw it then—and then when she observed it later, at other times: Edith's face was so closed and so selfcontained, so efficient and so careful: A girl that young just oughtnt to have that kind of a face, Agnes felt. And it had struck her, forcibly.

She did nothing at the time, and indeed thought nothing, actually. Was not even suspicious. But later on, when Edith bought herself a house on her grandmother's insurance money, the automatic calculator tumblers in Agnes' head suddenly seemed to fall into place, and a string of knowledge symbols poured out of it. In the first place, she was mildly surprised to find old Janie actually had that much insurance. It just didnt seem like Jane—although she always talked about insurance, and could indeed actually have had that much. But the second thing, even more disturbing to Agnes's rationality, was the fact that after Edith did buy and redecorate her house—she did not ask her father to come live in it with her! John Barclay continued to live in his own little cheap place out on Roosevelt Drive, and batched there with a housekeeper to cook and clean for him—presumably paid for by Edith's insurance money.

Agnes could not quite bring herself to believe that Frank would ever actually buy the girl a house, even if he was sleeping with her. —But how could he be? how could he be sleeping with her? after as close as they had been this past year— But even so: not a house. Not the way Frank liked money. And not the way he had been scraping everything together to put into his new Shopping Center. But then, that was largely a thing of the past now: the scraping; from now on it would be the collecting. And she had also become gradually aware that Frank had acquired really powerful contacts and supporters in Springfield. Much more than she had ever really given him credit for having —no matter how much he might talk—until just lately. All of this added up together to the fact that he *could* have bought the girl a house; though Agnes still doubted it, and felt a rather awed wonder to think that he might have.

But then, everything had changed, lately, for them: in the past year. And now with the Shopping Center going steadily up every day, was— and would be—changing even more. They had become really rich. And were really viewed as such, in the town. Frank had been saying it would be so for a year, and had told Dawnie so when she insisted on marrying, but Agnes had never really actually believed him—not, at least, to the extent which he maintained they would rise. But it had happened, just the same, just like he said, and there was no getting around it: It was clearly apparent from the invitations and offers of friendship she had been getting: They were moving right up in with the Wernzes and the Scotts and the Crowders.

When, after repeatedly—and sort of hopelessly—analyzing the knowledge her automatic calculator had presented her with, she finally decided to make her move to find proof—or disproof—she found it amazingly easy to do. Just about everybody was willing to help her—without even asking any questions, or wanting to know why. Agnes had discovered, finally, that she had almost limitless satellites.

She moved cautiously. First, there was the check Edith had received for the "insurance money." Almost certainly it would not be from Frank himself; he would surely have had someone send it—if it were indeed from him. Second, there was the insurance itself.

The check she found out about from Mrs Florence Duboise, who worked at the Second National Bank as a cashier. Mrs Florence Duboise had been a member of Agnes' former bridgeclub; and Agnes still saw her occasionally, though of course she could not see her as often as she used to, what with the flocks of new invitations she and Frank were getting now. But she had also been careful to keep Mrs Florence Duboise as a friend—as indeed, she had done all her old-time associates: no use antagonizing anybody. Mrs Florence Duboise, at tea, was most obsequiously anxious to tell Agnes everything she knew about everything. So obsequious in fact, that it rather disgusted Agnes; though of course she never let it be known. The talk, deftly, was brought around to poor old Janie Staley, who had used to work for Agnes, and her death. Agnes even wept a few tears: real tears they were; for Janie. She was so glad that Jane had been wise enough to have taken out insurance; which had turned out to be such a fine thing for her granddaughter. Edith would never have been able to buy herself such a darling little house if it had not been for the thoughtfulness of old Janie, and Agnes was very glad for her. When Mrs Florence Duboise left, Agnes had the name of the company upon which the rather large insurance check had been drawn—and had it without Mrs Florence Duboise even suspecting in the slightest that she had given any information which had been wanted or desired.

The insurance Agnes handled an entirely different way. Although in her techniques of doing so she employed the same forces: She merely wrote a letter to another very dear friend of hers like Mrs Florence Duboise in Indianapolis. Mrs Georgia Sheldon was a divorcee who had made a good settlement and moved to Indianapolis and employed herself with one of the oldest insurance houses in the city, as a private secretary. She was an excellent private secretary, and her boss could not do without her. She did not remarry.

Mrs Georgia Sheldon, while having moved to Indianapolis, still had relatives in Parkman and visited there often, and had up until just lately been a good close friend of Agnes, who had often entertained her. The situation was somewhat the same as with Mrs Florence Duboise: Agnes just had not had time to spend as much time with Georgia Shel-

don as formerly—but she had, nevertheless, been careful to keep her
as a friend just like she had Mrs Florence Duboise. And Georgia was
just as anxiously, if not as obsequiously, eager to be of help to Agnes as
Mrs Florence Duboise was—what with the turn the fortunes of the
Frank Hirshes had taken in the last year. In her letter to Georgia she
merely asked if Georgia could find out for her if any large insurance
policies had ever been issued to Mrs Jane Staley. (Georgia had told her
once, conversationally, that such information could always be had, if
one knew how to go about getting it.) Agnes did not tell her why she
wanted the information. She did not need to. Not with Georgia Sheldon:
Georgia had not been private secretary to a big important man for
years for nothing: She never said anything to anybody about *any*thing;
and she never asked anybody questions when questions were not needed.
In her letter, couched in the form of simply a friendly, newsy, conversational letter, Agnes also asked if Georgia knew anything at all—or
could find out anything—about an obscure little company in Springfield,
and gave the name of the company that had been on the check.

It was the answer to this letter that came back to her early in
August, nearly a month later. Whether it took that long because
Georgia Sheldon had had to hunt that long for the information, or
whether Georgia merely assumed the matter was not urgent from the
tone of Agnes's letter and was herself busy with other things, Agnes
didnt know. Anyway, it had been a bad long month for Agnes—and
not only because of the hot weather.

Most of the time, she felt guilty as hell. It was a shameful thing to
do to poor Frank—when he so obviously, she was quite sure, loved
her as much as he did. And in fact, she told herself, over and over, she
did not actually believe it herself—she *couldnt* believe it—that Frank
was actually having a hot and heavy love affair with some strip of a
girl—or with *any* other woman—when he and she had been so loving
and close for so long. It would have been a personal indignity, a personal affront, of such magnitude that no husband in the world would
have done it to his wife—not when he was loving her as much and
going to bed with her as often as Frank was. And Frank would not
do that to her. And actually, she told herself, she was only writing the
damned letter just to prove it to herself, and put her mind at ease—just
to *show* herself what a really foul, suspicious-minded bitch she was.
And she hated herself for doing it.

But there had, she knew, been a noticeable falling-off of their lovemaking the past month or two. And she knew, also, that this was
entirely her fault: She just was not as warm and ardent as she had
been. She couldnt be. She just couldnt help it. And she knew Frank
had sensed it, and was disturbed by it. Although he never said anything.
And most of all, she wanted to rectify this. To get things back to where

they had been. If she could just clear her own mind, they could get everything back to what it had been. Maybe, when she proved to herself how wrong she was, she would confess it to him. Would he be angry? Or would he only be amused? If she was sure he would only be amused—then it would clear the air: and they would have back their old warmth and closeness.

Most of the time, truthfully, Agnes was wanting to kick herself right in the tail, painfully, angrily, for being the kind of suspicious bitch she was.

But the rest of the time, other times, she would be filled with such a furious anger and indomitable rage at the thought that it *might* be true, that she would actually shake inside. If it *was* true— If it was true—and he had been actually doing this to her, secretly, while she had been giving herself, her whole soul to him— Well, it was such a personal indignity, an actual *physical* indignity, to her very body, that she could hardly bear to even think of it. It made her feel sickened all over. If it was true, she would think flamingly, then she would make him pay, make him pay and pay and pay, in some such horribly unspeakable way, that he would wish fervently that he had never ever even seen a woman before. *Any* woman. —But then the guilt would return and haunt her, at what an unspeakable suspicious bitch she was. It wasnt true. It just couldnt be true.

When the letter from Georgia Sheldon arrived, finally arrived, Agnes sat with it at her secretary, unopened. Feeling weak and shaky and already half sick from days of stewing, she sat for a long time with it that way, unopened, the seal not broken, and just looked at it. She was half way tempted to throw it away, to take it out and burn it, and not open it and find out whether her suspicions were right or wrong. She was, in fact, almost afraid to open it. Either way, whether she was right, or whether she was wrong, she was going to feel terrible. If she was right, she would feel horrible and hopeless, degraded, actually degraded in the dirt, at what he, Frank, her own husband had done to her. But if she was wrong, she would feel even worse, perhaps: She would have to face what a jealous, mean, suspicious old harridan of a bitch she really was. Actually, she wasnt sure which was worse, in a way. Right then, she promised herself religiously—before God—that if she was wrong, she would make a full confession of what she had done, make it to Frank this very night. —No, it couldnt be tonight; he was in Springfield again. Well, she would do it tomorrow when he returned. She promised herself that, as a penance. But even so, even after promising herself, she still sat and looked at the letter—with its neatly typed address, and the printed return of Georgia's company up in the corner—looked a long time, without opening it. Should she really burn it? But if she did, how would she ever *know?* for sure? Finally, her fingers trembling and awkward, she got her letter knife and slit it.

It was all there. Neatly typed by Georgia, and couched in the same friendly, newsy type of letter she herself had written, it was all there. —ridiculous, to get such black horrible news as that, in such a breezy happy friendly letter—— There had never been any large insurance policies issued to Mrs Jane Staley of Parkman Illinois by any company. There had been one small policy of $500 issued to her years ago by some obscure cheap firm. And the company in Springfield, which Agnes had mentioned, was *not* an insurance company but was an investment firm, bonds and real estate, and an insurance *agency*. Of course, Georgia did not know that she, Agnes, had even thought it was an insurance company; she was only telling the facts. She, Georgia, had had to go through a credit reference firm she knew to get this information, which was one reason she had not answered sooner. The firm was apparently a front organization, one of many, for a very wealthy speculator from Chicago and Springfield, and she gave the name of Frank's Greek friend, who was in with him and with Clark Hibbard's father in law in the building of the Shopping Center.

Agnes read it all through—at least, she read the parts with the information all through; she did not even bother to read the rest of the friendly letter—— —How could she bear to? a breezy happy letter—and then merely sat and looked at it. It was all there, and it was exactly what she had suspected. Her jealous, mean, bitchy, suspicious-minded mind had been accurately, and exactly, right.

Well, she tried to tell herself desperately—for a moment—well, maybe she was still wrong. This didnt prove that it was Frank who bought the house for her. Maybe it had been some other man, who also knew the Greek. It could be that. She tried to cling to this thought, desperately, for a moment; but it wasnt any good. Her mind wouldnt let her cling to it. She *knew*.

That was the worst. She did know. That he could do this to her—when they had been so very warm and close this past year. That was the most horrible, most exquisitely hurtful thing of all. That he could, behind her back, and while making ardent love to her, actually do this to her. Agnes could not even describe to herself what it made her feel. Once, not long ago, she had read a book on the Nazi War Crimes Trials and on the concentration camps, and in it had been a horrible picture of naked women being forced to run across a field in front of German soldiers. And that was how this made her feel. The indignity done to those poor women was not less than the personal indignity that had been done to her—by her own *husband*. That was how she felt. An actual violation of her person. A degradation no less strong than if she had been stripped naked and tied with a rope and dragged through all the filth and mire in the world.

Piecing it all together, while she sat staring at the news she would have given anything not to have had to learn, she figured back and decided, accurately, that he had actually in fact been sleeping with this young chit of a whore *before* he had even gone back to sleeping with *her,* with Agnes. It violated every concept of love that she had ever been taught or had learned or believed. She had broken him loose from that damned coldblooded Geneve Lowe; and he had sulked for months afterwards. And she had known he would come back to her, and had waited patiently. And now she knew the *real* reason why he had come back: He had gotten over his smart by taking up with this little chippy, when she Agnes did not know about it, and so had assuaged his vanity at being triumphed over; and that was why he had been willing to come back, magnanimously, to her. And all the time he had been— So really, in the true fact of the matter, it hadnt been love that had brought him back at all. Not love for her, Agnes, at all. What brought him back, really, was just that he thought he had outsmarted her, and could degrade her in that way. Yes, degrade her. So now, Agnes knew the whole truth of everything. Weak and shaky, she sat at the secretary and looked at the letter, unbelievingly.

And not only that, he had bought his whore a *house;* a *house* of her *own.* —And not only *that,* he had gone through his business friend the Greek—who had met Agnes herself, and had been right here in their home—to do it; had gotten this Greek man, whom Agnes knew and would be meeting again, to do this job for him.

Well, she was not going to have it. She was not going to put up with it, she was not going to have it. He had destroyed her; but he was not going to continue to destroy her.

But, as she sat thinking about it in a flaming pain and rage of hurt and indignation and humiliation, as she cast about in her mind for the best way to break this thing up, it suddenly dawned upon Agnes that there wasnt really much of anything she could do about it. If she did not intend to put up with it, and she did not, just what actually could she do to stop it? she asked herself. And immediately after that question, she discovered a big blank space. This situation was not the same as it had been with Geneve Lowe, not the same at all: Geneve had had her job and her reputation to look after. This girl, this Edith, held her job with Frank; only Frank could fire her. Also, what was more important, she had her house; and she could live in it forever if she wanted to. Her house, that was bought and was paid for and was in her own name.

You could not even go to her father about it. Although anyone who even considered going to John Barclay about *any*thing was already grasping at straws.

Frank had fixed it up pretty sharply, fixed it up so it was nearly ironclad. There were no handles sticking out anywhere for her to grasp. And that house—especially that damned house. That changed everything. He would never have been able to have done it, would never have been able to get this far along with it, go this far, if she had not been off her guard. But she had been off her guard. And for why? Because she had been fool enough, and soft enough, to think he really loved her, was really in love with her again. Oh, fool, fool!

Well, it had always been that way, hadnt it? Why did she let herself get taken in by him? The truth was, he had never loved her; never, even from the first. He had used her, just like he used everything and everybody in his life that he could get his fingers on. But most of all he had used *her*: her work, her energy, her time and thought and planning and managing, even her money: her own father's store, were all the things that had put him where he was today. And what did he do with his first success? Did he buy her something? Did he give her something? He did not. He went out and got himself a mistress, a cheap little mistress, granddaughter of a cleaning woman, and bought a house for her and installed her in it. And she, his wife, who had worked for him, and with him, and advised him all these years, was expected to simply sit back and accept this humiliation in the eyes of the town—while he happily visited his cheap little mistress in her house he had bought for her. *Bought* for her. Paid how many *thousands* of dollars out for?

Well, it was what she got for marrying beneath her: he was nothing but a bum, a jewelry store clerk, when she married him —and gave him, just *gave* him, her own father's store. Agnes had broken him away from one trashy woman after another, all these years she had done it, one right after the other, and now here was another one: only this time he had gone even further: had bought her a *house!* What kind of a woman was it, who would accept a *house* from a married man?

Oh, she knew who he was trying to imitate: old Al Dorner who had made all that oil money and installed his mistress in a house of her own: and Tony Wernz, whose mistress had an apartment in the best apartment house in town. And what did they have? Both of their wives hated their guts. If Al Dorner had dropped dead in front of old Lucy Dorner, she would have stood and laughed happily in his face. And those were the kind of people he was trying to imitate! God! Righteous outrage filled her.

But down underneath it, down underneath all this rage and mental tirade, was still the pain: the throbbing, aching, surging pain: that he would have done this to her: when they had been so close, so very close, and so happy. And had, in fact, actually started it even before they had been that happy. He had bastardized it, bastardized it all, before it was even begun. Had killed it. Before it even started. That pain was in her. And she knew it was something she would never, ever, get over.

Sitting at her secretary, still looking down at Georgia Sheldon's letter, her eyes full of tears of rage and misery and humiliation, and just plain helplessness, Agnes suddenly got up from the secretary, leaving the letter lying there, and walked shakily out into the diningroom and sat down at the table.

Well, there was nothing else for it. Shed have to accost him with it: with her proof: with the letter. There was no other way of handling this one, like there had been with Geneve Lowe. It would put her to bed sick, and be a horrible ordeal. But she was not going to live the life of a Lucy Dorner.

It never occurred to her that he would not give his mistress up. Agnes had done this same thing many times before. Oh, God, how many times? It always worked. Once she confronted him with incontrovertible proof—on paper; material solid proof—he always dropped them as if he had hold of a hot brick. And then, eventually, guiltily returned to the fold. Well, there would be no returning to *her* fold this time. She was through. She had had it. There would be no more of this "year of happy love" stuff—while all the time he was slipping out with some other woman behind her back. She would break him loose from his mistress; she had to do that; and she would remain his wife. But that was all, and damn him. Oh, damn him damn him. Never again would Agnes be able to trust her husband. Not after this one.

Already she was beginning to feel sick, just at the thought of accosting him. But she would do it. By God, she would do it. And just go ahead and get sick. She knew just exactly how. She had done it plenty of times. All she had to do was confront him with solid—on paper—proof, and he dropped them. Because he really got his pleasure from them, from these clandestine affairs, not out of the women themselves so much, as from the knowledge that he was putting something over on her, his wife, Agnes. What kind of hate was that to live with? live with all your life? Oh my God! she thought suddenly, agonizingly, how he must hate me! to do these things like that to me after all Ive done for him. How he must *hate* me! Well, other people could hate, too, Agnes thought coldly, and coldly she locked her mind down tight: The first thing she would do would be to break him loose from this little chit of a girl-whore, and let him sit and sweat and stew in his own damned juices.

But then, sitting there at the diningroom table, for the first time it occurred to her that Frank might refuse to give her up. Might just *refuse* to give up his mistress. He never had before. But things had changed so much lately, in the last year or so, what with all the money he was getting and the Shopping Center becoming the big thing it was.

Everything had changed. Agnes felt almost as if she were in a new place, in entirely new, and strange, surroundings. Where she did not know the predictable workings of things, any more; or what to expect. What if he did refuse? What if he looked her in the eyes, *dared* to look her in the eyes and just flatly refused to give up his little mistress?

Well, she thought, and she made her mind up coldly and harshly and indomitably: Well, if he refused, she would leave him. She would take little Walter and she would leave him. Go so far away he would never see either one of them again. That would hurt him. That would *really* hurt him: to take little Walter away from him. He loved little Walter—and the damned pompous smugness that it gave him—more than he had ever loved her. If he had ever loved her at all. —If he loved her, why did he always run out with other women? trashy women? all the time?— But to take little Walter away from him; that would cook him. And then let him live here then, alone, and with his damned lowclass mistress. Let him *marry* her, if he wanted to. Agnes knew him too well to believe that he would ever do that. He'd go out with them, but he would never marry them. He was too much of a damned snob.

Having made up her mind, Agnes got back up from the table, wearily, bone-tiredly, and went back to the secretary. She read the information in the letter over once more, her eyes blurring with hurt and mortally offended tears so much that she could hardly make the letters out, then she carefully filed it away where she would have it when he came home and went into the bathroom, weakly and shakily, and vomited up her breakfast. Then she went to bed.

Already, she was sick all over. Her nose was plugged up tighter than a drum. Her eyes ran water trying to relieve her congested sinuses. She was running a low fever, and her bones and joints ached. She had indigestion and she was constipated. And it was not any of it make-believe. It always did this to her when these things happened. She was really sick.

Little Walter was out playing somewhere, and she was alone in the house. Time enough to worry about his lunch when he came home from playing. Anyway, there was plenty in the icebox he could eat. He could fix his own lunch—and probably do it better than she could. Weakly, she reached over for the phone and called Doc Cost.

The big man arrived soon, his little MG sputtering up into the drive outside. As he always did, he only rapped lightly and came on in, right on into the bedroom where she was with just a sheet over her night-gown, carrying that same old battered old black bag. As he bent over her and then sat down on the bed edge, the smell of the whiskey on his breath wafted reassuringly about the room. And Agnes breathed it in comfortingly.

"Well, it looks like you really got it bad this time, Agnes," he said in his big awkward tender voice, after he had checked her pulse and temperature. "Little fever. Bones ache? Nose plugged up. Looks like you might have a touch of that summer flu thats been going the rounds." He reached for his black bag and handed her some pills, then he stood up and in that characteristic way he had, folded his big arms and looked down at her shrewdly.

"Frank out of town again?" he said soothingly.

Agnes only nodded, not even feeling like speaking.

For a moment he stood looking down at her, this big man who always instilled such confidence and reassurance in you that you actually felt he might be God, then he smiled slowly and affectionately.

"I have a pain right here in my side, too," Agnes said weakly.

"Right side?" He leaned over her and pressed her side just below the ribs. "Here?" he said, and straightened back up. "Might be having a little trouble with your gall bladder. Been eating a lot of greasy foods lately?"

"No," Agnes said, weakly, lassitude and a curious peace creeping over her.

"Ill go out the kitchen get you a glass of water for those pills," Doc Cost said and turned his big frame around in the small space beside the bed and ambled out through the door.

Agnes listened to his footsteps going away toward the kitchen comfortably. Nothing ever seemed so bad, nothing, when Doc Cost was around. All the real, genuine sympathy, the unspoken understanding, the *caring*, that she never seemed to get anywhere else in her life— from Frank, from her friends, from anybody—seemed to emanate to her from this big awkward sorrowful-looking man. Doc Cost. Suddenly Agnes wished she could just cuddle up to him, cuddle up against him, and have him stroke her head and tell her it would be all right like her father used to do. She could cry and tell him what the *real* trouble was and have him comfort her. There was so much kindness, so much real tenderness in him. What any woman, like that first wife of his: Louise, would want to leave him and run off with some other man for, Agnes couldnt understand. But maybe he hadnt been this way, back then, when he was young? She herself had lost everybody: her parents were both dead; Dawnie gone off now and married; Frank untrue to her once again—and for the *last* time; her only close relative was her sister in Kansas City, but they had drawn apart through the years until now they were hardly more than acquaintances: everybody. Lost everybody. Everybody except little Walter, who still loved her,—and Doc Cost. He came back through the door carrying a glass of water that looked midget-sized in his big hand.

"Here now," he said gently, and handed it to her carefully. "Take one of those every four hours or so. The other envelope is sedatives if you need them." He stepped back again, and folded the big arms, with those sausage fingers at the ends of them, and smiled at her kindly, affectionately. "I expect youll be all right in a day or two."

"I hope so," Agnes said weakly. "I have to take care of little Walter, you know."

"Do you want me to send you out a girl?" Doc said. "I can send you out a private nurse from the hospital for a couple days," he offered, "if you want."

"No," Agnes said weakly. "I guess Ill be all right."

Silently, his big arms still folded, he continued to stand, smiling down at her kindly;—and suddenly, for the first time in her life really, the first time consciously at any rate, Agnes realized with a kind of inward start that he was—available, she thought delicately. He was available to her, if she wanted him. Not out of lust, or salaciousness, or anything like that, but kindly, and warmly, and affectionately, because he liked her, and had sympathy for her, and because he thought she was attractive. Doc Cost was—available.

For a moment, she actually toyed with the idea. Savoring it, sort of. If she had ever felt it before, she didnt remember it; but then maybe she had sort of felt it, and not known it? He was a handsome man; not handsome like a movie star, but attractive in his bigness. And he was kind and tender. And suddenly Agnes realized that there were probably a large number of women in this town that Doc Cost had been to bed with in his career; a very large number, she bet; just how many she would probably never know. Nor would anybody else. He was discreet, Doc Cost. He was the soul of discretion. And he was a man who understood—and sympathized with—women. A whole lot of women, probably; women like herself. Not out of conquest, not out of lust, just out of simple friendliness and sympathy and liking. The thought astounded her; and even almost embarrassed her, and made her feel shy. And for a moment, she toyed with it. Why not? It certainly couldnt be said that she would be doing any injury to Frank that he did not deserve. That much was for sure. But then, she had never been that kind of woman, had not believed in that. Even though this, with Doc Cost, would not be that way, would only be friendly, and liking, and warm, a kind of comforting of each other by two human people. But she had always believed in loving one man only. And because of this, after toying with it for more than a moment, for several moments, she rejected it. Perhaps as much as anything she rejected it because of a certain ingrained, inarticulate shyness about herself and her person.

As if he read the look on her face, Doc Cost stood back up from the window sill and unfolded his big arms and smiled at her affectionately, and picked up his bag.

"Well, Agnes," he said, simply, kindly, "Ill stop back out tomorrow and have another look at you."

From the bed, impulsively, Agnes extended her hand to him. Doc Cost, smiling stepped forward and leaned over (the breath of whiskey emanating from him to her comfortingly) and took it.

"Thanks so much for coming out, Doc," Agnes said.

"Think nothing of it, Agnes," he said. And then he left.

Already feeling much better—must be that pill, she thought—and also feeling more attractive than she could remember having felt in years, Agnes rolled over and smiled at the wall. She wasnt really so big and fat after all. By noon she was able to get up and fix Walter's lunch for him.

But after that, after she had fed him and sent him on back out to play, she could not sustain the sense of feeling better; and the old depressive sickness, the horror, came back over her again in waves and she went back to bed. The momentary feeling of attractiveness, and the kindness of Doc Cost, was not enough to erase what Georgia Sheldon's letter had printed on her mind. The one man in the world she loved—*had* loved, she amended: used to love—the man she was married to, did not find her so very attractive, apparently; and she lay in the bed, bleakly and bitterly facing this fact. After a while she took another sedative. That made two already she had had today; and neither one of them had affected her a bit. She got no sleep, and no rest, out of either one of them. As she lay in the bed, sleeplessly, and rest-lessly, she heard young Walter come back in from outside and come toward the bedroom. Oh, God, she thought wearily, what does he want now? The weather was unbearably hot. Was she going to have to get up and do something else for him?

Walter, as if he had sensed in his perceptive way that something was wrong, his solemn little old man's face worried and distressed looking, came to the side of the bed and stood looking down at her; and suddenly Agnes's eyes filled with tears again.

"Mother, are you sick?" Walter said solicitously.

"No, honey," she said, "just tired. You go on back out and play."

Suddenly, abruptly, Walter leaned forward and put his arms around her and put his cheek against hers and hugged her. He did not say anything.

Despairfully, miserably, Agnes put her own arms around his little body and squeezed him. "Your mother loves you, Walter," she said tearfully. "Dont you ever forget that. Youre my son, my own son. Whatever else happens, youre *my* son."

Walter still did not say anything, and after a moment he stood back up, his little old man's face solemn and worried. "Please dont be sick," he said tremulously. "Please dont die."

"Oh, honey!" Agnes cried. "Dont you worry about me. Im all right."

Walter stared at her a moment longer, not saying anything, and then turned and went slowly out, and Agnes rolled back over in the bed, her face hardening at the thought of Frank.

She was ready for him when he came home from Springfield the next day. More than ready for him. Doc Cost had been and gone. She had not done anything, and had only got out of bed when she had to fix Walter's meals, and the rest of the time she spent in the bed planning savoringly just exactly how she was going to cut Frank up into little pieces.

He came in the house hustlingly and happily, carrying his bag, but when he found she was in bed, he stopped short.

"Why, honey!" Frank said. "Whats the matter? Are you sick?" He laid the bag down gingerly, almost fearfully, on his own bed. He knew. He knew she knew.

"Just tired," Agnes said shortly, and got up and put on her wrapper. "Ive got something I want to show you," she said, and went to the secretary and got the letter.

As he read it, at first puzzlingly and perplexed at why she should be showing him one of her newsy women's letters, and then guiltily when he came to the passage with the information, Agnes watched him coldly. Guilt seemed to roll down over his face like a curtain. If there had ever been any doubt in her mind, the look on his face erased it. He did not finish the letter.

"Well!" he said hollowly. "Well! This is interesting. But why show it to me?"

"The girl works for you, doesnt she?"

"Well," Frank said, guilt actually appearing to drip down off of his face in big wet bunches, "yes; she works for me. But what has that to do with this? Apparently old Janie didnt really have much insurance. So the girl—Edith—must have got the house some other way."

"Maybe some man got it for her."

"Well! I never thought of that," Frank said. "Hmm! That might be so."

"Do you want a girl like that working for you? in your place of business?"

"Well, her private life isnt of any concern to me, honey. Shes an efficient, hard-working girl."

"Yes, Ill bet shes efficient! And hard-working, too! Ill bet shes very efficient!" Agnes said caustically, twisting the word around.

Frank stared at her, trying to look puzzled by her implication, but the guilt on his face so strong that his attempted puzzled look hardly got through at all. Agnes stared back at him coolly, coldly, appraisingly. What a liar. What a *poor* liar! He wasnt even a good liar. What a cheap, sneaking, sniveling, guilty, little bad-liar.

"Well, she is," Frank said finally, still trying to pull off his act of puzzlement.

"Youre a poor liar," Agnes said coldly. "Did you notice the name of the company that paid her such a large check?"

"Why, yes," Frank said. "Thats one of the Greek's outfits in Springfield."

"And he did it for you, didnt he? It was *you* who bought her that damned house, wasnt it?" Agnes smiled. It was a contemptuous, very nearly murderous-looking, smile.

"Who?" Frank said. "Me?" He laughed hollowly, guilt all over his face. "My God! Is that whats been bothering you, honey? My God, the Greek handles all kinds of business for all kinds of people. He might have handled somethin like that for anybody here in Parkman. Hell, maybe its even Clark Hibbard whos keeping her! Who knows?"

"*I* know," Agnes said, in a clear—but low—voice like a trumpet. "And youre going to admit it! Youre going to admit it to *me*!"

Frank laughed, nervously. "Honey, honey! Why should I admit something I aint responsible for? Honey, youre just upset. You—"

"God!" Agnes cried trumpetingly. "What a cheap sniveling little creature you are! God! Frank Hirsh, the bigshot! Frank Hirsh, the *rich man*! who the moment he makes a little money has to run out and get himself a mistress and buy a house for her! And what a bigshot he thinks he is then! God, what a cheap sneaky sniveling little pipsqueak of a laughing-stock you are! Thats what you are; you know that dont you? A laughing-stock. All over Parkman. Running around like an ant, trying to be a bigshot; and everybody laughing at you behind your back!"

Frank stood and took it, still holding the letter, his jaw hardening a little, and anger replacing some of the guilt on his face. But not all of it. Not all of it, by any means.

Up to now it had all followed the same old, oh-so-familiar pattern. He would stand and take it, guilt written all over his face as plain as anything could be, and steadfastly, abjectly, he would refuse to admit it. Stubbornly, stolidly, he would stand there with his guilt sticking out eight feet, and never ever would he ever admit it. Then he would rush out and drop the women like a hot rock. He had never yet admitted to her that he had ever once been out with Geneve Lowe. Never once yet, in the two years since she had broken him off with her.

Well, this was *one* time he *was* going to admit it. Agnes stared at him, hate filling her up to the top of her very scalp and making it tingle; and keeping her voice low, and cold, and deadly, she went right on in the same vein. This time he was going to admit it to her. He owed her at least that much for what he had done to her. Slowly, and methodically, professionally and pleasurably, she peeled the skin right off of him down into a bloody bundle of ruptured ego lying on the floor about his feet, and left him standing with all his naked veins exposed: Carefully, she built up a picture of the reverse side of the coin of Frank Hirsh the success: Frank Hirsh, the pipsqueak, the front man for the real bigshots, who had done nothing, and deserved nothing—except what the real bigshots chose to dole out to him, for being their errand boy: Frank Hirsh, with his cheap trashy little mistress, the granddaughter of his own cleaning woman, the *clerk* and *office girl* in his own store: Frank Hirsh the laughing-stock of Parkman, whom everybody was giggling at behind his back everywhere he went. It was all of it true, too. Just equally and fully as true as the other side of the coin. And what was more, he knew it.

Frank stood and took it, in silence, still holding the letter until finally he remembered it and went and laid it on the secretary. Several times he tried to protest, unconvincingly. Looking convicted, totally convicted, he still stood and tried to deny it. When he went to lay the letter down, Agnes followed him, relentlessly, inexorably, her voice still cutting and slashing at him but not passionately: coldly, coolly, cruelly, appraisingly. He could stand and take it as long as he wanted to, she didnt give a damn. He could not outlast her. Flamingly, trumpetingly, but nonetheless coldly and lowly, she could go right on forever, if he wanted to stand and take it that long. And he knew it, too. And she would go on forever, if she had to. This time he was going to admit it to her. And she was right. Finally, when it got to be too much for even his tightened jaw and angry silence, he did admit it to her. And as soon as he admitted it, he changed.

"All right," he said, smiling almost dangerously, all guilt disappearing from his face, "its true. I did buy her the house; and she is my mistress. And has been for a year and a half now. So what? So what are you goin' to do about it?"

"Do?" Agnes said, coldly. "Do! Im going to demand that you leave her and never see her again."

"But you cant make me," Frank said, still smiling almost dangerously.

"No, I cant make you," Agnes said; "but if you dont, Ill leave you."

Frank's smile changed, into a grin, almost. He didnt believe that. "What?" he said soothingly. "Leave old Frank? Just when we're gettin' really rich. Why, we'll be livin' off the fat of the land in a year or so. We're liable to be millionaires. You mean you want to leave all that?"

"Yes," Agnes said. "I will."

Frank grinned at her disbelieving, and that was when he began to sweettalk her, almost confidently.

"I dont know," he said, hesitantly, making himself sound abject but not feeling it, where before he had *been* abject and trying to hide it. Agnes watched him closely: "I dont know. All I know is that I love you. Youre my wife and I love you and Ill always love you. You know that, too. No matter how mean you treat me, even. But I want a mistress. Almost all the men I know have mistresses; some of them more than one. And them and their wives love each other. Why do you and me have to be so different? I dont know," he said abjectly. "Maybe— Maybe all men are just—just—"

"Polygamous?" Agnes said coldly.

"Thats it," Frank said, smiling. "Polygamous. Im tryin' to be as honest as I can. But that *dont* mean—that polygamous—*dont* mean that I dont love *you*, my wife. I *do* love you, and I always have." He smiled again, a little more confidently. "But I want a mistress."

"And you love her, too," Agnes said.

Frank smiled again, more confidently still. "Well—" he said; "well— yes, I suppose you could say that. In a way. But not like I love you. It aint the same at all."

"And all the time we were so close and so happy," Agnes said coldly, "you were making love to this—this—" she restrained herself: "this *girl*, too."

"Shes a nice girl," Frank said, getting her meaning. "But I told you: It aint the same as when Im makin' love to you. I love you, and I want you. Youre my wife. It just aint the same at all."

"No man is going to love another woman while hes loving me," Agnes said flatly. "Not you, nor anybody else."

"Aw, now, honey," Frank said, and smiled again, confidently, easily. "If I loved her like I love you youd have a reason to be jealous. But you see I dont. Youre the only one for me really."

"Youve got to get rid of her," Agnes said coldly. "I demand that you get rid of her."

"What?" Frank said, smiling. "And what about the house? Hell, I spent over eight thousand dollars on that damned house. Dont be ridiculous, honey." He smiled at her again.

"I dont give a damn about the house," Agnes said narrowly, still studying him carefully. She had never seen him quite like this. "If you spent it, youve just lost it, thats all. But youve got to get rid of her."

Frank smiled at her again, his eyes thoughtful. "I cant do that, honey," he said.

"Then Ill leave you," Agnes said again.

Frank smiled, widely now. "Aw, now, honey. Youre just upset. Ive tried to explain it to you: it dont mean anything compared with you and me," he said joshingly. "You wouldnt leave me. Leave old Frank? Why, hell, just when we're really beginnin' to get into the big money? Just when we're really beginnin' to get rich?"

"I dont care about the money," Agnes said.

"Youre just mad, honey," Frank smiled. "Youll get over it. Look: Ive got three appointments waitin' on me right now downtown. Ive just got to get to them. Look, you go back to bed and rest a while, and when I come home we'll go out to the Club for dinner, and have ourselves a fine evening and then when we come home, we'll have us a 'party' like we use to do. A real one."

"Im telling you, Ill leave you," Agnes said. "Ill take Walter, and Ill leave you. Flat. For good."

Frank smiled at her confidently, almost cockily. "Aw, now, honey," he said softly, "you wouldnt do that." Smiling, he approached her—although he did not offer to touch her; her eyes forbade that—and began to talk softly and confidently, love talk almost, telling her how busy he was now he had to get to these appointments . . . how foolish she was to think all these things . . . etc. etc. etc.

And as he talked, she looked at him coolly, coldly, appraisingly, feeling more hatred for him than she had ever felt for anybody in her life before. He actually didnt think she would go. He thought he had her whipped. Had snatched victory from the jaws of defeat. He probably used these same loveterms, these same endearments, with Edith, with Geneve Lowe, all the same patter he had always used with her. Told them all, caressingly, fondly—and pompous and smug as hell inside— what great lovers they were, what they meant to him, how happy they were making him. Because, Agnes thought acidly, no woman will go out with a man and keep on going out with him unless he is building up her ego, unless he is telling her he loves her.

—And all this time, all the lovetalk he had talked to her, had tried to show her all this time, it had all been a farce, just like the others; and the same thing was being enacted night after night with his little whore.

Oh, God! If she had been way off someplace away from him, if she had refused to love him, if they hadnt been so full of love and happiness, hadnt been on their "second honeymoon", perhaps she could have understood it. Second honeymoon, hah! she thought acidly.

And then he stood there and had the gall and the stupidity to tell her that a mistress meant nothing to him, nothing at all, and that she was the only one he loved. Well, if a mistress meant nothing to him, then why was it so damned important that he have one?

Second honeymoon! And all that time they were deeply in love he was also out pawing, and murmuring and re-acting, and repeating the same things, the same acts, the same words—that he said to her—to another woman.

She could not stand the thought of it, and Agnes looked at her husband coldly and bitterly, behind the quiet mask of her face, and hated every inch of him. Every living inch, every movement, every silly little action he made, every little allusion about his having to get down to the office, so businesslike, and all ready to take off and do his playacting somewhere else. Did he think she was a fool? Did he think he could handle her like that? that easy? All right, go, she thought, and drop dead as you go. And suddenly she thought that she was like Lucy Dorner after all. However much she had wanted not to be. Old Lucy

Dorner, who could have stood and watched the old man, Al Dorner kick off at her feet and never have turned a hair, never felt a qualm. Agnes Hirsh felt the same identical way. And it was then that she made up her mind.

Frank put his hand on her shoulder, tentatively, smiling. But there was steel in his eyes, too, Agnes thought looking into them stormily. A curious kind of steel. That you could bend, and twist, and beat, and hammer, but that you could never break.

"Youll be all right in a little bit," he said gently, tenderly. "Youll get over this. Ill be back as soon as I can. And tonight we'll celebrate. Celebrate our love," he said softly. He still didnt think she would do it. Confidently, smiling, almost openly cocky, he looked at his watch; and as she stood immobile, kissed her on the cheek and hurried out. He thought she couldnt give up the money. Well, she could give up the damned money; as far as that went she could take damn near all of it away from him, if she wanted to; the law was on her side. But she didnt want to. She didnt want his damned money. If she took anything, it would be only what she had given him, the price of her father's store. She could give it up, even if he couldnt give up the girl. Well, let him have the girl. Let him move her right here into this house, and marry the damned whore.

Once she had made up her mind, Agnes acted swiftly. She went out in the back and got young Walter—who was sitting rather gloomily in his sand-dirt box, looking at his road equipment.

"Come on in here," she said. "We're going away on a visit."

She packed two bags for herself, and one for Walter. Then, carefully, her voice serene, she made her phone calls. Six or eight of them, to all her closest friends, and to the people they had dinner engagements with. She had had a hurry-up emergency call from her sister in Kansas City; yes, her sister was down sick; she just simply had to go to her. Serene, calm-voiced, the same perfect hostess and manager who had engineered Dawnie's wedding, she handled all of them.

There would be no talk, now. And that left it up to him. If he wanted the whore, let him make the choice. And in fact, she rather hoped he did. Really, she expected that he would. Except perhaps for Walter. But the whore could probably bear him some brats. Oh, God! she thought suddenly; a whole lifetime down the drain! Just like that! Well, let him choose.

So that he would be sure to know where to reach her, she left a little note, worded carefully so that it would not look like she had left it for that reason:

> *You didn't believe me. Walter and I are going to Mary Ellen's*
> *in Kansas City. I don't ever want to see or hear from you again.*

She left it prominently displayed, where he could not help but see it;

and leaving the house in a mess from the packing—and enjoying angrily the fact that she was doing so—she took Walter out to the little Ford and loaded up the bags.

"Are we getting separated?" Walter said gloomily, as she slid in behind the wheel. "Are we getting a divorce?"

"Did you hear what went on there in the house?" Agnes asked, startled.

"Well, I couldnt help but hear some of it," Walter said gloomily. "You both of you talked so loud."

"Well, you just forget you heard it," she commanded. "Yes, we probably are getting a divorce. But dont you worry. Youll always stay with me, honeybun." She started up the car.

As she pulled out of the drive, she looked back at the house where she had lived so long and tears filled her eyes. Just only a few months ago they had been talking about selling it and building a fine new home. And now she was leaving it for good. She couldnt help but cry. But then she shook the thoughts out of her mind and blinked away the tears and squared her shoulders positively.

What would Dawn think, when she found out? up there in Champaign where she and Jim were going to summer school? Well, she would write her a long letter as soon as she got out to Mary Ellen's in Kansas City.

And resolutely, stubborn-jawed, she drove away. But she could not resist driving past the other house: the house her husband had bought for his mistress. She knew where it was, and had seen it often enough— before Edith Barclay bought it. And something in her, some deliberate selfhurting painfulness, made her drive by and look at it. It was a pretty little green house, with white shutters and a pretty little yard. Once again tears filled her eyes so that she could hardly drive.

Driving out of her way to pass the other house had put her out of the way so that she had to turn back to get back on North Main the cross-street that led out to the bypass. Her eyes brimming with tears, she could hardly see where she was driving.

"Turn here," Walter said authoritatively, after they had gone a couple of blocks.

Blinking her eyes, Agnes pulled up and stopped at the corner. "Well, I dont know if I can," she said hesitantly. "All of these east-west streets are one-way streets now up here."

"Cant you see which way the cars are parked?" Walter said disgustedly.

Blinking again, Agnes looked and saw that the cars parked along the street were all headed east, and suddenly she laughed.

"Yes," she said. "Yes, of course." Suddenly, warmly, she leaned over and hugged the diminutive solemn-faced little boy. "Youre my boy, arent you?" she said tenderly. Then she turned the corner and went on down the street, resolutely, indomitably.

No man in the world was ever going to do something like that to her. Well, at least she did have little Walter.

CHAPTER 69

FRANK was feeling pretty chipper, when he left the house that afternoon, after talking to Agnes. For the first time in his life, really, he felt he had finally made Agnes understand just what the difference was, between a wife—a real wife—and a mistress. Naturally, he was elated. And as he drove downtown to the new offices to meet his appointments, with his new elation and enthusiasm boosting him up high, Frank began to plan ahead how he could get himself another, second mistress. In addition to Edith Barclay.

Hell, he should have talked to Agnes about this long ago. It would have saved them both all kinds of misery and trouble. She was mad now, of course. But she would get over that. In time. It had hurt her vanity a little, to find that a man could love one woman and still want to sleep with another: to find that men were really polygamous. But he thought he had made her understand it. And once she got over being mad, she would accept it. Agnes had always been one for accepting facts. She was a real realist. And as for her leaving him, well—Frank smiled. Of course she wouldnt leave him. Shed talk like that when she was mad, and blow off some steam, but as soon as she cooled down and her reasonable nature reasserted itself, shed forget it. She loved him too much to ever leave him. And she knew it as well as he did. She was a real woman—and a real wife. What, leave him? after theyd lived together for more than twenty years? And anyway, hell, shed be a fool— anybody would be a fool—to just up and leave the kind of setup she had here, with him, now; and Agnes was no fool. She wasnt about to leave him, and he knew it.

Hell, maybe hed even get himself *two* more. That would make three mistresses in all. One here, and one in Terre Haute, and the third one— where? Not Indianapolis; that was too far away. Hed be able to afford them all, all three, in another year or so. His heart squeezed in him with the joy of possession when he thought about it. Christ, why hadnt he talked to Agnes about it before? Hed get himself one in Terre Haute first, and buy that one a house there, in Terre Haute. Some nice young girl about like Edith—only a little older; hed prefer her a little older, and more experienced. It was really better to have them unmarried, like Edith, rather than have married women like Geneve Lowe, who had their own homes. Then you could set them up in a house and just go there whenever you pleased.

It would probably be better, he thought enthusiastically, to set this second one up in Terre Haute, rather than here in Parkman. He didnt want to make Edith jealous, too, and have to go through a scene like this with her too. Later on of course, he could let her know and bring her around. Just like he had Agnes. Then he could maybe set the third one up here in Parkman, too, like Edith. Or maybe he would set her up over in Israel where the Frenches lived. Now there was an idea!

Of course, that third one would have to wait a year or two. Until the Shopping Center and the rest of the enterprises really began paying off. But that *second* one! Hell, he could even start in on that second one this winter. Hed start looking around for some nice, professional gal, over there in Terre Haute, some gal who had her own job and her own work. That was the kind to get. Jesus! he thought enthusiastically; Christ, he was happy! He didnt know when he had felt so good! Three mistresses to go to, whenever he wanted, just take his pick. Hell, he felt like Midas!

Enthusiastically, happily, he parked the car and jauntily went upstairs to the office. Happily and energetically he bounced through his work with all the flare and energy Frank Hirsh was becoming noted for, anxious to get home to his wife. When he did get home that night, after his appointments, and found the note and the house messed up from the packing of the suitcases, he collapsed: stunned. Completely stunned, physically stunned, into disbelief and a state of shock; like an ox is stunned with a hammerblow between the eyes, before they slice his neck.

It took him fifteen minutes to really realize it, actually, in the numbed state he was in. Fifteen minutes to fully realize it. And eight seconds after that, he fell completely apart.

He had seen the note, of course, first thing after he had noticed all the clothes strewn around. The usually immaculate, spotless house was in a terrible state. There were clothes in the living room, there were clothes in the diningroom. In the kitchen, she had even left all the dirty dishes right on the table from lunch, with the food dried on them, congealed egg yolk on the plate of Walter who loved poached eggs on toast. One suitcase which she had decided not to take still lay open on his, Frank's, bed when he went in there. Frank pushed some clothes off a chair in the living room and sat down with the note and read it over and over. He would read it through, and then he would read it through again. He knew what it said, what the words said, he understood, but the meaning did not register on him with its full import. Along toward the end of the fifteen minutes, when his mind began to work again a little, he grasped craftily at the straw that she was only doing this to devil him, and had not left at all.

And with this in mind, he searched the house. He went upstairs, then down and into Walter's room, and into the laundry room, he even looked in the bathrooms and downstairs in the basement. Then, finally, he went out to the garage and checked to see if her car—her Ford; that he had given her himself—was gone.

It was when he came back inside from the garage, and saw again the clothes-strewn rooms and went and got the note and read it through again (it still read the same; he had hoped it wouldnt) that the full import of it all hit down on him. She had left him. She had really left him. His wife, his own wife, whom he had done more for and loved more than anybody else in the world, and *needed*, had actually left him. It made him come completely unstrung, and sitting in the clothes-strewn living room, the note dangling from his hand, he began to cry. That she could do this to him: so cruel and heartless a thing. Frank did not cry easily, had not cried for years, and he did not cry easily now. He had always believed men ought never to cry, and it was a broken, shattered, convulsive, shoulder-shaking kind of crying that came out of him, painful, abortive, awkward. The tears ran down his face and splashed on his dangling hands, and he held his mouth and nose tightened up against it, except when the convulsive little gasps for breath would shake him.

Still crying and unable to stop, he went about and aimlessly began to gather up the clothes. It seemed an endless and insurmountable task; there were so many of them. Finally he kicked them all together in a couple of piles and bent and picked them up and carried them in and dumped them all on her—on Agnes's; Agnes his wife's—bed, and then carefully laid the still open suitcase on top of them. Then he went out to the kitchen and took the dishes with food dried on them, the smell of the congealed egg yolk making him want to gag, and put them in the sink and ran water in them to soak them loose. That she would do this to him, deliberately, maliciously. And not only that: his son! His own little son! Walter! His son Walter! She had taken him, too! And after he had already had the signs changed on the store windows! That would make him look like an ass, wouldnt it! She had done that on purpose, he knew. At least, she could have left him Walter. But that she could do it at all, such a horribly cruel thing, to him, who had always loved her, and done so much for her—that was the worst of all! And he began to cry again, brokenly, shatteringly.

It was, in the end, the panic that finally made him stop the crying. Slowly, inexorably, it had been growing in him steadily all this time: the nameless, frightened, lonely panic: at the thought of living here all alone the rest of his life: at the thought of having to clean this house up himself: at the thought of having to keep it clean: at the thought of eating meals in restaurants, greasy spoons, all the rest of his life or of ineffectually trying to cook them himself: at the thought of the laundry room and of trying to run the mangle: how could he ever do that? who would he get to do that for him: but most of all at the thought of walking echoingly back and forth all through this house, alone, all the rest of his life. No Agnes. No Walter: no *son*! Gradually, unyieldingly, the panic grew until finally it was so powerfully strong that it superseded the crying and the feeling of selfsorrow and forced them both out of him.

Well, he would have to get her back, that was all! And suddenly he jumped up from where he sat, filled with a frantic energy to do something, to start acting, an energy which of course was only frustrated leaving him just that much more unstrung—because, he realized almost immediately, there wasnt anything he could start to do. At least not now. The sense of time drag was maddening. If she was going to her sister Mary Ellen's in Kansas City, they would not arrive there until some time tomorrow. He could not even call her, on the phone, until then. A wire would mean a long wait for an answer. And he couldnt send a wire anyway; not publicly in Parkman. And the thought of writing a letter and the long time lag before he would be able to get an answer back actually sickened him physically.

For a moment, the frustrated energy to do something, to start getting her back, burning and tormenting him, he thought of getting in the Cadillac and following them. Sure. That was what he could do. Agnes was a notoriously slow driver, and they couldnt have been gone over a couple of hours. Maybe he could catch them. —But then, what if he passed them, and missed them? And for that matter, how could he be sure which route she took? Almost certainly shed take Route 40 to St Louis;—but what if she didnt? And what if he should happen to catch up with them right in St Louis? He thought hed know Agnes's car anywhere, on sight,—he had known it so well—but driving in city traffic he might easily miss them. And on the other side of St Louis, both Route 40 and Route 50 went to Kansas City. How could he know which one she took? What if he was driving along one, frantically looking for her, and she was driving along the other one? The thought horrified him and he couldnt stand even the thought of it.

And for that matter, he thought craftily, how did he even know she was going to Mary Ellen's in Kansas City? Maybe she only told him that as a red herring to throw him off, while she was in fact going someplace else? She *might* be doing that.

No, there was nothing for it except to wait. To wait until tomorrow. And then call. It would mean waiting until almost tomorrow noon. The very thought was so agonizing, enhanced as it was by his frantic energy to do something to start getting her back, that he could hardly stand it. To relieve himself from it, from the unbearable tyranny of time, he went to the bar and shakily got out a full bottle of whiskey. He did not even bother with the pretense of mixing a drink, but took the bottle into the bedroom with him and lay down with it on the bed. But he could not stand the bedroom, with all those clothes there, on her bed—on Agnes's bed—and that open suitcase; and he got back up with it and went back out to sit in the living room. And there he sat, desperately, drinking the raw straight whiskey and looking at his watch every few minutes to see how much time had passed, until finally he drank himself to sleep there in the chair. He did not even think of going over to Edith Barclay's or of calling her; and if he had, the very thought would have been unbearable: he couldnt stand the thought of talking to anyone. And in fact, as far as that went, he had been supposed to go speak at a meeting again tonight, to a group of businessmen, about the Shopping Center; but it was utterly impossible even to consider it.

And so he sat, drinking the whiskey and peering at his watch every few minutes to see how much time had passed. He promised himself faithfully and devoutly that he would agree to anything she asked to get her to come back. He would give up Edith; hell, gladly. He hadnt known it meant that much to her, to Agnes. He hadnt had any idea. Sure, hed give up Edith and hed never take another mistress, as long as he lived. If that was what she wanted. My God, how could she do this to him! She was destroying his whole life! But if that was what she wanted, okay, hed give it to her: *Let* her destroy his life. Finally, he managed to get drunk enough to sleep. Anything. Anything she wanted. Agnes. Agnes.

He woke up in the morning, feeling dirty and greasy and unshaven and still in his now-rumpled business suit, just shortly after daylight. His watch, which he looked at immediately, said it was five o'clock. My God! that meant seven more hours he would have to wait! He didnt think he could stand it.

Maybe Agnes had driven all night? he thought suddenly and hopefully. If she had, she might be getting in there right about now or a little later. But no, never in her life would Agnes ever drive anywhere all night. No, he would just simply have to wait.

Only, he didnt think he could wait. Could stand to wait. Because how did he even know they were going there? If he knew for sure they were going there, it wouldnt be so bad. But he didnt even know that. And he would have to wait seven more hours just to find out, even. What if they didnt go to Mary Ellen's? What would he do then? How would he ever find them at all?

Getting a grip—a rather shaky grip; but still a grip—on himself, he made himself get up out of the chair to go shower and shave. And it was then he saw the whiskey bottle on the floor, where it had slipped out of his hand last night when he fell asleep; and as soon as he saw it he smelled the whiskey. Capless, the bottle had fallen over and most of its remaining contents had run out on the rug. Staring at it, the deep unnameable, unbearable panic seized him again. Frantically, he ran out to the kitchen and got the dishrag at the sink and wet it and grabbed some dishtowels and ran back in to try and sop and clean it up. The raw whiskey smell was strong in his nose as he knelt and rubbed and swabbed ineffectually. It was a very poor effort at cleaning, and it did not even assuage his conscience: Here he was, ruining their house, his and Agnes's house, almost before she had even left it. Guilt of a power and strength unknown to him before gripped him as he tried to clean it up. Ruining their house, his and Agnes's and Walter's house. My God! what would he do if she didnt come back? The whole place would sink into rack and ruin and decay; and he himself would descend into sloth and dirt and stagnation. A bum. She just had to come back! She just had to!

When he had cleaned it up as best he could—which was very poorly, and the whiskey still reeked in the room—he took the fine expensive dishtowels, soaked with whiskey and water now and dirt rubbed into them from the rug, into the laundry and threw them in a bunch on the floor, and looked down at them guiltily. Even his attempts at cleaning up had resulted in more destruction than good. Miserably, he forced himself to go shave and shower.

Afterwards, and dressed in clean clothes, he felt a little better. But it was still not yet six o'clock! Dejectedly, he ambled out in the kitchen and put some bread in the automatic toaster and made some coffee. At least, he could do that. But after he had made it, hopelessness and apathy made him unable to eat any of it, and he only sat and stared at it emptily. Agnes always made him such good breakfasts.

Finally, unable to think of anything else to do, he got up and went and got another bottle of whiskey and took it back to the kitchen table with him. He would have to be careful not to drink too much. He didnt want to be drunk when he called. And so, charily, sparingly, he drank whiskey and sat at the table with a deck of cards and tried to play solitaire and looked at his watch every few minutes to see how much time had passed.

Finally, he called Mary Ellen's in Kansas City at ten o'clock. Desperately, he tried to make his voice sound calm. No, she hadnt seen Agnes; or even had any word from her. She hadnt even known she was coming.

"Well, when she gets there you tell her I called," Frank said, striving to sound calm. "And that Ill call back. Or if she wants to, have her call me."

He went back to his whiskey and solitaire and his watch.

He called again at eleven. Still no word.

Then, at a quarter to twelve, he called again; and she was there.

"Just a minute," Mary Ellen said. "Here she is. They just got in."

Frank waited, breathless, half tight, filled with a desperate and hopeful despairfulness, and then Agnes's voice came on the phone.

"Hello?" she said. "Yes?"

"Youve got to come back," Frank babbled. "Youve got to come back right away. Youve got to come back."

"I told you I didnt ever want to see or hear from you again," Agnes said sharply.

"I dont care," Frank said. "I dont care. Youve got to come back."

There was a silence on the other end.

"Agnes?" he cried. "Agnes! Are you there? Weve been cut off!"

"No; Im here," she said.

"Oh," Frank said with relief. "Look: Ill do anything you say. Anything. Ill quit her. Ill tell her we're through, all washed up. And Ill never have another—"

"Dont talk over the phone!" Agnes said sharply.

"All right," he said eagerly, "all right. But anything. Anything you say. But youve got to come back. Look, I havent been to work. I was supposed to go to a meeting last night. But I couldnt go. And I havent been to work today. Youve got to come back, or we'll lose everything. And anyway I think Im sick," he said. "Ive got a fever, I think. And I havent got anybody to take care of me. I *need* you. What if I get down sick? I might die. I cant afford to get down sick now, with things going like they are. I got to be able to work. Youve *got* to come back!"

There was another silence on the other end.

"Hello?" he said hopefully.

"All right," Agnes said crisply, "Ill come back. But you know what the conditions are."

"All right," Frank said eagerly. "Anything. Anything. Ill tell her—"

"Dont talk over the *phone!*" Agnes said sharply. "Now, listen: Im willing to come back for little Walter's sake. He needs both his parents. So Ill come back. And Ill take care of both of you. But thats all, understand? Thats all. Itll be just a simple business arrangement."

"Anything," Frank said hopefully, "anything."

"But Im only doing it on account of little Walter," Agnes said. "Now listen: Its going to take you some time to get *everything*," she said meaningfully, "arranged back there. You know what I mean. At the store, too. And since we're already out here, I think we'll just stay for a while."

"Stay!" Frank said with dismay. "For how long?"

"For two weeks anyway," Agnes said. "Walter's never seen this part of the country. And anyway," she said, suddenly, in a peculiar, almost wailful tone, "I dont think Im equal to the drive back right now yet." Then her voice sharpened again. "So you get everything arranged back there. Itll take you that long to do it anyway, and we'll stay here and have ourselves a vacation. God knows we both need one."

"Well," Frank said miserably, "if you want to stay that long. But I can fix up everything here quicker than that. I can fix it all up in a minute. And I *need* you."

"Mrs Davis," Agnes said firmly, referring to the new cleaning woman who had replaced old Janie, "will take care of you while we're gone. Call her up and have her come clean up the house."

"All right," Frank said unhappily. Why the hell hadnt he thought of that himself? Of course.

"Shell probably even cook for you if you want her to," Agnes said. "But I want Walter to see some of this country, while we're out here, and get to know his cousins. And I want a rest myself."

"How is little Walter?" Frank said hopefully. "Is he all right?"

"Of course, hes all right."

"Does he miss his daddy?" Frank asked.

"Of course he misses you," Agnes said accusingly. "Youre his father, arent you?"

"Yeh," Frank said unhappily.

"Why shouldnt he miss you?" Agnes said condemningly. "Well," she said, "all right. Now be sure and tell everyone Mary Ellen is sick."

"Okay."

"Now, is there anything else?"

"No," he said lamely. "I guess not. Except that I love you."

"Yes," Agnes said; "well. Im sure you do. Well, goodby."

"Goodby," Frank said reluctantly. He waited until he heard the other phone click in his ear before he reluctantly hung up. Then he stood, looking around at the house, and feeling vastly relieved. The more he stood and looked, the more relieved he felt. She *was* coming back. Life would probably be hell on earth around here for a while, but she *was* coming back. And, more important, was bringing little Walter back home with her. Relief was like a vast relaxing sigh all through him. Then, suddenly, anger seized him. Damn her. God damn her. Damn her to hell.

Well, at least he could work this afternoon, anyway, now. Carefully, he dressed himself in another suit and clean white shirt and carefully he tied his tie. Then, as a last minute afterthought, went back into the bathroom and gargled with mouthwash to take the smell of whiskey off his breath so no one would think he was drinking before noon. There were still a lot of the leases to be taken care of. And now that they were starting to do the interiors of the units, he would have to consult with the architect and the contractors, together with the various lessees. They were having a restaurant in the unit, and this lease was already sold, but he and the Greek and the old man had agreed beforehand not to do anything special with the restaurant—it was just another typical long front-to-back unit like the other eleven—because later when they built the motel they wanted to include a restaurant in it, a really ritzy modern stone-and-glass one. Of course, the restaurant lessee in the Shopping Center didnt know this. Frank had all of these things to take care of, as well as more businessmen's meetings; and the half day he had lost would already throw him quite a ways behind. Still feeling the tremendous relief from the cessation of the panic, he got his new summer hat and went out to the Cadillac and left. He would call Mrs Davis from the office, and ask her to come out tomorrow. But he wasnt going to ask her to cook for him; hed eat out for two weeks and to hell with it.

The bigshots' errand boy, was he? Petty little laughing-stock, was he? He had had to do more real work in the past six months than he had ever done in all his life put together before. She didnt take any of that into account, when she started cussing him out. Hed like to see her do the work he had done in the past six months. It would kill her. Shed drop over dead. As he backed out of the drive, he wished momentarily, now, that he had waited a while before calling her out there. Why the hell didnt he think of Mrs Davis himself? Maybe, if he had waited a few days, she wouldnt have been so damned cocksure as she was. She might even have found she had decided to come back on her own, if he had waited long enough. Well, it was too late for that now. It was already done. And now he would have to go and talk to Edith. He hated to do it. But he had given her his word. It was going to be hard on Edith, poor kid.

But he did not go to see Edith that night; and in fact, had known all along, all afternoon while he was working, what he was going to do that night. All afternoon while he worked, hard and energetically, the excitement at the thought of it had been building up in him in the back of his mind: He was going out walking. The vague stirrings to get out and see adventure, see life—which he had not felt at all yesterday after he and Agnes talked there at the house; nor felt, either, after he had come home and found her gone—had come back in him now as a definite urge, with the cessation of his panic over Agnes and the ensuing sense of relief. As soon as he got home from work, he mixed himself a big batch of strong Manhattans and sat down with them at the dining-room table alone in the empty house and began to drink, the excitement mounting in him as he began to feel the liquor. The very silence and utter aloneness in the house added to his excitement, now that he was sure she was coming back. Why, hell, he could strip off all his clothes and caper about the house like one of them fauns or satyrs or whatever they called them, if he wanted to. Excitedly, tinglingly, he mixed himself another batch of Manhattans and sat back down at the table and drank them, slowly, savoringly, as the liquor began to hit him more, relishing excitedly the utter stillness, utter silence of the house. And finally,—at nine or nine thirty; ten or ten thirty it was, fast time— savoring the full three-quarter drunkenness in him, he got up to go out and walk. As a last minute afterthought, he went into the bedroom— where Agnes's clothes were still piled on the bed; damn her; Hah!

what would she think if she saw him now?—and tremblingly and excitedly exchanged his suit and shirt for darker ones and a darker hat. Then he walked out into the hot, quiet August night. Utterly alone. Utterly quiet in his heart, but with his stomach surging excitedly. Who knew what might lurk anywhere? along any of these streets? What adventures? What dangers?

He did not remember just exactly where he did walk. He merely walked the streets, sauntering along happily, and excitedly, looking at the houses, many of them still lighted, and wondering secretly to himself what might be going on in all of them? both the dark ones, and the lighted ones? He did not know how long he walked, either. He lost all track of time. But suddenly, startlingly, he came back to himself to realize that he was walking along the street where Edith lived, and was in fact just a few doors away from her little green and white house. More excitedly than ever, suddenly, he walked on along that way.

When he was in front of the little green house with its white shutters and pretty little lawn, he stopped on the sidewalk and stood, his hands behind his back, rocking back and forth from heel to toe. The house was still lighted. There was one light in the living room, and there was a light in the bedroom around on the north side. She was in there then, awake. The living room, with its one long latticed window, was unshuttered and he could see into it, but he could not see Edith. Where was she then? in the bedroom? Hell, maybe she had some man in there with her? he thought breathlessly. He had often wondered what she did on the nights he didnt come to see her? He knew the layout of this house like the back of his hand; he ought to, he had been in it often enough. Being in the middle of the block, which was lighted only at the street intersections with overhead streetlights, it was pretty dim around here—except for the light thrown out on the lawn by the front room window. Suddenly, after looking both ways up and down the street, Frank stepped silently off the public sidewalk onto the private grass, and walked noiselessly around to the north bedroom window. It was the first time he had ever approached a house.

But then what the hell? he thought breathlessly and excitedly, it was practically the same as his own house; he had bought and paid for it, hadnt he? And the woman living in it was his mistress. Anyway, his ex-mistress; or would be before long; although she didnt know it yet.

Around to the north side was a little stand of bushes, just at the corner, and he stood at the nearer, western end of them for a few moments, looking at the lighted window. The venetian blinds in it were closed, of course. Damn it. Or very nearly closed? Who did she have in there with her? That damned Alberson boy, maybe? Or did she have anybody with her? Just then the light in the livingroom went off, while the light in the bedroom stayed on. Aha! he thought to himself.

After a few moments, and feeling a tense sexual arousal surging as he stepped, Frank walked quietly up to the still-lighted bedroom window. The bottom of it was just chest high. And by raising and lowering his head, he could at this close range see in between the various slats of the blind. Edith was standing across the bed from himself at the window, disrobing herself to go to bed. Breathlessly, but hardly daring to breathe to relieve it, Frank watched her as she took off her clothes, until she was in her bra and panties. He could not see below her knees because she was beyond the bed, but Frank didnt give a damn about that. What he wanted to know was did she have someone with her? In a way, he almost wished she did. By craning his neck he could look down along the blind slats and see the rest of the bed, and that there was no one on it. Well, maybe they—he; whoever he was—was in the bathroom? Fascinatedly, excitedly, breathlessly, he watched between the slats as Edith slid her bra straps off her shoulders, and turned it around to the back so she could reach the fastener and unfasten it. Then she ran her hands down her thighs, shucking her panties down and stepped out of them, and he could see all of her. More excited by her now than he had ever been when he was in the same room with her, Frank drank her all in hungrily. Matter-of-factly, Edith stretched herself once, then went to massaging her legs where the elastic panties had cut into them. Then she turned, her long back toward him, and went into the bathroom and shut the door.

Leaving his vantage point, Frank slipped quietly around to the west side, the back, of the little house; but the bathroom window was too high for him to see into. He stood looking at it hungrily for a moment, then slipped back to his former place by the bedroom window. After a moment or two, Edith came back out and matter-of-factly—never realizing what beauty, what loveliness, what richness, she possessed; never even aware of it; he could tell—slipped into her pajamas. Frank was sure now there was no one with her. In a way, it was almost too bad. Then she reached for the light switch and flipped it off.

And just as she did so, Frank straightened up—his back was aching from his strained position—and knocked his knee against the side of the house. Almost immediately, the light went back on and Edith, her eyes narrowed, stood looking directly at him. (She couldnt see him, of course.) Then, swiftly, she came toward the window. Frank ducked down, wanting to laugh, and being careful to make no more noise, pressed himself on the ground against the house, his face averted. Above him, the venetian blind clattered as she raised it, and a square of light fell out beyond him into the yard. It stayed that way a moment or two, and then slowly Edith let the blind back down. Quickly, Frank slipped away from the house and back over behind the bushes and crouched down a little behind them, excitement pulsing through him, but she did not raise the blind again. After a moment, he stepped back out onto the sidewalk—the public sidewalk—and started walking leisurely away toward town, breathlessly excited, and having to hold his stomach muscles tight to keep from laughing spasmodically.

Only then did it occur to him that Edith might run in and call the police. More swiftly, but trying not to look hurried, he turned at the next corner and went two blocks west before he turned back toward town. Coldly, coolly, his brain working with a swift unfrightened sureness such as he seldom knew, he sauntered on along, taking the evening air, until he came out on West Wernz Avenue the mainstreet and then turned back east toward home.

Only when he was back safely in the house—just like that time in Springfield—did any fear enter him. But even the fear was itself stimulating and exciting this time. His hands trembling uncontrollably, he mixed himself still another batch of Manhattans, the third, and sat down with them in the diningroom, and proceeded to drink them—or almost all of them: He had had no dinner at all—although he was not in the least hungry—and he remembered his gastritis attacks; so he only finished about half of this third batch of Manhattans, though he would dearly have loved to have drunk the rest.

And while he sat and drank them—the half—he sat and savored his experience. It was the most completely satisfying sexual experience he had ever had in his life that he could remember. He had more completely and fully *had*, and dominated, this woman tonight than he had ever *had* or dominated her in bed; and yet he had not even touched her. He had merely seen her. He had *seen* her, naked, nude, while—all unsuspecting—she had not even known anyone was looking. He had *possessed* her. Tonight he had more completely possessed Edith Barclay than he had ever possessed any other woman in his entire life, even including his wife Agnes. And the feeling was exquisite. And even the fear—the fear that he might be *caught*—added to his passion. Looking wistfully at the half-pitcher of Manhattans he knew he mustnt drink, Frank got up and switched off the lights, and leaving the drinks there, went into his bedroom and undressed.

What would she say, Agnes? What would she say, if she could see him now? What if she suddenly walked in, right now, and came and stood in the bedroom door, and saw him, lying here flopping like a grotesque fish, and doing this? In his mind, wishfully, he could almost actually see her standing there, in the door. The thought excited him almost beyond physical bearability. The grotesqueness of himself excited him even more. What would she say? What would she do? What would she think?

God damn her.

Then he rolled over on his side and pulling the sheet up over him, went comfortably, satisfiedly, into a deep, sound sleep.

When he woke up next day, it all seemed like a strange wild dream. Like that time up at Springfield. Most of it he could not even remember, it seemed. But as he came more awake and thought about it more, it all came back, freshly, beautifully, as exciting as before. But it frightened him. Had it really happened after all? But there was the remaining half-pitcher of unfinished Mahattans to prove it. It frightened him badly;—and yet it did not really frighten him at all. But God! what if he had been *caught?* But even so, it did not really frighten him, not like the time in Springfield had, because the supreme satisfaction he had experienced this time still remained, overriding any fears. God, had it really happened, or had he only dreamed it? The Manhattans he poured distastefully down the sink. Then he dressed carefully and went downtown to eat breakfast and go to work. All day long, as he worked hard and energetically at all the myriad things he had to do, the night before receded more and more until finally he forgot it entirely in the press of business affairs and more important things. But the sense of supreme and delicious satisfaction, divorced now from its cause, remained with him all day. It was that night, that second night, that he went over to see Edith, and to tell her.

He fortified himself with several Manhattans at home before he went over there. He had called her from the office at the store during the day to let her know he was coming. And after he got there, while they sat around the nice little living room, he re-fortified himself with more Manhattans. He had thought, briefly, about going to bed with her before he told her; he knew there probably wouldnt be much chance after. He did not intend to repeat the humiliation to him that had happened with Geneve Lowe. But, also, he felt it would be a dirty trick to pull on her; and besides, he was considerably distressed by what he was going to have to tell her. Considerably. And anyway, he discovered, sitting there in the room with her, that he didnt have near as much desire to go to bed with her as formerly. Actually, if given a choice, he would have preferred to stand outside the bedroom window and watch her undress without her knowing like he had done last night, to the actual physical act of going to bed with her. Not entirely, though, however. Not, especially, when he thought about how he was going to have to give her up forever. Gee, he hated to have to do it. She was such a nice girl, really. And this was such a nice relaxing place for both of them. He hunted through his mind in vain for some gradual, easy way to bring it up, while they sat and drank.

"I think I had a visitor last night," Edith told him conversationally, amongst some other topics. She grinned a little, sheepishly: "A peeping tom."

"Oh?" Frank said. "Really? What makes you think so? Did you see him?"

"No; but after Id undressed getting ready for bed and turned off the light, I heard something bump against the house like a leg or a foot, right outside the bedroom window. I hadnt even got in bed yet, and I turned the light back on and went and raised the blinds. But I couldnt see anybody."

"Maybe you just imagined it," Frank said tranquilly.

"Maybe," Edith admitted. "But I dont think so."

"Who would be a peeping tom in Parkman?" Frank said. "In a little town like this?"

"I dont know. I havent the slightest idea. But its embarrassing."

"Did you call the police?" Frank asked.

"No," Edith said, and smiled ruefully. "It would look silly. Unmarried women are always supposed to be imagining they are seeing men. And I figured whoever it was, if it was anybody, was already gone—after I opened the blind."

"Probably was," Frank said; "if there was anybody. Didnt you have your blinds closed?"

"Yes. Thats what puzzled me. But maybe they could see in between the slats. I dont know if they were really fully closed."

"Well, you want to make sure you got your blinds all the way closed after this," Frank grinned, "when you get undressed."

"Yes," Edith said darkly. "I certainly intend to."

"But—well, why does it bother you so much?" Frank said after a moment. "What if somebody did see you naked for a minute or two; that wouldnt hurt you."

"But its embarrassing!"

"You dont care if I see you naked," Frank grinned.

"Thats different," Edith said. "God! I hate people like that. Peeping toms; windowpeepers."

"Why?" Frank grinned. "Hell, it wouldnt bother me if somebody looked in the window and saw me naked."

"Yes, but youre a man. Its different with a woman. Its—its sort of a personal indignity."

"What if it had been me?" Frank said, grinning, and then laughed. "Would it have upset you so if it had been me?"

"You!" Edith shrugged, then she frowned puzzledly. "Well, I dont know. No, I guess not. Not if I knew it *was* you. But it wouldnt *be* you. You can come inside."

Frank smiled. "Sure. I just wondered if it would have made any difference if it was me who saw you naked." Peeping tom, he thought to himself, windowpeeper; and such contempt. It made him suddenly secretly excited again almost. "Well, it probably wasnt anybody anyway, and it was probably all your imagination. I havent heard of any peeping toms in Parkman."

"I suppose not," Edith said. "I havent heard of any either. Though I remember hearing about several of them when I was little. But I never heard of any of them being caught. I didnt understand what it meant at the time, because I was so little. It seemed all so silly to me. But a woman—" she hesitated; "a woman just doesnt like to have some utter stranger staring at her naked. Its an indignity. —Well," she said, and smiled, "would you like another drink?"

And looking down at his nearly empty glass, Frank suddenly remembered what he was there for. He cleared his throat.

"Yes," he said; "yes, I would. —Listen, Edith," he said; "Ive got something to tell you. Something not very pleasant."

Edith who had started to get up, stopped, and sank back down and looked at him, directly, level-eyed, in that way she had. "Oh?" she said. "And whats that?"

"Lets have that drink first," Frank said awkwardly.

"All right," she said, and got up and went across the room to the little radio-bar to mix them. Frank watched her wistfully, the lithe way she walked, her perfectly molded hips, the slim waist from behind, enjoying her but remembering with a sudden excitation how she had looked last night, nude, through the slats of her venetian blind. He enjoyed that more. He really *had* possessed her, hadnt he? More than he knew. And more than he had ever done in bed. It was the first time in his life, really, that he had ever really possessed a woman, he thought suddenly with a kind of awe.

"All right," she said in her clear, direct voice when she brought the drinks back. She handed him his and sat back down in her chair and looked him squarely, directly in the eyes. "What is it?"

"Well, I dont exactly know how to begin," he said awkwardly.

"Why dont you just start?" Edith said.

"All right," he said, awkwardly. "Agnes has left me. She found out about you and me, and she—ahh—confronted me with it, and when I refused to give you up she took little Walter and went out to her sister's in Kansas City."

Edith suddenly smiled warmly. "You refused to give me up?"

"I did," he said. "I tried to explain to her the difference between a wife and a—a girlfriend; but you know Agnes."

Edith's smile faded as suddenly as it had come. "You mean different kinds of love?" she said.

"Well, yeh," Frank said awkwardly, "sort of, in a way."

Edith looked down at her drink. "And so what are you going to do now?"

"Well, that was what I wanted to talk to you about," Frank said awkwardly.

"And?"

"Well, to make a long story short," he said, "I called her up out there when she got there, and asked her to come back. She agreed to on one condition."

"That you give me up," Edith said.

Frank nodded, painfully. "Thats right." He paused a moment, then suddenly burst out. "Shes so damned old-fashioned," he said angrily.

Edith had sat back in her chair, and was looking at her drink. After a moment she sat back up again and looked at him squarely. She always had had such a disconcerting way of looking at you so squarely and directly. "So what are you going to do?" she said quietly.

"What can I do?" Frank said angrily. "Shes got little Walter. And as far as that goes, shes got me dead to rights as far as the law goes, too. She can get Walter, and damned near everything Ive got, too, if she wants to." Frank squirmed angrily and awkwardly in his chair, and very nearly upset his drink. God, he hated to have to go through things like this. God, he hoped she didnt cry.

Edith, leaning lightly on the elbow of the arm that held her drink on the chair arm, studied him squarely. "Well, Ive been expecting something like this, more or less," she said quietly after a moment. "It had to happen sometime. I guess I knew it would happen, eventually, when I took the house. You couldnt fool Agnes Hirsh forever. How did she find out?"

Frank squirmed unhappily. "It was the house," he admitted. "And putting you within the ribbons at the wedding. She checked up on the insurance and found there wasnt any."

Edith nodded, confirmingly. "I figured that she might. Well, if it hadnt of been that, it would have been something else, eventually. Maybe, in a way, I was even hoping it would happen, when I took this house."

"*Hoping?*" Frank said wonderingly.

"Yes," Edith said, and smiled. And suddenly she seemed to grow in stature, grow taller, before his very eyes. "Its freed me of something, too, you know. In a way," she said obscurely. Then she shook her head. "Not because of you, or anything like that. Something else." Then, before he could ask her what she meant by that, she spoke again: "Well, what do you want me to do?"

"Well, we'll have to stop seeing each other," Frank said awkwardly, and stopped.

"Youll want me to give up my job at the store, too, wont you?" Edith said, looking at him squarely.

Frank shrugged miserably. "I suppose youll have to, I guess," he said.

Edith looked at him levelly, efficiently, thoughtful. "Well, itll take me at least a couple of weeks to break in a new girl at the store—unless you just want me to drop it and let somebody start from scratch? I dont think I could do it in any less than that."

"Well, Agnes said she and Walter were goin to stay out there for a couple of weeks or so," Frank said awkwardly. "That would give us time to break somebody in, as it happens. And with Al runnin' the store we really need a good girl in there. But do you want to do it? Do you want to do that?"

"Of course," Edith said. "Of course I want to do it. The store needs it. I dont mind."

"Well, I appreciate it a lot," Frank said. He had never seen her look so strangely selfpossessed. All of a sudden like. It didnt seem to really be bothering her at all. "Its awful nice of you."

Suddenly she smiled at him. "And Ill sign the house back over to you," she said. "—Or," she added, "to anyone whom you designate. Like that company that sent me the check. Because I dont suppose Agnes let any of it get out and become public, did she?"

"No, I dont think anybody knows a thing about it," Frank said awkwardly. "But I want you to keep the house, Edith. Its yours. You own it. You paid for it."

"With your money," Edith smiled.

"Even so," Frank said, "I want you to keep the house." For a moment he thought he was going to get tears in his eyes. "Hell," he said gruffly, "I laid out eight thousand for this place for you. Thats a pretty sizable investment."

"But I wont have any use for it," Edith said simply. "Im not going to stay in Parkman."

"Youre not?"

"No. Of course not. Im beat," she said simply. "Agnes whipped me. I might as well admit it, hadnt I? No, I wont stay in Parkman."

"Well— Wherell you go?"

"I think Ill go to Chicago," Edith said. "Ive thought about it before, you know, planning ahead. I more or less figured this would happen someday. I think Chicago would be the best place for me; there ought to be a lot of openings for the kind of work I can do. Ive learned a lot about book-keeping and private-secretarying working for you." She smiled again, that strange resentmentless smile, that seemed so out of place to him, under the circumstances.

"Well, I want you to keep the house anyway, Edith," Frank said. "You—youve earned it. It belongs to you. I want you to keep it. It would make me feel a lot better."

"But what would I do with it?"

"Why, hell, its an investment. Rent it out to somebody and itll bring you in some income."

"I never thought of that," Edith said, her eyes widening thoughtfully. "Yes. Yes, I could do that. Would you handle it for me?"

"Well, I cant. Not very well," Frank said awkwardly. "Under the circumstances. But, well— Well—Judge Deacon would. Judge Deacon would handle it for you, and handle it well. He cant very well take you on anything like a simple house rental," he said, and smiled. "I could call him up about it."

"Yes," Edith said, and smiled back at him openly. "That would work out fine. What I want to do is fix it up so that the income from it would be paid to Daddy. Thatll give him a little money so he can afford to keep his housekeeper, that youve been paying for."

"It could be arranged like that," Frank said awkwardly.

"Yes," Edith said crisply, efficiently, "that would work out fine." And she sat and looked at him evenly, levelly. "Well, is there anything else to take care of?"

"No, I guess not," Frank said. "Ill send that little girl in my office over to you at the store tomorrow and you can start breakin' her in." He paused, awkwardly. "I wont come around the store any myself. In case it would bother you, or anything."

"That wouldnt bother me at all," Edith said.

"It wouldnt?"

"Not at all. You come any time you want."

"Well, okay," Frank said. He still couldnt understand this sudden, peculiar selfpossession she seemed to have. He had not thought she would take it in this way at all. Not after the way she had clung to him so, lately. Damn it. He tossed off the rest of his drink. Edith was still sitting, looking at him levelly, squarely.

"I didnt think youd take it this way," he said; "so nicely."

"In what way should I take it?" Edith said simply. "What would you want me to do? Weep and cry? Would you prefer that?"

"Oh, no," Frank said awkwardly. "No, no. I didnt mean nothing like that. Im glad. Im glad for you. Its better that it *dont* hurt you."

Edith gazed at him level-eyed. "Yes, it is better," she said simply. "That it doesnt hurt me. Isnt it?"

"Look, Edith," he said suddenly. "I—I know this is a terrible thing to ask. And you can tell me to go to hell, and kick me out if you want. But—well, would you go to bed with me one more time? a sort of farewell party?"

"Why, yes," Edith said, "if you want me to."

Frank was startled. He had not expected that answer at all; he had expected her to demur and not want to do it—only not do so in any nasty way like Geneve Lowe had done—and in fact, he didnt even know why he asked her. Why *had* he asked her? And he found himself suddenly remembering last night again, and the window.

"Well," he said awkwardly, "maybe it would be better if we didnt. I guess it would only make us both feel worse, instead of better." He paused. "Dont you think?" he said.

"Just as you wish," Edith said.

"Well, I guess I better go," he said and got up.

Edith walked with him to the door, and as he prepared to open it, she smiled. "Goodby, boss," she said.

Standing by the door with his hand already on the knob, Frank felt so unhappy that he thought he could not stand it, and he leaned straight over (she was almost as tall as he was, in her heels) and kissed her lightly on the cheek; but he did not touch her in any other way.

"Goodby, Edith," he said unhappily. "And if Ive caused you any unhappiness and hurt since you came to work for me, Im sorry. I never meant to. I truly never did." Then he opened the door and smiling sadly back at her went out and shut it.

And after he walked back uptown to where he had parked the Cadillac, he drove past the house twice, slowly. All the lights were still on.

And suddenly, as if making a sudden unexpected decision, but really having known all along that he was going to do it, he drove back home and put the car away in the garage and set out to walk back up there. When he arrived the lights in the bedroom were on; but when, after looking all around, he approached his vantage point beneath the window, he found the venetian blinds tightly closed this time. He could see nothing. Sadly and miserably, frustrated as it were in his attempt at a last farewell, he stood unhappily behind the screen of bushes until the bedroom light went off and then went on home. If only he hadnt knocked his damned knee against that wall!

That night, at home, he got *really* drunk. Really *really* drunk. He knew he had to work tomorrow, and that there were all kinds of things he ought to be taking care of, but something came over him and he just didnt give a damn. To hell with all of it, he thought selfinjuriously. Just what did he have really? A wife who didnt even love him; a mistress who was perforce leaving him; a son who probably didnt love him either; and he was making a lot of money. That was what he had. That: to show for nearly forty nine years of life. A hell of a lot, wasnt it? what he had?

But he had one more thing: luckily, just by chance, sheer lucky chance and no more—because what if the blinds had been closed last night, too?—luckily, he had a perfect memory of a woman. One woman. That he had possessed once in his lifetime. He knew he oughtnt to be drinking so much; and he kept telling himself so. But the more he drank, the more it became just rote words, as he reached for another, and he didnt care. The result, of course, what with all the other heavy drinking he had been doing lately, and as he himself had really anticipated, was another gastritis attack. And he didnt care. But when that hit him, the next day, he cared then. He cared plenty. When he got the heaves— which, as the liquid was swiftly all removed from his stomach, turned into the dry heaves—he kicked himself for having gotten drunk and caused it, as he had known—almost—that he would.

Had he maybe done it to himself deliberately? on purpose? he wondered dimly, as he lay in the bed fighting to keep from retching. What the hell? he didnt seem to know anything about anything any more. And with the sickness, and the rather rickety sobriety that came along with it, all the real terror and fear and horror that he had felt after that wild night in Springfield last year came booming down on him. Night before last he had been too drunk, and too excited over what he had seen, to really feel it; and most of yesterday he had been too busy to. But now it hit him full force. God, what if he had been *caught*, standing there in her yard peering through her bedroom window? Or what if she had called the police, and they had caught him before he got away? A guy like that son of a bitch Sherm Ruedy: hell, they might even have put him in jail. Even if she was his mistress.

What made him do it? What was it about it that excited him so? What made him *still*, even now, *still* want to do it some more? Women! Damn women. They didnt any of them ever care for you like you cared for them. None of them, not any of them, ever really allowed themselves to be possessed the way you wanted to possess them, the way a *man* should possess them. They might play at it a little bit—as long as you didnt rub them the wrong way and make them mad. But that was all. Naked women. What made him so hungry, so fascinated, so drawn to naked women? What was wrong with him? That Agnes. Damn that Agnes! Why didnt women ever have the urge to see naked men the way men wanted to see naked women? Damn them, they ought to have that urge, ought to have to suffer it like he did. It might be good for them. And what if Agnes ever found out? Of course, all the damned advertizing agencies were always throwing naked women at you—or near-naked women, anyway. Maybe that was it: They were never really naked. And the movies, too—while pretending to be so damned virtuous, but always throwing big-breasted near-naked women at you. Never really naked, any of them, though. That was one reason he hated going to the movies. Hell, even in the nude pictures in magazines they always blocked out the genitals. Maybe that was part of what caused his hunger to see naked women? He didnt attempt to understand it; but always all his life he had had thrown at him near-naked women, but never did you get to really see them naked. But what if Agnes should find out? My God! A peeping tom, a windowpeeper; at forty eight. Terror would grip him while he lay trying to stop himself from retching. What made him do it? What made him do it? And yet, even then, in the midst of this sheer chilling terror, never did the sense of excitement, the sheer deliciousness, he had felt that night as he stood there at the window and watched her undress herself, never did it abate or leave him. Well, never would he ever do it again. That was a promise. And anyway, that time it had been his own mistress he was watching.

So he would lie with his terror, trying to keep from gagging, until finally he would have to get up and creep to the bathroom again and heave and retch and gag, while nothing came out of him except saliva. Finally, when it got no better and showed no signs of getting any better, he called Doc Cost.

The big man came out right away, and gave him an injection of morphine, then made him swallow a powder that he poured out of a paper and mixed with water. He was not, Doc said, to get up any more that day. As if he even *could* have got up, for God's sake. Tomorrow when he felt a little better he could start out on some liquids and a few light solids. Starch was what he needed. Starch and carbohydrates. Feeling the morphine beginning to take hold of him, he watched the big man grow wavery, and finally he went to sleep.

The next day—Doc Cost had stopped back in the morning—he did exactly as he had been told; and by mid-afternoon he was able to go back down town to the office. Even though he had not shown up, Edith Barclay had taken care of everything: She had transferred the little blonde girl from the new offices over to the store, and had even hired a new girl for him: a brunette this time, but just as green as the other. God, they were all going to miss her, miss Edith. Shakily, Frank explained to the new girl what her duties were: there wasnt really much for a girl to do, up here. Afterwards, he went by the store to see how Edith was making out, and found her working with the little blonde girl and her same selfcontained, selfpossessed, quiet, efficient self. Al Lowe complained to him about Edith quitting: she said she could make more in Chicago, he said; and pleaded with Frank to talk to her and get her to not leave. Frank, of course, said he could do nothing. If she wanted to leave, it was her business. Looking back at her once longingly, he walked out past the crotchety old repairman, and went home. He did not drink anything at all that night, and because he could not sleep took one of the sedatives Doc had thoughtfully provided for him. Next day he felt pretty much like himself again, and was able to go to work, really go to work, this time.

During the next two weeks before Agnes and little Walter returned, while Edith was sturdily and efficiently training her little successor, Frank threw himself frenziedly and energetically into his work. He had never worked so hard, or so well. They were wanting to get all the leases wound up anyway, so that the lessees could get moved in and all set up for the big opening before cold weather. With this in mind, and with that other secret part of himself driving him also, he finished all the leases, and consulted with the lessees and the architect about their store layouts, and also made plans and purchases (while consulting with

Al Lowe) for his own new store, the jewelry store. Because he had to be over at both the old store and out at the new one, he saw Edith a number of times. Never once, though, in any way, was there any sign from her that they had ever been anything to each other, or had known each other in any way other than their official capacities there at the store. The new little blonde girl obviously looked up to him, to Frank, as if he was some sort of a tin god. But it was Edith that he watched. He could not understand her: He himself could not let go that easily, though he wished he could. And every time he looked at her, he would see her in his mind as she had looked that night, when he had stood and peered through her blinds, secretly, silently, and watched her undress herself there right down to the skin.

During those two weeks of hard hectic work, he only went out "walking" three times. He held himself down to that. That was what he always called it now anymore to himself: go out "walking." He could always feel it coming on him beforehand. As early as midafternoon he would begin to get that excited feeling, even when he was working. It seemed to come on him almost rhythmically, in a sort of definite cycle, the same way the desire to sleep with a woman used to hit him. He could go for a week without sex, sometimes even longer, before the desire would build up in him. And it was the same way with going out "walking". He could feel it gradually coming on him, day by day almost, until he knew on the day it reached its peak that he would not be able to stop it. Nothing would. And that evening he would go home and mix himself his Manhattans and get good and half drunk—though he was very careful now not to drink more than that—and with the liquor in him sit and savor what was coming until after it was good and dark and just about bed time for most people, and then he would go and change his clothes to darker ones and go out, that tremendous feeling of excitement and adventure—and of possible danger—rising in him powerfully. He could feel terror the next day, of course, every time; and horror, too, even; and he would promise himself never again; but the terror was never strong enough to completely offset the excitement, or the thought that this time he might actually see something *really* spectacular; and he knew, even when he promised himself never again, that it would not—when the cycle came to peak intensity—make any difference. He would go. He had to go. It was something he had no control over.

He knew, too, dimly—and perhaps not even so dimly—that in some strange way it was his way of getting even with Agnes. And for that matter, with all women. Getting even with all women. For the fact that they would never allow themselves to be possessed. This way he could possess them anyway, and they couldnt do anything about it because they didnt even know about it. Because never again did he, or would he, ever make a mistake like that first oafish error of knocking his knee against the wall. And, in fact as time went on, he became very accomplished and practiced in his new art. Because it was an art, just like business or anything else. He became very professional, and quickly.

He learned something else about this new art, too: Every night he went out was not going to be a spectacular, or even successful, evening. In fact, if he was any judge as he grew more practiced and gained more experience, it would only average out about one in ten nights that he would have any luck at all; even see anything. Long odds, for the risk involved, but he was willing to accept them. Because every night might be *the* one. Just like each new poker hand might be *the* one. But as far as that went, there wasnt really much risk involved. Nobody ever saw him. Nobody ever knew he was there. Unless they happened to see him sauntering along the sidewalks taking a respectable evening "constitutional". There was really very little risk. And always, tantalizingly, before his mind's eye, was that one night at Edith's.

On the three nights he did go out "walking" before Agnes returned, one time he walked—although pretty hopelessly—down past Edith's again; that was the first time. But the lights were already out anyway, when he got there. Either she wasnt home, or else had gone to bed. Damn! if he just hadnt knocked his knee against the wall that first time.

And then, on that same evening, with a sudden inspiration, he walked over east past Al and Geneve Lowe's house. He knew that house like the back of his hand, too. What, and where, every room was. And this time he had luck. As he stood screened by some bushes, peering into the side window of the long living room, where he could see Al sitting reading, Geneve came out of the hallway at the far end which led to both the bathroom and the bedroom. And Geneve was stark, mother naked. Lithely, she walked down the length of the long room directly toward him to where Al sat about a quarter of the way up; looking just exactly as she had when he had seen her so many other times, in Chicago, and other places. As he watched breathlessly, Geneve sat down on the arm of her husband's chair and kissed him. It didnt take her long. In a moment she was up and going back toward the hall, and Al was following her, his book lying forgotten on the floor. Cautiously, Frank slipped around to the back to where the bedroom window was, but it was dark. They had turned the lights off. Unhappily, almost wistfully, Frank stood for quite a while and looked at it. Then he went home himself, to his own empty house and bed, and self. Even so, though, he had had plenty of time to drink her, all of her, all in as she walked down the long room. That made two women now that he had completely possessed. He ought to start himself a score sheet. Someday, after they got home, he was going to spy on Agnes herself, by God!

But after that one, that first of the three nights, he didnt have much more luck. That night at Geneve's was the best. —Although, of course, not as good as that one perfect night at Edith's had been.—The second time, when the peak pitch reached him again and drove him out, he went back there, to Geneve's. But this time they had company, another young couple their own age, and all four of them were sitting around in the kitchen drinking. Nevertheless, he intended to put Geneve's house down on his permanent route. After he left there, he just walked around and saw nothing.

Yes, it was—as he progressed in his new hobby—becoming increasingly apparent that it was going to take a lot of leg work and a lot of nights of "walking" to get one even half-way decent result. But he was willing to accept the odds. Besides, his evening constitutionals were good exercise for him. He felt better physically than he had in years, in spite of the drinking. But then, of course, he had been playing golf all summer at the Country Club, too. And playing quite well, too, this year, he thought; if he did say so himself. He had come within one and two strokes of breaking par several times.

But if the results of 'walking' were so few, he was quite willing to accept that. High odds, yes; but every time he did get to see one, really and fully see one, it would be another woman he had possessed— whether she ever knew anything about it or not. And that was what he wanted: what he had always wanted: to possess women. Who would never allow themselves to be possessed. Ever. God, how he hated women sometimes! He had never realized how much he really did hate them. All except his mother, of course. He didnt hate her, of course. And, in fact, he had been visiting her a lot more often, since the Old Man died in July, and since all of this other—this going "walking"—had started. In spite of his heavy work schedule, he was visiting with her twice a week now almost every week, instead of just once. Which, of course, naturally pleased her.

But as for the rest of them: faugh! To hell with them. It was strange: anymore he saw almost every woman as a kind of double person: as mother, and as woman. When he saw them as mothers, or sometimes even as potential mothers, he admired and respected them. And would do almost anything for them. But then his mind would sort of shift gears on him—unless the woman in question was too old to see that way—and he would see them as women, instead of mothers, and he would hate their guts. Even on the street it happened; and if they were someone he knew, he would secretly place them on his growing list for future possession.

But when Agnes and Walter finally came home from their vacation, and he had them around the house there once again, he found it slowed him down a lot, and eased him. Instead of the frighteningly—and excitingly—lonely house there, with himself in it alone, they would be around, and it changed things. It eased him down, and the absolutely-uncontrollable urge to go out "walking" reached its peak less frequently—though still just as devastatingly, and irrepressibly, when it did come. And he was glad, too; because he didnt want to get himself to going out too often. That might increase his chances of getting caught. And as long as he stayed at home he was safe.

It wasnt much of a home anymore, he had to admit—except for little Walter—but at least it was better than it had been living there wholly alone. One thing Agnes made plain as soon as she got home, and that was that she had no intention of taking up "relations" with him again. She had told him over the phone from Kansas City that if she came back it was to be "strictly a business arrangement"—for the good of little Walter—and he had said yes yes anything, without even thinking about it one way or the other; he had been too upset to do more, or to think of the implications of what she said; but when she got home it became plain that she had meant it, exactly what she had said. As soon as she got home the very first thing she did was to move herself out of their joint bedroom. Immediately upon arrival, that first day,—with little Walter helping her—she moved all her clothes out of the closet and took all her things from the dresser, and moved them all upstairs to Dawnie's old room—vacated now by her marriage—and there she set up house. And immediately she had done so, she went to bed sick. It was her gall bladder. She had a constant nagging driving pain in her right side from it all the time; and had had, she said, for some time before she went on that exhausting trip to Kansas City. It was a miracle that she had even been able to make the drive both ways. There was a hint, unspoken, of a deep and abiding accusation of Frank for having forced her to do so when she was as ill as she was. She had, she said, gone to a specialist recommended to her by Mary Ellen in Kansas City who examined her and told her she ought to have her gall bladder out. She had not done so, because it was more than just a minor operation like an appendectomy, but she might have to do so yet.

Frank noted, rather sarcastically to himself, that her illness had not made her lose any weight, at any rate; if anything, she had gained a little. Nevertheless, she remained ill and in bed and in constant pain; and little Walter waited upon her like some miniature slave. Even Frank himself was forced to wait on her quite a bit himself, which he did with alacrity and ungrudgingly, because he was not even at all sure himself that she wasnt sick. She had Doc Cost out to examine her almost at once as soon as she was home and firmly ensconced upstairs—explaining to Doc that she had moved herself up there because of her illness with which she did not want to disturb Frank—and Doc's diagnosis, while more conservative than the Kansas City man, nevertheless confirmed that she might very easily have something wrong with her gall bladder, and probably did. It was, Doc admitted, hard to tell about these things sometimes. But he advised against taking it out unless absolutely necessary because it would make her a semi-invalid the rest of her life. Instead, he advised her to diet.

This was all right with Frank, who remained attentively present during Doc's visit, because Frank wanted to take care of her and didnt want anything to happen to her. But even so, he could not quite overcome a suspicion that a lot of it, including the constant pain, was more put-on than real. And yet, nevertheless, on two different occasions the first month she was home, she had acute attacks in the night, after dinner parties; and it looked to be damned real. Just the same, he noted that it never bothered her from getting out of bed to cook, or to go to some tea or club meeting somewhere; and it did not prevent her from going out and accepting all the flocks of high-toned dinner invitations they were still getting. And it did not prevent her from entertaining in return. But if that was what she wanted to do, if that was how she wanted to entertain herself, it was all right with him. As for the diet, there began to appear a lot more dishes of stewed vegetables and stewed fruit, a lot more "New England boiled dinners", amongst her cooking, and a lot less meat and potatoes; and Frank did not like that. But he did not say anything. He was willing to put up even with that, to have her home here with him and to look after him and Walter, damn her.

He didnt know what he was supposed to do. Perhaps she wanted him to come sit by her and hold her hand and wait on her and render her devotion, and gradually talk her back into being in love with him again and—after she finally got over her pique—get her to start sleeping with him again—although she herself had made it plain she never intended to again. Perhaps that was what she wanted: for him to talk her into it over her own protests. But if that was what she wanted, he was damned if he would. There was a limit to what even a loving husband could take, or could do. Damn her. She had ruined everything else, and ruined his damned life; he was damned if he would go and beg her for her damned affections. Let her be a damned invalid. And he would be a damned peeping tom. Oh, God! he thought terrifiedly; and yet there was still a high excitement in the thought, too: A peeping tom: A damned peeping tom. Let her stay upstairs. And he would stay downstairs. If she thought that hurt him: her moving up there: she couldnt have been more wrong. He was glad to have the downstairs bedroom to himself. It gave him more freedom than he had had in years, really; he could go out at night any time he wanted; and at the same time having her back home kept him from getting that curious panic.

God! Where had it gone, that year of happiness—such very real happiness—they had had? What had happened to it? What had happened to *them*? Why couldnt they get it back? Why couldnt they have kept it? He had never loved anyone or anything as much as he had loved her during that year. And now it was gone. Just faded completely out and away. She had forced him to give up his mistress—the having of which wasnt hurting her any; not a damned bit—and then she had come home, had agreed to come home, and had entrenched herself upstairs, giving nothing, not bending a damned inch, and he had entrenched himself downstairs, and the house in effect had become an armed camp—with little Walter the UN go-between. Except, of course, when there was company there; or they were out somewhere. Why did it have to be like that? If she was going to do that, she could at least have let him keep his mistress!

And an almost uncontainable outrage and humiliation and anger and sort of a dim vague selfdestructiveness would sweep over him. And the only way he could get rid of it was to put on dark clothes and go out "walking" and—whether he had luck or not—come home half drunk, maliciously, grindingly, viciously pleased at what he was taking away from her, God damn her. That, at least, was one thing no goddamned woman could make you give up or take away from you.

Edith, of course, was already gone by this time. There would be no more chances at her again, ever. And the thought of that—and the memory of that one perfect night—would make him catch his breath while his heart jumped, and hurt him with hunger that was almost unbearable. But she was gone. She had finished up her two weeks of training the new little girl—and done a pretty damned good job of it, considering—and then, three days before Agnes and Walter returned, she had gone. On the Saturday which was her last day she had come around to him where he was standing with Al Lowe discussing purchases for the new store, and had made her farewells to both of them. She shook hands with both of them, smiling affectionately, and once more—for the last time—she called him "boss". There was nothing whatever about her to indicate that she felt the least bit more bad about leaving him, or felt the least bit more affection for him, than she felt for Al. True to the last, Frank thought. True to the act, true to the role, that they had chosen—and been forced—to play. And he could not dampen a strong sense of admiration for her that made her leaving just that much more painful. She had gone on back to the office where the new little girl was, and he and Al had gone on up front and out, because they had to go out to the new store. What was she thinking, he wondered? What was she feeling? She certainly didnt show she was feeling *any*thing. That was the last time he had seen her.

And three days later, Agnes and little Walter arrived home.

Frank was downtown at his new offices working, when they got in that afternoon, and Agnes called him there from the house. Half deliberately—but half way honestly, too—he told her that he could not get away just now, that he was in an important conference about the Shopping Center. He was, in fact, in an important conference on the Shopping Center; but it was not any conference that he couldnt have got away from, or postponed, if he had really wanted to. It gave him considerable pleasure to tell her what he did. Damn her. He was still not entirely over Edith's leaving yet.

Later on, when he did wind everything up, and did get home, it was nearly evening and Agnes and little Walter were just finishing moving all of Agnes's things upstairs. Frank mixed himself a good stiff drink and came in through the living room to the foot of the stairs in the hall which they were going up and down with the things. He had not known what he was going to say when he went in there, and after they came back down the stairs from another trip, he still did not know what to say. Neither did they apparently. He and Agnes were both constrained. Everybody was constrained. Even little Walter was constrained. They all three stood in the hall looking at each other, Walter eyeing both of them carefully and thoughtfully out of a solemnly expressionless face. It seemed silly to merely say only the single word "Hello" to each other; but that was what they all said.

"Movin' upstairs?" Frank said thinly, finally.

"Yes," Agnes said crisply, with an added overtone of wailfulness in her voice. "Im not at all well." You wouldnt think anybody could speak crisply, and at the same time still sound wailful; but Agnes could.

"Im sorry to hear that," Frank said. Then he looked down at little Walter and emotion which he tried hard to disguise welled up in him, and he set his drink down and squatted down and put out his arms. "Well, hello there, buddy-boy," he grinned. "Hows it feel to be back home?"

Walter cast his mother one swift glance, as if checking to make sure she would not be offended, and then came into his arms and put his own arms around Frank.

"Fine, Dad," he said in his solemn way. "Im glad to be back. We're both of us glad to be home," he said diplomatically.

"Im sure you are," Frank said, patting him on the back. "And Im just as glad to have you both home." He looked up at Agnes and smiled, and she looked down at him and smiled too. Both were constrained, if not actually reserved.

"Did you get to see any ball games or anything while you were out there?" Frank said, patting the small back.

"We saw one game," Walter said. "But it wasnt bigleague. Me and Aunt Mary Ellen's boys went, by ourselves."

"Well, thats good," Frank said. "Thats good." Reluctantly, he released the little boy.

"Walter," Agnes said, "why dont you go out and play with your road equipment for a while? We'll finish all this later."

"Yes, mother," Walter said dutifully, and with another covert careful glance at both of them which Frank did not miss, he went out through the livingroom.

"I put all your road equipment away in the garage," Frank called after him, "to keep it out of the weather. Its on the big shelf at the back."

"Yes, sir," Walter said. "Thank you."

"Well, lets get it over with," Frank said thinly, after he was gone. He picked up his drink again.

"I just want to make it plain to you that Im not in good health," Agnes said, crisply-wailfully, "and also the conditions under which Im willing to come back. As far as you and I are concerned, its purely a business deal for the good of the child. I intend to sleep upstairs from now on, by myself."

"Okay," Frank said stolidly. "Anything else?"

"Yes," Agnes said. "Is that whore gone?"

"Shes gone," Frank said. "But shes not a whore. Shes a nice girl. I guess I done her more harm maybe even than I done you."

"I expect so," Agnes said thinly. "I expect so. What about the house?"

"Well," Frank said and hesitated; and then he lied. He couldnt help it. "She wanted to keep the house, and since it was in her name there wasnt very much I could do about it. Shes having Judge Deacon rent it for her and give the money to her father." He just couldnt bring himself to tell Agnes he had urged her to keep it.

"You mean shes not moved back out there with him?" Agnes said, looking a little surprised.

"No," Frank said. "Shes leaving town. Already left, in fact. Moved to Chicago."

"Well!" Agnes said. "And so she kept the house? Well, theres a pretty nice sum of money down the drain, isnt it?" she said bitterly.

Stolidly, Frank did not say anything for a moment. He pulled his chin down into his neck, like a man out in a hail storm. "We can afford it," he said shortly. "Theres plenty more where that came from. And going to be lots more."

"Eight thousand dollars!" Agnes said caustically.

"We can afford it," Frank said again.

"Well, at least the whore is gone!" Agnes said.

"Whats for supper?" Frank said, taking a drink.

"I dont know," Agnes said wailfully. "Ill have to look around. Well!" she said more crisply. "I guess youre pretty proud of yourself, arent you? Eight thousand dollars!"

Stolidly, Frank did not say anything, did not answer. If that was the way it was going to be, well, that was the way it was going to be. He had more or less expected it anyway. He turned to go and mix another drink. Hell, he had known what to expect, hadnt he?

Agnes followed him part way into the livingroom. "Yes, I can plainly see that that girl was no whore," she said bitterly. "I can see that by the way she insisted on keeping the house. Eight thousand dollars! Whoring's going up."

For a moment he debated telling her the truth: that Edith had in fact wanted to sign the house back over to him—and in fact had even been thoughtful enough to suggest signing it over to some company to avoid publicity; and that it was himself who had, because of his guilt, insisted on her keeping it. But what did it matter? That would only rile her up even more. And Edith was already gone. Had been, for three days now. Well, if this was the way it was going to be, this was the way it was going to be.

Edith Barclay, three days earlier, had been thinking almost exactly the same thing; but in a slightly different way: If that was the way it was going to be, that was the way it was going to be. And better so, really, she added to herself; better so. Better this way than some other way it might have all turned out. It was, she thought, somewhat similar to what the military analysts back during the war would have called "an untenable position". Hers and Frank's both; and always had been, really, from the first. She had always known, deep down, that if it ever came actually to the sticking point Frank would *stick* with Agnes. She had never thought it, consciously, but she had known. She had never *let* herself think it. She had never let herself think a lot of things. It was funny what one's mind could do to one if one allowed it to. The truth was, shibboleths were crashing down all over, for Edith Barclay. And she herself? She merely stood, and watched them smash, and felt nothing, really.

She never should have allowed herself to take the house. She had done that because of Jane. Old Jane. And she never should have let herself be seated "within the ribbon" at the wedding. She had done that because—? She didnt *know* why; because it was such a little trivial thing, she guessed. But even had she not allowed herself to do these two things, it would have made no difference. It would only have prolonged the agony. In the end, it would have all come down to the same thing. If not because of those two acts, then because of some others. Because it was, after all, an "untenable position"; and she had known it all along.

Love. What was love, after all? She didnt know. She couldnt analyze it. She only knew what she felt. But she had learned—the hard way— that what she felt was not the whole of it. Not by any means.

She did not wait around any, once the job at the store was done. That same Saturday that she received her last pay check from Al Lowe, she left. There was no point in staying—even a day longer—and prolonging the unpleasantness. The new little girl was adequate to handle the work at the store now; and she seemed bright enough. Probably in time, if she really worked, really liked it and wanted to work, she would modify Edith's own system Edith had built up into one that was uniquely her own, and would therefore be better for her. But she was adequate right now. So there was no point in staying any longer.

Her packing she had already done before, in the evenings after work. And her business with the house was already taken care of with Judge Deacon. Edith suspected, from the way the Judge looked, that he guessed the whole story pretty clearly; but he did not say anything to her, and was polite enough in his brusque crusty way—if he hadnt been, she wouldnt have stayed. He had agreed to handle it for her, and she had already given him two of the three keys. There was no need even to see him again. Her own key she was keeping, as a sort of souvenir. All she had to do was pack the one bag she was taking, lock the door, and go. The rest of her things she had, in the evenings during the past week, moved out to John's. They were all there ready, when she chose to send for them. Once she got settled in Chicago, and found an apartment, she would have John express them to her. The china and the inexpensive silverware and all the rest of the odds and ends that she had shopped for and bought so carefully, she simply left in the little house. If the new tenants wanted them, they were welcome. If not, they could do with them what they wanted.

The little house had grown increasingly empty the last week, as she packed and moved her things out to John's. Even so, while it caused a hollowness in the house and an unpleasant feeling in herself, she preferred doing it that way to spending two or three hectic days moving everything after she had quit the store. She was, she found, able to live with the hollowness in the house as easily and as well as she was able to live with all the thoughts that she used to not let herself think, but which now she did think. It was just a matter of adjustment, with the hollowness in the house, or with the thoughts.

It was all, of course, old Jane, really. Old Jane and her diverticulitis and her discharge she had so desperately tried to hide. That was, really, what had made her take the house in the first place. It was, in a way, a sort of penance to old Janie. Well, she had paid it; she had paid the penance, and so it had served its purpose. She was through with it. And she had felt that way ever since the night two weeks ago when Frank had come over to tell her about Agnes. She had been Frank Hirsh's "mistress"; Frank Hirsh's kept whore; and that was what she had wanted to be—because of Janie. Now it was over. Maybe in some private secret way that was partly why she had taken the house; just in order to bring this end about that much sooner.

Certainly, anyone who thought they could fool Agnes Hirsh indefinitely were only kidding themselves. And now with the humiliation of being kicked out forcibly by her lover's wife, she had in some obscure way, she felt, paid her debt to Janie. Old Jane. Old Janie Jane. She could not, however, resist the one last luxury of telling it all to John. Someone ought to know, she felt, and he was such a dull damned clod anyway. The last evening, Friday evening, when she took her last load of stuff out to his house, she sat and talked with him quite a little while, and explained quite carefully to him how she was being kicked out by Agnes. Agnes had left Frank, she explained to him. Over her: Edith. The only way Frank could get his wife back was to kick her, Edith, out. That meant out of her job at the store, too. Naturally, she was leaving town. There wasnt anything else for her to do.

John was, of course, naturally,—in his dull way—distressed over his daughter and what she had turned into. But more about the possibility of public scandal than anything else.

"I dont think youll have to worry about the publicity," she had told him. "Its all been kept very quiet.

"Of course," she added coolly, "it will all get around town eventually, Im sure. And everybody will hear about it. But it will never actually be *public* scandal; only *private* scandal."

That of course distressed him even more: her allusion to his fear of publicity; and in his dull way he tried to apologize to her. He was really a kind man; there wasnt really anything mean about him. In fact, he was just too damned dull to even be capable of being mean. Edith sat with him in the kitchen of the little old house—so full of memories of Jane for her—and drank a last cup of coffee with him, and told him she was leaving tomorrow. No, she would not be back out before she left. Then she kissed him and said goodby.

And so on Saturday there was nothing to keep her, once she got off work and got her one bag packed, nothing at all. That was the way she had planned it. And she was glad she had handled it this way, rather than waiting to do her moving. Life was so strange: there was such a time lag—and energy lag, too—between the making of a decision and the carrying of it out. You made up your mind to move, but you could not just move. All kinds of energy and work hours had to be expended to accomplish the material fact, once you had made up your mind. And it was so easy to make up your mind. It required no effort at all. All the effort came in the carrying of it out: in that time lag, and energy lag, before the mental decision became the material fact. Perhaps that was why most people changed their lives so seldom.

Carefully she went around the little house making sure there were no lights left on, no water running. Then she picked up her bag and went outside to where the taxi—Hirsh Bros. Taxi Service, only it wasnt

called that—she had called, was waiting. In its own right, apart from any
other consideration, she had really liked the little house; and had
enjoyed it; and enjoyed working on it, and fixing it up. Well, she could
do the same thing with an apartment in Chicago. The taxi took her
uptown, and she caught the evening bus to Terre Haute where she was
going to catch the train.

She had no regrets at all, and no fears. She had no sense of loss. If she
had it all to do over again, probably she would not have done it—knowing what she knew now. But then, how could she know now what she
knew, if she had not done it? There was a kind of fatality and inevitability about all of it. And as for going off to a strange city and looking
for work, she had no qualms whatever there. She was good at her work,
and she knew it; she had full confidence there; and she could *please*
a man with the best of them, now—whether she herself liked it or
not. She ought to make a nearly perfect private secretary.

Actually, she felt freer than she could remember having felt in a
long long time. Perhaps freer than she had ever felt in her life before.
Freer, and more unencumbered. And she could look forward with
equanimity, even adventure, to anything that came. Life wasnt like they
tried to teach you when you were little; but whatever it was, Edith felt
she was ready for it.

Only once, really, as she left, did she have any real feeling of pain and
unhappiness: After she got to Terre Haute on the bus and checked her
bag in the bus station lockers, knowing she had something over an
hour to wait for the evening Chicago train, she walked the block or so
up to the Marine Room bar in the Terre Haute House to have herself
a cocktail, and maybe a sandwich. And that was when she saw Dave
Hirsh.

He was sitting by himself over on the far side of the bar, having
dinner, obviously pretty tight, and kidding loudly and energetically with
the waitress. He did not see her. Edith gave up her idea of a sandwich
and sat down on the near side, in the little room where they served only
cocktails and ordered a Manhattan. To eat she would have had to go on
around to the other side, which meant Dave would see her. And she did
not want to have to speak to him. She had never liked him very well
anyway. But seeing him had momentarily stopped her. Round, blocky,
fat faced and ruddy, ball-headed and barrel-bodied, he looked so much
like his brother Frank that it made Edith's stomach fall away from
under her with the memory of him: of Frank. Poor old Frank. Frank
her lover. He rose up vividly in her mind. So many memories of him.
In so many different ways. And her sorrow and pity for him, in spite
of all his foibles that she knew so well, were still strong in her.
Stronger even than she had expected.

Toying with the stem of her glass as she drank her drink, the idea popped into her head that she could go over there and pick Dave up, pick him up quite easily, and get a hotelroom with him, and in that way—by sleeping with him—she could sleep one last time with—comfort for one last time, poor old Frank. A kind of private farewell, all her own. Dave looked so much like him.

But of course it was a silly idea. He wasnt Frank. He was Dave. And beyond a superficial resemblance there wasnt anything about them that was alike. It was a stupid, silly idea. And she did not even contemplate it beyond that first wild moment when it popped into her head. It did not even bother her that she had thought it. Once, it would have.

Quietly, strangely confident and selfcontained, she sat and sipped her drink. She knew one thing anyway: for sure: she would not want to be Frank and Agnes Hirsh, and have in store for her the life they had in store for them, for anything in this world. She felt sorry, deeply, sincerely sorry, for both of them.

Then she finished her drink and paid and walked out through the hotel lobby to catch a cab and pick up her bag and go out to the railroad station.

She could get her sandwich out there.

CHAPTER 70

When Edith Barclay, on her way out of Parkman for the last time, saw Dave Hirsh in Terre Haute without his seeing her, what she did not know was that Dave was out celebrating. He was having himself a sort of private bachelor dinner: He intended to get good and drunk and have himself a good big dinner and then make the rounds of the whorehouses one last time; after that, he was going to be a happily married man like everybody else. Dave had finally and at long last, after due and careful consideration, decided to marry Ginnie Moorehead; and tonight's solo party was a sort of symbol of the decision.

He hadnt told her yet, and he hadnt even told 'Bama; and that was why he was out doing his celebrating by himself. But as far as that went, he preferred to do his celebrating alone. What the hell, other people had bachelor dinners, didnt they? Why the hell shouldnt old Dave Hirsh have one? Actually of course, it wasnt a true bachelor dinner. It wasnt taking place the night before the marriage. But it was a bachelor dinner in the sense that it was taking place the night after the day of decision. Dave had looked it all over, and turned it around and around for a couple of weeks, and the more he looked it over and the more he turned it around, the more it seemed the most reasonable and rational out for him. After all, who the hell else would he—at his age, and with his prospects and looks—ever get to marry him? He wasnt in love with

Ginnie, at least not in the way he had once loved Gwen French; but in a way he did love her too, he guessed: she was so extremely pitiable. But more important was the fact that she would make him a good wife; a fine wife; the very kind of wife that a writer ought to have. She would take care of him. Carefully and methodically, he had looked it all over, had studied Ginnie herself closely the two weeks since she had been back from her Kansas fiasco, and finally he had decided. He couldnt very well see how he could go wrong.

Ginnie had—after he sent her the fifty dollars General Delivery in Kansas—taken nearly two weeks to get home to Parkman. Perhaps it had taken her that long to sneak away from her crazy ex-Marine, but on the other hand, Dave did not doubt but what she had picked up some guy on the bus—or stopped over in some town en route and picked one up—and had herself a several day brawling party. She probably wouldnt be Ginnie if she didnt. But if she had, and he suspected she had, that didnt bother him. Because after sending her the money, and with the idea already flirting around in the back of his head, during the nearly two weeks it took her to get home he had checked around Parkman at Smitty's and Ciro's and had found out definitely and for sure that she had been telling him the truth when she stated that she had not been out with anybody but him for nearly three months, before she took off with her ex-Marine. Discreetly, he had checked among the brassiere factory girls and the guys they ran around with—doing it so that they would not guess his reason—and everywhere the information he got was the same: Ginnie had indeed not been out with anybody but himself for three months. Naturally, this impressed him. But what impressed him even more was the Ginnie who arrived home chastened from Kansas.

Worn and wan after her three-months ordeal in the shack on the scorching treeless Kansas prairie, she came right down to the house on Lincoln Street as soon as she got off the afternoon bus. She had lost a considerable amount of weight—but lets face it, he thought: it hadnt done much for her figure, and never would. No matter how much she lost. She just didnt have the basic frame structure that losing weight, or anything else, would ever make into a beautiful—or even pretty—figure. If she only weighed 82 pounds, she would still look squat and fat and dumpy. But, after all, what the hell did that matter? She would never be long of thigh, and long of waist, and high of breast. But then that wasnt what he was marrying her for.

Nevertheless, she had lost quite a lot of weight, and it did make her a *little* more palatable. But mostly, more than that, it was the change in her personality that both impressed and touched Dave. And perhaps even flattered him a little, why not admit it? After she had arrived at the house, she sat down with him and 'Bama and a bottle of whiskey and, her eyes haunted-looking, told them the tale of her ordeal. Dull as she was by nature—(a good trait for a writer's wife;)—she was nevertheless considerably more sensitized by her recent unhappiness. Repeatedly, while she was living with her new husband in Kansas, at least half a dozen times, she said, she had been threatened by him with what was apparently a .45 Service Automatic—("a kind of square-looking gun it was," she said)—just on the mere suspicion that she might have been thinking about another man, or toying with the idea of leaving him. And his old father wasnt much better: a mean old son of a bitch, Ginnie said, dirty and unshaven, who wore nothing but ripe—very ripe—overalls, which she was forced to scrub by hand on a board in a big tub with water she heated on the old wood range, and whose sole opinion of women, apparently, from what she said, was that they were ordained by God and by law to work themselves to death for the men they married.

"Im scared," she admitted to them; "Im feared he'll come back here after me. He aint all there I dont think. All he can do is talk about the Marine Corps and when he was in the war. Hes really got all them medals he said, too. That was the only thing he told me the truth about. He showed 'em all to me. About a hundert times, in fact. Im jist scared to death he'll come back here after me."

"If he comes around here," 'Bama said with snorting relish, his eyes glittering hotly, "Ill kick his damned head in and take his Army automatic and shove it up his ——"

"Oh, but you dont know what hes like," Ginnie said nervously. "Hed kill ya."

'Bama made no answer, and only boredly took another drink. But Dave remembered the attempted holdup in Indianapolis;—and since then, since learning he had the diabetes, 'Bama had been more sour and mean than ever. If his own personal sympathies went out to anybody in this imagined fight, Dave felt it would be to the ex-Marine.

But Ginnie was not to be persuaded, nor her fears allayed. They didnt know what he was like, she kept repeating, they didnt know. And —as under this compulsion to talk, she kept on babbling out all the things that had happened to her and been done to her—she finally broke down and cried. She had to talk to somebody about it, she said, she just had to. Or she would bust. God she was glad to get back home—where there was trees, and people, and a town. Hell, the nearest town to where they lived out there (the one to which Dave had sent the money) was almost thirty miles away; and when you got there, it wasnt hardly any town anyway.

It was decided, that first afternoon, that Ginnie because of her fearful state, would move in there at the house with them. She had given up her room anyway, when she left. And 'Bama, strangely, because he had never liked her, was just about as gently solicitous over her predicament as Dave himself was. She was really a very pitiable object: nervous as a cat, and as jumpy; completely physically and mentally worn out from her ordeal.

"But by God, you can get yore old job back and go back to work," 'Bama added, "and start puttin some of it in the kitty. We aint livin off the fat of the land like we use to here."

"No," Dave said, adding his bit, "weve been losing more than weve been winning, gambling. Them old rich-livin days are gone."

Ginnie nodded eagerly. She was willing to do anything. And it was awful nice of them to take her in. She would, she said, be scared to death if she had to take her old room back and not have nobody around to protect her. She would see about the job tomorrow, and thank you both awful much. Then she broke down again.

"I dont know whatever made me do it," she wept unhappily. All the starch and pride and spine-stiffening she had gradually acquired after she had become Dave's "girlfriend" amongst the brassiere factory set was entirely gone out of her now, completely shaken out of her by her experience. "I just dont know whatever made me do it. And now Im *married* to him. Im his *wife*. Hes got me where he wants me. And I cant do *noth*ing."

"Hell, thats easy fixed," 'Bama snorted. "You never screwed him, did you?"

"Wha—what?" Ginnie said, her eyes widening frighteningly and guiltily.

"I say, you never slept with him did you?" 'Bama grinned sourly.

"Well, I—" Ginnie started, and then paused, guilt shining on her face like a coating of grease.

"What he means is that you never slept with the guy," Dave put in helpfully. He could see she wasnt getting the idea. "If you never slept with him, even though youre married, then you can get the marriage annulled."

"Annulled?" Ginnie said dumbly.

"Sure," Dave said encouragingly. "You know; like a divorce. Only easier to get, and quicker. And then its the same as if you were never married at all."

"Oh, no," Ginnie said quickly, "I never laid him." She held up her right hand. "Honest to God, I never did." She looked at both of them hopefully, looking as if she expected them to believe it too.

'Bama stared at her peculiarly, then sniffed. "It aint us you got to convince. Its the court."

"Court?" Ginnie said in an almost panicky voice. "Court! I dont want to go into no court for nothin!"

'Bama pulled his mouth around disgustedly in an impatient sneer.

"Well, its the only way youll ever get rid of the guy. You want to stay married to him all yore life?"

"No!" Ginnie said. "No, sir!"

"Well then, this is what you gotta do."

"Well—what would I have to do?" Ginnie said cautiously.

"Nothing," 'Bama said. "Except appear in court. We'll let Judge Deacon handle all of it."

"Well, I dont know," Ginnie said doubtfully.

"Go call him," Dave said. "Maybe he can explain it to her."

"Okay," 'Bama said disgustedly, and went to the phone.

The fat little roly-poly Judge, with his sardonic face, when he came out explained it not only to Ginnie but to all of them—and did it breezily enough that it instilled some measure, at least, of confidence in Ginnie. "Hell yes," he growled. "Ive got 'em for lots of people. Get 'em all the damned time. All you got to do is publish a notification in the paper for three consecutive weeks and send your husband a copy of it. Then thirty days after the publification you can take it into court. A week after the thirty days is up Ill take you in and the marriage will be declared null and void. Nothin to it."

"Is that all?" Ginnie said fearfully.

"Sure is," the Judge said breezily.

"Well, but what if he wants to fight it?"

"Then he could combat it. But I wouldnt worry about it." He grinned. "Maybe he'll never get the paper." Judge Deacon grinned sardonically.

"Shes afraid he'll come back here after her, Judge," Dave said.

"So what?" the Judge said briskly. "He cant take you away by force. Thats all there is to it. Well, you want me to go ahead with it?"

"Whatever Dave says," Ginnie said apprehensively, and tiredly. "What do you think, Dave?"

"Well, its the only chance you got about," Dave said, not without feeling a little flattered. "Sure, Id say go ahead with it. The Judge can handle it."

"Send me the goddamned bill," 'Bama said sneeringly.

"Okay," the Judge grinned. "Wont be much of a bill."

After he left, Ginnie broke down again and wept. "Whatever made me do it?" she wailed. "Whatever made me do it? I musta been plumb crazy." She wept into her little flowered hankerchief that Doris Fredric had once bought her. "I hate courts!" she said vehemently.

Dave and 'Bama had exchanged glances. She was, quite plainly, a truly pitiable object to both of them. "There, there," Dave said soothingly. "Dont cry. Its all going to be all right. What you need is to get good and half drunk and go to bed and get some sleep."

"You wont leave me if I do, will ya?" Ginnie said fearfully. "You wont go away if I do?"

"No," Dave said. "We'll stay right here."

"I wont," 'Bama said curtly. "Im goin down to the farhm tonight."

"Well, Ill stay," Dave said. "Ill stay here with you."

"Have you got a gun?" Ginnie said apprehensively.

"No," Dave said. "I dont need a gun."

"Oh yes you will!" Ginnie cried. "If he comes back lookin for me, youll need one."

"Ill leave you my thirty two," 'Bama said to Dave disgustedly. "All you have to do is point it and pull the damned trigger."

"Thatll make me feel a lot better," Ginnie said weepily, and looked about to cry again.

"Now dont cry," Dave said. And soothingly, after he had helped her to several more drinks, he had helped her upstairs to one of the extra rooms to go to bed.

Sitting in the Marine Room in Terre Haute, enjoying his solo bachelor dinner, Dave in thinking back over that first interview and the two weeks that followed still had the same strong sense of almost inarticulate pity for her that he had had then. She did need help; she was half scared to death. However, that was not the only reason he had finally decided on marrying her. Not by far. There were a number of others. He had been thinking on it and turning it all around in his mind for two weeks now.

One of the main ones was what happened that night, that first night —(and later nights, too)—after 'Bama had left for the farm, and after he had thought he had Ginnie in bed in her own room and asleep. He had had a few drinks himself and cooked himself a steak and made a few notes on the scene he wanted to work on tomorrow (he had gone back to working, if somewhat sporadically, after the letter from Ginnie came), and then had gone to bed himself. He had not been asleep more than an hour or so when he was startled awake by something moving beside him, and found that it was Ginnie. She didnt want to sleep in there by herself, she said; she was scared; she wanted to sleep in here with him. Then she began playing up to him. Whatever frights and unhappiness she had incurred out in Kansas, it sure hadnt diminished Ginnie's love of sex any; if anything she seemed to have more, rather than less. Three times in the night she woke him up to sleep with her by cuddling up against him, and all three times the sex he experienced was of a caliber and intensity greater than he had ever known existed. And after they had got up, without any prompting from him, Ginnie set to and made up the bed with fresh sheets, and fixed it all up fresh and clean and smooth. Then, she even offered to cook breakfast for him. Dave, who never ate breakfast when he was working, was tempted to refuse; but after all, this one time was a sort of an occasion, so he accepted. The bacon and eggs and coffee and toast were delicious, better than any he had ever cooked himself; things always seemed to taste better when you didnt have to cook them yourself. Yes, sir, whatever had happened before, or after, she went off to Kansas, it had not in any way changed Ginnie's love and zest for sex.

And after all, where was a man like him—a butterball of nearly forty —to get sex like that? Or sex of any kind, as far as that went? Whenever Dave would think of that, a kind of helpless panic would hit him. He had wasted—actually thrown away—his last two years of comparative youth on Gwen French, and without getting a damned thing for it. Now he had passed those prime years where women want to go out with you even if you dont have money. He was on the downhill grade side now. And from now on it would get worse, instead of better. There wasnt a woman anywhere in the country who would have him. And certainly not a woman who liked sex with him like Ginnie did. And that sex hadnt stopped with the first night, either; it had gone right on through the rest of these two weeks. That was, or should be, he thought, a principle reason for any man getting married. Married to her, he could look ahead to a number of years of sex like that. Completely apart from the panicky loneliness part of it. It was, to say the least, quite a strong inducement in favor.

But it was not the only one, by any means. There was Ginnie herself. It was a lot like the famous oldsoldier's saying about the fact that "whores make the best wives, because theyre grateful." But it went deeper than that. Here was Ginnie, who had never had anything in her life. Not anything. Not even one decent break from the society she lived in, from the moment she was born to the moment she married her crazy ex-Marine. Why should that be? Was that Justice? Ginnie was, in a way, a sort of female Raymond Cole. No one, neither her society nor any individual, had ever tested her capacities—or even thought about doing so. How did anyone know what she was capable of, if only given a chance? She had never had a chance to show what she was capable of. And she wasnt really dumb so much. She was pretty intelligent, really. It was just that she had never had a chance to develop what intelligence she had. Who knew what she might have amounted to—might still amount to—if she only had a decent chance? And Dave, with a warm deep overwhelming magnanimity of spirit, wanted to help her.

She was always talking—(rather hopelessly, it was true)—about the fact that she was a human being, that she had some rights, too. But who had ever treated her like one? Who had ever allowed her some of those human rights she was supposed to have? Who had ever treated her with the basic dignity that was her right? Nobody, and that even included himself. He was as guilty as everybody else. The truth was, it was more than just a personal or social problem; it was a moral issue. If he had ever believed in anything, Dave Hirsh believed fervently in the rights of the free individual. All his life he had espoused that cause. Every human being had the right to be treated *like* a human being, and not like some kind of animal or a member of some particular herd or other. Every human being had the right to some measure of dignity—no matter how unbeautiful that human being might be physically, or how low and undeveloped mentally. That human being still had the right to be treated optimistically and believingly, instead of pessimistically and cynically. It was that very thing that had so irritated him that time when he and 'Bama were getting ready to go to Florida, and 'Bama had talked about Ginnie so contemptuously, as if she were some kind of an animal. 'Bama had no right to talk about her like that. No human being had the right to talk that way about another. Everybody ought to be given their chance. Dave had believed this basic tenet, fierily and devoutly, all his life; and he still believed in it.

Hell, he had always been on the wrong side of the tracks himself, hadnt he? What better could he do than marry somebody from that same wrong side? Let the two fatties get together; the bums of the town; let the two bums marry each other.

All of these things were in his mind during the two weeks he toyed with it and finally made his decision; and not the least of these was 'Bama's wife Ruth, whom he had got to know so well those times 'Bama had taken him down there to the farm after that first hunting trip, and before he found out he had diabetes. (He had not taken him afterwards.) Ginnie would make him the same kind of wife as Ruth made 'Bama; and that was the kind of wife Dave wanted. Ruth Dillert came from the wrong side of the tracks, too. A Southern sharecropper's daughter. And you couldnt find a more perfect wife: she ran that farm, and took care of those people there, and she looked after her man and looked up to him and loved him. Maybe it wasnt the kind of wild passionate love the Gwen Frenches of the world indulged in; but maybe also, it was more important: this kind of love was productive. And that was the kind of wife Dave wanted, and needed: one that would help him with his work. That was the kind of wife old Ginnie would make him, and to hell with these rich, literary, neurotic, nymphomaniac ladies like Gwen French. Hed take a wife like Ruth or Ginnie any time.

—Only, after he married Ginnie, he wasnt going to be like 'Bama; Dave was going to be true to his wife.

And that was why he was over here in Terre Haute having his lone bachelor's dinner tonight: it was to be his last fling before putting on the harness of the faithful, happily married husband. And then he would tell them both, her and 'Bama both, tomorrow. There wasnt the slightest doubt in his mind that Ginnie would marry him, if he asked her; and there wasnt the slightest doubt that 'Bama would heartily approve.

Of course, there still remained another two or three weeks before the Judge could make the annulment final. Before they could actually get married in the fact. But Dave had never been one for following the letter of the contract: Once he had made up his mind and decided, as far as he was concerned it was the same as being married by the Law! He figured himself to be already morally and spiritually bound. Because in his mind he had given his own word of honor. And whatever else anybody might say about Dave Hirsh, by God, he could always say that his word was his Bond.

Sitting there in the Marine Room and eating his big steak and getting mellowly drunk and kidding with the pretty waitress, Dave felt that a truly momentous change was taking place in his life. The old life with 'Bama, and Dewey and Hubie, and Wally Dennis and Gwen French and Bob, was breaking up—already *had* broken up—and it would not be true to say that he did not in some ways regret it; but in its place he was getting a solid stable way of life where happily, contentedly, at peace, he could live and accomplish the kind of writing and volume of writing he wanted to do before he died. He wanted to write the truth about life. The real truth. Not all that crap that sentimental jerks crammed together into novels and tried to pretend was literature. The *real* truth, about life as it was *really* lived. And Ginnie was just the wife to help him do it.

And, the truth was, he loved Ginnie. Not in the same wild, flamboyant, passionate, crazy painful way he had loved Harriet Bowman and Gwen French—and, perhaps, still loved Gwen maybe, somewhat. A little bit. Loved the memory at least. He loved Ginnie, not like that, but in a paternal way: warm, and kindly, and fatherly, and with a strong desire to be helpful to her, and to teach and educate her. And, when you looked at it honestly,—without the benefit of the rose colored glasses of romance—this was the kind of love that successful marriages were founded on. Not that wild passionate unhappy other kind of love. And it was this kind of love, the kind he felt for Ginnie, that he wanted to write about. There were plenty of novels about the other kind; it was about time somebody wrote about the kindly, calm, helpful kind of love.

During the two weeks Dave had been carefully turning over in his mind this idea of marrying her, he had also been slowly developing a plan whereby he might work a love affair into his novel. He had toyed with the idea before, when he was in the deepest throes of his love affair with Gwen—if you could call it that; hah!—but both Bob and Gwen had vigorously warned him off of it; both had been against it. And that had held him off from doing it. Well, they werent either one of them working on this book with him now. He was doing it all on his own. If he wanted to put it in, by God he would put it in. But anyway, the love affair he was thinking about working in now was not that wild passionate unhappy miserable kind of love affair he had had with Gwen, but the kind of love affair he was having with Ginnie—which was just the opposite: kindly, calm, helpful: and the really desperate needing of two people, two down-and-out people, one for the other.

It was true that, in the original plan of the book, there had been no use—and no place—for a love affair; of any kind. The original plan— the original theme—had been the idea of a strictly combat novel: a strictly *comic* combat novel: which would show up and get away from all these horrible-horrors-of-war novels the world had been flooded with since 1920. But now Dave felt, and thought he could see, where a love affair—a simple gentle sorrowful love affair: between a commonplace private and a lowclass French peasant girl—might not only provide a supplemental theme, but would also heighten and contrast the really diabolic elements of the comedy of death.

It would certainly add affirmation to the book—an affirmation Dave was coming increasingly to feel the book needed. Ginnie had taught him that. Poor old Ginnie, who with nothing, not anything, the lowest of the lowly, could still go on and live and strive and hope, in her honest dumb way. Ginnie was a symbol of the whole human race, and its own affirmation. The love affair could take place during the central part of the book, after the breakout at St Lô and the Big Drive, during the relatively stable time that followed before the Battle of the Bulge. That way the commonplace little infantryman would have a chance to spend some time with his commonplace little peasant girl. It would all fit right in. In the central part he could work in isolated chapters on the love affair in between the various chapters on the combat. The peasant girl's father's little farm could be in the vicinity of Liége, and the love affair could begin with the liberation of Liége and continue on until after the jumpoff on Aachen. Not much time for the changing of a life through love, really; but enough. And sometime after Aachen—maybe during the Bulge—the little private would be killed.

Technically, he knew he could do it, and make it play. And as far as that went, it would be a healthy—if not actually brilliant—lyric contrast to the shocking comedy that was made of death. It would also help the sale of the book, too; a love affair always did. A novel without a love affair in it always had two strikes against it, sales-wise, from the start. —Not that that was why he was doing it: He wouldnt do that. Ever. He would never compromise his integrity for sales. He was doing it because he believed it, believed in what it said, sincerely and devoutly. And sitting in the Marine Room, full of enthusiasm over his decision to marry Ginnie, and full of the liquid lubricative confidence several drinks can impart, he went over it all again in his mind as he ate his steak, and decided happily that he was going to do it: was going to include the love affair. Man, that Hemingway! He sure had it right when he called alcohol the "giant killer."

It was when he got home late that night, after touring the whorehouses, that he found that Ginnie's ex-Marine had been there.

Ginnie was sitting at the kitchen table looking haggard and worn when he started to go in the house, and at the first sound of the screen-door opening she leaped up and backed away to the far side of the room against the counter, her eyes widening with fright and staring at the half-glassed door like a rabbit fascinated and hypnotized by a snake. Dave could see her through the door and wondered what the hell?

When he got inside and she saw who it was, her terrified face relaxed into a crumpled weeping relief and she ran across the room and grabbed him desperately and began to cry on his shoulder.

"Hey! Hey! What the hells the matter?" Dave demanded with slightly drunken expansiveness.

"He was here! He was here!" Ginnie cried.

"*Who* was here?"

"Rick! Rick was here!" She hugged herself against him selfprotectively.

"You mean your Marine?" Dave said. Well, the hell with him, he thought with drunken bloodthirstiness. If he was here, where was he? Let him show!

"Yes! Yes!" She could hardly even talk.

"Well, where is he?" Dave said.

"Hes gone! Hes gone! I sent him away."

"Wasnt 'Bama here?" Dave asked.

"No. He went down to the farm this afternoon," Ginnie cried, hugging him. "I was all by myself."

"Well, come on and sit down," Dave said. "Come on," he said soothingly. "Come on and sit down and tell me all about it. Did he have his gun?" Slowly, with Ginnie resisting him every step of the way as if she could not stand the thought of letting go of him, he led her to the table and sat her down and pulled her loose from him. "I say did he have his gun?"

"I dont know!" Ginnie cried. "I didnt see it!" She was still terrified.

"Here," Dave said, and went to the counter. "Let me mix us both a drink. You really need one."

"I dont know if he had his gun or not!" Ginnie cried. "But I bet he did! Whether he had his gun or not, he had a switch blade knife he kept flippin open and closin all the time! It was you he was after! He says hes going to kill you!"

Dave stopped, startled, in mid-pouring; then he had to laugh. The whole thing was ridiculous. Kill him! it was such a silly ridiculous thought it was like something out of a dime novel. Hell, even a one-armed ex-Marine couldnt be quite that bad!

"Well, where is he? Whered he go?"

"Dont go after him! Dont go after him! He'll kill you! He will!" Ginnie cried from the table.

"Here," Dave said, unable to keep from grinning. "Drink this. Nobodys going to kill me."

"*He* will! *He* will!" Ginnie cried, desperate to make him understand. "Oh, why did I ever git mixed up with him!"

"Now, listen," Dave said, "damn it; quiet down. Take it easy. Whered he go? Im not going after him. All I want to know is what *hap*pened!"

"Well, I sent him over to Professor French's," Ginnie said, a little more calmly.

Dave stared at her, his glass arrested half way to his mouth. "You did *what!*"

"I told you! I sent him over to Professor French's. In Israel," Ginnie said. "It was the first thing popped into my mind."

"But *why?* My God!" Dave protested, running his fingers through his hair. "You just cant go doing things like that, Ginnie! If the guy really is cracked and dangerous—! My *God!* You just *cant* go sending him off to somebody else who dont know anything about him! Just to get rid of him! You cant *do* things like that!"

"Well, it was the only thing I could think of," Ginnie said, almost placidly, now. "He sat here for over an hour, waiting for you to come home. Flippin and closin that switch blade all the time. What else could I do? I didnt want him sittin here all ready to knife you when you come home, did I? He was drunk and I couldnt talk no sense to him; you cant even talk sense to him when hes sober! It was the ony thing I could think of to do. I told him that you hung out a lot over there, that they was writer friends of yours, and probly that was where you was."

"My *God!*" Dave said, setting his drink down and grabbing his hair with both hands. "My *God,* Ginnie!" Then he turned and strode from the room.

"Where you goin?! Where you goin?!" Ginnie cried desperately, starting up.

"To the phone," Dave said. "Where else?"

Behind him, Ginnie started to follow him as if terrified to even let him out of her sight, and he stopped and turned back. "You go back and sit down and drink your drink," he said authoritatively. "Then mix yourself another one and drink it too. My God!" he said again, and grasped his hair.

Meekly, Ginnie did as she was told, and he picked up the phone in the hall and dialed long distance and asked for Bob French's number. Savagely, he listened to the ringing far away, and then after a few moments the phone was picked up and Bob's voice said: "Hello?"

"Bob, is that you?" he cried. "This is Dave."

"Ahh, yes. Hello, Dave," Bob's voice said rather faintly and tiredly "How are you?"

"How are *you*? Are you all right?"

"Ahhh— Yes. Quite all right," Bob's voice said tiredly. "And how are you?"

"Did that guy come over there?" Dave said urgently. "That one-armed Marine? Did he show up over there at your place?"

"Yes, as a matter of fact he did," Bob said. "We—ahh—had quite an interesting conversation, as a matter of fact."

Embarrassed already, Dave paused, caught up short by Bob's somewhat spare phraseology. "Well, but youre all right?" he said. "Youre okay, arent you?"

"Oh, yes. Quite all right," Bob's voice said a little faintly. "A little tired, perhaps."

"Well—I didnt wake you up, did I?" Dave said.

"Oh, no," Bob said. "I—ahh—rather didnt feel much like sleeping."

"Well, is he still there?" Dave said. "Is he there now?"

"No,—ahh—as a matter of fact, I rather expect hes on his way back to Kansas," Bob said. "Theres—ahh—a bus leaving, or rather one that *left,* at twelve thirty, I believe. Isnt that correct?"

"I dont know," Dave said, startledly, caught up short again. "Bob, Im coming over there. All right? Is that all right?"

"Why, yes. Do come," Bob's voice said. "Its been some time since weve seen each other, Dave. Ive been wondering how you were getting on. Do come, and we'll have a couple of drinks together."

"Ill be right there," Dave said urgently, trying to put into his voice all of the embarrassment and distress and need for apology that he felt.

"Fine," Bob said. "Do that."

He hung up and went back out to the kitchen and picked up his jacket—his loud Hollywood-style sports jacket he had bought so long ago in Indianapolis with 'Bama—and put it on.

"Youre not leavin me here?!" Ginnie cried frantically. "Youre not leavin me here?! Alone?!"

"Yes," Dave said firmly. "I am. Youll be all right. Bob says he left on the twelve thirty bus, for Kansas."

"He did?" Ginnie said disbelievingly, her eyes widening. Then her face crumpled up into fear again. "I dont believe it! I bet he didnt! Dont leave me, Dave! You cant leave me here alone!"

"Look," Dave said; "here." He went out into the hall and got 'Bama's little .32 out of the phone table drawer and brought it back and laid it in front of her. "Thatll protect you."

"I dont know how to use one of them things," Ginnie said, staring at it fearfully.

"All you got to do is point it and pull the trigger," Dave said, quoting 'Bama. "Now lock all the doors and turn off the lights and go to bed, if youre still scared. Have a couple more drinks. And take the gun up with you. But I simply have to go there and talk to Bob and apologize."

"But you dont know him!" Ginnie cried. "Hed bust the glass and reach in and unlock it!"

"Then take the key out."

"Hed knock out all the glass and climb in over it!" Ginnie said. "You dont know him!"

"Bob says hes already gone, and if Bob says hes gone Ill bet my bottom dollar he *is* gone," Dave said, soothingly. "Now you go on up to bed. Everything's perfectly all right now. But I simply have to go over there and apologize. My *God,* Ginnie!" he said again, seizing his hair at the thought of it. "You just cant *do* things like that!"

"It was the ony thing I could think of to do," Ginnie said defensively.

"Well, there are just some things that youve got to learn you *cant* do. No matter what," Dave said. "What if he had been really dangerous? My God!" he said again.

"I was ony tryin to think of you," Ginnie said. "Please dont leave me here alone, Dave."

"Im sorry. I cant help it. Now, you lock the door after me, if thatll make you feel any better," he said. "Ive got my own key. —Now, for Christ's sake dont shoot *me* when I come home!"

"I wont touch that thing," Ginnie said fervently.

"Then Ill put it back in the drawer," Dave said, and did. "Now lock the door after me." He went out to the little Plymouth, aware of Ginnie staring after him beseechingly. My God! he thought once again anguishedly.

When he drove up into the crushed-rock drive and shut off the lights and motor and rushed inside, he found the tall spare white-haired crew-cut poet sitting sprawled out at the big table in one of the ladder-backs, his long legs stretched out before him, and holding a tall high-ball glass of whiskey and water.

"Come in," he said. "Come in, Dave." He looked a little bit worn and tired under his eyes and around his mouth, but other than that he appeared perfectly sound. "Come right on in. The whiskey and ice are on the cabinet. Or if youd prefer a Martini—"

Dave ignored the liquor, and rushed on across the long room up to him, and then, not knowing what to do when he got there, stopped himself short. "My God, Bob!" he said abjectly. "I dont know what to say. I just dont know what to say!"

"No, no," Bob said. "Not at all, not at all. Quite all right, quite all right." Suddenly he smiled brightly, that eager smile of his. "As a matter of fact, it was quite an interesting experience."

"Someone—someone else sent him over here from Parkman," Dave said. "I didnt know a damned thing about it. I wasnt even home."

"Yes, I rather gathered that," Bob said. He took a tired relaxed pull at his glass. "Dear Dave, mix yourself a drink and come sit down, and we'll discuss it. Ive been sitting here analyzing it by myself. For heaven's sake, dont look so perturbed! Its really been a most interesting evening.

"—Now you mix yourself a drink," he commanded, "and come sit down."

Dave did as he was told, mixing himself a stiff whiskey and water like Bob had, and came back and sat down in another of the ladderbacks alongside him, turned slightly toward him, and stretched out his own legs. They were shaky, and tired.

"Its really a most interesting thing," Bob said. "Most interesting. I wouldnt really have missed it for anything really."

"Well, what did he do?" Dave said urgently. "What the hell happened?"

"Well, first let me give it to you in sequence," Bob said analyzingly; "a description." And he proceeded to tell the story of what had happened.

When he heard the knock on the side door he had, in fact, been just about ready to go to bed. He had no idea who it might be, since both the ministerial student and the polio girl had stopped coming over since Gwen left, as well as Dave himself. "I really dont know why he picked the side door," he said wonderingly, "rather than the front door. It just must have been that when he got out of the cab, it was the closest one, and in his state he instinctively made a beeline for it. —Of course," he added thoughtfully, "the lights in the kitchen were still on; the only lights, in fact." Well, he had gone down to the landing and opened the door, but before he could say anything, even a single word, this tall lean one-armed young man had given him one wild searching look, then shoved him aside and charged in and up the steps into the middle of the kitchen, his empty sleeve flapping—(he rather expected, Bob said parenthetically, that most of the time, in moments of—ahh—comparative repose, the empty sleeve remained tucked into the pocket of his coat; but now it was out and flapping)—and the young man was shouting: "Where is he! I know hes here! And I know exactly what he looks like, too! You cant hide him! Ill find him! Where is he!" And he began charging all around the kitchen.

"Naturally, I was rather astonished," Bob said.

He himself, after getting over his astonishment somewhat, had followed the young man up the steps and into the kitchen. That was when he saw he had the knife.

"One of these—ahh—?" Bob said, looking at Dave questioningly.

"Switch blades?" Dave said.

"Thats the term! Ive read it in the newspapers, you know; but I couldnt remember it," Bob said. Well, he had this knife, and he kept closing it against his leg and then pushing the button and flipping it open again. Then he'd close it against his thigh and flip it open again. "Really vicious looking," Bob said analytically; "not the blade itself, but the way it snicks open there in the hand when you push the button. Very interesting." But, while the knife itself looked dangerous enough, one of the things that had struck Bob immediately was that if the young man was in fact prepared to use his knife immediately, then why did he keep closing it? It would have been more reasonable to expect him to have held it at the ready with the blade open ready to use, would it not? Actually, it was this that gave him the key, really.

But of course, he himself was still completely in the dark, Bob said, and had no idea who the young man was, or why he was there, nor whom he was in fact looking for. And until he could find out just what exactly was going on, he felt it would be better to keep quiet and stay fairly far away from him so as not to antagonize or frighten him. So Bob had remained standing at the counter just inside the cellar door while the young man charged all around the kitchen knocking over chairs and kicking them looking for whomever it was he was chasing. He yanked one of the ladderbacks away from the table and flung it down ("Fortunately, it didn't break that one," Bob said; "though he later broke another when he kicked it out of his way") and peered in under the table; then he went and dragged out the big chair and turned it over and looked behind it, and then in the corner around the end of the cabinet. And finally, still cursing to himself, he came back and stood in the middle of the floor again, knocking over two more ladderbacks as he did so, and stared accusingly at Bob.

"I know he's here," he said wildly. "I got information. I know he's here. So dont try to hide him from me, see?" he said menacingly. It was quite easy to see, and did not require the professional eye of an expert psychiatrist to note, that he had lost all rationality. And a person in that kind of state could not be handled with reason.

"Well, what did you do?" Dave said urgently. "What did you do?"

"Why, I talked to him," Bob said simply, raising his eyebrows. "What would you have done?"

"I dont know," Dave said.

"As a matter of fact, we talked for very nearly three hours," Bob said; "as a matter of fact. After he got quieted down enough to talk, and allowed me to mix him some drinks." He sighed tiredly. "It was really very interesting."

The first thing, of course, was to find out who he was and whom he was looking for; and to convince him that there was no one in the house but Bob himself—whoever it was he was hunting. It looked as if that might be a hard task to accomplish. But, when after standing wild-eyed in the middle of the floor a few moments the young man charged the diningroom door, Bob had an opportunity to at least get a word in and get started with it.

"Whats in there?" the boy demanded when he stopped in front of it.

"My library," Bob had said, and when he saw the young man looked puzzled he elucidated: "Thats where I keep my books, in other words. Also, its sort of a diningroom of sorts. But we never use it. We eat out here."

"You eat in the kitchen? here?" the young man had asked interestedly, and jabbed with his knife toward the table.

"Thats correct," Bob had said. He would have gone on. But then the interest faded out of the young man's face, and the wild-eyed irrationality replaced it.

"I know hes here," he had said again. "I got information. I know hes here. And Im going to find him if I have to take your whole damned house apart. And when I find him, by God Ill kill him. And Ill kill you too if I have to. How do I know hes not hidin right in there?" he demanded, jabbing with his knife at the diningroom door.

"Youre welcome to look," Bob had said. "The light switch is just to the left inside the door."

The young man had gone in there and looked—or rather, had just stuck his head in and turned on the light, while keeping one eye as it were on Bob all the time, as if afraid Bob might try to spirit his prey out while he was looking. "Well, there aint nobody in there," he had said, coming back.

"Youll find its that way through the whole house," Bob had said. "There is no one here but myself."

"How do I know you aint lyin?"

"Ill take you on a tour of the entire house, if you wish," Bob had said. "But after all, dont you think its only fair to tell me whom youre looking for? and why? I dont even know *that* yet."

"That was when he found out it was Dave he was looking for. Cursing savagely, the young man explained that Dave Hirsh had stolen his girl —and not just his girl, his *wife,* his own *wife,* that he was *married* to, his *Ginnie.* And when he found him, by God he was going to kill him. He had killed a lot of other men in his life—for a lot less reason. He might as well kill one more.

"He was, I noted," Bob said to Dave, "strangely proud of his killing abilities. He talked a lot about that later on." He hesitated a moment, almost apologetically. "You see, Im not used to young men like that young man. Oh, I know they exist, you know; I mean, I know *intellectually* that they exist. But I have almost no personal contact with them. And living the rather retiring type of life I live, I rather tend to forget about them. Meeting and talking with one is an entirely different thing. It was very interesting. Well," he said, "to proceed."

To make a long story short, the upshot of it was that once the young man got to talking about himself, he wanted to go on talking about himself. Bob noted that immediately.

"Naturally, I encouraged him," he smiled wanly. "I offered once again to take him all through the house; but after a moment's laborious thought he said no, he would take my word for it that I was alone: and anyway. if he *was* here,—the man he was seeking; which was you— he could slip ahead of him from room to room and theyd just keep going around in a circle and hed never catch up with him." Bob smiled. "A rather astonishing mental analysis, for a man of so obviously little intellectual capacities, dont you think? It rather intrigued me. —Anyway, he refused the grand tour. So then I offered him a drink. This he accepted. And we sat down to talk about him."

This the young man had enjoyed highly, in his peculiar fashion. And naturally, Bob smiled tiredly, he had plied him with drink, as the saying was; all he could get down him in fact. He himself had rather nursed his own drink, feeling that perhaps it was better if he kept his wits as keen as possible; but the young man noticed this after a while and insisted emphatically that Bob finish his drink and get another, and drink with him drink for drink; and he got his knife out again and laid it on the table. Bob was able to circumvent the drink-for-drink compact to some extent, but not entirely. Probably, he judged, the young man had two or possibly three to his one. "Amazing capacity!" Bob said in a somewhat awed voice. And the more the young man drank, the more eager he became to talk about himself, and—and this was noteworthy— to ask advice about his problems and himself and what did Bob—("an utter stranger, remember," Bob said)—what did Bob think he ought to do? Consequently, during the next three hours Bob heard the entire story of his life, plus a very detailed and worshipful history of the United States Marine Corps, not to mention a great many astonishing combat episodes and killings of various types that took place during the war.

"He was really quite proud of his killing abilities," Bob said, "and of all the Japanese men he had killed—which was a considerable number. He was at Tarawa. Have you ever read about Tarawa, dear Dave? You have? Amazing thing!—Well, by the end, dear Dave, he was on a regular crying jag. Especially about not being able to stay in his beloved Marine Corps. It was really rather amazing. Several times he offered to fight me, there and then—with fists, with knives, with rocks, with guns. One of which he had tucked in his belt. He showed me. But he seemed to prefer his—ahh—switch blade, for some reason. Anyway, he offered to fight me in any or all of these ways, and was, he said, willing to spot me his missing arm. And inbetween times of offering to fight me, all of which I modestly declined, he would tell me that I was in reality the best—if not the only—friend he had in the world." He smiled, tiredly.

"So when he left I helped him back on with his coat and tucked his sleeve back in his pocket for him and called a cab over from Parkman for him and when it came we put our arms around each other and swore our undying friendship and he promised to write me a letter as soon as he got home to Kansas." Bob shook his head, a little awedly. "Amazing! Amazing!" he said, and smiled again. "It was really a most intensely interesting experience. —Not one, however," he added, "that I would look forward to having every day.

"And, well, thats the story," he finished. Then he added, "I expect I now know more about the United States Marine Corps than anyone in the United States except its commandant and members."

"But how the hell did you get him to go back to Kansas?" Dave asked.

"Well—I must admit—that was on a rather flimsy moral pretext," Bob said. "I told him that if he really loved his wife, he would want her to be happy. Therefore, if she were happier with another man—or without any man at all, perhaps—including him—then, if he really loved her, he would want her to do just that: do whatever would make her most happy. And he agreed to this.

"Of course, as you know, dear Dave, all that was quite untrue. When a person is really in love with another, that person is not concerned with the beloved's happiness at all; he is concerned, first, foremost and solely, with his own happiness. Of course, very few like to admit this, and I sized this young man up as being one of those who would not admit it. Also, he had told me about how he was always—ahh—'bucking heads,' as he called it, with his father; and also how dearly he had loved his beloved mother—who, he said, died of overwork on their little farm when he himself was still quite young. So you can see how I tricked him with his own beliefs. It was a rather unfair advantage to take of the young man, in a way. But still I felt it was justified if it would get him to return to Kansas without—ahh—blooding his knife.

"Of course, once he admitted the initial premise that one who loves wants most of all the happiness of the beloved, he had no recourse but to admit he should return home. His own sentimentality and his desire to be a fine, likeable, admirable person forced him to it. He had no other choice."

Dave was forced to laugh, though he felt a little ashamed of doing so. Bob however did not laugh, and did not even look amused, but only looked thoughtful, and a little sad.

"Do you suppose he actually will write me a letter?" he said.

"God, I dont know, Bob," Dave said. "He might. But Im inclined to think once he gets home he'll forget the whole episode with you."

"If he does write, I suppose I shall have to answer and strike up a correspondence and continue further to advise him," Bob said unhappily.

"Do you think he'll ever come back?" Dave asked. "And try to look me up again?"

"That I wouldnt know," Bob said, thoughtfully. "I rather think not, not for some time anyway. But of course its very hard to tell about these overly emotional people who have no real capacity for selfanalysis. They change their minds according to whatever emotion they happen to be feeling at the moment, and believe today what they just as devoutly disbelieved yesterday. I rather think he wont be back for some time though, because it will take him quite a while to free himself of the mental picture of himself which I forced upon him by the misuse of logic. He had a very highly developed moralism in him, I think, that young man; and he wants to be right, not wrong; good, not evil; and very strongly. And as long as he believes it immoral to interfere with his 'wife's' happiness, he wont. No, I should say it would be some time before he comes back. If he ever does come back at all. In general, I believe, persons of his type quickly fall deeply in love with someone else while telling them of their unhappiness in their current love. Perhaps that is what our young man will do. Let us hope so.

"Its amazing!" he said once again, and once again shook his head. "I almost never meet young people of this type. Oh, of course I did, when I was younger. But one tends to forget how very mentally backward the majority of people really are—unless one is forced to be amongst them all the time. Hes really a very brave young man, that one," Bob said; "and hes had a most interesting and adventurous and painful life, too." Then he shrugged, slowly, almost elaborately for him. "But then, after all, what is bravery?"

Bob took a sad thoughtful swallow of his drink.

"Their lives," he said. "Their lives are governed by such fantastic illusions about what is 'good' and what is 'bad' and what is 'manly.' Or 'womanly.' Utterly fantastic. Has nothing to do with what life really is at all." He took another thoughtful swallow.

"You know, dear Dave," he said, almost apologetically. "I have a sort of a theory about killing. —Outside of wartime, of course, I mean.— I believe there is not ever a murder committed that is not—ahh—requested, shall we say, right at the time. In other words, for every murderer there must also be a murderee; otherwise there would be no murder. Now that young man might very easily—considering the state he was in—have killed me, had I made one false move or false step in handling him. Or if I had panicked, or something like that. Because, you see, he was scared, too. But even more than that it was that his pride was involved. He really didnt want to kill anyone; but he felt he should want to kill someone, and that way he would prove he was a man, you see. In other words, had I done anything so foolish as to laugh at him, had I done anything that would have in his own eyes—in his own pride

—made him look bad or futile or ridiculous, I should have been forcing him to kill me. You see? Even when he didnt want to, really; and all he really wanted to do was show off a bit.

"—Of course, I admit," he added, "that there are circumstances when the theory doesnt apply. For instance, should he have struck me with the knife right there at the door before I got a chance to talk to him. Or, perhaps, say, if he were a hired killer, hired expressly to kill me for some reason. Ive never had any experience with—ahh—?" he looked at Dave questioningly.

"Hoods?" Dave said.

"Yes, thats it. Hoods. Ive never had any experience with that type. Who do it as a job. Thats a field of research in itself. But this young man didnt want to kill anybody, and was in fact really afraid that someone would call his braggadocio bluff, and force him to back it up. That was the key to the whole situation when I noted how he kept opening and closing his knife against his leg. I think if he were really bent on killing, he would not have done that. However, if *you* had been here, he might have felt impelled to go ahead with it, just to prove he wasnt backing down. It would have been exceedingly foolish, but he might have done it."

He stopped, and took another swallow of his drink. "Amazing!" he said again. "Very interesting!"

"Im going to marry that girl he came over here after me for," Dave said suddenly.

"Oh?" Bob said slowly. Still sitting relaxedly and tiredly in the ladderback, his long legs sprawled out before him, his face still worn looking from his evening's work, he turned his thoughtful gaze onto Dave slowly with a look both of deep interest and surprise. "You are?"

"Yes," Dave said. "Shes getting an annulment from the boy who was over here to see you. Im paying for it. She just up and married him on the spur of the moment, and got herself into a trap. Actually, shed only known him three or four days before she married him."

"I see," Bob said, still watching him thoughtfully.

"I—uh—Ive done a great deal of thinking about it the past few weeks," Dave said. "Everything between me and Gwen is over. You told me that yourself; and Gwen made it plain to you. And I need a wife. I— Her name is Ginnie Moorehead."

Bob did not say anything for a moment. Then he nodded noncommittally. "Ah, yes. I know of the young woman."

"You probly do. She used to be the biggest whore—not whore, but the biggest free romp in Parkman. She never got beyond the sixth grade in school; and shes not very bright. And that in itself is one of the main reasons I think shell make me a perfect wife: dumb, preoccupied with her housework, etcetera; but goodnatured; I think its the perfect kind of a wife for a writer to have."

"Yes, there is a lot to be said for that school of thought on writers' wives," Bob said. For a long moment he stared at Dave, a little sadly perhaps but otherwise expressionless, and Dave was unable to read the meaning of it. "Of course," Bob said finally, after taking another pull at his glass, "one must be quite sure that they *are* dumb; and that they *are* goodnatured."

"Those are two things I *am* sure of," Dave said.

"Well then," Bob said, and suddenly he raised himself back up in his chair somewhat, and bent his long legs. "Then you have no worries, do you? I want to wish you the best of luck and happiness with it, dear Dave."

"Thanks," Dave said. "You know, its probably better that it all turned out as it did. With Gwen and me, and all. I was completely thrown for a while; but maybe in the end this was how it was supposed to be."

"Yes," Bob said thinly, his voice curiously veiled, curiously expressionless. "I expect in the end that just about everything happens as it was supposed to happen."

"More of your Karma?" Dave said. "More Yog-h?" He pronounced it very precisely.

Bob grinned, then laughed, and Dave laughed with him. Then Bob's face sobered again. "No," he said, "not exactly. Karma doesnt exactly work like that, I guess. Theres always the matter of free choice, you know? But then, if everyone free-chooses as they perforce must—" He shrugged. "Perhaps it is the same in the end, in a way. One must wear out one thing before he is ready—or capable—of going on to some other. So perhaps it is somewhat the same in the end: Its all for learning lessons. One lesson, or another lesson. Eventually, we learn them."

"Damn it! I wish I could be *sure*: the way you always sound," Dave said explosively. "I wish I *knew* something: the way you do. I wish I could *believe* like you seem to. You have belief. Positive, downright belief."

"Dear Dave," Bob said, and smiled sadly, "dear Dave. I dont *know* anything. I just surmise. —But then, I dont even surmise. I just guess— and hope. I read, and I wonder. Im really far less ahead of *you* than you seem to think."

"Well, you always seem to know," Dave said almost irritably. "You always sound so damned positive."

"Theorizing," Bob said. "Pure theorizing. I *know* nothing. —And," he added, "I expect I never shall *know* anything. I have a theory about that, too," he smiled, but not apologetically this time; pleasantly. "I believe that the way of the artist—the artist type; such as you and I—is *never* to know. The Way, the Path," he said, capitalizing the words with his voice, "of the artist is actually based upon that very point, I think: to *not* know. If he *knew* what God was, he would be too sure. And the very nature of an artist, a great artist, is that he must never *know;* must never be *sure.* That is why he works so hard, and so painfully, and hungers so hard and painfully. If he *knew—*" He smiled. "Well, I dont suppose he would ever produce anything, would he? He wouldnt *need* to." He finished off the last of the tall drink he held in his hand. "So youre going to marry Ginnie Moorehead?" he said.

"Yes," Dave said. "Ive made up my mind. Ive thought it all over very carefully and logically."

"Im sure you have," Bob said softly.

"Ill tell you something else Im going to do," Dave said positively, and reluctantly: He didnt want to have to tell him this, because he didnt want an argument; but at the same time he felt honorbound to tell him, since Bob—as well as Gwen—had worked with him on the book so much. "Im going to write that love affair into the novel like I once talked to you about. Remember?"

"Dear Dave," Bob said gently. "I may be unable to advise you on things of the spirit; but this is one thing I can advise you on. If you do, youll ruin it."

"I dont think so," Dave said stubbornly. "Let me explain it to you, before you jump in with both feet. Its not the kind of wildly passionate love affair we talked about and that I meant to write when I talked to you about it before. This is a different love affair: a small sad pathetic little love affair between a commonplace little private and a commonplace little peasant girl." And he went ahead to explain in full detail the theory of the love affair for the novel that he had worked out during the past weeks. He talked at some length, because he wanted to convince him; he himself knew he was right, but he wanted Bob to agree. But Bob only listened silently. "So you see," Dave wound up, "not only will it be a true sad little love affair of two little people caught in the mills of war—for which read also: life—but it will also provide a heightening contrast with the combat stuff. Technically, it will be a *vast* improvement.

"Well," he said confidently, "what do you think?"

"You really want to know?" Bob said.

"Yes," Dave said. "I do."

"Its terrible," Bob said. "Its not only terrible, its ghastly. It makes me shudder all over. And then shudder again, to think what it will do to your book. Even the other love affair you talked of—which certainly had no place in your book at all, either—would have been better than this. But this—this—this mawkish, sentimental, tear-jerking trash— well, its just simply horrible. It will ruin your novel. In the first place, no one is ever 'caught in the mills' of anything that he himself doesnt bring upon himself; there are no onerous blows struck that are not invited."

"But thats just the point!" Dave said. "They *do* invite it. And thats their very heroism!"

"Not at all," Bob said positively. "What you have outlined to me will make them *victims*. And that makes it philosophically wrong right there. And in the second place, it is diametrically opposite to the theme and purpose of the book you started out to write."

"But I think thats its virtue," Dave said stubbornly. "Dont you?"

"Certainly not," Bob said. "That kind of contrast will only destroy the very effect you started out to achieve."

"Well, maybe I didnt make it clear to you, when I told you about it," Dave said.

"You made it exceedingly clear."

"Well, Im sorry, Bob," he said; "I just dont agree with you."

"Dear Dave," Bob said and smiled. "Then you must write it as you wish to write it. Its your book. You must do what you have to do. So must I. So must we all. But dont expect to receive moral support from me by getting me to agree to something that I feel is totally wrong."

"Well," Dave said lamely, "maybe thats what I was doing, hunh? I didnt mean to be. I *thought* I was telling you out of a sense of honor—because you, and Gwen too, have worked with me so patiently and helped me so much on this book. But—maybe I was seeking moral support?"

Bob said nothing, and did not answer. Instead, he got up—almost briskly—and went back over to the counter to fix himself another drink. "Im afraid Im going to get rather tight tonight," he said after a moment, with a smile. "Rather tight. Its too bad its so late and there is no poker game on at the Club.

"Would you like another drink?" he said.

"No, I guess not," Dave said, and looked at his watch. He could not help feeling a little piqued and hurt that Bob refused to understand and see what he was driving at. "Its after two. I better be getting back home. Have you heard anything from Gwen?"

"I had one letter," Bob said carefully. "After I wrote her what you said about your sister."

"Whats she going to do?"

"Well, shes nearly finished with the book," Bob said. "So shes going ahead and finish it, but shes not going to submit it until after shes come home and weve gone into the whole thing thoroughly."

"Then shes coming home?"

"Eventually, I expect," Bob said, carefully. "But not at all soon, I dont think. She has made no plans to teach this fall. And if she does come, it may only be for a visit to discuss the book."

"Well—" Dave said inconclusively. He got up. Bob seemed almost crisp. "You know, I have no hard feelings, Bob, about Gwen any more at all. I want to wish her the best of everything."

"Thats very fine of you," Bob said, staring over the edge of his highball glass somberly into its dark depths. "Im sure she feels the same about you."

"Gwen wouldnt want me to include this love affair in the book either, I expect," Dave said.

"No, Dave; Im sure she wouldnt. But then, as I said, its your book. Not hers or mine." Bob got up himself.

"Well, I believe in it," Dave said. "And I think the book needs it. I have to do it." He walked down to the end of the kitchen, and slowly Bob followed. "I guess you dont think I ought to marry this girl, either, do you?" he said, after he had gone down to the landing.

Bob stared down at him for a moment, narrowly, thoughtfully, then he shrugged and smiled. "Dear Dave," he said. "Who am I to say what you should do? or what anyone should do? I dont even know what I myself should do, most of the time. As Ive so often said, we all do as we must. As our desires make us do. Most of the time, I dont know if Ive done right," he said somberly, thoughtfully, almost to himself. "Even right now, I dont know."

"Yes," Dave said. "Well—" He opened the door, then turned back one last time, urgently. "You see, Im not getting any younger. And Im certainly not getting any more palatable. And I need somebody. Somebody to take care of me, somebody to—somebody to sleep with," he said bluntly. "If I dont marry this one, Ill probably never get a chance at any other woman again." It was the first time he had ever spoken of sex, of copulation, outright with Bob; but he had to do it. He had to make it plain.

"Yes," Bob said from above him. "Well, we all need something or other, I guess. I wish you the best of luck with your attempt, Dave."

"Thanks," Dave said sourly. But once he was outside, and also all of the rest of the way back home to Parkman, he knew he was right. He had studied it all over—not passionately; but carefully, *dis*passionately— and he knew that logically and rationally he was right, in both the marriage and the putting of the love affair in the book; and Bob's disagreements did not touch him.

But before he left, he turned back one more time. "Well, anyway, Im glad you were all right, Bob, after your visit with the US Marines. That was what I really came over for."

"Oh, him," Bob said musingly from the head of the stairs. "I had forgotten all about him."

"Im sorry it happened," Dave said; "and—Ill try to see it doesnt happen again."

"I dont think it will," Bob said musingly. "I truly dont. Goodby, dear Dave."

And so that was that. All the way home in the car Dave studied it over and over again. The book's love affair, and his marriage to

Ginnie. Bob French was a wise man, perhaps the wisest he had ever known; and his disagreements were not to be taken lightly. But as Bob himself was so prone to say so often: he *could* be wrong; he *didnt* know. And this was one time Dave felt he must be. Never in his life before, Dave was sure, had he ever approached anything, any decision, with such complete objectivity—with such absolute dispassion. Always before his important decisions about his life had been made on the spur of the moment, when he was in the throes of—and influenced by —some screwy emotion or other. Just like the time he had decided suddenly to stay in Parkman because of Gwen; and look what that had got him into. But this time it was not like that. It was a cool calm collected logical decision. Bob just had to be wrong. There wasnt any other answer. Perhaps he was influenced in his attitude toward Dave because of his strong feeling for Gwen?

There remained nothing else to do but inform Ginnie and 'Bama, and the first of these he did next day. She was asleep when he got home, and did not even wake up when he crawled into bed beside her. Evidently she had gotten over her fear of Rick; or else had drunk herself out of it. So he waited till next day to tell her he was going to marry her.

He told her that morning, before he went to work. 'Bama was still gone and had not returned yet. Ginnie was immediately and obviously delighted, if not a little awed.

"You mean youll *marry* me?" she said, almost disbelievingly. "You mean your really willin to marry me? Oh, Dave! I dont know what to say, honey! I jus dont know what to say."

They agreed that she would keep her job at the brassiere factory, and Dave would continue to work on his book. That way she could support them here with 'Bama, at least until the book was done and sold. Then they would show them; they would show all of them! Frank and Agnes and everybody else: when the book was done. It would be still another three weeks or so before the Judge could get the annulment through the courts; and they would just continue to live here like they were till then;—and afterwards too, after they were married too, as far as that went. There was no reason why they should move. And that night Ginnie gave him one of the best and most satisfying parties he had ever had.

But it all did not, however, turn out quite exactly as they had planned it all out ahead of time: 'Bama came home two days later from the farm, and Dave told him. He came in in the morning—luckily; very luckily, Dave thought later—when Dave was at work and Ginnie was gone to her job at the brassiere factory, carrying his little diabetic's case, and Dave sat down with him in the kitchen to tell him over coffee. It was, Dave thought protectively afterwards, a damn good thing

Ginnie was working and wasnt there. Because he did not get at all the type of reaction he had expected to get from 'Bama.

What he had expected was that 'Bama would be pleased and happy for him, and would immediately see the really important and worthwhile similarity between Dave and Ginnie's marriage and his own with Ruth. 'Bama was not, and did not. At all.

"Jesus Christ!" the gambler sneered disgustedly and slammed his cup down on the table and tugged at his hatbrim, when Dave told him the news of his decision. "Jesus *H* Christ! Of all the screwy, hairbrained ideas I eveh heard! Of all the screwy, hair-brained ways to commit *suicide!*"

"Hey! Hey!" Dave said, completely caught up short. "Wait a minute! Wait a minute!"

"Wait for what?" 'Bama said. "Jesus Christ!" he snorted again disgustedly.

"Well, dont you want to hear my reasons even?"

'Bama opened his mouth sneeringly to say something, then snapped it shut and stared at Dave disbelievingly. "Okay," he said with patient disgust. "Okay, all right. Lets hear yore reasons." But then, before Dave could begin to give them, the tall man raised his hand and slapped it down stingingly on his leg and rubbed it slowly back and forth: Damn! I admit I never have understood you. A screwball artist, and all that. I never did know what you were goin to do from one minute to another. I admit it. —But Jesus *Christ!*" he said disgustedly. "All right. Okay. Lets hear yore reasons."

Dave went through them for him, ticking them off one at a time on his fingers for him, still somewhat numbly startled by the unexpected explosion he had touched off, going through them just like he had done with Bob: how he was too old to probably ever get a chance at another woman, and too fat and ugly and too broke; how there was a really valuable kindliness between him and Ginnie; how her working could help support him; how all of it was conducive to helping his work: all the same things he had told Bob; and then he added on the extra point, which he had not bothered to tell Bob who did not know her, about how he wanted a wife who would do for him and work with him and take care of him like 'Bama's own wife Ruth did for him.

'Bama sat and listened through all of it, only shaking his head disbelievingly and disgustedly, and now and then snorting through his nose.

"All right," he said when Dave had finished and sat looking at him expectantly for acquiescence, "all right. Them are all good reasons. Fine reasons. Now for Christ sake put it away and forget all about it and lets get drunk, what do you say?"

"But no!" Dave said, unbelievingly. "Im serious, 'Bama. I really mean it."

"You do?" 'Bama said equally unbelievingly.

Dave nodded emphatically. "Hell yes."

"Well— You havent asked her to marry you yet, have you now?" 'Bama said hopefully.

"Hell yes Ive asked her!" Dave said angrily. "And shes all for it."

"Christ, yes! why wouldnt she be?" 'Bama snorted. "Well, you can still get out of it. Ill help you. Shes scared to death of me."

"I dont *want* out of it!" Dave yelled. "Damn it!"

"Look, Dave," 'Bama said patiently and with great selfcontrol. "I dont know if yore crazy or not. But listen to me." But then he exploded again. "Why, God *damn!*" he cried. "Look, you dumb bastard!" But then he caught hold, and pulled himself down again, at least partially. "Look, as far as getting or not getting women is concerned, all you got to do is finish yore book and sell the damned thing and move away out of this town, and youll have all the goddamned women you want after you! You can pick and choose. If you *got* to get married, if you feel for some damned reason you *got* to get married, you can marry some *rich* woman, then! Some damn millionaire's daughter or somebody! And live the high life!"

"'Bama, 'Bama," Dave said; "you overestimate the influence this novel's going to have. It wont be a drop in the bucket, when it comes out, and itll make a noise just about as big."

'Bama rubbed his hand over his face irritably. "Okay, all right," he said. "I dont know the damned literary world. But, for Christ's sake, why marry a *bum!*"

"Why *not* marry her?" Dave said, stubborn anger growing in him; this wasnt the reaction he had expected at all. "Shell make me a good *wife*. Why *not* marry her?"

"Because shes a pig!" 'Bama cried. "Thats why! Because shes a pig!"

"Well, I dont agree with you that shes a pig," Dave said stubbornly. "People can change. I can *help* her to change. But supposing she is a pig, so what? So am I."

"No," 'Bama said seriously, shaking his head slowly. "No, yore not, Dave. You may look like a pig, but you aint one. You may even act like one, sometimes, but you still aint one. But she is. And she always will be, whether she acts like a pig or acts like something else.

"And another thing," 'Bama cried; "you talkin about Ruth all the time. Ruth this and Ruth that. Why the hell shouldnt Ruth be glad to 'take care of me', as you put it? Ruth's got what she wants: Shes got the farm, and them kids and that family of Clint's. Thats what she really wants. And shes got it. She can sit down there and run that place like a little queen; and thats what she wants, and thats what shes got. But let me ask you something? What if I was to sell that farm and move her up here, to live the kind of life you and me live? And how long do you think shed hang around then? If I did that? Hunh?

Answer me that. Shed take off and leave me so goddamned quick itd make yore head swim, thats what! But she can afford to 'take care of me', as long as shes got a setup like that that she wants. And dont you think she wouldnt have me in bed as an invalid, where she could really 'take care of me', if I just give her half a damned chance!" The tall man stopped and caught his breath:

"All right," he said, "answer me this. What do you think Ginnie wants? What do you think *Ginnie* wants like Ruth wants that farm?"

"How the hell do I know?" Dave said angrily. "I dont know. I dont think she wants anything."

"Probably not," 'Bama snorted. "Shes probly too damned dumb to want anything."

"Ill tell you what she wants," Dave said. "She wants to be *loved*, thats what. One person in the world who will love her."

"Oh, nuts!" 'Bama snorted. "No, thats not what she wants. But Ahll tell you what she wants. More than anything else in the world, Ginnie Moorehead wants to be *respectable*.

"Oh," he said sarcastically, at the look on Dave's face. "Dont believe that, hunh?"

"I dont know," Dave said sullenly. "Maybe she does. So what? I want to be respectable, too. Theres no problem there."

"There aint, hunh?" 'Bama said. "I dont know how its goin to affect yore life after you marry her, but by God, its goin to affect it some way."

"You aint told me a damn thing," Dave said. "You aint said a god-damned thing."

"I—" 'Bama stopped and scratched his jaw jitterishly. "Look: are you really goin through with this heah? You really really got yore mind made up and you really goin to do it?"

"Yes," Dave said emphatically. "I am."

"Okay," 'Bama said angrily. "Then you and me are through. We're quits."

"Well, if thats the way you want it," Dave said sullenly.

Pausing for a moment, 'Bama ran his hand over his face again and got hold of himself, and when he spoke again it was no longer angrily, or irritably, but more a sort of solemn sad reasonability. "Look, Dave," he said, warmly. "Weve washed this thing up already a long time ago, and you know it. We both know it. Why try to hang onto somethin that dont exist any more? Hunh? Dewey and Hubie's gone; Wally's gone; you and me aint makin any more money any more gamblin. The whole thing's washed up, and we both know it. It has been for six months now, damn near."

"Ever since you found out you had diabetes," Dave said sullenly.

"All right. Okay," 'Bama said. "And thats part of it, too. But why do we try to hang onto something that is changed, and isnt the same any more, and dont mean anything any more. Lets finish it up. Lets give her the old coup de grace; and be done with it. Hunh? What do you say?"

Dave felt a sudden deep really painful sadness stealing over him, at the words his buddy spoke, replacing the stubborn sullenness that had been in him. He was right, of course. 'Bama was right, as he usually was—in everything but one or two like Ginnie. "I guess youre right," he said. "I guess thats really what we ought to do."

"Shore it is," 'Bama said. "And you know it as well as I do. Okay. You want to marry Ginnie, go ahead and marry her. Go live someplace else with her, and we'll turn this old house back over to the Judge to lease to somebody else. Weve wore it out—for us. Ill git me back a room somewhere in town, and go back to livin like I use to. What do you say?

"—Hell," he said, before Dave could answer, "I know how you feel about me bein sick with this damned diabetes and all. How do you think that makes me feel? knowin yore worryin about me half the time? You want to marry Ginnie: Okay. I want to keep on gettin drunk: Okay, too. Dont you worry about me, and I wont worry about you. Lets just close up shop and call it a day. What do you say?"

"I guess youre right," Dave said lowly. "Okay," he said, "thats okay with me."

"And we'll bust up friends just like we always was," 'Bama said. And after he said it, he grinned, a sharp, sour, bitter, acid grin—a grin which told Dave more about him, and about his diabetes, than any words that 'Bama himself could say.

"Sure," Dave said. "Thats the way it ought to be, old buddy."

"Fine!" 'Bama said, and straightened up and stuck out his hand.

Dave took it. And for a moment, not a long one, because both of them were embarrassed now before the other, but nevertheless for a moment, they looked straight and square into each other's eyes, and—Dave was sure—the same things rose up in both their minds; at least he knew they did in his: the old games of peapool and fourteen ball; General Nathan Bedford Forrest and the long wild ride to Florida; James Frye and his nephew Jim Custis and the cabin back in the scrub pine; Miami; the gambling; Winnie's Little Club; the Jai alai games; the drive home; the house; the gambling here; Dave's book and the two stories; the garden they had all of them worked so hard on all one summer; all these things rose up in Dave's mind, and he was sure they did in 'Bama's. Then, embarrassedly, as if by mutual consent, both of them let go of the other's hand and looked away.

"But what about the annulment?" Dave said suddenly. "That wont be through for three more weeks. Me and Ginnie cant just go to settin up housekeeping somewhere, while thats still in the works."

'Bama moved his head back and forth emphatically. "Stay here," he said. "Stay right here till its all worked out. Stay here until youve

found yoreself a place where you can move, after you git married.—"
He paused, and looked momentarily disbelieving again. "Jesus!" he
said. Then he shook his head. "—Stay here; and Ill start lookin for me
a place, too. And if you need any money—you know?—why just let me
know. I aint broke yet. Not by quite a little ways."

"I dont want to take any money off you," Dave said, awkwardly.
"You know? Not when you feel like you feel. You know; not personal or
anything, you know?"

"Sure," 'Bama said. "Okay."

And that was the way they left it. By the end of September when
the leaves were turning brown again, Judge Deacon took a frightened
Ginnie into court for a brief session and the annulment was granted.
Two days later they got married, at the JP's basement office, just like
Mildred Pierce had done. They found a little apartment, a nice cozy
little place, Dave thought, even if it was cheap, out in the East End
not far from where Ginnie had once had her room: right out there
where that definite but undecipherable dividing line was, that marked
the first beginnings of Parkman's "Hollywood." It was a nice little two
room place, upstairs, with its own outside entrance that went down a
flight of open stairs. They moved in and set up housekeeping, mostly
with stuff from the house on Lincoln Street, and Ginnie kept on with
her job and Dave went back to work on his book. They were very
happy. There was a small piece, very small, just a recorded mention
along with five other marriage licenses, in the *Oregonian* about their
marriage license being issued. Dave wondered, not without a certain
satisfaction, whether Frank had seen it, and if so, what he thought.

CHAPTER 71

FRANK saw it, right enough. But after he did see it, and did read it in
the *Oregonian,* he didnt think anything about it one way or the
other. It didnt please him, and it didnt disturb him. It did not even
embarrass him. Since the Old Man had died—and, he guessed, too,
since he himself had become so successful with the Shopping Center—
a great deal of the pressure about the family had gone off of Frank. With
the Old Man safely dead and decently buried, where he couldnt do
any more damned outlandish vindictive things, the old scandal could
be allowed to die too, and be forgotten. And as far as Dave went,
Frank had given him his chance; and he had refused it. Frank did not
even feel that he was his brother any more, his kid brother that he
had used to have to take care of—and had received so little gratitude
for in return. Frank had marked Dave off his list for good. He understood, from the little bit he heard around, that Dave was still working

on some kind of a book he was supposed to be writing; but then, he had been supposed to be working on that same book for over two years now, ever since he first came back to Parkman. And so far there had been no book. And nothing else, as far as that went, except that one story in that little pocketbook. Probably, there wouldnt ever be. Frank was quite sure of that, in his own mind. He read the marriage license notice in the *Oregonian* and forgot it, and he put his former brother out of his mind and forgot him too. He had his own business, and his own problems, to worry about.

That winter, that winter of 1949-and-50, after Frank had seen the notice of his brother's marriage, that winter and the following spring, up until the Korean War began, were in some ways and simultaneously both the happiest and the *un*happiest period of Frank's whole life. And it was easy to separate the two: Frank was happy, supremely joyously happy, at three times, and three times only: one, when he was working —as he often was—so hard that he forgot himself completely; and two, when he was out at some football game or basketball game with little Walter; and three, when he was out "walking." He was unhappy: one, whenever he was at home; two, whenever he was out at some social dinner or engagement that he had to make with Agnes; and three, when he was thinking—which was just about all the rest of the time. Even when he was drunk, he wasnt happy, any more. Because no matter how drunk he was—unless he drank himself totally and completely unconscious, which he sometimes did—he could not stop thinking. Only when he was working, or at a game with Walter, or out "walking", could he stop thinking about himself long enough to forget who and what he was; and when he did he was supremely, almost unbelievably, happy. The rest of the time, he wasnt. The rest of the time he was supremely, almost unbelievably, miserably *un*happy. Certainly, he could not stop thinking or forget himself when he was around Agnes. Even if he did, and could have, which he couldnt, Agnes certainly would never have allowed it. It was amazing what a happy, pleased, loving act they could put on out in public—and then to see it fall off of both of them to the floor like a discarded overcoat, the minute they got home and were alone.

Little Walter obviously could tell it, although he very carefully never said anything, or made any recriminations. And they both, both he and Agnes, managed to pretty well control themselves around the boy. Not that that made any difference. He could sense it just the same. It was like a sort of tacit unspoken mutual pact between the three of them: that they would be polite and "happy" and "loving" whenever Walter was present. But when Walter wasnt there, whenever for some reason he was gone: in bed, or out playing, or at school, and the two of them were alone together in the house, it was, Frank was sure, one of the most devastatingly miserable experiences that could happen to any human being. Even when they didnt talk, the resentment, the *hatred*, the battle, hung heavy in the air like smoke. —And, in the end, Agnes had defeated him. Finally and conclusively defeated him, and driven his army from the field in rout, total rout. All except, that is, for his going "walking" which she could do nothing about because she didnt know about it—or even guess at it. But other than that, she had won. A complete and total victory.

Agnes had, during the course of that winter and after considerable consultation and searching thought, finally decided to have her gall bladder out. She had decided—more or less in conflict with Doc Cost's advice; though not entirely, because Doc said that it *might* be a good thing, *might* help her—that that was the only thing that would do her any good. She was in constant pain, she said; and the pain she suffered was not worth it, and so she had it out. Doc Cost performed the operation. And Agnes had triumphed, had won a victory of the first magnitude over him, and over Walter, and over everybody else. It cost her a lot—her gall bladder, in fact, Frank thought sourly—but she had won. The magnitude of just how conclusively she had won became apparent as soon as she came home from the hospital and took to her bed.

And so, for two weeks in November when she was out in Doc Cost's hospital, and then for another six weeks that it took her to recover from the surgery, Mrs Davis—old Jane's successor—moved in and took over and took care of him and of little Walter. It was a most miserable two months for Frank. Not only could Mrs Davis not cook worth a damn, but as soon as Agnes was out of the house and no longer there, Frank's frightened objectless unreasonable panic came back over him again, and the urge to go out "walking" got noticeably stronger. He had been holding himself down pretty well, up to then, only going out one or two nights a month. Now, with Agnes gone, he found himself going out twice a week. That in itself scared him. But the thought that Agnes might die during her operation—Doc Cost assured him that she would not; but doctors always said that—just that thought that she might die drove him nearly frantic. It was winter, too, now: cold hard winter in November: and several times Frank desperately feared he was going to freeze off both his ears, when he was out "walking". Finally, he was forced to buy himself a pair of earmuffs to wear on his "walking" junkets. And that distressed him even more so, because what if some cop or somebody should walk up behind him when he had his earmuffs on, and he wouldnt be able to hear them in time? After a while, he took to wearing his earmuffs only when he was on the sidewalk, and took them off as soon as he stepped into somebody's yard. As long as he was on that sidewalk, that *public* sidewalk, he was all right; only when he stepped off that *public* sidewalk onto the *private* yard was he really in any danger. It got so it became a definite dividing line for him, that he was powerfully aware of, every time he took that step, that single step, off the sidewalk onto the winter grass.

Actually, in all that time—those two weeks when Agnes was in Doc's hospital, and then the first two weeks after she was home but still very sick before she began to mend, and at which time his urge began to fade somewhat—actually in all that time, he had only one real delicious experience: only one anywhere near approaching that so wonderful memory of Edith. But that one, that one successful one, was a real beaut: a real honey. He got to see Clark Hibbard's wife Betty Lee completely naked. He didnt really know what made him go over there, to *Clark's;* and afterwards it terrified him: he was risking his own business contacts and business future, to go to *Clark's.* But he had always hungered to see what Betty Lee looked like naked, and had looked at her covetously that way many times, in Springfield, and at the Country Club—as far back and before, in fact, the very beginning of the bypass deal. So this one night he had ambled over there. They had a modern one storey house, newly built since the war, in one of the best sections of town. (Frank had come to actively and passionately hate two-storey houses in the past few months; and in fact, had debated buying himself some high-powered binoculars but had decided against it since to carry them at night would look suspicious.) And not only was Clark's house one-storey, it was also a house that he knew well from the inside. What he did not know, but discovered that night, was that Clark and Betty Lee had separate bedrooms. Just like him and Agnes now, in fact, by God. But, hell, they were lots younger! He knew, of course, that there were two bedrooms separated by a short hall and bath at the east end of the house; but he had always guessed, without thinking, that one was simply a guest room. Such, however, he discovered was not the case. Lights were on in both bedrooms when he approached the house, and took that one frightening, always-decisive step off the sidewalk onto the yard, and the first one he approached had Clark in it, Clark in his pajamas. And nobody but Clark. And when he slipped across to the other window on the east end, there was Betty Lee!

In a great many ways it was an even better experience than the one with Edith had been, though of course he would always remember that one as his first.

But then, as if all of this were not luck enough, not windfall enough, as he watched her Betty Lee turned her nude self to the full length mirror on the door and inspected herself and ran her hands lovingly over her body. For a moment, Frank thought fearfully he might fall over on the ground in a dead faint. Then she put on her pajamas, and turned out the light, and went to bed.

Frank walked away. His knees were trembling so with excitement by then, that he didnt even know whether he could walk home or not. Hell, he might have to stop somewhere and call up one of his own taxis. But he made it. He made it home. —On the public sidewalk where he was always safe.— But, of course, the next day terror—even stronger than his customary terror afterwards—attacked him viciously: my God! not only was Clark, her husband, his partner in the Shopping Center, but her father, her own *father,* was the man who put up most of the money for it! My God, if either one of them had seen him—or if anybody else had—and the old man in Springfield found out about it, what the hell terrible results might not have come from it! But then, gradually, he calmed himself. After all, nobody had seen him. But after that, he tried very hard to hold himself down and not go out any more.

And—after Agnes's return from the hospital; and those two very bad weeks after that when she was really very sick and he had been afraid that she might die—after those four weeks, when she clearly began to mend, the urge to go out "walking" tapered down in him considerably; and for that he was grateful. Because when it hit him, he had no control over it, just no control at all. Frank was *glad* he didnt want to go out oftener. And anyway, he had finally added one new and fully complete possession to his list: and a magnificent one at that: Betty Lee Hibbard! He now had possessed Betty Lee Hibbard, as well as Edith and Geneve. He was willing to rest on that. For quite a while. And whenever he saw her after that, in Springfield or out at the Country Club where she still played the slotmachines passionately, or uptown on the street, he could look at her in whatever clothes she was wearing and wonder at the magnificence of his own good luck, while the delicious secret knowledge of possession filled him. Whatever her troubles with her husband Clark, that made them sleep in separate bedrooms, she was—Frank felt—about as unhappy in her married life as he was himself in his.

He was aware that his urge to go out "walking" was all tied in with Agnes someway, and in more than just one way. He did it to get even with her, secretly and in his own private way, and he knew that. But there was something else in it too, because the urge became stronger— unbearably stronger, in fact—whenever Agnes went away or was gone a while and that peculiar strange objectless panic hit him. Frank didnt attempt to understand it—and in fact strove mightily not even to think about it at all—but in some way the urge to "walk" tied in with his panic over Agnes' absences. Even if she just went away for a few days, on a visit, which she began doing after she recovered from the operation, even then, he would feel it begin to grow in him. And yet when she was home now—and after a month at home she had begun to get around, more and more and better and better, until by February they were going out again to dinners and parties together—when she was home, the old grinding resentment between them both, like a tangible presence, was just as strong as always.

Only, Agnes had the upper hand now. Whenever she didnt like it, or didnt like anything, and everything didnt just go to suit her, she could always have an attack and have to go to bed with her operation. And he, and Walter, were more or less forced to run around and wait on her and fetch and carry, and get Mrs Davis in to run the house. My God, it wasnt a very bright future prospect, was it? for the rest of your whole life? No wonder he wanted so desperately not to *think*.

The work with the Shopping Center had tapered off some after the grand opening in September. The stores were all moved in now and running, and while there was still a good bit for him to do—arbitrating, handling this or that for this or that lessee—it was nevertheless a far cry from the heavy work schedule he had followed all summer. And, almost panicky when he thought about it, Frank regretted it and was sorry it had slacked off. His own new store was set up and running, too, now—and making more money than the old jewelry store had ever made—and Al Lowe was running it, and needed no help. More in selfdefense than for any other reason, Frank took over the management of the old store again himself: at least it helped keep him busy. Business had fallen off everywhere around the square: not entirely, but noticeably: since the opening of the Shopping Center—just as everyone had known it would, in spite of all his talks to the businessmen—and it was Frank's plan to downgrade the store on the square into a cheaper outfit that offered cheaper merchandise, so that in a way at least it was becoming almost what it had been when he first took it over after Agnes's father died: a notion store. Not entirely, because he still offered jewelry—the cheaper sort—and watch repair and the line of figurines and stuff he had built up. But most of the real business was being done for him by Al at the new store in the Shopping Center. So methodically, carefully, Frank began to lower the level of the merchandise in the store uptown on the square, working at it carefully, grateful for the opportunity to even do the work, planning it thoughtfully to appeal to the cheaper type of buying. Lots of the poorer people in town were even afraid and embarrassed to go into the ritzy new stores in the Shopping Center. His plan was to capture all that business here with the old store. And it worked, too. And he was glad of the opportunity to do it. He had really moved up in the last year. There was already talk among the inner circle of electing him vice-president of the Country Club next year. But it was strange, and somehow odd, to actually be downgrading this store he had worked so long to build up: down into—almost—what it had been when he first took it over.

It wasnt really much work, actually. But Frank made more work of it than there was in it, deliberately. Just in selfdefense. Doing all the listing and the buying and everything by himself, while at the same time he was breaking in a new man to later on take over the management of it. He dreaded to look forward to that moment: when the new man would take it over.—But, along with that, there was nevertheless an important silver lining: Next spring, as soon as the weather opened up again, the Greek and the old man and he were planning on starting the motel out next to the Shopping Center—the motel-and-restaurant. And when that happened, Frank told himself hopefully all winter, he would be right back into it up to his neck again. And he planned, with the Greek's and the old man's agreement, to take over the overall management of the motel and of the restaurant—which would be under separate sub-managers—himself, and coordinate the whole thing into one whole. He kept telling himself that all winter, hopefully, while he fiddled around at the old store on the square to keep his mind from thinking.

And, sure enough, when the spring did open up and the weather did break, that was what accurately happened. And gratefully, Frank plunged into it—into the volumes of work he had to do to first make the motel a reality, and then to run it. And more so than he had been since the Shopping Center opened, more than he had been all that winter, he was happy—and not only happy, but proud, and successful. Almost all the time—except, of course, when he was home:

A new plan had interested him during the winter, and he had brought it up with Agnes. This was the building of their big new home they had talked about all during the year before—when they had been so happy. He hoped, secretly, it would at least give Agnes an interest—if she would only go into it, and start the handling of it by herself. He, he told her, would not be able to do it; there was just too much coming up for him to do with the motel. And, in fact, Agnes had decided to do it and go into it, and had started checking plans and talking with architects. But it did not change the atmosphere at home any.

But then, when the Korean War came up in June, it scotched the house plans, and Agnes went back to watching the new TV set in the living room most of the time, although the only station they could get was Bloomington Indiana's WTTV, and only get it poorly at that.

But the Korean War, in June, did not really affect the motel-restaurant. Not, anyway, like it had affected their own house plans. Luckily, they had got started with the building early in the spring, before the crisis came. Actually, after June, there was quite a while when they could not get materials to finish it. But the Greek, with his ubiquitous hand in so many, many pies was able to expedite this by August. There were always ways and means of getting materials, if you knew where to go. Steels, of course, were the hardest to come by. But almost all their framing on the motel-restaurant—a really beautiful modern angular low-lying structure—was already completed by the time the war broke out. So they were able to go ahead and complete the job.

Frank, working frenetically and in high gear all the time, worked with them on it—with the Greek and the old man. It necessitated many trips to Springfield. And each time he went he was of course always invited out to the old man's for dinner, and as often as not—more often, in fact—Clark and Betty Lee would be there. Needless to say, Frank enjoyed that tremendously, and deliciously. The secret picture was still there, emblazoned—branded, even—on his mind. And every time he looked at Betty Lee he would not see her in her clothes; he'd see her, once again, in the nude, as he had seen her that one time.

It took a lot of work, up there in Springfield, to keep the motel-building going—for which, of course, Frank was very grateful. But actually, outside of that, the Korean War had almost no effect on him at all. Indeed, he was almost unaware of it. It didn't touch his personal life at all. How could it? He had too much misery of his own, at home, to occupy him. He felt sorry for the boys dying over there, but—to him —it was really nothing compared to the misery he suffered.

He would come home, dead beat and dead tired, after a hectic drive-drive-driving day of work at his offices, or out at the motel, and Agnes— back upon her feet and in good shape now (except when she wanted to be sick)—would be there to meet him and stare at him accusingly. Or else, which was worse, would suddenly burst forth over nothing in some vituperous tirade that would surgically disjoint him completely —and then take to her bed, in pain from the gall bladder she no longer had. So he would put up with it. What else was there to do? He had to get drunk every night to do it, but he put up with it. And this was his life. She had taken everything, destroyed everything—both him and herself. He was making more money than he had ever made in his life before—was, in fact, well on his way to becoming—magic word—a millionaire—and yet what did it avail him? He had not slept with a woman in almost a year. He could not escape a feeling that he had his neck in an as-yet-untightened hangman's noose clutched tightly in the hands of the Law, just waiting to catch him, just waiting to tighten up. And whenever he was home he was miserable.

Marriage, he thought bitterly; the happy marriage of two years ago. Hah! What a lie. This was the *real* marriage. This was what marriage *really* was. He knew it now; he knew the truth now. And he had it stretching away out ahead of him to look forward to for the rest of his life. The marriage. The real marriage.

What a winter! What a *year!*

How *could* the Korean War possibly affect him personally, or mean anything to him, when he was faced with a situation like he was faced with?

BOOK SIX

THE RELEASE

CHAPTER 72

For a man working in a defense plant, however, the Korean War could not help but be something important, and affect him personally. And, after a year of married life, that was where Dave Hirsh was working: in a defense plant. And making more cash money than he had ever made in his life before, too. Except when he and 'Bama had been at their very peak, gambling.

The shell factory—for that was what it was: they made forty millimeter anti-aircraft shells—was located just south of Terre Haute not far from the big Federal prison there; and in fact, whenever you stepped outside the plant you could see the prison in the distance, across the flat Indiana fields. Dave, however, didnt like to look at it; it always disturbed him some way. The shell factory itself was a newer installation, built right at the end of World War II; and in August of 1950 Dave was a paint foreman in it. His job was to operate the automatic painting machine that painted the unprimed shell casings, and to oversee the two women who fed the casings into the conveyer belt unpainted and took them off after they came out of the dryer. He had not started out like that, of course; he had started out cleaning shells —cleaning the casings with an acid bath before they were to be painted—but he had been promoted quickly, back in May before the war had even started, because his predecessor had been a man who arrived at work drunk too often.

Every day he and five other men with whom he pooled his car would drive the fifteen miles to Terre Haute and then the seven and a half miles south to the shell factory in order to go to work. And every evening after work they would drive back to Parkman together. Not an especially long trip, actually. Compared to some of the people who came to work there. Some came from as far as fifty miles away, driving both ways: a hundred miles: every day. And after June, after the war in Korea started, it became even more hectic and more fantastic as they put on more and more people to boost the production into an around-the-clock schedule.

It was a strange thing to think about, really. And Dave never failed to have a sense of strangeness, a sense of mild astonishment and near-disbelief, every time he got up so early in the morning and went out and crawled into the little Plymouth to go and pick up the other men and make the trip. They were all strangers to him, actually. Oh, he knew them, even knew the wives of three of them, but they were strangers. While they talked and laughed and joked all the way over to the shell factory, or back, they were still strangers. Strangers to his life, and to what his life had always been, to what he himself had always

1201

been. Dave had, somehow or other, in the year he had been married, become respectable: a respectable workingman. It was such a far cry from the life he had used to live with 'Bama in the house on Lincoln Street that he could not help but feel a sense of strangeness. And with it, also, a definite sense of shame: at being so respectable. But when he stood beside his automatic paint machine, wearing the new glasses he had bought recently to improve his eyesight, while the shell casings set up by the women revolved by on their spindles tripping the automatic sprays that coated them with lacquer both inside and out and then went on into the baking dryer, he could not help but feel a sense of greater strangeness still. And, whenever he stepped outside and saw again the big Federal prison buildings in the distance across the fields, he would wonder darkly how all those nameless prisoners who were in there had come to be there? what had they done? just as he wondered how he himself had ever come to be *here?*

Oh, he knew. He knew the factual events that had, step by step, brought it about. That is, he could recall—and clearly—the factual progression of the events themselves: each time when outwardly a change, a definite change, easily discernible, was made. Because after all each was an event, a physical event, you participated in. What he could not see, or understand, were the reasons which brought each physical, material event about: the small nuances inbetween the events of change, and which led to them. Because, after all, it *neednt* have turned out like it did. And yet it had.

As far as the money went, that was fine. He was actually making more money than he had ever made. After June and the crisis and the war which came from it, he was working sometimes as much as ninety and ninety two hours a week: fifty hours of overtime a week at time-and-a-half. This was because he and his two women did the painting of all of the factory's output. The plant did not carry an extra painting crew, because the output of shell casings varied so from week to week because of shutdowns and errors that as often as not there wasnt really enough work to keep even one crew busy for a full forty hour week. So Dave was doing it all; and making that much more because of it, from the overtime. But then he was spending it just as fast, too. Payments on the little house that he and Ginnie had bought, payments on the furniture and furnishings they had had to buy for it; and now he was getting ready to incur further payments, because Ginnie wanted a new car: the Plymouth was no longer in keeping with their raised financial status. So as far as that went, actually, the money didnt really make much difference: Ginnie was spending it just as fast as he made it, spending it on something or other. It was almost kind of ridiculous, in a way.

Once, working—standing in his new, expensive glasses beside his steadily moving, steadily clicking painting machine and watching nearly thoughtlessly to see that nothing upset or broke the rhythm— all of a sudden it was as if he seemed to be standing outside of himself looking at him from the vantage point of another person, and what he saw was such a strange apparition that it shocked him into motionlessness: this was not the Dave Hirsh he had lived with all his life at all. And he had raised up his head and through the glasses that still felt new on his face had looked all around at this strange unearthly interior of the plant, and a feeling of such strangeness came over him that he could not even describe it to himself. Dave Hirsh: paint foreman. The paint machine was working well—(actually all he had to do was mix the paint carefully and see that no dirt got in it to clog the sprays and to keep the nozzles clean)—and he had walked away from it for a moment, over to the big well-lighted window complex and looked out across at the prison in the distance, wondering again with a kind of awe how all those men—those prisoners—had come to be over there? How come? Why? How had each man's particular, personal crisis come about? And then he remembered again that night that seemed so long ago: when he, drunk and lying beside Ginnie out on the porch, had heard Lois Wallup crying inside the house on Lincoln Street.

Oh, he knew how it had all come about. The factual events, anyway. Really, it had started when the novel had been rejected in New York. That was the first "factual-event" of change. He had, working hard and steadily and well, finished the novel up three months after they got married in September, while Ginnie worked at the brassiere factory and supported them. Then he had sent it off to the *NLL* lady editor in New York. By that time that second story "The Peons" had come out in the fall paperback anthology: and with an added biographical note on him which lauded him highly as a new and coming voice. The other paperback, the lady editor's short novel anthology, had come out with "The Confederate" in it again shortly before that. (And this time, both these times, Ginnie had brought her copies of both that she had bought to *him* to autograph to her friends, instead of doing it herself.) With both stories out like that, he had been full of confidence when he sent the novel in—completely full of confidence. He had worked on it hard, deftly working in the sad little love affair, finishing and toning up the really diabolic humor of the combat and death. Why shouldnt he have been full of confidence?

And so when he heard from it—and it was a long time before he did hear: two whole months of total silence, all of November and December: puzzled silence it was, he was to realize later—and found it had been rejected by them, the seeming confidence made the news even more shocking to him. It threw him into a state of near terror. The *NLL* lady editor wrote him a puzzled letter. She could not, she said, just exactly point out what was wrong with the book. But something was. She had analyzed it carefully, going through the whole thing two or three times in fact, and she still could not place her finger on the flaw. But somehow the book just did not come off. She herself felt it had to do somehow with the combat material: in spite of the really rich humor of some of it, it was just almost too horrible to take, that humor, especially when contrasted with the really beautiful little love affair which she had liked exceedingly. She, herself, felt he had over-done the humor of the combat—perhaps unwittingly—and it ought to be toned down she felt. Perhaps if the diabolical humor of the com-bat were toned down, and the love affair heightened more—perhaps starting sooner in the book and continuing on through it further—perhaps that would fix it up. She thought it might. But perhaps even that wouldnt do it. She did, in fact, she said, feel so really unsure about the whole novel that she did not feel *NLL* could even offer him an advance on revising it.

This was not, the lady editor wrote, entirely a woman's opinion, either. She had had the book read by several of her male associates. Without exception they all agreed with her: both about the love affair and about the too-strong combat. She would, she said, since he had done so well with them the last year, be glad to send the novel around to some other publishers, if Dave wanted her to. Because she herself was really so unsure as to what was wrong that she thought it might be best to get other opinions. Perhaps some other publisher would see something more in it than she did, and would want to take it. But in the state it was in now, she could not honestly accept it; and indeed, could not even offer him an advance to do further work on it.

This was the first "factual event". Dave had, hopefully, agreed for her to send it around, in his answer. This time the answers came back quickly: Nobody knew just what was wrong with it, but some-thing was; and nobody wanted it. Without exception, everyone liked the love affair part of it the best. With these comments, she had re-turned the manuscript to him.

It was an awful, and a terrifying, blow to Dave. He had put more than two years of his life into it, and a great deal of his heart's blood. Pretty hopelessly, he got it out and tried to go back to work on it. But he didnt know what to do to it. It was, virtually, from his stand-point, complete. He couldnt see anything to do to it. Perhaps Bob French had been right about the love affair after all, all along. And yet without exception every editor and publisher in New York who read it, liked the love affair the best. As for the combat material, if he "toned that down" as the lady editor had suggested—and as the others had suggested—he wouldnt have the same book at all; he wouldnt, in fact, have any book—except for the love affair itself.

And it was then, in January of 1950, that the second "factual-event" happened. Ginnie quit her job and disappointedly refused to support him any more. If he couldnt write and sell his book, she said emphatically, and unhappily, then he could get a job and support *her*, like other men did their wives. Of course, it had been coming on for some time. It didnt just happen suddenly. She had been making nasty, bitterly disappointed cracks at him about it: about her working while he didnt: ever since the first rejection came from NLL. And, in a way, Dave could see her side of it, too. And so it was then, in January, that he had gone and got the job (more to keep Ginnie quiet than for any other reason; but to allay his own desperate feeling of terror, too), and had started cleaning shell casings—but determined in the evenings to work on the book, to go back over and do something—although he didnt know what—with it.

Maybe he shouldnt ever have gone and got the first job? But in some odd way, ever since they had been married, Ginnie had the Indian sign on him in a way she had never had before. He couldnt even put his finger on just what it was. But she could always make him do what *she* wanted. In the beginning she had wanted him to finish the book and make a lot of money; now she didnt care if he finished it or not because she had lost faith in it. What she wanted now was for him to take the job. So he had taken it. Thank God, at least, they didnt have to worry about having any damned kids, too; Ginnie's gonorrhea when she was a kid had made her sterile, so at least they didnt have to worry about that, thank God. But Dave had—without realizing it; because he had never had experience with it—become afflicted with and subject to that peculiar odd pointless sense of panic that married men who are settled get whenever they think of being without their wives. Later on, when he did understand it, it was already too late: he had it, this panic, waiting there to rise, always waiting, and understanding it did not in the least free him of it.

Of course, he could see Ginnie's side of it, too; and that very thing —his ability to see her side—made him even more incapable of being able to defend his own. She had had such large and rosy dreams about what they were going to do when they sold the novel and got all that money. He had tried once or twice to delicately get across to her that if the novel did sell, it still wasnt going to make anywhere near the kind of money she was dreaming of getting from it. But it was almost the same thing as trying to talk to a sleepwalker: wrapped up in her own dreams of their forthcoming riches, she didnt even hear what he said. No wonder she became so bitter and disappointed when it was turned down. So you couldnt blame Ginnie really, and he knew it; and that fact also added to his inability to argue with her. And added to that was his own panic over the rejection. So, he had gone and got the job; and that was the third "factual-event" in the series. The fourth was that he got promoted. And the fifth was that they, at Ginnie's insistence, moved out of the cheap apartment and bought the house.

And that brought him up to date: a clean and bespectacled man who painted forty millimeter shell casings with an automatic painting machine in a shell factory south of Terre Haute—near the Federal prison. Strange? Yes, very strange.

And yet, there was much more to it than that, too. And that was where all those little nuances came in—those little nuances that slipped out from between your fingers like blobs of mercury that you could not pick up. A lot more to it.

Almost from the first, not right away—not for those first few weeks of marriage when they were so happy—but increasing gradually once it had got started, Ginnie came more and more to putting him off whenever he wanted to go to bed with her. You would think she—Ginnie: Ginnie Moorehead: who had slept with just about every man she could get her hands on for years—you would almost think she actually disliked sex. Actually, by the time the first rejection of the book came from *NLL,* which was in December, Dave was almost never sleeping with her more than twice a week. And after the rejection, when she was really bitterly disappointed and unhappy, that had dwindled down to no more than once a week, and during some weeks not at all. He would ask her, and try to play up to her; and Ginnie would irritably put him off.

"Is that all you ever think about?" she would say crossly. "Cant you ever think about anything else?"

He could not understand it. He was not stepping out on her. And after he took the job in January, he wouldnt even have had time to, what with trying to work the job and then work on the book in the evenings. But even that irritated her: They never went out evenings, like her friends did; they never went to parties, never went to the movies: all they did was sit here at home while he worked on that damned old book that wouldnt sell anyway. She had a really active resentment against the book itself now anymore, as if she held the book itself responsible for not having sold itself and made them all the money she had dreamed of so happily. But she *knew,* she *must* know, that he wasnt stepping out on her. Then why had she taken such a dislike to sleeping with him?

And so here he was: a man who had married first for sex, and second for stability and peace; and third for someone to help him with his work: and he had none of them. And in addition, he was working as a paint foreman in a forty millimeter shell factory—in order to keep all these things that he already didnt have. And he knew she wasnt stepping out on him; Ginnie had become very, very careful of her reputation since she had become a respectable married woman. Sometimes it made him mad, blindly, furiously mad,—but never quite furiously enough that he could bring himself to do anything, or say anything, or argue with her: never quite furiously enough that it burned away or superceded that married man's settled panic at the thought of being without his wife.

Marriage. It was really a funny thing, very funny. All it was actually was a piece of legal paper, that could be unlegalized almost about as easily as it had been done. And yet it was more than that; and its real power of holding people came from something else, not just the legal paper. Perhaps from a sense of responsibility, maybe? Some, maybe. But the real power of marriage lay somewhere else yet. Dave thought perhaps it lay in the *mental* acceptance of the otherwise meaningless legal fact: it was something you had done, something you had bound yourself to, and this knowledge bound you to it more. That, and the fact that other people knew you had committed this legal act.

She became much better for a while, after they got the little house. Although it did not make her want to sleep with him any oftener. They had bought it right away after he got promoted at the plant in May, and Ginnie immediately went to work to fix it all up the best they could afford—better than they could afford, really. But then came the Korean War and Dave's paychecks jumped as high as a hundred and forty percent some weeks. But of course he was working all those extra hours. And the book, which he had tried to struggle with all those evenings when he came home dog-tired from work, the book he had had to finally put away entirely.

Once they had got the little house—it wasnt a very expensive one; a prefab; but it was very nice—Ginnie began, once she had spent the money on fixing it up, to entertain her friends more. They almost never went out to Ciro's or Smitty's any more. They did all their partying at home, or at the little homes of one of Ginnie's friends. Mildred Bell (nee Pierce) and her husband were two of their most frequent guests; just as they were theirs. And Lois Wallup who had married a man named Wills and finally got that home for her two kids. But gradually Ginnie began to draw away from these. Several times she invited Doris Fredric down for dinner, and Doris always came—though she never returned the invitation to her parents' big home on East Wernz, which was understandable enough. Doris, in that same still-virginal way of hers, looked at Dave as though he were a man she had never even known before at all. Dave never had liked her, and still didnt. But even worse than Doris Fredric, Ginnie started taking up with his mother: inviting her frequently to the house for dinner and forcing Dave to go with her up to the old gal's apartment to eat that horrible food with her. The two of them, his mom and Ginnie, would sit around either in their living room or the apartment's living room and watch the television all evening, while Dave, totally and deathly bored, would sit out in the kitchen by himself and try to read—the sound of the yacking voices of the television keeping him from even doing that adequately.

Not long after she started inviting his mom to dinner, Ginnie had suddenly—after talking with the old lady—decided to join her church, the Church of Christ, Saved, out in the East End; and had insisted on Dave attending Sunday morning with her. That was one place, the first, where he flatly set his foot down and refused. He was not going to spend his Sunday mornings being bored in some damned church.

But Ginnie's interest in the Church of Christ, Saved, did not last long. Less than a month, in fact. This was because she decided that the Methodist Church was the one she wanted to belong to, and there was an elderly lady down the street who lived just a few doors from them and was still a member of it. This elderly lady had once been rather influential in the town—before her husband died and lost most of his money—and now she was all alone, but she still belonged to the Methodist. She liked to spend afternoons sitting with Ginnie drinking coffee and talking, telling Ginnie stories of the old days, before her husband died and lost most of his money. And she was quite willing to take them along to the Methodist Church and introduce them to the minister. Once again Dave flatly refused, but this time Ginnie wasnt taking any no for answer and they went to the mat with it—their first real *fight,* first real conflict in which neither side would give, in the year they had been married. Dave refused to go, and Ginnie insisted that he must. Belonging to the Methodist Church was one of the most important things in the whole town of Parkman, she said; even his brother Frank and his wife Agnes with all their money belonged to it; and she couldnt go alone, without her husband, could she? Dave, in his turn, said that if she went it would certainly be with*out* her husband. It turned into a very recriminatory verbal match before it was over—with Ginnie doing most of the recriminating, however; Dave still couldnt get his nerve up. But in the end he won: he did not go to the Methodist Church with her, then or at any other time, and she went by herself with the elderly lady to meet the preacher. Probably, Dave thought afterwards, the reason he was able to win, this once, was because after all it was really a negative action he was taking rather than a positive one: in other words, all he had to do was just sit, and stay sat. Whereas Ginnie had to move him. Inertia was on his side. The victory, however, did not give him much confidence, or satisfaction.

The pattern was beginning to emerge, and he could see it. He wished he didnt. The truth was, it was just about exactly what old 'Bama had said at the house that last time, when they had argued over him marrying her: 'Bama had pretty accurately called the turn: Ginnie wanted more than anything else in the world to be *respectable.* Neither he nor 'Bama—as 'Bama had also said at the time—had been able to foresee just what the pattern would be that this desire of hers would take. But Dave could see it now. And in fact, once it began to be clear to him, he could understand for the first time why it was that Ginnie —who had once been so sexy all the time—now appeared to almost dislike sex, and no longer liked to sleep with him: It wasnt, to Ginnie's mind, ladylike to like sex. And being a lady now, by God, a respectable married lady, she just wasnt going to be unladylike. Old 'Bama, the son of a bitch, Dave thought sourly and glumly, 'Bama had been right all along. But who could have foreseen it?—that it would take this course?

Dave didnt see his old gambling buddy much any more. He was too busy working at the shell factory and staying home to help Ginnie entertain her newer, slightly higher up, friends which had replaced Mildred Bell and Lois Wallup. Once or twice downtown Dave saw him close enough to speak to—which they both did, and then rather embarrassedly went their separate ways; and once when he was downtown Dave had passed by the Ath Club poolroom and seen in through the big plate window the tall Southerner sneeringly engaged in beating a bunch of the local sharpies at fourteen ball. Dave had intended to go in. But after seeing 'Bama he just didnt have the heart. Not only because of the past, but also because while he didnt see him often, he nevertheless heard about him from guys at the plant who sometimes played poker with him: 'Bama had gone downhill badly in the last year. He still drank his fifth or more of whiskey a day, and half the time when he played poker he actually seemed to be deliberately throwing his money away, the guys said. Also, a thing which all of them had noticed too, 'Bama was wearing both gauze and elastic bandages on both legs up to the knees. He didnt mind talking about it in the least, and laughingly showed the bandages around. The gauze was for the open sores that had started breaking out on his legs, and the elastic bandages were to try and keep new sores from breaking out. And he still would not give up his heavy drinking or his unhealthy night life gambling. It was almost frightening, the guys said. Knowing all of this, that day he saw him at the Ath Club Dave had turned and sorrowfully gone away. He saw him a few times after that, in town, at a distance.

Dave also saw—just twice; just two times only—Gwen French in Parkman during that summer of 1950. So, evidently, she had finally returned. Both times that he saw her he suspected that she saw him, too. Anyway, both of them—at a distance of a block or so—turned off and went different ways so that they would not meet. Dave could stand meeting and speaking to 'Bama, even though it embarrassed both of them; but Gwen he could not.

Another thing that happened during that first year of his "marriage"

—back during the middle of the winter this was, in February—was that Ginnie's Marine ex-husband showed up again in Parkman. Dave did not see him. He was far too busy working at the shell factory and staying home, and even though they did not have the house yet Ginnie had stopped them from going to Smitty's and Ciro's. But he heard about it afterwards. Not everybody in town knew about him; but some did. It was Gus Nernst, Dewey Cole's old buddy, who told him. Gus worked at the shell plant too now, and sometimes they saw each other. Evidently Rick the ex-Marine had come in town on the bus pretty drunk. He had hung around Ciro's and Smitty's a couple of days, sullenly drinking himself drunker. Then he had just disappeared again. He had, Gus said, while in his cups made a few threats about Dave; he was looking for him, he said. Gus thought Dave ought to know. Dave had to grin, remembering the wild night the ex-Marine had spent with Bob French. After that night, and Bob's description of it, Dave could no longer take the guy seriously. If the guy was still wanting to look him up, it should have been easy enough for him to find out where they lived, shouldnt it? Why hadnt he done it? Apparently he was just blowing like he had that time with Bob. Apparently he didnt want to look him up, really. Maybe he only wanted to return to the scenes of his past "love", poor guy. And he did not say anything about it to Ginnie: it would only have meant that she would have jumped on *him* and given him hell, out of her new-found respectability, for always throwing up her past to her to insult her. Dave was getting to know her pretty well now, any more, after a year.

If Ginnie desired respectability so strongly, she also wanted to get ahead, too. This was another bone of contention between them. Even the money Dave was making with all the extra overtime because of the war, was not enough. For some time now, just lately, the past month or two, Ginnie had begun twitting him about his brother Frank. Why couldnt he be friends with Frank? Why did he always have to antagonize him? Dave had always refused to shop out at the new Shopping Center, just because he might run into Frank, and he didnt want to. But Ginnie shopped there all the time. And now with the new motel and its ritzy modern restaurant going up out there too, Ginnie's recrimination with him about Frank got even more pointed and stinging. He could have been in on all of that,—still could be in on it. Frank was well on his way to being the most important and richest man in Parkman. Why couldnt Dave make up with him? Then, someday, they might have a chance of joining the Country Club. Ginnie knew about Dave's near-forty percent interest in the taxi service which he still owned, and the money from it—insignificant as it was—was still coming in every month to them; and she would not let up on that point either. Why couldnt he have gotten in on some of the other things, too? The bigger things? Why just the damned taxi service? *Why couldnt he make up with Frank?* Inadvertently, in a moment of vain boasting, Dave had once told her—long before they were married—that Frank had once offered to take him in with him as a partner, and that he had refused. Now that statement returned to haunt him increasingly, all out of proportion to its importance. He was learning to regret ever having said it more and more every week: If Frank had once offered him a partnership, what was to keep him from offering it again? Ginnie demanded. He *should* have taken it then. But at least there was no reason why he couldnt take it now. —It was useless to try and tell her that things had changed since then; that now he and Frank both hated each other's guts. She just simply refused to see it: If he could have been his partner once, she insisted, damn fool that he was to refuse, he could still be his partner now. Why werent they ever invited out to Frank and Agnes's for dinner, like other people? Only because he refused—just stubbornly, bullheadedly refused—*to make up with Frank.*

It became such an increasing theme whenever he was home that in sheer desperation Dave took to running out of the house and just walking up and down the streets. More than once he ran out through the door with his hands above his head, while that stinging rebuking voice followed him like some actual physical weapon beating him about the ears. Then he would just walk up and down the streets, alone, glad for the momentary peace, the temporary cessation of that noise. He no longer went to Smitty's or Ciro's; didnt want to; and anyway Ginnie would have raised hell with him if he did. He was, in fact, drinking almost nothing any more, at all. Ginnie saw to that, too: a cocktail before dinner was all right, was sophisticated, but any more than that—no, sir; it was *out.* So he just walked the streets, the summer streets, thinking sadly of that novel lying back there on the closet shelf that he did not know what to do with.

Once, in a sheer wild hope born of desperation, he went downtown in Terre Haute to the Post Office during his lunch hour and tried to enlist back in the Army. He was, of course, refused: Forty years old, and fat as a butterball, and with weak eyes—what else could he expect? It was a wild shot in the dark at best. Anyway, he was told, he was more important to the war effort in his job of painting shells at the defense plant. Driving back out to the plant after his rejection, Dave asked himself why he didnt just up and leave? Just go away? Let her have the house, and everything that went with it? Why not? If he was willing to go back in the Army to get away from it? But he couldnt face the prospect: it was an entirely different thing: in the Army there was at least the companionship of other men and similar interests. Going off alone, with no friends, not even knowing where to go, and with very little money or none—it was a different thing. And he just couldnt face that loneliness. And the married man's panic rose up in him again, at the thought of the loss of his wife. Was this why most marriages remained intact maybe?

Actually, that was really how she kept the upper hand over him so much: that old, settled, married man's panic. But why didnt she have some of that? some female equivalent of it? Apparently, she didnt. Apparently she never worried that he might leave *her*, that—just because of that constant harping and dinging and carping at him—he might just suddenly decide to up and take off. Why didnt she?

The only recourse, the only possible escape, in any way, seemed to be to get that damned novel back out again and try to fix it up. Hell, if he could only sell the book, maybe she would stop. And so, in spite of the extra hours he was already working at the shell plant, and in spite of the sleep and rest it cost him, he pulled the novel down off its shelf in the closet and—in spite of Ginnie's sneering stinging remarks about it —in desperation locked himself away in the one little room in the house where he could work, and started in to revise it—some way, some *how*. Night after night he would sit up with it, and with his same old typewriter—his same old portable—and many times would fall asleep over it right there in the chair and not wake up until it was nearly dawn and almost time to get up and go back to work at the plant. Ginnie bitched and carped about this, too; but—silently, doggedly, stubbornly—he stuck with it. He had to. It was his only out. He knew, of course, that the caliber of the work was not—could not be—up to the caliber of the work he used to turn out. But it was his only out. If he gave that up, there was nothing left.

God! It was a far cry from the marriage he had once envisioned for himself, wasnt it? He couldnt blame Ginnie really, and maybe that was the very source of his lack of strength. But he knew how badly disappointed she had been when it was turned down, knew how badly she was disappointed by his not getting back in with Frank, knew how badly she wanted all those things which she had always been denied all her life: money, respectability, the right friends, a chance to really be somebody. He understood. But they just wanted different things.

He could do an awful lot with that "sad pathetic little love affair" now, he thought sourly. God, what an ass he had been. God, no wonder Bob French was so emphatic about it ruining the book! Leaving the combat stuff strictly alone for fear he might damage its excellence, he started working—on those late nights—on the love affair, having in mind to change the peasant girl. His new little peasant girl was going to be more like women really were: his new little peasant girl was going to take up with her little private to get chocolate bars and food for the rest of her family on the farm; and from her little private she was going to move up, whenever she got the chance: first to a corporal, then a sergeant, then finally even to a major or captain. He worked at rewriting it doggedly, and he was able to relieve himself of a great deal of the vindictiveness and malice and just sheer flaming dislike that he felt for Ginnie in the doing of it. —Even though he felt guilty about it, too.— But when he was done, it would be about as devastating as the combat stuff, by God!

Marriage. Happy, happy marriage. What was wrong with him? Why did his marriage have to be so different from other peoples'? Frank and Agnes were happily married, very happily,—even though Frank did— or at least used to—step out on his wife. And yet they were happy for Christ's sake. What the hell was wrong with *him*?

Why, for Christ's sake even Dawnie, even little Dawnie his damned niece, who was just a green kid, and whom he had not even seen since almost a year before her marriage, even she green as she was had a happy marriage, at least to all intents and purposes she did. She and Jim Shotridge were still living up there in Champaign, still going to college, and apparently they were still completely happy. Why couldnt he be? What was wrong with him? And now hed heard theyd had a baby.

Marriage. Happy, happy marriage. He would sit up at night, dog-tired from the ten and sometimes even fourteen hours he was putting in at the shell factory,—while Ginnie went to the movies by herself, or went to visit other people, or even had people in to visit her and he could hear them in the other room and the television—and he would drive himself to work on the book. Because it was his only out. His only hope. Without that, there was—: nothing. Nothing left.

Marriage. Happy, happy marriage. And even little Dawnie: had a baby: those kids: those damned green kids: had a baby.

CHAPTER 73

THEY had. And it was the sweetest, cutest, cuddliest, most beautiful, most delicious baby that had ever been born on the face of the earth. Both Mrs Dawn Hirsh Shotridge and her husband James H Shotridge were thoroughly agreed on that—(and, Dawnie thought to herself deliciously and warmly, thoroughly agreed on everything else, too)—but most of all they were agreed on Diana Sue: Miss Diana Sue Shotridge, age six months. And on that afternoon in late August of 1950 when Dave Hirsh had thought of them briefly and in passing, but bitterly, while résuméing his own troubles, they were both engaged in showing Diana Sue off to an interviewer from *Weight* Inc. and having their pictures taken by the photographer who accompanied him, for an article in *Weight* magazine on young married college students.

The streets of Champaign-Urbana where the campus imperceptibly shades into the residential section are wide and shaded by beautiful big old trees, but Dawnie and Shotridge did not live there. They lived further back in on the campus, where a Quonset hut village had been set up for married students. Originally, the Quonset village had been set up to house exclusively the married World War II veterans going to school on the GI Bill and under Public Law 16; but gradually, as more and more students who were not veterans got married, and as more and more of the veterans graduated, its clientele was extended to include all married students. And in the summer of 1949 when they had first moved to the campus Dawnie and Shotridge had decided immediately that they would rather live there—if they could get in—than to take an apartment. They could easily have afforded an apartment in town, and a fine one, because both Harry Shotridge and Frank would gladly have financed them in it. But Dawnie and Shotridge had chosen the Quonset village anyway. Because, after all, with all the myriads of beautiful wedding gifts they had, they could decorate their little three room Quonset apartment as beautifully as an apartment in town; and here, they were able to be amongst their own set: the young married students. As Dawnie so often said, the young married students, being naturally more stable and mature than the unmarried kids,—and, actually, most of them already parents of kids of their own—naturally preferred to live amongst themselves. And it was a wonderful way of life: They entertained for each other, and helped each other out with their chores and babysitting, and lived a quiet mature stay-at-home simple life different from the rather frantic kiddishness of the unmarrieds. And, in fact, this very thing was the subject of the *Weight* magazine series of articles.

They, Dawnie and Shotridge, had—as Dawnie later told the *Weight* magazine man, smiling sparklingly at him with amusement—come up to school for the summer course of 1949 more or less out of necessity: when she had been going to Western Reserve Shotridge had spent so much time over there courting her that hed flunked out three subjects and had to make them up. But then, having attended one summer term, they both liked it so well they had decided to go right on this summer too. Most of the married kids were doing that. After all, when you were married—and with the added responsibility of a baby—it made you look differently at the idea of spending your summers loafing. You wanted to get your schooling over with the quickest and best way possible and get out and assume your position in society. Because after all, look at her: she was in her second semester junior year now; this fall, she would be a senior and graduate next spring. Without those two summer terms she would only be a first semester junior this fall. As for Shotridge, after he had made up those three dropped subjects, he had—after getting married —risen steadily up in his class, and he would graduate at mid-term this coming year. He intended to stay over and pick up some more, extra credits the next semester until Dawnie graduated. Then, as he was Air Force Administrative ROTC, and high up in his class—(Dawnie had seen to this; to both of these, in fact; although she did not tell the *Weight* man that)—they would probably have to do their stint in Service. They hoped to be able to spend their two years in Paris. Or at least in France. All this information they imparted to the *Weight* Inc. man, as the photographer moved around the place clicking his two Leicas.

Weight: The Magazine of Opinion was—as both Dawnie and Shotridge knew, of course—the biggest as well as the first of all the big picture-story magazines. There were a lot of more or less secondrate imitations floating around now, but there was only one *Weight*. And now *Weight* had decided to do a big series of picture stories on this peculiar new phenomenon of American colleges and universities: the young married students, and their young families. And Dawnie and Shotridge and their Quonset village at the University of Illinois had been selected as one of their examples.

Sitting in her expensively decorated living room with its curving Quonset walls and the Oriental rug on the floor that Agnes had given them, while the *Weight* interviewer fired his questions at them and the photographer continued to go around snapping his two Leicas, Dawnie could not help but feel that they—she and Shotridge and little Diana Sue—were a pretty excellent example for their story. Most of the kids didnt have quite as much money to lay out as they did, and there they were perhaps an exception. However, no one would have known it to look at them. They very carefully hid it and kept it in the background —in everything except the decoration of the little apartment, and the real parties they threw for their friends who didnt have as much, and whom they wanted to do things for—but other than that, it was unnoticeable and they preferred it that way, not only because they liked living in the Quonset village, but also because they did not want to embarrass their friends. But beyond that little bit of extra money, Dawnie felt *Weight* Inc. could not have picked a better example of college marriage, and what it could do for young people. And as the *Weight* man questioned Shotridge interestedly and intently, and Shotridge sensitively and amiably expounded his views and descriptions of what their life was like, Dawnie looked contentedly at her husband and then over at her daughter, playing in her playpen. Little Diana Sue with her little pink bow tying up her wispy hair, looked back at her with her wide blue eyes and then grinned and gurgled happily, and everything in

Dawnie—her happiness, her contentment, her pleasure—swelled up powerfully.

"Hold it!" the photographer said. "I missed that. Look that way again. Here: look back at the baby and think just exactly what you were thinking before."

So Dawnie looked back at Diana Sue, and thought about her baby and everything that it entailed. There just was no experience in a woman's life that compared with motherhood. A woman who hadnt become a mother just wasnt a complete woman. At all. She was only half a woman. And Dawnie could not help feeling sorry for all the poor women who had never had the delicious experience of motherhood. Looking at Baby Diana Sue, Dawnie already knew what her baby was going to be, when she grew up. Diana Sue was going to be a prima ballerina: she already had, at six months, all the qualifications: the potential beauty, the coordination, the intelligence, and not only all of that the little imp was a natural born actress. And she tried to prance on her toes too, only Dawn knew it wasnt wise to allow her to try standing yet; her little legs werent strong enough yet. And Diana Sue knew her picture was being taken, dont think she didnt: she posed and primped herself with all the aplomb of a successful prima ballerina already! Dawnie had been going into ballet vigorously since she and Shotridge had moved to the UI campus the summer before. All the major ballet troupes, both foreign and homegrown, made the UI campus for one- or two-night stands; and while she had seen some of them before in Cleveland, ballet had never struck her with the passionate interest it smote her with after she moved here. She had seen Fonteyn and Somes of the Sadler's Wells, and Tallchief of the New York Ballet, the previous winter—and, not only had she seen them dance, but had been able to talk with them—a little bit, at least—since she was on the student committee that expedited the putting on of the shows. And after that she had started reading everything she could get hold of on the subject. And she could not help but feel that all this, occurring when she was still carrying little Diana Sue, had had some effect on the child. Why else would she want to try to dance? when she couldnt even walk yet? Yes, she knew what her baby was going to be. And she was deliciously proud and pleased.

"Fine!" the photographer said enthusiastically. "Thats just fine! Exactly what I wanted! Now, if youll just pick the baby up. You know, just hold it, like you would every day if you were doing something for it. Maybe we could get a shot of you changing it."

"Well, wouldnt that be—sort of . . ." Dawn said hesitantly.

"Oh, no. Wed shoot it right, you know. And itd make a good picture for us."

"All right," Dawnie smiled. "We're completely at your disposal." She picked her up out of the playpen, while Diana Sue chortled happily and mugged for the camera shamelessly, and carried her in on the bed in the little bedroom where she always changed her.

"Fine!" the photographer said, encouragingly. "Fine!—We wont use all of these pictures, you see. May not use any of you folks, actually, even. But we have to have a lot of variety to choose from."

"We dont care if we're not pictured in your magazine, Mr Beckett," Dawnie smiled, and went to changing her little baby, her beloved own little baby—though at present Diana Sue didnt actually need it. "We're just about as happy as we could be, I think," she smiled; "and I dont think anything could add or detract from it."

"Yeah, sure," the photographer said, and smiled encouragingly. "Now, if youll just stand a little more this way. Fine!" He began clicking his Leica vigorously. "Maybe later on, after you get through talking, we can get a shot of you all in your car out front. Is that your new red Dodge out there in front?"

"Yes," Dawnie smiled. "It was a wedding present from my father."

"Your father's Frank Hirsh, isnt he?" the photographer said muffledly from behind his camera, still clicking. "From down in Parkman?"

"Why, yes! Do you know Daddy?"

"I met 'im once, in Springfield," the photographer said, still clicking away. "When I was shooting a big important businessman's meeting there." And he mentioned the names of the Greek and Clark Hibbard's father in law. "Your father's got influential friends."

"I wouldnt know about that," Dawnie smiled; "but hes very nice to us."

"Yeah, sure," the photographer said and took his camera down and smiled encouragingly. "Well, I guess thatll do for that one. We went through the President's office, you know, to get permission to do the article; and they recommended that you and Mr Shotridge might be fine typical examples for what we wanted."

"Well, I think thats very flattering," Dawn smiled blushingly. "I do rather think we *are* pretty typical, of what happy married college students are like."

"Yeah, sure," the photographer said and smiled encouragingly. He looked all around the rest of the bedroom thoughtfully.

"You know, you mentioned my father," Dawnie smiled. "We'll be going down there to Parkman soon, after the term's out, for the Centennial Week Festival of Parkman's hundredth birthday."

"Yeah, sure," the photographer said and smiled encouragingly. "You are? Well now, lets see, what else do I need? You do the cooking yourself of course, dont you?"

Dawn could not help but smile at that. "Yes," she said simply.

Outside in the living room the *Weight* writer was just finishing up

talking to Shotridge—or rather, had already finished. He came over to
them, as they came back through the door and Dawnie put little Diana
Sue back in the playpen. "You take him for a while," he said, "and
let me talk to her. Then we'll get some shots of them together—and
then some with all three."

"Okay," the photographer said, and Dawnie sat down with the writer.

It was a very interesting interview she had with him. He was obviously
an extremely intelligent man. Tall and spare with a long nose and
glasses and a crewcut, talking in a clipped way through his long nose,
he sat beside her on the divan—asking question after question, encouraging her to talk about her own ideas of her life. And as a result,
Dawnie was able to air—and even to further develop—a lot of her own
ideas about college marriages and marriage in general. All of her own
theories that she had gradually acquired and worked out for herself in
the past year. Yes, she thought marriage helped college students; helped
them immensely, in fact; helped to stabilize them and to give them a
sense of really mature responsibility: after all, she smiled, looking over
at Diana Sue, when one had a little helpless human soul to look out for,
it was very sobering. No, she didnt think a college marriage had a bad
effect upon students' grades; in fact, they had found it just the reverse:
it helped to *raise* the grades she thought: by giving the students a
maturity that young, and unmarried, people often did not have. She
wouldnt have traded her marriage, and her husband and her little Diana
Sue, for any other situation on the face of the globe. And actually, as far
as the work part of it went, it wasnt really very much worse than one
would have if one were single: a few days off to have the baby, of course,
she smiled; but those missed classes were easily made up; and the colleges and universities themselves, she felt, were taking an increasing
interest in obstetrical care for married students. As a matter of fact,
the being married—even with the little baby—was even easier than
living singly. She and her husband staggered their courses pretty well,
so that whenever one was in class the other could be home with Diana
Sue; and on those few occasions when they both couldnt be there, one
of their friends in the Quonset village would babysit for them—a favor
which of course they themselves reciprocated. As compared to this, on
the other hand, when one was single there was the expense and time
wasted dating, and the consequent loss of study time. But married, she
and her husband shared the household chores, and had lots of study time,
since they preferred staying at home. But when you were single, if one
didnt date—at least somewhat—one wound up lonely and without
friends. So there you were. Whereas, when you were married you didnt
want to go out; you stayed at home and helped each other with the work
and with each other's studies. On the whole, she was all for college
marriages.

Dating? Oh, of course, there was lots of dating—before you were married. Everyone did. That was just life. Petting? Oh, of course there were a few kisses after dates. No, she didnt honestly feel that the un-married dating ever went much further than that. In spite of Doctor Kinsey, she smiled, she felt that there was really very little pre-marital sexuality in American colleges. Oh, of course there were always a few bad apples in every barrel. But not very many: no, the generation of American youth to which she belonged was pretty level-headed about sex, she thought. Could he quote that? Why, yes. Of course. Everybody was always getting alarmed about American youth and its morals, she smiled; but after all this wasnt the Flaming 'Twenties: this was—well— the 'Fifties already, actually—now—wasnt it? The "Level-headed Fifties" they might be called, someday, Dawnie thought.

The *Weight* man scribbled notes in his rapidly filling notebook, and looked at her penetratingly, and fired more questions at her and scrib-bled down her answers, and smiled at her encouragingly to talk. And under his sympathetic—if somewhat rather detached—impetus Dawnie found herself expanding, and going more and more into what her ideas of marriage and motherhood really were. Women matured more quickly nowadays, she thought, and so there was a sooner need in them today for the fulfillment that only marriage and motherhood can bring. Then, too, with the world in the state it was in today, sitting on the edge of an atomic bomb, young people were maturing and sobering more quickly, and seeing the place that they as citizens and family-upbringers must fill.

Finally, the *Weight* man closed his notebook and said that they were done. He had all that he needed, he thought. After that, they took the other pictures: the family group pictures, and the pictures of her and Shotridge together, and the pictures of her in the kitchen, and the car picture, and then they left.

Dawnie and Shotridge both—once that encouraging sympathetic im-petus of the *Weight* man and his photographer were gone—discovered that they were limp as dishrags. They sat, while Baby Diana Sue played unconcernedly in her playpen between them, and smiled at each other wornly but happily.

"Dawnie, you were wonderful," Shotridge said finally, and came over to her and put his arms around her. "Just simply wonderful. Especially when you were talking about marriage and maturity and the world and all. I was awful proud of you, Dawnie."

"You were pretty good yourself, Shotridge," she said. "I was proud of you, too."

"Yes, but not like you I wasnt," Shotridge protested mildly. "When you were talking about motherhood, and how the college students were so much more level-headed—well, I thought I was just going to have to come over to you and put my arms around you right in front of them. You actually looked to me as if you had a halo, a real halo, around your head."

"Well, I only told them the truth to the best of my ability," Dawnie said gently. "What I felt to be the real truth, and what our lives are like, and what theyll always be like. I think as long as you tell people the truth, youll always be safe."

"Thats true," Shotridge said fervently. "Thats very true. But nobody but you would ever think of it, Dawnie."

After they had rested a little while, they talked about the trip to Parkman as soon as classes were over. It would be early September and they would be arriving just in time for the Parkman Centennial Week: the big celebration of the hundredth birthday of the founding of the city of Parkman named after the old Western explorer and writer Francis Parkman. It was going to be a week long festival, with street booths and street dancing and everything. And, since neither of their folks had been able to see Baby Diana Sue more than a couple of times, it would be doubly nice to take her home with them and let her get to know her grandparents.

"Cant you just see our lives stretching away ahead of us, Shotridge?" Dawnie said passionately and happily. "Always just like this: so happy, and so wonderful: and never changing. People have to earn that kind of happiness, Shotridge; it isnt just handed to them on a silver platter. They have to earn it; like weve earned it."

"They sure do," Shotridge said fervently, and put his arms around her again. "Just like we did."

They decided, after discussing it thoughtfully, not to say anything about the *Weight* magazine article now just yet, at home. Not until they found out whether or not any of their pictures would be in it. Because after all, there was no use in building the folks' hopes up and then having them fall flat. And *Weight: The Magazine of Opinion* was a pretty big, important outfit. But wouldnt it be nice to be home for the big hundredth year Centennial Festival? They could spend part of the time with Frank and Agnes and part with Harry and Eleanor.

CHAPTER 74

THE Parkman Centennial Festival was indeed a big thing in Parkman. It was also a big operation. It had been planned ahead for the second week of September for over a year. All the businessmen's clubs and organizations and the College had worked on it together with remarkable amicability as co-sponsors: at the really mammoth preparations that were required to bring it off; and Frank Hirsh, as one of the officers of

the Chamber of Commerce—as well as being the newly respected entre-
preneur and manager of the bypass Shopping Center and the new
motel-restaurant—was right in the thick of it from the very start.

There was really a tremendous lot to be done by everybody. There
were the rides and games concessions, first of all, to be handled—although this was actually more easily done than the rest: Because an
apparently entirely new profession had grown up in Southern Illinois
in the last couple of years: that of "Festival Impresario". Whether this
was true in other states and other parts of the country nobody knew, but
in Southern Illinois it was certainly true. In the past three summers—
'48, '49 and '50—there had been a rash of "Festivals" all over Southern
Illinois: Harvest Festivals, Summer Festivals, Spring Festivals, Fiftieth
Year Anniversary Festivals, Apple Festivals, Grape Festivals, an Anni-
versary-of-the-Founding-of-the-First-Wagon-Train-to-the-West-Festival,
Seventy Fifth Year Anniversary Festivals, Lincoln Festivals, Pioneer
Festivals, even one Sixty Seventh Year Anniversary Festival—although
no one, even the revelers themselves, knew exactly what this signified,
and of course the really bona fide Hundredth Year Centennial Festivals.
But whatever they were called, and whyever they were initiated, almost
every town and city in Southern Illinois had had some kind of a Festival
or other in the past three years. And, for every Festival, there must be
a Festival Impresario. Mostly these were ex-carnival managers, who
simply switched over because there was more money to be made in
Festivals any more than there was in old-fashioned carnivals.

Parkman, however, was an exception. They had had no Festivals—
although in the three years the Chamber of Commerce must have been
approached by a full fifty "Festival Impresarios" wanting to sell them
on some kind of festival. But the businessmen of Parkman had wisely
decided to wait—despite impatience, and a number of dissenting votes—
for their bona fide Centennial Festival. There was something not only
satisfying, but actually spiritually reassuring, at looking at those round
zeros after that one, and knowing that your city—your own town where
you lived—had actually existed for a full hundred years. So they were
all glad they had waited—even including the dissenting votes. And now
that it *was* here they were going to give it the really full treatment, and
let the sky be the limit.

The entire square and courthouse was to be fully lighted up with
strings of blazing lights, at city expense. And three whole sides of the
square were to be blocked off to traffic for the entire week. That in itself
lent an excitement and holiday air to the whole thing: In an age of
automobiles where almost everybody owned one and it was extremely
hazardous to walk in the street—if not actually downright illegal—
there was something extremely pleasing about being able to walk up
and down the middle of the street with impunity and in safety.

The rides and games concessions wisely had been farmed out to the "Festival Impresario" the business organizations had finally chosen, who of course would receive his flat-price profit, and he in turn would dispose of the concessions and rides through his own contacts. That in turn saved the Parkman businessmen untold work, because the three blocked-off sides of the square would be lined with booths and concessions and games of all kinds: places to eat, places to buy soft drinks, cider booths, pastry booths, a kissing booth sponsored by the Professional Women's Club for charity at a buck a throw, dart games, baseball throwing games, rifle shooting booths, wheel of fortune booths. In short, just about every variation of all the carny games booths. And in fact, that was what it really resembled more than anything else: a mammoth carnival. Or a super county fair. Only, instead of being held at the fair grounds it was being held right up town on the square. The rides themselves, which needed staking out and guying for safety's sake, were being set up on the courthouse lawn—a Ferris wheel, a bullet, an octopus, a bump-car ride, and of course a merry-go-round—and in fact it was fully two years afterwards before the courthouse lawn ever fully recovered from the stakeholes and the seemingly inescapable sawdust and the trampling of thousands of feet. In addition, every businessman's organization—the Kiwanis, the Lions, the Rotary, the Elks, the Moose, the Eagles—were all of them setting up their own particular cider booth or lemonade booth or hotdog stand, to be run by the businessmen members themselves—who would, naturally, regard this as a great lark. Also, the College was sponsoring a large historical display of artifacts and tools and weapons and clothes from a hundred years ago, to be run by the students and professors. In fact, there was almost nothing that wasnt thought of and attempted.

The joint Festival committee, composed of small committees from all the various organizations, at their first meeting back early in the summer had—naturally—decided to elect a Festival Queen. There would also be a parade of floats across the still-open fourth side of the square, sponsored by the various organizations and businesses and whose motif would be "Pioneer Days", and a prize would be given for the best one. Also, the joint committee decided, since the motif was to be "Pioneer Days", this ought to apply to everybody—to the citizens, as well. Consequently, proclamations were printed and prominently displayed in town to the effect that beginning the Monday of Festival Week until the following Sunday at midnight any male or female found on the square in unsuitable attire would be arrested and jailed on the old-fashioned pole stockade which would be set up on the northeast corner of the square for this purpose, for a period of two hours. Also, the proclamations read, any male found without a beard or mustachios or some suitable hirsute adornment would be locked up in the stocks set up alongside the stockade for a period of one hour. Consequently, as far back as six to eight weeks before official Festival Week, men began laughingly to appear at work unshaven, starting their beards, and as Festival Week approached began to trim and tidy them up into all sorts of variations. Sensing the trend, the joint committee issued a further proclamation that a prize would also be given for the best or most unusual beard or combination of hirsute adornments. As a result, there were Mormon type beards, Quaker type beards, Amish beards, Wyatt Earp (an ex-Illinois boy, himself) mustachios, all kinds of chin beards and goatees and bulging sideburns. And as Festival Week approached the laughing feverish excitement grew apace with it: for one week, for just one week, everybody was going to be able to forget themselves, and the world they hadnt made but had to live in,—forget it all, everything, and be happy, for just one week. And a stranger, visiting the Country Club for dinner and seeing all the astonishing hirsute variations, might—except for the modern clothes—have thought himself transported back into the middle of the 19th Century. Where men were braver—or at least the wars were less murderous and efficient. By the first of September a kind of insanely happy hysteria—not unlike an American Legion National Convention— seemed to have seized the whole of Parkman: for a while—for a week at least—Korea and the Russians could be forgotten. Large bets were made on various superior-looking beards. The drugstores and the news-stand (since there were no bookstores) stocked in large supplies of Francis Parkman's *The Oregon Trail* and smaller supplies of his other books, when they could be had. The clothing stores sold out almost as soon as they could get them in, all their supplies of Western shirts and levis and narrow-legged gambler's pants. A large platform was to be erected in the southwest corner of the square for round dancing; two hillbilly bands were to play for those who wanted to indulge in square dancing. All the stores around the square planned to stay open during Festival Week as long as there were potential customers available, all night if necessary, and Frank Hirsh decided that the Parkman Village Shopping Center would also stay open for shoppers, if any of the individual store proprietors wished to. Naturally, they all did: Frank Hirsh's new restaurant adjoining the motel, as soon as it opened in late August, immediately—since it had a bar—became the most popular dinner place in town—people were even forsaking the Country Club to have dinner there—so naturally there would be a string of people out there during Festival Week.

The setting up was, of course—once the administrative work was all out of the way—the hardest job. Saturday night at midnight after the stores had all closed, trucks began to move in the equipment: the rides, and the concession booths and their contents. All night and all the next day countless nameless hordes of tough leathery carnies labored to get everything set up for the official opening Sunday evening, while the citizenry stood around on the sidewalks and watched excitedly. The Chamber of Commerce had already appointed their private police force for the inspection of beards and costumes, and while their authority did not go into force until midnight Sunday they were able, amid much laughing, to go about warning offenders of what they would do to them after midnight. The warm crazy laughing near-hysteria spread like a contagion from one to another all over town. It was going to be a gala occasion, and a gala week. Just about everybody in the county, as well as in Parkman, was expected to turn out, and spend money, and be happy.

There was, however, at least one man in Parkman who had no intention of turning out and participating. Dave Hirsh was still working ten to fourteen hours a day at the shell plant—where in the last few weeks they had been setting up to make rifle grenade casings as well as the forty millimeters; and he was still trying to work at night on his goddamned novel—which by now he had come to hate more than he had ever hated anything in his whole life. It wasnt right, and he knew it. The trouble still lay with the damned love affair. It just didnt play right. It could; he could see clearly where it could, but he just couldnt write it right somehow. If he cut it out entirely, which he had been thinking of more and more lately, it would leave a book of only some five hundred manuscript pages: not a very big book at all; in fact, a rather slim one. And anyway, he still felt it was—or could be— an integral part of the whole novel. But he still could not write it right. And he had no intention of going out nights to some damn carnival— which was all it was; and he had lived as a carny too damned much in his life, to be able to be excited by a carnival—and trying to be gay and happy: the way he felt, about this book, and about everything else, he would only be a killjoy to everybody he came in contact with with his boredom, and his unhappiness he could not get rid of.

But it was not only the book and the rest of it that made him unable to participate in the sense of forthcoming gaiety: He was working ten and sometimes fourteen hours a day in the shell factory painting forty millimeter shells—and now rifle grenades too—and he could not forget that as soon as all of these were finished up and primed, and fused, and loaded, they were being swiftly shipped off to Korea—where men were using them, and perhaps being killed in using them. And he could sense the quality of rising hysteria in the whole town as Festival Week approached: whenever he went downtown he felt it: to forget! just to forget! just for a little while! It was in the shrill laughter, and the happy ridiculous beards on everybody. But he could not forget: he worked with it every day, always in his mind, and it was not a question of whether he *wanted* to forget or not: he could not. He just did not belong down there downtown, not the way he felt. The heavy portentous ominous feeling of being in at the end of the Roman Empire which he had felt so strongly over Dewey and Hubie down at the house on Lincoln Street came back over him, as he watched the growing hysteria-to-forget as the Festival Week approached. The trouble was, he knew the reason for it. He felt it too: that fear. But he knew what it was. And consequently, he could not participate.

But if Dave wanted nothing to do with what, in his mind, he could only call the Tragedy of Festival Week, Ginnie did not feel that way at all. She was looking forward to it eagerly. In fact, she talked about little else for an entire month before. Dave had slept with her once, just once, in the past whole month. He had tried half-heartedly several times, but when she put him off, he just gave up and didnt keep on trying as hard as he had used to. But in spite of that, Ginnie was making eager plans for all that they were going to do together Festival Week. And, in the end, it was this that brought on the crisis, and the final blowup, between them.

For the first two days of Festival Week he refused to go out and go downtown with her. He hated to do it, he knew how much she wanted him to go, but he couldnt help it. In the first place, he hadnt grown a beard or mustachios—though Ginnie had tried to devil him into doing so—and he did not feel equal to spending an hour in those damned stocks: something like that was possible, and even fun, if you were in the proper gay and carefree mood for it. But he wasnt; and to go without being in the proper mood would only be an unpleasant experience for everybody. Ginnie, of course, could not understand this. And in fact, he made no very strong effort at trying to explain it to her. She would only have said, angrily: Well, why cant you *be* in the proper mood? and what would he have said? So he had stayed home alone those first two nights, working on the book alone in the little house, and it had been one of the pleasantest most peaceful experiences he had had in some time—even though he couldnt get the writing on the love affair going very much better. He was beginning to think perhaps he was being too calumnious with this love affair because of his irritation with Ginnie—perhaps even to the point of losing his objectivity. Anyway, it was worthwhile staying home and working on it and thinking about it. And so Ginnie had gone on by herself with some of her friends. Reluctantly, and irritably, and angrily hurt at him—but she had gone.

But on the third night, when he came home from work, he found Ginnie already waiting for him with a wad of false hair which several of the stores had picked up a good bit on by selling to those who for one reason or another had not grown, or else could not grow, beards.

"Look!" she said eagerly. "Look what I bought you! Now we can fix you up some sideburns and a beard. Then you can go and be all right.

You wont get picked up. We'll have a lot of fun," she said eagerly. "Theres a big dance on tonight on the platform at the southwest corner."

"Ah, look honey," Dave said sadly; he was incredibly touched by the false hair. "You go ahead. You go ahead and go with your friends, and have a good time. I dont want to go. If I go, Ill only be a wet blanket and spoil the fun. And Id really rather stay here."

Ginnie looked at the false hair in her hand disappointedly and let her arm drop to her side. Her own costume was an old-fashioned calico dress and long-billed sunbonnet she had picked up God knew where, and her round moon face stared out from under the sunbonnet at him— at first pensively, then irritably, then finally angry.

"Whats the matter with you?" she demanded. "You dont never want to go out anywhere with me; or do anything with me. All you do is stay here at home with that damned book. You dont love me at all any more. —If you ever did love me."

"Ah, honey, its not that," Dave said. "I just dont feel like going, thats all. Its— Well, all those people— Well, you know?— Theyre—" He didnt want to say hysterical, but it was the only word that fit. "Theyre not having fun, theyre— Well, theyre just hysterical."

"Hys-terical!" Ginnie cried. "Hys-terical, hell! You and your damn big writer's words! Those people are having *fun*. Theyre laughing, and theyre playing, and theyre having *fun*. Why cant you ever laugh, and play, and have fun? You dont never do nothing. Not with me, anyway. —How do you think I feel? havin to go down to the Festival all the time without my husband?" Suddenly, convulsively, disappointedly she threw the wad of false hair forcibly on the floor. "All my friends, their husbands go with them. And *they* have fun. And what do you think they say about me? always goin by myself? Hunh? You never want to do anything with me, damn you. You just dont want to *do* anything with me, because its *me*."

"Ah, no, honey," Dave said lamely. "It aint that. Its just that— Well, its just gloomy. The whole damn thing makes me sad. Id only spoil the fun."

"I know what it is!" Ginnie cried suddenly, furiously, her disappointment at the failure of the false hair shining on her moonlike face beneath the sunbonnet. "Its that damned book! That damned book, that damned book! You sit and work and work and beat your damned brains out on it—and what do you get? Nothing, thats what! That damned book! You cant sell it to nobody and you know it! It wont *never* sell! And you keep wastin time on it when you could be livin! With *me*! That damned book!"

They were standing in the kitchen, just inside the kitchen door, around the corner from which was the door to the little room Dave had fixed up as a writing room and to which Dave had gradually retreated, hoping to get in and shut the door, hoping to get her to go on without getting angry, until he was fully inside of it now with his hand resting on the corner of the table he used for a desk.

"That damned book!" Ginnie screamed suddenly and, herself still in the kitchen, seized up a heavy thick-walled aluminum saucepan—of the type given away for coupons by the Kroger Company, and for which she had carefully saved her coupons up to get a full set of—and taking a step toward him beyond the doorway, threw it with all her strength through the door. She didnt throw it at him, and in fact didnt throw it at anything particularly—but the big deep-bottomed saucepan hit Dave's typewriter sitting on the table beside which he stood, and hit it squarely, and both typewriter and saucepan slid off the table and crashed to the floor.

For a moment there was complete silence in the little house, as both of them stood staring at each other and looking startled and surprised. Then Dave bent and picked up the typewriter and set it back on the table to see what damage had been done to it. The platen had been knocked completely off of it, and the carriage itself was bent. The thin back of the little portable had been deeply dented. It wasnt anything that couldnt be fixed, it could be repaired, but Dave felt his face growing white with anger. And as his own face grew white, Ginnie's face under the long floppy-brimmed old sunbonnet grew correspondingly redder with sullen guilt.

"Well, Im *glad* I done it," she said sullenly and guiltily. "Im glad, I say. Maybe now youll throw that old thing away and start actin and livin like a reglar human being." She stared at him, wide-eyed with both start and fright, sullenly, guiltily.

"Get out!" Dave hissed at her through his teeth. "Get out of here!" Suddenly, loomingly, he took a stride toward her beyond the doorway. "I said *get out!*"

And Ginnie, her eyes wide with both guilt and fear, as well as surprise at what she herself had done, backed away and then put her hands up over her face and began to cry and ran out through the back door.

Dave, his face still deathly pale, merely stood looking after her, feeling sorry for her, and for himself. For both of them.

———Ginnie Moorehead, Ginnie Moorehead *Hirsh*, was crying so hard she could hardly see the path as she ran around to the front of the house, her hands up over her nose and mouth to stifle her sobs. He wasnt comin after her. She knew that. If he was, she would of heard the screendoor slam. But that wasnt why she was runnin. She was runnin because she had just done the very thing she had promised herself she wouldnt never do: She had acted unbecomin to a lady. She had, she had. And that was what she was runnin from. Only, there wasnt noplace to run to. When she got out to the sidewalk, breathing heavily from the dash down the side yard, she stopped and stood looking back at the little house sadly. Then, finally, she started to walk to town.

She had tried. God knew she had tried. Takin all them cookin lessons. And she kept that house immaculately clean. She had washed and ironed. She had bought nice things for that house. She had fixed it up real pretty. And she had changed all her friends. She had done everything she knew. She had even watched her language, always saying "taking" instead of "takin"—except maybe when she got mad or excited, and then she might forget. —Takin! Takin! she thought wildly, suddenly: what the hell difference did it make if you said "takin" instead of "taking"? What the hell difference? Damn them! All of them! She had done everything she knew. But most of all she had tried to be a lady for him, because she knew ladies was what he liked—real ladies, like that schoolteacher Gwen French over there in Israel. She had tried to be one. —And it was right there, right just exactly there, that she had failed, and she guessed she knew it. And she wasnt no lady. She was a bum. And always had been, she thought sorrowfully and guiltily. A pig! A pig!—like 'Bama Dillert was always callin her behind her back. Oh, she knew what he said about her: a pig. A bum. A pig! a pig! All right, damn them! All of them! She hadnt done nothing, hadnt been out with nobody, ever since she got home from way out there in Kansas. She had tried her very level best.

But it wasnt good enough, was it? All right then, shed show them. All of them! And wiping her eyes carefully dry on her little lacy handkerchief she headed on up to town—but not for the Festival Week: she headed for Ciro's. And after that, by God, shed go out to Smitty's too if she had to. Because, if she went to the Festival tonight, by God, it would be with a man. Shed show them! All of them!

It wasnt Dave's fault. It was hers. And she guessed she knew it. Something in her somehow or other had done it, no matter how hard she had tried, and kept her from bein a lady; and sick at heart and hating herself for whatever it was in her that had done it—had always done it, all her life—she went resolutely on uptown to Ciro's. Told her to get out: just up and told her to get out! Of her own home! But it wasnt his fault. It was hers.

If she could only of been as lady-like as Doris Fredric—then Dave would of been proud of her and would of loved her *really*. But she couldnt be, she just didnt have what it took to be like Doris, and she had failed.

Two or three times as she walked along she felt like somebody was following her and thought she heard footsteps, but when she looked around there was nothing.————

Dave sat for a long time at the kitchen table after she had gone, thinking it all over, the whole year, and all the rest that had gone before it. Something had happened; some light had gone out; and he could feel it. It wasnt the busting of the typewriter so much, he didnt care about that, it was the way both of them had reacted to the *act*, afterwards. He shouldnt have told her to get out like that, and he was sorry for that. And she shouldnt have thrown the saucepan, and she was probably— was undoubtedly—sorry for that. But neither one of them had reacted like they really felt: sorry. Why? Vanity? Pride? Stubbornness? Yes, but also no. Basically, they had both reacted as they did because both of them possessed—were afflicted with—certain—ahh—desires. They each of them had in them a sort of superimposed picture, like a celluloid overlay on a map, of life—and of what life was, or was not, and also of what it should be: or, rather, what they *wanted* it to be. *Expected* it to be. And actually, if you set these two pictures side by side they would be so totally different that it would be as if they were actually two different planets. Neither one actually coincided with the *real* planet, really. And yet each saw his own picture—his own planet—so clearly and positively that they actually made them exist: They did actually exist, these two separate planets—just as much as, and as actually, as the real planet neither of them could see—(because each could see only his own)—existed also. And it was when these two private planets clashed and collided and overlapped each other that all the trouble came,—just simply because Ginnie's picture of the world and his picture of the world could not be made to coincide: they *could* not be: because both of them existed just as factually and as materially as the *real* world existed. And so it was just exactly like the physical impossibility of two bodies trying to inhabit the same space at the same time.

Perhaps—no, not perhaps; almost undoubtedly—he thought elaborating it as he sat there sadly,—undoubtedly no two humans on earth ever lived in identical worlds. So he was probably wrong when he had thought Frank and Agnes were happily married, and that Dawnie and Shotridge were happily married—or, anyway, would continue to be. Because each had his own private world, and what was more wanted to keep it. And not only that, wanted to if possible impose it upon everyone else that he possibly could, in order to prove to himself that it did in fact exist. And that was always where the trouble came. Because the other man—or woman—or nation, for that matter—was doing the same identical thing. Consequently, only clash resulted—and with the clash, trouble.

And from the trouble came the pain: the pain of defeat, the pain of victory and the hate it brought, but most of all the pain of being forced to relinquish part or all of that illusory world each has built up for himself.

Ginnie: poor old Ginnie: with her illusory world of what she thought a happy respectable marriage ought to be: Ginnie, who—as old 'Bama had once said—wanted to be respectable more than anything else in the world: so much so that she even convinced herself that it was distasteful for a "lady" to even sleep with her own husband—after she finally got one.

And him: was he any better? with his illusory world of what he thought would be a safe, sane, quiet, peaceful, work-producing life being married to a good dumb writer's wife, like some said a writer ought to have. But who knew what went on between *any* man and his wife when they were alone?

For the first time, really,—sitting there at the little kitchen table sadly, smoking a slow thoughtful cigarette—Dave thought he could get a glimpse of what Bob French had been driving at when he talked about "illusions" all the time.

And for the first time in his life, as this window opened up just a little, giving him a glimpse beyond the frosted pane into the cold wintry scene outside, Dave Hirsh realized fully and with complete finality just how much he was, after all, alone—and would always be alone. Just how alone it was almost ghastly to contemplate: because no one would ever just exactly see the illusory world he lived in, nor would he ever be able to get out of it. But perhaps you could: could get out; partially, at least: in writing, in creating. It wouldnt make you less alone, but it *would* at least make other people's illusory world more real—to you. But even so, such utter and complete loneliness—(loneliness wasnt even the term: it was too weak: *aloneness* was; bone cold aloneness)—such aloneness was almost physically unbearable to contemplate. And no way out of it; not through love, not through work, not through play, not through courage, not through fear. No way.

And the *real* world: what about it? *Was* there even a real world? Who could tell? If there was, no ordinary human—or for that matter extraordinary human—would ever see it. To all intents and purposes there was no real world, only a sharply jostling collection of private spheres. You could love a million women, and be loved by the million in return, and never—ever—would you be able to show them your private world, or have them show you theirs; never would either of you be able to escape from your private illusory world. It was not only frightening, it was devastating.

Sitting there with fear and terror quivering and running all through him like mercury, Dave thought he could realize—a little bit, at least— what Bob French had been driving at when he spoke of "Glamours". Everything that exists is "Glamours"; because there isnt anything but "Glamours". And simultaneously, he thought perhaps he understood— a little bit anyway—of what Bob meant by Karma that he was always talking about. He didnt understand it clearly, or anything about how it worked. But he had made Karma with Ginnie, and simultaneously made Karma *in* Ginnie. By clashing his private illusory world against hers. He had shaken her illusion, just as she had shaken his. Just like he had made Karma with and also *in* everyone he had come in contact with since he first came back to Parkman. Frank, and Agnes, Gwen and Bob and 'Bama, Dewey, Hubie, Wally. And that Karma would stay with all of them, himself and them too, until the day they died. And perhaps, as Bob maintained, would stay with them afterwards, too. And, as Bob also said so often, perhaps they had all met before somewhere, too? It *could* be. And perhaps, if it was so, they were all also working out *old* Karma, at the same time they were making new. He wished he knew. He wished there was just some way he could actually *know*. Some Sign, some Voice, some Something that would speak to him. But nothing did.

Poor old Ginnie: with her illusory world of what respectability should be. And him, with his "Glamour" of the safe calm productive life. Man, what a match they were! In his illusory picture he had desirously tried to bring about, he had caused her pain: and in so doing, had caused "Karma". She had caused him pain, too; but he was more responsible than she was because he was smarter. He knew more, or should have. But no, perhaps that wasnt true: was a sentimental judgment. Are we responsible for the pain we cause in others? or are we only responsible for the pain *that others cause in us*? That really sounded more reasonable, didnt it? Because if we were not susceptible to our illusions and our Glamours, no one could cause pain in us. Anyway, and even so, he felt responsible—sorely, and sadly, and hopelessly responsible. Whatever Ginnie did or hadnt done, he was responsible for his own illusions. He had run to her and, in a wildly selfimposed illusion, had taken her on—because he was afraid after having lost Gwen, afraid of being alone. And whatever Ginnie had to do with the whole thing just simply did not count. Only what he did—as far as he himself was concerned. What she did was her problem.

"Each man must find his salvation in himself alone. It is not to be found outside. In another person." Bob French's statement came back in his mind clearly, almost bell-like, with an understanding of it he had never had before. It was really very simple: There just wasnt *any other way*. It was as simple as that. There just wasnt any other place to find it. And nothing that anyone did *to* you, or *for* you, made one damn bit of difference, in the end. It was the one alone. And Bob's other statement—and a clear picture of Bob's sad smile as he said it—came back too: "It was the most terribly painful thing I ever had to learn in my life, dear Dave."

Tonight, somehow—perhaps only as a culmination of a year's effort and pain of trying to live to separate illusions—had broken two illusions:

God knew how many more both of them had: but tonight had broken two: Ginnie's illusion of what a happy respectable marriage was;—and his own illusion—which was an even greater one—that there existed a way in which a man need not be alone. Whatever happened from now on to either of them was not the other's responsibility any more. And perhaps, never had been.

Stubbing out his cigarette—his third since she had gone—Dave got up resolutely and went to pack. The fear and terror that had slid mercurially along his veins and nerves had subsided somewhat—subsided completely, actually. And in their place was left only that bone-cold aloneness, frozen as the moon. He packed only one bag—and, after looking at all his clothes in the closet, wondered why he even packed that much? He looked, once, at all his war ribbons; then left them in their drawer. In the bag, with the few clothes he was taking, he carefully packed the stack of manuscript: all the untouched combat parts, and the two or three versions of the love affair. And as he did so, he knew something else: that love affair didnt belong in this book at all; Bob French had been right all along; and if it made a slim volume, why it made it a slim volume and to hell with it; and if it didnt sell because there wasnt enough sex in it, why to hell with that too: that love affair didnt belong in there. It had taken him an awfully long time to see it, but now he knew; and he was sure. And when he got settled in someplace, wherever it might be, he would start working on it from that theory. And after that? Well, there was that novel about his childhood and Parkman that he wanted to write: he could probably do that one an awful lot better away from Parkman where he couldnt see it, anyway. And then there was that novel on Ginnie's life that he wanted to write: that one would certainly be an awful lot better now than if he had written it when he first conceived it. And then, in addition to those, there was still the *true* novel he wanted to write about Francine and the group in Hollywood—not that crap like he had once written. He figured, as he packed, that he would have plenty to keep him busy. Keep him busy quite a while. Keep him busy all the time he had left, probably.

The only other thing he packed was his broken typewriter in its battered little case. He could leave it and buy another one somewhere wherever he was going but somehow—sentimentally, perhaps, and he grinned ruefully at himself for doing it—he did not want to leave it. He did not want to leave it here. After all, it had been through as much with him as his head had, the past two years. The broken platen he padded into the case with rags—sparklingly clean rags, from Ginnie's rag drawer—then he set it on the floor of the kitchen with the bag and looked all around to see if there wasnt something else he wanted to take. There wasnt. Not a damn thing. He was ready to go.

But then, just as he was ready to pick them up and go, a sort of an idea struck him: Only God knew where he might be the next few weeks until he got settled in, or what might happen to him. And lighting another cigarette he sat down again at the kitchen table and decided to write himself out a Last Will and Testament. —What was it the guy said? "Last Will and Testamony." Really, he didnt know what made him do it—probably the manuscript more than anything else, he didnt want anything to happen to it; but after he had done it he felt strangely better. There really wasnt much to leave: the house, and its contents: his little old Plymouth: and his little share of the taxi service: that was all. He left all of these to Ginnie: she deserved them; and, maybe she might even have some use for them. The manuscript he left to Bob and Gwen French jointly. It didnt take very long to write it out. But then, with still another cigarette, and sitting looking at it, he had an afterthought and wrote out two more exact copies of it. One he put in an envelope and addressed to Judge Deacon, and the other he put in another envelope and addressed it to Gwen French. He would like to see her—and old Bob—once more before he left; but there was really no point: it would only be painful to them all. —Could a man, any human, really live and not cause pain? Dave wondered; live his whole lifetime and cause no one any pain? It was an interesting thought, anyway. Old Bob would probably say: No; we were all *supposed* to cause each other pain.— In the envelope addressed to Gwen he stuck an added little note:

> *Should anything happen to me—which I am not expecting— the love affair should come out—entirely.*

The two letters he put in his pocket to drop in the mailbox on his way out of town, and the third Will he left lying on the table. Then he picked up the bag and typewriter and left the house.

There was a mailbox on the corner of Wernz Avenue the mainstreet, and he dropped the letters in. It was only a couple of blocks up Wernz to town, and from where he stood he could see all the bright lights decorating the square for Festival Week and hear the loud laughter and the music of the bands, and the voices of the pitchmen in the booths, the whine and grind of the ride machines, and like a thin tart salad dressing over all the rest binding it together and giving it cohesion the tinny music of the merry-go-round. For a moment he stood and looked up the hill at it, sadly. Was it really the Decline and Fall of the Roman Empire, after all? being enacted over again? Perhaps not. Perhaps that was only another of his illusions. God, he had so many. Anyway, he hoped it wasnt. He loved this country—and this town, too —loved them deeply: this big broad expanse of country that was called America; and this little town perched on its little hilltop in the flat Illinois prairie. But perhaps that was an illusion, too? Why should a man love one country—or one town—or one person—more than he loved another? Well, he certainly hoped, sincerely and devoutly hoped, we werent living in the beginning of the Decline and Fall.

He did not want to go up through town, with all the festivities and lights going full blast, and so he crossed Wernz Avenue the mainstreet and went two blocks north before he turned back west. That street would bring him out just at the end of the business district on North Main the crossstreet, and from there he could go on back out north on North Main to the bypass and catch himself a ride with some trucker riding west. He only had fifty bucks on him and he didnt intend to waste any of that on a bus ticket. It wouldnt be the first time hed hitched a ride in his day. In his Forty Years. He didnt feel brave, or courageous, or even adventurous at the prospect of getting out and seeing "life". In fact, he felt scared and full of fear, if not actually terrified: he knew enough of the road and of job-hunting to know it wasnt going to be any lark of a picnic for him. But he did feel free. And, with the kind of bone-cold aloneness that was in him now, mere loneliness was hardly even a bother. A mere gnat or mosquito in the eyes of a man being crushed by a bear.

Steadily, but taking his time because he didnt have too much wind anymore, he walked west toward North Main the crossstreet, and all the time two blocks over he could hear the tinkle of the tinny music from the merry-go-round and the conflicting music of the bands, the voices of the pitchmen, and now and then a loud laugh or whoop of gaiety rising above the mass of noise of Festival Week. It did not seem incongruous to him. Not at all. In a way, it was the best time to be leaving. Once, he felt as though someone were following him and thought he heard footsteps, but when he turned around there was nothing there.

But then, when he emerged on North Main and turned north away from town along the last dingy block of little jerrybuilt stores—as far from the gaiety and light behind him as another planet—he saw the man step out of the shadow of the alley in front of him about fifteen feet away and the glint of white metal in his hand, and he knew; instantaneously. His heart leaped up into his throat—not from fear, there wasnt even time for that, just from sheer adrenalin. It was the first time they had ever actually seen each other, but Dave recognized the lanky figure and the prominent cheekbones and the lips drawn back in a simultaneous sneer-grin. Since the forty-five Service automatic glinted white, instead of blue, he must have had it nickel-plated after he got home. If you can talk to them, Bob French had said tiredly that night, if you can talk to them. But there wasnt time for that. There wasnt even time to laugh at the supreme irony of it. Poor guy, Dave thought, poor guy.

"I know you, you son of a bitch," the lanky young man said with his sneer-grin. That was all that was said. Then the gun bucked and flashed in his hand—shooting from the hip, too, he was, Dave had time to think—and simultaneously a larger, greater flame exploded in his own face and head. As he fell, he let the suitcase go and tried to twist sideways so that instead of lighting on the fragile little typewriter case, it would light on him. It was more or less an instinctive motion of protection, but it was rather silly, and completely pointless, because he never reached the ground. The last thing he heard was the thin, tinny, sprightly music of the merry-go-round.

CHAPTER 75

FRANK HIRSH sat at the nearly-deserted Country Club main bar two weeks later, squinting carefully through one eye at the bottle racks on the back bar to gauge how drunk he was, and the thought that was uppermost in his mind was the unhappy realization that before long it would be midnight and they would close the Club, and he would have to go home. To Agnes.

Damn it all.

Festival Week was over: Festival Week that he had worked so hard on, and that Agnes had not even gone uptown to see, and Frank had shaved his little beard off. Dave's funeral was over, too: Dave's funeral which he Frank had given him—the very best funeral that he could give him—and which, of course, Agnes had attended: wild horses couldnt have kept her away from Dave's funeral, considering how it would look if she didnt go, and so she had gone and wept with the best of them. The business about Dave's will, which Frank had had a hand in, was over also. And, although they had not taken him away yet, the law's handling of Dave's murderer was over, too: they had expedited that mess quickly: he was being shipped under guard to a Veterans' Hospital as a lockup mental patient. He was crazy—a crazy killer—there wasnt any doubt of that; everybody knew it. So probably that was the best way of handling it, after all. Especially when it came out that he was a Congressional Medal of Honor winner in the last war. But just the same Frank hated to see him get off scot-free like that.

Frank looked at his watch—(11:15; only forty five minutes left)—and squinted again at the back bar bottle racks, and then did what he had known he was going to do all along: motioned for Les the pro to fix him another highball. The little red-Irishman came running up quickly, smiling. And Frank studied him, grinning back. They were getting so they treated Frank Hirsh with quite a bit of deference any more. Not like they used to treat him. Especially now, now that his election as vice-president of the Club for next year was practically a foregone conclusion. Of course, he always tipped old Les good and heavy before he left, too. But even so, he was getting to be a pretty big man around this town any more. Everywhere, that is, except one place, he thought with a curious kind of irascible hopelessness: his own damned home. He wasnt treated like *any*thing there. Except of course by Walter, who really loved him. Reminded, Frank looked at his watch again—(11:16 now; only forty four minutes left before hed have to go)—and hopelessly thought about going home. She had been having another attack today; he only hoped she was in bed and asleep when he got there. If she wasnt, it would mean he would be up half the night fetching and carrying for her, since little Walter would be asleep.

Frank had taken more and more lately to eating at the Club alone in the evenings. He would come out straight from work at the office around five or five thirty for the cocktail hour and then just stay on and eat. Usually, he would also stay right on until closing, too, at midnight. As long as there were people around him and he could talk, he didnt feel quite so bad and could forget—for a while—that eventually he would have to go home.

Les the pro set his fresh drink in front of him and waited attentively and half-expectantly to see if he didnt want to talk; but this time Frank just said thanks and fell again to thinking of the crazy killer: the crazy killer who had murdered his brother Dave.

He must have found out about the house, and just where it was, from someone who didnt know about him and then had hidden himself out there and stalked first Ginnie and then gone back and stalked Dave, and when he saw him turn north away from town had slipped across behind the building on the corner so that he would be in front of him in the alley. Anyway, that was the way they had reconstructed it; and, in fact, that was what he himself had told them, too—later, when they finally got him to talk.

Frank hadnt even known about the guy, and apparently most of the people in town hadnt either. He hadnt known that Ginnie Moorehead —God! what a whore!—had actually gone off with him to Kansas and married him, and then run away and come back here to Dave. All that came out at the inquest when she told her damned story.

God, that woman! If you could even call her a woman. Whatever would have made Dave marry a lowlife like that Frank simply couldnt understand. He had brought it all on himself, Dave had: every damned bit of it: getting mixed up with a bum like that.

Well, he had given him a good funeral, Frank thought sorrowfully. By God, he had given his kid brother a fine funeral. He had given the Old Man a good funeral, too, but compared to the funeral he had given

Dave it wasnt nothing. They had buried him out there in the family plot with the Old Man—where all of them would wind up eventually. And Frank was sure Dave would have been pleased by that.

You just didnt ever think of a murder—for that was what it was: coldblooded murder; whether the guy was crazy or not—you just didnt ever think of a murder like that happening in your own little home town. Chicago, yes; or New York or some other city; or some nameless little hamlet in some distant state. But not your hometown, not Parkman Illinois. And especially not to your own blood relatives—your own *brother*. Of course, the soldier had not been from Parkman, and that made some difference.

Maybe they had had their differences, him and Dave, maybe they had disagreed about a lot of things. Yes, and actually fought over them—with hard feelings. But by God they *were* brothers; and always had been. If Dave only had of come to him for help, it might none of it have happened. Hell, he would of helped him! Dave should have known that—and would have, if only he wasnt so damned bullheaded and stubborn. He would have helped him out. But that damned bullheaded stubbornness that had got him mixed up with that damned Ginnie Moorehead, and had got him *married* to her, had also got him killed. He just wouldnt learn; he never would.

Now that it was all over, now that he was dead and buried, it was funny but Frank never thought of him as he had been the last few years. Whenever he thought of Dave, Frank saw him as the little kid brother who had always depended on him so much, and that he had always taken such careful care of. That was the way he always saw him: the little towheaded kid he had loved so much and worked so hard to put through school. Poor old Dave, he guessed he must have been having a pretty bad time of it the last year or two, but he himself hadnt known it. Dave wouldnt come to him; and he had been so busy with all his own work on the bypass. And with Agnes sick and all, it had been impossible to have him out to dinner like Frank would have liked to. So it had all just slipped up on him: on Dave. Well, Frank was sure that Dave, wherever he was, understood.

The thought of Agnes sent a sharp note through Frank's melancholy revery and reminded him again that she was home sick now. He looked at his watch again—(11:30 now; only thirty minutes left now)—and took a big pull at his highball. In a kind of desperation he called Les over to talk about the closing baseball season. What did he think of those damned amazing Phils? Werent they something this year? It looked like the race might go all the way down to closing Sunday, and what was more, that the Phils might win it unless Brooklyn played some mighty heads-up ball. The Yankees of course had fooled everybody and only just yesterday had clinched the American League when

Cleveland—already eliminated mathematically—had beat the Tigers.

Well— But it didnt do him much good. Les was a good listener; he guessed golf pros had to be; but they had already talked about the National League race once this evening, and after a few moments of energetically worked-up enthusiasm, the whole thing fell flat for Frank and he sent Les to fix him another drink.

Anyway, baseball had set him to thinking of Dave again, and that one book Dave had written about a ball player—years and years ago. Why hadnt he written more stuff like that? It was the only thing Dave had ever written that Frank had ever thought much of, or enjoyed reading. And now old Dave was dead. Frank had talked to Bob and Gwen French—the day that they all met in the Judge's office to probate the will—about this new book, the manuscript of which Dave had left to them, and had learned enough about it to know it was some kind of a combat novel about the war but that was all; but both Bob and Gwen seemed to think it could be published—that it was good enough—with a little work of cutting on it. Something about a love affair. Well, it would be nice for old Dave if they could publish it—posthumously. Frank only hoped that they would use his right name—Hirsh—if they did publish it, instead of making his name Herschmidt like Dave himself had done on those two stories.

It had been an unpleasant scene for all of them, that day they all met in the Judge's office in connection with the will. Largely because of that damned Ginnie Moorehead. (Frank simply could not think of her as *Hirsh;* just simply could not.) The Judge had called him right away the next day after Dave was killed, as soon as he got the will through the mail. And when Bob and Gwen learned about it that evening in the *Oregonian,* Bob had called him from Israel about the copy Dave had mailed to them. Frank had put them all off and asked that they wait until after Festival Week was over before doing anything. Just as he had waited to have Dave's funeral till after Festival Week was over. The whole affair damn near ruined the whole Centennial Festival that everybody had worked so hard on, as it was. But when they finally did get together in the Judge's office, Ginnie Moorehead had kicked up a rumpus about Dave's manuscript being given to the Frenches. It belonged to her, she said. It made a very unpleasant scene. And it didnt do her a damned bit of good. Because the Judge was just as strong on that point as he was on all the rest. It was just a simple will, ironbound; Dave had clearly intended that the book be left to the Frenches, and to them it was going, and if Ginnie wanted to go to court and try to get it, that was up to her. Of course, she didnt. Any more than Frank himself went to court about the taxi service. He couldnt have made it stick —certainly not against Judge Deacon—and he knew it.

Funny thing: when, afterwards, Frank asked the Judge about what his fee would be in connection with the will and offered to pay it, the Judge simply said: "Im being paid. Dont worry about it." Frank couldn't figure out who it would be that was paying him. Unless it was that damned gambler 'Bama Dillert. That must have been who it was. It certainly wouldnt be the Judge himself.

The leaving of Dave's share of the taxi service to Ginnie Moorehead was the only thing that upset Frank about the will. That meant that now Frank would have that lowlife bum as a partner! In spite of his sadness over Dave's death, he still couldnt help but feel that Dave shouldnt have done that to him. Of course, the only thing left for him to do was to buy her out. Which he had done. Christ, he couldnt have *Ginnie Moorehead* for a partner! And, apparently, when she sensed that, that day there in the Judge's office after the Frenches had taken their manuscript and left, she held him up on the price and refused to sell. Whether Judge Deacon with his sarcastic brain had advised her to do that or not, Frank didnt know. He wouldnt have put it past him. But she obviously wasnt as dumb as she looked. Christ, probably nobody in the damned world could be! So he had had to pay through the nose— but he had been glad to: to get rid of Ginnie Moorehead as a partner. He had had to pay her $7500 for Dave's near-forty percent share. But then, he hadnt expected to get it for what Dave himself had paid. Ginnie Moorehead had used the money to pay off the house she and Dave had bought, so now she had a house and Dave's old car, and she was pretty well set up. It wouldnt be long, Frank figured sarcastically, before she married some other joker. She had had her little taste of respectability, and now she wanted more. Not that he was against respectability—but God! a bum like that. He had already heard she was going with some young guy who worked for Sternutol Chemical as a day laborer.

Well, anyway, he had gotten rid of her, and cheap at the price he figured. She had been there at the funeral, too, weeping and wailing. It had been all Frank could do to keep from getting up and going over and kicking her in the tail. Agnes wouldnt even sit on the same side of the church with her. And rightly so. It was her who was the cause of the whole damned tragedy and scandal.

And once again the thought of Agnes impinged upon him like a red-hot spear through the belly and he looked at his watch. —(11:45 now: only fifteen minutes left till closing)—Frank swung around on his stool and looked around the bar, but there were only two couples left in it now: both young guys with their wives. They wouldnt want to be talking to him. He turned back around to his drink. Probably they were laughing at him behind his back: at him sitting here by himself night after night.

Well, let them! he thought fierily. Let them and to hell with it. He could afford to let them laugh at him. He had earned all the prestige and respect—and power, too—in this town that he had once told Dave he would. He had earned it. Himself. Even the original idea had been his. And by God he could afford to sit back and let the sons of bitches laugh at him if he wanted to.

If he wanted to come out to the Country Club and eat by himself and sit and drink by himself, it was his business. —And, as far as that went, he thought with a touch of the old terror—just a touch of it—rising in him at the thought: as far as that went, it was good for him. Because when he was around people and could talk he thought a lot less about going out "walking"; and that uncontrollable desire, that uncontrollable-when-it-hit-him urge, hit him a lot less often this way. But when he sat home and drank alone— . . . There had been a lot of talk around Parkman lately about a nocturnal windowpeeper, a peeping tom. He didnt know where it had got started, but he had begun to listen to all of it carefully—and even add his own bit of indignation and amusement, whenever it seemed warranted. Perhaps Edith had started it, before she left; because that was the only time that anybody knew someone was watching them, as far as he knew. But Edith had been gone—what, now?—a little over a year; and this talk had only started going around the last couple of months or so. In the past few months—during this past summer—Frank had added two new conquests—two new *possessions*—to his growing list of naked women, one of them a pretty woman he saw every evening out here at the Club. But the delicious pleasure of the added conquests—these two made five altogether, now—could not offset the terror and the sense of unreality he got when he thought about getting *caught*. Probably, if he ever was caught, they wouldnt do anything to him. He had enough pull and prestige and power in this town any more that he could hush it up, he thought. But the very idea of the scandal and embarrassment, of being *caught*—while at some times, in certain moods, it actually seemed enticing to him: to be *caught*: to be *exposed*— still nevertheless created in him the rest of the time a terror and a sense of sheer unreality: of everything being a figment of a dream: that he could not even describe to himself. And *that* was why he sat out here at the Club alone every night, talking to whoever was around to talk to. He did it to protect himself from going out. Out here the prestige and power and respect he had earned in Parkman —as he had once fervently promised Dave he would—was tendered to him, and was given freely.

And by God he *had* earned it. Whatever anybody said. Let them hate him for his success, the sons of bitches. He had *earned* it, what he had, all of it. Just the getting of the cocktail lounge into the motel's restaurant was a perfect example of it. He had really pulled off a brilliant bit of business, getting that bar in the restaurant. In a dry county like Cray was: or, at least, was supposed to be. Actually, Cray County wasnt dry;

Parkman was dry, but there was no law in the County that stated that liquor (except for beer) could not be sold over the bar; and it was up to the discretion of the county officers and county law-enforcement officers as to whether hard liquor could be sold over the bar out in the county. All of them were against it, and against the issuing of licenses, and so was most of the citizenry—the influential citizenry, anyway. And, as far as that went, Frank was against it himself: he had never believed it was a good policy, either in the town precincts of Parkman —where there was an actual law against it—or whether out in the county, to allow whiskey and hard liquor to be served by the drink to the lower elements. But, as he explained to the county officers when he contacted them about it, his place—his restaurant—was not intended to cater to that lower element class: his restaurant was a high class dinner place, catering to tourists and to the better people of Parkman—like themselves, and himself—and that very fact would keep most of the lower class people in town from even entering it and eliminate trouble and brawls. But, to cater to the type of people he wanted it to cater to, he had to have a cocktail lounge. Just like they themselves, he told the meeting laughingly: would they patronize his new high class dinner place if they couldnt get a drink or two before they ate? Certainly not; and neither would *he!* It got quite a good laugh.

And—it had been easy enough to make them see the difference, especially when he pointed out that nobody would be admitted without a coat and tie—and even then, certain undesirables would not be admitted. They had all of them seen it easily enough, and in fact all of them—as his guests; including the sheriff—had been there the night of the big opening. And all of them were enthusiastic about the place, and felt he had been wise, and were glad they had let him have the license. Why hell, he thought—not without a certain pride—he may have established—all by himself—a new precedent in the issuing of liquor licenses in the County: there were liable to be all kinds of nice dinner places going up someday, and a good thing for the better class of people too. And—something not to be looked at lightly either, he grinned to himself—it had made the restaurant. The place was pulling in money hand over fist ever since it opened.

So let all the sons of bitches laugh at him, it they wanted to, he thought fiercely. Calculating it all up once again, as he often did, he figured that—with all his holdings in the bypass venture, and the rest of his investments: not the least of which was the new filling-station 99-year lease he had just sold the other bypass corner for to Standard Oil: the corner which he himself owned privately—calculating all that in and adding it all up, he was worth, now, today, something over $900,000. And, before another year was out, he would be—oh, that magic word—A Millionaire. In the Millionaire class. He would be worth $1,000,000. And he hadnt forgotten about all his plans for future factory sites, either. So let all the sons of bitches laugh, if they wanted to.

Dawnie was impressed with what he had done. If *nobody* else was. Dawnie and her Shotridge—(Frank found he called him that now all the time; instead of Jim; both in his mind and out loud; everybody seemed to call him that now, any more, since Dawnie had started it)— Dawnie and her Shotridge were both impressed: when he drove them out there and showed them all of it while they were home for Festival Week. But of course, they were gone now, back to school, he thought lamely.

Out of the corner of his eye, Frank saw the other two couples remaining in the bar were leaving; and then he saw Les approaching him. Les had that apologetic look. Frank looked at his watch again. It was just exactly twelve.

Damn it all.

Tossing off the rest of his last drink, Frank got up—holding himself carefully and steadily so as not to stagger any—and prepared to go home to his wife. He hoped she was asleep. If she wasnt, it would mean that he would be up half the night preparing compresses for her.

CHAPTER 76

MOST all of what the Frenches learned about Dave's death they got from Frank; all of it, in fact. Because there was very little printed about it in the *Oregonian*, both because of Festival Week and because Clark Hibbard was a good friend of Frank's and wanted to help him keep it quiet. So there wasnt really much of anywhere to get information, except from Frank. And the day they all met in Judge Deacon's office in connection with the will,—before Ginnie Moorehead arrived—, Bob and Gwen had sat with Frank for quite a while and he had told them all he knew about it. And Gwen, sitting and listening to it agonizingly, had to fight herself hard to keep from crying.

Of course, he Frank had been in on the whole thing, he told them: the handling of the soldier, the removal of Dave's body, everything. The shot had been heard uptown, and when Sherm Ruedy and his deputy cop get there the one-armed soldier boy had stepped out grinning and dropped his gun. Sherm and his deputy cop had roughed him up a little bit, getting him to the jail. But the guy just grinned at them in silence. Probably Sherm and his helper were a little teed off at him upsetting the peace of their town with a murder. It didnt make them look too good: a murder in their town. And as far as that went, Frank himself figured a little bit of pistol-whipping wouldnt hurt him a damned bit. Especially since later he got off scot-free and was sent to a Veterans' Hospital.

Of course, they had called him—Frank—right away. He had been working the Rotary Club hotdog stand on the square that night. He had got somebody to take over for him and had gone down there right away. It was hard to tell it was even Dave: the .45 slug had hit him right square in the face. And, in fact, they had had to identify him from cards in his wallet before they called Frank. Later on, after the undertaker had worked on him, he had sewed his head up in some kind of velvet bag. Of course, not everybody saw that, because at the funeral itself they—as Bob and Gwen knew—had kept the casket closed, but Frank had seen it at the undertaker's beforehand. He had told them, down there on North Main where Dave still lay when he got there, what undertaker to take him to: the best in town, of course. And he had stayed and waited for the ambulance and helped them load him in and had ridden down to the undertaker's with him. He had, Frank told them, felt that was little enough to do for poor old Dave.

Dave had evidently been on his way out of town, when this guy shot him. Because he was carrying both a suitcase and a portable typewriter. The typewriter, when they opened it and looked in it later, had evidently been broken when he dropped it as he fell. Of course, he hadnt opened it or the suitcase then but had only taken them home and kept them, unopened, until the Judge called him next day after having received the will through the mail, and then he had turned them both over to the Judge here. The manuscript, of course, as they knew, which he had left to them, had been in the suitcase. Later on, at the inquest, Ginnie Moorehead had said that she hadnt known that Dave was leaving and, indeed, knew no reason why he should want to leave. She herself had been uptown at the festivities with some friends, and Dave had stayed home by himself as he had all week, and when she left him he seemed perfectly happy and contented. But then, Frank said, that damned woman was liable to say anything and would probably lie under oath and tell any damned thing that came into her head. And, well, that was the whole story.

Gwen sat and heard it out, although it was exquisitely painful to her and she didnt want to. Bob evidently felt the same way, from the look she caught on his face. But curiosity is just too strong, no matter how painful the information. And anyway Gwen felt in some obscure way it was her duty to do it: to sit and take it and hear all the gory details. And after Frank had finished, still fighting to keep from crying and keep her voice down, Gwen told him calmly about the note Dave had included with the copy of the will he sent to her, and showed it to him.

Frank, of course, didnt know anything about it or what it meant—or, for that matter, what it symbolized, either. Bob did, of course; they had talked about it earlier, that same day they received the will. That note, together with the will itself and the fact that he was leaving town, meant for both of them that Dave had come to some momentous decision—about his life, and about his writing—in his own mind; just exactly what it was, of course, they would never know. But there was no point in trying to explain any of all this to Frank. He wouldnt have understood it anyway; and anyway, Frank was having a hard enough time as it was over his brother dying, Gwen thought looking at him as he sat there solemnly: short and blocky and with his round face and balding head shining in the light. The manuscript itself lay on the Judge's desk, stacked neatly in a single pile the height of a man's hand, where the Judge himself had placed it. They would, she said, attempt to put it into shape for him and see if they couldnt get it published.

When Ginnie Moorehead finally came in, the homogeneity of the group seemed to disintegrate immediately. Gwen could not help but feel sorry for her: she was so obviously scared and ill at ease before the solemn fact of legality in any form. But when, later, she raised a fuss and insisted that the manuscript belonged to her, Gwen could not help feeling anger and total disgust for her, either: just as strongly as she had felt sorry earlier. The Judge handled it, of course, and handled it very definitely and with dispatch. But before he did, Gwen had made up her mind to fight Ginnie Moorehead through every court in the land— to keep her from getting that manuscript. What on earth would she have done with it anyway?

His wife, Gwen kept saying to herself with exquisite pain: *his wife*: *Dave's wife*. It was such an agonizing thought, as she sat looking at the gross ignorant acquisitiveness of her, that Gwen thought she could not bear it. Bob, from his face, apparently knew what she was feeling; but she didnt think any of the others did. She covered it up well. She didnt think she was still in love with Dave; she thought she had whipped that out; out there in Arizona; but she did still feel love for his talent—and for his work. And that this ignorant woman would sit there and try to claim his manuscript—which he had clearly left to herself and Bob— was insufferable. But what on earth—what on *earth*—would ever have made him *do* it? a man of his exquisite sensibilities? to marry a creature like this woman? to *marry* her?

When the decision about the manuscript was made—which was quite quickly, with the Judge's cold-steel voice—and Ginnie had backed down, Gwen collected Bob and the manuscript and got them out of there as quickly as she could. They had no further business there; they were not concerned, and did not want to be, with any of the rest of it; and she wanted to get out. Bob, sensing her anxiousness to leave, expedited their departure in that beautiful suave way that nobody had but him, whenever he wanted to use it.

So they had taken the manuscript home. But once they got there, neither one of them wanted to talk about it—or even to look at it; and they had simply put it carefully away. It was still too soon yet, would be too painful, to try to do anything with it now. And in the same way they both felt about the manuscript, they also felt about talking about Dave: by a kind of tacit agreement they did not discuss him either. The manuscript lay in its file, and the thought of Dave lay filed in their minds, for nearly another two months, while the pain of his violent death gradually diminished and faded away, before they ever took it out again.

Gwen had been home nearly a year before Dave died. She had come home in October of 1949, and he was killed in September of 1950. The school year, of course, was already started when she got back to Illinois; but then she had no more desire to teach at the College any more, anyway; not anywhere else. It had just faded out of her out there in the desert sun of Arizona. She knew about his marriage, of course; but she had cleansed herself in Arizona. She had, in effect, operated on herself: taken up the knife and reached in and taken hold of the painful canker and cut it off and removed it and sewed up the gaping wound. Then she had recuperated in the hot desert sun of Arizona. She had ridden, and swum, and gone for long walks in the foothills of the Catalinas on the edge of Tucson, and whenever she wanted it she had had access to Cousin Wilson Ball's jeep to make long trips out into the desert country: down to Tombstone, up to Coolidge and Casa Grande, and out into the back country roads to little places like Sells and Sonoita and Oracle and Mammoth: driving in the open topless jeep in just shorts and halter until she was as brown as any Indian, and the sun had cleansed her: that hot dry baking sun, that reached right down into your very bones themselves, baking and baking you, until you were clean and serene all through. She had arrived too late to catch the snow on Mt Lemmon; but she didnt mind not skiing. The sun was what she needed. The sun, and her own strong mind, had cooked Dave—or at least the pain of Dave— right out of her. Every day she was out in that sun, dazzling, blinding, baking, and it changed her. Every day she looked forward to it, to being out in it, after she finished work.

The letter from Bob about Dave's sister Francine had caught her just as she was finishing up the book. It was the one letter she had from Bob, and its answer was the only one she sent him. She had been suspecting something of this kind might come up over the book: the further she got into it, the closer to the bone it got. But spending her cool early mornings working on it, and the rest of the day out in that glorious cleansing sun, she went ahead and finished it anyway. It was really a shame, she thought looking at the last page as she finished, in a way;

because it was really a small masterpiece of the analysis of sexual drives in writers, in its own small way; and now she wouldnt be able to publish it—someday it might be published after all the participants were long dead; but certainly not now. Then she put it away and forgot about it until such time as she should go home. Because she knew, by then, that she was going home. Eventually. Home to Parkman and home to Israel. Home to Bob and the *Last Retreat*.

And with the book done, and back home now, there really wasnt much for her to do: she still had no desire at all to teach any more; somehow that had gone completely out of her; and she just simply refused to read anything the young ministerial student and the polio girl brought over to her, as soon as they discovered she was home. Finally, after a long enough period of discouragement, they became aware she really meant it and stopped coming. So, in lieu of anything else to do, she started in on a research on Hawthorne—something she had always planned to do someday, anyway—and began writing more conventional articles on that work, and some others on Whitman, whom she had always admired and studied. All of them were sold, to one little college publication or another, and especially the Hawthorne pieces got an enthusiastic reception among the academics whose works and theories —so little read by the general public—both she and Bob knew and read; and she began toying with the idea of expanding them into a book on Hawthorne. He was really a fascinating and enigmatic personality. And a wise one. And, with all of this, she was reasonably happy. She had seen Dave just twice, over in Parkman, on the street; and both times as if by tacit agreement they had both turned off so as not to meet. Perhaps it hurt her? Yes, perhaps it did; but not really very strongly.

She was, somehow a changed person; and she knew it herself. She could tell it just in her driving. She had, from a rather timid always-ill-at-ease driver, become a really excellent one. So much so that she had had to train herself to always be on the lookout for the cops—after she began to collect a few speeding tickets over in Indiana. Perhaps this driving thing was due to all those long hours of herding Cousin Wilson Ball's jeep over the back roads—and the highways—of Arizona. She had certainly had plenty of practice. But there was more to it than just that, too. Her driving had become more forceful, more a dominating of the car, and she herself had become more forceful, too; she could feel it in herself. She was just—changed. And she was happy.

And that was the way she was—the *person* she was—when she picked up the *Oregonian* that evening in September and was shocked to a standstill by the news of Dave's killing by the ex-Marine from Kansas: a small, very small, little item down at the bottom of the front page.

She knew all about the one-armed ex-Marine and Ginnie Moorehead, how Ginnie Moorehead had gone off to Kansas with him and then come back to Dave, and Bob's subsequent visit from the unhappy lover. He had told her all of it—reluctantly: it was clear he did not want to tell her; but she wanted to know, and insisted on knowing, and so he had told her. And so, when she had read it in the paper, the evening of that same day when Dave's Will and Testament had come in through the mail—another surprise, in itself—she had known the whole story. Whatever it was that Ginnie Moorehead had, it must be something. She couldnt see it herself, at all—but then she was not a man. But Ginnie Moorehead must have *something*—to keep so many men interested so long, and chasing after her so long.

She had, of course, shown the piece to Bob and had him phone Frank right away. And, later, after the unpleasant scene in Judge Deacon's office, and they had returned home with the manuscript, she found that another change of some sort had taken place in her: the Hawthorne work no longer interested her, and she laid the book aside. She could not free herself of a deep, obsessive guilt that—somehow, in some way, that she could not even isolate—she herself was responsible for Dave's death. More so than Ginnie Moorehead. More so than the boy who pulled the trigger.

She could not talk to Bob about it. And during those near-two months —a little over six weeks it was: from the tail end of September to just past the middle of November—while both his manuscript and the thought of Dave lay quietly put aside in both of them, and the shocked pain at his death faded away and abated somewhat, she brooded about it. Was she responsible? Or wasnt she?

But when, finally, in the middle of November, they got the manuscript out and began going through it, she and Bob, and the picture of Dave's mind and thought and phraseology—all of it already dead and gone—suddenly emerged from it, freshly, and clearly, and shockingly alive, as if *he* were still alive, she could not keep quiet any longer.

There really wasnt too awfully much work to do on the manuscript. Most of the love affair chapters were separate entities, and those had only to be just pulled out entire. But, within the narrative and characterizations there were, as they read it through, various small allusions to the "little private" and the "little peasant girl": all of these needed to be cut, too, because they all became non sequiturs once the love affair chapters were pulled out, and they both read it very carefully to make sure they missed none of them. And once this was done, the book was finished; complete. So there really wasnt too much to do, but they were both very careful to change nothing else: when they started on it, it was with the principle of not adding or changing even one word or comma that was not Dave's own; and this they held to: whenever an occasion came up, as just a few did, that a transition was obscure because of a cut or of a missing love affair chapter, they solved it by more minor cutting rather than by adding anything. In all, it took them just a little over a week to do it all. That was how little there was to do: one week's work. And it was one of the most deeply pleasing and satisfying—as well as one of the most exquisitely painful—experiences Gwen had ever had in her life.

And, after it was done and mailed in to NLL, and they finally heard from them, Gwen told Bob about her forebodings and her broodings over Dave and her sense of responsibility for his death. She felt that, honorably, she had to, now.

She did not know just exactly what it was that made her do it: made her feel she *had* to do it. Perhaps, more than anything else, it was the simple fact that Dave had sent that copy of his will to them and had left them the manuscript, and that little note he had stuck in with it: *Should anything happen to me—which I am not expecting—the love affair should come out—entirely.* All of this—coupled to the fact that he was apparently leaving town—and leaving Ginnie—indicated that some large change had taken place in Dave. It was also a vindication of herself and Bob: of the faith and the hope they had had in him; and, in the end, a proof of Dave's own trust in them. He had left *them* the manuscript, not someone else. Because he knew that they sympathized with and shared—perhaps alone of all people—his ideas and his beliefs. And because he knew he could trust them to edit it according to his purpose and his meaning. And this meant a great deal to Gwen. It was also, as she realized, the cause—and the measure—of her guilt. She did not know what miseries of selfsearching he had had to go through in order to arrive at this change of viewpoint. There just wasnt any way of knowing—ever, now. But she did feel—and strongly— that if she herself had not failed him, he might not even have ever had to go through them; and even more important: he might still be here now to write other, greater books. That was the worst of all: he was dead now, and he would never write the things he might have written. And Gwen felt that that was her responsibility.

God, how she hated being a woman! A silly, lying, vain, preening woman: playing spiritual, playing at being the Pedestal: the universal "Conscience"—and all the time being sly and deceitful underneath the thin veneer of sweet and soulful respectability. And that was just what she had been! All her life she had worked at *not* being, and had promised herself she would *not* be, that kind of woman. She had seen Dawnie with her Shotridge—that same Dawnie she had once wept and thrown a tantrum over, when she had read the handwriting on the wall. And she had seen Doris Fredric, with her sly lying so-virginal act she played to such perfection. Even Agnes—once so strong; and now a selfpitying semi-invalid—even Agnes, in her perpetual handling of Frank, had lived and worked mainly by deceit. Perhaps all women *had* to live like this; but Gwen did not believe this—she *refused* to believe it; and she had promised herself that *she* would never be like that.

And yet, when it had come down to it—when, in her own situation, with her own man—(the only man she had ever really loved)—she had been confronted with her own need to act—she had reacted just like all the rest. She had lied—about her virginity; and even more deceitfully than they: because hers was a tacit lie: she simply let him believe what he already thought. And out of what: out of vanity, vanity and sheer pride. Out in Tucson she had hated him: hated him violently and shakingly, every time the thought of him crossed her mind. She had not stayed at home all the time, she had been out some—quite a lot. And she had seen them: the tall willowy exquisitely beautiful call girls that you find in every city and big resort town: with their expensive furs and exquisitely done hair and faces. She had had at least six known ones pointed out to her by Cousin Wilson Ball and his wife, and she had studied them in the bars and clubs. She had even contemplated getting herself up and taking a crack at it herself. Tall, exquisitely kept figures, beautiful expensive clothes, perfectly kept and perfectly preserved, cold, reserved, almost contemptuous even. To be so perfectly kept, so perfectly dressed, never a single hair out of place, they had to spend hours and hours every day, just dressing, just getting ready to go out; and in fact, as Cousin Wilson Ball said, they did just exactly that: hours and hours each and every day. But take the makeup, and the expensive clothes, and the perfect hair-dos off of them and they wouldnt be much different from herself. Get herself a builtup bra, make her mouth up exquisitely perfectly—but about twice its actual size, spend the hours on the hair-do, she could be just like them. And many times, when she was hating Dave so violently, she seriously contemplated doing it: No man in the world ever touched those girls, no matter how many times they slept with them.

And then, when she got back home, and found out that he actually had *married* her, had married that pig Ginnie, she hated him even more violently. Like those two times she had seen him on the street. And so, after promising herself never to do so, or be so, she had reacted just exactly like all the rest: like Agnes, and like Dawn, and like Doris Fredric: a lying, vain, preening, petty, jealous, *deceitful* woman.

She had been reading some in some of Bob's occult books and in one of them, a thin little volume called *Light on the Path*, she had read a phrase that leaped out at her from the page "*Shun not the cloak of evil, for if you do it will be yours to wear.*" It leaped out bodily at her and into her heart and mind and she read on: "*And if you turn with horror from it, when it is flung upon your shoulders, it will cling the more closely to you.*" It was almost like some personal message to her, and she had closed the book. Because this was what she had done. And it was the measure of her guilt, and the measure also—after that evening she talked to Bob—of the penance she imposed upon herself.

Bob had already, when they were first starting the work on Dave's manuscript, written to their lady editor friend at *NLL*, asking if she would not like to reconsider the book and explaining the circumstances of Dave's death and their own posthumous editing of his manuscript. They had got back from her one of her typical letters that they both knew so well and always were so warmly amused by—(she was a good friend of Gwen's; and Gwen always stayed with her when she was in New York)—saying that of course if they requested it she would be glad to look at it again, but from the condition of the book as she remembered it she couldnt see how just simple cutting would ever help it. Bob had written her back, when he sent the manuscript, a—for him—extremely forceful letter praising it, and which in effect put his own reputation as a critic and a judge of writing, and even as a writer himself, on the block.

And they had, in a remarkably short time—just under two weeks, in fact—gotten back a letter enthusiastically accepting the book for publication. There were reservations in the letter from the lady editor: She thought, as the book now stood—without the love affair—it was so *very* shocking, both in its implied attitude about the human race, and also in its technique of making death so comic and unheroic, that it might be almost completely unpalatable to an ordinary average American reader: it was *so* bitter, and so *very* strong, that she herself had been almost unable to read it. Nevertheless, she felt, as did her associates and the publisher himself, that it was a true work of genius—a twisted, distorted genius perhaps: but nevertheless genius. And now, with the love affair cut completely out of it—something she herself would never have even considered doing; and, in fact, had been surprised by—it did nevertheless have a peculiar unity that it had not had before. It was, she said, good enough that they intended to do it in a hardback edition first.

Gwen and Bob stared at each other triumphantly, after reading the letter, and then grinned victoriously.

"Well, you pushed them into it," Gwen smiled.

"On the contrary, dear Gwen," Bob said earnestly; "on the contrary, the manuscript and its merit pushed them into it. You know as well as I, that no one—myself or anybody else—can push a publisher into publishing a meritless book." He smiled slyly. "Despite all our lady editor friend's reservations—which I suspect she goes on about much more than she actually in truth feels—she herself knows that it is a truly unique and outstanding book. As do her superiors and the publisher himself."

"I think Dave would be pleased," she said softly.

"Im sure he would," Bob said gently.

Gwen, looking at him lovingly, felt tears want to come up into her eyes. But calmly she blinked them back, clear eyed. And suddenly she knew that now was the time to tell him: to talk to him: about what she had been feeling—that guilt, and that sense of responsibility for Dave's death. Her own sense of integrity made her know that she would have to tell him sometime; and it wouldnt do any good to tell anybody else, because Bob was the only one who could understand it—And, for that matter, was the only one who would even be interested, now— now that Dave was dead.

They were both of them sitting in the kitchen, after she had gone down for the evening mail. The big long old-fashioned kitchen with its fireplace: Bob in his big chair down by the fireplace, herself in one of the ladderbacks at the big table: the same kitchen which Dave had used to stand and admire so many times. It seemed that they were always sitting here, here in this kitchen, whenever they talked seriously.

"You know, Bob, you told me once—once before I left for Tucson—" Gwen said clearly, and forcefully, "that you thought it would be a bad thing for me to leave. You really wanted me to stay, didnt you? Do you still feel that way? —Wait," she said calmly, clear eyed, before he could answer; "this is of tremendous importance to me: what you answer. Do you still feel that way?"

Bob smiled sadly, and made a movement approaching a small shrug. "Dear Gwen, who am I to say? I just dont know."

"In other words, you do still feel I shouldnt have left; but you just dont want to say so to me."

Bob spread his hands out helplessly. "Who am I to judge? Who is anyone to judge?"

"You mustnt have reservations with me," Gwen said clearly; she felt completely cool, completely calm, completely rational, inside. "Youve always been honest with me. —More honest than Ive been with you, in fact," she added obscurely. Bob raised his eyebrows questioningly, but she only shook her head. "I want to know your opinion," she said. "Do you believe that had I stayed Dave wouldnt have been killed?"

"Perhaps not," Bob said. "Perhaps not by that boy at any rate. —But," he shrugged, "who knows? He might have been hit by a truck and killed even sooner."

"Thats another ambiguous answer," Gwen said, refusing still to be put off. "You told me—back then; at that same time—that you believed Dave would not ever finish his book if I left. And you were right: he didnt. We did."

"Dave did finish it," Bob said. "It was finished when it came into our hands. He just didnt know it was finished. But then again, perhaps he did know it was finished. Because he wrote you that the love affair must come out."

"No," Gwen said stubbornly; "it was *not* finished. It was not finished because it still needed work done on it. Luckily, it was work of a type you and I were able to do on it. Or it would never have been finished."

"Dear Gwen, I fear youre quibbling," Bob said from his chair. "What is it that is bothering you?"

"I feel a very strong responsibility for Dave's death," Gwen said calmly. "Ive thought and thought about it. To try and find out if I really am. I feel a *very* strong sense of responsibility for it, and a great guilt about it."

"Dear Gwen," Bob said slowly, and also sadly. "You are not alone in that. I feel the same thing. There is so much more I could have done, perhaps. But that I did not do. Everyone always feels that after a death." He smiled; but Gwen stared back at him squarely, and shook her head. She was not about to be put off, or eased out of what she had to say.

"I dont mean that," she said; "and you know it. —And also, if I *am* responsible for his death," she said unflinchingly, "I am then also responsible for all the work he did not do—but might have done, had he lived." She was glad—very glad; and very relieved—that they were at last getting this out in the open.

"Dear Gwen," Bob said; he had laid both the *NLL* letter and his book he had been reading when she brought it, aside; "is anyone ever *really* responsible for another's death. *If the red slayer think he slays, Or if the slain think he is slain, They know not well the subtle ways I keep, and pass, and turn again*," Bob said, quoting Emerson's poem "Brahma." "Perhaps no one is ever responsible for one's death except the one himself."

"You know," Gwen said resolutely, and took a deep breath, "you know, Dad, you and I have never talked much about ourselves to each other, about our own private lives, our sexual lives."

"Need we?" Bob said.

"Yes," she said clearly; "right now we must. I have something I feel I must tell you. I dont want to embarrass you with anything; but this is something Im—well—more or less morally obligated to tell you, I feel."

"Very well," Bob said, and folded his hands together.

Gwen tood another deep breath. "You see, Dad," she said simply, and looking at him squarely, "Im a virgin. I never slept with Dave Hirsh. At all." It took a great deal out of her, even now, to say it: to just say the words—a great deal more than she had thought it would, even. And yet she felt strangely very calm, too, at the same time.

"Dear Gwen," Bob said helplessly from his chair, "dear Gwen Im sorry."

"Why sorry?" Gwen demanded quickly. "Why do you say that?"

"Well, I—" Bob said confusedly. "Well, I guess, because I instinctively felt that you had wanted to, and that you yourself regretted that you hadnt." He paused, still confusedly. "But, I guess, more than that, because Im sorry, and embarrassed for you, that you should feel you had to tell me."

"It changes everything, doesnt it?" Gwen said calmly.

"No-o," Bob said helplessly; "no. I dont think it changes any of it. It does give me the missing element: the missing element in this whole affair that Ive never just been able to put my finger on."

"You thought I was sleeping with him," Gwen said. "I know it from things you said to me. But you see I wasnt. And never had been. —Although I let you think it."

"The missing element," Bob said again, sadly. "The missing element I never was able to put my finger on. —Ahhh, dear Gwen. Poor dear Gwen. I had no idea."

"No," Gwen said. "Nor does anybody else. Its always been my secret, my closely guarded secret. Dave didnt know either. Hes always thought I was almost promiscuous. He even accused me of being a nymphomaniac once. Nobody knows. Nobody has any idea that Im a virgin. And all those other men, those former lovers, and all the hot and heavy love affairs, all that sophisticated woman-of-the-world routine:—all an act: a part of my secret lie."

"But why?!"

"Because I was ashamed of anybody finding out. Doubly ashamed, after becoming known as such a 'woman of the world'. I was afraid of being laughed at."

"The missing element," Bob said sadly. He straightened up in his chair, suddenly looking very tired. "It is I, dear Gwen, not you, who am responsible for Dave's death, my dear. I should have known. I should have been intelligent enough, smart enough, perceptive enough, to have figured it out. Had I done that, I would have reacted very differently, I think. I would have told Dave about that girl Ginnie Moorehead coming over here and talking to you—even when you didnt want me to; and that would have changed everything. That girl knew *exactly* what she was doing. Dumb as she appears to be, with her sly animal cunning she outsmarted us all." He paused, and shrugged, the corner of his mouth pulled up sadly. "But I: I, with all my books Id read: I, with my notion of trying not to interfere, and to avoid new Karma: I, in always saying 'Thy will be done, not mine', in trying to follow 'God's Will' and not interfere, or let my own feelings interfere—*I* refused to be a *part* of God's Will. I refused to *act*. I refused to be a part of *life*." The corner of his mouth pulled itself up still tighter, into a still deeper sadness. "If Dave had only known that that girl had come over here—" It tapered off into silence. "I really am the villain of the piece," he said.

"No," Gwen said positively. "It wasnt you. It was me. I was the one who lied."

"When Dave came over here, and kept coming, and kept coming, he was asking for something—and I didnt give it to him," Bob said sorrowfully.

"Ive read your books, too, you know," Gwen said. "And when you get so far along, you dont make Karma any more. You come in a class where you just dont *make* Karma. I quote you back your quote from Emerson."

"My dear," Bob said sorrowfully. "None of us are in that class. Nor are we likely to be for some time, and many lives, I fear. And I expect I made more future Karma for myself in my refusal to act than I should ever have done had I acted and tried to help you and Dave. One simply cannot *withdraw* from life, and refuse to *live*. Not without dire consequences. No, I am the one who is responsible, if anyone is responsible."

"Dont forget Dave comes into this for some responsibility, too," Gwen said sharply. "Dont forget that in your guilt."

"No; and dont you forget it either, in yours." He paused, musingly. "Yes, of course. He does. He was an almost living proof of your theory in your book, wasnt he?" he said with a sad smile. "Here was a man who on the one hand had his work—his art—and had companionship and love, too, though not physical, sexual love; and on the other he had just that: sexual love and nothing more. He had to choose between. He chose the sex."

"Perhaps he wouldnt have, if I had not left," Gwen said calmly. "Thats been my whole point."

Bob merely shook his head, almost as if he had not even heard her. "Dear Gwen," he said, "while we are confessing —and Ive always been told confession is good for the soul— I have something to confess myself: I have felt—oh, for some quite long time now—that it is I who have taken away your life from you. I kept you here, quite selfishly actually, just to take care of *me*, and look after *me*. What you told me just a moment ago makes me more sure of it than ever now."

"I chose to stay," Gwen said; "you didnt keep me."

"Ahh, but in subtle ways I did," Bob said. "In subtle ways I did. What I should have done was to have forced you out. Out into life. Out on your own. Then life would have forced you to—ahh—love. And in loving, in giving yourself, you would have been hurt—as love hurts us all. And in being hurt, you would have grown—either better; or worse—as you were meant to do. Yes, I have done you great harm, dear Gwen."

"Youve just given me my answer," Gwen said crisply. "The answer Ive been asking you for—about me; and about my guilt—since we started talking." The peculiar calmness in her seemed to grow even stronger, expanding outward until it filled not only all of her but everything she came in contact with. And suddenly she knew what she was going to do: Now: Now when it was too late, and meant nothing: meant nothing to anyone but herself at any rate. And at the same time she felt a strange protectiveness toward Bob, not like any protectiveness she had ever felt for him before, but more like the feeling of a parent for a child. Feeling very strange, she smiled at her father's bent, still-musing head sadly. He still had great work in him though, despite the age, despite the change, despite everything. But, she thought suddenly, she had great work in her, too—perhaps even greater; though she didnt know just what.

But she knew what she was going to do. In fact, she had contemplated doing it out in Tucson, even; and also in the year since she had been back here. But then that had been out of hatred. This was not. There had been plenty of chances, out there in Tucson—and plenty of chances back here, too. She had seen a lot of men who would be quite obviously willing—more than willing—to seduce her, both out there and here; and she had even contemplated a few of them. But even then—even with the hatred—she could never just bring herself to come in contact with them.—Physical contact. It was just too—too intimate a thing to do—without love. And she could not. She would have felt degraded. But then there was no need to have a man to do it. It could be done professionally by a doctor. And it was this that, just now, when Bob had given her—unwittingly, on his part—her answer she had wanted to know, that she had decided to do—to have done.

It really meant nothing: not now, when it was too late. And once it could have meant so much. But whether it meant anything to anybody else or not—and whether it might seem ridiculous to anybody else or not—it meant something to her. Something very important. Cold-bloodedly, calmly, clear eyed, she was going over to Indianapolis to see a doctor. An act of gynecological surgery could accomplish for her what in their ignorance and silly stupidity neither she—nor Dave—could ever quite get done.

It wouldnt do her any good especially, or serve any useful purpose. Not physically, at any rate. She had no desire for any men now any more, at all. If indeed she ever had had—except possibly that one brief few weeks period with Dave. And it would not bring back what was gone, or change anything. But whether it served any external purpose or not, any physical purpose, it served a purpose in her soul, and in her spirit: It would not only be a penance. It would, she felt, in some way, also be a redemption.

She didnt think she still loved him now. And in fact she was sure she didnt. But she did still love what he *could* have been, and what he might have done. And because of this, she felt it was her right—even her duty; but certainly her right—to pay off her debt to what she knew she had destroyed.

Why had she never thought of a doctor before? All those times? When it might have meant something? Probably she hadnt wanted to, that was why. Probably, in all her champings and cageshakings and miseries and wild outcries, she had nevertheless been proud of it. Down somewhere in the very deepest bottoms of herself: Proud of the ancient shibboleth, the ageold touchstone, the mystic symbol; the Vestal's purity: all that time she had been playing the "Pedestal", the "Great Conscience" of the males. And all that time she had been just like the rest. Only she had been the greatest whore of all. Well, damn it all, it was possible for a woman to be honest like a man. It must be. It *had* to be.

For a moment, she looked over at her father's bent still-musing head and thought of telling him what she meant to do—to have done, to herself. But that was pointless: and in fact it might even be sheer vanity and bravado: and anyway, Gwen realized suddenly, he was so concerned with his own guilt that he no longer had any concern for hers. If he had ever had. What was it he was always saying: "Each man must find his salvation within himself alone. It is not to be found outside. In another person." Well, he would have to find his own. She had found—or was finding—hers.

As if he was aware of her looking at him, Bob suddenly raised his head from where he had been staring at the floor.

"Yes?" he said. "You do have your answer? And what is it?"

"That Im guilty," Gwen said simply.

"We both are guilty, dear Gwen, I think," Bob said. "I might say we *all* are guilty. You, me, Dave, that girl, everyone. And yet at the same time we all are also *un*guilty. We suffer, and we learn; and then we grow. —Though growth may often seem like 'Sin' to others; to the ignorant. Do you remember the end of Hawthorne's *Marble Faun*?" He straightened up in his chair and laced his hands together. "And what do you plan to do now? now that you have your answer? What are your plans? Do you intend to go back to teaching?"

"No," Gwen said positively. "I dont think Ill ever want to try to teach anybody anything again. —If," she added, "in all these years I ever have."

Bob was looking at her carefully, almost strangely she thought. "You know, Dave used to tell me," he said suddenly, "used to tell me many times, that you didnt have a critical work in your book, dear Gwen, you had a novel. From what he said I gather that he had told you this, too. I had forgotten it until just now," he added almost slyly.

"Yes, he did say that," Gwen said. She felt suddenly startled; almost breathless. A sudden strange high excitement began to rise in her.

"Yes, he did say that, didnt he! As a matter of fact, he told me that that first night we met, there at Frank's and Agnes's for dinner."

Bob just merely looked at her, strangely, almost penetratingly, almost calculatingly. "Perhaps it might provide a way out of your dilemma with your book," he said softly, gently.

Gwen stared back at him thoughtfully, hardly seeing him. "You know, I believe hes right!" she said excitedly. "I could very *easily* novelize it. It wouldnt be an academic work, then; and consequently would be no *proof*; but what do I care for *proof*? Why would I give a damn about academic *proof*? —And, if I novelized it," she went on enthusiastically, "I could develop and expand it in ways I know about—in my mind— but never had the research proof to do, as long as it was supposed to be a critical work. Why, yes!" she said excitedly. "Its a perfect answer! And, more than that, I have a lot of other novels I might do, someday, too, I think."

Bob said nothing and merely continued to watch her, eyes brimming with some private emotion of his own, apparently. Whatever it might be, Gwen thought in her excitement. His guilt over Dave, probably.

"Well," he said finally, "you do already know a good bit about novel writing after all, dont you?"

Gwen turned to look at him. "He gave us something too; didnt he?" she said softly. "Dave gave *us* something, too."

Bob did not answer. But after a moment he said, gently: "I think you should move away from here, too, dear Gwen."

"Yes," Gwen said thoughtfully. "Yes, I expect I should."

"Of course this place will always be yours, you know," Bob added. "It isnt as if you were losing it. It will be left to you. And you will always be able to come back to it, when you want."

Gwen nodded vaguely, but she did not answer this remark. She sat for a moment looking at her father, realizing suddenly that if she did not tell him what she meant to do—and have done to herself—she would once again be lying, be parading under false pretenses—just as she once done before, in just the opposite way. And he, whenever he saw or heard from her, would go right on thinking she was still that virgin, that same virgin—who had, she was convinced, caused so much damage with her virginity—whether he believed that or not.

So she told him, calmly, coolly, clear eyed, what she meant to do—and have done, to herself.

Once more Bob made his old familiar apologetic near-shrugging motion. "Well, dear Gwen, I cannot advise you. If that is what you think you must do, then you must—" But then he stopped himself. And suddenly he smiled. And then he said: "Yes, dear Gwen. I think that is just exactly what you should do," and smiled at her tiredly. "If you want my opinion, and for its share of the responsibility, I would advise you to do just that."

And so it was that three days later, Gwen French with three bags packed and loaded in her new sedan she had bought out in Tucson and driven home —(in just slightly less than three and one half days)— was on Route 40 driving east and keeping a sharp eye out for the Indiana cops. She was headed for New York, where she would put up with their lady editor friend until she could get an apartment and get settled in, and she planned a stopover in Indianapolis.

She picked one of the nicest of the business buildings, and there were three gynecologists on the wall directory. She chose the first one, which began with a G: a Doctor Goster. When she was ushered into his consulting room, she pointedly waited until the nurse had gone out and closed the door. She had come in figuring that if she did not like his looks, she would just get up and go right back out; but she didnt mind this doctor's looks. He had a heavy florid face, but he also had sensitive eyes. Okay. So far so good. But how did you begin? How did you say it? Just how did you go about picking out just what words to say?

A half an hour later she was back out on the road, on Route 40, and heading eastward toward Ohio, driving eighty and keeping a weather eye out for cops.

It really had been nothing. One small sharp pain, and that was all. Such a simple thing. Just nothing. Just practically nothing at all. Well, she was what she was now, at least, at any rate. Perhaps someday she might find a man. Who knew? She wasnt looking for one; and she wasnt expecting one. She didnt even want one. But who knew? She might: one who was sensitive, and kind, and gentle, and intelligent. She just might. But he would certainly have to be all of those things, and be them damned plainly and clearly. But mostly what she was thinking about was the work she was going to get done, and the thought of it filled her with a rising, burgeoning high excitement of just living.

Then, across the screen of her eyesight as her eyes moved about watching the road and the driving almost automatically, a picture of Bob superimposed itself on the windshield in front of her: Bob as he had looked this morning when she left. She had looked back in the rearview mirror after she turned around before she pulled out of the drive, and had seen him standing in the cellar doorway. He had been leaning on the door, his hand high up on its edge, with his white crew-cut and heavy gray moustache, and he had been smiling, actually smiling happily, and there had been that other, strange look on his face too. Old Bob. Well, she wouldnt be gone forever. Someday she would be coming back. Coming back home.

Leaning over, she switched on the car's radio just in time to hear a news broadcast that the Chinese Communists had invaded North Korea and that our armies were in full retreat. She had heard from Wally's mother that he was over there, had been from the very first—(he had never written to herself or Bob)—and that his outfit had been one of the first sent there from Japan, and suddenly her heart went out to him, painfully, warmly.

EPILOGUE

They came running through the paddy fields across the snow, dog-trotting, their rifles held at a rigid precise Port Arms, in their quilted uniforms or large long overcoats and the quilted boots, the conspicuous white bandoliers crossing their chests, and you shot them down. Sometimes, later, —on those occasions when the Company held— you could count upwards of a hundred bodies lying on the slope up which they came in front of the position. Other times —on those occasions when the Company did not hold; and these were in the majority— you did not know how many the all of you might have killed. But then it didnt seem to matter, really. There were so many of them that no matter how many hundreds of them you might kill, it was never enough. They swarmed around like ants or termites, everywhere, coming from every direction, all around you, all over you. And on those times the Company would finally, under the constant never-wavering overpowering pressure, have to fall back as best they could to another hilltop and regroup and reform and set up another perimeter.

They did not always run. Sometimes they walked. In long thin evenly spaced lines, those rifles held at that rigid Port like on parade, right up the slope at you. At other times they would come ramming down a draw, all running in unison and in step in their quilted boots, rifles at rigid Port, in a regular column of fours, close packed. Trying to out-flank, of course. And usually they did. Those were the best for shooting. But—much more often than not, of course—it would be at night.

In the evening, as dusk came on, if the wind was right, you could sometimes hear them on the next hill: that strange weird out-of-tune chant; they were death-singing: getting ready to die. Ought to do some death-singing ourselves, somebody would say. Then, with the dark, the bugles and the shepherd's pipes and the whistles and the cymbals and the rattles would start making their weird ungodly noises, and the attack would begin again. And if the night was light enough, or if some house or something was burning somewhere, you could see those widely spaced lines of widely spaced men—strange, alien, totally foreign and un-understandable—coming down their own hill, crossing the frozen paddy fields, beginning to mount your hill below you. They seemed to always prefer the gentlest slope—for their main attack, at least. Sometimes,—if the BARs and LMGs didnt jam, or freeze, or just simply burn

1260

out—the fire would be too much for them and they would go to ground among the rocks. Then the grenading and countergrenading and the firefight would begin, while they tried to work up close enough to rush. They had a trick of —when they thought they were close enough— three men rushing in a V —point first— the two men behind firing to cover the one in front. Lots of times, small knots would break inside the perimeter in their rushes. But they fought funny. Once they were inside, most of them didnt seem to know what to do and just sort of ran around aimlessly until somebody cut them down. Although all of them didnt do that though. So far the Company had kept its unity, as Regiment withdrew slowly westward back onto Division. They had never quite been caught bad enough to be broken up entirely. But if they had kept their unity, attrition was thinning them out swiftly and dangerously.

The pattern was set—had been set for some days now. After the first big battle at the Chongchon —which we had lost, so badly; and which the Company had only got a very little of— it was withdraw and fight, withdraw and fight. Luckily, moving back on their own Division to the west, they had not had to run "The Gauntlet". But they were catching hell of their own kind, just the same. The trouble was, in these damned hills that nearly overlapped each other and this damned weather, nobody knew where anybody else was most of the time. They might be behind you in a big column, they might be ahead, they might be on either side. You just had to set up as tight a perimeter as you could, and fight. Then when they drew off next day to eat and bury their dead, as they always seemed to do, take the road and withdraw. That was the pattern. There wasnt much question any more of trying to attack.

Wally Dennis: Wallace French Dennis: former holder of the Parkman College Fellowship for the novel: could, as he cleaned his piece and saw that his squad was altogether, think back wryly to his former life in Parkman Illinois—so many thousands of miles and thousands of years away. That just hadnt been him, that was all: it had been another guy. When he thought of Gwen French, and of Dave Hirsh, and of 'Bama Dillert, and of old Bob—they just werent real. They were only a dream, and this, here, now, was all that was real. Funny, had he once been in love with some girl named Dawn? he would think wryly; some girl who had been the cause of him enlisting in the goddamned Army? Funny. How funny people were. Howlingly funny. But the only people he knew existed anywhere were, and in that order: one, his squad that he had to take care of all the time and check them to see they changed their socks; and two, the Company and the Captain—Captain Hewitt—whom they all of them loved desperately, and who was the main instrument that up to now had kept the Company together—he wasnt scared of anything that lived, Captain Hewitt wasnt; and three, a long line of unknown men behind him up through Regiment and Division whom he had never seen and would never know, but who were governing with their strategy the continued existence of his life. And that was all. His bad ear had been running for some time now, with him unable to take proper care of it. But little things like that just didnt matter any more. Not now. Wally had been at the Pusan Perimeter—was the only one left in his squad who had, in fact—but the Pusan Perimeter had never been anything like this. He had long ago—on November 25th, to be exact, when he saw all the antlike hordes pouring in—given up the idea of ever getting out of this alive.

"Here they come," someone would say, and he would get his little pile of M1 clips ready and at hand. Nobody had any helmets any more; you just couldnt wear them in this cold without freezing off your ears; and it was always a funny feeling to stick your head up over the edge of the hole in the big pile cap. But you had to do it. It was just something that had to be done.

He still had his Randall #1, and in fact had carried it all through— from Pusan Perimeter on through. He had rigged a prong-hook on the sheath so he could wear it on his ammo belt like a canteen, and he kept it bright and shining clean. Every time he cleaned his piece—which in this freezing weather had to be frequently—he also got out the Randall #1 and cleaned it too and wiped it carefully with the oily rag he carried in his shirt. Oil, of course, could not be put on the gun at all, in this weather: it would thicken and lock it in a minute. But the Randall #1 had no working parts—unless you wanted to count his own right arm —and the oil was good for it: it still looked as bright and shining clean as when it used to lie on his dresser at home. And he loved it. It had saved his life on more than one occasion. He bet he had sold a couple of hundred knives for that W.D. Randall. Guys were always coming up to look at and handle it. Most all of them said they were going to order one;—and back before all this bugout started, a lot of them probably had. Well, if he had helped sell a bunch of Randall knives, he was glad: because more than anything else, more than any other thing any- where, his Randall #1 gave him a sense of comfort and luck. It was funny, in times of stress, what things men cadged onto to believe in and superstitiously hang their hopes on as luckypieces. Wally's was his knife: If he could just keep his knife with him, and keep it clean and in good shape, he felt he might still yet get out—be one of those who wouldnt have to be hauled out like cordwood in the trucks, dead. Be- sides, it was beautiful: a lethally beautiful work of art: the only piece of beauty he had been able to hang on to—except for some snatch pictures he had picked up in Japan. He had killed eight Gooks with it.

Funny, even now that fact was still almost unbelievable. It took a lot more force to drive a sharp knife into a man's body than he had antici- pated. The shock in your arm was about the same as punching a guy in the head. It didnt take much effort to slash their throats—if you could get at them—but even then there was more pull against the knife than he had ever thought there would be. The flesh clung to it. And he had killed eight with it. Unbelievable. Eight Gooks. Eight ants. Only, they werent ants; they were men.

They were so different from us, these Asiatics. They had no idea of the individual importance of the separate human life. And in that, they were like ants. It was like fighting the terrifying Mongol hordes of Genghis Khan. Apparently they had no thought at all about killing one man, or five, like we did. They were terribly poor equipped. Their quilted uniforms were almost completely inadequate to the cold. The rice bags they lived off of would not have sustained our men at all. Their Russian rifles were evidently not of the best grade, either. —Of course, now, lots and lots of them were equipped with captured American equipment: our own M1s and grenades, being used against us.— But the others: some of them even attacked uphill without any weapons at all. And yet none of them seemed to mind all this much at all, not one twentieth that we would. You couldnt help feeling sorry for the poor bastards sometimes—or would have, if there were not so many of them all around you—trying so hard to kill you.

"Here they come," somebody would say, and he would stick his head up over the edge of his hole—with that extraordinary feeling of complete nakedness it gave you—and then would, as soon as he could pick out targets, begin to fire.

They want what we got, was the phrase that always jumped into Wally's head as he squinted through the sights at targets. They want what we got. Our bread, our food, our guns, our ammo, our grenades, our warm clothes. And more than that they want all of that that weve got behind us back home: the luxuries theyve never dreamed of: the richness of America: they want what we got, he would think, and fire. And we want to keep it, and thats why we're here: we mean to keep it. We built it, we made and invented it, why shouldnt we want to keep it? Squint and fire. Squint and fire. Pick your targets. Dont waste ammo. Squint and fire.

And still they kept on coming, dogtrotting up the slopes at the perimeter. Or walking, in the slow thin widely spaced lines. You could go on killing them forever, Wally sometimes thought, with all the ammunition of the whole world, and you just couldnt kill them all: and they would still keep on running, dogtrotting uphill in their funny quilted uniforms, silently, stubbornly, endlessly. It was like some new kind of way of life, he would think. Without justice for either side; no law; no courts; no police forces; and only The Company existed truly. They want what we got. They want what I got. But I intend to keep it. If I can.

"*They're going back,*" somebody would say, and the firefight would slack off and once again you could hear the bugles in the night, and the funny shepherd's pipes blowing, and the cymbals and weird rattles that sounded like Hallowe'en.

"*They're going back!*"

Or—

"*Bug out! They're gettin in! we got to pull out. Fall back, fall back. Bug out, bug out.*" And shepherding his squad, what was left of it, they would try to work their way back, and reform again, on some other hill. Almost every time they would lose at least a man or two in the platoon; sometimes more.

Dead tired. Dead asleep. Almost all the time, except when the firefight started. They want what we got. And mean to take it. And we got to keep it. Squint and fire. Squint and fire. Keep them out. And still they kept on coming. They werent like people, not like people we know anyway, they were more like animals.

The ROKs were the ones he felt sorry for the most. The Chinese did not hesitate to shoot them, without compunction, most of the times when they took ROKs prisoners. They didnt shoot nearly so many of the Americans, though they did shoot some; a lot. But the ROKs also shot the Chinese when they took them prisoner—unless forcibly detained by some American—shot them even when prisoners were wanted for information. And yet they were your close friends. But they were like children. They just werent like us, that was all. They were Asiatics, of the most primitive sort. One man just wasnt important. Wally had read Harold Lamb's Genghis Khan and The March of the Barbarians—long ago, in some other life—and they chilled his spine then. And they chilled his spine now, these inheritors of Genghis Khan.

"*They're turning back!*"

Or—

"*Pull out, pull out! Fall back, fall back! Bug out!*"

What was it Napoleon had once said? when asked of China? "There lies a sleeping dragon, let it sleep." Maybe someday, in some faroff future, the Russians themselves would be turned upon and destroyed by this Frankenstein they had created so cavalierly. That would be nice, he thought drowsily. Squint and fire.

—"*They're turning back!*"—

—"*Pull out, pull out!*"—

The last time, the time he had somehow always known was coming, he shepherded his dwindling squad—four men now, besides himself— ahead of him toward the rearward crest and off the hill, and it was then that the burp gun firing from somewhere near took him through the ass and legs with a prolonged burst and he fell. Am I dead? No, not dead. But he couldnt move his legs much, and when he did it hurt so much he had to quit. Must have got him through the hips. The remnants of his carefully shepherded squad—good boys; good boys—were a good little ways ahead of him, running hard. Maybe they would notice he was gone, and somebody would try to come back for him. But maybe they wouldnt, either. And maybe they wouldnt even notice, in the confusion, until later. Much later.

Working hard with his arms and sweating with pain in the cold, Wally squirmed himself around until he was facing the other way: toward the enemy: the "enemy." Such a funny word. He had dropped his rifle when he fell running, and it had bounced away somewhere; he couldnt see it, and he could not go and look for it. He had no pistol. All he had left now was his knife.

He got it out, then held it comfortingly in his hand against his side. There was no describing the enormous comfort that it gave him, holding it. And it was still razor-shaving-sharp, too. The little stone in its pocket on the sheath assured that. Grinning, wryly, briefly, Wally thought suddenly of the time he had slashed his finger with it, and the scar. The scar he had been so proud of.

Was anybody coming back? Had they found out he was gone yet? —Well, maybe they wouldnt come this way. The Chinks. Maybe theyd go on around the other side of the position. They might. They might bypass him completely. That had happened to guys lots of times, and they were collected later.

Then he heard the jabbering voices, talking in their funny droning firecracker talk, dead ahead of him. Raising his head, he saw several Chinese appear over the crest, their heads showing first, then their quilted shoulders, then their waists. All but one of them were to his left. But that one saw him, and stopped. He must have been eight or ten yards away. And for a moment they simply looked at each other, the Chink standing, him lying there on his belly with his head up, two foreigners, two total aliens, two men. Then the Chink approached him cautiously. He wasnt carrying any rifle. And Wally raised the knife and menaced him with it. The Chink stopped again.

He might have tried playing dead. But hell, they shot most of the dead ones again anyway, just to make sure. Maybe it was a mistake not to have tried it, but then the Chink had seen him looking right at him as his head came over the hill. Once again the Chink started to approach him, cautiously, curiously, and once again Wally menaced him with the knife and he stopped. Then, fumbling with his uniform he took out a grenade—an American grenade—and pulled the pin and tossed it over at Wally. There was the loud, familiar pop, as the spoon flew loose, and then the fizz. Then he and the others with him who had been watching all this jumped back down over the crest grinning.

Wally lay, staring at the fizzing hand grenade fascinatedly. It was

*only just a few feet in front of him. But of course he couldnt reach it.
Not in time. At least hed got the squad out.*

*Wally Dennis. Sgt Wally F. Dennis, Infantryman. And he thought
suddenly of the unfinished manuscript locked up in his bureau drawer
back there at home. He did not even drop his head down or close his
eyes, he just stared fascinatedly. Then the whole world blew up; blew
up in his face.*

*The several Chinese came back up over the crest after the grenade
exploded, and the one who had tossed it walked grinning and curiously
over to the blackened figure. The American grenade had not torn the
figure up much, but the whole head was blackened. The Chinese
approached it cautiously and rolled it over with his foot, then he stepped
on the wrist and pried the long beautiful knife out of the hand and
looked at it curiously. Squatting on one knee, he pushed the chin back
and drew the knife sharply across the throat, cutting the big artery
which pumped blood out in a gush. Looking down at the body, the
Chinese stood up grinning happily, and inspected his new knife. Then
he unfastened the ammobelt around the waist with its sheath hanging
on it and jerked it loose. Putting it around his own waist, he swaggered
back to his companions jabbering excitedly, proudly flourishing the
blood-covered knife he had taken as a prize. All of them looked at it
enviously. Then one man, more acquisitive than the others, reached out
and made a grab for it. The new owner merely flicked his wrist, and the
envious one drew back a badly cut hand. Except for him, everybody
laughed. Then the proud new owner jammed the bloody knife down
into its sheath without bothering, or having the slightest notion, to wipe
it off; and the four of them walked on.*

ACKNOWLEDGMENT

ONCE again upon looking back over the six years it took to write this novel, I find no other term applicable to the writing of it than to call it all a collective enterprise. This time though, having had the experience once before, I no longer find it a startling development. I was prepared for it.

Grateful acknowledgment is here tendered to Mr & Mrs Harry E Handy for their unfailing confidence and help, both financial and spiritual, and particularly to Lowney Handy herself for her invaluable editorial and creative aid and advice; to Mr Burroughs Mitchell for his unflagging faith and belief and his remarkably astute editorial aid in cutting; to Mr Horace S Manges for his tenderly careful care of a rather unstable 'artist' like myself; and to Mr Ned Brown, agent, of Beverly Hills California who kept a repeatedly cramping finger on the pulse of it for six long and often grueling years.